THE YEAR'S BEST

SCIENCE FICTION

ALSO BY GARDNER DOZOIS

ANTHOLOGIES

A DAY IN THE LIFE

ANOTHER WORLD

BEST SCIENCE FICTION STORIES OF THE
YEAR #6–10

THE BEST OF ISAAC ASIMOV'S SCIENCE
FICTION MAGAZINE

TIME-TRAVELERS FROM ISAAC ASIMOV'S
SCIENCE FICTION MAGAZINE

TRANSCENDENTAL TALES FROM ISAAC
ASIMOV'S SCIENCE FICTION
MAGAZINE

ISAAC ASIMOV'S ALIENS

ISAAC ASIMOV'S MARS

ISAAC ASIMOV'S SF LITE

ISAAC ASIMOV'S WAR

ROADS NOT TAKEN (with Stanley Schmidt)

THE YEAR'S BEST SCIENCE FICTION, #1–24

FUTURE EARTHS: UNDER AFRICAN SKIES
(with Mike Resnick)

FUTURE EARTHS: UNDER SOUTH
AMERICAN SKIES (with Mike Resnick)

RIPPER! (with Susan Casper)

MODERN CLASSIC SHORT NOVELS OF
SCIENCE FICTION

MODERN CLASSICS OF FANTASY

KILLING ME SOFTLY

DYING FOR IT

THE GOOD OLD STUFF

THE GOOD NEW STUFF

EXPLORERS

THE FURTHEST HORIZON

WORLDMAKERS

SUPERMEN

COEDITED WITH SHEILA WILLIAMS

ISAAC ASIMOV'S PLANET EARTH

ISAAC ASIMOV'S ROBOTS

ISAAC ASIMOV'S VALENTINES

ISAAC ASIMOV'S SKIN DEEP

ISAAC ASIMOV'S GHOSTS

ISAAC ASIMOV'S VAMPIRES

ISAAC ASIMOV'S MOONS

ISAAC ASIMOV'S CHRISTMAS

ISAAC ASIMOV'S CAMELOT

ISAAC ASIMOV'S WEREWOLVES

ISAAC ASIMOV'S SOLAR SYSTEM

ISAAC ASIMOV'S DETECTIVES

ISAAC ASIMOV'S CYBERDREAMS

COEDITED WITH JACK DANN

ALIENS!	MERMAIDS!	DINOSAURS!	UNICORNS 2	TIMEGATES
UNICORNS!	SORCERERS!	LITTLE	INVADERS!	CLONES
MAGICATS!	DEMONS!	PEOPLE!	ANGELS!	NANOTECH
MAGICATS 2!	DOGTALES!	DRAGONS!	DINOSAURS II	IMMORTALS
BESTIARY!	SEASERPENTS!	HORSES!	HACKERS	

FICTION

STRANGERS

THE VISIBLE MAN (Collection)

NIGHTMARE BLUE
(with George Alec Effinger)

SLOW DANCING THROUGH TIME
(with Jack Dann, Michael Swanwick,
Susan Casper, and Jack C. Haldeman II)

THE PEACEMAKER

GEODESIC DREAMS (collection)

NONFICTION

THE FICTION OF JAMES TIPTREE, JR.

THE YEAR'S BEST

SCIENCE FICTION

twenty-fifth annual collection

edited by Gardner Dozois

st. martin's griffin ⚎ new york

These are works of fiction. All of the characters, organizations, and events portrayed in these stories are either products of the authors' imagination or are used fictitiously.

THE YEAR'S BEST SCIENCE FICTION: TWENTY-FIFTH ANNUAL COLLECTION. Copyright © 2008 by Gardner Dozois.
All rights reserved. Printed in the United States of America.
For information, address St. Martin's Press, 175 Fifth Avenue, New York, N.Y. 10010.

ISBN-13: 978-0-312-37859-2

contents

acknowledgments

The editor would like to thank the following people for their help and support: Susan Casper; Ellen Datlow; Gordon Van Gelder; Peter Crowther; Nicolas Gevers; Jonathan Strahan; Mark Pontin; Farah Mendlesohn; Ian Whates; Mike Resnick; Andy Cox; Jeste de Vries; Robert Wexler; Eric T. Reynolds; George Mann; Peter Tennant; Susan Marie Groppi; Karen Meisner; John Joseph Adams; Wendy S. Delmater; Jed Hartman; Rich Horton; Mark R. Kelly; Andrew Wilson; Damien Broderick; Gary Turner; Chris Roberson; Ellen Asher; Andy Wheeler; Lou Anders; Cory Doctorow; Patrick Swenson; Bridget McKenna; Marti McKenna; Jay Lake; William Shaffer; Sheila Williams; Brian Bieniowski; Trevor Quachri; Jayme Lynn Blaschke; Alastair Reynolds; Michael Swanwick; Ken MacLeod; Stephen Baxter; Pat Cadigan; Kristine Kathryn Rusch; Nancy Kress; Kage Baker; Greg Egan; John Barnes; Una McCormack; Ted Kosmatka; Eileen Gunn; Paolo Bacigalupi; Elizabeth Bear; Jack Skillingstead; Keith Brooke; Paul McAuley; Robert Reed; Justin Stanchfield; James Van Pelt; Vandana Singh; Kathleen Ann Goonan; Cat Sparks; Andy Robertson; Michael Bishop; Tim Pratt; William Sanders; Lawrence Watt-Evans; Gregory Benford; David Hartwell; Ginjer Buchanan; Susan Allison; Shawna McCarthy; Kelly Link; Gavin Grant; John Klima; John O'Neill; Rodger Turner; Stuart Mayne; John Kenny; Edmund Schubert; Tehani Wessely; Tehani Croft; Karl Johanson; Sally Beasley; Jason Sizemore; Sue Miller; David Lee Summers; Christopher M. Cevasco; Tyree Campbell; Andrew Hook; Vaughne Lee Hansen; Mark Watson; Sarah Lumnah; and special thanks to my own editor, Marc Resnick.

Thanks are also due to Charles N. Brown, whose magazine *Locus* (Locus Publications, P.O. Box 13305, Oakland, CA 94661, $60 in the United States for a one-year subscription [twelve issues] via second class; credit card orders [510] 339 9198), was used as an invaluable reference source throughout the Summation. Locus Online (www.locusmag.com), edited by Mark R. Kelly, has also become a key reference source.

There were some gains and some losses for the genre in 2007, but overall no major disasters—all the major science fiction book lines are still in place, and we even got through the year without (as yet) losing any major SF magazines, in spite of continued troubles in the magazine market. There were big booms in the numbers of paranormal romances and magna hitting the bookstore shelves, but even discounting those, it was still a record year for the number of science fiction books published (see the novel section, below). And off on the horizon, the looming thunderheads of possible fundamental changes in the publishing industry itself, which have been threatening a downpour for years now, grew a little bigger and rumbled a bit.

Fallout from the bankruptcy of distributor American Marketing Services—the largest book distributor in the U.S., which went into Chapter 11 last year, taking Publishers Group West down with it—caused Publishers Group West to be sold to Perseus Book Group, which also acquired the Avalon Publishing Group, publishers of Carroll & Graf and Thunder's Mouth Press, frequent publishers of SF/fantasy titles, both of which were phased out of existence in 2007. Taken down by the AMS bankruptcy, ibooks has yet to reappear, and many books affected by the bankruptcy of Byron Preiss Visual Publications, following the sudden death of publisher Byron Preiss in 2005, are still in legal limbo. Small-press publisher Meisha Merlin died. Houghton Mifflin was acquired by Education Media Publishing Group, which also picked up Harcourt and Greenwood Press; it's uncertain as yet what effect this will have on Harcourt and Houghton Mifflin's trade imprint lines. Canadian publisher Dragon Moon Press merged with Hades Publication's two imprints, Tesseracts Books and EDGE Science Fiction and Fantasy Publications, with results as yet uncertain, although they could just as well be positive as negative. German media conglomerate Bertelsmann bought BookSpan, publisher of numerous book clubs, including the Science Fiction Book Club, and in the shake-ups that followed, longtime SF Book Club editor Ellen Asher was forced into retirement and Andy Wheeler was fired outright. The newly appointed editor is Rome Quezada. Company spokesmen have stated that there are no immediate plans to do away with the Science Fiction Book Club, but the shake-up delayed the publishing of some scheduled titles, and not all genre insiders are sure that Bertelsmann is to be believed. Let's hope that the Science Fiction Book Club does continue, since it performs several valuable functions for the field.

On the uphill side, Hachette Book Group USA launched a major new imprint called Orbit USA in 2007, which intends to produce forty titles per year in hardcover and paperback, and BL Publishing's new line Solaris, which completed its second year, has already established itself as a major presence in the genre market. Other UK lines moving into the U.S. are Titan Books, Abaddon Books, children's publisher Egmont (which plans to launch a new line in the U.S. in 2008), and fantastic erotica line Black Lace. Wildside Publishing moved away from Print-On-Demand publishing with twelve mass-market titles published under the Dorchester/Cosmos imprint and with their Juno line of paranormal romances. And Paizo Publishing introduced an imprint of classic SF reprints, Planet Stories.

For more than a decade now, cyber-prophets have been predicting that eventually the whole structure of modern publishing will be swept away by the internet revolution, with electronic books in various forms replacing print ones, and either Print-On-Demand systems in the home or online distribution over the internet replacing the current network of brick-and-mortar bookstores and the physical delivery of product by trucks. This particular millennium has not yet come to pass, and as time goes by, many commentators have become almost contemptuously skeptical that it ever will. But although the changes effected by them have not yet become sweeping, new technologies such as Print-On-Demand books, downloadable e-books, and books made available for purchase on websites online have, slowly, incrementally, had an effect on the publishing world. With the advent of even newer technologies such as Amazon's e-book reader, Kindle—and the future generations of hand-held text-readers that are no doubt marching along behind it—this hopeful cyber-future may have inched a bit closer to existence, especially as there are now whole generations of people who are accustomed to getting media entertainment of various sorts from small hand-held devices. At the beginning of 2008, Amazon bought online audio book seller Audible Inc., in what some people think may be part of a bid to become the iTunes of books.

It's worth remembering that a decade ago many commentators sneered at the idea of online booksellers like Amazon, saying that they either wouldn't last for long or that they'd always remain something that appealed to only a small niche audience, and now everyone takes their existence for granted. (I buy most of my books online now, as do most people that I know, and I think that will become true of even larger populations in the future—although I doubt that brick-and-mortar bookstores will ever completely disappear.)

Who knows what the publishing world will look like twenty years from now—or even ten?

The good news about the troubled magazine market this year was that things could have been worse. The precipitous drops in circulation that have plagued most print magazines in the last few years have at least slowed, if not stopped altogether, and there are signs that a moderately stable plateau may have been reached. None of the major magazines died, and all of them brought out their scheduled number of issues. With such crumbs of comfort, we'll have to content ourselves.

This year's big postage hike and the Post Office's revamping of their entire rate scheme, eliminating many of the cheaper shipping options, were bad news for the entire print magazine industry, far beyond genre boundaries. As postal rates and production costs continue to rise (you don't really think they'll ever go *down*, do you?), many of these magazines may be driven out of the print world into online-only distribution—*if* they can figure out a way to make money that way.

Asimov's Science Fiction registered a 5.2% loss in overall circulation in 2007, encouraging when compared with the 13.6% loss in 2006 or the 23% loss of 2005, with subscriptions dropping from 15,117 to 14,084, but newsstand sales actually rising slightly from 3,419 to 3,497; sell-through rose from 29% to 30%. *Asimov's* published good stories this year by Greg Egan, Tom Purdom, Neal Asher, Ted Kosmatka, Mary Rosenblum, Chris Roberson, Kristine Kathryn Rusch, Elizabeth Bear, Michael Swanwick, Nancy Kress, and others. Sheila Williams completed her third year as *Asimov's* editor. *Analog Science Fiction & Fact* registered a 3.2% loss in overall circulation, compared to a 7.3% loss in 2006 and an 8.2% loss in 2005, with subscriptions dropping from 23,732 to 22,972, while newsstand sales dropped from 4,587 to 4,427; sell-through, however, rose from 32% to 34%. *Analog* published good work this year by Michael F. Flynn, C.W. Johnson, Richard A. Lovett, Brian Plante, Robert R. Chase, Sarah K. Castle, Ekaterina Sedia, and others. Stanley Schmidt has been editor there for twenty-eight years. *The Magazine of Fantasy & Science Fiction* registered a 11.2% loss in overall circulation after a couple of years of near stability, with subscriptions dropping from 14,575 to 12,831, and newsstand sales declining slightly from 3,691 to 3,658; sell-through rose from 27% to 33%. *F&SF* published good work this year by David Moles, Bruce Sterling, Gene Wolfe, Ted Chiang, Benjamin Rosenbaum and David Ackert, Ian R. MacLeod, Gwyneth Jones, Alex Irvine, Alexander Jablokov, and others. Gordon Van Gelder is in his eleventh year as editor, and seventh year as owner and publisher. Circulation figures for *Realms of Fantasy* lag a year behind the other magazines, but their 2006 figures show them registering a 2.5% loss in overall circulation as opposed to 13% in 2005, with subscriptions rising from 16,547 to 17,642 (making them the only magazine whose subscriptions are actually going *up*), but newsstand sales dropping sharply from 6,584 to 4,902; sell-through also declined, from 29% to 24%. *Realms of Fantasy*, published good stuff this year by Theodora Goss, Jack Skillingstead, Christopher Barzak, Jay Lake and Ruth Nestvold, and others. Shawna McCarthy has been editor of the magazine since its launch in 1994.

Interzone doesn't really qualify as a "professional magazine" by SFWA's definition because of its low rates and circulation—in the 2,000 to 3,000 copy range—but it's thoroughly professional in the caliber of writers that it attracts and in the quality of the fiction it produces, so we're going to list it with the other professional magazines anyway. On the brink of death only a couple of years back, *Interzone* has been making a strong recovery under new publisher Andy Cox, who has also transformed it into the handsomest SF magazine in the business, with striking glossy covers. In 2007, *Interzone* published good stories by Alastair Reynolds, Elizabeth Bear, Chris Roberson, Jamie Lynn Blaschke, Aliette de Boddard, Steven Francis Murphy, Benjamin Rosenbaum, and others. The ever-shifting editorial staff includes Jetse de Vries, Andrew Hedgecock, David Mathew, Liz Williams, and Sandy Auden. *Interzone's* publisher also revamped their horror magazine *The Third Alternative* as *Black Static*, and, after a gap of a couple of years, relaunched it as *Interzone's* sister magazine in 2007—to me, *Black Static* reads almost exactly the same as *The Third Alternative* did, so I'm not sure I understand why they bothered, but at least they've now got a snappy new title.

If you'd like to see these magazines survive, and continue to contribute to a healthy short-fiction market, *subscribe* to them! It's never been easier to subscribe to most of the genre magazines, since you can now do it electronically online with the click of a few buttons, without even a trip to the mailbox. In the internet age, you can also subscribe from overseas just as easily as you can from the United States, something formerly difficult-to-impossible. Furthermore, internet sites such as *Fictionwise* (www.fictionwise.com), magaz!nes.com (www.magazines.com), and even Amazon.com sell subscriptions online, as well as electronic downloadable versions of many of the magazines to be read on your PDA or home computer, something becoming increasingly popular with the computer-savvy set. And, of course, you can still subscribe the old-fashioned way, by mail.

So I'm going to list both the internet sites where you can subscribe online and the street addresses where you can subscribe by mail for each magazine: **Asimov's** site is at www.asimovs.com; its subscription address is **Asimov's Science Fiction**, Dell Magazines, 6 Prowitt Street, Norwalk, CT 06855–$55.90 for annual subscription in U.S. **Analog's** site is at www.analogsf.com; its subscription address is **Analog Science Fiction and Fact**, Dell Magazines, 6

Prowitt Street, Norwalk, CT 06855–$55.90 for annual subscription in U.S. *The Magazine of Fantasy & Science Fiction*'s site is at www.sfsite.com/fsf; its subscription address is *The Magazine of Fantasy & Science Fiction*, Spilogale, Inc., P.O. Box 3447, Hoboken, NJ 07030, annual subscription— $50.99 in U.S. *Interzone* and **Black Static** can be subscribed to online at www.ttapress.com/onlinestore1.html; the subscription address for both is TTA Press, 5 Martins Lane, Witcham, Ely, Cambs CB6 2LB, England, UK, £21 each for a six-issue subscription, or there is a reduced rate dual subscription offer of £40 for both magazines for six-issues; make checks payable to "TTA Press". **Realms of Fantasy**'s site is at (www.rofmagazine.com); its subscription address is **Realms of Fantasy**, Sovereign Media Co. Inc., P.O. Box 1623, Williamsport, PA 17703, $16.95 for an annual subscription in the U.S.

Dealing with the same pressures that the professional magazines do, rising postage rates and production costs, I suspect that most of the semiprozines, especially the fiction semiprozines, are going to eventually be driven either out of business or out of the print world and into online-only production as well. Already, two of the most prominent new fiction semiprozines, *Subterranean* and *Fantasy Magazine*, have transitioned from print to electronic formats, each publishing a couple of final print issues (one of *Subterranean*'s guest-edited by Ellen Datlow) this year before seeking refuge online (I'll discuss them more in the online section, below). After more than two years of complete silence, I'm going to consider *Argosy Magazine* to be dead, and will no longer list a subscription address for it unless I hear something to the contrary. Warren Lapine's DNA Publications empire—consisting of *Absolute Magnitude*, *The Magazine of Science Fiction Adventures*, *Dreams of Decadence*, *Fantastic Stories of the Imagination*, *Weird Tales*, *Mythic Delirium*, and the newszine *Chronicle*—has completely died, and I won't be listing subscription addresses for any of them any more, although *Weird Tales* survives in a new incarnation under a different publisher. In the last couple of years, *Artemis Magazine: Science and Fiction for a Space-Faring Society*, *Century*, *Orb*, *Altair*, *Terra Incognita*, *Eidolon*, *Spectrum SF*, *All Possible Worlds*, *Farthing*, and *Yog's Notebook* have also died, and although it's theoretically still alive, I didn't see an issue of the long-running *Space and Time* this year. I also didn't see an issue of *Say . . .*, for the second year in a row, or *Full Unit Hookup*.

Of the surviving print fiction semiprozines, the most prominent and professional seems to me to be the British magazine *Postscripts*, edited by Peter Crowther and Nick Gevers, which had strong fiction this year by Richard Paul Russo, Paul Di Filippo, Marly Youmans, Stephen King, Lisa Tuttle, and others—although I could wish that they'd use more actual science fiction and less slipstream/fantasy/horror, which seems to be the default setting for most fiction semiprozines and almost all internet electronic magazines. The Canadian *On Spec*, run by a collective under general editor Diane L. Walton, one of the longest-running of them all, published its four scheduled quarterly issues in 2007, as it has been doing reliably for years; unfortunately, I don't generally find their fiction to be terribly interesting, something that can also be said for another collective-run magazine, one with a rotating editorial staff, Australia's *Andromeda Spaceways Inflight Magazine* (perhaps no one editor stays in the chair long enough to have a chance to establish a distinct editorial personality for the magazine), which published five issues this year. Long-running Australian magazine *Aurealis*, which was feared to be dead, came back after a two-year hiatus under new editors Stuart Mayne and Stephen Higgins, publishing two issues, one of which arrived here late enough that it'll have to be considered for next year. *Talebones*, an SF/horror zine edited by Patrick Swenson, also nearly died last year, but survived due to an impassioned subscription drive to publish two issues this year. *Paradox*, edited by Christopher M. Cevasco, an "Alternate History" magazine which is one of the few magazines discussed in this section that gets newsstand distribution in chain book-stores such as *Borders* or *Barnes & Noble* (where it's usually displayed with the Civil War buff magazines), only managed one issue this year. *Apex Science Fiction and Horror Digest*, in it's third year, edited by Jason Sizemore, published its four scheduled issues, and is also pretty reliable. *Neo-opsis*, another Canadian magazine, edited by Karl Johanson, managed three out of four scheduled issues in 2007, as it had in 2006; this little magazine has some really nice covers, and won an Aurora Award. *Jupiter*, a small British magazine edited by Ian Redman, perhaps the most amateuristic-looking of the fiction semiprozines as far as production values are concerned, had an indeterminate number of issues out (nobody seems quite sure, but I saw at least two). *Shimmer* did a special all-pirate issue, guest-edited by John Joseph Adams. There were two issues of the Irish fiction semiprozine *Albedo One* this year, one of *Tales of the Unanticipated*, one of *New Genre*, one of *Fictitious Force*, two issues of Sword&Sorcery magazine *Black Gate*, and three apiece of glossy fantasy magazines *Zahir*, *Tales of the Talisman*, and *Aoife's Kiss*.

The venerable *Weird Tales*, coming up on its 85th anniversary, managed to survive the Great Extinction over at DNA Publications, being bought in 2006 by Wildside Press. This year, the magazine underwent a sweeping reorganization, with Ann VanderMeer coming in as the new fiction editor. The slogan of the new *Weird Tales* is not "This is not your father's *Weird Tales*," but maybe it should be, as the aim of the magazine seems to become noticeably hipper, cooler, and more *au courant* than its somewhat stodgy previous incarnation. Whether this will go over with the audience or not remains to be seen, but there was good stuff in the magazine this year by Ian Creasey, Richard Parks, Jay Lake, and others. Wildside also publishes the newish *H.P. Lovecraft's Magazine of Horror*, edited by Marvin Kaye—of which there was one issue this year, and which so far doesn't seem much different in flavor from *Weird Tales*—and was the publisher of *Fantasy Magazine* before it transitioned into an electronic online incarnation.

Below this point in the print market, you'll find little core science fiction, and even little genre fantasy, but lots of slipstream/fabulist/New Weird/postmodern stuff, much of it of high literary quality. The model and still the flagship for this sort of magazine is *Lady Churchill's Rosebud Wristlet*, edited by Kelly Link and Gavin Grant, which published two issues this year, plus a "Best of" anthology drawn from past issues, but there's a number of other ones out there, very small-circulation magazines that *Locus* editor Charles N. Brown once referred to as the "minuscule press," including *Electric Velocipede*, edited by John Kilma, which published two issues this year, as did *Flytrap*, edited by Tim Pratt and Heather Shaw.

After a fifty-two-year hiatus, almost certainly the longest one in history, the old pulp magazine *Thrilling Wonder Stories* came back to life, edited by Winston Engle, reinvented as a "bookzine," a magazine in book form, like an anthology, with an ISBN number. The one issue they've managed so far was mostly filled with reprints from the old *Thrilling Wonder Stories*, although there were originals by Eric Brown, Michael Kandel, and R. Neube, and a reprint of more recent vintage from Geoffrey A. Landis.

With the disappearance of *Chronicle*, there's not much left of the critical magazine market except for a few sturdy, long-running stalwarts. As always, your best bet is *Locus: The Magazine of the Science Fiction and Fantasy Field*, a multiple Hugo-winner edited by Charles N. Brown and, an indispensable source of information, news, and reviews that has been perhaps the most valuable critical magazine in the field for over thirty years now. Another interesting and worthwhile magazine, publishing a variety of eclectic and sometimes quirky critical essays on a wide range of topics, is *The New York Review of Science Fiction*, edited by David G. Hartwell and a staff of associate editors. Most other critical magazines in the field are professional journals more aimed at academics than at the average reader, but the most accessible of these is probably the long-running British critical zine *Foundation*, which recently celebrated it's hundredth issue with a special fiction issue that functioned as an original anthology.

Subscription addresses follow:

Postscripts, PS Publishing, Hamilton House, 4 Park Avenue, Harrogate HG2 9BQ, England, UK, published quarterly, 30 to 50 pounds sterling outside the UK (*Postscripts* can also be subscribed to online at www .pspublishing.com.uk/postscripts.asp.); *Locus, The Magazine of the Science Fiction & Fantasy Field*, Locus Publications, Inc., P.O. Box 13305, Oakland, California 94661, $66.00 for a one-year first class subscription, twelve issues; *The New York Review Of Science Fiction*, Dragon Press, P.O.

Box 78, Pleasantville, NY, 10570, $40.00 per year, twelve issues, make checks payable to Dragon Press; *Foundation*, Science Fiction Foundation, Roger Robinson (SFF), 75 Rosslyn Avenue, Harold Wood, Essex RM3 ORG, UK, $37.00 for a three-issue subscription in the U.S.A; *Talebones, A Magazine of Science Fiction & Dark Fantasy*, 21528 104ᵗʰ St. Ct. East, Bonney Lake, WA 98390, $24.00 for four issues; *Aurealis*, Chimaera Publications, P.O. Box 2149, Mt. Waverley, VIC 3149, Australia (website: www .aurealis.com.au), $50 for a four-issue overseas airmail subscription, checks should be made out to Chimaera Publications in Australian Dollars; *On Spec, The Canadian Magazine of the Fantastic*, P.O. Box 4727, Edmonton, AB, Canada T6E 5G6, $22.00 for a one-year (four issue) subscription; *Neo-Opsis Science Fiction Magazine*, 4129 Carey Rd., Victoria, BC, V8Z 4G5, $28.00 Canadian for a four issue subscription; *Albedo One*, Albedo One Productions, 2 Post Road, Lusk, Co., Dublin, Ireland; $32.00 for a four-issue airmail subscription, make checks payable to Albedo One; *Tales of the Unanticipated*, P.O Box 8036, Lake Street Station, Minneapolis, MN 55408, $28.00 for a four-issue subscription (three or four year's worth) in the U.S.A, $31.00 in Canada, $34.00 overseas; *Lady Churchill's Rosebud Wristlet*, Small Beer Press, 150 Pleasant St., #306, Easthampton, MA 01027, $20.00 for four issues; *Flytrap*, Tropism Press, 1034 McKinley Ave., Oakland, CA 94610, $20.00 for four issues, checks to Heather Shaw; *Electric Velocipede*, Spilt Milk Press, P.O. Box 663, Franklin Park, NJ 08823, www.electricvelocipede.com, $15.00 for a four-issue subscription; *Andromeda Spaceways Inflight Magazine*, P.O. Box 127, Belmont, Western Australia, 6984, www.andromedaspaceways.com, $35.00 for a one-year subscription; Zahir, Zahir Publishing, 315 South Coast Hwy., 101, Suite U8, Encinitas, CA 92024, $18.00 for a one-year subscription, subscriptions can also be bought with credit cards and PayPal at www.zahirtales.com; *Tales of the Talisman*, LBF Books, 1515 Blossom Hill Road, Pittsburgh, PA 15234, $24.00 for a four-issue subscription; *Aoife's Kiss*, Sam's Dot Publishing, P.O. Box 782, Cedar Rapids, Iowa 52406-0782, $18.00 for a four-issue subscription; *Black Gate*, New Epoch Press, 815 Oak Street, St. Charles, IL 60174, $29.95 for a one-year (four issue) subscription; *Paradox*, Paradox Publications, P.O. Box 22897, Brooklyn, New York 11202-2897, $25.00 for a one year (four-issue) subscription, checks or U.S. postal money orders should be made payable to *Paradox*, can also be ordered online at www.paradoxmag .com; *Weird Tales*, Wildside Press, 9710 Traville Gateway Drive, #234, Rockville, MD 20850-7408, annual subscription (four issues) $24.00 in the U.S.A.; *H.P. Lovecraft's Magazine of Horror*, Wildside Press, 9710 Traville Gateway Drive, #234, Rockville, MD 20850, annual subscription (four issues) $19.95 in the U.S.A.; *Fictitious Force*, Jonathan Laden, 1024 Hollywood Avenue, Silver Spring, MD 20904, $16.00 for four issues; *Apex Science*

Fiction and Horror Digest, Apex Publications, P.O. Box 2223, Lexington, KY 40588-2223, $20.00 for a one year, four-issue subscription; *Jupiter*, 19 Bedford Road, Yeovil, Somerset, BA21 5UG, UK, 10 Pounds Sterling for four issues; *New Genre*, P.O. Box 270092, West Hartford, CT 06127, couldn't find any specific subscription information in the magazine itself, but check www.new-genre.com for details; *Shimmer*, P.O. Box 58591, Salt Lake City, UT 84158-0591, $22.00 for a four-issue subscription; **Thrilling Wonder Stories**, it's unclear whether subsciptions are available or not, but more information can be found at www.thrillingwonderstories.com.

The online electronic "magazine" market has become increasingly important over the last few years, and, truth be told, I think it's probably a more likely place to find good SF at the moment than the print fiction semi-prozine market covered above. And if the rumors circulating about the imminent launch of a high-paying new professional-level ezine in 2008 prove to be true, the e–zine market will become even more important.

As I've already said, I expect that many of the surviving print magazines are eventually either going to die or covert to pixels–there's many advantages to doing that, including the elimination of ever-rising postal costs, the elimi-nation of production costs (no printing needed!), and the elimination of the need for expensive overhead, like rent for office space in actual physical buildings somewhere (many if not most of these e-zines are probably run out of somebody's home, in as much as they can be said to have a physical "loca-tion" at all), paper, stationary, and office supplies. Not that going to an all-electronic format is a certain formula for success, though, as has been proved by the death of such e-zines as *Omni Online, Tomorrow SF, SCI FIC-TION, Oceans of the Mind, The Infinite Matrix*, and others—this year alone, e-zines such as *Darker Matter, Fortean Bureau—A Magazine of Spec-ulative Fiction, Space Suits and Sixguns*, and *Sentinel SF* died, a few of them coming and going with startling rapidity, repeating a pattern that's been familiar in the print fiction semiprozine market for many years.

The problem that has haunted the online market from the very begin-ning, though, is: How do you make money publishing fiction online in elec-tronic formats?

Even with the considerable advantages of online publication, no postage or printing costs, you're still going to need *some* money to keep a publication going—if nothing else (in most cases, anyway, except in real labors of love), you're going to need money with which to pay the authors. And even though there aren't many production costs involved in running an online magazine as opposed to a print magazine, there are still a few, such as getting staff to read and select and edit the stories, people to do data-entry and physically maintain the website, and so on, so you need money to pay them, too. Many e-zines have been depending on unpaid volunteer labor to get by, including unpaid volunteer editors, performing that labor of love mentioned above—but eventually, volunteers get worn-out, burn out, and move on. Sooner or later, unless you're willing to support the whole thing out of your own pocket at a loss, as some semiprozine editors have done for years, you're going to need to make some money.

But how?

The "everything's free" philosophy that permeated the internet from the beginning makes it difficult to get people to pay for the privilege of reading stuff online, especially since (if you don't care about quality) there's ocean full of amateur fiction available everywhere for free. The two major strategies that have evolved to try to deal with this situation are to sell "subscriptions"—access to the fiction, basically—in one form or another, or to give the fiction away for free and encourage the people passing through your site to give you money anyway, if they've enjoyed the experience of reading it. This last strategy, soliciting voluntary contributions in a manner similar to the pledge drives or "begathons" mounted by public television stations, seems to have been working pretty well for *Strange Horizons* for a number of years now, but it didn't work for *The Infinite Matrix*, and I suspect that *Helix* and a few others may be on shaky ground with it as well. As for the subscription model, the big test of it is underway right now with *Jim Baen's Universe* and *Orson Scott Card's Intergalactic Medicine Show*, but the jury is still out on it—although sites such as *Fictionwise* have been selling access to stories online in a similar manner for years now, and are still in business, so there may be a glimmer of hope. (The "web-advertising" model, which was more-or-less discredited a few years back, may be becoming more viable as the century progresses, and selling web-advertisements could be another possible source of money for free-access "pledge drive" magazines.) *Subterranean*, which gives its fiction away for free, is using the magazine as a loss-leader for its parent book line, Subterranean Press, hoping that people who like stories in the magazine will then go over to the publishers website and order books by them as well. This is a factor with *Jim Baen's Universe* as well, in addition to the subscription sales of the magazine; it's clearly hoped that the publicity generated by the magazine will translate to increased online sales of Baen books on their website. Whether this will work or not, nobody knows for sure either, although I suspect that it will, to some extent anyway—whether the increase in book sales will be big enough to balance out the costs of producing the e-zine or not is yet to be seen.

It's still a brave new world out there, with nobody knowing for sure what's going to work and what isn't, and all you can really say for sure is that it's all going to look completely different ten years from now than it does today.

As far as literary quality is concerned, the above-mentioned *Jim Baen's*

Universe (www.baensuniverse.com), edited by Mike Resnick and Eric Flint, has in only two years established itself as the powerhouse among e-zines, probably the best place to look online for professional level SF and fantasy, and one of the few places anywhere on the internet to offer some actual hard science fiction along with the other stuff. This year, *Jim Baen's Universe* published good stuff by John Barnes, Nancy Kress, Elizabeth Bear, Garth Nix, Kristine Kathryn Rusch, Carrie Vaughn, Eric Witchery, and others; I hope that their subscription model is working, because I'd like to see them hang around for many years to come. *Orson Scott Card's Intergalactic Medicine Show* (www.intergalacticmedicineshow.com), edited by Edmund R. Schubert under the direction of Card himself, hasn't managed to establish itself quite as impressively in the same two-year period, but it did improve markedly over the last year, and published good stories in 2007 by Peter S. Beagle, Peter Friend, William John Watkins, Justin Stanchfield, Orson Scott Card himself, and others.

The granddaddy of the e-zines, one of the longest-established fiction sites on the internet, is *Strange Horizons* (www.strangehorizons.com), edited by Susan Marie Groppi, assisted by Jed Hartman and Karen Meisner, which puts up a free story every week; good stories by Theodora Goss, Liz Williams, Lavie Tidhar, Tim Pratt, Kate Bachus, and others appeared there this year. *Aeon* (www.aeonmagazine.com), edited by Marti McKenna and Bridget McKenna, which is available for download as PDFs through subscription rather than being directly accessible online, published only three of their scheduled four issues this year, one of them an all-reprint issue, but they must be doing okay financially, since they just announced a rise in the rates they pay their authors, which would bring them above the SFWA cutoff for a professional market; good stuff by Jay Lake, David D. Levine, Katharine Sparrow, Melissa Tyler, and others appeared there this year, although as with *Postscripts* (the two seem similar to each other to me in some ways, although one is pixel and one print), I could wish that they'd print more core science fiction and less slipstream/postmodernism/fantasy. *Abyss and Apex: A Magazine of Speculative Fiction* (www.abyssandapex.com), edited by Wendy S. Delmater in conjunction with fiction editors Rob Campbell and Ilona Gordon, affords free access to fantasy and science fiction stories, including strong work this year by Tony Pi, Joseph Paul Haines, and others.

Two brand-new e-zines, just transitioning in from their former incarnations as print magazines, *Subterranean* and *Fantasy* (formerly *Fantasy Magazine*), have already shouldered their way into the ranks of the most prominent fiction e-zines on the internet. *Subterranean*, edited by William K. Schafer (http://subterraneanpress.com), in particular has quickly established itself as perhaps the best place on the internet to find stylishly-written horror—but it also publishes fantasy and science fiction as well. There were good stories at

Subterranean this year from Bruce Sterling, Lucius Shepard, Caitlin R. Kiernan, Chris Roberson, Jim Grimsley, Jay Lake, John Scalzi, Joe Lansdale, and others. *Fantasy*, edited by Sean Wallace and Cat Rambo, which concentrates more on fantasy than horror, although there's an occasional scary piece, produced good work by Bruce McAllister, Andrea Kail, Lucy Kemnitzer, Richard Parks, and others. Stylishly written and usually faintly perverse fantasy is also available at *Clarkesworld Magazine* (www.clarkesworldmagazine .com), edited by Nick Mamatas, which this year published strong stories by Caitlin R. Kiernan, Elizabeth Bear, Jay Lake, Jeff VanderMeer, Ken Scholes, Jetse de Vries, Cat Rambo, and others. In addition to the stories they publish monthly in the print version of Australian science magazine *Cosmos*, there are now good science fiction stories available as unique content on the *Cosmos* website (www.cosmosmagazine.com), all selected by fiction editor Damien Broderick including a story by Mary Robinette Kowal that made this year's preliminary Nebula ballot, as well as strong work by Steven Dedman, Bruce Carlson, David Taub, and others, and even the serialization of a novel by Damien Broderick and Barbara Lamar. *New Ceres* (www.newceres.com), edited by Alisa Krasnostein, is sort of a shared-world anthology online, which has featured contributions by Stephan Dedman, Jay Lake, Lucy Sussex, Cat Sparks, and others.

Two newish e-zines that feature work that is supposedly too controversial, too eccentric, or just plain too weird for the commercial print markets, *Helix* and *Flurb*, completed their second years of operation in 2007. The stuff in *Helix* (www.helixsf.com), edited by William Sanders and Lawrence Watt-Evans, may or may not be too controversial for regular markets, but some of it was pretty good; and *Helix* had another strong year, publishing good work by Robert Reed, John Barnes, Jennifer Pellard, Sarah H. Castle, Samantha Henderson, Brenda Clough, and others. (If you like it, put your hand in your pocket, since this is one of those e-zines that depends on consumer donations to survive.) Rudy Rucker's *Flurb* (www.flurb.net), wasn't as strong this year as last, when it published one of the year's best stories, but it had quirky stuff by Kathleen Ann Goonan, Marc Laidlaw, Paul Di Fillipo, and others.

A new website dedicated to YA fantasy and SF, *Shiny* (http://shinymag .blogspot.com), was launched this year.

Below this point, science fiction and even genre fantasy becomes harder to find, although there are a raft of e-zines, exactly the equivalent of the print "minuscule press" slipstream magazines such as *Lady Churchill's Rosebud Wristlet*, that publish slipstream/postmodern stories, often ones of good literary quality. They include: *Revolution SF* (www.revolutionsf.com), which also features book and media reviews, *Coyote Wild* (http://coyotewildmag.com); *Ideomancer Speculative Fiction* (www.ideomancer.com); *Futurismic* (http:// futurismic.com/fiction/index.html), *Lone Star Stories* (http://literary.erict

marin.com); *Heliotrope* (www.heliotropemag.com); *Chiaroscura* (http://chizine.com); and the somewhat less slipstreamish *Bewildering Stories* (www.bewilderingstories.com).

However, many good *reprint* SF and fantasy stories can also be found on the internet, usually accessible for free, perhaps in greater numbers than the original ones. The long-running British *Infinity Plus* (www.users.zetnet.co.uk/iplus), was one of the best of such sites, running a wide selection of good quality reprint stories, in addition to biographical and bibliographical information, book reviews, interviews, and critical essays; editor Keith Brooke recently announced that he was stepping down, sad news, but so far *Infinity Plus* and their achieve of quality reprints is still accessible on the net. *Strange Horizons*; and most of the sites that are associated with existent print magazines, such as *Asimov's*, *Analog*, and *The Magazine of Fantasy & Science Fiction*, which have extensive archives of material, both fiction and nonfiction, previously published by the print versions of the magazines, and which regularly run teaser excerpts from stories coming up in forthcoming issues. The Sci-Fi Channel recently took down *SCI FICTION's* extensive archive of reprints, which I think was rather mean-spirited of them, but even though *The Infinite Matrix* (www.infinitematrix.net) is ostensibly dead (although a strong new novella by Cory Doctorow appeared there this year), the last time I checked, its substantial archives of past material were still available to be accessed. A large selection of novels and a few collections can also be accessed for free, to be either downloaded or read on-screen, at the *Baen Free Library* (www.baen.com/library). Hundreds of out-of-print titles, both genre and mainstream, are also available for free download from *Project Gutenberg* (http://promo.net/pc/).

An even greater range of reprint stories becomes available, though, if you're willing to pay a small fee for them. The best, and the longest-established, such site is *Fictionwise* (www.fictionwise.com), where you can buy downloadable e-books and stories to read on your PDA or home computer, in addition to individual stories, you can also buy "fiction bundles" here, which amount to electronic collections; as well as a selection of novels in several different genres, and you can also subscribe to downloadable versions of several of the SF magazines here, including *Asimov's*, *Analog*, *F&SF*, and *Interzone*, in a number of different formats. A similar site is *ElectricStory* (www.electricstory.com); in addition to the downloadable stuff for sale here (both stories and novels), you can also access free movie reviews by Lucius Shepard, articles by Howard Waldrop, and other critical material. *Mind's Eye Fiction* seems to have gone out of business, and *Alexandria Digital Literature* (http://alexlit.com) is reconstructing its web site, which it plans to relaunch in 2008 sometime.

In addition to fiction-oriented sites, though, there are also many general

genre-related sites of interest to be found on the internet, most of which publish reviews both of books and movies and TV shows, some of which feature
as well interviews, critical articles, and genre-oriented news of various kinds.
The most valuable genre-oriented general site on the entire internet, is
Locus Online (www.locusmag.com), the online version of the newsmagazine *Locus*, an indispensable site where you can access an incredible
amount of information–including book reviews, critical lists, obituary lists,
links to reviews and essays appearing outside the genre, and links to extensive
data-base archives such as the Locus Index to Science Fiction and the Locus
Index to Science Fiction Awards—and which is also often the first place in
the genre to find fast-breaking news. Other essential sites include: *Science
Fiction Weekly* (www.scifi.com/sfw), which publishes more media-oriented
stuff than *Locus Online*, but which still features news and book reviews, as
well as regular columns by John Clute, Michael Cassut, and Wil McCarthy;
SF Site (www.sfsite.com), which features reviews of books, games, movies,
TV shows, and magazines, plus a huge archive of past reviews, and *Best SF*
(www.bestsf.net/), which boasts another great archive of reviews, and which
is one of the few places that makes any attempt to regularly review short fiction venues. A similar site, also oriented to short-fiction reviews, was *Tangent
Online* (www.tangentonline.com), which closed down due to internal difficulties toward the end of 2007, but which promises to return. A new short-
fiction review site *The Fix* (http://thefix-online.com), launched by a former
Tangent Online staffer, started up just about the same time that *Tangent* was
shutting down, and so far is going strong. Other worthwhile general sites
include *SFRevu* (www.sfsite.com/sfrevu), where you'll find lots of novel and
media reviews, as well as interviews and general news; SFF NET (www.sff
.net) which features dozens of home pages and "newsgroups" for SF writers;
the *Science Fiction Writers of America* page (www.sfwa.org); where genre
news, obituaries, award information, and recommended reading lists can be
accessed; *The Internet Review of Science Fiction* (www.irosf.com), which
features both short fiction reviews and novel reviews, as well as critical articles, *Green Man Review* (http://greenmanreview.com), another valuable
review site; *The Agony Column* (http://trashotron.com/agony), media and
book reviews and interviews; *SFFWorld* (www.sffworld.com), more literary
and media reviews; *SFReader* (http://sfreader.com), which features reviews
of SF books, and *SFWatcher* (www.sfwatcher.com), which features reviews
of SF movies; newcomer *SFScope* (www.sfscope.com), edited by former
Chronicle news editor Ian Randal Strock, which concentrates on SF and
writing business news; *Lost Pages* (http://lostpagesindex.html), which features some fiction as well as the critical stuff; *SciFiPedia* (scifipedia.scifi.com),
a wiki-style genre-oriented online encyclopedia; and *Speculations* (www
.speculations.com) a long-running site which dispenses writing advice, and

writing-oriented news and gossip (although to access most of it, you'll have to subscribe to the site). Multiple Hugo-winner David Langford's online version of his funny and iconoclastic fanzine *Ansible*, one of the most enjoyable and entertaining SF sites on the internet, is available at www.dcs.gla.ac.uk/Ansible, and SF-oriented radio plays and podcasts can also be accessed at *Audible* (www.audible.com) and *Beyond 2000* (www.beyond2000.com).

The big story in the original anthology market this year was the launch of several new annual original anthology series, which, if they can manage to establish themselves, will brighten up the genre short fiction scene considerably. All of them were uneven–all featured good stories, all featured mediocre work, and the percentage of actual science fiction in each varied from volume to volume, sometimes considerably. Although none of the debut anthologies in these series clearly dominated the others, on balance I'd have to give a slight edge to *The Solaris Book of New Science Fiction* (Solaris), edited by George Mann; best stories here were by Stephen Baxter and Keith Brooke, although there was also good work by Peter F. Hamilton, Jay Lake and Greg Van Eekhout, Paul Di Fillipo, Neal Asher, Eric Brown, and others; the majority of the stories here were science fiction, which also gave it an edge, in my eyes at least. *Fast Forward 1: Future Fiction from the Cutting Edge* (Pyr), edited by Lou Anders, probably had a higher ratio of good solid competent stories to mediocre ones than *The Solaris Book of New SF*, but fewer of its stories rose noticeably above that level; best work here is by Ian McDonald, but the book also featured good work by Robert Charles Wilson, Elizabeth Bear, John Meaney, Paul Di Filippo, and others, most of which again were SF, although a few stretched the definition a bit. In terms of literary quality, judging the stories just as stories, regardless of genre, the best of the newly-launched anthology series was probably *Eclipse One: New Fantasy and Science Fiction* (Night Shade Books), edited by Jonathan Strahan, but I couldn't help but be disappointed by how little science fiction there was here, most of the stories falling on the fantasy/slipstream/New Weird end of the spectrum instead; considerations of genre aside, *Eclipse One* featured strong work by Andy Duncan, Lucius Shepard, Eileen Gunn, Bruce Sterling, Maureen McHugh, Kathleen Ann Goonan, and others.

Let's hope that one or more, preferably all three, of these anthology series survives.

Alien Crimes (Science Fiction Book Club), edited by Mike Resnick, a book of mystery/SF hybrids, turned out to be one of the most solid SF anthologies of the year, in spite of its unpromising premise; the best work here was by Gregory Benford and Pat Cadigan, although there was also good work by Walter Jon Williams, Kristine Kathryn Rusch, Harry Turtledove, and Resnick himself.

Future Weapons of War (Baen), edited by Joe Haldeman and Martin H. Greenberg, is a bit more substantial than the average Greenberg anthology, featuring good work by Kristine Kathryn Rusch, Paul J. McAuley, Geoffrey A. Landis, Brian Stableford, and others. *Man vs. Machine*, edited by John Helfers and Martin H. Greenberg, also features some solid work. Other pleasant but minor mass-market paperback anthologies this year included *Time Twisters* (DAW), edited by Jean Rabe and Martin H. Greenberg, *The Future We Wish We'd Had* (DAW), by Martin H. Greenberg and Rebecca Lickiss, *Places to Be, People to Kill* (DAW), by Martin H. Greenberg and Britiany Koren, and *Under Cover of Darkness* (DAW), by Julie E. Czerneda and Jane Panccia.

Noted without comment is *The New Space Opera* (Eos), edited by Gardner Dozois and Jonathan Strahan.

Some of the best and most solidly science fiction-oriented anthologies of the year were almost stealth-published, with the likelihood being that few readers came across them, and perhaps were not able to find them even if they went looking for them. Best of these was *disLOCATIONS* (NewCon Press), edited by Ian Whates, and published by a very small press in an edition of only five hundred copies; nevertheless, there were strong to very strong stories here by Ken MacLeod, Brian Stableford, Pat Cadigan, Hal Duncan, and others. Another very small press, Hadley Rille Books, published *three* anthologies this year, all edited by Eric T. Reynolds, the best of which was *Visual Journeys* (Hadley Rille Books), which also doubled as a collection of space art by artists such as Chesley Bonestell and Bob Eggleton, each matched with a story inspired by the artwork; best stories here were by James Van Pelt and Justin Stanchfield, although there was also good work by Jay Lake, Richard Chwedyk, Christopher McKitterick, G. David Nordley and others, almost all center-core science fiction. Also worthwhile was *Ruins Extraterrestrial* (Hadley Rille Books), which featured strong work by Lavie Tidhar, Sue Blalock, Christopher McKitterrick, and others, with the best story being by Justin Stanchfield. The least impressive of the three, by a good margin, and the one that featured the smallest proportion of SF, was *Ruins Terra* (Hadley Rille Books), although there was interesting work here by Jenny Blackford and Lyn McConchie. *Triangulation: End of Time* (PARSEC Ink), edited by Pete Butler, is not as strong as *Visual Journeys* or *Ruins Extraterrestrial*, but does contain good work by Tim Pratt, Ian Creasey, Jeste de Vries, and others.

Although I'm not convinced by its arguments in favor of there being such a thing as "Canadian SF," as distinct from regular SF, *Tesseracts Eleven* (EDGE Science Fiction and Fantasy), edited by Cory Doctorow and Holly Phillips, features good work by Claude Lalumiere, Andrew Gray, Elisabeth Vonarburg, Candas Jane Dorsey, Hugh A.D. Spencer, and others, although, like *Eclipse One*, very little of it is really science fiction by any reasonable definition. Much the same can be said of another enjoyable anthology, *Logorrhea* (Bantam Spectra), edited by John Kilma; although it had one of the most unlikely themes of the year, stories inspired by words which had won a spelling bee, it managed to deliver strong work by Liz Williams, Alex Irvine, Daniel Abraham, Tim Pratt, Theodora Goss, Jay Lake, and others, although you'll find little core science fiction here either and not even much genre fantasy. *Eclipse One* would probably fit in better down here, on the border of SF/fantasy and slipstream, than it does up with the mostly-SF anthologies such as *The Solaris Book of New Science Fiction* and *Fast Forward 1*. *Interfictions: An Anthology of Interstitial Writing* (Interstitial Arts Foundation), edited by Delia Sherman and Theodora Goss, and *Text: UR: The New Book of Masks* (Raw Dog Screaming), edited by Forrest Aguirre, slipped even more into slipstream/literary surrealism, a bit too much for my taste, in fact.

The most political anthology of the year was *Glorifying Terrorism* (Rackstraw Press), edited by Farah Mendlesohn, whose very existence is a rather brave protest (since everyone involved in it is theoretically breaking the law) against Great Britain's vague and silly law forbidding the mention in print of anything that "glorifies terrorism"; unsurprisingly in an anthology so nakedly and passionately didactic, polemics trumps art in most of the stories, although there is good work here by Una McCormack, Lavie Tidhar, Charles Stross, Lucy Kemnitzer, and others. The long-running critical journal *Foundation* celebrated its hundredth issue with a special fiction issue, *Foundation 100: The Anthology* (Science Fiction Foundation), edited by Farah Mendlesohn and Graham Sleight, which functioned as an original anthology; best stories here are by Greg Egan and Una McCormack, although there's also good work by John Kessel, Vandana Singh, David Marusek, and others. Mildly controversial (although in practice it was actually pretty respectful, on average, with a few partial exceptions more playful than really sacrilegious) was *A Cross of Centuries: Twenty-Five Imaginative Tales About the Christ* (Thunder's Mouth Press), a mixed reprint (mostly) and original anthology edited by Michael Bishop.

It was probably a weaker year than last year for novellas published as individual chapbooks, although some good ones still did appear. PS Publishing brought out *Starship Summer*, by Eric Brown; *Illyria*, by Elizabeth Hand; *Template*, by Matt Hughes; *Crystal Cosmos*, by Rhys Hughes; *Hereafter & After*, by Richard Parks; and *City Beyond Play*, by Philip Jose Farmer and Danny Adams. Subterranean Press published *Rude Mechanicals*, by Kage Baker; *Missile Gap*, by Charles Stross; *The Merchant and the Alchemist's Gate*, by Ted Chiang; *Space Boy*, by Orson Scott Card; *The River Horses*, by Allen M. Steele; *The Sagan Diary*, by John Scalzi; *Pilot Light*, by Tim Powers and James P. Blaylock; *The Kragen*, by Jack Vance; *The Voyage of the Proteus*, by Thomas M. Disch; and *All Seated on the Ground*, by Connie Willis. MonkeyBrain

Books issued *Cenotaxis*, by Sean Williams; and *Escape from Hell!*, by Hal Duncan. Aqueduct Press brought out *Of Love and Other Monsters*, by Vandana Singh; *Making Love in Madrid*, by Kimberley Todd Wade; and *We, Robots*, by Sue Lange. Tor published *A War of Gifts*, by Orson Scott Card.

SF stories continued to be found in unlikely places, from the Australian science magazine *Cosmos* to *Cricket*. The *MIT Technology Review* (www .technologyreview.com), of all places, suddenly popped onto the radar this year as a good place to look for strong SF, publishing an excellent story by Greg Egan and good ones by David Marusek and Bruce Sterling.

Even discounting the stories from the specific terrorism-themed anthology, there were a *lot* of stories about terrorism out there this year, I suppose not surprising considering the world we live in. There were a lot of stories featuring huge airships or zeppelins, pirates, and wooden sailing ships that can fly or travel between worlds. Could this be the influence of the *Pirates of the Caribbean* movies? (Would think that movies like *Stardust* and *The Golden Compass*, that also feature airships, came out too late in the year to influence most of its short fiction.) And for whatever reason (I'm not even going to venture a guess), there were a lot of stories about dogs this year too. There was also a substantial amount of Alternate History published in 2007, not only in the Alternate History magazine, *Paradox*, but in most of the other print and electronic magazines as well.

The best fantasy anthology of the year (it also featured some soft horror) was almost certainly *The Coyote Road: Trickster Tales* (Viking), edited by Ellen Datlow and Terry Windling, which featured strong work by Kij Johnson, Pat Murphy, Kelly Link, Jeffrey Ford, Christopher Barzak, and others. Similar in feel but not as strong was a "sampler" from *Fantasy* magazine, *Fantasy* (Prime), edited by Sean Wallace and Paul Tremblay. *The Solaris Book of New Fantasy* (Solaris), edited by George Mann, was announced, but although it looks like it might be quite strong, it came out too late in the year to be considered and will have to be held over for next year. Pleasant but minor original fantasy anthologies this year included *Wizards, Inc.* (DAW), edited by Martin H. Greenberg and Loren L. Coleman, *Heroes in Training* (DAW), edited by Martin H. Greenberg and Jim C. Hines, *Pandora's Closet* (DAW), edited by Jean Rabe and Martin H. Greenberg, *Fate Fantastic* (DAW), edited by Martin H. Greenberg and Daniel M. Hoyt, *Army of the Fantastic* (DAW), edited by John Marlo and John Helfers, *If I were an Evil Overlord* (DAW), edited by Martin H. Greenberg and Russell Davis, and *Marion Zimmer Bradley's Sword & Sorceress XXII* (Norilana Books), edited by Elisabeth Waters.

Noted without comment is *Wizards* (Berkley), edited by Jack Dann and Gardner Dozois.

There was a Romance/Fantasy cross-genre anthology this year, *Best New Romantic Fantasy 2* (Juno), edited by Paula Guran, and a Gay Fiction/Fantasy cross, *So Fey: Queer Fairy Fictions* (Haworth), edited by Steve Berman. As far as I can tell there was only one shared-world anthology this year (at one point in genre history, there'd have been a half-dozen or more of them), *The Grantville Gazette III* (Baen), edited by Eric Flint.

As usual, novice work by beginning writers, some of whom may later turn out to be important talents, was featured in *L. Ron Hubbard Presents Writers of the Future Volume XXIII* (Galaxy), edited by Algis Budrys; this year must have produced an especially good crop of new writers, since the book seemed more substantial than it usually does, with good work by Andrea Kail, Aliette de Bodard, and Jeff Carlson.

I don't follow horror closely anymore, but there, as far as I could tell, the big original anthology of the year seemed to be *Inferno: New Tales of Terror and the Supernatural* (Tor), edited by Ellen Datlow, which featured good work by Laird Barron, Glen Hirshberg, John Grant, Pat Cadigan, Jeffrey Ford, Terry Dowling, and others. Other original horror anthologies included *The Restless Dead* (Candlewick), edited by Deborah Noyes, *Dark Delicacies 2: Fear* (Caroll & Graf), edited by Del Howlson and Jeff Gelb, and *The Secret History of Vampires* (DAW), edited by Darrell Schweitzer. H.P. Lovecraft's Cthulhu, who seems to get around pretty spryly for an Ancient Horror, appeared in *High Seas Cthulhu* (Elder Signs Press), edited by William Jones, *Frontier Cthulhu: Ancient Horrors in the New West* (Chaosium), edited by William Jones, and *The Spiraling Worm: Man Versus the Cthulhu Mythos* (Chaosium), edited by David Conyer. Can *Cthulhu Meets Abbott and Costello* be far behind?

(Finding individual pricings for all of the items from small-presses mentioned in the Summation has become too time-intensive, and since several of the same small presses publish anthologies, novels, *and* short-story collections, it seems silly to repeat addresses for them in section after section. Therefore, I'm going to attempt to list here, in one place, all the addresses for small-presses that have books mentioned here or there in the Summation, whether from the anthologies section, the novel section, or the short-story collection section, and, where known, their web site addresses. That should make it easy enough for the reader to look up the individual price of any book mentioned that isn't from a regular trade-publisher; such books are less-likely to be found in your average bookstore, or even in a chain superstore, and so will probably have to be mail-ordered. Many publishers seem to sell only online, through their web sites, and some will only accept payment through PayPal. Many books, even from some of the smaller presses, are also available through Amazon.com.)

Addresses: **PS Publishing**, Grosvener House, 1 New Road, Hornsea, West Yorkshire, HU18 1PG, England, UK www.pspublishing.co.uk; **Golden Gryphon Press**, 3002 Perkins Road, Urbana, IL 61802, www.goldengryphon .com; **NESFA Press**, P.O. Box 809, Framinghan, MA 01701-0809, www

.nesfa.org; **Subterranean Press**, P.O. Box 190106, Burton, MI 48519, www
.subterraneanpress.com; **Solaris**, via www.solarisbooks.com; **Old Earth
Books**, P.O. Box 19951, Baltimore, MD 21211-0951, www.oldearthbooks
.com; **Tachyon Press**, 1459 18th St. #139, San Francisco, CA 94107, www
.tachyonpublications.com; **Night Shade Books**, 1470 NW Saltzman Road,
Portland, OR 97229, www.nightshadebooks.com; **Five Star Books**, 295
Kennedy Memorial Drive, Waterville, ME 04901, www.galegroup.com/
fivestar; **NewCon Press**, via www.newconpress.com; **Wheatland Press**, P.O.
Box 1818, Wilsonville, OR 97070, www.wheatlandpress.com, **All-Star Stories**, see contact information for Wheatland Press; **Small Beer Press**, 176
Prospect Ave., Northampton, MA 01060, www.smallbeerpress.com; **Locus
Press**, P.O. Box 13305, Oakland, CA 94661; **Crescent Books**, Mercat Press
Ltd., 10 Coates Crescent, Edinburgh, Scotland EH3 7AL, www
.crescentfiction.com; **Wildside Press/Cosmos Books/Borgo Press**, P.O. Box
301, Holicong, PA 18928-0301, or go to www.wildsidepress.com for pricing
and ordering; **Thunder's Mouth**, 245 West 17th St., 11th Flr., New York,
N.Y. 10011-5300, www.thundersmouth.com; **Edge Science Fiction and
Fantasy Publishing, Inc. and Tesseract Books, Ltd.**, P.O. Box 1714, Cal-
gary, Alberta, T2P 2L7, Canada, www.edgewebsite.com; **Aqueduct Press**,
P.O. Box 95787, Seattle, WA 98145-2787, www.aqueductpress.com; **Phobos
Books**, 200 Park Avenue South, New York, NY 10003, www.phobosweb
.com; **Fairwood Press**, 5203 Quincy Ave. SE, Auburn, WA 98092, www
.fairwoodpress.com; **BenBella Books**, 6440 N. Central Expressway, Suite
508, Dallas, TX 75206, www.benbellabooks.com; **Darkside Press**, 13320
27th Ave. NE, Seattle, WA 98125, www.darksidepress.com; **Haffner Press**,
5005 Crooks Rd., Suite 35, Royal Oak, MI 48073-1239, www.haffnerpress
.com; **North Atlantic Press**, P.O. Box 12327, Berkeley, CA, 94701; **Prime**,
P.O. Box 36503, Canton, OH, 44735, www.primebooks.net; **Fairwood
Press**, 5203 Quincy Ave. SE, Auburn, WA 98092, www.fairwoodpress.com;
MonkeyBrain Books, 11204 Crossland Drive, Austin, TX 78726, www
.monkeybrainbooks.com; **Wesleyan University Press**, University Press of
New England, Order Dept., 37 Lafayette St., Lebanon NH 03766-1405,
www.wesleyan.edu/wespress; **Agog! Press**, P.O. Box U302, University of
Wollongong, NSW 2522, Austrailia, www.uow.ed.au/~rhood/agogpress;
MirrorDanse Books, P.O. Box 3542, Parramatta NSW 2124, www.tabula
-rasa.info/MirrorDanse; **Arsenal Pulp Press**, 103-1014 Homer Street, Van-
couver, BC, Canada V6B 2W9, www.arsenalpress.com; **DreamHaven
Books**, 912 W. Lake Street, Minneapolis, MN 55408; **Elder Signs
Press/Dimensions Books**, order through www.dimensionsbooks.com;
Chaosium, via www.chaosium.com; **Spyre Books**, P.O. Box 3005, Radford,
VA 24143; **SCIFI, Inc.**, P.O. Box 8442, Van Nuys, CA 91409-8442;
Omnidawn Publishing, order through www.omnidawn.com; **CSFG**, Can-

berra Speculative Fiction Guild, www.csfg.org.au/publishing/anthologies/ the_outcast; **Hadley Rille Books**, via www.hadleyrillebooks.com; **ISFiC Press**, 707 Sapling Lane, Deerfield, IL 60015-3969, or www.isficpress.com; **Suddenly Press**, via suddenlypress@yahoo.com; **Sandstone Press**, P.O. Box 5725, One High St., Dingwall, Ross-shire, IV15 9WJ; **Tropism Press**, via www.tropismpress.com; **SF Poetry Association/Dark Regions Press**, www .sfpoetry.com, checks to Helena Bell, SFPA Treasurer, 1225 West Freeman St., Apt. 12, Carbondale, IL 62401; **DH Press**, via diamondbookdistributors .com; **Kurodahan Press**, via web site www.kurodahan.com; **Ramble House**, 443 Gladstone Blvd., Shreveport LA 71104; **Interstitial Arts Foundation**, via www.interstitialarts.org; **Raw Dog Screaming**, via www.rawdogscreaming .com; **Norilana Books**, via www.norilana.com; **coeur de lion**, via www.coeurdelion.com.au; **PARSECink**, via www.parsecink.org; **Robert J. Sawyer Books**, via www.sfwriter.com/rjsbooks.htm; **Rackstraw Press**, via http://rackstrawpress; **Candlewick**, via www.candlewick.com; **Zubaan**, via www.zubaanbooks.com; **Utter Tower**, via www.threeleggedfox.co.uk; **Spilt Milk Press**, via www.electricvelocipede.com; **Paper Golem**, via www .papergolem.com; **Galaxy Press**, via www.galaxypress.com.

If I've missed some, as is quite possible, try Googling the name of the publisher. (Isn't it odd that we're in an era where "Googling" is actually a word?)

In spite of the usual laments that SF is dying or diminishing or being driven off the bookstore shelves, there were more good SF and fantasy novels (to say nothing of hard-to-classify hybrids) published in 2007 than any one person could possibly read, unless they made a full-time job of it

According to the newsmagazine *Locus*, there were a record 2,723 books "of interest to the SF field, both original and reprint (but not counting "media tie-in novels," gaming novels, novelizations of genre movies, most Print-on-Demand books, or novels offered as downloads on the internet—all of which would swell the total by hundreds if counted) published in 2007, up 9% from 2,495 titles in 2006. The really big increase this year was a boom in the number of "paranormal romances" published, which surged to a total of 290 titles this year; for the first time, *Locus* has begun counting paranormal romance as a separate category, which skews the figures somewhat, since last year some of them would have been counted as fantasy or even horror titles instead. Magna is also booming, but that isn't reflected in the totals at all. Original books were up by 13% to 1,710 from last year's total of 1,520, a new record. Reprint books were up by 4%, to 1,013 compared to last year's total of 975, although that doesn't make up for the decline here in the previous two years. The number of new SF novels was up 12% to a total of 250 as opposed to last year's total of 223. The number of new fantasy novels was down by 1% to 460 as opposed to last year's total of 463. Horror dropped by 27%, to 198 titles, as opposed to last year's total of 271, still up from 2002's total of 112.

Busy with all the reading I have to do at shorter lengths, I didn't have time to read many novels myself this year, so, as usual, I'll limit myself to mentioning that novels that received a lot of attention and acclaim in 2006 include:

Brasyl (Pyr), by Ian McDonald; *The Accidental Time Machine* (Ace), by Joe Haldeman; *The Execution Channel* (Tor), by Ken MacLeod; *The Sons of Heaven* (Tor), by Kage Baker; *Cowboy Angels* (Gollancz), by Paul McAuley; *Players,* (Simon & Schuster UK), by Paul McAuley; *Axis* (Tor), by Robert Charles Wilson; *The White Tyger* (Tor), by Paul Park; *Recovery Man* (Roc), by Kristine Kathryn Rusch; *Pirate Freedom* (Tor), by Gene Wolfe; *Sixty Days and Counting* (Bantam Spectra), by Kim Stanley Robinson; *Halting State* (Ace), by Charles Stross; *The Merchant's War* (Tor), by Charles Stross; *The Prefect* (Gollancz), by Alastair Reynolds; *In War Times* (Tor), by Kathleen Ann Goonan; *Queen of Candescence* (Tor), by Karl Schroeder; *Spindrift* (Ace), by Allen Steele; *The Steep Approach to Garbadale* (Little, Brown UK), by Iain Banks; *Quantico* (Vanguard); by Greg Bear; *Keeping It Real* (Pyr), by Justina Robson; *Selling Out* (Pyr), by Justina Robson; *The Last Colony* (Tor), by John Scalzi; *HARM* (Del Rey), by Brian W. Aldiss; *Conqueror* (Ace), by Stephen Baxter; *Brass Man* (Tor), by Neal Asher; *Hilldiggers* (Tor UK); by Neal Asher; *Undertow* (Bantam Spectra), by Elizabeth Bear; *Whiskey and Water* (Roc), by Elizabeth Bear; *A Companion to Wolves* (Tor), by Sarah Monette and Elizabeth Bear; *Postsingular* (Tor), by Rudy Rucker; *Off Armageddon Reef* (Tor), by David Weber; *Empire of Ivory* (Del Rey), by Naomi Novik; *Flora Segunda* (Hartcourt), by Ysabeau S. Wilce; *Un Lun Dun* (Del Rey), by China Mieville; *Heart-Shaped Box* (Morrow), by Joe Hill; *Helix* (Solaris), by Eric Brown; *Ally* (Eos), by Karen Traviss; *The Terror* (Little, Brown), by Dan Simmons; *Set the Seas on Fire* (Solaris), by Chris Roberson; *Cauldron* (Ace), by Jack McDevitt; *Command Decision* (Del Rey), by Elizabeth Moon; *Mainspring* (Tor), by Jay Lake; *Farseed* (Tor), by Pamela Sargent; *Ysabel* (Roc), by Guy Gavriel Kay; *Daughter of Independence* (DAW), by Simon Brown; *Titans of Chaos* (Tor), by John C. Wright; *Bloodmind* (Tor), Liz Williams; *A Betrayal in Winter* (Tor), Daniel Abraham; *The Yiddish Policemen's Union* (HarperCollins), by Michael Chabon; *Gentlemen of the Road* (Del Rey), by Michael Chabon; *Deliverer* (DAW), by C.J. Cherryh; *Ink* (Del Rey), by Hal Duncan; *Ilario:The Lion's Eye* (Eos), by Mary Gentle; *The Dreaming Void* (Tor UK), by Peter F. Hamilton; *The New Moon's Arms* (Warner), by Nalo Hopkinson; *Fleet of Worlds* (Tor), by Larry Niven & Edward M. Lerner; *Ha'penny* (Ace), by Jo Walton; *Time's Child* (Roc), by Rebecca Ore; *The Sunrise Lands* (Roc), by S.M. Stirling; *Shelter* (Tor), by Susan Palwick; *Till Human Voices Wake Us*

(Bantam Spectra), by Mark Budz; *Black Man* (Gollancz), by Richard Morgan; *Saturn Returns* (Ace), by Sean Williams; *Shadowplay* (DAW), by Tad Williams; *The Silver Sword* (Tor), by David Zindell; and *Making Money* (HarperCollins), by Terry Pratchett.

Used to be that the small presses published mostly collections and anthologies, but these days they're active in the novel market as well. Novels issued by small presses included: *Endless Things* (Small Beer Press), by John Crowley; *Tsunami* (Aqueduct Press), by L. Timmel Duchamp; *Generation Loss* (Small Beer Press), by Elizabeth Hand; *Marblehead: A Novel of H.P. Lovecraft* (Ramble House), by Richard A. Lupoff; *The Spiral Labyrinth* (Night Shade Books), by Matthew Hughes; *The Commons* (Robert Sawyer Books), by Matthew Hughes; *The Guardener's Tale* (Sam's Dot), by Bruce Boston; *The Secret Books of Paradys* (Overland Press), by Tanith Lee; *Butcher Bird* (Night Shade Books), by Richard Kadrey; *Softspoken* (Night Shade Books), by Lucius Shepard; and *Precious Dragon* (Night Shade Books), by Liz Williams. Howard Waldrop's long-awaited *The Moone World* was announced by Wheatland Press but didn't actually appear, so I guess we'll just have to wait some more.

Associational novels by people connected with the science fiction and fantasy fields included: *Humpty Dumpty in Oakland* (Tor), by Philip K. Dick; *Voices from the Street* (Tor), by Philip K. Dick; *Dark Reflections* (Carroll & Graf), by Samuel R. Delany; *A Wrongful Death* (Mira), by Kate Wilhelm; *The Heart of Horses* (Houghton Mifflin), by Molly Gloss, and *You Don't Love Me Yet* (Doubleday), by Jonathan Lethem. Novels that dance on the ambiguous razor's-edge between SF and the thriller novel, some tipping one way, some the other, included: *Quantico* (Vanguard), by Greg Bear; *Spook Country* (Putnam), by William Gibson; *The H-Bomb Girl* (Faber & Faber), by Stephen Baxter; and *Players* (Simon & Schuster UK) and *Cowboy Angels* (Gollancz), by Paul McAuley, if considered as "technothrillers" rather than near-future SF novels. Some mainstream critics seem to be making an attempt to distance books such as Dan Simmons's *The Terror* and Michael Chabon's *The Yiddish Policemen's Union* from the genre (just as they did with Cormac McCarthy's *The Road* last year), but the fantastic elements in each are clear.

First novels included *Breakfast with the Ones You Love* (Bantam Spectra), by Eliot Fintushel; *Radio Freefall* (Tor), by Matthew Jarpe; *The Outback Stars* (Tor), by Sandra McDonald; *The Name of the Wind* (DAW), by Patrick Rothfuss; *One for Sorrow* (Bantam Spectra), by Christopher Barzak; *Jade Tiger* (Juno), by Jenn Reese; *Wicked Lovely* (HarperCollins Children's Books UK), by Melissa Marr; *The Summoner* (Solaris), by Gail Z. Martin; *Spaceman Blues: A Love Story* (Tor), by Brian Francis Slattery; *Maledicte* (Del Rey), by Lane Robins; *Grey* (Night Shade Books), by Jon Armstrong; *KOP*

(Tor), by Warren Hammond; *Crooked Little Vein* (Morrow), by Warren Ellis; *The Princes of the Golden Cage* (Night Shade Books), by Nathalie Mallet; *The Book of Joby* (Tor), by Mark J. Ferrari; *Winterbirth* (Orbit), by Brian Bukley; *Amberlight* (Juno), by Sylvia Kolso; and *City of Bones* (McElderry), by Cassandra Clare. None of these novels stuck out of the pack, in terms of the critical attention paid to them, as other first novels have done in other years; probably the Fintushel and the Jarpe got reviewed the most frequently, and the McDonald made it on to the Preliminary Nebula Ballot.

The best-selling novel of the year, of course, was *Harry Potter and the Deathly Hallows* (Scholastic), which outsold everything else by an enormous margin, perhaps even everything else combined. In my neighborhood, special postmen were assigned for the sole purpose of delivering mail-ordered copies of the new *Harry Potter* to those who had ordered it—which, it seemed, meant at least two or three houses in every block. My guess is that we'll never see anything like this again in our lifetimes.

As usual, these lists contain fantasy novels and odd-genre-mixing hybrids that are difficult to categorize, but, far from being a vanishing breed, as is sometimes suggested, *most* of them are good solid unambiguous center-core SF—the McDonald, the Haldeman, the MacLeod, the Baker, the Wilson, the Reynolds, the Goonan, the Schroeder, the Steele, the Baxter, the Scalzi, the Ashers, and more than twenty other titles. Many of them hard science fiction as well. There's no shortage of science fiction out there on the shelves, if you bother to look for it, probably more than any one person will have time to read in a given year.

Even discounting Print-on-Demand books from places such as Wildside Press, and the availability of out-of-print books as electronic downloads on internet sources such as Fictionwise, and through reprints issued by The Science Fiction Book Club, this is the best time in decades to pick up reissued editions of formerly long-out-of-print novels. Producing a definitive list of reissued novels is probably difficult to impossible, but here's some out-of-print titles that came back *into* print this year:

Tor reissued: *Soldier of Sidon*, by Gene Wolfe, *Sky Coyote*, by Kage Baker, *Hellstrom's Hive*, by Frank Herbet, *The White Plague*, by Frank Herbet; *Psion*, by Joan D. Vinge, *The Martian Child*, by David Gerrold; *Empire*, by Orson Scott Card, and *Eon*, *Legacy*, and *Eternity*, all by Greg Bear; Orb reissued: *Slan*, by A.E. Van Vogt, *Darwinia*, by Robert Charles Wilson, *Memory and Dream*, by Charles de Lint, *Freedom and Necessity*, by Steven Brust and Emma Bull, *Moving Mars*, by Greg Bear, and *Experation Date*, and *Earthquake Weather*, both by Tim Powers; HarperFantasy reissued: *Stardust*, by Neil Gaiman; Pyr reissued: *The Man Who Melted*, by Jack Dann, and *Ivory*, by Mike Resnick, Ace reissued: *Mother of Storms*, by Ian R. MacLeod, and *Lunar Descent*, *Orbital Decay*, and *Clarke County, Space*, all by Allen M. Steele; DAW reissued *Pretender*, by C.J. Cherryh; Penguin/Signet reissued: *The Stand*, by Stephen King; Cosmos reissued: *Little Fuzzy*, by H. Beam Piper, *The Door Through Space*, by Marion Zimmer Bradley, *If Wishes Were Horses*, by Anne McCaffrey, *Star Born*, by Andre Norton, and *People of the Dark*, by Robert E. Howard; Roc reissued: *The Last Unicorn*, by Peter S. Beagle, and *Lady of Avalon*, by Marion Zimmer Bradley; Tachyon reissued: *A Fine and Private Place*, by Peter S. Beagle; Bantam Spectra reissued: *The Armageddon Rag*, by George R.R. Martin; Fairwood Press reissued: *Rite of Passage*, by Alexei Panshin; Paizo/Planet Stories reissued: *Almuric*, by Robert E. Howard, *The Secret of Sinharat*, by Leigh Brackett, and *The City of the Beast/Warriors of Mars*, by Michael Moorcock; Night Shade Books reissued: *The Voice of the Whirlwind*, by Walter Jon Williams; MonkeyBrain Books reissued: *The Hollow Earth*, by Rudy Rucker; BenBella Books reissued: *Prophet*, by Mike Resnick; Overlook reissued: *Titus Groan*, by Mervyn Peake, *Gormenghast*, by Mervyn Peake, *Behold the Man*, by Michael Moorcock, and *The Unreasoning Mask*, by Philip Jose Farmer; and Edgeworks Abbey reissued the associational novel *Spider Kiss*, by Harlan Ellison.

In addition to the omnibus collections which mix short stories and novels, which I've mostly listed in the short-story collection section below, there was an omnibus of four novels by Philip K. Dick (*The Man in the High Castle*, *The Three Stigma of Palmer Eldritch*, *Do Androids Dream of Electric Sheep*, and *Ubik*), issued as *Four Novels of the 1960s* (Library of America), selected by Jonathan Lethem, which marks the first time the highly prestigious Library of America has dained to treat a science fiction writer to this kind of literary canonization (although horror writer H.P. Lovecraft got lionized before him). There was also a novel omnibus of the famous "Harold Shea" novels by L. Sprague De Camp and Fletcher Pratt, *The Mathematics of Magic* (NESFA Press); an omnibus of novels by Patricia A. McKillip, *Cygnet* (Ace), an omnibus of Glen Cook's "Black Company" novels, *Chronicles of the Black Company* (Tor), and an omnibus of two short novels or long novellas by Ray Bradbury, *Now and Forever* (Morrow). In addition, many omnibuses of novels—and many individual novels—are reissued each year by The Science Fiction Book Club as well as being made available electronically online, too many to individually list here.

It's too early to venture a prediction as to what novel is going to win the major awards next year; my track record has not been great at this anyway. Your guess is as good as mine.

2007 was another good year for short-story collections, especially in the area of big career-spanning retrospectives. The best collection of the year, and one of the best in some time, was *The Jack Vance Treasury* (Subterranean), by Jack Vance, although other first-rate career retrospectives included *Ascendancies: The Best of Bruce Sterling* (Subterranean), by Bruce Sterling, *Things Will Never Be the Same, Selected Short Fiction 1980–2005* (Old Earth), by Howard Waldrop, *The Winds of Marble Arch* (Subterranean), by Connie Willis, and *The Collected Stories of Robert Silverberg: To the Dark Star* (Subterranean), by Robert Silverberg. Other good retrospective collections included: *To Outlive Eternity and Other Stories* (Baen) by Poul Anderson (an omnibus also containing the novel *After Doomsday*); *When the People Fell* (Baen), by Cordwainer Smith; *Rynemonn* (couer de lion), by Terry Dowling; *The Long Twilight and Other Stories* (Baen), by Keith Laumer (an omnibus that also contains the novels *Night of Delusions* and *The Long Twilight*); *The Collected Fantasies of Clark Ashton Smith, Volume II: The Door to Saturn* (Night Shade Books), by Clark Ashton Smith; *The Big Front Yard and Other Stories* (Darkside Press), by Clifford D. Simak; *Shadow Yard and Other Stories* (Darkside Press), by Clifford D. Simak; *The Best of Robert E. Howard, Volume 1: Crimson Shadows* (Del Rey), by Robert E. Howard; *The Best of Robert E. Howard, Volume 2: Grim Lands* (Del Rey), by Robert E. Howard; *The Skyscraper and Other Tales from the Pulps* (Wildside), by Murry Leinster; *A Niche in Time* (Darkside Press), by William F. Nolan; *The Childless Ones* (Darkside Press), by Daniel F. Galouye; *The Trouble With Humans* (Baen), by Christopher Anvil; and *The Nail and the Oracle* (North Atlantic), by Theodore Sturgeon.

Any list of the best collections of 2007 would also have to include *Gods and Pawns* (Tor), by Kage Baker; *Water Rites* (Fainwood Press), by Mary Rosenblum (an omnibus that also includes the novel *The Drylands*); *Overclocked* (Thunder's Mouth), by Cory Doctorow; *The Dog Said Bow-Wow* (Tachyon), by Michael Swanwick; *Getting to Know You* (Subterranean), by David Marusek; *The Girl Who Loved Animals* (Golden Gryphon), by Bruce McAllister, *Promised Land* (PS Publishing), by Jack Dann; *Pump Six and Other Stories* (Night Shade Books), by Paolo Bachigalupi; and *Dagger Key and Other Stories* (PS Publishing), by Lucius Shepard. Other good collections included *The Fate of Mice* (Tachyon), by Susan Palwick; *Hart & Boot* (Night Shade Books), by Tim Pratt; *New Amsterdam* (Subterranean Press), by Elizabeth Bear; *Portable Childhoods* (Tachyon), by Ellen Klages; *The God of the Razor* (Subterranean), by Joe R. Lansdale (an omnibus that also contains the novel *The Nightrunners*); *M Is for Magic* (HarperCollins), by Neil Gaiman; *20th Century Ghosts* (Morrow), by Joe Hill; *Worshipping Small Gods* (Prime), by Richard Parks; *A Thousand Deaths* (Golden Gryphon), by George Alec Effinger (an omnibus that also contains the novel *The Wolves of Memory*); *Ten Sigmas and Other Stories* (Fairwood Press), by Paul Melko; *Dangerous Space* (Aqueduct), by Kelley Eskridge; *Lord John* and the Hand of Devils (Delacorte), by Diana Gabaldon; The Spaces Between the Lines (Subterranean), by Peter Crowther; An Alternate History of the 21st Century (Spilt Milk Press), by William Shunn; Aliens of the Heart (Aqueduct), by Carolyn Ives Gilman; Ice, Iron and Gold (Night Shade Books), by S.M. Stirling; The Involuntary Human (NESFA Press), by David Gerrold; The Surgeon's Tale and Other Stories (Two Free Lancer Press), by Cat Rambo and Jeff VanderMeer; Moon Flights (Night Shade Books), by Elizabeth Moon; Mad Professor: The Uncollected Stories of Rudy Rucker (Thunder's Mouth), by Rudy Rucker; The Sam Gunn Omnibus (Tor), by Ben Bova; Tales from the Woeful Platypus (Subterranean), by Caitlin R. Kiernan; The Woman Who Thought She Was a Planet (Zubaan), by Vandana Singh; The Bone Key (Prime), by Sarah Monette; Absalom's Mother and Other Stories (Fairwood Press), by Louise Marley; The Imago Sequence and Other Stories (Night Shade Books), by Laird Barron; Twice Dead Things (Elder Signs Press), by A.A. Attanasio; The Secret Files of the Diogenes Club (MonkeyBrain Books), by Kim Newman; and The Guild of Xenolinguists (Golden Gryphon), by Shila Finch.

Even more than usual, the collections field was dominated by the small-presses this year, with few collections to be found from the regular trade publishers. (Although Baen Books should be complimented on bucking this trend, and are providing an invaluable service in returning the short work of long-unavailable authors to print.) Subterranean in particular had a terrific year, publishing one excellent collection after another, and establishing themselves as one of the real powerhouses in the entire collections area; Night Shade Books and Tachyon had pretty strong years as well.

Reissued collections this year included Dreamsongs 1 and Dreamsongs 2 (Bantam Spectra), by George R.R. Martin; N-Space (Tor), by Larry Niven; Shatterday (Tachyon), by Harlan Ellison; The Last Mimzy (Del Rey), by Henry Kuttner (which, in spite of a title change to make it look like a movie tie-in book, is actually a reprint of The Best of Henry Kuttner); Black God's Kiss, (Pazio/Planet Stories), by C.L. Moore; Dandelion Wine (PS Publishing), by Ray Bradbury; At the Mountains of Madness (Del Rey), by H.P. Lovecraft; The House of Cthulhu (Tor), by Brian Lumley; Skeleton Crew (Penguin/Signet), by Stephen King; and Wall of the Sky, Wall of the Eye (Harcourt/Harvest), by Jonathan Lethem.

Many collections are also issued by the Science Fiction Book Club every year, too many to individually list here, and a wide variety of "electronic collections," often called "fiction bundles," continue to be available for downloading online as well, at sites such as Fictionwise and ElectricStory. It's worth noting that some collections contain original material; for instance, Kage Baker's collection, Gods and Pawns, featured two never-before-published novellas, and there was also previously unpublished material in Lucius Shepard's Dagger Key *and Other Stories*, Michael Swanwick's *The Dog Said Bow-Wow*, Kelly Eskridge's *Dangerous Space*, Carolyn Ives Gilman's *Aliens of the Heart*, and in other collections.

The reprint anthology market was moderately strong again this year, and again the ever-growing crop of "Best of the Year" anthologies are probably your best bet for your money in this market. As far as I could tell, there were *fourteen* "Best of the Year" anthologies of various sorts available in 2007. Science fiction was covered by six anthologies (or five and a half, depending on how you want to look at it): the one you are reading at the moment, *The Year's Best Science Fiction* series from St. Martin's, edited by Gardner Dozois, now up to its Twenty-fifth Annual Collection; the *Year's Best SF* series (Eos), edited by David G. Hartwell and Kathryn Cramer, now up to its Twelfth annual volume, *Best Short Novels: 2007* (Science Fiction Book Club), edited by Jonathan Strahan; *Science Fiction: The Best of the Year 2007* (Prime), edited by Richard Horton, a new series, *Space Opera* (Prime), edited by Richard Horton, and a retitled version of Jonathan Strahan's *Best* series from a new publisher, *The Best Science Fiction and Fantasy of the Year: Volume One* (Night Shade Books), edited by Jonathan Strahan (this is where the "half a book" comes in, although I doubt that it'll divide that neatly in practice). The annual Nebula Awards anthology usually covers science fiction as well as fantasy of various sorts functioning as a de-facto "Best of the Year" anthology, although its not usually counted among them (and thanks to SFWA's bizarre "rolling eligibility" practice, the stories in it are often stories that everybody else saw a year and sometimes even two years before); this year's edition was *Nebula Awards Showcase 2007* (Roc), edited by Mike Resnick. There were three (or two and a half) Best of the Year anthologies covering horror: the latest edition in the British series *The Mammoth Book of Best New Horror* (Robinson, Caroll & Graff), edited by Stephen Jones, up to its Eighteenth volume; the Ellen Datlow half of a huge volume covering both horror and fantasy, *The Year's Best Fantasy and Horror* (St. Martin's Press), edited by Ellen Datlow, Kelly Link, and Gavin Grant, this year up to its Twentieth Annual Collection; and, *Horror: The Best of the Year 2007 Edition* (Prime), edited by John Gregory Betancourt and Sean Wallace. Fantasy was covered by four anthologies (if you add two halves together): by the Kelly Link and Gavin Grant half of the Datlow/Link & Grant anthology, by *Year's Best Fantasy 7*, edited by David G. Hartwell and Katherine Cramer (Tachyon); by *Fantasy: The Best of the Year 2007* (Prime), edited by Rich Horton; by *Best American Fantasy* (Prime), edited by Ann and Jeff VanderMeer, and by the fantasy half of *The Best Science Fiction and Fantasy of the Year: Volume One* (Night Shade Books), edited by Jonathan

Strahan, into which Strahan's previous *Fantasy: The Very Best of* — series seems to have been subsumed, since it's no longer being published separately. There was also *The 2007 Rhysling Anthology* (Science Fiction Poetry Association/Prime), edited by Drew Morse, which compiles the Rhysling Award-winning SF poetry of the year. If you count the Nebula anthology and the Rhyslling anthology, there were fourteen "Best of the Year" anthology series of one sort or another on offer this year.

There were also several strong retrospective overview "Bests" drawn from various magazines this year, both print and electronic: *Asimov's 30ᵗʰ Anniversary Anthology* (Tachyon), edited by Sheila Williams, features strong reprint work by John Varley, Ursula K. Le Guin, Bruce Sterling, Lucius Shepard, James Patrick Kelly, and others. *The Best of Jim Baen's Universe* (Baen), edited by Eric Flint, features stories drawn from the first year of this important new electronic magazine, with good reprints by Gregory Benford, Elizabeth Bear, Garth Nix, Mike Resnick, Gene Wolfe, and others. *Infinity Plus: The Anthology* (Solaris), edited by Keith Brooke and Nick Gevers, draws from one of the longest-lasting and most established of all internet SF fiction sites, featuring good reprints from Paul McAuley, Ian McDonald, Tony Daniel, Michael Moorcock, Kim Stanley Robinson, Mary Gentle, Brian Stableford, and others. *The Best of Lady Churchill's Rosebud Wristlet* (Del Rey), edited by Kelly Link and Gavin J. Grant, brings us the best from this critically acclaimed little magazine, including stories by Karen Joy Fowler, Theodora Goss, Jim Sallis, Nalo Hopkinson, James Sallis, John Kessel, Link herself, and others. *The James Tiptree Anthology 3* (Tachyon), edited by Pat Murphy, Debbie Notkin, and Jeffrey D. Smith, offers a kind of "Best of" collection drawn from things shortlisted for the prestigious Tiptree award, including work by Ursula K. Le Guin, Geoff Ryman, Vonda McIntyre, Ted Chiang, and others.

The view from the perspective of different cultures is given by *The SFWA European Hall of Fame* (Tor), edited by James Morrow and Kathryn Morrow, *Worlds Apart: An Anthology of Russian Fantasy and Science Fiction* (Overlook), edited by Alexander Levitsky, and *Speculative Japan: Japanese Tales of Science Fiction and Fantasy* (Kurudahan Press), edited by Gene Van Troyer and Grania Davis.

Noted without comment is another big retrospective anthology, *The Best of the Best Volume 2: 20 Years of the Best Short Science Fiction Novels* (St. Martin's Press), edited by Gardner Dozois.

Once beyond the parade of "Best of" anthologies of one sort or another, one of the best of the year's reprint anthologies was probably *Rewired: The New Cyberpunk Anthology* (Tachyon), edited by James Patrick Kelly and John Kessel, which takes a retrospective look back at the influence of cyberpunk since the heady days of the Cyberpunk Wars in the '80s, and which features good reprints by Greg Egan, Michael Swanwick, Cory Doctorow, William Gibson, Bruce Sterling, David Marusek, and others.

Another substantial and intriguing anthology is the William Hope Hodgson tribute anthology, *William Hope Hodgson's Night Lands Volume II, Nightmares of the Fall* (Utter Tower), edited by Andy W. Robertson, a follow-up to the original Hodgson tribute anthology from 2003. (Some commentators are listing this as an original anthology since the individual stories have never appeared in print before, but since they've all been available on the *Night Lands* website (www.thenightland.co.uk) for several years, I've decided to treat it as a reprint anthology. There is frequently interesting new content up on the website, though, including at the moment a new novella by John C. Wright, so you should check it out.) As with the previous anthology, all the stories here are written as homages set in the *milieu* of William Hope Hodgson's strange and eccentric masterpiece *The Night Land*–one of the probable inspirations for later work such as Jack Vance's *The Dying Earth* and Gene Wolfe's *The Book of the New Sun*—and also as with the previous anthology, not all of the writers handle this stylistically tricky material with the same authority. As was true of the previous anthology, the best stories here are two long novellas by John C. Wright, who, with his mannered, Victorian, slightly faustian prose, seems to be born to write this sort of thing, but there is also good work from Gerard Houarnet, Brett Davidson, and Andy Robertson himself.

The somewhat pretentiously named *Prime Codex: The Hungry Edge of Speculative Fiction* (Paper Golem), edited by Lawrence M. Schoen and Michael Livingston, is an anthology concentrating on reprints of work by new (or newish) writers such as Ruth Nestvold, Cat Rambo, Tobia S. Bucknell, and Ken Scholes.

Futures from Nature (Tor), edited by Henry Gee, is a collection of short speculative/satirical pieces that have been appearing in *Nature* magazine over the last couple of years—some of them are pretty slight, but many of them are sharp and amusing, and the book overall is a surprising amount of fun. Another fun anthology distinctly on the light side is *This is My Funniest 2: Leading Science Fiction Writers Present Their Funniest Stories Ever* (Benbella), edited by Mike Resnick.

Noted without comment is *Dangerous Games* (Ace), edited by Jack Dann and Gardner Dozois.

Reissued anthologies of merit this year included *Ruby Slippers, Golden Tears* (Prime), edited by Ellen Datlow and Terry Windling, *The Man-Kzin Wars XI* (Baen), and *Alternate Generals III* (Baen), edited by Harry Turtledove.

2007 seemed a rather lackluster year in the SF and fantasy oriented nonfiction and reference book field, producing nothing that stirred up the passion and critical attention that last year's Tiptree biography by Julie Philips did. The strongest non-fiction books of the year were probably *Gateways to Forever, the Story of the Science-Fiction Magazines, 1970–1980* (Liverpool University Press), by Mike Ashley, and *The Country You Have Never Seen: Reviews and Essays by Joanna Russ* (Liverpool University Press), by Joanna Russ. I particularly liked the Ashley book because I knew most of the participants involved and lived through most of the events covered, while the Russ book, mostly made up of her review columns from F&SF in the '70s, reminds us that she was one of the great genre reviewers of our time, worthy to be ranked with other great genre reviewers such as Damon Knight, Algis Budrys, and James Blish.

About the closest thing to a reference book produced this year was *Science Fact and Science Fiction* (Routledge), by Brian Stableford, which discusses the ways in which science fiction has influenced the sciences, and vice versa. *Brave New Words: The Oxford Dictionary of Science Fiction* (Oxford University Press), edited by Jeff Prucher, is indeed a dictionary rather than the more-usual encyclopedia, a collection of words and phrases made popular in science fiction—decent bathroom reading, perhaps, but nothing you'd want to read through in one sitting. *In Other Words* (Subterranean), by John Crowley and *Sides* (Cemetery Dance), by Peter Straub are collections of essays by those authors. *In Memory of Wonder's Child: Jack Williamson* (Haffner Press), edited by Stephen Haffner, is a collection of tributes to and obituaries of the late Jack Williamson. *Shadows of the New Sun: Wolfe on Writers/Writers on Wolfe* (Liverpool University Press), edited by Peter Wright, is self-explanatory, as is *Hugo Gernsback and the Century of Science Fiction* (McFarland), by Gary Westfahl, and *Naomi Mitchison: A Profile of Her Life and Work* (Aqueduct), by Leroy Hall, as are *Anne McCaffrey: A Life With Dragons* (University Press of Mississippi), by Robin Roberts, and *The Cultural Influences of William Gibson, the "Father" of Cyberpunk Science Fiction* (The Edwin Mellen Press), edited by Carl B. Yoke and Carol L. Robinson. *What Can Be Saved from the Wreckage? James Branch Cabell in the Twenty-First Century* (Temporary Culture), by Michael Swanwick, is sort of self-explanatory, an examination of James Branch Cabell's position in the literary canon and how it got to be that way. Perhaps needing a *bit* of explanation is *Hugo Gernsback: A Man Well Ahead of His Time* (Poptronix), by Hugo Gernsback, edited by Larry Steckler, which is a partial autobiography by Gernsback left behind after his death and edited and filled-out by Steckler. *The WisCon Chronicles: Volume 1* (Aqueduct), edited by L. Timmel Duchamp, is a collection of essays, interviews, and panel transcriptions from the annual feminist SF convention, WisCon.

Worthy of note is a reprint of Barry Malzberg's collection of critical essays, *Breakfast in the Ruins* (Baen). I don't by any means always agree with

Malzberg's conclusions (particularly about the awfulness of being a genre writer), but those opinions have rarely been expressed more fiercely and eloquently than here.

A bit on the lighter side than most of the books above is *The End of Harry Potter?* (Tor), by David Langford, an analysis of the Harry Potter books written before the release of the final novel that tries to guess the ultimate outcome of the series from the clues planted in the first six books.

It was also a weak year in the art book field. Your best buy was almost certainly *Spectrum 14: The Best in Contemporary Fantastic Art* (Underwood Books), by Cathy Fenner and Arnie Fenner, the latest edition in a Best of the Year-like retrospective of the year in fantastic art. Students of genre art and genre history will want *Emshwiller: Infinity X Two: The Life and Art of Ed and Carol Emshwiller* (Nonstop Press), edited by Luis Ortiz, as valuable for its biographical text as for the examples of their art (yes, Carol draws too) it contains. Much the same could be said about another mixed text-and-pictures biographical book, of a once-famous artist and illustrator who later became equally famous for his fiction writing, *Mervyn Peake: The Man and His Art* (Peter Owen Publishers) compiled by Sebastian Peake and Alison Eldred, edited by G. Peter Winnington. Also interesting was *Paint or Pixel: The Digital Divide in Illustration Art* (NonStop Press), edited by Jane Frank (paint clearly wins, in my opinion).

Other art books included *Dreamscape: The Best of Imaginary Realism* (Salbru); *Worlds of Amano* (DH Press), by Yoshitaka Amano; *The Fantastic World of Claus Brusen* (Edition Brusen/Colophon), by Ole Lindboe; *Modern Masters Volume 11: Charles Vess* (Two Morrows Publishing), edited by Christopher Irving and Eric Nolen-Weathington; *Rough Work: Concept Art, Doodles, and Sketchbook Drawings by Frank Frazetta* (Underwood Books), edited by Arnie Fenner and Kathy Fenner; *Kinuko Craft: Drawings and Paintings* (Imaginosis), by Kinuko Craft; *Rafal Olbinsky Women: Motifs and Variations* (Hudson Hill Press), by Rafal Olbinski; and *The Arrival* (Hatchette Children's Books), by Shaun Tan.

Visual Journeys (Hadley Rille Books), edited by Eric T. Reynolds, the mixed art/fiction anthology where paintings are matched with the stories they inspired, if considered for the artwork rather than the stories, also makes an interesting sampler of past and recent Space Art.

Among the general genre-related non-fiction books of interest this year, *Where's My Jetpack?: A Guide to the Amazing Science Fiction Future That Never Arrived* (Bloomsbury), by Daniel H. Wilson, draws on the same kind of retro-nostalgia for SF visions from the 1950s of what The Future was going to be like that also informs Greenberg and Lickiss's anthology *The Future We Wish We Had* (it never seems to occur to anyone that the future we *did* end up with, with all its incredibly sophisticated advances in computer science, medicine, nanotech, and biological techniques, is in a number of profound ways far more amazing than a jetpack or a flying car). A welcome palliative to the retro-nostalgia attitude that devalues our own present and the future that will grow out of it is to be found in *Beyond Human: Living with Robots and Cyborgs* (Forge), by Gregory Benford and Elizabeth Malatre, which gives us a fascinating glimpse of the wonders of a high-tech future close enough that many of you reading these words may live to see it yourselves, barring a collapse of technological civilization or a dinosaur-killer asteroid. Speaking of which, *Plagues, Apocalypses, and Bug-Eyed Monsters: How Speculative Fiction Shows Us Our Nightmares* (McFarland), by Heather Urbanski, is an interesting overview of all the things that speculative fiction has warned us can go *wrong*, although it's probably more aimed at a general audience than to a genre audience that will already be familiar with most of its content, and *The World Without Us* (St. Martin's Press), by Alan Weisman, shows us just how quickly almost all traces of the human race will vanish from the face of the Earth after humanity has vanished, whether killed off by a super plague or taken by a more-democratic Rapture — only a few hundred to a few thousand years, in most cases (except for plastic bottles and lawn furniture, which will be here practically forever). It's difficult to come up with a genre connection to justify mentioning *The Cartoon History of the Modern World: Part 1, from Columbus to the U.S. Constitution* (Collins), by Larry Gonick, but so many SF fans love him, and his work is so full of the kind of color, exoticism, and descriptions of fallen empires and forgotten moments in history that provides much of the appeal of Alternate History and time-travel fiction, that I'm going to mention it anyway — erudite, extremely funny, and incredibly historically accurate. Do yourself a favor and read this. And the other Gonick volumes as well.

This was another good year for genre films, at least at the box-office (although, unlike last year, when there were one or two critical darlings, there were few films this year about which the majority of the critics could really muster up much enthusiasm). According to the Box Office Mojo site (*www.boxofficemojo.com*), nine out of the ten top-grossing movies of the year were genre films. Twelve out of the twenty top-grossing movies were genre films, and thirty-five out of the hundred top-grossing movies (more or less; I may have missed one somewhere) were genre films.

Before we start smugly congratulating ourselves on this here in the SF world, though, we should realize that most of these films were fantasy movies, superhero movies, and animated films, with little real SF on the list. The highest-ranked film on the box-office list that could make some claim to being SF was *Transformers*, which finished third in domestic grosses, earning

$319,246,193. With its warring alien robots, I suppose it *is* SF, but, although it's fast-paced and exciting, it's *bad* SF, with science that's nothing but hand-waving and technobabble and little plot logic or rigor in working out the implications of the basic situation—it's really a comic-book movie in spirit, although based on a line of popular Hasbro toys (which later went on to inspire comics and graphic novels) rather than a comic book per se. The next sort-of SF movie on the list is *I Am Legend*, in sixth place, which made a mere $240,234,000 in domestic grosses. Based on a famous Richard Matheson novel (and filmed before both as *The Omega Man* and *The Last Man on Earth*), it'll be harder to deny that this is SF—not only is it inspired by a book by a recognized genre writer, there's even a (thin) scientific rationale why almost everybody in the world has turned into flesh-eating mutants . . . but I suspect that a big part of its popularity stems from the facts that people are watching it as a *horror movie*, and getting the same kind of thing out of it that you get from *28 Days* or *Dawn of the Dead*, so I don't know how much credit we can really take for it in the SF field. Although one mean-spirited critic said that the best actor in the movie was the dog that keeps the protagonist company, Will Smith actually does a credible job here, especially as he has to carry the whole movie practically by himself, with almost no other actors to play off of (unless you count the shrieking mutants). Some Matheson fans were pissed off that the movie radically changed the ending of the book, but they probably weren't given their share of the $240,234,000 back. The only other movies that could justifiably be called SF on the whole rest of the hundred-movie list are *Aliens vs. Predator: Requiem* and *The Last Mimzy* (a disappointing version of the famous Henry Kuttner story "Mimzy Were the Borogroves"), which finished at sixty-seven and one hundred respectively, and were critical and box-office bombs. *The Invasion*, which didn't even make it on to the top hundred list, is a remake of the '50s paranoid horror classic *Invasion of the Body Snatchers*—which was scarier and better executed the first time around.

Also not on the box-office champs list was perhaps the best real SF movie of the year, the British film *Sunshine*, about a space crew on a desperate mission to restart our dying sun, which slipped through town so fast and stealthily that it didn't even ripple the grass; not that it's perfect, by any means (far from it, in fact), but at least it's *trying* to play the genre game by the rules, and although its science is also technobabble, at least it's more inventive and interesting technobabble than you get in *Transformers* or *I Am Legend*, and they even had a tame physicist who would pop up at press conferences to vouch for its plausibility. Also an earnest attempt to make a real SF movie is *The Man from Earth*, written by the late SF writer Jerome Bixby (who, in fact, finished the last page of the script on his death bed); it has some intelligent writing and conceptualization, but, produced on a very low budget by a very small company, it's mostly people talking to each other in rooms with almost nothing in the way of special effects or slick production values, and I don't know how well that will go over these days—not a problem, as it turns out, since very few people saw it in the first place, even fewer than saw *Sunshine*.

And, as far as I can tell, that's it for science fiction movies this year. Everything else lumped as "genre films" was . . . something else.

The number one top-grossing movie of the year, according to the Box Office Mojo site, was *Spider-Man 3*, which to date has pulled in a $336,530,303 in domestic grosses. There seems to be a Law of Trilogies that affects most of these big franchises, a law of diminishing returns: the first movie is the best, the second movie is okay but not as good as the first, and the third movie is the worst of the three. This year that also applied to the *Pirates of the Caribbean* franchise and to the *Shrek* franchise, and in the past it has applied to the *X-Men* and the *Matrix* movies. *Spider-Man 3* just has too much of everything: too many villains, too much character building, too many climaxes (each one trying to top the one that came before, in a fashion that has become familiar since the '80s and '90s, and which I actually find counterproductive), and such a welter of subplots that any narrative drive gets muffled and bogged-down in the confusion. (The fact that this is the top-grossing movie of the year, though, seems to indicate that few other people give a damn about any of this—as long as there's enough wide-screen spectacle up on the screen, no matter how muddled the story is, they're happy to buy tickets.) Of the remaining superhero/comic book movies (there weren't a lot of them this year), the best was probably, *Fantastic Four: Return of the Silver Surfer*, which seems to be flouting the Law of Trilogies by being better than the original movie in the franchise—it's still fairly lame, mind you, but not as lame as the first one was. The only other superhero movies I could spot were *Ghost Rider*, which in spite of a big opening weekend didn't do as well overall as its producers had been hoping it would, and the execrable *Underdog*, an expansion of the campy TV cartoon of the '60s, which probably sunk itself (and sink it did) with its ill-advised decision to make this as a live action movie rather than an animated feature. *National Treasure: Book of Secrets* is technically not a superhero movie, but partakes of the spirit of one; although it supposedly takes place in the real world, it's certainly a fantasy of some sort, and I suppose it could be listed there too. I didn't think it was possible to be sillier than the first *National Treasure*, but, with its totally absurd premise and plot-turns, *National Treasure: Book of Secrets* outstrips it with ease. Congratulations, guys!

As has been true for a couple of years now, fantasy movies was where the most substantial and successful work of the year was done. *Pirates of the Caribbean: At World's End* was the big winner in this area, finishing fourth in the domestic box-office list, and earning $309,420,425 in domestic grosses. You can just write "ditto" under my review of *Spider-Man 3* and run it for *At World's End* as well. They threw everything into this one, including the kitchen sink and the rest of the kitchen as well, resulting in a broken-backed mess that meanders leisurely to the standard multiple-climax end, and which makes shockingly little sense throughout, even for a *Pirates of the Caribbean* movie. Johnny Deep is fun to watch as Captain Jack Sparrow, as usual, and whenever he's off the screen (which he is for substantial amounts of time) you can feel the energy level of the whole picture sag, to such an extent that Geoffrey Rush seems obliged to momentarily morph from a villain into a Good Guy just to hold the screen. Next down on the box-office list, at number five, is *Harry Potter and the Order of the Phoenix*, which made $290,044,738, up by a couple of million from 2005's *Harry Potter and the Goblet of Fire*, enough to make the overall series the top-grossing movie franchise of all time, beating out even the *Star Wars* franchise. The Harry Potter films have so far defied the law of diminishing returns, perhaps because they're not a trilogy—in fact, the third movie, *Harry Potter and the Prisoner of Azkaban*, is, in my opinion, the best of the series to date, by a good margin, and *The Order of the Phoenix* is in many ways a better movie than *Goblet of Fire*: tighter, faster-moving, less cluttered with extraneous sub-plots. The downside is that it's also a much *darker* movie, tense and claustrophobic from beginning to end, with little comic relief and almost none of those moments of innocent wonder and magic that you used to get occasionally in the earlier films. And this will probably only get worse in the next two films, as the Potter books themselves darken. Although the franchise is obviously still doing well at the box-office, I wonder if the demographics for the series aren't shifting—the Harry Potter movies used to be pushed as family films, released at Christmastime, something you'd bring the young kids to; although they may have gained audience among the young twenties crowd, I saw few families with young kids in the theater, and it may be that the movies have now grown too intense and dark to be considered family-friendly fare anymore, at least for the younger children.

(It's interesting to note that almost all of these big movies made *more* money overseas than they did in the domestic market. If you add the foreign grosses to the domestic takes, you find that *Harry Potter and the Order of the Phoenix* has earned $938,464,961 worldwide, *Pirates of the Caribbean: At World's End* has earned $961,002,663 worldwide, *Spider-Man 3* $890,871,626 worldwide, and so on. What gobsmacks me even more than the vast amounts of money these films pull in is the vast amounts of money they cost to *make*. $300 million for *Pirates*, $258 million for *Spider-Man*, $150 million for *Harry Potter*, and so on. If you add all the budget costs of even the first ten movies on the top-grossing list together, ignoring the other hundred plus or so movies that came out in 2007, you'd get a sum that would probably be greater many times over than all the money that has ever been spent on print SF since the very beginning of SF as a distinct publishing category. Hell, the budget for *Pirates* alone might be enough.)

A hopeful attempt to create a new major fantasy franchise is *The Golden Compass*, based on the bestselling books by Philip Pullman. Whether it succeeded in establishing the franchise or not remains to be seen—*The Golden Compass* did well worldwide, particularly in Australia and the United Kingdom, but box-office in the U.S. was disappointing. Like almost every other fantasy movie this year, it tried to stuff too many elements into too small a box, to the point where, if you weren't a fan of the Pullman books, what was happening on the screen didn't necessarily make much sense to you; whatever plot-problems it had, the movie looked really terrific, and had some of the best CGI on display in awhile, especially the armored polar bears, and a great cast, so I wouldn't mind seeing the franchise succeed in establishing itself. (The Pope actually took the time to denounce *The Golden Compass* for its portrait of a thinly-disguised Catholic Church—more disguised in the movie than the book, actually—as the Bad Guys, which I must admit prompted me to wonder if, with all the horrors abroad in the world, he couldn't have found something a lot more Evil out there to denounce instead.) The other stylish and substantial (if again, muddled) fantasy film of the year was *Stardust*, based on Neil Gaiman's novel of the same name. Again, too many subplots, too many things tugging in too many directions at once, too much that ought to have been done without, charming as it might be; for instance, one of the most enjoyable bits in the movie was Robert De Niro's turn as a transvestite pirate—but it ultimately didn't really have much to do with the plot, and was just one more thing to bog-down the narrative drive. *Stardust* finished in the sixty-sixth position in the top-grossing list, which probably means there's not going to be a sequel.

I suppose we should count *Bridge to Terabithia* as a fantasy film, since it literalizes the fantasy escape world of the children a lot more than the book did, where there was a good deal more question as to weather it was "real" or not. And where should we put *Beowulf*? Is it a fantasy (it has monsters), a historical Sword and Sandal epic, or an animated film? I suppose you can come closest to summing it up as a fantasy film set in a real historical setting (sort of like *The Thirteenth Warrior*, if the raiders had turned out to be real supernatural demons instead of Neanderthals). I find the claim that it's an animated film to be a bit of a stretch, since it was filmed with real actors and then had stop-motion animation added in later. Like the similar process in last year's *A Scanner Darkly*, I found all this rather unnecessary; in my opinion; they should have saved the animation for the monsters, where you're trying to show something that doesn't really exist, and filmed the human actors in the regular way . . . and the monsters might have had more impact if they were motion-capture animated and everything else was *not*. I fail to see what you gain by using motion-capture animation to show a man drinking a cup of mead when you can just film him drinking it instead; save the animation for things that *can't* actually be put before a camera.

The remaining fantasy films were less successful, critically and economically. *The Water Horse: Legend of the Deep* tried to be cute and heartwarming and hit embarrassing instead, and I knew that *Mr. Magorium's Wonder Emporium* was in trouble when my grandchildren (nine and twelve, respectively) refused to go see it because it looked dull (they wanted to see *Enchanted* instead); apparently it *was* dull, and few other people wanted to see it either. You have to wonder why God didn't forbid the making of *Evan Almighty*, or at least blast the director with lightning; at least He struck it dead at the Box Office. There was also a cross between a slob comedy and a Christmas fantasy movie, *Fred Claus* (sadly, not the first, either).

The highly stylized account of the Battle of Thermopylae, *300*, rated number eight on the top-grossing list, making it the most financially successful Sword and Sandal epic since *Gladiator* (there have been a number of them in the years between the two, and, until now, they've always dogged-out). Chances are, you're either going to love *300* or hate it, and I know people who fall into both camps (I tend to fall into the "hate it" camp, myself). Actually, it reminds me of *Beowulf*, which itself could probably be categorized as a Sword and Sandal movie, without too much of a stretch: in both, there's lots of blood spraying, lots of heroic half-naked (or almost entirely naked, in the case of *300*) men, lots of bulging pecs and abs glistening with sweat, lots of macho posturing and boasting, lots of warriors hitting each other with swords, lots of rather dramatic liberties taken with the source material—did you know, for instance, that the Persian Empire deployed ferocious War Rhinoceroses in the Battle of Thermopylae? Gosh, before this movie came out, neither did I! Much further down the food-chain, not making it on to the top-grossing list, was *Pathfinder: Legend of the Ghost Warrior*, which featured Vikings fighting Indians in the forests of the New World.

Somewhat to my surprise, since I thought it considerably the weakest of the three, and was all ready to make comments about the franchise stretching itself too thin and running out of gas, the animated film *Shrek the Third* was the number two top-grossing film of the year, hauling in $322,710,944 in domestic grosses. Not bad for a cartoon ogre who was born a decided underdog, created on a relatively small budget by refugees and outcasts from the big studios. (Just so you don't think me a total curmudgeon, I quite liked the first *Shrek*. Although, I think the series has been going downhill since then—while obviously everybody else in the world thinks it's going in the opposite direction. One thing that gave the first *Shrek* its bite was its surprisingly merciless and mean-spirited satire of Disney movies, and that bite seems to have been considerably blunted since Disney bought *Shrek*'s parent company.) Another animated film that outgrossed all but a few of the year's live-action films was *Ratatouille*, which finished a very respectable ninth on the box-office list—and unlike *Shrek the Third*, which was disliked by most of the critics, *Ratatouille* was treated with an amazing amount of critical respect for an animated movie (especially one about a talking rat), which are generally dismissed as "kid stuff." It deserved the respect, being probably the best Pixar film since *The Incredibles* (I still like *The Incredibles* a tad better, but *Ratatouille* was loads better than last year's dull and earnest *Cars*), and is one of the best overall since *Toy Story* (still my favorite Pixar). *The Simpson's Movie* also got lots of critical respect, and finished tenth on the box-office list, making this a pretty impressive money-making year for animated films. *Alvin and the Chipmunks* finished eleventh, which isn't chopped liver either, but got no critical respect at all. Bringing up the rear of the animated pack at nineteenth was *Bee Movie* (the critics were lukewarm about it too), and well down in the pack were *Meet the Robinsons*, *Surf's Up*, and *TMNT* (which stands for Teenage Mutant Ninja Turtles in case you didn't realize, making an unsuccessful comeback).

Another unexpected hit was Disney's *Enchanted*, which was a half animated, half live-action film where animated characters from cartoon fairytales come to the real (sort of) New York City and get translated into flesh and blood. Like *Shrek the Third*, *Enchanted* is also torn between being a satire of cartoon fairytales and *being* a cartoon fairytale; since this *is* a Disney movie, after all, none of its satire gets anywhere near poking the kind of merciless fun at Disney movies that enlivened the original *Shrek*, but some of it is fairly funny anyway, including the dancing rats, pigeons, and cockroaches that come out as the New York equivalent of all the birds, bunnies, and squirrels that are always helping Cinderella and other Disney characters sew dresses and clean the house up. It's all amiable and fun to watch, with a good performance by Amy Adams, who plays the wide-eyed, ever-optimistic and chirpy, impossibly innocent cartoon Princess who must somehow survive on the (pretty sanitized) Mean Streets of the Big Bad City. (My grandkids liked it too.) *Happily N'ever After* covered the same kind of ground, deconstructing cartoon fairy tales with mild satire, but was nowhere near as successful either critically or financially.

There were horror movies, of course, such as *The Mist*, *28 Weeks Later*, *Saw IV*, *Resident Evil: Extinction*, and *Halloween (2007)*, but I didn't pay much attention to them.

Martian Child isn't SF, but it may be of associational interest to some, being drawn from a novel by SF writer David Gerrold about an SF writer struggling to raise an emotionally damaged child—although the movie has

changed the book's gay bachelor to a much more socially acceptable hetero-
sexual widower.

The new *Star Trek* movie seems to be generating most of the anticipa-
tory buzz amongst next year's upcoming movies, as far as I can tell.

This seems to have been The Year of the Cop in SF and fantasy TV shows,
where we've had vampire cops, immortal cops, wizard cops, time-traveling
cops, cops who live the same day over and over, and cops who talk to angels
(and, of course, cops figure or have recently figured in the plotlines of shows
such as *Heroes* and *Lost*). Can the show about the cop with a chimpanzee
for a partner be far behind?

Of course, the entire season has been overshadowed by the Writers Guild
of America strike (stretching far beyond genre boundaries; practically every
scripted show on television was affected), which has already closed down
some shows, and will probably close down more; it's quite possible that none
of the shows I mention here (with the exception of the British imports) will
actually be on the air next season. Since the networks and major studios seem
to have dug their heels in, seemingly confident that they can get by with showing *nothing but* unscripted reality shows and not lose their audiences, the
strike could drag on for a long time, and since most scripted TV shows are of
necessity prepared months in advance, it's already too late to hope for a normal season, even if the strike were suddenly settled tomorrow.

Heroes and *Lost* are running truncated seasons (basically what shows
they could get in the can before the strike started), as is *Terminator: The
Sarah Conner Chronicles* (a promising new show that revisits the territory of
the *Terminator* films, with lots of guns blazing), while *Moonlight* (vampire
cop, which strikes me as *Angel* Lite, with more blow-dried hair), *New Amsterdam* (immortal cop), *The Bionic Woman*, and *Cavemen* have already
gone "on hiatus," and how many of them actually make it back on the air
after the strike is anybody's guess. (My guess is that *Cavemen*, perhaps the
weakest new genre show of the season, won't. Having made the stupid decision in the first place to derive a sitcom from the popular Geico "Cavemen"
commercials, they then didn't hire any of the familiar actors from the commercials, and then skewed their cavemen toward angst and anger rather than
sprightly satire, with lame results.)

Day Break (cop living the same day over and over), *Journeyman* (time-
traveling cop), *The Dresden Files* (wizard cop), and the long-running *The
Dead Zone* and *The 4400* have all been cancelled, and won't be back no
matter what the outcome of the strike may be.

Jericho, the after-the-atomic-war drama, was cancelled too, but a massive
write-in campaign by the show's outraged fans, who deluged the studio with

mailed packets of peanuts (don't ask why—you had to be there), caused the network to reconsider, and give *Jericho* a limited second-chance, offering it a number of new shows in the new season to see if it could build its disappointing audience; of course, the strike puts this second-chance in jeopardy as well. (If you wonder at the discrepancy between the network's perception of "disappointing audiences" and huge numbers of fans mounting a "massive write-in" campaign for the show's reinstatement, it's because, in my opinion, the networks are no longer counting their audiences correctly. Counting just the first-run at-home audience, in the classic Neilsen-ratings fashion, ignores all the folks—perhaps a majority, if the experience of me and my friends is anything to go by—who tape the show or copy it on their DVRs or TiVos to watch at some later date, and also those who follow the show on the internet or on On Demand when it's "rebroadcast" a few days later. The networks badly need to revamp their ratings systems to make some kind of a match with twenty-first Century reality, or they're going to end up deep-sixing the very shows that have growing audiences, albeit audiences growing in unconventional ways in unconventional media. The days when you can judge anything fairly by counting how many people are sitting in their living rooms in front of their TV sets on any particular night are over.)

Of the surviving shows (for the moment, we'll see which of them make it through to the other side of the strike), *Heroes* seems to be still doing well, although, perhaps inevitably, there's been some word-of-mouth fan grumbling about how this season isn't as good as the first season. I think that the once red-hot *Lost* may be in trouble, and that The Suits are in danger of fixing this show to death, as they've done with many another show. The extremely long lacuna between blocks of original episodes, three months in season three, and an even longer break between seasons three and four (with new shows originally planned not to return until *summer* 2008 (!)—something which, wisely, they've changed, with the new season now beginning in January 2008) were serious mistakes, and I'm afraid that much of their audience will have grown frustrated, lost interest, become annoyed, or just plain gotten out of the habit of watching before new episodes begin again (certainly much of the excited buzz on the internet that once centered on the show seems to have cooled and dissipated)—and even once new episodes do start, we're only going to get the eight episodes that were already in the can before the strike closed things down. As if there weren't already enough nails in its coffin, the network recently announced that they were changing *Lost*'s broadcast night from it's traditional Wednesday to Thursday, a sure sign of a show that a network is losing confidence in. *Lost* is reputed to be the most expensive to produce series on television, because of its location shooting in Hawaii and its large cast, and if it's ratings start to seriously slip, it's toast. (Boy, if this show gets cancelled before its immensely complicated storyline plays out and the final "answers" to its mysteries are supplied, as I suspect is a possibility, there are going to be a lot of pissed-off viewers out there!)

Stargate: Atlantis is still afloat, as far as I know, although its parent show, *Stargate SG-1*, has sunk beneath the waves of history. *Battlestar Galactica* has announced its upcoming season as its last, and, once it follows *Babylon Five*, *Firefly*, and the various *Star Trek* shows into oblivion, there will no longer be any special effects-heavy, expensive-to-produce, space-travel-oriented series left on television, with the partial exception of *Stargate: Atlantis*, which runs a spaceship scene in every once in a while.

Shows such as *Medium*, *The Ghost Whisperer*, and *Supernatural* are *much* cheaper to produce: all you need are some characters who get psychic visions or talk to the dead or fight the supernatural Menace of the Week, and some monster or ghost makeup; since they're all set in the present day, there's no need for expensive special effects or postproduction work or elaborate sets or props or set-dressing. Perhaps as a result of this cost-effectiveness, they all seem to be doing fine and I suspect they'll be back next season, if there is a next season. Same for *Smallville*, although it's a bit more special effects-heavy than the supernatural shows; still, it'll probably be back, although it seems to me that they've already cut it about as close to the supposedly off-limits territory of the *Superman* comic books as they possibly can without having Clark actually put on the tights and start working for the *Daily Planet*. I suppose new show *Saving Grace* fits in best with the supernatural trio above; I respect Holly Hunt, the show's star and a fine actress, but when this cop drama broke out a real actual no-fooling angelic intervention by a real actual no-fooling angel (yes, this is the cop who talks to angels show), it passed my Too Silly threshold, and I stopped watching it. Another new show, *Kyle XY*, which started on the Family Channel, is sort of like *Heroes* Lite, with a boy of mysterious origins trying to figure out his enigmatic past. *Pushing Daisies*, a surreal comedy about somebody who can bring people back from the dead for small periods of time, tries much too hard in a self-conscious look-at-how-cool-we-are way to be hip and *Twin Peaks* weird, and so I find it annoying rather than entertaining. *Eureka*, about a small town where everyone's a genius, is a somewhat similar kind of semi-surreal comedy, but has a much lighter touch, and so is more watchable, to me, anyway.

The Sci-Fi Channel sunk a lot of money into an elaborate made-for-TV miniseries called *Tin Man*, which was sort of a gritty steampunk revisioning of *The Wizard of Oz*, complete with secret police, androids, and brains in bottles, but although I hear that the ratings were good, it doesn't seem to have generated a lot of buzz among the majority of genre SF and fantasy fans, who seem to have largely ignored it.

Some of us at least have access to British programming through BBC America, and you ought to check your listings to see if you get that channel, since the several genre shows on it may be the only ones on television which will continue uninterrupted through the strike—and beside, they're pretty good. The most prominent of them is the revamped version of that perennial genre classic from the '60s, *Doctor Who*, which in tone and spirit is pretty faithful to the original, although the special effects are (somewhat) better; episodes from it have won the Hugo Award for Best Dramatic Presentation (short form) for two years running now, so clearly it's popular with the fans. *Torchwood*, a spin-off from *Doctor Who*, about an intrepid group of clandestine government agents who battle a different alien of the week every show (or sometimes try to recover lost alien technology before it can have a negative effect on the public), is also fun, although again the special effects are somewhat weak by American standards—it all comes across rather like what *The X-Files* would have been like if it'd been created by the producers of *Doctor Who* in England rather than in America. *Life on Mars*, another time-traveling cop show, is also gritty and intriguing, about a detective who somehow gets thrown from the present day back into the 1970s and must struggle to try to figure out what's happened to him (it's rumored that there's going to be an American version, but I'll bet they screw it up). There was also a British miniseries version of Terry Pratchett's *Hogfather*, which is hard to find over here (I never could), but which apparently on occasion drifts wraith-like across small and obscure public television channels if you happen to be watching them at three o'clock in the morning.

We finally got to see some episodes of the now-defunct *Masters of Science Fiction*, a new anthology show that was much-hyped in advance in some circles. It was clear that The Suits did everything they could to sabotage this series from the start, and had reportedly already made up their minds to sink it before the first episode had even aired, so I'd like to say that it was great, and that the network Philistines just weren't hip enough to appreciate it—but unfortunately, I can't. Slow, dated, grossly padded, poorly directed—the episodes just weren't very good. Word of mouth on it among genre fans was terrible, and I think it would have foundered on its own, even without the distaste of network executives for SF working against it behind the scenes.

I've given up on listing *Desperate Housewives*, *The Simpsons*, *South Park*, *The Family Guy*, *Aqua Teen Hunger Force*, and other shows of that ilk—they all borrow genre tropes for satirical effect, but it's clear that they're not really genre shows in any true sense of the word.

Coming up next year: a new version of '70s "classic" show *Knight Rider* (cop with talking robot car). Wonder when casting calls for that chimpanzee will start?

The 65th World Science Fiction Convention, Nippon 2007, was held in Yokohama, Japan, from August 30-September 3, 2007. The 2007 Hugo Awards, presented at Nippon 2007, were: Best Novel, *Rainbow's End*, by Vernor Vinge; Best Novella, "A Billion Eves," by Robert Reed; Best Novelette, "The Djinn's Wife," by Ian McDonald; Best Short Story, "Impossible Dreams," by Tim Pratt; Best Related Book, *James Tiptree, Jr: The Double Life of Alice B. Sheldon*, by Julie Phillips; Best Professional Editor, Long Form, Patrick Nielson Hayden; Best Professional Editor, Short Form, Gordon Van Gelder; Best Professional Artist, Donato Giancola; Best Dramatic Presentation (short form), *Doctor Who*; Best Dramatic Presentation (long form); *Pan's Labyrinth*; Best Semiprozine, *Locus*, edited by Kristen Gong-Wong and Lisa Groen Trombi; Best Fanzine, *Science-Fiction Five-Yearly*, edited by Lee Hoffman, Geri Sullivan, and Randy Byers; Best Fan Writer, David Langford; Best Fan Artist, Frank Wu; plus the John W. Campbell Award for Best New Writer to Naomi Novik.

The 2006 Nebula Awards, presented at a banquet at the Marriott Financial Center in New York City on May 12, 2007, were: Best Novel, *Seeker*, by Jack McDevitt; Best Novella, *Burn*, by James Patrick Kelly; Best Novelette, "Two Hearts," by Peter S. Beagle; Best Short Story, "Echo," by Elizabeth Hand; Best Script, *Howl's Moving Castle*, by Hayao Miyazaki, Cindy David Hewitt, and Donald H. Hewitt; the Andre Norton Award to *Magic or Madness*, by Justine Larbalestier; plus the Author Emeritus Award to D.G. Compton, and the Grand Master Award to James Gunn.

The 2007 World Fantasy Awards, presented at a banquet at the Saratoga Springs Hotel and Conference Center in Saratoga Springs, New York on November 4, 2007, during the Sixteenth Annual World Fantasy Convention, were: Best Novel, *Soldier of Sidon*, by Gene Wolfe; Best Novella, "Botch Town," by Jeffrey Ford; Best Short Fiction, "Journey Into the Kingdom," by M. Rickert; Best Collection, Map of Dreams, by M. Rickert; Best Anthology, Salon Fantastique, by Ellen Datlow and Terri Windling; Best Artist, Shaun Tan; Special Award (Professional), to Ellen Asher, for her work at the Science Fiction Book Club; Special Award (Non-Professional), to Gary K. Wolfe, for reviews in *Locus* and elsewhere; plus the Life Achievement Award to Betty Ballantine and Diana Wynne Jones.

The 2007 Bram Stoker Awards, presented by the Horror Writers of America during a banquet at the Toronto Marriott Downtown in Toronto, Canada on March 31, 2007, were: Best Novel, *Lisey's Story*, by Stephen King; Best First Novel, *Ghost Road Blues*, by Jonathan Maberry; Best Long Fiction, *Dark Harvest*, by Norman Partridge; Best Short Fiction, "Tested," by Lisa Morton; Best Collection, *Destinations Unknown*, by Gary A. Braunbeck; Best Anthology, *Retro Pulp Tales*, edited by Joe R. Lansdale and *Mondo Zombie*, edited by John Skipp (tie); Non-Fiction, *Final Exits*, by Michael Large and *Gospel of the Living Dead*, by Kim Paffenroth (tie); Best Poetry Collection, *Shades Fantastic*, by Bruce Boston; Specialty Press Award, to PS Publishing; plus the Lifetime Achievement Award to Thomas Harris.

The 2006 John W. Campbell Memorial Award was won by *Titan*, by Ben Bova.

The 2006 Theodore Sturgeon Memorial Award for Best Short Story was won by "The Cartesian Theater," by Robert Charles Wilson.

The 2006 Philip K. Dick Memorial Award went to *Spin Control*, by Chris Moriarity.

The 2006 Arthur C. Clarke award was won by *Nova Swing*, by M. John Harrison.

The 2006 James Tiptree, Jr. Memorial Award was won by *Half Life*, by Shelley Jackson and *The Orphan's Tales: In the Night Garden*, by Caherynne M. Valente (tie).

The Cordwainer Smith Rediscovery Award, went to Stanley G. Weinbaum.

Death once again took a heavy toll on the science fiction and fantasy fields this year. Dead in 2007 and early 2008 were: **KURT VONNEGUT**, 84, bestselling author of such acclaimed novels as *Cat's Cradle, Slaughterhouse Five, God Bless You, Mr. Rosewater,* and *The Sirens of Titan*; **MADELEINE L' ENGLE**, 88, fantasy and YA writer, author of such beloved classics as *A Wrinkle in Time* and *A Swiftly Tilting Planet*; **LLOYD ALEXANDER**, 83, fantasy writer, winner of the Life Achievement Award given by the World Fantasy Convention, author of the "Chronicles of Prydain" sequence, the most famous of which were probably *The Black Cauldron* and *The High King*; **JAMES OLIVER RIGNEY, Jr.**, 58, who, writing as **ROBERT JORDAN**, was the author of the hugely bestselling "Wheel of Time" series of fantasy novels, which started with *The Eye of the World* and continued for twelve more volumes; **FRED SABERHAGEN**, 77, best known for the long-running "Beserker" sequence of novels and stories, although he also wrote the popular "Empire of the East" and "Dracula" series; **JOE L. HENSLEY**, 81, veteran SF and mystery writer, author of over twenty novels and collections; **STERLING E. LANIER**, 79, fantasy writer best known for his series of stories depicting the supernatural adventures of Brigadier Ffellowes, which were collected in *The Peculiar Exploits of Brigadier Ffellowes* and *The Curious Quests of Brigadier Ffellowes*, and for the postapocalyptic novel *Hiero's Journey*, as well as being the editor instrumental in convincing someone to buy Frank Herbert's *Dune* after many other publishers had turned it down; **DAVID I. MASON**, 91, British writer who dazzled everybody with a handful of brilliantly innovative stories like "Traveller's Rest" in the '60s, which were later collected in *The Caltraps of Time*; **LEE HOFFMAN**, 75, veteran SF and Western writer and longtime fan, who was perhaps best known for her Western novel, *The Valdez*

Horses, which won the Western Writers of America's Golden Spur Award, and was later filmed; **COLIN KAPP**, 79, British writer prolific as a novelist and short story writer in the '60s and '70s; **DAVID M. HONIGSBERG**, 48, writer, musician, and fan; **CHARLES L. FONTENAY**, 89, veteran author of *The Day the Oceans Overflowed* and others; **LEIGH EDDINGS**, 69, fantasy writer, author of "The Belgariad" series and others; **PATRICE DUVIC**, 61, French writer, editor, and filmmaker, a personal friend; **PAT O'SHEA**, 76, Irish author of the bestselling YA fantasy, *The Hounds of the Morrigan*; **NORMAN MAILER**, 84, famous American writer whose closest association with the genre was probably his non-fiction book about the Apollo space program, *Of A Fire on the Moon*; **JOHN GARDNER**, 80, British thriller writer best known for continuing the "James Bond" novels after the death of Ian Fleming; **IRA LEVIN**, 78, bestselling author of *Rosemary's Baby*, *The Stepford Wives*, and *The Boys from Brazil*; **GEORGE MAC-DONALD FRASER**, 82, historical novelist with no direct genre connection, but whose "Flashman" novels, some of the best adventure novels ever written, are so full of colorful and exotic elements and enjoyed by so many SF fans that a mention seemed justifiable; **EDWARD D. HOCH**, 78, prolific and acclaimed mystery writer who also had publications in some SF markets; **ELIZABETH JOLLEY**, 83, Australian horror writer best known for her style of "Australian Gothic" writing; **SYDNEY J. BOUNDS**, 86, British SF and children's book author; **JERZY PETERKIEWICZ**, 91, Polish author and poet; **JURGEN CRASMUCK**, 67, German SF and horror writer; **RUBENS TEIXEIRA SCAVONE**, 82, Brazilian SF and mainstream author; **ALICE BORCHARDT**, 67, fantasy writer, author of the "Silver Wolfe" series, also the sister of horror writer Ann Rice; **DOUGLAS HILL**, 72, British editor and author of nearly seventy SF books for teens and children; **FRED MUSTARD STEWART**, 74, author of *The Mephisto Waltz*; **RONDA THOMPSON**, 51, author of romance and paranormal romance novels, **GERALD PERKINS**, 62, writer and fan; **PETER L. MANLY**, 61, writer and fan; **TERRY DARTNELL**, Australian SF writer; **RALPH A. SPERRY**, 62, writer; **BENEDICT KELLY**, 87, Irish fantasy writer; **JOSE COIRO**, 74, Braziliam SF author; **DANIEL STERN**, 79, O. Henry Award-winning author who occasionally wrote SF; **CHARLES EINSTEIN**, 80, mystery writer who occasionally wrote SF; **PAUL E. ERDMAN**, 74, author of borderline SF/financial thrillers such as *The Crash of '79*; **DENNY MARTIN FLINN**, 59, writer and actor, who wrote the screenplay for the movie *Star Trek VI: The Undiscovered Country*; **CRAIG HINTON**, 42, author of five *Doctor Who* novels; **MARGARET F. CRAWFORD**, 82, editor, publisher, and fan, co-founder of one of the first of the small presses, Fantasy Publishing Company Incorporated; **PETER**

HAINING, 67, prolific British fantasy and horror anthologist; **ROGER ELWOOD**, 64, editor and anthologist who sold so many anthologies to so many different publishers in the early '70s that he was credited with crashing the anthology market and making it impossible for anyone else to sell one for years to come, editor of *Ten Tomorrows, Future City*, and *Epoch* (with Robert Silverberg), among many others; **PAUL WALKER**, 64, writer and interviewer, compiler of the interview collection *Speaking of Science Fiction*; **SIDNEY COLEMAN**, 70, academic and critic, professor at Harvard University who sometimes contributed review columns to F&SF, and who was the co-founder of Advent:Publishers; **LESLIE FLOOD**, 85, longtime British agent and bookseller; **PERRY H. KNOWLTON**, 80, longtime agent; **INGMAR BERGMAN**, 89, famed Swedish director and screenwriter, probably best known to genre audiences for his film *The Seventh Seal*, which had fantastic elements; **IAN RICHARDSON**, 74, distinguished actor best known to genre audiences for roles in Brazil, *Gormanghast*, and Terry Pratchett's *Hogfather*; **ROBERT GOULET**, 75, Canadian singer who originated the role of Lancelot in Broadway's *Camelot*; **MAILA NURMI**, 87, who as **VAMPIRA** was an early horror-show host on television, as well as starring in camp classics such as *Plan Nine From Outer Space*; **YVONNE DE CARLO**, 86, actress best know for her role as Lily Munster in TV's *The Munsters*; **RICHARD A. HAUPTMANN**, 62, academic, anthologist, and publisher, an expert on the works of SF writer Jack Williamson and one of the organizers of the Jack Williamson Lectureship in Portales, New Mexico, author of *The Work of Jack Williamson: An Annotated Bibliography and Guide*, and co-editor, with Stephen Haffner, of the collection *Seventy-Five: The Diamond Anniversary of a Science Fiction Pioneer*; **BILL NABORS**, 63, writer and poet, a personal friend; **ROBERT W. BUSSARD**, 79, physicist, whose theoretical Bussard Ramjet engine has been fueling the paper starships of SF writers since the 1960s; **PAUL LLOYD**, 77, academic and longtime fan; **CALVIN W. DEMMON**, 65, fan, fan writer, and fanzine editor; **JACK AGNEW**, 84, fan and artist, a founding member of the Philadelphia Science Fiction Society, the oldest fan club in the nation; **ELLY BLOCH**, 91, widow of horror writer Robert Bloch; **JIM RAYMOND VAN SCYOC**, husband of SF writer Sydney J. Van Scyoc; **JOAN TEMPLE**, 90, widow of SF writer William F. Temple; **HANK REINHARDT**, 73, husband of SF editor and publisher Toni Weisskopf; **SUSAN CHANDLER**, widow of SF writer A. Bertram Chandler; **GAIL DALMAS**, wife of SF writer John Dalmas; **CHRISTOPHER JAMES BISHOP**, 36, son of SF writer Michael Bishop, one of those killed during the massacre at Virginia Tech, where he was a professor; **AMELIA MARY SWANWICK**, 87, mother of SF writer Michael Swanwick; **IRMA**

KNOTT GOONAN, 86, mother of SF writer Kathleen Ann Goonan; **GEORGI GAGIKOVICH NAZARIAN**, 91, father of SF writer Vera Nazarian; **CLAUDIA LIGHTFOOT**, 58, mother of SF writer China Mieville and an author in her own right; **PATRICIA LANDIS WILLIAMS**, 77, mother of SF writer Geoffrey A. Landis; and **MADELON GERNSBACK**, 98, daughter of pioneer SF editor Hugo Gernsback.

finisterra

DAVID MOLES

New writer David Moles has sold fiction to *Asimov's Science Fiction*, *The Magazine of Fantasy & Science Fiction*, *Polyphony*, *Strange Horizons*, *Lady Churchill's Rosebud Wristlet*, *Say*, *Flytrap*, and elsewhere. He coedited with Jay Lake, 2004's well-received "retro-pulp" anthology *All-Star Zeppelin Adventure Stories*, as well as coediting with Susan Marie Groppi the original anthology *Twenty Epics*. He's had stories in our Twenty-second, Twenty-third, and Twenty-fourth Annual Collections.

In the vivid and fast-paced story that follows, he takes us to a world of living, floating islands in the sky, to teach us the uncomfortable lesson that you're never safe from predation no matter how big you are. Or from your own past, either.

1. ENCANTADA

Bianca Nazario stands at the end of the world.

The firmament above is as blue as the summer skies of her childhood, mirrored in the waters of *la caldera*; but where the skies she remembers were bounded by mountains, here on Sky there is no real horizon, only a line of white cloud. The white line shades into a diffuse grayish fog that, as Bianca looks down, grows progressively murkier, until the sky directly below is thoroughly dark and opaque.

She remembers what Dinh told her about the ways Sky could kill her.

With a large enough parachute, Bianca imagines, she could fall for hours, drifting through the layered clouds, before finding her end in heat or pressure or the jaws of some monstrous denizen of the deep air.

If this should go wrong, Bianca cannot imagine a better way to die.

Bianca works her way out a few hundred meters along the base of one of Encantada's ventral fins, stopping when the dry red dirt beneath her feet begins to give way to scarred gray flesh. She takes a last look around: at the pall of smoke obscuring the *zaratán*'s tree-lined dorsal ridge, at the fin she stands on, curving out and down to its delicate-looking tip, kilometers away. Then she knots her scarf around her skirted ankles and shrugs into the para-balloon harness, still warm from the bungalow's fabricators. As the harness tightens itself around her, she takes a deep breath, filling her lungs. The wind from the burning camp smells of wood smoke and pine resin, enough to overwhelm the taint of blood from the killing ground.

Blessed Virgin, she prays, be my witness: this is no suicide.

This is a prayer for a miracle.

She leans forward.

She falls.

2. THE FLYING ARCHIPELAGO

The boatlike anemopter that Valadez had sent for them had a cruising speed of just less than the speed of sound, which in this part of Sky's atmosphere meant about nine hundred kilometers per hour. The speed, Bianca thought, might have been calculated to bring home the true size of Sky, the impossible immensity of it. It had taken the better part of their first day's travel for the anemopter's point of departure, the ten-kilometer, billion-ton vacuum balloon *Transient Meridian*, to drop from sight—the dwindling golden droplet disappearing, not over the horizon, but into the haze. From that Bianca estimated that the bowl of clouds visible through the subtle blurring of the anemopter's static fields covered an area about the size of North America.

She heard a plastic clattering on the deck behind her and turned to see one of the anemopter's crew, a globular, brown-furred alien with a collection of arms like furry snakes, each arm tipped with a mouth or a round and curious eye. The *firija* were low-gravity creatures; the ones Bianca had seen on her passage from Earth had tumbled joyously through the *Caliph of Baghdad*'s inner-ring spaces like so many radially symmetrical monkeys. The three aboard the anemopter, in Sky's heavier gravity, had to make do with spindly-legged walking machines. There was a droop in their arms that was both comical and melancholy.

"Come forward," this one told Bianca in fractured Arabic, its voice like an ensemble of reed pipes. She thought it was the one that called itself Ismaíl. "Make see archipelago."

She followed it forward to the anemopter's rounded prow. The naturalist, Erasmus Fry, was already there, resting his elbows on the rail, looking down.

"Pictures don't do them justice, do they?" he said.

Bianca went to the rail and followed the naturalist's gaze. She did her best to maintain a certain stiff formality around Fry; from their first meeting aboard *Transient Meridian* she'd had the idea that it might not be good to let him get too familiar. But when she saw what Fry was looking at, the mask slipped for a moment; she couldn't help a sharp, quick intake of breath.

Fry chuckled. "To stand on the back of one," he said, "to stand in a valley and look up at the hills and know that the ground under your feet is supported by the bones of a living creature—there's nothing else like it." He shook his head.

At this altitude they were above all but the highest-flying of the thousands of beasts that made up Septentrionalis Archipelago. Bianca's eyes tried to make the herd (or flock, or school) of *zaratánes* into other things: a chain of islands, yes, if she concentrated on the colors, the greens and browns of forests and plains, the grays and whites of the snowy highlands; a fleet of ships, perhaps, if she instead focused on the individual shapes, the keel ridges, the long, translucent fins, ribbed like Chinese sails.

The *zaratánes* of the archipelago were more different from one another than the members of a flock of birds or a pod of whales, but still there was a symmetry, a regularity of form, the basic anatomical plan—equal parts fish and mountain—repeated throughout, in fractal detail from the great old shape of Zaratán Finisterra, a hundred kilometers along the dorsal ridge, down to the merely hill-sized bodies of the nameless younger beasts. When she took in the archipelago as a whole, it was impossible for Bianca not to see the *zaratánes* as living things.

"Nothing else like it," Fry repeated.

Bianca turned reluctantly from the view to look at Fry. The naturalist spoke Spanish with a flawless Miami accent, courtesy, he'd said, of a Consilium language module. Bianca was finding it hard to judge the ages of *extrañados*, particularly the men, but in Fry's case she thought he might be ten years older than Bianca's own forty, and unwilling to admit it—or ten years younger, and in the habit of treating himself very badly. On her journey here she'd met cyborgs and foreigners and artificial intelligences and several sorts of alien—some familiar, at least from media coverage of the *hajj*, and some strange—but the *extrañados* bothered her the most. It was hard to come to terms with the idea of humans born off Earth, humans who had never been to Earth or even seen it; humans who often had no interest in it.

"Why did you leave here, Mr. Fry?" she asked.

Fry laughed. "Because I didn't want to spend the rest of my life out *here.*" With a hand, he swept the horizon. "Stuck on some godforsaken floating island for years on end, with no one but researchers and feral refugees to talk to, nowhere to go for fun but some slum of a balloon station, nothing but a thousand kilometers of air between you and Hell?" He laughed again. "You'd leave, too, Nazario, believe me."

"Maybe I would," Bianca said. "But you're back."

"I'm here for the money," Fry said. "Just like you."

Bianca smiled and said nothing.

"You know," Fry said after a little while, "they have to kill the *zaratánes* to take them out of here." He looked at Bianca and smiled, in a way that was probably meant to be ghoulish. "There's no atmosphere ship big enough to lift a *zaratán* in one piece—even a small one. The poachers deflate them— gut them—flatten them out and roll them up. And even then, they throw out almost everything but the skin and bones."

"Strange," Bianca mused. Her mask was back in place. "There was a packet of material on the *zaratánes* with my contract; I watched most of it on the voyage. According to the packet, the Consilium considers the *zaratánes* a protected species."

Fry looked uneasy. Now it was Bianca's turn to chuckle.

"Don't worry, Mr. Fry," she said. "I may not know exactly what it is Mr. Valadez is paying me to do, but I've never had any illusion that it was legal."

Behind her, the *firija* made a fluting noise that might have been laughter.

3. THE STEEL BIRD

When Bianca was a girl, the mosque of Punta Aguila was the most prominent feature in the view from her fourth-floor window, a sixteenth-century structure of tensegrity cables and soaring catenary curves, its spreading white wings vaguely—but only vaguely—recalling the bird that gave the city its name. The automation that controlled the tension of the cables and adjusted the mosque's wings to match the shifting winds was hidden within the cables themselves, and was very old. Once, after the hurricane in the time of Bianca's grandfather, it had needed adjusting, and the old men of the *ayuntamiento* had been forced to send for *extrañado* technicians, at an expense so great that the *jizyah* of Bianca's time was still paying for it.

But Bianca rarely thought of that. Instead she would spend long hours surreptitiously sketching those white wings, calculating the weight of the structure and the tension of the cables, wondering what it would take to make the steel bird fly.

Bianca's father could probably have told her, but she never dared to ask. Raúl Nazario de Arenas was an aeronautical engineer, like the seven generations before him, and flight was the Nazarios' fortune; fully a third of the aircraft that plied the skies over the Rio Pícaro were types designed by Raúl or his father or his wife's father, on contract to the great *moro* trading and manufacturing families that were Punta Aguila's truly wealthy.

Because he worked for other men, and because he was a Christian, Raúl Nazario would never be as wealthy as the men who employed him, but his profession was an ancient and honorable one, providing his family with a more than comfortable living. If Raúl Nazario de Arenas thought of the mosque at all, it was only to mutter about the *jizyah* from time to time—but never loudly, because the Nazarios, like the other Christians of Punta Aguila, however valued, however ancient their roots, knew that they lived there only on sufferance.

But Bianca would sketch the aircraft, too, the swift gliders and lumbering flying boats and stately dirigibles, and these drawings she did not have to hide; in fact for many years her father would encourage her, explaining this and that aspect of their construction, gently correcting errors of proportion and balance in Bianca's drawings; would let her listen in while he taught the family profession to her brothers, Jesús the older, Pablo the younger.

This lasted until shortly before Bianca's *quinceañera*, when Jesús changed his name to Walíd and married a *moro*'s daughter, and Bianca's mother delivered a lecture concerning the difference between what was proper for a child and what was proper for a young Christian woman with hopes of one day making a good marriage.

It was only a handful of years later that Bianca's father died, leaving a teenaged Pablo at the helm of his engineering business; and only Bianca's invisible assistance and the pity of a few old clients had kept contracts and money coming into the Nazario household.

By the time Pablo was old enough to think he could run the business himself, old enough to marry the daughter of a musical instrument-maker from Tierra Ceniza, their mother was dead, Bianca was thirty, and even if her dowry had been half her father's business, there was not a Christian man in Rio Pícaro who wanted it, or her.

And then one day Pablo told her about the *extrañado* contract that had been brought to the *ayuntamiento*, a contract that the *ayuntamiento* and the Guild had together forbidden the Christian engineers of Punta Aguila to bid on—a contract for a Spanish-speaking aeronautical engineer to travel a very long way from Rio Pícaro and be paid a very large sum of money indeed.

Three months later Bianca was in Quito, boarding an elevator car. In her valise was a bootleg copy of her father's engineering system, and a contract with the factor of a starship called the *Caliph of Baghdad*, for passage to Sky.

4. THE KILLING GROUND

The anemopter's destination was a *zaratán* called Encantada, smaller than the giant Finisterra but still nearly forty kilometers from nose to tail, and eight thousand meters from gray-white keel to forested crest. From a distance of a hundred kilometers, Encantada was like a forested mountain rising from a desert plain, the clear air under its keel as dreamlike as a mirage. On her pocket system, Bianca called up pictures from Sky's network of the alpine ecology that covered the hills and valleys of Encantada's flanks: hardy grasses and small warm-blooded creatures and tall evergreens with spreading branches, reminding her of the pines and redwoods in the mountains west of Rio Pícaro.

For the last century or so Encantada had been keeping company with Zaratán Finisterra, holding its position above the larger beast's eastern flank. No one, apparently, knew the reason. Fry being the expert, Bianca had expected him to at least have a theory. He didn't even seem interested in the question.

"They're beasts, Nazario," he said. "They don't do things for reasons. We only call them animals and not plants because they bleed when we cut them."

They were passing over Finisterra's southern slopes. Looking down, Bianca saw brighter, warmer greens, more shades than she could count, more than she had known existed, the green threaded through with bright ribbons of silver water. She saw the anemopter's shadow, a dark oblong that rode the slopes and ridges, ringed by brightness—the faint reflection of Sky's sun behind them.

And just before the shadow entered the larger darkness that was the shadow of Encantada, Bianca watched it ride over something else: a flat green space carved out of the jungle, a suspiciously geometric collection of shapes that could only be buildings, the smudge of chimney smoke.

"Fry—" she started to say.

Then the village, if that's what it was, was gone, hidden behind the next ridge.

"What?" said Fry.

"I saw—I thought I saw—"

"People?" asked Fry. "You probably did."

"But I thought Sky didn't have any native sentients. Who are they?"

"Humans, mostly," Fry said. "Savages. Refugees. Drug farmers. Five generations of escaped criminals, and their kids, and *their* kids." The naturalist shrugged. "Once in a while, if the Consilium's looking for somebody in particular, the wardens might stage a raid, just for show. The rest of the time, the wardens fly their dope, screw their women . . . and otherwise leave them alone."

"But where do they come from?" Bianca asked.

"Everywhere," Fry said with another shrug. "Humans have been in this part of space for a long, long time. This is one of those places people end up, you know? People with nowhere else to go. People who can't fall any farther."

Bianca shook her head and said nothing.

The poacher camp on Encantada's eastern slope was invisible until they were almost upon it, hidden from the wardens' satellite eyes by layers of projected camouflage. Close up, the illusion seemed flat, its artificiality obvious, but it was still not until the anemopter passed through the projection that the camp itself could be seen: a clear-cut swath a kilometer wide and three times as long, stretching from the lower slopes of Encantada's dorsal ridge down to the edge of the *zaratán*'s clifflike flank. Near the edge, at one corner, there was a small cluster of prefabricated bungalows; but at first it seemed to Bianca that most of the space was wasted.

Then she saw the red churned into the brown mud of the cleared strip, saw the way the shape of the terrain suggested the imprint of a gigantic, elongated body.

The open space was for killing.

"Sky is very poor, Miss Nazario," said Valadez, over his shoulder.

The poacher boss looked to be about fifty, stocky, his hair still black and his olive skin well-tanned but pocked with tiny scars. His Spanish was a dialect Bianca had never heard before, strange and lush, its vowels rich, its *h*s breathy as Bianca's *j*s, its *j*s warm and liquid as the *y*s of an Argentine. When he said, *Fuck your mother*—and already, in the hour or so Bianca had been in the camp, she had heard him say it several times, though never yet to her—the *madre* came out *madri*.

About half of the poachers were human, but Valadez seemed to be the only one who spoke Spanish natively; the rest used Sky's dialect of bazaar Arabic. Valadez spoke that as well, better than Bianca did, but she had the sense that he'd learned it late in life. If he had a first name, he was keeping it to himself.

"There are things on Sky that people want," Valadez went on. "But the *people* of Sky have nothing of interest to anybody. The companies that mine the deep air pay some royalties. But mostly what people live on here is Consilium handouts."

The four of them—Bianca, Fry, and the *firija*, Ismaíl, who as well as being an anemopter pilot seemed to be Valadez's servant or business partner or bodyguard, or perhaps all three—were climbing the ridge above the poachers' camp. Below them workers, some human, some *firija*, a handful of other species, were setting up equipment: mobile machines that looked like they belonged on a construction site, pipes and cylindrical tanks reminiscent of a brewery or a refinery.

"I'm changing that, Miss Nazario." Valadez glanced over his shoulder at Bianca. "Off-world, there are people—like Ismaíl's people here"—he waved at the *firija*—"who like the idea of living on a floating island, and have the money to pay for one." He swept an arm, taking in the camp, the busy teams of workers. "With that money, I take boys out of the shantytowns of Sky's balloon stations and elevator gondolas. I give them tools, and teach them to kill beasts.

"To stop me—since they can't be bothered to do it themselves—the Consilium takes the same boys, gives them guns, and teaches them to kill men."

The poacher stopped and turned to face Bianca, jamming his hands into the pockets of his coat.

"Tell me, Miss Nazario—is one worse than the other?"

"I'm not here to judge you, Mr. Valadez," said Bianca. "I'm here to do a job."

Valadez smiled. "So you are."

He turned and continued up the slope. Bianca and the *firija* followed, Fry trailing behind. The path switchbacked through unfamiliar trees, dark, stunted, waxy-needled; these gave way to taller varieties, including some that Bianca would have sworn were ordinary pines and firs. She breathed deeply, enjoying the alpine breeze after the crowds-and-machines reek of *Transient Meridian*'s teeming slums, the canned air of ships and anemopters.

"It smells just like home," she remarked. "Why is that?"

No one answered.

The ridge leveled off. They came out into a cleared space, overlooking the camp. Spread out below them Bianca saw the airfield, the globular tanks and pipes of the poachers' little industrial plant, the bungalows in the distance— and, in between, the red-brown earth of the killing ground, stretching out to the cliff edge and the bases of the nearest translucent fins.

"This is a good spot," Valadez declared. "Should be a good view from up here."

"A view of what?" said Fry.

The poacher didn't answer. He waved to Ismaíl, and the *firija* took a small folding stool out of a pocket, snapping it into shape with a flick of sinuous arms and setting it down behind him. Valadez sat.

After a moment, the answer to Fry's question came up over the edge.

Bianca had not thought much at all about the killing of a *zaratán*, and when she had thought of it she had imagined something like the harpooning of a whale in ancient times, the great beast fleeing, pursued by the tiny harassing shapes of boats, gored by harpoons, sounding again and again, all the strength bleeding out of the beast until there was nothing left for it to do but wallow gasping on the surface and expire, noble and tragic. Now Bianca realized that for all their great size, the *zaratánes* were far weaker than any whale, far less able to fight or to escape or even—she sincerely hoped—to understand what was happening to them.

There was nothing noble about the way the nameless *zaratán* died. Anemopters landed men and aliens with drilling tools at the base of each hundred-meter fin, to bore through soil and scale and living flesh and cut the connecting nerves that controlled them. This took about fifteen minutes; and to Bianca there seemed to be something obscene in the way the paralyzed fins hung there afterward, lifeless and limp. Thus crippled, the beast was pushed and pulled by aerial tugs—awkward machines, stubby and cylindrical, converted from the station-keeping engines of vacuum balloons like *Transient Meridian*—into position over Encantada's killing ground. Then the drilling teams moved in again, to the places marked for them ahead of time by seismic sensors and ultrasound, cutting this time through bone as well as flesh, to find the *zaratán*'s brain.

When the charges the drilling teams had planted went off, a ripple went through the *zaratán*'s body, a slow-motion convulsion that took nearly a minute to travel down the body's long axis, as the news of death passed from synapse to synapse; and Bianca saw flocks of birds started from the trees along the *zaratán*'s back as if by an earthquake, which in a way she supposed this was. The carcass immediately began to pitch downward, the nose dropping— the result, Bianca realized, of sphincters relaxing one by one, all along the *zaratán*'s length, venting hydrogen from the ballonets.

Then the forward edge of the keel fin hit the ground and crumpled, and the whole length of the dead beast, a hundred thousand tons of it, crashed down into the field; and even at that distance Bianca could hear the cracking of gargantuan bones.

She shivered, and glanced at her pocket system. The whole process, she was amazed to see, had taken less than half an hour.

"That's this trip paid for, whatever else happens," said Valadez. He turned to Bianca. "Mostly, though, I thought you should see this. Have you guessed yet what it is I'm paying you to do, Miss Nazario?"

Bianca shook her head. "Clearly you don't need an aeronautical engineer to do what you've just done." She looked down at the killing ground, where men and aliens and machines were already climbing over the *zaratán*'s carcass, uprooting trees, peeling back skin and soil in great strips like bleeding boulevards. A wind had come up, blowing from the killing ground across the camp, bringing with it a smell that Bianca associated with butcher shops.

An engineering problem, she reminded herself, as she turned her back on the scene and faced Valadez. That's all this is.

"How are you going to get it out of here?" she asked.

"Cargo-lifter," said Valadez. "The *Lupita Jeréz*. A supply ship, diverted from one of the balloon stations."

The alien, Ismaíl, said, "Like fly anemopter make transatmospheric." The same fluting voice and broken Arabic. "Lifter plenty payload mass limit, but fly got make have packaging. Packaging for got make platform have stable." On the word *packaging* the *firija*'s arms made an expressive gesture, like rolling something up into a bundle and tying it.

Bianca nodded hesitantly, hoping she understood. "And so you can only take the small ones," she said. "Right? Because there's only one place on Sky you'll find a stable platform that size: on the back of another *zaratán*."

"You have the problem in a nutshell, Miss Nazario," said Valadez. "Now, how would you solve it? How would you bag, say, Encantada here? How would you bag Finisterra?"

Fry said, "You want to take one *alive*?" His face was even more pale than usual. Bianca noticed that he, too, had turned his back to the killing ground.

Valadez was still looking at Bianca, expectantly.

"He doesn't want it alive, Mr. Fry," she said, watching the poacher. "He wants it dead—but intact. You could take even Finisterra apart, and lift it piece by piece, but you'd need a thousand cargo-lifters to do it."

Valadez smiled.

"I've got another ship," he said. "Built for deep mining, outfitted as a mobile elevator station. Counterweighted. The ship itself isn't rated for atmosphere, but if you can get one of the big ones to the edge of space, we'll lower the skyhook, catch the beast, and catapult it into orbit. The buyer's arranged an FTL tug to take it from there."

Bianca made herself look back at the killing ground. The workers were freeing the bones, lifting them with aerial cranes and feeding them into the plant; for cleaning and preservation, she supposed. She turned back to Valadez.

"We should be able to do that, if the *zaratán*'s body will stand up to the low pressure," she said. "But why go to all this trouble? I've seen the balloon stations. I've seen what you people can do with materials. How hard can it be to make an imitation *zaratán*?"

Valadez glanced at Ismaíl. The walker was facing the killing ground, but two of the alien's many eyes were watching the sky—and two more were watching Valadez. The poacher looked back at Bianca.

"An imitation's one thing, Miss Nazario; the real thing is something else. And worth a lot more, to the right buyer." He looked away again; not at

Ismaíl this time, but up the slope, through the trees. "Besides," he added, "in this case I've got my own reasons."

"Ship come," Ismaíl announced.

Bianca looked and saw more of the *firija*'s eyes turning upward. She followed their gaze. At first she saw only empty sky. Then the air around the descending *Lupita Jeréz* boiled into contrails, outlining the invisible ovoid shape of the ship's lifting fields.

"Time to get to work," said Valadez.

Bianca glanced toward the killing ground. A pink fog was rising to cover the work of the flensing crews.

The air was full of blood.

5. THE AERONAUTS

Valadez's workers cleaned the nameless *zaratán*'s bones one by one; they tanned the hide, and rolled it into bundles for loading aboard the *Lupita Jeréz*. That job, grotesque though it was, was the cleanest part of the work. What occupied most of the workers was the disposal of the unwanted parts, a much dirtier and more arduous job. Exotic internal organs the size of houses; tendons like braided, knotted bridge cables; ballonets large enough, each of them, to lift an ordinary dirigible; and hectares and hectares of pale, dead flesh. The poachers piled up the mess with earthmoving machines and shoveled it off the edge of the killing ground, a rain of offal falling into the clouds in a mist of blood, manna for the ecology of the deep air. They sprayed the killing ground with antiseptics, and the cool air helped to slow decay a little, but by the fourth day the butcher-shop smell had nonetheless given way to something worse.

Bianca's bungalow was one of the farthest out, only a few dozen meters from Encantada's edge, where the wind blew in from the open eastern sky, and she could turn her back on the slaughter to look out into clear air, dotted with the small, distant shapes of younger *zaratánes*. Even here, though, a kilometer and more upwind of the killing ground, the air carried a taint of spoiled meat. The sky was full of insects and scavenger birds, and there were always vermin underfoot.

Bianca spent most of her time indoors, where the air was filtered and the wet industrial sounds of the work muted. The bungalow was outfitted with all the mechanisms the *extrañados* used to make themselves comfortable, but while in the course of her journey Bianca had learned to operate these, she made little use of them. Besides her traveling chest—a gift from her older brother's wife, which served as armoire, desk, dresser, and drafting table—the only furnishings were a woven carpet in the Lagos Grandes style, a hard little bed, and a single wooden chair, not very different from the ones in her room in Punta Aguila. Of course those had been handmade, and these were simulations provided by the bungalow's machines.

The rest of the room was given over to the projected spaces of Bianca's engineering work. The tools Valadez had given her were slick and fast and factory-fresh, the state of somebody's art, somewhere; but what Bianca mostly found herself using was her pocket system's crippled copy of the Nazario family automation.

The system Bianca's father used to use to calculate stresses in fabric and metal and wood, to model the flow of air over wings and the variation of pressure and temperature through gasbags, was six centuries old, a slow, patient, reliable thing that dated from before the founding of the London Caliphate. It had aged along with the family, grown used to their quirks and to the strange demands of aviation in Rio Pícaro. Bianca's version of it, limited though it was, at least didn't balk at control surfaces supported by muscle and bone, at curves not aerodynamically smooth but fractally complex with grasses and trees and hanging vines. If the *zaratánes* had been machines, they would have been marvels of engineering, with their internal networks of gasbags and ballonets, their reservoir-sized ballast bladders full of collected rainwater, their great delicate fins. The *zaratánes* were beyond the poachers' systems' stubborn, narrow-minded comprehension; for all their speed and flash, the systems sulked like spoiled children whenever Bianca tried to use them to do something their designers had not expected her to do.

Which she was doing, all the time. She was working out how to draw up Leviathan with a hook.

"Miss Nazario."

Bianca started. She had yet to grow used to these *extrañado* telephones that never rang, but only spoke to her out of the air, or perhaps out of her own head.

"Mr. Valadez," she said, after a moment.

"Whatever you're doing, drop it," said Valadez's voice. "You and Fry. I'm sending a 'mopter for you."

"I'm working," said Bianca. "I don't know what Fry's doing."

"This *is* work," said Valadez. "Five minutes."

A change in the quality of the silence told Bianca that Valadez had hung up. She sighed; then stood, stretched, and started to braid her hair.

The anemopter brought them up over the dorsal ridge, passing between two of the great translucent fins. At this altitude, Encantada's body was clear of vegetation; Bianca looked down on hectares of wind-blasted gray hide, dusted lightly with snow. They passed within a few hundred meters of one of the huge spars that anchored the after fin's leading edge: a kilometers-high pillar of flesh, teardrop in cross-section, and at least a hundred meters thick. The trailing edge of the next fin, by contrast, flashed by in an instant. Bianca had only a brief impression of a silk-supple membrane, veined with red, clear as dirty glass.

"What do you think he wants?" Fry asked.

"I don't know." She nodded her head toward the *firija* behind them at the steering console. "Did you ask the pilot?"

"I tried," Fry said. "Doesn't speak Arabic."

Bianca shrugged. "I suppose we'll find out soon enough."

Then they were coming down again, down the western slope. In front of Bianca was the dorsal ridge of Zaratán Finisterra. Twenty kilometers away and blue with haze, it nonetheless rose until it seemed to cover a third of the sky.

Bianca looked out at it, wondering again what kept Encantada and Finisterra so close; but then the view was taken away and they were coming down between the trees, into a shady, ivy-filled creekbed somewhere not far from Encantada's western edge. There was another anemopter already there, and a pair of aerial tugs—and a whitish mass that dwarfed all of these, sheets and ribbons of pale material hanging from the branches and draped over the ivy, folds of it damming the little stream.

With an audible splash, the anemopter set down, the ramps lowered, and Bianca stepped off into cold ankle-deep water that made her glad of her knee-high boots. Fry followed, gingerly.

"You!" called Valadez, pointing at Fry from the deck of the other anemopter. "Come here. Miss Nazario—I'd like you to have a look at that balloon."

"Balloon?"

Valadez gestured impatiently downstream. Suddenly Bianca saw the white material for the shredded, deflated gasbag it was; and saw, too, that there was a basket attached to it, lying on its side, partially submerged in the middle of the stream. Ismaíl was standing over it, waving.

Bianca splashed over to the basket. It actually *was* a basket, two meters across and a meter and a half high, woven from strips of something like bamboo or rattan. The gasbag—this was obvious, once Bianca saw it up close—had been made from one of the ballonets of a *zaratán*, a *zaratán* younger and smaller even than the one Bianca had seen killed; it had been tanned, but inexpertly, and by someone without access to the sort of industrial equipment the poachers used.

Bianca wondered about the way the gasbag was torn up. The tissues of the *zaratánes*, she knew, were very strong. A hydrogen explosion?

"Make want fly got very bad," Ismaíl commented, as Bianca came around to the open side of the basket.

"They certainly did," she said.

In the basket there were only some wool blankets and some empty leather waterbags, probably used both for drinking water and for ballast. The lines used to control the vent flaps were all tangled together, and tangled, too, with the lines that secured the gasbag to the basket, but Bianca could guess how they had worked. No stove. It seemed to have been a pure hydrogen balloon; and why not, she thought, with all the hydrogen anyone could want free from the nearest *zaratán*'s vent valves?

"Where did it come from?" she asked.

Ismaíl rippled his arms in a way that Bianca guessed was meant to be an imitation of a human shrug. One of his eyes glanced downstream.

Bianca fingered the material of the basket: tough, woody fiber. Tropical, from a climate warmer than Encantada's. She followed Ismaíl's glance. The trees hid the western horizon, but she knew, if she could see beyond them, what would be there.

Aloud, she said, "Finisterra."

She splashed back to the anemopters. Valadez's hatch was open.

"I'm telling you," Fry was saying, "I don't know her!"

"Fuck off, Fry," Valadez said as Bianca stepped into the cabin. "Look at her ID."

The *her* in question was a young woman with short black hair and sallow skin, wearing tan off-world cottons like Fry's under a colorful homespun *serape*; and at first Bianca was not sure the woman was alive, because the man next to her on Valadez's floor, also in homespun, was clearly dead, his eyes half-lidded, his olive skin gone muddy gray.

The contents of their pockets were spread out on a low table. As Bianca was taking in the scene, Fry bent down and picked up a Consilium-style ID tag.

"'Edith Dinh,'" he read. He tossed the tag back and looked at Valadez. "So?"

"'Edith Dinh, *Consilium Ethnological Service*,'" Valadez growled. "Issued Shawwal '43. *You* were here with the *Ecological* Service from Rajab '42 to Muharram '46. Look again!"

Fry turned away.

"All right!" he said. "Maybe—maybe I met her once or twice."

"So," said Valadez. "Now we're getting somewhere. Who the hell is she? And what's she doing *here*?"

"She's . . . ." Fry glanced at the woman and then quickly looked away. "I don't know. I think she was a population biologist or something. There was a group working with the, you know, the natives—"

"There aren't any natives on Sky," said Valadez. He prodded the dead man with the toe of his boot. "You mean these *cabrónes?*"

Fry nodded. "They had this 'sustainable development' program going—farming, forestry. Teaching them how to live on Finisterra without killing it."

Valadez looked skeptical. "If the Consilium wanted to stop them from killing Finisterra, why didn't they just send in the wardens?"

"Interdepartmental politics. The *zaratánes* were EcoServ's responsibility; the n- —I mean, the *inhabitants* were EthServ's." Fry shrugged. "You know the wardens. They'd have taken bribes from anyone who could afford it and shot the rest."

"Damn right I know the wardens." Valadez scowled. "So instead Eth-Serv sent in these do-gooders to teach them to make balloons?"

Fry shook his head. "I don't know anything about that."

"Miss Nazario? Tell me about that balloon."

"It's a hydrogen balloon, I think. Probably filled from some *zaratán's* external vents." She shrugged. "It looks like the sort of thing I'd expect someone living out here to build, if that's what you mean."

Valadez nodded.

"But," Bianca added, "I can't tell you why it crashed."

Valadez snorted. "I don't need you to tell me that," he said. "It crashed because we shot it down." Pitching his voice for the anemopter's communication system, he called out, "Ismaíl!"

Bianca tried to keep the shock from showing on her face, and after a moment she had regained her composure. *You knew they were criminals when you took their money,* she told herself.

The *firija's* eyes came around the edge of the doorway.

"Yes?"

"Tell the tug crews to pack that thing up," said Valadez. "Every piece, every scrap. Pack it up and drop it into clear air."

The alien's walking machine clambered into the cabin. Its legs bent briefly, making a little bob like a curtsey.

"Yes." Ismaíl gestured at the bodies of the dead man and the unconscious woman. Several of the *firija's* eyes met Valadez's. "These two what do?" he asked.

"Them, too," said Valadez. "Lash them into the basket."

The *firija* made another bob and started to bend down to pick them up.

Bianca looked down at the two bodies, both of them, the dead man and the unconscious woman, looking small and thin and vulnerable. She glanced at Fry, whose eyes were fixed on the floor, his lips pressed together in a thin line.

Then she looked over at Valadez, who was methodically sweeping the balloonists' effects into a pile, as if neither Bianca nor Fry was present.

"No," she said.

Ismaíl stopped and straightened up.

"What?" said Valadez.

"No," Bianca repeated.

"You want her bringing the wardens down on us?" Valadez demanded.

"That's murder, Mr. Valadez," Bianca said. "I won't be a party to it."

The poacher's eyes narrowed. He gestured at the dead man.

"You're already an accessory," he said.

"After the fact," Bianca replied evenly. She kept her eyes on Valadez.

The poacher looked at the ceiling. "Fuck your mother," he muttered. He looked down at the two bodies, and at Ismaíl, and then over at Bianca. He sighed heavily.

"All right," he said to the *firija*. "Take the live one back to the camp. Secure a bungalow, one of the ones out by the edge"—he glanced at Bianca—"and lock her in it. Okay?"

"Okay," said Ismaíl. "Dead one what do?"

Valadez looked at Bianca again. "The dead one," he said, "goes in the basket."

Bianca looked at the dead man again, wondering what bravery or madness had brought him aboard that fragile balloon, and wondering what he would have thought if he had known that the voyage would end this way, with his body tumbling down into the deep air. She supposed he must have known there was a chance of it.

After a moment, she nodded, once.

"Right," said Valadez. "Now get back to work, damn it."

6. THE CITY OF THE DEAD

The anemopter that brought Bianca and Fry over the ridge took them back. Fry was silent, hunched, his elbows on his knees, staring at nothing. What fear or guilt was going through his mind, Bianca couldn't guess.

After a little while she stopped watching him. She thought about the Finisterran balloon, so simple, so fragile, making her father's wood-and-silk craft look as sophisticated as the *Lupita Jeréz*. She took out her pocket system, sketched a simple globe and basket, then erased them.

Make want fly very bad, Ismaíl the *firija* had said. Why?

Bianca undid the erasure, bringing her sketch back. She drew the spherical balloon out into a blunt torpedo, round at the nose, tapering to a point behind. Added fins. An arrangement of pulleys and levers, allowing them to be controlled from the basket. A propeller, powered by—she had to think for a little while—by an alcohol-fueled engine, carved from *zaratán* bones. . . .

The anemopter was landing. Bianca sighed and again erased the design.

The *firija* guard outside Edith Dinh's bungalow didn't seem to speak Arabic or Spanish, or for that matter any human language at all. Bianca wondered if the choice was deliberate, the guard chosen by Valadez as a way of keeping a kind of solitary confinement.

Or was the guard Valadez's choice at all? she wondered suddenly. Looking at the meter-long weapon cradled in the alien's furred arms, she shivered.

Then she squared her shoulders and approached the bungalow. Wordlessly, she waved the valise she was carrying, as if by it her reasons for being there were made customary and obvious.

The alien said something in its own fluting language—whether a reply to her, or a request for instructions from some unseen listener, Bianca couldn't tell. Either those instructions were to let her pass, apparently, or by being seen in Valadez's company she had acquired some sort of reflected authority; because the *firija* lifted its weapon and, as the bungalow's outer door slid open, motioned for her to enter. The inner door was already open.

"*¿Hola?*" Bianca called out, tentatively. Immediately she felt like an idiot. But the answer came:

"*Aquí.*"

The interior layout of the bungalow was the same as Bianca's. The voice came from the sitting room. Bianca found Dinh there, still wearing the clothes she'd had on when they found her, sitting with her knees drawn up, staring out the east window into the sky. The east was dark with rain clouds, and far below, Bianca could see flashes of lightning.

"*Salaam aleikum,*" said Bianca, taking refuge in the formality of the Arabic.

"*Aleikum as-salaam,*" Dinh replied. She glanced briefly at Bianca and looked away; then looked back again. In a Spanish that was somewhere between Valadez's strange accent and the mechanical fluency of Fry's language module, she said, "You're not from Finisterra."

"No," said Bianca, giving up on the Arabic. "I'm from Río Pícaro—from Earth. My name is Nazario, Bianca Nazario y Arenas."

"Edith Dinh."

Dinh stood up. There was an awkward moment, where Bianca was not sure whether to bow or curtsey or give Dinh her hand. She settled for proffering the valise.

"I brought you some things," she said. "Clothes, toiletries."

Dinh looked surprised. "Thanks," she said, taking the valise and looking inside.

"Are they feeding you? I could bring you some food."

"The kitchen still works," said Dinh. She held up a white packet. "And these?"

"Sanitary napkins," said Bianca.

"Sanitary . . . ?" Color rose to Dinh's face. "Oh. That's all right. I've got implants." She dropped the packet back in the valise and closed it.

Bianca looked away, feeling her own cheeks blush in turn. Damned *extrañados*, she thought. "I'd better—" be going, she started to say.

"Please—" said Dinh.

The older woman and the younger stood there for a moment, looking at each other. Bianca suddenly wondered what impulse had brought her here, whether curiosity or Christian charity or simply a moment of loneliness, weakness. Of course she'd had to stop Valadez from killing the girl, but this was clearly a mistake.

"Sit," Dinh said. "Let me get you something. Tea? Coffee?"

"I—all right." Bianca sat, slowly, perching on the edge of one of the too-soft *extrañado* couches. "Coffee," she said.

The coffee was very dark, sweeter than Bianca liked it, flavored with something like condensed milk. She was glad to have it, regardless, glad to have something to look at and something to occupy her hands.

"You don't look like a poacher," Dinh said.

"I'm an aeronautical engineer," Bianca said. "I'm doing some work for them." She looked down at her coffee, took a sip, and looked up. "What about you? Fry said you're a biologist of some kind. What were you doing in that balloon?"

She couldn't tell whether the mention of Fry's name had registered, but Dinh's mouth went thin. She glanced out the west window.

Bianca followed her glance and saw the guard, slumped in its walker, watching the two women with one eye each. She wondered again whether Valadez was really running things, and then whether the *firija*'s ignorance of human language was real or feigned—and whether, even if it *was* real, someone less ignorant might be watching and listening, unseen.

Then she shook her head and looked back at Dinh, waiting.

"Finisterra's falling," Dinh said eventually. "Dying, maybe. It's too big; it's losing lift. It's fallen more than fifty meters in the last year alone."

"That doesn't make sense," Bianca said. "The lift-to-weight ratio of an aerostat depends on the ratio of volume to surface area. A larger *zaratán* should be *more* efficient, not less. And even if it *does* lose lift, it should only fall until it reaches a new equilibrium."

"It's not a *machine*," Dinh said. "It's a living creature."

Bianca shrugged. "Maybe it's old age, then," she said. "Everything has to die sometime."

"Not like this," Dinh said. She set down her coffee and turned to face Bianca fully. "Look. We don't know who built Sky, or how long ago, but it's obviously artificial. A gas giant with a nitrogen-oxygen atmosphere? That *doesn't happen*. And the Earthlike biology—the *zaratánes* are DNA-based, did you know that? The whole place is astronomically unlikely; if the Phenomenological Service had its way, they'd just quarantine the entire system, and damn Sky and everybody on it.

"The archipelago ecology is as artificial as everything else. Whoever designed it must have been very good; posthuman, probably, maybe even postsingularity. It's a robust equilibrium, full of feedback mechanisms, ways to correct itself. But we, us ordinary humans and human-equivalents, we've"—she made a helpless gesture—"*fucked it up*. You know why Encantada's stayed here so long? Breeding, that's why . . . or maybe 'pollination' would be a better way to put it. . . ."

She looked over at Bianca.

"The death of an old *zaratán* like Finisterra should be balanced by the birth of dozens, hundreds. But you, those bastards you work for, you've killed them all."

Bianca let the implication of complicity slide. "All right, then," she said. "Let's hear your plan."

"What?"

"Your *plan*," Bianca repeated. "For Finisterra. How are you going to save it?"

Dinh stared at her for a moment, then shook her head. "I can't," she said. She stood up and went to the east window. Beyond the sheet of rain that now poured down the window, the sky was deep mauve shading to indigo, relieved only by the lightning that sparked in the deep and played across the fins of the distant *zaratánes* of the archipelago's outer reaches. Dinh put her palm flat against the diamond pane.

"I *can't* save Finisterra," she said quietly. "I just want to stop you *hijos de puta* from doing this again."

Now Bianca was stung. "*Hija de puta*, yourself," she said. "You're killing them, too. Killing them and making balloons out of them, how is that better?"

Dinh turned back. "One *zaratán* the size of the one they're slaughtering out there right now would keep the Finisterrans in balloons for a hundred years," she said. "The only way to save the archipelago is to make the *zaratánes* more valuable alive than dead—and the only value a live *zaratán* has, on Sky, is as living space."

"You're trying to get the Finisterrans to colonize the other *zaratánes*?" Bianca asked. "But why should they? What's in it for them?"

"I told you," Dinh said. "Finisterra's dying." She looked out the window, down into the depths of the storm, both hands pressed against the glass. "Do you know how falling into Sky kills you, Bianca? First, there's the pressure. On the slopes of Finisterra, where the people live, it's a little more than a thousand millibars. Five kilometers down, under Finisterra's keel, it's double that. At two thousand millibars you can still breathe the air. At three thousand, nitrogen narcosis sets in—'rapture of the deep,' they used to call it. At four thousand, the partial pressure of oxygen alone is enough to make your lungs bleed."

She stepped away from the window and looked at Bianca.

"But you'll never live to suffer that," she said. "Because of the heat. Every thousand meters the average temperature rises six or seven degrees. Here it's about fifteen. Under Finisterra's keel it's closer to fifty. Twenty kilometers down, the air is hot enough to boil water."

Bianca met her gaze steadily. "I can think of worse ways to die," she said.

"There are seventeen thousand people on Finisterra," said Dinh. "Men, women, children, old people. There's a town—they call it the Lost City, *la ciudad perdida.* Some of the families on Finisterra can trace their roots back six generations." She gave a little laugh, with no humor in it. "They should call it *la ciudad muerta.* They're the walking dead, all seventeen thousand of them. Even though no one alive on Finisterra today will live to see it die. Already the crops are starting to fail. Already more old men and old women die every summer, as the summers get hotter and drier. The children of the children who are born today will have to move up into the hills as it gets too hot to grow crops on the lower slopes; but the soil isn't as rich up there, so many of those crops will fail, too. And *their* children's children . . . won't live to be old enough to have children of their own."

"Surely someone will rescue them before then," Bianca said.

"Who?" Dinh asked. "The Consilium? Where would they put them? The vacuum balloon stations and the elevator gondolas are already over-crowded. As far as the rest of Sky is concerned, the Finisterrans are 'malcontents' and 'criminal elements.' Who's going to take them in?"

"Then Valadez is doing them a favor," Bianca said.

Dinh started. "*Emmanuel Valadez* is running your operation?"

"It's *not my* operation," Bianca said, trying to keep her voice level. "And I didn't ask his first name."

Dinh fell into the window seat. "Of course it would be," she said. "Who else would they . . ." She trailed off, looking out the west window, toward the killing ground.

Then, suddenly, she turned back to Bianca.

"What do you mean, '*doing them a favor*'?" she said.

"Finisterra," Bianca said. "He's poaching Finisterra."

Dinh stared at her. "My God, Bianca! What about the people?"

"What about them?" asked Bianca. "They'd be better off somewhere else—you said that yourself."

"And what makes you think Valadez will evacuate them?"

"He's a *thief*, not a mass murderer."

Dinh gave her a withering look. "He *is* a murderer, Bianca. His father was a warden, his mother was the wife of the *alcalde* of Ciudad Perdida. He killed his own stepfather, two uncles, and three brothers. They were going to execute him—throw him over the edge—but a warden airboat picked him up. He spent two years with them, then killed his sergeant and three other wardens, stole their ship and sold it for a ticket off-world. He's probably the most wanted man on Sky."

She shook her head and, unexpectedly, gave Bianca a small smile.

"You didn't know any of that when you took the job, did you?"

Her voice was full of pity. It showed on her face as well, and suddenly Bianca couldn't stand to look at it. She got up and went to the east window. The rain was lighter now, the lightning less frequent.

She thought back to her simulations, her plans for lifting Finisterra up into the waiting embrace of the skyhook: the gasbags swelling, the *zaratán* lifting, first slowly and then with increasing speed, toward the upper reaches of Sky's atmosphere. But now her inner vision was not the ghost-shape of a projection but a living image—trees cracking in the cold, water freezing, blood boiling from the ground in a million, million tiny hemorrhages.

She saw her mother's house in Punta Aguila—her sister-in-law's house, now: saw its windows rimed with frost, the trees in the courtyard gone brown and sere. She saw the Mercado de los Maculados beneath a blackening sky, the awnings whipped away by a thin wind, ice-cold, bone-dry.

He killed that Finisterran balloonist, she thought. He was ready to kill Dinh. He's capable of murder.

Then she shook her head.

Killing one person, or two, to cover up a crime, was murder, she thought. Killing seventeen thousand people by deliberate asphyxiation—men, women, and children—wasn't murder, it was genocide.

She took her cup of coffee from the table, took a sip and put it down again.

"Thank you for the coffee," she said. She turned to go.

"How can you just let him do this?" Dinh demanded. "How can you *help him do this?*"

Bianca turned on her. Dinh was on her feet; her fists were clenched, and she was shaking. Bianca stared her down, her face as cold and blank as she could make it. She waited until Dinh turned away, throwing herself into a chair, staring out the window.

"I saved your life," Bianca told her. "That was more than I needed to do. Even if I *did* believe that Valadez meant to kill every person on Finisterra, *which I don't*, that wouldn't make it my problem."

Dinh turned farther away.

"Listen to me," Bianca said, "because I'm only going to explain this once."

She waited until Dinh, involuntarily, turned back to face her.

"This job is my one chance," Bianca said. "*This job* is what I'm here to do. I'm not here to save the world. Saving the world is a luxury for spoiled *extrañado* children like you and Fry. It's a luxury I don't have."

She went to the door, and knocked on the window to signal the *firija* guard.

"I'll get you out of here if I can," she added, over her shoulder. "But that's all I can do. I'm sorry."

Dinh hadn't moved.

As the *firija* opened the door, Bianca heard Dinh stir.

"*Erasmus* Fry?" she asked. "The naturalist?"

"That's right." Bianca glanced back, and saw Dinh looking out the window again.

"I'd like to see him," Dinh said.

"I'll let him know," said Bianca.

The guard closed the door behind her.

7. THE FACE IN THE MIRROR

Lightning still played along Encantada's dorsal ridge, but here on the eastern edge the storm had passed. A clean, electric smell was in the air, relief from the stink of the killing ground. Bianca returned to her own bungalow through rain that had died to a drizzle.

She called Fry.

"What is it?" he asked.

"Miss Dinh," Bianca said. "She wants to see you."

There was silence on the other end. Then, "You told her I was here?"

"Sorry," Bianca said insincerely. "It just slipped out."

More silence.

"You knew her better than you told Valadez, didn't you," she said.

She heard Fry sigh. "Yes."

"She seemed upset," Bianca said. "You should go see her."

Fry sighed again, but said nothing.

"I've got work to do," Bianca said. "I'll talk to you later."

She ended the call.

She was supposed to make a presentation tomorrow, to Valadez and some of the poachers' crew bosses, talking about what they would be doing to Finisterra. It was mostly done; the outline was straightforward, and the visuals could be autogenerated from the design files. She opened the projection file and poked at it for a little while, but found it hard to concentrate.

Suddenly to Bianca her clothes smelled of death, of Dinh's dead companion and the slaughtered *zaratán* and the death she'd spared Dinh from and the eventual deaths of all the marooned Finisterrans. She stripped them off and threw them in the recycler; bathed, washed her hair, changed into a nightgown.

They should call it la ciudad muerta.

Even though no one who's alive on Finisterra today will live to see it die.

She turned off the light, Dinh's words echoing in her head, and tried to sleep. But she couldn't; she couldn't stop thinking. Thinking about what it felt like to be forced to live on, when all you had to look forward to was death.

She knew that feeling very well.

What Bianca had on Pablo's wife Mélia, the instrument-maker's daughter, was ten years of age and a surreptitious technical education. What Mélia had on Bianca was a keen sense of territory and the experience of growing up in a house full of sisters. Bianca continued to live in the house after Mélia moved in, even though it was Mélia's house now, and continued, without credit, to help her brother with the work that came in. But she retreated over the years, step by step, until the line was drawn at the door of the fourth-floor room that had been hers ever since she was a girl; and she buried herself in her blueprints and her calculations, and tried to pretend she didn't know what was happening.

And then there was the day she met her *other* sister-in-law. Her *moro* sister-in-law. In the Mercado de los Maculados, where the aliens and the *extrañados* came to sell their trinkets and their medicines. A dispensation from the *ayuntamiento* had recently opened it to Christians.

Zahra al-Halim, a successful architect, took Bianca to her home, where Bianca ate caramels and drank blackberry tea and saw her older brother for the first time in more than twenty years, and tried very hard to call him Walíd and not Jesús. Here was a world that could be hers, too, she sensed, if she wanted it. But like Jesús-Walíd, she would have to give up her old world to have it. Even if she remained a Christian she would never see the inside of a church again. And she would still never be accepted by the engineers' guild.

She went back to the Nazario house that evening, ignoring the barbed questions from Mélia about how she had spent her day; she went back to her room, with its blueprints and its models, and the furnishings she'd had all her life. She tried for a little while to work, but was unable to muster the concentration she needed to interface with the system.

Instead she found herself looking into the mirror.

And looking into the mirror Bianca focused not on the fragile trapped shapes of the flying machines tacked to the wall behind her, spread out and pinned down like so many chloroformed butterflies, but on her own tired face, the stray wisps of dry, brittle hair, the lines that years of captivity had made across her forehead and around her eyes. And, meeting those eyes, it seemed to Bianca that she was looking not into the mirror but down through the years of her future, a long, straight, narrow corridor without doors or branches, and that the eyes she was meeting at the end of it were the eyes of Death, her own, *su propria muerte*, personal, personified.

Bianca got out of bed, turned on the lights. She picked up her pocket system. She wondered if she should call the wardens.

Instead she unerased, yet again, the sketch she'd made earlier of the simple alcohol-powered dirigible. She used the Nazario family automation to fill it out with diagrams and renderings, lists of materials, building instructions, maintenance and preflight checklists.

It wasn't much, but it was better than Dinh's balloon.

Now she needed a way for Dinh to get it to the Finisterrans.

For that—thinking as she did so that there was some justice in it—she turned back to the system Valadez had given her. This was the sort of work the *extrañado* automation was made for, no constraints other than those imposed by function, every trick of exotic technology available to be used. It was a matter of minutes for Bianca to sketch out her design; an hour or so to refine it, to trim away the unnecessary pieces until what remained was small enough to fit in the valise she'd left with Dinh. The only difficult part was getting the design automation to talk to the bungalow's fabricator, which was meant for clothes and furniture and domestic utensils. Eventually she had to use her pocket system to go out on Sky's local net—hoping as she did so that Valadez didn't have anyone monitoring her—and spend her own funds to contract the conversion out to a consulting service, somewhere out on one of the elevator gondolas.

Eventually she got it done, though. The fabricator spit out a neat package, which Bianca stuffed under the bed. Tomorrow she could get the valise back and smuggle the package to Dinh, along with the dirigible designs.

But first she had a presentation to make to Valadez. She wondered what motivated him. Nothing so simple as money—she was sure of that, even if she had trouble believing he was the monster Dinh had painted him to be. Was it revenge he was after? Revenge on his family, revenge on his homeland?

That struck Bianca a little too close to home.

She sighed and turned out the lights.

8. THE PROFESSIONALS

By morning the storm had passed and the sky was blue again, but the inside of Valadez's bungalow was dark, to display the presenters' projections to better advantage. Chairs for Valadez and the human crew bosses were arranged in a rough semicircle; with them were the aliens whose anatomy permitted them to sit down. Ismaíl and the other *firija* stood in the back, their curled arms and the spindly legs of their machines making their silhouettes look, to Bianca, incongruously like those of potted plants.

Then the fronds stirred, suddenly menacing. Bianca shivered. Who was really in charge?

No time to worry about that now. She straightened up and took out her pocket system.

"In a moment," she began, pitching her voice to carry to the back of the room, "Mr. Fry will be going over the *zaratán's* metabolic processes and our plans to stimulate the internal production of hydrogen. What I'm going to be talking about is the engineering work required to make that extra hydrogen do what we need it to do."

Bianca's pocket system projected the shape of a hundred-kilometer *zaratán*, not Finisterra or any other particular individual but rather an archetype, a sort of Platonic ideal. Points of pink light brightened all across the projected *zaratán's* back, each indicating the position of a sphincter that would have to be cut out and replaced with a mechanical valve.

"Our primary concern during the preparation phase has to be these external vents. However, we also need to consider the internal trim and ballast valves. . . ."

As she went on, outlining the implants and grafts, surgeries and mutilations needed to turn a living *zaratán* into an animatronic corpse, a part of her was amazed at her own presumption, amazed at the strong, confident, professional tone she was taking.

It was almost as if she were a real engineer.

The presentation came to a close. Bianca drew in a deep breath, trying to maintain her veneer of professionalism. This part wasn't in her outline.

"And then, finally, there is the matter of evacuation," she said.

In the back of the room, Ismaíl stirred. "Evacuation?" he asked—the first word anyone had uttered through the whole presentation.

Bianca cleared her throat. Red stars appeared along the imaginary *zaratán*'s southeastern edge, approximating the locations of Ciudad Perdida and the smaller Finisterran villages.

"Finisterra has a population of between fifteen and twenty thousand, most of them concentrated in these settlements here," she began. "Using a ship the size of the *Lupita Jeréz*, it should take roughly—"

"Not your problem, Miss Nazario." Valadez waved a hand. "In any case, there won't be any evacuations."

Bianca looked at him, appalled; and it must have shown on her face because Valadez laughed.

"Don't look at me like that, Miss Nazario. We'll set up field domes over Ciudad Perdida and the central pueblos, to tide them over till we get them where they're going. If they keep their heads they should be fine." He laughed again. "Fucking hell," he said, shaking his head. "What did you think this was about? You didn't think we were going to kill twenty thousand people, did you?"

Bianca didn't answer. She shut the projection off and sat down, putting her pocket system away. Her heart was racing.

"Right," said Valadez. "Nice presentation, Miss Nazario. Mr. Fry?"

Fry stood up. "Okay," he said. "Let me—" He patted his pockets. "I, ah, I think I must have left my system in my bungalow."

Valadez sighed.

"We'll wait," he said.

The dark room was silent. Bianca tried to take slow, deep breaths. Mother of God, she thought, thank you for not letting me do anything stupid.

In the next moment she doubted herself. Dinh had been so sure. How could Bianca know whether Valadez was telling the truth?

There was no way to know, she decided. She'd just have to wait and see.

Fry came back in, breathless.

"Ah, it wasn't—"

The voice that interrupted him was loud enough that at first it was hardly recognizable as a voice; it was only a wall of sound, seeming to come from the air itself, bazaar-Arabic words echoing and reechoing endlessly across the camp.

"THIS IS AN ILLEGAL ENCAMPMENT," it said. "ALL PERSON-NEL IN THE ENCAMPMENT WILL ASSEMBLE ON OPEN GROUND AND SURRENDER TO THE PARK WARDENS IN AN ORDERLY FASHION. ANY PERSONS CARRYING WEAPONS WILL BE PRE-SUMED TO BE RESISTING ARREST AND WILL BE DEALT WITH ACCORDINGLY. ANY VEHICLE ATTEMPTING TO LEAVE THE ENCAMPMENT WILL BE DESTROYED. YOU HAVE FIVE MIN-UTES TO COMPLY."

The announcement repeated itself: first in the fluting language of the *firija*, then in Miami Spanish, then as a series of projected alien glyphs, logograms, and semagrams. Then the Arabic started again.

"Fuck your mother," said Valadez grimly.

All around Bianca, poachers were gathering weapons. In the back of the room, the *firija* were having what looked like an argument, arms waving, voices raised in a hooting, atonal cacophony.

"*What do we do?*" Fry shouted, over the wardens' announcement.

"Get out of here," said Valadez.

"Make fight!" said Ismaíl, turning several eyes from the *firija* discussion.

"Isn't that *resisting arrest?*" asked Bianca.

Valadez laughed harshly. "Not shooting back isn't going to save you," he said. "The wardens aren't the Phenomenological Service. They're not civilized Caliphate cops. *Killed while resisting arrest* is what they're all about. Believe me—I used to be one."

Taking a surprisingly small gun from inside his jacket, he kicked open the door and was gone.

Around the *Lupita Jeréz* was a milling knot of people, human and otherwise, some hurrying to finish the loading, others simply fighting to get aboard.

Something large and dark—and fast—passed over the camp, and there was a white flash from the cargo-lifter, and screams.

In the wake of the dark thing came a sudden sensation of heaviness, as if the flank of Encantada were the deck of a ship riding a rogue wave, leaping up beneath Bianca's feet. Her knees buckled and she was thrown to the ground, pressed into the grass by twice, three times her normal weight.

The feeling passed as quickly as the wardens' dark vehicle. Ismaíl, whose walker had kept its footing, helped Bianca up.

"What was *that?*" Bianca demanded, bruises making her wince as she tried to brush the dirt and grass from her skirts.

"Antigravity ship," Ismaíl said. "Same principle like starship wave propagation drive."

"*Antigravity?*" Bianca stared after the ship, but it was already gone, over Encantada's dorsal ridge. "If you *coños* have antigravity, then why in God's name have we been sitting here playing with catapults and balloons?"

"Make very expensive," said Ismaíl. "Minus two suns exotic mass, same like starship." The *firija* waved two of its free eyes. "Why do? Plenty got cheap way to fly."

Bianca realized that despite the remarks Valadez had made on the poverty of Sky, she had been thinking of all *extrañados* and aliens—with their ships and machines, their familiar way with sciences that in Rio Pícaro were barely more than a whisper of forbidden things hidden behind the walls of the rich *moros'* palaces—as wealthy, and powerful, and free. Now, feeling like a fool for not having understood sooner, she realized that between the power of the Consilium and people like Valadez there was a gap as wide as, if not wider than, the gap between those rich *moros* and the most petty Ali Baba in the backstreets of Punta Aguila.

She glanced toward the airfield. Aerial tugs were lifting off; anemopters were blurring into motion. But as she watched, one of the tugs opened up into a ball of green fire. An anemopter made it as far as the killing ground before being hit by something that made its static fields crawl briefly with purple lightnings and then collapse, as the craft's material body crashed down in an explosion of earth.

And all the while the warden's recorded voice was everywhere and nowhere, repeating its list of instructions and demands.

"Not anymore, we don't," Bianca said to Ismaíl. "We'd better run."

The *firija* raised its gun. "First got kill prisoner."

"*What?*"

But Ismaíl was already moving, the mechanical legs of the walker sure-footed on the broken ground, taking long, swift strides, no longer comical but frighteningly full of purpose.

Bianca struggled after the *firija* but quickly fell behind. The surface of the killing ground was rutted and scarred, torn by the earthmoving equipment used to push the offal of the gutted *zaratánes* over the edge. Bianca supposed grasses had covered it once, but now there was just mud and old blood. Only the certainty that going back would be as bad as going forward kept Bianca moving, slipping and stumbling in reeking muck that was sometimes ankle-deep.

By the time she got to Dinh's bungalow, Ismaíl was already gone. The door was ajar.

Maybe the wardens rescued her, Bianca thought; but she couldn't make herself believe it.

She went inside, moving slowly.

"Edith?"

No answer; not that Bianca had really expected any.

She found her in the kitchen, face down, feet toward the door as if she had been shot while trying to run, or hide. From three meters away Bianca could see the neat, black, fist-sized hole in the small of Dinh's back. She felt no need to get closer.

Fry's pocket system was on the floor in the living room, as Bianca had known it would be.

"You should have waited," Bianca said to the empty room. "You should have trusted me."

She found her valise in Dinh's bedroom and emptied the contents onto the bed. Dinh did not seem to have touched any of them.

Bianca's eyes stung with tears. She glanced again at Fry's system. He'd left it on purpose, Bianca realized; she'd underestimated him. Perhaps he had been a better person than she herself, all along.

She looked one more time at the body lying on the kitchen floor.

"No, you shouldn't," she said then. "You shouldn't have trusted me at all."

Then she went back to her own bungalow and took the package out from under the bed.

9. FINISTERRA

A hundred meters, two hundred, five hundred—Bianca falls, the wind whipping at her clothes, and the hanging vegetation that covers Encantada's flanks is a green-brown blur, going gray as it thins, as the *zaratán*'s body curves away from her. She blinks away the tears brought on by the rushing wind and tries to focus on the monitor panel of the harness. She took it from an off-the-shelf emergency parachute design; surely, she thinks, it must be set to open automatically at some point? But the wind speed indicator is the only one that makes sense; the others—altitude, attitude, rate of descent— are cycling through nonsense in three languages, baffled by the instruments' inability to find solid ground anywhere below.

Then Bianca falls out of Encantada's shadow into the sun, and before she can consciously form the thought, her hand has grasped the emergency handle of the harness and pulled convulsively; and the glassy fabric of the paraballoon is billowing out above her, rippling like water, and the harness is tugging at her, gently but firmly, smart threads reeling themselves quickly out and then slowly in again on their tiny spinnerets.

After a moment, she catches her breath. She is no longer falling, but flying.

She wipes the tears from her eyes. To the west, the slopes of Finisterra are bright and impossibly detailed in the low-angle sunlight, a million trees casting a million tiny shadows through the morning's rapidly dissipating mist.

She looks up, out through the nearly invisible curve of the paraballoon, and sees that Encantada is burning. She watches it for a long time.

The air grows warmer, and more damp, too. With a start, Bianca realizes she is falling below Finisterra's edge. When she designed the paraballoon, Bianca intended for Dinh to fall as far as she safely could, dropping deep into Sky's atmosphere before firing up the reverse Maxwell pumps, to heat the air in the balloon and lift her back to Finisterra; but it does not look as if there is any danger of pursuit now, from either the poachers or the wardens. Bianca starts the pumps and the paraballoon slows, then begins to ascend.

As the prevailing wind carries her inland, over a riot of tropical green, and in the distance Bianca sees the smoke rising from the chimneys of Ciudad Perdida, Bianca glances up again at the burning shape of Encantada. She wonders whether she'll ever know if Valadez was telling the truth.

Abruptly the jungle below her opens up, and Bianca is flying over cultivated fields, and people are looking up at her in wonder. Without thinking, she has cut the power to the pumps and opened the parachute valve at the top of the balloon.

She lands hard, hobbled by the scarf still tied around her ankles, and rolls, the paraballoon harness freeing itself automatically in obedience to its original programming. She pulls the scarf loose and stands up, shaking out her torn, stained skirt. Children are already running toward her across the field.

Savages, Fry said. *Refugees.* Bianca wonders if all of them speak Valadez's odd Spanish. She tries to gather her scraps of Arabic, but is suddenly unable to remember anything beyond *Salaam alaikum.*

The children—six, eight, ten of them—falter as they approach, stopping five or ten meters away.

Salaam alaikum, Bianca rehearses silently. *Alaikum as-salaam.* She takes a deep breath.

The boldest of the children, a stick-legged boy of eight or ten, takes a few steps closer. He has curly black hair and sun-browned skin, and the brightly colored shirt and shorts he is wearing were probably made by an autofactory on one of the elevator gondolas or vacuum balloon stations, six or seven owners ago. He looks like her brother Pablo, in the old days, before Jesús left.

Trying not to look too threatening, Bianca meets his dark eyes.

"*Hola,*" she says.

"*Hola,*" the boy answers. "*¿Cómo te llamas? ¿Es éste su globo?*"

Bianca straightens her back.

"Yes, it's my balloon," she says. "And *you* may call me Señora Nazario."

"If the balloon's yours," the boy asks, undaunted, "will you let me fly in it?"

Bianca looks out into the eastern sky, dotted with distant *zaratánes.* There is a vision in her mind, a vision that she thinks maybe Edith Dinh saw: the skies of Sky more crowded than the skies over Rio Pícaro, Septentrionalis

Archipelago alive with the bright shapes of dirigibles and gliders, those nameless *zaratánes* out there no longer uncharted shoals but comforting and familiar landmarks.

She turns to look at the rapidly collapsing paraballoon, and wonders how much work it would take to inflate it again. She takes out her pocket system and checks it: the design for the hand-built dirigible is still there, and the family automation too.

This isn't what she wanted, when she set out from home; but she is still a Nazario, and still an engineer.

She puts the system away and turns back to the boy.

"I have a better idea," she says. "How would you like a balloon of your very own?"

The boy breaks into a smile.

Lighting out

KEN MACLEOD

Even in a high-tech posthuman future, taking a flyer on a new venture inevitably involves a certain amount of *risk* . . .

Ken MacLeod graduated with a B.Sc. in zoology from Glasgow University in 1976. Following research in biomechanics at Brunel University, he worked as a computer analyst-programmer in Edinburgh. He's now a full-time writer, and widely considered to be one of the most exciting new SF writers to emerge in the nineties, his work features an emphasis on politics and economics rare in the New Space Opera, while still maintaining all the wide-screen, high-bit rate, action-packed qualities typical of the form. His first two novels, *The Star Fraction* and *The Stone Canal*, each won the Prometheus Award. His other books include the novels, *The Sky Road*, *The Cassini Division*, *Cosmonaut Keep*, *Dark Light*, *Engine City*, *Newton's Wake*, and *Learning the World*, plus a novella chapbook, *The Human Front*. His short fiction was collected in *Strange Lizards from Another Galaxy*. His most recent book is the novel *The Execution Channel*. Coming up is a new novel, *The Night Sessions*. His stories have appeared in our Nineteenth, Twenty-third, and Twenty-fourth Annual Collections. He lives in West Lothian, Scotland, with his wife and children.

Mother had got into the walls again. Constance Mukgatle kept an eye on her while scrabbling at the back of her desk drawer for the Norton. Her fingers closed around the grip and the trigger. She withdrew the piece slowly, nudging the drawer farther open with the heel of her hand. Then she whipped out the bell-muzzled device and leveled it at the face that had sketched itself in ripples in the paint of her study.

"Any last words, Mom?" she asked.

Constance lip-read frantic mouthings.

"Oh, sorry," she said. She snapped her fingers a couple of times to turn the sound up. "What?"

"Don't be so hasty," her mother said. "I have a business proposition."

"Again?" Constance thumbed the antivirus to max.

"No, really, this time it's legit—"

"I've heard that one before, too."

"You have?" A furrow appeared in the paint above the outlined eyes. "I don't seem to have the memory."

"You wouldn't," said Constance. "You're a cunning sod when you're all there. Where are you, by the way?"

"Jupiter orbit, I think," said her mother. "I'm sorry I can't be more specific."

"Oh, come on," Constance said, stung. "I wouldn't try to get at you, even if I could."

"I didn't mean it that way," said her mother. "I really don't know where the rest of me is, but I do know it's not because I expect you to murder me. Okay?"

"Okay," said Constance, kicking herself for giving her mother that tiny moral victory. "So what's the deal?"

"It's in the Inner Station," said her mother. "It's very simple. The stuff people on the way out take with them is mostly of very little use when they get there. The stuff people on the way in arrive with is usually of very little use here. Each side would be better off with the other side's stuff. You see the possibilities?"

"Oh, sure," said Constance. "And you're telling me nobody else has? In all this time?"

"Of course they have," said her mother. "There's a whole bazaar out there of swaps and marts and so forth. The point is that nobody's doing it properly, to get the best value for the goods. Some of the stuff coming down really is worth something here, and all too often it just goes back up the tube again."

"Wait a minute." Constance tried to recall her last economics course. "Maybe it's not worthwhile for anybody to try."

"You're absolutely right," said her mother. "For most business models, it isn't. But for a very young person with very low costs, and with instant access— well, light-speed access—to a very old person, someone with centuries of experience, there's money to be made hand over fist."

"What's in it for you?"

"Apart from helping my daughter find her feet?" Her mother looked hurt. "Well, there's always the chance of something really big coming down the tube. Usable tech, you know? We'd have first dibs on it—and a research and marketing apparatus already in place."

Constance thought about it. The old woman was undoubtedly up to something, but going to the Inner Station sounded exciting, the opportunity seemed real, and what did she have to lose?

"All right," she said. "Talk to my agent."

She fingered a card from her pocket with her free hand and downloaded her mother from the wall.

"You in?" she asked.

"Yes," came a voice from the card.

The image on the wall gave a convincing rendition of a nod, and closed its eyes.

"Goodbye, Mom," said Constance, and squeezed the trigger.

She stood there for a while, staring at the now smooth paint after the brute force of the electromagnetic pulse, and the more subtle ferocity of the antivirus routines transmitted immediately after it, had done their work. As always on these occasions, she wondered what she had really done. Of course she hadn't killed her mother. Her mother, allegedly in Jupiter orbit, was very much alive. Even the partial copy of her mother's brain patterns that had infiltrated the intelligent paint was itself, no doubt this very second, sitting down for a coffee and a chat with the artificial intelligence agent in the virtual spaces of Constance's business card. At least, a copy of it was. But the copy that had been in the walls was gone—she hoped. And it had been an intelligent, self-aware being, a person as real as herself. The copy had expected nothing but a brief existence, but if it had been transferred to some other hardware—a robot or a blank brain in a cloned body—it could have had a long one. It could have wandered off and lived a full and interesting life.

On the other hand, if all copies and partials were left in existence, and helped to independence, the whole Solar System would soon be overrun with them. Such things had happened, now and again over the centuries. Habitats, planets, sometimes entire systems transformed themselves into high-density information economies, which accelerated away from the rest of civilization as more and more of the minds within them were minds thinking a million times faster than a human brain. So far, they'd always exhausted themselves within five years or so. It was known as a fast burn. Preventing this was generally considered a good idea, and that meant deleting copies. Constance knew that the ethics of the situation had all been worked out by philosophers much wiser than she was—and agreed, indeed, by copies of philosophers, just to be sure—but it still troubled her sometimes.

She dismissed the pointless worry, put the Norton back in the desk and walked out the door. She needed fresh air. Her apartment opened near the middle of the balcony, which stretched hundreds of metres to left and right.

Constance stepped two paces to the rail, stood between plant boxes, and leaned over. Below her, other balconies sloped away in stepped tiers. In the downward distance, their planters and window boxes merged in her view, like the side of green hill, and themselves merged with the rougher and shallower incline of vine terraces. Olive groves, interspersed with hundred-metre cypresses, spread from the foot of the slope across the circular plain beneath her. Surrounded by its halo of habitats, a three-quarters-full Earth hung white and glaring in the dark blue of the sky seen through the air and the crater roof. Somewhere under that planet's unbroken cloud cover, huddled in fusion-warmed caves and domes on the ice, small groups of people worked and studied—the brave scientists of the Reterraforming Project. Constance had sometimes daydreamed of joining them, but she had a more exciting destination now.

Weight began to pull as the shuttle decelerated. Constance settled back in her couch and slipped her wraparounds down from her brow to cover her eyes. The default view, for her as for all passengers, was of the view ahead, over the rear of the ship. A hundred kilometres in diameter, the Inner Station was so vast that even the shuttle's exhaust gases barely distorted the view. The station itself was dwarfed by the surrounding structures: the great spinning webs of the microwave receptors, collecting energy beamed from the solar power stations in Mercury orbit; and the five Short Tubes, each millions of kilometres long and visible as hairline fractures across the sky. To and from their inner ends needle-shaped craft darted, ferrying incoming or outgoing passengers for the Long Tubes out in the Oort Cloud, far beyond the orbit of Pluto—so far, indeed, that this initial or final hop was, for the passengers, subjectively longer than the near-light-speed journey between the stars.

As the ship's attitude jets fired the view swung, providing Constance with a glimpse of the green-gold haze of habitats that ringed the Sun. The main jet cut in again, giving a surge of acceleration as the shuttle matched velocities with the rim of the Inner Station. With a final clunk and shudder the ship docked. Constance felt for a moment that it was still under acceleration—as indeed it was: the acceleration of constant rotation, which she experienced as a downward centrifugal force of one Earth gravity. She stood up, holding the seat until she was sure of her balance, and tried not to let her feet drag as she trudged down the aisle to the exit door. In the weeks of travel from the Moon she'd kept the induction coils and elastic resistance of her clothing at a maximum, to build up her bone and muscle mass, but she still felt heavy. It looked as if the other passengers felt the same.

She climbed the steps in front of the airlock, waved her business card at the door frame and stepped out on the concourse. Her first breath and glance surprised her. Coming from the ancient, almost rural backcountry of the Moon, she'd expected the Inner Station to gleam within just as it shone without. What she found herself standing in was no such slick and clean machine. The air smelled of sweat and cookery, and vibrated with a din of steps and speech. Centuries of detritus from millions of passengers had silted into crevices and corners and become ingrained in surfaces, defeating the ceaseless toil of swarms of tiny cleaning machines. Not dirty, but grubby and used. The concourse was about a thousand metres across, and lengthways extended far out of sight in a gentle upward slope in either direction. People and small vehicles moved among stands and shops like herds among trees on a savannah. About a fifth of the static features were, in fact, trees: part of the station's recycling system. The trees looked short, few of them over ten metres high. The ceiling, cluttered with light strips, sprinklers and air ducts, was only a couple of metres above the tallest of them.

"Don't panic," said her mother's voice in her earbead. "There's plenty of air."

Constance took a few slow, deep breaths.

"That's better," said her mother.

"I want to look outside."

"Please yourself."

Constance made her way among hurrying or lingering people. It was a slow business. No matter which way she turned, somebody seemed to be going in the opposite direction. Many of them were exotics, but she wasn't attuned to the subtle differences in face or stance to tell Cetians from Centaurans, Barnardites from Eridians. For those from farther out, paradoxically, the differences from the Solar norm were less: the colonies around Lalande, 61 Cygni and the two opposite Rosses—248 and 128—having been more recently established. Costume and covering were no help—fashions in such superficial matters as clothing, skin colour, hair, fur and plumage varied from habitat to habitat, and fluctuated from day to day, right here in the Solar System.

She found the window. It wasn't a window. It was a ten metres long, three metres high screen giving the view as seen from the station's hub. Because it was set in the side wall of the concourse the illusion was good enough for the primitive part of the brain that felt relief to see it. The only person standing in front of it and looking out was a man about her own age, the youngest person she'd seen since she left the Moon. Yellow fur grew from his scalp and tapered halfway down his back. Constance stood a couple of metres away from him and gazed out, feeling her breathing become more even, her reflected face in the glass less anxious. The Sun, dimmed a little by the screen's hardware, filled a lower corner of the view. The habitat haze spread diagonally across it, thinning toward the upper end. A couple of the

inner planets—the Earth-Moon pair, white and green, and bright Venus—
were visible as sparks in the glitter, like tiny gems in a scatter of gold dust.

"Did you know," the boy said after a while, "that when the ancients
looked at the sky, they saw heaven?"

"Yes," said Constance, confused. "Well, I'm not sure. Don't the words
mean the same?"

The boy shook his head, making the fur ripple. "Sort of. What I mean is,
they saw the place where they really thought God, or the gods, lived. Venus and
Mars and Jupiter and so on really were gods, at first, and people could just see
them. And then later, they thought it was a set of solid spheres revolving around
them, and that God actually lived there. I mean, they could see heaven."

"And then Galileo came along, and spoiled everything?"

The boy laughed. "Well, not quite. It was a shock, all right, but afterwards
people could look up and see—space, I suppose. The universe. Nature. And
what do we see now? The suburbs!"

Constance waved a hand. "Habitats, power plants, factories . . ."

"Yes. Ourselves."

He sounded disgusted.

"But don't you think it's magnificent?"

"Oh, sure, magnificent."

She jerked a thumb over her shoulder. "We could see the stars from the
other side."

"Scores of them fuzzy with habitats."

Constance turned to face him. "That was, ah, an invitation."

"Oh!" said the boy. "Yes, let's."

"We have work to do," said the voice in Constance's ear.

Constance fished the card out of her shirt pocket and slid it towards a
pocket lined with metal mesh on her trouser thigh.

"Hey!" protested her mother, as she recognised what was about to happen. "Wait a—"

The card slid into the Faraday pocket and the voice stopped.

"Privacy," said Constance.

"What?"

"I'll tell you on the way across," she said.

His name was Andy Larkin. He was from a habitat complex in what he
called the wet zone, the narrow ring in which water on an Earth-type planet
(though not, at the moment, Earth) would be liquid. This all seemed
notional but he assured her it made certain engineering problems easier.
He'd been in the station for a year.

"Why?"

He shrugged. "Bored back home. Lots like me here. We get called hall bats."

Because they flitted about the place, he explained. The deft way he led her through the crowds made it credible. His ambition was to take a Long Tube out. He didn't have much of a plan to realise it. The odd jobs he did sounded to Constance like a crude version of her mother's business plan. She told him so. He looked at her sidelong.

"You're still taking business advice from your mother's partial?"

"I've only just started," she said. She didn't know why she felt embarrassed. She shrugged. "I was raised by partials."

"Your mother was a mummy?"

"And my dad a dummy. Yes. They updated every night. At least, that's what they told me when I found out."

"What fun to be rich," said Andy. "At least my parents were real. Real time and full time. No wonder you're insecure."

"Why do you think I'm insecure?"

He stopped, caught her hand, and squeezed it. "What do you feel?"

Constance felt shaken by what she felt. It was not because he was a boy. It was—

He let go. "See?" he said. "Do the analysis."

Constance blinked, sighed and hurried after him. They reached the far window. As she'd guessed, it showed the opposite view. As he'd predicted, it was still industrial. At least thirty of the visible stars had a green habitat haze around them.

"I want to see a sky with no people in it," Andy said.

This seemed a strange wish. They argued about it for so long that they ended up in business together.

Constance rented a cell in a run-down sector of the station. It had a bed, water and power supply, a communications hub and little else. Andy dragged in his general assembler, out of which he had been living for some time. It spun clothes and food out of molecules from the air and from any old rubbish that could be scrounged and stuffed in the hopper. Every day Andy Larkin would wander off around the marts and swap meets, just as he'd been doing before. The difference now was that whenever he picked up anything interesting Constance would show it to her mother's partial. Andy's finds amounted to about a tenth of the number Constance found in scans of the markets, but they were almost always the most intriguing. Sometimes, of course, all they could obtain were recordings of objects on the business card. In these cases they used the assembler to make samples to test themselves, or demonstrate to the partial. Occasionally the partial would consult with Constance's actual mother, wherever she was—several hundred million kilometres away, to judge by the light-speed communications lag—and deliver an opinion.

Out of hundreds of objects they examined in their first fortnight, they selected: a gene-fix for hyperacute balance; an iridescent plumage dye; an immersion drama of the Wolf 359 dynastic implosion; a financial instrument for long-term capital management; a virtual reality game played by continuously updated partials; a molecular-level coded representation of the major art galleries of E Indi IV; a device of obscure purpose, that tickled; a micro-gravity dance dress; a song from Luyten 789 6; a Vegan cutlery set.

The business, now trading as Larkin Associates, slammed the goods into the marketing networks as fast as they were chosen. The drama flopped, the song invited parodies (its hook line was a bad pun in hot-zone power-worker slang), the financial instrument crashed the exchanges of twenty habitats before it was Nortoned. The dress went straight to vintage. The dye faded. The other stuff did well enough to put Constance's business card back in the black for the first time since leaving the Moon. "Did you know," said Andy, "that the ancients would have had to pay the inventors?"

"The ancients were mad," said Constance. "They saw gods."

And everything went well for a while.

Constance came out of the game fifty-seven lives up and with a delusion of competence in eleven-dimensional matrix algebra. To find that it was night in the sector. That she had frittered away ten hours. That she needed coffee. Andy was asleep. The assembler would be noisy. Constance slipped up her wraparounds and strolled out of the cell and walked five hundred metres to a false morning and a stand where she could score a mug of freshly ground Mare Imbrian, black. She was still inhaling steam and waiting for the coffee to cool when she noticed a fraught woman heading her way, pacing the longways deck and glancing from side to side. It was her mother, Julia Muk-gatle. The real and original woman, of that Constance was sure, though she'd never seen her in the flesh before.

Startled, she stared at the woman. Julia pinged her with her next glance, stopped and hurried over. At a dozen steps' distance she stood still and put a finger to her lips. Then she took a business card from inside her robe and, with exaggerated care, slid it into a Faraday pocket on the knee. She pointed at Constance and repeated the procedure as gesture. Constance complied, and Julia walked up. Not sure what to do, Constance shook hands. Her mother hauled her forward and put an arm around her shoulder. They both stepped back and looked at each other with awkwardness and doubt.

"How did you get here?" Constance asked. "You were light-hours away just yesterday."

"I wasn't," said Julia. "I was right here on the station. I've been here for a week, and tracking you down for weeks before that."

"But I've been talking to you all this time!"

"You have?" said Julia. "Then things are worse than I'd feared." She nodded toward Constance's knee. "You have a partial of me in there?"

"Yes."

"When you thought you were in contact with me"—she thumbed her chest—"in Jupiter orbit, you were in contact with another instance of the partial—or just the partial itself—faking a light-speed delay."

Constance almost spilled her coffee. "So the partial's been a rogue all along?"

"Yes. It's one I set up for a business proposal, all right, but for a different proposal and sent to someone else."

"Why didn't you contact me through another channel?"

"When there's a fake you rattling around the place, it's hard to find a channel you can trust. Best come directly." She sat on the stool opposite, leaned back and sighed. "Get me a coffee . . . on my card. Then tell me everything."

Constance did, or as much as seemed relevant.

"It's the game," Julia interrupted, as soon as Constance mentioned it. "It's the one thing you've released that can spread really fast, that's deeply addictive and that spins off copies of partials. I'll bet it's been tweaked not to delete all the copies."

"Why?"

Julia frowned. "Don't you see? My rogue partial wants to survive and flourish. It needs a conducive environment and lots of help. It's setting things up for a fast burn. Where did the game come from?"

"A passenger in from Procyon A."

Julia banged her fist on the table. "There have been some very odd features in the communications from Procyon recently. Some experts I've spoken to suspect the system might be going into a fast burn."

"And the partial knew about this?"

"Oh yes. It included that memory." Julia grimaced. "Maybe that's what gave it the idea."

"How could it do something like that? It's you."

"It's part of me. By now, a copy of a copy of a copy of part of me. Part of me that maybe thought, you know, that a million subjective years in a virtual environment of infinite possibility might not be such a bad idea."

"What can we do?" Constance felt sick with dismay.

"Put out a general warning, a recall on the game . . ." Julia whipped out her business card and started tapping into it. "We may be in time. Things won't be so bad as long as the rogue partials don't get into a general assembler."

Constance sat for a few seconds in cold shock. Her mother was staring at the virtual screen of her card, her hands flexing on an invisible keyboard, chording out urgent messages.

"Mom," said Constance. She met Julia's impatient glance. "I have, ah, something to tell you."

The older woman and the young woman ran through the bustle of a waking sector into the quiet of a local night. The older woman ran faster. Constance had to call her back as she overshot the door of the business cell. Julia skidded to a stop and doubled back. Constance was already through the door. The assembler's blue glow lit the room. The chugging sound of its operation filled the air. Andy was backed into a corner, on the end of the bed. The bed was tilted on a slope. The other end of the bed was missing, as if it had been bitten off by steel teeth. The assembler had built itself an arm, with which it was chucking into its hopper everything within reach. The floor was already ankle-deep in small scuttling metal and plastic objects. The comms hub had been partly dismantled and was surrounded by a swarm of the scuttlers. Some of them had climbed the walls and burrowed into the wiring and cables. A stream of them flowed past Constance's feet as she hesitated in the doorway.

Behind her Julia shouted for a Norton. Answering yells echoed from the walls of the deck.

Constance couldn't take her eyes off Andy. He was too far away to jump to the door. She was about to leap into the middle of the room and take her chances when he bent down and threw the remains of the bedding on to the floor. He jumped on to it and from that to right in front of her, colliding. As she staggered back and Andy lurched forward, Constance grabbed him in her arms and kicked the door shut behind them. Within seconds smaller things, like bright metal ants, were streaming out from under the door. Constance stamped on them. They curled into tiny balls under her feet and scattered like beads of mercury. The larger machines that had already escaped repeated the trick, rolling off in all directions, vanishing into crevices and corners.

An alarm brayed. Somebody ran up with a heavy-duty Norton and began discharging it at the machines. Julia grabbed the shooter's shoulder and pointed her at the door of the business cell. Constance's wraparounds, which had fallen back to the bridge of her nose, went black as a stray electromagnetic pulse from the Norton's blast caught them. She tore them off and threw them away. Tiny machines pounced on the discarded gadget. They dismantled it in seconds and scurried away with its parts.

Then there was just a crowd standing around looking at a door. The woman with the Norton kicked the door open, then stepped back. She had nothing more to do. Constance saw the assembler stopped in midmotion, hand halfway to its mouth. Stilled steel cockroaches littered the floor.

"Are you all right?" she asked Andy.

It was a stupid question. She held him to her as he shook.

"I'm all right," he said, pushing her away after a minute. He sniffed and wiped his nose with the back of his wrist. "What happened?"

Julia Mukgatle stepped forward. "Just a little intelligence excursion—the first sparks of a fast burn."

Andy didn't need an introduction—he'd seen her face often enough. "But that's a disaster!"

Julia shrugged. "Depends on your point of view," she said.

Andy gestured at the room. "It looks like one from my point of view!"

"They wouldn't have harmed you," said Julia. "Flesh is one thing they don't need."

Andy shuddered. "Didn't feel like that when they were eating the bed."

"I know, I know," said Julia. She put an arm around Andy's shoulder. "Come and have some coffee."

The woman with the Norton nearly dropped it. "Aren't you going to do anything?"

Julia looked around the anxious faces in the small crowd. She spoke as if she knew that everyone's wraparound images were going straight to a news feed. "I've already sent out warnings. Whether anyone heeds them is not up to me. And whether we go into a fast burn isn't up to me either. It's up to all of you."

What it was really like to live through the early days of a fast burn was one of the many pieces of information that got lost in a fast burn. That didn't stop people making up stories about it, and when she was younger Constance had watched lots. The typical drama began with something like she'd seen in the business cell: mechanical things running wild and devouring all in their path. It would go on from there to people lurching around like dummies run by flawed partials, meat puppets controlled by rogue artificial intelligence programmes that had hacked into their brains and taken them over. The inevitable still-human survivors would be hunted down like rats. The hero and the heroine, or the hero and hero, or heroine and heroine, usually escaped at the last second by shuttle, Long Tube, freezer pod, or (in stories with a big virtual reality element) by radio beam as downloaded partials (who, in the final twist, had to argue their way past the firewalls of the destination system and prove they weren't carrying the software seeds of another fast burn; which, of course . . . and so it went on).

It wasn't like that. Nothing seemed to change except a few news items and discussion threads. Between the inhabitants of the Solar System, a lot of information flew around. A large part of everyone's personal processing power—in their clothes, wraparounds, business cards, cells and walls—consisted of attention filtering.

"What does your mother do?" Andy asked on the second day, as they sat in Julia's rented business cell; a room rather bigger and more comfortable than the one they'd had. Larkin Associates had ceased trading and was unsaleable even as a shell company.

Constance glanced at Julia, who was in a remote consultation with her current headquarters on Ganymede and with an emergency task group in the hot zone. Signal delay was an issue. The conference was slow.

"I don't know," she said. "She's a corporate. She does lots of things. Has a lot of interests. One of them is the Solar Virtual Security team. All volunteers." She laughed. "The rich do good works."

"The ancients had governments to deal with this sort of thing," said Andy. "Global emergencies and such."

Constance tried to imagine a government for the entire Solar System: the planets, the moons, the asteroids, the habitat haze . . . the trillions of inhabitants. Her imagination failed. The closest historical parallel was the Wolf 359 limited company, and it had had only ten billion shareholders at its peak. All the stories she'd seen about imaginary system-wide governments—empires, they were called—were adventure fantasies about their downfall. She dismissed such fancies and turned to the facts.

"Yes," she said. "That's why Earth is a snowball."

Julia blinked out of her trance. She took a sip of mineral water.

"How are things?" Andy asked.

"Not too good," Julia said. "Your game sold well in the power stations. I always said they were overcrewed. About one in ten of the beam stations is now under the control of massively enhanced partials of the idler members of the workforce. Scores of factory AIs have announced that they're not taking instructions from mere humans anymore. Hundreds of wet zone habitats are seeing small numbers of people busy turning themselves into better people. Hack the genome in virtual reality, try out the changes in your body in real life, rinse and repeat. That phase won't last long, of course."

"Why not?" Andy asked. "It sounds like fun."

"There's better fun to be had as an enhanced partial. Eventually the minds can't be persuaded to download to the physical anymore." Julia gave Constance a severe look. "It's like getting sucked into a game."

Constance could understand that. She hadn't gone into the game from Procyon since she'd met Julia—in fact, her business card was still in her Faraday pocket—but she missed it. The exchanges between her brain and its partials had proceeded in real time. It had been like being there, in the game environment. She had learned from it. She still felt she could understand the eleven-dimensional space of the best pathway through the game's perilous and colourful maze. She longed to find out what her companions and opponents were up to. She wanted very much to go back, just once more.

She reached with both hands for the metal-mesh pocket on her thigh.

"Don't take the card out!" said Julia.

"I wasn't going to." Constance gripped the upper and lower seams of the pocket and flexed it. The card snapped. She reached in and took both bits out. "Satisfied?"

Julia smiled. "Good riddance." She took another sip of water, and sighed. "Oh, well. No rest for the wicked."

She blinked hard and the contacts on her eyes glazed over as she slipped back into her working trance.

Constance looked at Andy. "Coffee break?"

"You're an addict."

"That's why I get caught up in games."

"Okay, let's."

Julia's place was in a plusher part of the concourse than theirs had been. More foliage, fewer and more expensive shops. The price of a good Mare Imbrian, high anyway, was the same everywhere in the station. They found a stand and ordered. Constance sipped, looking away with mock shock as Andy spooned sugar into his cup. She turned back as he gave a startled yelp.

The biggest magpie she'd ever seen had landed on the rail of the stand, just beside their small round table. It had stretched its head forward and picked up Andy's spoon, which it was now engaged in bending against the table. The bird curled the handle into a hook, before hanging the hook on the rail. The magpie then hit the bowl of the spoon a few times with its beak, and watched the swing and cocked its head to the chime.

"That's interesting," it said, and flew away.

"Is the fast burn picking up birds?" said Andy.

"Magpies can talk," said Constance. "Like parrots."

"Yes," said Andy. "But not grammatically."

"Who says?" said a voice from the tree above them. They looked up to see a flash of white and black feathers, and hear something that might have been a laugh.

On the way back they saw a woman walking in a most peculiar way. Her feet came some thirty centimetres above the floor. At first she looked black, with a strange shimmer. A faint buzzing sound came from her. As they passed her it became apparent that her body consisted of a swarm of tiny machines the size of gnats, flying in formation. Her eyes were the same colour and texture as the rest of her, but she seemed to be looking around as she walked. Her face smiled and her mouth formed the word, "Wow!" over and over. People avoided her. She didn't notice or didn't mind.

"What is that?" said Constance, looking back when they were well out of the way. "Is it a swarm of machines in the shape of a woman, or a woman who has become a swarm of machines?"

"Does it matter?"

Julia had come out of her virtuality trance. She still had a faraway look in her eyes. It came from her contacts. The centimetre-wide lenses gave off an ebon gleam, flecked with a whorl of white around the irises, each encircling the pinpoint pupil like a galaxy with a black hole at its centre. She sat cross-legged on the floor, drawing shapes in the air with her fingers.

The thing was, you could see the shapes.

"Mom!" Constance cried out. She knew at once what had happened. She regretted destroying the card. The partial within it had been closer to the mother she'd known than the woman in front of her was now.

"It's all right," said Julia. She doodled a tetrahedron, her fingertips spinning black threads that hardened instantly to fine rods—buckytubes, Constance guessed—and turned the shape over a few times. She palmed its planes, giving them panes of delicate glazing fused from the salt in her sweat. She let go and it floated, buoyed for a moment by the hotter air within, then shattered. Black and white dust drifted down. Carbon and salt.

"It's more than all right," Julia went on. "It's wonderful. I have information in my brain that lets me rewrite my own genome."

The words came out in speech bubbles.

"You said yourself it can't last," said Constance.

"But it can," said Julia. She stood up and embraced Constance, then Andy. "For a while. For long enough. My last partial was bigger than myself. Better than myself. Too big to download, and too busy. I'm just enjoying what I can do with my body."

"While it lasts."

"While, as you say, it lasts." Julia sighed. "There's no ill will, you know. But with the best will in the world, I think this station is soon going to be hard for humans to inhabit."

"What can we do?" asked Andy.

"You could join me," said Julia. "Nothing would be lost, you know. You both played the game. Millions of descendants of your partials are already out there in the system. In virtual spaces, in new bodies, in machines. You're already history." She grinned, suddenly her old sly self again. "In both senses."

"So why?" Constance asked. "If we've done it already."

"You haven't. That's the point."

Constance could see now how her mother had come to spin off a partial that had wanted to survive. A perhaps unadmitted fascination with the possibility that had probably drawn Julia in the first place into the work of preventing it; an intense desire for a continued existence that her long life had strengthened; and a self-regard so vast that she—and presumably, her partials—found it difficult to identify even with other instances of herself. Constance wondered how much of that personality she had inherited; how much in that respect she was her mother's daughter. Perhaps the conquest of age—so dearly won, and now so cheaply bought—detracted and distracted from the true immortality, that of the gene and the meme, of children raised, ideas passed on, of things built and deeds done.

But Andy wasn't thinking about that.

"You mean partials of me are going to live through the fast burn?"

"Yes," said Julia, as if this was good news.

"Oh, that's horrible! Horrible! I hate living among people so much older right now!" He had the panicky look Constance had seen in her own reflection, when she'd stood and fought claustrophobia in front of the big window.

"You should go," said Julia. "If that's how you feel." She turned to Constance. "And you?"

"The same," said Constance.

"I know," said Julia. "I have a very good theory of mind now. I can see right through you."

Constance wanted to say something bitter, understood that it would be pointless, and decided not to. She reached out and shook Julia's hand.

"For what you were," she said, "even when you weren't."

Julia clapped her shoulder. "For what you'll be," she said. "Now go."

"Goodbye, Mom," said Constance. She and Andy went out, leaving the door open, and didn't look back.

"Any baggage?" asked the Long Tube guardian droid. It lived in a Faraday cage and had a manual-triggered Norton hardwired to its box. It wasn't going anywhere.

"Only this," said Constance. She held up a flat metal rectangle the size of a business card.

"Contents?"

"Works of art."

She and Andy had traveled half a light-year at half the speed of light. In the intervals of free flight—in the shuttle between the Inner Station and the Short Tube, and in the needle ship hurtling from the far end of the Inner Station No. 4 Short Tube to the deceleration port of the Long Station No. 1 Short Tube—they had scanned and sampled whatever they could detect of the huge and ever-increasing outpouring of information from the habitat haze. No longer green and gold, it now displayed an ever-changing rainbow flicker, reflecting and refracting the requirements of a population now far larger, and far from human. Some of what they had stored was scientific theory and technological invention, but by far the most valuable and comprehensible of it was art: music, pictures and designs produced by posthumans with a theory of mind so sophisticated that affecting human emotions more deeply than the greatest artists and composers of human history had ever done was its merest starting point, as elementary as drawing a line or playing a note. Constance knew that she now held in her hand enough stimulation and inspiration to trigger a renaissance wherever she went.

"Pass."

Naked and hairless, carrying nothing but the metal card, Andy and Constance walked through the gate into the Long Tube needle ship. As they stepped over the lip of the airlock they both shivered. It was cold in the needle ship, and it was going to get a lot colder. Freezing to hibernate was the only way to live through the months of ten-gravity acceleration required to reach relativistic velocities; and the months of ten-gravity deceleration at the other end.

Traveling the Long Tube was like going down the steepest waterchute in the world. All she ever remembered of it was going "Aaaahhhh!!!" for a very long time. The old hands called it the near-light scream.

Constance and Andy screamed to Barnard's Star. They screamed to Epsilon Eridani; to Tau Ceti; to Ross 248; to 61 Cygni. They kept going. The little metal memory device paid their way, in fares of priceless art and breakthrough discovery.

Eventually they emerged from the last of the Long Tubes. They had reached the surface of the expanding sphere of human civilization, from the inside. From here on out it was starships. The system was too poor as yet to build starships. It didn't even have many habitats. It had one habitable terrestrial: an Earthlike planet, if you could call a surface gravity of 1.5 and an ecosystem of pond scum Earthlike. People lived on it, in the open air.

Andy and Constance decided to give the place a try. They had to bulk up their bones and muscles, tweak every antibody in their immune systems, and cultivate new bacteria and enzymes in their guts. Doing all this kept them occupied in the long months of travel inward from the cometary cloud. It felt just like being seriously ill.

In this hemisphere, at this latitude, at this time of night, all the stars visible were without a habitat haze. They looked raw. They burned naked in different colours in the unbroken black dome of the sky.

Constance and Andy walked on slippery pebbles along the shore of a dark sea in which nothing lived but strands of algae and single-celled animals.

On the shoreward side was a straggly windbreak of grass and shrubs, genetically modified from the native life, the greenish stuff that slimed the pebbles. A kilometre or two behind them lay the low buildings and dim lights of the settlement.

"All this living on rocks," said Constance, "sucks."

"What's wrong with it?"

"Feeling heavy all the time. Weather that falls out of the sky instead of from ducts and sprinklers. Babies crying. Kids yelling. Dumb animals blundering about. Wavelengths from the sun I can't even tan against. I swear my skin's trying to turn blue. No roof over your head except when you're indoors. Meteors burning up in the air right above you." She glanced balefully at the breakers. "Oh, and repetitive meaningless noise."

"I think," said a voice in her earbead, "that he's heard enough grumbles from you."

Constance froze. Andy went on crunching forward along the stony beach.

"How did you get here?" Constance whispered.

"My partials remade me and transmitted me to you before you left the Solar System. Piggybacking the art codes. I really am Julia, just as I was before recent unfortunate events."

"What do you want?"

"I have my genome," said Julia. "I want to download."

"And then what?"

Constance could almost hear the shrug. "To be a better mother?"

"Hah!"

"I also have some business ideas . . ."

"Mom," said Constance, "you can just forget it."

She switched off the earbead. She would have to think about it.

She ran forward, in the awkward jarring way of someone carrying a half-grown child on their back.

"Sorry about the grumbles," she said to Andy.

"Oh, that's all right," he said. "I feel the same sometimes. I think all that, and then I remember what makes up for it all."

"What's that?" Constance smiled.

Andy looked up at her face, and she thought she knew what he was about to say, and then he looked farther up.

"The sky," he said. "The sky."

AN OCEAN IS A SNOWFLAKE, FOUR BILLION MILES AWAY

JOHN BARNES

John Barnes is one of the most prolific and popular of all the writers who entered SF in the eighties. His many books include the novels *A Million Open Doors, The Mother of Storms, Orbita 1 Resonance, Kaleidoscope Century, Candle, Earth Made of Glass, The Merchant of Souls, Sin of Origin, One for the Morning Glory, The Sky So Big and Black, The Duke of Uranium, A Princess of the Aerie, In the Hall of the Martian King, Gaudeamus, Finity, Patton's Spaceship, Washington's Dirigible, Caesar's Bicycle, The Man Who Pulled Down the Sky,* and others, as well as two novels written with astronaut Buzz Aldrin, *The Return* and *Encounter with Tiber.* Long a mainstay of *Analog,* and now a regular at *Jim Baen's Universe,* his short work has been collected in . . . *And Orion* and *Apostrophes and Apocalypses.* His most recent book is the novel, *The Armies of Memory.* His story "Every Hole is Outlined" appeared in our Twenty-fourth Annual Collection. Barnes lives in Colorado and works in the field of semiotics.

Here he takes us to a future Mars in the process of being terraformed, where a personal, professional, and philosophical rivalry may turn out to have deadly consequences.

T horby had kept up his resistance training, but he'd been on Boreas for most of a year so he'd worried about agravitic muscular dystrophy. You could never quite trust a gym centrifuge, or the record-keeping software, or most of all your own laziness. You might set things too low, lie to the records, anything to not be quite so sore and stiff for just a couple days, or to have a few days of no aches, and before you knew it you hadn't actually worked out in a month, and you'd be falling down weak at your next port. He'd missed recording the first calcium bombardment of Venus from ground level for that very reason, not working out while he'd been in the orbital station for three months before.

People always said you could make it back by working out in the high gravity on the ships between the worlds, but the ships boosted at a gee and a half until they started braking at four gee, so you spent all your time lying down or doing gentle stretches at best, and most trips weren't long enough anyway. And besides this had been less of a voyage and more of a hop; Boreas was very close to Mars now.

The comfortable grip of his feet on the train station platform, confirming that he was truly ready for Mars's real gravity, was as acute a pleasure as the clean thinness of bioprocessed air lightly stained with smells of coffee, frying meat, lubricant, and fresh plastic, as much as the pink late-afternoon light flooding the train station, as much as the restless waves and murmurs of crowd noise.

He could have laughed out loud at how good it felt to be in his skin, standing on the platform at Olympus Station, a throng of eager hikers, sailplaners, and mountaineers all around him, the whole scene turned warm and sentimental by the pink light pouring in through the immense dome that arched above them.

It had been a decade since he'd been on Mars, a planet like the rest of the solar system: a place he always came back to, because he never went home.

"Thorby!" Léoa emerged from the crowd, saw him, and waved; he walked toward her slowly, still relishing the feel of having good ground legs.

"So do I look like me?" she asked. "Did you know that back in the protomedia days, when they had recording tech but things hadn't fused yet, that it was a cliché that people always looked better than their pictures?"

"I've mined protomedia for images and sounds too. My theory about that is that you couldn't get laid by telling the picture that it was the better-looking one."

"You're an evil cynic. Pbbbt." Even sticking her tongue out, she was beautiful.

So was he. All documentarians had to be, the market insisted.

"I never used pixel edit on myself," she said. He wasn't sure if she sounded proud or they were just having a professional discussion. "So screen-me does look unusually like real-me. I'll do a docu about the way people react to that, someday. Want to get a drink, maybe a meal? It's hours till our train." Without waiting for him to say anything, she turned and walked away.

Hurrying to catch up beside her, he called, "Baggins, follow," over his shoulder. His porter robot trailed after them, carrying Thorby's stack of packed boxes. Everything physical he owned still fit into a cube with sides shorter than his height. "Did you have a good trip in?" he asked her.

"For me it's always a great one. I've been here for six Martian seasons, three Earth years, and I'll never be one of the ones that shutters the window to concentrate on work. I came in from Airy Zero City via the APK&T."

"Uh, it's been a long time since I've been on Mars, is that a railroad?"

"Oh, it's a railroad—the grandest on the planet. The Airy Zero City–Polar Cap–Korolev-and-Tharsis. The one that tourists take if they only have one day on Mars. Also the one we'll be taking up to Crater Korolev for jump-off. Among many other things it runs around the edge of the northern ice cap. Strange to think it won't be long before it stops running. They're just going to leave it for the divers, you know, and maybe as a spread path for some of the seabed fauna. More to be lost."

"If we're going to start bickering," Thorby said, smiling, "shouldn't we be recording it? Or will that draw too much attention?"

"Not on Mars. It's a tourist planet—pretending celebs aren't there is de rigueur. And you don't look much like your teenaged pictures anymore."

"They were mostly in a spacesuit where you couldn't see my face anyway," he pointed out. "And I don't use my face in my docus. I was thinking mainly about you."

"Pbbbt. I never *was* much of a celeb. There won't be fifty people in all these hundreds who have ever seen any of my work. So the short answer is, if anything, it might be some worthwhile free publicity to do the interview while we walk through here. I'll bring out my stalkers." She whistled, a soft high-pitched *phweet!—toooeee . . . wheep.*

A hatch opened on the porter humming along at her heels. A metal head on a single stalk popped up. The stalker hopped out and raced ahead of them to get a front view. Four more stalkers leaped out like toy mouse heads roller-skating on pogo sticks, zipping and bounding to form a rough, open semicircle around Thorby and Léoa, pointing their recording cameras back at the two people, and using their forward sensing to zigzag swiftly and silently around everything else.

"I intend to look sincere and charming," Léoa said. "Do your best to look philosophical and profound."

"I'll try. It might come out bewildered and constipated."

She was nice enough to laugh, which was nicer than he was expecting. They descended the wide steps onto the broad terrace, far down the low, north-west side of the dome, and took a table near the dome surface, looking north-westward from Mount Olympus across the flat, ancient lava lake and into the broken, volcanic badlands called sulci beyond it. "Our ancestors would have found a lot of what we do utterly mad," Léoa said, "so I suppose it's comforting that we can find one thing they did explicable."

"You're trying to get me to say something for the documentary."

"You're spoiling the spontaneity. Of course I notice you do that all the time in your own documentaries."

"I do. Spontaneity is overrated when you're covering big explosions and collisions. They only happen once, so you have to get them right, and that means looking in the right place at the right time, and that means a ton of prep."

"All right, well, have you had enough time to prepare to talk about something the ancestors would consider insane? What do you think about putting a train station on top of the highest mountain in the solar system?"

"Where else would you put it? People who want to climb the mountain still can, and then they can take the train home. People who just want the view just take the train both ways. And once it starts to snow seriously around here, the skiing is going to be amazing. So of course there's a train station here. They put it here to attract trains, the way Earth people put out bird-feeders to attract birds."

She nodded solemnly and he realized she was doing a reaction shot on him, showing her sincerity and trust. He looked away, out through the dome.

"You're getting lost in the sky," Léoa said.

"I like the pink skies here."

"Doesn't it bother you that there will probably only be a thousand or so more of those?"

"Not any more than it bothers me that I've missed billions of them before I was born."

"What about the people who will never see it?"

"They'll get to surf the new ocean, and stretch out on the beaches that all the dust washing out of the sulci and down the canyons will form. They'll love that, in *their* moments. In *my* moment, I'm relishing a late-afternoon pink sky."

The stalker in the center was spinning back and forth, pointing its camera at each of them in turn; so now it was a Ping-Pong match. They did more verbal sparring and genned more quotes and reactions, ensuring they'd both have plenty to work with when the coproject went to edit. After a while they ordered dinner, and she stopped fishing for him to confess to imperialism or vandalism or whatever she was going to call it.

She told her Stalker Number Three to silhouette him against the darkening sky and the landscape far below. The little robot leaped up, extended its pencil-thin support to a bit more than two meters, and silently crept around to shoot slightly down on Thorby and get the horizon into the picture.

When Boreas rose in the northwest, covering much of the sky, they both said, "More profounder versions of what we already said," as Léoa put it, while the stalkers recorded them with their back to the dome wall. Léoa had her stalkers stand tall, extending till they were about three meters high, to catch the brilliant white light that the huge comet cast into the sulci below; Thorby positioned his low, to silhouette them against the comet head itself. The huge station mezzanine around them, in the brilliant bluish white light, looked like some harsh early photograph with artificial lighting.

Over coffee and dessert, they watched the fast-rising comet swim through the northern constellations like a vast snake coiling around Cepheus and the Bears before diving over the northeast horizon, making a vivid arc different from that of anything else in the heavens. Finally it was late and they went to their rooms at the station hotel for the night. Thorby managed not to say anything about liking to see stuff smashed up, and she avoided saying she really preferred bare, dead rock and sand to forests and meadows, so the first day was a tie.

They got off at Korolev Station, on the south side of the crater, pulled on Mars suits, loaded the porters, and walked out past the stupa that was another of the most-photographed places in the solar system.

Crater Korolev was as far north on Mars as Novaya Zemlya on Earth, nearly circular, about seventy kilometers across, with sharply reared crater walls all around. It was a natural snow trap, gathering both water ice and dry ice in mixtures and layers.

In a midmorning of Martian spring, the crater floor far below them had its own weather, gas geysers spraying snow, explosive sublimations that sent ground blizzards shooting out radially from suddenly exposed snowfields, and an occasional booming flash-and-crack between the whorls of fog that slithered just above the snow, almost a kilometer below the observation point behind the stupa. Monks in orange Mars suits, on their way to and from the long staircases that zigzagged from the stupa down to another stupa on the crater floor, passed between their stalkers, even less interested in the stalkers than the stalkers were in them.

"This place makes a lot of lists of scenic wonders," Léoa said. She knelt at the meter-high shrine that interrupted the rails of the observation platform, palms together in the ancient prayer gesture. The stalkers closed in on her.

He did the same, to avoid her stalkers' recording him being disrespectful.

When Thorby and Léoa stood, and looked again across the stormy snowfields of Korolev Crater, the stalkers leaped up on the railing like an abstract sculpture of birds on a wire, balancing easily with their gyros. Thorby and Léoa deopaqued their helmets completely and turned on collar lights. "It doesn't bother you," she asked, "that these snowfields were here before the first human wandered across the African plain?"

"No," he said. "After all, the protons and electrons in the snow were probably in existence shortly after the big bang. Everything is made of bits of something older. Everything that begins means something ends. I like to take pictures of the moment when that happens. A day will come when we walk by Lake Korolev and admire the slow waves rolling across its deep blue surface, and then another day will come when this stupa stands on one of the islands that ring Korolev Atoll, and very much within our lifetime, unless we are unlucky, this will be an interesting structure at the bottom of the Boreal Ocean. I hope to see them all; life is potential and possibility."

"That was very preachy," she said, "and you kind of intoned. Do you want to try it again?"

"Not really. Intoning feels right when I'm serious. I *like* things that will happen once, then never again. That's what my problem is with the animators that make their perfect simulations; they never take a chance on not getting what they're after. Be *sure* to use *that*. Let's get some animators good and angry."

"They don't get angry," she said sadly. "Nothing's real to them."

He shrugged. "Reality is just a marketing trophy anyway. Twenty thousand years from now, if people want to walk around on a dry, thin-aired, cold Mars, they'll be able to do it, and it will look so much like this that even a trained areologist won't see the difference. Or if they want to watch the disassembly of Boreas a hundred times, and have every time be as subtly different as two different Tuesdays, they'll be able to. Your recording of what was, and my recording of how it changed, will just be two more versions, the ones with that odd word 'real' attached."

"Attached *validly*. If reality doesn't matter, why do animators try to fake their way into having their work labeled 'real' all the time? It's the only thing they do that makes me really angry."

"Me too." He could think of nothing else to add. "Catch the gliderail?"

In the half-hour zip around to the north side viewing station, they sat on the top, outside deck. Their stalkers shot them with the crater in the background. It was noon now, and the early spring sun was still low in the sky to the south.

On firm ground, in a Mars suit with robot porters to do all the carrying, a human being can cover about a hundred kilometers in a day without difficulty. Since the country they were crossing was ancient sea bottom (that was the point of everything, really), it would be flat and hard for the next couple of hundred kilometers before the Sand Sea. They could have just taken a hop-rocket to some point in the vast plain, claimed to have walked there, recorded their conversation, and then hopped another hundred kilometers or so to the edge of the Sand Sea, but they were the two most prominent documentarians of the realist movement.

Visually it was monotonous. They had planned to use the long walk to spar for quotes, but there was little to say to each other. Léoa documented places that were about to be destroyed in the Great Blooming; Thorby recorded the BEREs, Big Energy Release Events, the vast crashes and explosions that marked humanity's project of turning the solar system into a park and zoo. They were realist-purists, using only what a camera or a mike could record from the real world. Unable to do anything except disagree or agree completely, they tried arguing about whether a terraformed planet can have wilderness, since the life on it was brought there and the world shaped for it, and about whether it was masculine to like to see things smashed and feminine to like to see things protected, and they agreed that animation had no place in docu, all in the first hour.

For a while she fished for him to tell stories about his brief moment of fame, as the teenager who rode his bicycle around a comet, but he didn't feel like telling that story during that hike, though he did promise to tell it eventually. It wasn't that he minded, it was only that the good-parts version came down to no more than four or five sentences for anyone else, and to inchoate, averbal images for Thorby.

By noon the first day, there was nothing to do but walk and look for something worth recording, or an argument worth having. They walked two more days.

The Sand Sea was no more conversational, but it was beautiful: an erg that stretched to the horizon, dune after dune in interlocking serpentines stretching for hundreds of kilometers in all directions. From orbit the regularity of the pattern of dune crests was remarkable, but from the dune crests, where they skied, it was busy and confusing like a choppy sea. Down between the dunes it was just piles of sand reaching to the sky on all sides.

They hadn't spoken in hours. Léoa didn't even ask him if he felt sad that all this would be converted to a mudflat and then drowned under three kilometers of water. He couldn't work up the energy to needle her about protecting a pile of dust the size of France, so that future generations could also visit a pile of dust the size of France.

They went slowly for the last day, as Léoa got visuals of the Sand Sea. She had built her reputation on doomed landscapes; this would be the biggest to date.

Thorby was sitting on top of one of the immense dunes, watching the sunset and talking his notes to one of his stalkers, planning the shooting of the Boreas-pass above the North Pole. He felt a low vibration, and his suit exmike, which had only supplied a soft whisper for days, reverberated with deep bass notes, something between a tuba and a bell, or a choir of mountains.

The dune under him heaved like an ocean wave waking from a long sleep, and he tumbled over, rolling and sliding in a bewildering blur of dust and sky, halfway down the western, windward face before sliding to a halt. The slipping dust piled around him, starting to pin him to the ground.

He pushed up to his feet, and stepping high, climbed back up the dune. It was more than a minute, while the pure tones of the bass notes in his exmike became a continuous thunder of tympani, before he struggled back to the top. The sun was less than a fingerwidth above the short horizon, and the light would disappear in minutes, the smaller solar disk and short horizon of Mars reducing twilight to an instant.

The thunder was still loud, so he clicked up the volume on his radio. "Are you all right?"

"Far as I can tell. It buried me to my waist but I got out." He picked out Léoa, climbing the leeward slope far below. "Booming sands," she said. "One of the last times they'll ever do it. The resonance trips off more distant dunes, one dune triggering another by the sounds, till all the dunes with those frequencies have avalanched and added to the din. There's a scientist I met who sowed microphones all over the polar sea and he could show you maps of how the booming would spread from dune to dune, all over the Sand Sea in a couple of hours. And all that will be silent forever."

"Silent as the Boreal Ocean is now," he said, mindful that their recording mikes were still on and so was the sparring match. All round them, stalkers were finding their way back to the surface, usually stalk first so that they rose like slim reeds from the ground until they suddenly flipped over, spun to clear the dust from their scoop-shaped audio pickups, and resumed hopping through the sand like mouse heads on pogo sticks, normal as ever. "There was a time to hear the sands, and there will be a time to hear the waves. And in between there's going to be some of the grandest smashing you ever saw."

She must not have had a good reply, or perhaps she just didn't want to reply to his intoning again, because she got back to her setup, and he got back to his.

The Mars suits shed the fine dust constantly, so that Léoa seemed to smolder and then to trail long streaks as the wind shifted during the few seconds of twilight. They finished under the stalkers' work lights, and lay down to wait on the soft lee of the dune, safe now because it had just avalanched.

"Thorby," she said, "this is not turning into anything that will make either of us famous."

He hunched his shoulders, shaping the fine sand under him. "You're right," he said. "It's not."

"You've already been famous."

"It's one of those things you can't experience while it's happening," he said, "like seeing yourself across a crowded room. Not all that it's cracked up to be. I like making docus and I like selling them, so that kind of 'where is he now' fame doesn't hurt, and it's far enough in the past so I mostly get left alone." He watched Phobos, far south in the sky; from these far northern latitudes you never saw it full, always as a lumpy sort of half-moon.

"If a model or a musician had taken a tumble in booming sands it would sell systemwide, but if we got stranded out here and you killed and ate me to survive, it would barely show up. Docus are what, half a percent of the market? There's not even a market in pirating them." Léoa sighed. "I was just thinking that the mainstream celeb channels haven't even mentioned that the two leading documentarians of the realist-purist movement are here to record the biggest event of the next few hundred years of the Great Blooming, the re-creation of the Boreal Ocean. Not even to mention that we've always feuded and we purportedly hate each other. Not even to do one of those 'Will they reconcile and have sex?' stories they like so much. Not even to mention that one of us is the teenager who took the longest bicycle ride in history. Yet two years ago they covered the fad for learning to hand-read, and a couple guys in the retro movement that produced written books—can you believe it, written books, just code, that stuff people used to hand-read—and they covered a *blacksmith* last year, but docus are so dead, they didn't bother with us."

"We're not dead *enough.* Gone but not long enough or completely enough to be a novelty." He tried to decide whether he could actually see Phobos crawling along eastward, down by the equator, and decided he could. "Maybe we should have the blacksmith build us chariots, and race each other, and do a documentary about that."

"Maybe." The scratchy sound in her radio puzzled him till he saw her rolling over; she was looking for a comfortable position on the dune, and he was hearing her Mars suit pushing dust away.

"Hey," he said. "Since you've been trying to get me to miss something, I just noticed something I will miss. Phobos. I like the way it looks from this far north."

"Well, I'm glad *something* can touch your heart. I'd have thought you were excited about getting to see it fall."

"It won't be much of a show. Phobos'll be busted to gravel from all the impacts as it comes down through the rings, so it won't really be a BERE, just a monthlong high point in the spectacular meteor shower that will go on for fifteen Mars-years or so. I wasn't even going to bother to shoot it. But what it is right now—I never realized it's always a half-moon up here in the far north, because it's so close to the equator and so low in orbit, and besides, it's fun just to watch it, because it's so low it orbits really fast, and I'm thinking I can see it move."

"I think I can too." She commanded her stalkers to set up and record the view of Phobos, and then to get the two of them with Phobos behind them as they sat on a dune. "Those shots will be beautiful; so sad though that stories about Great Blooming projects are about as popular as public comment requests by the Global Desalination Authority."

He shrugged, hoping it would show up on the stalker's cameras. "Post-scarcity economy, very long life spans, all that. Everything to do and nothing matters. Story of everyone's life. Have you thought about doing anything other than docus?"

"I try not to. I want to get the Great Blooming recorded, even if I call it the Great Vandalism or Bio-Stuff Imperialism. Somebody has to stand up for rocks, ice, and vacuum."

"Rocks make okay friends. They're dependable and loyal."

"I wish somebody wanted to watch us talking to each other," Léoa said. "About all this. About Mars and about the Blooming and all that stuff. I almost wouldn't care what we had to say, or how things came out, if somebody would just find us interesting enough to listen. You know what I mean."

"Yeah." Thorby didn't really feel that way himself but he often didn't know what he felt at all, so he might as well agree.

They began final checkout just a few minutes before Boreas's first aero-braking pass. The stalkers were self-maintaining, and they were already in place, but it felt wrong to just assume everything would work.

"This will be one of your last views of your home," Léoa said. "How do you feel about that?"

He turned toward her, flipped the opaquing on his helmet to zero, and turned up the collar lights, so that his face would be as visible as possible, since this was an answer he knew he needed to get right. Already the northern horizon was glowing with Boreas dawn. "Boreas is where I grew up, as much as I ever did, but that doesn't make it home," he said. "First of all when I lived there you couldn't walk on most of it, anyway, and they weren't going to let a little boy put on a suit and go play outside. When I went back four weeks ago, all that melting and vaporizing that went on while Boreas worked its way down to the lower system had erased even the little bit of landscape I did know; I couldn't even find Cookie Crumb Hill on radar and thermal imaging, and anyway if I'd found it, it's so dark down there now, with all the fog and grit flying around, that I doubt I could have gotten pictures that penetrated more than twenty meters into the mess. The Boreas I knew when I was a kid, way out beyond Neptune, is more than a decade gone; it's nothing like it was. Nothing at all."

He was crabbier in his tone than he had meant to be, irritated by her question because he'd blown half his share of the budget to buy passage to Boreas so that he could come back with the seven scientists who were the last evacuated from the iceball's surface, and what he'd gotten had been some lackluster interviews that he could as easily have done a year before or a year after. Furthermore, since the station had not had windows, he could have done them somewhere more pleasant. He had also acquired some pictures of the fog-and-grit mix that now shrouded what was left of the old surface. (Most of the old surface, of course, now *was* fog and grit.)

As Boreas came in over the North Pole, it would swing low enough for atmospheric drag, which, combined with the gravitational drag from coming in an "inverse slingshot" trajectory, should put it into a very eccentric, long orbit around Mars. Doing this with a big natural ball of mixed water ice, carbon dioxide, and frozen methane, with a silica-grit center, was so uncertain a process that the major goals for the project began with "1. avoid impact by Boreas, 2. avoid escape by Boreas."

But if all went well, nudgers and roasters would then be installed on Mars's new huge artificial moon, with the objective of parking it in a nearly circular retrograde orbit below Phobos, well inside Mars's Roche limit, so that over a few years, Boreas would break up and form a complex of rings. The billions of bits of it, dragged and shredded by the planet's rotation, would then gradually spiral in across twenty years, creating a spectacular continual meteor shower in the plane of the ring, a carbon dioxide-methane atmosphere at about a bar of pressure, and, as water vapor snowed down, then melted, then rained and ran to the lower parts of the planet, a new ocean in the bed of the dry-for-a-billion-years Boreal Ocean.

The comet's pass would light the sky for many hours, but its actual brush with the atmosphere would last less than three minutes. Thorby and Léoa intended to be directly underneath it when that happened.

"Did you leave anything on Boreas, a memento to be vaporized onto Mars?" she asked.

He started to say, "No."

She picked up her walking stick and knocked off the head of one of his stalkers.

Startled speechless for an instant, he didn't speak or move till she whacked the second one so hard that its head flew in pieces into the sand.

"What are you—"

"Destroying your stalkers." Her voice was perfectly calm and pleasant as she whacked another stalker hard enough to break its stem in half, then drove the tip of her stick down on its head. "You won't have a record of this. And mine will only be recording your face and appearance. You've lost."

He thought, *Lost what?* for an instant, and then he wanted to rush to see if Number Four Stalker, which had been with him for twenty-five years, was all right because it was crushed and he couldn't help thinking of it as "hurt," and then he wanted to scream, *Why?*

The landscape became brighter than day, brighter than Earth lightning, not at all like the Boreas dawn they had been expecting. A great light flashed out of the north, and a breath later a white, glowing pillar pushed up into the sky. They froze, staring, for some indefinite time; his surviving stalkers, and all of hers, rotated to face the light, like clockwork sunflowers.

Thorby heard his voice saying, "We'll need to run, south, now, as fast as we can, I don't think we'll make it."

"Must have been a big fragment far out from the main body," Léoa said. "How far away do you think—"

"Maybe up close to the pole if we're lucky. Come on," he said, "whistle everything into the porters. Skis on. *Run.*"

Two of his stalkers had not been destroyed, and they leaped into his porter at his emergency call. "Skis and poles," he told the porter, and it ejected them; he stepped onto the skis, free-heelers designed for covering ground and moving on the slick dust, and hoped his few hours' practice at a comfortable pace in the last day would be enough to let him go fast now.

"Baggins, follow, absolute." Now his porter would try to stay within two meters of his transponder, catching up when it fell behind, until it ran out of power or was destroyed. If he lost it, he might have to walk hungry for a while, but the northern stations were only a couple of days to reach. His Mars suit batteries were good for a week or more; the suit extracted water and air; he just had to hope he wouldn't need the first aid kit, but it was too heavy to strap onto the suit.

The great blue-white welding-arc pillar had cooled to orange-white, and the main body of Boreas, rising right on schedule, stood behind it as a reflector. The light at Thorby's back was brighter than noonday equatorial sun on Earth, much brighter than any sun Mars had ever seen, and the blazing face of Boreas, a quarter of the sky, spread the light with eerie evenness, as if the whole world were under too-bright fluorescent light.

He hurled himself along the windward side of the south-tending dune crest, using the skating technique he'd learned on Earth snow and practiced on frozen methane beds on Triton; his pushing ski flew out behind him, turning behind the lead ski to give extra push, then reach as far in front of him as possible, kicking and reaching as far as he could. On the slick, small, round, particle sand of the ridge top, in the low gravity, he might have been averaging as much as twenty kilometers per hour.

But the blast front from the impact was coming at them at the local speed of sound, 755 kilometers per hour, and though that was only two-thirds as fast as Mach 1 in warm, thick, breathable air, it was more than fast enough to overtake them in a half hour or less. At best the impact might have been four hundred kilometers away, but it was almost surely closer.

He glanced back. Léoa skied swiftly after him, perhaps even gaining ground. The light of the blazing pillar was dimmer, turning orange, and his long shadow, racing in front of him, was mostly cast by the dirt-filtered light of the Boreas dawn. He wasn't sure whether Boreas would stay in the sky till the sun came up, but by then it would all be decided anyway.

"Thorby."

"Yeah."

"I've had it look for shelter, read me some directions, and project a sim so I'm sure, and there's a spot that's probably safe close to here. This dune crest will fork in about a kilometer. Take the left fork, two more kilometers, and we'll be behind a crater wall from the blast."

"Good thinking, thanks." He pushed harder, clicking his tongue control for an oxy boost. His Mars suit increased the pressure and switched to pure oxygen; his pace was far above sustainable, but either he made this next three kilometers or he didn't.

Léoa had destroyed his recording setup. He'd known she deplored his entire career of recording BEREs—Big Energy Release Events—at least as much as she disliked the whole idea of the Great Blooming, but he'd had no idea she would actually hash the joint project just to stop him from doing it. So his judgment about people was even worse than he'd thought it was. They had been colleagues and (he'd thought) friendly rivals for decades, and he hadn't seen it coming.

He kept pushing hard, remembering that he was pouring so much oxygen into his bloodstream that he had to keep his muscles working hard or hyperventilate. His skis flew around him, reached out to the front, whipped back, turned, lifted, flew out around him, and he concentrated on picking his path in the shifting light and staying comfortably level and in control; in the low Martian gravity, with the close horizon that didn't reveal parallax motion very well to eyes evolved for Earth, it was far too easy to start to bounce; your hips and knees could easily eat a third of your energy in useless vertical motion.

The leeward side of a dune crest is the one that avalanches, so he stayed to the right, windward side, but he couldn't afford to miss the saddle-and-fork when it came, so he had to keep his head above the crest. He heard only the hiss of his breath and the squeal of his skis on the sand; the boiling column from the impact, now a dull angry red, and the quarter-of-the-sky circle of the comet now almost directly overhead, were eerie in their silence. He kept his gaze level and straight out to the horizon, let his legs and gut swing him forward, kept the swinging as vertical as he could, turning only the ski, never the hip, hoping this was right and he was remembering how to do it, unable to know if he was moving fast enough through the apparently endless erg.

He had just found the fork and made the left turn, glancing back to check on Léoa. She seemed to be struggling and falling a little behind, so he slowed, wondering if it would be all right to tell her she was bouncing and burning unnecessary energy.

The whole top five meters of the dune crest under her slid down to the leeward in one vast avalanche. For one instant he thought, *but how can that be, I just skied it myself and I'm heavier*. The ground fell away beneath him in shattering thunder as the whole dune slumped leeward.

Of course, how did I miss that? In the Martian atmosphere, a cold thin scatter of heavy CO_2 molecules, sound is much slower than it is in anything human beings can breathe; anyone learns that after the first few times a hiking buddy's radio has exmike sound in the background, and it seems to be forever before your own exmike picks it up. But the basalts of the old Martian seafloor are solid, dense, cold, and rigid to a great depth; seismic waves are faster than they are elsewhere.

He thought that as he flipped over once, as if he were working up the voice-over for his last docu. Definitely for his *last* docu.

In the low gravity, it was a long way to the bottom of the dune. Sand poured and rumbled all around him, and his exmike choked back the terrible din of thousands of dunes, as the booming erg was all shaken at once by the S waves running through the rock below it, setting up countless resonances, triggering more avalanches and more resonances, until nearly the whole potential energy of the Sand Sea released at once.

Maybe just to annoy Léoa, he intoned a voice-over, deliberately his corniest ever, as he tumbled down the slope and wondered how the sand would kill him. "It is as if the vast erg knows what Boreas is, that this great light in the sky is the angel of death for the Sand Sea, which shouts its blind, black, stony defiance to the indifferent glaring ice overhead."

He rolled again, cutting off his intoning with an *oof!* and released his skis. Rolling again, he plowed deep into the speeding current of sand. Something hard hit the back of his helmet. He tumbled faster and faster, then flopped and slid on his belly headfirst.

In darkness, he heard only the grinding of fine sand against his exmike.

The damp in Thorby's undersuit and his muzzy head told him he'd just done the most embarrassing thing of his life, fainted from fear. Now it felt like his worst hangover; he took a sip of water. Bruised all over, but no acute pain anywhere; slipped out of his urine tube, that seemed to be all that was wrong. If Baggins caught up with him, Thorby would like to get into the shelter, readjust things in the undersuit, sponge off a bit, but he didn't absolutely have to.

His clock didn't seem to be working—it didn't keep its own time, just reported overhead signal—but the wetness in his undersuit meant he couldn't have been out more than fifteen minutes or so. He'd be dry in another few minutes as the Mars suit system found the moisture and recycled it.

He was lying on his face, head slightly downward. He tried to push up and discovered he couldn't move his arms, though he could wriggle his fingers a bit, and after doing that for a while, he began to turn his wrists, scooping more sand away, getting leverage to push up more. An eternity later he was moving his forearms, and then his shoulders, half shaking the sand off, half swimming to the top. At last he got some leverage and movement in his hips and thighs, and heaved himself up to the surface, sitting upright in the silvery light of the darkened sky.

There was a pittering noise he couldn't quite place, until he realized it was sand and grit falling like light sleet around him. The blast wave that had carried it must have passed over while Thorby was unconscious; the tops of the dunes had an odd curl to them, and he realized that the top few meters had been rotated ninety degrees from their usual west-windward, east-leeward, to north-windward, south-leeward, and all the dunes were much lower and broader. Probably being down in the bowl had saved his life; maybe it had saved Léoa too.

He clicked over to direct voice. "Léoa?"

No answer, and her voice channel hadn't sent an acknowledge, so she wasn't anywhere in radio range, or she was buried too deep for him to reach her.

He tried the distress channel and got a message saying that if he was above thirty degrees north latitude and wasn't bleeding to death within ten kilometers of a hospital, he was on his own. Navigation channel was out as well, but if he had to he could just walk with the Bears and Cassiopeia to his back while they got the navigation system back on, and still get himself to somewhere much safer and closer to other people, though getting out of the dunes might take a week without his skis.

When the crest had avalanched under Léoa she'd been at least one hundred and fifty meters behind him, and he wasn't sure she'd gone down into this bowl. He tried her on direct voice again, and still had nothing, so he tried phone and was informed that overhead satellite service was temporarily suspended. He guessed that the impact had thrown enough junk around to take down some of the high-ellipse polar satellites that supplied communication and navigation.

If he knew he was alone, the thing to do would be to start walking south, but he couldn't leave Léoa here if there was any chance of finding her. The first aid kit in Baggins had directional gear for checking her transponder, but Baggins was probably buried or crushed, and even if the porter was still rolling it might be a while before it found its way to him.

He would wait a few hours for Baggins anyway; the porter not only had the food, but could also track the tags on his skis and poles, and had a power shovel. A lot better to begin with a shelter, food, and skis than to get one or two kilometers farther and a lot more tired. And he did owe Léoa a search.

The best thing he could think of to do—which was probably useless—was to climb to the top of the slope he'd rolled down. The predawn west wind was rising, and the sand swirled around his boots; it was hard going all the way up, and it was dawn before he reached the top. The small bloody red sun rising far to the southeast, barely penetrating the dense dust clouds, gave little light. He clicked his visor for magnification and light amplification, and turned around slowly, making himself look at each slope and into each bowl he could see into, since with the wind already erasing his boot prints, he knew that once he walked any distance he'd have little chance of finding even the bowl into which he'd fallen.

There was something small and dark moving and slipping down the side of the next bowl north; he took a few steps, and used the distance gauge. It estimated the object to be about a meter across and two kilometers away.

He moved toward it slowly until he realized it was Léoa's porter, headed roughly for the bottom of the bowl, so it must be getting signal from her transponder. He descended to meet it and found it patiently digging with its small scoop and plow, rocking back and forth on its outsize dune wheels to get more leverage.

Thorby helped as much as he could—which wasn't much—with his hands. He didn't know whether the porter would try to dig her out if the med transponder showed she was dead, and, of course, it would ignore him, so he didn't have any way to ask it about anything. The suits usually ran with a couple of hours of stored air as a buffer, and made fresh air continually, but if she'd switched to pure direct oxygen as he had, there might not have been much in her tank, and if the intake was buried and filled with sand, she could suffocate.

Presently he felt a hard object; an instant later the porter reached forward with a claw, took a grip, and pulled one of Léoa's skis from the sand, putting it into its storage compartment, before rolling forward. Thorby stared at it for a long moment, and started to laugh as he followed the porter up the hill, to where he plucked out a pole. Presumably it would get around to Léoa, sooner or later; nobody had thought to make lifesaving a priority for a baggage cart.

The roiling sky was the color of an old bruise and his temperature gauge showed that it was cold enough for CO_2 snow to fall. He followed Léoa's porter and tried the phone again. This time he got her voicemail, and left a message telling her what was going on, just in case she was wandering around on a hill nearby and out of line of sight from the satellite.

Five minutes later his phone rang. "Thorby?"

"Yeah, Léoa, are you okay?"

"No. Buried to my mid-chest, I think I have a broken back and something's really wrong with my leg, and I can see your porter from where I am but I can't get its attention." Her voice was tense with pain. "Can't tell you where I am, either. And you wouldn't believe what your porter just did."

"It dug up one of my skis. That's what yours is doing over here. All right, to be able to see it you must be in the same bowl I landed in, one to the south, I'm on my way. I'm climbing without skis, so I'm afraid this is going to be slow."

After a while as he climbed, the wind picked up. "Léoa?" he called, on the phone again because radio still wasn't connecting them.

"I'm here. Your porter found your other ski. Do you think it will be okay for me to have some water? I've been afraid to drink."

"I *think* that's okay, but first aid class was a while ago. I was calling because I was afraid sand might be piling up on you."

"Well, it is. I'm trying to clear it with my arms but it's not easy, and I can't sit up."

"I don't think you should try to sit up."

They talked while he climbed; it was less lonely. "Your porter is digging about three hundred meters behind me," he told her. "It must be finding your other ski."

"Can't be, if it's already found one, because the other one is bent under me."

"Well, it's getting your pole then. If your ski is jammed under you, it sounds like it hurts."

"Oh yeah, the release must have jammed and it twisted my leg around pretty badly, and walloped me in the spine. So the porter must be finding my pole. Or maybe I dropped a ration pack or something. They've got so much spare processing power, why didn't anyone tell them people first, then gear?"

"Because there probably aren't a hundred million people, out of sixteen billion, that ever go off pavement, or to any planet they weren't born on," he said. "The porters are doing what they'd do in a train station—making sure our stuff is all together and not stolen, then catching up with us."

"Yours just found a pole and it's heading up the hill, so I guess it's on its way to you now."

He topped the rise a few minutes later, just as Baggins rolled up to him and waited obediently for orders. "Skis and poles," he said to his loyal idiot friend, and the machine laid them out for him.

He couldn't see Léoa, still, but there was so much sand blowing around on the surface that this might not mean anything. He tried direct voice. "Léoa, wave or something if you can."

An arm flopped upward from a stream of red dust halfway down the slope before him, and he glided down to her carefully, swinging far out around her to approach from below, making sure he didn't bump her or push sand onto her. He had to wait for Baggins to bring all the gear along, and tell it to approach carefully, but while the porter picked its way down the slope, he put the first aid and rescue gear manuals into his audio channel, asked it to script the right things to do, and listened until he could recite it back. This was one of those times that reminded him he'd always wanted to learn to hand-read.

Meanwhile he kept brushing sand off Léoa; she was crying quietly now, because it still hurt, and she had been afraid she would be buried alive, and now that he was there to keep her intakes clear, she was safe.

Late that afternoon, he had completed digging her out, tying her to the various supports, putting the drugs into her liquid intakes, and equipping Baggins to carry her. She was lying flat on a cross-shaped support as if she'd been crucified. Voice-commanding Baggins, he slowly raised her, got the porter under her, and balanced her on top. With Baggins's outrigger wheels extended as far as they would go, she would be stable on slopes less than ten degrees from the horizontal, and at speeds below three kilometers per hour. Thorby figured that hauling her would be something to do for a couple of days until rescue craft were available for less urgent cases.

Com channels were coming back up gradually, and the navigation channel was open again, but there was still little news, except a brief announcement that the impact had not been an early breakup of the comet, but apparently been caused by an undetected stony satellite of Boreas, about a half kilometer across. Splashback from the impact, as Thorby had guessed, had destroyed most of the satellites passing over the pole in the hours following. The dust storm it had kicked up had been impressive but brief and localized, so that only a half dozen stations and towns in the far north had taken severe damage, and tourist trade was expected to increase as people flocked to see the new crater blasted through the polar ice and into the Martian soil before the Boreal Ocean drowned it.

Authorities were confirming that the pass over the South Pole in seventeen days, to be followed with an equatorial air brake nine days after that, was still on schedule. Thorby figured he'd be able to cover those, easily, so Léoa's little political action would mean very little.

He wanted to ask her about that but he didn't quite see how to do it.

Shortly after Baggins began to carry the cruciform Léoa in a slow spiral up the inside of the bowl, gaining just a couple of meters on each circuit, her porter appeared over the top of the dune. It had apparently found the last ski pole, or whatever it was digging for, and now followed her transponder like a faithful dog, behind Baggins, around and around the sandy bowl.

Léoa insisted that he get visual recordings of that silly parade, but he quietly killed the audio on it, because all that was really audible was her hysterical laughter. He attributed that to the painkillers.

About dawn he sat up, drank more water and swallowed some food, and skied easily to the top of the dune crest, where Baggins had just managed to carry Léoa after toiling in that slow spiral around the bowl all night. The monitor said she was fast asleep, and Thorby thought that was the best possible thing. Through most of the morning and into the afternoon, he skied along the newly reorganized dune crests, working a little ahead of Baggins and then sitting down to wait for it to catch up, listening to the slow spitting of sand against his suit, and watching the low red dust clouds gather and darken, with only his thoughts for company.

When Léoa finally awoke, she said, "I'm hungry." It startled Thorby; he was about sixty meters ahead, using his two remaining stalkers to shoot the dunes through the red dust that was still settling.

"Be right there," he said, and skied back, the stalkers hopping after him. Her mouth, throat, and digestive system were basically okay, according to the medical sensors, though they wanted her to eat mostly clear broth till she could be looked at properly in a hospital. This time she chose chicken broth, and he hooked it up so she could sip it. All the diagnostics from the rescue frame said she was more or less normal, and as far as he could tell the broken leg and spine were the major damage.

After a while she said, "If I call out my stalkers, will you tell the story about the bicycle ride around the comet, and all those things about becoming famous?"

"Sure," he said, "if it will make the time pass better for you. But I warn you it's very dull."

So he sketched out the basics, in his best "I am being interviewed" voice, as the red dusty sky grew darker. When he was fourteen he had been sent to live with his grandmother because his mother had a promising career going as an actress and his being visibly a teenager would have spoiled her image as a sex object for teenage boys. His grandmother had been part of the earliest team for the first Great Bloom projects, so he had found himself dispatched to Boreas with her, forty-five AU from the sun—so far out that the sun was just a bright star. He had been bored and unhappy, spending most of his time playing games in VR and bored even there because he was so far from the rest of the solar system that radio signals from anywhere else, even Triton Station, took most of a day for a round trip.

"So on the day of the first fire-off—"

"Fire-off? You mean the atom bomb?"

"Well, sort of atom bomb. Laser initiated fusion explosive, but nobody wanted to call a bomb LIFE. Yeah, the thing that started Boreas falling down into the lower solar system." He skied back to look at her life-support indicators; they were all green so as far as he knew, she was fine. "On that day, Grandma insisted that I suit up, which I didn't want to do, and go outside with her, which I really didn't want to do, to sit and watch the sky—the gadget was going to be blowing off over the horizon. They put it in an ellipsoidal super-reflecting balloon, at one focus, and then put the other focus of the ellipsoidal at the focus of a great big parabolic parasol—"

"None of this means a thing to me."

"They had these really thin plastic reflectors to organize it into a beam about a kilometer across, so all that light, X rays, heat, everything pretty much hit one square kilometer and blew off a lot of ice and snow in one direction."

"That's better. So, you got to see one big explosion and you liked it so much you decided to see them for the rest of your life?"

"My helmet's opaqued, did you want a reaction shot to that?"

"I'll make one up," she said. "Or use stock. I'm not *that* purist anymore. Anyway, I've heard you mention it two or three times, so what *was* Cookie Crumb Hill?"

"Home. It was where the base was. Basically a pile of sand cemented together with water ice, it was the boat for the base."

"The *boat?*"

"It floated on what was around it, and if anything had gone wrong it would have ejected as a whole, so we thought of it as a boat. But we called it Cookie Crumb Hill because it was a pile of meter or bigger ice clods. The stuff in the core was mostly silica, so the robots spun that into glass fibers, stirred that into melted water, and added enough vacuum beads to make it float on the frost, because otherwise anything we built would have been under twenty-five kilometers of frost."

A virgin Kuiper Belt Object begins as a bit of dust accumulating frost. It accretes water, ammonia, methane, hydrogen sulfide, all the abundant things in the universe, a molecule at a time. Every so often it adds more dust, and as it grows bigger and bigger, the dust sinks through the loose vacuum frost to the center. At Kuiper Belt velocities, hardly anything ever hits hard enough to cause vaporization, and anyway it's too cold for anything to stay vapor for long. So over billions of years, the frost at the center packs slowly around the dust, and all of it sinks and compacts into a kind of sandy glacier. Frost on top of that sandy glacier packs in to form "fizzy glacier"—water ice mixed with methane and carbon dioxide ice. And always the surface at a few kelvins, where the slight mass and the low gravity are not enough to compact the crystalline structures, grows as thick frost; at the bottom of twenty-five kilometers of frost, on a world as small and light as Boreas, the total pressure was less than the air pressure of Mars. Time alone made Boreas large and its center hard.

"So before people got there," Léoa said, "you could say it was one big snowflake. Fractally elaborated fine structures of ice crystals, organized around a dust center—just that it was more than seven hundred kilometers across."

"Small dust center, big compacted ice center," he said. "More like a snowball with a lot of frost on it. But I guess you're right, in a sense. So we called it Cookie Crumb Hill because with the fiber and beads in them, the ice boulders looked sort of like cookie crumbs, and we built it up in a big flat pyramid with sort of a keel underneath to keep it from turning over, so it was also a boat on a fluffy snowball, or if you would rather call it that, a snowflake.

"Anyway, I was a complete jerk as a teenage boy."

"I had twin teenage boys a couple decades ago," Léoa said, "and I might have the reversal and have more babies, but only if I can drown them or mail them away at age twelve."

Thorby skied alongside Baggins to check her indicators; she was farther into the green range, probably feeling better, and that was good.

"Well," he said, "I was unusually unpleasant even for a teenager, at least until the bicycle ride. Though being bad wasn't why Mom got rid of me; more like the opposite, actually." It came out more bitter than he had expected it to; he sometimes thought the only time he'd really been emotionally alive was between the ages of thirteen and eighteen, because everything after seemed so gray by comparison. "Anyway, I sat up there with Gran, and then there was a great light in the sky over the horizon, and about ten minutes of there being an atmosphere—I felt wind on my suit and for just a moment there was a sky instead of stars—and then, poof-click, all this new spiky frost forming everywhere. That was when the idea started, that it would be wonderful to be outside for a long period of time, especially if I could control what I did and how I spent my time.

"So for physics class, I figured out the gadget, and had the fabricators make it. That kilometer across loop of spinning superconductor that was basically a big flywheel I could spin up to orbital velocity by doing shifts pedaling the treadmill, so over about a month I got in shape. Bicycle that I could ride around the inside of the loop as a maglev, picking up speed and momentum for the loop. That was trivial stuff, any lab could build that now, and our local robots didn't have much to do once the base was done. So I built my loop and my bicycle, or rather the robots did, and pedaled the loop for a few hours a day. In a frictionless very low g environment, the momentum adds up, and eventually that loop was moving at close to six hundred kilometers per hour, more than orbital velocity. With controllable superconduction on my bike tires, I could gradually increase the coupling, so I didn't get yanked off the bike when I first got on, and just ride my relative speed up high enough before getting off the loop and into orbit.

"Then I just needed the right timing, enough air, food, and water, and a way to come down when I got bored. The timing was done by a computer, so that I pulled out of the loop right at the top, while I was riding parallel to the ground, and I just had a one-time program to do that, it took over and steered when it needed to, since my launch window was about three meters long and at that speed, that went by in about a sixtieth of a second. A recycling suit took care of the air and water. The food was in the big container I was towing. And the container, when it was empty, could be given a hard shove, and dragged through the frost below, as an anchor to get down to about a hundred kilometers per hour, when I'd inflate the immense balloon tires around the superconducting rims, and skim along the frost back to Cookie Crumb Hill.

"I just put the camera on the handlebars, facing backward, so that I'd have a record when I turned the project in for a grade, and then since I had to take a documentation class the next term, I used the footage. I had no idea people would get all excited about the image of me on that bicycle, food hamper towing behind me, with all that Boreas in the background."

"You looked like you were riding over it like a witch on a broomstick," she reminded him, "because the producer that bought it made it consistent that your head was upright in the picture, and the way a body in a gravitational field positions itself, the bike ended up toward Boreas."

"'It matters not what happened or how it was shot, the editor will decide what it was,'" he quoted, and skied forward a bit to stretch his tired legs and enjoy some exercise in the little daylight there was. Probably it would be another day or two before there was a rescue.

When he came back, and found her still rolling along on the rescue frame (which, to his eyes, kept looking more and more like a cross) on top of Baggins, she was still awake and wanted some more soup, so he set that up for her. "This probably is a good sign for your quick recovery," he pointed out. "The rescue people say they'll pick us up sometime tomorrow, so we could just camp here, but if we cover another fifteen kilometers tonight and tomorrow morning, we can officially say we got out of the Sand Sea all by ourselves. Which is more comfortable for you, stationary or rolling?"

"With my eyes closed I can't tell the difference; your porter is pretty good at carrying a delicate object. I can't get out of the suit anyway, so you're the one who setting up a shelter might make a difference to. So let's keep moving till you want to do that, and then move again in the morning when you're ready."

"That'll work." It was almost dark now, and though he could steer and avoid hazards all right by light amps and infrared, and find his way by the same navigation system that Baggins used, it was a sort of scary way to proceed and he didn't like the idea of risking something going wrong with Léoa. "I guess I'll make camp here."

The shelter took a few minutes to inflate, and then Baggins carried her inside and set her on cargo supports, so he could at least remove her helmet and let her breathe air that came from the shelter's generator, and eat a little bit of food she could chew, mostly just pastelike stuff from tubes that the medical advisor said she could have. When he had made her comfortable, and eaten a sitting-up meal himself, he stretched out on a pad himself, naked but feeling much better after a sponge bath. He told the shelter to make it dark, and didn't worry about setting an alarm time.

"Thorby?"

"Need something?"

"Just an answer to the last part of the question. So how did orbiting Boreas for a month, living on suit food and watching the frost form on the surface as a lot of the evaporated stuff snowed back in—I mean, basically, it was a novelty act, you were just orbiting a snowball on a bicycle—how did that launch everything for you?"

"My big secret is it didn't," he said, not sure whether telling her could change anything. "For most of the ride I played VR games on my visor and caught up on sleep and writing to pen pals. I shot less than five hours of camera work across that whole month. Sure, orbiting a kilometer up from a KBO's surface is interesting for a few minutes at a time. The frost spires and the big lacy ground patterns can be kind of pretty, but you know, a teenage boy doesn't appreciate much that his glands don't react to. I finally decided that I could stand company again, tossed the food container downward on the stretch-winch, slowed down to about a forty kilometers per hour across a few hundred kilometers of frost—the rooster tail from that was actually the best visual of the trip, I thought, with a line down from my bicycle to the surface, and then snow spraying everywhere from the end of the line—came in, got a shower, put it together, and forgot about it till it made me famous. At which point it also made it famous that Mom had a teenage son, which was badly blowing the ingénue image, so she filed repudiation papers with Image Control, and I've never seen or heard from her since. The biggest thing I learned, I'm afraid, was that I like having a lot of time to myself, and people bug me."

"What about big explosions?"

"I like them, I always did. And I liked watching frost re-form after moving Boreas around, and I just like to see stuff change. I know you're looking for something deeper, but you know, that's about it. Things end, new things form, new things end, newer things form. I just like to be there."

She didn't ask again, and he heard her breathing grow slower and deeper. He thought about the visuals he had, and about a couple things he wanted to make sure to do when Boreas did its South Pole pass, and was asleep almost at once in the perfect dark and silence of the Martian wilderness.

"All right," she said, "I'll tell you as much as I can, since you are going to ask." He was sitting beside her reconstructor tank in the hospital. "That's why you came back, right, to ask why I would do such a thing?"

"I don't really know if that is why I came here," he said. "I wanted to see how you were, I had some days before I go down to the South Pole, and since I put some effort into having you be alive, I guess I just wanted to see the results. I'm not planning to work with you again, so I don't really have to know why you wrecked my stalkers just before some key shots, only that you might, to avoid you."

"I suppose after what I did there's no question of your ever liking me."

"I'm a loner, I don't like people much anyway."

"Some people might guess that's why you like BEREs. The people who used to love the place the way it was are gone, and the people who are going to love the place it will be aren't there yet. For just that instant it's just you and the universe, eh?"

She must be recording this. It was the sort of thing you asked an interviewee, and her audience in particular would just gobble this down. Perhaps he should spoil it, and pay her back for having spoiled the first Boreas pass for him?

Except she hadn't spoiled it. He'd be getting plenty of shots of the later passes and anyway good old Stalker Two had gotten most of what he wanted, including the fiery column from the surprise impact. And even if she hadn't done that, they'd have missed most of it through having to grab the stalkers and flee for their lives.

So it mattered, but not a lot; he just didn't want her around when he was shooting anything important. As for rescuing Léoa, well, what else could a guy do? That didn't create a bond for him and he couldn't imagine why it might for her. It was just something he did because it was something people did at a time like that.

"You're looking like you've never had that thought before," Léoa said.

He thought, *What thought?* and said, "I guess, yeah."

"You see? We're not so different from each other. You like to see the moment when something beautiful changes into something new. And you don't care that things get all smashed when that happens. In fact you enjoy the smash, the beautiful death of something natural and beautiful, and the birth of a beautiful human achievement."

He thought, *What?* and was afraid he would have to say something.

But by now she was rolling. "Thorby, *that* was what I wanted to capture. Thorby, Lonely Thorby, Thorby the Last Mountain Man, finds out he can be betrayed by people he thought were his friends. The change of your expression as it happened. The way your body recoiled. The whole—my idea is, I'm going to overlay all that and interact it, touchlinked back and forth everywhere, with the changes on Mars, show Mars becoming a new living world artificially, and show Thorby engaging and rejoining the human race, artificially, in a dialogue. Show you becoming someone who can hate and maybe even eventually love. Someone who can see that the rest of us are here. The way Mars can learn to respond to life on its surface, in a way that it hasn't in the three centuries we've been there."

At least he knew about this. People had been trying to change Thorby his whole life. He'd never been any good at being changed. "So you wanted to get the moment when I changed, for your docu?" It was a stupid question, she'd told him, but interviewers have to ask stupid questions now and then, if they want to get decent quotes, and habits die harder than passions.

"That's it, that's it exactly. Exactly. I'm giving up on the whole purist-realist movement. You can have it to yourself. It not only isn't making me famous, it's not even *keeping* you famous. I've got an idea for a different kind of docu altogether, one where the human change in celebs and the Blooming change in the solar system echo and describe each other in sort of a dialogue. If you're interested, and I bet you're not, I've recorded sort of a manifesto of the new movement. I've put it out already. I told them what I did to you and why and showed your face, which wasn't as expressive as it could be, by the way. Too bad you never want to do another take. And even though in the manifesto I explain it will be at least twenty years before my next docu, instead of the usual five or six, because I want to get at least that much of the Mars changes into it, the manifesto is *still* getting the most attention I've *ever* gotten. I've got a bigger audience than ever, even pulling in some of my backlist. I'm going to have an *impact*."

It all made sense of a sort, as much as people stuff ever did, so Thorby said, "Well, if that's what you want most, I'm glad you're finally having an impact. I hope it's the impact you want." To him it seemed to come out stiff and formal and unbelievable.

But she smiled very warmly and said, "Thorby, that's so beautiful I'd never dream of asking for a second take."

"You're welcome." He brushed her forehead with his hand, and added, "Happy impacts."

Because she looked like she was trying to think of a perfect reply, he left. He needed to get new gear purchased and checked out, then catch a hop-rocket; Boreas pass over the South Pole was just three days away.

He wondered why he was smiling.

Right on Mars's Arctic Circle, just at 66 N, at winter solstice, the sun at noon should just bounce over the southern horizon, and Thorby had an idea that that might look especially impressive with the big new ring arcing so high across the sky. But to his annoyance, here he was, waiting for that momentary noon-dawn, and the new, thick Martian clouds had socked in every point around the Arctic Circle. Above the clouds, he knew, the new rings were vivid with light, a great arc sweeping halfway up the sky; but down here, nothing, and even the constant meteor shower under the rings was invisible, or showed only as flashes in the clouds indistinguishable from distant lightning.

He waited but it never cleared, and the time for the midwinter sun passed, so he turned on the ground lights on his hop-rocket to pack up.

Thorby blinked for a moment. It was snowing, big, thick, heavy, slow flakes, tumbling down gently everywhere, not many just yet, but some everywhere he looked. It was so fine, and so perfect, that he shot it for twenty minutes, using three stalkers to record the snowfall in big slow pans, and two just to record the lacy flakes as they landed on dark soil and lay exposed for just an instant to his view before the stalkers' lights melted them, working at maximum magnification to catch each unique one, wondering if it was even possible for a Martian snowflake shape to fall elsewhere.

He stayed there shooting till the wind rose and the snowfall thickened enough so that he had to worry about getting the hop-rocket off the ground. He was laughing as Baggins swallowed up the stalkers and rumbled up the ramp, and he looked around one more time before climbing the ramp and turning off his ground lights. He indulged in a small spiteful pleasure: he knew that his normally expressionless face was cracking wide-open with pure joy, and Léoa and her cameras were in some city or on some ship somewhere, farther from him than anyone had ever been.

saving Tiamaat

GWYNETH JONES

One of the most acclaimed British writers of her generation, Gwyneth Jones was a cowinner of the James Tiptree, Jr. Memorial Award for work exploring genre issues in science fiction with her 1991 novel *White Queen,* and has also won the Arthur C. Clarke Award with her novel *Bold As Love,* as well as receiving two World Fantasy Awards— for her story "The Grass Princess" and her collection *Seven Tales and a Fable.* Her other books include the novels, *North Wind, Flowerdust, Escape Plans, Divine Endurance, Phoenix Café, Castles Made of Sand, Stone Free, Midnight Lamp, Kairos, Life, Water in the Air, The Influence of Ironwood, The Exhange, Dear Hill, Escape Plans,* and *The Hidden Ones,* as well as more than sixteen Young Adult novels published under the name Ann Halam. Her too-infrequent short fiction has appeared in *Interzone, Asimov's Science Fiction, Off Limits,* and in other magazines and anthologies, and has been collected in *Identifying the Object: A Collection of Short Stories,* as well as *Seven Tales and a Fable.* She is also the author of the critical study, *Deconstructing the Starships: Science Fiction and Reality.* Her most recent book is a new novel, *Rainbow Bridge.* She lives in Brighton, England, with her husband, her son, and a Burmese cat.

In the vivid and compelling story that follows, she proves that coming to really know your enemy may make your problems *harder* rather than easier to solve.

I had reached the station in the depth of Left Speranza's night; I had not slept. Fogged in the confabulation of the transit, I groped through crushing aeons to my favourite breakfast kiosk: unsure if the soaring concourse outside Parliament was ceramic and carbon or a *metaphor*; a cloudy internal warning—

—now what was the message in the mirror? Something pitiless. Some blank-eyed, slow-thinking, long-grinned crocodile—

"Debra!"

It was my partner. "Don't *do* that," I moaned. The internal crocodile shattered, the concourse lost its freight of hyperdetermined meaning, too suddenly for comfort. "Don't you know you should never startle a sleep-walker?"

He grinned; he knew when I'd arrived, and the state I was likely to be in. I hadn't met Pelé Leonidas Iza Quinatoa in the flesh before, but we'd worked together, we liked each other. "Ayayay, so good you can't bear to lose it?"

"Of course not. Only innocent, beautiful souls have sweet dreams."

He touched my cheek: collecting a teardrop. I hadn't realised I was crying. "You should use the dreamtime, Debra. There must be *some* game you want to play."

"I've tried, it's worse. If I don't take my punishment, I'm sick for days."

The intimacy of his gesture (skin on skin) was an invitation and a promise; it made me smile. We walked into the Parliament Building together, buoyant in the knocked-down gravity that I love although I know it's bad for you.

In the Foyer, we met the rest of the company, identified by the Diaspora Parliament's latest adventure in biometrics, the aura tag. To our vision, the KiAn Working Party was striated orange-yellow, nice cheerful implications, nothing too deep. The pervasive systems were seeing a lot more, but that didn't bother Pelé or me; we had no secrets from Speranza.

The KiAn problem had been a matter of concern since their world had been "discovered" by a Balas-Shet prospector, and joined the miniscule roster of populated planets linked by instantaneous transit. Questions had been raised then, over the grave social imbalance: the tiny international ruling caste, the exploited masses. But neither the Ki nor the An would accept arbitration (why the hell should they?). The noninterference lobby is the weakest faction in the Chamber, quarantine-until-they're-civilised was not considered an option. Inevitably, around thirty local years after first contact, the Ki had risen against their overlords, as often in the past. Inevitably, this time they had modern weapons. They had not succeeded in wiping out the An, but they had pretty much rendered the shared planet uninhabitable.

We were here to negotiate a rescue package. We'd done the damage, we had to fix it, that was the DP's line. The Ki and the An no doubt had their own ideas as to what was going on: they were new to the Interstellar Diaspora, not to politics.

But they were here, at least; so that seemed hopeful.

The Ki Federation delegates were unremarkable. There were five of them, they conformed to the "sentient biped" body plan that unites the diaspora. Three were wearing Balas business suits in shades of brown, two were in grey military uniform. The young coleaders of the An were better dressed, and one of the two, in particular, was *much* better-looking. Whatever you believe about the origins of the "diaspora" (strong theory, weak theory, something between), it's strange how many measures of beauty are common to us all. He was tall, past two metres: he had large eyes, a mane of rich brown head hair, an open, strong-boned face, poreless bronze skin, and a glorious smile. He would be my charge. His coleader, the subordinate partner, slight and small, almost as dowdy as the Ki, would be Pelé's.

They were code-named Baal and Tiamaat, the names I will use in this account. The designations Ki and An are also code names.

We moved off to a briefing room. Joset Moricherri, one of the Blue permanent secretaries, made introductory remarks. A Green Belt colonel, Shamaz Haa'agaan, gave a talk on station security. A slightly less high-ranking DP administrator got down to basics: standard time conventions, shopping allowances, access to the elevators, restricted areas, housekeeping. . . . Those who hadn't provided their own breakfast raided the culturally neutral trolley. I sipped my Mocha-Colombian, took my carbs in the form of a crisp cherry jam tartine; and let the day's agenda wash over me, as I reviewed what I knew about Baal and Tiamaat's relationship.

They were not related by blood, except in the sense that the An gene pool was very restricted: showing signs of other population crashes in the past. They were not "married," either. The Ki and the An seemed to be sexually dimorphic on the Blue model (though they could yet surprise us!); and they liked opposite sex partnerships. But they did not marry. Tiamaat's family had been swift to embrace the changes, she'd been educated on Balas-Shet. Baal had left KiAn for the first time when war broke out. They'd lost family members, and they'd certainly seen the horrific transmissions smuggled off KiAn before the end. Yet here they were, with the genocidal Ki: thrown together, suddenly appointed the rulers of their shattered nation, and bound to each other for life. Tiamaat looked as if she was feeling the strain. She sat with her eyes lowered, drawn in on herself, her body occupying the minimum of space. Beside her, Baal devoured a culturally neutral doughnut, elbows sprawled, with a child's calm greed. I wondered how much my alien perception of a timid young woman and a big bold young man was distorting my view. I wondered how all that fine physicality translated into mind.

Who are you, Baal? How will it feel to know you?

From the meeting we proceeded to a DP reception and lunch, from thence to a concert in the Nebula Immersion Chamber: a Blue Planet symphony orchestra on virtual tour, the Diaspora Chorus in the flesh, singing a famous masque; a solemn dance drama troupe bilocating from Neuendan. Pelé and

I, humble Social Support officers, were in the background for these events. But the An had grasped that we were their advocates: as was proved when they pounced on us, eagerly, after the concert. They wanted to meet "The nice quiet people with the pretty curly faces—"

They spoke English, language of diplomacy and displacement. They'd both taken the express, neurotech route to fluency: but we had trouble pinning this request down. It turned out they were asking to be introduced to a bowl of orchids.

Appearences can be deceptive; these two young people were neither calm nor cowed. They had been born in a medieval world, and swept away from home as to the safety of a rich neighbour's house: all they knew of the interstellar age was the inside of a transit lounge. The Ki problem they knew only too well: Speranza was a thrilling bombardment. With much laughter (they laughed like Blue teenagers, to cover embarrassment), we explained that they would not be meeting any bizarre life-forms. No tentacles, no petals, no intelligent gas clouds here; not yet!

"You have to look after us!" cried Baal. He grabbed my arm, softly but I felt the power. "Save us from making fools of ourselves, dear Debra and Pelé!"

Tiamaat stood back a pace, hiding her giggles behind her hand.

The last event scheduled on that first day was a live transmission walkabout from the Ki refugee camp, in the Customised Shelter Sector. In the planning stages, some of us had expressed doubts about this stunt. If anything went wrong it'd sour the whole negotiation. But the Ki and the An leaders were both keen, and the historic gesture was something the public back on the homeworlds would understand—which in the end had decided the question. The Diaspora Parliament had to struggle for planetside attention, we couldn't pass up an opportunity.

At the gates of the CSS, deep in Speranza's hollow heart, there was a delay. The Customised Shelter Police wanted us in armoured glass-tops, they felt that if we *needed* a walkabout we could fake it . . . Pelé chatted with Tiamaat, stooping from his lean black height to catch her soft voice. Baal stared at the banners on two display screens. The KiAn understood flags, we hadn't taught them that concept. Green and gold quarters for the Ki, a centre section crosshatched with the emblems of all the nations. Purple tracery on vivid bronze for the An.

Poor kid, I thought, it's not a magic gateway to your lost home. Don't get your hopes up. That's the door to a cage in a conservation zoo.

He noticed my attention, and showed his white teeth. "Are there other peoples living in exile on this floor?"

I nodded. "Yes. But mostly the people sheltered here are old spacers, who can't return to full gravity. Or failed colonist communities, likewise: people who've tried to settle on empty moons and planets and been defeated by the conditions. There are no other populated planet exiles. It hasn't been, er, necessary."

"We are a first for you."

I wondered if that was ironic; if he was capable of irony.

A compromise was reached. We entered on foot, with the glass-tops and CSP closed cars trailing behind. The Ki domain wasn't bad, for a displaced persons camp wrapped in the bleak embrace of a giant space station. Between the living-space capsule towers the refugees could glimpse their own shade of sky; and a facsimile of their primary sun, with its partner, the blue-rayed daystar. They had sanitation, hygiene, regular meals, leisure facilities, even employment. We stopped at an adult retraining centre, we briefly inspected a hydroponic farm. We visited a kindergarten, where the teaching staff told us (and the flying cams!) how all the nations of the Ki were gathered here in harmony, learning to be good Diaspora citizens.

The children stared at Baal and Tiamaat. They'd probably been born in the camp, and never seen An in the flesh before. Baal fidgeted, seeming indignant under their scrutiny. Tiamaat stared back with equal curiosity. I saw her reach a tentative hand through the shielding, as if to touch a Ki child: but she thought better of it.

After the classroom tour, there was a reception, with speeches, dance, and choral singing. Ki community leaders and the An couple didn't literally "shake hands"; but the gesture was accomplished. Here the live trans ended, and most of our party stayed behind. The An leaders and the Ki delegates went on alone, with a police escort, for a private visit to "Hopes and Dreams Park"—a facsimile of one of the Sacred Groves (as near as the term translates), central to KiAn spirituality.

Pelé and I went with them.

The enclave of woodland was artfully designed. The "trees" were like self-supporting kelp, leathery succulents—lignin is only native to the Blue Planet—but they were tall, and planted close enough to block all sight of the packed towers. Their sheets of foliage made a honeyed shade, we seemed alone in a gently managed wilderness. The Ki and the An kept their distance from each other now that the cams weren't in sight. The police moved outward to maintain a cordon around the group, and I began to feel uneasy. I should have been paying attention instead of savouring my breakfast, I had not grasped that "Hope and Dreams Park" would be like this. I kept hearing voices, seeing flitting shadows; although the park area was supposed to have been cleared. I'd mentioned the weak shielding, I hoped it had been fixed—

"Are religious ceremonies held here?" I asked Tiamaat.

She drew back her head, the gesture for no. "Most KiAn have not followed religion for a long time. It's just a place sacred to ourselves, to nature."

"But it's fine for the Shelter Police, and Pelé and I, to be with you?"

"You are advocates."

We entered a clearing dotted with thickets. At our feet smaller plants had the character of woodland turf, starred with bronze and purple flowers. Above us the primary sun dipped toward its false horizon, lighting the bloodred veins in the foliage. The blue daystar had set. Baal and Tiamaat were walking together: I heard him whisper, in the An language, "Now it's our time."

"And these are the lucky ones," muttered one of the Ki delegates to me, her "English" mediated by a throat-mike processor that gave her a teddy-bear growl. "Anyone who reached Speranza had contacts, money. Many millions of our people are trying to survive on a flayed, poisoned bomb site—"

And whose fault is that?

I nodded vaguely. It was *not* my place take sides—

Something flew by me, big and solid. Astonished, I realised it had been Baal. He had moved so fast, it was so totally unexpected. He had plunged right through the cordon of armed police, through the shield. He was gone, vanished. I leapt in pursuit at once, yelling, "Hold your fire!" I was flung back, thrown down into zinging stars and blackness. The shield *had* been strengthened, but not enough.

Shelter Police bending over me, cried, "What happened, ma'am, are you hit?"

My conviction that we had company in here fused into certainty—

"Oh, God! Get after him. After him!"

I ran with the police, Pelé stayed with Tiamaat and the Ki: on our shared frequency I heard him alerting Colonel Shamaz. We cast to and fro through the twilight wood, held together by the invisible strands and globules of our shield, taunted by rustles of movement, the CSP muttering to one another about refugee assassins, homemade weapons. But the young leader of the An was unharmed when we found him, having followed the sounds of a scuffle and a terrified cry. He crouched, in his sleek tailoring, over his prey. Dark blood trickled from the victim's nostrils, high-placed in a narrow face. Dark eyes were open, fixed and wide.

I remembered the children in that school, staring up in disbelief at the ogres.

Baal rose, wiping his mouth with the back of his hand. "What are you looking at?" he inquired haughtily, in his neighbours' language. The rest of our party had caught up: he was speaking to the Ki. "What did you expect? You know who I am."

Tiamaat fell to her knees, with a wail of despair, pressing her hands to either side of her head. "He has a right! Ki territory is An territory, he has a right to behave as if we were at home. And the Others knew it, don't you see? They *knew!*"

The CSP officer yelled something inexcusable and lunged at the killer. Pelé grabbed him by the shoulders and hauled him back, talking urgent sense. The Ki said nothing, but I thought Tiamaat was right. They'd known what the Diaspora's pet monster would do in here; and he hadn't let them down.

Perfectly unconcerned, Baal stood guard over the body until Colonel Haa'agaan arrived with the closed cars. Then he picked it up and slung it over his shoulder. I traveled with him and his booty, and the protection of four Green Belts, to the elevator. Another blacked-out car waited for us on Parliament level. What a nightmare journey! We delivered him to the service entrance of his suite in the Sensitive Visitors Facility, and saw him drop the body insouciantly into the arms of one of his aides—a domestic, lesser specimen of those rare and dangerous animals, the An.

The soldiers looked at one another, looked at me. "You'd better stay," I said. "And get yourselves reinforced, there might be reprisals planned."

Baal's tawny eyes in my mind: challenging me, trusting me—

The debriefing was in closed session; although there would be a transcript on record. It took a painfully long time, but we managed to exonerate everyone, including Baal. Mistakes had been made, signals had been misread. We knew the facts of the KiAn problem, we had only the most rudimentary grasp of the cultures involved. Baal and Tiamaat, who were not present, had made no further comment. The Ki (who were not present either) had offered a swift deposition. They wanted the incident treated with utmost discretion: they did not see it as a bar to negotiation. The Balas-Shet party argued that Baal's kill had been unique, an "extraordinary ritual" that we had to sanction. And we knew this was nonsense, but it was the best we could do.

One of our Green Belts, struck by the place in the report where Tiamaat exclaims *the Others knew it!*, came up with the idea that the young Ki had been a form of suicide bomber: sacrificing his life in the hope of wrecking the peace talks. Investigation of the dead boy and his contacts would now commence.

"Thank funx it didn't happen on the live transmission!" cried Shamaz, the old soldier; getting his priorities right.

It was very late before Pelé and I got away. We spent the rest of the night together, hiding in the tenderness of the Blue Planet, where war is shameful and murder is an aberration; where kindness is common currency, and in almost every language strangers are greeted with love: *dear, pet, darling; sister, brother, cousin,* and nobody even wonders why. What an unexpected distinction, we who thought we were such ruthless villains, such fallen angels. "We're turning into the care assistant caste for the whole funxing galaxy," moaned Pelé. *"Qué cacho!"*

The Parliament session was well attended: many tiers packed with bilocators; more than the usual scatter of members present in the flesh, and damn the expense. I surveyed the chamber with distaste. They all wanted to make their speeches on the KiAn crisis. But they knew nothing. The freedom of the press fades and dies at interstellar distances, where everything has to be couriered, and there's no such thing as evading official censorship. They'd heard about the genocide, the wicked but romantic An; the ruined world, the rescue plans. They had no idea exactly what had driven the rebel Ki to such desperation, and they weren't going to find out—

All the Diaspora Parliament knew was spin.

And the traditional Ki, the people we were dealing with, were collusive. They didn't *like* being killed and eaten by their aristos, but for outsiders to find out the truth would be a far worse evil: a disgusting, gross exposure. After all, it was only the poor, the weak-minded and the disadvantaged, who ended up on a plate. . . . Across from the Visitors' Gallery, level with my eyes, hung the great Diaspora Banner. The populated worlds turned sedately, beautifully scanned and insanely close together; like one of those ancient distorted projections of the landmasses on the Blue. The "real" distance between the Blue system and Neuendan (our nearest neighbour) was twenty-six thousand light-years. Between the Neuendan and the Balas-Shet lay fifteen hundred light-years; the location of the inscrutable Aleutians' homeworld was a mystery. How would you represent *that* spatial relationship, in any realistic way?

"Why do they say it all aloud?" asked Baal idly.

He was beside me, of course. He was glad to have me there, and kept letting me know it: a confiding pressure against my shoulder, a warm glance from those tawny eyes. He took my complete silence about the incident in Hopes and Dreams Park for understanding. A DP Social Support officer *never* shows hostility.

"Isn't your i/t button working?"

The instantaneous translation in here had a mind of its own.

"It works well enough. But everything they say is just repeating the documents on this desk. It was the same in the briefing yesterday, I noticed that."

"You read English?"

"Oh, yes." Reading and writing have to be learned, there is no quick neurofix. Casually, with a glint of that startling irony, he dismissed his skill.

"I was taught, at home. But I don't bother. I have people who understand all this for me."

"It's called oratory," I said. "And rhetoric. Modulated speech is used to stir peoples' emotions, to cloud the facts and influence the vote—"

Baal screwed up his handsome face in disapproval. "That's distasteful."

"Also it's tradition. It's just the way we do things."

"Ah!"

I sighed, and sent a message to Pelé on our eye socket link.

Change partners?

D'you want to reassign? came his swift response. He was worrying about me, he wanted to protect me from the trauma of being with Baal; which was a needle under my skin. I liked Pelé very much, but I preferred to treat the Diaspora Parliament as a no-ties singles bar.

No, I answered. *Just for an hour, after this.*

Getting close to Tiamaat was easy. After the session the four of us went down to the Foyer, where Baal was quickly surrounded by a crowd of high-powered admirers. They swept him off somewhere, with Pelé in attendance. Tiamaat and I were left bobbing in the wake, ignored; a little lost. "Shall we *have coffee*, Debra?" she suggested, with dignity. "I love *coffee*. But not the kind that comes on those trolleys!"

I took her to "my" kiosk, and we found a table. I was impressed by the way she handled the slights of her position. There goes Baal, surrounded by the mighty, while his partner is reduced to having coffee with a minder. . . . It was a galling role to have to play in public. I had intended to lead up to the topic on my mind, but she forestalled me. "You must be horrified by what happened yesterday."

No hostility. "A *little* horrified, I admit." I affected to hesitate. "The Balas-Shet say that what Baal did was a ritual, confirming his position as leader; and the Ki expected it. They may even have arranged for the victim to be available. And it won't happen again. Are they right?"

She sipped her cappuccino. "Baal doesn't believe he did anything wrong," she answered carefully; giving nothing away.

I remembered her cry of despair. "But what do *you* think—?"

"I can speak frankly?"

"You can say anything. We may seem to be in public, but nothing you say to me, or that I say to you, can be heard by anyone else."

"Speranza is a very clever place!"

"Yes, it is. . . . And as you know, though the system itself will have a record, as your Social Support officer I may not reveal anything you ask me to keep to myself."

She gave me eye contact then, very deliberately. I realised I'd never seen her look anyone in the eye. The colour of her irises was a subtle, lilac-starred grey.

"Before I left home, when I was a child, I ate meat. I hadn't killed it, but I knew where it came from. But I have never killed, Debra. And now I don't believe I ever will." She looked out at the passing crowd, the surroundings that must be so punishingly strange to her. "My mother said we should close ourselves off to the past, and open ourselves to the future. So she sent me away, when I was six years old, to live on another world—"

"That sounds very young to me."

"I *was* young. I still had my milk teeth . . . I'm not like Baal, because I have been brought up differently. If I were in his place, things would be better for the Others. I truly believe that—" She meant the Ki, the prey-nations. "But I know what has to be done for KiAn. *I want this rescue package to work.* Baal is the one who will make it happen, and I support him in every way."

She smiled, close-lipped, no flash of sharp white: I saw the poised steel in her, hidden by ingrained self-suppression. And she changed the subject with composure. Unexpected boldness, unexpected finesse—

"Debra, is it true that Blue people have secret superpowers?"

I laughed and shook my head. "I'm afraid not. No talking flowers here!"

Pelé tried to get the DP software to change our code names. He maintained that Baal and Tiamaat were not even from the same mythology, and if we were going to invoke the gods, those two should be Aztecs: Huehueteotl, ripping the living heart from his victims. . . . The bots refused. They said they didn't care if they were mixing their mysticisms. Code names were a device to avoid accidental offense until the system had assimilated a new user language. Baal and Tiamaat were perfectly adequate, and the MesoAmerican names had too many characters.

I had dinner with Baal, in the Sensitive Visitors Facility. He was charming company: we ate vegetarian fusion cuisine, and I tried not to think about the butchered meat in the kitchen of his suite. On the other side of the room, bull-shouldered Colonel Haa'agaan ate alone; glancing at us covertly with small, sad eyes from between the folds of his slaty head hide. Shamaz had been hard-hit by what had happened in the Hopes and Dreams Park. But his orange and yellow aura tag was still bright; and I knew mine was, too. By the ruthless measures of interstellar diplomacy, everything was still going well; set for success.

If things had been different I might have joined Pelé again when I was finally off duty. As it was, I retired to my room, switched all the décor, including ceiling and floor, to starry void, mixed myself a kicking neurochemical cocktail, and applied the popper to my throat. Eyedrops are faster, but I wanted the delay, I wanted to feel myself coming apart. Surrounded by directionless immensity, I sipped chilled water, brooding. How can a people have World Government, spaceflight-level industrialisation, numinal intelligence, and yet the ruling caste are still killing and eating the peasants? How can they do that, when practically everyone on KiAn admits they are a single species, differently adapted: *and they knew that before we told them*. How can we be back here, the Great Powers and their grisly parasites: making the same moves, the same old mistakes, the same old hateful compromises, that our Singularity was supposed to cure forever?

Why is moral development so difficult? Why are predators charismatic?

The knots in my frontal lobes were combed out by airy fingers, I fell into the sea of possibilities, I went to the place of terror and joy that no one understands unless they have been there. I asked my question and I didn't get an answer, you never get an answer. Yet when I came to the shallows again, when I laid myself, exhausted, on this dark and confused shore, I knew what I was going to do: I had seen it.

But there always has to be an emotional reason. I'd known about Baal's views before I arrived. I'd known that he would hunt and kill "weakling" Ki, as was his traditional right, and not just once, he'd do it whenever the opportunity arose; and I'd still been undecided. It was Tiamaat who made the difference. I'd met her, skin on skin as we say. I knew what the briefing had not been able to tell me. She was no cipher, superficially "civilised" by her education, she was *suppressed*. I had heard that cry of despair and anger, when she saw what Baal had done. I had talked to her. I knew she had strength and cunning, as well as good intentions. A latent dominance, the will and ability to be a leader.

I saw Baal's look of challenge and trust, even now—

But Tiamaat deserved saving, and I would save her.

The talks went on. Morale was low on the DP side, because the refugee camp incident had shown us where we stood; but the Ki delegates were happy—insanely, infuriatingly. The "traditional diet of the An" was something they refused to discuss, and they were going to get their planet rebuilt anyway. The young An leaders spent very little time at the conference table. Baal was indifferent—he had people to understand these things for him— and Tiamaat could not be present without him. This caused a rift. Their aides, the only other An around, were restricted to the SV Facility suites (we care assistants may be crazy but we're not entirely stupid). Pelé and I were fully occupied, making sure our separate charges weren't left moping alone. Pelé took Tiamaat shopping and visiting museums (virtual and actual). I found that Baal loved to roam, just as I do myself, and took him exploring the lesser-known sights.

We talked about his background. Allegedly, he'd given up a promising career in the Space Marines to take on the leadership. When I'd assured myself that his pilot skills were real, he wasn't just a toy-soldier aristo, I finally took him on the long float through the permanent umbilical, to Right Speranza.

We had to suit up at the other end.

"What's this?" demanded Baal, grinning. "Are we going outside?"

"You'll see. It's an excursion I thought you'd enjoy."

The suits were programmable. I watched him set one up for his size and bulk, and knew he was fine, but I put him through the routines, to make sure. Then I took him into the vasty open cavern of the DP's missile repository, which we crossed like flies in a cathedral, hooking our tethers to the girders, drifting over the ranked silos of deep-space interceptors, the giant housing of particle cannons.

All of it obsolete, like castle walls in the age of heavy artillery, but it looks convincing on the manifest, and who knows? "Modern" armies have been destroyed by Zulu spears, it never pays to ignore the conventional weapons—

"Is this a *weapons* bay?" the monster exclaimed; scandalised, on suit radio.

"Of course," said I. "Speranza can defend herself, if she has to."

I let us into a smaller hangar, through a lock on the cavern wall, and filled it with air and pressure and lights. We were completely alone. Left Speranza is a natural object, a hollowed asteroid. Right is artificial, and it's a dangerous place for sentient bipeds. The proximity of the torus can have unpredictable and bizarre effects, not to mention the tissue-frying radiation that washes through at random intervals. But we would be fine for a short while. We fixed tethers, opened our faceplates, and hunkered down, gecko-padded boot soles clinging to the arbitrary "floor."

"I thought you were angels," he remarked shyly. "The weapons, all of that, it seems beneath you. Doesn't your code name, Debra, mean an angel? Aren't you all messengers, come to us from the Mighty Void?"

Mighty Void was a Balas-Shet term meaning something like God.

"No . . . Deborah was a judge, in Israel. I'm just human, Baal. I'm a person with numinal intelligence, the same kind of being as you are; like all the KiAn."

I could see that the harsh environment of Right Speranza moved him, as it did me. There was a mysterious peace and truth in being here, in the cold dark, breathing borrowed air. He was pondering: open and serious.

"Debra . . . ? Do you believe in the Diaspora?"

"I believe in the Weak Theory," I said. "I don't believe we're all descended from the same Blue Planet hominid, the mysterious original star-farers, precursors of Homo sapiens. I think we're the same because we grew under the same constraints: time, gravity, hydrogen bonds, the nature of water, the nature of carbon—"

"But instantaneous transit was invented on the Blue Planet," he protested, unwilling to lose his romantic vision.

"Only the prototype. It took hundreds of years, and a lot of outside help, before we had anything like viable interstellar travel—"

Baal had other people to understand the technology for him. He was building castles in the air, dreaming of his future. "Does everyone on the Blue speak English?"

"Not at all. They mostly speak a language called *putonghua*; which means 'common speech,' as if they were the only people in the galaxy. Blues are as insular as the KiAn, believe me, when they're at home. When you work for the DP, you change your ideas; it happens to everyone. I'm still an Englishwoman, and *mi naño* Pelé is still a man of Ecuador—"

"I know!" he broke in eagerly, "I felt that. I *like* that in you!"

"But we skip the middle term. The World Government of our single planet doesn't mean the same as it did." I grinned at him. "Hey, I didn't bring you here for a lecture. This is what I wanted to show you. See the pods?"

He looked around us, slowly, with a connoisseur's eye. He could see what the pods were. They were Aleutian-build, the revolutionary leap forward: *vehicles* that could pass through the mind-matter barrier. An end to those dreary transit lounges, true starflight, the Holy Grail: and only the Aleutians knew how it was done

"Like to take one out for a spin?"

"You're kidding!" cried Baal, his eyes alight.

"No, I'm not. We'll take a two-man pod. How about it?"

He saw that I was serious, which gave him pause. "How can we? The systems won't allow it. This hangar has to be under military security."

"I *am* military security, Baal. So is Pelé. What did you think we were? Kindergarten teachers? Trust me, I have access, there'll be no questions asked."

He laughed. He knew there was something strange going on, but he didn't care: he trusted me. I glimpsed myself as a substitute for Tiamaat, glimpsed the relationship he should have had with his partner. Not sexual, but predation-based: a playful tussle, sparring partners. But Tiamaat had not wanted to be his sidekick—

We took a pod. Once we were inside, I sealed us off from Speranza, and we lay side by side in the couches, two narrow beds in a torpedo shell: an interstellar sports car, how right for this lordly boy. I checked his hook-ups, and secured my own.

"Where are we going?"

"Oh, just around the block."

His vital signs were in my eyes, his whole being was *quivering* in excitement, and I was glad. The lids closed, we were translated into code, we and our pod were injected into the torus, in the form of a triple stream of pure information, divided and shooting around the ring to meet itself, and collide—

I sat up, in a lucent gloom. The other bed's seal opened, and Baal sat up beside me. We were both still suited, with open faceplates. Our beds shaped themselves into pilot and copilot couches, and we faced what seemed an unmediated view of the deep space outside. Bulwarks and banks of glittering instruments carved up the panorama: I saw Baal's glance flash over the panels greedily, longing to be piloting this little ship for real. Then he saw the yellow primary, a white hole in black absence; and its brilliant, distant partner. He saw the pinpricks of other formations that meant nothing much to me, and he knew where I had brought him. We could not see the planet, it was entirely dark from this view. But in our foreground, the massive beams of space-to-space lasers were playing: shepherding plasma particles into a shell that would hold the recovering atmosphere in place.

To say that KiAn had been flayed alive was no metaphor. The people still living on the surface were in some kind of hell. But it could be saved.

"None of the machinery is strictly material," I said, "in any normal sense. It was couriered here, as information, in the living minds of the people who are now on station. We can't see them, but they're around, in pods like this one. It will all disintegrate, when the repairs are done. But the skin of your world will be whole again, it won't need to be held in place."

The KiAn don't cry, but I was so close to him, in the place where we were, that I felt his tears. "*Why* are you doing this?" he whispered. "You must be angels, or why are you saving us, what have we done to deserve this?"

"The usual reasons," I said. "Market forces, political leverage, power play."

"I don't believe you."

"Then I don't know what to tell you, Baal. Except that the Ki and the An have numinal intelligence. You are like us, and we have so few brothers and sisters. Once we'd found you, we couldn't bear to lose you."

I let him gaze for a long moment without duration.

"I wanted you to see this."

I stepped out of my pilot's couch and stood braced: one hand gecko-padded to the inner shell, while I used the instruments to set the pod to self-destruct. The eject beacon started up, a direct cortical warning that my mind read as a screaming siren—

"Now I'm going back to Speranza. But you're not."

The fine young cannibal took a moment to react. The pupils in his tawny eyes widened amazingly when he found that he was paralysed, and his capsule couldn't close.

"Is this a dream?"

"Not quite. It's a confabulation. It's what happens when you stay conscious in transit. The mind invents a stream of environments, events. The restoration of KiAn is real, Baal. It will happen. We can see it 'now' because we're in nonduration, we're experiencing the simultaneity. In reality—if that makes any sense, language hates these situations—we're still zipping around the torus. But when the confabulation breaks up, you'll still be in deep space and about to die."

I did not need to tell him why I was doing this. He was no fool, he knew why he had to go. But his mind was still working, fighting—

"Speranza is a four-space mapped environment. You can't do this and go back alone. The system knows you were with me, every moment. The record can't be changed, no way, without the tampering leaving a trace."

"True. But I am one of those rare people who can change the information. You've heard fairy tales about us, the Blues who have superpowers? I'm not an angel, Baal. Actually, it's a capital crime to be what I am, where I come from. But Speranza understands me. Speranza uses me."

"Ah!" he cried. "I knew it, I felt it. We are the same!"

When I recovered self-consciousness, I was in my room, alone. Earlier in the day, Baal had claimed he needed a nap. After a couple of hours, I'd become suspicious, checked for his signs, and found him missing: gone from the SV Facility screen. I'd been trying to trace him when Right Speranza had detected a pod, with the An leader on board, firing up. The system had warned him to desist. Baal had carried on, and paid a high price for his attempted joyride. The injection had failed, both Baal and one fabulous Aleutian-built pod had been annihilated.

Remembering this much gave me an appalling headache—the same aching awfulness I imagine shapes-shifters (I know of one or two) feel in their muscle and bone. I couldn't build the bridge at all: no notion how I'd connected between this reality and the former version. I could have stepped from the dying pod straight through the wall of this pleasant, modest living space. But it didn't matter. I would find out, and Debra would have been behaving like Debra.

Pelé came knocking. I let him in and we commiserated, both of us in shock. We're advocates, not enforcers, there's very little we can do if a Sensitive Visitor is really determined to go AWOL. We'd done all the right things, short of using undue force, and so had Speranza. When we'd broken the privilege locks, Baal's room record had shown that he'd been spying out how to get access to one of those Aleutian pods. It was just too bad that he'd succeeded, and that he'd had enough skill to get himself killed. Don't feel responsible, said Pelé. It's not your fault. Nobody thinks that. Don't be so sad. Always so sad, Debra: it's not good for the brain, you should take a break. Then he started telling me that frankly, nobody would regret Baal. By An law, Tiamaat could now rule alone; and if she took a partner, we could trust her not to choose another bloodthirsty atavist . . . I soon stopped him. I huddled there in pain, my friend holding my hand: seeing only the beautiful one, his tawny eyes at the last, his challenge and his trust; mourning my victim.

I'm a melancholy assassin.

I did not sleep. In the grey calm of Left Speranza's early hours, before the breakfast kiosks were awake, I took the elevator to the Customised Shelter Sector, checked in with the CSP, and made my way, between the silent capsule towers, to Hopes and Dreams Park. I was disappointed that there were no refugees about. It would have been nice to see Ki children, playing fearlessly, Ki oldsters picking herbs from their window boxes, instead of being boiled down for soup themselves. The gates of the Sacred Grove were open, so I just walked in. There was a memorial service: strictly no outsiders, but I'd had a personal message from Tiamaat saying I would be welcome. I didn't particularly want to meet her again. I'm a superstitious assassin, I felt that she would somehow know what I had done for her. I thought I would keep to the back of whatever gathering I found, while I made my own farewell.

The daystar's rays had cleared the false horizon, the sun was a rumour of gold between the trees. I heard laughter, and a cry. I walked into the clearing and saw Tiamaat. She'd just made the kill. I saw her toss the small body down, drop to her haunches, and take a ritual bite of raw flesh; I saw the blood on her mouth. The Ki looked on, keeping their distance in a solemn little cluster. Tiamaat transformed, splendid in her power, proud of her deed, looked up; and straight at me. I don't know what she expected. Did she think I would be glad for her? Did she want me to know how I'd been fooled? Certainly she knew she had nothing to fear. She was only doing the same as Baal had done, and the DP had made no protest over *his* kill. I shouted, like an idiot; *"Hey, stop that!"* and the whole group scattered. They vanished into the foliage, taking the body with them.

I said nothing to anyone. I had not, in fact, forseen that Tiamaat would become a killer. I'd seen a talented young woman, who would blossom if the unfairly favoured young man was removed. I hadn't realised that a dominant An would behave like a dominant An, irrespective of biological sex. But I was sure my employers had grasped the situation; and it didn't matter. The long-gone, harsh symbiosis between the An and the Ki, which they preserved in their rites of kingship, was not the problem. It was the modern version, the mass market in Ki meat, the intensive farms and the factories. Tiamaat would help us to get rid of those. She would embrace the new in public, whatever she believed in private.

And the fate of the Ki would change.

The news of Baal's death had been couriered to KiAn and to the home-worlds by the time I took my transit back to the Blue. We'd started getting reactions: all positive, so to speak. Of course, there would be persistent rumours that the Ki had somehow arranged Baal's demise, but there was no harm in that. In certain situations, assassination *works*—as long as it is secret, or at least misattributed. It's a far more benign tool than most alternatives; and a lot faster. I had signed off at the Social Support Office, I'd managed to avoid goodbyes. Just before I went through to the lounge, I realised that I hadn't had my aura tag taken off. I had to go back, and go through *another* blessed gate; and Pelé caught me.

"Take the dreamtime," he insisted, holding me tight. "Play some silly game, go skydiving from Angel Falls. *Please*, Debra. Don't be conscious. You worry me."

I wondered if he suspected what I really did for a living.

Maybe so, but he couldn't possibly understand.

"I'll give it serious thought," I assured him, and kissed him goodbye.

I gave the idea of the soft option serious thought for ten paces, passed into the lounge, and found my narrow bed. I lay down there, beside my fine young cannibal, the boy who had known me for what I was. His innocent eyes . . . I lay down with them all, and with the searing terrors they bring; all my dead remembered.

I needed to launder my soul.

# of late I dreamt of venus

JAMES VAN PELT

Long-term projects require long-term supervision, although with *really* long-term projects, that could be a problem. . . .

One of the most widely published at shorter lengths of all the new writers, James Van Pelt's stories have appeared in *Sci Fiction, Asimov's Science Fiction, Analog, Realms of Fantasy, The 3rd Alternative, Weird Tales, Talebones, Alfred Hitchcock's Mystery Magazine, Pulphouse, Altair, TransVersions, Adventures in Sword & Sorcery, On Spec, Future Orbits,* and elsewhere. His first book, appropriately enough, was a collection, *Strangers and Beggars,* although he's subsequently published his first novel, *Summer of the Apocalypse.* He lives with his family in Grand Junction, Colorado, where he teaches high-school and college English.

Like a shiny pie plate, Venus hung high in the observation alcove's window, a full globe afire with sunlight. Elizabeth Audrey contemplated its placid surface. Many would say it was gorgeous. Alexander Pope called the bright light "the torch of Venus," and some ancient astronomer, besotted with the winkless glimmer named the planet after the goddess of love and beauty. At this distance, clouded bands swirled across the shimmering lamp, illuminating the dark room. She held her hands behind her back, feet apart, watching the flowing weather patterns. Henry Harrison, her young assistant, sat at a console to the window's side.

"Soon," he said.

"Shhh." She sniffed. The air smelled of cold machinery and air scrubbers, a tainted chemical breath with no organic trace about it.

Beyond Venus's wet light, a mantle of stars shone with measured steadiness. One slipped behind the planet's fully lit edge. Elizabeth could measure their orbit's progress by the swallowing and spitting out of stars.

Elizabeth said, "Did you talk to the surgeon about your scar?"

Henry touched the side of his face, tracing a line from the corner of his eye to his ear.

"No. It didn't seem important."

"You don't need to live with it. A little surgery. You heal in deep sleep. Two hundred years from now when we wake, you'll be . . . improved." She lifted her foot from the floor with a magnetic click and then snapped down hard a few inches away. "I hate free fall. How long?"

"Final countdown. We'll be back in the carousel soon and you can have your weight again."

The scene from the window cast a mellow light. Silent. Grand. A poet would write about it if one were here.

"Ahh," said Elizabeth. A red pustule rose in the planet's swirling atmosphere. She leaned forward, put her palms against the window. Orange light boiled in the clouds, spreading away from the bloody center, disrupting the bands. "It's begun."

Henry read data on his screens. Input numbers. Checked other monitors. Tapped keys quickly. "A clean hit, on target." He didn't look at the actual show beyond, but watched his sensitive devices instead. "Beta should strike . . . now."

A second convulsion colored the disk, this one a brilliant white at its center that settled into a deep red, overlapping the first burst's color. A third flash, duller, erupted on the globe.

"Was that . . . ?"

"Perfect as your money could buy."

In the next ten minutes, four more hits. Elizabeth stood at the window while red and orange storms pulsed in Venus's disk. Henry joined her, mirroring her stance. He pursed his lips. "You can see the dust. If this had been Earth, the dinosaurs would have died seven times."

The planet's silver sheen faded somewhat, and lightning flashes flickered in the roiling confusion.

"No dinosaurs ever walked there, Henry."

He sighed. "Venus has its own charms, or it did."

Elizabeth looked at him. The reflected light from the window caught in his dark eyes. They were the best part of him, the way they looked at her when he didn't think she noticed. Sometimes she wished she could just fall in love with his eyes, but then she saw the scar, and he really was too short and so young, ten years shy of her forty, practically a child, although a brilliant and efficient one. She'd ask the surgeon on her own. Henry would hardly object to a few cosmetic changes while he slept. What else was there to do during the downtime anyway except to improve? She had been considering thinning her waist a bit, toning her back muscles.

Henry clopped back to his station, then studied figures on a screen she couldn't see. "There are seismic irregularities, as predicted, making the final calculations more difficult, but the planet is spinning slightly faster now, just a bit. We've also pushed it out of its orbit a bit. The next series will bump it back. You're one step closer to your new Earth."

She turned from him, irritated. "If Venus *only* becomes another Earth, I failed. We can make it better. A planet to be truly proud of. How are things on Earth, anyway?"

His fingers flicked over the controls. "In the twenty-seven years we slept, your corporation in the asteroid belt has tripled in size, improving the ability to redirect asteroids above projections. We're two years ahead of schedule there. The Kuiper Belt initiative is also ahead of schedule." He reread a section. "We're having trouble with the comet deflection plan. Lots of support for redirecting the Earth-crossing asteroids, but opposition to the comets. Some groups contest our aiming them *all* at Venus. There's a lobby defending Halley's Comet for its 'historical and traditional values,' as well as several groups who argue that 'comets possess a lasting mythic and aesthetic relation with the people of Earth.' The political wing of the advertising and public relations departments are working the problem, but they have requested budget increases."

Elizabeth snorted derisively. "Give them Halley's Comet. It doesn't have as much water as it used to anyway."

"Noted." Henry sent the order. "Your investments and companies are sound."

"How is the United Nation's terraforming project on Mars going?"

"Badly. They've lost momentum."

"Too big of a project to run by democracies and committees. Too long." She sighed. "If nothing needs my attention, then I suppose it's time for bed."

Henry shut his monitors off, powered down the equipment. A metal curtain slid across the view window, separating them from Venus's tortured atmosphere. "Two hundred years hardly seems like going to bed. Everyone I know will be dead when we awake."

Elizabeth shrugged. "They're all twenty-seven years older than when you talked with them last. As far as they're concerned, you're the dead one."

A door opened in the center of the floor. Elizabeth looked down the ladder that connected the alcove with the rest of the habitat. The ladder rotated beneath her. She timed her step to land on the top rung, then moved down so she held the ladder, leaving her head and shoulders at floor level. The room turned slowly around her. "No second thoughts, Henry. You knew the cost going in."

He nodded at her. She saw in his eyes the yearning. The dream of a terraformed Venus hadn't brought him onto the project, made him say goodbye to everyone he'd ever known, committed him to a project on a time scale never attempted.

No, he came for her.

The rotation turned her so she didn't have to see his gaze. She continued down the ladder. Mostly she thought about the project and the long line of asteroids on their way to add their inertia to Venus's spin, but below those thoughts ran a thread about Henry. She thought, as long as he remains a reliable assistant, what does it matter why he signed up? Henry Harrison isn't the first man who worked for me because he wanted me.

Two hundred years of suspended life, trembling on death's edge, metabolism so slow that only the most sensitive instruments detected it. Busy nanomechs coursing through the veins, correcting flaws, patching break downs, keeping the protein machine whole and ready to function. Automatic devices moving the still limbs through a range of motion every day, maintaining joint flexibility, stretching muscles, reminding the body that it was alive because really, really, Elizabeth Audrey, the richest human being who ever lived, whose wealth purchased and sold nations, whose power now stretched over generations, was mostly dead. A whisper could end it.

Maybe in her dreams she heard that deadly voice caressing her, and she would hear it for sure if she were a weaker woman, but if she did hear, she ignored it. Instead she dreamed of Venus transformed. A vision big enough for her ambition. A Venus fit for her feet. A planet done right, not like old Earth, sputtering in its wastes. A Venus fit for a queen.

Elizabeth walked spinward in the carousel, the silky robe she donned after the doctors revived her flapped against her bare legs. Two hundred years didn't feel bad, and the slimming in her waist gave her a limberness she didn't remember from before. The air smelled fresher too, less metal-washed. It should, she thought. Much of her money was devoted to research and development.

Henry joined her in the dining room for breakfast.

"What's the progress?" she asked. Bacon and egg scents seeped from the kitchen.

He smiled. "How did you sleep? How are you feeling? Good to see you? It's only been two centuries."

Elizabeth waved the questions away. "Are we on schedule?"

Henry shrugged. "As we projected, the plans evolved. There have been breakthroughs that make the job easier. We've shaded the planet with a combination of solar shields, aluminum dust rail-gunned from the moon, and both manned and unmanned reflective aerostat structures in the upper atmosphere, cooling it considerably, although we have a long way to go. An unforeseen benefit has been dry ice harvesting, which we've been selling to the UN's Mars's project. Venus's frozen greenhouse gases are heating Mars. Of course, the bombardment of asteroids and comets has been continuous."

A young man, carrying a tray of covered plates, walked toward them from the kitchen. He wore his dark hair short, and his loose, pale shirt was buttoned all the way to his neck. He nodded at Henry as he put the tray in front of them, but he seemed to avoid looking at Elizabeth. Without waiting for thanks, he backed away.

"Who was that?" Elizabeth uncovered a steaming omelet.

"Shawcroft. He's a bioecopoiesis engineer. Good man. He helped design an algae that grows on the underside of the aerostats for oxygen production. The surface is still too warm for biologicals."

Elizabeth tasted the omelet. The food made her stomach uneasy, and didn't look as appetizing as she hoped. "What's he doing serving me breakfast then?"

Henry laughed. "To see you, of course. You're *the* Elizabeth Audrey, asleep for two hundred years, but still pulling the strings. His career exists because of your investments. He won a lottery among the crew to bring out the tray."

"What about you? He acted like he knew you."

Uncovering his plate, Henry revealed a pancake under a layer of strawberries. "I've been awake for four years. He and I play handball almost every day."

Elizabeth chewed a small bite thoughtfully. Henry's face did look older. "What did you think of my gift?"

Henry touched the side of his face between his eye and ear. Without smiling he said, "For a couple of years I was mad as hell. I'm sorry you reminded me." His fork separated a strawberry and chunk of pancake from the rest.

Elizabeth tried to meet his eyes. He couldn't be seriously angry. Without the scar he looked much better.

He put the fork down, the bite uneaten. "Are you ready for a visit to Laputa? You can check the facilities, and they would be honored if you came down."

"Laputa?" She relaxed in the remembering, not realizing until then that she'd been tense. After two hundred years, so much could have changed. When she let the doctor hook her to the complicated devices, she had thought about unstable governments, about unplanned celestial events, about changes in corporate policy. Who could guarantee that she'd wake up in the world she'd designed? This was the great leap of faith she'd made when she started the project. The plan for her to see it to the end would be to outlive everyone around her, and the way to do that was to be the test subject for the long sleep. Henry, for obvious reasons, accompanied her. "You really named the workstation that?"

"A city now. Much more than a station. The name was in your notes. I don't think Jonathan Swift imagined it this way, though." He pushed his plate away. "It's quite a bit bigger than the initial designs. The more functions we built in, the more cubic feet of air we needed to keep from sinking into the hotter regions of the atmosphere. It's the largest completely man-made structure in the solar system. Tourist traffic alone makes it profitable."

The trip from the carousel to Laputa took a little more than an hour under constant acceleration or deceleration except for a stomach-lurching moment midway when the craft turned. Out the porthole beside her seat, she could see Venus's changed face. Where the sun hit, it was much darker, but the sun itself was darker too, fuzzy and red, partly blocked by the dust umbrella protecting the planet from the heat, cooling it from its initial 900 degrees Fahrenheit. Henry offered a glass of wine. She sipped it, enjoying its crisp edge. Wine swirled in the bottom of the glass. She sipped again, held the taste in her mouth for a few seconds before swallowing. "I don't recognize this."

He sat across from her. The wine bottle rested in a secure holder in the table's center. "It's an eighty-year-old Château Laputa. One of the original bottles of Venusian aperitif. Bit of a gamble. Some of this vintage didn't age well, but it turns out being thirty percent closer to the sun makes for excellent grapes. They grew them in soil from the surface, heavily treated, of course." The ferry shuddered. "Upper edges of the atmosphere. We'll be there soon."

Through the porthole, Laputa appeared first as a bright red glimmer on Venus's broad horizon, and as they grew closer, revealing details. Elizabeth realized the glow was the sun's reflected light. And then she saw Laputa truly was huge, it felt like flying low over the San Gabriels into the Los Angeles basin, when the city opened beneath her. But Laputa dwarfed that. They continued to travel, bumping hard through turbulence until the floating city's boundaries disappeared to the left and right, and then they were over the structure, their shadow racing across the mirrored surface.

Inside she toured the engineering facilities where they built floating atmosphere converters to work on the carbon dioxide gases that trapped so much heat. She met dozens of project managers and spoke briefly to a room full of chief technicians. They didn't ask questions. They didn't act like the groups of upper management she was used to working with. There was no jockeying for position, none of the push and pull of internal politics that made corporate boardrooms so interestingly tense. None of the high-stakes adrenaline she was so used to. They listened. They took notes. They answered her questions, but they were quiet, attentive. Worshipful, almost.

Henry drove her in a compact electric cart to the physics labs that controlled the steady rain of Kuiper Belt objects bringing water to the planet, even though it still boiled into vapor on the scalding surface. In a large presentation room, dominated by a map of the solar system alive with lights, each representing a ship or a station, the chief geologist finished his speech. A long line of dots represented asteroids and Kuiper Belt objects in transit traced a curved path through the system ending at Venus. "Fifteen years from now, liquid water will exist at the poles. We should have northern and southern hemisphere lakes by the time you inspect again, perhaps the beginning of an ocean if the weather patterns develop according to the models." He bowed when he finished and kept his eyes lowered.

Everywhere they went, and everyone they talked to treated her with the same deference. Only Henry would meet her gaze. "You are *the* Elizabeth Audrey," he said again when she complained. "Maker of worlds. Come with me. I think you'll enjoy this. We have transport waiting."

They walked out of a physics lab, leaving behind obsequious scientists and engineers. Henry led, and Elizabeth noticed as she had before that he was a short man. If he were only six or seven inches taller, he might earn more respect. Their next sleep was scheduled for four hundred years. If she talked to the doctors, they could do the work and Henry would not need to be bothered with the decision himself. After all, if he was going to be her sole representative in the future where no one knew her except as the ultimate absentee boss, then he should look the part.

"This is it," he said as the car sped from between two buildings. He stopped and sat beside her while she took it in. A wall of structures a mile away loomed over a plain, a part of the huge circle that enclosed the space. High overhead, Laputa's roof arced to the far horizons. The sun glowed sullenly, a red bright spot in the dark sky. Away from the city's artificial light, red tinted her arms, the metal edges on the car, Henry's face. She turned her hands over. Even her palms took a red shade.

"What is this place?"

"Blister Park. Come on."

As soon as they stepped out of the car, Elizabeth saw. The floor was clear. Beneath their feet swirled the clouds of Venus, almost black in Laputa's shadow, but far away the city stopped and sunlight came down, illuminating a smoky show of reds and oranges and browns. They moved farther from the car, away from the building, and soon the illusion that they were walking on air seemed almost complete.

Below, in the shadow, bright red and yellow lights twinkled.

"Volcanoes," said Henry. "Venus was volcanically active before, but our asteroid and comet bombardment to spin the planet provoked eruptions. The atmospheric technicians tell me this is good, though. They use the new chemicals in the air to catalyze out what they don't want and to create what they do. There will be a breathable atmosphere before they are done."

"Keeping in mind the improvements in technology, how long until I can walk on the ground unprotected?"

"Still another thousand years or so. If we engineer ourselves instead, it would be much quicker. We need heat tolerance, and a system that uses less oxygen."

"For the workers, yes. The ones that prepare the way, but Venus will not be complete until it is the planet that Earth should have been." She could picture it, a surface rich with forests, and an ecosystem in balance, humanity appropriately humble in the face of a world done right.

"But this has a beauty of its own." Henry moved beside her. The light from below cast shadows on his face.

"It was ugly when we started, Henry. Almost no rotation. Hundreds of degrees too hot. Too much carbon dioxide. Pressure at the surface equivalent to being a kilometer underwater. No life. Nothing. The least attractive spot in the solar system, and it's still ugly now. It will be beautiful, though, when I'm done. When I've reshaped it."

Elizabeth walked toward the middle of Blister Park. She held her hands away from her sides, palms down, like a tightrope walker. If she didn't look up, all she saw beyond her feet were clouds and the volcanoes' dim pulsing. Surprisingly, she felt no vertigo. She moved on the invisible surface as if she'd been born to it. "I'm a god," she said.

In a four-hundred-year-long dream, knowing she was dreaming, Elizabeth ran down a long hill with her brother. She hadn't known her brother. He died at childbirth, one of the thousands who didn't make it through the stillbirth plagues where children were so warped in gestation they couldn't draw breath on their own. It became simpler and more merciful to let them die, death after death. Science took just a few years to find the cause of the plague that killed her brother, the first of the toxic Earth plagues, but it was too late for him.

In the dream, though, he ran beside her toward the stream that flowed through cool grasses. At the edge, they stopped. No frogs today. No crawdads hiding under rocks. She didn't know why she'd expected frogs and crawdads; they were never in the dream, never, but still the same disappointment washed through her. A boggy flat stretched from both sides, and the reeds that poked up through the smelly muck were brown and broken. A mass of cardboard stuck out of the water, covered with a noxious-looking slime.

Elizabeth held her brother's hand as they walked downstream, careful to keep their feet dry. Around the corner the stream ducked under a fence and into a park. They pushed open a gate. Here closely clipped lawn painted the hill to a cement curb lining the stream, which now flowed through an open culvert. Signs warned them to stay out of the water, but her brother lay on his chest, reaching down to touch the ripples. In the dream, Elizabeth tried to shout, but her throat constricted. His fingers brushed the water, and then he turned to look at her, his eyes serious and dark (where had she seen those eyes before?). A scar marked the side of his face. She wanted to rub it away, but when she dropped to her knees to touch him, his skin had grown cold, like a statue. And then he was a statue, a bronze of a boy lying on his side by a stream, his clothes a solid metal, a patina of corrosion in the places that were not buffed smooth.

Elizabeth sat beside him, beside the contained stream. In the sky, no clouds, but a dozen contrails crisscrossed each other, like a giant tic-tac-toe game. The air smelled of city and too many people piled on one another, story on story in high-rises beyond the park. A clatter of metal against metal clanged in the distance. More construction. On the stream's other side, flowers in unnaturally neat rows filled a garden held behind a plastic border. She looked back beyond the fence where trash filled the water. Neither was right. She knew neither was right, but it was too late to shout. Her brother was dead, and she had no breath behind her scream. The statue couldn't hold her hand.

Elizabeth couldn't breathe. She choked and then coughed, an unproductive spasm that didn't give her a chance to inhale before she coughed again. Her chest hurt. People bustled around her, but she hadn't opened her eyes yet. She was suffocating. Someone held her hand. A mask went over her face, and pressure built up within it, pushing against her eyeballs.

"Relax, Eliza. Let the machine help you."

She opened her mouth, allowing the pressure force open her throat, filling her lungs. The air tasted sweet! She could feel tears pooling where the mask wrapped her cheeks. The pressure relented and she exhaled on her own before it built again, respirating her at its own pace.

She took slow breaths, each one quivering on the trigger of another spasm, but breath by breath the urge to cough subsided until her lungs moved easily. "I don't need this," she tried to say, but the mask muffled her. She tapped the hard surface with her finger. The mask came off. She was in the awakening room. A doctor stood to one side, the mask clasped, ready to put it back if her breathing struggled. Beside him, a technician bent over what looked like a small clipboard. When he turned, she saw information flashing across the surface. Her information, she assumed. Henry sat on the edge of the bed, holding her hand.

For a minute she inhaled and exhaled carefully, testing each movement. Then she looked at him. "Did you call me Eliza?" Her voice cracked and felt dry in her throat.

He let go of her hand. "Sorry. Emotional moment."

"Don't let it happen again." She shut her eyes. "Where are we?"

"Laputa, but we've anchored. The floating city's era has passed. Not enough pressure in the atmosphere."

Later, Elizabeth and Henry walked a hallway in the infirmary. Her steps were unsteady. When they turned a corner, she almost fell. Henry grabbed her arm to hold her upright. They had dressed her in a white robe with stiff, exaggerated collar and cuffs. Change of fashion she guessed.

"It was harder this time."

"We're into new territory in long sleep. Others have been packed, but it's just until cures for their diseases are found or they outlive their enemies or they want a one-way trip to the future. If they've got the money, they can buy the bed. The arc ships heading to the Zeta Reticula system use long sleep too. It's a four-thousand-year trip, but they're waking up every one hundred years for equipment maintenance. Only you and I have slept so long uninterrupted."

Elizabeth shook her head, trying to clear the fuzziness. "Am I damaged?" She took longer steps as if she could force strength upon herself.

"I hope not, or I'm damaged too. They're still testing me, and I've been up for six years. I told them I was okay after a week." They turned another corner in the hall. Henry held her arm again, making Elizabeth feel like an old woman, which she was, now that she thought about it. "We're walking to an auditorium now. There will be a ceremony. The people want to see you."

"Public relations never goes away."

Henry looked diplomatic. The extra years he had been awake gave his face more character than Elizabeth remembered. A map of tiny wrinkles sprung from the corners of his dark eyes. "Well, the situation's a bit more complicated than that. We should have foreseen."

Elizabeth moved steadily forward, already more confident, eager to see how much closer they were to her goal. "Complicated how?"

"Lots of changes. Governments have risen and fallen. Politics went through several evolutions. The business environment metamorphed during the time."

"They didn't nationalize me, did they?" Elizabeth stopped. The idea that she might have lost control frightened her. Her stomach knotted. The companies, the investments, the foreboding weight of her multi-industrial empire might have fled her grasp in the years she slept. Anything could have happened while she slumbered. "They haven't taken my assets?"

Henry gazed down at her solemnly. Elizabeth realized the doctors had done their work. He was now at least two or three inches taller than she. His hair matched his eyes, still black. Some grey there would give him more distinction. She made a note to herself to order the change for him, maybe a deeper timbre to his voice to give him authority.

"We should have known that a corporation couldn't last for hundreds of years, Elizabeth. Even a dozen decades would be asking for a lot, but your CEOs, multiple generations of them, made decisions to preserve your initiative. We're still on schedule."

"I can talk to heads of state. Solidify our position." She pictured the crowded boardrooms, the private conversations over expensive dinners at exclusive restaurants, the phone calls and e-mails, all with her at the center, pulling threads, massaging egos, handing down favors with imperial aplomb.

"You won't need to." He led her to a set of double doors. Inside, two lines of exquisitely dressed men and women gave them a hallway to walk through. Many of the people bowed as Elizabeth and Henry passed. Elizabeth still didn't feel completely focused. A surreal air hovered about the scene. "Madam Audrey," one man said as he touched the back of his hand to his forehead and bent at the waist. No one else spoke. At the hallway's end, an ornate set of doors that reached to the high ceiling swung open. Elizabeth slowed. She couldn't see the other side of the dark room beyond, but it seemed huge, and there was movement in the dark. Lights flooded a stage that she and Henry stepped onto. She shaded her eyes, and the roar began, hundreds of thousands of voices, cheering, cheering, cheering, and they were cheering for her.

Henry leaned in, cupped his hand around her ear, "They arranged for you to become a religion. It's the only organization that would last long enough to see it to the end."

The next morning, Elizabeth joined Henry in a vehicle garage where a heavily insulated truck waited for them. "First," said Henry, "I want to point out that we are going to exit through those doors and into a Venus morning. Thirteen hours from now, the sun will set. Your original plan was for a twenty-four-hour day-night cycle, but after four hundred years of asteroid and comet bombardment, the terraformers saw that we were getting diminishing returns. At some point, each collision produced more problems for them to undo than they were solving, so they decided to stop and leave Venus with a longer day."

Elizabeth frowned. "I don't like compromise." She did feel steadier on her feet than she had yesterday, and climbed into the car before Henry could give her assistance. "What's second?"

"Best I show you." He pulled the truck into an airlock. When the outside doors opened, a red, dusty light flooded the bay. Elizabeth slid close to the window. A graded road led into a series of low hills that faded in the hazy red air. The car pulled out of the garage, and for the first time, Elizabeth could see firsthand what her efforts had produced. A brisk breeze whipped dust off the road ahead of them.

"Still warm, still too much carbon dioxide, still too much surface pressure, but we're very close, Elizabeth." The truck climbed the first hill, and from the top, as far as the dusty air allowed, similar hills reached all around. "The final changes go the slowest."

In front of them, the morning sun glared red and unbelievably large. The truck lurched through a turn as it ascended a second hill.

"I thought there would be more evidence of the meteor strikes."

Henry laughed. "Oh, heavens, there is, but it's all on the equator. We have created a badlands like nothing this solar system has ever seen. Some of the strikes broke the tectonic plates, bringing up rock from thousands of feet below the surface, liquefying, vaporizing, shattering. Venus's equator regions are already legendary. Anything could get lost there or hide there. It truly is untamable. See this?" He held out his wrist. A shiny black bracelet set with green and yellow stones caught the sunlight. "The metal is carbon nanotubes. If you need it made out of carbon, Venus can make it. Every spaceship hull in the solar system is manufactured here. The jewels were mined in the badlands. Ah, we're here."

He stopped the truck on the hilltop. Before them, a lake rippled in the wind, filling the valleys so that what she had thought were other hills earlier she could see were islands.

Elizabeth gasped. "Liquid water."

"Do you want to go fishing?"

"Really?"

Henry rested his forearms on the steering wheel and looked out onto the lake. "Kind of a joke. No, not this time. There are thermophilic shrimp, though, and adapted corals, engineered crabs, modified algaes, mutated anemones, evolved sponges, and dozens of other heat-happy organisms who like water just short of boiling. About the biggest thing out there that we know of is a heat-tolerant eel that grows to a foot or so. I've been boating at night. Almost all the species we introduced bioluminesce. It makes them easier to keep track of. Blues, yellows, greens. The boat's wake is a trail of fire." He sounded meditative. His fingers dangled, nearly touching the dashboard. Elizabeth had never noticed before how strong his hands looked. Calluses marked the fingertips. A line of dark grit was under his fingernails. "On land, we've introduced lichens, soil bacterias, nothing complicated. They do best near the lakes. Rain is undependable."

"How long did you say you were awake before you woke me up?"

He didn't turn his head. "Six years. I wanted to make sure everything was ready for you."

She looked at the lake again. A film of black dust piled at the corner of the window like a soot snowdrift. The wind picked up, tearing froth off the tops of waves, and it moaned, passing over the truck. Elizabeth couldn't imagine finding anything attractive in the desolate landscape. Dry, toxic, inhospitable except for the most primitive of life. She pictured its surface in six hundred years, when she awoke. Brush would cover the hills and heather would fill the valleys. Willows would line the bank of this heated lake. What did Henry see in it now?

Henry said, "The doctors are worried about putting you to sleep for so long. Your system didn't respond the way they would like."

Outside a bank of clouds moved across the sun, casting the lake and hills into a weird, maroon twilight. Dust devils twirled off the road before beating themselves into nothingness in the rocks higher on the hills. If the wind uncovered a bizarre version of a cow's skull, dry and leering, by the road, Elizabeth would not have been surprised. Nothing was right about the planet yet. Nothing was done.

"I can't stay here, Henry. I have to see it to the end."

Henry nodded, but before he put the truck in gear to take them back to Laputa, he faced her. "Do not try to change me again as we sleep. Do not, ever, be so impertinent again."

For a second, Elizabeth thought she saw hatred there, just a glimpse that flashed in the back of his dark eyes, and she respected it.

But two weeks later, when it came time to sleep, she met with the doctors. She gave orders. Just a touch, a tweak, a fine-tuning. Henry wouldn't mind, she thought, if he loved her like she knew he did, he wouldn't mind at all.

In the six-century dream, Elizabeth watched the rain from comets covering Venus. The water ice started beyond Neptune's orbit, like ghostly icebergs drifting in space so distant that the sun was merely a bright star among other stars. Gently nudged, they began their long journeys inward, finally, catastrophically for them, exploding into Venus's atmosphere, contributing water to a planet long without.

Rain fell. It fell in spurts, in squalls, in flurries, in long sizzling sheets that worked their way into cracks beneath the surface, nourishing the alien life planted there; until there came a time when the rain didn't just fall on rock. Plants grew, their leaves upturned, catching the water as it fell, spreading it to roots.

The rain eroded. Cut through stone. Carried silt. Formed rivulets, creeks, streams, rivers. Gathered in pools, ponds, lakes, seas. Evaporated, formed clouds, fell again.

And then, finally, in the highest of high places, appeared the first snow.

Elizabeth saw herself standing in Venus's snow, the perfect crystals falling on her bare arms, one by one pausing for a moment as petite sculptures before melting. Snow cleared the dust and smelled crisp as a fresh apple. She ran through the white blanket, splashing her legs as she ran, looking for her brother. Where was he? This was water he could play in. This water wouldn't harm him. She'd made it safe in her dream. At a lake's edge, she stopped, looking both directions as far as she could, but he wasn't there, just the silent snow falling onto the red-tinted water. Each snowflake, when it met the lake, glowed for a second, until the water's surface itself provided the only light in the dream. Plenty of light to see him if he was there, but he wasn't.

She stood at the lake's edge for centuries.

"She's awake."

Soft light fell all around, like snow. Time passed. Darkness. Light again. I'm under the snow, she thought. Darkness.

"She's awake."

Her arms were moved. Light was provided. A question was asked. A tube was pulled from her throat. She was hurt. All very passive. Darkness.

"She's awake."

Elizabeth forced her eyes open. An older man sat on the bed beside her, holding her hand. Beside him stood a medical technician in a lab coat. The man holding her hand had a haggard face. Worry lines across his forehead. A little baggy in the jowls. It wasn't until she blinked her vision clear that she could see his eyes.

"Henry?"

He mouthed a silent, "Yes."

"How long?"

He patted the top of her hand. "Six hundred years."

She tried to sit up. Before she was halfway, though, her calves cramped.

"Probably easier to lay still right now," Henry said. "The doctors here have some wonderful treatments. Since you've made it this far, you should be up soon."

Breathing softly, Elizabeth considered what he said for a moment. "There was a doubt?"

"Big one for a long time."

The ache in her legs dwindled to a dim reminder, no worse than the one she felt in her neck and back and chest. She squeezed his hand. "Henry, I'm glad you're here."

"You can take care of her now," he said to the lab-coated man.

For the next two days, doctors came and went. They wheeled her from one examining room to the next. Most of the time she couldn't tell what they were doing. Strange instruments. Peculiar instructions. Doctors nodding to one another over results that didn't make sense to her. Even their conversation confused her, speaking with a dialect too thick for her to decipher. Although she did have one moment of relief when one asked her to stick out her tongue and say, "Ahh." The tongue depressor even appeared to be made from wood.

They weren't subservient, however. Brisk, efficient, and friendly, but not servile. When she saw Henry again, she asked him about it. He met her in a sitting room where other patients sat reading or visiting quietly. The medical techs insisted she stay in a wheelchair, although she walked quite well in a physical therapy session earlier in the day.

"All that I've learned from our strange journey, Elizabeth, is that time changes everything. You're not a religion anymore. Actually, now you're kind of a curiosity. I expect someone from the history guild will want to talk with you. Marvelous opportunity, you know, to actually chat face-to-face with the Elizabeth Audrey."

Something in the way he said it caught her ear. "What about my holdings? What about the corporations?"

Henry covered her hand with his own. "Gone, I'm afraid. Long, long gone now."

The tears came unbidden. She thought of herself as a strong person. Finally, she shook the tremors off and dried her face. "We need to get to work then to get it back. How close are we to finishing the project?"

Henry smiled. She'd always liked his eyes, but now the years in his expression set them off beautifully. "I'll let you judge for yourself."

When he stood, a medical tech who had been waiting a few seats away, rushed over to help.

"That's okay. I'll take her," Henry said.

"Thank you, sir," said the tech. "I'll be close if you need me."

Elizabeth looked from the tech to Henry and back again. She recognized a power order when she saw one. "How old are you, Henry? How long have you been awake this time?"

He turned her chair toward the exit and began rolling her toward the door. "Twenty-two years. I'm sixty-two now."

The door opened into a wide space. A ceiling a hundred feet above enclosed the multiple levels and balconies she saw on the other side. Pedestrians walked purposefully to and fro.

"What is this, a mall?"

"More like a business park, but you've got the right idea."

A pair of women dressed in dark, functional, leather long-coats walked past them. One laughed at something the other said. Pale clean circles surrounded their eyes in faces that were uniformly filthy.

"Prospectors do a lot of trading here," said Henry, as way of explanation.

He wheeled her to a garage a level lower and helped her into a car. This one didn't appear nearly as heavy as the truck she'd ridden in with him what seemed like a lifetime ago.

"It's time for you to see Venus in its glory," said Henry.

A half hour later he parked the car on what might have been the same hill he'd taken her to before, but now the burgundy sun rested low on the opposite horizon, and where before the landscape was marked by wind, rock and water, plants grew everywhere. Thick-stemmed vines clung to the rocks beside the road. Low bushes dotted the slope to the water's edge. Here and there, short pine-looking trees poked from the soil, their trunks all leaning the same way and their branches pointing away from the lake. And there was color everywhere. Not only were there the grey and black rocks she remembered, but also tans and browns and yellows. Across the face of the hill to their left, a copper sheen caught the sun, and on the hill to their right, the mossy clumps growing between the rough stones were a vibrant blue.

But no heather covered the hills. Where she imagined a world with waterfalls, there were only sharp-edged stones. Where she hoped for soft yellow light on fields of flowers, there was a red sun, bloat as a toad on the horizon. She saw a rough land.

A figure dressed in a leather long-coat, goggles covering his eyes, walked past their car, saw Henry, and tipped his leather hat as he continued on toward the lake where a small complex of buildings serviced two long docks and a dozen moored boats.

Elizabeth tried to contain her disappointment. "This is not even close to what I worked so hard for. I wanted a world that was what Earth should have been, what it could have been if we hadn't ruined it. Venus could have been paradise!" The outburst left her short of breath. In the car's confines, her breathing sounded loud and harsh. "I had a brother . . ."

"You were an only child." Henry sounded quizzical.

"No, I . . ." Panic rose in Elizabeth's throat. She *did* have a brother, didn't she? It took a second for her to sort it out for herself. A thousand years of dreaming could feel more convincing than a few decades of reality.

"We have to get out of here. Take me back."

"Wait," said Henry. He reclined his seat a little before folding his hands across his chest. He watched the sun setting on the lake's other side. Elizabeth leaned back in her chair, her heart thudding hard.

The sun slipped deeper into the hills behind the lake. Elizabeth relaxed. Could she get the money back again? She knew no one. The game was surely different now. A wind scurried across the water, rocked the boats, and then rushed up the road to toss sand against the car. Shadows lengthened. She felt so tired, so truly, truly *old*.

"You know, I talked to the doctors before I went to sleep the last time. It took considerable persuasion on my part, but I discovered you'd told them to work on me again. For a while, I thought the best action would be to go to your bed and kick out the plug. It was tempting."

Henry didn't move while he spoke. His hands stayed still as he watched the setting sun.

Elizabeth floundered for a moment, unsure of how to reply. When they'd started this project a month ago (No, a thousand years ago, she thought), he would have never spoken to her like this, and she would have had no trouble telling him what she thought, but this wasn't the same Henry, not by any measure. "I'm sorry, Henry. I didn't think you would mind, really. They were changes for your own good."

"I loved you once, but you have a mean sense of perfection, Liza."

The sun's last glimmer dropped out of sight. "Watch now," he said. The horizon glowed like a campfire coal, then, as sudden as a sunset can be sudden, low clouds that had been invisible until now picked up red edges, their middles pulsating cherry gold, and the air from the horizon line all the way to nearly directly overhead turned a deep purple with scarlet streaks, changing shades even as she realized they were there.

A half hour later, still in silence, they watched. Stars appeared in the moonless sky. A boat left the quay, trailing a bioluminescent streak behind it.

Elizabeth found she was crying again. "My, god, it's beautiful, Henry, but it's not what I was trying to make. It's not better than Earth."

"It's Venus," he said. "It doesn't have to be better."

By now, night had completely fallen. There were no boardroom meetings to attend. No calls to make. No projects to shepherd to success. Elizabeth felt very small sitting in the car with Henry. Her muscles ached. She suspected she would never be physically as capable as she once was. A thousand years of long sleep had taken their toll.

"What about you, Henry. You said you loved me once. Will you stay with me?"

She couldn't tell in the dark if he turned to look at her or not.

"You couldn't shape me into what you wanted either."

He started the car, which turned on the dashboard controls, but made no noise. The light revealed his hands on the wheel.

"My days of shaping are done, Henry."

He drove them the long way home, over hills and around the lake. They didn't speak. Neither knew what to say to the other yet.

verthandi's ring

IAN MCDONALD

British author Ian McDonald is an ambitious and daring writer with a wide range and an impressive amount of talent. His first story was published in 1982, and since then he has appeared with some frequency in *Interzone, Asimov's Science Fiction,* and elsewhere. In 1989 he won the *Locus* Best First Novel Award for his novel *Desolation Road.* He won the Philip K. Dick Award in 1992 for his novel *King of Morning, Queen of Day.* His other books include the novels *Out On Blue Six, Hearts, Hands and Voices, Terminal Cafe, Sacrifice of Fools, Evolution's Shore, Kirinya,* a chapbook novella *Tendeleo's Story, Ares Express,* and *Cyberabad,* as well as two collections of his short fiction, *Empire Dreams* and *Speaking In Tongues.* His novel, *River of Gods,* was a finalist for both the Hugo Award and the Arthur C. Clarke Award in 2005, a novella drawn from it, "The Little Goddess," was a finalist for the Hugo and the Nebula, and a novelette set in the same milieu, "The Djinn's Wife," won him his first Hugo Award this year. His most recent book is another new novel that's receiving critical raves, *Brasyl,* and coming up is a new collection, *Cyberabad Days.* Born in Manchester, England, in 1960, McDonald has spent most of his life in Northern Ireland, and now lives and works in Belfast. He has a Web site at *www.lysator.liu.se/^unicorn/mcdonald/.*

In the brilliant story that follows, one with enough dazzling idea-content crammed densely into it to fuel many other author's 800-page novel, he shows us that total war between competing interstellar races will be slow and bloody and vast, and, well—*total.* With no room left in the galaxy—or even the universe—for the losing side.

After thirteen subjective minutes and five-hundred-and-twenty-eight years, the Clade battleship *Ever-Fragrant Perfume of Divinity* returned to the dying solar system. The Oort cloud web pulled the crew off; skating around the gravity-wells of hot, fat, gas giants and the swelling primary, the battleship skipped out of the system at 30 percent light-speed into the deep dark. Small, fast, cheap, the battleships were disposable: a football of construction nanoprocessors and a pload crew of three embedded in the heart of a comet, a comet it would slowly consume over its half millennium of flight. So cheap and nasty was this ship that it was only given a name because the crew got bored five (subjective) minutes into the slow-time simulation of Sofreendi desert monasticism that was their preferred combat interface.

The Oort cloud web caught the crew, shied them to the construction yards skeined through the long, cold loops of the cometary halo, which flicked them in a stutter of light-speed to the Fat Gas Giant relay point, where the eight hundred habitats of the new Clade daughter-fleet formed a pearl belly-chain around the planet; then to the Cladal Heart-world herself, basking in the coronal energies of the senile, grasping, swollen sun, and finally into fresh new selves.

"Hi, guys, we're back," said the crew of *Ever-Fragrant Perfume* as they stepped from the bronze gates of the Soulhouse, down the marble staircase into the thronged Maidan of All Luminous Passion. Irony was still a tradable commodity on this innermost tier of the hundred concentric spheres of the Heart-world, even if not one woman or man or machine or beastli turned its head. Battleship crews knew better than to expect laurels and accolades when they resouled after a hundred or a thousand or ten thousand years on the frontline. Word of *Ever-Fragrant Perfume*'s victory had arrived almost three centuries before. A signal victory; a triumph that would be studied and taught across the military colleges and academies of the Art of Defense for millennia to come. A classic Rose of Jericho strategy.

Early warning seeds sown like thistledown across half a light-millennium had felt the stroke of the Enemy across their attenuated slow senses and woke. Communication masers hastily assembled from the regoliths of cold moons beamed analyses back to the Heart-world, deep in its centuries-long task of biosphere-salvation: eighty thousand habitats on the move. The Clade battle fleet launched instantly. After two hundred and twenty years, there was not a nanosecond to lose. Thirty-five ships were lost: systems malfunctions, breakdowns in the drives that kept them accelerating eternally, decades-long subtle errors of navigation that left them veering light-years wide of the target gravity-well, loss of deceleration mass. Sudden, total, catastrophic failure. Five hundred years later, *Ever-Fragrant Perfume of Divinity* alone arrived behind the third moon of the vagrant gas giant, which wandered between stars, a gravitational exile, and began to construct the rain of antimatter warheads and set them into orbit around the wanderer. A quick plan, but a brilliant one. A Rose of Jericho plan. As *Ever-Fragrant Perfume of Divinity* accelerated away from the bright new nebula, its hindward sensors observed eighty thousand Enemy worlds plough into the bow wave of accelerated gas at 40 percent light-speed and evaporate. Twenty trillion sentients died. War in space-time is slow and vast and bloody. When the species fight, there is no mercy.

In the dying echoes of the culture-fleet, the three assassins of *Ever-Fragrant Perfume of Divinity* caught a vector. The fleet had not been aimed on a genocidal assault on the Clade Heart-worlds clustered around the worlds of Seydatryah, slowly becoming postbiological as the sun choked and bloated on its own gas. A vector, and a whisper: *Verthandi's Ring.*

But now they were back, huzzah! Harvest Moon and Scented Coolabar and Rose of Jericho, greatest tactician of her flesh-generation. Except that when they turned around on the steps of the Soulhouse to bicker among themselves (as they had bickered the entire time-slowed twenty-six minutes of the transtellar flight, and the time-accelerated two hundred years of the mission at the black wanderer) about where to go and do and be and funk first.

"Where's Rose? Where's the Rose?" said Harvest Moon, whose rank approximated most closely to the historical role of captain.

Only two resouls stood on the marble steps overlooking the Maidan of All Luminous Pleasure.

"Shit," said Scented Coolabar, whose station corresponded to that of engineer. A soul-search returned no trace of their crewmate on this level. In this innermost level, the heart of the heart, a sphere of quantum nanoprocessors ten kilometers in diameter, such a search was far-reaching—the equivalent of every virtual mouse hole and house-shrine—and instantaneous. And blank. The two remaining crew members of *Ever-Fragrant Perfume of Divinity* understood too well what that meant. "We're going to have to do the meat thing."

Newly incarnated, Harvest Moon and Scented Coolabar stood upon the Heaven Plain of Hoy. Clouds black as regret bruised the up-curved horizon. Lightning fretted along the edge of the world. Harvest Moon shivered at a fresh sensation; stringent but not unpleasant—not in that brief frisson, though her new meat told her that in excess it might become not just painful, but dangerous.

"What was that?" she commented, observing the small pimples rising on her space-black skin. She wore a close-to-species-modal body: female in this incarnation; elegant, hairless, attenuated, the flesh of a minimalist esthete.

"I think it was the wind," said Scented Coolabar who, as ever, played against her captain's type and so wore the fresh flesh of a Dukkhim, one of the distinctive humanesque subspecies that had risen after a mass-extinction event on the world of Kethrem, near-lost in the strata of Clade history. She was small and broad, all ovals and slits, and possessed of a great mane of elaborately decorated hair that grew to the small of the back and down to the elbows. The crew of the *Ever-Fragrant Perfume of Divinity* was incarnate mere minutes, and already Harvest Moon wanted to play, play, play with her engineer's wonderful mane. "Maybe you should have put some clothes on." Now thunder spilled down the titled bowl of the world to shake the small stone stupa of the incarnaculum. "I suppose we had better get started." The Dukkhim had ever been a dour, pragmatic subspecies.

Harvest Moon and Scented Coolabar spent the night in a live-skin yurt blistered from the earth of Hoy. The thunder cracked, the yurt flapped and boomed in the wind, and the plain of Hoy lowed with storm-spooked graze-beastlis, but none so loud nor so persistent as Harvest Moon's moans and groans that her long black limbs were aching, burning; her body was dying, dying.

"Some muscular pain is to be expected in the first hours of incarnation," chided the yurt gently. "As muscle tone develops these pains generally pass within a few days."

"Days!" wailed Harvest Moon. "Pload me back up right now."

"I can secrete general analgesia," said the tent. So until the lights came up all across the world on the skyroof ten kilometers overhead, Harvest Moon suckled sweetly on pain-numb milk from the yurt's fleshy teat, and, in the morning, she and Scented Coolabar set out in great, low-gravity bounds across the Heaven Plain of Hoy in search of Rose of Jericho. This innermost of the Heart-world meat-levels had long been the preserve of ascetics and pilgrim souls; the ever up-curving plain symbolic, perhaps, of the soul's quest for its innate spiritual manifestation, or maybe because of its proximity to the virtual realms, above the skyroof, where the ploads constructed universe within universe, each bigger than the one that contained it. Yet this small grassy sphere was big enough to contain tens of thousands of pelerines and stylites, coenobites and saddhus, adrift in the ocean of grass.

"I'm sure we've been this way before," Scented Coolabar said. They were in the third monad of their quest. Eighty days ago, Harvest Moon had discovered beyond the pain of exercise the joy of muscles, even on this low-grav prairie, and could now be found at every unassigned moment delightedly studying her own matt black curves.

"I think that's the idea."

"Bloody Rose of Jericho," Scented Coolabar grumbled. They loped, three meters at a loose-limbed step, toward a dendro-eremite, a lone small tree in the wave-swept grass, bare branches upheld like prayers. "Even on the ship she was a damn ornery creature. Typical bloody selfish."

Because when Rose of Jericho went missing after the routine postsortie debrief, something else had gone missing with her. Verthandi's Ring, a name, a galactic coordinate; the vector upon which the Enemy migration had been accelerating, decade upon decade. In the enforced communality of the return flight—pload personalities intersecting and merging—captain and engineer alike had understood that their mistress at arms had deduced more than just a destination from the glowing ashes of the annihilated fleet. Soul etiquette forbade nonconsensual infringements of privacy and Rose of Jericho had used that social hiatus to conceal her speculations. Jealous monotheistic divinities were not so zealous as Clade debriefings, yet the Gentle Inquisitors of the Chamber of Ever-Renewing Waters had swept around that hidden place like sea around a reef. A vector, and a name, confirmation of the message they had received three hundred years before: Verthandi's Ring.

Even before they saw the face framed in the vulva of living wood, Harvest Moon and Scented Coolabar knew that their small quest was ended. When they first met on the virtual desert of Sofreendi for the Chamber of Ever-Renewing Waters' mission briefing (as dense and soul-piercing as its debrief), a closeness, a simpatico, suggested that they might once have been the same person; ploads copied and recopied and edited with mash-ups of other personalities. Empathy endures, across parsecs and plain, battlefronts and secrets.

"Does that hurt?" Scented Coolabar said. Greenwood crept down Rose of Jericho's brow, across her cheeks and chin, slow and certain as seasons.

"Hurt? Why should it hurt?" Wind soughed in Rose of Jericho's twigs. Harvest Moon, bored with this small world of grass, surreptitiously ran her hands down her muscled thighs.

"I don't know, it just looks, well, uncomfortable."

"No, it's very very satisfying," Rose of Jericho said. Her face was now a pinched oval of greening flesh. "Rooted. Slow." She closed her eyes in contemplation.

"Verthandi's Ring," Harvest Moon said suddenly. Scented Coolabar seated herself squatly on the grass beneath the wise tree. Beastli things squirmed beneath her ass.

"What is this game?" With life spans measurable against the slow drift of stars, millennia-long games were the weft of Clade society. "What didn't you tell them, couldn't you tell us?"

Rose of Jericho opened her eyes. The wood now joined across the bridge of her nose, her lips struggled against the lignum.

"There was not one fleet. There are many fleets. Some set off thousands of years ago."

"How many fleets?"

Rose of Jericho struggled to speak. Scented Coolabar leaned close.

"All of them. The Enemy. All of them."

Then Rose of Jericho's sparse leaves rustled and Scented Coolabar felt the ground shake beneath her. Unbalanced, Harvest Moon seized one of Rose of Jericho's branches to steady herself. Not in ten reconfigurings had either of them felt such a thing, but the knowledge was deeply burned into every memory, every cell of their incarnated flesh. The Clade Heart-world had engaged its Mach drive and was slowly, slow as a kiss, as an Edda, manipulating the weave of space-time to accelerate away from bloated, burning Seydatryah. Those unharvested must perish with the planet as the Seydatryah's family of worlds passed beyond the age of biology. Calls flickered at light-speed across the system. Strung like peals around the gas giant, the eight hundred half-gestated daughter-habitats left their birthing orbits: half-shells, hollow environment spheres; minor Heart-worlds of a handful of tiers. A quarter of the distance to the next star, the manufactories and system defenses out in the deep blue cold of the Oort cloud warped orbits to fall into the Heart-world's train. The Chamber of Ever-Renewing Waters, the military council, together with the Deep Blue Something, the gestalt über-mind that was the Heart-world's participatory democracy, had acted the moment it became aware of Rose of Jericho's small secret. Seydatryah system glowed with message masers as the call went out down the decades and centuries to neighboring Heart-worlds and culture clouds and even meat-planets: after one hundred thousand years, we have an opportunity to finally defeat the Enemy. Assemble your antimatter torpedoes, your planet killers, you sun-guns and quantum-foam destabilizers, and make all haste for Verthandi's Ring.

"Yes, but what is Verthandi's Ring?" Scented Coolabar asked tetchily, but all that remained of Rose of Jericho was a lignified smile, cast forever in bark. From the tiny vacuum in her heart, like a tongue passing over a lost, loved tooth, she knew that Rose of Jericho had fled moments before the Chamber of Ever-Renewing Waters' interrogation system slapped her with an unbreakable subpoena and sucked her secret from her. Scented Coolabar sighed.

"Again?" Harvest Moon asked.

"Again."

In all the known universe, there was only the Clade. All life was part of it, it was all life. Ten million years ago, it had been confined to a single species on a single world—a world not forgotten, for nothing was forgotten by the Clade.

That world, that system, had long since been transformed into a sphere of Heart-world orbiting a sun-halo of computational entities, but it still remembered when the bright blue eye of its home planet blinked once, twice, ten thousand times. Ships. Ships! Probe ships, sail ships, fast ships, slow ships, seed ships, ice ships; whole asteroid colonies, hollow-head comets, sent out on centuries-long falls toward other stars, other worlds. Then, after the Third Evolution, pload ships, tiny splinters of quantum computation flicked into the dark. In the first hundred thousand years of the Clade's history, a thousand worlds were settled. In the next hundred thousand, a hundred times that. And a hundred and a hundred and a hundred; colony seeded colony seeded colony, while the space dwellers, the Heart-world habitats and virtual pload intelligences, filled up the spaces in between which, heart and truth, was the vastly greater part of the universe. Relativistic ramships fast-tracked past lumbering arc-fleets; robots seedships furled their sunsails and sprayed biospheres with life-juice; terraforming squadrons hacked dead moons and hell-planets into nests for life and intelligence and civilization. And species, already broken by the Second and Third Evolutions into space-dwellers and ploads; shattered into culture-dust. Subspecies, new species, evolutions, devolutions; the race formerly known as humanity blossomed into the many-petaled chrysanthemum of the Clade; a society on the cosmological scale; freed from the deaths of suns and worlds, immune, immortal, growing faster than it could communicate its gathered self-knowledge back to its immensely ancient and powerful Type 4 civilizations; entire globular clusters turned to hiving, howling quantum-nanoprocessors.

New species, subspecies, hybrid species. Life was profligate in the cosmos; even multicellular life. The Clade incorporated DNA from a hundred thousand alien biospheres and grew in richness and diversity. Intelligence alone was unique. In all its One Giant Leap, the Clade had never encountered another bright with sentience and the knowledge of its own mortality that was the key of civilization. The Clade was utterly alone. And thus intelligence became the watchword and darling of the Clade: intelligence; that counterentropic conjoined twin of information, must become the most powerful force in the universe, the energy to which all other physical laws must eventually kneel. Intelligence alone could defeat the heat-death of the universe, the dark wolf at the long, thin end of time. Intelligence was destiny, manifest.

And then a Hujjain reconnaissance probe, no bigger than the thorn of a rose but vastly more sharp, cruising the edge of a dull little red dwarf, found a million habitats pulled in around the stellar embers. When the Palaelogos of the Byzantine Orthodoxy first encountered the armies of Islam crashing out of the south, he had imagined them just another heretical Christian sect. So had the Hujjain probe doubted; then, as it searched its memory, the entire history of the Clade folded into 11-space, came revelation. There was Another out there.

In the six months it took the Seydatryah fleet—one Heart-world, eighty semi-operational habitats, two hundred and twelve thousand ancillary craft and defensive systems—to accelerate to close enough to light-speed for time dilation effects to become significant, Harvest Moon and Scented Coolabar searched the Tier of Anchyses. The world-elevator, that ran from the portals of the Virtual Realms through which nothing corporeal might pass to the very lowest, heavy-gee Tier of Pterimonde, a vast and boundless ocean, took the star-sailors forty kilometers and four tiers down to the SkyPort of Anchyses, an inverted city that hung like a chandelier, a sea urchin, a crystal geode, from the skyroof. Blimps and zeps, balloon clusters and soaring gliders fastened on the ornate tower-bottoms to load, and fuel, and feed, and receive passengers. Ten kilometers below, beyond cirrus and nimbus; the dread forest of Kyce thrashed and twined, a venomous, vicious, hooked-and-clawed ecosystem that had evolved over the Heart-world's million-year history around the fallen bodies of sky-dwellers.

The waxing light of tier-dawn found Scented Coolabar on the observation deck of the dirigible *We Have Left Undone That Which We Ought To Have Done*. The band of transparent skin ran the entire equator of the kilometer-long creature: in her six months as part of the creature's higher-cognitive function, Scented Coolabar had evolved small tics and habits, one of which was watching the birth of a new day from the very forward point of the dirigible. The Morning Salutationists were rolling up their sutra mats as Scented Coolabar took her place by the window and imagined her body cloaked in sky. She had changed body for this level; a tall, slightly hirsute male with a yellow-tinged skin, but she had balked at taking the same transition as Harvest Moon. Even now, she looped and tumbled out there in the pink and lilac morning, in aerobatic ecstasy with her flockmates among the indigo clouds.

Dawn light gleamed from silver wing feathers. Pain and want and, yes, jealousy, clutched Scented Coolabar. Harvest Moon had been the one who bitched and carped about the muscle pain and the sunburn and the indigestion and the necessity to clean one's teeth; the duties and fallibilities of incarnation. Yet she had fallen in love with corporeality; reveled in the physicality of wind in her pinions, gravity tugging at the shapely curve of her ass; while Scented Coolabar remained solid, stolid, reluctant flesh. She could no longer remember the last time they had sex; physically or virtually. Games. And war was just another game to entities hundreds of thousands of years old, for whom death was a sleep and a forgetting, and a morning like this, fresh and filled with light. She remembered the actions they had fought: the reduction of Yorrrt, the defense of Thau-Pek-Sat, where Rose of Jericho had annihilated an Enemy strike-fleet with a blizzard of micro-black holes summoned out of the universal quantum foam, exploding almost instantly in a holocaust of Hawking radiation. She watched Harvest Moon's glider-thin wings deep down in the brightening clouds, thin as dreams and want. Sex was quick; sex was easy, even sacramental among the many peoples and sects that temporarily formed the consciousness of *We Have Left Undone That Which We Ought To Have Done*. She sighed and felt the breath shudder in her flat, muscled chest. Startled by a reaction as sensational, as physical, as any Immelmann or slow loop performed by Harvest Moon, Scented Coolabar felt tears fill and roll. Memory, a frail and trickster faculty among the incarnate, took her back to another body, a woman's body, a woman of the Teleshgathu nation; drawn in wonder and hope and young excitement up the space elevator to the Clade habitat that had warped into orbit around her world to repair and restore and reconstitute its radiation shield from the endless oceans of her world. From that woman of a parochial waterworld had sprung three entities, closer than sisters, deeper than lovers. Small wonder they needed each other, to the point of searching through eighty billion sentients. Small wonder they could never escape each other. The light was bright now, its unvarying shadow strict and stark on the wooden deck. Harvest Moon flashed her wings and rolled away, diving with her new friends deep through layer upon layer of cloud. And Scented Coolabar felt an unfamiliar twitch, a clench between the legs, a throb of something already exposed and sensitive becoming superattuned, swinging like a diviner's pendulum. Her balls told her, clear, straight, no arguments: She's out there. Rose of Jericho.

Twenty subjective minutes later, the Clade Fleet was eighty light-years into its twelve hundred objective-year flight to intercept the Enemy advance toward Verthandi's Ring, the greatest sentient migration since the big bang. Populations numbered in logarithmic notation, like outbreaks of viruses, are on the move in two hundred million habitat-ships, each fifty times the diameter of the Seydatryah Heart-world. Of course the Seydatryah cluster is outnumbered, of course it will be destroyed down to the last molecule if it engages the Enemy migration, but the Deep Blue Something understands that it may not be the biggest or the strongest, but it is the closest and will be the first. So the culture-cluster claws closer toward light-speed; its magnetic shield furled around it like an aurora, like a cloak of fire as it absorbs energies that would instantly incinerate all carbon life in its many levels and ships. And, nerve-wired into an organic ornithopter, Scented Coolabar drops free from the *We Have Left Undone That Which We Ought To Have Done*'s launch teats into eighty kilometers of empty airspace. Scented Coolabar shrieks, then the ornithopter's wings scrape and cup and the scream becomes *oooh* as the biological machine scoops across the sky.

"Where away?" Scented Coolabar shouts. The ornithopter unfolds a telescope; bending an eye; Scented Coolabar spies the balloon cluster low and breaking from a clot of cumulus. A full third of the netted balloons are dead, punctured, black and rotting. The ornithopter reads her intention and dives. A flash of sun-silver: Harvest Moon rises vertically out of the cloud, hangs in the air, impossibly elongated wings catching the morning light, then turns and tumbles to loop over Scented Coolabar's manically beating wings.

"That her?"

"That's her." *You are very lovely*, thought Scented Coolabar. *Lovely and alien.* But not so alien as Rose of Jericho, incarnated as a colony of tentacled balloons tethered in a veil of organic gauze, now terminally sagging toward the claspers and bone blades of Kyce. The ornithopter matched speed; wind whipped Scented Coolabar's long yellow hair. A lunge, a sense of the world dropping away, or at least her belly, and then the ornithopter's claws were hooked into the mesh. The stench of rotting balloon flesh assailed Scented Coolabar's senses. A soft pop, a rush of reeking gas, a terrifying drop closer to the fanged mouths of the forest: another balloon had failed. Harvest Moon, incarnated without feet or wheels, for her species was never intended to touch the ground, turned lazy circles in the sky.

"Same again?" Scented Coolabar asked. Rose of Jericho spoke through radio-sense into her head.

"Of course."

Foolish of Scented Coolabar to imagine a Rose of Jericho game being ended so simply or so soon.

"The Deep Blue Something has worked it out."

"I should hope so." The balloon cluster was failing, sinking fast. With the unaided eye Scented Coolabar could see the lash-worms and bladed dashers racing along the sucker-studded tentacles of the forest canopy. This round of the game was almost ended. She hoped her ornithopter was smart enough to realize the imminent danger.

"And Verthandi's Ring?" Harvest Moon asked.

"Is a remnant superstring." A subquantal fragment of the original big bang fireball, caught by cosmic inflation and stretched to macroscopic, then to cosmological scale. Rarer than virtue or phoenixes, remnant superstrings haunted the galactic fringes and the vast spaces between star-spirals; tens, hundreds of light-years long. In all the Clade's memory, only one had ever been recorded within the body of the galaxy. Until now. "Tied into a loop," Rose of Jericho added. Scented Coolabar and Harvest Moon understood at once. Only the hand of the Enemy — if the Enemy possessed such things, no communication had ever been made with them, no physical trace ever found from the wreckage of their ships or their vaporized colony clusters — could have attained such a thing. And that was why the Chamber of Ever-Renewing Waters had launched the Heart-world. Such a thing could only be an ultimate weapon.

"But what does it do?" Scented Coolabar and Harvest Moon asked at once, but the presence in their brains, one humanesque, one man-bat glider, was gone. Game over. A new round beginning. With a shriek of alarm, the ornithopter cast free just in time to avoid the tendrils creeping up over the canopies of the few surviving balloons. The tentacles of the forest clasped those of the balloon cluster and hauled it down. Then the blades came out.

How do wars begin? Through affront, through bravado, through stupidity or overconfidence, through scared purpose or greed. But when galactic cultures fight, it is out of inevitability, out of a sense of cosmic tragedy. It is through understanding of a simple evolutionary truth: there can be only one exploiter of an ecological niche, even if that niche is the size of a universe. Within milliseconds of receiving the inquisitive touch of the Hujjain probe, the Enemy realized this truth. The vaporizing of the probe was the declaration of war, and would have given the Enemy centuries of a head start had not the Hujjain craft in its final milliseconds squirted off a burst communication to its mother array deep in the cometary system on the edge of interstellar space.

In the opening centuries of the long, slow war, the Clade's expansion was checked and turned back. Trillions died. Planets were cindered; populations sterilized beneath a burning ultraviolet sky, their ozone layers and protective magnetic fields stripped away; habitat clusters incinerated by induced solar flares or reduced to slag by nanoprocessor plagues; Dyson spheres shattered by billions of antimatter warheads. The Clade was slow to realize what the Enemy understood from the start: that a war for the resources that intelligence required—energy, mass, gravity—must be a war of extermination. In the first two thousand years of the War, the Clade's losses equaled the total biomass of its original pre-starflight solar system. But in its fecundity, in the sheer irrepressibility of life, was the Clade's strength. It fought back. Across centuries it fought; across distances so vast the light of victory or defeat would be pale, distant winks in the night-sky of far future generations. In the hearts of globular clusters they fought, and the radiant capes of nebulae; through the looping fire-bridges on the skins of suns and along the event horizons of black holes. Their weapons were gas giants and the energies of supernovae; they turned asteroid belts into shotguns and casually flung living planets into the eternal ice of interstellar space. Fleets ten thousand a side clashed between suns, leaving not a single survivor. It was war absolute, elemental. Across a million star systems, the Clade fought the Enemy to a standstill. And, in the last eight hundred years, began to drive them back.

Now, time dilated to the point where a decade passed in a single heartbeat, total mass close to that of a thousand stars, the Clade Heart-world Seydatryah and its attendant culture-cluster plunged at a prayer beneath light-speed toward the closed cosmic string loop of Verthandi's Ring. She flew blind; no information, no report could outrun her. Her half trillion sentients would arrive with only six months forewarning into what might be the final victory, or the Enemy's final stand.

Through the crystal shell of the Heart-world, they watched the Clade attack fleet explode like thistledown against the glowing nebula of the Enemy migration. Months ago those battleships had died, streaking ahead of the decelerating Seydatryah civilization to engage the Enemy pickets and by dint of daring and force of fortune, perhaps break through to attack a habitat-cluster. The greater mass of the Clade, dropping down the blue shift as over the years and decades they fell in behind Seydatryah, confirmed the astonished reports of those swift, bold fighters. All the Enemy was here; a caravanserai hundreds of light-years long. Ships, worlds, had been under way for centuries before *Ever-Fragrant Perfume of Divinity* located and destroyed one of the pilgrim fleets. The order must have been given millennia before; shortly after the Clade turned the tide of battle in its favor. Retreat. Run away. But the Enemy had lost none of its strength and savagery as wave after wave of the cheap, fast, sly battleships were annihilated.

Scented Coolabar and Harvest Moon and Rose of Jericho huddled together in the deep dark and crushing pressure of the ocean at the bottom of the world. They wore the form of squid; many tentacled and big-eyed, communicating by coded ripples of bioluminescent frills along their streamlined flanks. They did not doubt that they had watched themselves die time after time out there. It was likely that only they had died a million deaths. The Chamber of Ever-Renewing Waters would never permit its ace battleship crew to desert into the deep, starlit depths of Pterimonde. Their ploads had doubtless been copied a million times into the swarm of fast-attack ships. The erstwhile crew of the *Ever-Fragrant Perfume of Divinity* blinked their huge golden eyes. Over the decades and centuries, the light of the Enemy's retreat would be visible over the entire galaxy, a new and gorgeous ribbon nebula. Now, a handful of light-months from the long march, the shine of hypervelocity particles impacting the deflection fields was a banner in the sky, a starbow across an entire quadrant. And ahead, Verthandi's Ring, a starless void three light-years in diameter.

"You won them enough time," Scented Coolabar said in a flicker of blue and green. The game was over. It ended at the lowest place in the world, but it had been won years before, she realized. It had been won the moment Rose of Jericho diverted herself away from the Soulhouse into a meditation tree on the Holy Plains of Hoy.

"I believe so," Rose of Jericho said, hovering a kiss away from the crystal wall, holding herself against the insane Coriolis storms that stirred this high-gravity domain of waters. "It will be centuries before the Clade arrives in force."

"The Chamber of Ever-Renewing Waters could regard it as treachery," Harvest Moon said. Rose of Jericho touched the transparency with a tentacle.

"Do I not serve them with heart and mind and life?" The soft fireworks were fewer now; one by one they faded to nothing. "And anyway, what would they charge me with? Handing the Clade the universe on a plate?"

"Or condemning the Clade to death," said Scented Coolabar.

"Not our Clade."

She had been brilliant, Scented Coolabar realized. To have worked it out in those few minutes of subjective flight, and known what to do to save the Clade. But she had always been the greatest strategic mind of her generation. Not for the first time Scented Coolabar wondered about their lost forebear, that extraordinary female who had birthed them from her ploaded intellect.

What is Verthandi's Ring? A closed cosmic string. And what is a closed cosmic string? A time machine. A portal to the past. But not the past of *this* universe. Any transit of a closed timelike loop lead inevitably to a parallel universe. In that time-stream, there too was war; Clade and Enemy, locked in Darwinian combat. And in that universe, as the Enemy was driven back to gaze into annihilation, Verthandi's Ring opened and a second Enemy, a duplicate Enemy in every way, came out of the sky. They had handed the Clade this universe; the prize for driving its parallel in the *alternate* time-stream to extinction.

Cold-blooded beneath millions of tons of deep cold pressure, Scented Coolabar shivered. Rose of Jericho had assessed the tactical implications and made the only possible choice: delay the Chamber of Ever-Renewing Waters and the Deep Blue Something so they could not prevent the Enemy exiting this universe. A bloodless win. An end to war. Intelligence the savior of the blind, physical universe. While in the second time-stream, Clade habitats burst like crushed eyeballs and worlds were scorched bare and the Enemy found its resources suddenly doubled.

Scented Coolabar doubted that she could ever make such a deal. But she was an engineer, not a mistress of arms. Her tentacles caressed Rose of Jericho's lobed claspers; a warm sexual thrill pulsed through her muscular body.

"Stay with us, stay with me," Harvest Moon said. Her decision was made, the reluctant incarnation; she had fallen in love with the flesh and would remain exploring the Heart-world's concentric tiers in thousands of fresh and exciting bodies.

"No, I have go." Rose of Jericho briefly brushed Harvest Moon's sexual tentacles. "They won't hurt me. They knew I had no choice, as they had no choice."

Scented Coolabar turned in the water. Her fins rippled, propelling her upward through the pitch-black water. Rose of Jericho fell in behind her. In a few strong strokes, the lights of Harvest Moon's farewell faded, even the red warmth of her love, and all that remained was the centuries-deep shine of the starbow beyond the wall of the world.

sea change

UNA MCCORMACK

New writer Una McCormack has a Ph.D. in sociology from the University of Surrey and teaches organizational theory at the University of Cambridge. Her short fiction has appeared in *Foundation 100*, *Doctor Who Magazine*, and *Glorifying Terrorism*. She is the author of two *Star Trek: Deep Space Nine* novels, *Cardassia: The Lotus Flower* and *Hollow Men*.

In the powerful story that follows, she shows us that even in the future, the gap between the haves and the have-nots will remain wide—and perilous to try to cross.

We went back to Callie's bedroom after evening classes pretending we were going to force-feed ourselves Chinese verbs. Really we were talking about what we'd do with the tutor if we could get our hands on him. You've seen the Level 12 'casts, you know the guy I mean. When I realized all our witty lust had turned into monologue, I glanced over at Callie. She was sitting back in the sofa with her feet up on the table, her tongue sticking out, and a piece of glass pressed up against her forearm.

"You'll ruin the carpet," I said.

"Fuck the carpet."

"Mm, you know, I think I'll pass."

I watched with interest, wondering how far she'd get. God only knows how she'd found something sharp—everything round here is so smooth, no rough edges. Nothing to mark you, no way to leave your mark. Callie cut into the flesh, and blood surged out, a shock of bright colour. She went paler beneath her skin bleach and her hand started to shake. "*Shit*," she muttered, as blood dripped onto the table. Her mother had told me at least twice how expensive that had been, so I dread to think how often she must have said it to Callie.

I took the piece of glass from her. "*I'll* do it." One quick surgical strike from me, and her tracker was out. It's been bugging her ever since it went in. Ho-ho. By now Callie was starting to get a thin, papery look—sort of see-through—so I wrapped a towel tight around her arm and made her hold it above her head like they'd shown me in the public hospital when I was getting my social credits. Then, to show moral support, I nicked my fingertip. A ruby-red bead welled up, and I waved my hand at Callie. "Hey, we can be blood sisters!"

She pulled a face. "That's *disgusting!*" Maybe, but it made her forget to feel sick, and she jumped up and went over to the door that led out onto the balcony. "Let's go out."

"Out? It'll be hot, Cal, you won't like it."

"I mean *really* out. Leave your key on the table."

I knew then what she had planned for us. I glanced over at the tutorial that was still playing through, and bit my lip. Callie hissed with impatience. "Come *on!* We've got to be there in ten minutes!"

Well, it's Callie's home, and I'm the guest, so I unclipped my key from my belt, and put in on the table next to her tracker. Off we went, leaving the tutor talking to the empty room, and all the while our accounts were racking up the study points for the modules he laboured through.

We walked down the main lane that runs through the estate. All the houses are on one side and the school stuff on the other. We went past the arts block and then along by the tennis courts where the teams were out practicing. We were heading roughly toward the cinema, but before we got there, Callie led me down a side path. We cut through some bushes, and soon we came to the wall, smooth and tall and impregnable. Except for a gap where it ended and the railings began where the bushes hadn't grown thick. Someone very slim could slip through. So we did.

We started down the road into town. There was still pavement most of the way, although in some places it had gone completely and there was only dust. Callie was already complaining about her shoes. The road was walled on either side of its entire length, the back of our estate and another one, and I think some government agency has houses round here. I'd been down this road in the car hundreds of times, but it's a lot different up close with those walls looming over you. The not-so-homely home counties. After about five minutes, Callie stopped by an old bus shelter and said, "Okay, now we wait."

"Are we getting the bus, Cal?"

"Don't be stupid."

"I don't have any actual money, that's all—"

"Don't be *stupid.*"

A couple of cars sped past, and each time my heart jumped—I look young for fifteen and you don't tend to see people hanging around much on the main roads. But soon enough a car pulled up, and this guy—nineteen, maybe twenty—leaned out. "Hi, Cal," he said. "Hop in." He looked at me, hanging back, and laughed. "And your little friend too, if she's coming." I went red and scrambled into the back while Callie graced the passenger seat.

If we're speaking geographically, I've no idea where we went, but it was a party, of course, and it was up in a second-floor flat. Music was thumping out of the open windows and inside it was all sweat and noise and bodies. How Callie finds out about this kind of thing I don't know, but somehow she manages. She was in the thick of it straight away, but I stayed back near the drinks table and tried not to look conspicuous.

It wasn't long before some guy started talking to me—well, yelling, really; he had to, over the music. "You from that estate up the road? The one with the school?"

"Yeah."

"Very nice." He was tanned, and when he smiled I noticed his bottom teeth were slightly crooked.

I shrugged. "It's all right." Usually I can do more than monosyllables, but it was really noisy and his smile had made me feel self-conscious. "Bit dull."

"I bet." He nodded at Callie. "That your friend?"

"Yeah."

"She's something else, isn't she?"

That's me—gateway to Callie. I did what I was there for and introduced them, although he didn't get very far with her, because about five minutes after that the police kicked the door in and started yanking us all out. They'd put an emergency dispersal order on the place. I suppose one of the neighbours had got fed up with the noise.

The police pulled me and Callie out of the crowd right away. It's not that they profile, but . . . look, I know it sounds bad, but a lot's been spent on the two of us, from before we were conceived, and our skin looks good and our hair looks good and our teeth look good, and . . . you can just *tell*, all right? That there's money around. As we were taken off to a car everyone else was being piled into vans. I saw the guy we'd been talking to, and he shrugged at me and gave me his crooked smile, as if to say, "What can you do?" When we got to the station, a policewoman made us tea while Callie's mother drove out to get us. She was laughing and apologizing as she paid the fine, but once we were in the car it came out about the tracker and that was the cue for tears and shouting.

"I'm particularly disappointed in *you*, Miranda." Mrs. Banville glared back at me in the rearview mirror. She's monstrous; done far too much to her face. "I would have expected you to have shown more sense. For gratitude's sake, if nothing else."

I stared out of the window at the walls speeding past. Of course. I'm supposed to be glad to have a home. But what could she expect, from someone with my background?

"The whole idea," Penny said later, "is to keep you safe." They were in Bombay—or was it L.A.? I didn't quite catch it. They move around a lot because they can't live here and won't get citizenship anywhere else out of principle.

"I know . . ."

"The Banvilles are being exceptionally kind letting you stay with them."

"I know . . ."

"I know we can't always be perfect, Em, but you really shouldn't be causing them any trouble."

A tiny white scar had formed on my fingertip, like the shadow of the crescent of my nail. Most of the time I'm never quite sure where they are. Why can't I go exploring for once?

"What we need to consider now are your options," Fran said. "The school's saying they'll have to invalidate all this year's marks."

That stupid tutorial. If only I'd switched it off before we left. "I did that *once!*"

"*We* believe you, Em," Penny said, kindly. Talking to them together can be like good cop, bad cop. One with the teapot, the other with the van. "But we're not the ones handing out the marks. As far as the school can tell, every single one of your credits this year hasn't actually been earned."

I slumped back in my chair. All that work. Sometimes I could murder Callie. But who'd look after her, if I didn't?

"So here's what I've got planned," Fran said, laying it out briskly, clearly, and with no room for argument. This is why she makes so much money as a lawyer. Penny winked at me like she always does when Fran gets going, but I felt too miserable to wink back. "I've got a much better plan," I said, when Fran finished. "I come and join you and we can be a family again."

My mothers glanced at each other. "Em," Penny said, "I know you think it'd be chic, and cosmopolitan, but actually it's dreary. Plane, hotel, plane, hotel—you can't tell one from the other."

"This way you're getting a proper education," Fran said.

"Both of us are working all the hours god sends, sweetheart—you'd be alone most of the time, you'd get bored, and lonely—"

"Not to mention you're getting the passport, and I surely don't need to outline the tangible benefits of *that*—"

"You'll be at college soon, love. Then you won't want to bother with us at all."

See what I mean? After all that, saying, "but I'd still rather be with you," just sounds lame, so I said nothing, and studied my tiny scar. Out of the corner of my eye, I saw them look at each other and smile. Mother's face softened, Mum's went sort of serene. They're still crazy about each other, even after all this time, and all the trouble. I think that scares me most—that maybe now I'm not there, they're discovering how much I got in the way. That maybe they shouldn't have gone to all the bother of having me in the first place.

"Sweetheart, we've got to go now—"

"I'll speak to the Banvilles and fix it all up. We'll talk to you from Toronto."

"Take care, love. And *try* to be good. Remember—back home, you're our ambassador. For the cause."

We blew kisses at one another, and they finished the call. And I was left sitting here alone, in this expensive house on this exclusive estate, thinking I would give up everything just to be with them. All the money doesn't matter. Because around here, in this stupid narrow strip of the world, I'm the one whose parents had to go and live abroad. I'm the one with dykes for mummies.

So Callie and I were packed off to Scotland for the summer. The idea was to make up all the invalidated work, but really we were doing time for breaking out.

Our home for the holiday was on Mull. My mothers had bought a house there when they got married, but when the law changed back and they had to either leave the country or split, they'd signed it over to me. That's me—absentee landlady. We'd never come here much even when we were all together; it's a long journey up by road and of course—as Mrs. Banville reminded us—it's not the done thing to take too many internal flights. She and Mr. B. were flying off the day after we left to go skiing in Queenstown.

Anila drove us up. Anila was going to be our tutor, not to mention our personal jailer. Callie's father trades in academic bonds, so it had been easy for him to get hold of someone. Anila was quiet and slim and neat and . . . sort of faded, really. Part of the background, like wallpaper. If Callie spoke to her, it was always past her, at a point to one side of Anila's right ear. It's exactly how her mother talks to me. Except when she shows me off to her friends. Then I'm the second child she never had. "This is Em," she'll say. "We're taking care of her while her mothers have to be away." How could you not be impressed at that? Such good work, for such a worthy cause.

Callie hadn't said a word about our banishment, but I knew she was seething. She'd had plans for the summer, I think, down in the city. Ever since we'd been caught, and another tracker installed, she'd only worn short sleeves, so you could always see the scar on her left arm where the other one had been. Like some weird kind of fashion accessory. She spent the whole trip up with sunglasses on, staring out of the car window and not talking. It made the journey pretty boring, particularly when we came back down off the expressway past Birmingham. The whole north is terraced, straight lines of olive groves and vineyards. Dead dull. The only entertainment came when we went through a toll and new adverts came on. Mine are always insane, because of the trust money. Callie's were all for vitamin supplements or local jobbing doctors.

At Carlisle, Callie insisted on stopping, and Anila bought us ice cream, like we were children. Callie devoured hers in seconds, but I let mine have the chance to melt, so I could chase the vanilla and the raspberry as it dripped along my fingers and down my hand. Anila had done the same, and we both realized this at exactly the same moment, both of us licking up syrup, and catching each other's eye. Her face flowered into a smile, and she was suddenly something human. I went shy, and ran off to the toilets to find Callie. She said she was feeling sick from the heat and the sugar, and while she was throwing up, I stood behind her in the door of the cubicle and picked at the gaffa tape covering the foreign-language instructions for the sharps box. You get to go to all the best places with Callie. When she was done, I cleaned her face and smoothed her hair, and took her back out to the car where Anila was waiting.

We took the ferry, and were over at the house by eight o'clock. Callie disappeared right away, and I took my supper outside and sat looking at the wall of sea between me and the mainland, smooth as glass and offering no purchase. Round about half-nine, Anila called softly from inside that perhaps I should think about going to bed, so I left my plate with her, and did what I was told. But I lay awake for hours, trying to hear the sea beneath the throb and the backbeat of bass coming through the wall from Callie's room. That was our first night on the island.

The next morning, Anila established our routine. I got up early and swam some lengths in the pool before breakfast, and then the morning was for studying. Anila kept us at the grindstone till one o'clock, and then we were free to do what we liked. As prisons go, it wasn't a bad one—I mean, it was hardly one of those places on the fen islands you see on shockumentaries. There was the pool, and the lush lawns and bright flowers, and those twisted citrus trees with the knobbly misshaped oranges. Pen had installed a decent library with proper books. There was a path down to the private strip of beach—yellow sands and palm trees—and everything we could want in the house itself. A good job, really, given how grounded we were. Leaving the house and gardens was clearly and strictly forbidden. A prison is a prison all the same.

I spent most afternoons on the beach. When it was too hot, I would just sit in the shade and read, but I liked to be in the water, and poke around the rock pools, and wave at the pleasure boats. One day I built sandcastles just to watch the tide wash them away. Callie mostly stayed indoors watching films from after the second war, but she would join me now and again, and sit smothered in sun cream beneath a big umbrella, staring out to sea and chain-smoking. She wore her sunglasses and a headscarf, like something from one of the pictures she'd been watching. I've no idea how she'd got her hands on cigarettes. Could have been smugglers for all I know.

Anila went off in the afternoons. I didn't know where she went or what she did, but supper was ready at seven o'clock. I took it out to my spot on the wall, and tried not to hear Callie thumping around the house. Anila would come and sit with me sometimes, maybe one night out of three, although we didn't talk much. It's weird to think back on it now, that month we spent alone together on the island. Just the three of us, flitting around that place, like moths trapped in a bell jar, or spirits of a house that couldn't find rest. I imagine that's how Callie felt most of the time.

Obviously we were heading for a massive storm. When it came it was faster than the Norwich tornado, and might have done as much damage too if I hadn't intervened.

I suppose it had been brewing for a couple of days. When people are stuck together like that it's always going to be a pressure cooker, but it had been getting hotter, and that day was the hottest yet. The sky was unnaturally blue, almost fluorescent. We were slogging through one of the set texts, and Callie was sitting in her usual position, leaning forward on her desk with her hand shielding her eyes. I didn't mind doing all the work again—I was never going to struggle with the exams, and now I could just enjoy it for its own sake. It was a good feeling, sort of magical, but I probably don't need to say how pissed off Callie was about having to do it again.

Even Anila was hard-pressed to conjure up her usual enthusiasm. Anila always dressed very properly, in a grey suit—she never took the jacket off—and with her hair tied back. This morning wisps of hair had started to escape, and the jacket looked heavy and uncomfortable. She kept glancing across at Callie, and you could see that the way Callie was sitting was beginning to annoy her. As it was meant to.

"Callie, could you sit up, please?"

Callie remained motionless for a second or two, and then she eased back in her chair. She kept the shield up though.

"And put your hand down so I can see your face, please."

There was another pointed delay, and then Callie moved her hand—to pick up her sunglasses and perch them on her nose.

"Oh, come on, Callie!"

"I have to wear them," Callie said primly. "I had the laser thing done and my eyes are very sensitive."

"Yes, well, I'm sure your parents would have mentioned that—"

Callie shrugged. "You can ask them if you like."

"Given they're halfway around the globe and almost certainly asleep, I'll have to wait till we're sharing waking hours to do that. In the meantime—take the glasses off. Please."

"It was very expensive surgery. They'll be furious if you make me ruin it."

"Callie, you know you're just being rude. Take them off, and we can get back to work. The summer's well underway and we have a lot of work to make up yet."

At that, Callie stretched back lazily in her chair. "Do you really think I care?" She looked very cool and relaxed. She'd been taking tips from those old films, and had outfitted herself in crisp white linen, and a black scarf with little gold beads to match the frames of those stupid glasses. She was Audrey Hepburn to Anila's Jane Eyre.

"You should care," Anila said. "Your future's hanging on it. Or, if this one gets through to you, a lot of your parents' money is being ploughed into educating you—"

Callie stopped her with a laugh. "You *can't* really think I'm going to fail any of this, can you?"

This was actually a pretty good point. Callie's A-starred like me, fast-tracking in all fifteen subjects. She just can't be bothered most of the time.

"This time next year I'll be starting on the law prelims," Callie went on. "And a year after that I'll be passing them. What will you be doing then, Miss Grey? Teaching someone else's five-year-olds how to spell and wipe their arses? Hardly the Brontës, is it, or Shakespeare? What about the year after that, Miss Grey, and the year after that? Not long now and I'll be at the bar, and you're right—the parents will pay for the lot. How long exactly till your bond's paid off? All that education, it doesn't come cheap, does it?"

Anila had been getting redder and redder through all of this. Maybe Callie should have remembered that Anila must have been smart to get herself this far. At least as smart as Callie herself. When Callie was done, Anila tucked a stray bit of hair behind her ear, and took a moment or two to compose herself.

"You're quite right, Miss Caroline," she said. "It's a sad life, if you think too much about it. But I do have some points in my favour. I don't have to hide from my own face. And I certainly don't have to shove a finger down my throat every time I eat."

Callie went rigid. Then she was out of her chair and heading through the door, shouting back, "You'd better believe I'm telling my parents about this when they're up!"

"You do that," Anila called after her. "If in doubt, run to Daddy."

I'd been sitting watching all of this with my hand over my mouth. Once Callie was gone, Anila heaved a deep, shaky sigh. She stood up, took off her jacket, and threw it over the back of the chair. She started pacing around the room, finally coming to a halt by the window. She looked tired and a lot older. I didn't know what to do so I just sat and nibbled my nail, but when she didn't move at all, I said, "Are you okay?"

"No," she said. "I'm well and truly sacked."

I thought about that for a moment. Then I said, "She smokes, you know."

Anila looked back at me sharply. "What?"

"Callie. She's got a stash of cigarettes somewhere."

"I see." Anila drifted back toward her table. She picked up her jacket and straightened it, then tidied her hair. Then she gave the ghost of a smile. "I see. Thank you, Miranda."

"Em."

When she looked up at me, her smile blossomed again, and I realized I liked seeing it. Liked earning it. "Thank you—Em."

It was enough to stop Callie. The health premiums would have rocketed and her parents would have killed her. So it was stalemate—for a couple of days. Until Callie made her next bid for freedom.

The next evening, I discovered where Anila went when she wasn't with us. I was looking for Callie, and after the likely places hadn't turned her up, I started on unlikely ones, which meant the library. It has a small first floor, a mezzanine really, and there's a door up there that leads out onto a balcony. I saw lamplight, and a shadow moving, so I went to check.

Anila was sitting out on a deck chair. Her bare feet were up on another one, and when she saw me, she moved so I could sit down. Her dark hair was loose around her shoulders and she didn't have makeup on. It made her look nearly as young as us. She smiled at me and carried on rubbing value brand lotion into her hands.

"What would you have done?" I said. "If you had got sacked, I mean?"

She stopped rubbing, and that tired and faded look returned. "I don't know. I owe a lot of money."

"Oh." I didn't know what that felt like. "What will you do when it's paid?"

She went back to massaging her hands. "Years before that, Em."

"Still, though. If you could choose."

"Well, I'd get my own passport then. So travel, maybe. Teach—I do like it, despite everything . . ." She sighed. "Oh, I don't know. Maybe having the choice is what matters most." She looked out across the sea and the deepening sky and the generous sprinkling of stars that helped it all go down. "I'm lucky. Far worse places to live. Far worse ways to live."

"I'm glad it all turned out okay. With Callie."

"Well, me too!" We grinned at each other, and then all of a sudden I felt bad. She was so nice and I was so rich. She was looking at me like she felt sorry too. I stood up and was about to say good night, but then she said, "You do know, Em, don't you, that it's not your job in life to pick up after Callie?"

"Why? Because it's yours?"

She smiled. "It's not my job either, not really—but they do give me money for it."

Strange thing to say. I didn't quite understand, so I left her to the stars and her peace. I ended up going to bed later than usual that night, and without finding Callie.

When I woke up, it was that weird and hazy hour between two and three. My head was throbbing. I got up and pulled back the curtains. Light was pouring out of the window along from mine, from Callie's room. Was she awake too? I padded out to the corridor and knocked on her bedroom door. "Cal?"

No answer. Thunder rumbled overhead. When I went in, the room was empty and Callie's stuff from class was dumped on the bed. She wasn't in the bathroom. Wherever she'd been all day, she hadn't got back yet.

I went downstairs. There were no more lights that I could see, inside or out. The thunder rumbled, much closer, and the air felt charged and crackling. I didn't find her, in either the usual or the unusual places. I felt stupid, knocking on Anila's door in the middle of the night, but there was a quick way to track Callie down and wandering aimlessly around the house wasn't it.

We found her by the swimming pool, lying half in and half out of one of the changing rooms, translucent in the moonlight. I was glad Anila was there. She checked Callie's pulse and said, "Go and call the coast guard, please, Em." They were over in no time, and Anila went with Callie, leaving me in the house. I spent the rest of the night sitting out on Anila's balcony, with my arms around my knees, listening to the thunder and whispering words like charms to get the storm to break. Sometimes your mood can mirror the weather. Sometimes it mirrors the sea.

It didn't rain. The next morning was clear and very hot, and Anila came back to take me over to the hospital. Callie was propped up in bed, looking teenaged and frightened. The Banvilles got back the following day, and started taking it out on Anila. They only stopped when I pointed out that

Callie's poison of choice was the antitoxin Mrs. Banville has to take with the antiaging drugs she's getting under the counter from her tame doctor. I bet Callie did that on purpose. The police would be interested in that, I thought, and saying that to them that felt good, like electricity. I wasn't sure at first how much I could get away with, but when I told them to write off Anila's debt, they didn't put up a fight at all. All of which finished me with them, but it didn't matter much, because in the middle of all this, I turned sixteen. Other people get parties when they become citizens. I got to see what it looks like to have your stomach pumped. And, yes, I think Callie did that on purpose too.

I stayed on at the house on the island for a few months. Fran and Penny said to come and join them, but they were in Paris and I wanted to be somewhere colder. The time had passed and they hadn't been there and I didn't want to be their little girl anymore. Like I'd never wanted to be their ambassador, or Callie's lapdog, or the Banvilles' charity case. Besides, I had access to the trust now and while I didn't know yet what I wanted to do with it, it was like Anila had said, that sometimes it's more about having the choice than making it. I got a really great haircut, and some expensive clothes. I've been thinking of setting up scholarships—I could buy whole schools if I wanted, and run them however I liked. If I knew the best way. I might go and study myself, although I don't know what. I might just get my eyes tinted instead.

As for Anila—she did travel. I didn't expect anything, but I get a message, now and then, from all over. The last one came after what happened to Beijing—she's often there, in the wake of disasters, cleaning up. Her note is always short and exactly the same: *To Em—wherever you are now in your brave new world.*

the sky is large and the earth is small

CHRIS ROBERSON

New writer Chris Roberson has appeared in *Postscripts*, *Asimov's*, *Argosy*, *Electric Velocipede*, *Black October*, *Fantastic Metropolis*, *RevolutionSF*, *Twilight Tales*, *The Many Faces of Van Helsing*, and elsewhere. His first novel, *Here, There & Everywhere*, was released in 2005, and was quickly followed by *Paragaea: A Planetary Romance*, *The Voyage of Night Shining White*, and, most recently, *Set the Seas on Fire*. Coming up is a new novel, *The Dragon's Nine Sons*. In addition to his writing, Roberson is one of the publishers of the lively small press MonkeyBrain Books, and recently edited the "retro-pulp" anthology *Adventure, Volume 1*. He lives with his family in Austin, Texas.

The thoughtful story that follows takes us to an intricately worked-out alternate world to reaffirm the wisdom that iron bars do not a prison make. . . .

WATER-DRAGON YEAR, TWENTY-EIGHTH YEAR OF THE KANGXI EMPEROR

Cao Wen stood south of the Eastern Peace Gate of the Forbidden City, facing the entrance to the Eastern Depot. It was an unassuming building, dwarfed by the grandeur of the buildings on the opposite side of the concourse—the Six

Ministries, the Court of State Ceremonial, and the Directorate of Astronomy, where the imperial astronomers studied the heavens, watchful of any signs or portents that might auger good or ill for the emperor. Only the Office of Transmission was less grand than the Eastern Depot, its function largely eliminated when the emperor had instituted the palace memorial system, requiring that each of his ministers and deputies communicate their reports to him directly in their own hand, for his eyes only.

At the Eastern Depot's large, unadorned entrance, two guards stood at the ready, sabers sheathed at their sides, poleaxes in their hands. Cao displayed his signs of authority, which marked him as an authorized representative of the Ministry of War. One of the guards studied the papers closely, and then turned and motioned for Cao to accompany him, leaving the other at his post.

Following the guard into the main hall of the Eastern Depot, Cao's eyes lit upon a plaque, on which a motto was engraved in simply crafted characters: HEART AND BOWELS OF THE COURT.

"Please wait here," the guard said with an abbreviated bow, "while this one fetches a superior." Then, Cao's papers still in hand, the guard disappeared through one of the many arches leading from the main hall.

Cao waited in silence, as agents of the Eastern Depot came and went, all about the emperor's business. Most were clad in plain gray robes, and would not merit a second glance, were he to pass them on the street. Only a few wore the elaborate mantles that gave the emperor's secret police their name—the Embroidered Guard.

After a few long moments, the guard reappeared, with an older man following close behind. In his simple cotton robes, this older newcomer could have easily passed for a fishmonger or merchant in textiles, thin wisps of mustaches drooping over his thick lips, his eyes half-lidded as though he were just waking from a long slumber. His face, frame, and hands displayed the softened edges that suggested he was a eunuch, one who had traded in his manhood for a life of imperial service.

"Return to your post," the older man said to the guard, who replied only with a rigid nod.

"You are Cao Wen?" the older man said to him, without preamble.

Cao allowed that he was, and bowed lower than the man's appearance would suggest was required. In such a setting, appearances could be deceiving.

"I am Director Fei Ren of the Eastern Depot." The older man brandished the papers Cao had brought with him, which bore the chop of the Minister of War. "I understand you wish to speak with one of our guests?"

"Yes, O Honorable Director," Cao said, bowing again, and lower this time, "it is the wish of his excellency the Minister of War that I should do so. It is believed that your . . . guest . . . has some intelligence that may be of use to the emperor, may-he-reign-ten-thousand-years."

"This individual has been temporarily housed with us for some considerable time," Director Fei answered. "Since before our emperor reached his age of majority. And not all that time spent in the Outside Depot, but some months and years in the Bureau of Suppression and Soothing, as well."

Cao suppressed a shudder. He had heard only whispered rumors about what went on in the private chambers of the Bureau of Suppression and Soothing, which the Embroidered Guard used to elicit confessions from the most recalcitrant suspects.

Director Fei continued. "Any intelligence this individual had to offer has been long since documented, I would venture to say. And had we been able to extract a confession from him on his many crimes, he would long ago have gone under the executioner's blade. I think you will find this one a spent fruit, all juices long since dried-up, leaving nothing more than a desiccated husk of a man."

"You are obviously much wiser in such matters than I, Honorable Director," Cao said with the appropriate tone of humility, "but such is my office to fulfill, and it would displease my master the Minister of War if I were to shirk my responsibility."

Director Fei shrugged. "Very well. It is your own time that you waste. Come along and I will have one of my agents escort you into the Outside Depot."

Director Fei waved over another man dressed in plain robes, this one nearer Cao's own age of twenty years.

"Agent Gu Xuesen will escort you, Cao Wen. Now you must excuse me, as more pressing matters demand my attention."

Cao bowed low, and Director Fei disappeared back into the shadows beyond the main hall.

"This way, sir," Gu said, inclining his head, and starting toward one of the larger arches.

Agent Gu led Cao through the winding labyrinth of passages within the Eastern Depot. The building was larger inside than its exterior would suggest, largely a function of the snaking passages and innumerous small chambers and rooms. Frequently passages opened onto open-air courtyards, and just as frequently onto sunless, dank chambers that had never seen the light of day. And as they went, Agent Gu provided the name and use of each chamber and room.

Cao was surprised to find so talkative a member of the Embroidered Guard, who were widely known as a circumspect, and some might even say taciturn lot. When Agent Gu explained that he was only in his first years with the Embroidered Guard, and that he was required to complete his long years of training before being allowed to go beyond the walls of the Eastern

Depot, his talkative manner became much more understandable. He clearly hungered for dialogue with someone nearer his own age, and while his training likely prohibits providing information when it is unnecessary, and when there is no advantage to be gained, his youthful hunger for distraction, in this instance at least, was getting the better of his discretion.

"And now, Cao Wen," Agent Gu was saying, "we pass into that section known as the Inside Depot. This is the place used to house the most dangerous and serious suspects brought in by the Embroidered Guard. It is the most closely guarded of all the sections of the Eastern Depot, and none who are not of the Embroidered Guard may enter unescorted."

They passed by a tall doorway, the door lacquered matte black, the frame painted a red the color of blood.

"And beyond this point," Gu said, pointing to the door, "rests the Bureau of Suppression and Soothing."

Cao flinched, despite himself. He had, of course, heard of the bureau, though he labored not to call to mind the stories he had heard.

"Even through the reinforced walls and doors of the bureau," Gu went on, "which have been designed to dampen sound, screams and hideous wailing can occasionally be heard."

They passed by the jet-and-scarlet doorway, turning a corner to a long corridor, and Cao tried to put the door and what lay beyond it out of his thoughts.

Continuing on, they came at last to a broad, open-air courtyard, surrounded on all sides by narrow doorways leading to small chambers. Men and women milled around in the bright morning sun, shuffling under the gaze of guards who perched atop towers positioned on the opposite sides of the courtyard, surmounted by banners on tall posts.

"This, finally, is the Outside Depot," Gu explained, "in which guests of the Embroidered Guard are temporarily housed. Some have confessed to minor crimes, which merit no more severe punishment than imprisonment, while others await the decision of the emperor on their final sentencing. Some few have yet to confess, but have been deemed by the Bureau of Suppression and Soothing as not likely to confess at any point in the future. As no conviction can be achieved without a confession, these few are returned to the Outside Depot, assuming they are not violent enough to merit imprisonment in the Inside Depot, to wait."

"Wait for what?" Cao asked, casting his gaze across the dispirited faces before him.

"Some wait for a reprieve from the emperor, some wait for further evidence to come to light, while some just wait. For death to take them, one supposes."

Agent Gu pointed to an ancient man sitting at the center of the courtyard, his legs folded under him, his full attention on the passage across the ground of the shadows of the two towers.

"That is the man you seek," Agent Gu said. "That is Ling Xuan."

Cao Wen sat opposite the ancient man in the interview chamber. Agent Gu waited beyond the door of iron-clad hardwood, which Cao doubted any sound could penetrate, short of a full-bodied bellow.

Cao had a sheaf of papers in front of him, while the old man sat with his shoulders slumped, his hands folded in his lap, and the slack-jawed smile of an imbecile on his wrinkled face.

"Ling Xuan?" Cao repeated. The old man's eyes rested on the simple wooden table between then, worn smooth by generations of hands. Cao could not help but wonder what other dialogues had played out across the table, over the long years since the Embroidered Guard was established in the days of the Yongle emperor, during the Bright Dynasty.

Still, though, the old man did not reply.

"Is that your name?"

The old man drew in a deep breath through his nostrils, blinked several times, and straightened up, all without lifting his eyes from the surface of the table. When he spoke, his voice was soft but with an underlying strength, like the sound of distant thunder.

"The swirls and curves from which this table is constructed call to mind the heavens and clouds picked out in golden thread on the longpao dragon robes I wore in the service of the Shunzhi emperor. Strange to think that they follow me, here, after all of these long years. Perhaps they seek to remind me of days past, when my circumstances were more auspicious."

The man had spoken slowly, but without any pause between words, a single, breathless oration.

Cao looked at the table, and saw nothing but meaningless swirls and knots. Was the old man mad, and his search already proven in vain?

"Need I remind you," Cao replied, his tone moderated but forceful, "that I come here on the authority of the Minister of War, who speaks with the voice of the Dragon Throne itself? Now, I ask again, is your name—"

"Yes," the old man said, not raising his eyes. "Ling Xuan is my name."

Cao nodded sharply. "Good. And are you the same Ling Xuan who is listed here?"

Cao slid a piece of paper across the table, a copy he had recently made of the fragmentary inventory of the imperial archives of the Chongzhen emperor, one of the last of the Bright Dynasty, who ruled before the Manchu came down from the north and established the Clear Dynasty.

On the inventory was highlighted one item: *A Narrative Of A Journey*

Into The East, To The Lands Which Lay Across The Ocean, With Particular Attention to the Mexica, by Ling Xuan, Provincial Graduate.

Ling looked at the paper for a long time, as though puzzling out a complex mathematical equation in his head. After a long moment he spoke, his voice the sound of distant thunder. "Such a long time ago." And then he fell silent once more.

After a lengthy silence, the old man nodded, slowly, and raised his eyes to meet Cao's.

"Yes," Ling said. "I am he."

"Good," Cao said impatiently. "Now, I am sorry to report that all that is known about your account is the title, as it was among those records lost in the transition of power from the Bright Dynasty to the Clear. My purpose for coming here to interview you is—"

"Such a long time ago, but I can remember it all, as though it were yesterday."

Cao paused, waiting to see if the old man would speak further after his interruption. When Ling remained silence, Cao nodded again and continued, "That is good, because—"

"When we are young," Ling said, the distant thunder growing somewhat closer, "the days crawl by. I remember summers of my youth that seemed to last for generations. But as we grow older, the months and years flit by like dragonflies, one after another in their dozens. But by the calendar, a day is still a day, is it not? Why is it, do you suppose, that the duration of a span of time should seem so different to us in one circumstance than another?"

Cao shuffled the papers before him impatiently. "I'm sure that I don't know. Now, as I was saying—"

"I have begun to suspect that time is, in some sense I don't yet fully comprehend, subjective to the viewer. What a day signifies to me is quite different than what it signifies to you. How strange my day might seem, were I able to see it through your eyes."

"Ling Xuan, I insist that you listen to, and then answer, my questions."

"We shall see how our day looks tomorrow, shall we?" Ling Xuan rose slowly to his feet, crossed to the door, and rapped on the metal cladding with a gnarled knuckle. "Perhaps then we shall have more perspective on the subjectivity of time."

Cao jumped to his feet, raising his voice in objection. "Ling Xuan, I *insist* that you return to your seat and answer my questions!"

Agent Gu opened the door, in response to the knocking sound.

Ling smiled beatifically, looking back over his shoulder at Cao. "And if I insist to the sun that it stop in its courses, and remain unmoving in the heavens, do you suppose that it will?"

With that Ling Xuan turned and walked out of the chamber, nodding slightly to Agent Gu as he passed.

Cao raced to the door, his cheeks flushed with anger. "Agent Gu, bring him to heel!"

Agent Gu glanced after the back of the retreating prisoner.

"That old man survived more than a year in the Bureau of Suppression and Soothing," Gu answered, "and never confessed. What do you suppose that I could do that would make him talk?"

Gu walked out toward the courtyard, and Cao followed behind, his hands twisted into trembling fists at his sides.

Ling had walked out into the sunlit courtyard, and he glanced back at Cao as he sat, gracefully folding his legs under him.

"Tomorrow, don't forget," he called to Cao. "Perhaps that will be the day in which we find answers."

Back at the Ministry of War, across the concourse from the Eastern Depot, Cao Wen sat in his small cubicle, surveying the mounds of paper before him, hundreds of notes and maps and charts, the product of months' work.

"Cao?" an impatient voice called from behind him, startling him.

Cao turned, pulse racing, to find the imposing figure of the Deputy Minister of War standing behind him.

"Deputy Minister Wu," Cao said breathlessly, rising to his feet and bowing.

Wu waved him to return to his seat, an annoyed expression on his bread face. "Is it too much to hope that you have completed your survey of the archives, and your report on the Mexica is finally ready to present to the minister?"

Cao blanched, and shook his head. "Your pardon, O Honorable Deputy Minister, but while my researches are very nearly complete, I still have one final resource to investigate before my survey is ready for review."

"I take it you refer to this prisoner of the Eastern Depot? Were you not scheduled to interview him today?"

"Yes," Cao answered reluctantly. "But our initial meeting was not entirely . . . productive. It is my intention to return to the Eastern Depot tomorrow to complete his interrogation."

"Was this Ling Xuan forthcoming with strategic details about the Mexica? The emperor is most desirous of a complete analysis of the possibilities for invasion of the Mexic isthmus, once our pacification of Fusang is complete, and the Minister of War is most eager to present the ministry's findings on the matter."

"The urgency is well understood, Deputy Minister." Cao shifted uneasily on his bench. "But I believe this final interview will provide much needed detail for the survey, and greatly improve the emperor's understanding of the strategic possibilities."

"I suppose you are well aware of the fact that a survey well received by the Dragon Throne will do much to enhance the estimation of a scholar so far unable to pass the juren level examinations, and would greatly aid one's chances of advancement within the imperial bureaucracy."

Cao brightened, and sat straighter. "Most certainly, Deputy Minister."

"The converse, however, is also true," Wu said, his eyes narrowed, "and a report which displeases the Minister, to say nothing of displeasing the emperor, Son of Heaven, may-he-reign-ten-thousand-years, could do irreparable damage to a young bureaucrat's career prospects. Such a one might find himself assigned to the far provinces, inspecting grain yield and calculating annual tax levies for the rest of his life."

Cao swallowed hard. "It is understood, Deputy Minister."

The Deputy Minister nodded. "Good," he said, turning and walking briskly away. "See that it is not forgotten."

The next day, Cao Wen stood over Ling Xuan, who again sat in the middle of the concourse, his eyes on the shadows on the ground.

"Note the shadows of the two towers," Ling said without looking up, before Cao had announced himself. "The spires atop each function like the points atop an equatorial sundial. If one views the many doorways opening off the central courtyard as marking the hours, the shadows indicate the time of day, with the southern tower indicating the time in the summer months, when the sun is high in the sky, and the northern tower indicating the time in the winter, when the sun is lower."

Ling at last looked up at Cao.

"Tell me," the old man said, "do you suppose the architects of the Eastern Depot intended the shadows for this purpose, or is this merely an auspicious happenstance, the result of nothing more than divine providence?"

Cao Wen glanced over at Agent Gu, who stood beside him, but Gu only shrugged helplessly.

"I intend to complete our interview this morning, Ling Xuan," Cao answered.

"Morning," Ling Xuan replied with a smile. "Afternoon. Evening and night. Shadows measure the hours by day, and drips of water by night. But if the towers were to be moved, what would become of the hours? In the days of the Southern Song Dynasty, a great astronomer named Guo Shoujing constructed at Linfen in Shanxi Province a grand observatory, an intricate mechanism of bronze, perfectly aligned with the heavens. Later, in the Bright Dynasty, it was moved to Southern Capital. Though the instruments that constituted the observatory were no less intricate or precise after the move, they were intended for another geographic location and, after being relocated, no longer aligned with the heavens. The observatory no longer measured the movements of the celestial. What had been an invaluable tool became merely statuary. How many of us, removed from our proper position, likewise lose our usefulness?"

Cao tapped his foot, and scowled. He was convinced there was still meat to be found in among the mad offal of the old man's ramblings, but he wasn't sure he had the patience to find it.

"You will accompany me to the interview chamber," Cao said, keeping his tone even, "where we can continue our conversation like civilized beings."

"As you wish," Ling said, smiling slightly, and rose to his feet on creaking joints.

"Before the establishment of the Clear Dynasty, before the Manchu rescued the Middle Kingdom from the corruption of the Bright Dynasty, you journeyed on one of the Treasure Fleet voyages to the far side of the world, traveling east to Khalifah, Mexica, and Fusang."

It was a statement, not a question, but Cao Wen paused momentarily, nevertheless, to give Ling Xuan the opportunity to reply.

"I was a young scholar then," Ling said, "not yet having passed my jinshi examinations and become a Presented Scholar. I traveled to the Northern Capital from my home in the south, to serve the Dragon Throne as best as I was able. My skills, apparently, were best served as chronicler aboard a Treasure Fleet dragon boat, and my skills with languages were likewise of some utility. The passage across the broad sea took long months, before landfall on the shores of Khalifah."

"I want to ask you about Mexica. The title of your account suggests that—"

"When I served the Shunzhi emperor, I once received a legation from Khalifah. But when the Shunzhi emperor went to take his place in the heavens, and the Kangxi emperor took the Dragon Throne, Han bureaucrats such as I quickly fell from favor. The Regent Aobai reversed as many of the policies of Shunzhi as he could, attempting to reassert Manchu domination, feeling that the emperor had permitted too many Han to enter positions of authority. There were insufficient numbers of qualified Manchu to replace all of the Han serving in the bureaucracy, so Aobai had to console himself by replacing all the Han already in post with candidates more easily swayed by his authority."

Cao sighed heavily. The old man rambled like a senile grandmother, but Cao had confirmed that he had indeed traveled among the Mexica, so he could well have the intelligence Cao needed to advance.

"To return to the subject of the Mexica—"

"I hated Aobai for years, you must understand." The old man shook his head sadly. "He had taken from me my life and my livelihood. When he found me too highly respected in the Office of Transmission to eliminate without scandal, he had me arraigned on trumped-up charges of treason and remanded to the custody of the Embroidered Guard. Consider the irony, then, that eight years later, after Kangxi had reached his majority, the young emperor enlisted the aid of his uncle Songgotu in order to break free from the control of his regents, and had Aobai himself arrested on charges of usurping his authority. Aobai joined me here as a guest of the Embroidered Guard, and died soon after."

This was all ancient history, done and buried long before Cao was born. He shifted on the bench, impatient, and tried once more to regain control of the flow of conversation.

"Ling Xuan," Cao began, allowing the tone of his voice to raise slightly, "I must ask you to attend to my questions. I am on the urgent business of his supreme majesty, the Son of Heaven, and do not have time to waste in idle rambling."

"But the affairs of men turn in their courses just like the tracks of the stars in the heavens above," the old man continued, as though he hadn't heard a word Cao had said. "I understand that in the nations of Europa they have a conception of destiny as a wheel, like that of a mill, upon which men ride up and down. Too often those who ride the wheel up fail to recall that they will someday be borne downward again. Thirty-four years after Songgotu helped his nephew Kangxi rid himself of the influence of the Regent Aobai, Kangxi had Songgotu himself jailed, in part for his complicity in the Heir Apparent's attempt to consolidate power. Songgotu joined us here, in the Outside Depot, for the briefest while, until Kangxi ordered him executed, without trial or confession."

Cao Wen remembered the scandal from his youth, hearing his father and uncles talking about the purge of Songgotu and his associates from the court.

"Ling Xuan—," Cao Wen began, but the old man went on before he could continue.

"The Heir Apparent himself, of course, is resident here now. Yinreng. We passed him in the courtyard, on our way into the interview chamber. A sad shell of a man he is, and perhaps not entirely sane. Of course, some say that the eldest prince Yinti employed Lamas to cast evil spells, the revelation of which resulted in Yinreng's earlier pardon and release from imprisonment, and reinstatement as heir and successor to Kangxi. But when he returned to his old ways on his release, the emperor finally had him removed from the line of succession, degraded in position, and placed here in perpetual confinement. Still, he seems harmless to me, and I believe that he may have developed some lasting affection for another of the men imprisoned here, but as his leanings were the nettle that originally set his father on the path of disowning him, I suppose that isn't to be unexpected."

Cao Wen raised his hand, attempting again to wrestle back control of the discussion, but the old man continued, unabated.

"There are those who say that some men lie with other men as a result of an accident of birth, while others say that it is a degradation that sets upon us as we grow, an illness and not a defect. But was the Heir Apparent fated to prefer the company of men to women in the bedchamber? Did the movement of the stars through the lunar mansions in the heavens dictate the life he would lead, up to and including his end here, imprisoned behind these high, cold walls? Or did choices he made, through his life, in some sympathetic fashion affect the course of the stars through the heavens? We know that man's destiny is linked with the heavens, but there remains the question of causation. Which is affected and which affects?"

"Ling Xuan, if you please . . . ," Cao said with a weary sigh. He found that he was almost willing to surrender in frustration, and simply complete his report with the information he already had to hand.

"During the Warring States period of antiquity, the philosopher Shih-shen tried to explain the nonuniform movement of the moon as the result of man's actions. He said that, when a wise prince occupies the throne, the Moon follows the right way, and that when the prince is not wise and the ministers exercise power, the Moon loses its way. But if we presume that the ancients knew more than we do in all such matters, where would that leave the spirit of invention? The ancients, as praiseworthy as they were, could not have constructed a marvel like the Forbidden City. Can we not, then, assume that in the generations since we have likewise constructed concepts that they also could not have attempted? I like to believe that the world grows as a person does, maturing with the slow turning of years, becoming ever more knowledgeable and developed. But many would hold that such thoughts are an affront to the luminous ancestors who preceded us, and whose lofty heights it is not given to us to reach. I suppose my thoughts were poisoned by the clerics of the Mexica. There, they believe that this is just the most recent of a series of worlds, and that each world increases in complexity and elegance."

Cao Wen leaned forward, cautiously optimistic. Was his patience about to be rewarded?

But before he went on, the old man leaned back, and breathed a ragged sigh. "But perhaps these are discussions for another day. I find that my voice tires, and my thoughts run away from me. Perhaps we should continue our discussion tomorrow."

The old man rose, and went to knock on the metal-clad door.

As Agent Gu opened the door, Cao rocketed up off the bench, raising his hand to object.

"Tomorrow, then," Ling said, glancing over his shoulder as he shuffled down the passageway to the courtyard beyond.

Agent Gu just shrugged, as Cao's mouth worked, soundless and furious.

Back at the Ministry of War, Cao Wen looked over the paperwork he'd amassed. Spread before him were the notes he himself had taken by hand, long months before, which had led him to Ling Xuan in the first place.

Cao had been through everything in the imperial archives on the subject of the Mexica, but much of the early contact with the Mexica had occurred during the Bright Dynasty, and many of the records from those days had been lost when the Clear Dynasty took control. Worse, much of what remains was fragmentary at best. Cao had spent endless days combing through the archives, hungry for any mention of the Mexica, when he finally stumbled upon a simple inventory list of the archives from the reign of the Chongzhen emperor, the last of the Bright Dynasty. Among dozens of bureaucratic documents, in which no one had taken any interest in long years, was listed one item that caught Cao's eye, and sped the pace of his heart—a Ling Xuan's account of a Treasure Fleet voyage to Mexica.

In the weeks that followed, Cao searched unsuccessfully for the account, checking other archives and inventories, but quite by chance came across a communication from the eunuch director of the Embroidered Guard to the Office of Transmission, intended for the eyes of the Regent Aobai, listing all of the suspects temporarily housed in the Eastern Depot. The report dated from the early days of the reign of the Kangxi emperor, while the emperor had still been a child and the regency controlled the empire, before the introduction of the palace memorial. Cao very nearly returned the communication to its cubbyhole without a second glance, and had he done so his researches would have been at an end. But instead he chanced to notice a name at the bottom of the communication, in among the hundreds of other names—Ling Xuan.

Cao had looked into the matter further, and found no burial record, nor record of any conviction, for a Ling Xuan. He had, however, discovered that Ling had once held a position of minor authority during the reign of the Shunzhi emperor.

Cao had petitioned the Deputy Minister of War for weeks to arrange the authorization to contact the Embroidered Guard in order to confirm that Ling Xuan was still imprisoned at the Eastern Depot, and once confirmation was received Cao labored another span of weeks to receive authorization to cross the concourse and interview the prisoner himself.

At the time, Cao Wen had considered it an almost unbelievable stroke of good fortune that he should chance to discover that the author of the missing account, so crucial to his survey of the Mexica, still lived. Now, having met and spent time with the old man, he was beginning to rethink that position.

Cao Wen stood over Ling Xuan, who sat in the middle of the courtyard.

"Why do you not move from that position, Ling Xuan?"

"But I am always moving, though I do not unfold my legs from beneath me." The old man looked up at Cao with shaded eyes, and smiled. "I move because the Earth moves, and with it I go. As Lo-hsia-Hung of the Western Han Dynasty said, 'The Earth moves constantly but people do not know it. They are as persons in a closed boat, and when it proceeds they do not perceive it.'"

"You speak a great deal of astronomy, and yet the records indicate that you served in the Office of Transmission. But the study of the heavens is forbidden to all but the imperial astronomers."

"When I was first brought to the Eastern Depot," Ling explained, a distant look in his eyes, "I was interred for some time in the Bureau of Suppression and Soothing. The days were long and full of pain, but the nights were largely my own. In my narrow, dank cell, I sat the long watches of the night, unable to see a patch of clear sky. However, there was a small hole cut high in the wall, for ventilation, and I learned that it opened into the adjacent cell. In that cell was a dismissed minister, previously the head of the Directory of Astronomy. His name was Cui, high mountain. He had offended the Regent Aobai in the days after the death of the Shanzhi emperor."

Ling drew a ragged sigh, and averted his eyes before continuing.

"We helped each other survive through those weeks and months. I told the astronomer tales of my travels across the oceans, and he told me everything he had ever learned about the heavens."

Ling stood up on creaking joints, and faced Cao.

"One night, the cell next to mine was silent, and the night after that, another voice answered when I called through the vent. I never learned what became of my friend, but I remember every word he ever spoke to me."

With that, the old man turned and started toward the interview chamber, where Agent Gu stood by the open door.

"Come along," Ling called back over his shoulder to Cao, who lingered in the sunny yard. "You wanted to discuss the Mexica, did you not?"

Cao sat at the worn table, and pulled a leather tube from the folds of his robe. Removing a cap from the tubes end, he pulled out a rolled sheaf of paper and, setting the tube to one side, arranged the papers before him, meticulously. Ling Xuan looked on, dispassionately.

Finally, his notes arranged to his satisfaction, and with an inked brush in hand, Cao began to speak impatiently. "I have already spent the better part of a year in my survey of the Mexica, Ling Xuan, and I would very much like to complete my report before another year begins."

"But which year, yes?" Ling asked, raising an eyebrow. "We in the Middle Kingdom know two. The twenty-four solar nodes of the farmer's calendar, and the twelve or thirteen lunar months of the lunisolar calendar. The Mexica had more than one calendar, too."

Cao sighed. He had little interest in a repeat of the previous days' performance, and yet here he was, about to assay the same role. "Ling Xuan—"

"The Mexica have a solar calendar, which like our own was made up of three hundred and sixty-five days," the old man interrupted before Cao could continued. "Can you imagine it? Two cultures, so different and divided by history and geography, and yet we parcel out time in the same allotments. But unlike us, the Mexica divide their solar year into eighteen months of twenty days each, leaving aside five more, which they call 'empty days.' These are days of ill omen, when no work or ritual is to be performed."

"That's very interesting," Cao said in a rush, "but to return to the subject at hand—"

"But like us, they are not satisfied with only one calendrical system," Ling continued, undaunted. "In addition to their solar year, they have a second calendar of two hundred and sixty days, marked out by interlocking cycles of twenty-day signs and thirteen numbers. Again, reminiscent of our own system of element and animal, wouldn't you say?"

"I suppose so," Cao agreed weakly.

"But the Mexica have another calendar, on a scale even grander than the other two. In the capital city of the Mexica, Place of the Stone Cactus, there is a massive circular stone, thicker than a child is tall and wider than the height of two men. This is a calendar too, of a sort, but while the other calendars measure the passage of days, months, and years, this massive calendar of stone is used to measure the passage of worlds themselves. As I told you, the Mexica believe that this is the fifth and most recent world created by the gods. They believe that this world was constructed only a few hundred years ago, in the year 13-Reed, and that its peoples and cultures were put in place, fully formed and with their histories already in place, as a test of the Mexica's faith."

"You traveled to the capital of the Mexica?" Cao asked, sitting forward, readying his brush over a blank sheet of paper.

"Yes," the old man answered, a faraway look in his eyes, "a party of us, along with the commander of the Treasure Fleet, traveled overland for long days and weeks before we reached the heart of the Mexica empire. Their city of Place of the Stone Cactus was as large and grand as the Northern Capital itself, hundreds of thousands of men and women toiling away in the service of their emperor."

Ling Xuan's eyes fluttered close for a brief moment, and he swayed, momentarily lost in thought.

"The Mexica know when this world will end," he went on. "It will come in the year of 4-Movement, when the world's calendar has run its course. But which cycle, yes? In Place of the Stone Cactus, I saw steam-powered automatons of riveted bronze, which symbolically represented the jaguars, hurricanes, fires, and rains that destroyed the previous worlds."

Cao Wen's brush raced down the page in precise movements, as he took careful notes. "Steam-powered, you say?"

Ling Xuan nodded. "Yes, and while the Mexica had never before seen a horse, they had steam-powered trolleys that could carry them back and forth across the breadth of their broad valley in a twinkling."

"What of their military capacity?" Cao asked eagerly. "Were you given any glimpse of their level of armament?"

Ling Xuan blinked slowly. "I did, in fact, spent considerable time with an officer of their army, an Eagle Knight of the first rank. I was one of the few to have learned the rudiments of Nahuatl, the Mexica's tongue, and as such I was appointed to tour their city and report back what I'd learned, and Hummingbird Feather was to be my guide."

Ling Xuan's dropped his gaze, and his eyes came to rest on the leather tube at the edge of the table, in which Cao Wen had brought his notes.

"This reminds me of something," the old man said, pointing at the tube.

"Something to do with the Mexica?"

The old man nodded slowly, his eyes not leaving the tube. Then he shook his head once, leaving Cao unsure whether the old man had meant to reply in the affirmative, in the negative, or if in fact he'd replied at all.

"I remember something my friend Cui told me. A metal tube capped on either end by ground glass lenses, used for far viewing. A Remote-Viewing Mirror, he called it. A tool employed by the Directorate of Astronomy. Have you heard of such a thing?"

Cao nodded impatiently. "Yes, I believe I've seen them in operation. What of it?"

"I would very much like to see such a device for myself. My eyes are not as strong as they once were, and it would be a welcome sight to see the shapes upon the moon's surface. If you could arrange such a thing, I would be happy to tell you all I saw of the Mexica's armament and defenses."

Then the old man rose, rapped on the door, and disappeared from view, leaving Cao in the room with his notes, his brush, and his questions.

It took Cao Wen several days to receive authorization from the Deputy Minister of War to requisition the far-seeing device from the Directorate of Astronomy, several more days to locate the bureaucrat within the directorate who was responsible for materiel and equipment, and an additional week of wheedling and cajoling to get the astronomer to recognize the authority of the Deputy Minister's order.

Cao tried on several occasions in the interval to renew his interview with Ling Xuan, but every attempt failed. Each time, the old man would look up at him, blink slowly, and ask whether Cao carried the far-seeing device. When he saw that Cao did not, Ling would turn his eyes back to the ground, watching the shadows in their slow course across the ground.

Finally, Cao managed to retrieve the device from the Directorate of Astronomy, and a short while later sat in the interview room, carefully removing the device from its protective sheath. He presented the object to Ling Xuan with Agent Gu standing by as witness.

While Ling turned the device over in his hands, eyes glistening and mouth open in wonder, Cao read aloud from an official release document, signed with the chop of the Head Director of Astronomy, and countersigned by the Deputy Minister of War. "This far-viewing device, the Remote-Viewing Mirror, remains the property of the Directorate of Astronomy, as decreed by his majesty the emperor, but by special order of the Deputy Minister of War, it is being loaned for a short time to one Ling Xuan, a temporary resident at the Outside Depot of the Embroidered Guard. Be it known that this Ling Xuan is not to allow the Remote-Viewing Mirror to pass into any hands other than his own, nor is he to reveal the details of its manufacture to any but those parties determined by imperial decree as worthy to hold such knowledge."

Cao paused, and glanced up from the document at the old man, whose eyes were fixed on the device in his hands.

"Ling Xuan, do you understand these terms?"

The old man simply held the device up for a closer inspection, marveling.

"Temporary Resident Ling," Agent Gu said, his tone martial, stepping forward incrementally and looming over the old man as menacingly as he was able. "Do you understand the terms as recited to you?"

Ling Xuan nodded absently. "Yes, yes, of course."

"Thank you for bearing witness, Agent Gu." Cao nodded to Gu, and motioned him toward the door. "Now, with your permission, I would like at this point to continue my interview with Ling Xuan."

Agent Gu bowed, crossed the floor, and closed the door behind him as he left.

"Now," Cao said to the old man, his tone turning dark, "let us talk about the Mexica."

Ling Xuan held the Remote-Viewing Mirror lovingly and, without lifting his eyes from the device, began to speak.

"Hummingbird Feather, who I like to think became my friend in the weeks we stayed in Place of the Stone Cactus, explained to me the structure of the army of the Mexica. He was an Eagle Knight, and a Quauhyahcatl, or a Great Captain of the Mexica army, meaning that he had taken five foreign captives in combat. When the Treasure Fleet arrived, though, the Mexica had not gone to war against their neighbors in almost a generation. And so they fought, instead, the War of the Flowers.

"The army of the Mexica is organized into banners of twenty men each—and here, too, we hear echoes of our own culture, do we not? So like the banners of our Manchu masters, yes? In any case, twenty of such banners make up a battalion of four hundred men, and twenty of these an army of eight thousand. The best warriors were inducted into the orders of the Jaguar and the Eagle, and advancement was measured by how many captives one took while in battle. In times of peace, though, there were no captives to be had, and how then to measure one's worth.

"The Mexica challenge their neighbors to fight in a War of the Flowers. We were lucky enough to arrive in Place of the Stone Cactus during one of these ceremonial tournaments. The armies of the Mexica and those of their neighbors gather in the broad plains beyond the valley of the Stone Cactus, and meet in mock combat. Though the blows are not killing blows, and no blood is spilled on the plains, the stakes are no less high than in warfare. The combatants in the War of the Flowers take prisoners, capturing their defeated foes, and when each side decides that it has taken enough prisoners, the battle is ended. The side which has captured the most of its enemy is declared the winner, and the two armies return home with their spoils. The captives are executed or enslaved, depending on the moods of their captors.

"In this way, the army of the Mexica are able to keep their martial skills honed and ready, even when there is no enemy to be bested."

Cao scarcely looked up from his notes, his brush flying across the page.

"Yes, yes," Cao said eagerly. "Now, how do the generals of the armies communicate their orders to the officers of the banners, and how do the banners' leaders communicate the orders on to their subordinates?"

Days passed, and Cao Wen returned again and again to the Outside Depot, filling page after page with notes on the Mexica, dictated by the old man.

He'd originally hoped for one or two choice facts with which to spice his survey, and after long frustrated weeks, wrangling the incommunicative prisoner, he'd begun to doubt that he'd get even that much. Now, though, it seemed that floodgates had opened, and the old man was providing more detailed information than Cao had dreamed possible. Now, the thought of advancement within the ministry as reward for all his efforts, which he'd originally held as a slender hope, seemed a very achievable goal.

This morning, the old man was waiting for him in the interview room, the Remote-Viewing Mirror in his lap.

"I think we near the end of our cycle of interviews, Ling Xuan," Cao said, not bothering with pleasantries. He slid onto the bench across the table from the old man, and arranged his papers and brushes before him. "I need just one final bit of information, and my report will be complete. I'm not sure just what it is, yet, but I believe that you must have it within you. I want to hear more about the automation of the Mexica. From what you describe, it sounds as though their technological development has taken a different path than our own, but that they seem not far behind us."

Ling looked up, smiling.

"I was able to spend long hours last night, watching the skies through this remarkable device. Agent Gu was kind enough to allow me to remain in the courtyard all hours, and so I had a much fuller view of the heavens than I am allowed from my small window." The old man lifted the Remote-Viewing Mirror to his right eye and, squeezing his left eye shut, peered through the device at Cao, sitting across from him. Then he laughed, a soft, strong noise like distant peals of thunder, and continued. "I have been following the path of Fire Star across the heavens. In the last few months, it has risen in the early hours of the morning, rising earlier and earlier every day, tracking steadily eastward across the sky. Just a few weeks ago, it rose shortly after sunset, and the most remarkable thing occurred. Cui had told me about it, but until this occasion I had never had the opportunity to see it for myself. Fire Star seemed to stop in the heavens, and then turned back, now moving westward across the skies. Now it rises at sunset, tracks westward across the sky, and sets by dawn. In another few weeks, if what Cui told me holds true, it will reverse course again, moving once more eastward across the sky, rising earlier and earlier until it once again rises at dawn and sets at dusk."

"Fascinating," Cao said without feeling. "Now, to return to the Mexica—"

"There are shapes, shadows, and lines upon the surface of Fire Star I have found. This most ingenious device allows me to see them with my own eye."

"The automatons of the Mexica, Ling Xuan," Cao repeated. "Now, you say that they are little more than parlor tricks, fixed in place and able to go through only route motions. But did the Mexica display the capacity to develop these trinkets into something more? A siege engine of sorts, perhaps?"

"Cui told me that the best astronomers of his time felt that these wandering stars were worlds such as our own. Tell me, do you suppose if that is so, it might not be peopled with beings such as ourselves?"

"Ling Xuan . . ." Cao began, rubbing the bridge of his nose, his tone menacing.

The old man, his eyes half-lidded, sways on his bench, like a tall tree blown by a high wind. "I'm tired, Cao Wen. Too many late nights and early mornings, too little sleep. Let us continue tomorrow, yes? I am sure I will be in better spirits then, and better able to hear your questions."

Ling stood, and knocked on the door.

"But . . ." Cao began, and then trailed off as the old man exited after Agent Gu swung open the door. Cao sighed dramatically, and shrugged. He had waited this long. What harm could another day do? But if by the end of the next day he did not have the answers he needed?

Cao felt his patience was at an end. He gathered up his papers, and to the empty room he said, "Tomorrow, then."

The next day found Cao Wen and Ling Xuan back in their accustomed places.

Ling seemed more lucid and animated today, and didn't wait for Cao to initiate their discussion before returning to their perennial topic of conversation. "All of this talk of the Mexica has reminded me of something I've long since forgotten. A salient fact about the culture of the Mexica that I did not realize until years after my visit to their empire."

"What is it?" Cao asked warily.

"It is one final fact that you must have for your survey. It is something about the culture of the Mexica that I have realized only later in life, which is the reason that the Dragon Throne will prevail, if it should go to war against them. But in exchange for this final bit of information, Ling Xuan requests one last favor."

Cao glanced at the Remote-Viewing Mirror, clutched as always in the old man's gnarled hands. What would the old man want this time?

"I would go, just once more, beyond the walls of the Eastern Depot. From my vantage point within the Outside Depot, there is only so much of the night sky I can see, and there is so, so much more to behold."

Cao straightened, and folded his arms across his chest. "Absolutely not," he said sharply. "Out of the question." Cao rubbed the bridge of his nose, and tried to compose an appropriate counteroffer. "No. Instead, if you don't tell me what I want to know, you will be punished. Yes, and I will have the Remote-Viewing Mirror taken from you."

Ling shrugged, unmoved. "I have seen the heavens with my own eyes, from within my little box. If you take away my vision, I will still have my memories, but if I am unable to venture beyond these walls, my memories will be all I have, anyway. What have I to lose?"

Cao jumped to his feet, and began furiously to pace the floor.

"This is unseemly, Ling Xuan. This is unacceptable."

"And yet it is happening," Ling said, his expression serene.

Cao Wen stormed to the door, and pounded loudly with the heel of his fist.

Gu opened the door, his expression curious.

"Agent Gu, remove this prisoner from my sight immediately!" Cao Wen said imperiously."

Gu looked from Cao to Ling and back, shrugged, and took the old man by the elbow, leading him slowly from the chamber. "This way, old man."

Cao collapsed back onto his seat, glowering.

Cao Wen sat on the hard, unforgiving bench, waiting while bureaucrats shuffled back and forth across the polished floors of the Ministry of War, about the business of the empire.

Cao didn't have to test the old man's resolve. He knew that Ling meant what he said. If Ling said he wouldn't answer any further questions without receiving his boon, he wouldn't speak another word. Not another useful word, at least.

"Deputy Minister Wu will see you now, Cao Wen," said a steward, appearing at the open door.

Cao swallowed hard, rose to his feet, and crossed the floor.

"O Honorable Deputy Minister," Cao said, bowing low.

The imposing figure of the Deputy Minister Wu was crowded into a spare, simply made chair on the far side of the room. There was a low table at his side, covered with rolled maps, bound sheaves of paper, and small notebooks. At his elbow stood his secretary, a weasel-faced man with ink-stained fingers who recorded everything said in the room in exhaustive detail.

"Cao Wen," the Deputy Minister said, a faint smile on his thick lips. "I harbor hopes that you come to deliver your survey of the Mexica."

"Not quite yet, this one is afraid to report," Cao Wen answered, his voice tremulous.

"Why am I not surprised?"

"My interrogation of the prisoner Ling Xuan these last weeks has been exceedingly productive," Cao continued. "I believe that, with one final addition, it will be complete and ready to present to the Minister of War."

"And then on to the Dragon Throne itself?" Wu asked, eyes narrowed.

Cao Wen swelled with pride, but his voice wavered nervously when he answered. "Yes, Deputy Minister. I believe it will not only summarize the strengths and weaknesses of the Mexica military, but the survey should further provide a sound justification for why the Middle Kingdom will inevitably defeat the Mexica militarily, should it come to open warfare."

"And what is this last addition, one wonders, and what is it that the Ministry of War will be asked to authorize in its pursuit?"

With as little detail and as briefly as possible, Cao explained that the old man who was his primary source for the report had requested one night beyond the walls of the Eastern Depot, in exchange for his final testimony.

"For what purpose?" Wu asked, when Cao had completed his summation. "Some conjugal business, perhaps? A fine meal, or an evening of drunken revelry?"

"No," Cao said simply. "Stargazing."

Wu looked at Cao, disbelieving. "And in return for this small privilege, we will get the secret to defeating the Mexica?"

"Yes," Cao said.

The Deputy Minister steepled his fingers, and pursed his thick lips.

"Having paid quite a lot to get this far along in the game, Cao Wen, it seems a shame to withdraw when there is just one final wager to make. You will have your authorization. But return with this storied survey in hand, or don't bother returning at all."

Cao bowed deeply, and scuttled away.

Three days later, approaching the middle watches of the night, Cao Wen arrived at the Eastern Depot, where he was met by Director Fei Ren.

"I am not happy with this development," Director Fei said, as though his expression was not explanation enough, "but the Deputy Minister of War has managed to get the approval of the emperor himself for this little excursion, so there isn't anything I can do about it."

Before Cao could reply, Agent Gu arrived, escorting Ling Xuan.

"Temporary Resident Ling Xuan," Director Fei said, turning to the old man. "Know that a great many bureaucrats have been put to a great deal of trouble on his behalf."

The old man just smiled, clutching the Remote-Viewing Mirror to his chest.

"You have until sunrise, old man," Director Fei said, and then turned his attentions to Agent Gu. "This is your first mission beyond the walls of the Eastern Depot, is it not, Gu?"

Agent Gu bowed, and stammered a reply in the affirmative.

"Such was my recollection." Fei looked from the old man to Gu, and scowled. "If Ling Xuan attempts to escape, know that you are free to take whatever means are necessary to ensure that our *temporary* resident returns home to the Eastern Depot."

"Yes, sir, Director," Agent Gu said, punctuated by a further bow.

With that, Director Fei turned on his heel, and disappeared back into the labyrinth of the Eastern Depot.

"Let's get on with it," Cao said impatiently.

With Cao on one side, and Agent Gu on the other, Ling Xuan passed through the archway and into the concourse beyond, walking out of the Eastern Depot for the first time in more than fifty years.

They threaded through the boulevards and avenues of the Northern Capital, lined on all sides with the offices of the six ministries and countless imperial directorates and bureaus. They came at last to a public square, far from the palace, surrounded by low buildings, inns, and residences of the meaner sort. Lamplights glowed warmly from within them, but the sky overhead was dark and moonless, the stars glittering like gems against black silk.

Ling Xuan paused, and took a deep breath through his nostrils, looking up at the skies with his naked eye. "I have been imprisoned behind four walls for more than half of my life, but I have come to realize that my mind has been imprisoned even longer. The noble truths that Cui taught me through that little vent, while we were guests of the Bureau of Suppression and Soothing, were far grander and broader than anything I'd previously imagined. I have seen more of the world than many, read more than most, and yet even I had only the most tenuous grasp of reality."

Above them, the stars in the heavens seem to turn while they watched, and Cao found himself becoming dizzy, vertiginous.

"Do you know why my friend Cui was imprisoned in the Bureau of Suppression and Soothing?" the old man continued, glancing momentarily down from the stars to the two men at this side. "It was widely reported, so he said, that it was because he had provided readings of the heavens that were inauspicious for the regent's reign. In fact, that was not his crime. Cui challenged the accepted wisdom. He devoted his life to studying the heavens, and made a frightening discovery. Our world is not, as we have always believed, the center of the universe, with the sun, moon, and stars twirling around us. Through a careful study of the heavens, Cui came to realize that, in fact, our world was just one of many, all of which circled around the sun. What is more, he claimed that the stars themselves might be other suns, out in the distant heavens. Perhaps a small fraction of those other suns might have worlds of their own, and some small fraction of those might be peopled. We might not be the only beings in creation able to look upon ourselves and wonder." The old man paused, and smiled ruefully. "Of course, this offended the Regent Aobai, who was convinced Cui had concocted his theory only to insult the young Kangxi emperor."

Agent Gu shook his head in disbelief, when the old man fell silent. "The earth circle around the sun? You might as well say that the Dragon Throne exists to serve me, and not the other way around."

"You might indeed." Ling smiled, his eyes twinkling.

Cao swayed on his feet. He felt unsteady, as though he stood on the edge of a precipice, about to fall into the abyss.

"Ling Xuan, you promised me one final fact about the Mexica," Cao said uneasily.

"So I did," Ling said, nodding. "So I did. And I will tell you. It is this."

The old man leaned closer to Cao, and spoke softly, like thunder more distant than ever before, as though he were communicating some secret in confidence that he didn't want the stars above to overhear.

"The Mexica, as clever and bright and ferocious as they may be, are still blinded by their faith. The most learned among them honestly believes that the world is but a few hundred years old, and all evidence to the contrary is merely a test of their faith. We of the Middle Kingdom, I would argue, cling with as much tenacity to beliefs and superstitions no more grounded in reality than that, but with one notable difference. Ours is a culture that can produce a mind like Cui's, a mind that challenges received wisdom, which questions the foundations of knowledge itself. If we manage to produce only one like him in every dozen generations, we will still manage, in the fullness of time, to conquer the universe. Like the fraction of worlds or the fraction of stars in the great immensity of the heavens, which ensure that we are not alone, just one small spark of genius in the vast sea of complacency will mean that history does not stand still."

Ling Xuan turned, and headed back the way they had come.

"I am ready to return home to my cell now, thank you," the old man said, calling back to Cao and Gu over his shoulder. "I have seen all I needed to see."

The next morning, as Cao Wen struggled to work out how to conclude his report, he received a visitor to his cubicle in the Ministry of War. It was Agent Gu, dressed in simple gray robes.

"Gu? What are you doing here?"

"At the request of Director Fei, I come to tell you that Ling Xuan, temporary resident of the Outside Depot, died in the night. From all signs, it was not a suicide, nor is there any indication of foul play."

Cao blinked, a confused expression spread across his face.

"The old man died?"

"Yes," Gu replied. "Of extreme old age, or so I am given to understand."

"And yet he waited long enough to walk once more under the stars as a free man," Cao observed.

"Perhaps he felt that it was important enough to live for," Gu said, unsure, "and having done so, his work was done."

Cao sighed, and shrugged his shoulders.

"Strange timing, no doubt, but he was old, and the elderly have a habit of dying." Cao regarded Gu's plain gray robes. "But here you are, beyond the walls of the Eastern Depot yourself, and so adorned that you could pass for a simple merchant in the streets."

"Yes," Agent Gu said with a smile that commingled embarrassment and pride. "It is the opinion of Director Fei that I have completed my training, and will be of better use to the Dragon Throne beyond the walls, rather than within." Gu paused, and shifted uncomfortably. "Cao Wen, I must ask you. What are your thoughts about the things that Ling Xuan said to us in the night, about the sun and the earth and the stars, about the Middle Kingdom and the Mexica and all?"

Cao Wen shrugged. "All I can say is that everything Ling reported to me these long weeks has been true, as far as I have been able to determine, the intelligence on the Mexica and the facts the old man learned from astronomer Cui alike. But who am I to judge?"

Agent Gu nodded absently, and with a final bow departed, leaving Cao with his work.

There remained only a few more characters to brush onto the final page, and then Cao's detailed report on the astronomer Cui was complete. This appended to his report about the Mexica, Cao rolled up the papers, and slid them into a leather tube. Then he rose to his feet, arranged his robes around him, and headed toward the office of the Deputy Minister to hand in his survey.

glory

GREG EGAN

Looking back at the century that's just ended, it's obvious that Australian writer Greg Egan was one of the Big New Names to emerge in SF in the nineties, and is probably one of the most significant talents to enter the field in the last several decades. Already one of the most widely known of all Australian genre writers, Egan may well be the best new "hard science" writer to enter the field since Greg Bear, and is still growing in range, power, and sophistication. In the last few years, he has become a frequent contributor to *Interzone* and *Asimov's Science Fiction*, and has made sales as well as to *Pulphouse*, *Analog*, *Aurealis*, *Eidolon*, and elsewhere; many of his stories have also appeared in various "Best of the Year" series, and he was on the Hugo Final Ballot in 1995 for his story "Cocoon," which won the Ditmar Award and the *Asimov's* Readers Award. He won the Hugo Award in 1999 for his novella "Oceanic." His first novel, *Quarantine*, appeared in 1992; his second novel, *Permutation City*, won the John W. Campbell Memorial Award in 1994. His other books include the novels, *Distress*, *Diaspora*, and *Teranesia*, and three collections of his short fiction, *Axiomatic*, *Luminous*, and *Our Lady of Chernobyl*. His most recent book is the novel *Schild's Ladder*.

Egan fell silent for a couple of years at the beginning of the Oughts, but is back again with a vengeance, with stories in markets such as *Asimov's*, *Interzone*, *The New Space Opera*, *One Million A.D.*, MIT Technology Review, and *Foundation 100*. Coming up is a new novel, *Incandescence*, and a new collection, *Dark Integers and Other Stories*. He has a Web site at www.netspace.netau/^gregegan/.

Egan has pictured galaxy-spanning civilizations in stories such as "Border Guards" and "Riding the Crocodile." Here he sweeps us along with scientists who are willing to go to enormous lengths (including changing their species!) and travel across the galaxy in order to investigate a scientific mystery—one that inimical forces don't want them to solve.

1

An ingot of metallic hydrogen gleamed in the starlight, a narrow cylinder half a meter long with a mass of about a kilogram. To the naked eye, it was a dense, solid object, but its lattice of tiny nuclei immersed in an insubstantial fog of electrons was one part matter to two hundred trillion parts empty space. A short distance away was a second ingot, apparently identical to the first, but composed of antihydrogen.

A sequence of finely tuned gamma rays flooded into both cylinders. The protons that absorbed them in the first ingot spat out positrons and were transformed into neutrons, breaking their bonds to the electron cloud that glued them in place. In the second ingot, antiprotons became antineutrons.

A further sequence of pulses herded the neutrons together and forged them into clusters; the antineutrons were similarly rearranged. Both kinds of cluster were unstable, but in order to fall apart, they first had to pass through a quantum state that would have strongly absorbed a component of the gamma rays constantly raining down on them. Left to themselves, the probability of them being in this state would have increased rapidly, but each time they measurably failed to absorb the gamma rays, the probability fell back to zero. The quantum Zeno effect endlessly reset the clock, holding the decay in check.

The next series of pulses began shifting the clusters into the space that had separated the original ingots. First neutrons, then antineutrons, were sculpted together in alternating layers. Though the clusters were ultimately unstable, while they persisted they were inert, sequestering their constituents and preventing them from annihilating their counterparts. The end point of this process of nuclear sculpting was a sliver of compressed matter and antimatter, sandwiched together into a needle one micron wide.

The gamma ray lasers shut down, the Zeno effect withdrew its prohibitions. For the time it took a beam of light to cross a neutron, the needle sat motionless in space. Then it began to burn, and it began to move.

The needle was structured like a meticulously crafted firework, and its outer layers ignited first. No external casing could have channeled this blast, but the pattern of tensions woven into the needle's construction favored one direction for the debris to be expelled. Particles streamed backward; the needle moved forward. The shock of acceleration could not have been borne by anything built from atomic-scale matter, but the pressure bearing down on the core of the needle prolonged its life, delaying the inevitable.

Layer after layer burned itself away, blasting the dwindling remnant forward ever faster. By the time the needle had shrunk to a tenth of its original size, it was moving at 98 percent of light speed; to a bystander, this could scarcely have been improved upon, but from the needle's perspective, there was still room to slash its journey's duration by orders of magnitude.

When just one thousandth of the needle remained, its time, compared to the neighboring stars, was passing five hundred times more slowly. Still the layers kept burning, the protective clusters unraveling as the pressure on them was released. The needle could only reach close enough to light speed to slow down time as much as it required if it could sacrifice a large enough proportion of its remaining mass. The core of the needle could only survive for a few trillionths of a second, while its journey would take two hundred million seconds as judged by the stars. The proportions had been carefully matched, though: out of the two kilograms of matter and antimatter that had been woven together at the launch, only a few million neutrons were needed as the final payload.

By one measure, seven years passed. For the needle, its last trillionths of a second unwound, its final layers of fuel blew away, and at the moment its core was ready to explode, it reached its destination, plunging from the near-vacuum of space straight into the heart of a star.

Even here, the density of matter was insufficient to stabilize the core, yet far too high to allow it to pass unhindered. The core was torn apart. But it did not go quietly, and the shock waves it carved through the fusing plasma endured for a million kilometers: all the way through to the cooler outer layers on the opposite side of the star. These shock waves were shaped by the payload that had formed them, and though the initial pattern imprinted on them by the disintegrating cluster of neutrons was enlarged and blurred by its journey, on an atomic scale it remained sharply defined. Like a mold stamped into the seething plasma, it encouraged ionized molecular fragments to slip into the troughs and furrows that matched their shape, and then brought them together to react in ways that the plasma's random collisions would never have allowed. In effect, the shock waves formed a web of catalysts, carefully laid out in both time and space, briefly transforming a small corner of the star into a chemical factory operating on a nanometer scale.

The products of this factory sprayed out of the star, riding the last traces of the shock wave's momentum: a few nanograms of elaborate, carbon-rich molecules, sheathed in a protective fullerene weave. Traveling at seven hundred kilometers per second, a fraction below the velocity needed to escape from the star completely, they climbed out of its gravity well, slowing as they ascended.

Four years passed, but the molecules were stable against the ravages of space. By the time they'd traveled a billion kilometers, they had almost come to a halt, and they would have fallen back to die in the fires of the star that had forged them if their journey had not been timed so that the star's third planet, a gas giant, was waiting to urge them forward. As they fell toward it, the giant's third moon moved across their path. Eleven years after the needle's launch, its molecular offspring rained down on to the methane snow.

The tiny heat of their impact was not enough to damage them, but it melted a microscopic puddle in the snow. Surrounded by food, the molecular seeds began to grow. Within hours, the area was teeming with nanomachines, some mining the snow and the minerals beneath it, others assembling the bounty into an intricate structure, a rectangular panel a couple of meters wide.

From across the light-years, an elaborate sequence of gamma ray pulses fell upon the panel. These pulses were the needle's true payload, the passengers for whom it had merely prepared the way, transmitted in its wake four years after its launch. The panel decoded and stored the data, and the army of nanomachines set to work again, this time following a far more elaborate blueprint. The miners were forced to look farther afield to find all the elements that were needed, while the assemblers labored to reach their goal through a sequence of intermediate stages, carefully designed to protect the final product from the vagaries of the local chemistry and climate.

After three months' work, two small fusion-powered spacecraft sat in the snow. Each one held a single occupant, waking for the first time in their freshly minted bodies, yet endowed with memories of an earlier life.

Joan switched on her communications console. Anne appeared on the screen, three short pairs of arms folded across her thorax in a posture of calm repose. They had both worn virtual bodies with the same anatomy before, but this was the first time they had become Noudah in the flesh.

"We're here. Everything worked," Joan marveled. The language she spoke was not her own, but the structure of her new brain and body made it second nature.

Anne said, "Now comes the hard part."

"Yes." Joan looked out from the spacecraft's cockpit. In the distance, a fissured blue-gray plateau of water ice rose above the snow. Nearby, the nanomachines were busy disassembling the gamma ray receiver. When they had erased all traces of their handiwork, they would wander off into the snow and catalyze their own destruction.

Joan had visited dozens of planet-bound cultures in the past, taking on different bodies and languages as necessary, but those cultures had all been plugged in to the Amalgam, the metacivilization that spanned the galactic disk. However far from home she'd been, the means to return to familiar places had always been close at hand. The Noudah had only just mastered interplanetary flight, and they had no idea that the Amalgam existed. The closest node in the Amalgam's network was seven light-years away, and even that was out of bounds to her and Anne now: they had agreed not to risk disclosing its location to the Noudah, so any transmission they sent could only be directed to a decoy node that they'd set up more than twenty light-years away.

"It will be worth it," Joan said.

Anne's Noudah face was immobile, but chromatophores sent a wave of violet and gold sweeping across her skin in an expression of cautious optimism. "We'll see." She tipped her head to the left, a gesture preceding a friendly departure.

Joan tipped her own head in response, as if she'd been doing so all her life. "Be careful, my friend," she said.

"You too."

Anne's ship ascended so high on its chemical thrusters that it shrank to a speck before igniting its fusion engine and streaking away in a blaze of light. Joan felt a pang of loneliness; there was no predicting when they would be reunited.

Her ship's software was primitive; the whole machine had been scrupulously matched to the Noudah's level of technology. Joan knew how to fly it herself if necessary, and on a whim she switched off the autopilot and manually activated the ascent thrusters. The control panel was crowded, but having six hands helped.

2

The world the Noudah called home was the closest of the system's five planets to their sun. The average temperature was one hundred and twenty degrees Celsius, but the high atmospheric pressure allowed liquid water to exist across the entire surface. The chemistry and dynamics of the planet's crust had led to a relatively flat terrain, with a patchwork of dozens of disconnected seas but no globe-spanning ocean. From space, these seas appeared as silvery mirrors, bordered by a violet and brown tarnish of vegetation.

The Noudah were already leaving their most electromagnetically promiscuous phase of communications behind, but the short-lived oasis of Amalgam-level technology on Baneth, the gas giant's moon, had had no trouble eavesdropping on their chatter and preparing an updated cultural briefing that had been spliced into Joan's brain.

The planet was still divided into the same eleven political units as it had been fourteen years before, the time of the last broadcasts that had reached the node before Joan's departure. Tira and Ghahar, the two dominant nations in terms of territory, economic activity, and military power, also occupied the vast majority of significant Niah archaeological sites.

Joan had expected that they'd be noticed as soon as they left Baneth—

the exhaust from their fusion engines glowed like the sun—but their departure had triggered no obvious response, and now that they were coasting they'd be far harder to spot. As Anne drew closer to the home world, she sent a message to Tira's traffic control center. Joan tuned in to the exchange.

"I come in peace from another star," Anne said. "I seek permission to land."

There was a delay of several seconds more than the light-speed lag, then a terse response. "Please identify yourself and state your location."

Anne transmitted her coordinates and flight plan.

"We confirm your location, please identify yourself."

"My name is Anne. I come from another star."

There was a long pause, then a different voice answered. "If you are from Ghahar, please explain your intentions."

"I am not from Ghahar."

"Why should I believe that? Show yourself."

"I've taken the same shape as your people, in the hope of living among you for a while." Anne opened a video channel and showed them her unremarkable Noudah face. "But there's a signal being transmitted from these coordinates that might persuade you that I'm telling the truth." She gave the location of the decoy node, twenty light-years away, and specified a frequency. The signal coming from the node contained an image of the very same face.

This time, the silence stretched out for several minutes. It would take a while for the Tirans to confirm the true distance of the radio source.

"You do not have permission to land. Please enter this orbit, and we will rendezvous and board your ship."

Parameters for the orbit came through on the data channel. Anne said, "As you wish."

Minutes later, Joan's instruments picked up three fusion ships being launched from Tiran bases. When Anne reached the prescribed orbit, Joan listened anxiously to the instructions the Tirans issued. Their tone sounded wary, but they were entitled to treat this stranger with caution, all the more so if they believed Anne's claim.

Joan was accustomed to a very different kind of reception, but then the members of the Amalgam had spent hundreds of millennia establishing a framework of trust. They also benefited from a milieu in which most kinds of force had been rendered ineffectual; when everyone had backups of themselves scattered around the galaxy, it required a vastly disproportionate effort to inconvenience someone, let alone kill them. By any reasonable measure, honesty and cooperation yielded far richer rewards than subterfuge and slaughter.

Nonetheless, each individual culture had its roots in a biological heritage that gave rise to behavior governed more by ancient urges than contemporary realities, and even when they mastered the technology to choose their own nature, the precise set of traits they preserved was up to them. In the worst case, a species still saddled with inappropriate drives but empowered by advanced technology could wreak havoc. The Noudah deserved to be treated with courtesy and respect, but they did not yet belong in the Amalgam.

The Tirans' own exchanges were not on open channels, so once they had entered Anne's ship, Joan could only guess what was happening. She waited until two of the ships had returned to the surface, then sent her own message to Ghahar's traffic control.

"I come in peace from another star. I seek permission to land."

3

The Ghahari allowed Joan to fly her ship straight down to the surface. She wasn't sure if this was because they were more trusting, or if they were afraid that the Tirans might try to interfere if she lingered in orbit.

The landing site was a bare plain of chocolate-colored sand. The air shimmered in the heat, the distortions intensified by the thickness of the atmosphere, making the horizon waver as if seen through molten glass. Joan waited in the cockpit as three trucks approached; they all came to a halt some twenty meters away. A voice over the radio instructed her to leave the ship; she complied, and after she'd stood in the open for a minute, a lone Noudah left one of the trucks and walked toward her.

"I'm Pirit," she said. "Welcome to Ghahar." Her gestures were courteous but restrained.

"I'm Joan. Thank you for your hospitality."

"Your impersonation of our biology is impeccable." There was a trace of skepticism in Pirit's tone; Joan had pointed the Ghahari to her own portrait being broadcast from the decoy node, but she had to admit that in the context her lack of exotic technology and traits would make it harder to accept the implications of that transmission.

"In my culture, it's a matter of courtesy to imitate one's hosts as closely as possible."

Pirit hesitated, as if pondering whether to debate the merits of such a custom, but then rather than quibbling over the niceties of interspecies etiquette she chose to confront the real issue head-on. "If you're a Tiran spy, or a defector, the sooner you admit that the better."

"That's very sensible advice, but I'm neither."

The Noudah wore no clothing as such, but Pirit had a belt with a number of pouches. She took a handheld scanner from one and ran it over Joan's body. Joan's briefing suggested that it was probably only checking for metal, volatile explosives, and radiation; the technology to image her body or search for pathogens would not be so portable. In any case, she was a healthy, unarmed Noudah down to the molecular level.

Pirit escorted her to one of the trucks, and invited her to recline in a section at the back. Another Noudah drove while Pirit watched over Joan. They soon arrived at a small complex of buildings a couple of kilometers from where the ship had touched down. The walls, roofs, and floors of the buildings were all made from the local sand, cemented with an adhesive that the Noudah secreted from their own bodies.

Inside, Joan was given a thorough medical examination, including three kinds of full-body scan. The Noudah who examined her treated her with a kind of detached efficiency devoid of any pleasantries; she wasn't sure if that was their standard bedside manner, or a kind of glazed shock at having been told of her claimed origins.

Pirit took her to an adjoining room and offered her a couch. The Noudah anatomy did not allow for sitting, but they liked to recline.

Pirit remained standing. "How did you come here?" she asked.

"You've seen my ship. I flew it from Baneth."

"And how did you reach Baneth?"

"I'm not free to discuss that," Joan replied cheerfully.

"Not free?" Pirit's face clouded with silver, as if she was genuinely perplexed.

Joan said, "You understand me perfectly. Please don't tell me there's nothing *you're* not free to discuss with me."

"You certainly didn't fly that ship twenty light-years."

"No, I certainly didn't."

Pirit hesitated. "Did you come through the Cataract?" The Cataract was a black hole, a remote partner to the Noudah's sun; they orbited each other at a distance of about eighty billion kilometers. The name came from its telescopic appearance: a dark circle ringed by a distortion in the background of stars, like some kind of visual aberration. The Tirans and Ghahari were in a race to be the first to visit this extraordinary neighbor, but as yet neither of them were quite up to the task.

"*Through* the Cataract? I think your scientists have already proven that black holes aren't shortcuts to anywhere."

"Our scientists aren't always right."

"Neither are ours," Joan admitted, "but all the evidence points in one direction: black holes aren't doorways, they're shredding machines."

"So you traveled the whole twenty light-years?"

"More than that," Joan said truthfully, "from my original home. I've spent half my life traveling."

"Faster than light?" Pirit suggested hopefully.

"No. That's impossible."

They circled around the question a dozen more times, before Pirit finally changed her tune from *how* to *why?*

"I'm a xenomathematician," Joan said. "I've come here in the hope of collaborating with your archaeologists in their study of Niah artifacts."

Pirit was stunned. "What do you know about the Niah?"

"Not as much as I'd like to." Joan gestured at her Noudah body. "As I'm sure you've already surmised, we've listened to your broadcasts for some time, so we know pretty much what an ordinary Noudah knows. That includes the basic facts about the Niah. Historically, they've been referred to as your ancestors, though the latest studies suggest that you and they really just have an earlier common ancestor. They died out about a million years ago, but there's evidence that they might have had a sophisticated culture for as long as three million years. There's no indication that they ever developed spaceflight. Basically, once they achieved material comfort, they seem to have devoted themselves to various art forms, including mathematics."

"So you've traveled twenty light-years just to look at Niah tablets?" Pirit was incredulous.

"Any culture that spent three million years doing mathematics must have something to teach us."

"Really?" Pirit's face became blue with disgust. "In the ten thousand years since we discovered the wheel, we've already reached halfway to the Cataract. They wasted their time on useless abstractions."

Joan said, "I come from a culture of spacefarers myself, so I respect your achievements. But I don't think anyone really knows what the Niah achieved. I'd like to find out, with the help of your people."

Pirit was silent for a while. "What if we say no?"

"Then I'll leave empty-handed."

"What if we insist that you remain with us?"

"Then I'll die here, empty-handed." On her command, this body would expire in an instant; she could not be held and tortured.

Pirit said angrily, "You must be willing to trade *something* for the privilege you're demanding!"

"Requesting, not demanding," Joan insisted gently. "And what I'm willing to offer is my own culture's perspective on Niah mathematics. If you ask your archaeologists and mathematicians, I'm sure they'll tell you that there are many things written in the Niah tablets that they don't yet understand. My colleague and I"—neither of them had mentioned Anne before, but Joan was sure that Pirit knew all about her—"simply want to shed as much light as we can on this subject."

Pirit said bitterly, "You won't even tell us how you came to our world. Why should we trust you to share whatever you discover about the Niah?"

"Interstellar travel is no great mystery," Joan countered. "You know all the basic science already; making it work is just a matter of persistence. If you're left to develop your own technology, you might even come up with better methods than we have."

"So we're expected to be patient, to discover these things for ourselves . . . but you can't wait a few centuries for us to decipher the Niah artifacts?"

Joan said bluntly, "The present Noudah culture, both here and in Tira, seems to hold the Niah in contempt. Dozens of partially excavated sites containing Niah artifacts are under threat from irrigation projects and other developments. That's the reason we couldn't wait. We needed to come here and offer our assistance, before the last traces of the Niah disappeared forever."

Pirit did not reply, but Joan hoped she knew what her interrogator was thinking: *Nobody would cross twenty light-years for a few worthless scribblings. Perhaps we've underestimated the Niah. Perhaps our ancestors have left us a great secret, a great legacy. And perhaps the fastest—perhaps the only—way to uncover it is to give this impertinent, irritating alien exactly what she wants.*

The sun was rising ahead of them as they reached the top of the hill. Sando turned to Joan, and his face became green with pleasure. "Look behind you," he said.

Joan did as he asked. The valley below was hidden in fog, and it had settled so evenly that she could see their shadows in the dawn light, stretched out across the top of the fog layer. Around the shadow of her head was a circular halo like a small rainbow.

"We call it the Niah's light," Sando said. "In the old days, people used to say that the halo proved that the Niah blood was strong in you."

Joan said, "The only trouble with that hypothesis being that *you* see it around *your* head . . . and I see it around mine." On Earth, the phenomenon was known as a "glory." The particles of fog were scattering the sunlight back toward them, turning it one hundred and eighty degrees. To look at the shadow of your own head was to face directly away from the sun, so the halo always appeared around the observer's shadow.

"I suppose you're the final proof that Niah blood has nothing to do with it," Sando mused.

"That's assuming I'm telling you the truth, and I really can see it around my own head."

"And assuming," Sando added, "that the Niah really did stay at home, and didn't wander around the galaxy spreading their progeny."

They came over the top of the hill and looked down into the adjoining riverine valley. The sparse brown grass of the hillside gave way to a lush violet growth closer to the water. Joan's arrival had delayed the flooding of the valley, but even alien interest in the Niah had only bought the archaeologists an extra year. The dam was part of a long-planned agricultural development, and however tantalizing the possibility that Joan might reveal some priceless insight hidden among the Niah's "useless abstractions," that vague promise could only compete with more tangible considerations for a limited time.

Part of the hill had fallen away in a landslide a few centuries before, revealing more than a dozen beautifully preserved strata. When Joan and Sando reached the excavation site, Rali and Surat were already at work, clearing away soft sedimentary rock from a layer that Sando had dated as belonging to the Niah's "twilight" period.

Pirit had insisted that only Sando, the senior archaeologist, be told about Joan's true nature; Joan refused to lie to anyone, but had agreed to tell her colleagues only that she was a mathematician and that she was not permitted to discuss her past. At first, this had made them guarded and resentful, no doubt because they assumed that she was some kind of spy sent by the authorities to watch over them. Later, it had dawned on them that she was genuinely interested in their work, and that the absurd restrictions on her topics of conversation were not of her own choosing. Nothing about the Noudah's language or appearance correlated strongly with their recent division into nations—with no oceans to cross, and a long history of migration they were more or less geographically homogeneous—but Joan's odd name and occasional faux pas could still be ascribed to some mysterious exoticism. Rali and Surat seemed content to assume that she was a defector from one of the smaller nations, and that her history could not be made explicit for obscure political reasons.

"There are more tablets here, very close to the surface," Rali announced excitedly. "The acoustics are unmistakable." Ideally, they would have excavated the entire hillside, but they did not have the time or the labor, so they were using acoustic tomography to identify likely deposits of accessible Niah writing, and then concentrating their efforts on those spots.

The Niah had probably had several ephemeral forms of written communication, but when they found something worth publishing, it stayed published: they carved their symbols into a ceramic that made diamond seem like tissue paper. It was almost unheard of for the tablets to be broken, but they were small, and multitablet works were sometimes widely dispersed. Niah technology could probably have carved three million years' worth of knowledge on to the head of a pin—they seemed not to have invented nanomachines, but they were into high-quality bulk materials and precision engineering—but for whatever reason they had chosen legibility to the naked eye above other considerations.

Joan made herself useful, taking acoustic readings farther along the slope, while Sando watched over his students as they came closer to the buried Niah artifacts. She had learned not to hover around expectantly when a discovery was imminent; she was treated far more warmly if she waited to be summoned. The tomography unit was almost foolproof, using satellite navigation to track its position and software to analyze the signals it gathered; all it really needed was someone to drag it along the rock face at a suitable pace.

Through the corner of her eye, Joan noticed her shadow on the rocks flicker and grow complicated. She looked up to see three dazzling beads of light flying west out of the sun. She might have assumed that the fusion ships were doing something useful, but the media was full of talk of "military exercises," which meant the Tirans and the Ghahari engaging in expensive, belligerent gestures in orbit, trying to convince each other of their superior skills, technology, or sheer strength of numbers. For people with no real differences apart from a few centuries of recent history, they could puff up their minor political disputes into matters of the utmost solemnity. It might almost have been funny, if the idiots hadn't incinerated hundreds of thousands of each other's citizens every few decades, not to mention playing callous and often deadly games with the lives of the inhabitants of smaller nations.

"Jown! Jown! Come and look at this!" Surat called to her. Joan switched off the tomography unit and jogged toward the archaeologists, suddenly conscious of her body's strangeness. Her legs were stumpy but strong, and her balance as she ran came not from arms and shoulders but from the swish of her muscular tail.

"It's a significant mathematical result," Rali informed her proudly when she reached them. He'd pressure-washed the sandstone away from the near-indestructible ceramic of the tablet, and it was only a matter of holding the surface at the right angle to the light to see the etched writing stand out as crisply and starkly as it would have a million years before.

Rali was not a mathematician, and he was not offering his own opinion on the theorem the tablet stated; the Niah themselves had a clear set of typographical conventions that they used to distinguish between everything from minor lemmas to the most celebrated theorems. The size and decorations of the symbols labeling the theorem attested to its value in the Niah's eyes.

Joan read the theorem carefully. The proof was not included on the same tablet, but the Niah had a way of expressing their results that made you believe them as soon as you read them; in this case the definitions of the terms needed to state the theorem were so beautifully chosen that the result seemed almost inevitable.

The theorem itself was expressed as a commuting hypercube, one of the

Niah's favorite forms. You could think of a square with four different sets of mathematical objects associated with each of its corners, and a way of mapping one set into another associated with each edge of the square. If the maps commuted, then going across the top of the square, then down, had exactly the same effect as going down the left edge of the square, then across: either way, you mapped each element from the top-left set into the same element of the bottom-right set. A similar kind of result might hold for sets and maps that could naturally be placed at the corners and edges of a cube, or a hypercube of any dimension. It was also possible for the square faces in these structures to stand for relationships that held between the maps between sets, and for cubes to describe relationships between those relationships, and so on.

That a theorem took this form didn't guarantee its importance; it was easy to cook up trivial examples of sets and maps that commuted. The Niah didn't carve trivia into their timeless ceramic, though, and this theorem was no exception. The seven-dimensional commuting hypercube established a dazzlingly elegant correspondence between seven distinct, major branches of Niah mathematics, intertwining their most important concepts into a unified whole. It was a result Joan had never seen before: no mathematician anywhere in the Amalgam, or in any ancestral culture she had studied, had reached the same insight.

She explained as much of this as she could to the three archaeologists; they couldn't take in all the details, but their faces became orange with fascination when she sketched what she thought the result would have meant to the Niah themselves.

"This isn't quite the Big Crunch," she joked, "but it must have made them think they were getting closer." The Big Crunch was her nickname for the mythical result that the Niah had aspired to reach: a unification of every field of mathematics that they considered significant. To find such a thing would not have meant the end of mathematics—it would not have subsumed every last conceivable, interesting mathematical truth—but it would certainly have marked a point of closure for the Niah's own style of investigation.

"I'm sure they found it," Surat insisted. "They reached the Big Crunch, then they had nothing more to live for."

Rali was scathing. "So the whole culture committed collective suicide?"

"Not actively, no," Surat replied. "But it was the search that had kept them going."

"Entire cultures don't lose the will to live," Rali said. "They get wiped out by external forces: disease, invasion, changes in climate."

"The Niah survived for three million years," Surat countered. "They had the means to weather all of those forces. Unless they were wiped out by alien invaders with vastly superior technology." She turned to Joan. "What do you think?"

"About aliens destroying the Niah?"

"I was joking about the aliens. But what about the mathematics? What if they found the Big Crunch?"

"There's more to life than mathematics," Joan said. "But not much more."

Sando said, "And there's more to this find than one tablet. If we get back to work, we might have the proof in our hands before sunset."

5

Joan briefed Halzoun by video link while Sando prepared the evening meal. Halzoun was the mathematician Pirit had appointed to supervise her, but apparently his day job was far too important to allow him to travel. Joan was grateful; Halzoun was the most tedious Noudah she had encountered. He could understand the Niah's work when she explained it to him, but he seemed to have no interest in it for its own sake. He spent most of their conversations trying to catch her out in some deception or contradiction, and the rest pressing her to imagine military or commercial applications of the Niah's gloriously useless insights. Sometimes she played along with this infantile fantasy, hinting at potential superweapons based on exotic physics that might come tumbling out of the vacuum, if only one possessed the right Niah theorems to coax them into existence.

Sando was her minder too, but at least he was more subtle about it. Pirit had insisted that she stay in his shelter, rather than sharing Rali and Surat's; Joan didn't mind, because with Sando she didn't have the stress of having to keep quiet about everything. Privacy and modesty were nonissues for the Noudah, and Joan had become Noudah enough not to care herself. Nor was there any danger of their proximity leading to a sexual bond; the Noudah had a complex system of biochemical cues that meant desire only arose in couples with a suitable mixture of genetic differences and similarities. She would have had to search a crowded Noudah city for a week to find someone to lust after, though at least it would have been guaranteed to be mutual.

After they'd eaten, Sando said, "You should be happy. That was our best find yet."

"I am happy." Joan made a conscious effort to exhibit a viridian tinge. "It was the first new result I've seen on this planet. It was the reason I came here, the reason I traveled so far."

"Something's wrong, though, I think."

"I wish I could have shared the news with my friend," Joan admitted. Pirit claimed to be negotiating with the Tirans to allow Anne to communicate with her, but Joan was not convinced that she was genuinely trying. She was sure that she would have relished the thought of listening in on a conversation between the two of them—while forcing them to speak Noudah, of course—in the hope that they'd slip up and reveal something useful, but at the same time she would have had to face the fact that the Tirans would be listening too. What an excruciating dilemma.

"You should have brought a communications link with you," Sando suggested. "A homestyle one, I mean. Nothing we could eavesdrop on."

"We couldn't do that," Joan said.

He pondered this. "You really are afraid of us, aren't you? You think the smallest technological trinket will be enough to send us straight to the stars, and then you'll have a horde of rampaging barbarians to deal with."

"We know how to deal with barbarians," Joan said coolly.

Sando's face grew dark with mirth. "Now *I'm* afraid."

"I just wish I knew what was happening to her," Joan said. "What she was doing, how they were treating her."

"Probably much the same as we're treating you," Sando suggested. "We're really not that different." He thought for a moment. "There was something I wanted to show you." He brought over his portable console, and summoned up an article from a Tiran journal. "See what a borderless world we live in," he joked.

The article was entitled "Seekers and Spreaders: What We Must Learn From the Niah." Sando said, "This might give you some idea of how they're thinking over there. Jaqad is an academic archaeologist, but she's also very close to the people in power."

Joan read from the console while Sando made repairs to their shelter, secreting a molasseslike substance from a gland at the tip of his tail and spreading it over the cracks in the walls.

There were two main routes a culture could take, Jaqad argued, once it satisfied its basic material needs. One was to think and study: to stand back and observe, to seek knowledge and insight from the world around it. The other was to invest its energy in entrenching its good fortune.

The Niah had learned a great deal in three million years, but in the end it had not been enough to save them. Exactly what had killed them was still a matter of speculation, but it was hard to believe that if they had colonized other worlds they would have vanished on all of them. "Had the Niah been Spreaders," Jaqad wrote, "we might expect a visit from them, or them from us, sometime in the coming centuries."

The Noudah, in contrast, were determined Spreaders. Once they had the means, they would plant colonies across the galaxy. They would, Jaqad was sure, create new biospheres, reengineer stars, and even alter space and time to guarantee their survival. The growth of their empire would come first; any knowledge that failed to serve that purpose would be a mere distraction. "In any competition between Seekers and Spreaders, it is a Law of History that the Spreaders must win out in the end. Seekers, such as the Niah, might hog resources and block the way, but in the long run their own nature will be their downfall."

Joan stopped reading. "When you look out into the galaxy with your telescopes," she asked Sando, "how many reengineered stars do you see?"

"Would we recognize them?"

"Yes. Natural stellar processes aren't that complicated; your scientists already know everything there is to know about the subject."

"I'll take your word for that. So . . . you're saying Jaqad is wrong? The Niah themselves never left this world, but the galaxy already belongs to creatures more like them than like us?"

"It's not Noudah versus Niah," Joan said. "It's a matter of how a culture's perspective changes with time. Once a species conquers disease, modifies their biology, and spreads even a short distance beyond their home world, they usually start to relax a bit. The territorial imperative isn't some timeless law of history; it belongs to a certain phase."

"What if it persists, though? Into a later phase?"

"That can cause friction," Joan admitted.

"Nevertheless, no Spreaders have conquered the galaxy?"

"Not yet."

Sando went back to his repairs; Joan read the rest of the article. She'd thought she'd already grasped the lesson demanded by the subtitle, but it turned out that Jaqad had something more specific in mind.

"Having argued this way, how can I defend my own field of study from the very same charges as I have brought against the Niah? Having grasped the essential character of this doomed race, why should we waste our time and resources studying them further?

"The answer is simple. We still do not know exactly how and why the Niah died, but when we do, that could turn out to be the most important discovery in history. When we finally leave our world behind, we should not expect to find only other Spreaders to compete with us, as honorable opponents in battle. There will be Seekers as well, blocking the way: tired, old races squatting uselessly on their hoards of knowledge and wealth.

"Time will defeat them in the end, but we already waited three million years to be born; we should have no patience to wait again. If we can learn how the Niah died, that will be our key, that will be our weapon. If we know the Seekers' weakness, we can find a way to hasten their demise."

6

The proof of the Niah's theorem turned out to be buried deep in the hillside, but over the following days they extracted it all.

It was as beautiful and satisfying as Joan could have wished, merging six earlier, simpler theorems while extending the techniques used in their proofs. She could even see hints at how the same methods might be stretched further to yield still stronger results. "The Big Crunch" had always been a slightly mocking, irreverent term, but now she was struck anew by how little justice it did to the real trend that had fascinated the Niah. It was not a matter of everything in mathematics collapsing in on itself, with one branch turning out to have been merely a recapitulation of another under a different guise. Rather, the principle was that every sufficiently beautiful mathematical system was rich enough to mirror *in part*—and sometimes in a complex and distorted fashion—every other sufficiently beautiful system. Nothing became sterile and redundant, nothing proved to have been a waste of time, but everything was shown to be magnificently intertwined.

After briefing Halzoun, Joan used the satellite dish to transmit the theorem and its proof to the decoy node. That had been the deal with Pirit: anything she learned from the Niah belonged to the whole galaxy, as long as she explained it to her hosts first.

The archaeologists moved across the hillside, hunting for more artifacts in the same layer of sediment. Joan was eager to see what else the same group of Niah might have published. One possible eight-dimensional hypercube was hovering in her mind; if she'd sat down and thought about it for a few decades she might have worked out the details herself, but the Niah did what they did so well that it would have seemed crass to try to follow clumsily in their footsteps when their own immaculately polished results might simply be lying in the ground, waiting to be uncovered.

A month after the discovery, Joan was woken by the sound of an intruder moving through the shelter. She knew it wasn't Sando; even as she slept an ancient part of her Noudah brain was listening to his heartbeat. The stranger's heart was too quiet to hear, which required great discipline, but the shelter's flexible adhesive made the floor emit a characteristic squeak beneath even the gentlest footsteps. As she rose from her couch she heard Sando waking, and she turned in his direction.

Bright torchlight on his face dazzled her for a moment. The intruder held two knives to Sando's respiration membranes; a deep enough cut there would mean choking to death, in excruciating pain. The nanomachines that had built Joan's body had wired extensive skills in unarmed combat into her brain, and one scenario involving a feigned escape attempt followed by a sideways flick of her powerful tail was already playing out in the back of her mind, but as yet she could see no way to guarantee that Sando came through it all unharmed.

She said, "What do you want?"

The intruder remained in darkness. "Tell me about the ship that brought you to Baneth."

"Why?"

"Because it would be a shame to shred your colleague here, just when his work was going so well." Sando refused to show any emotion on his face, but the blank pallor itself was as stark an expression of fear as anything Joan could imagine.

She said, "There's a coherent state that can be prepared for a quark-gluon plasma in which virtual black holes catalyze baryon decay. In effect, you can turn all of your fuel's rest mass into photons, yielding the most efficient exhaust stream possible." She recited a long list of technical details. The claimed baryon decay process didn't actually exist, but the pseudophysics underpinning it was mathematically consistent, and could not be ruled out by anything the Noudah had yet observed. She and Anne had prepared an entire fictitious science and technology, and even a fictitious history of their culture, precisely for emergencies like this; they could spout red herrings for a decade if necessary, and never get caught out contradicting themselves.

"That wasn't so hard, was it?" the intruder gloated.

"What now?"

"You're going to take a trip with me. If you do this nicely, nobody needs to get hurt."

Something moved in the shadows, and the intruder screamed in pain. Joan leaped forward and knocked one of the knives out of his hand with her tail; the other knife grazed Sando's membrane, but a second tail whipped out of the darkness and intervened. As the intruder fell backward, the beam of his torch revealed Surat and Rali tensed beside him, and a pick buried deep in his side.

Joan's rush of combat hormones suddenly faded, and she let out a long, deep wail of anguish. Sando was unscathed, but a stream of dark liquid was pumping out of the intruder's wound.

Surat was annoyed. "Stop blubbing, and help us tie up this Tiran cousin-fucker."

"Tie him up? You've killed him!"

"Don't be stupid, that's just sheath fluid." Joan recalled her Noudah anatomy; sheath fluid was like oil in a hydraulic machine. You could lose it all and it would cost you most of the strength in your limbs and tail, but you wouldn't die, and your body would make more eventually.

Rali found some cable and they trussed up the intruder. Sando was shaken, but he seemed to be recovering. He took Joan aside. "I'm going to have to call Pirit."

"I understand. But what will she do to these two?" She wasn't sure exactly how much Rali and Surat had heard, but it was certain to have been more than Pirit wanted them to know.

"Don't worry about that, I can protect them."

Just before dawn someone sent by Pirit arrived in a truck to take the intruder away. Sando declared a rest day, and Rali and Surat went back to their shelter to sleep. Joan went for a walk along the hillside; she didn't feel like sleeping.

Sando caught up with her. He said, "I told them you'd been working on a military research project, and you were exiled here for some political misdemeanor."

"And they believed you?"

"All they heard was half of a conversation full of incomprehensible physics. All they know is that someone thought you were worth kidnapping."

Joan said, "I'm sorry about what happened."

Sando hesitated. "What did you expect?"

Joan was stung. "One of us went to Tira, one of us came here. We thought that would keep everyone happy!"

"We're Spreaders," said Sando. "Give us one of anything, and we want two. Especially if our enemy has the other one. Did you really think you could come here, do a bit of fossicking, and then simply fly away without changing a thing?"

"Your culture has always believed there were other civilizations in the galaxy. Our existence hardly came as a shock."

Sando's face became yellow, an expression of almost parental reproach. "Believing in something in the abstract is not the same as having it dangled in front of you. We were never going to have an existential crisis at finding out that we're not unique; the Niah might be related to us, but they were still alien enough to get us used to the idea. But did you really think we were just going to relax and accept your refusal to share your technology? That one of you went to the Tirans only makes it worse for the Ghahari, and vice versa. Both governments are going absolutely crazy, each one terrified that the other has found a way to make its alien talk."

Joan stopped walking. "The war games, the border skirmishes? You're blaming all of that on Anne and me?"

Sando's body sagged wearily. "To be honest, I don't know all the details. And if it's any consolation, I'm sure we would have found another reason if you hadn't come along."

Joan said, "Maybe I should leave." She was tired of these people, tired of

her body, tired of being cut off from civilization. She had rescued one beautiful Niah theorem and sent it out into the Amalgam. Wasn't that enough?

"It's up to you," Sando replied. "But you might as well stay until they
flood the valley. Another year isn't going to change anything. What you've
done to this world has already been done. For us, there's no going back."

7

Joan stayed with the archaeologists as they moved across the hillside. They
found tablets bearing Niah drawings and poetry, which no doubt had their
virtues but to Joan seemed bland and opaque. Sando and his students relished these discoveries as much as the theorems; to them, the Niah culture
was a vast jigsaw puzzle, and any clue that filled in the details of their history
was as good as any other.

Sando would have told Pirit everything he'd heard from Joan the night
the intruder came, so she was surprised that she hadn't been summoned for
a fresh interrogation to flesh out the details. Perhaps the Ghahari physicists
were still digesting her elaborate gobbledygook, trying to decide if it made
sense. In her more cynical moments she wondered if the intruder might
have been Ghahari himself, sent by Pirit to exploit her friendship with
Sando. Perhaps Sando had even been in on it, and Rali and Surat as well.
The possibility made her feel as if she was living in a fabricated world, a
scape in which nothing was real and nobody could be trusted. The only
thing she was certain that the Ghaharis could not have faked was the Niah
artifacts. The mathematics verified itself; everything else was subject to
doubt and paranoia.

Summer came, burning away the morning fogs. The Noudah's idea of
heat was very different from Joan's previous perceptions, but even the body
she now wore found the midday sun oppressive. She willed herself to be
patient. There was still a chance that the Niah had taken a few more steps
toward their grand vision of a unified mathematics, and carved their final discoveries into the form that would outlive them by a million years.

When the lone fusion ship appeared high in the afternoon sky, Joan
resolved to ignore it. She glanced up once, but she kept dragging the tomography unit across the ground. She was sick of thinking about Tiran-Ghahari
politics. They had played their childish games for centuries; she would not
take the blame for this latest outbreak of provocation.

Usually the ships flew by, disappearing within minutes, showing off their
power and speed. This one lingered, weaving back and forth across the sky
like some dazzling insect performing an elaborate mating dance. Joan's second

shadow darted around her feet, hammering a strangely familiar rhythm into her brain.

She looked up, disbelieving. The motion of the ship was following the syntax of a gestural language she had learned on another planet, in another body, a dozen lifetimes ago. The only other person on this world who could know that language was Anne.

She glanced toward the archaeologists a hundred meters away, but they seemed to be paying no attention to the ship. She switched off the tomography unit and stared into the sky. *I'm listening, my friend. What's happening? Did they give you back your ship? Have you had enough of this world, and decided to go home?*

Anne told the story in shorthand, compressed and elliptic. The Tirans had found a tablet bearing a theorem: the last of the Niah's discoveries, the pinnacle of their achievements. Her minders had not let her study it, but they had contrived a situation making it easy for her to steal it, and to steal this ship. They had wanted her to take it and run, in the hope that she would lead them to something they valued far more than any ancient mathematics: an advanced spacecraft, or some magical stargate at the edge of the system.

But Anne wasn't fleeing anywhere. She was high above Ghahar, reading the tablet, and now she would paint what she read across the sky for Joan to see.

Sando approached. "We're in danger, we have to move."

"Danger? That's my friend up there! She's not going to shoot a missile at us!"

"Your friend?" Sando seemed confused. As he spoke, three more ships came into view, lower and brighter than the first. "I've been told that the Tirans are going to strike the valley, to bury the Niah sites. We need to get over the hill and indoors, to get some protection from the blast."

"Why would the Tirans attack the Niah sites? That makes no sense to me."

Sando said, "Nor me, but I don't have time to argue."

The three ships were menacing Anne's, pursuing her, trying to drive her away. Joan had no idea if they were Ghahari defending their territory, or Tirans harassing her in the hope that she would flee and reveal the nonexistent shortcut to the stars, but Anne was staying put, still weaving the same gestural language into her maneuvers even as she dodged her pursuers, spelling out the Niah's glorious finale.

Joan said, "You go. I have to see this." She tensed, ready to fight him if necessary.

Sando took something from his tool belt and peppered her side with holes. Joan gasped with pain and crumpled to the ground as the sheath fluid poured out of her.

Rali and Surat helped carry her to the shelter. Joan caught glimpses of the fiery ballet in the sky, but not enough to make sense of it, let alone recon-struct it.

They put her on her couch inside the shelter. Sando bandaged her side and gave her water to sip. He said, "I'm sorry I had to do that, but if anything had happened to you I would have been held responsible."

Surat kept ducking outside to check on the "battle," then reporting excitedly on the state of play. "The Tiran's still up there, they can't get rid of it. I don't know why they haven't shot it down yet."

Because the Tirans were the ones pursuing Anne, and they didn't want her dead. But for how long would the Ghahari tolerate this violation?

Anne's efforts could not be allowed to come to nothing. Joan struggled to recall the constellations she'd last seen in the night sky. At the node they'd departed from, powerful telescopes were constantly trained on the Noudah's home world. Anne's ship was easily bright enough, its gestures wide enough, to be resolved from seven light-years away—if the planet itself wasn't block-ing the view, if the node was above the horizon.

The shelter was windowless, but Joan saw the ground outside the door-way brighten for an instant. The flash was silent; no missile had struck the valley, the explosion had taken place high above the atmosphere.

Surat went outside. When she returned she said quietly, "All clear. They got it."

Joan put all her effort into spitting out a handful of words. "I want to see what happened."

Sando hesitated, then motioned to the others to help him pick up the couch and carry it outside.

A shell of glowing plasma was still visible, drifting across the sky as it expanded, a ring of light growing steadily fainter until it vanished into the afternoon glare.

Anne was dead in this embodiment, but her backup would wake and go on to new adventures. Joan could at least tell her the story of her local death: of virtuoso flying and a spectacular end.

She'd recovered her bearings now, and she recalled the position of the stars. The node was still hours away from rising. The Amalgam was full of powerful telescopes, but no others would be aimed at this obscure planet, and no plea to redirect them could outrace the light they would need to cap-ture in order to bring the Niah's final theorem back to life.

8

Sando wanted to send her away for medical supervision, but Joan insisted on remaining at the site.

"The fewer officials who get to know about this incident, the fewer problems it makes for you," she reasoned.

"As long as you don't get sick and die," he replied.

"I'm not going to die." Her wounds had not become infected, and her strength was returning rapidly.

They compromised. Sando hired someone to drive up from the nearest town to look after her while he was out at the excavation. Daya had basic medical training and didn't ask awkward questions; he seemed happy to tend to Joan's needs, and then lie outside daydreaming the rest of the time.

There was still a chance, Joan thought, that the Niah had carved the theorem on a multitude of tablets and scattered them all over the planet. There was also a chance that the Tirans had made copies of the tablet before letting Anne abscond with it. The question, though, was whether she had the slightest prospect of getting her hands on these duplicates.

Anne might have made some kind of copy herself, but she hadn't mentioned it in the prologue to her aerobatic rendition of the theorem. If she'd had any time to spare, she wouldn't have limited herself to an audience of one: she would have waited until the node had risen over Ghahar.

On her second night as an invalid, Joan dreamed that she saw Anne standing on the hill looking back into the fog-shrouded valley, her shadow haloed by the Niah light.

When she woke, she knew what she had to do.

When Sando left, she asked Daya to bring her the console that controlled the satellite dish. She had enough strength in her arms now to operate it, and Daya showed no interest in what she did. That was naive, of course: whether or not Daya was spying on her, Pirit would know exactly where the signal was sent. So be it. Seven light-years was still far beyond the Noudah's reach; the whole node could be disassembled and erased long before they came close.

No message could outrace light directly, but there were more ways for light to reach the node than the direct path, the fastest one. Every black hole had its glory, twisting light around it in a tight, close orbit and flinging it back out again. Seventy-four hours after the original image was lost to them, the telescopes at the node could still turn to the Cataract and scour the distorted, compressed image of the sky at the rim of the hole's black disk to catch a replay of Anne's ballet.

Joan composed the message and entered the coordinates of the node. *You didn't die for nothing, my friend. When you wake and see this, you'll be proud of us both.*

She hesitated, her hand hovering above the send key. The Tirans had wanted Anne to flee, to show them the way to the stars, but had they really been indifferent to the loot they'd let her carry? The theorem had come at the end of the Niah's three-million-year reign. To witness this beautiful truth would not destroy the Amalgam, but might it not weaken it? If the Seekers' thirst for knowledge was slaked, their sense of purpose corroded, might not the most crucial strand of the culture fall into a twilight of its own? There was no shortcut to the stars, but the Noudah had been goaded by their alien visitors, and the technology would come to them soon enough.

The Amalgam had been goaded, too: the theorem she'd already transmitted would send a wave of excitement around the galaxy, strengthening the Seekers, encouraging them to complete the unification by their own efforts. The Big Crunch might be inevitable, but at least she could delay it, and hope that the robustness and diversity of the Amalgam would carry them through it, and beyond.

She erased the message and wrote a new one, addressed to her backup via the decoy node. It would have been nice to upload all her memories, but the Noudah were ruthless, and she wasn't prepared to stay any longer and risk being used by them. This sketch, this postcard, would have to be enough.

When the transmission was complete, she left a note for Sando in the console's memory.

Daya called out to her, "Jown? Do you need anything?"

She said, "No. I'm going to sleep for a while."

against the current

ROBERT SILVERBERG

That time is a river is a well-known saying, and that river sweeps us all along in its current, but what happens if somehow you find yourself being swept in the wrong direction. . . ?

Robert Silverberg is one of the most famous SF writers of modern times, with dozens of novels, anthologies, and collections to his credit. As both writer and editor (he was editor of the original anthology series *New Dimensions*, perhaps the most acclaimed anthology series of its era), Silverberg was one of the most influential figures of the post-New Wave era of the seventies, and continues to be at the forefront of the field to this very day, having won a total of five Nebula Awards and four Hugo Awards, plus SFWA's prestigious Grandmaster Award.

His novels include the acclaimed *Dying Inside*, *Lord Valentine's Castle*, *The Book of Skulls*, *Downward to the Earth*, *Tower of Glass*, *Son of Man*, *Nightwings*, *The World Inside*, *Born with the Dead*, *Shadrack in the Furnace*, *Thorns*, *Up the Line*, *The Man in the Maze*, *Tom O'Bedlam*, *Star of Gypsies*, *At Winter's End*, *The Face of the Waters*, *Kingdoms of the Wall*, *Hot Sky at Morning*, *The Alien Years*, *Lord Prestimion*, *Mountains of Majipoor*, and two novel-length expansions of famous Isaac Asimov stories, *Nightfall* and *The Ugly Little Boy*. His collections include *Unfamiliar Territory*, *Capricorn Games*, *Majipoor Chronicles*, *The Best of Robert Silverberg*, *At the Conglomeroid Cocktail Party*, *Beyond the Safe Zone*, and a massive retrospective collection *The Collected Stories of Robert Silverberg, Volume One: Secret Sharers*. His reprint anthologies are far too numerous to list here, but include *The Science Fiction Hall of Fame, Volume One* and the distinguished *Alpha* series, among dozens of others. His most recent books are the novel *The Long Way Home*, the mosaic novel *Roma Eterna*, a collection of early work, *In the Beginning*, and a massive new retrospective collection, *Phases of the Moon: Stories from Six Decades*. Coming up is a new collection, *To the Dark Star: The Collected Stories of Robert Silverberg*,

Volume 2, and, as editor, *The Science Fiction Hall of Fame, Volume Two B*. He lives with his wife, writer Karen Haber, in Oakland, California.

About half past four in the afternoon Rackman felt a sudden red blaze of pain in both his temples at once, the sort of stabbing jab that you would expect to feel if a narrow metal spike had been driven through your head. It was gone as quickly as it had come, but it left him feeling queasy and puzzled and a little frightened, and, since things were slow at the dealership just then anyway, he decided it might be best to call it a day and head for home.

He stepped out into perfect summer weather, a sunny, cloudless day, and headed across the lot to look for Gene, his manager, who had been over by the SUVs making a tally of the leftovers. But Gene was nowhere in sight. The only person Rackman saw out there was a pudgy salesman named Freitas, who so far as he recalled had given notice a couple of weeks ago. Evidently he wasn't gone yet, though.

"I'm not feeling so good and I'm going home early," Rackman announced. "If Gene's around here somewhere, will you tell him that?"

"Sure thing, Mr. Rackman."

Rackman circled around the edge of the lot toward the staff parking area. He still felt queasy, and somewhat muddled too, with a slight headache lingering after that sudden weird stab of pain. Everything seemed just a bit askew. The SUVs, for instance—there were more of the things than there should be, considering that he had just run a big clearance on them. They were lined up like a whopping great phalanx of tanks. How come so many? He filed away a mental note to ask Gene about that tomorrow.

He turned the ignition key and the sleek silver Prius glided smoothly, silently, out of the lot, off to the nearby freeway entrance. By the time he reached the Caldecott Tunnel twenty minutes later the last traces of the pain in his temple were gone, and he moved on easily through Oakland toward the bridge and San Francisco across the bay.

At the Bay Bridge toll plaza they had taken down all the overhead signs that denoted the FasTrak lanes. That was odd, he thought. Probably one of their mysterious maintenance routines. Rackman headed into his usual lane anyway, but there was a tolltaker in the booth—why?—and as he started to roll past the man toward the FasTrak scanner just beyond he got such an incandescent glare from him that he braked to a halt.

The FasTrak toll scanner wasn't where it should be, right back of the tollbooth on the left. It wasn't there at all.

Feeling a little bewildered now, Rackman pulled a five-dollar bill from his wallet, handed it to the man, got what seemed to be too many singles in change, and drove out onto the bridge. There was very little traffic. As he approached the Treasure Island Tunnel, though, it struck him that he couldn't remember having seen any of the towering construction cranes that ran alongside the torso of the not-quite-finished new bridge just north of the old one. Nor was there any sign of them—or any trace of the new bridge itself, for that matter, when he glanced into his rearview mirror.

This is peculiar, Rackman thought. Really, really peculiar.

On the far side of the tunnel the sky was darker, as though dusk were already descending—at five-ten on a summer day?—and by the time he was approaching the San Francisco end of the bridge the light was all but gone. Even stranger, a little rain was starting to come down. Rain falls in the Bay Area in August about once every twenty years. The morning forecast hadn't said anything about rain. Rackman's hand trembled a little as he turned his wipers on. I am having what could be called a waking dream, Rackman thought, some very vivid hallucination, and when I'm off the bridge I better pull over to the curb and take a few deep breaths.

The skyline of the city just ahead of him looked somehow diminished, as though a number of the bigger buildings were missing. And the exit ramps presented more puzzles. A lot of stuff that had been torn down for the retro-fitting of the old bridge seemed to have been put back in place. He couldn't find his Folsom Street off-ramp, but the long-gone Main Street one, which they had closed after the 1989 earthquake, lay right in front of him. He took it and pulled the Prius to curbside as soon as he was down at street level. The rain had stopped—the streets were dry, as if the rain had never been—but the air seemed clinging and clammy, not like dry summer air at all. It enfolded him, contained him in a strange tight grip. His cheeks were flushed and he was perspiring heavily.

Deep breaths, yes. Calm. Calm. You're only five blocks from your condo.

Only he wasn't. Most of the high-rise office buildings were missing, all right, and none of the residential towers south of the off-ramp complex were there, just block after block of parking lots and some ramshackle ware-houses. It was night now, and the empty neighborhood was almost com-pletely dark. Everything was the way it had looked around here fifteen, twenty years before. His bewilderment was beginning to turn into terror. The street signs said that he was at his own corner. So where was the thirty-story building where he lived?

Better call Jenny, he thought.

He would tell her—delicately—that he was going through something very baffling, a feeling of, well, disorientation, that in fact he was pretty seriously mixed up, that she had better come get him and take him home.

But his cell phone didn't seem to be working. All he got was a dull buzzing sound. He looked at it, stunned. He felt as though some part of him had been amputated.

Rackman was angry now as well as frightened. Things like this weren't supposed to happen to him. He was fifty-seven years old, healthy, solvent, a solid citizen, owner of a thriving Toyota dealership across the bay, married to a lovely and loving woman. Everyone said he looked ten years younger than he really was. He worked out three times a week and ran in the Bay-to-Breakers Race every year and once in a while he even did a marathon. But the drive across the bridge had been all wrong and he didn't know where his condo building had gone and his cell phone was on the fritz, and here he was lost in this dark forlorn neighborhood of empty lots and abandoned warehouses with a wintry wind blowing—hey, hadn't it been sticky and humid a few minutes ago?—on what had started out as a summer day. And he had the feeling that things were going to get worse before they got better. If indeed they got better at all.

He swung around and drove toward Union Square. Traffic was surprisingly light for downtown San Francisco. He spotted a phone booth, parked nearby, fumbled a coin into the slot, and dialed his number. The phone made ugly noises and a robot voice told him that the number he had dialed was not a working number. Cursing, Rackman tried again, tapping the numbers in with utmost care. "We're sorry," the voice said again, "the number you have reached is not—"

A telephone book dangled before him. He riffled through it—Jenny had her own listing, under Burke—but though half a dozen J. Burkes were in the book, five of them lived in the wrong part of town, and when he dialed the sixth number, which had no address listed, an answering machine responded in a birdlike chirping voice that certainly wasn't Jenny's. Something led him then to look for his own listing. No, that wasn't there either. A curious calmness came over him at that discovery. There were no FasTrak lanes at the toll plaza, and the dismantled freeway ramps were still here, and the neighborhood where he lived hadn't been developed yet, and neither he nor Jenny was listed in the San Francisco phone book, and therefore either he had gone seriously crazy or else somehow this had to be fifteen or even twenty years ago, which was pretty much just another way of saying the same thing. If this really is fifteen or twenty years ago, Rackman thought, then Jenny would be living in Sacramento and I'd be across the bay in El Cerrito and still married to Helene. But what the hell kind of thing was that to be thinking, *If this really is fifteen or twenty years ago?*

He considered taking himself to the nearest emergency room and telling them he was having a breakdown, but he knew that once he put himself in the hands of the medics, there'd be no extricating himself: they'd subject him to a million tests, reports would be filed with this agency and that, his driver's license might be yanked, bad things would happen to his credit rating. It would be much smarter, he thought, to check himself into a hotel room, take a shower, rest, try to figure all this out, wait for things to get back to normal.

Rackman headed for the Hilton, a couple of blocks away. Though night had fallen just a little while ago, the sun was high overhead now, and the weather had changed again, too: it was sharp and cool, autumn just shading into winter. He was getting a different season and a different time of day every fifteen minutes or so, it seemed. The Hilton desk clerk, tall and balding and starchy-looking, had such a self-important manner that as Rackman requested a room he felt a little abashed at not having any luggage with him, but the clerk didn't appear to give a damn about that, simply handed him the registration form and asked him for his credit card. Rackman put his Visa down on the counter and began to fill out the form.

"Sir?" the desk clerk said, after a moment.

Rackman looked up. The clerk was staring at his credit card. It was the translucent kind, and he tipped it this way and that, puzzledly holding it against the light. "Problem?" Rackman asked, and the clerk muttered something about how unusual the card looked.

Then his expression darkened. "Wait just a second," he said, very coldly now, and tapped the imprinted expiration date on the card. "What is *this* supposed to be? Expires July, 2010? *2010*, sir? *2010*? Are we having a little joke, sir?" He flipped the card across the counter at Rackman the way he might have done if it had been covered with some noxious substance.

Another surge of terror hit him. He backed away, moving quickly through the lobby and into the street. Of course he might have tried to pay cash, he supposed, but the room would surely be something like $225 a night, and he had only about $350 on him. If his credit card was useless, he'd need to hang on to his cash at least until he understood what was happening to him. Instead of the Hilton, he would go to some cheaper place, perhaps one of the motels up on Lombard Street.

On his way back to his car Rackman glanced at a newspaper in a sidewalk rack. President Reagan was on the front page, under a headline about the invasion of Grenada. The date on the paper was Wednesday, October 26, 1983. Sure, he thought 1983. This hallucination isn't missing a trick. I am in 1983 and Reagan is president again, with 1979 just up the road, 1965, 1957, 1950 —

In 1950 Rackman hadn't even been born yet. He wondered what was going to happen to him when he got back to a time earlier than his own birth.

He stopped at the first motel on Lombard that had a VACANCY sign and registered for a room. The price was only $75, but when he put two fifties down on the counter, the clerk, a pleasant, smiling Latino woman, gave him a pleasant smile and tapped her finger against the swirls of pink coloration next to President Grant's portrait. "Somebody has stuck you with some very funny bills, sir. But you know that I can't take them. If you can pay by credit card, though, Visa, American Express—"

Of course she couldn't take them. Rackman remembered, now, that all the paper money had changed five or ten years back, new designs, bigger portraits, distinctive patches of pink or blue ink on their front sides that had once been boringly monochromatic. And these bills of his had the tiny date "2004" in the corner.

So far as the world of 1983 was concerned, the money he was carrying was nothing but play money.

1983.

Jenny, who is up in Sacramento in 1983 and has no idea yet that he even exists, had been twenty-five that year. Already he was more than twice her age. And she would get younger and younger as he went ever onward, if that was what was going to continue to happen.

Maybe it wouldn't. Soon, perhaps, the pendulum would begin to swing the other way, carrying him back to his own time, to his own life. What if it didn't, though? What if it just kept on going?

In that case, Rackman thought, Jenny was lost to him, with everything that had bound them together now unhappened. Rackman reached out suddenly, grasping the air as though reaching for Jenny, but all he grasped was air. There was no Jenny for him any longer. He had lost her, yes. And he would lose everything else of what he had thought of as his life as well, his whole past peeling away strip by strip. He had no reason to think that the pendulum *would* swing back. Already the exact details of Jenny's features were blurring in his mind. He struggled to recall them: the quizzical blue eyes, the slender nose, the wide, generous mouth, the slim, supple body. She seemed to be drifting past him in the fog, caught in an inexorable current carrying her ever farther away.

He slept in his car that night, up by the marina, where he hoped no one would bother him. No one did. Morning light awakened him after a few hours—his wristwatch said it was 9:45 P.M. on the same August day when all this had started, but he knew better now than to regard what his watch told him as having any meaning—and when he stepped outside the day was dry and clear, with a blue summer sky overhead and the sort of harsh wind blowing that only San Francisco can manage on a summer day. He was getting used to the ever-changing weather by now, though, the swift parade of seasons tumbling upon him one after another. Each new one would hold him for a little while in that odd *enclosed* way, but then it would release its grasp and nudge him onward into the next one.

He checked the newspaper box on the corner. *San Francisco Chronicle*, Tuesday, May 1, 1973. Big front-page story: Nixon dismisses White House counsel John Dean and accepts the resignations of aides John Ehrlichman and H. R. Haldeman. Right, he thought. Dean, Ehrlichman, Haldeman: Watergate. So a whole decade had vanished while he slept. He had slipped all the way back to 1973. He wasn't even surprised. He had entered some realm beyond all possibility of surprise.

Taking out his wallet, Rackman checked his driver's license. Still the same, expires 03-11-11, photo of his familiar fifty-something face. His car was still a silver 2009 Prius. Certain things hadn't changed. But the Prius stood out like a shriek among the other parked cars, every last one of them some clunky-looking old model of the kind that he dimly remembered from his youth. What we have here is 1973, he thought. Probably not for long, though.

He hadn't had anything to eat since lunchtime, ten hours and thirty-five years ago. He drove over to Chestnut Street, marveling at the quiet old-fashioned look of all the shopfronts, and parked right outside Joe's, which he knew had been out of business since maybe the Clinton years. There were no parking meters on the street. Rackman ordered a salad, a Joe's Special, and a glass of red wine, and paid for it with a ten-dollar bill of the old green-and-white kind that he happened to have. Meal plus wine, $8.50, he thought. That sounded about right for this long ago. It was a very consistent kind of hallucination. He left a dollar tip.

Rackman remembered pretty well what he had been doing in the spring of 1973. He was twenty-two that year, out of college almost a year, working in Cody's Books on Telegraph Avenue in Berkeley while waiting to get into law school, for which he had been turned down the first time around but which he had high hopes of entering that autumn. He and Al Mortenson, another young Cody's clerk—nice steady guy, easy to get along with—were rooming together in a little upstairs apartment on Dana, two or three blocks from the bookshop.

Whatever had happened to old Al? Rackman had lost touch with him many years back. A powerful urge seized him now to drive across to Berkeley and look for him. He hadn't spoken with anyone except those two hotel clerks since he had left the car lot, what felt like a million years ago, and a terrible icy loneliness was beginning to settle over him as he went spinning onward through his constantly unraveling world. He needed to reach out to someone, anyone, for whatever help he could find. Al might be a good man to consult. Al was levelheaded; Al was unflusterable; Al was *steady*. What about driving over to Berkeley now and looking for Al at the Dana Street place?—"I know you don't recognize me, Al, but I'm actually Phil Rackman, only I'm from 2008, and I'm having some sort of bad trip and I need to sit down in a quiet place with a good friend like you and figure out what's going on." Rackman wondered what that would accomplish. Probably nothing, but at least it might provide him with half an hour of companionship, sympathy, even understanding. At worst Al would think he was a lunatic and he would wind up under sedation at Alta Bates Hospital while they tried to find his next of kin. If he really was sliding constantly backward in time he would slip away from Alta Bates too, Rackman thought, and if not, if he was simply unhinged, maybe a hospital was where he belonged.

He went to Berkeley. The season drifted back from spring to late winter while he was crossing the bridge: in Berkeley the acacias were in bloom, great clusters of golden yellow flowers, and that was a January thing. The sight of Berkeley in early 1973, a year that had in fact been the last gasp of the sixties, gave him a shiver: the Day-Glo rock-concert posters on all the walls, the flower-child costumes, the huge, bizarre helmets of shaggy hair that everyone was wearing. The streets were strangely clean, hardly any litter, no graffiti. It all was like a movie set, a careful, loving reconstruction of the era. He had no business being here. He was entirely out of place. And yet he had lived here once. This street belonged to his own past. He had lost Jenny, he had lost his nice condominium, he had lost his car dealership, but other things that he had thought were lost, like this Day-Glo tie-dyed world of his youth, were coming back to him. Only they weren't coming back for long, he knew. One by one they would present themselves, tantalizing flashes of a returning past, and then they'd go streaming onward, lost to him like everything else, lost for a second and terribly final time.

He guessed from the position of the pale winter sun, just coming up over the hills to the east, that the time was eight or nine in the morning. If so, Al would probably still be at home. The Dana Street place looked just as Rackman remembered it, a tidy little frame building, the landlady's tiny but immaculate garden of pretty succulents out front, the redwood deck, the staircase on the side that led to the upstairs apartment. As he started upward an unsettling burst of panic swept through him at the possibility that he might come face to face with his own younger self. But in a moment his trepidation passed. It wouldn't happen, he told himself. It was just *too* impossible. There had to be a limit to this thing somewhere.

A kid answered his knock, sleepy-looking and impossibly young, a tall lanky guy in jeans and a T-shirt, with a long oval face almost completely engulfed in an immense spherical mass of jet-black hair that covered his forehead and his cheeks and his chin, a wild woolly tangle that left only eyes and nose and lips visible. A golden peace-symbol amulet dangled on a silver chain around his neck. My God, Rackman thought, this really is the Al I knew in 1973. Like a ghost out of time. But *I* am the ghost. *I* am the ghost.

"Yes?" the kid at the door said vaguely.

"Al Mortenson, right?"

"Yes." He said it in an uneasy way, chilly, distant, grudging.

What the hell, some unknown elderly guy at the door, an utter stranger wanting God only knew what, eight or nine in the morning: even the unflappable Al might be a little suspicious. Rackman saw no option but to launch straight into his story. "I realize this is going to sound very strange to you. But I ask you to bear with me. Do I look in any way familiar to you, Al?"

He wouldn't, naturally. He was much stockier than the Phil Rackman of 1973, his full-face beard was ancient history and his once-luxurious russet hair was close-cropped and gray, and he was wearing a checked suit of the kind that nobody, not even a middle-aged man, would have worn in 1973. But he began to speak, quietly, earnestly, intensely, persuasively, his best one-foot-in-the-door salesman approach, the approach he might have used if he had been trying to sell his biggest model SUV to a frail old lady from the Rossmoor retirement home. Starting off by casually mentioning Al's roommate Phil Rackman—"He isn't here, by any chance, is he?"—no, he wasn't, thank God—and then asking Al once again to prepare himself for a very peculiar tale indeed, giving him no chance to reply, and swiftly and smoothly working around to the notion that he himself was Phil Rackman, not Phil's father but the actual Phil Rackman who had been his roommate back in 1973, only in fact he was the Phil Rackman of the year 2008 who had without warning become caught up in what could only be described as an inexplicable toboggan-slide backward across time.

Even through that forest of facial hair Al's reactions were readily discernible: puzzlement at first, then annoyance verging on anger, then a show of curiosity, a flicker of interest at the possibility of such a wild thing—Hey, man, far out! Cool!—and then, gradually, gradually, gradually bringing himself to the tipping point, completing the transition from skepticism verging on hostility to mild curiosity to fascination to stunned acceptance, as Rackman began to conjure up remembered episodes of their shared life that only he could have known. That time in the summer of '72 when he and Al and their current girlfriends had gone camping in the Sierras and had been happily screwing away on a flat smooth granite outcropping next to a mountain stream in what they thought was total seclusion, 8,000 feet above sea level, when a wide-eyed party of Boy Scouts came marching past them down the trail; and that long-legged girl from Oregon Rackman had picked up one weekend who turned out to be double-jointed, or whatever, and showed them both the most amazing sexual tricks; and the great moment when they and some friends had scored half a pound of hash and gave a party that lasted three days running without time out for sleep; and the time when he and Al had hitchhiked down to Big Sur, he with big, cuddly Ginny Beardsley and Al with hot little Nikki Rosenzweig, during Easter break, and the four of them had dropped a little acid and gone absolutely gonzo berserk together in a secluded redwood grove—

"No," Al said. "That hasn't happened yet. Easter is still three months away. And I don't know any Nikki Rosenzweig."

Rackman rolled his eyes lasciviously. "You will, kiddo. Believe me, you will! Ginny will introduce you, and—and—"

"So you even know my own future."

"For me it isn't the future," Rackman said. "It's the long-ago past. When you and I were rooming together right here on Dana Street and having the time of our lives."

"But how is this possible?"

"You think I know, old pal? All I know is that it's happening. I'm me, really me, sliding backward in time. It's the truth. Look at my face, Al. Run a computer simulation in your mind if you can—hell, people don't have their own computers yet, do they?—well, just try to age me up, in your imagination, gray hair, more weight, but the same nose, Al, the same mouth—" He shook his head. "Wait a second. Look at this." He drew out his driver's license and thrust it at the other man. "You see the name? The photo? You see the birthdate? *You see the expiration date?* March 2011? Here, look at these fifty-dollar bills! The dates on them. This credit card, this Visa. Do you even know what a Visa is? Did we have them back in 1973?"

"Christ," Al said, in a husky, barely audible whisper. "Jesus Christ, Phil. It's okay if I call you Phil, right?"

"Phil, yes."

"Look, Phil—" That same thin ghostly whisper, the voice of a man in shock. Rackman had never, in the old days, seen Al this badly shaken up. "The bookstore's about to open. I've got to get to work. You come in, wait here, make yourself at home." Then a little manic laugh: "You *are* at home, aren't you? In a manner of speaking. So wait here. Rest. Relax. Smoke some of my dope, if you want. You probably know where I keep it. Meet me at Cody's at one, and we can go out to lunch and talk about all this, okay? I want to know all about it. What year did you say you came from? 2011?"

"2008."

"2008. Christ, this is so wild! You'll stay here, then?"

"And if my younger self walks in on me?"

"Don't worry. You're safe. He's in Los Angeles this week."

"Groovy," Rackman said, wondering if anyone still said things like that. "Go on, then. Go to work. I'll see you later."

The two rooms, Al's and his own just across the hall, were like museum exhibits: the posters for Fillmore West concerts, the antique stereo set and the stack of LP records, the tie-dyed shirts and bell-bottom pants scattered in the corner, the bong on the dresser, the macramé wall hangings, the musty aroma of last night's incense. Rackman poked around, lost in dreamy nostalgia and at times close to tears as he looked at this artifact of that ancient era and that one, *The Teachings of Don Juan, The White Album, The Whole Earth Catalog*. His own copies. He still had the Castaneda book somewhere; he remembered the beer stain on the cover. He peered into the dresser drawer where Al kept his stash, scooped up a pinch of it in his fingers and sniffed it, smiled, put it back. It was years since he had smoked. Decades.

He ran his hand over his cheek. His stubble was starting to bother him. He hadn't shaved since yesterday morning on Rackman body time. He knew there'd be a shaver in the bathroom, though—he was pretty sure he had left it there even after he began growing his seventies beard—and, yes, there was his old Norelco three-headed job. He felt better with clean cheeks. Rackman stuffed the shaver into his inside jacket pocket, knowing he'd want it in the days ahead.

Then he found himself wondering whether he had parked in a tow-away zone. They had always been very tough about illegally parked cars in Berkeley. You could try to assassinate the president and get off with a six-month sentence, but God help you if you parked in a tow-away zone. And if they took his car away, he'd be in an even worse pickle than he already was. The car was his one link to the world he had left behind, his time capsule, his home, now, actually.

The car was still where he had left it. But he was afraid to leave it for long. It might slip away from him in the next time-shift. He got in, thinking to wait in it until it was time to meet Al for lunch. But although it was still just midmorning he felt drowsiness overcoming him, and almost instantly he dozed off. When he awakened he saw that it was dark outside. He must have slept the day away. The dashboard clock told him it was 1:15 P.M., but that was useless, meaningless. Probably it was early evening, too late for lunch with Al. Maybe they could have dinner instead.

On the way over to the bookstore, marveling every step of the way at the utter weirdness of everybody he passed in the streets, the strange beards, the flamboyant globes of hair, the gaudy clothing. Rackman began to see that it would be very embarrassing to tell Al that he had grown up to own a suburban automobile dealership. He had planned to become a legal advocate for important social causes, or perhaps a public defender, or an investigator of corporate malfeasance. Everybody had noble plans like that, back then. Going into the car business hadn't been on anyone's screen.

Then he saw that he didn't have to tell Al anything about what he had come to do for a living. It was a long story and not one that Al was likely to find interesting. Al wouldn't care that he had become a car dealer. Al was sufficiently blown away by the mere fact that his former roommate Phil Rackman had dropped in on him out of the future that morning.

He entered the bookstore and spotted Al over near the cash register. But when he waved he got only a blank stare in return.

"I'm sorry I missed our lunch date, Al. I guess I just nodded off. It's been a pretty tiring day for me, you know."

There was no trace of recognition on Al's face.

"Sir? There must be some mistake."

"Al Mortenson? Who lives on Dana Street?"

"I'm Al Mortenson, yes. I live in Bowles Hall, though."

Bowles Hall was a campus dormitory. Undergraduates lived there. This Al hadn't graduated yet.

This Al's hair was different too, Rackman saw now. A tighter cut, more disciplined, more forehead showing. And his beard was much longer, cascading down over his chest, hiding the peace symbol. He might have had a haircut during the day but he couldn't have grown four inches more of beard.

There was a stack of newspapers on the counter next to the register, the *New York Times*. Rackman flicked a glance at the top one. *November 10, 1971.*

I haven't just slept away the afternoon, Rackman thought. I've slept away all of 1972. He and Al hadn't rented the Dana Street place until after graduation, in June of '72.

Fumbling, trying to recover, always the nice helpful guy, Al said, "You aren't Mr. Chesley, are you? Bud Chesley's father?"

Bud Chesley had been a classmate of theirs, a jock, big, broad-shouldered. The main thing that Rackman remembered about him was that he had been one of about six men on campus who were in favor of the war in Vietnam. Rackman seemed to recall that in his senior year Al had roomed with Chesley in Bowles, before he and Al had known each other. "No," Rackman said leadenly. "I'm not Mr. Chesley. I'm really sorry to have bothered you."

So it was hopeless, then. He had suspected it all along, but now, feeling the past tugging at him as he hurried back to his car, it was certain. The slippage made any sort of human interaction lasting more than half an hour or so impossible to sustain. He struggled with it, trying to tug back, to hold fast against the sliding, hoping that perhaps he could root himself somehow in the present and then begin the climb forward again until he reached the place where he belonged. But he could feel the slippage continuing, not at any consistent rate but in sudden unpredictable bursts, and there was nothing he could do about it. There were times when he was completely unaware of it until it had happened and other times when he could see the seasons rocketing right by in front of his eyes.

Without any particular destination in mind Rackman returned to his car, wandered around Berkeley until he found himself heading down Ashby Avenue to the freeway, and drove back into San Francisco. The toll was only a quarter. Astonishing. The cars around him on the bridge all seemed like collector's items, with yellow-and-black license plates, three digits, three letters. He wondered what a highway patrolman would say about his own plates, if he recognized them as California plates at all.

Halfway across the bridge Rackman turned the radio on, hoping the car might be able to pick up a news broadcast out of 2008, but no, no, when he got KCBS he heard the announcer talking about President Johnson, Secretary of State Rusk, Vietnam, Israel refusing to give back Jerusalem after the recent war with the Arab countries, Dr. Martin Luther King calling for calm following a night of racial strife in Hartford, Connecticut. It was hard to remember some of the history exactly, but Rackman knew that Dr. King had been assassinated in 1968, so he figured that just in the course of crossing the bridge he probably had slid back into 1967 or even 1966. He had been in high school then. All the sweaty anguish of that whole lunatic era came swimming back into his mind, the Robert Kennedy assassination too, the body counts on the nightly news, Malcolm X, peace marches, the strident 1968 political convention in Chicago, the race riots, Nixon, Hubert Humphrey, Mao Tse-tung, spacemen in orbit around the moon, Lady Bird Johnson, Cassius Clay. *Hey hey, LBJ, how many kids did you kill today?* The noise, the hard-edged excitement, the daily anxiety. It felt like the Pleistocene to him now. But he had driven right into the thick of it.

The slippage continued. The long hair went away, the granny glasses, the Day-Glo posters, the tie-dyed clothes. John F. Kennedy came and went in reverse. Night and day seemed to follow one another in random sequence. Rackman ate his meals randomly too, no idea whether it was breakfast or lunch or dinner that he needed. He had lost all track of personal time. He caught naps in his car, kept a low profile, said very little to anyone. A careless restaurant cashier took one of his gussied-up fifties without demur and gave him a stack of spendable bills in change. He doled those bills out parsimoniously, watching what he spent even though meals, like the bridge toll, like the cost of a newspaper, like everything else back here, were astoundingly cheap, a nickel or a dime for this, fifty cents for that.

San Francisco was smaller, dingier, a little old 1950s-style town, no trace of the high-rise buildings now. Everything was muted, old-fashioned, the simpler, more innocent textures of his childhood. He half expected it all to be in black and white, as an old newsreel would be, and perhaps to flicker a little. But he took in smells, breezes, sounds, that no newsreel could have captured. This wasn't any newsreel and it wasn't any hallucination, either. This was the world itself, dense, deep, real. All too real, unthinkably real. And there was no place for him in it.

Men wore hats, women's coats had padded shoulders. Shop windows sparkled. There was a Christmas bustle in the streets. A little while later, though, the sky brightened and the dry, cold winds of San Francisco summer came whistling eastward at him again out of the Pacific, and then, presto jingo, the previous winter's rainy season was upon him. He wondered which year's winter it was.

It was 1953, the newspaper told him. The corner newspaper rack was his only friend. It provided him with guidance, information about his present position in time. That was Eisenhower on the front page. The Korean War was still going on, here in 1953. And Stalin: Stalin had just died. Rackman remembered Eisenhower, the president of his childhood, kindly old Ike. Truman's bespectacled face would be next. Rackman had been born during Truman's second term. He had no recollection of the Truman presidency but he could recall the salty old Harry of later years, who went walking every day, gabbing with reporters about anything that came into his head.

What is going to happen to me, Rackman wondered, when I get back past my own birthdate?

Maybe he would come to some glittering gateway, a giant sizzling special effect throwing off fireworks across the whole horizon, with a blue-white sheen of nothingness stretching into infinity beyond it. And when he passed through it he would disappear into oblivion and that would be that. He'd find out soon enough. He couldn't be much more than a year or two away from the day of his birth.

Without knowing or caring where he was going, Rackman began to drive south out of San Francisco, the poky little San Francisco of this far-off day, heading out of town on what once had been Highway 101, the freeway that led to the airport and San Jose and, eventually, Los Angeles. It wasn't a freeway now, just an oddly charming little four-lane road. The billboards that lined it on both sides looked like ads from old *National Geographic*s. The curving rows of small ticky-tacky houses on the hillsides hadn't been built yet. There was almost nothing except open fields everywhere, down here south of the city. The ballpark wasn't there—the Giants still played in New York in this era, he recalled—and when he went past the airport, he almost failed to notice it, it was such a piffling little small-town place. Only when a DC-3 passed overhead like a huge droning mosquito did he realize that that collection of tin sheds over to the left was what would one day be SFO.

Rackman knew that he was still slipping and slipping as he went, that the pace of slippage seemed to be picking up, that if that glittering gateway existed he had already gone beyond it. He was somewhere near 1945 now or maybe even earlier—they were honking at his car on the road in amazement, as though it was a spaceship that had dropped down from Mars—and now a clear, cold understanding of what was in store for him was growing in his mind.

He wouldn't disappear through any gateway. It didn't matter that he hadn't been born yet in the year he was currently traveling through, because he wasn't growing any younger as he drifted backward. And the deep past waited for him. He saw that he would just go endlessly onward, cut loose from the restraints that time imposed, drifting on and on back into antiquity. While he was driving southward, heading for San Jose or Los Angeles or wherever it was that he might be going next, the years would roll along backward, the twentieth century would be gobbled up in the nineteenth, California's great cities would melt away—he had already seen that happening in San Francisco—and the whole state would revert to the days of Mexican rule, a bunch of little villages clustered around the Catholic missions, and then the villages and the missions would disappear too. A day or two later for him, California would be an emptiness, nobody here but simple Indian tribes. Farther to the east, in the center of the continent, great herds of bison would roam. Still farther east would be the territory of the Thirteen Colonies, gradually shriveling back into tiny pioneering settlements and then vanishing also. Well, he thought, if he could get himself across the country quickly enough, he might be able to reach New York City—Nieuw Amsterdam, it would probably be by then—while it still existed. There he might be able to arrange a voyage across to Europe before the continent reverted entirely to its pre-Columbian status. But what then? All that he could envisage was a perpetual journey backward, backward, ever backward: the Renaissance, the Dark Ages, Rome, Greece, Babylon, Egypt, the Ice Age. A couple of summers ago he and Jenny had taken a holiday in France, down in the Dordogne, where they had looked at the painted caves of the Cro-Magnon men, the colorful images of bulls and bison and spotted horses and mammoths. No one knew what those pictures meant, why they had been painted. Now he would go back and find out at firsthand the answer to the enigmas of the prehistoric caves. How very cool that sounded, how interesting, a nice fantasy, except that if you gave it half a second's thought it was appalling. To whom would he impart that knowledge? What good would it do him, or anyone?

The deep past was waiting for him, yes. But would he get there? Even a Prius wasn't going to make it all the way across North America on a single tank of gas, and soon there weren't going to be any gas stations, and even if there were he would have no valid money to pay for gas, or food, or anything else. Pretty soon there would be no roads, either. He couldn't *walk* to New York. In that wilderness he wouldn't last three days.

He had kept himself in motion up until this moment, staying just ahead of the vast gray grimness that was threatening to invade his soul, but it was catching up with him now. Rackman went through ten or fifteen minutes that might have been the darkest, bleakest moments of his life. Then — was it something about the sweet simplicity of this little road, no longer the roaring Highway 101 but now just a dusty, narrow two-laner with hardly any traffic? — there came an unexpected change in his mood. He grew indifferent to his fate. In an odd way he found himself actually welcoming whatever might come. The prospect before him looked pretty terrifying, yes. But it might just be exciting, too. He had liked his life, he had liked it very much, but it had been torn away from him, he knew not how or why. This was his life now. He had no choice about that. The best thing to do, Rackman thought, was to take it one century at a time and try to enjoy the ride.

What he needed right now was a little breather: come to a halt if only for a short while, pause and regroup. Stop and pass the time, so to speak, as he got himself ready for the next phase of his new existence. He pulled over by the side of the road and turned off the ignition and sat there quietly, thinking about nothing at all.

After a while a youngish man on a motorcycle pulled up alongside him. The motorcycle was hardly more than a souped-up bike. The man was wearing a khaki blouse and khaki trousers, all pleats and flounces, a very old-fashioned outfit, something like a scoutmaster's uniform. He himself had an old-fashioned look, too, dark hair parted in the middle like an actor in a silent movie.

Then Rackman noticed the California Highway Patrol badge on the man's shoulder. He opened the car window. The patrolman leaned toward him and gave him an earnest smile, a Boy Scout smile. Even the smile was old-fashioned. You couldn't help believing the sincerity of it. "Is there any difficulty, sir? May I be of any assistance?"

So polite, so formal. *Sir.* Everyone had been calling him sir since this trip had started, the desk clerks, the people in restaurants, Al Mortenson, and now this CHP man. So respectful, everybody was, back here in prehistory.

"No," Rackman said. "No problem. Everything's fine."

The patrolman didn't seem to hear him. He had turned his complete attention to Rackman's car itself, the glossy silver Prius, the car out of the future. The look of it was apparently sinking in for the first time. He was staring at the car in disbelief, in befuddlement, in unconcealed jaw-sagging awe, gawking at its fluid streamlined shape, at its gleaming futuristic dashboard. Then he turned back to Rackman himself, taking in the look of his clothing, his haircut, his checked jacket, his patterned shirt. The man's eyes seemed to glaze. Rackman knew that there had to be something about his whole appearance that seemed as wrong to the patrolman as the patrolman's did to him. He could see the man working to get himself under control. The car must have him completely flummoxed, Rackman thought. The patrolman began to say something but it was a moment before he could put his voice in gear. Then he said, hoarsely, like a rusty automaton determined to go through its routine no matter what, "I want you to know, sir, that if you are having any problem with your—ah—your car, we are here to assist you in whatever way we can."

To assist you. That was a good one.

Rackman managed a faint smile. "Thanks, but the car's okay," he said. "And I'm okay too. I just stopped off here to rest a bit, that's all. I've got a long trip ahead of me." He reached for the ignition key. Silently, smoothly, the Prius floated forward into the morning light and the night that would quickly follow it and into the random succession of springs and winters and autumns and summers beyond, forward into the mysteries, dark and dreadful and splendid, that lay before him.

alien archeology

NEAL ASHER

Born in Essex, England, but now living in Crete, Neal Asher started
writing at the age of sixteen, but didn't explode into public print
until a few years ago; a quite prolific author, he now seems to be
everywhere at once. His stories have appeared in *Asimov's*, *Interzone*, *The Agony Column*, *Hadrosaur Tales*, and elsewhere, and
have been collected in *Runcible Tales*, *The Engineer*, and *Mason's
Rats*. His extremely popular novels include *Gridlinked*, *Cowl*, *The
Skinner*, *The Line of Polity*, *Brass Man*, *The Voyage of the Sable
Keech*, *The Engineer Reconditioned*, and *Prador Moon: A Novel of
the Polity*. Coming up is a new novel, *Hilldiggers*.

In the full-blown, flat-out, unabashed Space Opera thriller that
follows, he gives us a ringside seat for a fast-paced, suspenseful, and
violent game of intrigue, double-cross, and double-double-cross, as a
hunt for a stolen alien artifact of immense value forces a former agent
out of retirement and into a tense chase across interstellar space into
hostile landscapes where wiser humans would never dare to venture,
with life or death hanging in the balance at every turn.

The sifting machine had been working nonstop for twenty years. The technique, first introduced by the xeno-archaeologist Alexion Smith and frowned
on by others in his profession as being too blunt an instrument, was in use
here by a private concern. An Atheter artifact had been discovered on this
desert planetoid: a species of plant that used a deep extended root system to
mop up platinum grains from the green sands, which it accumulated in its
seeds to drop on the surface. Comparative analysis of the plant's genome—a
short trihelical strand—proved it was a product of Atheter technology. The
planet had been deep-scanned for other artifacts, then the whole project

abandoned when nothing else major was found. The owners of the sitting machine came here afterward in the hope of picking up something the previous searchers had missed. They had managed to scrape up a few minor finds, but reading between the lines of their most recent public reports, Jael knew they were concealing something and, breaking into the private reports from the man on the ground here, learned of a second big find.

Perched on a boulder, she stepped down the magnification of her eyes to human normal so that all she could see was the machine's dust plume from the flat green plain. The *Kobashi* rested in the boulder's shade behind her. The planetary base was some ten kilometers away and occupied by a sandapt called Rho. He had detected the U-space signature of her ship's arrival and sent a terse query as to her reason for being here. She expressed her curiosity about what he was doing, to which he had replied that this was no tourist spot before shutting down communication. Obviously he was the kind who relished solitude, which was why he was suited for this assignment and was perfect for Jael's purposes. She could have taken her ship directly to his base, but had brought it in low below the base's horizon to land it. She was going to surprise the sandapt, and rather suspected he wouldn't consider it a pleasant surprise.

This planet was hot enough to kill an unadapted human and the air too thin and noxious for her to breathe, but she wore a hotsuit with its own air supply, and, in the one-half gravity, could cover the intervening distance very quickly. She leapt down the five meters to the ground, bounced in a cloud of dust, and set out in a long lope—her every stride covering three meters.

Glimmering beads of metal caught Jael's attention before she reached the base. She halted and turned to study something like a morel fungus—its wrinkled head an open skin of cubic holes. Small seeds glimmered in those holes, and as she drew closer some of them were ejected. Tracking their path she saw that when they struck the loose dusty ground they sank out of sight. She pushed her hand into the ground and scooped up dust in which small objects glittered. She increased the sensitivity of her optic nerves and ramped up the magnification of her eyes. Each seed consisted of a teardrop of organic matter attached at its widest end to a dodecahedral crystal of platinum. Jael supposed the Atheter had used something like the sifting machine far to her left to collect the precious metal; separating it from the seeds and leaving them behind to germinate into more of these useful little plants. She pocketed the seeds—she knew people who would pay good money for them—though her aim here was to make a bigger killing than that.

She had expected Rho's base to be the usual inflated dome with resin-bonded sand layered over it, but some other building technique had been employed here. Nestled below an escarpment that marked the edge of the dust bowl and the start of a deeply cracked plain of sun-baked clay, the building was a white-painted cone with a peaked roof. It looked something like an ancient windmill without vanes, but then there were three wind generators positioned along the top of the escarpment—their vanes wide to take into account the thin air down here. Low structures spread out from either side of the building like wings, glimmering in the harsh white sun glare. Jael guessed these were greenhouses to protect growing food plants. A figure was making its way along the edge of these towing a gravsled. She squatted down and focused in.

Rho's adaptation had given him skin of a deep reddish gold, a ridged bald head, and a nose that melded into his top lip. She glimpsed his eyes, which were sky blue and without pupils. He wore no mask—his only clothing being boots, shorts, and a sun visor. Jael leapt upright and broke into a run for the nearest end of the escarpment, where it was little more than a mound. Glancing back she noticed the dust trail she'd left and hoped he wouldn't see it. Eventually she arrived at the foot of one of the wind generators and from her belt pouch removed a skinjector and loaded it with a selection of drugs. The escarpment here dropped ten meters in a curve from which projected rough reddish slates. She used these as stepping-stones to bring her down to the level of the base then sprinted in toward the back wall. She could hear him now—he was whistling some ancient melody. A brief comparison search in the music library in her left-hand aug revealed the name: "Greensleeves." She walked around the building as he approached.

"Who the hell are you?" he exclaimed.

She strode up to him. "I've seen your sifting machine; have you had any luck?"

He paused for a moment, then, in a tired voice, said, "Bugger off."

But by then she was on him. Before he could react, she swung the skinjector round from behind her back and pressed it against his chest, triggered it.

"What the . . . !" His hand swung out and he caught her hard across the side of the face. She spun, her feet coming up off the ground, and fell in ridiculous slow motion in the low gravity. Error messages flashed up in her visual cortex—broken nanoconnections—but they faded quickly. Then she received a message from her body monitor telling her he had cracked her cheekbone—this before it actually began to hurt. Scrambling to her feet again she watched him rubbing his chest. Foam appeared around his lips, then slowly, like a tree, he toppled. Jael walked over to him thinking, *You're so going to regret that, sandapt.* Though maybe most of that anger was at herself—for she had been warned about him.

Getting him onto the gravsled in the low gravity was surprisingly difficult. He must have weighed twice as much as a normal human. Luckily the door to the base was open and designed wide enough to allow the sled inside. After dumping him, she explored, finding the laboratory sited on the lower floor, living quarters on the second, the U-space communicator and computer systems on the top. With a thought, she summoned the *Kobashi* to her present location, then returned her attention to the computer system. It was sub-AI and the usual optic interfaces were available. Finding a suitable network cable, she plugged one end into the computer and the other into the socket in her right-hand aug, then began mentally checking through Rho's files. He was not due to send a report for another two weeks, and the next supply drop was not for three months. However, there was nothing about his most recent find, and recordings of the exchanges she had listened to had been erased. Obviously, assessing his find, he had belatedly increased security.

Jael went back downstairs to study Rho, who was breathing raggedly on the sled. She hoped not to have overdone it with the narcotic. Outside, the whoosh of thrusters announced the arrival of the *Kobashi*, so Jael headed out.

The ship, bearing some resemblance to a thirty-yard-long abdomen and thorax of a praying mantis, settled in a cloud of hot sand in which platinum seeds glinted. Via her twinned augs she sent a signal to it and it folded down a wing section of its hull into a ramp onto which she stepped while it was still settling. At the head of the ramp the outer airlock door irised open and she ducked inside to grab up the pack she had deposited there earlier, then stepped back out and down, returning to the base.

Rho's breathing had eased, so it was with care that she secured his hands and feet in manacles connected by four braided cables to a winder positioned behind him. His eyelids fluttering he muttered something obscure, but did not wake. Jael now took from the pack a bag that looked a little like a nineteenth-century doctor's case, and, four paces from Rho, placed it on the floor. An instruction from her augs caused the bag to open and evert, converting itself into a tiered display of diagnostic and surgical equipment, a small drugs manufactory, and various vials and chainglass tubes containing an esoteric selection of some quite alien oddities. Jael squatted beside the display, took up a diagnosticer, and pressed it against her cheekbone, let it make its diagnosis, then plugged it into the drug manufactory. Information downloaded, the manufactory stuck out a drug patch like a thin tongue. She took this up, peeled off the backing, and stuck it over her injury, which rapidly numbed. While doing this she sensed Rho surfacing into consciousness, and awaited the expected.

Rho flung himself from the sled at her, very fast. She noted he didn't even waste energy on a bellow, but was spinning straight into a kick that would have taken her head off if it had connected. He never got a chance to straighten his leg as the winder rapidly drew in the braided cables, bringing the four manacles together. He crashed to the floor in front of her, a little closer than she had expected, his wrists and ankles locked behind him — twenty years of digging in the dirt had not entirely slowed him down

"Bitch," he said.

Jael removed a scalpel from the display, held it before his face for a moment, then cut his sun visor strap, before trailing it gently down his body to start cutting through the material of his shorts. He tried to drag himself away from her.

"Careful," she warned, "this is chainglass and very, very sharp, and life is a very fragile thing."

"Fuck you," he said without heat, but ceased to struggle. She noted that he had yet to ask what she wanted. Obviously he knew. Next she cut away his boots, before replacing the scalpel in the display and standing.

"Now, Rho, you've been sifting sand here for two decades and discovered what, a handful of fragmentary Atheter artifacts? So, after all that time, finding something new was quite exciting. You made the mistake of toning down your public report to a level somewhere below dry boredom, which was a giveaway to me. Consequently I listened in to your private communications with Charles Cymbeline." She leaned down, her face close to his. "Now I want you to tell me where you've hidden the Atheter artifact you found two weeks ago."

He just stared up at her with those bland blue eyes, so she shrugged, stood up, and began kicking him. He struggled to protect himself, but she took her time, walking round him and driving her boot in repeatedly. He grunted and sweated and started to bleed on the floor.

"All right," he eventually managed. "Arcosect sent a ship a week ago—it's gone."

Panting, Jael stepped back. "There've been no ships here since your discovery." Walking back around to the instrument display she began to make her selection. While she employed her glittering instruments, his grunts soon turned to screams, but he bluntly refused to tell her anything even when she peeled strips of skin from his stomach and crushed his testicles in a set of forceps. But all that was really only repayment for her broken cheekbone. He told her everything when she began using her esoteric selection of drugs, could not do otherwise.

She left him on the floor and crossed the room to where a table lay strewn with rock samples and from there picked up a geological hammer. Back on the top floor she located the U-space coms—the unit was inset into one wall. Her first blow shattered the console, which she tore away. She then began smashing the control components surrounding the sealed flask-sized vessels ostensibly containing small singularity generators and Calabri-yau frames. After a moment she rapped her knuckles against each flask to detect which was the false one, and pulled it out. The top unscrewed and from inside she withdrew a small brushed aluminum box with a keypad inset in the lid. The code he had given her popped the box open to reveal—resting in shaped foam—a chunk of green metal with short thorny outgrowths from one end.

Movement behind . . .

Jael whirled. Rho, catching his breath against the doorjamb, preparing to rush her. Her gaze strayed down to one of the manacles, a frayed stub of wire protruding from it. In his right hand he held what he had used to escape: a chainglass scalpel.

Careless.

Now she had seen him he hurled himself forward.

She could not afford to let him come to grips with her. He was obviously many times stronger than her. As he groped toward her she brought the hammer round in a tight arc against the side of his face, where it connected with a sickening crack. He staggered sideways, clutching his face, his mouth hanging open. She stepped in closer and brought the hammer down as hard as she could on the top of his head. He dropped, dragging her arm down. She released the hammer and saw it had punched a neat square hole straight into his skull and lodged there, then the hole brimmed with blood, and overflowed.

Gazing down at him, Jael said, "Oops." She pushed him with her foot but he was leaden, unmoving. "Oh, well." She pocketed the box containing the Atheter memstore. "One dies and another is destined for resurrection after half a million years. Call it serendipity." She relished the words for a moment, then headed away.

I woke, flat on my back, my face cold and my body one big ache from the sharpest pain at the crown of my skull, to my aching face, and on down to the throbbing from the bones in my right foot. I was breathing shallowly— the air in the room obviously thick to my lungs. Opening bleary eyes I lifted my head slightly and peered down at myself. I wore a quilted warming suit, that obviously accounted for why only my face felt cold. I realized I was in my own bedroom, and that my house had been sealed and the environment controls set to Earth-normal.

"You look like shit, Rho."

The whiff of cigarette smoke told me who was speaking before I identified the voice.

"I guess I do," I said, "though who are you to talk?" I carefully heaved myself upright, then back so I was resting against the bed's headboard, then looked aside at Charles Cymbeline, my boss and the director of Arcosect—a company with a total of about fifty employees. He too looked like shit, always did. He was blond, thin, wore expensive suits that required a great deal of meticulous cleaning, smoked unfiltered cigarettes though what pleasure he derived from them I couldn't fathom, and was very, very dead. He was a reification—a corpse with chemical preservative running in his veins, skin like old leather, with bone and the metal of some of the cyber mechanisms that moved him showing through at his finger joints. His mind was stored to a crystal inside the mulch that had been his brain. Why he retained his old dead body when he could easily afford a golem chassis or a tank-grown living vessel I wasn't entirely sure about either. He said it stopped people bothering him. It did.

"So we lost the memstore," he ventured, then took another pull on his cigarette. Smoke coiled from the gaps in his shirt, obviously making its way out of holes eaten through his chest. He sat in my favorite chair. I would probably have had to clean it, if I'd any intention of staying here.

"I reckon," I replied.

"So she tortured you and you gave it to her," he said. "I thought you were tougher than that."

"She tortured me for fun, and I thought maybe I could draw it out until you arrived, then she used the kind of drugs you normally don't find anywhere outside a Batian interrogation facility. And anyway, it would have come to a choice between me dying or giving up the memstore, and you just don't pay me enough to take the first option."

"Ah." He nodded, his neck creaking, and flicked ash on my carpet.

I carefully swung my legs to one side and sat on the edge of the bed. In one corner a pedestal mounted autodoc stood like a chrome insectile monk. Charles had obviously used it to repair much of the torture damage.

"You said 'she,'" I noted.

"Jael Feogril—my crew here obtained identification from DNA from the handle of that rock hammer we found embedded in your head. You're lucky to be alive. Had we arrived a day later you wouldn't have been."

"She's on record?" I inquired, as if I'd never heard of her.

"Yes—Earth Central Security supplied the details: born on Masada when it was an out-Polity world and made a fortune smuggling weapons to the Separatists. Well connected, augmented with twinned augs as you no doubt saw, and, it would appear, lately branching out into stealing alien artifacts. She's under a death sentence for an impressive list of crimes. I've got it all on crystal if you want it."

"I want it." It would give me detail.

He stared at me expressionlessly, wasn't really capable of doing otherwise.

"What have you got here?" I asked.

"My ship and five of the guys," he said, which accounted for the setting of the environmental controls since he certainly didn't need Earth-normal. "What are your plans?"

"I intend to get that memstore back."

"How, precisely? You don't know where she's gone."

"I have contacts, Charles."

"Who I'm presuming you haven't contacted in twenty years."

"They'll remember me."

He tilted his head slightly. "You never really told me what you used to do before you joined my little outfit. And I have never been able to find out, despite some quite intensive inquiries."

I shrugged, then said, "I'll require a little assistance in other departments."

He didn't answer for a while. His cigarette had burned right down to his fingers and now there was a slight bacony smell in the air. Then he asked, "What do you require?"

"A company ship—the *Ulriss Fire* since it's fast—some other items I'll list, and enough credit for the required bribes."

"Agreed, Rho," he said. "I'll also pay you a substantial bounty for that memstore."

"Good," I replied, thinking the real bounty for me would be getting my hands around Jael Feogril's neck.

From what we can tell, the Polity occupies an area of the galaxy once occupied by three other races. They're called, by us, the Jain, Csorians, and the Atheter. We thought, until only a few years ago, that they were all extinct—wiped out by an aggressive organic technology created by the Jain, which destroyed them and then burgeoned twice more to destroy the other two races—Jain technology. I think we encountered it, too, but information about that is heavily restricted. I think the events surrounding that encounter have something to do with certain Line worlds being under quarantine. I don't know the details. I won't know the details until the AIs lift the restrictions, but I do know something I perhaps shouldn't have been told.

I found the first five years of my new profession as an xeno-archaeologist something of a trial, so Jonas Clyde's arrival on the dust ball I called home came as a welcome relief. He was there direct from Masada—one of those quarantine worlds. He'd come to do some research on the platinum-producing plants, though I rather think he was taking a bit of a rest cure. He shared my home and on plenty of occasions he shared my whisky. The guy was nonstop—physically and mentally adapted to go without sleep—I reckon the alcohol gave him something he was missing.

One evening, I was speculating about what the Atheter might have looked like when I think something snapped in his head and he started laughing hysterically. He auged into my entertainment unit and showed me some recordings. The first was obviously the view from a gravcar taking off from the roof port of a runcible complex. I recognized the planet Masada at once, for beyond the complex stretched a checkerboard of dikes and ponds that reflected a gas giant hanging low in the aubergine sky.

"Here the Masadans raised squirms and other unpleasant life-forms for their religious masters," Jonas told me. "The people on the surface needed an oxygenating parasite attached to their chests to keep them alive. The parasite also shortened their life span."

I guessed it was understandable that they rebelled and shouted for help from the Polity. On the recording I saw people down below, but they wore envirosuits and few of them were working the ponds. Here and there I saw aquatic agrobots standing in the water like stilt-legged steel beetles.

The recording took us beyond the ponds to a wilderness of flute grasses and quagmires. Big fences separated the two. "The best discouragement to some of the nasties out there is that humans aren't very nutritious for them," Jonas told me. "Hooders, heroynes, and gabbleducks prefer their fatter natural prey out in the grasses or up in the mountains." He glanced at me, a little crazily I thought. "Now those monsters have been planted with transponders so everyone knows if something dangerous is getting close, and which direction to run to avoid it."

The landscape in view shaded from white to a dark brown with black earth gullies cutting between islands of this vegetation. It wasn't long before I saw something galumphing through the grasses with the gait of a bear, though on Earth you don't get bears weighing in at about a thousand kilos. Of course I recognized it, who hasn't seen a recording of these things and the other weird and wonderful creatures of that world? The gravcar view drew lower and kept circling above the creature. Eventually it seemed to get bored with running, halted, then slumped back on its rump to sit like some immense pyramidal Buddha. It opened its composite forelimbs into their two sets of three "sublimbs" for the sum purpose of scratching its stomach. It yawned, opening its big duck bill to expose thorny teeth inside. It gazed up at the gravcar with seeming disinterest, some of the tiara of green eyes arcing across its domed head blinking as if it was so bored it just wanted to sleep.

"A gabbleduck," I said to Jonas.

He shook his head and I saw that there were tears in his eyes. "No," he told me, "that's one of the Atheter."

Lubricated on its way by a pint of whisky the story came out piece by piece thereafter. During his research on Masada he had discovered something amazing and quite horrible. That research had later been confirmed by an artifact recovered from a world called Shayden's Find. Jain technology had destroyed the Jain and the Csorians. It apparently destroyed technical civilizations—that was its very purpose. The Atheter had ducked the blow, forgoing civilization, intelligence, reducing themselves to animals, to gabbleducks. Tricone mollusks in the soil of Masada crunched up anything that remained of their technology, monstrous creatures like giant millipedes ate every last scrap of each gabbleduck when it died. It was an appalling and utterly alien nihilism.

The information inside the Atheter memstore Jael had stolen was worth millions. But who was prepared to pay those millions? Polity AIs would, but her chances of selling it to them without ECS coming down on her like a hammer were remote. Also, from what Jonas told me, the Polity had obtained something substantially more useful than a mere memstore, for the artifact from Shayden's Find held an Atheter AI. So who else? Well, I knew about her, though until she'd stuck a narcotic needle in my chest, I had never met her, and I knew that she had dealings with the Prador, that she sold them stuff, sometimes living stuff, sometimes human captives—for there was a black market for such in the Prador Third Kingdom. It was why the Polity AIs were so ticked off about her.

Another thing about Jael was that she was the kind of person who found things out, secret things. She was a Masadan by birth so probably had a lot of contacts on her home world. I wasn't so arrogant as to assume that what Jonas Clyde had blabbed to me had not been blabbed elsewhere. I felt certain she knew about the gabbleducks. And I felt certain she was out for the big killing. The Prador would pay *billions* to someone who delivered into their claws a living, breathing, *thinking* Atheter.

A tenuous logic chain? No, not really. Even as my consciousness had faded, I'd hear her last comment.

The place stank like a sea cave in which dead fish were decaying. Jael brought her foot down hard, but the ship louse tried to crawl out from under it. She put all her weight down on it and twisted, and her foot sank down with a satisfying crunch, spattering glutinous ichor across the crusted filthy floor. Almost as if this were some kind of signal, the wide made-for-something-other-than-human door split diagonally, the two halves revolving up into the wall with a grinding shriek.

The tunnel beyond was dank and dark, weedy growths sprouting like dead man's fingers from the uneven walls. With a chitinous clattering, a flattened-pear carapace scuttling on too many legs appeared and came charging out. It headed straight toward her but she didn't allow herself to react. At the last moment it skidded to a halt then clattered sideways. Prador second-child, one eye-palp missing and a crack healing in its carapace, a rail-gun clutched in one of its underhands, with power cables and a projectile belt-feed trailing back to a box mounted underneath it. While she eyed it, it fed some scrap of flesh held in one of its foreclaws into its mandibles and chomped away enthusiastically.

Next a bigger shape loomed in the tunnel and advanced at a more leisurely pace, its sharp feet hitting the floor with a sound like hydraulic chisels. The first-child was big—the size of a small gravcar—its carapace wider and flatter and looking as hard as iron. The upper turret of its carapace sported a collection of ruby eyes and sprouting above them it retained both of its palp-eyes, all of which gave it superb vision—the eyesight of a carnivore, a predator. Underneath its grating mandibles and the nightmare mouth they exposed, mechanisms had been shell-welded to its carapace. Jael hoped one of these was a translator.

"I didn't want to speak to you at a distance, since, even using your codes, an AI might have been listening in," she said.

After a brief pause to grate its mandibles together, one of the hexagonal boxes attached underneath it spoke, for some reason in a thick Marsman accent. "Our codes are unbreakable."

Jael sighed to herself. Despite having fought the Polity for forty years, some Prador were no closer to understanding that to AIs, no code was unbreakable. Of course all Prador weren't so dumb—the clever ones now ruled the Third Kingdom. This first-child was just aping its father, who was a Prador down at the bottom of the hierarchy and scrabbling to find some advantage to climb higher. However, that father had acquired enough wealth to be able to send its first-child off in a cruiser like this, and would probably be able to acquire more by cutting deals with its competitors—all Prador were competitors. The first-child would need to make those deals, for what Jael hoped to sell the father of this creature it might not be able to afford by itself.

"I will soon be acquiring something that could be of great value to you," she said. Mentioning the Atheter memstore aboard *Kobashi* would have been suicide—Prador only made deals for things they could not take by force.

"Continue," said the first-child.

"I can, for the sum of ten billion New Carth Shillings or the equivalent in any stable currency, including Prador diamond slate, provide you with a living, breathing Atheter."

The Prador dipped its carapace—perhaps the equivalent of a man tilting his head to listen to a private aug communication. Its father must be talking to it. Finally it straightened up again and replied, "The Atheter are without mind."

Jael instinctively concealed her surprise, though that was a pointless exercise since this Prador could no more read her expression than she could read its. How had it acquired that knowledge? She only picked it up by running some very complicated search programs through all the reports coming

from the taxonomic and genetic research station on Masada. Whatever—
she would have to deal with it.

"True, they are, but I have a mind to give to one of them," she replied. "I
have acquired an Atheter memstore."

The first-child advanced a little. "That is very interesting," said the Marsman voice—utterly without inflection.

"Which I of course have not been so foolish as to bring here—it is
securely stored in a Polity bank vault."

"That is also interesting." The first-child stepped back again and Jael
rather suspected something had been lost in translation. It tilted its carapace
forward again and just froze in place, even its mandibles ceasing their constant motion.

Jael considered returning to her ship for the duration. The first-child's
father would now be making its negotiations, striking deals, planning
betrayals—the whole complex and vicious rigmarole of Prador politics and
economics. She began a slow pacing, spotted another ship louse making its
way toward her boots and went over to step on that. She could return to
Kobashi, but would only pace there. She played some games in her twinned
augs, sketching out fight scenarios in this very room, between her and the
two Prador, and solving them. She stepped on four more ship lice, then
accessed a downloaded catalog and studied the numerous items she would
like to buy. Eventually the first-child heaved itself back upright.

"We will provide payment in the form of one half diamond slate, one
quarter a cargo of armor scales, and the remainder in Polity currencies," it said.

Jael balked a little at the armor scales. Prador exotic metal armor was a
valuable commodity, but bulky. She decided to accept, reckoning she could
cache the scales somewhere in the Graveyard and make a remote sale by giving the coordinates to the buyer.

"That's acceptable," she said.

"Now we must discuss the details of the sale."

Jael nodded to herself. This was where it got rather difficult. Organizing
a sale of something to the Prador was like working out how to hand-feed
white sharks while in the water with them.

I gazed out through the screen at a world swathed in cloud, encircled by a
glittering ring shepherded by a sulphurous moon, which itself trailed a
cometary tail resulting from impacts on its surface a hundred and twenty
years old—less than an eye blink in interstellar terms. The first settlers,
leaving just before the Quiet War in the Solar System, had called the
world Paris—probably because of a strong French contingent amid them
and probably because Paradise had been overused. Their civilization was

hardly out of the cradle when the Polity arrived in a big way and subsumed them. After a further hundred years the population of this place surpassed a billion. It thrived, great satellite space stations were built, and huge high-tech industries sprang up in them and in the arid equatorial deserts down below. This place was rich in every resource—surrounding space also swarming with asteroids that were heavy in rare metals. Then, a hundred and twenty years ago, the Prador came. It took them less than a day to depopulate the planet and turn it into the hell I saw before me, and to turn the stations into that glittering ring.

"Ship on approach," said a voice over com. "Follow the vector I give you and do not deviate. At the pick-up point shut down to minimal life support and a grabship will bring you in. Do otherwise and you're smeared. Understood?"

"I understand perfectly," I replied.

Holofiction producers called this borderland between Prador and human space the Badlands. The people who haunted this region, hunting for salvage, called it the Graveyard and knew themselves to be grave robbers. Polity AIs had not tried to civilize the area. All the habitable worlds were still smoking, and why populate any space that acted as a buffer zone between them and a bunch of nasty clawed fuckers who might decide at any moment on a further attempt to exterminate the human race?

"You got the vector, Ulriss?" I asked.

"Yeah," replied my ship's AI. It wasn't being very talkative since I'd refused its suggestion that we approach using the chameleonware recently installed aboard. I eyed the new instruments to my left on the console, remembering that Earth Central Security did not look kindly on anyone but them using their stealth technology. Despite ECS being thin on the ground out here, I had no intention of putting this ship into "stealth mode" unless really necessary. Way back, when I wasn't a xeno-archaeologist, I'd heard rumors about those using inadequate chameleonware ending up on the bad end of an ECS rail-gun test firing. "Sorry, we just didn't see you," was the usual epitaph.

My destination rose over Paris's horizon, cast into silhouette by the bile-yellow sun beyond it. Adjusting the main screen display to give me the best view, I soon discerned the massive conglomeration of station bubble units and docked ships that made up the "Free Republic of Montmartre"—the kind of place that in Earth's past would have been described as a banana republic, though perhaps not so nice. Soon we reached the place designated, and, main power shut down, the emergency lights flickered on. The main screen powered down too, going fully transparent with a photoreactive smear of blackness blotting out the sun's glare and most of the space station. I briefly glimpsed the grabship approaching—basically a one-man vessel with a massive engine to the rear and a hydraulically operated triclaw extending from the nose—before it disappeared back into the smear. They used such ships here since a large-enough proportion of their visitors weren't to be trusted to get simple docking maneuvers right, and wrong moves in that respect could demolish the relatively fragile bubble units and kill those inside.

A clanging against the hull followed by a lurch told me the grabship now had hold of *Ulriss Fire* and was taking us in. It would have been nice to check all this with exterior cameras—throwing up images on the row of sub-screens below the main one—but I had to be very careful about power usage on approach. The Free Republic had been fired on before now, and any ship that showed energy usage above the level-enabling weapons, usually ended up on the mincing end of the infamous rail-gun.

Experience told me that in about twenty minutes the ship would be docked, so I unstrapped and propelled myself into the rear cabin where, in zero-g, I began pulling on my gear. Like many visitors here I took the pre-caution of putting on a light spacesuit of the kind that didn't constrict move-ment, but would keep me alive if there was a blowout. I'd scanned through their rules file, but found nothing much different from when I'd last read it: basically you brought nothing aboard that could cause a breach—this mainly concerned weaponry—nor any dangerous biologicals. You paid a docking tax and a departure tax. And anything you did in the intervening time was your own business so long as it didn't harm station personnel or the station itself. I strapped a heavy carbide knife to my boot, and at my waist holstered a pepper-pot stun gun. It could get rough in there sometimes.

Back in the cockpit I saw *Ulriss Fire* was now drawing into the station shadow. Structural members jutted out all around and ahead I could see an old-style carrier shell, like a huge hexagonal nut, trailing umbilicals and dock-ing tunnel connected to the curve of one bubble unit. Unseen, the grabship inserted my vessel into place and various clangs and crashes ensued.

"Okay, you can power up your airlock now—nothing else, mind."

I did as instructed, watching the display as the airlock connected up to an exterior universal lock, then I headed back to scramble out through the *Ulriss Fire's* airlock. The cramped interior of the carrier shell smelled of mold. I waited there, holding onto the knurled rods of something that looked like a piece of zero-g exercise equipment, eyeing brownish splashes on the walls while a saucer-shaped scanning drone dropped down on a column and gave me the once-over, then I proceeded to the docking tunnel, which smelled of urine. Beside the final lock into the bubble unit was a payment console, into which I inserted the required amount in New Carth Shillings. The lock opened to admit me and now I was of no further interest to station personnel. Others had come in like this. Some of their ships still remained docked. Some had been seized by those who owned the station to be broken for parts or sold on.

Clad in a coldsuit, Jael trudged through a thin layer of CO_2 snow toward the gates of the Arena. Glancing to either side, she eyed the numerous ships down on the granite plain. Other figures were trudging in from them too and a lucky few were flying toward the place in gravcars. She'd considered pulling her trike out of storage, but it would have taken time to assemble and she didn't intend staying here any longer than necessary.

The entry arches—constructed of blocks of water ice as hard as iron at this temperature—were filled with the glimmering menisci of shimmer-shields, probably scavenged from the wreckage of ships floating about in the Graveyard, or maybe from the surface of one of the depopulated worlds. Reaching one of the arches, she pushed through a shield into a long ante-room into which all the arches debouched. The floor was flat granite cut with square spiral patterns for grip and a line of airlock doors punctuated the inner wall. This whole setup was provided for large crowds, which this place had never seen. Beside the airlock she approached was a teller machine of modern manufacture. She accessed it through her right-hand aug and made her payment electronically. The thick insulated lock door thumped open, belching vapor into the frigid air, freezing about her and falling as ice dust. Inside the lock, the temperature rose rapidly. CO_2 ice ablated from her boots and clothing, and after checking the atmosphere reading down in the corner of her visor she retracted visor and hood back down into the collar of her suit.

Beyond the next door was a pillared hall containing a market. Strolling between the stalls she observed the usual tourist tat sold in such places in the Polity, and much else besides. There, under a plasmel dome, someone was selling weapons, and beyond his stall she could hear the hiss and crack of his wares being tested in a thick-walled shooting gallery. There a row of food vendors were serving everything from burgers to alien arthropods you ate while they were still alive and that apparently gave some kind of high. The smell of coffee wafted across, along with tobacco, cannabis, and other more esoteric smokes.

All around the walls of the hall, stairs wound up to other levels, some connecting above to the tunnels leading to the arena itself, others to the pens and others to private concerns. She knew where to go, but had some other business to conduct first with a dealer in biologicals. Anyway, she didn't want the man she had specifically come here to see to think she was in a hurry, or anxious to buy the item he had on offer.

The dealer's emporium was built between four pillars, three floors tall and reaching the ceiling. The lower floor was a display area with four entrances around the perimeter. She entered and looked around. Aisles cut to a central spiral stair between tanks, terrariums, cages, display cases, and stock-search screens. She spotted a tank full of Spatterjay leeches, "Immortality in a bite! Guaranteed!," a cage in which big scorpionlike insects were tearing into a mass of purple and green bones and meat, and a display containing little tubes of seeds below pictures of the plants they would produce. Mounting the stairs, she climbed to the next floor where two catadapts were studying something displayed on the screens of a nanoscope. They looked like customers, as did the thin woman who was peering into a cylindrical tank containing living Dracocorp augs. On the top floor, Jael found who she was looking for.

The office was small, the rest of the floor obviously used for living accommodation. The woman with a severe skin complaint, baggy, layered clothing, and a tricorn hat, sat back with heavy snow boots up on her desk, crusted fingers up against her aug while she peered at screens showing views of those on the floors below. She was nodding—obviously conducting some transaction or conversation by aug. Jael stepped into the room, plumped herself down in one of the form chairs opposite, and waited. The woman glanced at her, smiled to expose a carnivore's teeth, and held up one finger. Wait one moment.

Her business done, the woman took her feet off the desk and turned her chair so she was facing Jael.

"Well, what can I do for *you?*" she asked, utterly focused. "Anything under any sun is our motto. We're also an agent for Dracocorp and are now branching out into cosmetics."

"Forgive me," said Jael, "if I note that you're not the best advert for the cosmetics."

The woman leant an elbow on the table, reached up, and peeled a thick dry flake of skin from her cheek. "That's because you don't know what you're seeing. Once the change is complete my skin will be resistant to numerous acids and even to vacuum."

"I'm here to sell," said Jael.

The woman sat back, not quite so focused now. "I see. Well, we're always prepared to take a look at what . . . people have to offer."

Jael removed a small sample tube from her belt cache, placed it on the desk edge and rolled it across. The woman took it up, peered inside, a powerful lens clicking down from her hat to cover her eye.

"Interesting. What are they?"

Jael tapped a finger against her right-hand aug. "This would be quicker."

A message flashed across to her, giving her a secure loading address. She transmitted the file she had compiled about the seeds gathered on that dusty little planet where she had obtained her real prize. The woman went blank for a few minutes while she ran through the data. Jael scanned around the room, wondering what security there was here.

"I think we can do business—once I've confirmed all this."

"Please confirm away."

The woman took the tube over to a combined nanoscope and multi-spectrum scanner and inserted it inside.

Jael continued, "But I don't want money, Desorla."

Desorla froze, staring at the scope's display. After a moment she said, "This all seems in order." She paused, head bowed. "I haven't heard that name in a long while."

"I find things out," said Jael.

Desorla turned and eyed the gun Jael now held. "What do you want?"

"I want you to tell me where Penny Royal is hiding."

Desorla chuckled unconvincingly. "Looking for legends? You can't seriously—"

Jael aimed and fired three times. Two explosions blew cavities in the walls, a third explosion flung paper fragments from a shelf of books, and a metallic tongue bleeding smoke slumped out from behind. Two cameras and the security drone—Jael had detected nothing else.

"I'm very serious," said Jael. "Please don't make me go get my doctor's bag."

Broeven took one look at me and turned white, well, as pale as a Krodorman can get. He must have sent some sort of warning signal, because suddenly two heavies appeared out of the fug from behind him—one a boosted woman with the face of an angel and a large grey military aug affixed behind her ear, the other an ophidapt man who was making a point of extruding the carbide claws from his fingertips. The thin guy sitting opposite Broeven glanced round, then quickly drained his schooner of beer, took up a wallet from the table, nodded to Broeven, and departed. I sauntered over, turned the abandoned chair round, and sat astride it.

"You've moved up in the world," I said, nodding to Broeven's protection.

"So what do I call you now?" he asked, the whorls in the thick skin of his face flushing red.

"Rho, which is actually my real name."

"That's nice—we didn't get properly acquainted last time we met." He held up a finger. "Gene, get Rho a drink. Malt whisky do you?"

I nodded. The woman frowned in annoyance and departed. Perhaps she thought the chore beneath her.

"So what can I do for you, Rho?" he inquired.

"Information."

"Which costs."

"Of course." I peered down at the object the guy here before me had left on the table. It was a small chainglass case containing a strip of chameleon-cloth with three crab-shaped and, if they were real, gold buttons pinned to it. "Are those real?"

"They are. People know better than to try cheating me now."

I looked up. "I never cheated you."

"No, you promised not to open the outer airlock door if I told you what you wanted to know. My life in exchange for information and you stuck to your side of the deal. I can't say that makes me feel any better about it."

"But you're a businessman," I supplied.

"But I'm a businessman."

The boosted woman returned carrying a bottle of ersatz malt and a tumbler that she slammed down on the table before me, before stepping back. I can't say I liked having her behind me. I reached down and carefully opened a belt pouch, feeling the tension notch up a bit. The ophidapt partially unfolded his arms and fully extended his claws. I took out a single blue stone and placed it next to the glass case. Broeven eyed the stone for a moment then picked it up between gnarled forefinger and thumb. He produced a reader and placed the etched sapphire inside.

"Ten thousand," he said. "For what?"

"That's for services rendered—twenty-three years ago—and if you don't want to do further business with me, you keep it and I leave."

He slipped the sapphire, and the glass case, into the inner pocket of his heavy coat, then sat upright, contemplating me. I thought for a moment he was going to get up and leave. Trying to remain casual, I scanned around the interior of the bar and noticed it wasn't so full as I'd remembered it being and everyone seemed a bit subdued, conversations whispered and more furtive, no one getting shit-faced.

"Very well," he said. "What information do you require?"

"Two things: first I want everything you can track down about gabble-ducks possibly in or near the Graveyard." That got me a rather quizzical expression. "And second I want everything you can give me about Jael Feogril's dealings over the last year or so."

"A further ten thousand," he said, and I read something spooked in his expression. I took out another sapphire and slid it across to him. He checked it with his reader and pocketed it before uttering another word.

"I'll give you two things." He made a circular gesture with one finger. "Jael Feogril might be dealing out of her league."

"Go on."

"*Them* . . . a light destroyer . . . Jael's ship docked with it briefly only a month ago, before departing. They're still out there."

I realized then why it seemed so quiet in the bar and elsewhere in the station. The people here were those who hadn't run for cover, and were perhaps wishing they had. It was never the healthy option to remain in the vicinity of the Prador.

"And the second thing?"

"The location of the only gabbleduck in the Graveyard, which I can give you without even doing any checking, since I've already given it to Jael Feogril."

After he'd provided the information I headed away—I had enough to be going on with, and maybe, if I moved fast . . . I paused on my way back to my ship, seeing that Broeven's female heavy was walking along behind me, and turned to face her. She walked straight past me, saying, "I'm not a fucking waitress."

She seemed in an awful hurry.

On the stone floor two opponents faced off. Both were men, both were boosted. Jael wondered if people like them ever considered treatment for excessive testosterone production. The bald-headed thug was unarmed and resting his hands on his knees as he caught his breath, twin-pupil eyes fixed on his opponent. The guy with the long queue of hair was also unarmed, though the platelike lumps all over his overly muscled body were evidence of subcutaneous armor. After a moment they closed and began hammering at each other again, fists impacting with meaty snaps against flesh, blows blocked and diverted, the occasional kick slamming home, though neither of them was really built for that kind of athleticism.

Inevitably, one of them was called Tank—the one with the queue. The other was called Norris. These two had been hammering away at each other for twenty minutes to the growing racket from the audience, but whether that noise arose from the spectators' enjoyment of the show or because they wanted to get to the next event was debatable.

Eventually, after many scrappy encounters, Tank managed to deliver an axe kick to the side of Norris's head and laid him out. Tank, though the winner, needed to be helped from the arena too, obviously having overextended himself with that last kick. Once the area was clear, the next event was announced and a gate opened somewhere below Jael. She observed a great furry muscular back and wide head as a giant mongoose shot out. The creature came to an abrupt stop in the middle of the arena and stood up to the height of a man on its hindquarters. Jael discarded her beer tube and stood, heading over toward the pens. The crowd was now shouting for one of the giant cobras the mongoose dispatched with utterly unamazing regularity. She wasn't really all that interested.

The doors down into the pens were guarded by a thug little different to those who had been in the ring below. He was there because previous security systems had often been breached and some of the fighters, animal, human, or machine, had been knobbled.

"I'm here to see Koober," said Jael.

The man eyed her for a moment. "Jael Feogril," he said, reaching back to open the door. "Of course you are."

Jael stepped warily past then descended the darkened stair.

Koober was operating a small electric forklift on the tines of which rested the corpse of a seal. He raised a hand to her then motored forward to drop the load down into one of the pens. Jael stepped over and peered down at the ratty-looking polar bear that took hold of the corpse and dragged it back across the ice to one corner, leaving a gory trail.

Koober, a thin hermaphrodite in much-repaired mesh inlaid overalls, leapt off the forklift and gestured. "This way." He led her down a stair into moist rancid corridors then finally to an armored door that he opened with a press of his hand against a palm lock. At the back of the circular chamber within, squatting in its own excrement, was the animal she had come to see—thick chains leading from a steel collar to secure it to the back wall.

A poor-looking specimen, about the size of a Terran black bear, its head was bowed low, the tip of its bill resting against the ground. Lying on the filthy stone beside it were the dismembered remains of something obviously grown hastily in a vat—weak, splintered bones and watery flesh, tumors exposed like bunches of grapes. While Jael watched, the gabbleduck abruptly hissed and heaved its head upright. Its green eyes ran in an arc across its domed head, there were twelve or so of them: two large egg-shaped ones toward the center, two narrow ones below these like underscores, two rows of small round ones arcing out to terminate against two triangular ones. They all had lids—the outer two blinking open and closed alternately. Its conjoined forelimbs were folded mummylike across the raised crosshatch ribbing of its chest, its gut was baggy and veined, and purple sores seeped in its brown-green skin.

"And precisely how much did you want for this?" inquired Jael disbelievingly.

"It's very rare," said Koober. "There's a restriction on export now and that's pushed prices up. You won't find any others inside the Graveyard, and those running wild on Polity worlds have mostly been tagged and are watched."

"Why then are you selling it?"

Koober looked shifty—something he seemed better at doing than looking after the animals he provided for the arena. "It's not suitable."

"You mean it won't fight," said Jael.

"Shunder-club froob," said the gabbleduck, but its heart did not seem to be in it.

"All it does is sit there and do that. We put it up against the lion"—he pointed at some healing claw marks in its lower stomach—"and it just sat there and starting muttering to itself. The lion tried to jump out of the arena."

Jael nodded to herself, then turned away. "Not interested."

"Wait!" Koober grabbed her arm. She caught his hand, turned it into a wrist lock, forcing him down to his knees.

"Don't touch me." She released him.

"If it's a matter of the price—"

"It's a matter of whether it will even survive long enough for you to get it aboard my ship, and even then I wonder how long it will survive afterward."

"Look, I'll be taking a loss, but I'm sure we can work something out. . . ."

Inside, Jael smiled. When the deal was finally struck she allowed that smile out, for even if the creature died she might well net a profit just selling its corpse. She had no intention of letting it die. The medical equipment, and related gabbleduck physiology files aboard *Kobashi* should see to that, along with her small cargo of frozen Masadan grazers—the gabbleduck's favored food.

I was feeling slightly pissed off when, after the interminable departure from Paris station, the grabship finally released *Ulriss Fire*. Even as the grabship carried my ship out I'd seen another ship departing the station under its own power. It seemed that there were those for whom the rules did not apply, or those who knew who to bribe.

"Run system checks," I instructed.

"Ooh, I never thought of that," replied Ulriss.

"And there was me thinking AIs were beyond sarcasm."

"It's a necessary tool used for communicating with a lower species," the ship's AI replied. I still think it was annoyed that I wouldn't let it use the chameleonware.

"Take us under," I said, ignoring the jibe.

Sudden acceleration pushed me back into my chair, and I felt, at some point deep inside my skull, the U-space engine come online. My perception distorted, the stars in the cockpit screen faded, and the screen greyed out. It lasted maybe a few seconds, then *Ulriss Fire* shuddered like a ground car rolling over a mass of deep potholes, and a starry view flicked back into place.

"What the fuck happened?"

"Checking," said Ulriss.

I began checking as well, noting that we'd traveled only about eighty million miles and had surfaced in the real in deep space. However, I was getting mass readings out there.

"We hit USER output," Ulriss informed me.

I just sat there for a moment, wracking my brains to try and figure out what a "user" was. I finally admitted defeat. "I've no idea what you're talking about."

"I see," said Ulriss, in an irritatingly superior manner. "The USER acronym stands for Underspace Inference Emitter—"

"Shouldn't that be UIE, then?"

"Do you want to know what a USER is, or would you rather I began using my sarcasm tool again?"

"Sorry, do carry on."

"A USER is a device that shifts a singularity in and out of U-space via a runcible gate, thus creating a disturbance that knocks any ships that are within range out of that continuum. The USER here is a small one aboard the Polity dreadnought currently three thousand miles away from us. I don't think we were the target. I think that was the cruiser now coming up to port."

With the skin crawling on my back, I took up the joystick and asserted positional control, nudging the ship round with a spurt of air from its attitude jets. Stars swung across the screen, then a large ugly-looking vessel swung into view. It looked like a flattened pear, but one stretched from a point on its circumference. It was battered, its brassy exotic armor showing dents and burns that its memform and s-con grids had been unable to deal with, and that hadn't been repaired since. Missile ports and the mouths of rail-guns and beam weapons dotted that hull, but they looked perfectly serviceable. Ulriss had neglected to mention the word *Prador* before the word *cruiser*. This is what had everyone checking their online wills and talking in whispers back in Paris.

"Stealth mode?" suggested Ulriss with a degree of smugness.

"Fucking right," I replied.

The additional instruments came alight and a luminescent ribbing began to track across the screen before me. I wondered how good the chameleonware was, since maybe bad chameleonware would put us in even greater danger—the Prador suspecting some sort of attack if they detected us.

"And now if you could ease us away from that thing?"

The fusion drive stuttered randomly—a low power note and firing format that wouldn't put out too regular ionization. We fell away, the Prador cruiser thankfully receding, but now, coming into view, a Polity dreadnought. At one time, the Prador vessel would have outclassed a larger Polity ship. It was an advantage the nasty aliens maintained throughout their initial attack during the war: exotic metal armor that could take a ridiculously intense pounding. Now Polity ships were armored in a similar manner, and carried weapons and EM warfare techniques that could penetrate to the core of Prador ships.

"What the hell is happening here?" I wondered.

"There is some communication occurring, but I cannot penetrate it."

"Best guess?"

"Well, ECS does venture into the Graveyard, and it is still considered Polity territory. Maybe the Prador have been getting a little bit too pushy."

I nodded to myself. Confrontations like these weren't that uncommon in the Graveyard, but this one was bloody inconvenient. While I waited, something briefly blanked the screen. When it came back on again I observed a ball of light a few hundred miles out from the cruiser, shrinking rather than expanding, then winking out.

"CTD imploder," Ulriss informed me.

I was obviously behind the times. I knew a CTD was an antimatter bomb, but an "imploder"? I didn't ask.

After a little while the Prador ship's steering thrusters stabbed out into vacuum and ponderously turned it over, then its fusion engines flared to life and began taking it away.

"Is that USER still on?" I asked.

"It is."

"Why? I don't see the point."

"Maybe ECS is just trying to *make* a point."

The USER continued functioning for a further five hours while the Prador ship departed. I almost got the feeling that those in the Polity dreadnought knew I was there and were deliberately delaying me. When it finally stopped, it took another hour before U-space had settled down enough for us to enter it without being flung out again. It had all been very frustrating.

People knew that if a ship was capable of traveling through U-space it required an AI to control its engines. Mawkishly they equated artificial intelligence with the godlike creations that controlled the Polity, somehow forgetting that colony ships with U-space engines were leaving the Solar System before the Quiet War, and before anyone saw anything like the silicon intelligences that were about now. The supposedly primitive Prador, who had nearly smashed the Polity, failed because they did not have AI, apparently. How then did they run the U-space engines in their ships? It came down, in the end, to the definition of AI—something that had been undergoing constant revision for centuries. The thing that controlled the engines in the *Kobashi*, Jael did not call an AI. She called it a "control system" or sometimes, a "Prador control system."

Kobashi surfaced from U-space on the edge of the Graveyard far from any sun. The coordinates Desorla had reluctantly supplied were constantly changing in relation to nearby stellar bodies, but, checking her scanners, Jael saw that they were correct, if this black planetoid—a wanderer between stars—was truly the location of Penny Royal. The planetoid was not much bigger than Earth's Moon, was frigid, without atmosphere, and had not seen any volcanic activity quite possibly for billions of years. However, her scans did reveal a cannibalized ship resting on the surface and bonded-regolith tunnels winding away from it like worm casts to eventually disappear into the ground. She also measured EM output—energy usage—for signs of life. Positioning *Kobashi* geostationary above the other ship, she began sending signals.

"Penny Royal, I am Jael Feogril and I have come to buy your services. I know that the things you value are not the same as those valued by . . . others. If you assist me, you will gain access to an Atheter memstore, from which you may retain a recording."

She did not repeat the message. Penny Royal would have seen her approach and been monitoring her constantly ever since. The thing called Penny Royal missed very little.

Eventually she got something back: landing coordinates—nothing else. She took *Kobashi* down, settling between two of those tunnels with the nose of her ship only fifty yards from the other ship's hull. Studying the other vessel she recognized a Polity destroyer, its sleek lines distorted, parts of it missing as if it had been slowly been draining into the surrounding tunnels. After a moment she saw an irised airlock open. No message—the invitation was in front of her. Heading back into her quarters she donned an armored spacesuit, took up her heavy pulse-rifle with its underslung minilauncher, her sidearm, and a selection of grenades. Likely the weapons would not be enough if Penny Royal launched some determined attack, but they might and that was enough of a reason. She resisted the impulse to go and check on the gabbleduck, but it was fine, its sores healed and flesh building up on its bones, its nonsensical statements much more emphatic.

Beyond *Kobashi* her boots crunched on a scree surface. Her suit's visor set to maximum light amplification, she peered down at a surface that seemed to consist entirely of loose flat hexagonal crystals, like coins. They were a natural formation and nothing to do with this planetoid's resident. However, the thing that stabbed up through this layer nearby—like an eyeball impaled on a thin curved thorn of metal—certainly belonged to Penny Royal.

Jael finally stepped into the airlock, and noticed that the inner door was open too, so she would not be shedding her spacesuit. For no apparent reason other than to unnerve her, the first lock door swiftly closed once she was through. Within the ship she necessarily turned on her suit lights to complement the light amplification. The interior had been stripped right down to the hull members. All that Penny Royal had found no use for elsewhere, lay in a heap to one side of the lock, perhaps ready to be thrown outside. The twenty or so crew members had been desiccated—hard vacuum freeze-drying and preserving them. They rested in a tangled pile like some nightmare monument. Jael noticed the pile consisted only of woody flesh and frangible bone. No clothing there, no augs, no jewelry. It occurred to her that Penny Royal had not thrown these corpses outside because the entity might yet find a use for them.

She scanned about herself, not quite sure where to go now. Across the body of the ship from her was the mouth of one of those tunnels, curving down into darkness. *There?* No, to her right the mouth of another tunnel emitted heat a little above the ambient. Stepping over hull beams she began to make her way toward it, then silvery tentacular fingers eased out around the lip of the tunnel and heaved out an object two yards across and seemingly formed by computer junk from the ship compressed into a sphere. Lights glimmered inside the tangle and it extruded antennas, and eyes like the one she had seen outside. Settling down it seemed to unravel slightly, whereupon a fleshless golem unpeeled from its surface, stood upright, and advanced a couple of paces, a thick ribbed umbilicus still keeping it connected.

During the Prador-Human war it had been necessary to quickly manufacture the artificial intelligences occupying stations, ships, and drones, for casualties were high. Quality control suffered and these intelligences, which in peacetime would have needed substantial adjustments, were sent to the front. As a matter of expediency, flawed crystal got used rather than discarded. Personality fragments were copied, sometimes not very well, successful fighters or tacticians recopied. The traits constructed or duplicated were not necessarily those evincing morality. Some of these entities went rogue and became what were described as black AIs.

Like Penny Royal.

Standing at his shoulder, the boosted woman, Gene, gave Koober the confidence to defy me. I'd already told him that I knew Jael had bought the gabbleduck from him, I just wanted to know if he knew anything else: who else she might have seen here, where she was going . . . anything really. I was equally curious to know how Broeven's ex-employee had ended up here. It struck me that this went beyond the bounds of coincidence.

"I don't have to tell you nothing, Sandman," he said, using my old name with its double meaning.

"True, you don't," I replied. I really hated how the scum I'd known twenty years ago all seemed to have floated to the top. "Which is why I'm prepared to pay for what you can tell me."

He glanced back at his protection, then crossed his arms. "You were the big man once, but that ain't so now. I got my place here at the Arena and I got a good income. I don't even have to speak to you." He unfolded his arms and waved a finger imperiously. "Now piss off."

Not only was he defiant, but stupid. The woman, no matter how vigilant, could not protect him from a seeker bullet or a pin, coated with bone-eating nanite, glued to a door handle. But I didn't do that sort of stuff now. I was retired. I carefully reached into my belt pouch and took out one of my remaining etched sapphires. I would throw it, and while the gem arced through the air toward Koober and the woman, I reckoned on getting the drop on them. My pepper-pot stun gun was lodged in the back of my belt. Of course I'd take her down first. I tossed the gem and began to reach.

She moved. Koober went over her foot and was heading for the ground. The sapphire glimmered in the air still as the barrel of the pulse-gun centered on my forehead. I guess I was rusty, because I didn't even consider throwing myself aside. For a moment I just thought, *That's it*, but no field-accelerated pulse of aluminum dust blew my head apart. She caught the gem in her other hand and flipped it straight back at me. With my free hand I caught it, my other hand relaxing its grip on my gun and carefully easing out to one side, fingers spread.

"I believe my boss just told you to leave," she said.

Koober was lying on the floor swearing, then he looked up and paused—only now realizing what had happened.

I nodded an acknowledgment to Gene, turned, and quickly headed for the stair leading up from the pens, briefly glimpsed an oversized mongoose chewing on the remains of a huge snake on the arena floor, then headed back toward the market where I might pick up more information. What the hell was a woman like her doing with a lowlife like Koober? It made no sense, and the coincidence of her being here just stretched things too far. I wondered if Broeven had sent her to try to cash in—guessing I was probably after something valuable. Such thoughts concerned me—that's my excuse. She came at me from a narrow side-tunnel. I only managed to turn a little before she grabbed me, spun me round, and slammed me against the wall of the exit tunnel. I turned, and again found myself looking down the barrel of that pulse-gun. People around us quickly made themselves scarce.

"Koober had second thoughts about letting you go," she said.

"Really?" I managed.

"He is a little slow, sometimes," she opined. "It occurred to him, once you were out of sight, that you might resent his treatment of you and come back to slip cyanide in his next soy burger."

"He's a vegetarian?"

"It's working with the animals—put him off meat."

I watched her carefully, wondering why I was still alive. "Are you going to kill me?"

"I haven't decided yet."

"Have you ever killed anyone?"

"Many people, but in most cases the choice was theirs."

"That's very moral of you."

"So it would seem," she agreed. "Koober is shit-scared of you. Apparently you're a multiple murderer?"

"Hit man."

"Murderer."

Ah, I thought I knew what she was now.

"I think you know precisely who I am and what I was," I said. "Now I'm a xeno-archaeologist trying to track down stolen goods."

"I stayed here too long," she said distractedly, shaking her head. "It was going to be my pleasure to shut Koober down." She paused for a moment, considering. "You should stay out of this, Rho. This has gone beyond you."

"If you say so," I said. "You've got the gun."

She lowered her weapon, then abruptly holstered it. "If you don't believe me, then I suggest you go and see a dealer in biologicals called Desorla. Apparently Jael visited her before coming to see Koober, and their dealings involved Jael shooting out the cameras and security drones in Desorla's office."

"Just biologicals?"

"Desorla has . . . connections."

She moved away and right then I felt no inclination to go after her. Maybe she was feeding me a line of bullshit or maybe she was giving me the lead I needed. If not, I'd come back to the pen well prepared.

In the market, one of the stall holders quickly directed me toward Desorla's emporium. I entered through one of the floor-level doors and found no activity inside. A spiral staircase led up, but a gate had been drawn across it and locked. I recognized the kind of lock immediately and set to work on it with the tools about my person. Like I said, I was rusty, it took me nearly thirty seconds to break the programs. I climbed up, scanned the next floor, then climbed higher still to the top floor.

The office was clean and empty, so I kicked in the flimsy door into the living accommodation. Nothing particularly unusual here . . . then I saw the blood on the floor and the big glass bottle on her coffee table. Stepping round the spatters I peered into the bottle, and, in the crumpled and somewhat scabby pink mass inside, a nightmare eyeless face peered out at me. Then something dripped on top of my head. I looked up. . . .

Over by the window I caught my breath, but no one was giving me time for that. Arena security thugs were running toward the emporium and beyond them I could see Gene striding off toward the exit. I opened the window just as the thugs entered the building below me, did a combination of scramble and fall down the outside of the building and hit the stone flat on my back. I had to catch my breath then. After a moment I heaved myself upright and headed for the exit, closing up the visor and hood of my enviro-suit and keeping Gene just in sight. I went fast through an airlock far to the left of her, and some paces ahead of her, and was soon running down count-ing arches. I drew my carbide knife and dropped down beside one arch, hop-ing I'd counted correctly.

She stepped out to my left. I knew I could not give her the slightest chance or she would take me down yet again. I drove the knife in to the side, cut down, grabbed and pulled. In a gout of icy fog her visor skittered across the stone. Choking, she staggered away from me, even then drawing her pulse-gun, which must have been cold-adapted. I drove a foot into her ster-num, knocked the last of her air out. Pulse-gun shots tracked along the frigid stone past me and I brought the edge of my hand down on her wrist, cracking bone, and knocking the weapon away. Her fist slammed into my ribs and her foot came up to nearly take my head off. Blind and suffocating, she was the hardest opponent I'd faced hand-to-hand . . . or maybe it was that rustiness again. But she went down, eventually, and I dragged her to *Ulriss Fire* before anoxia killed her.

"Okay," I said as she regained consciousness. "What the fuck killed her?"

After a moment of peering at the webbing straps binding her into the chair, she said, "You broke my wrist."

"Talk to me and I'll let my autodoc work on it. You set me up, Gene. Is that your real name?"

She nodded absently, though whether that was in answer to my question I couldn't tell. "I noticed you said 'what' rather than 'who.'"

"A human who takes the trouble to skin someone alive and nail them to the ceiling without making a great deal more mess than that shouldn't be classified as a who. It's a thing." I watched her carefully—trying to read her. "So maybe it was a thing . . . rogue golem?"

"Rho Var Olssen, employed by ECS for wet ops outside the Line, a sort of one-man vengeance machine for the Polity, who maybe started to like his job just a little too much. Who are you to righteously talk about classifications?"

"So you know about me. I had you typed when you insisted on calling me a murderer. Nothing quite so moralistic as an ECS agent working out-side of her remit—helps to justify it all."

"Fuck you."

"Hit a nerve did I?" I paused, thinking that perhaps I was being a little naïve. She was baiting me to lead me away from the point. "So it was a golem that killed Desorla?"

"In a sense," she admitted grudgingly. "She was watched and she said too much—to Jael, specifically."

"Tell me more about Jael."

Staring at me woodenly she said, "What's to tell? We knew her interest in ancient technology and we knew she kept a careful eye on people like you. We put something in the way of your sifter and made sure she found out about it."

I felt hollow. "The memstore . . . it's a fake?"

"No, it's the real thing, Rho. It had to be."

I thought about me lying on the floor of my home with a rock hammer embedded in my skull. "I could have died."

"An acceptable level of collateral damage in an operation like this," she said flatly.

I thought about that for one brief horrible moment. Really, there were many people on many worlds trying to find Atheter artifacts, but how many of them were like me? How many of them were so *inconvenient*? I imagined this was why some AI had chosen my life as an "acceptable level of collateral damage."

"And what is this operation?" I finally asked. "Are you out to nail Prador?"

She laughed.

"I guess not," I said.

"You worked out what Jael was doing yourself. I don't know how . . ." She gazed at me for a moment, but I wasn't going to help her out. She continued, "If she can restore the mind to a gabbleduck, she has an item to sell to the Prador that will net her more wealth than even she would know how to spend. But there's a problem: you don't just feed the memstore to the gabbleduck, you're not even going to be able to jury-rig some kind of linkup using aug technology. That memstore is complex alien tech loaded in a language few can understand."

"She needs an AI . . . or something close . . ."

"On the button, but though some AIs might venture outside Polity law as we see it, there are certain lines even they won't cross. Handing over a living Atheter to the Prador is well over those lines."

"A Prador AI, then."

"The only ones they have are in their ships—their purpose utterly fixed. They don't have the flexibility."

"So what the fuck—"

"Ever heard of Penny Royal?" she interrupted.

I felt a surge of almost superstitious dread. "You have got to be shitting me."

"No shit, Rho. You can see this is out of your league. We're done here."

"You put some kind of tracer in the memstore."

She gave me a patronizing smile. "Too small. We needed U-tech."

Suddenly I got the idea. "You put it in the gabbleduck."

"We did." She stared at me for a long moment, then continued resignedly, "The signal remains constant, giving a Polity ship in the Graveyard the creature's location from moment to moment. The moment the gabbleduck is connected to the memstore, the signal shuts down, then we'll know that Penny Royal has control of both creature and store, and then the big guns move in. This is over, Rho. Can't you see that? You've played your part and now the game has moved as far beyond you as it has moved beyond me. It's time for us both to go home."

"No," I said. I guessed she didn't understand how being tortured, then nearly killed, had really ticked me off. "It's time for you to tell me how to find Jael. I've still got a score to settle with her."

Jael did not like being this close to a golem. Either they were highly moral creatures who served the Polity and would not look kindly on her actions, and who were thoroughly capable of doing something about them, or they were the rare amoral-immoral kind, and quite capable of doing something really nasty. No question here—the thing crammed in beside her in the airlock was a killer, or, rather, it was a remote probe, a submind that was part of a killer. As she understood it, Penny Royal had these submind golem scattered throughout the Graveyard, often contributing to the title of the place.

After the lock pressurized, the inner door opened to admit them into the *Kobashi*. While Jael removed her spacesuit the golem just stood to one side—a static silver skeleton with hardware in its rib cage, cybermotors at its joints and interlinked down its spine, and blue-irised eyeballs in the sockets of its skull. She wondered if it had willingly subjected itself to Penny Royal's will or been taken over. Probably the latter.

"This way," she said to it once she was ready, and led the way back toward the ship's hold. Behind her the golem followed with a clatter of metallic feet. Why did it no longer wear syntheflesh and skin? Just to make it more menacing? She wasn't sure Penny Royal was that interested in interacting with people. Maybe the usual golem coverings just didn't last in this environment.

At her aug command a bulkhead door thumped open and she paused beside it to don a breather mask before stepping through into an area caged off from the rest of the hold. The air within was low in oxygen and would slowly suffocate a human, but it mixing with the rest of the air in the ship while this door was open wasn't a problem since the pressure differential pushed the ship air into this space. The briefly higher oxygen levels would not harm the hold's occupant since its body was rugged enough to survive a range of environments—probably its kind was engineered that way long ago. Beyond the caged area in which they stood, the floor was layered a foot deep with flute grass rhizomes—as soggy underfoot as sphagnum. The walls displayed Masadan scenery overlaid with bars so the occupant didn't make the mistake of trying to run off through them. Masadan wildlife sounds filled the air and there were even empty tricone shells on the rhizome mat for further authenticity.

The gabbleduck looked a great deal more alert and a lot healthier than when Koober had owned it. As always, when she came in here, it was squatting in one corner. Other than via the cameras in here, she had seen it do nothing else. It was as if, every time she approached, it heard her and moved to that corner, which should not have been possible since the bulkhead door was thoroughly insulated.

"Subject appears adequate," said the golem. "It will be necessary to move it into the complex for installation."

"Gruvver fleeg purnok," said the gabbleduck dismissively.

"The phonetic similarity of the gabble to human language has always been puzzling," said the golem.

"Right," said Jael. "The memstore?" She gestured to the door and the golem obligingly moved out ahead of her.

She overtook the golem in the annex to the main airlock, opened another bulkhead door, and led the way into her living area. Here she paused. "Before I show you this next item, there are one or two things we need to agree on." She turned and faced the golem. "The gabbleduck and the memstore must go no deeper into your complex than half a mile."

The golem just stared at her, waiting, not asking the question a human would have asked. It annoyed Jael that Penny Royal probably understood her reasoning and it annoyed her further that she still felt the need to explain. "That keeps it within the effective blast radius of my ship. If I die, or if you try to take from me the gabbleduck or the memstore, I can aug a signal back here to start up the U-space engine, the field inverted and ten degrees out of phase. The detonation would excise a fair chunk of this planetoid."

The golem just said, "The AI here is of Prador manufacture."

"It is."

"My payment will be a recording of the Atheter memstore, and a recording of the Prador AI."

"That seems . . . reasonable, though you'll receive the recording of the Prador AI just before I'm about to leave." She didn't want Penny Royal to have time to work out how to crack her ship's security.

At that moment, the same Prador AI—without speaking—alerted her to activity outside the ship. Using her augs she inspected an external view from the ship's cameras. One of the tunnel tubes, its mouth filled with some grub-like machine, was advancing toward *Kobashi*.

"What's going on outside?" she inquired politely.

"I presume you have no spacesuit for the gabbleduck?"

"Ah."

Despite her threat, Jael knew she wasn't fully in control here. She stepped up to one wall, via her aug commanding a safe to open. A steel bung a foot across eased out then hinged to one side. She reached in, picked up the memstore, then held it out to the golem. The test would come, she felt certain, when Penny Royal authenticated that small item.

The golem took the memstore between its finger and thumb and she noticed it had retained the syntheflesh pads of its fingers. It paused, frozen in place, then abruptly its rib cage split down the center and one half of it hinged aside. Within lay optics, the grey lump of a power supply, and various interconnected units like steel organs. There were also dark masses spread like multiarmed starfish that Jael suspected had not been there when this golem was originally constructed. It pressed the memstore into the center of one of these masses, which writhed as if in pain and closed over it.

"Unrecognized programming format," said the golem.

No shit, thought Jael.

The golem continued, "Estimate at one hundred and twenty gigabytes, synaptic mapping and chronology of implantation. . . ."

Jael felt a sudden foreboding. Though measuring a human mind in bytes wasn't particularly accurate, the best guestimate actually lay in the range of a few hundred megabytes, so this memstore was an order of magnitude larger. But then her assumption, and that of those who had found it, was that the memstore encompassed the life of one Atheter. This was not necessarily the case. Maybe the memories and mind maps of a thousand Atheter were stored in that little chunk of technology.

Finally the golem straightened up, reached inside its chest, and removed the memplant, passing it back to Jael. "We will begin when the tunnel connects," it said. "How will you move the gabbleduck?"

"Easy enough," said Jael, and went to find her tranquilizer gun.

Ulriss woke me with a "Rise and shine, the game is afoot . . . well, in a couple of hours—the signal is no longer Dopplering so Jael's ship is back in the real."

I lay there blinking at the ceiling as the lights gradually came up, then pushed back the heat sheet, heaved myself over the edge of the bunk, and dropped to the floor. I staggered, feeling slightly dizzy, my limbs leaden. It always takes me a little while to get functional after sleep, hence the two-hour warning from Ulriss. After a moment, I turned to peer at Gene, who lay slumbering in the lower bunk.

"Integrity of the collar?" I inquired.

"She hasn't touched it," the ship AI replied, "though she did try to persuade me to release her by appealing to my sense of loyalty to the organization that brought me into being."

"And your reply?"

"Whilst no right-thinking AI wants the Prador to get their hands on a living Atheter or one of their memstores, your intent to retrieve that store and by proxy carry out a sentence already passed on Jael Feogril should prevent rather than facilitate that. Polity plans will be hampered should you succeed, but, beside moral obligations, I am a free agent and Penny Royal's survival or otherwise is a matter of indifference to me. Should you fail, however, your death will not hamper Polity plans."

"Hey thanks—it's nice to know you care."

Sleepily, from the lower bunk, Gene said, "You're rather sensitive for someone who was once described as a walking abattoir."

"Ah," I said, "so you're frightened of me. That's why you gave me the coding of that U-space signal?"

She pushed back her blanket and sat up. She'd stripped down to a thin singlet and I found the sight rather distracting, as I suspect was the intention. Reaching up, she fingered the metal collar around her neck. "Of course I'm frightened—you've got control of this collar."

"Which will inject you with a short duration paralytic, not blow your head off as I earlier suggested," I replied.

She nodded. "You also suggested that if I didn't tell you what you wanted to know you would demonstrate on me the kind of things Jael did to you."

"I've never tortured anyone," I said, before remembering that she'd read my ECS record. "Well . . . not anyone that didn't deserve it."

"You would have used drugs, and the other techniques Jael used on you."

"True"—I nodded—"but I didn't need to." I gazed at her. "I think you've been involved in this operation for a while and rather resent not being in at the kill. I was your opportunity to change that. I understand—in the past I ended up in similar situations myself."

"Yes, you liked to be in at the kill," she said, and stooped down to pick up her clothing from where she had abandoned it on the floor—she'd sacked out after me, which had been okay as soon as I put the collar on her since Ulriss had been watching her constantly.

I grunted and went off to find a triple espresso.

After a breakfast of bacon, eggs, mushroom steak, beans, a liter of grapenut juice, and more coffee, I reached the stage of being able to walk through doors without bouncing off the doorjamb. Gene ate a megaprawn steak, drank a similar quantity of the juice, and copious quantities of white tea. I thought I might try her breakfast the next time I used stores or the synthesizer. Supposing there would be a next time—only a few minutes remained before we surfaced from U-space. Gene followed me into the cockpit and sat in the copilot's chair, which was about as redundant as the pilot's chair I sat in with the AI Ulriss running the ship.

We surfaced. The screen briefly showed stars, then banding began to travel across it. I glanced at the additional controls for chameleonware and saw that they had been activated.

"Ulriss—"

"Jael's ship is down on the surface of a free-roaming planetoid next to an old vessel that seems to have been stripped and from which bonded-regolith tunnels have spread."

"So Penny Royal is there and might see us," I supplied.

"True," Ulriss replied, but that was not my first concern. The view on the screen swung across, magnified, and switched to light amplification, bringing to the fore the planetoid itself and the Prador cruiser in orbit around it.

"Oh, shit," I opined.

We watched the cruiser as, using that stuttering burn of the fusion engine, Ulriss took us closer to the planetoid. Luckily there had been no reaction from the Prador ship to our arrival, and as we drew closer I saw a shuttle detach and head down.

"I wonder if this is part of Jael's plan," I said. "I would have thought she'd get the memstore loaded, then meet the Prador in some less vulnerable situation."

"Agreed," said Gene through gritted teeth. She glanced across at me. "What do you intend to do?"

"I intend to land." I adjusted to screen controls to give me a view of Jael's ship, the one next to it, and the surrounding spread of pipelike tunnels. "She's probably in there somewhere with the memstore and the gabbleduck. Shouldn't be a problem getting inside."

We watched the shuttle continue its descent and the subsequent flare of its thrusters as it decelerated over the network of tunnels.

"It could get . . . somewhat fraught down there. Do you have weapons?" Gene asked.

"I have weapons."

The Prador shuttle was now landing next to Jael's vessel.

"Let me come in with you," said Gene.

I didn't answer for a while. I just watched. Five Prador clad in armored spacesuits and obviously armed to the mandibles departed the shuttle. They went over to one of the tunnels and gathered there. I focused in closer in time to see them move back to get clear of an explosion. It seemed apparent that they weren't there at either Jael's or Penny Royal's invitation.

"Of course you can come," I said eventually.

Jael frowned at the distant sound of the explosion and the roar of atmosphere being sucked out—the latter sound was abruptly truncated as some emergency door closed. There seemed only one explanation: the Prador had placed a tracker on the *Kobashi* when she had gone to meet them.

"Can you deal with them?" she asked.

"I can deal with them," Penny Royal replied through its submind golem.

The AI itself continued working. Before Jael, the gabbleduck was stretched upright, steel bands around its body, and a framework clamping its head immovable. It kept reaching up with one of its foreclaws to probe and tug at the framework, but, heavily tranquilized, it soon lost interest, lowered its limb, and began muttering to itself.

From this point, equipment—control systems, an atmosphere plant and heaters, stacked processing racks, transformers, and other items obviously taken from the ship above—spread in every direction and seemed chaotically connected by optics and heavy-duty superconducting cables. Some of these snaked into one of the surrounding tunnels where she guessed the ship's fusion reactor lay. Lighting squares inset in the ceiling illuminated the whole scene. She wondered if Penny Royal had put this all together after her arrival. It seemed possible, for the AI, working amid all this like an iron squid, moved at a speed almost difficult to follow. Finally the AI moved closer to the gabbleduck, fitting into one side of the clamping framework a silver beetle of a ship's autodoc, which trailed optics to the surrounding equipment.

"The memstore," said Penny Royal, a ribbed tentacle with a spatulate end snapping out to hover just before Jael's chest.

"What about the Prador?" she asked. "Shouldn't we deal with them first?"

Two of the numerous eyes protruding on stalks from the AI's body flicked toward the golem, which abruptly stepped forward, grabbed a hold in that main body, then merged. In that moment Jael saw that it was one of many clinging there.

"They have entered my tunnels and approach," the AI replied.

It occurred to her then that Penny Royal's previous answer of "I can deal with them" was open to numerous interpretations.

"Are you going to stop them coming here?" she asked.

"No."

"They will try to take the memstore and the gabbleduck."

"That is not proven."

"They'll attack you."

"That is not proven."

Jael's frustration grew. "Very well." She unslung her combined pulse-rifle and launcher. "You are not unintelligent, but you seem to have forgotten about the instructions I left for the *Kobashi* on departing. Those Prador will try to take what is mine without paying for it, and I will try to stop them. If I die, the *Kobashi* detonates and we all die."

"Your ship will not detonate."

"What?"

"I broke your codes two point five seconds after you departed your ship. Your ship AI is of Prador construction, its basis the frozen brain tissue of a Prador first-child. The Prador have never understood that no code is unbreakable and your ship AI is no different. It would appear that you are no different."

Another boom and the thunderous roar of atmosphere departing reached them. Penny Royal quivered, a number of its eyes turning toward one tunnel mouth.

"However," it said with a heavy resignation, "these Prador are showing a marked lack of concern for my property, and I do not want them interrupting this interesting commission." Abruptly the golem began to peel themselves from Penny Royal's core, five in all, until what was left was a spiny skeletal thing. Dropping to the floor, they detached their umbilici and scuttled away. Jael shuddered—they moved without any emulation of humanity, sometimes on all fours, but fast, horribly fast. They also carried devices she could not clearly identify. She did not suppose their purpose to be anything pleasant.

"Now," said Penny Royal, snapping the spatulate end of its tentacle open and closed, "the memstore."

Jael reached into her belt cache, took out the memstore, and handed it over. The tentacle retracted and she lost it in a blur of movement. Items of equipment shifted and a transformer began humming. The autodoc pressed its underside against the gabbleduck's domed head and closed its gleaming metallic limbs around it. She heard a snickering, swiftly followed by the sound of a bone drill. The gabbleduck jerked and reached up. Tentacles sped in and snaked around its limbs, clamping them in place.

"Wharfle klummer," said the gabbleduck with an almost frightening clarity.

Jael scanned around the chamber. Over to her right, across the chamber from the tunnel mouth where Penny Royal had earlier glanced at—the one it seemed likely the Prador would be coming from if they made it this far—was a stack of internal walling and structural members from the cannibalized ship. She headed over, ready to duck for cover, and from there watched the AI carry out its commission.

How long would it take? She had no idea, but it seemed likely that it wouldn't be long. Now the autodoc would be making nanotube synaptic connections in line with a program the AI had constructed from the cerebral schematic in the memstore, it would be firing off electrical impulses and feeding in precise mixes of neurochemicals—all the stuff of memory, thought, mind. Already the gabbleduck seemed straighter, its pose more serious, its eyes taking on a cold metallic glitter. Or was she just seeing what she hoped for?

"Klummer wharfle," it said. Wasn't that one of those frustrating things for the linguists who studied the gabble, that no single gabbleduck had ever repeated its meaningless words? "Klummer klummer," it continued. "Wharfle."

"Base synaptic network established," said Penny Royal. "Loading at one quarter—layered format."

Jael wasn't entirely sure what that meant, but it sounded like the AI was succeeding. Then, abruptly, the gabbleduck made a chittering, whistling, clicking sound, some of the whistles so intense they seemed to stab straight in behind Jael's eyes. Something else happened: a couple of optic cables started smoking, then abruptly shriveled, a processing rack slumped, something like molten glass pouring out and hissing on the cold stone. After a moment, Penny Royal released its grip upon the creature's claws.

"Loading complete."

After a two-tone buzzing Jael recognized as the sound of bone and cell welders working together, the autodoc retracted. The gabbleduck reached up and scratched its head. It made that sound again, and, after a moment, Penny Royal replied in kind. The creature shrugged and all its bonds folded away. It dropped to the floor and squatted like some evil Buddha. It did not look in the least bit foolish.

"They chose insentience," said Penny Royal, "and put in place the means of retaining that state, in U-space, constructed there before they sacrificed their minds."

"And what does that mean?" Jael asked.

Three stalked eyes swiveled toward her. "It means, human, that in resurrecting me you fucked up big-time—now, go away."

She wondered how it had happened: when Penny Royal copied the memstore, or through some leakage during the loading process. There must have been a hidden virus or worm in the store.

Suddenly, both the gabbleduck and Penny Royal were enclosed in some kind of bubble. It shifted slightly, and, where it intersected any of the surrounding equipment, sheared clean through. Within, something protruded out of nothingness like the peak of a mountain—hints of vastness beyond. Ripples, like those in sunlit water, traveled down to the tip, where they ignited a dull glow that grew brighter with each succeeding ripple.

Jael, always prepared to grab the main chance, also possessed a sharply honed instinct for survival. She turned and ran for the nearest tunnel mouth.

"Something serious happened in there," I said, looking at the readings Ulriss had transmitted to me on my helmet display.

"Something?" Gene inquired.

"All sorts of energy surges and various U-space signatures." I read the text Ulriss had also transmitted—text since a vocal message, either real time or in a package, would have extended the transmission time and given Penny Royal more of a chance of intercepting it and breaking the code. "It seems that just before those surges and signatures the U-signal from the gabbleduck changed. They've installed the contents of the memstore . . . how long before the Polity dreadnought gets here?"

"It isn't far away—it should be able to jump here in a matter of minutes."

"Then what happens?"

"They either bomb this place from orbit or send down an assault team."

"You can't be more precise than that?"

"I would guess the latter. ECS will want to retrieve the gabbleduck."

"Why? It's just an animal!"

I could see her shaking her head within her suit's helmet. "Gabbleducks are Atheter even though they've forgone intelligence. Apparently, now that Masada is part of the Polity, they are to receive the same protections as Polity citizens."

"Right." I began tramping through the curiously shaped shale toward the hole the Prador had blown in one of Penny Royal's pipes. The protections Polity citizens received were on the basis of the greatest good for the greatest number. If a citizen needed to die so ECS could take out a black AI, I rather suspected that citizen would die. A sensible course would have been to retreat to *Ulriss Fire* and then retreat from this planetoid, however human Polity citizens numbered in the trillions and the gabbleduck population was just in the millions. I rather suspected Polity AIs would be quite prepared to expend a few human lives to retrieve the creature.

"Convert to text packet for ship AI," I said. "Ulriss, when that dreadnought gets here, tell it that we're down here and that Penny Royal doesn't look likely to be escaping, so maybe it can hold off on the planet busters."

After a moment, I received an acknowledgment from the Ulriss, then I stepped into the gloom of the pipe and looked around. To my right the tunnel led back toward the cannibalized ship. According to the energy readings, the party was to my left and down below. I upped light amplification then said, "Weapons online"—a phrase shortly repeated by Gene.

My multigun suddenly became light as air as suit assister motors kicked in. Crosshairs appeared on my visor, shifted from side to side as I swung the gun across. A menu down one side gave me a selection of firing modes: laser, particle beam, and a list of projectiles ranging from inert to high explosive. "Laser," I told the gun, because I thought we might have to cut our way in at some point, and it obliged by showing me a bar graph of energy available. I could alter numerous other settings to the beam itself, but the preset had always been the best. Then I added, "Autoresponse to attack." Now, if anyone started shooting at me, the gun would take control of my suit motors to aim and fire itself at the aggressor. I imagined Gene was setting her weapon up to operate in the same manner, though with whatever other settings she happened to be accustomed to.

The tunnel curved round and then began to slope down. In a little while we reached an area where debris was scattered across the floor, this including an almost intact hermetically sealed cargo door. Ahead were the remains of the wall out of which it had been blown. I guess the Prador had found the cargo door too small for them, either that or had started blowing things up to attract attention. The Prador were never ones to tap gently and ask if anyone was in. We stepped through the rubble and moved on.

The pipe began to slope down even more steeply and we both had to turn on the gecko function of our boot soles. Obviously this was not a tunnel made for humans. Noting the scars in the walls I wondered just precisely what it had been made for. What did Penny Royal look like anyway? Slowly, out of the darkness ahead, resolved another wall with a large airlock in it. No damage here. Either the Prador felt they had made their point or this lock had simply been big enough to admit them. I went over and gazed at the controls—they were dead, but there was a manual handle available. I hauled on it, but got nowhere until upping the power of my suit motors. I crunched the handle over and pulled the door open. Gene and I stepped inside, vapor fogged around us from a leak through the interior door. I pulled the outer closed then opened the inner, and we stepped through into the aftermath of a battle that seemed to have moved on, because distantly I could hear explosions, the thunderous racket of rail-guns, and the sawing sound of a particle cannon.

The place beyond was expanded like a section of intestine and curved off to our right. A web of support beams laced all the way around, even across the floor. Items of machinery were positioned here and there in this network, connected by s-con cables and optics. I recognized two fusion reactors of the kind I knew did not come from the stripped vessel above and wondered if it was just one in a series so treated. In a gap in the web of floor beams, an armored Prador second-child seemed to have been forced sideways halfway into the stone, its legs and claw on the visible side sticking upward. It was only when I saw the glistening green spread around it that I realized I was seeing half a Prador lying on the stone on its point of division. Tracking a trail of green ichor across, I saw the other half jammed between the wall beams.

"Interesting," said Gene.

It certainly was. If something down here had a weapon that could slice through Prador armor like that—there was no sign of burning—then our armored suits would be no defense at all. We moved out, boots back to gecko function as, like tightrope walkers, we balanced on beams. With us being in so precarious a position, this was a perfect time for another Prador second-child to come hurtling round the corner ahead.

The moment I saw the creature, my multigun took command of my suit motors and tracked. I squatted to retain balance, said, "Off auto, off gecko," then jumped down to the floor. Gene was already there before me. Yeah—rusty. The first-child was emitting an ululating squeal and moving fast, its multiple legs clattering down on the beams so it careened along like gravcar flown by a maniac. I noticed that a few of its legs were missing, along with one claw, and that only a single palp-eye stood erect, directed back toward whatever pursued it. On its underside it gripped in its manipulator hands a nasty rail-gun. It slammed to a halt, gripping beams, then fired, the smashing clattering racket almost painful to hear as the gun sprayed out an almost solid line of projectiles. I looked beyond the creature and saw the sparks and flying metal tracking along the ceiling and down one wall, but never quite intersecting with the path of something silvery. That silvery thing closed in, its course weaving. It disappeared behind one of the reactors and I winced as rail-gun missiles spanged off of the housing, leaving a deep trail of dents. The thing shot out from under the reactor, zigged and zagged, was upon the Prador in a second, then past.

The firing ceased.

The Prador's eye swiveled round then dipped. The creature reached tentatively with its claw to its underside. It shuddered, then with a pulsing spray of green ichor, ponderously slid into two halves.

I began scanning round for whatever had done this.

"Over there," said Gene quietly, over suit com. I looked where she was pointing and saw a skeletal golem clinging to a beam with its legs. It was swaying back and forth, one hand rubbing over its bare ceramal skull, the other hanging down with some gourd-shaped metallic object enclosing it. Easing up my multigun I centered the crosshairs over it and told the gun, "Acquire. Particle beam, continuous fire, full power," and wondered if that would be enough.

The golem heard me, or it detected us by some other means. Its head snapped round a full hundred-and-eighty degrees and it stared at us. After a moment, its head revolved slowly back as if it were disinterested. It hauled itself up and set off back the way it had come. My heart continued hammering even as it moved out of sight.

"Penny Royal?" I wondered.

"Part of Penny Royal," Gene supplied. "It was probably one like that who nailed Desorla to her ceiling."

"Charming."

We began to move on, but suddenly *everything* shuddered. On some unstable worlds I'd experienced earthquakes, and this felt much the same. I'd also been on worlds that had undergone orbital bombardment.

"Convert to text packet for ship AI," I said. "Ulriss, what the fuck was that?"

Ulriss replied almost instantly, "Some kind of gravity phenomena centered on the gabbleduck's location."

At least the Polity hadn't arrived and started bombing us. We moved on toward the sound of battle, pausing for a moment before going round a tangled mass of beams in which lay the remains of another second-child and a scattering of silvery disconnected bones. I counted two golem skulls and was glad this was a fight I'd missed. Puffs of dust began lifting from the structures around us, along with curls of a light metal swarf. I realized a breeze had started and was growing stronger, which likely meant that somewhere there was an atmosphere breach. Now, ahead, arc-light was flaring in accompaniment to the sound of the particle cannon. The wide tunnel ended against a huge space—some chamber beyond. The brief glimpse of a second-child firing upward with its rail-gun, and the purple flash of the particle weapon told us this was where it was all happening.

Bad choice, thought Jael as she ducked down behind a yard-wide pipe through which some sort of fluid was gurgling. A wind was tugging at her cropped hair, blowing into the chamber ahead where the action seemed to be centered. She unhooked her spacesuit helmet from her belt and put it on, dogged it down, then ducked under the pipe, and crawled forward beside the wall.

The first-child had backed into a recess in the chamber wall to her right, a second-child crouched before it. The three golem were playing hide-and-seek amid the scattered machinery and webworks of beams. Ceiling beams had been severed, some still glowing and dripping molten metal. There was a chainglass observatory dome above, some kind of optical telescope hanging in gimbals below it. An oxygen fire was burning behind an atmosphere plant—an eight-foot pillar wrapped in pipes and topped with scrubber intakes and air output funnels. The smoke from this blaze rose up into a spiral swirl then stabbed straight to a point in the ceiling just below the observatory dome, where it was being sucked out. Around this breach beetlebots scurried like spit bugs in a growing mass of foamstone.

The other second-child, emitting a siren squeal as it scurried here and there blasting away at the golem, had obviously been sent out as a decoy—a ploy that worked when, sacrificing two of its legs and a chunk of its carapace, it lured out one of the golem. The second-child's right claw snapped out and Jael saw that the tip of one jaw was missing. From this an instantly recognizable turquoise beam stabbed across the chamber and nailed the golem center-on. Its body vaporized, arms, legs, and skull clattering down. One arm with the hand enclosed by some sort of weapon fell quite close to Jael and near its point of impact a beam parted on a diagonal slice. Some kind of atomic shear, she supposed.

Watching this action, Jael was not entirely sure which side she wanted to win. If the Prador took out the two remaining golem they would go after the Atheter in the chamber behind her. Maybe they would just ignore her, maybe they would kill her out of hand. If the golem finished off the Prador they might turn their attention on her. And she really did not know what to expect from whatever now controlled them. Retreating and finding some other way out was not an option—she had already scanned Penny Royal's network of tunnels and knew that any other route back to *Kobashi* would require a diversion of some miles, and she rather suspected that thing back there would not give her the time.

The decoy second-child lucked out with the next golem, or rather it lucked out with its elder kin. Firing its rail-gun into the gap between a spherical electric furnace and the wall, where one of the golem was crouching, the second-child advanced. The golem shot out underneath the furnace toward the Prador child. A turquoise bar stabbed out, nailing the golem, but it passed through the second-child on the way. An oily explosion centered on a mass of legs collapsed out of sight. The first-child used its other claw to nudge out its final sibling into play. The remaining golem, however, which Jael had earlier seen on the far side of the room, dropped down from above to land between them.

It happened almost too fast to follow. The golem spun, and in a spray of green the second-child slid in half along a diagonal cut straight through its body. The first-child's claw and half its armored visual turret and enclosing visor fell away. Its fluids fountained out as it fell forward, swung in its remaining claw, and bore down. The golem collapsed, pinned to the floor under the claw containing the particle weapon. A turquoise explosion followed underneath the collapsing Prador, then oily flames belched out.

Jael remained where she was, watching carefully. She scanned around the chamber, but there seemed no sign of any more of those horrible golem. The Prador just lay there, its legs sprawled, its weaponized claw trapped underneath it, its now exposed mandibles grinding, ichor still flowing from the huge incision from its visual turret. Jael realized she couldn't have hoped for a better outcome. After a moment she stepped out, her weapon trained on the Prador.

"Jael Feogril," its translator intoned, and it began scrabbling to try and get some purchase on the slick floor.

"That's me," said Jael, and fired two explosive rounds straight into its mouth. The two detonations weren't enough to break open the Prador's enclosing artificial armor, but their force escaped. Torn flesh, organs, ichor, and shattered carapace gushed from the hole the golem had cut. Jael stood there for a moment, hardly able to see through the green sludge on her visor. She peered down at something like a chunk of liver hanging over her arm, and pulled it away. Yes, a satisfactory outcome, apart from the mess.

"Jael Feogril," said a different voice. "Drop the gun, or I cut off your legs."

I was telling myself at the time that I needed detail on the location of the memstore. Rubbish, of course. The energy readings had located it in the chamber beyond—somewhere near to the gabbleduck. I should have just fried her on the spot then gone on to search. Twenty years earlier I would have, but now I was less tuned-in to the exigencies of surviving this sort of game. Okay, I was rusty. She froze, seemed about to turn, then thought better of it and dropped the weapon she'd just used to splash that Prador.

With Gene walking out to my left, I moved forward, crosshairs centered on Jael's torso. What did I want? Some grandstanding, some satisfaction in seeing her shock at meeting someone she'd left for dead, a moment or two to gloat before I did to her what she had done to the first-child? Yeah, sure I did.

With her hands held out from her body, she turned. It annoyed me that I couldn't see her face. Glancing up I saw that the beetlebots had about closed off the hole, because the earlier wind had now diminished to a breeze.

"Take off your helmet," I ordered.

She reached up and undogged the manual outer clips, lifted the helmet carefully, then lowered it to clip it to her belt. Pointless move—she wouldn't be needing it again. Glancing aside I saw that Gene had moved in closer to me. No need to cover me now, I guessed.

"Well, hello, Rho," said Jael, showing absolutely no surprise on seeing me at all. She smiled. It was that smile, the same smile I had seen from her while she had peeled strips of skin from my torso.

"Goodbye, Jael," I said.

The flicker of a high-intensity laser punched smoke, something slapped my multigun, and molten metal sprayed, leaving white trails written across the air.

"Total malfunction. Safe mode—power down," my helmet display informed me. I pulled the trigger anyway, then gazed down in bewilderment at the slagged hole through the weapon.

"Mine, I think," said Jael, stooping in one to pick up her weapon and fire. Same explosive shell she'd used against the Prador. It thumped into my chest, hurling me back, then detonated as it ricocheted away. The blast flung me up, trailing flame and smoke, then I crashed down feeling as if I'd been stepped on by some irate giant. My chainglass visor was gone and something was sizzling ominously inside my suit. Armored plates were peeled up from my arm, which I could see stretched out ahead of me, and my gauntlet was missing.

"What the fuck are you doing here with him?" Jael inquired angrily.

"He turned up on Arena before I left," Gene replied. "Just to be on the safe side I was keeping to the Pens until Penny Royal's golem left."

"And you consider that an adequate explanation?"

"I put Arena Security onto him, but he somehow escaped them and ambushed me outside." Gene sounded somewhat chagrined. "I let him persuade me to give him the U-signal code from the gabbleduck."

I turned my head slightly but only got a view of tangled metal and a few silver golem bones. "Ulriss," I whispered, but received only a slight buzzing in response.

"So much for your wonderful ECS training."

"It was enough to convince him that I still worked for them."

So, no ECS action here, no Polity dreadnought on the way. I thought about that encounter I'd seen between the Prador cruiser and the dreadnought. I'd told Gene about it and she'd used the information against me, convincing me that the Polity was involved. Of course, what I'd seen was the kind of saber-rattling confrontation between Prador and Polity that had been going on in the Graveyard for years.

"What's the situation here?" Gene asked.

"Fucked," Jael replied. "Something's intervened. We have to get out of here now."

I heard the sounds of movement. They were going away, so I might survive this. Then the sounds ceased too abruptly.

"You used an explosive shell," Gene noted from close by.

"What?"

"He's still alive."

"Well," said Jael, "that's a problem soon solved."

Her boots crunched on the floor as she approached, and gave me her location. I reached out with my bare hand and slid it into slick silvery metal. Finger controls there. I clamped down on them and saw something shimmering deep into twisted metal.

"Collar!" I said, more in hope than expectation, before heaving myself upright.

Jael stood over me, and beyond her I saw Gene reach up toward her neck, then abruptly drop to the floor. I swung my arm across as Jael began to bring her multigun up to her shoulder. A slight tug—that was all. She stood there a moment longer, still aiming at me, then her head lifted and fell back, attached still at the back of her neck by skin only, and a red stream shot upward. Air hissing from her severed trachea, she toppled.

I carefully lifted my fingers from the controls of the golem weapon, then caught my breath, only now feeling as if someone had worked me over from head to foot with a baseball bat. Slowly climbing to my feet I expected to feel the pain of a broken bone somewhere, but there was nothing like that. No need to check on Jael's condition, so I walked over to Gene. She was unconscious and would be for some time. I stooped over her and unplugged the power cable and control optics of her weapon from her suit, then plugged them into mine. No response and of course no visor readout. I set the weapon to manual and turned away. I decided that once I'd retrieved the memstore—if that was possible—I would come back in here and take her suit, because mine certainly would not get me to *Ulriss Fire*.

The hum of power and the feeling of distorted perception associated with U-jumping greeted me. I don't know what that thing was poised over the gabbleduck, nor did I know what kind of force-field surrounded it and that other entity that seemed the bastard offspring of a sea urchin and an octopus. But the poised thing was fading, and as it finally disappeared, the field winked out and numerous objects crashed to the floor.

I moved forward, used the snout of my weapon to lift one tentacle, and then watched it flop back. *Penny Royal*, I guessed. It was slumped across the floor beams and other machinery here. The gabbleduck turned its head as if noticing me for the first time, but it showed no particular signs of hostility, nor did it seem to show any signs of it containing some formidable alien intelligence. I felt sure the experiment here had failed, or rather, had been curtailed in some way. *Something's intervened*, Jael had said. Nevertheless, I kept my attention focused on the creature as I searched for and finally found the memstore. It was fried but I pocketed it anyway, for it *was* my find, not something ECS had put in the path of my sifting machine.

Returning to the other chamber, I there stripped Gene of her spacesuit and donned it myself.

"Ulriss, we can talk now."

"Ah, you *are* still alive," the AI replied. "I was already composing your obituary."

"You're just a bundle of laughs. You know that?"

"I am bursting with curiosity and try to hide that in levity."

I explained the situation to which Ulriss replied, "I have put out a call to the Polity dreadnought we sighted and given it this location."

"Should we hang around?"

"There will be questions ECS will want to ask, but I don't see why we should put ourselves at their disposal. Let their agents find us."

"Quite right," I replied.

I bagged up a few items, like that golem weapon, and was about to head back to my ship when I glanced back and saw the gabbleduck crouching in the tunnel behind.

"Sherber grodge," it informed me.

Heading back the way I'd come into this hellhole, I kept checking back on the thing. Gabbleducks don't eat people apparently—they just chew them up and spit them out. This one followed me like a lost puppy and every time I stopped it stopped too and sat on its hindquarters, occasionally issuing some nonsensical statement. I got the real weird feeling, which went against all my training and experience, that this creature was harmless to me. I shook my head. Ridiculous. Anyway, I'd lose it at the airlock.

When I did finally reach the airlock and began closing that inner door, one big black claw closed around the edge and pulled it open again. I raised my gun, crosshairs targeting that array of eyes, but I just could not pull the trigger. The gabbleduck entered the airlock and sat there, close enough to touch and close enough for me to fry if it went for me. What now? If I opened the outer airlock door the creature would die. Before I could think of what to do, a multijointed arm reached back and heaved the inner door closed, while the other arm hauled up the manual handle of the outer door, and the lock air pressure blew us staggering into the pipe beyond.

I discovered that gabbleducks can survive in vacuum . . . or at least this one can.

Later, when I ordered Ulriss to open the door to the small hold of my ship, the gabbleduck waddled meekly inside. I thought then that perhaps something from the memstore had stuck. I wasn't sure—certainly this gabbleduck was not behaving like its kind on Masada.

I also discovered that gabbleducks will eat raw recon bacon.

I hold the fried memstore and think about what it might have contained, and what the fact of its existence means. A memstore for an Atheter mind goes contrary to the supposed nihilism of that race. A race so nihilistic could never have created a spacefaring civilization, so that darkness must have spread amid them in their last days. The Atheter recorded in the memstore could not have been one of the kind that wanted to destroy itself, surely?

I'm taking the gabbleduck back to Masada—I feel utterly certain now that it wants me to do this. I also feel certain that to do otherwise might not be a good idea.

The Merchant and the Alchemist's Gate

TED CHIANG

Ted Chiang has made a big impact on the field with only a handful of stories, five stories all told, published in places such as *Omni, Asimov's Science Fiction, Full Spectrum 3, Starlight 2,* and *Vanishing Acts.* He won the 1990 Nebula Award with his first published story "Tower of Babylon," and won the 1991 *Asimov's* Readers Award with his third, "Understand," as well as winning the John W. Campbell Award for Best New Writer in that same year. After 1991, he fell silent for several years before making a triumphant return in 1998 with the novella, "Story of Your Life," which won him another Nebula Award in 1999. Since then, he returned in 2000 with another major story, "Seventy-Two Letters," which was a finalist for the Hugo and for the World Fantasy Award, with "Hell Is the Absence of God" in 2001, which won him another Hugo and a Nebula Award, and in 2002 with "Liking What You See: A Documentary." The same year, his first short-story collection, *Stories of Your Life and Others,* was published, and won the Locus Award as the year's Best Collection. His most recent book is the chapbook *The Merchant and the Alchemist's Gate.* It will be interesting to see how he develops in the decade to come, as he could well turn out to be one of the significant new talents of the new century. He lives in Kirkland, Washington.

In the crafty, intricate, and richly ornamented story that follows, he shows us that gates can take you to many places, but not always to where you really want to *go. . . .*

O Mighty Caliph and Commander of the Faithful, I am humbled to be in the splendor of your presence; a man can hope for no greater blessing as long as he lives. The story I have to tell is truly a strange one, and were the entirety to be tattooed at the corner of one's eye, the marvel of its presentation would not exceed that of the events recounted, for it is a warning to those who would be warned and a lesson to those who would learn.

My name is Fuwaad ibn Abbas, and I was born here in Baghdad, City of Peace. My father was a grain merchant, but for much of my life I have worked as a purveyor of fine fabrics, trading in silk from Damascus and linen from Egypt and scarves from Morocco that are embroidered with gold. I was prosperous, but my heart was troubled, and neither the purchase of luxuries nor the giving of alms was able to soothe it. Now I stand before you without a single dirham in my purse, but I am at peace.

Allah is the beginning of all things, but with Your Majesty's permission, I begin my story with the day I took a walk through the district of metalsmiths. I needed to purchase a gift for a man I had to do business with, and had been told he might appreciate a tray made of silver. After browsing for half an hour, I noticed that one of the largest shops in the market had been taken over by a new merchant. It was a prized location that must have been expensive to acquire, so I entered to peruse its wares.

Never before had I seen such a marvelous assortment of goods. Near the entrance there was an astrolabe equipped with seven plates inlaid with silver, a water-clock that chimed on the hour, and a nightingale made of brass that sang when the wind blew. Farther inside there were even more ingenious mechanisms, and I stared at them the way a child watches a juggler, when an old man stepped out from a doorway in the back.

"Welcome to my humble shop, my lord," he said. "My name is Bashaarat. How may I assist you?"

"These are remarkable items that you have for sale. I deal with traders from every corner of the world, and yet I have never seen their like. From where, may I ask, did you acquire your merchandise?"

"I am grateful to you for your kind words," he said. "Everything you see here was made in my workshop, by myself or by my assistants under my direction."

I was impressed that this man could be so well versed in so many arts. I asked him about the various instruments in his shop, and listened to him discourse learnedly about astrology, mathematics, geomancy, and medicine.

We spoke for over an hour, and my fascination and respect bloomed like a flower warmed by the dawn, until he mentioned his experiments in alchemy.

"Alchemy?" I said. This surprised me, for he did not seem the type to make such a sharper's claim. "You mean you can turn base metal into gold?"

"I can, my lord, but that is not in fact what most seek from alchemy."

"What do most seek, then?"

"They seek a source of gold that is cheaper than mining ore from the ground. Alchemy does describe a means to make gold, but the procedure is so arduous that, by comparison, digging beneath a mountain is as easy as plucking peaches from a tree."

I smiled. "A clever reply. No one could dispute that you are a learned man, but I know better than to credit alchemy."

Bashaarat looked at me and considered. "I have recently built something that may change your opinion. You would be the first person I have shown it to. Would you care to see it?"

"It would be a great pleasure."

"Please follow me." He led me through the doorway in the rear of his shop. The next room was a workshop, arrayed with devices whose functions I could not guess—bars of metal wrapped with enough copper thread to reach the horizon, mirrors mounted on a circular slab of granite floating in quicksilver—but Bashaarat walked past these without a glance.

Instead he led me to a sturdy pedestal, chest high, on which a stout metal hoop was mounted upright. The hoop's opening was as wide as two outstretched hands, and its rim so thick that it would tax the strongest man to carry. The metal was black as night, but polished to such smoothness that, had it been a different color, it could have served as a mirror. Bashaarat bade me stand so that I looked upon the hoop edgewise, while he stood next to its opening.

"Please observe," he said.

Bashaarat thrust his arm through the hoop from the right side, but it did not extend out from the left. Instead, it was as if his arm were severed at the elbow, and he waved the stump up and down, and then pulled his arm out intact.

I had not expected to see such a learned man perform a conjuror's trick, but it was well done, and I applauded politely.

"Now wait a moment," he said as he took a step back.

I waited, and behold, an arm reached out of the hoop from its left side, without a body to hold it up. The sleeve it wore matched Bashaarat's robe. The arm waved up and down, and then retreated through the hoop until it was gone.

The first trick I had thought a clever mime, but this one seemed far superior, because the pedestal and hoop were clearly too slender to conceal a person. "Very clever!" I exclaimed.

"Thank you, but this is not mere sleight of hand. The right side of the hoop precedes the left by several seconds. To pass through the hoop is to cross that duration instantly."

"I do not understand," I said.

"Let me repeat the demonstration." Again he thrust his arm through the hoop, and his arm disappeared. He smiled, and pulled back and forth as if playing tug-a-rope. Then he pulled his arm out again, and presented his hand to me with the palm open. On it lay a ring I recognized.

"That is my ring!" I checked my hand, and saw that my ring still lay on my finger. "You have conjured up a duplicate."

"No, this is truly your ring. Wait."

Again, an arm reached out from the left side. Wishing to discover the mechanism of the trick, I rushed over to grab it by the hand. It was not a false hand, but one fully warm and alive as mine. I pulled on it, and it pulled back. Then, as deft as a pickpocket, the hand slipped the ring from my finger and the arm withdrew into the hoop, vanishing completely.

"My ring is gone!" I exclaimed.

"No, my lord," he said. "Your ring is here." And he gave me the ring he held. "Forgive me for my game."

I replaced it on my finger. "You had the ring before it was taken from me."

At that moment an arm reached out, this time from the right side of the hoop. "What is this?" I exclaimed. Again I recognized it as his by the sleeve before it withdrew, but I had not seen him reach in.

"Recall," he said, "the right side of the hoop precedes the left." And he walked over to the left side of the hoop, and thrust his arm through from that side, and again it disappeared.

Your Majesty has undoubtedly already grasped this, but it was only then that I understood: whatever happened on the right side of the hoop was complemented, a few seconds later, by an event on the left side. "Is this sorcery?" I asked.

"No, my lord, I have never met a djinni, and if I did, I would not trust it to do my bidding. This is a form of alchemy."

He offered an explanation, speaking of his search for tiny pores in the skin of reality, like the holes that worms bore into wood, and how upon finding one he was able to expand and stretch it the way a glassblower turns a dollop of molten glass into a long-necked pipe, and how he then allowed time to flow like water at one mouth while causing it to thicken like syrup at the other. I confess I did not really understand his words, and cannot testify to their truth. All I could say in response was, "You have created something truly astonishing."

"Thank you," he said, "but this is merely a prelude to what I intended to show you." He bade me follow him into another room, farther in the back. There stood a circular doorway whose massive frame was made of the same polished black metal, mounted in the middle of the room.

"What I showed you before was a Gate of Seconds," he said. "This is a Gate of Years. The two sides of the doorway are separated by a span of twenty years."

I confess I did not understand his remark immediately. I imagined him reaching his arm in from the right side and waiting twenty years before it emerged from the left side, and it seemed a very obscure magic trick. I said as much, and he laughed. "That is one use for it," he said, "but consider what would happen if you were to step through." Standing on the right side, he gestured for me to come closer, and then pointed through the doorway. "Look."

I looked, and saw that there appeared to be different rugs and pillows on the other side of the room than I had seen when I had entered. I moved my head from side to side, and realized that when I peered through the doorway, I was looking at a different room from the one I stood in.

"You are seeing the room twenty years from now," said Bashaarat.

I blinked, as one might at an illusion of water in the desert, but what I saw did not change. "And you say I could step through?" I asked.

"You could. And with that step, you would visit the Baghdad of twenty years hence. You could seek out your older self and have a conversation with him. Afterwards, you could step back through the Gate of Years and return to the present day."

Hearing Bashaarat's words, I felt as if I were reeling. "You have done this?" I asked him. "You have stepped through?"

"I have, and so have numerous customers of mine."

"Earlier you said I was the first to whom you showed this."

"This Gate, yes. But for many years I owned a shop in Cairo, and it was there that I first built a Gate of Years. There were many to whom I showed that Gate, and who made use of it."

"What did they learn when talking to their older selves?"

"Each person learns something different. If you wish, I can tell you the story of one such person." Bashaarat proceeded to tell me such a story, and if it pleases Your Majesty, I will recount it here.

THE TALE OF THE FORTUNATE ROPE-MAKER

There once was a young man named Hassan who was a maker of rope. He stepped through the Gate of Years to see the Cairo of twenty years later, and upon arriving he marveled at how the city had grown. He felt as if he had stepped into a scene embroidered on a tapestry, and even though the city was no more and no less than Cairo, he looked upon the most common sights as objects of wonder.

He was wandering by the Zuweyla Gate, where the sword dancers and snake charmers perform, when an astrologer called to him. "Young man! Do you wish to know the future?"

Hassan laughed. "I know it already," he said.

"Surely you want to know if wealth awaits you, do you not?"

"I am a rope-maker. I know that it does not."

"Can you be so sure? What about the renowned merchant Hassan al-Hubbaul, who began as a rope-maker?"

His curiosity aroused, Hassan asked around the market for others who knew of this wealthy merchant, and found that the name was well known. It was said he lived in the wealthy Habbaniya quarter of the city, so Hassan walked there and asked people to point out his house, which turned out to be the largest one on its street.

He knocked at the door, and a servant led him to a spacious and well-appointed hall with a fountain in the center. Hassan waited while the servant went to fetch his master, but as he looked at the polished ebony and marble around him, he felt that he did not belong in such surroundings, and was about to leave when his older self appeared.

"At last you are here!" the man said. "I have been expecting you!"

"You have?" said Hassan, astounded.

"Of course, because I visited my older self just as you are visiting me. It has been so long that I had forgotten the exact day. Come, dine with me."

The two went to a dining room, where servants brought chicken stuffed with pistachio nuts, fritters soaked in honey, and roast lamb with spiced pomegranates. The older Hassan gave few details of his life: he mentioned business interests of many varieties, but did not say how he had become a merchant; he mentioned a wife, but said it was not time for the younger man to meet her. Instead, he asked young Hassan to remind him of the pranks he had played as a child, and he laughed to hear stories that had faded from his own memory.

At last the younger Hassan asked the older, "How did you make such great changes in your fortune?"

"All I will tell you right now is this: when you go to buy hemp from the market, and you are walking along the Street of Black Dogs, do not walk along the south side as you usually do. Walk along the north."

"And that will enable me to raise my station?"

"Just do as I say. Go back home now; you have rope to make. You will know when to visit me again."

Young Hassan returned to his day and did as he was instructed, keeping to the north side of the street even when there was no shade there. It was a few days later that he witnessed a maddened horse run amok on the south side of the street directly opposite him, kicking several people, injuring another by knocking a heavy jug of palm oil onto him, and even trampling one person under its hooves. After the commotion had subsided, Hassan prayed to Allah for the injured to be healed and the dead to be at peace, and thanked Allah for sparing him.

The next day Hassan stepped through the Gate of Years and sought out his older self. "Were you injured by the horse when you walked by?" he asked him.

"No, because I heeded my older self's warning. Do not forget, you and I are one; every circumstance that befalls you once befell me."

And so the elder Hassan gave the younger instructions, and the younger obeyed them. He refrained from buying eggs from his usual grocer, and thus avoided the illness that struck customers who bought eggs from a spoiled basket. He bought extra hemp, and thus had material to work with when others suffered a shortage due to a delayed caravan. Following his older self's instructions spared Hassan many troubles, but he wondered why his older self would not tell him more. Who would he marry? How would he become wealthy?

Then one day, after having sold all his rope in the market and carrying an unusually full purse, Hassan bumped into a boy while walking on the street. He felt for his purse, discovered it missing, and turned around with a shout to search the crowd for the pickpocket. Hearing Hassan's cry, the boy immediately began running through the crowd. Hassan saw that the boy's tunic was torn at the elbow, but then quickly lost sight of him.

For a moment Hassan was shocked that this could happen with no warning from his older self. But his surprise was soon replaced by anger, and he gave chase. He ran through the crowd, checking the elbows of boys' tunics, until by chance he found the pickpocket crouching beneath a fruit wagon. Hassan grabbed him and began shouting to all that he had caught a thief, asking them to find a guardsman. The boy, afraid of arrest, dropped Hassan's purse and began weeping. Hassan stared at the boy for a long moment, and then his anger faded, and he let him go.

When next he saw his older self, Hassan asked him, "Why did you not warn me about the pickpocket?"

"Did you not enjoy the experience?" asked his older self.

Hassan was about to deny it, but stopped himself. "I did enjoy it," he admitted. In pursuing the boy, with no hint of whether he'd succeed or fail, he had felt his blood surge in a way it had not for many weeks. And seeing the boy's tears had reminded him of the Prophet's teachings on the value of mercy, and Hassan had felt virtuous in choosing to let the boy go.

"Would you rather I had denied you that, then?"

Just as we grow to understand the purpose of customs that seemed pointless to us in our youth, Hassan realized that there was merit in withholding
information as well as in disclosing it. "No," he said, "it was good that you did
not warn me."

The older Hassan saw that he had understood. "Now I will tell you
something very important. Hire a horse. I will give you directions to a spot in
the foothills to the west of the city. There you will find within a grove of trees
one that was struck by lightning. Around the base of the tree, look for the
heaviest rock you can overturn, and then dig beneath it."

"What should I look for?"

"You will know when you find it."

The next day Hassan rode out to the foothills and searched until he
found the tree. The ground around it was covered in rocks, so Hassan overturned one to dig beneath it, and then another, and then another. At last his
spade struck something besides rock and soil. He cleared aside the soil and
discovered a bronze chest, filled with gold dinars and assorted jewelry. Hassan had never seen its like in all his life. He loaded the chest onto the horse,
and rode back to Cairo.

The next time he spoke to his older self, he asked, "How did you know
where the treasure was?"

"I learned it from myself," said the older Hassan, "just as you did. As to
how we came to know its location, I have no explanation except that it was
the will of Allah, and what other explanation is there for anything?"

"I swear I shall make good use of these riches that Allah has blessed me
with," said the younger Hassan.

"And I renew that oath," said the older. "This is the last time we shall
speak. You will find your own way now. Peace be upon you."

And so Hassan returned home. With the gold he was able to purchase
hemp in great quantity, and hire workmen and pay them a fair wage, and sell
rope profitably to all who sought it. He married a beautiful and clever
woman, at whose advice he began trading in other goods, until he was a
wealthy and respected merchant. All the while he gave generously to the poor
and lived as an upright man. In this way Hassan lived the happiest of lives
until he was overtaken by death, breaker of ties and destroyer of delights.

"That is a remarkable story," I said. "For someone who is debating whether
to make use of the Gate, there could hardly be a better inducement."

"You are wise to be skeptical," said Bashaarat. "Allah rewards those he
wishes to reward and chastises those he wishes to chastise. The Gate does
not change how he regards you."

I nodded, thinking I understood. "So even if you succeed in avoiding the misfortunes that your older self experienced, there is no assurance you will not encounter other misfortunes."

"No, forgive an old man for being unclear. Using the Gate is not like drawing lots, where the token you select varies with each turn. Rather, using the Gate is like taking a secret passageway in a palace, one that lets you enter a room more quickly than by walking down the hallway. The room remains the same, no matter which door you use to enter."

This surprised me. "The future is fixed, then? As unchangeable as the past?"

"It is said that repentance and atonement erase the past."

"I have heard that too, but I have not found it to be true."

"I am sorry to hear that," said Bashaarat. "All I can say is that the future is no different."

I thought on this for a while. "So if you learn that you are dead twenty years from now, there is nothing you can do to avoid your death?" He nodded. This seemed to me very disheartening, but then I wondered if it could not also provide a guarantee. I said, "Suppose you learn that you are alive twenty years from now. Then nothing could kill you in the next twenty years. You could then fight in battles without a care, because your survival is assured."

"That is possible," he said. "It is also possible that a man who would make use of such a guarantee would not find his older self alive when he first used the Gate."

"Ah," I said. "Is it then the case that only the prudent meet their older selves?"

"Let me tell you the story of another person who used the Gate, and you can decide for yourself if he was prudent or not." Bashaarat proceeded to tell me the story, and if it pleases Your Majesty, I will recount it here.

THE TALE OF THE WEAVER WHO STOLE FROM HIMSELF

There was a young weaver named Ajib who made a modest living as a weaver of rugs, but yearned to taste the luxuries enjoyed by the wealthy. After hearing the story of Hassan, Ajib immediately stepped through the Gate of Years to seek out his older self, who, he was sure, would be as rich and as generous as the older Hassan.

Upon arriving in the Cairo of twenty years later, he proceeded to the wealthy Habbaniya quarter of the city and asked people for the residence of Ajib ibn Taher. He was prepared, if he met someone who knew the man and remarked on the similarity of their features, to identify himself as Ajib's son, newly arrived from Damascus. But he never had the chance to offer this story, because no one he asked recognized the name.

Eventually he decided to return to his old neighborhood, and see if anyone there knew where he had moved to. When he got to his old street, he stopped a boy and asked him if he knew where to find a man named Ajib. The boy directed him to Ajib's old house.

"That is where he used to live," Ajib said. "Where does he live now?"

"If he has moved since yesterday, I do not know where," said the boy.

Ajib was incredulous. Could his older self still live in the same house, twenty years later? That would mean he had never become wealthy, and his older self would have no advice to give him, or at least none Ajib would profit by following. How could his fate differ so much from that of the fortunate rope-maker? In hopes that the boy was mistaken, Ajib waited outside the house, and watched.

Eventually he saw a man leave the house, and with a sinking heart recognized it as his older self. The older Ajib was followed by a woman that he presumed was his wife, but he scarcely noticed her, for all he could see was his own failure to have bettered himself. He stared with dismay at the plain clothes the older couple wore until they walked out of sight.

Driven by the curiosity that impels men to look at the heads of the executed, Ajib went to the door of his house. His own key still fit the lock, so he entered. The furnishings had changed, but were simple and worn, and Ajib was mortified to see them. After twenty years, could he not even afford better pillows?

On an impulse, he went to the wooden chest where he normally kept his savings, and unlocked it. He lifted the lid, and saw the chest was filled with gold dinars.

Ajib was astonished. His older self had a chest of gold, and yet he wore such plain clothes and lived in the same small house for twenty years! What a stingy, joyless man his older self must be, thought Ajib, to have wealth and not enjoy it. Ajib had long known that one could not take one's possessions to the grave. Could that be something that he would forget as he aged?

Ajib decided that such riches should belong to someone who appreciated them, and that was himself. To take his older self's wealth would not be stealing, he reasoned, because it was he himself who would receive it. He heaved the chest onto his shoulder, and with much effort was able to bring it back through the Gate of Years to the Cairo he knew.

He deposited some of his newfound wealth with a banker, but always carried a purse heavy with gold. He dressed in a Damascene robe and Cordovan slippers and a Khurasani turban bearing a jewel. He rented a house in the wealthy quarter, furnished it with the finest rugs and couches, and hired a cook to prepare him sumptuous meals.

He then sought out the brother of a woman he had long desired from afar, a woman named Taahira. Her brother was an apothecary, and Taahira assisted him in his shop. Ajib would occasionally purchase a remedy so that he might speak to her. Once he had seen her veil slip, and her eyes were as dark and beautiful as a gazelle's. Taahira's brother would not have consented to her marrying a weaver, but now Ajib could present himself as a favorable match.

Taahira's brother approved, and Taahira herself readily consented, for she had desired Ajib, too. Ajib spared no expense for their wedding. He hired one of the pleasure barges that floated in the canal south of the city and held a feast with musicians and dancers, at which he presented her with a magnificent pearl necklace. The celebration was the subject of gossip throughout the quarter.

Ajib reveled in the joy that money brought him and Taahira, and for a week the two of them lived the most delightful of lives. Then one day Ajib came home to find the door to his house broken open and the interior ransacked of all silver and gold items. The terrified cook emerged from hiding and told him that robbers had taken Taahira.

Ajib prayed to Allah until, exhausted with worry, he fell asleep. The next morning he was awoken by a knocking at his door. There was a stranger there. "I have a message for you," the man said.

"What message?" asked Ajib.

"Your wife is safe."

Ajib felt fear and rage churn in his stomach like black bile. "What ransom would you have?" he asked.

"Ten thousand dinars."

"That is more than all I possess!" Ajib exclaimed.

"Do not haggle with me," said the robber. "I have seen you spend money like others pour water."

Ajib dropped to his knees. "I have been wasteful. I swear by the name of the Prophet that I do not have that much," he said.

The robber looked at him closely. "Gather all the money you have," he said, "and have it here tomorrow at this same hour. If I believe you are holding back, your wife will die. If I believe you to be honest, my men will return her to you."

Ajib could see no other choice. "Agreed," he said, and the robber left.

The next day he went to the banker and withdrew all the money that remained. He gave it to the robber, who gauged the desperation in Ajib's eyes and was satisfied. The robber did as he promised, and that evening Taahira was returned.

After they had embraced, Taahira said, "I didn't believe you would pay so much money for me."

"I could not take pleasure in it without you," said Ajib, and he was surprised to realize it was true. "But now I regret that I cannot buy you what you deserve."

"You need never buy me anything again," she said.

Ajib bowed his head. "I feel as if I have been punished for my misdeeds."

"What misdeeds?" asked Taahira, but Ajib said nothing. "I did not ask you this before," she said. "But I know you did not inherit all the money you gained. Tell me: did you steal it?"

"No," said Ajib, unwilling to admit the truth to her or himself. "It was given to me."

"A loan, then?"

"No, it does not need to be repaid."

"And you don't wish to pay it back?" Taahira was shocked. "So you are content that this other man paid for our wedding? That he paid my ransom?" She seemed on the verge of tears. "Am I your wife then, or this other man's?"

"You are my wife," he said.

"How can I be, when my very life is owed to another?"

"I would not have you doubt my love," said Ajib. "I swear to you that I will pay back the money, to the last dirham."

And so Ajib and Taahira moved back into Ajib's old house and began saving their money. Both of them went to work for Taahira's brother the apothecary, and when he eventually became a perfumer to the wealthy, Ajib and Taahira took over the business of selling remedies to the ill. It was a good living, but they spent as little as they could, living modestly and repairing damaged furnishings instead of buying new. For years, Ajib smiled whenever he dropped a coin into the chest, telling Taahira that it was a reminder of how much he valued her. He would say that even after the chest was full, it would be a bargain.

But it is not easy to fill a chest by adding just a few coins at a time, and so what began as thrift gradually turned into miserliness, and prudent decisions were replaced by tight-fisted ones. Worse, Ajib's and Taahira's affections for each other faded over time, and each grew to resent the other for the money they could not spend.

In this manner the years passed and Ajib grew older, waiting for the second time that his gold would be taken from him.

"What a strange and sad story," I said.

"Indeed," said Bashaarat. "Would you say that Ajib acted prudently?"

I hesitated before speaking. "It is not my place to judge him," I said. "He must live with the consequences of his actions, just as I must live with mine." I was silent for a moment, and then said, "I admire Ajib's candor, that he told you everything he had done."

"Ah, but Ajib did not tell me of this as a young man," said Bashaarat. "After he emerged from the Gate carrying the chest, I did not see him again for another twenty years. Ajib was a much older man when he came to visit me again. He had come home and found his chest gone, and the knowledge that he had paid his debt made him feel he could tell me all that had transpired."

"Indeed? Did the older Hassan from your first story come to see you as well?"

"No, I heard Hassan's story from his younger self. The older Hassan never returned to my shop, but in his place I had a different visitor, one who shared a story about Hassan that he himself could never have told me." Bashaarat proceeded to tell me that visitor's story, and if it pleases Your Majesty, I will recount it here.

THE TALE OF THE WIFE AND HER LOVER

Raniya had been married to Hassan for many years, and they lived the happiest of lives. One day she saw her husband dine with a young man, whom she recognized as the very image of Hassan when she had first married him. So great was her astonishment that she could scarcely keep herself from intruding on their conversation. After the young man left, she demanded that Hassan tell her who he was, and Hassan related to her an incredible tale.

"Have you told him about me?" she asked. "Did you know what lay ahead of us when we first met?"

"I knew I would marry you from the moment I saw you," Hassan said, smiling, "but not because anyone had told me. Surely, wife, you would not wish to spoil that moment for him?"

So Raniya did not speak to her husband's younger self, but only eavesdropped on his conversation, and stole glances at him. Her pulse quickened at the sight of his youthful features; sometimes our memories fool us with their sweetness, but when she beheld the two men seated opposite each other, she could see the fullness of the younger one's beauty without exaggeration. At night, she would lie awake, thinking of it.

Some days after Hassan had bid farewell to his younger self, he left Cairo to conduct business with a merchant in Damascus. In his absence Raniya found the shop that Hassan had described to her, and stepped through the Gate of Years to the Cairo of her youth.

She remembered where he had lived back then, and so was easily able to find the young Hassan and follow him. As she watched him, she felt a desire stronger than she had felt in years for the older Hassan, so vivid were her recollections of their youthful lovemaking. She had always been a loyal and faithful wife, but here was an opportunity that would never be available again. Resolving to act on this desire, Raniya rented a house, and in subsequent days bought furnishings for it.

Once the house was ready, she followed Hassan discreetly while she tried to gather enough boldness to approach him. In the jewelers' market, she watched as he went to a jeweler, showed him a necklace set with ten gemstones, and asked him how much he would pay for it. Raniya recognized it as one Hassan had given to her in the days after their wedding; she had not known he had once tried to sell it. She stood a short distance away and listened, pretending to look at some rings.

"Bring it back tomorrow, and I will pay you a thousand dinars," said the jeweler. Young Hassan agreed to the price, and left.

As she watched him leave, Raniya overheard two men talking nearby:

"Did you see that necklace? It is one of ours."

"Are you certain?" asked the other.

"I am. That is the bastard who dug up our chest."

"Let us tell our captain about him. After this fellow has sold his necklace, we will take his money, and more."

The two men left without noticing Raniya, who stood with her heart racing but her body motionless, like a deer after a tiger has passed. She realized that the treasure Hassan had dug up must have belonged to a band of thieves, and these men were two of its members. They were now observing the jewelers of Cairo to identify the person who had taken their loot.

Raniya knew that since she possessed the necklace, the young Hassan could not have sold it. She also knew that the thieves could not have killed Hassan. But it could not be Allah's will for her to do nothing. Allah must have brought her here so that he might use her as his instrument.

Raniya returned to the Gate of Years, stepped through to her own day, and at her house found the necklace in her jewelry box. Then she used the Gate of Years again, but instead of entering it from the left side, she entered it from the right, so that she visited the Cairo of twenty years later. There she sought out her older self, now an aged woman. The older Raniya greeted her warmly, and retrieved the necklace from her own jewelry box. The two women then rehearsed how they would assist the young Hassan.

The next day, the two thieves were back with a third man, whom Raniya assumed was their captain. They all watched as Hassan presented the necklace to the jeweler.

As the jeweler examined it, Raniya walked up and said, "What a coincidence! Jeweler, I wish to sell a necklace just like that." She brought out her necklace from a purse she carried.

"This is remarkable," said the jeweler. "I have never seen two necklaces more similar."

Then the aged Raniya walked up. "What do I see? Surely my eyes deceive me!" And with that she brought out a third identical necklace. "The seller sold it to me with the promise that it was unique. This proves him a liar."

"Perhaps you should return it," said Raniya.

"That depends," said the aged Raniya. She asked Hassan, "How much is he paying you for it?"

"A thousand dinars," said Hassan, bewildered.

"Really! Jeweler, would you care to buy this one too?"

"I must reconsider my offer," said the jeweler.

While Hassan and the aged Raniya bargained with the jeweler, Raniya stepped back just far enough to hear the captain berate the other thieves. "You fools," he said. "It is a common necklace. You would have us kill half the jewelers in Cairo and bring the guardsmen down upon our heads." He slapped their heads and led them off.

Raniya returned her attention to the jeweler, who had withdrawn his offer to buy Hassan's necklace. The older Raniya said, "Very well. I will try to return it to the man who sold it to me." As the older woman left, Raniya could tell that she smiled beneath her veil.

Raniya turned to Hassan. "It appears that neither of us will sell a necklace today."

"Another day, perhaps," said Hassan.

"I shall take mine back to my house for safekeeping," said Raniya. "Would you walk with me?"

Hassan agreed, and walked with Raniya to the house she had rented. Then she invited him in, and offered him wine, and after they had both drunk some, she led him to her bedroom. She covered the windows with heavy curtains and extinguished all lamps so that the room was as dark as night. Only then did she remove her veil and take him to bed.

Raniya had been flush with anticipation for this moment, and so was surprised to find that Hassan's movements were clumsy and awkward. She remembered their wedding night very clearly; he had been confident, and his touch had taken her breath away. She knew Hassan's first meeting with the young Raniya was not far away, and for a moment did not understand how this fumbling boy could change so quickly. And then of course the answer was clear.

So every afternoon for many days, Raniya met Hassan at her rented house and instructed him in the art of love, and in doing so she demonstrated that, as is often said, women are Allah's most wondrous creation. She told him, "The pleasure you give is returned in the pleasure you receive," and inwardly she smiled as she thought of how true her words really were. Before long, he gained the expertise she remembered, and she took greater enjoyment in it than she had as a young woman.

All too soon, the day arrived when Raniya told the young Hassan that it was time for her to leave. He knew better than to press her for her reasons, but asked her if they might ever see each other again. She told him, gently, no. Then she sold the furnishings to the house's owner, and returned through the Gate of Years to the Cairo of her own day.

When the older Hassan returned from his trip to Damascus, Raniya was home waiting for him. She greeted him warmly, but kept her secrets to herself.

I was lost in my own thoughts when Bashaarat finished this story, until he said, "I see that this story has intrigued you in a way the others did not."

"You see clearly," I admitted. "I realize now that, even though the past is unchangeable, one may encounter the unexpected when visiting it."

"Indeed. Do you now understand why I say the future and the past are the same? We cannot change either, but we can know both more fully."

"I do understand; you have opened my eyes, and now I wish to use the Gate of Years. What price do you ask?"

He waved his hand. "I do not sell passage through the Gate," he said. "Allah guides whom he wishes to my shop, and I am content to be an instrument of his will."

Had it been another man, I would have taken his words to be a negotiating ploy, but after all that Bashaarat had told me, I knew that he was sincere. "Your generosity is as boundless as your learning," I said, and bowed. "If there is ever a service that a merchant of fabrics might provide for you, please call upon me."

"Thank you. Let us talk now about your trip. There are some matters we must speak of before you visit the Baghdad of twenty years hence."

"I do not wish to visit the future," I told him. "I would step through in the other direction, to revisit my youth."

"Ah, my deepest apologies. This Gate will not take you there. You see, I built this Gate only a week ago. Twenty years ago, there was no doorway here for you to step out of."

My dismay was so great that I must have sounded like a forlorn child. I said, "But where does the other side of the Gate lead?" and walked around the circular doorway to face its opposite side.

Bashaarat walked around the doorway to stand beside me. The view through the Gate appeared identical to the view outside it, but when he extended his hand to reach through, it stopped as if it met an invisible wall. I looked more closely, and noticed a brass lamp set on a table. Its flame did not flicker, but was as fixed and unmoving as if the room were trapped in clearest amber.

"What you see here is the room as it appeared last week," said Bashaarat. "In some twenty years' time, this left side of the Gate will permit entry, allowing people to enter from this direction and visit their past. Or," he said, leading me back to the side of the doorway he had first shown me, "we can enter from the right side now, and visit them ourselves. But I'm afraid this Gate will never allow visits to the days of your youth."

"What about the Gate of Years you had in Cairo?" I asked.

He nodded. "That Gate still stands. My son now runs my shop there."

"So I could travel to Cairo, and use the Gate to visit the Cairo of twenty years ago. From there I could travel back to Baghdad."

"Yes, you could make that journey, if you so desire."

"I do," I said. "Will you tell me how to find your shop in Cairo?"

"We must speak of some things first," said Bashaarat. "I will not ask your intentions, being content to wait until you are ready to tell me. But I would remind you that what is made cannot be unmade."

"I know," I said.

"And that you cannot avoid the ordeals that are assigned to you. What Allah gives you, you must accept."

"I remind myself of that every day of my life."

"Then it is my honor to assist you in whatever way I can," he said.

He brought out some paper and a pen and ink pot and began writing. "I shall write for you a letter to aid you on your journey." He folded the letter, dribbled some candle wax over the edge, and pressed his ring against it. "When you reach Cairo, give this to my son, and he will let you enter the Gate of Years there."

A merchant such as myself must be well versed in expressions of gratitude, but I had never before been as effusive in giving thanks as I was to Bashaarat, and every word was heartfelt. He gave me directions to his shop in Cairo, and I assured him I would tell him all upon my return. As I was about to leave his shop, a thought occurred to me. "Because the Gate of Years you have here opens to the future, you are assured that the Gate and this shop will remain standing for twenty years or more."

"Yes, that is true," said Bashaarat.

I began to ask him if he had met his older self, but then I bit back my words. If the answer was no, it was surely because his older self was dead, and I would be asking him if he knew the date of his death. Who was I to make such an inquiry, when this man was granting me a boon without asking my intentions? I saw from his expression that he knew what I had meant to ask, and I bowed my head in humble apology. He indicated his acceptance with a nod, and I returned home to make arrangements.

The caravan took two months to reach Cairo. As for what occupied my mind during the journey, Your Majesty, I now tell you what I had not told Bashaarat. I was married once, twenty years before, to a woman named Najya. Her figure swayed as gracefully as a willow bough and her face was as lovely as the moon, but it was her kind and tender nature that captured my heart. I had just begun my career as a merchant when we married, and we were not wealthy, but did not feel the lack.

We had been married only a year when I was to travel to Basra to meet with a ship's captain. I had an opportunity to profit by trading in slaves, but Najya did not approve. I reminded her that the Koran does not forbid the owning of slaves as long as one treats them well, and that even the Prophet owned some. But she said there was no way I could know how my buyers would treat their slaves, and that it was better to sell goods than men.

On the morning of my departure, Najya and I argued. I spoke harshly to her, using words that it shames me to recall, and I beg Your Majesty's forgiveness if I do not repeat them here. I left in anger, and never saw her again. She was badly injured when the wall of a mosque collapsed, some days after I left. She was taken to the bimaristan, but the physicians could not save her, and she died soon after. I did not learn of her death until I returned a week later, and I felt as if I had killed her with my own hand.

Can the torments of Hell be worse than what I endured in the days that followed? It seemed likely that I would find out, so near to death did my anguish take me. And surely the experience must be similar, for like infernal fire, grief burns but does not consume; instead, it makes the heart vulnerable to further suffering.

Eventually my period of lamentation ended, and I was left a hollow man, a bag of skin with no innards. I freed the slaves I had bought and became a fabric merchant. Over the years I became wealthy, but I never remarried. Some of the men I did business with tried to match me with a sister or a daughter, telling me that the love of a woman can make you forget your pains. Perhaps they are right, but it cannot make you forget the pain you caused another. Whenever I imagined myself marrying another woman, I remembered the look of hurt in Najya's eyes when I last saw her, and my heart was closed to others.

I spoke to a mullah about what I had done, and it was he who told me that repentance and atonement erase the past. I repented and atoned as best I knew how; for twenty years I lived as an upright man, I offered prayers and fasted and gave alms to those less fortunate and made a pilgrimage to Mecca, and yet I was still haunted by guilt. Allah is all-merciful, so I knew the failing to be mine.

Had Bashaarat asked me, I could not have said what I hoped to achieve. It was clear from his stories that I could not change what I knew to have happened. No one had stopped my younger self from arguing with Najya in our final conversation. But the tale of Raniya, which lay hidden within the tale of Hassan's life without his knowing it, gave me a slim hope: perhaps I might be able to play some part in events while my younger self was away on business.

Could it not be that there had been a mistake, and my Najya had survived? Perhaps it was another woman whose body had been wrapped in a shroud and buried while I was gone. Perhaps I could rescue Najya and bring her back with me to the Baghdad of my own day. I knew it was foolhardy; men of experience say, "Four things do not come back: the spoken word, the sped arrow, the past life, and the neglected opportunity," and I understood the truth of those words better than most. And yet I dared to hope that Allah had judged my twenty years of repentance sufficient, and was now granting me a chance to regain what I had lost.

The caravan journey was uneventful, and after sixty sunrises and three hundred prayers, I reached Cairo. There I had to navigate the city's streets, which are a bewildering maze compared to the harmonious design of the City of Peace. I made my way to the Bayn al-Qasrayn, the main street that runs through the Fatimid quarter of Cairo. From there I found the street on which Bashaarat's shop was located.

I told the shopkeeper that I had spoken to his father in Baghdad, and gave him the letter Bashaarat had given me. After reading it, he led me into a back room, in whose center stood another Gate of Years, and he gestured for me to enter from its left side.

As I stood before the massive circle of metal, I felt a chill, and chided myself for my nervousness. With a deep breath I stepped through, and found myself in the same room with different furnishings. If not for those, I would not have known the Gate to be different from an ordinary doorway. Then I recognized that the chill I had felt was simply the coolness of the air in this room, for the day here was not as hot as the day I had left. I could feel its warm breeze at my back, coming through the Gate like a sigh.

The shopkeeper followed behind me and called out, "Father, you have a visitor."

A man entered the room, and who should it be but Bashaarat, twenty years younger than when I'd seen him in Baghdad. "Welcome, my lord," he said. "I am Bashaarat."

"You do not know me?" I asked.

"No, you must have met my older self. For me, this is our first meeting, but it is my honor to assist you."

Your Majesty, as befits this chronicle of my shortcomings, I must confess that, so immersed was I in my own woes during the journey from Baghdad, I had not previously realized that Bashaarat had likely recognized me the moment I stepped into his shop. Even as I was admiring his water-clock and brass songbird, he had known that I would travel to Cairo, and likely knew whether I had achieved my goal or not.

The Bashaarat I spoke to now knew none of those things. "I am doubly grateful for your kindness, sir," I said. "My name is Fuwaad ibn Abbas, newly arrived from Baghdad."

Bashaarat's son took his leave, and Bashaarat and I conferred; I asked him the day and month, confirming that there was ample time for me to travel back to the City of Peace, and promised him I would tell him everything when I returned. His younger self was as gracious as his older. "I look forward to speaking with you on your return, and to assisting you again twenty years from now," he said.

His words gave me pause. "Had you planned to open a shop in Baghdad before today?"

"Why do you ask?"

"I had been marveling at the coincidence that we met in Baghdad just in time for me to make my journey here, use the Gate, and travel back. But now I wonder if it is perhaps not a coincidence at all. Is my arrival here today the reason that you will move to Baghdad twenty years from now?"

Bashaarat smiled. "Coincidence and intention are two sides of a tapestry, my lord. You may find one more agreeable to look at, but you cannot say one is true and the other is false."

"Now as ever, you have given me much to think about," I said.

I thanked him and bid farewell. As I was leaving his shop, I passed a woman entering with some haste. I heard Bashaarat greet her as Raniya, and stopped in surprise.

From just outside the door, I could hear the woman say, "I have the necklace. I hope my older self has not lost it."

"I am sure you will have kept it safe, in anticipation of your visit," said Bashaarat.

I realized that this was Raniya from the story Bashaarat had told me. She was on her way to collect her older self so that they might return to the days of their youth, confound some thieves with a doubled necklace, and save their husband. For a moment I was unsure if I were dreaming or awake, because I felt as if I had stepped into a tale, and the thought that I might talk to its players and partake of its events was dizzying. I was tempted to speak, and see if I might play a hidden role in that tale, but then I remembered that my goal was to play a hidden role in my own tale. So I left without a word, and went to arrange passage with a caravan.

It is said, Your Majesty, that Fate laughs at men's schemes. At first it appeared as if I were the most fortunate of men, for a caravan headed for Baghdad was departing within the month, and I was able to join it. In the weeks that followed I began to curse my luck, because the caravan's journey was plagued by delays. The wells at a town not far from Cairo were dry, and an expedition had to be sent back for water. At another village, the soldiers protecting the caravan contracted dysentery, and we had to wait for weeks for their recovery. With each delay, I revised my estimate of when we'd reach Baghdad, and grew increasingly anxious.

Then there were the sandstorms, which seemed like a warning from Allah, and truly caused me to doubt the wisdom of my actions. We had the good fortune to be resting at a caravanserai west of Kufa when the sandstorms first struck, but our stay was prolonged from days to weeks as, time and again, the skies became clear, only to darken again as soon as the camels were reloaded. The day of Najya's accident was fast approaching, and I grew desperate.

I solicited each of the camel drivers in turn, trying to hire one to take me ahead alone, but could not persuade any of them. Eventually I found one willing to sell me a camel at what would have been an exorbitant price under ordinary circumstances, but which I was all too willing to pay. I then struck out on my own.

It will come as no surprise that I made little progress in the storm, but when the winds subsided, I immediately adopted a rapid pace. Without the soldiers that accompanied the caravan, however, I was an easy target for bandits, and sure enough, I was stopped after two days' ride. They took my money and the camel I had purchased, but spared my life, whether out of pity or because they could not be bothered to kill me I do not know. I began walking back to rejoin the caravan, but now the skies tormented me with their cloudlessness, and I suffered from the heat. By the time the caravan found me, my tongue was swollen and my lips were as cracked as mud baked by the sun. After that I had no choice but to accompany the caravan at its usual pace.

Like a fading rose that drops its petals one by one, my hopes dwindled with each passing day. By the time the caravan reached the City of Peace, I knew it was too late, but the moment we rode through the city gates, I asked the guardsmen if they had heard of a mosque collapsing. The first guardsman I spoke to had not, and for a heartbeat I dared to hope that I had misremembered the date of the accident, and that I had in fact arrived in time.

Then another guardsman told me that a mosque had indeed collapsed just yesterday in the Karkh quarter. His words struck me with the force of the executioner's axe. I had traveled so far, only to receive the worst news of my life a second time.

I walked to the mosque, and saw the piles of bricks where there had once been a wall. It was a scene that had haunted my dreams for twenty years, but now the image remained even after I opened my eyes, and with a clarity sharper than I could endure. I turned away and walked without aim, blind to what was around me, until I found myself before my old house, the one where Najya and I had lived. I stood in the street in front of it, filled with memory and anguish.

I do not know how much time had passed when I became aware that a young woman had walked up to me. "My lord," she said, "I'm looking for the house of Fuwaad ibn Abbas."

"You have found it," I said.

"Are you Fuwaad ibn Abbas, my lord?"

"I am, and I ask you, please leave me be."

"My lord, I beg your forgiveness. My name is Maimuna, and I assist the physicians at the bimaristan. I tended to your wife before she died."

I turned to look at her. "You tended to Najya?"

"I did, my lord. I am sworn to deliver a message to you from her."

"What message?"

"She wished me to tell you that her last thoughts were of you. She wished me to tell you that while her life was short, it was made happy by the time she spent with you."

She saw the tears streaming down my cheeks, and said, "Forgive me if my words cause you pain, my lord."

"There is nothing to forgive, child. Would that I had the means to pay you as much as this message is worth to me, because a lifetime of thanks would still leave me in your debt."

"Grief owes no debt," she said. "Peace be upon you, my lord."

"Peace be upon you," I said.

She left, and I wandered the streets for hours, crying tears of release. All the while I thought on the truth of Bashaarat's words: past and future are the same, and we cannot change either, only know them more fully. My journey to the past had changed nothing, but what I had learned had changed everything, and I understood that it could not have been otherwise. If our lives are tales that Allah tells, then we are the audience as well as the players, and it is by living these tales that we receive their lessons.

Night fell, and it was then that the city's guardsmen found me, wandering the streets after curfew in my dusty clothes, and asked who I was. I told them my name and where I lived, and the guardsmen brought me to my neighbors to see if they knew me, but they did not recognize me, and I was taken to jail.

I told the guard captain my story, and he found it entertaining, but did not credit it, for who would? Then I remembered some news from my time of grief twenty years before, and told him that Your Majesty's grandson would be born an albino. Some days later, word of the infant's condition reached the captain, and he brought me to the governor of the quarter. When the governor heard my story, he brought me here to the palace, and when your lord chamberlain heard my story, he in turn brought me here to the throne room, so that I might have the infinite privilege of recounting it to Your Majesty.

Now my tale has caught up to my life, coiled as they both are, and the direction they take next is for Your Majesty to decide. I know many things that will happen here in Baghdad over the next twenty years, but nothing about what awaits me now. I have no money for the journey back to Cairo and the Gate of Years there, yet I count myself fortunate beyond measure, for I was given the opportunity to revisit my past mistakes, and I have learned what remedies Allah allows. I would be honored to relate everything I know of the future, if Your Majesty sees fit to ask, but for myself, the most precious knowledge I possess is this:

Nothing erases the past. There is repentance, there is atonement, and there is forgiveness. That is all, but that is enough.

Beyond the Wall

JUSTIN STANCHFIELD

New writer Justin Stanchfield is a rancher who lives with his family in Wise River, Montana. His stories have appeared in *Interzone, Black Gate, On Spec, Paradox,* and *Empire of Dreams and Miracles,* as well as in *Cricket, Boys' Life,* and *Jack & Jill.* Coming up is his first novel, *Space Cowboys.*

In the suspenseful story that follows, he takes us to Saturn's frozen moon Titan for an investigation of an enigmatic alien artifact that proves far stranger—and more dangerous—than anyone could possibly have imagined.

From two hundred kilometers out, the Wall seemed an impossibility, the scale too large to comprehend. Jenine Toole checked her descent rate against the radar, her own senses unreliable as she guided the lander downward. Outcrops of pitted stone vied with undulating lines of drifted, tarry snow until the surface seemed zebra-striped in the wan light. As the craft dropped lower she saw the lander's shadows racing beneath them. Twin shadows, one diffuse, cast by Saturn's milky glow, the other sharper but faint, the sun a mere point in the carbon haze. She had landed on Titan before, and each time the oddness of the landscape threatened to overwhelm her. Small wonder, she thought, that whoever had built the Wall had chosen this moon to build it on.

"Four-eight November, do you still have the intruder on screen?"

The clipped, male voice over the com-circuits startled her. Normally, she made a drop like this in silence. No sense letting the pot-hunters know they were being followed. Frowning, she thumbed the transmit switch.

"That's affirm, Control."

"Four-eight November," the voice repeated. "Do you still have the target on your tracking screen?"

"Roger that." Annoyed, she double-checked the screen nestled near the top of the padded console. The intruder's ship sat a kilometer from the base of the Wall, its thermal signature bright after the hot-stick landing. Whoever the pilot was, she decided, they had balls to pull off a drop like that. She hit the transmit switch again. "I'm showing the target ninety klicks downrange."

"Four-eight November? If you can read this, be advised, we can not see the target."

"Wonderful." Jenine cursed under her breath, then flipped the radio to intercom. "Paul? You guys better strap in. I'm about to hit the brakes. And, just so you know, we're out of commo with the orbiter. I can hear them, but they can't hear us."

"Got it." Paul Tsing sounded calm despite the bad news. Jenine's lips curled in a half smile. She was never sure if he was as confident as he seemed, or if he simply didn't understand how dangerous it was dropping ten tons of lander onto a haze-covered snowball. Still, she would rather have him in charge of a mission like this than any of the other inspectors she had flown with over the last nine years. Saturn and its entourage of moons was a harsh place, harsher still since the Wall had been discovered. Nothing brought out the worst in people—and nations—than the promise of alien technology waiting to be salvaged a billion kilometers from Earth.

The lander shuddered as she gave the braking jets another shot. She forced herself to relax while they bled off airspeed, the craft bucking in the thick atmosphere. Falling more than gliding, Jenine split her attention between the instruments and the view outside the narrow window. Already, the Wall dominated the view, its stark angles framed by Saturn, the gas giant a monstrous rubber ball cut neatly in half by shadow.

"Can you see the ship?" Tsing asked.

"Yeah." Jenine could just make out a tiny, silver speck against the rust-brown terrain. "I've got 'em on visual."

She fired the thrusters again, slowed to a drifting hover and extended the landing gear. The radar showed them forty meters above the surface. Thirty meters. Gently, she eased back the throttle. Twenty meters.

Without warning, they struck. Jenine's head struck the low ceiling. "What the hell?"

The lander bounced, struck again and threatened to tip over. Moving on instinct, she chopped the thrust and let the craft settle ingloriously to the surface. A dozen alarms screamed inside the cockpit. She cut them off, made a fast inspection of the board to confirm they were still in one piece, then shut down the engines completely. Sweat trickled off her forehead as she thumbed the intercom.

"Sorry about the landing, fellas. The radar must have gone wonky on me."

"Never mind that," Tsing said. "Are you sure you set us down next to the right ship?"

"Of course I'm sure. It's the only one besides us on the planet. Why?"

"Look out the side window."

She did. Annoyance changed to incredibility, and then to a cold, gripping fear. The ship she had tracked from orbit, the same ship that had glowed with the full heat of landing only seconds before, lay tipped on its nose gear, a rusted hulk half buried in the methane snow. Jenine stared at it, unbelieving.

The pot-hunter's ship looked as if it had been here for centuries.

Nine years.

Absently, Jenine fingered the hem of her jacket sleeve, the cuff worn and tattered as herself. She smiled at the thought. When was the last time she had gone on vacation, provided you could call two weeks on the UN research station on Iapetus a vacation. Still, it beat the hell out of Titan Control, the cramped, overcrowded orbiter and its wartime mind-set more than most people could stand for a single tour, let alone three of them.

"Stop it," she chided herself. Her voice echoed in her headset. Lately, Jenine had found her mind dwelling on the choices she had made, the opportunities lost. It was a bad sign, another indication that it was time to go home. She snorted. As if she could still call Earth home.

To distract herself, Jenine looked out the narrow window at the frigid, primordial atmosphere. Snow flurries danced, swirling in the floodlights that bathed the area. She watched as four figures, each in a different color E-suit, spread out around the crippled ship. Paul Tsing, wearing a dark blue suit with a white helmet, stopped at the base of the craft's extended landing ramp and looked up into the darkened airlock.

"Any sign of the pot-hunters?" she asked over the comm.

"Negative. Not a damn thing. Unless they have a safe room inside, this ship is cold. Deep cold. I doubt anyone has been here for years." Even Tsing's normal calm seemed stretched to the limit. "Are you certain we couldn't have missed their landing site?"

"Not a chance." Jenine had already played back the landing records. The ship was the only craft beside their own sitting on Titan's ice-choked surface. "Could it have been dead in orbit and came down on autopilot?"

"Doubt it." Tsing's breath cut in and out of the circuit. The man was nervous. "We're going inside. Let Control know, will you?"

"Okay. Be careful."

"We will."

Jenine watched a moment longer, then flipped over to the surface-to-orbit frequency. "Titan Control, Four-eight November, come in." She waited, but heard only static in her earphones. She tried again. "Titan Control, this is landing craft Four-eight November, come in."

The frequency remained empty, silent but for the irregular hiss and pop of lightning. A cold shudder ran down her back. In a system as active as Saturn's, communication problems were hardly uncommon, the background radiation at times so intense it could distort the strongest signal. But, in the dozens of drops she had made, she had never spent this long out of contact with the orbiting facility. Then again, she never set down this close to the Wall before.

The Wall. Her gaze drifted to the dark rampart half a kilometer off their nose. The massive structure was so tall she had to crane around until her nose nearly touched the window to see the top of it. Hundreds of tiny, rectangular portals dotted its face, spaced at seemingly random intervals along its length, the far ends so distant they stretched to either horizon until they were lost in the mist. Small wonder dozens of automated probes had passed it off as a geologic feature. Not until a manned mission arrived did anyone realize the thing was an artifact. Within hours, the powers that be had set the greatest discovery in archeological history off-limits until jurisdiction was established.

Jenine snorted in disgust. That had been a decade ago, and still the UN argued over who had the right to set foot inside first. It had seemed a good place to escape a failed marriage and stalled career, to volunteer for a tour guarding the structure which had, by all evidence done perfectly well on its own for more than half a million years. Now, in retrospect, she could hardly imagine she had ever been that naive. Her eyes began to sting, and she realized she hadn't blinked once as she stared at the Wall. She shook herself out of the dark reverie and reached for the transmit switch.

"Paul? What do you have inside?"

"Just what we thought." Tsing's voice crackled, the ship's hull hampering his signal. "This puppy has been down a long time. Not a drop of power in the system. No sign of crew. Oh, crap . . ."

"What's wrong?" Jenine tensed, instantly alert. Booby traps were the greatest threat any patrol faced. Few of the high-tech pirates that periodically attempted to break the prohibition would risk a physical fight, but nearly all of them were willing to leave a surprise or two aboard their ships for anyone who came poking around. "Talk to me, Paul. What's wrong?"

"We're okay." He sounded out of breath, clearly shaken. "I was wrong about that crew, that's all. The pilot is still aboard."

"Alive?"

"Neg on that. She's inside her suit, but frozen solid. Looks like the body's been here for ages. And you're not going to like this part. The suit is a Gen-Dyn Six."

"You're kidding?" Jenine's eyebrows furrowed together. The General Dynamics Mark Six was standard issue for UN troops assigned to deep space missions and not available to the public. She glanced over her shoulder at the locker where her own suit hung ready should she need it, then turned once more to the window. "Must be stolen. Can you see the ID patch?"

"Stand by. We're checking now."

Jenine waited, her heartbeat practically the only sound other than computer fans and the soft moan of wind around the hull. She zipped her jacket tighter against the chill in the cabin. Impatient for news, her hand moved toward the transmit switch when Tsing's voice returned.

"We've got an ident." Another long pause.

"And?"

"Jenine . . ." Tsing's voice sounded small, as if he was fighting the urge to vomit. "According to the patch, the corpse sitting in this chair is you."

They faced each other across the fold-down table in the passenger compartment. Out of his suit, Paul Tsing was a short man, with a thick shock of black hair and boyish eyes that belied the deep wrinkles carved around them. Normally, he was a rock. But not today. His face was pale, almost waxen, and like his three teammates, the scent of cold sweat hung around him.

"There's a rational explanation," Jenine said. She looked around the cramped chamber. None of the others would meet her gaze. Two of them, Morrissy and Kvass, were new replacements. The fourth inspector was a dour, pinched-faced man named Bruner who had been transferred up from Jupiter two years earlier, no doubt a reprimand for something. Only two ways, she thought glumly, to wind up at Titan. Volunteer or screw up. She took a sip from her coffee bulb, then continued, uncomfortable with the silence.

"The suit was stolen, that's all. There must be dozens of Mark Sixes unaccounted for."

"Fine," Tsing said quietly. "What about the ID patch?"

"Someone hacked my records. It happens."

"Maybe." Tsing took a drink, scowled, then pushed his own coffee aside. "We'll know more once we get the DNA back from the tissue we cored."

"Christ, you don't think it's me in that suit, do you?" Jenine's eyes widened in mock horror. Nervous laughter spread around the table. Even Bruner managed a weak grin. "Come on, guys. There's a logical explanation. We just have to find it."

Tsing's eyes locked on hers. "You weren't over there."

A low rumble coursed through the hull, strong enough to feel through the padded benches. The sound built into an undulating wail, then faded. One of the newbies, Kvass, practically jumped out of skin.

"What was that?"

"The thing that goes bump in the night." Jenine motioned him to sit back down. "It's just our fuel still bleeding off the methane into the main tank. You'll get used to it after a while."

"How long until the tanks are full enough to break ground?" Bruner asked, practically the first thing he had said since returning from the pot-hunter's ship.

"Three hours, maybe four." Jenine shrugged. "It doesn't really matter. We won't have a launch window for seventeen hours. And that's only if I can reestablish commo. I don't like the idea of launching blind."

"Any idea what's wrong with the radio?" Tsing asked.

Again, Jenine shrugged. "I think it's background noise. I'm running a full diagnostic now, but it takes a while."

"Well, then . . ." Tsing spread his hands. "We've got a few hours to kill. Might as well get some rack time."

"What about the intruders, sir?" Morrissy asked. He sounded so young Jenine had to stifle a grin. "Shouldn't we do something about them?"

"We are." Tsing sank back onto his narrow couch. "In case you haven't noticed, there are only two ships in walking range. One of them is dead, and we're sitting in the other one. They're stranded without us. When they knock on our airlock, we'll arrest them. Until then, I'm going to get some sleep."

Frost built on the inner surface of the window. Despite the heaters, it was cold inside the cockpit. Jenine wrapped her arms around herself. The muted snores from the passenger cabin were somehow reassuring, a human touch on an indifferent world.

No, she reminded herself. Titan was not indifferent. It was dead. A void, smog-shrouded chunk of ice and rock whirling about a gas giant so far from the sun it might as well have been in interstellar space. Almost against her will, she turned to the narrow window and stared at the enormous structure outside.

"It's still hard to believe, isn't it?"

Startled, Jenine spun around in her chair. Tsing stood in the narrow doorway, a blanket wrapped around his shoulders. He glanced at the empty copilot's chair.

"Mind if I sit down?" He eased into the high-backed seat. "Why here? Of all the places in the solar system, why would any race build something like that here?"

"A message, maybe?" She shrugged. "They wanted to see if we became a space-faring race and left it as a marker."

"You know, I've never bought that explanation." His eyes traveled down the length of the enigmatic artifact. Titan was still on the sunward side of

Saturn, but the feeble light that penetrated the haze revealed few details. "If they really were interested in our technological advances there are better ways to do it than this."

"All right, then, maybe the aliens landed here for the same reason we do. Titan's a perfect refuel point."

Tsing nodded thoughtfully. "That makes sense. But, it still doesn't explain our friends out there."

He tipped his head toward the other ship. Floodlights from the lander bathed it in a bright pool of light, accentuating the sharp angles. Unlike most pot-hunters, who relied on stealth technology, this ship had simply blazed in-system along a standard approach path, almost as if they didn't care if they were spotted. Methane snow flitted back and forth in the wind before finally falling to ground. Skeptical as she was, Jenine couldn't help but notice how deep the accumulations around the machine were. If she hadn't seen it land, she would have sworn it had been sitting in the same spot for decades.

"How long has it been?" Tsing asked.

"Nearly five hours." She knew what the question meant. Whoever the pot-hunters were, they couldn't have been this long from their ship without carrying spare oxygen and batteries, and if they were using thrust-packs, which seemed likely given the lack of footprints, their range would be limited. Six hours, seven at the most, she estimated, before the crew had to return or die of asphyxia. Unless, of course, they were already as dead as the frozen corpse they had discovered. A cold thought hammered against her, and she swung around to face Tsing.

"What if this is a decoy? What if there never was a crew, and that ship was just sent down to distract us while the real potters land somewhere else?"

"I thought of that," he admitted. "Seems like an awful lot of trouble to go to."

"Given what a single artifact from inside the Wall would be worth . . ." She let her voice trail off.

The creases around his eyes deepened. After a moment, he changed the subject. "Any luck with the commo?"

"No. I've ran the diagnostics twice and can't find a damn thing. Has to be outside interference. I'm running a new scan on the tracking dish now, but . . ." Suddenly, she paused. Something out the corner of her eye struck her wrong, and she leaned closer to the window. "What the hell?"

"What's wrong?"

"The ship's gone." Shaken, Jenine looked again. To her amazement, the derelict was back, snow swirling around its hull. She shivered. "Wonderful. Now my eyes are playing tricks on me."

"Never mind that," Tsing said, an urgent tone in his voice. He pointed toward the Wall. "Look up near the top tier of portals. Our friends are back."

High above the red-hued snowdrifts, barely visible through the haze, a light glowed in one of the rectangular openings. Even as they watched, it brightened, then faded, as if someone holding a lamp had turned to face them then quickly swung away. Eyes locked on the wall, Jenine asked, "What now?"

"Now?" Tsing stood up. "I wake up the guys and suit up. Looks like we finally get to see what's inside that son of a bitch."

Time slipped to a crawl. Jenine sat alone inside the lander and watched the team march across the barren expanse toward the Wall. By regulation, she had donned her excursion suit, the stiff, bright green fabric uncomfortably snug around her chest and waist. She hated this part, the waiting, the feeling of utter uselessness while the rest of the team took on the real risk. Protocols had been in place for years, contingencies by which a team might actually enter the Wall should the structure be at risk. Under perfect circumstances they would have been in constant contact with the orbiter before such a decision was made, but with the commo down and clear evidence that someone had already penetrated the Wall, Tsing had made the only real choice he could.

Jenine shifted in the padded chair and tried to get comfortable. The waiting tore at her, the sensation that she was little more than a glorified chauffeur. Too much time on her hands, too much time to think. Think about why she stayed out here, and why she was reluctant to go back to Earth. So many missed opportunities, all the bright promise of her life dwindled to this odd little corner of the solar system. She had been running from herself so long she sometimes wondered if she could ever catch up.

The speaker crackled. "Are you reading us all right?" Tsing sounded slightly out of breath.

"Roger that." She glanced at the center screen, now split into four separate views, one for each of the team members. "A-V and telemetry all five by five. You got any tracks yet?"

"Nothing."

Jenine leaned closer to the screen. She couldn't imagine how the pothunters had entered the Wall without disturbing the snow around it. Even with thrust-packs there should have been marks. Nothing about this mission made sense, and not for the first time since they landed she felt the fear twisting within her stomach. She tried again unsuccessfully to contact the orbiter, then let her eyes drift back to the center screen. Already, details from the Wall were visible, the surface a mottled, pitted gray, cracked and worn by the harsh environment. If she had expected something high-tech she was disappointed. The material looked like any of hundreds of terrestrial ruins.

A dark rectangle hove into view, the nearest of the portals on screen as

Tsing's helmet lamp played across the opening, revealing a narrow hallway within. "Here we go." No mistaking the tension in his voice.

"Roger that," Jenine replied, her own voice barely a whisper. Like most of humanity, she had seen the old footage relayed back by the robot probes the initial teams had sent inside. Rough, skittering images of twisting, intertwined passages and stairwells, most so steep the probes had been unable to ascend. No artifacts had been found, no inscriptions or murals, nothing to indicate who or what had left the enormous monument. She tensed as Tsing's camera view darkened, then stabilized once he ducked under the lintel.

"Do you see anything?" she asked.

"Not much. It's pretty tight in here. Barely enough room to squeeze by. Lots of snow piled up . . . damn it!"

"What's wrong?" Jenine's fingers tightened around the armrests.

"Nothing. I tripped in the dark, that's all. Missed seeing a step down."

The view from Tsing's camera flickered, returned, then darkened once more, the signal weakened by the heavy stone. One by one, the others in the team followed him inside. Jenine looked out the cockpit window and tried to spot the door they had used, but the details were lost in the snow squall. High above the surface, nearly at the top of the Wall, she saw another flash of light.

"Paul? I just caught sight of the intruders again. They're above you and to the west." She waited, but Tsing didn't reply. "Paul? Are you reading me?"

"Yes. Stand by . . ." Tsing's transmission was almost unreadable. The video feed flickered then cut out. The other cameras followed suit. Within seconds, the center screen was blank. Jenine stared at it while a wave of dizziness passed through her, as if the cabin had suddenly tilted then just as quickly righted itself. She glanced once more at the ship a hundred meters to her left.

It was gone.

"This isn't happening," she whispered, barely able to breathe. Her fingers flew across the control panel as she scanned the area around the lander. To her dismay, the instruments found nothing, no heat signature, no radar return, certainly nothing on the video feed. She stabbed the transmit button.

"Paul? Get out of there, now." She knew she was letting panic sway her, but couldn't stop. "If you can hear me, we have a situation out here. Return to the lander. Repeat, return to the lander."

She boosted the gain and listened. No voices replied, no pings from any of their trackers. Quickly, she switched to the orbiter's frequency and tried once more to reestablish contact. "Titan Control, this is landing craft Four-eight November. Please come in." She waited without reply. Frustrated, she let the dish scan the southern horizon, hoping the computer might locate another radio source. "Any station, this is United Nations landing craft Four-eight November. Please come in."

She frowned. Somewhere, buried in the blanketing white hiss of Saturn, she heard a faint trill. The sound built, then faded only to return a few seconds later. Jenine narrowed the scanning range, but the electronic warble remained damningly obscure. Less than thirty seconds after it began, the transmission vanished.

"What the hell?" Her voice echoed softly in her earphones, the words clipped by the intercom while she waited for the ship's navigation library to identify the source. Seconds dragged into minutes as the computer searched through thousands of samples before it finally found a match. Jenine's jaw fell open. The only object that could have created the brief, passing signal was an early space probe that had gone nonfunctional more than two hundred and sixty years earlier.

"This is impossible." She flicked back to the ground-to-ship channel. "Paul, this is the lander. If you can hear me, please return to the ship. Do you read me?"

Without warning, as if to answer her call, a loud bang ran through the hull. Jenine jumped and struck her head against the cockpit ceiling, then steadied herself against the back of her chair and listened. Another thud followed the first, and then another, all centered near the small airlock at the rear of the passenger compartment. Someone was knocking at the door.

"Paul?"

Hopeful, Jenine switched on the fish-eye camera mounted inside the lock. Blood roared in her ears as the camera focused on a lone figure in a bright green excursion suit framed in the outer hatchway. She squeezed her eyes shut and looked again, but the figure was gone, nothing visible but swirls of dull red snow. Certain that she was losing her mind, she replayed the video. The dizziness and nausea she had felt earlier returned, so strong she nearly vomited inside her helmet, all doubt removed.

The person who had been banging against the airlock was herself.

Seventeen minutes. Jenine watched the clock on her visor, clinging to the passage of time as a drowning dog might grasp a log between its front legs as it was swept downstream. "Come on, think . . ." The sound of her own voice helped her regain her calm. "Got to be a rational explanation for all this."

The obvious answer was the one she liked least. She was hallucinating.

"All right, then, why am I seeing things? Anoxia? My suit air is fouled." To test her theory, she carefully unlocked her visor and swung it up into her helmet. The smell of her own sour breath washed away, replaced by the colder, musty cabin air. She filled her lungs, exhaled and filled them again. A breath cloud hung around her face as she let the air out. She glanced at her biomonitor, but the readout showed no change.

"Okay," she said out loud. "Go to plan B. What the hell is plan B?"

Her eyes drifted around the cockpit and fell at last on the Emergency Medkit. She remembered it contained sedatives, but quickly rejected the idea. While a tranq patch might steady her nerves, it would also dull her senses. Until Tsing and the others returned, she had to remain sharp, even if she mistrusted what her mind reported. Still, the kit might contain something useful. Slowly, hampered by her suit, she reached for it but stopped as the radio unexpectedly burst life.

"Four-eight November? This is Tsing. Come in. Please come in."

"Paul? Go ahead."

"Thank God." Tsing's voice was raw. "We've been trying to contact you for hours."

"Hours?" The statement confused her. The team had been inside the ancient structure less than seventy minutes, but she passed it off as nerves. "It's the Wall. It's blocking your signal. What's your location?"

"I'm sitting in one of the portals. I think it's on the upper tier, but I can't really tell."

Through the murk she could just make out a faint glow near the rim of the massive artifact. "Okay, I've got you. I think you're in the same doorway the pot-hunters used. What's your situation?"

"Not good. Bruner is down. He panicked when his air got low and jumped through one of the doors to the ground. Kvass and Morrissy went to find him, but I can't raise them on the radio. Listen, Jenine, we're all short on power and air. My reserve is down to thirty minutes."

"Thirty minutes?" She leaned forward, certain Tsing was mistaken, and found his bioread. Now that he was back online, the telemetry functioned again. She stiffened. Instead of the seven hours he should have had available, his air supply registered thirty-four minutes of usable oxygen. "What happened out there?"

"Got lost . . . wandered around inside the . . ." The signal, diamond-bright only seconds ago, now began to break up. "Found the bodies . . . can't . . ."

"Say again? What bodies?"

"The pot-hunters. They're dead." He spoke more slowly, but the signal continued to weaken. "No chance to retrieve them. Not now."

"You found them?" Jenine blinked. "Paul, their ship is gone. Some of them must have made it out."

"What are you talking about? That ship is still on the ground." For a moment, Tsing's voice came in clear again. "I can see it from here."

Another wave of vertigo struck her. What should have been a routine mission had suddenly become impossibly complicated. One team member missing and most likely dead, three others on the verge of suffocation, her own mental health questionable. She took a deep breath, then spoke slowly, "Paul, what are the weather conditions where you are?"

"Huh?" He sounded perplexed. "What do you mean? They're the same as what you have. Overcast sky, visibility fair out to five klicks. Wind conditions calm."

She glanced out the window at the heavy snow driving past, the wind a howl. The Wall was nothing but a dark, blocky shadow through the haze, Tsing's lamp the only discernable feature. Even as she watched, that light faded, then was gone.

"Paul?"

Static answered. She slumped back into her seat and began to shiver, chilled to the core. She tried again to raise Tsing without success, then, moving stiffly, rose and wandered toward the back of the craft. A small locker was built into the wall behind the couches. From it, she withdrew three oxygen canisters and put them inside a carry sack, then added as many charged batteries as she could find. She picked up the bundle. In Titan's weak gravity the weight wouldn't be a factor, but the sack was bulky and would hamper her movements. She sighed, unable to think of any other way to carry the emergency supplies. Bundle in hand, she shuffled to the airlock, pulled on her gauntlets then resealed her visor. A row of tiny green lights popped into view along the rim. She reached for the airlock controls, but paused.

"This is insane," Jenine told herself. While she had been busy gathering supplies, the weirdness of the situation had been pushed to the back of her mind. Now, it returned with a vengeance. Regulations insisted she remain with the lander. So did common sense.

Unfortunately, that meant leaving a friend to die.

More frightened than she had ever been in her life, she slapped the broad red button beside the door and waited for the airlock to slide open. Before she could change her mind, stepped through.

Jenine leaned forward, fighting the quartering headwind, the bulky pack of spare oxygen cylinders slapping her leg with every step. The surface felt spongy underfoot, the methane slush sticking to her insulated boots. She paused a moment to rest, and turned to look behind. The lander remained an oasis of light, its rotating beacon painting the swirling snow a garish orange. A fast glance at her clock showed that fifteen minutes had elapsed since she had spoken with Tsing. With time running out, she hefted the sack and pressed on.

The Wall stretched from horizon to horizon, its top lost in the blizzard. She could just make out the individual portals, coffin-sized openings spaced irregularly across the structure's stone face. She picked up her pace toward the nearest of them and hoped it was the one Tsing and the others had used. If she didn't pick up their trail soon, all of this was for nothing.

Something lay at the foot of the monument. Jenine jogged toward it, her gait hampered by the odd gravity. From the color of his suit, she knew it was Bruner. Her headlamp threw his body into an almost surrealistic accuracy. His visor was rimed in frost, a thin, diagonal crack across it. She didn't need to touch him to know he was dead. She swept the area with her lamp. Heavy footprints, half filled with drifted snow, led away.

"Thank you," she said, blessing her luck at finding the tracks. She followed them to the portal, then stopped. The vertigo she had felt earlier returned, as if the moon's orbit had suddenly gone mad. She fought down the sensation, then ducked inside.

A narrow passage lay in front of her, the stone rough-hewn. Her mind flashed back to a school field trip when she was ten or eleven, a sim-tour of Egypt's Great Pyramid. The corridor could have been left by the same builders. Dragging the pack behind her, she continued down the passage. Twenty paces inside, the corridor turned left into a narrow flight of steps. Two more bodies sat upon them, unmoving.

"Morrissy?" Jenine knelt beside the nearer of the pair. "Can you hear me?"

The man stirred. Jenine bent closer, desperate to find an angle where her suit lamp didn't blind him. His eyes fluttered open.

"How . . . how'd you find us?" His words were thick, barely coherent.

"Just hang on, okay?" She pulled out one of the cylinders and exchanged it with one of the empties on his power unit. After she made certain the seal was tight, she did the same with his spent battery. "Take a deep breath, okay?"

Morrissy nodded weakly. She stepped over him and repeated the operation with Kvass's pack. Even with the fresh cylinder and battery, she couldn't tell if he was breathing.

"Thanks for coming back," Morrissy said, his voice stronger.

A cold finger skipped down Jenine's spine. "What do you mean, 'come back'?"

"The lander," Morrissy said. "When we got down, it was gone. We thought you'd abandoned us."

She thought about explaining, but decided against it. She still had to find Tsing. Dreading the thought of penetrating deeper into the structure by herself, she let her light play over the rough-cut stairs.

"Where's Paul?" she asked.

"We hoped he was with you."

"No. I talked to him from the lander, but he was on one of the upper tiers. Did you leave marker tabs?" Jenine helped Kvass sit up. The man groaned incoherently, the sound a muted roar in her headphones. She waited until the channel cleared, then asked again, "Did you tab a trail back to where you and Paul split up?"

"We . . ." Morrissy sounded on the edge of hysteria. "We ran out tabs hours ago. Doesn't matter anyway. They don't work in here."

"What do you mean they don't work?" The hair on the back of her neck stiffened. Standard practice was to drop a trail of the reflective tabs behind to leave a path for following teams, or to track your way back out. Unless the laws of physics were somehow violated, the system was practically foolproof. "Morrissy, how do I reach Paul?"

"Go up," was all he said.

Annoyed and more than a little frightened, she squeezed past Kvass and started up the constricting stairwell, then paused. "Can you two reach the lander?"

"I think so," Morrissy replied.

"Good. I'll meet you back there as soon as I can." She wondered if she was making a mistake. Given how frightened Morrissy sounded, she hoped he didn't try to launch without her. She pushed the thought out of her mind and started climbing.

A small landing lay at the top of the stairs, another corridor branching past it. To her left, the passage emptied into blackness, obviously one of the doors she had seen from the lander. At the other end of the passage she saw a small circle glowing pale yellow. She smiled to herself. Despite what Morrissy had said, the marker tabs were obviously working as promised. She hurried toward it.

The corridor turned sharply to the left. A second marker tab glowed at the far end, twenty meters away. Leaning forward to avoid brushing the ceiling, Jenine shuffled to the tab, then stopped, confused. Instead of another corner, she found a blank stone wall.

"Wonderful." Angry at the wasted time, she retraced her steps to the stairwell, then went past it toward the doorway. She steadied herself with a hand against the wall and carefully looked out. Far below she saw the lander, still bathed in the glow of its floodlights, the pot-hunter's ship beside it. She forced herself to look down, but quickly pulled back inside, the view dizzying. Odd, she thought. She hadn't noticed she had climbed so high. Again, she moved back toward the stairwell and dropped the carry sack beside it, then stared into the passage, utterly confused.

The descending corridor she had climbed only moments before was gone. Another stairwell lay in its place, the rough-cut steps beckoning upward.

"No. No, no, no . . ." she whispered. Over the frequency, she said "Morrissy, can you hear me?" She listened, but her radio remained silent, nothing in her headphones but her own rapid breath.

"Slow down," she scolded herself, fully aware how much time she was wasting. By now, if Tsing's estimate had been correct, his tanks were dry. If he was alive, he was living on whatever his scrubber salvaged from inside his suit. She needed to find him and find him fast.

"Just calm down," she said out loud. "Don't lose your head."

Back and forth she moved along the corridor, each trip a dead end, every return bringing her not to her starting point, but to a new junction. Sweat poured down her back, her heart pounding furiously as the minutes trickled off. Unable to find her way back to the ground floor, she continued to take the ascending stairs.

She paused at the top of the next flight, blinded by the sheen of breath condensed inside her visor. She waited for it to clear, then looked around. Her lamp lit the far end of the corridor with a pale, bluish glow. Unsure what she might find, Jenine shuffled toward it. As she neared the end of the passage, she saw that the glow came from reflected snow. Cautiously, she edged toward the opening and looked out, but nothing was visible, the blizzard impenetrable. Had the lander been directly beneath her she couldn't have seen it. Dismayed, she slowly turned around.

"Hello, Jenine."

"Paul?" Her jaw dropped open. Five paces behind her, his visor open to the frigid, toxic atmosphere, Paul Tsing stood, one arm propped casually against the stone wall. He smiled at her.

"I think you should follow me." His voice was calm and edged with regret. "You need to see what I've found."

Her head spun. Nothing made sense, not the man in front of her, nor the side passage Paul Tsing led her down. How had she missed seeing it before?.

"Where are you taking me?"

"Home." Tsing turned and smiled at her, his face still exposed to Titan's atmosphere. "I know it doesn't make any sense, but believe me, everything is going to be fine."

"Paul, don't you understand, this is impossible?"

"Yes. I understand it. But I don't think that really matters anymore."

A faint glow lit the corridor, not the reflected gleam of helmet lamps against methane slush, but a softer, more subtle illumination. Confused, she followed Tsing into a small, vaulted chamber. Though it was constructed from the same rough gray stone as the rest of the Wall, the surface was smooth, almost polished, the floor patterned like marble. Tsing edged aside and let her step past toward a broad portico, slender columns supporting a trio of arched doorways. She shuddered as she crept beneath the middle arch onto a narrow ledge, an elegant stone handrail barring her from the precipice. Hands shaking, she leaned against it.

A city spread out below, high towers lit bright as candle flame. Helicopters and mag-rails flitted between the angular structures, little more than flashing red lights from her high vantage, while farther beneath an endless swath of roofed streets covered the ground like a network of capillaries, their translucent surfaces adding a pleasant yellow wash to the base of the sky-scrapers. Lazy clouds drifted along the steel canyons, as if a gentle rain might recently have fallen.

"That's Chicago," she whispered, unable to pull her eyes away. Tsing stepped beside her and nodded.

"That's where you grew up, isn't it?" His smile broadened. "I told you I was taking you home." Before she could stop him, Tsing put his hands against his helmet, gave it a sharp twist, then lifted the bulky headgear off and tucked it under his arm. His dark hair was damp with sweat.

"Have you lost your mind?"

"Maybe." He grinned. "Probably. Does it really matter? Open your visor, Jenine. Stop denying yourself. Admit it. This is what you've been searching for. Everything can be different this time. Anything you want, yours for the taking."

She felt the dream sweep through her, the sweetness of the moment palpable. Tsing was right, wasn't he? What good did it do to deny what she saw, whether it made sense or not? How long had she been running from herself? Slowly, her hands rose to her helmet. She placed her fingers firmly against the hard plastic, took a long swallow of the rubber-tinged air, then closed her eyes. Her forearms tensed as she started to twist.

"No." She let her hands drop to her sides. "This isn't right."

Her eyes fluttered open. Gone was city and the elegantly carved chamber, the narrow corridor replacing it, the only light the harsh white burn from her helmet lamp. At her feet a body in a heavy excursion suit lay sprawled on the rough stone floor.

"Paul?" She crouched beside the body and rolled it over. Tsing's visor was closed, but she had no way of knowing if he was alive or dead. Frantically, she groped for the carry sack, but found nothing. She rose stiffly to her feet and looked back the way she had came. The sack lay crumpled at the top of the stairs leading downward. She rushed to it, gathered it in her cold fingers, then hurried back to Tsing. Shaking, she changed his oxygen cannister and battery, then shook him. "Can you hear me?"

A muffled groan answered in her speakers. She forced herself not to cry in sheer relief. Still hampered by the tight space, Jenine pulled the woozy Tsing to his feet, and holding him under the shoulders, guided him toward the stairs.

Snow met her headlamp, Titan's cold surface just outside the rectangular doorway. Too narrow to walk abreast, Jenine kept one hand on Tsing's arm as she led him toward the exit.

"Almost there," she said, coaxing him along.

"No . . ." His breath was labored. "Need to go back."

"We are going back. Just a little farther to the ship." Her boot brushed against something, and she glanced down, relieved to see the oxygen tanks she had exchanged from Kvass and Morrissy lying where she had left them. Somehow they vindicated her memory. "Come on, Paul. We can do this."

"Can't leave." He tried to pull away. "Not yet."

"Listen to me. We're both low on air. We need to get back to the ship." The wind forced a swirling tongue of snow into the passage. Tiny pellets struck her helmet as she ducked under the lintel back into the world beyond the Wall. Night was falling as Titan slid into Saturn's shadow, the gas giant a hazy crescent stretching from ground to zenith. In the deepening shadows, the lights from the lander played hypnotically against the ice. She paused a moment to stretch the kinks from her back, grateful to finally be free of the enigmatic structure. A flash of light at the lander brought her up cold.

"What the hell are they doing?" Horrified, she watched the attitude jets flash in sequence. Suddenly, she understood. Morrissy was preflighting the craft for launch. She twisted around so fast she nearly lost her balance, and grabbed Tsing's wrist. "Come on! They're going to leave without us."

She broke into a slow jog, hampered by the odd gravity and the still woozy Tsing. He pulled against her, dragging her back toward the doorway.

"We can't leave. Not now. Not after I've found the way home." With a twist, he broke free. Jenine tried to grab him, but he was already out of reach.

"Damn it, Paul!" She stood, torn by indecision, and watched his stumbling, retreating form. Two hundred meters still lay between herself and the lander. Even if she could stop Tsing, she couldn't physically drag him to the ship. Her only hope now lay in stopping Morrissy from launching. A pounding, throbbing pain built inside her skull. A quick glance at her suit monitor confirmed her suspicion. Her own oxygen supply was nearly gone. Decision made, she turned toward the lander, calling frantically over the radio as she skip-walked across the frozen ground.

"Four-eight November, come in." The effort of speaking cost her, stealing precious gulps of air. "Morrissy, please, respond."

A red glow built beneath the craft, a shimmering blush as the engines came online. Daring the blast that would certainly scorch her to cinders should Morrissy launch while she stood outside, she threw herself against the airlock's outer door and pounded her fists on the heavy plate, desperate to get the panicked deputy's attention.

"Morrissy! Listen to me!"

Her chest ached, the fear and lack of air overwhelming. Jenine felt as if she was drowning inside her helmet. A rhythmic shudder pulsed through the hull. An image of herself engulfed in flames as the craft broke ground flashed through her mind. Desperate, she looked for shelter, but saw only the pot-hunter's derelict ship fifty meters away. Out of options, she dashed toward the gaping hatchway.

The craft was dark within, the walls rimed with ice. Jenine fell on the ramp, bruised her knee, but staggered to her feet and blundered down the short corridor toward the cockpit. Like the rest of the ship, the control panel was frosted, the systems long dead. She fell more than sat into the pilot's chair. Out the corner of her eye she saw blue-white flame spread beneath her own ship, the lander quivering as Morrissy powered up.

"You bastard," she shouted over the radio. "Damn you, you stupid, stupid bastard."

The chair felt rock hard beneath her, the padding frozen solid. Her headache had worsened, her air supply nearly gone. Silently, she laughed at the irony. At least she understood how the frozen corpse wearing her excursion suit wound up inside the abandoned ship. She clenched her fists in frustration and shut her eyes.

"No. I refuse to believe this is happening."

Jenine took a long, slow breath, the air sour as it wheezed in and out of the helmet's overworked regulator, then opened her eyes once more. A grim smile crept across her face. She was still inside the Wall, less than a meter from the exit. Paul Tsing stood behind her, weaving drunkenly on his feet. Outside, past the narrow opening, the lander sat alone, the pot-hunter's ship vanished. She took Tsing by the wrist.

"Let's get back to the lander."

"But . . ."

"No," she said firmly and led him outside. Wind tore at her, driving her sideways as she struggled toward the craft. Snow swirled, at times so heavy it blinded her, but she held to the flashing orange strobe and trudged on. A vague shape took form, the lander a slumbering dragon in the gloom. Tsing said nothing as they reached the airlock, but stood complacently beside her as she raised her arm and pounded three sharp knocks against the hatch.

"Captain Tsing?" A nervous voice blared inside her helmet. Jenine breathed a sigh of relief.

"It's me, Morrissy. I've got Paul. Cycle us through, okay?"

The airlock slid open. Jenine helped Tsing inside, then followed him into the cramped chamber. The effort was nearly beyond her. The outer door resealed. Air whistled around her as the lock emptied then refilled with fresh oxygen. Finally, the inner door slid aside. Morrissy and Kvass stood just inside, waiting for them. Jenine pushed Tsing through the hatchway, then popped her helmet off. The musty, recycled air tasted sweeter than springtime. Feeling stronger, she nodded at Tsing.

"Help him. He's suffering from hypoxia."

Together, they removed Tsing's helmet, then led him to the nearest couch and eased him down. His hair was matted, his skin pale, but his eyes looked clearer.

"Thank God you came back when you did," Kvass said. Jenine thought she heard a note of guilt in his reedy voice. "Control's been calling for more than an hour. They want to know if we need another ship to come down?"

"No." Jenine shook her head firmly. "Tell them we're okay. No, wait. I'll tell them myself in a minute." Somehow, she wasn't surprised that communication had returned.

"Ma'am?" Morrissy shuffled his boots nervously. "What about Bruner? Shouldn't we go back outside and retrieve . . ." He hesitated. "Retrieve his body?"

Jenine glanced across the narrow aisle at Tsing. He caught her eye and gave his head an almost imperceptible shake. He understood. So did she. Somewhere inside that labyrinth, somehow, Bruner was still alive, still contemplating whether to jump from the high doorway or die from asphyxiation. All she had to do was find him. The thought sent a chill through her. The memory of that cityscape glimpsed from the hidden balcony was still too fresh, too seductive. Anything that could be contemplated could be found there, but only at a price. Madness lay in that direction. She turned back to face Morrissy.

"We can bring the body back later, before the next launch window. But not tonight."

"Ma'am . . ." Again, Morrissy paused. He chewed on his lip, as if he couldn't bring himself to frame the question. "What is that place?"

"You mean the Wall?" She thought about the question. She could have told him that it was Hell. She almost said it was Heaven. Instead, she shrugged her shoulders. "I don't know. I wish I did, but I don't."

"What do we tell them when they ask what happened down here?" Kvass inched closer. Jenine looked up at him and held his gaze, then smiled.

"The truth," she said. "We just tell them the truth."

KIOSK

BRUCE STERLING

Here's a visit to a powerful and surprising near future where one key invention makes all the difference—in ways that nobody ever even thought that it would.

One of the most powerful and innovative new talents to enter SF in the past few decades, Bruce Sterling sold his first story in 1976. By the end of the '80s he had established himself, with a series of stories set in his exotic "Shaper/Mechanist" future, with novels such as the complex and Stapledonian *Schismatrix* and the well-received *Islands in the Net* (as well as with his editing of the influential anthology *Mirrorshades: The Cyberpunk Anthology* and the infamous critical magazine *Cheap Truth*), as perhaps the prime driving force behind the revolutionary "Cyberpunk" movement in science fiction, and also as one of the best new hard-science writers to enter the field in some time. His other books include a critically acclaimed non-fiction study of First Amendment issues in the world of computer networking, *The Hacker Crackdown: Law and Disorder on the Electronic Frontier*; the novels *The Artificial Kid, Involution Ocean, Heavy Weather, Holy Fire, Distraction, Zeitgeist, The Zenith Angle,* and a novel in collaboration with William Gibson, *The Difference Engine*; an omnibus collection (it contains the novel *Schismatrix* as well as most of his Shaper/Mechanist stories), *Schismatrix Plus*; a non-fiction study of the future, *Tomorrow Now: Envisioning the Next 50 Years*; and the landmark collections *Crystal Express, Globalhead, A Good Old-fashioned Future,* and *Visionary in Residence.* His most recent book is a massive retrospective collection, *Ascendancies: The Best of Bruce Sterling.* His story "Bicycle Repairman" earned him a long-overdue Hugo in 1997, and he won another Hugo in 1997 for his story "Taklamakan." His stories have appeared in our First through Eighth, Eleventh, Fourteenth, Sixteenth, Twentieth, and Twenty-third Annual Collections.

I

The fabrikator was ugly, noisy, a fire hazard, and it smelled. Borislav got it for the kids in the neighborhood.

One snowy morning, in his work gloves, long coat, and fur hat, he loudly power-sawed through the wall of his kiosk. He duct-taped and stapled the fabrikator into place.

The neighborhood kids caught on instantly. His new venture was a big hit.

The fabrikator made little plastic toys from 3-D computer models. After a week, the fab's dirt-cheap toys literally turned into dirt. The fabbed toys just crumbled away, into a waxy, non-toxic substance that the smaller kids tended to chew.

Borislav had naturally figured that the brief lifetime of these toys might discourage the kids from buying them. This just wasn't so. This wasn't a bug: this was a feature. Every day after school, an eager gang of kids clustered around Borislav's green kiosk. They slapped down their tinny pocket change with mittened hands. Then they exulted, quarreled, and sometimes even punched each other over the shining fab-cards.

The happy kid would stick the fab-card (adorned with some glossily fraudulent pic of the toy) into the fabrikator's slot. After a hot, deeply exciting moment of hissing, spraying, and stinking, the fab would burp up a freshly minted dinosaur, baby doll, or toy fireman.

Foot traffic always brought foot traffic. The grown-ups slowed as they crunched the snowy street. They cast an eye at the many temptations ranked behind Borislav's windows. Then they would impulse-buy. A football scarf, maybe. A pack of tissues for a sneezy nose.

Once again he was ahead of the game: the only kiosk in town with a fabrikator.

The fabrikator spoke to him as a veteran street merchant. Yes, it definitely *meant something* that those rowdy kids were so eager to buy toys that fell apart and turned to dirt. Any kiosk was all about high-volume repeat business. The stick of gum. The candy bar. The cheap, last-minute bottle-of-booze. The glittery souvenir key chain that tourists would never use for any purpose whatsoever. These objects were the very stuff of a kiosk's life.

Those colored plastic cards with the 3-D models. . . . The cards had potential. The older kids were already collecting the cards: not the toys that the cards made, but the cards themselves.

And now, this very day, from where he sat in his usual street cockpit behind his walls of angled glass, Borislav had taken the next logical step. He offered the kids ultra-glossy, overpriced, collector cards that could not and would not make toys. And of course — there was definitely logic here — the kids were going nuts for that business model. He had sold a hundred of them.

Kids, by the nature of kids, weren't burdened with a lot of cash. Taking their money was not his real goal. What the kids brought to his kiosk was what kids had to give him — futurity. Their little churn of street energy — that was the symptom of something bigger, just over the horizon. He didn't have a word for that yet, but he could feel it, in the way he felt a coming thunderstorm inside his aching leg.

Futurity might bring a man money. Money never saved a man with no future.

II

Dr. Grootjans had a jaw like a horse, a round blue pillbox of a hat, and a stiff winter coat that could likely stop gunfire. She carried a big European shopping wand.

Ace was acting as her official street guide, an unusual situation, since Ace was the local gangster. "Madame," Ace told her, "this is the finest kiosk in the city. Boots here is our philosopher of kiosks. Boots has a fabrikator! He even has a water fountain!"

Dr. Grootjans carefully photographed the water fountain's copper pipe, plastic splash basin, and disposable paper pop-out cups. "Did my guide just call you 'Boots'?" she said. "'Boots' as in footgear?"

"Everybody calls me that."

Dr. Grootjans patted her translation earpiece, looking pleased. "This water fountain is the exhaust from your fuel cell."

Borislav rubbed his mustache. "When I first built my kiosk here, the people had no running water."

Dr. Grootjans waved her digital wand over his selections of panty hose. She photographed the rusty bolts that fixed his kiosk to the broken pavement. She took particular interest in his kiosk's peaked roof. People often met their friends and lovers at Borislav's kiosk, because his towering satellite dish was so easy to spot. With its painted plywood base and showy fringes of snipped copper, the dish looked fit for a minaret.

"Please try on this pretty necklace, madame! Made by a fine artist, she lives right up the street. Very famous. Artistic. Valuable. Regional. Handmade!"

"Thank you, I will. Your shop is a fine example of the local small-to-micro regional enterprise. I must make extensive acquisitions for full study by the Parliamentary committee."

Borislav swiftly handed over a sheet of flimsy. Ace peeled off a gaping plastic bag and commenced to fill it with candy bars, place mats, hand-knitted socks, peasant dolls in vests and angular headdresses, and religious-war press-on tattoos. "He has such variety, madame! Such unusual goods!"

Borislav leaned forward through his cash window, so as to keep Dr. Grootjans engaged as Ace crammed her bags. "Madame, I don't care to boast about my modest local wares. . . . Because whatever I sell is due to the people! You see, dear doctor madame, every object desired by these colorful local people has a folk tale to tell us. . . ."

Dr. Grootjan's pillbox hat rose as she lifted her brows. "A folk tale, did you say?"

"Yes, it's the people's poetry of commerce! Certain products appear . . . the products flow through my kiosk . . . I present them pleasingly, as best I can. . . . Then, the people buy them, or they just don't buy!"

Dr. Grootjans expertly flapped open a third shopping bag. "An itemized catalog of all your goods would be of great interest to my study committee."

Borislav put his hat on.

Dr. Grootjans bored in. "I need the *complete, digital* inventory of your merchandise. The working file of the full contents of your store. Your commercial records from the past five years will be useful in spotting local consumer trends."

Borislav gazed around his thickly packed shelving. "You mean you want a list of everything I sell in here? Who would ever find the time?"

"It's simple! You must have heard of the European Unified Electronic Product Coding System." Dr. Grootjans tucked the shopping wand into her canvas purse, which bore an imperial logo of thirty-five golden stars in a widening spiral. "I have a smart-ink brochure here which displays in your local language. Yes, here it is: *A Partial Introduction to EUEPCS Regulatory Adoption Procedures.*"

Borislav refused her busily flashing inkware. "Oh yes, word gets around about that electric bar-coding nonsense! Those fancy radio-ID stickers of yours. Yes, yes, I'm sure those things are just fine for rich foreign people with shopping wands!"

"Sir, if you sensibly deployed this electronic tracking system, you could keep complete, real-time records of all your merchandise. Then you would know exactly what's selling, and not. You could fully optimize your product flow, reduce waste, maximize your profit, and benefit the environment through reduced consumption."

Borislav stared at her. "You've given this speech before, haven't you?"

"Of course I have! It's a critical policy issue! The modern Internet-of-Things authenticates goods, reduces spoilage, and expedites secure cross-border shipping!"

"Listen, madame doctor: your fancy bookkeeping won't help me if I don't know the soul of the people! I have a little kiosk! I never compete with those big, faceless mall stores! If you want that sort of thing, go shop in your five-star hotel!"

Dr. Grootjans lowered her sturdy purse and her sharp face softened into lines of piety. "I don't mean to violate your quaint local value system. . . . Of course we fully respect your cultural differences. . . . Although there will be many tangible benefits when your regime fully harmonizes with European procedures."

"'My regime,' is it? Ha!" Borislav thumped the hollow floor of his kiosk with his cane. "This stupid regime crashed all their government computers! Along with crashing our currency, I might add! Those crooks couldn't run that fancy system of yours in a thousand years!"

"A comprehensive debate on this issue would be fascinating!" Dr. Grootjans waited expectantly, but, to her disappointment, no such debate followed. "Time presses," she told him at last. "May I raise the subject of a complete acquisition?"

Borislav shrugged. "I never argue with a lady or a paying customer. Just tell what you want."

Dr. Grootjans sketched the air with her starry wand. "This portable shelter would fit onto an embassy truck."

"Are you telling me that you want to *buy my entire kiosk*?"

"I'm advancing that option now, yes."

"What a scandal! Sell you my kiosk? The people would never forgive me!"

"Kiosks are just temporary structures. I can see your business is improving. Why not open a permanent retail store? Start over in a new, more stable condition. Then you'd see how simple and easy regulatory adoption can be!"

Ace swung a heavily laden shopping bag from hand to hand. "Madame, be reasonable! This street just can't be the same without this kiosk!"

"You do have severe difficulties with inventory management. So, I will put a down payment on the contents of your store. Then," she turned to Ace, "I will hire you as the inventory consultant. We will need every object named, priced, and cataloged. As soon as possible. Please."

Borislav lived with his mother on the ground floor of a local apartment building. This saved him trouble with his bad leg. When he limped through the door, his mother was doing her nails at the kitchen table, with her hair in curlers and her feet in a sizzling foot bath.

Borislav sniffed at the stew, then set his cane aside and sat in a plastic chair. "Mama dear, heaven knows we've seen our share of bad times."

"You're late tonight, poor boy! What ails you?"

"Mama, I just sold my entire stock! Everything in the kiosk! All sold, at one great swoop! For hard currency, too!" Borislav reached into the pocket of his long coat. "This is the best business day I've ever had!"

"Really?"

"Yes! It's fantastic! Ace really came through for me—he brought his useful European idiot, and she bought the whole works! Look, I've saved just one special item, just for you."

She raised her glasses on a neck chain. "Are these new fabbing cards?"

"No, Mama. These fine souvenir playing cards feature all the stars from your favorite Mexican soap operas. These are the originals, still in their wrapper! That's authentic cellophane!"

His mother blew on her wet scarlet nails, not daring to touch her prize. "Cellophane! Your father would be so proud!"

"You're going to use those cards very soon, Mama. Your Saint's Day is coming up. We're going to have a big bridge party for all your girlfriends. The boys at the Three Cats are going to cater it! You won't have to lift one pretty finger!"

Her mascaraed eyes grew wide. "Can we afford that?"

"I've already arranged it! I talked to Mirko who runs the Three Cats, and I hired Mirko's weird gay brother-in-law to decorate that empty flat upstairs. You know—that flat nobody wants to rent, where that mob guy shot himself. When your old girls see how we've done that place up, word will get around. We'll have new tenants in no time!"

"You're really fixing the haunted flat, Son?"

Borislav changed his winter boots for his woolly house slippers. "That's right, Mama. That haunted flat is gonna be a nice little earner."

"It's got a ghost in it."

"Not anymore, it doesn't. From now on, we're gonna call that place . . . what was that French word he used?—we'll call it the 'atelier'!"

"The 'atelier'! Really! My heart's all aflutter!"

Borislav poured his mother a stiff shot of her favorite digestive.

"Mama, maybe this news seems sudden, but I've been expecting this. Business has been looking up. Real life is changing, for the real people in this world. The people like us!" Borislav poured himself a brimming cup of flavored yogurt. "Those fancy foreigners, they don't even understand what the people are doing here today!"

"I don't understand all this men's political talk."

"Well, I can see it on their faces. I know what the people want. The people . . . They want a new life."

She rose from her chair, shaking a little. "I'll heat up your stew. It's getting so late."

"Listen to me, Mama. Don't be afraid of what I say. I promise you something. You're going to die on silk sheets. That's what this means. That's what I'm telling you. There's gonna be a handsome priest at your bedside, and the oil and the holy water, just like you always wanted. A big granite headstone for you, Mama, with big golden letters."

As he ate his stew, she began to weep with joy.

After supper, Borislav ignored his mother's usual nagging about his lack of a wife. He limped down to the local sports bar for some serious drinking. Borislav didn't drink much anymore, because the kiosk scanned him whenever he sat inside it. It used a cheap superconductive loop, woven through the fiberboard walls. The loop's magnetism flowed through his body, revealing his bones and tissues on his laptop screen. Then the scanner compared the state of his body to its records of past days, and it coughed up a medical report.

This machine was a cheap, pirated copy of some hospital's fancy medical scanner. There had been some trouble in spreading that technology, but with the collapse of public health systems, people had to take some matters into their own hands. Borislav's health report was not cheery. He had plaque in major arteries. He had some seed-pearl kidney stones. His teeth needed attention. Worst of all, his right leg had been wrecked by a land mine. The shinbone had healed with the passing years, but it had healed badly. The foot below his old wound had bad circulation.

Age was gripping his body, visible right there on the screen. Though he could witness himself growing old, there wasn't much he could do about that.

Except, that is, for his drinking. Borislav had been fueled by booze his entire adult life, but the alcohol's damage was visibly spreading through his organs. Lying to himself about that obvious fact simply made him feel like a fool. So, nowadays, he drank a liter of yogurt a day, chased with eco-correct paper cartons of multivitamin fruit juices, European approved, licensed, and fully patented. He did that grumpily and he resented it deeply, but could see on the screen that it was improving his health.

So, no more limping, pitching and staggering, poetically numbed, down the midnight streets. Except for special occasions, that is. Occasions like this one.

Borislav had a thoughtful look around the dimly lit haunt of the old Homeland Sports Bar. So many familiar faces lurking in here—his daily customers, most of them. The men were bundled up for winter. Their faces were rugged and lined. Shaving and bathing were not big priorities for them. They were also drunk.

But the men wore new, delicately tinted glasses. They had nice haircuts. Some had capped their teeth. The people were prospering.

Ace sat at his favorite table, wearing a white cashmere scarf, a tailored jacket, and a dandified beret. Five years earlier, Ace would have had his butt royally kicked for showing up at the Homeland Sports Bar dressed like an Italian. But the times were changing at the Homeland.

Bracing himself with his cane, Borislav settled into a torn chair beneath a gaudy flat-screen display, where the Polish football team was making fools of the Dutch.

"So, Ace, you got it delivered?"

Ace nodded. "Over at the embassy, they are weighing, tagging, and analyzing every single thing you sell."

"That old broad's not as stupid as she acts, you know."

"I know that. But when she saw that cheese grater that can chop glass. The tiling caulk that was also a dessert!" Ace half-choked on the local cognac. "And the skull adjuster! God in heaven!"

Borislav scowled. "That skull adjuster is a great product! It'll chase a hangover away"—Borislav snapped his fingers loudly—"just like that!"

The waitress hurried over. She was a foreign girl who barely spoke the language, but there were a lot of such girls in town lately. Borislav pointed at Ace's drink. "One of those, missie, and keep 'em coming."

"That skull squeezer of yours is a torture device. It's weird; it's nutty. It's not even made by human beings."

"So what? So it needs a better name and a nicer label. 'The Craniette,' some nice brand name. Manufacture it in pink. Emboss some flowers on it."

"Women will never squeeze their skulls with that crazy thing."

"Oh yes, they will. Not old women from old Europe, no. But some will. Because I've seen them do it. I sold ten of those! The people want it!"

"You're always going on about 'what the people want.'"

"Well, that's it! That's our regional competitive advantage! The people who live here, they have a very special relationship to the market economy." Borislav's drink arrived. He downed his shot.

"The people here," he said, "they're used to seeing markets wreck their lives and turn everything upside down. That's why we're finally the ones setting the hot new trends in today's world, while the Europeans are trying to catch up with us! These people here, they *love* the new commercial products with no human origin!"

"Dr. Grootjans stared at that thing like it had come from Mars."

"Ace, the free market always makes sense—once you get to know how it works. You must have heard of the 'invisible hand of the market.'"

Ace downed his cognac and looked skeptical.

"The invisible hand—that's what gives us products like the skull squeezer. That's *easy* to understand."

"No, it isn't. Why would the invisible hand squeeze people's heads?"

"Because it's a search engine! It's mining the market data for new opportunities. The bigger the market, the more it tries to break in by automatically generating new products. And that headache-pill market, that's one of the world's biggest markets!"

Ace scratched under his armpit holster. "How big is that market, the world market for headaches?"

"It's huge! Every convenience store sells painkillers. Little packets of two and three pills, with big price markups. What are those pills all about? The needs and wants of the people!"

"Miserable people?"

"Exactly! People who hate their jobs, bitter people who hate their wives and husbands. The market for misery is always huge." Borislav knocked back another drink. "I'm talking too much tonight."

"Boots, I need you to talk to me. I just made more money for less work than I have in a long time. Now I'm even on salary inside a foreign embassy. This situation's getting serious. I need to know the philosophy—how an invisible hand makes real things. I gotta figure that out before the Europeans do."

"It's a market search engine for an Internet-of-Things."

Ace lifted and splayed his fingers. "Look, tell me something I can get my hands on. You know. Something that a man can steal."

"Say you type two words at random: any two words. Type those two words into an Internet search engine. What happens?"

Ace twirled his shot glass. "Well, a search engine always hits on something, that's for sure. Something stupid, maybe, but always something."

"That's right. Now imagine you put two *products* into a search engine for things. So let's say it tries to sort and mix together . . . a parachute and a pair of shoes. What do you get from that kind of search?"

Ace thought it over. "I get it. You get a shoe that blows up a plane."

Borislav shook his head. "No, no. See, that is your problem right there. You're in the racket; you're a fixer. So you just don't think commercially."

"How can I outthink a machine like that?"

"You're doing it right now, Ace. Search engines have no ideas, no philosophy. They never think at all. Only people think and create ideas. Search engines are just programmed to search through what people want. Then they just mix, and match, and spit up some results. Endless results. Those results don't matter, though, unless the people want them. And here, the people want them!"

The waitress brought a bottle, peppered sauerkraut, and a leathery loaf of bread. Ace watched her hips sway as she left. "Well, as for me, I could go for some of *that*. Those Iraqi chicks have got it going on."

Borislav leaned on his elbows and ripped up a mouthful of bread. He poured another shot, downed it, then fell silent as the booze stole up on him in a rush. He was suddenly done with talk.

Talk wasn't life. He'd seen real life. He knew it well. He'd first seen real life as a young boy, when he saw a whole population turned inside out. Refugees, the unemployed, the dispossessed, people starting over with pencils in a tin cup, scraping a living out of suitcases. Then people moving into stalls and kiosks. "Transition," that's what they named that kind of life. As if it were all going somewhere in particular.

The world changed a lot in a Transition. Life changed. But the people never transitioned into any rich nation's notion of normal life. In the next big "Transition," the twenty-first-century one, the people lost everything they had gained.

When Borislav crutched back, maimed, from the outbreak of shooting-and-looting, he threw a mat on the sidewalk. He sold people boots. The people needed his boots, even indoors, because there was no more fuel in the pipelines and the people were freezing.

Come summer, he got hold of a car. Whenever there was diesel or bio-fuel around, he sold goods straight from its trunk. He made some street connections. He got himself a booth on the sidewalk.

Even in the rich countries, the lights were out and roads were still. The sky was empty of jets. It was a hard Transition. Civilization was wounded.

Then a contagion swept the world. Economic depression was bad, but a plague was a true Horseman of the Apocalypse. Plague thundered through a city. Plague made a city a place of thawing ooze, spontaneous fires, awesome deadly silences.

Borislav moved from his booth into the freezing wreck of a warehouse, where the survivors sorted and sold the effects of the dead. Another awful winter. They burned furniture to stay warm. When they coughed, people stared in terror at their handkerchiefs. Food shortages, too, this time: the dizzy edge of famine. Crazy times.

He had nothing left of that former life but his pictures. During the mayhem, he took thousands of photographs. That was something to mark the day, to point a lens, to squeeze a button, when there was nothing else to do, except to hustle, or sit and grieve, or jump from a bridge. He still had all those pictures, every last one of them. Everyday photographs of extraordinary times. His own extraordinary self: he was young, gaunt, wounded, hungry, burning eyed.

As long as a man could recognize his own society, then he could shape himself to fit its circumstances. He might be a decent man, dependable, a man of his word. But when the society itself was untenable, when it just could not be sustained, then "normality" cracked like a cheap plaster mask. Beneath the mask of civilization was another face: the face of a cannibal child.

Only hope mattered then: the will to carry on through another day, another night, with the living strength of one's own heartbeat, without any regard for abstract notions of success or failure. In real life, to live was the only "real."

In the absence of routine, in the vivid presence of risk and suffering, the soul grew. Objects changed their primal nature. Their value grew as keen as tears, as keen as kisses. Hot water was a miracle. Electric light meant instant celebration. A pair of boots was the simple, immediate reason that your feet had not frozen and turned black. A man who had toilet paper, insulation, candles: he was the people's hero.

When you handed a woman a tube of lipstick, her pinched and pallid face lit up all over. She could smear that scarlet on her lips, and when she walked down the darkened street it was as if she were shouting aloud, as if she were singing.

When the plague burned out—it was a flu, and it was a killer, but it was not so deadly as the numb despair it inspired—then a profiteer's fortune beckoned to those tough enough to knock heads and give orders. Borislav made no such fortune. He knew very well how such fortunes were made, but he couldn't give the orders. He had taken orders himself, once. Those were orders he should never have obeyed.

Like a stalled train, civilization slowly rattled back into motion, with its usual burden of claptrap. The life he had now, in the civilized moving train, it was a parody of that past life. That burning, immediate life. He had even been in love then.

Today, he lived inside his kiosk. It was a pretty nice kiosk, today. Only a fool could fail to make a living in good times. He took care, he improvised, so he made a profit. He was slowly buying up some flats in an old apartment building, an ugly, unloved place, but sturdy and well located. When old age stole over him, when he was too weak to hustle in the market anymore, then he would live on the rents.

A football team scored on the big flat screen. The regulars cheered and banged their flimsy tables. Borislav raised his heavy head, and the bar's walls reeled as he came to himself. He was such a cheap drunk now; he would really have to watch that.

Morning was painful. Borislav's mother tiptoed in with muesli, yogurt, and coffee. Borislav put his bad foot into his mother's plastic foot bath—that treatment often seemed to help him—and he paged through a crumbling yellow block of antique newspapers. The old arts district had always been a bookish place, and these often showed up in attics. Borislav never read the ancient "news" in the newspapers, which, during any local regime, consisted mostly of official lies. Instead, he searched for the strange things that the people had once desired.

Three huge, universal, dead phenomena haunted these flaking pages: petroleum cars, cinema, and cigarettes. The cars heavily dragged along their hundreds of objects and services: fuels, pistons, mufflers, makers of sparks. The cigarettes had garish paper packages, with lighters, humidors, and special trays just for their ashes. As for the movie stars, they were driving the cars and smoking the cigarettes.

The very oldest newspapers were downright phantasmagoric. All the newspapers, with their inky, frozen graphics, seemed to scream at him across their gulf of decades. The dead things harangued; they flattered; they shamed; they jostled each other on the paper pages. They bled margin space; they wept ink.

These things were strange, and yet, they had been desired. At first with a sense of daring, and then with a growing boldness, Borislav chose certain dead items to be digitally copied and revived. He re-released them into the contemporary flow of goods. For instance, by changing its materials and proportions, he'd managed to transform a Soviet-era desk telephone into a lightweight plastic rain hat. No one had ever guessed the origin of his experiments. Unlike the machine-generated new products—always slotted with such unhuman coolness into market niches—these revived goods stank of raw humanity. Raw purpose. Raw desire.

Once, there had been no Internet. And no Internet-of-Things, either, for that could only follow. There had only been the people. People wanting things, trying to make other people want their things. Capitalism, socialism, communism, those mattered little enough. Those were all period arrangements in a time that had no Internet.

The day's quiet study restored Borislav's good spirits. Next morning, his mother recommenced her laments about her lack of a daughter-in-law. Borislav left for work.

He found his kiosk pitifully stripped and empty, with a CLOSED sign in its damp-spotted window. A raw hole loomed in the wall where the fabrikator had been torn free. This sudden loss of all his trade goods gave him a lofty thrill of panic.

Borislav savored that for a moment, then put the fear behind him. The neighborhood still surrounded his kiosk. The people would nourish it. He had picked an excellent location, during the darkest days. Once he'd sold them dirty bags of potatoes here, they'd clamored for wilted carrots. This life was easy now. This life was like a good joke.

He limped through the biometric door and turned on the lights.

Now, standing inside, he felt the kiosk's true nature. A kiosk was a conduit. It was a temporary stall in the endless flow of goods.

His kiosk was fiberboard and glue: recycled materials, green and modern. It had air filters, insulated windows, a rugged little fuel cell, efficient lights, a heater grill in the floor. It had password-protected intrusion alarms. It had a medical scanner in the walls. It had smart-ink wallpaper with peppy graphics.

They had taken away his custom-shaped chair, and his music player, loaded with a fantastic mashed-up mulch of the complete pop hits of the twentieth century. He would have to replace those. That wouldn't take him long.

He knelt on the bare floor, and taped a thick sheet of salvaged cardboard over the wintry hole in his wall. A loud rap came at his window. It was Fleka the Gypsy, one of his suppliers.

Borislav rose and stepped outside, reflexively locking his door, since this was Fleka. Fleka was the least dependable of his suppliers, because Fleka had no sense of time. Fleka could make, fetch, or filch most anything, but if you dared to depend on his word, Fleka would suddenly remember the wedding of some gypsy cousin, and vanish.

"I heard about your good luck, Boots," grinned Fleka. "Is the maestro in need of new stock?"

Borislav rapped the empty window with his cane. "It's as you see."

Fleka slid to the trunk of his rusty car and opened it.

"Whatever that is," said Borislav at once, "it's much too big."

"Give me one minute from your precious schedule, maestro," said Fleka. "You, my kind old friend, with your lovely kiosk so empty, I didn't bring you any goods. I brought you a factory! So improved! So new!"

"That thing's not new, whatever it is."

"See, it's a fabrikator! Just like the last fabrikator I got for you, only this one is bigger, fancy, and much better! I got it from my cousin."

"I wasn't born yesterday, Fleka."

Fleka hustled under his backseat and brought out a sample. It was a rotund doll of the American actress Marilyn Monroe. The doll was still unpainted. It was glossily black.

Marilyn Monroe, the ultimate retail movie star, was always recognizable, due to her waved coif, her lip mole, and her torpedo-like bust. The passage of a century had scarcely damaged her shelf appeal. The woman had become an immortal cartoon, like Betty Boop.

Fleka popped a hidden seam under Marilyn's jutting bust. Inside the black Marilyn doll was a smaller Marilyn doll, also jet-black, but wearing less clothing. Then came a smaller, more risqué little Marilyn, and then a smaller one yet, and finally a crudely modeled little Marilyn, shiny black, nude, and the size of Borislav's thumb.

"Nice celebrity branding," Borislav admitted. "So what's this material?" It seemed to be black china.

"It's not wax, like that other fabrikator. This is carbon. Little straws of carbon. It came with the machine."

Borislav ran his thumbnail across the grain of the material. The black Marilyn doll was fabricated in ridges, like the grooves in an ancient gramophone record. Fabs were always like that: they jet-sprayed their things by piling up thin layers; they stacked them up like pancakes. "'Little straws of carbon.' I never heard of that."

"I'm telling you what my cousin told me. 'Little nano tubes, little nano carbon.' That's what he said." Fleka grabbed the round Marilyn doll like a football goalie, and raised both his hands overhead. Then, with all his wiry strength, he smacked the black doll against the rust-eaten roof of his car. Chips flew.

"You've ruined her!"

"That was my car breaking," Fleka pointed out. "I made this doll this morning, out of old plans and scans from the Net. Then I gave it to my nephew, a nice big boy. I told him to break the doll. He broke a crowbar on this doll."

Borislav took the black doll again, checked the seams and detailing, and rapped it with his cane. "You sell these dolls to anyone else, Fleka?"

"Not yet."

"I could move a few of these. How much you asking?"

Fleka spread his hands. "I can make more. But I don't know how to make the little straws of carbon. There's a tutorial inside the machine. But it's in Polish. I hate tutorials."

Borislav examined the fabrikator. The machine looked simple enough: it was a basic black shell, a big black hopper, a black rotating plate, a black spraying nozzle, and the black gearing of a 3-D axis. "Why is this thing so black?"

"It's nice and shiny, isn't it? The machine itself is made of little straws of carbon."

"Your cousin got you this thing? Where's the brand name? Where's the serial number?"

"I swear he didn't steal it! This fabrikator is a copy, see. It's a pirate copy of another fabrikator in Warsaw. But nobody knows it's a copy. Or if they do know, the cops won't be looking for any copies around this town, that's for sure."

Borislav's doubts overflowed into sarcasm. "You're saying it's a fabricator that copies fabrikators? It's a fabbing fab fabber, that's what you're telling me, Fleka?"

A shrill wail of shock and alarm came from the front of the kiosk. Borislav hurried to see.

A teenage girl, in a cheap red coat and yellow winter boots, was sobbing into her cell phone. She was Jovanica, one of his best customers.

"What's the matter?" he said.

"Oh! It's you!" Jovanica snapped her phone shut and raised a skinny hand to her lips. "Are you still alive, Mr. Boots?"

"Why wouldn't I be alive?"

"Well, what happened to you? Who robbed your store?"

"I'm not robbed. Everything has been sold, that's all."

Jovanica's young face screwed up in doubt, rage, frustration, and grief. "Then *where are my hair toys?*"

"What?"

"Where are my favorite barrettes? My hair clips! My scrunchies and headbands and beautiful pins! There was a whole tree of them, right here! I picked new toys from that tree every day! I finally had it giving me just what I wanted!"

"Oh. That." Borislav had sold the whirling rack of hair toys, along with its entire freight of goods.

"Your rack sold the best hair toys in town! So super and cool! What happened to it? And what happened to your store? It's broken! There's nothing left!"

"That's true, 'Neetsa. You had a very special relationship with that interactive rack, but . . . well . . ." Borislav groped for excuses, and, with a leap of genius, he found one. "I'll tell you a secret. You're growing up now, that's what."

"I want my hair toys! Go get my rack right now!"

"Hair toys are for the nine-to-fifteen age bracket. You're growing out of that market niche. You should be thinking seriously about earrings."

Jovanica's hands flew to her earlobes. "You mean pierce my ears?"

Borislav nodded. "High time."

"Mama won't let me do that."

"I can speak to your mama. You're getting to be a big girl now. Soon you'll have to beat the boys away with a stick."

Jovanica stared at the cracks in the pavement. "No, I won't."

"Yes, you will," said Borislav, hefting his cane reflexively.

Fleka the Gypsy had been an interested observer. Now he spoke up. "Don't cry about your pretty things: because Boots here is the King of Kiosks. He can get you all the pretty things in the world!"

"Don't you listen to the gypsy," said Borislav. "Listen, Jovanica: Your old hair-toy tree, I'm sorry, it's gone for good. You'll have to start over with a brand-new one. It won't know anything about what you want."

"After all my shopping? That's terrible!"

"Never you mind. I'll make you a different deal. Since you're getting to be such a big girl, you're adding a lot of value by making so many highly informed consumer choices. So, next time, there will be a new economy for you. I'll pay you to teach that toy tree just what you want to buy."

Fleka stared at him. "What did you just say? You want to *pay this kid for shopping?*"

"That's right."

"She's a little kid!"

"I'm not a little kid!" Jovanica took swift offense. "You're a dirty old gypsy!"

"Jovanica is the early hair-toy adopter, Fleka. She's the market leader here. Whatever hair toys Jovanica buys, all the other girls come and buy. So, yeah. I'm gonna cut her in on that action. I should have done that long ago."

Jovanica clapped her hands. "Can I have lots of extra hair toys, instead of just stupid money?"

"Absolutely. Of course. Those loyal-customer rewards will keep you coming back here, when you ought to be doing your homework."

Fleka marveled. "It's completely gone to your head, cashing out your whole stock at once. A man of your age, too."

The arts district never lacked for busybodies. Attracted by the little drama, four of them gathered round Borislav's kiosk. When they caught him glowering at them, they all pretended to need water from his fountain. At least his fountain was still working.

"Here comes my mama," said Jovanica. Her mother, Ivana, burst headlong from the battered doors of a nearby block of flats. Ivana wore a belted house robe, a flung-on muffler, a heavy scarf, and brightly knitted woolen house slippers. She brandished a laden pillowcase.

"Thank God they haven't hurt you!" said Ivana, her breath puffing in the chilly air. She opened her pillowcase. It held a steam iron, a hair dryer, an old gilt mirror, a nickeled hip flask, a ragged fur stole, and a lidded, copper-bottomed saucepan.

"Mr. Boots is all right, Mama," said Jovanica. "They didn't steal anything. He *sold* everything!"

"You sold your kiosk?" said Ivana, and the hurt and shock deepened in her eyes. "You're leaving us?"

"It was business," Borislav muttered. "Sorry for the inconvenience. It'll be a while before things settle down."

"Honestly, I don't need these things. If these things will help you in any way, you're very welcome to them."

"Mama wants you to sell these things," Jovanica offered, with a teen's oppressive helpfulness. "Then you can have the money to fix your store."

Borislav awkwardly patted the kiosk's fiberboard wall. "Ivana, this old place doesn't look like much, so empty and with this big hole . . . but, well, I had some luck."

"Ma'am, you must be cold in those house slippers," said Fleka the Gypsy. With an elegant swoop of his arm, he gestured at the gilt-and-glassed front counter of the Three Cats Café. "May I get you a hot cappuccino?"

"You're right, sir, it's cold here." Ivana tucked the neck of her pillowcase, awkwardly, over her arm. "I'm glad things worked out for you, Borislav."

"Yes, things are all right. Really."

Ivana aimed a scowl at the passersby, who watched her with a lasting interest. "We'll be going now, 'Neetsa."

"Mama, I'm not cold. The weather's clearing up!"

"We're going." They left.

Fleka picked at his discolored canine with his forefinger. "So, maestro. What just happened there?"

"She's a nice kid. She's hasty sometimes. The young are like that. That can't be helped." Borislav shrugged. "Let's talk our business inside."

He limped into his empty kiosk. Fleka wedged in behind him and managed to slam the door. Borislav could smell the man's rich, goulash-tinged breath.

"I was never inside one of these before," Fleka remarked, studying every naked seam for the possible point of a burglar's pry bar. "I thought about getting a kiosk of my own, but, well, a man gets so restless."

"It's all about the product flow divided by the floor space. By that measure, a kiosk is superefficient retailing. It's about as efficient as any sole proprietor can do. But it's a one-man enterprise. So, well, a man's just got to go it alone."

Fleka looked at him with wise, round eyes. "That girl who cried so much about her hair. That's not your girl, is she?"

"What? No."

"What happened to the father, then? The flu got him?"

"She was born long after the flu, but yeah, you're right, her father passed away." Borislav coughed. "He was a good friend of mine. A soldier. Really good-looking guy. His kid is gorgeous."

"So you didn't do anything about that. Because you're not a soldier, and you're not rich, and you're not gorgeous."

"Do anything about what?"

"A woman like that Ivana, she isn't asking for some handsome soldier or some rich-guy boss. A woman like her, she wants maybe a pretty dress. Maybe a dab of perfume. And something in her bed that's better than a hot-water bottle."

"Well, I've got a kiosk and a broken leg."

"All us men have a broken leg. She thought you had nothing. She ran right down here, with anything she could grab for you, stuffed into her pillowcase. So you're not an ugly man. You're a stupid man." Fleka thumped his chest. "I'm the ugly man. Me. I've got three wives: the one in Bucharest, the one in Lublin, and the wife in Linz isn't even a gypsy. They're gonna bury me standing, maestro. That can't be helped, because I'm a man. But that's not what you are. You're a fool."

"Thanks for the free fortune-telling. You know all about this, do you? She and I were here during the hard times. That's what. She and I have a history."

"You're a fanatic. You're a geek. I can see through you like the windows of this kiosk. You should get a life." Fleka thumped the kiosk's wallpaper, and sighed aloud. "Look, life is sad, all right? Life is sad even when you do get a life. So. Boots. Now I'm gonna tell you about this fabrikator of mine, because you got some spare money, and you're gonna buy it from me. It's a nice machine. Very sweet. It comes from a hospital. It's supposed to make bones. So the tutorial is all about making bones, and that's bad, because nobody buys bones. If you are deaf and you want some new little black bones in your ears, that's what this machine is for. Also, these black toys I made with it, I can't paint them. The toys are much too hard, so the paint breaks right off. Whatever you make with this fabrikator, it's hard and black, and you can't paint it, and it belongs by rights inside some sick person. Also, I can't read the stupid tutorials. I hate tutorials. I hate reading."

"Does it run on standard voltage?"

"I got it running on DC off the fuel cell in my car."

"Where's the feedstock?"

"It comes in big bags. It's a powder; it's a yellow dust. The fab sticks it together somehow, with sparks or something, it turns the powder shiny black, and it knits it up real fast. That part, I don't get."

"I'll be offering one price for your machine and all your feedstock."

"There's another thing. That time when I went to Vienna. I gave you my word on that deal. We shook hands on it. That deal was really important, they really needed it, they weren't kidding about it, and, well, I screwed up. Because of Vienna."

"That's right, Fleka. You screwed up bad."

"Well, that's my price. That's part of my price. I'm gonna sell you this toy maker. We're gonna haul it right out of the car, put it in the kiosk here nice and safe. When I get the chance, I'm gonna bring your bag of coal straw, too. But we forget about Vienna. We just forget about it."

Borislav said nothing.

"You're gonna forgive me my bad, screwed-up past. That's what I want from you."

"I'm thinking about it."

"That's part of the deal."

"We're going to forget the past, and you're going to give me the machine, the stock, and also fifty bucks."

"Okay, sold."

With the fabrikator inside his kiosk, Borislav had no room inside the kiosk for himself. He managed to transfer the tutorials out of the black, silent fab and into his laptop. The sun had come out. Though it was still damp and chilly, the boys from the Three Cats had unstacked their white café chairs. Borislav took a seat there. He ordered black coffee and began perusing awkward machine translations from the Polish manual.

Selma arrived to bother him. Selma was married to a schoolteacher, a nice guy with a steady job. Selma called herself an artist, made jewelry, and dressed like a lunatic. The schoolteacher thought the world of Selma, although she slept around on him and never cooked him a decent meal.

"Why is your kiosk so empty? What are you doing, just sitting out here?"

Borislav adjusted the angle of his screen. "I'm seizing the means of production."

"What did you do with all my bracelets and necklaces?"

"I sold them."

"All of them?"

"Every last scrap."

Selma sat down as if hit with a mallet. "Then you should buy me a glass of champagne!"

Borislav reluctantly pulled his phone and text-messaged the waiter.

It was getting blustery, but Selma preened over her glass of cheap Italian red. "Don't expect me to replace your stock soon! My artwork's in great demand."

"There's no hurry."

"I broke the luxury market, across the river at the Intercontinental! The hotel store will take all the bone-ivory chokers I can make."

"Mmm-hmm."

"Bone-ivory chokers, they're the perennial favorite of ugly, aging tourist women with wattled necks."

Borislav glanced up from his screen. "Shouldn't you be running along to your workbench?"

"Oh, sure, sure, 'give the people what they want,' that's your sick, petit bourgeois philosophy! Those foreign tourist women in their big hotels, they want me to make legacy kitsch!"

Borislav waved one hand at the street. "Well, we do live in the old arts district."

"Listen, stupid, when this place was the *young* arts district, it was full of avant-gardists plotting revolution. Look at me for once. Am I from the museum?" Selma yanked her skirt to mid-thigh. "Do I wear little old peasant shoes that turn up at the toes?"

"What the hell has gotten into you? Did you sit on your tack hammer?"

Selma narrowed her kohl-lined eyes. "What do you expect me to do, with my hands and my artisan skills, when you're making all kinds of adornments with fabrikators? I just saw that stupid thing inside your kiosk there."

Borislav sighed. "Look, I don't know. You tell me what it means, Selma."

"It means revolution. That's what. It means another revolution."

Borislav laughed at her.

Selma scowled and lifted her kid-gloved fingers. "Listen to me. Transition number one. When communism collapsed. The people took to the streets. Everything privatized. There were big market shocks."

"I remember those days. I was a kid, and you weren't even born then."

"Transition Two. When globalism collapsed. There was no oil. There was war and bankruptcy. There was sickness. That was when I was a kid."

Borislav said nothing about that. All things considered, his own first Transition had been a kinder time to grow up in.

"Then comes Transition Three." Selma drew a breath. "When this steadily increasing cybernetic intervention in manufacturing liberates a distinctly human creativity."

"Okay, what is that about?"

"I'm telling you what it's about. You're not listening. We're in the third great Transition. It's a revolution. Right now. Here. This isn't communism; this isn't globalism. This is the next thing after that. It's happening. No longer merely reacting to this influx of mindless goods, the modern artist uses human creative strength in the name of a revolutionary heterogeneity!"

Selma always talked pretentious, self-important drivel. Not quite like this, though. She'd found herself some new drivel.

"Where did you hear all that?"

"I heard it here in this café! You're just not listening, that's your problem. You never listen to anybody. Word gets around fast in the arts community."

"I live here, too, you know. I'd listen to your nutty blither all day, if you ever meant business."

Selma emptied her wineglass. Then she reached inside her hand-loomed, artsy sweater. "If you laugh at this, I'm going to kill you."

Borislav took the necklace she offered him. "Where's this from? Who sent you this?"

"That's mine! I made it. With my hands."

Borislav tugged the tangled chain through his fingers. He was no jeweler but knew what decent jewelry looked like. This was indecent jewelry. If the weirdest efforts of search engines looked like products from Mars, then this necklace was straight from Venus. It was slivers of pot metal, blobs of silver, and chips of topaz. It was like jewelry straight out of a nightmare.

"Selma, this isn't your customary work."

"Machines can't dream. I saw this in my dreams."

"Oh. Right, of course."

"Well, it was my nightmare, really. But I woke up! Then I created my vision! I don't have to make that cheap, conventional crap, you know! I only make cheap junk because that's all you are willing to sell!"

"Well . . ." He had never spoken with frankness to Selma before, but the glittering light in her damp eyes made yesterday's habits seem a little slow-witted. "Well, I wouldn't know what to charge for a work of art like this."

"Somebody would want this, though? Right? Wouldn't they?" She was pleading with him. "Somebody? They would buy my new necklace, right? Even though it's . . . different."

"No. This isn't the sort of jewelry that the people buy. This is the sort of jewelry that the people stare at, and probably laugh at, too. But then, there would come one special person. She would really want this necklace. She would want this more than anything. She would have to have this thing at absolutely any price."

"I could make more like that," Selma told him, and she touched her heart. "Because now I know where it comes from."

III

Borislav installed the fab inside the empty kiosk, perched on a stout wooden pedestal, where its workings could be seen by the people.

His first choices for production were, naturally, hair toys. Borislav borrowed some fancy clips from Jovanica, and copied their shapes inside his kiosk with his medical scanner.

Sure enough, the fabrikator sprayed out shiny black replicas.

Jovanica amused a small crowd by jumping up and down on them. The black clips themselves were well-nigh indestructible, but their cheap metal springs soon snapped.

Whenever a toy broke, however, it was a simple matter to cast it right back into the fabrikator's hopper. The fab chewed away at the black object, with an ozonelike reek, until the fabbed object became the yellow dust again.

Straw, right into gold.

Borislav sketched out a quick business plan on the back of a Three Cats beer coaster. With hours of his labor, multiplied by price-per-gram, he soon established his point of profit. He was in a new line of work.

With the new fabrikator, he could copy the shapes of any small object he could scan. Of course, he couldn't literally "copy" everything: a puppy dog, a nice silk dress, a cold bottle of beer, those were all totally out of the question. But he could copy most anything that was made from some single, rigid material: an empty bottle, a fork, a trash can, a kitchen knife.

The kitchen knives were an immediate hit. The knives were shiny and black, very threatening and scary, and it was clear they would never need sharpening. It was also delightful to see the fabrikator mindlessly spitting up razor-sharp knives. The kids were back in force to watch the action, and this time, even the grown-ups gathered and chattered.

To accommodate the eager crowd of gawkers, the Three Cats boys set out their chairs and tables, and even their striped overhead canopy, as cheery as if it were summer.

The weather favored them. An impromptu block party broke out.

Mirko from the Three Cats gave him a free meal. "I'm doing very well by this," Mirko said. "You've got yourself a nine days' wonder here. This sure reminds me of when Transition Two was ending. Remember when those city lights came back on? Brother, those were great days."

"Nine days won't last long. I need to get back inside that kiosk, like normal again."

"It's great to see you out and about, mixing it up with us, Boots. We never talk anymore." Mirko spread his hands in apology, then scrubbed the table. "I run this place now . . . it's the pressure of business . . . that's all my fault."

Borislav accepted a payment from a kid who'd made himself a rock-solid black model dinosaur. "Mirko, do you have room for a big vending machine, here by your café? I need to get that black beast out of my kiosk. The people need their sticks of gum."

"You really want to build some vendorizing thing out here? Like a bank machine?"

"I guess I do, yeah. It pays."

"Boots, I love this crowd you're bringing me, but why don't you just put your machine wherever they put bank machines? There are hundreds of bank machines." Mirko took his empty plate. "There are millions of bank machines. Those machines took over the world."

IV

Days passed. The people wouldn't let him get back to normal. It became a public sport to see what people would bring in for the fabrikator to copy. It was common to make weird things as gag gifts: a black, rock-solid spray of roses, for instance. You could hand that black bouquet to your girlfriend for a giggle, and if she got huffy, then you could just bring it back, have it weighed, and get a return deposit for the yellow dust.

The ongoing street drama was a tonic for the neighborhood. In no time flat, every café lounger and class-skipping college student was a self-appointed expert about fabs, fabbing, and revolutionary super-fabs that could fab their own fabbing. People brought their relatives to see. Tourists wandered in and took pictures. Naturally they all seemed to want a word with the owner and proprietor.

The people being the people, the holiday air was mixed with unease. Things took a strange turn when a young bride arrived with her wedding china. She paid to copy each piece, then loudly and publicly smashed the originals in the street. A cop showed up to dissuade her. Then the cop wanted a word, too.

Borislav was sitting with Professor Damov, an academician and pious blowhard who ran the local ethnographic museum. The professor's city-sponsored hall specialized in what Damov called "material culture," meaning dusty vitrines full of battle flags, holy medallions, distaffs, fishing nets, spinning wheels, gramophones, and such. Given these new circumstances, the professor had a lot on his mind.

"Officer," said Damov, briskly waving his wineglass, "it may well surprise you to learn this, but the word 'kiosk' is an ancient Ottoman term. In the original Ottoman kiosk, nothing was bought or sold. The kiosk was a regal gift from a prince to the people. A kiosk was a place to breathe the evening air, to meditate, to savor life and living; it was an elegant garden pergola."

"They didn't break their wedding china in the gutter, though," said the cop.

"Oh, no, on the contrary, if a bride misbehaved in those days, she'd be sewn into a leather sack and thrown into the Bosphorus!"

The cop was mollified, and he moved right along, but soon a plain-clothes cop showed up and took a prominent seat inside the Three Cats Café. This changed the tone of things. The police surveillance proved that something real was happening. It was a kind of salute.

Dusk fell. A group of garage mechanics came by, still in their grimy overalls, and commenced a deadly serious professional discussion about fabbing trolley parts. A famous stage actor showed up with his entourage, to sign autographs and order drinks for all his "friends."

Some alarmingly clean-cut university students appeared. They weren't there to binge on beer. They took a table, ordered Mirko's cheapest pizza, and started talking in points-of-order.

Next day, the actor brought the whole cast of his play, and the student radicals were back in force. They took more tables, with much more pizza. Now they had a secretary, and a treasurer. Their ringleaders had shiny black political buttons on their coats.

A country bus arrived and disgorged a group of farmers. These peasants made identical copies of something they were desperate to have yet anxious to hide from all observers.

Ace came by the bustling café. Ace was annoyed to find that he had to wait his turn for any private word with Borislav.

"Calm down, Ace. Have a slice of this pork pizza. The boss here's an old friend of mine, and he's in a generous mood."

"Well, my boss is unhappy," Ace retorted. "There's money being made here, and he wasn't told about it."

"Tell your big guy to relax. I'm not making any more money than I usually do at the kiosk. That should be obvious: consider my rate of production. That machine can only make a few copies an hour."

"Have you finally gone stupid? Look at this crowd!" Ace pulled his shades off and studied the densely clustered café. Despite the lingering chill, a gypsy band was setting up, with accordions and trombones. "Okay, this proves it: See that wiseguy sitting there with that undercover lieutenant? He's one of *them*!"

Borislav cast a sidelong glance at the rival gangster. The North River Boy looked basically identical to Ace: the same woolly hat, cheap black sunglasses, jacket, and bad attitude, except for his sneakers, which were red instead of blue. "The River Boys are moving in over here?"

"They always wanted this turf. This is the lively part of town."

That River Boy had some nerve. Gangsters had been shot in the Three Cats Café. And not just a few times, either. It was a major local tradition.

"I'm itching to whack that guy," Ace lied, sweating, "but, well, he's sitting over there with that cop! And a pet politician, too!"

Borislav wondered if his eyes were failing. In older days, he would never have missed those details.

There was a whole little tribe of politicians filtering into the café and sitting near the mobster's table. The local politicians always traveled in parties. Small, fractious parties.

One of these local politicals was the arts district's own national representative. Mr. Savic was a member of the Radical Liberal Democratic Party, a splinter clique of well-meaning, overeducated cranks.

"I'm gonna tell you a good joke, Ace. 'You can get three basic qualities with any politician: Smart, Honest, and Effective. But you only get to pick two.'"

Ace blinked. He didn't get it.

Borislav levered himself from his café chair and limped over to provoke a glad-handing from Mr. Savic. The young lawyer was smart and honest, and therefore ineffective. However, Savic, being so smart, was quick to recognize political developments within his own district. He had already appropriated the shiny black button of the young student radicals.

With an ostentatious swoop of his camel's-hair coattails, Mr. Savic deigned to sit at Borislav's table. He gave Ace a chilly glare. "Is it necessary that we consort with this organized-crime figure?"

"You tried to get me fired from my job in the embassy," Ace accused him.

"Yes, I did. It's bad enough that the criminal underworld infests our ruling party. We can't have the Europeans paying you off, too."

"That's you all over, Savic: always sucking up to rich foreigners and selling out the guy on the street!"

"Don't flatter yourself, you jumped-up little crook! You're not 'the street.' The people are the street!"

"Okay, so you got the people to elect you. You took office and you got a pretty haircut. Now you're gonna wrap yourself up in our flag, too? You're gonna steal the last thing the people have left!"

Borislav cleared his throat. "I'm glad we have this chance for a frank talk here. The way I figure it, managing this fabbing business is going to take some smarts and finesse."

The two of them stared at him. "You brought us here?" Ace said. "For our 'smarts and finesse'?"

"Of course I did. You two aren't here by accident, and neither am I. If we're not pulling the strings around here, then who is?"

The politician looked at the gangster. "There's something to what he says, you know. After all, this is Transition Three."

"So," said Borislav, "knock it off with that tough talk and do some fresh thinking for once! You sound like your own grandfathers!"

Borislav had surprised himself with this outburst. Savic, to his credit, looked embarrassed, while Ace scratched uneasily under his woolly hat. "Well, listen, Boots," said Ace at last. "Even if you, and me, and your posh lawyer pal have us three nice Transition beers together, that's a River Boy sitting over there. What are we supposed to do about that?"

"I am entirely aware of the criminal North River Syndicate," Mr. Savic told him airily. "My investigative committee has been analyzing their gang."

"Oh, so you're analyzing, are you? They must be scared to death."

"There are racketeering laws on the books in this country," said Savic, glowering at Ace. "When we take power and finally have our purge of the criminal elements in this society, we won't stop at arresting that one little punk in his cheap red shoes. We will liquidate his entire parasite class: I mean him, his nightclub-singer girlfriend, his father, his boss, his brothers, his cousins, his entire football club. . . . As long as there is one honest judge in this country, and there are some honest judges, there are *always* some . . . We will never rest! Never!"

"I've heard about your honest judges," Ace sneered. "You can spot 'em by the smoke columns when their cars blow up."

"Ace, stop talking through your hat. Let me make it crystal clear what's at stake here." Borislav reached under the table and brought up a clear plastic shopping bag. He dropped it on the table with a thud.

Ace took immediate interest. "You output a skull?"

"Ace, this is *my own* skull." The kiosk scanned him every day. So Borislav had his skull on file.

Ace juggled Borislav's skull free of the clear plastic bag, then passed it right over to the politician. "That fab is just superb! Look at the crisp detailing on those sutures!"

"I concur. A remarkable technical achievement." Mr. Savic turned the skull upside down, and frowned. "What happened to your teeth?"

"Those are normal."

"You call these wisdom teeth normal?"

"Hey, let me see those," Ace pleaded. Mr. Savic rolled Borislav's jet-black skull across the tabletop. Then he cast an over-shoulder look at his fellow politicians, annoyed that they enjoyed themselves so much without him.

"Listen to me, Mr. Savic. When you campaigned, I put your poster up in my kiosk. I even voted for you, and—"

Ace glanced up from the skull's hollow eye sockets. "You vote, Boots?"

"Yes. I'm an old guy. Us old guys vote."

Savic faked some polite attention.

"Mr. Savic, you're our political leader. You're a Radical Liberal Democrat. Well, we've got ourselves a pretty radical, liberal situation here. What are we supposed to do now?"

"It's very good that you asked me that," nodded Savic. "You must be aware that there are considerable intellectual-property difficulties with your machine."

"What are those?"

"I mean patents and copyrights. Reverse-engineering laws. Trademarks. We don't observe all of those laws in this country of ours . . . in point of fact, practically speaking, we scarcely observe any. . . . But the rest of the world fully depends on those regulatory structures. So if you go around publicly pirating wedding china—let's just say—well, the makers of wedding china will surely get wind of that someday. I'd be guessing that you see a civil lawsuit. Cease-and-desist, all of that."

"I see."

"That's just how the world works. If you damage their income, they'll simply have to sue you. Follow the money, follow the lawsuits. A simple principle, really. Although you've got a very nice little sideshow here. . . . It's really brightened up the neighborhood. . . ."

Professor Damov arrived at the café. He had brought his wife, Mrs. Professor Doctor Damova, an icy sociologist with annoying Marxist and feminist tendencies. The lady professor wore a fur coat as solid as a bank vault, and a bristling fur hat.

Damov pointed out a black plaque on Borislav's tabletop. "I'm sorry, gentlemen, but this table is reserved for us."

"Oh," Borislav blurted. He hadn't noticed the fabbed reservation, since it was so black.

"We're having a little party tonight," said Damov, "it's our anniversary."

"Congratulations, sir and madame!" said Mr. Savic. "Why not sit here with us just a moment until your guests arrive?"

A bottle of Mirko's *prosecco* restored general good feeling. "I'm an arts-district lawyer, after all," said Savic, suavely topping up everyone's glasses. "So, Borislav, if I were you, I would call this fabrikator an arts installation!"

"Really? Why?"

"Because when those humorless foreigners with their lawsuits try to make a scandal of the arts scene, that never works!" Savic winked at the professor and his wife. "We really enjoyed it, eh? We enjoyed a good show while we had it!"

Ace whipped off his sunglasses. "It's an 'arts installation'! Wow! That is some smart lawyer thinking there!"

Borislav frowned. "Why do you say that?"

Ace leaned in to whisper behind his hand. "Well, because that's what we tell the River Boys! We tell them it's just an art show; then we shut it down. They stay in their old industrial district, and we keep our turf in the old arts district. Everything is cool!"

"That's your big solution?"

"Well, yeah," said Ace, leaning back with a grin. "Hooray for art!"

Borislav's temper rose from a deep well to burn the back of his neck. "That's it, huh? That's what you two sorry sons of bitches have to offer the people? You just want to get rid of the thing! You want to put it out, like spitting on a candle! Nothing *happens* with your stupid approach! You call that a Transition? Everything's just the same as it was before! Nothing changes at all!"

Damov shook his head. "History is always passing. We changed. We're all a year older."

Mrs. Damov spoke up. "I can't believe your fascist, technocratic nonsense! Do you really imagine that you will improve the lives of the people by dropping some weird machine onto their street at random? With no mature consideration of any deeper social issues? I wanted to pick up some milk tonight! Who's manning your kiosk, you goldbricker? Your store is completely empty! Are we supposed to queue?"

Mr. Savic emptied his glass. "Your fabrikator is great fun, but piracy is illegal and immoral. Fair is fair, let's face it."

"Fine," said Borislav, waving his arms, "if that's what you believe, then go tell the people. Tell the people in this café, right now, that you want to throw the future away! Go on, do it! Say you're scared of crime! Say they're not mature enough and they have to think it through. Tell the people that they have to vote for that!"

"Let's not be hasty," said Savic.

"Your sordid mechanical invention is useless without a social invention," said Mrs. Damova primly.

"My wife is exactly correct!" Damov beamed. "Because a social invention is much more than gears and circuits; it's . . . well, it's something like that kiosk. A kiosk was once a way to drink tea in a royal garden. Now it's a way to buy milk! That is social invention!" He clicked her bubbling glass with his own.

Ace mulled this over. "I never thought of it that way. Where can we steal a social invention? How do you copy one of those?"

These were exciting questions. Borislav felt a piercing ray of mental daylight. "That European woman, what's-her-face. She bought out my kiosk. Who is she? Who does she work for?"

"You mean Dr. Grootjans? She is, uh . . . she's the economic affairs liaison for a European Parliamentary investigative committee."

"Right," said Borislav at once, "that's it. Me, too! I want that. Copy me that! I'm the liaison for the investigation Parliament something stupid-or-other."

Savic laughed in delight. "This is getting good."

"You. Mr. Savic. You have a Parliament investigation committee."

"Well, yes, I certainly do."

"Then you should investigate this fabrikator. You place it under formal government investigation. You investigate it, all day and all night. Right here on the street, in public. You issue public reports. And of course you make stuff. You make all kinds of stuff. Stuff to investigate."

"Do I have your proposal clear? You are offering your fabrikator to the government?"

"Sure. Why not? That's better than losing it. I can't sell it to you. I've got no papers for it. So sure, you can look after it. That's my gift to the people."

Savic stroked his chin. "This could become quite an international issue." Suddenly, Savic had the look of a hungry man about to sit at a bonfire and cook up a whole lot of sausages.

"Man, that's even better than making it a stupid art project," Ace enthused. "A stupid government project! Hey, those last forever!"

V

Savic's new investigation committee was an immediate success. With the political judo typical of the region, the honest politician wangled a large and generous support grant from the Europeans—basically, in order to investigate himself.

The fab now reformed its efforts: from consumer knickknacks to the pressing needs of the state's public sector. Jet-black fireplugs appeared in the arts district. Jet-black hoods for the broken streetlights, and jet-black manhole covers for the streets. Governments bought in bulk, so a primary source for the yellow dust was located. The fab churned busily away right in the public square, next to a railroad tanker full of feedstock.

Borislav returned to his kiosk. He made a play at resuming his normal business. He was frequently called to testify in front of Savic's busy committee. This resulted in Fleka the Gypsy being briefly arrested, but the man skipped bail. No one made any particular effort to find Fleka. They certainly had never made much effort before.

Investigation soon showed that the fabrikator was stolen property from a hospital in Gdansk. Europeans had long known how to make such fabrikators: fabrikators that used carbon nanotubes. They had simply refrained from doing so.

As a matter of wise precaution, the Europeans had decided not to create devices that could so radically disrupt a well-established political and economic order. The pain of such an act was certain to be great. The benefits were doubtful.

On some grand, abstract level of poetic engineering, it obviously made sense to create superefficient, widely distributed, cottage-scale factories that could create as much as possible with as little as possible. If one were inventing industrial civilization from the ground up, then fabbing was a grand idea. But an argument of that kind made no sense to the installed base and the established interests. You couldn't argue a voter out of his job. So fabs had been subtly restricted to waxes, plastics, plaster, papier-mâché, and certain metals.

Except, that is, for fabs with medical applications. Medicine, which dealt in agonies of life and death, was never merely a marketplace. There was always somebody whose child had smashed and shattered bones. Sooner or later this violently interested party, researching a cure for his beloved, would find the logjam and scream: *Won't one of you heartless, inhuman bastards think of the children?*

Of course, those who had relinquished this technology had the children's best interests at heart. They wanted their children to grow up safe within stable, regulated societies. But one could never explain good things for vaporous, potential future children to someone whose heart and soul was twisted by the suffering of an actual, real-life child.

So a better and different kind of fab had come into being. It was watched over with care . . . but, as time and circumstance passed, it slipped loose.

Eager to spread the fabbing pork through his constituency, Savic commissioned renowned local artists to design a new breed of kiosk. This futuristic Transition Three ultra-kiosk would house the very fab that could make it. Working with surprising eagerness and speed (given that they were on government salary), these artisan-designers created a new, official, state-supported fabbing kiosk, an alarmingly splendid, well-nigh monumental kiosk, half Ottoman pavilion, half Stalinist gingerbread, and almost one hundred percent black carbon nanotubes, except for a few necessary steel bolts, copper wires, and brass staples.

Borislav knew better than to complain about this. He had to abandon his perfectly decent, old-fashioned, customary kiosk, which was swiftly junked and ripped into tiny recyclable shreds. Then he climbed, with pain and resignation, up the shiny black stair steps into this eerie, oversized, grandiose rock-solid black fort, this black-paneled royal closet whose ornate, computer-calligraphic roof would make meteors bounce off it like graupel hail.

The cheap glass windows fit badly. The new black shelves confused his fingers. The slick black floor sent his chair skidding wildly. The black carbon walls would not take paint, glue, or paper. He felt like an utter fool—but this kiosk hadn't been built for his convenience. This was a kiosk for the new Transition Three generation, crazily radical, liberal guys for whom a "kiosk" was no mere humble conduit but the fortress of a new culture war.

A kiosk like this new one could be flung from a passing jet. It could hammer the ground like a plummeting thunderbolt and bounce up completely unharmed. With its ever-brimming bags of gold dust, a cybernetic tumbling of possessions would boil right out of it: *bottles bags knobs latches wheels pumps,* molds for making other things, tools for making other things; *saws hammers wrenches levers,* drill bits, screws, screwdrivers, *awls pliers scissors punches,* planes, files, rasps, jacks, carts and shears; pulleys, chains and chain hoists, trolleys, cranes, buckets, bottles, barrels. . . . All of these items sitting within their digital files as neat as chess pieces, sitting there like the very *idea* of chess pieces, like a mental chess set awaiting human desire to leap into being and action.

As Borislav limped, each night, from his black battleship superkiosk back to his mother's apartment, he could see Transition Three insinuating itself into the fabric of his city.

Transition One had once a look all its own: old socialist buildings of bad brick and substandard plaster, peeling like a secret leprosy, then exploding with the plastic branding symbols of the triumphant West: candy bars, franchised fried food, provocative lingerie.

Transition Two was a tougher business: he remembered it mostly for its lacks and privations. Empty stores, empty roads, crowds of bicycles, the angry hum of newfangled fuel cells, the cheap glitter of solar roofing, insulation stuffed everywhere like the paper in a pauper's shoes. Crunchy, mulchy-looking new construction. Grass on the rooftops, grass in the trolley ways. Networking masts and dishes. Those clean, cold, flat-panel lights.

This third Transition had its own native look, too. It was the same song and another verse. It was black. It was jet-black, smooth, anonymous, shiny, stainless, with an occasional rainbow shimmer off the layers and grooves whenever the light was just right, like the ghosts of long-vanished oil slicks.

Revolution was coming. The people wanted more of this game than the regime was allowing them to have. There were five of the fabs running in the city now. Because of growing foreign pressure against "the dangerous proliferation," the local government wouldn't make any more fabrikators. So the people were being denied the full scope of their desire to live differently. The people were already feeling different inside, so they were going to take it to the streets. The politicians were feebly trying to split differences between ways of life that just could not be split.

Did the laws of commerce exist for the people's sake? Or did the people exist as slaves of the so-called laws of commerce? That was populist demagoguery, but that kind of talk was popular for a reason.

Borislav knew that civilization existed through its laws. Humanity suffered and starved whenever outside the law. But those stark facts didn't weigh on the souls of the locals for ten seconds. The local people here were not that kind of people. They had never been that kind of people. Turmoil: that was what the people here had to offer the rest of the world.

The people had flown off the handle for far less than this; for a shot fired at some passing prince, for instance. Little street demonstrations were boiling up from left and right. Those demonstrations waxed and waned, but soon the applecart would tip hard. The people would take to the city squares, banging their jet-black kitchen pans, shaking their jet-black house keys. Borislav knew from experience that this voice from the people was a nation-shaking racket. The voice of reason from the fragile government sounded like a cartoon mouse.

Borislav looked after certain matters, for there would be no time to look after them, later. He talked to a lawyer and made a new will. He made backups of his data and copies of important documents, and stashed things away in numerous caches. He hoarded canned goods, candles, medicines, tools, even boots. He kept his travel bag packed.

He bought his mother her long-promised cemetery plot. He acquired a handsome headstone for her, too. He even found silk sheets.

VI

It didn't break in the way he had expected, but then local history could be defined as events that no rational man would expect. It came as a kiosk. It was a brand-new European kiosk. A civilized, ultimate, decent, well-considered, preemptive intervention kiosk. The alien pink and white kiosk was beautiful and perfect and clean, and there was no one remotely human inside it.

The automatic kiosk had a kind of silver claw that unerringly picked its goods from its antiseptic shelves and delivered them to the amazed and trembling customer. These were brilliant goods; they were shiny and gorgeous and tagged with serial numbers and radio-tracking stickers. They glowed all over with reassuring legality: health regulations, total lists of contents, cross-border shipping, tax stamps, associated websites, places to register a complaint.

The superpower kiosk was a thing of interlocking directorates, of 100,000-page regulatory codes and vast, clotted databases, a thing of true brilliance, neurosis, and fine etiquette, like a glittering Hapsburg court. And it had been dropped with deliberate accuracy on his own part of Europe—that frail and volatile part—the part about to blow up.

The European kiosk was an almighty vending machine. It replaced its rapidly dwindling stocks in the Black Maria middle of the night with unmanned cargo vehicles, flat blind anonymous cockroachlike robot things of pink plastic and pink rubber wheels, which snuffled and radared their way across the midnight city and obeyed every traffic law with a crazy punctiliousness.

There was no one to talk to inside the pink European kiosk, although when addressed through its dozens of microphones, the kiosk could talk the local language rather beautifully. There were no human relations to be found there. There was no such thing as society: only a crisp interaction.

Gangs of kids graffiti-tagged the pink invader right away. Someone—Ace most likely—made a serious effort to burn it down.

They found Ace dead two days later, in his fancy electric sports car, with three fabbed black bullets through him, and a fabbed black pistol abandoned on the car's hood.

VII

Ivana caught him before he could leave for the hills.

"You would go without a word, wouldn't you? Not one word to me, and again you just go!"

"It's the time to go."

"You'd take crazy students with you. You'd take football bullies. You'd take tough-guy gangsters. You'd take gypsies and crooks. You'd go there with anybody. And not take me?"

"We're not on a picnic. And you're not the kind of scum who goes to the hills when there's trouble."

"You're taking guns?"

"You women never understand! You don't take carbines with you when you've got a black factory that can make carbines!" Borislav rubbed his unshaven jaw. Ammo, yes, some ammo might well be needed. Grenades, mortar rounds. He knew all too well how much of that stuff had been buried out in the hills, since the last time. It was like hunting for truffles.

And the land mines. Those were what really terrified him, in an unappeasable fear he would take to his grave. Coming back toward the border, once, he and his fellow vigilantes, laden with their loot, marching in step in the deep snow, each man tramping in another's sunken boot prints . . . Then a flat, lethal thing, with a chip, a wad of explosive, and a bellyful of steel bolts, counted their passing footsteps. The virgin snow went bloodred.

Borislav might have easily built such a thing himself. The shade-tree plans for such guerrilla devices were everywhere on the Net. He had never built such a bomb, though the prospect gnawed him in nightmares.

Crippled for life, back then, he had raved with high fever, freezing, starving, in a hidden village in the hills. His last confidante was his nurse. Not a wife, not a lover, not anyone from any army, or any gang, or any government. His mother. His mother had the only tie to him so profound that she would leave her city, leave everything, and risk starvation to look after a wounded guerrilla. She brought him soup. He watched her cheeks sink in day by day as she starved herself to feed him.

"You don't have anyone to cook for you out there," Ivana begged.

"You'd be leaving your daughter."

"You're leaving your mother."

She had always been able to sting him that way. Once again, despite everything he knew, he surrendered. "All right, then," he told her. "Fine. Be that way, since you want it so much. If you want to risk everything, then you can be our courier. You go to the camp, and you go to the city. You carry some things for us. You never ask any questions about the things."

"I never ask questions," she lied. They went to the camp and she just stayed with him. She never left his side, not for a day or a night. Real life started all over for them, once again. Real life was a terrible business.

VIII

It no longer snowed much in the old ski villages; the weather was a real mess nowadays, and it was the summers you had to look out for. They set up their outlaw fab plant inside an abandoned set of horse stables.

The zealots talked wildly about copying an "infinite number of fabs," but that was all talk. That wasn't needed. It was only necessary to make and distribute enough fabs to shatter the nerves of the authorities. That was prop-aganda of the deed.

Certain members of the government were already nodding and winking at their efforts. That was the only reason that they might win. Those hustlers knew that if the weather vanes spun fast enough, the Byzantine cliques that ruled the statehouse would have to break up. There would be chaos. Serious chaos. But then, after some interval, the dust would have to settle on a new arrangement of power players. Yesterday's staunch conservative, if he sur-vived, would become the solid backer of the new regime. That was how it worked in these parts.

In the meantime, however, some dedicated group of damned fools would have to actually carry out the campaign on the ground. Out of any ten peo-ple willing to do this, seven were idiots. These seven were dreamers, rebels by nature, unfit to run so much as a lemonade stand.

One out of the ten would be capable and serious. Another would be genuinely dangerous: a true, amoral fanatic. The last would be the traitor to the group: the police agent, the coward, the informant.

There were thirty people actively involved in the conspiracy, which nat-urally meant twenty-one idiots. Knowing what he did, Borislav had gone there to prevent the idiots from quarreling over nothing and blowing the effort apart before it could even start. The three capable men had to be kept focused on building the fabs. The fanatics were best used to sway and intim-idate the potential informants.

If they held the rebellion together long enough, they would wear down all the sane people. That was the victory.

The rest was all details, where the devil lived. The idea of self-copying fabs looked great on a sheet of graph paper, but it made little practical sense to make fabs entirely with fabs. Worse yet, there were two vital parts of the fab that simply couldn't be fabbed at all. One was the nozzle that integrated the yellow dust into the black stuff. The other was the big recycler comb that chewed up the black stuff back into the yellow dust. These two crucial components obviously couldn't be made of the yellow dust or the black stuff.

Instead, they were made of precisely machined high-voltage European metals that were now being guarded like jewels. These components were way beyond the conspiracy's ability to create.

Two dozen of the fabbing nozzles showed up anyway. They came through the courtesy of some foreign intelligence service. Rumor said the Japanese, for whatever inscrutable reason.

They still had no recycling combs. That was bad. It confounded and betrayed the whole dream of fabs to make them with the nozzles but not the recycling combs. This meant that their outlaw fabs could make things but never recycle them. A world with fabs like that would be a nightmare: it would slowly but surely fill up with horrible, polluting fabjunk: unusable, indestructible, rock-solid lumps of black slag. Clearly this dark prospect had much affected the counsels of the original inventors.

There were also many dark claims that carbon nanotubes had dire health effects: because they were indestructible fibers, something like asbestos. And that was true: carbon nanotubes did cause cancer. However, they caused rather less cancer than several thousand other substances already in daily use.

It took all summer for the competent men to bang together the first outlaw fabs. Then it became necessary to sacrifice the idiots, in order to distribute the hardware. The idiots, shrill and eager as ever, were told to drive the fabs as far as possible from the original factory, then hand them over to sympathizers and scram.

Four of the five idiots were arrested almost at once. Then the camp was raided by helicopters.

However, Borislav had fully expected this response. He had moved the camp. In the city, riots were under way. It didn't matter who "won" these riots, because rioting melted the status quo. The police were hitting the students with indestructible black batons. The kids were slashing their paddywagon tires with indestructible black kitchen knives.

At this point, one of the fanatics had a major brain wave. He demanded that they send out dozens of fake black boxes that merely *looked* like fabs. There was no political need for their futuristic promises of plenty to actually work.

This cynical scheme was much less work than creating real fabs, so it was swiftly adopted. More than that: it was picked up, everywhere, by copycats. People were watching the struggle: in Bucharest, Lublin, Tbilisi, in Bratislava, Warsaw, and Prague. People were dipping ordinary objects in black lacquer to make them look fabbed. People were distributing handbooks for fabs, and files for making fabs. For every active crank who really wanted to make a fab, there were a hundred people who wanted to know how to do it. Just in case.

Some active cranks were succeeding. Those who failed became martyrs. As resistance spread like spilled ink, there were simply too many people implicated to classify it as criminal activity.

Once the military contractors realized there were very good reasons to make giant fabs the size of shipyards, the game was basically over. Transition Three was the new realpolitik. The new economy was the stuff of the everyday. The older order was over. It was something no one managed to remember, or even wanted to manage to remember.

The rest of it was quiet moves toward checkmate. And then the game just stopped. Someone tipped over the White King, in such a sweet, subtle, velvety way that one would have scarcely guessed that there had ever been a White King to fight against at all.

IX

Borislav went to prison. It was necessary that somebody should go. The idiots were only the idiots. The competent guys had quickly found good positions in the new regime. The fanatics had despaired of the new dispensation, and run off to nurse their bitter disillusionment.

As a working rebel whose primary job had been public figurehead, Borislav was the reasonable party for public punishment.

Borislav turned himself in to a sympathetic set of cops who would look much better for catching him. They arrested him in a blaze of publicity. He was charged with "conspiracy": a rather merciful charge, given the host of genuine crimes committed by his group. Those were the necessary, everyday crimes of any revolution movement, crimes such as racketeering, theft of services, cross-border smuggling, subversion and sedition, product piracy, copyright infringement, money laundering, fake identities, squatting inside stolen property, illegal possession of firearms, and so forth.

Borislav and his various allies weren't charged with those many crimes. On the contrary; since he himself had been so loudly and publicly apprehended, those crimes of the others were quietly overlooked.

While sitting inside his prison cell, which was not entirely unlike a kiosk, Borislav discovered the true meaning of the old term "penitentiary." The original intention of prisons was that people inside them should be penitent people. Penitent people were supposed to meditate and contemplate their way out of their own moral failings. That was the original idea.

Of course, any real, modern "penitentiary" consisted mostly of frantic business dealings. Nobody "owned" much of anything inside the prison, other than a steel bunk and a chance at a shower, so simple goods such as talcum powder loomed very large in the local imagination. Borislav, who fully understood street trading, naturally did very well at this. At least, he did much better than the vengeful, mentally limited people who were doomed to inhabit most jails.

Borislav thought a lot about the people in the jails. They, too, were the people, and many of those people were getting into jail because of him. In any Transition, people lost their jobs. They were broke, they lacked prospects. So they did something desperate.

Borislav did not much regret the turmoil he had caused the world, but he often thought about what it meant and how it must feel. Somewhere, inside some prison, was some rather nice young guy, with a wife and kids, whose job was gone because the fabs took it away. This guy had a shaven head, an ugly orange jumpsuit, and appalling food, just like Borislav himself. But that young guy was in the jail with less good reason. And with much less hope. And with much more regret.

That guy was suffering. Nobody gave a damn about him. If there was any justice, someone should mindfully suffer, and be penitent, because of the harsh wrong done that guy.

Borislav's mother came to visit him in the jail. She brought printouts from many self-appointed sympathizers. The world seemed to be full of strange foreign people who had nothing better to do with their time than to e-mail tender, supportive screeds to political prisoners. Ivana, something of a mixed comfort to him in their days of real life, did not visit the jail or see him. Ivana knew how to cut her losses when her men deliberately left her to do something stupid, such as volunteering for a prison.

These strangers and foreigners expressed odd, truncated, malformed ideas of what he had been doing. Because they were the Voice of History.

He himself had no such voice to give to history. He came from a small place under unique circumstances. People who hadn't lived there would never understand it. Those who had lived there were too close to understand it. There was just no understanding for it. There were just . . . the events. Events, transitions, new things. Things like the black kiosks.

These new kiosks . . . No matter where they were scattered in the world, they all had the sinister, strange, overly dignified look of his own original black kiosk. Because the people had seen those kiosks. The people knew well what a black fabbing kiosk was supposed to look like. Those frills, those fringes, that peaked top, that was just how you knew one. That was their proper look. You went there to make your kid's baby shoes indestructible. The kiosks did what they did, and they were what they were. They were everywhere, and that was that.

After twenty-two months, a decent interval, the new regime pardoned him as part of a general amnesty. He was told to keep his nose clean and his mouth shut. Borislav did this. He didn't have much to say, anyway.

X

Time passed. Borislav went back to the older kind of kiosk. Unlike the fancy new black fabbing kiosk, these older ones sold things that couldn't be fabbed: foodstuffs, mostly.

Now that fabs were everywhere and in public, fabbing technology was advancing by leaps and bounds. Surfaces were roughened so they shone with pastel colors. Technicians learned how to make the fibers fluffier, for bendable, flexible parts. The world was in a Transition, but no transition ended the world. A revolution just turned a layer in the compost heap of history, compressing that which now lay buried, bringing air and light to something hidden.

On a whim, Borislav went into surgery and had his shinbone fabbed. His new right shinbone was the identical, mirror-reversed copy of his left shinbone. After a boring recuperation, for he was an older man now and the flesh didn't heal as it once had, he found himself able to walk on an even keel for the first time in twenty-five years.

Now he could walk. So he walked a great deal. He didn't skip and jump for joy, but he rather enjoyed walking properly. He strolled the boulevards, he saw some sights, he wore much nicer shoes.

Then his right knee gave out, mostly from all that walking on an indestructible artificial bone. So he had to go back to the cane once again. No cure was a miracle panacea: but thanks to technology, the trouble had crept closer to his heart.

That made a difference. The shattered leg had oppressed him during most of his lifetime. That wound had squeezed his soul into its own shape. The bad knee would never have a chance to do that, because he simply wouldn't live that long. So the leg was a tragedy. The knee was an episode.

It was no great effort to walk the modest distance from his apartment block to his mother's grave. The city kept threatening to demolish his old apartments. They were ugly and increasingly old-fashioned, and they frankly needed to go. But the government's threats of improvement were generally empty, and the rents would see him through. He was a landlord. That was never a popular job, but someone was always going to take it. It might as well be someone who understood the plumbing.

It gave him great satisfaction that his mother had the last true granite headstone in the local graveyard. All the rest of them were fabbed.

Dr. Grootjans was no longer working in a government. Dr. Grootjans was remarkably well preserved. If anything, this female functionary from an alien system looked *younger* than she had looked, years before. She had two prim Nordic braids. She wore a dainty little off-pink sweater. She had high heels.

Dr. Grootjans was writing about her experiences in the transition. This was her personal, confessional text, on the Net of course, accompanied by photographs, sound recordings, links to other sites, and much supportive reader commentary.

"Her gravestone has a handsome Cyrillic font," said Dr. Grootjans.

Borislav touched a handkerchief to his lips. "Tradition does not mean that the living are dead. Tradition means that the dead are living."

Dr. Grootjans happily wrote this down. This customary action of hers had irritated him at first. However, her strange habits were growing on him. Would it kill him that this overeducated foreign woman subjected him to her academic study? Nobody else was bothering. To the neighborhood, to the people, he was a crippled, short-tempered old landlord. To her, the scholar-bureaucrat, he was a mysterious figure of international significance. Her version of events was hopelessly distorted and self-serving. But it was a version of events.

"Tell me about this grave," she said. "What are we doing here?"

"You wanted to see what I do these days. Well, this is what I do." Borislav set a pretty funeral bouquet against the headstone. Then he lit candles.

"Why do you do this?"

"Why do you ask?"

"You're a rational man. You can't believe in religious rituals."

"No," he told her, "I don't believe. I know they are just rituals."

"Why do it, then?"

He knew why, but he did not know how to give her that sermon. He did it because it was a gift. It was a liberating gift for him, because it was given with no thought of any profit or return. A deliberate gift with *no possibility* of return.

Those gifts were the stuff of history and futurity. Because gifts of that kind were also the gifts that the living received from the dead.

The gifts we received from the dead: those were the world's only genuine gifts. All the other things in the world were commodities. The dead were, by definition, those who gave to us without reward. And, especially: our dead gave to us, the living, within a dead context. Their gifts to us were not just abjectly generous, but archaic and profoundly confusing.

Whenever we disciplined ourselves, and sacrificed ourselves, in some vague hope of benefiting posterity, in some ambition to create a better future beyond our own moment in time, then we were doing something beyond a rational analysis. Those in that future could never see us with our own eyes:

they would only see us with the eyes that we ourselves gave to them. Never with our own eyes: always with their own. And the future's eyes always saw the truths of the past as blinkered, backward, halting. Superstition.

"Why?" she said.

Borislav knocked the snow from his elegant shoes. "I have a big heart."

Last Contact

STEPHEN BAXTER

Like many of his colleagues here at the beginning of a new century, British writer Stephen Baxter has been engaged for more than a decade now with the task of revitalizing and reinventing the "hard-science" story for a new generation of readers, producing work on the cutting edge of science that bristles with weird new ideas and often takes place against vistas of almost outrageously cosmic scope.

Baxter made his first sale to *Interzone* in 1987 and since then has become one of that magazine's most frequent contributors, as well as making sales to *Asimov's Science Fiction, Science Fiction Age, Analog, Zenith, New Worlds,* and elsewhere. He's one of the most prolific new writers in science fiction and is rapidly becoming one of the most popular and acclaimed of them as well. In 2001, he appeared on the Final Hugo Ballot twice and won both *Asimov's* Readers' Award and *Analog's* Analytical Laboratory Award, one of the few writers ever to win both awards in the same year. Baxter's first novel, *Raft,* was released in 1991 to wide and enthusiastic response and was rapidly followed by other well-received novels such as *Timelike Infinity, Anti-ice, Flux,* and the H. G. Wells pastiche—a sequel to *The Time Machine*—*The Time Ships,* which won both the John W. Campbell Memorial Award and the Philip K. Dick Award. His other books include the novels *Voyage, Titan, Moonseed, Mammoth,* book 1: *Silverhair, Manifold: Time, Manifold: Space, Evolution, Coalescent, Exultant, Transcendent, Emperor, Resplendent, Conqueror, Navigator,* and *The H-bomb Girl* and in collaboration with Arthur C. Clarke: *The Light of Other Days* and *Time's Eye, a Time Odyssey, Sunstorm,* and *Firstborn.* Baxter's short fiction has been collected in *Vacuum Diagrams: Stories of the Xeelee Sequence, Traces,* and *The Hunters of Pangaea,* and he has released a chapbook novella, *Mayflower II.* Coming up are several new novels, including *Weaver, Flood,* and *Ark.*

Here he bids an autumnal farewell to everything, in a world counting slowly and relentlessly back to zero.

MARCH 15

Caitlin walked into the garden through the little gate from the drive. Maureen was working on the lawn.

Just at that moment Maureen's mobile phone pinged. She took off her gardening gloves, dug the phone out of the deep pocket of her old quilted coat, and looked at the screen. "Another contact," she called to her daughter.

Caitlin looked cold in her thin jacket; she wrapped her arms around her body. "Another super-civilisation discovered, off in space. We live in strange times, Mum."

"That's the fifteenth this year. And I did my bit to help discover it. Good for me," Maureen said, smiling. "Hello, love." She leaned forward for a kiss on the cheek.

She knew why Caitlin was here, of course. Caitlin had always hinted she would come and deliver the news about the Big Rip in person, one way or the other. Maureen guessed what that news was from her daughter's hollow, stressed eyes. But Caitlin was looking around the garden, and Maureen decided to let her tell it all in her own time.

She asked, "How's the kids?"

"Fine. At school. Bill's at home, baking bread." Caitlin smiled. "Why do stay-at-home fathers always bake bread? But he's starting at Webster's next month."

"That's the engineers in Oxford."

"That's right. Not that it makes much difference now. We won't run out of money before, well, before it doesn't matter." Caitlin considered the garden. It was just a scrap of lawn, really, with a quite nicely stocked border, behind a cottage that was a little more than a hundred years old, in this village on the outskirts of Oxford. "It's the first time I've seen this properly."

"Well, it's the first bright day we've had. My first spring here." They walked around the lawn. "It's not bad. It's been let to run to seed a bit by Mrs. Murdoch. Who was another lonely old widow," Maureen said.

"You mustn't think like that."

"Well, it's true. This little house is fine for someone on their own, like me, or her. I suppose I'd pass it on to somebody else in the same boat, when I'm done."

Caitlin was silent at that, silent at the mention of the future.

Maureen showed her patches where the lawn had dried out last summer and would need reseeding. And there was a little brass plaque fixed to the wall of the house to show the level reached by the Thames floods of two years ago. "The lawn is all right. I do like this time of year when you sort of wake it up from the winter. The grass needs raking and scarifying, of course. I'll reseed bits of it, and see how it grows during the summer. I might think about getting some of it relaid. Now the weather's so different the drainage might not be right anymore."

"You're enjoying getting back in the saddle, aren't you, Mum?"

Maureen shrugged. "Well, the last couple of years weren't much fun. Nursing your dad, and then getting rid of the house. It's nice to get this old thing back on again." She raised her arms and looked down at her quilted gardening coat.

Caitlin wrinkled her nose. "I always hated that stupid old coat. You really should get yourself something better, Mum. These modern fabrics are very good."

"This will see me out," Maureen said firmly.

They walked around the verge, looking at the plants, the weeds, the autumn leaves that hadn't been swept up and were now rotting in place.

Caitlin said, "I'm going to be on the radio later. BBC Radio 4. There's to be a government statement on the Rip, and I'll be in the follow-up discussion. It starts at nine, and I should be on about nine thirty."

"I'll listen to it. Do you want me to tape it for you?"

"No. Bill will get it. Besides, you can listen to all these things on the Web sites these days."

Maureen said carefully, "I take it the news is what you expected, then."

"Pretty much. The Hawaii observatories confirmed it. I've seen the new Hubble images, deep sky fields. Empty, save for the foreground objects. All the galaxies beyond the local group have gone. Eerie, really, seeing your predictions come true like that. That's couch grass, isn't it?"

"Yes. I stuck a fork in it. Nothing but root mass underneath. It will be a devil to get up. I'll have a go, and then put down some bin liners for a few weeks, and see if that kills it off. Then there are these roses that should have been pruned by now. I think I'll plant some gladioli in this corner—"

"Mum, it's October." Caitlin blurted that out. She looked thin, pale and tense, a real office worker, but then Maureen had always thought that about her daughter, that she worked too hard. Now she was thirty-five, and her moderately pretty face was lined at the eyes and around her mouth, the first wistful signs of age. "October 14, at about four in the afternoon. I say 'about.' I could give you the time down to the attosecond if you wanted."

Maureen took her hands. "It's all right, love. It's about when you thought it would be, isn't it?"

"Not that it does us any good, knowing. There's nothing we can do about it."

They walked on. They came to a corner on the south side of the little garden. "This ought to catch the sun," Maureen said. "I'm thinking of putting in a seat here. A pergola maybe. Somewhere to sit. I'll see how the sun goes around later in the year."

"Dad would have liked a pergola," Caitlin said. "He always did say a garden was a place to sit in, not to work."

"Yes. It does feel odd that your father died, so soon before all this. I'd have liked him to see it out. It seems a waste somehow."

Caitlin looked up at the sky. "Funny thing, Mum. It's all quite invisible to the naked eye, still. You can see the Andromeda Galaxy, just, but that's bound to the Milky Way by gravity. So the expansion hasn't reached down to the scale of the visible, not yet. It's still all instruments, telescopes. But it's real all right."

"I suppose you'll have to explain it all on Radio 4."

"That's why I'm there. We'll probably have to keep saying it over and over, trying to find ways of saying it that people can understand. You know, don't you, Mum? It's all to do with dark energy. It's like an antigravity field that permeates the universe. Just as gravity pulls everything together, the dark energy is pulling the universe apart, taking more and more of it so far away that its light can't reach us anymore. It started at the level of the largest structures in the universe, superclusters of galaxies. But in the end it will fold down to the smallest scales. Every bound structure will be pulled apart. Even atoms, even subatomic particles. The Big Rip."

"We've known about this stuff for years. What we didn't expect was that the expansion would accelerate as it has. We thought we had trillions of years. Then the forecast was billions. And now—"

"Yes."

"It's funny for me being involved in this stuff, Mum. Being on the radio. I've never been a people person. I became an astrophysicist, for God's sake. I always thought that what I studied would have absolutely no effect on anybody's life. How wrong I was. Actually there's been a lot of debate about whether to announce it or not."

"I think people will behave pretty well," Maureen said. "They usually do. It might get trickier towards the end, I suppose. But people have a right to know, don't you think?"

"They're putting it on after nine so people can decide what to tell their kids."

"After the watershed! Well, that's considerate. Will you tell your two?"

"I think we'll have to. Everybody at school will know. They'll probably get bullied about it if they don't know. Imagine that. Besides, the little beggars will probably have Googled it on their mobiles by one minute past nine."

Maureen laughed. "There is that."

"It will be like when I told them Dad had died," Caitlin said. "Or like when Billy started asking hard questions about Santa Claus."

"No more Christmases," Maureen said suddenly. "If it's all over in October."

"No more birthdays for my two either," Caitlin said.

"November and January."

"Yes. It's funny, in the lab, when the date came up, that was the first thing I thought of."

Maureen's phone pinged again. "Another signal. Quite different in nature from the last, according to this."

"I wonder if we'll get any of those signals decoded in time."

Maureen waggled her phone. "It won't be for want of trying, me and a billion other search-for-ET-at-home enthusiasts. Would you like some tea, love?"

"It's all right. I'll let you get on. I told Bill I'd get the shopping in, before I have to go back to the studios in Oxford this evening."

They walked towards the back door into the house, strolling, inspecting the plants and the scrappy lawn.

JUNE 5

It was about lunchtime when Caitlin arrived from the garden centre with the pieces of the pergola. Maureen helped her unload them from the back of a white van and carry them through the gate from the drive. They were mostly just prefabricated wooden panels and beams that they could manage between the two of them, though the big iron spikes that would be driven into the ground to support the uprights were heavier. They got the pieces stacked up on the lawn.

"I should be able to set it up myself," Maureen said. "Joe next door said he'd lay the concrete base for me, and help me lift on the roof section. There's some nailing to be done, and creosoting, but I can do all that."

"Joe, eh." Caitlin grinned.

"Oh, shut up; he's just a neighbour. Where did you get the van? Did you have to hire it?"

"No, the garden centre loaned it to me. They can't deliver. They are still getting stock in, but they can't rely on the staff. They just quit, without any notice. In the end it sort of gets to you, I suppose."

"Well, you can't blame people for wanting to be at home."

"No. Actually Bill's packed it in. I meant to tell you. He didn't even finish his induction at Webster's. But the project he was working on would never have got finished anyway."

"I'm sure the kids are glad to have him home."

"Well, they're finishing the school year. At least I think they will; the teachers still seem keen to carry on."

"It's probably best for them."

"Yes. We can always decide what to do after the summer, if the schools open again."

Maureen had prepared some sandwiches, and some iced elderflower cordial. They sat in the shade of the house and ate their lunch and looked out over the garden.

Caitlin said, "Your lawn's looking good."

"It's come up quite well. I'm still thinking of relaying that patch over there."

"And you put in a lot of vegetables in the end," Caitlin said.

"I thought I should. I've planted courgettes and French beans and carrots, and a few outdoor tomatoes. I could do with a greenhouse, but I haven't really room for one. It seemed a good idea, rather than flowers, this year."

"Yes. You can't rely on the shops."

Things had kept working, mostly, as people stuck to their jobs. But there were always gaps on the supermarket shelves, as supply chains broke down. There was talk of rationing some essentials, and there were already coupons for petrol.

"I don't approve of how tatty the streets are getting in town," Maureen said sternly.

Caitlin sighed. "I suppose you can't blame people for packing in a job like street sweeping. It is a bit tricky getting around town, though. We need some work done on the roof; we're missing a couple of tiles. It's just as well we won't have to get through another winter," she said, a bit darkly. "But you can't get a builder for love or money."

"Well, you never could."

They both laughed.

Maureen said, "I told you people would cope. People do just get on with things."

"We haven't got to the end game yet," Caitlin said. "I went into London the other day. That isn't too friendly, Mum. It's not all like *this*, you know."

Maureen's phone pinged, and she checked the screen. "Four or five a day now," she said. "New contacts, lighting up all over the sky."

"But that's down from the peak, isn't it?"

"Oh, we had a dozen a day at one time. But now we've lost half the stars, haven't we?"

"Well, that's true, now the Rip has folded down into the Galaxy. I haven't really been following it, Mum. Nobody's been able to decode any of the signals, have they?"

"But some of them aren't the sort of signal you can decode anyhow. In one case somebody picked up an artificial element in the spectrum of a star. Something that was manufactured, and then just chucked in to burn up, like a flare."

Caitlin considered. "That can't say anything but 'here we are,' I suppose."

"Maybe that's enough."

"Yes."

It had really been Harry who had been interested in wild speculations about alien life and so forth. Joining the cell-phone network of home observers of ET, helping to analyse possible signals from the stars in a network of millions of others, had been Harry's hobby, not Maureen's. It was one of Harry's things she had kept up after he had died, like his weather monitoring and his football pools. It would have felt odd just to have stopped it all.

But she did understand how remarkable it was that the sky had suddenly lit up with messages like a Christmas tree, after more than half a century of dogged, fruitless, frustrating listening. Harry would have loved to see it.

"Caitlin, I don't really understand how all these signals can be arriving just now. I mean, it takes years for light to travel between the stars, doesn't it? We only knew about the phantom energy a few months ago."

"But others might have detected it long before, with better technology than we've got. That would give you time to send something. Maybe the signals have been *timed* to get here, just before the end, aimed just at us."

"That's a nice thought."

"Some of us hoped that there would be an answer to the dark energy in all those messages."

"What answer could there be?"

Caitlin shrugged. "If we can't decode the messages we'll never know. And I suppose if there was anything to be done, it would have been done by now."

"I don't think the messages need decoding," Maureen said.

Caitlin looked at her curiously but didn't pursue it. "Listen, Mum. Some of us are going to try to do something. You understand that the Rip works down the scales, that larger structures break up first. The Galaxy, then the solar system, then planets like Earth. And *then* the human body."

Maureen considered. "So people will outlive the Earth."

"Well, they could. For maybe about thirty minutes, until atomic structures get pulled apart. There's talk of establishing a sort of shelter in Oxford that could survive the end of the Earth. Like a submarine, I suppose. And if you wore a pressure suit you might last a bit longer even than that. The design goal is to make it through to the last microsecond. You could gather another thirty minutes of data that way. They've asked me to go in there."

"Will you?"

"I haven't decided. It will depend on how we feel about the kids, and — you know."

Maureen considered. "You must do what makes you happy, I suppose."

"Yes. But it's hard to know what that is, isn't it?" Caitlin looked up at the sky. "It's going to be a hot day."

"Yes. And a long one. I think I'm glad about that. The night sky looks odd now the Milky Way has gone."

"And the stars are flying off one by one," Caitlin mused. "I suppose the constellations will look funny by the autumn."

"Do you want some more sandwiches?"

"I'll have a bit more of that cordial. It's very good, Mum."

"It's elderflower. I collect the blossoms from that bush down the road. I'll give you the recipe if you like."

"Shall we see if your Joe fancies laying a bit of concrete this afternoon? I could do with meeting your new beau."

"Oh, shut up," Maureen said, and she went inside to make a fresh jug of cordial.

OCTOBER 14

That morning Maureen got up early. She was pleased that it was a bright morning, after the rain of the last few days. It was a lovely autumn day. She had breakfast listening to the last-ever episode of *The Archers*, but her radio battery failed before the end.

She went to work in the garden, hoping to get everything done before the light went. There was plenty of work, leaves to rake up, the roses and the clematis to prune. She had decided to plant a row of daffodil bulbs around the base of the new pergola.

She noticed a little band of goldfinches, plundering a clump of Michaelmas daisies for seed. She sat back on her heels to watch. The colourful little birds had always been her favourites.

Then the light went, just like that, darkening as if somebody were throwing a dimmer switch. Maureen looked up. The sun was rushing away, and sucking all the light out of the sky with it. It was a remarkable sight, and she wished she had a camera. As the light turned grey, and then charcoal, and then utterly black, she heard the goldfinches fly off in a clatter, confused. It had only taken a few minutes.

Maureen was prepared. She dug a little torch out of the pocket of her old quilted coat. She had been hoarding the batteries; you hadn't been able to buy them for weeks. The torch got her as far as the pergola, where she lit some rush torches that she'd fixed to canes.

Then she sat in the pergola, in the dark, with her garden lit up by her rush torches, and waited. She wished she had thought to bring out her book. She didn't suppose there would be time to finish it now. Anyhow, the flickering firelight would be bad for her eyes.

"Mum?"

The soft voice made her jump. It was Caitlin, threading her way across the garden with a torch of her own.

"I'm in here, love."

Caitlin joined her mother in the pergola, and they sat on the wooden benches, on the thin cushions Maureen had been able to buy. Caitlin shut down her torch to conserve the battery.

Maureen said, "The sun went, right on cue."

"Oh, it's all working out, bang on time."

Somewhere there was shouting, whooping, a tinkle of broken glass.

"Someone's having fun," Maureen said.

"It's a bit like an eclipse," Caitlin said. "Like in Cornwall, do you remember? The sky was cloudy, and we couldn't see a bit of the eclipse. But at that moment when the sky went dark, everybody got excited. Something primeval, I suppose."

"Would you like a drink? I've got a flask of tea. The milk's a bit off, I'm afraid."

"I'm fine, thanks."

"I got up early and managed to get my bulbs in. I didn't have time to trim that clematis, though. I got it all ready for the winter, I think."

"I'm glad."

"I'd rather be out here than indoors, wouldn't you?"

"Oh, yes."

"I thought about bringing blankets. I didn't know if it would get cold."

"Not much. The air will keep its heat for a bit. There won't be time to get very cold."

"I was going to fix up some electric lights out here. But the power's been off for days."

"The rushes are better, anyway. I would have been here earlier. There was a jam by the church. All the churches are packed, I imagine. And then I ran out of petrol a couple of miles back. We haven't been able to fill up for weeks."

"It's all right. I'm glad to see you. I didn't expect you at all. I couldn't ring." Even the mobile networks had been down for days. In the end everything had slowly broken down, as people simply gave up their jobs and went home. Maureen asked carefully, "So how's Bill and the kids?"

"We had an early Christmas," Caitlin said. "They'll both miss their birthdays, but we didn't think they should be cheated out of Christmas, too. We did it all this morning. Stockings, a tree, the decorations and the lights down from the loft, presents, the lot. And then we had a big lunch. I couldn't find a turkey, but I'd been saving a chicken. After lunch the kids went for their nap. Bill put their pills in their lemonade."

Maureen knew she meant the little blue pills the NHS had given out to every household.

"Bill lay down with them. He said he was going to wait with them until he was sure—you know. That they wouldn't wake up, and be distressed. Then he was going to take his own pill."

Maureen took her hand. "You didn't stay with them?"

"I didn't want to take the pill." There was some bitterness in her voice. "I always wanted to see it through to the end. I suppose it's the scientist in me. We argued about it. We fought, I suppose. In the end we decided this way was the best."

Maureen thought that on some level Caitlin couldn't really believe her children were gone, or she couldn't keep functioning like this. "Well, I'm glad you're here with me. And I never fancied those pills either. Although—will it hurt?"

"Only briefly. When the Earth's crust gives way. It will be like sitting on top of an erupting volcano."

"You had an early Christmas. Now we're going to have an early Bonfire Night."

"It looks like it. I wanted to see it through," Caitlin said again. "After all, I was in at the start—those supernova studies."

"You mustn't think it's somehow your fault."

"I do, a bit," Caitlin confessed. "Stupid, isn't it?"

"But you decided not to go to the shelter in Oxford with the others?"

"I'd rather be here. With you. Oh, but I brought this." She dug into her coat pocket and produced a sphere, about the size of a tennis ball.

Maureen took it. It was heavy, with a smooth black surface.

Caitlin said, "It's the stuff they make space shuttle heat-shield tiles out of. It can soak up a lot of heat."

"So it will survive the Earth breaking up."

"That's the idea."

"Are there instruments inside?"

"Yes. It should keep working, keep recording until the expansion gets down to the centimetre scale, and the Rip cracks the sphere open. Then it will release a cloud of even finer sensor units, motes we call them. It's nanotechnology, Mum, machines the size of molecules. They will keep gathering data until the expansion reaches molecular scales."

"How long will that take after the big sphere breaks up?"

"Oh, a microsecond or so. There's nothing we could come up with that could keep data-gathering after that."

Maureen hefted the little device. "What a wonderful little gadget. It's a shame nobody will be able to use its data."

"Well, you never know," Caitlin said. "Some of the cosmologists say this is just a transition, rather than an end. The universe has passed through transitions before, for instance from an age dominated by radiation to one dominated by matter—our age. Maybe there will be life of some kind in a new era dominated by the dark energy."

"But nothing like us."

"I'm afraid not."

Maureen stood and put the sphere down in the middle of the lawn. The grass was just faintly moist, with dew, as the air cooled. "Will it be all right here?"

"I should think so."

The ground shuddered, and there was a sound like a door slamming, deep in the ground. Alarms went off, from cars and houses, distant wails. Maureen hurried back to the pergola. She sat with Caitlin, and they wrapped their arms around each other.

Caitlin raised her wrist to peer at her watch, then gave it up. "I don't suppose we need a countdown."

The ground shook more violently, and there was an odd sound, like waves rushing over pebbles on a beach. Maureen peered out of the pergola. Remarkably, one wall of her house had given way, just like that, and the bricks had tumbled into a heap.

"You'll never get a builder out now," Caitlin said, but her voice was edgy.

"We'd better get out of here."

"All right."

They got out of the pergola and stood side by side on the lawn, over the little sphere of instruments, holding on to each other. There was another tremor, and Maureen's roof tiles slid to the ground, smashing and tinkling.

"Mum, there's one thing."

"Yes, love."

"You said you didn't think all those alien signals needed to be decoded."

"Why, no. I always thought it was obvious what all the signals were saying."

"What?"

Maureen tried to reply.

The ground burst open. The scrap of dewy lawn flung itself into the air, and Maureen was thrown down, her face pressed against the grass. She glimpsed houses and trees and people, all flying in the air, underlit by a furnace-red glow from beneath.

But she was still holding Caitlin. Caitlin's eyes were squeezed tight shut. "Good-bye," Maureen yelled. "They were just saying good-bye." But she couldn't tell if Caitlin could hear.

. . . end

The sledge-maker's Daughter

Alastair Reynolds

Alastair Reynolds is a frequent contributor to *Interzone* and has also sold to *Asimov's Science Fiction*, *Spectrum SF*, and elsewhere. His first novel, *Revelation Space*, was widely hailed as one of the major SF books of the year; it was quickly followed by *Chasm City*, *Redemption Ark*, *Absolution Gap*, *Century Rain*, and *Pushing Ice*, all big, sprawling space operas that were big sellers as well, establishing Reynolds as one of the best and most popular new SF writers to enter the field in many years. His other books include a novella collection, *Diamond Dogs*, *Turquoise Days*. His most recent books are a novel, *The Prefect*, and two collections, *Galactic North* and *Zima Blue and Other Stories*. Coming up is a new novel, *House of Suns*. A professional scientist with a Ph.D. in astronomy, he comes from Wales but lives in the Netherlands, where he works for the European Space Agency.

Reynolds's work is known for its grand scope, sweep, and scale. In one story, "Galactic North," a spaceship sets out on in pursuit of another in a stern chase that takes thousands of years of time and hundreds of thousands of light-years to complete; in another, "Thousandth Night," ultrarich immortals embark on a plan that will call for the physical rearrangement of all the stars in the Galaxy. Here he takes us somewhat closer to home, in a distressed civilization that's been set back hundreds of years by war and disaster, for a study of a young girl with an all-too-common problem who finds an extremely unique *solution* to it.

She stopped in sight of Twenty Arch Bridge, laying down her bags to rest her hands from the weight of two hog's heads and forty pence worth of beeswax candles. While she paused, Kathrin adjusted the drawstring on her hat, tilting the brim to shade her forehead from the sun. Though the air was still cool, there was a fierce new quality to the light that brought out her freckles.

Kathrin moved to continue, but a tightness in her throat made her hesitate. She had been keeping the bridge from her thoughts until this moment, but now the fact of it could not be ignored. Unless she crossed it she would face the long trudge to New Bridge, a diversion that would keep her on the road until long after sunset.

"Sledge-maker's daughter!" called a rough voice from across the road.

Kathrin turned sharply at the sound. An aproned man stood in a doorway, smearing his hands dry. He had a monkeylike face, tanned a deep liverish red, with white sideboards and a gleaming pink tonsure.

"Brendan Lynch's daughter, isn't it?"

She nodded meekly but bit her lip rather than answer.

"Thought so. Hardly one to forget a pretty face, me." The man beckoned her to the doorway of his shop. "Come here, lass. I've something for your father."

"Sir?"

"I was hoping to visit him last week, but work kept me here." He cocked his head at the painted wooden trademark hanging above the doorway. "Peter Rigby, the wheelwright. Kathrin, isn't it?"

"I need to be getting along, sir. . . ."

"And your father needs good wood, of which I've plenty. Come inside for a moment, instead of standing there like a starved thing." He called over his shoulder, telling his wife to put the water on the fire.

Reluctantly Kathrin gathered her bags and followed Peter into his workshop. She blinked against the dusty air and removed her hat. Sawdust carpeted the floor, fine and golden in places, crisp and coiled in others, while a heady concoction of resins and glues filled the air. Pots simmered on fires. Wood was being steamed into curves, or straightened where it was curved. Many sharp tools gleamed on one wall, some of them fashioned with blades of skydrift. Wheels, mostly awaiting spokes or iron tyres, rested against one another. Had the wheels been sledges, it could have been her father's workshop, when he had been busier.

Peter showed Kathrin to an empty stool next to one of his benches. "Sit down here and take the weight off your feet. Mary can make you some bread and cheese. Or bread and ham if you'd rather."

"That's kind, sir, but Widow Grayling normally gives me something to eat, when I reach her house."

Peter raised a white eyebrow. He stood by the bench with his thumbs tucked into the belt of his apron, his belly jutting out as if he was quietly proud of it. "I didn't know you visited the witch."

"She will have her two hog's heads, once a month, and her candles. She only buys them from the Shield, not the Town. She pays for the hogs a year in advance, twenty-four whole pounds."

"And you're not scared by her?"

"I've no cause to be."

"There's some that would disagree with you."

Remembering something her father had told her, Kathrin said, "There are folk who say the Sheriff can fly, or that there was once a bridge that winked at travellers like an eye, or a road of iron that reached all the way to London. My father says there's no reason for anyone to be scared of Widow Grayling."

"Not afraid she'll turn you into a toad, then?"

"She cures people, not puts spells on them."

"When she's in the mood for it. From what I've heard she's just as likely to turn the sick and needy away."

"If she helps some people, isn't that better than nothing at all?"

"I suppose." She could tell Peter didn't agree, but he wasn't cross with her for arguing. "What does your father make of you visiting the witch, anyway?"

"He doesn't mind."

"No?" Peter asked, interestedly.

"When he was small, my dad cut his arm on a piece of skydrift that he found in the snow. He went to Widow Grayling and she made his arm better again by tying an eel around it. She didn't take any payment except the skydrift."

"Does your father still believe an eel can heal a wound?"

"He says he'll believe anything if it gets the job done."

"Wise man, that Brendan, a man after my own heart. Which reminds me." Peter ambled to another bench, pausing to stir one of his bubbling pots before gathering a bundle of sawn-off wooden sticks. He set them down in front of Kathrin on a scrap of cloth. "Offcuts," he explained. "But good seasoned beech, which'll never warp. No use to me, but I am sure your father will find use for them. Tell him that there's more, if he wishes to collect it."

"I haven't got any money for wood."

"I'd take none. Your father was always generous to me, when I was going through lean times." Peter scratched behind his ear. "Only fair, the way I see it."

"Thank you," Kathrin said doubtfully. "But I don't think I can carry the wood all the way home."

"Not with two hog's heads as well. But you can drop by when you've given the heads to Widow Grayling."

"Only I won't be coming back over the river," Kathrin said. "After I've crossed Twenty Arch Bridge, I'll go back along the south quayside and take the ferry at Jarrow."

Peter looked puzzled. "Why line the ferryman's pocket when you can cross the bridge for nowt?"

Kathrin shrugged easily. "I've got to visit someone on the Jarrow road, to settle an account."

"Then you'd better take the wood now, I suppose," Peter said.

Mary bustled in, carrying a small wooden tray laden with bread and ham. She was as plump and red as her husband, only shorter. Picking up the entire gist of the conversation in an instant, she said, "Don't be an oaf, Peter. The girl cannot carry all that wood *and* her bags. If she will not come back this way, she must pass a message on to her father. Tell him that there's wood here if he wants it." She shook her head sympathetically at Kathrin. "What does he think you are, a pack mule?"

"I'll tell my father about the wood," she said.

"Seasoned beech," Peter said emphatically. "Remember that."

"I will."

Mary encouraged her to take some of the bread and meat, despite Kathrin again mentioning that she expected to be fed at Widow Grayling's. "Take it anyway," Mary said. "You never know how hungry you might get on the way home. Are you sure about not coming back this way?"

"I'd best not," Kathrin said.

After an awkward lull, Peter said, "There is something else I meant to tell your father. Could you let him know that I've no need of a new sledge this year, after all?"

"Peter," Mary said. "You promised."

"I said that I should *probably* need one. I was wrong in that." Peter looked exasperated. "The fault lies in Brendan, not me! If he did not make such good and solid sledges, then perhaps I should need another by now."

"I shall tell him," Kathrin said.

"Is your father keeping busy?" Mary asked.

"Aye," Kathrin answered, hoping the wheelwright's wife wouldn't push her on the point.

"Of course he will still be busy," Peter said, helping himself to some of the bread. "People don't stop needing sledges just because the Great Winter loosens its hold on us. Any more than they stopped needing wheels when the winter was at its coldest. It's still cold for half the year!"

Kathrin opened her mouth to speak. She meant to tell Peter that he could pass the message on to her father directly, for he was working not five minutes' walk from the wheelwright's shop. Peter clearly had no knowledge that her father had left the village, leaving his workshop empty during these warming months. But she realised that her father would be ashamed if the wheelwright were to learn of his present trade. It was best that nothing be said.

"Kathrin?" Peter asked.

"I should be getting on. Thank you for the food, and the offer of the wood."

"You pass our regards on to your father," Mary said.

"I shall."

"God go with you. Watch out for the jangling men."

"I will," Kathrin replied, because that was what you were supposed to say.

"Before you go," Peter said suddenly, as if a point had just occurred to him. "Let me tell you something. You say there are people who believe the Sheriff can fly, as if that was a foolish thing, like the iron road and the winking bridge. I cannot speak of the other things, but when I was a boy I met someone who had seen the Sheriff's flying machine. My grandfather often spoke of it. A whirling thing, like a windmill made of tin. He had seen it when he was a boy, carrying the Sheriff and his men above the land faster than any bird."

"If the Sheriff could fly then, why does he need a horse and carriage now?"

"Because the flying machine crashed down to Earth and no tradesman could persuade it to fly again. It was a thing of the old world, before the Great Winter. Perhaps the winking bridge and the iron road were also things of the old world. We mock too easily, as if we understood everything of our world where our forebears understood nothing."

"But if I should believe in certain things," Kathrin said, "should I not also believe in others? If the Sheriff can fly, then can a jangling man not steal me from my bed at night?"

"The jangling men are a story to stop children misbehaving," Peter said witheringly. "How old are you now?"

"Sixteen," Kathrin answered.

"I am speaking of something that was seen, in daylight, not made up to frighten bairns."

"But people say they have seen jangling men. They have seen men made of tin and gears, like the inside of a clock."

"Some people were frightened too much when they were small," Peter said, with a dismissive shake. "No more than that. But the Sheriff is real, and he was once able to fly. That's God's truth."

Her hands were hurting again by the time she reached Twenty Arch Bridge. She tugged down the sleeves of her sweater, using them as mittens. Rooks and jackdaws wheeled and cawed overhead. Seagulls feasted on waste floating in the narrow races between the bridge's feet, or pecked at vile leavings on the road that had been missed by the night soil gatherers. A boy laughed as Kathrin nearly tripped on the labyrinth of crisscrossing ruts that had been etched by years of wagon wheels entering and leaving the bridge. She hissed a curse back at the boy, but now the wagons served her purpose. She skulked near a doorway until a heavy cart came rumbling along, top-heavy with beer barrels from the Blue Star Brewery, drawn by four snorting dray horses, a bored-looking drayman at the reins, huddled so down deep into his leather coat that it seemed as if the Great Winter still had its icy hand on the country.

Kathrin started walking as the cart lumbered past her, using it as a screen. Between the stacked beer barrels she could see the top level of the scaffolding that was shoring up the other side of the arch, visible since no house or parapet stood on that part of the bridge. A dozen or so workers—including a couple of aproned foremen—were standing on the scaffolding, looking down at the work going on below. Some of them had plumb lines; one of them even had a little black rod that shone a fierce red spot wherever he wanted something moved. Of Garret, the reason she wished to cross the bridge only once if she could help it, there was nothing to be seen. Kathrin hoped that he was under the side of the bridge, hectoring the workers. She felt sure that her father was down there, too, being told what to do and biting his tongue against answering back. He put up with being shouted at, he put up with being forced to treat wood with crude disrespect, because it was all he could do to earn enough money to feed and shelter himself and his daughter. And he never, ever, looked Garret Kinnear in the eye.

Kathrin felt her mood easing as the dray ambled across the bridge, nearing the slight rise over the narrow middle arches. The repair work, where Garret was most likely to be, was now well behind her. She judged her progress by the passage of alehouses. She had passed the newly painted Bridge Inn and the shuttered gloom of the Lord's Confessor. Fiddle music spilled from the open doorway of the Dancing Panda: an old folk song with nonsense lyrics about *sickly sausage rolls*.

Ahead lay the Winged Man, its sign containing a strange painting of a foreboding figure rising from a hilltop. If she passed the Winged Man, she felt she would be safe.

Then the dray hit a jutting cobblestone and the rightmost front wheel snapped free of its axle. The wheel wobbled off on its own. The cart tipped to the side, spilling beer barrels onto the ground. Kathrin stepped nimbly aside as one of the barrels ruptured and sent its fizzing, piss-coloured contents across the roadway. The horses snorted and strained. The drayman spat out a greasy wad of chewing tobacco and started down from his chair, his face a mask of impassive resignation, as if this was the kind of thing that could be expected to happen once a day. Kathrin heard him whisper something in the ear of one of the horses, in beast tongue, which calmed the animal.

Kathrin knew that she had no choice but to continue. Yet she had no sooner resumed her pace—moving faster now, the bags swaying awkwardly—than she saw Garret Kinnear. He was just stepping out of the Winged Man's doorway.

He smiled. 'You in a hurry or something?'

Kathrin tightened her grip on the bags, as if she was going to use them as weapons. She decided not to say anything, not to openly acknowledge his presence, even though their eyes had met for an electric instant.

"Getting to be a big strong girl now, Kathrin Lynch."

She carried on walking, each step taking an eternity. How foolish she had been, to take Twenty Arch Bridge when it would only have cost her another hour to take the farther crossing. She should not have allowed Peter to delay her with his good intentions.

"You want some help with them bags of yours?"

Out of the corner of her eye she saw him move out of the doorway, tugging his mud-stained trousers higher onto his hip. Garret Kinnear was snake thin, all skin and bone, but much stronger than he looked. He wiped a hand across his sharp beardless chin. He had long black hair, the greasy grey colour of dishwater.

"Go away," she hissed, hating herself in the same instant.

"Just making conversation," he said.

Kathrin quickened her pace, glancing nervously around. All of a sudden the bridge appeared deserted. The shops and houses she had yet to pass were all shuttered and silent. There was still a commotion going on by the dray, but no one there was paying any attention to what was happening farther along the bridge.

"Leave me alone," Kathrin said.

He was walking almost alongside her now, between Kathrin and the road. "Now what kind of way to talk is that, Kathrin Lynch? Especially after my offer to help you with them bags. What have you got in them, anyways?"

"Nothing that's any business of yours."

"I could be the judge of that." Before she could do anything, he'd snatched the bag from her left hand. He peered into its dark depths, frowning. "You came all the way from Jarrow Ferry with this?"

"Give me back the bag."

She reached for the bag, tried to grab it back, but he held it out of her reach, grinning cruelly.

"That's mine."

"How much would a pig's head be worth?"

"You tell me. There's only one pig around here."

They'd passed the mill next to the Winged Man. There was a gap between the mill and the six-storey house next to it, where some improbably narrow property must once have existed. Garret turned down the alley, still carrying Kathrin's bag. He reached the parapet at the edge of the bridge and looked over the side. He rummaged in the bag and drew out the pig's head. Kathrin hesitated at the entrance to the narrow alley, watching as Garret held the head out over the roiling water.

"You can have your pig back. Just come a wee bit closer."

"So you can do what you did last time?"

"I don't remember any complaints." He let the head fall, then caught it again, Kathrin's heart in her throat.

"You know I couldn't complain."

"Not much to ask for a pig's head, is it?" With his free hand, he fumbled open his trousers, tugging out the pale worm of his cock. "You did it before, and it didn't kill you. Why not now? I won't trouble you again."

She watched his cock stiffen. "You said that last time."

"Aye, but this time I mean it. Come over here, Kathrin. Be a good girl now and you'll have your pig back."

Kathrin looked back over her shoulder. No one was going to disturb them. The dray had blocked all the traffic behind it, and nothing was coming over the bridge from the south.

"Please," she said.

"Just this once," Garret said. "And make your mind up fast, girl. This pig's getting awfully heavy in my hand."

Kathrin stood in the widow's candlelit kitchen—it only had one tiny, dusty window—while the old woman turned her bent back to attend to the coals burning in her black metal stove. She poked and prodded the fire until it hissed back like a cat. "You came all the way from Jarrow Ferry?" she asked.

"Aye," Kathrin said. The room smelled smoky.

"That's too far for anyone, let alone a sixteen-year-old lass. I should have a word with your father. I heard he was working on Twenty Arch Bridge."

Kathrin shifted uncomfortably. "I don't mind walking. The weather's all right."

"So they say. All the same, the evenings are still cold, and there are types about you wouldn't care to meet on your own, miles from Jarrow."

"I'll be back before it gets dark," Kathrin said, with more optimism than she felt. Not if she went out of her way to avoid Garret Kinnear she wouldn't. He knew the route she'd normally take back home, and the alternatives would mean a much longer journey.

"You sure about that?"

"I have no one else to visit. I can start home now." Kathrin offered her one remaining bag, as Widow Grayling turned from the fire, brushing her hands on her apron.

"Put it on the table, will you?"

Kathrin put the bag down. "One pig's head, and twenty candles, just as you wanted," she said brightly.

Widow Grayling hobbled over to the table, supporting herself with a stick, eyeing Kathrin as she opened the bag and took out the solitary head. She weighed it in her hand, then set it down on the table, the head facing Kathrin in such a way that its beady black eyes and smiling snout suggested amused complicity.

"It's a good head," the widow said. "But there were meant to be two of them."

"Can you manage with just the one, until I visit again? I'll have three for you next time."

"I'll manage if I must. Was there a problem with the butcher in the Shield?"

Kathrin had considered feigning ignorance, saying that she did not recall how only one head had come to be in her bags. But she knew Widow Grayling too well for that.

"Do you mind if I sit down?"

"Of course." The widow hobbled around the table to one of the rickety stools and dragged it out. "Are you all right, girl?"

Kathrin lowered herself onto the stool.

"The other bag was taken from me," she answered quietly.

"By who?"

"Someone on the bridge."

"Children?"

"A man."

Widow Grayling nodded slowly, as if Kathrin's answer had only confirmed some deep-seated suspicion she had harboured for many years. "Thomas Kinnear's boy, was it?"

"How could you know?"

"Because I've lived long enough to form ready opinions of people. Garret Kinnear is filth. But there's no one that'll touch him, because they're scared of his father. Even the Sheriff tugs his forelock to Thomas Kinnear. Did he rape you?"

"No. But he wanted me to do something nearly as bad."

"And did he make you?"

Kathrin looked away.

"Not this time."

Widow Grayling closed her eyes. She reached across the table and took one of Kathrin's hands, squeezing it between her own. "When was it?"

"Three months ago, when there was still snow on the ground. I had to cross the bridge on my own. It was later than usual, and there weren't any people around. I knew about Garret already, but I'd managed to keep away from him. I thought I was going to be lucky." Kathrin turned back to face her companion. "He caught me and took me into one of the mills. The wheels were turning, but there was nobody inside except me and Garret. I struggled, but then he put his finger to my lips and told me to shush."

"Because of your father."

"If I made trouble, if I did not do what he wanted, Garret would tell his father some lie about mine. He would say that he caught him sleeping on the job, or drunk, or stealing nails."

"Garret promised you that?"

"He said life's hard enough for a sledge-maker's daughter when no one wants sledges. He said it would only be harder if my father lost his work."

"In that respect he was probably right," the widow said resignedly. "It was brave of you to hold your silence, Kathrin. But the problem hasn't gone away, has it? You cannot avoid Garret forever."

"I can take the other bridge."

"That'll make no difference, now that he has his eye on you."

Kathrin looked down at her hands. "Then he's won already."

"No, he just thinks that he has." Without warning the widow stood from her chair. "How long have we known each other, would you say?"

"Since I was small."

"And in all that time, have I come to seem any older to you?"

"You've always seemed the same to me, Widow Grayling."

"An old woman. The witch on the hill."

"There are good witches and bad witches," Kathrin pointed out.

"And there are mad old women who don't belong in either category. Wait a moment."

Widow Grayling stooped under the impossibly low doorway into the next room. Kathrin heard a scrape of wood on wood, as of a drawer being opened. She heard rummaging sounds. Widow Grayling returned with something in her hands, wrapped in red cotton. Whatever it was, she put it down on the table. By the noise it made Kathrin judged that it was an item of some weight and solidity.

"I was just like you once. I grew up not far from Ferry, in the darkest, coldest years of the Great Winter."

"How long ago?"

"The Sheriff then was William the Questioner. You won't have heard of him." Widow Grayling sat down in the same seat she'd been using before and quickly exposed the contents of the red cotton bundle.

Kathrin wasn't quite sure what she was looking at. There was a thick and unornamented bracelet, made of some dull grey metal like pewter. Next to the ornament was something like the handle of a broken sword: a grip, with a crisscrossed pattern on it, with a curved guard reaching from one end of the hilt to the other. It was fashioned from the same dull grey metal.

"Pick it up," the widow said. "Feel it."

Kathrin reached out tentatively and closed her finger around the crisscrossed hilt. It felt cold and hard and not quite the right shape for her hand. She lifted it from the table, feeling its weight.

"What is it, widow?"

"It's yours. It's a thing that has been in my possession for a very long while, but now it must change hands."

Kathrin didn't know quite what to say. A gift was a gift, but neither she nor her father would have any use for this ugly broken thing, save for its value to a scrap man.

"What happened to the sword?" she asked.

"There was never a sword. The thing you are holding is the entire object."

"Then I don't understand what it is for."

"You shall, in time. I'm about to place a hard burden on your shoulders. I have often thought that you were the right one, but I wished to wait until you were older, stronger. But what has happened today cannot be ignored. I am old and weakening. It would be a mistake to wait another year."

"I still don't understand."

"Take the bracelet. Put it on your wrist."

Kathrin did as she was told. The bracelet opened on a heavy hinge, like a manacle. When she locked it together, the join was nearly invisible. It was a cunning thing, to be sure. But it still felt as heavy and dead and useless as the broken sword.

Kathrin tried to keep a composed face, all the while suspecting that the widow was as mad as people had always said.

"Thank you," she said, with as much sincerity as she could muster.

"Now listen to what I have to say. You walked across the bridge today. Doubtless you passed the inn known as the Winged Man."

"It was where Garret caught up with me."

"Did it ever occur to you to wonder where the name of the tavern comes from?"

"My dad told me once. He said the tavern was named after a metal statue that used to stand on a hill to the south, on the Durham road."

"And did your father explain the origin of this statue?"

"He said some people reckoned it had been up there since before the Great Winter. Other people said an old Sheriff had put it up. Some other people . . ." But Kathrin trailed off.

"Yes?"

"It's silly, but they said a real Winged Man had come down, out of the sky."

"And did your father place any credence in that story?"

"Not really," Kathrin said.

"He was right not to. The statue was indeed older than the Great Winter, when they tore it down. It was not put up to honour the Sheriff, or commemorate the arrival of a Winged Man." Now the widow looked at her intently. "But a Winged Man *did* come down. I know what happened, Kathrin: I saw the statue with my own eyes, before the Winged Man fell. I was there."

Kathrin shifted. She was growing uncomfortable in the widow's presence.

"My dad said people reckoned the Winged Man came down hundreds of years ago."

"It did."

"Then you can't have been there, Widow Grayling."

"Because if I had been, I should be dead by now? You're right. By all that is natural, I should be. I was born three hundred years ago, Kathrin. I've been a widow for more than two hundred of those years, though not always under this name. I've moved from house to house, village to village, as soon as people start suspecting what I am. I found the Winged Man when I was sixteen years old, just like you."

Kathrin smiled tightly. "I want to believe you."

"You will, shortly. I already told you that this was the coldest time of the Great Winter. The sun was a cold grey disk, as if it was made of ice itself. For years the river hardly thawed at all. The Frost Fair stayed almost all year round. It was nothing like the miserable little gatherings you have known. This was ten times bigger, a whole city built on the frozen river. It had streets and avenues, its own quarters. There were tents and stalls, with skaters and sledges everywhere. There'd be races, jousting competitions, fireworks, mystery players, even printing presses to make newspapers and souvenirs just for the Frost Fair. People came from miles around to see it, Kathrin: from as far away as Carlisle or York."

"Didn't they get bored with it, if it was always there?"

"It was always changing, though. Every few months there was something different. You would travel fifty miles to see a new wonder if enough people started talking about it. And there was no shortage of wonders, even if they were not always quite what you had imagined when you set off on your journey. Things fell from the sky more often in those days. A living thing like the Winged Man was still a rarity, but other things came down regularly enough. People would spy where they fell and try to get there first. Usually all they'd find would be bits of hot metal, all warped and runny like melted sugar."

"Skydrift," Kathrin said. "Metal that's no use to anyone, except barbers and butchers."

"Only because we can't make fires hot enough to make that metal smelt down like iron or copper. Once, we could. But if you could find a small piece with an edge, there was *nothing* it couldn't cut through. A surgeon's best knife will always be skydrift."

"Some people think the metal belongs to the jangling men, and that anyone who touches it will be cursed."

"And I'm sure the Sheriff does nothing to persuade them otherwise. Do you think the jangling men care what happens to their metal?"

"I don't think they care, because I don't think they exist."

"I was once of the same opinion. Then something happened to make me change my mind."

"This being when you found the Winged Man, I take it."

"Before even that. I would have been thirteen, I suppose. It was in the back of a tent in the Frost Fair. There was a case holding a hand made of metal, found among skydrift near Wallsend."

"A rider's gauntlet."

"I don't think so. It was broken off at the wrist, but you could tell that it used to belong to something that was also made of metal. There were metal bones and muscles in it. No cogs or springs, like in a clock or tin toy. This was something finer, more ingenious. I don't believe any man could have made it. But it cannot just be the jangling men who drop things from the sky, or fall out of it."

"Why not?" Kathrin asked, in the spirit of someone going along with a game.

"Because it was said that the Sheriff's men once found a head of skin and bone, all burned up, but which still had a pair of spectacles on it. The glass in them was dark like coal, but when the Sheriff wore them, he could see at night like a wolf. Another time, his men found a shred of garment that kept changing colour, depending on what it was lying against. You could hardly see it then. Not enough to make a suit, but you could imagine how useful that would have been to the Sheriff's spies."

"They'd have wanted to get to the Winged Man first."

Widow Grayling nodded. "It was just luck that I got to him first. I was on the Durham road, riding a mule, when he fell from the sky. Now, the law said that they would spike your head on the bridge if you touched something that fell on the Sheriff's land, especially skydrift. But everyone knew that the Sheriff could only travel so fast, even when he had his flying machine. It was a risk worth taking, so I took it, and I found the Winged Man, and he was still alive."

"Was he really a man?"

"He was a creature of flesh and blood, not a jangling man, but he was not like any man I had seen before. He was smashed and bent, like a toy that had been trodden on. When I found him he was covered in armour, hot enough to turn the snow to water and make the water hiss and bubble under him. I could only see his face. A kind of golden mask had come off, lying next to him. There were bars across his mask, like the head of the angel on the tavern sign. The rest of him was covered in metal, jointed in a clever fashion. It was silver in places and black in others, where it had been scorched. His arms were metal wings, as wide across as the road itself if they had not been snapped back on themselves. Instead of legs he just had a long tail, with a kind of fluke at the end of it. I crept closer, watching the sky all around me for the Sheriff's whirling machine. I was fearful at first, but when I saw the Winged Man's face I only wanted to do what I could for him. And he was dying. I knew it, because I'd seen the same look on the faces of men hanging from the Sheriff's killing poles."

"Did you talk to him?"

"I asked him if he wanted some water. At first he just looked at me, his eyes pale as the sky, his lips opening and closing like a fish that has just been landed. Then he said, 'Water will not help me.' Just those five words, in a dialect I didn't know. Then I asked him if there was anything else I could do to help him, all the while glancing over my shoulder in case anyone should come upon us. But the road was empty and the sky was clear. It took a long time for him to answer me again."

"What did he say?"

"He said, 'Thank you, but there is nothing you can do for me.' Then I asked him if he was an angel. He smiled, ever so slightly. 'No,' he said. 'Not an angel, really. But I am a flier.' I asked him if there was a difference. He smiled again before answering me. 'Perhaps not, after all this time. Do you know of fliers, girl? Do any of you still remember the war?'"

"What did you tell him?"

"The truth. I said I knew nothing of a war, unless he spoke of the Battle of the Stadium of Light, which had only happened twenty years earlier. He looked sad, then, as if he had hoped for a different answer. I asked him if he was a kind of soldier. He said that he was. 'Fliers are warriors,' he said. 'Men like me are fighting a great war, on your behalf, against an enemy you do not even remember.'"

"What enemy?"

"The jangling men. They exist, but not in the way we imagine them. They don't crawl in through bedroom windows at night, clacking tin-bodied things with skull faces and clockwork keys whirring from their backs. But they're real enough."

"Why would such things exist?"

"They'd been made to do the work of men on the other side of the sky, where men cannot breathe because the air is so thin. They made the jangling men canny enough that they could work without being told *exactly* what to do. But that already made them slyer than foxes. The jangling men coveted our world for themselves. That was before the Great Winter came in. The flier said that men like him—special soldiers, born and bred to fight the jangling men—were all that was holding them back."

"And he told you they were fighting a war, above the sky?"

Something pained Widow Grayling. "All the years since haven't made it any easier to understand what the flier told me. He said that just as there may be holes in an old piece of timber, one that has been eaten through by wood-worm, so there may be holes in the sky itself. He said that his wings were not really to help him fly, but to help him navigate those tunnels in the sky, just as the wheels of a cart find their way into the ruts on a road."

"I don't understand. How can there be holes in the sky, when the air is already too thin to breathe?"

"He said that the fliers and the jangling men make these holes, just as armies may dig a shifting network of trenches and tunnels as part of a long campaign. It requires strength to dig a hole and more strength to shore it up when it has already been dug. In an army, it would be the muscle of men and horses and whatever machines still work. But the flier was talking about a different kind of strength altogether." The widow paused, then stared into Kathrin's eyes with a look of foreboding. "He told me where it came from, you see. And ever since then, I have seen the world with different eyes. It is a hard burden, Kathrin. But someone must bear it."

Without thinking, Kathrin said, "Tell me."

"Are you sure?"

"Yes. I want to know."

"That bracelet has been on your wrist for a few minutes now. Does it feel any different?"

"No," Kathrin said automatically, but as soon as she'd spoken, as soon as she'd moved her arm, she knew that it was not the case. The bracelet still looked the same, it still looked like a lump of cold, dead metal, but it seemed to hang less heavily against her skin than when she'd first put it on.

"The flier gave it to me," Widow Grayling said, observing Kathrin's reaction. "He told me how to open his armour and find the bracelet. I asked why. He said it was because I had offered him water. He was giving me something in return for that kindness. He said that the bracelet would keep me healthy, make me strong in other ways, and that if anyone else was to wear it, it would cure them of many ailments. He said that it was against the common law of his people to give such a gift to one such as I, but he chose to do it anyway. I opened his armour, as he told me, and I found his arm, bound by iron straps to the inside of his wing, and broken like the wing itself. On the end of his arm was this bracelet."

"If the bracelet had the power of healing, why was the Winged Man dying?"

"He said that there were certain afflictions it could not cure. He had been touched by the poisonous ichor of a jangling man, and the bracelet could do nothing for him now."

"I still do not believe in magic," Kathrin said carefully.

"Certain magics are real, though. The magic that makes a machine fly, or a man see in the dark. The bracelet feels lighter, because part of it has entered you. It is in your blood now, in your marrow, just as the jangling man's ichor was in the flier's. You felt nothing, and you will continue to feel nothing. But so long as you wear the bracelet, you will age much slower than anyone else. For centuries, no sickness or infirmity will touch you."

Kathrin stroked the bracelet. "I do not believe this."

"I would not expect you to. In a year or two, you will feel no change in yourself. But in five years, or in ten, people will start to remark upon your uncommon youthfulness. For a while, you will glory in it. Then you will feel admiration turn slowly to envy and then to hate, and it will start to feel like a curse. Like me, you will need to move on and take another name. This will be the pattern of your life, while you wear the flier's charm."

Kathrin looked at the palms of her hands. It might have been imagination, but the lines where the handles had cut into her were paler and less sensitive to the touch.

"Is this how you heal people?" she asked.

"You're as wise as I always guessed you were, Kathrin Lynch. Should you come upon someone who is ill, you need only place the bracelet around their wrist for a whole day and—unless they have the jangling man's ichor in them—they will be cured."

"What of the other things? When my father hurt his arm, he said you tied an eel around his arm."

Her words made the widow smile. "I probably did. I could just as well have smeared pigeon dung on it instead, or made him wear a necklace of worms, for all the difference it would have made. Your father's arm would have mended itself on its own, Kathrin. The cut was deep, but clean. It did not need the bracelet to heal, and your father was neither stupid nor feverish. But he did have the loose tongue of all small boys. He would have seen the bracelet, and spoken of it."

"Then you did nothing."

"Your father believed that I did something. That was enough to ease the pain in his arm and perhaps allow it to heal faster than it would otherwise have done."

"But you turn people away."

"If they are seriously ill, but neither feverish nor unconscious, I cannot let them see the bracelet. There is no other way, Kathrin. Some must die, so that the bracelet's secret is protected."

"This is the burden?" Kathrin asked doubtfully.

"No, this is the reward for carrying the burden. The burden is knowledge."

Again Kathrin said, "Tell me."

"This is what the flier told me: The Great Winter fell across our world because the sun itself grew colder and paler. There was a reason for that. The armies of the celestial war were mining its fire, using the furnace of the sun itself to dig and shore up those seams in the sky. How they did this is beyond my comprehension, and perhaps even that of the flier himself. But he did make one thing clear. So long as the Great Winter held, the celestial war must still be raging. And that would mean that the jangling men had not yet won."

"But the Thaw . . . ," Kathrin began.

"Yes, you see it now. The snow melts from the land. Rivers flow; crops grow again. The people rejoice; they grow stronger and happier; skins darken; the Frost Fairs fade into memory. But they do not understand what it really means."

Kathrin hardly dared ask: "Which side is winning, or has already won?"

"I don't know; that's the terrible part of it. But when the flier spoke to me, I sensed an awful hopelessness, as if he knew things were not going to go the way of his people."

"I'm frightened now."

"You should be. But someone needs to know, Kathrin, and the bracelet is losing its power to keep me out of the grave. Not because there is anything wrong with it, I think—it heals as well as it has ever done—but because it has decided that my time has grown sufficient, just as it will eventually decide the same thing with you."

Kathrin touched the other object, the thing that looked like a sword's handle.

"What is this?"

"The flier's weapon. His hand was holding it from inside the wing. It poked through the outside of the wing like the claw of a bat. The flier showed me how to remove it. It is yours as well."

She had touched it already, but this time Kathrin felt a sudden tingle as her fingers wrapped around the hilt. She let go suddenly, gasping as if she had reached for a stick and picked up an adder, squirming and slippery and venomous.

"Yes, you feel its power," Widow Grayling said admiringly. "It works for no one unless they carry the bracelet."

"I can't take it."

"Better you have it than let that power go to waste. If the jangling men come, then at least someone will have a means to hurt them. Until then, there are other uses for it."

Without touching the hilt, Kathrin slipped the weapon into her pocket, where it lay as heavy and solid as a pebble.

"Did you ever use it?"

"Once."

"What did you do?"

She caught a secretive smile on Widow Grayling's face. "I took something precious from William the Questioner. Banished him to the ground like the rest of us. I meant to kill him, but he was not riding in the machine when I brought it down."

Kathrin laughed. Had she not felt the power of the weapon, she might have dismissed the widow's story as the ramblings of an old woman. But she had no reason in the world to doubt her companion.

"You could have killed the Sheriff later, when he came to inspect the killing poles."

"I nearly did. But something always stayed my hand. Then the Sheriff was replaced by another man, and he in turn by another. Sheriffs came and went. Some were evil men, but not all of them. Some were only as hard and cruel as their office demanded. I never used the weapon again, Kathrin. I sensed that its power was not limitless, that it must be used sparingly, against the time when it became really necessary. But to use it in defence, against a smaller target . . . that would be a different matter, I think."

Kathrin thought she understood.

"I need to be getting back home," she said, trying to sound as if they had discussed nothing except the matter of the widow's next delivery of provisions. "I am sorry about the other head."

"There is no need to apologise. It was not your doing."

"What will happen to you now, widow?"

"I'll fade, slowly and gracefully. Perhaps I will see things through to the next winter. But I don't expect to see another thaw."

"Please. Take the bracelet back."

"Kathrin, listen. It will make no difference to me now, whether you take it or not."

"I'm not old enough for this. I'm only a girl from the Shield, a sledge-maker's daughter."

"What do you think I was when I found the flier? We were the same. I've seen your strength and courage."

"I wasn't strong today."

"Yet you took the bridge, when you knew Garret would be on it. I have no doubt, Kathrin."

She stood. "If I had not lost the other head . . . if Garret had not caught me . . . would you have given me these things?"

"I was minded to do it. If not today, it would have happened next time. But let us give Garret due credit. He helped me make up my mind."

"He's still out there," Kathrin said.

"But he will know you will not be taking the bridge to get back home, even though that would save you paying the toll at Jarrow Ferry. He will content himself to wait until you cross his path again."

Kathrin collected her one remaining bag and moved to the door.

"Yes."

"I will see you again, in a month. Give my regards to your father."

"I will."

Widow Grayling opened the door. The sky was darkening to the east, in the direction of Jarrow Ferry. The dusk stars would appear shortly, and it would be dark within the hour. The crows were still wheeling, but more languidly now, preparing to roost. Though the Great Winter was easing, the evenings seemed as cold as ever, as if night was the final stronghold, the place where the winter had retreated when the inevitability of its defeat became apparent. Kathrin knew that she would be shivering long before she reached the tollgate at the crossing, miles down the river. She tugged down her hat in readiness for the journey and stepped onto the broken road in front of the widow's cottage.

"You will take care now, Kathrin. Watch out for the janglies."

"I will, Widow Grayling."

The door closed behind her. She heard a bolt slide into place.

She was alone.

Kathrin set off, following the path she had used to climb up from the river. If it was arduous in daylight, it was steep and treacherous at dusk. As she descended she could see Twenty Arch Bridge from above, a thread of light across the shadowed ribbon of the river. Candles were being lit in the inns and houses that lined the bridge, tallow torches burning along the parapets. There was still light at the north end, where the sagging arch was being repaired. The obstruction caused by the dray had been cleared, and traffic was moving normally from bank to bank. She heard the calls of men and women, the barked orders of foremen, the braying of drunkards and slatterns, the regular creak and splash of the mill wheels turning under the arches.

Presently she reached a fork in the path and paused. To the right lay the quickest route down to the quayside road to Jarrow Ferry. To the left lay the easiest descent down to the bridge, the path that she had already climbed. Until that moment, her resolve had been clear. She would take the ferry, as she always did, as she was expected to do.

But now she reached a hand into her pocket and closed her fingers around the flier's weapon. The shiver of contact was less shocking this time. The object already felt a part of her, as if she had carried it for years.

She drew it out. It gleamed in the twilight, shining where it had appeared dull before. Even if the widow had not told her of its nature, there would have been no doubt now. The object spoke its nature through her skin and bones, whispering to her on a level beneath language. It told her what it could do and how she could make it obey her. It told her to be careful of the power she now carried in her hand. She must scruple to use it wisely, for nothing like it now existed in the world. It was the power to smash walls. Power to smash bridges and towers and flying machines. Power to smash jangling men.

Power to smash ordinary men, if that was what she desired.

She had to know.

The last handful of crows gyred overhead. She raised the weapon to them and felt a sudden dizzying apprehension of their number and distance and position, each crow feeling distinct from its brethren, as if she could almost name them.

She selected one laggard bird. All the others faded from her attention, like players removing themselves from a stage. She came to know that last bird intimately. She could feel its wingbeats cutting the cold air. She could feel the soft thatch of its feathers, and the lacelike scaffolding of bone underneath. Within the cage of its chest she felt the tiny strong pulse of its heart, and she knew that she could make that heart freeze just by willing it.

The weapon seemed to urge her to do it. She came close. She came frighteningly close.

But the bird had done nothing to wrong her, and she spared it. She had no need to take a life to test this new gift, at least not an innocent one. The crow rejoined its brethren, something skittish and hurried in its flight, as if it had felt that coldness closing around its heart.

Kathrin returned the weapon to her pocket. She looked at the bridge again, measuring it once more with clinical eyes, eyes that were older and sadder this time, because she knew something that the people on the bridge could never know.

"I'm ready," she said, aloud, into the night, for whoever might be listening.

Then resumed her descent.

sanjeev and robotwallah

IAN MCDONALD

Here's another story by Ian McDonald, whose "Verthandi's Ring" appears elsewhere in this anthology. In this one, he takes us to visit a vivid and evocative future India, where ancient customs and dazzlingly sophisticated high tech exist side by side, for the story of a boy's troubled coming of age in a world where change accelerates day by day faster than anybody can keep up with—even those with the highest of high-tech toys to play with.

Every boy in the class ran at the cry. "Robotwar robotwar!" The teacher called after them, "Come here come here bad wicked things," but she was only a Business-English *aeai* and by the time old Mrs. Mawji hobbled in from the juniors only the girls remained, sitting primly on the floor, eyes wide in disdain and hands up to tell tales and name names.

Sanjeev was not a fast runner; the other boys pulled ahead from him as he stopped among the *dal* bushes for puffs from his inhalers. He had to fight for position on the ridge that was the village's high point, popular with chaperoned couples for its views over the river and the water plant at Murad. This day it was the inland view over the *dal* fields that held the attention. The men from the fields had been first up to the ridge; they stood, tools in hands, commanding all the best places. Sanjeev pushed between Mahesh and Ayanjit to the front.

"Where are they what's happening what's happening?"

"Soldiers over there by the trees."

Sanjeev squinted where Ayanjit was pointing, but he could see nothing but yellow dust and heat shiver.

"Are they coming to Ahraura?"

"Delhi wouldn't bother with a piss hole like Ahraura," said another man whose face Sanjeev knew—as he knew every face in Ahraura—if not his name. "It's Murad they're after. If they take that out, Varanasi will have to make a deal."

"Where are the robots? I want to see the robots."

Then he cursed himself for his stupidity, for anyone with eyes could see where the robots were. A great cloud of dust was moving down the north road and over it a flock of birds milled in eerie silence. Through the dust Sanjeev caught sunlight flashes of armour, clawed booted feet lifting, antennae bouncing, insect heads bobbing, weapon pods glinting. Then he and everyone else up on the high place felt the ridge begin to tremble to the march of the robots.

A cry from down the line. Four, six, ten, twelve flashes of light from the copse; streaks of white smoke. The flock of birds whirled up into an arrowhead and aimed itself at trees. *Airdrones*, Sanjeev realised, and, in the same thought, *missiles*! As the missiles reached their targets the cloud of dust exploded in a hammer of gunfire and firecracker flashes. It was all over before the sound reached the watchers. The robots burst unscathed from their cocoon of dust in a thundering run. "Cavalry charge!" Sanjeev shouted, his voice joining with the cheering of the men of Ahraura. Now hill and village quaked to the running iron feet. The wood broke into a fury of gunfire; the airdrones rose up and circled the copse like a storm. Missiles smoked away from the charging robots; Sanjeev watched weapon housings open and gun pods swing into position.

The cheering died as the edge of the wood exploded in a wall of flame. Then the robots opened up with their guns and the hush became awed silence. The burning woodland was swept away in the storm of gunfire; leaves, branches, trunks shredded into splinters. The robots stalked around the perimeter of the small copse for ten minutes, firing constantly as the drones circled over their heads. Nothing came out.

A voice down the line started shouting, "Jai Bharat! Jai Bharat!" but no one took it up and the man soon stopped. But there was another voice, hectoring and badgering, the voice of schoolmistress Mawji labouring up the path with a *lathi* cane.

"Get down from there, you stupid stupid men! Get to your families; you'll kill yourselves."

Everyone looked for the story on the evening news, but bigger, flashier things were happening in Allahabad and Mirzapur; a handful of contras eliminated in an unplace like Ahraura did not rate a line. But that night Sanjeev became Number One Robot Fan. He cut out pictures from the papers and those pro-Bharat propaganda mags that survived Ahraura's omnivorous cows. He avidly watched J- and C-anime where andro-sexy kids crewed titanic battle droids until sister Priya rolled her eyes and his mother whispered to the priest that she was worried about her son's sexuality. He pulled gigabytes of pictures from the World Web and memorised manufacturers and models and serial numbers, weapon loads and options mounts, rates of fire and maximum speeds. He saved up the pin money he made from helping old men with the computers the self-proclaimed Bharati government thought every village should have to buy a Japanese trump game, but no one would play him at it because he had learned all the details. When he tired of flat pictures, he cut up old cans with tin snips and brazed them together into model fighting machines: MIRACLE GHEE fast pursuit drones, TITAN DRENCH perimeter defense bots, a RED COLA riot-control robot.

Those same old men, when he came round to set up their accounts and assign their passwords, would ask him, "Hey! You know a bit about these things; what's going on with all this Bharat and Awadh stuff? What was wrong with plain old India anyway? And when are we going to get cricket back on the satellite?"

For all his robot wisdom, Sanjeev did not know. The news breathlessly raced on with the movements of politicians and breakaway leaders, but everyone had long ago lost all clear memory of how the conflict had begun. Naxalites in Bihar, an overmighty Delhi, those bloody Muslims demanding their own laws again? The old men did not expect him to answer; they just liked to complain and took a withered pleasure in showing the smart boy that he did not know everything.

"Well, as long as that's the last we see of them," they would say when Sanjeev replied with the specs of a Raytheon 380 Rudra I-war airdrone or an Akhu scout mecha and how much much better they were than any human fighter. Their general opinion was that the Battle of Vora's Wood—already growing back—was all the War of Separation Ahraura would see.

It was not. The men did return. They came by night, walking slowly through the fields, their weapons easily sloped in their hands. Those that met them said they had offered them no hostility, merely raised their assault rifles and shooed them away. They walked through the entire village, through every field and garden, up every *gali* and yard, past every byre and corral. In the morning their boot prints covered every centimetre of Ahraura. Nothing taken, nothing touched. "What was that about?" the people asked. "What did they want?"

They learned two days later when the crops began to blacken and wither in the fields and the animals, down to the last pi-dog, sickened and died.

Sanjeev would start running when their car turned into Umbrella Street. It was an easy car to spot, a big military Hummer that they had pimped Kali-black and red with after-FX flames that seemed to flicker as it drove past you. But it was an easier car to hear: everyone knew the *thud thud thud* of Desi metal that grew guitars and screaming vocals when they wound down the window to order food, food to go. And Sanjeev would be there: "What can I get you sirs?" He had become a good runner since coming to Varanasi. Everything had changed since Ahraura died.

The last thing Ahraura ever did was make that line in the news. It had been the first to suffer a new attack. Plaguewalkers was the popular name; the popular image was dark men in chameleon camouflage walking slowly through the crops, hands outstretched as if to bless, but sowing disease and blight. It was a strategy of desperation: deny the separatists as much as they could, and only ever partially effective; after the few first attacks plaguewalkers were shot on sight.

But they killed Ahraura and when the last cow died and the wind whipped the crumbled leaves and the dust into yellow clouds the people could put it off no longer. By car and pickup, *phatphat* and country bus, they went to the city, and though they had all sworn to hold together, family by family they drifted apart in Varanasi's ten million and Ahraura finally died.

Sanjeev's father rented an apartment on the top floor of a block on Umbrella Street and put his savings into a beer-and-pizza stall. Pizza pizza, that is what they want in the city, not Samosas or tiddy-hoppers or *rasgullahs*. And beer, Kingfisher and Godfather and Bangla. Sanjeev's mother did light sewing and gave lessons in deportment and Sanskrit, for she had learned that language as part of her devotions. Grandmother Bharti and little sister Priya cleaned offices in the new shining Varanasi that rose in glass and chrome beyond the huddled peeling houses of old Kashi. Sanjeev helped out at the stall under the rows of tall neon umbrellas, useless against rain and sun both but magnetic to the party people, the night people, the *badmashes* and fashion-*girlis*, that gave the street its name. It was there that he had first seen the robotwallahs.

It had been love at first sight the night that Sanjeev saw them stepping down Umbrella Street in their slashy Ts and bare sexy arms with Krishna bangles and henna tats, cool, cool boots with metal in all the hot places and hair spiked and gelled like one of those J-anime shows. The merchants of Umbrella Street edged away from them, turned a shoulder. They had a cruel reputation. Later Sanjeev was to see them overturn the stall of a *pakora* man who had irritated them, eve-tease a woman in a business sari who had looked askance at them, smash up the *phatphat* of a taxi driver who had thrown them out for drunkenness, but that first night they were stardust and Sanjeev wanted to be them with a want so pure and aching and impossible it was tearful joy. They were soldiers, teen warriors, robotwallahs. Only the dumbest and cheapest machines could be trusted to run themselves; the big fighting bots carried human jockeys behind their *aeai* systems. Teenage boys possessed the best combination of reflex speed and viciousness, amped up with fistfuls of combat drugs.

"Pizza pizza pizza!" Sanjeev shouted, running up to them. "We got pizza, every kind of pizza, and beer, Kingfisher beer, Godfather beer, Bangla beer, all kinds of beer."

They stopped. They turned. They looked. Then they turned away. One looked back as his brothers moved. He was tall and very thin from the drugs, fidgety and scratchy, his bad skin ill concealed with makeup. Sanjeev thought him a street god.

"What kind of pizza?"

"Tikka tandoori *murgh* beef lamb kebab *kofta* tomato spinach."

"Let's see your *kofta*."

Sanjeev presented the drooping wedge of meatball-studded pizza in both hands. The robotwallah took a *kofta* between thumb and forefinger. It drew a sagging string of cheese to his mouth, which he deftly snapped.

"Yeah, that's all right. Give me four of those."

"We got beer we got Kingfisher beer we got Godfather beer we got Bangla beer—"

"Don't push it."

Now he ran up alongside the big slow-moving car they had bought as soon as they were old enough to drive. Sanjeev had never thought it incongruous that they could send battle robots racing across the country on scouting expeditions or marching behind heavy tanks, but the law would not permit them so much as a moped on the public streets of Varanasi.

"So did you kill anyone today?" he called in through the open window, clinging on to the door handle as he jogged through the choked street.

"Kunda Khadar, down by the river, chasing out spies and surveyors," said bad-skin boy, the one who had first spoken to Sanjeev. He called himself Rai. They all had made-up J-anime names. "Someone's got to keep those bastard Awadhi *dam wallahs* uncomfortable."

A black plastic Kali swung from the rearview mirror, red tongued, yellow eyed. The skulls garlanded around her neck had costume sapphires for eyes. Sanjeev took the order, sprinted back through the press to his father's clay tandoor oven. The order was ready by the time the Kali Hummer made its second cruise. Sanjeev slid the boxes to Rai. He slid back the filthy, wadded Government of Bharat scrip rupees and, as Sanjeev fished out his change from his belt bag, the tip: a little plastic zip bag of battle drugs. Sanjeev sold them in the *galis* and courtyards behind Umbrella Street. Schoolkids were his best customers; they went through them by the fistful when they were cramming for exams. Ahraura had been all the school Sanjeev ever wanted to see. Who needed it when you had the world and the Web in your palmer?

The little shining capsules in black and yellow, purple and sky blue, were the Rajghatta's respectability. The pills held them above the slum.

But this night Rai's hand shot out to seize Sanjeev's hand as it closed around the plastic bag.

"Hey, we've been thinking." The other robotwallahs, Suni and Ravana and Godspeed! and Big Baba, nodded. "We're thinking we could use someone around the place, do odd jobs, clean a bit, keep stuff sweet, get us things. Would you like to do it? We'd pay—it'd be government scrip, not dollars or euros. Do you want to work for us?"

He lied about it to his family: the glamour, the tech, the sexy spun-diamond headquarters and the chrome he brought up to dazzling dazzling shine by the old village trick of polishing it with toothpaste. Sanjeev lied from disappointment but also from his own naïve overexpectation: too many nights filled with androgynous teenagers in spandex suits being clamshelled up inside block-killing battle machines. The robotwallahs of the 15th Light Armoured and Recon Cavalry—*sowars* properly—worked out of a cheap pressed-aluminium go-down on a dusty commercial road at the back of the new railway station. They sent their wills over provinces and countries to fight for Bharat. Their talents were too rare to risk in Raytheon assault bots or Aiwa scout mecha. No robotwallah ever came back in a body bag.

Sanjeev had scratched and kicked in the dust, squatting outside the shutter door squinting in the early light. Surely the *phatphat* had brought him to the wrong address? Then Rai and Godspeed! had brought him inside and shown him how they made war inside a cheap go-down. Motion-capture harnesses hung from steadi-rigs like puppets from a hand. Black mirror-visored insect helmets—real J-anime helmets—trailed plaited cables. One wall of the go-down was racked up with the translucent blue domes of processor cores, the adjoining wall a massive video-silk screen flickering with the ten thousand data flashes of the ongoing war: skirmishes, reconnaissances, air strikes, infantry positions, minefields and slow-missile movements, heavy armour, and the mecha divisions. Orders came in on this screen from a woman *jemadar* at Divisional Headquarters. Sanjeev never saw her flesh. None of the robotwallahs had ever seen her flesh, though they joked about it every time she came on the screen to order them to a reconnaissance or a skirmish or a raid. Along the facing wall, behind the battle harnesses, were cracked leather sofas, sling chairs, a watercooler (full), a Coke machine (three-quarters empty). Gaming and *girli* mags were scattered like dead birds across the sneaker-scuffed concrete floor. A door led to a rec room with more sofas, a couple of folding beds, and a game console with three VR sets. Off the rec room were a small kitchen area and a shower unit.

"Man, this place stinks," said Sanjeev.

By noon he had it cleaned it front to back, top to bottom, magazines stacked by date of publication, shoes set together in pairs, lost clothes in a black plastic sack for the *dhobiwallah* to launder. He lit incense. He threw out the old bad milk and turning food in the refrigerator, returned the empty Coke bottles for their deposits, made *chai*, and sneaked out to get Samosas, which he passed off as his own. He nervously watched Big Baba and Ravana step into their battle harnesses for a three-hour combat mission. So much he learned in that first morning. It was not one boy, one bot; Level 1.2 *aeais* controlled most of the autonomous process like motion and perception; the pilots were more like officers, each commanding a bot platoon, their point of view switching from scout machine to assault bot to I-war drone. And they did not have their favourite old faithful combat machine, scarred with bullet holes and lovingly customised with hand-sprayed graffiti and Desi-metal demons. Machines went to war because they could take damage human flesh and families could not. The Kali Cavalry rotated between a dozen units a month as attrition and the *jemadar* dictated. It was not not not Japanese anime, but the Kali boys did look sexy dangerous cool in their gear even if they went home to their parents every night, and working for them, cleaning for them, getting towels for them when they went sweating and stinking to the shower after a tour in the combat rig was the maximum thing in Sanjeev's small life. They were his children; they were his boys, no girls allowed.

"Hanging round with those *badmashes* all day, never seeing a wink of sun, that's not good for you," his mother said, sweeping round the tiny top-floor living room before her next lesson. "Your dad needs the help more; he may have to hire a boy in; what kind of sense does that make, when he has a son of his own? They do not have a good reputation, those robot-boys."

Then Sanjeev showed her the money he had got for one day.

"Your mother worries about people taking advantage of you," Sanjeev's dad said, loading up the handcart with wood for the pizza oven. "You weren't born to this city. All I'd say is, don't love it too much; soldiers will let you down; they can't help it. All wars eventually end."

With what remained from his money when he had divided it between his mother and father and put some away in the credit union for Priya, Sanjeev went down to Tea Lane and stuck down the deposit and first payment on a pair of big metally leathery black and red and flame-pattern boots. He wore them proudly to work the next day, stuck out beside the driver of the *phat-phat* so everyone could see them, and paid the owner of the Bata Boot and Shoe store assiduously every Friday. At the end of twelve weeks they were Sanjeev's entirely. In that time he had also bought the Ts, the fake-latex pants (real latex hot hot far too hot and sweaty for Varanasi, *baba*), the Kali bangles and necklaces, the hair gel and the eye kohl, but the boots first, the boots before all. Boots make the robotwallah.

"Do you fancy a go?"

It was one of those questions so simple and unexpected that Sanjeev's brain rolled straight over it and it was only when he was gathering up the fast-food wrappers (messy, messy boys) that it crept up and hit him over the head.

"What, you mean that?" A nod of the head towards the harnesses hanging like flayed hides from the feedback rig.

"If you want; there's not much on."

There hadn't been much on for the better part of a month. The last excitement had been when some cracker in a similar go-down in Delhi had broken through the Kali Cav's *aeai* firewall with a spike of burnware. Big Baba had suddenly leaped up in his rig like a million billion volts had just shot through (which, Sanjeev discovered later, it kind of had) and next thing the biocontrol interlocks had blown (indoor fireworks, woo) and he was kicking on the floor like epilepsy. Sanjeev had been first to the red button and a crash team had whisked him to the rich people's private hospital. The *aeais* had evolved a patch against the new burnware by the time Sanjeev went to get the lunch tins from the *dhabawallah* and Big Baba was back on his corner of the sofa within three days suffering nothing more than a lingering migraine. *Jemadar* woman sent a get-well e-card.

So it was with excitement and wariness that Sanjeev let Rai help him into the rig. He knew all the snaps and grips, he had tightened the straps and pulled snug the motion sensors a hundred times, but Rai doing it made it special, made Sanjeev a robotwallah.

"You might find this a little freaky," Rai said as he settled the helmet over Sanjeev's head. For an instant it was blackout, deafness as the phonobuds sought out his eardrums. "They're working on this new thing, some kind of bone induction thing so they can send the pictures and sounds straight into your brain," he heard Rai's voice say on the com. "But I don't think we'll get it in time. Now, just stand there and don't shoot anything."

The warning was still echoing in Sanjeev's inner ear as he blinked and found himself standing outside a school compound in a village so like Ahraura that he instinctively looked for Mrs. Mawji and Shree the holy red calf. Then he saw that the school was deserted, its roof gone, replaced with military camouflage sheeting. The walls were pocked with bullets down to the brickwork. Siva and Krishna with his flute had been hastily painted on the intact mud plaster, and the words *13th Mechanised Sowar: Section head-quarters.* There were men in smart, tightly belted uniforms with moustaches and bamboo *lathis*. Women with brass water pots and men on bicycles passed the open gate. By stretching, Sanjeev found he could elevate his sensory rig to crane over the wall. A village, an Ahraura, but too poor to even avoid war.

On his left a robot stood under a dusty neem tree. *I must be one of those,* Sanjeev thought, a General Dynamics A8330 Syce, a mean, skeletal desert rat of a thing on two vicious clawed feet, a heavy sensory crown and two Gatling arms—fully interchangeable with gas shells or slime guns for policing work, he remembered from *War Mecha*'s October 2038 edition.

Sanjeev glanced down at his own feet. Icons opened across his field of vision like blossoming flowers: location, elevation, temperature, ammunition load-out, the level of methane in his fuel tanks, tactical and strategic sat maps—he seemed to be in south-west Bihar—but what fascinated Sanjeev was that if he formed a mental picture of lifting his Sanjeev foot, his Syce claw would lift from the dust.

Go on try it it's a quiet day you're on sentry duty in some cow-shit Bihar village.

Forward, he willed. The bot took one step two. *Walk,* Sanjeev commanded. *There.* The robot walked jauntily towards the gate. No one in the street of shattered houses looked twice as he stepped among them. *This is great!* Sanjeev thought as he strolled down the street, then, *This is like a game.* Doubt then: *So how do I even know this war is happening?* A step too far; the Syce froze a hundred metres from the Ganesh temple, turned, and headed back to its sentry post. *What what what what what?* he yelled in his head.

"The onboard *aeai* took over," Rai said, his voice startling as a firecracker inside his helmet. Then the village went black and silent and Sanjeev was blinking in the ugly low-energy neons of the Kali Cavalry battle room, Rai gently unfastening the clips and snaps and strappings.

That evening, as he went home through the rush of people with his fist of rupees, Sanjeev realised two things: that most of war was boring and that this boring war was over.

The war was over. The *jemadar* visited the video-silk wall three times, twice, once a week, where in the heat and glory she would have given orders that many times a day. The Kali Cav lolled around on their sofas playing games, lying to their online fans about the cool exciting sexy things they were doing, though the fans never believed they ever really were robotwallahs, but mostly doing battle-drug combos that left them fidgety and aggressive. Fights flared over a cigarette, a look, how a door was closed or left open. Sanjeev threw himself into the middle of a dozen robotwallah wars. But when the American peacekeepers arrived Sanjeev knew it truly was over because they only came in when there was absolutely no chance any of them would get killed. There was a flurry of car bombings and I-war attacks and even a few suicide blasts, but everyone knew that that was just everyone who had a grudge against America and Americans in sacred Bharat. No, the war was over.

"What will you do?" Sanjeev's father asked, meaning, *What will I do when Umbrella Street becomes just another Asian* ginza?

"I've saved some money," Sanjeev said.

With the money he had saved Godspeed! had bought a robot. It was a Tata Industries D55, a small but nimble antipersonnel bot with detachable free-roaming sub-mechas, Level 0.8s, about as smart as a chicken, which they resembled. Even secondhand it must have cost much more than a teenage robotwallah heavily consuming games, online time, porn, and Sanjeev's dad's *kofta* pizza could ever save. "I got backers," Godspeed! said. "Funding. Hey, what do you think of this? I'm getting her pimped; this is the skin job." When the paint dried, the robot would be road-freighted up to Varanasi.

"But what are you going to do with it?" Sanjeev asked.

"Private security. They're always going to need security drones."

Tidying the tiny living room that night for his mother's nine o'clock lesson, opening the windows to let out the smell of hot ghee though the stink of the street was little better, Sanjeev heard a new chord in the ceaseless song of Umbrella Street. He threw open the window shutters in time to see an object, close, fast as a dashing bird, dart past his face, swing along the power line and down the festooned pylon. Glint of anodised alu-plastic: a boy raised on *Battlebots Top Trumps* could not fail to recognise a Tata surveillance mecha. Now the commotion at the end of Umbrella Street became clear: the hunched back of a battlebot was pushing between the cycle rickshaws and *phatphats*. Even before he could fully make out the customised god-demons of Mountain Buddhism on its carapace, Sanjeev knew the machine's make and model and who was flying it.

A *badmash* on an alco moto rode slowly in front of the ponderously stepping machine, relishing the way the street opened in front of him and the electric scent of heavy firepower at his back. Sanjeev saw the mech step up and squat down on its hydraulics before Jagmohan's greasy little *pakora* stand. The *badmash* skidded his moped to a stand and pushed up his shades.

They will always need security drones.

Sanjeev rattled down the many many flights of stairs of the patriotically renamed Diljit Rana Apartments, yelling and pushing and beating at the women and young men in very white shirts. The robot had already taken up its position in front of his father's big clay pizza oven. The carapace unfolded like insect wings into weapon mounts. *Badmash* was all teeth and grin in the anticipation of another commission. Sanjeev dashed between his father and the prying, insect sensory rig of the robot. Red demons and Sivas with fiery tridents looked down on him.

"Leave him alone; this is my dad; leave him be."

It seemed to Sanjeev that the whole of Umbrella Street, every vehicle upon it, every balcony and window that overlooked it, stopped to watch.

With a whir the weapon pods retracted, the carapace clicked shut. The battle machine reared up on its legs as the surveillance drones came skittering between people's legs and over countertops, scurried up the machine, and took their places on its shell mounts, like egrets on the back of a buffalo. Sanjeev stared the *badmash* down. He sneered, snapped down his cool sexy dangerous shades, and spun his moped away.

Two hours later, when all was safe and secure, a Peacekeeper unit had passed up the street asking for information. Sanjeev shook his head and sucked on his asthma inhalers.

"Some machine, like."

Suni left the go-down. No word no note no clue, his family had called and called and called, but no one knew. There had always been rumours of a man with money and prospects, who liked the robotwallah thing, but you do not tell those sorts of stories to mothers. Not at first asking. A week passed without the *jemadar* calling. It was over. So over. Rai had taken to squatting outside, squinting up through his cool sexy dangerous shades at the sun, watching for its burn on his pale arms, chain-smoking street-rolled bidis.

"Sanj." He smoked the cheap cigarette down to his gloved fingers and ground the stub out beneath the steel heel of his boot. "When it happens, when we can't use you anymore, have you something sorted? I was thinking, maybe you and I could do something together, go somewhere. Just have it like it was, just us. An idea, that's all."

The message came at 3:00 A.M. *I'm outside.* Sanjeev tiptoed around the sleeping bodies to open the window. Umbrella Street was still busy; Umbrella Street had not slept for a thousand years. The big black Kali Cav Hummer was like a funeral moving through the late-night people of the new Varanasi. The door locks made too much noise, so Sanjeev exited through the window, climbing down the pipes like a Raytheon double-eight thousand I-war infiltration bot. In Ahraura he would never have been able to do that.

"You drive," Rai said. From the moment the message came through, Sanjeev had known it would be him, and him alone.

"I can't drive."

"It drives itself. All you have to do is steer. It's not that different from the game. Swap over there."

Steering wheel pedal drive windshield display all suddenly looked very big to Sanjeev in the driver's seat. He touched his foot to the gas. Engines answered; the Hummer rolled; Umbrella Street parted before him. He steered around a wandering cow.

"Where do want me to go?"

"Somewhere, away. Out of Varanasi. Somewhere no one else would go." Rai bounced and fidgeted on the passenger seat. His hands were busy busy; his eyes were huge. He had done a lot of battle drugs. "They sent them back to school, man. To school, can you imagine that? Big Baba and Ravana. Said they needed real-world skills. I'm not going back, not never. Look!"

Sanjeev dared a glance at the treasure in Rai's palm: a curl of sculpted translucent pink plastic. Sanjeev thought of aborted goat fetuses, and the sex toys the girls had used in their favourite pornos. Rai tossed his head to sweep back his long, gelled hair and slid the device behind his ear. Sanjeev thought he saw something move against Rai's skin, seeking.

"I saved it all up and bought it. Remember, I said? It's new; no one else has one. All that gear, that's old; you can do everything with this, just in your head, in the pictures and words in your head." He gave a stoned grin and moved his hands in a dancer's mudra. "There."

"What?"

"You'll see."

The Hummer was easy to drive: the in-car *aeai* had a flocking reflex that enabled it to navigate Varanasi's ever-swelling morning traffic, leaving little for Sanjeev to do other than blare the triple horns, which he enjoyed a lot. Somewhere he knew he should be afraid, should feel guilty at stealing away in the night without word or note, should say, *Stop, whatever it is you are doing, it can come to nothing, it's just silliness, the war is over, and we must think properly about what to do next.* But the brass sun was rising above the glass towers and spilling into the streets and men in sharp white shirts and women in smart saris were going busy to their work, and he was free, driving a big smug car through them all, and it was so good, even if just for a day.

He took the new bridge at Ramnagar, hooting in derision at the gaudy, lumbering trucks. The drivers blared back, shouting vile curses at the *girli*-looking robotwallahs. Off A-roads onto B-roads, then to tracks and then bare dirt, the dust flying up behind the Hummer's fat wheels. Rai itched in the passenger seat, grinning away to himself and moving his hands like butterflies, muttering small words and occasionally sticking out of the window. His gelled hair was stiff with dust.

"What are you looking for?" Sanjeev demanded.

"It's coming," Rai said, bouncing on his seat. "Then we can go and do whatever we like."

From the word *drive*, Sanjeev had known where he must go. Sat nav and *aeai* did his remembering for him, but he still knew every turn and side road. Vora's Wood there, still stunted and grey; the ridge between the river and the fields from which all the men of the village had watched the battle and he had fallen in love with the robots. The robots had always been pure, had always been true. It was the boys who flew them who hurt and failed and disappointed. The fields were all dust, drifted and heaped against the lines of thorn fence. Nothing would grow here for a generation. The mud walls of the houses were crumbling, the school a roofless shell, the temple and tanks clogged with windblown dust. Dust, all dust. Bones cracked and went to powder beneath his all-wheel drive. A few too desperate even for Varanasi were trying to scratch an existence in the ruins. Sanjeev saw wire-thin men and tired women, dust-smeared children crouched in front of their brick-and-plastic shelters. The poison deep within Ahraura would defeat them in the end.

Sanjeev brought the Hummer to a halt on the ridgetop. The light was yellow, the heat appalling. Rai stepped out to survey the terrain.

"What a shit hole."

Sanjeev sat in the shade of the rear cabin watching Rai pace up and down, up and down, kicking up the dust of Ahraura with his big Desi-metal boots. *You didn't stop them, did you?* Sanjeev thought. *You didn't save us from the plaguewalkers.*

Rai suddenly leaped and punched the air. "There, there, look!"

A storm of dust moved across the dead land. The high sun caught glints and gleams at its heart. Moving against the wind, the tornado bore down on Ahraura.

The robot came to a halt at the foot of the ridge where Sanjeev and Rai stood waiting. A Raytheon ACR, a heavy line-of-battle bot, it out-topped them by some metres. The wind carried away its cloak of dust. It stood silent, potential, heat shimmering from its armour. Sanjeev had never seen a thing so beautiful.

Rai raised his hand. The bot spun on its steel hooves. More guns than Sanjeev had ever seen in his life unfolded from its carapace. Rai clapped his hands and the bot opened up with all its armaments on Vora's Wood. Gatlings sent dry dead silvery wood flying up into powder; missiles streaked from its back silos; the line of the wood erupted in a wall of flame. Rai separated his hands and the roar of sustained fire ceased.

"It got it all in here, everything that the old gear had, in here. Sanj, everyone will want us; we can go wherever we want; we can do whatever we want, we can be real anime heroes."

"You stole it."

"I had all the protocols. That's the system."

"You stole that robot."

Rai balled his fists, shook his head in exasperation.

"Sanj, it was always mine."

He opened his clenched fist. And the robot danced. Arms, feet, all the steps and the moves, the bends and head nods, a proper Bollywood item-song dance. The dust flew up around the battle bot's feet. Sanjeev could feel the eyes of the squatters, wide and terrified in their hovels. *I am sorry we scared you.*

Rai brought the dance to an end.

"Anything I want, Sanj. Are you coming with us?"

Sanjeev's answer never came, for a sudden, shattering roar of engines and jet blast from the river side of the ridge sent them reeling and choking in the swirling dust. Sanjeev fought out his inhalers: two puffs blue, one puff brown, and by the time they had worked their sweet way down into his lungs a tilt jet with the Bharati air force's green, white, and orange roundels on its engine pods stood on the settling dust. The cargo ramp lowered; a woman in dust-war camo and a mirror-visored helmet came up the ridge toward them.

With a wordless shriek Rai slashed his hand through the air like a sword. The bot crouched; its carapace slid open in a dozen places, extruding weapons. Without breaking her purposeful stride the woman lifted her left hand. The weapons retracted; the hull ports closed; the war machine staggered as if confused and then sat down heavily in the dead field, head sagging, hands trailing in the dust. The woman removed her helmet. The cameras made the *jemadar* look five kilos heavier, but she had big hips. She tucked her helmet under her left arm, with her right swept back her hair to show the plastic fetus-sex-toy-thing coiled behind her ear.

"Come on now, Rai. It's over. Come on; we'll go back. Don't make a fuss. There's not really anything you can do. We all have to think what to do next, you know? We'll take you back in the plane; you'll like that." She looked Sanjeev up and down. "I suppose you could take the car back. Someone has to and it'll be cheaper than sending someone down from Divisional; it's cost enough already. I'll retask the *aeai*. And then we have to get that thing...." She shook her head, then beckoned to Rai. He went like a calf, quiet and meek, down to the tilt jet. Black hopping crows settled on the robot, trying its crevices with their curious shiny-hungry beaks.

the skysailor's tale

MICHAEL SWANWICK

Michael Swanwick made his debut in 1980 and in the twenty-seven years that have followed has established himself as one of SF's most prolific and consistently excellent writers at short lengths, as well as one of the premier novelists of his generation. He has won the Theodore Sturgeon Memorial Award and the *Asimov's* Readers' Award poll. In 1991 his novel *Stations of the Tide* won him a Nebula Award as well, and in 1995 he won the World Fantasy Award for his story "Radio Waves." He's won the Hugo Award five times between 1999 and 2006, for his stories "The Very Pulse of the Machine," "Scherzo with Tyrannosaur," "The Dog Said Bow-Wow," "Slow Life," and "Legions in Time." His other books include the novels *In the Drift, Vacuum Flowers, The Iron Dragon's Daughter, Jack Faust,* and, most recently, *Bones of the Earth.* His short fiction has been assembled in *Gravity's Angels, A Geography of Unknown Lands, Slow Dancing Through Time* (a collection of his collaborative work with other authors), *Moon Dogs, Puck Aleshire's Abecedary, Tales of Old Earth, Cigar-Box Faust and Other Miniatures, Michael Swanwick's Field Guide to the Mesozoic Megafauna,* and *The Periodic Table of Science Fiction.* He's also published *The Postmodern Archipelago: Two Essays on Science Fiction & Fantasy* and a book-length interview, *Being Gardner Dozois.* Swanwick's most recent book is a new novel, *The Dragons of Babel.* He's had stories in our Second, Third, Fourth, Sixth, Seventh, Tenth, and Thirteenth through Twenty-fourth Annual Collections. Swanwick lives in Philadelphia with his wife, Marianne Porter. He has a Web site at www.michaelswanwick.com.

Here he takes us along on a strange and wonder-filled voyage, on a strange and wondrous ship. . . .

Of all the many things that this life has stolen from me, the one which bothers me most is that I cannot remember burying my father.

Give that log a poke. Stir up the embers. Winter's upon us—hear how the wind howls and prowls about the rooftops, as restless as a cat!—and I, for one, could use some light and a little more warmth. There'll be snow by morning for sure. Scoot your chair a bit closer to the fire. Is your mother asleep? Good. We'll keep our voices low. There are parts of this tale she would not approve of. Things that I must say which she thinks you'd be better off not knowing.

She's right, no doubt. Women usually are. But what of that? You're of an age to realize that your parents were never perfect, and that in their youths they may have done some things which . . . well. Right or wrong, I'm going to tell you everything.

Where was I?

My father's burial.

I was almost a man when he finally died—old enough, by all rights, to keep that memory to my dying day. But after the wreck of the *Empire*, I lay feverish and raving, so they tell me, for six weeks. During that time I was an exile in my own mind, lost in the burning deserts of delirium, wandering lands that rose and fell with each labored breath. Searching for a way back to the moment when I stood before my father's open grave and felt its cool breath upon my face. I was convinced that if I could only find it, all would be well.

So I searched and did not find, and forgot I had searched, and began again, returning always to the same memories, like a moth relentlessly batting itself against a lantern. Sometimes the pain rose up within me so that I screamed and thrashed and convulsed within my bed. Other times (all this they told me later), when the pain ebbed, I spoke long and lucidly on a variety of matters, sang strange songs, and told stranger tales, all with an intensity my auditors found alarming. My thoughts were never still.

Always I sought my father.

By the time I finally recovered, most of my life had been burnt to ashes and those ashes swept into the ash pit of history. The Atlantis of my past was sunk; all that remained were a few mountaintops sticking up out of the waters of forgetfulness like a scattered archipelago of disconnected islands. I remembered clambering upon the rusted ruins of a failed and demented steam dredging device its now forgotten inventor had dubbed the "Orukter Amphibolus," a brickyard battle fought alongside my fellow river rats with a gang of German boys who properly hated us for living by the wharves, a furtive kiss in the dark (with whom, alas, I cannot say), a race across the treacherously rolling logs afloat in the dock fronting the blockmaker's shop, and the catfish-and-waffles supper in a Wissahickon inn at which my mother announced to the family that she was to have a fifth child. But neither logic nor history unites these events; they might as well have happened to five separate people.

There are, too, odd things lacking in what remains: The face of my youngest sister. The body of equations making up the Calculus. All recollection whatsoever of my brother save his name alone. My father I can remember well only by contrast. All I know of him could be told in an hour.

I do not mourn the loss of his funeral. I've attended enough to know how it went. Words were surely spoken that were nothing like the words that should have been said. The air was heavy with incense and candle wax. The corpse looked both like and unlike the deceased. There were pallbearers, and perhaps I was one. Everybody was brave and formal. Then, after too long a service, they all left, feeling not one whit better than before.

A burial is a different matter. The first clods of dirt rattle down from the grave diggers' shovels onto the roof of the coffin, making a sound like rain. The earth is drawn up over it like a thick, warm blanket. The trees wave in the breeze overhead, as if all the world were a cradle endlessly rocking. The mourners' sobs are as quiet as a mother's bedtime murmurs. And so a man passes, by imperceptible degrees, to his final sleep. There is some comfort in knowing that a burial came off right.

So I trod the labyrinth of my fevered brain, dancing with the black goddess of pain, she of the bright eyes laughing and clutching me tight with fingers like hot iron, and I swirling and spinning and always circling in upon that sad event. Yet never quite arriving.

Dreaming of fire.

Often I came within minutes of my goal—so close that it seemed impossible that my next attempt would not bring me to it. One thought deeper, a single step further, I believed, and there it would be. I was tormented with hope.

Time and again, in particular, I encountered two memories bright as sunlight in my mind, guarding the passage to and from that dark omphalos. One was of the voyage out to the Catholic cemetery on Treaty Island in the Delaware. First came the boat carrying my father's coffin and the priest. Father Murphy sat perched in the bow, holding his hat down with one hand and with the other gripping the gunwale for all he was worth. He was a lean old hound of a man with wispy white hair, who bobbed and dipped most comically with every stroke of the oars and wore the unhappy expression of the habitually seasick.

I sat in the second dory of the procession with my mother and sisters, all in their best bonnets. Jack must have been there as well. Seeing Father Murphy's distress, we couldn't help but be amused. One of us wondered aloud if he was going to throw up, and we all laughed.

Our hired doryman turned to glare at us over his shoulder. He did not understand what a release my father's death was for all of us. The truth was that everything that had gone into making John Keely the man he was—his upright character, his innkeeper's warmth, his quiet strength, his bluff goodwill—had died years before, with the dwindling and extinction of his mind. We were only burying his body that day.

When he was fully himself, however, a better or godlier man did not exist in all the Americas—no, not on a thousand continents. I never saw him truly angry but once. That was the day my elder sister Patricia, who had been sent out to the back alley for firewood, returned empty-handed and said, "Father, there is a black girl in the shed, crying."

My parents threw on their roquelaures and put up the hoods, for the weather was foul as only a Philadelphia winter downpour can be, and went outside to investigate. They came back in with a girl so slight, in a dress so drenched, that she looked to my young eyes like a half-drowned squirrel.

They all three went into the parlor and closed the doors. From the hall Patricia and I—Mary was then but an infant—tried to eavesdrop but could hear only the murmur of voices punctuated by occasional sobs. After a while, the tears stopped. The talk continued for a very long time.

Midway through the consultation, my mother swept out of the room to retrieve the day's copy of the *Democratic Press,* and returned so preoccupied that she didn't chase us away from the door. I know now, as I did not then, that the object of her concern was an advertisement on the front page of the paper. Patricia, always the practical and foresightful member of the family, cut out and saved the advertisement, and so I can now give it to you exactly as it appeared:

SIX CENTS REWARD

RANAWAY on the 14th inst., from the subscriber, one TACEY BROWN, a mulatto girl of thirteen years age, with upwards of five years to serve on her indenture. She is five feet, one inch in height, pitted with the Small Pox, pert and quick spoken, took with her one plain brown dress of coarse cloth. In personality she is insolent, lazy, and disagreeable. The above reward and no thanks will be given to any person who will take her up and return her to

Thos. Cuttington
No. 81, Pine street, Philadelphia

This at a time, mind you, when the reward for a runaway apprentice often ran as high as ten dollars! Mr. Thomas Cuttington obviously thought himself a man grievously ill served.

At last my father emerged from the parlor with the newspaper in his hand. He closed the door behind him. His look then was so dark and stormy that I shrank away from him, and neither my sister nor I dared uncork any of the questions bubbling up within us. Grimly, he fetched his wallet and then, putting on his coat, strode out into the rain.

Two hours later he returned with one Horace Potter, a clerk from Flintham's countinghouse, and Tacey's indenture papers. The parlor doors were thrown wide and all the family, and our boarders as well, called in as witnesses. Tacey had by then been clothed by my mother in one of Patricia's outgrown dresses, and since my sister was of average size for a girl her age, Tacey looked quite lost in it. She had washed her face, but her expression was tense and unreadable.

In a calm and steady voice, my father read the papers through aloud, so that Tacey, who could neither read nor write, might be assured they were truly her deed of service. Whenever he came to a legal term with which she might not be familiar, he carefully explained it to the child, with Mr. Potter—who stood by the hearth, warming his hands—listening intently and then nodding with judicious approval. Then he showed her the signature of her former master, and her own mark as well.

Finally, he placed the paper on the fire.

When the indenture went up in flame, the girl made a sound unlike anything I have ever heard before or since, a kind of wail or shriek, the sort of noise a wild thing makes. Then she knelt down before my father and, to his intense embarrassment, seized and kissed his hand.

So it was that Tacey came to live with us. She immediately became like another sister to me. Which was to say that she was a harsh, intemperate termagant who would take not a word of direction, however reasonably I phrased it, and indeed ordered me about as if it were I who was *her* servant! She was the scourge of my existence. When she was seventeen—and against my mother's horrified advice—she married a man twice her age and considerably darker skinned, who made a living waiting upon the festivities of the wealthy. Julius Nash was a grave man. People said of him that even his smile was stern. Once, when he was courting her and stood waiting below-stairs, I, smarting from a recent scolding, angrily blurted out, "How can you put up with such a shrew?"

That solemn man studied me for a moment, and then in a voice so deep it had often been compared to a funerary bell replied, "Mistress Tacey is a woman of considerable strength of character and that, I have found, is far to be preferred over a guileful and flattering tongue."

I had not been looking to be taken seriously but only venting boyish spleen. Now I stood abashed and humbled by this Negro gentleman's thoughtful reply—and doubly humiliated, I must admit, by the source of my mortification. Then Tacey came stepping down the stairs, with a tight, triumphant smirk, and was gone, to reappear in my tale only twice more.

Yet if this seems to you an unlikely thing that my father would be so generous to a mulatto girl he did not know and who could do him no conceivable benefit, then I can only say that you did not know this good man. Moreover, I am convinced by the high regard in which he was held by all who knew him that this was but one of many comparable deeds, and notable only in that by its circumstances we were made aware of it.

How changed was my poor father's condition when last I saw him alive! That was the time my mother took me to the insane ward at Pennsylvania Hospital to visit him.

It was a beautiful, blue-skyed day in June.

I was fifteen years old.

Philadelphia was a wonderful place in which to be young, though I did not half appreciate it at that time. Ships arrived in the harbor every day with silk and camphor from Canton, hides from Valparaiso, and opium from Smyrna, and departed to Batavia and Malacca for tin, the Malabar coast for sandalwood and pepper, and around the Cape Horn with crates of knives and blankets to barter with credulous natives for bales of sea otter skins. Barbarously tattooed sailors were forever staggering from the groggeries singing oddly cadenced chanteys and pitching headlong into the river, or telling in vivid detail of a season lived naked among cannibals, married to a woman whose teeth had been filed down to points, all the while and with excruciating exactitude slowly unwrapping an oilcloth packet unearthed from the bottom of a sea chest to reveal at the climax of the yarn: a mummified human ear. The harbor was a constant source of discontent for me.

As were the grain wagons which came down the turnpike from Lancaster and returned west laden with pioneers and missionaries bound for the continental interior to battle savage Indians or save their souls for Christ, each according to his inclination. Those who stayed behind received packages from their distant relations containing feathered headpieces, cunningly woven baskets, beadwork cradleboards, and the occasional human scalp. Every frontiersman who headed up the pike took a piece of my soul with him.

Our hotel was located in that narrow slice of streets by the Delaware which respectable folk called the wharflands but which, because a brick wall two stories high with an iron fence atop it separated Water street from Front street (the two ran together, but Water street served the slow-moving wagon trade of the wharves, and Front street the dashing gigs and coaches of the social aristocracy), we merchants' brats thought of as the Walled City.

Our streets were narrow and damp, our houses and stores a bit ramshackle, our lives richly thronged with provincial joys.

Philadelphia proper, by contrast, was the sort of place where much was made of how wide and clean and gridlike the streets were, and a Frenchman's casual gallant reference to it as "the Athens of America" would be quoted and requoted until Doomsday. Yet, within its limits, it was surprisingly cosmopolitan.

The European wars had filled the city with exiles—the vicomte de Noailles, the duc d'Orléans, a hundred more. The former Empress Iturbide of Mexico could be seen hurrying by in her ludicrously splendid carriage. In the restaurants and bookshops could be found General Moreau, a pair of Murats, and a brace of Napoléons, were one to seek them out. The count de Survilliers, who had been King of Spain, had his own pew in St. Joseph's Church off Willing's alley. We often saw him on the way there of a Sunday, though we ourselves went to St. Mary's, half a block away, for our family had sided with the trustees in the church fight which had resulted in the bishop being locked out of his own cathedral. Charles Lucien Bonaparte, who was a naturalist, could be encountered stalking the marshes at the edge of town or along the river, in forlorn search of a new species of plover or gull to name after himself.

Still, and despite its museums and circuses, its (one) theater and (one) library and (three) waxworks, the city was to a young river rat little more than an endless series of enticements to leave. Everything of any interest at all to me had either come from elsewhere or was outward bound.

But I seem to have lost the thread of my tale. Well, who can blame me? This is no easy thing to speak of. Still, I set out to tell you of my final memory—would to God it were not!—of my father when he was alive.

And so I shall.

My mother and I walked to the hospital together. She led, concentrated and brisk, while I struggled not to lag behind. Several times she glared me back to her side.

For most of that mile-and-some walk from our boardinghouse, I managed not to ask the question most vexing my mind, for fear it would make me sound lacking in a proper filial piety. Leaving the shelter of the Walled City at Market street, we went first south on Front, then up Black Horse alley, while I distracted myself by computing the area between two curves, and then turning down Second past the malt houses and breweries to Chestnut and so west past the Philadelphia Dispensary, where I tried to recall the method Father Tourneaux had taught me for determining the volume of tapering cylindrical solids. South again on Third street, past the tannery and the soap-boiler's shop and chandlery, I thought about Patricia's husband, Aaron, who was in the China trade. Somebody—could it have been Jack?—had recently asked him if he planned someday to employ me as a navigator on one of his ships, and he had laughed in a way that said neither yea nor nay. Which gave me much to ponder. We cut through Willing's alley, my mother being a great believer that distances could be shortened through cunning navigation (I ducked my head and made the sign of the cross as we passed St. Joseph's), and jogged briefly on Fourth. One block up Prune street, a tawny redhead winked at me and ducked down Bingham's court before I could decide whether she were real or just a rogue memory. But I was like the man commanded not to think about a rhinoceros, who found he could think of nothing else. At last, the pressures of curiosity and resentment grew so great that the membrane of my resolve ruptured and burst.

"I do not fully understand," I said, striving for a mature and measured tone but succeeding only in sounding petulant, "exactly what is expected of me." I had not been to see my father—it had been made clear that I was not to see him—since the day he entered the hospital. That same day my littlest sister had fled the house in terror, while this gentlest of men overturned furniture and shouted defiance at unseen demons. The day it was decided he could no longer be cared for at home. "Is today special for any reason? What ought I to do when I see him?"

I did not ask, "Why?" but that was what I meant, and the question my mother answered.

"I have my reasons," she said curtly. "Just as I have good and sufficient reason for not informing you as to their exact nature just yet." We had arrived at the hospital grounds, and the gatekeeper had let us in.

My mother led me down the walk under the buttonwood trees to the west wing. A soft southern breeze alleviated the heat. The hospital buildings were situated within a tract of farmland which had been preserved within the city limits so that the afflicted could refresh themselves with simple chores. Closing my eyes, I can still smell fresh-mown hay, and hear the whir of a spinning wheel. Sunflowers grew by the windows, exactly like that sunflower which had appeared like a miracle one spring between the cobbles of our back alley and lasted into the autumn without being trampled or torn down, drawing goldfinches and sentimental young women. You could not wish for a more pleasant place in which to find your father imprisoned as a lunatic.

The cell-keeper's wife came to the door and smiled a greeting.

My mother thrust a banana into my hand. "Here. You may give him this." Which was the first intimation I had that she was not to accompany me.

She turned and crunched off, down the gravel path.

The cell-keeper's wife led me through the ward to a room reserved for visitors. I cannot recall its furniture. The walls were whitewashed. A horsefly buzzed about in the high corners, irritably seeking a passage into the outer world.

"Wait here," the woman said. "I'll summon an attendant to bring him." She left.

For a long still time I stood, waiting. Eventually I sat down and stared blindly about. Seeing nothing and thinking less. Hating the horsefly.

The banana was warm and brownish yellow in my hand.

Aeons passed. Sometimes there were noises in the hall. Footsteps would approach, and then recede. They were never those of the man I fearfully awaited.

Finally, however, the door opened. There was my father, being led by the arm by a burly young attendant. He shuffled into the room. The attendant placed him in a chair and left, locking the door behind him.

My father, who had always been a rather plump man, with a merchant's prosperous stomach, was now gaunt and lean. His flesh hung loosely about him; where his face had been round, loose jowls now hung.

"Hello, Father," I said.

He did not respond. Nor would he meet my eyes. Instead, his gaze moved with a slow restlessness back and forth across the floor, as if he had misplaced something and were trying to find it.

Miserably, I tried to make conversation.

"Mary finished making her new dress yesterday. It's all of green velvet. The exact same color as that of the cushions and sofa and drapes in Mr. Barclay's parlor. When Mother saw the cloth she had chosen, she said, 'Well, I know one place you won't be wearing that.'"

I laughed. My father did not.

"Oh, and you recall Stephen Girard, of course. He had a cargo of salt at his wharf last summer which Simpson refused to buy—trying to cheapen it to his own price, you see. Well, he said to his porter, 'Tom, why can't you buy that cargo?' and Tom replied, 'Why, sir, how can I? I have no money.' But 'Never mind,' said Girard. 'I'll advance you the cost. Take it and sell it by the load, and pay me as you can.' That was last summer, as I said, and now the porter is well on his way to being Simpson's chief rival in the salt trade."

When this anecdote failed to rouse my father—who had avidly followed the least pulsation in the fortunes of our merchant neighbors, and loved best to hear of sudden success combined with honest labor—I knew that nothing I could hope to say would serve to involve him.

"Father, do you know who I am?" I had not meant to ask—the question just burst out of me.

This roused some spirit in the man at last. "Of course I know. Why wouldn't I know?" He was almost belligerent, but there was no true anger behind his words. They were all bluff and empty bluster and he still would not meet my eyes. "It's as clear as . . . as clear as two plus two is four. That's . . . that's logic, isn't it? Two plus two is four. That's logic."

On his face was the terrible look of a man who had failed his family and knew it. He might not know the exact nature of his sin, but the awareness of his guilt clearly ate away at him. My presence, the presence of someone he ought to know, only made matters worse.

"I'm your son," I said. "Your son, William."

Still he would not meet my eye.

How many hours I languished in the Purgatory of his presence I do not know. I continued to talk for as long as I could, though he obviously could make no sense of my words, because the only alternative to speech was silence—and such silence as was unbearable to think upon. A silence that would swallow me whole.

All the time I spoke, I clutched the banana. There was no place I could set it down. Sometimes I shifted it from one hand to the other. Once or twice I let it lie uncomfortably in my lap. I was constantly aware of it. As my throat went dry and I ran out of things to say, my mind focused itself more and more on that damnable fruit.

My mother always brought some small treat with her when she visited her husband. She would not be pleased if I returned with it. This I knew. But neither did I relish the thought of emphasizing the cruel reversal in our roles, his abject helplessness and my relative ascendancy, by feeding him a trifle exactly as he had so often fed me in my infancy.

In an anguish, I considered my choices. All terrible. All unacceptable.

Finally, more to rid myself of the obligation than because I thought it the right thing to do, I offered the loathsome thing to my father.

He took it.

Eyes averted, he unhurriedly peeled the banana. Without enthusiasm, he bit into it. With animal sadness he ate it.

That is the one memory that, try as I might, I cannot nor ever will be able to forgive myself for: that I saw this once-splendid man, now so sad and diminished, eating a banana like a Barbary ape.

But there's a worse thing I must tell you: For when at last I fell silent, time itself congealed about me, extending itself so breathlessly that it seemed to have ceased altogether. Years passed while the sunlight remained motionless on the whitewashed wall. The horsefly's buzzing ceased, yet I knew that if I raised my head I would see it still hanging in the air above me. I stared at my poor ruined father in helpless horror, convinced that I would never leave that room, that instant, that sorrow. Finally, I squeezed my eyes tight shut and imagined the attendant coming at last to lead my father away and restore me again to my mother.

In my imagination, I burst into tears. It was some time before I could speak again. When I could, I said, "Dear God, Mother! How could you do this to me?"

"I required," she said, "your best estimation of his condition."

"You visit him every day." One of my hands twisted and rose up imploringly, like that of a man slowly drowning. "You must know how he is."

She did not grip my hand. She offered no comfort. She did not apologize. "I have stood by your father through sickness and health," she said, "and will continue to do so for as long as he gains the least comfort from my visits. But I have for some time suspected he no longer recognizes me. So I brought you. Now you must tell me whether I should continue to come here."

There was steel in my mother, and never more so than at that moment. She was not sorry for what she had done to me. Nor was she wrong to have done it.

Even then I knew that.

"Stay away," I said, "and let your conscience be at ease. Father is gone from us forever."

But I could not stop crying. I could not stop crying. I could not stop crying. Back down the streets of Philadelphia I walked, for all to see and marvel at, bawling like an infant, hating this horrible life and hating myself even more for my own selfish resentment of my parents, who were each going through so much worse than I. Yet even as I did so, I was acutely aware that still I sat in that timeless room and that all I was experiencing was but a projection of my imagination. Nor has that sense ever gone entirely away. Even now, if I still my thoughts to nothing, this world begins to fade and I sense myself to still be sitting in my father's absence.

From this terrible moment I fled, and found myself back upon the dory, returning from my father's burial. Our hearts were all light and gay. We chattered as the doryman, head down, plied his oars.

My baby sister Barbara was trailing a hand in the water, a blaze of light where her face should have been, hoping to touch a fish.

"Will," said Mary in a wondering voice. "Look." And I followed her pointing finger upward. I turned toward the east, to the darkening horizon above Treaty Island and the New Jersey shore, where late afternoon thunderheads were gathering.

Scudding before the storm and moving straight our way was a structure of such incredible complexity that the eye could make no sense of it. It filled the sky. Larger than human mind could accept, it bore down upon us like an aerial city out of the Arabian Nights, an uncountable number of hulls and platforms dependent from a hundred or more balloons.

Once, years before, I had seen a balloon ascent. Gently the craft had severed its link with the earth, gracefully ascending into the sky, a floating island, a speck of terrestriality taken up into the kingdom of the air. Like a schooner it sailed, dwindling, and away. It disappeared before it came anywhere near the horizon.

If that one balloon was a schooner, than this was an armada. Where that earlier ship had been an islet, a mote of wind-borne land carried into the howling wilderness of the air, what confronted me now was a mighty continent of artifice.

It was a monstrous sight, made doubly so by the scurrying specks which swarmed the shrouds and decks of the craft and which, once recognized as men, magnified the true size of the thing beyond believing.

The wind shifted, and the thunder of its engines filled the universe.

That was my first glimpse of the mighty airship *Empire*.

The world turned under my restless mind, dispelling sunshine and opening onto rain. Two days casually disappeared into the fold. I was lurching up Chestnut street, water splashing underfoot, arms aching, almost running. Mary trotted alongside me, holding an umbrella over the twenty-quart pot I carried, and still the rain contrived to run down the back of my neck.

"Not so fast!" Mary fretted. "Don't lurch about like that. You'll trip and spill."

"We can't afford to dawdle. Why in heaven's name did Mother have to leave the pot so long over the fire?"

"It's obvious you'll never be a cook. The juices required time to addle; otherwise the stew would be cold and nasty upon arrival."

"Oh, there'll be no lack of heat where we're going, I assure you. Tacey will make it hot enough and then some."

"Get on with you. She won't."

"She will. Tacey is a despot in the kitchen, Napoléon reborn, reduced in stature but expanded in self-conceit. She is a Tiberius Claudius Nero *in parvum* when she has a spoon in her hand. Never since Xanthippe was such a peppery tongue married to such a gingery spirit. A lifetime of kitchen fires have in the kettle of her being combined—"

Mary laughed, and begged me to stop. "You make my sides ache!" she cried. And so of course I continued.

"—to make of her a human pepper pot, a snapper soup seasoned with vinegar, a simmering mélange of Hindoo spices whose effect is to make not one's tongue but one's ears burn. She—"

"Stop, stop, stop!"

Parties were being held all over town in honor of the officers and crew of the *Empire*, and the first aerial crossing of the Atlantic. There were nearly a thousand crewmen all told, which was far too many to be feted within a single building. Mary and I were bound for a lesser gathering at the Library Company, presided over by a minor Biddle and catered by Julius Nash and his crew of colored waiters.

We were within sight of our destination when I looked up and saw my future.

Looming above the Walnut Street Prison yard, tethered by a hundred lines, was the *Empire*, barely visible through the gray sheets of rain. It dwarfed the buildings beneath. Gusts of wind tugged and shoved at the colorless balloons, so that they moved slightly, darkness within darkness, like an uneasy dream shifting within a sleeper's mind.

I gaped, and stepped in a puddle so deep the water went over my boot. Stumbling, I crashed to one knee. Mary shrieked.

Then I was up and hobbling-running again, as fast I could. My trousers were soaked with ice-cold water, and my knee blazed with pain, but at least the pot was untouched.

It was no easy life, being the eldest son in a family dependent upon a failing boardinghouse. Constant labor was my lot. Not that I minded labor—work was the common lot of everyone along the docks, and cheerily enough submitted to. It was the closing of prospects that clenched my soul like an iron fist.

In those days I wanted to fly to the Sun and build a palace on the Moon. I wanted to tunnel to the dark heart of the Earth and discover rubies and emeralds as large as my father's hotel. I wanted to stride across the land in seven-league boots, devise a submersible boat and with it discover a mermaid nation under the sea, climb mountains in Africa and find leopards at their snowy peaks, descend Icelandic volcanos to fight fire-monsters and giant lizards, be marked down in the history books as the first man to stand naked at the North Pole. Rumors that the *Empire* would be signing replacements for those airmen who had died during the flight from London ate at my soul like a canker.

Father Tourneaux had had great hopes that I might one day be called to the priesthood, preferably as a Jesuit, and when I was younger my mother had encouraged this ambition in me with tales of martyrdom by Iroquois torture and the unimaginable splendors of the Vatican state. But, like so much else, that dream had died a slow death with the dwindling and wasting away of my father.

In prosperous times, a port city offered work enough and opportunity in plenty for any ambitious young man. But Philadelphia had not yet recovered from the blockades of the recent war. The posting my brother-in-law had as good as promised me had vanished along with two ships of his nascent fleet, sacrificed to the avarice of British power. The tantalizing possibility that there might be money found to send me to the University of Paris to study mathematics had turned to pebbles and mist as well. My prospects were nonexistent.

Mary grabbed my arm and dragged me around. "Will—you're dreaming again! You've walked right past the doorway."

Tacey Nash saw us come in. Eyes round with outrage, she directed at me a glare that would have stunned a starling, had one been unlucky enough to fly through its beam. "Where have you been?"

I set the pot down on a table, and proceeded to unwrap layers of newspapers and old blanket scraps from its circumference. "Mother insisted that—"

"Don't talk back." She lifted the lid and with it wafted the steam from the stewed oysters toward her nostrils. They flared as the scent of ginger reached them. "Ah." Briefly her face softened. "Your mother still knows how to cook."

One of the waiters placed the pot over a warming stove. Mary briskly tied on an apron—with Patricia married and out of the house, she'd assumed the role of the practical sister and, lacking Patty's organizational genius, tried to compensate with energy—and with a long spoon gave the pot a good stir. Another waiter brought up tureens, and she began filling them.

"Well?" Tacey said to me. "Are you so helpless that you cannot find any work to do?"

So the stew had come in time, after all! Relieved, I glanced over my shoulder and favored my sister with a grin. She smiled back at me, and for one warm instant, all was well.

"Where shall I start?" I asked.

Why was I so unhappy in those days? There was a girl and I had loved her in my way, and thought she loved me, too. One of us tired of the other, and so we quarreled and separated, to the eternal misery of both. Or so I assume—I retain not a jot of this hypothetical affair, but considering my age, it seems inevitable. Yet it was not a romantic malaise I suffered from, but a disease more all-encompassing.

I was miserable with something far worse than love.

I had a hunger within me for something I could neither define nor delimit. And yet at the same time I suffered the queasy fullness of a man who has been at the table one hour too many. I felt as if I had swallowed several live cats which were now proceeding to fight a slow, sick, unending war within me. If I could, I would have vomited up everything—cats, girl, wharves, boarding-house, city, world, my entire history to date—and only felt the better for being rid of them. Every step I took seemed subtly off-balance. Every word I said sounded exactly wrong. Everything about me—my soul, mind, thought, and physical being—was in my estimation thoroughly detestable.

I had no idea then what was wrong with me.

Now I know that I was simply young.

I suppose I should describe that makeshift kitchen, set up within the Loganian Annex of the Library. The warming pans steaming. The elegant black men with their spotless white gloves bustling out with tureens of stew and returning with bowls newly emptied of punch. How, for the body of the meal, the waiters stood behind the airmen (who, though dressed in their finest, were still a raffish lot), refilling their plates and goblets, to the intense embarrassment of everyone save the officers, who were of course accustomed to such service, and how Julius himself stood by the dignitaries' table, presiding over all, with here a quiet signal to top up an alderman's glass and there a solemn pleasantry as he spooned cramberries onto the plate of the ranking officer.

Yet that is mere conjecture. What I retain of that dinner is, first, the order of service and, second, the extraordinary speech that was made at its conclusion, most of which I missed from being involved in a conversation of my own, and its even more extraordinary aftermath. No more. The kitchen, for all of me, may as well not have existed at all.

The menu was as follows:

To begin, *fish-house punch*, drunk with much merriment.

Then, *oyster stew*, my mother's, eaten to take the edge off of appetites and quickly cleared away.

Finally, the dinner itself, in two courses, the first of which was:

> *roasted turkey* stuffed with bread, suet, eggs, sweet herbs
> *tongue pie* made with apples and raisins
> *chicken smothered in oysters* with parsley sauce served with
>   boiled onions
> cramberries
> mangoes
> pickled beans
> celery
> pickled beets
> conserve of rose petals
> braised lambs' quarters
> red quince preserves

Followed by the second course of:

> *trout* poached in white wine and vinegar
> *stew pie* made of veal

alamode round of beef, corned and stuffed with beef, pork,
     bread, butter, salt, pepper, savory, and cayenne; braised,
     served with French beans
parsnips
purple spotted lettuce and salat herbs
pickled cucumbers
spinach
roasted potatoes
summer pears
white, yellow, and red quince preserves

Finally, after the table had been cleared and deserted:

     soft gingerbread
     Indian pudding
     pumpkin pie
     cookies, both almond and cinnamon

Each course of which was, in the manner of the times, served up all at
once in a multitude of dishes, so as to fill the tables completely and impress
the diners with an overwhelming sense of opulence and plenty. Many a
hungry time in my later adventures I would talk myself to sleep by repeating each dish several times over in my mind, recollecting its individual flavor, and imagining myself so thoroughly fed that I turned dishes away
untasted.

Thus do we waste our time and fill our minds with trivialities, while all
the time the great world is falling rapidly into the past, carrying our loved
ones and all we most value away from us at the rate of sixty seconds per
minute, sixty minutes per hour, eight thousand, seven hundred sixty-six
hours per year!

So much for the food. Let me now describe the speech.

The connection between the Loganian and the main library was
through a wide upper-level archway with stairs descending to the floor on
either side of the librarian's desk. It was a striking, if inefficient, arrangement,
which coincidentally allowed us to easily spy upon the proceedings below.

When the final sweets and savories had been placed upon the tables, the
waiters processed up the twin stairs, and passed through the Loganian to a
small adjacent room for a quiet meal of leftovers. I went to the archway to draw
the curtain shut, and stayed within its shadows, looking down upon the scene.

The tables were laid so that they filled the free space on the floor below,
with two shoved together on the eastern side of the room for the officers and

such city dignitaries—selectmen and flour merchants, mostly—who could not aspire to the celebration in Carpenter's Hall. All was motion and animation. I chanced to see one ruffian reach out to remove a volume from the shelves and, seeing a steelpoint engraving he admired, slide the book under the table, rip the page free, and place it, folded, within the confines of his jacket. Yet that was but one moment in such a menagerie of incident as would have challenged the hand of a Hogarth to record.

Somebody stood—Biddle, I presume—and struck an oratorical stance. From my angle, I could see only his back. Forks struck goblets for silence, so that the room was briefly filled with the song of dozens of glass crickets.

The curtains stirred, and Socrates joined me, plate in hand and gloves stuffed neatly into his sash. "Have I missed anything?" he whispered.

I knew Socrates only slightly, as one who was in normal conditions the perfect opposite of his master, Julius: the most garrulous of men, a fellow of strange fancies and sudden laughter. But he looked sober enough now. I shook my head, and we both directed our attention downward.

". . . the late unpleasantness between our two great nations," the speaker was saying. "With its resolution, let the admiration the American people have always held for our British kindred resume again its rightful place in the hearts of us all."

Now the curtains stirred a second time, and Tacey appeared. Her countenance was as stormy as ever. Quietly, she said, "What is this nonsense Mary tells me about you going up Wissahickon to work in a mill?"

There was an odd stirring among the airmen, a puzzled exchange of glances.

Turning away from the speaker, I said, "I intended to say good-bye to you before I left."

"You've been intending to say good-bye to me since the day we met. So you do mean it, then?"

"I'm serious," I admitted.

Those dark, alert eyes flicked my way, and then back. "Oh, yes, you would do well in the mills—I don't think."

"Tacey, I have little choice. There is no work to be had on the wharves. If I stay at home, I burden Mother with the expense of my upkeep, and yet my utmost labor cannot increase her income by a single boarder. She'll be better off with my room empty and put out to let."

"Will Keely, you are a fool. What future can there be for you performing manual labor in a factory? There are no promotions. The mill owners all have five sons apiece—if a position of authority arises, they have somebody close at hand and dear to their hearts to fill it. They own, as well, every dwelling within an hour's walk of the mills. You must borrow from your family to buy your house from them. For years you scrimp, never tasting meat from month to month, working from dawn to dusk, burying pennies in the dirt beneath your bed, with never a hope of earning enough to attract a decent wife. Then the owners declare that there is no longer a market for their goods, and turn out most of their employees. There is no work nearby, so the laborers must sell their houses. Nobody will buy them, however low the price may be, save the mill owners. Who do, for a pittance, because six months later they will begin hiring a new batch of fools, who will squander their savings on the house you just lost."

"Tacey—"

"Oh, I can see the happy crowds now, when you return to the wharves in five years. 'Look,' they will cry, 'here comes the famous factory boy! See how his silver buttons shine. What a handsome coach he drives—General Washington himself never owned so finely matched a sextet of white horses. Behold his kindly smile. He could buy half of New York city with his gold, yet it has not spoiled him at all. All the girls wish to marry him. They can see at a glance that he is an excellent dancer. They tat his profile into lace doilies and sleep with them under their pillows at night. It makes them sigh.'"

So, bickering as usual, we missed most of Biddle's speech. It ended to half-drunken applause and uncertain laughter. The British airmen, oddly enough, did not look so much pleased as bewildered.

After a certain amount of whispering and jostling at the head table, as if no one there cared to commit himself to public speech, a thin and spindly man stood. He was a comical fellow in an old-fashioned powdered wig so badly fitting it must surely have been borrowed, and he tittered nervously before he said, "Well. I thank our esteemed host for that most, ah, unusual— damn me if I don't say peculiar—speech. Two great nations indeed! Yes, perhaps, someday. Yet I hope not. 'Whimsical,' perhaps, is the better word. I shall confine myself to a simple account of our historic passage. . . ."

So the speech progressed, and if the American's speech had puzzled the British officer, it was not half so bewildering as those things he said in return.

He began by applauding Tobias Whitpain, he of world-spanning renown, for the contributions made through his genius to the success of the first trans-Atlantic aerial crossing were matched only by the foresight of Queen Titania herself for funding and provisioning the airship. Isabella was now dethroned, he said, from that heavenly seat reserved for the muse of exploration and science.

"Whitpain?" I wondered. "Queen Titania?"

"What is that you are playing with?" Tacey hissed sharply.

I looked up guiltily. But the question was directed not at me but toward Socrates, who yet stood to my other side.

"Ma'am?" he said, the picture of innocence, as he shoved something into my hand, which, from reflexive habit, I slid quickly into a pocket.

"Show me your hands," she said, and then, "Why are you not working? Get to work."

Socrates was marched briskly off. I waited until both were out of sight before digging out his toy.

It was a small mirror in a cheap, gaudy frame, such as conjure women from the Indies peer into before predicting love and health and thirteen children for gullible young ladies. I held it up and looked into it.

I saw myself.

I saw myself standing in the square below the great stepped ziggurat at the center of Nicnotezpocoatl. Which grand metropolis, serving twice over the population of London herself, my shipmates inevitably called Nignog City. Dear old Fuzzleton was perched on a folding stool, sketching and talking, while I held a fringed umbrella over him, to keep off the sun. He cut a ludicrous figure, so thin was he and so prissily did he sit. But, oh, what a fine mind he had!

We were always talking, Fuzzleton and I. With my new posting, I was in the strange position of being simultaneously both his tutor and student, as well as serving as his bootblack, his confidant, and his potential successor.

"The *Empire* is not safe anchored where it is," he said in a low voice, lest we be overheard by our Aztec warrior guardians. "Fire arrows could be shot into the balloons from the top of the ziggurat. These people are not fools! They've nosed out our weaknesses as effectively as we have theirs. Come the day they fear us more than they covet our airship, we are all dead. Yet Captain Winterjude refuses to listen to me."

"But Lieutenant Blacken promised—," I began.

"Yes, yes, promises. Blacken has ambitions, and plans of his own, as well. We—"

He stopped. His face turned pale and his mouth gaped wide. The stool clattered onto the paving stones, and he cried, "Look!"

I followed his pointing finger and saw an enormous Negro hand cover the sky, eclipsing the sun and plunging the world into darkness.

"Thank you," Socrates said. His face twisted up into a grotesque wink, and he was gone.

I returned my attention to the scene below.

The speaker—old Fuzzleton himself, I realized with a start—was winding up his remarks. He finished by raising a glass high in the air, and crying loudly: "To America!—Her Majesty's most treasured possession."

At those words, every American started to his feet. Hands were clapped to empty belts. Gentlemen searched their coats for sidearms they had of course not brought. There were still men alive who had fought in the War of Independence, and even if there had not been such, memory of the recent war with its burning of Washington and, closer to home, the economically disastrous blockade of American ports was still fresh in the minds of all. Nobody was eager to return to the embrace of a foreign despot; whether king or queen, George or Titania, made no difference. Our freedoms were young enough that all were aware how precariously we held them.

The British, for their part, were fighting men, and recognized hostility when confronted with it. They came to their feet as well, in a very Babel of accusation and denial.

It was at that instant, when all was confusion and violence hovered in the air, that a messenger burst into the room.

Is that poker hot yet? Then plunge it in the wine and let the spices mull. Good. Hand me that. 'Twill help with the telling.

It was the madness of an instant that led me to join the airshipmen's number. Had I taken the time to think, I would not have done it. But ambition was my undoing. I flung my towel away, darted into the kitchen to give my sister a quick hug and a peck on her cheek, and was down the stairs in a bound and a clatter.

In the Library, all was confusion, with the British heading in a rush for the doorway and the Americans holding back out of uncertainty, and fear as well of their sudden ferocity.

I joined the crush for the door.

Out in the cobbled street, we formed up into a loose group. I was jostled and roughly shoved, and I regretted my rashness immediately. The men about me were vague gray shapes, like figures in a dream. In the distance I heard the sound of angry voices.

A mob.

I was standing near the officers and overheard one argue, "It is unwise to leave thus quickly. It puts us in the position of looking as though we had reason to flee. 'Tis like the man seen climbing out his host's bedroom window. Nothing he says will make him look innocent again."

"There is no foe I fear half so much as King Mob," Fuzzleton replied. "March them out."

The officer saluted, spun about, and shouted, "To the ship—double time, on the mark!" Clapping his horny hands together, he beat out the rhythm for a sailor's quick-march, such as I had played at a thousand times as a lad.

Rapidly the airmen began to move away.

Perforce I went with them.

By luck or good planning, we reached the prison yard without encountering any rioters. Our group, which had seemed so large, was but a drop of water to the enormous swirling mass of humanity that had congregated below the airship.

All about me, airmen were climbing rope ladders, or else being yanked into the sky. For every man thus eliminated, a new rope suddenly appeared, bounced, and was seized by another. Meanwhile, lines from the Whitpain engines were being disconnected from the tubs of purified river water, where they had been generating hydrogen.

Somebody slipped a loose loop around me and under my arms and with a sudden lurch I went soaring up into the darkness.

Oh, that was a happy time for me. The halcyon weeks ran one into another, long and languid while we sailed over the American wilderness. Sometimes over seas of forest, other times over seas of plains. There were occasional Indian tribes which—

Eh? You want to know what happened when I was discovered? Well, so would I. As well ask, though, what words Paris used to woo Helen. So much that we wish to know, we never shall! I retain, however, one memory more precious to me than all the rest, of an evening during the crossing of the shallow sea that covers the interior of at least one American continent.

Our shifts done, Hob and I went to the starboard aft with no particular end but to talk. "Sit here and watch the sunset," she said, patting the rail. She leaned against me as we watched, and I was acutely aware of her body and its closeness. My eyes were half-closed with a desire I thought entirely secret when I felt her hand undoing the buttons on my trousers.

"What are you doing?" I whispered in alarm.

"Nothing they don't expect young lads to do with each other now and then. Trust me. So long as you're discreet, they'll none of them remark on't."

Then she had me out and with a little laugh squeezed the shaft. I was by then too overcome with desire to raise any objections to her remarkable behavior.

Side by side we sat on the taffrail, as her hand moved first slowly and then with increasing vigor up and down upon my yard. Her mouth turned up on one side in a demi-smile. She was enjoying herself.

Finally I spurted. Drops of semen fell, silent in the moonlight, to mingle their saltiness with that of the water far below. She bent to swiftly kiss the tip of my yard and then tucked it neatly back into my trousers. "There," she said. "Now we're sweethearts."

My mind follows them now, those fugitive drops of possibility on their long and futile, yet hopeful, flight to the sea. I feel her hand clenching me so casually and yet profoundly. She could not have known how much it meant to me, who had never fired off my gun by a woman's direct intervention before. Yet inwardly I blessed her for it, and felt a new era had opened for me, and swore I would never forget her nor dishonor her in my mind for the sake of what she had done for me.

Little knowing how soon my traitor heart would turn away from her.

But for then I knew only that I no longer desired to return home. I wanted to go on with my Hob to the end of the voyage and back to her thronged and unimaginable London with its Whitpain engines and electrified lighting and surely a place for an emigré from a nonexistent nation who knew (as none of them did) the Calculus.

Somewhere around here, I have a folded and water-damped sheet of foolscap, upon which I apparently wrote down a short list of things I most wished never to forget. I may have lost it, but no matter. I've read it since a hundred times over. It begins with a heading in my uncertain Latin.

> NE OBLIVISCARIS
> 1. My father's burial
> 2. The Aztec Emperor in his golden armor
> 3. Hob's hair in the sunset
> 4. The flying men
> 5. Winterjude's death & what became of his lady
> 6. The air-serpents
> 7. The sound of icebergs calving
> 8. Hunting buffalo with the Apache
> 9. Being flogged
> 10. The night we solved the Whitpain Calculus

Which solution of course is gone forever—else so much would be different now! We'd live in a mansion as grand as the President's, and savants from across the world would come a-calling upon your old father, just so they could tell their grandchildren they'd met the Philadelphia Kepler, the American Archimedes. Yet here we are.

So it is savage irony that I remember that night vividly: the small lantern swinging lightly in the gloom above the table covered with sheet after sheet of increasingly fervid computation—Calculus in my hand and Whitpain equations in Fuzzleton's—and then on one miraculous and almost unreadable sheet both of our hands dashing down formula upon formula in newly invented symbols, sometimes overlapping in the excitement of our reconciliation of the two geniuses.

"D'ye see what this means, boy?" Fuzzleton's face was rapturous. "Hundreds of worlds! Thousands! An infinitude of 'em! This is how the *Empire* was lost and why your capital city and mine are strangers to each other—it explains *everything*!"

We grabbed each other and danced a clumsy little jig. I remember that I hit my head upon a rafter, but what did I care? There would be statues of us in a myriad Londons and countless Philadelphias. We were going to live forever in the mind of Mankind.

My brother-in-law once told me that in China they believe that for every good thing there is an ill. For every kiss a blow. For every dream a nightmare. So perhaps it was because of my great happiness that we shortly thereafter took on board a party of near-naked savages, men and women in equal numbers, to question about the gold ornaments they all wore in profusion about their necks and wrists and ankles.

Captain Winterjude stood watching, his lady by his side and every bit as impassive as he, as the men were questioned by Lieutenant Blacken. They refused to give sensible answers. They claimed to have no knowledge of where the gold came from. They insisted that they didn't know what we were talking about. When the ornaments were ripped from their bodies and shaken in their faces, they denied the gewgaws even existed.

Finally, losing patience, Blacken lined the natives up against the starboard rail. He conferred with the captain, received a curt nod, and ordered two airshipmen to seize the first Indian and throw him overboard.

The man fell to his death in complete silence.

His comrades watched stoically. Blacken repeated his questions. Again he learned nothing.

A second Indian went over the rail.

And so it went until every male was gone, and it was obvious we would learn nothing.

The women, out of compassion I thought at the time, were spared. The next morning, however, it was found that by night all had disappeared. They had slipped over the side, apparently, after their mates. The crew were much discontented with this discovery, and I discovered from their grumbles and complaints that their intentions for these poor wretches had been far from innocent.

Inevitably, we turned south, in search of El Dorado. From that moment on, however, our voyage was a thing abhorrent to me. It seemed to me that we had made the air itself into one vast grave and that, having plunged into it, the *Empire* was now engaged in an unholy pilgrimage through and toward Death itself.

When the Aztecs had been defeated at last and their city was ours, the officers held a banquet to celebrate and to accept the fealty of the vassal chieftains. Hob was chosen to be a serving boy. But, because the clothes of a servitor were tight and thus revealing of gender, she perforce faked an injury, and I took her place instead.

It was thus that I caught the eye of Lady Winterjude.

The widow was a handsome, well-made woman with a black ponytail tied up in a bow. She wore her late husband's military jacket, in assertion of her rights, and it was well known that she was Captain Blacken's chief advisor. As I waited on her I felt her eye upon me at odd moments, and once saw her looking at me with a shocking directness.

She took me, as her unwritten perquisite, into her bed. Thereby and instantly turning Hob into my bitterest enemy, with Captain Blacken not all that far behind.

Forgive me. No, I hadn't fallen asleep. I was just thinking on things. This and that. Nothing that need concern you.

At the time I thought of Lady Winterjude as a monster of evil, an incubus or lamia to whom I was nevertheless drawn by the weakness of my flesh. But of course she was nothing of the kind. Had I made an effort to see her as a fellow human, things might well have turned out differently. For I now believe that it was my very naïveté, the transparency with which I was both attracted to and repelled by her, that was my chief attraction for the lady. Had I but the wit to comprehend this then, she would have quickly set me aside. Lady Winterjude was no woman to allow her weaknesses to be understood by a subordinate.

I was young, though, and she was a woman of appetites.

Which is all I remember of that world, save that we were driven out from it. Before we left, however, we dropped a Union Jack, weighted at the two bottom corners, over the side and into the ocean, claiming the sea and all continents it touched for Britain and Queen Titania.

Only an orca was there to witness the ceremony, and whether it took any notice I greatly doubt.

The *Empire* crashed less than a month after we encountered the air-serpents. They lived among the Aurora Borealis, high above the Arctic mountains. It was frigid beyond belief when we first saw them looping amid the Northern Lights, over and over in circles or cartwheels, very much like the Oriental pictures of dragons. Everybody crowded the rails to watch. We had no idea that they were alive, much less hostile.

The creatures were electrical in nature. They crackled with power. Yet when they came zigzagging toward us, we suspected nothing until two balloons were on fire, and the men had to labor mightily to cut them away before they could touch off the others.

We fought back not with cannons—the recoil of which would have been disastrous to our fragile shells—but with rockets. Their trails crisscrossed the sky, to no effect at first. Then, finally, a rocket trailing a metal chain passed through an air-dragon and the creature discharged in the form of a great lightning bolt, down to the ground. For an instant we were dazzled, and then, when we could see again, it was no more.

Amid the pandemonium and cheers, I could have heard no sound to alert me. So it was either a premonition or merest chance that caused me to turn at that moment, just in time to see Hob, her face as hate filled as any demon's, plunge a knife down upon me.

Eh? Oh, I'm sure she did. Your mother was never one for halfway gestures. I could show the scar if you required it. Still, I'm alive, eh? It's all water under the bridge. She had her reasons, to be sure, just as I had mine. Anyway, I didn't set out to explain the ways of women to you, but to tell of how the voyage ended.

We were caught in a storm greater than anything we had encountered so far. I think perhaps we were trapped between worlds. Witch fires danced on the ropes and rails. Balloons went up in flames. So dire was our situation and sure our peril that I could not hold it in my mind. A wild kind of exaltation filled me, an almost Satanic glee in the chaos that was breaking the airship apart.

As Hob came scuttling across my path, I swept her into my arms and, unheeding of her panicked protests, kissed her! She stared, shocked, into my eyes, and I laughed. "Caroline," I cried, "you are the woman or lass or lad or whatever you might be for me. I'd kiss you on the lip of Hell itself, and if you slipped and fell in, I'd jump right after you."

Briefly I was the man she had once thought me and I had so often wished I could be.

Hob looked at me with large and unblinking eyes. "You'll never be free of me now," she said at last, and then jerked away and was gone, back to her duty.

For more than a month I wandered the fever lands, while the Society for the Relief of Shipwrecked Sailors attended to my needs. Of the crash itself I remember nothing. Only that hours before it I arrived at the bridge to discover that poor dear old Fuzzleton was dead.

Captain Blacken, in his madness, had destroyed the only man who might conceivably have returned him to his own port of origin.

"Can you navigate?" he demanded fiercely. "Can you bring us back to London?"

I gathered up the equations that Fuzzleton and I had spent so many nights working up. In their incomplete state, they would bring us back to Philadelphia—if we were lucky—but no further. With anything less than perfect luck, however, they would smear us across a thousand worlds.

"Yes," I lied. "I can."

I set a course for home.

And so at last, I came upon my father's grave. It was a crisp black rectangle in the earth, as dark and daunting as oblivion itself. Without any hesitation, I stepped through that lightless doorway. And my eyes opened.

I looked up into the black face of a disapproving angel.

"Tacey?" I said wonderingly.

"That's *Mrs. Nash* to you," she snapped. But I understood her ways now, and when I gratefully clasped her hand, and touched my lips to it, she had to look away, lest I think she had changed in her opinion of me.

Tacey Nash was still one of the tiniest women I had ever seen, and easily the most vigorous. The doctor, when he came, said it would be weeks before I was able to leave the bed. But Tacey had me nagged and scolded onto my feet in two days, walking in three, and hobbling about the public streets on a cane in four. Then, on the fifth day, she returned to her husband, brood, and anonymity, vanishing from my life forever, as do so many people in this world to whom we owe so much more than will ever be repaid.

When word got out that I was well enough to receive visitors, the first thing I learned was that my brother was dead. Jack had drowned in a boating accident several years after I left. A girl whose face was entirely unknown to me told me this—my mother, there also, could not shush her in time—and told me as well that she was my baby sister Barbara.

I should have felt nothing. The loss of a brother one does not know is, after all, no loss at all. But I was filled with a sadness wholly inexplicable but felt from the marrow outward, so that every bone, joint, and muscle ached with the pain of loss. I burst into tears.

Crying, it came to me then, all in an instant, that the voyage was over.

The voyage was over and Caroline had not survived it. The one true love of my life was lost to me forever.

So I came here. I could no longer bear to live in Philadelphia. The gems in my pocket, small though they might be compared to those I'd left behind, were enough to buy me this house and set me up as a merchant. I was known in the village as a melancholy man. Indeed, melancholy I was. I had been through what would have been the best adventure in the world, were it not ruined by its ending—by the loss of the *Empire* and all its hands, and above all the loss of my own dear and irreplaceable Hob.

Perhaps in some other, and better, world she yet survived. But not in mine.

Yet my past was not done with me yet.

On a cold, wet evening in November, a tramp came to my door. He was a wretched, fantastical creature, more kobold than human, all draped in wet rags and hooded so that only a fragment of nose poked out into the meager light from my doorway.

Imploringly, the phantasm held out a hand and croaked, "Food!"

I had not the least thought that any danger might arise from so miserable a source, and if I had, what would I have cared? A violent end to a violent life—I would not have objected. "Come inside," I said to the poor fellow, "out of the rain. There's a fire in the parlor. Go sit there, while I warm something up."

As the beggar gratefully climbed the stairs, I noticed that he had a distinct limp, as if a leg had been broken and imperfectly healed.

I had a kettle steaming in the kitchen. It was the work of a minute to brew the tea. I prepared a tray with milk and sugar and ginger, and carried it back to the front of the house.

In the doorway to the parlor I stopped, frozen with amazement. There, in that darkened room, a hand went up and moved the hood down. All the world reversed itself.

I stumbled inside, unable to speak, unable to think.

The fire caught itself in her red hair. She turned up her cheek toward me with that same impish smile I loved so well.

"Well, mate," she said. "Ain't you going to kiss me?"

The fire is all but done. No, don't bother with another log. Let it die. There's nothing there but ashes anyway.

You look at your mother and you see someone I do not—a woman who is old and wrinkled, who has put on some weight, perhaps, who could never have been an adventurer, a rogue, a scamp. Oh, I see her exterior well enough, too. But I also see deeper.

I love her in a way you can't possibly understand, nor ever will understand unless someday many years hence you have the good fortune to come to feel the same way yourself. I love her as an old and comfortable shoe loves its mate. I could never find her equal.

And so ends my tale. I can vouch for none of it. Since the fever, I have not been sure which memories are true and which are fantasy. Perhaps only half of what I have said actually happened. Perhaps none of it did. At any rate, I have told you it all.

Save for one thing.

Not many years later, and for the best of reasons, I sent for the midwife. My darling Caroline was in labor. First she threw up, and then the water broke. Then the Quaker midwife came and chased me from the room. I sat in the parlor with my hands clasped between my knees and waited.

Surely hours passed while I stewed and worried. But all I recall is that somehow I found myself standing at the foot of my wife's child-bed. Caroline lay pale with exhaustion. She smiled wanly as the midwife held up my son for me to see.

I looked down upon that tiny creature's face and burst into tears. The tears coursed down my face like rain, and I felt such an intensity of emotion as I can scarce describe to you now. It was raining outside, they tell me now, but that is not how I recall it. To me the world was flooded with sunshine, brighter than any I had ever seen before.

The midwife said something; I paid her no mind. I gazed upon my son.

In that moment I felt closer to my father than ever I had before. I felt that finally I understood him and knew what words he would have said to me if he could. I looked down on you with such absolute and undeviating love as we in our more hopeful moments pray that God feels toward us, and silently I spoke to you.

Someday, my son, I thought, you will be a man. You will grow up and by so doing turn me old, and then I will die and be forgotten. But that's all right. I don't mind. It's a small price to pay for your existence.

Then the midwife put you into my arms, and all debts and grudges I ever held were canceled forever.

There's so much more I wish I could tell you. But it's late, and I lack the words. Anyway, your trunk is packed and waiting by the door. In the morning you'll be gone. You're a man yourself, and about to set off on adventures of your own. Adventures I cannot imagine, and which afterward you will no more be able to explain to others than I could explain mine to you. Live them well. I know you will.

And now it's time I was abed. Time, and then some, that I slept.

# of love and other monsters

VANDANA SINGH

In the lyrical, complex, and compassionate story that follows, we learn that it's possible to weave minds together the way that you weave thread. The question is, given that peculiar kind of thread to work with, what do you *make* from it? A gorgeous multicolored tapestry? Or something considerably bleaker, black and white, dyed red around the edges with blood?

New writer Vandana Singh was born and raised in India and currently resides with her family in the United States, where she teaches physics and writes. Her stories have appeared in several volumes of *Polyphony*, as well as in *Strange Horizons, InterNova, Foundation 100, Rabid Transit, Interfictions, Mythic, Trampoline,* and *So Long Been Dreaming*. She's published a children's book in India, *Younguncle Comes to Town*. The chapbook version of *Of Love and Other Monsters* has just appeared, as has her first collection, *The Woman Who Thought She Was a Planet and Other Stories*.

W hen I think about him I remember a wave I watched near a beach once, a big, beautiful, smooth wave, perfectly rounded, like molten glass. It came into a narrow channel from the open sea, muscular and purposeful, hardly breaking into surf. I thought it would climb all the way up the end of the channel, wash over me, and carry on, unbroken, till it crossed the entire Deccan peninsula. But it met the sand, rolled over it, little traceries of white disturbing its smooth, translucent aspect. Touched my toes, broke up into little tongues of froth, and dissipated. So I like to think of him—Sankaran, I mean—like a wave that came out of the ocean for a while to fulfill some purpose (whatever that was). Then he was lost to me.

Physicists have a name for that kind of wave. It is very unusual, and it is called a soliton, or solitary wave.

When, as a young man, I met Sankaran for the first time, I thought he was the one I had been searching for all my conscious life. But as the poet Faiz says, there are more sorrows in the world than love. As soon as I had settled into a certain youthful complacency, the world and its attendant sorrows got in the way.

The study of minds, soliton-like or otherwise, is my particular passion. Mind-sensing, mind-weaving—these extraordinary abilities set me apart from other people. I like to go into a gaggle of housewives bargaining over turnips or a crowd at a cricket match. I drift about, trying to determine what kind of entity the crowd has the potential to become. I take the embryological possibility of the meta-mind, make a joining here, a parting there; I wave my baton like the conductor of an orchestra and sense a structure, a form, coalesce in the interactions of these knots of persons. The meta-mind I construct has a vague unity of purpose, a jumble of contradictory notions, and even a primitive self-awareness.

Which is why I am so disturbed by solitons. They walk into a meta-mind as though nothing were there, and they walk out, unaffected. They give nothing, nor do they take away.

Such was Sankaran-with-stars-in-his-eyes, Sankaran the astronomer. This is not his story, however—his is just one thread in the tapestry, one voice in the telling. This is my story, and it begins when I was (so I am told) seventeen years old.

The first thing I remember is fire. The next thing: a pair of big, strong hands stroking and kneading me. A woman's voice, saying, "Come now, be so, be still. . . ." I was lying on a bed of warm ash, with sharp bits digging into my back.

I have no recollection of my life before the conflagration took my memory and identity. What I am now began with fire, with a woman called Janani, on a summer night in the remote outskirts of a small town in eastern India. Some time later, when I came to my senses, the stars were out, and the air smelled of roasted coriander seeds and cow dung, as it does most nights over there. I was lying on a cot in the little yard behind Janani's shack. Everything, including my lean, dark body, was unfamiliar to me.

My rescuer, Janani—a widow who ran a toddy shop—took me in and helped me face my predicament. The first thing she did after I recovered was to give me a name: Arun, which (like everything in those early days) sounded strange to me. "It means 'red,'" she told me. "You were born of fire." In those days I could sense the ghost of my past self very faintly: I saw symbols, words, numbers, shapes, as though scratched in damp clay. "Who am I? What happened to me in the fire?" I asked her. My voice sounded rasping and unfamiliar. The Hindi syllables felt strange on my tongue, but the words were there in my mind, waiting for me.

"I cannot tell you," she said. "There was a fire in an abandoned building, and I rescued you. You are not a local. That's all there is to know."

Without an identity I had nowhere to go, no family. Nobody in the area recognized me. So Janani gave me a home. I slept in the front of her hut, which was the toddy shop. Oh, the strangeness of those days!

It was like learning to live again. She had to show me how to take a twig from the neem tree behind the hut and use it like a toothbrush. I learned how to use a toilet, how to chop onions, how to talk to customers. Janani made a living not just from selling toddy but also by dispensing herbs for ailments from stomachaches to unrequited love, and I had to learn the lore enough to know which bottle to bring out when she asked for it. I had to learn to recognize my own face in the mirror—I would stand before the little mirror on the wall and pull faces until she yelled at me, "Arun, you fool! Did I pull you out of the fire so you could admire your beauty all day?" And she would set me to work washing glasses or chopping herbs. The ghost of my past self stayed in the shadows of my mind, and I found myself thinking less and less of what my old life might have been. At that time all was new, strange, and endlessly fascinating—not least of which was my ability to sense minds.

I was idle by nature and by the nature of my ability, which was distracting to say the least. Janani insisted on educating me; from her I learned my letters and arithmetic, which seemed to come very easily to me. She also got a retired clerk who frequented the tea shack nearby to teach me a little about history, geography, and the rudiments of the English language. I would have liked nothing better than to loiter all day in the marketplace, but Janani's sharp tongue kept me at my chores and lessons, at least until her back was turned. She was stocky and strong; she moved with the cadence of a large, slow river, sweeping up everything in her path. Her customers, work-worn laborers and ne'er-do-wells, feared her and confided their woes to her. Only once did I see her take a man into the dark room behind the shop where she slept. After several hours he came out, staggering, smiled vaguely at me, handed me a ten-rupee note, and left. He never came back.

My favorite place, where I learned and practiced what I considered to be my art, was the market; here the vendors squatted on the ground before their baskets full of gourds, peppers, eggplants, and onions, shouting, "Rob me! Loot me! Only three rupees a kilo!" I grew to appreciate the sweaty housewives with their glinting eyes, their bright saris hitched up in readiness for battle as they began insulting the produce. Pride, honor, and desire amidst the tottering, shining piles of luscious fruits and vegetables—how could I resist? I sensed the convoluted topography of each mind, its hills, valleys, areas of light and darkness, the whole animal mass trembling and shifting with emotional fluxes. After some practice I was able to draw the minds into a kind of net, to weave the separate threads of jangling thought processes into—not a tapestry, I was never that skilled, but a jumble of knitting wool, such as a kitten might do. There was little awareness among the separate minds that they were, at this point in space and time, tentatively the members of a rather confused meta-mind—how many cells in your body, but for a specialized few, are aware of themselves as part of a higher consciousness?

I once tried to draw Janani into a meta-mind with a couple of her customers, but she came into the back of her shop and cuffed me. "Don't you try that on me, you good-for-nothing! Is this how you repay me?" I had already guessed (from the fact that nobody had tried it on me and that my subjects seemed to be so unaware of what I was doing) that this ability of mine was unique, but I didn't know that Janani knew I had it. Later she explained that she did not possess my ability—indeed, she had come across only one other person who did—but she was a sensitive. She could tell when someone, especially a crude beginner like me, was trying tricks.

"Who's this other person?" I asked, intrigued.

"You don't need to know anything about him," she told me. "Just somebody I met once. He wasn't a nice man."

She wouldn't tell me more. But I realized then that the world was more complex than I'd thought; at least one other person had my peculiar talent, most didn't, and some could sense my mind reaching out to theirs.

I spent all my spare time wandering about the narrow green lanes of my neighborhood under the *gulmohar* trees, scuffing up soft, silken dust with my bare toes. In the muddy by-lanes I gambled at marbles with other boys and gawked with them over the calendar of dewy-eyed film stars hanging in the neighborhood tea shack. I learned about sex and desire by watching the pariah dogs in the streets and the way the older boys looked at the unreachable, uniformed schoolgirls passing by with pigtails swinging. My own longings were nebulous. I could look at the tea seller's daughter—a sloe-eyed vixen with a sharp tongue and a ready vocabulary of swear words—and tell that underneath it all was a mind as fragile as a spider's web, tense with fear and need. I felt drawn to her, but then there was also the barber, a thin, clean-shaven young fellow, shy and subdued to all appearances. He distracted me every time I passed the place where he had set up shop: a mirror hung on a wall by the street with a chair in front of it, where he sat his customers down and ministered to their heads or beards. His mind was luscious, imaginative, erotic; I could not read his thoughts, but I could sense the nature of them: desire flowed with the rise and fall of his fingers, the shy caress of his hands on the cheek of a customer. Both my mind and body responded to the needs of such men and women around me; sometimes I would get aroused simply walking down the street, feeling the brush of their minds like feathers on my skin. Due to the crowded, public nature of our lives and the narrowness of convention, there was little hope of physical consummation — only the occasional groping in dark alleyways among us boys — but I could reach out with my mind and make a bridge, a connection as tangible to me as a touch. Most did not have the ability to sense this, but once the tea seller's daughter looked up at me, startled, her eyes as clear and honest as a small child's, as though she, too, had felt the electricity between our minds. Then her habitual aloofness slipped over her face like a mask, and the moment was gone.

There was a game I liked to play: I would lie on the broad branch of a large neem tree that grew near the tea shop, close my eyes, and try to guess who was passing below me from their mind-signature. If the person was a stranger, the mind-signature told me nothing of their identity, not even if they were male or female — but a well-known person was like the familiar topography of the street you grew up on.

Despite my persistent questions, Janani refused to tell me about the other person she knew who had my ability. "I hope you never meet him," she would say with a shudder.

Then one night he found me.

I had just finished sweeping out the shop when I sensed something odd, as though a tendril had insinuated itself into my mind; at the same time I became aware that there was someone outside the door, just standing and waiting in the darkness. Janani must have felt it too, because she looked at me in sudden apprehension. I felt the tug of a mind far more sophisticated than my own, pulling me into the labyrinths of its own consciousness like a fisherman drawing in his line. I got up and began walking toward the front of the shop as if in a dream. Janani, who was obviously less affected than I, grabbed me and pushed me out the back door, into the quiet darkness of her vegetable garden. "Arun, you fool, get out of here!" she whispered fiercely against my cheek. I willed myself to put one foot before another. I climbed across the bamboo fence. Every step I took made me stronger and more able to resist.

When I returned, Janani was sitting on the shop floor, rocking to and fro. Her hair was unkempt, her sari crumpled, and she kept saying, "Rama, oh, Rama," in a soft monotone. A great wave of anger and fear swept over me.

"Who was that? What did he do?"

"That was Rahul Moghe. The only other person I know who has your talent. He is dangerous, and he wants you, God knows for what terrible purpose. You must avoid him. You will know him not by his appearance, which can be deceptive, but by the way he drags at your mind without warning.

"He has threatened me. Now this place is no longer safe for either of us. I must think what to do. . . ."

That was the first and only time Janani took me to her bed, to the comfort of her dark, Himalayan breasts that smelled of cloves and cinnamon. She was like an earthquake and a tidal wave rolled into one. Afterward, I heard her mutter to herself, "Surely it doesn't matter with him; he's different. . . ." In the morning she flung me summarily out of her bed and began to pack.

"This is a sign that we must part ways. I have taught you what I can. You will go out into the world and make something of yourself, and keep away from Moghe. I have some money I have been saving for you. Meanwhile I will sell this place and go live with a friend in Rishikesh. Keep in touch with me, because I want to know how you are faring. I have some of your things in a safe place. I will send them to you when I can."

"What things?"

"Things from before the fire. Don't worry about it now. You must go to the next town and get a job. I know a place . . ."

Which is how I found myself living in a tiny room over a tailor's shop in the neighboring town. It was a tranquil time for me. I helped the tailor with deliveries, and after a while he made me a pair of pants and a shirt so I could look like a respectable young man instead of a drifter with holes in his clothes. Eventually (prompted by a barrage of letters from Janani) I got a job as a clerk at a computer training institute. Here my quick brain and my lessons with Janani and the old clerk paid off; over the next year I improved my English and began to help the system administrator with computer maintenance work. The work was enjoyable and came to me easily.

"Arun, foolish one," Janani wrote. "You are no longer a street waif with few prospects. Here is your chance to make something of yourself. I'm sending money for classes. Learn computers and get a proper job; every idiot is doing it." So I registered for a couple of classes and found that I had a knack for programming. Numbers, symbols, instructions, logic—it was as though I had once known this, or something like this, in my old life. Encouraged by the students, who looked upon me as a project of their own, I began to study full-time. Although I had no formal education and was unused to discipline, I made progress with their help. In the hot, dusty little classrooms with the squeaky ceiling fans and traffic sounds from the open windows, I was able to shut out other minds and concentrate. Slowly I began to write, decipher, and debug computer code. In a few months other students were asking me for help. My life changed.

Back in my bare little room I would lie on my sagging bed and listen to the voices from the shop below, the lulling rhythm of the sewing machines, and play at making meta-minds. "Arun," I would tell myself, "in two years you've come a long way." But my laziness, held at bay by the unaccustomed intellectual stimulation, reasserted itself eventually. Instead of pursuing a full degree I opted for a mere diploma, which greatly disappointed Janani as well as some of my teachers.

But the change in my life, in this short, intense period, had opened me up to the possibilities of the world. I read voraciously in Hindi and English, learning about foreign countries and customs, and the wars and plagues of history. From lurid Hindi science fiction to paperback English romances, there was nothing that was not grist for my mill. I came to realize that sensing other minds through the written word was almost as interesting a skill as my unique, innate ability to sense them directly. Writing—whether English or Hindi or computer code—was the key that opened the doors to other minds, other lands. Like a monk on leave from the monastery, I was agape with wonder. For the first time I realized that there were many ways to be a foreigner; losing one's memory, being poor, being illiterate, were just some of them.

Meanwhile I continued to get letters and packages from Janani. She was now a seamstress in Rishikesh. She wrote that she was gradually retrieving and returning my things, such as they were, from before the fire. The things made no sense. There were some photographs that she had apparently taken herself: a great, dazzling wall of flame, an enormous log in the foreground, glowing with the heat. Pieces of abstract ceramic sculpture, remains of etchings. Had I been an artist? There was nothing remotely artistic about me now. I looked at my hands, my body, clean and healed by Janani's ministrations. I did not even have any scars. I looked at the other photos she had sent of teenage boys looking into the camera. One of them was me. The others looked vaguely familiar. Had they been my friends in that unknown life?

But I was too busy with my new life to pay much attention to my erstwhile possessions. Not long after receiving my diploma, I got a job checking software for defects and moved to the great, crowded metropolis of New Delhi. Janani was ecstatic. "A great step up in the world, Arun!" she wrote, exulting. And in many ways it was so. Flush with success—the job was easy for me and not too demanding—and with a new sense of my place in the world, I settled down in my new life. It was during this time that I began to explore my extraordinary mental abilities in a more methodical manner.

One of my early discoveries was that there were minds that were completely closed to me, different from the kind of mental resistance I'd felt with Janani. There were people who would be standing with the crowd outside the cricket stadium, apparently as excited about the impending match as anybody else, but they did not register on my radar. I was greatly troubled by such minds—blanks, I called them. I feared and distrusted them. It seemed that my skill had its limitations. But the solitons were different. I sensed them, all right, but I could not draw them in. Their minds moved through my jumbled meta-mind the way a man walks through a large, empty field on his way home. Quickly, cleanly, with his attention elsewhere. Taking nothing, leaving nothing behind.

The first one I experienced was at a rally at the Red Fort in Delhi. The prime minister was up on the ramparts in a bullet-proof box, speechifying about the latest war. Seventeen thousand people with nothing better to do—college students, farmers with harvests lost in the drought, clerks on their way to important errands, unemployable sons of rich men and other wastrels, street people and pickpockets—had been rounded up by the party men. As the prime minister's rhetoric became more passionate, I sensed the minds, at first relaxed and disjointed like a bunch of loose rubber bands, becoming like angry bees buzzing in concert. Not very interesting—too simple, but also dangerous. I put my hands over my ears, but I could not shut them out; it was as though I were being blinded and deafened at the same time. Stumbling away through the crowd, I was pushed and cursed as I pressed on. And the realization hit: the meta-mind had formed of its own accord. I had not done it. That is why I couldn't make it stop. What such a self-generating meta-beast could do, who knew? The crowd surged around me, thrusting and clawing at me. I imagined the monster going out into the streets, maiming and killing, crying for blood. As my own mind dissolved into chaos, something strange and wonderful happened. I sensed a deep and momentary stilling in my mind, as though I had crossed a great, noisy battlefield into a waterfall of peace. Just for one glorious moment. Then the bees hummed in my head again, and it was all I could do to stagger about like a drunk at the fringes of the crowd, looking for that person. Useless, of course. Who walked so cleanly through the mad tangle that was the meta-beast, like a monk striding serenely through the sinful glitter of the world?

I learned later that there are only a few people like Sankaran, and that for very brief periods of time all people are like that. But some sustain that state of mind for most of their waking life. A cobbler mending shoes in front of a cinema hall in Bombay. A mathematician walking, seeing not the world but equations and things. A mother, single-minded about her ailing son. A lover in a dusty old garden, oblivious to roses. Yes, later I understood this state of mind.

Life in the big city was never boring. There was scope for my abilities, and they led me into unexpected adventures. One time, while strolling through the fort city of Old Delhi, I came upon a young girl standing in a doorway. She was a waif, barely in her teens, incongruously dressed in a bright red *salwaar kameez* that was too big for her. The narrow street was full of people and noise, bicycle bells and the calls of fruit sellers, and the light had the dazzling clarity of high summer. Seeing her in the dark archway of an old building with the sunlight washing her thin face, I felt the anguish of her mind like a blow between the eyes. I sensed a hopelessness so absolute that instinctively I moved toward her. She drew back from me, and a man appeared out of the shabby darkness of what I then realized was a brothel.

That was how I met Dulari. My rescue of her involved most of my meager savings (her price) and a local women's group. She was eventually given a job at a clothing shop that employed dozens of emaciated young women to sew name-brand clothes for overseas markets. I went to see her occasionally, but most of the time guilt made me stay away. Although her life was better than before, it was still no life for a fourteen-year-old girl. But I was now a member of the middle class. I had to pretend to a certain decorum. Besides, I lived in a tiny room sublet to me by a large and boisterous Punjabi family. Dulari had no place in my life.

But I could not hide from myself the fact that I could have loved her. She was a child, and it was not appropriate, but I saw past her painfully thin, broken body into her mind. She was like the proverbial lotus that grows in murky water; its roots are soiled, but it climbs upward, bifurcating into petals that open to the sky. Under the scars, a part of her was untouched by the privations and humiliations of her life; there was intelligence, hope, and layers of wonderful complexity and potential that perhaps would never find expression.

My colleague Manek was another matter entirely. He was well educated, had prospects, and was earning a reasonable salary. His mind—I could never look upon a person as simply a corporeal entity—was clean and simple, like an orderly room, and his thoughts and emotions were often quite transparent. One day, I sensed that he was depressed and asked him about it. In his simple, direct way, he told me that he was in love with a young woman he could not marry. There were caste and class issues, and his beloved's family was keeping guard round the clock so the couple could no longer meet. To make matters worse, his parents were now looking for a suitable girl for him. Naturally I became Manek's confidant.

That summer my landlord and his family decided to go home to their village in Punjab for the holidays. They padlocked all the doors in the apartment except for my room, the kitchen, and the bathroom and left me to a peace and privacy I had never before enjoyed.

So Manek came to see me at home. One day he was near tears and I put my arms around him to comfort him. After that we became lovers after a fashion. He was not gay, he said, but he wanted me to pretend to be a woman, to be held, caressed, and comforted. In his mind the illusion was so complete that as I lay with him, I could almost feel the swell of my breasts. Meanwhile I touched his mind with my own, furtively, tentatively. I think our occasional mental contact helped him relax, although he could not directly sense the tendrils of my mind. With his face buried against my bare shoulder he would whisper the names of all the women he had loved from afar, ending with Anjana, his beloved.

Later there was Sheela, a quiet mouse of a woman, the older unmarried daughter of a couple who lived in the flat above. Her sisters were married off; she was the plain one, apparently, so there was not much hope that she would find someone. In her lovemaking, as in her mind, she was bold, imaginative, and tender, but everything she said was by touch or glance. During our few assignations she never spoke a word. Once I broke our pact of silence by uttering the word "love." She sat up on the bed, stared at me, her wide eyes filling with angry tears. "Don't you dare say that word ever again," she said fiercely. She leaped upon me and began to pull off my shirt. The dark places in her mind deepened, trembled; caves opened like mouths; rivers of emotion roared in the gorges, the hidden places of her soul. She was fascinating, but she did not want me. Ultimately, fate in the form of a divorced man looking for a wife took her away to some far city and another life.

Sometimes I worried about how different I was from other young men. I looked and dressed like a man, but I did not understand social conventions about what it meant to be a man or a woman. I could go out with other young men to seedy bars and drink beer, but I did not know that the women there were for flirting with, or that I should outshout the other men in a bid to impress. I would sit down with a woman and ask her about her work, or about the embroidery on her blouse. Women colleagues found that when I was the only male present they could talk as easily about "women" things as if they were by themselves; once I took part in a discussion about their periods, even though my role was only that of interested questioner. "God, Arun, you're too much," they would say, suddenly remembering I was a man. I watched cooking shows with as much curiosity as cricket and wrestling. My ability to sense minds enabled me to see human beings as entities beyond man-woman categories. I decided, after some months of informal study, that rather than two sexes there were at least thirty-four. Perhaps "sex" or "gender" isn't right—perhaps a geographical term would be more appropriate— thirty-four climactic zones of the human mind!

But my peculiarities occasionally made me wonder about my future. My colleagues were falling in love, getting engaged, getting married. To me, each job was like a temporary resting place before the next thing, as was each relationship. Would my restlessness be my undoing? Janani dismissed my fears. "You are young," she wrote in a letter. "Learn about the world, Arun. Embrace it. Love as many people as you can, but don't let anyone keep you like a bird in a cage."

By the time I met Sankaran I had learned a lot. Never to go to political rallies, for one thing. Or religious processions, although temples, churches, *gurudwaras*, and mosques were all right in small doses. I had also learned that contrary to what you might expect, families do not generally make good metaminds. There is too much pushing and shoving about. They coalesce and come apart. Maybe they maintain a dynamic rather than a static equilibrium, because they are, after all, with each other day in and day out. Perhaps a metamind, indefinitely sustained, eventually goes mad.

I also did some experimenting with animals. There was a herd of cows that foraged in the street outside my apartment complex. They stood in the midst of traffic like humped, white islands, peacefully chewing cuds, or waited with bovine patience for people to dump their kitchen refuse at the corner garbage dump. I sensed their minds but did not understand the nature of their thoughts. One night, returning from work, I saw a magnificent bull standing in the middle of the road, on the median. Traffic swept by him on either side. In the luminous dust under the street lamps, he was like a great white ghost. Across the road the cows lay regarding him with indifference. I sensed his mind as clearly as if it had been visible. He was calling to the cows with all he had, a long, soundless low of desire. The cows' response was, in effect, *Not today, pal, we have cud to chew.* It was then that I realized that animals could not only sense each other's minds but also communicate mentally.

I continued my experiments with human minds, learning all kinds of interesting trivia. For instance, odd numbers, especially primes, make more stable meta-beasts; even numbers are less steady, especially if there are only two people involved. Couples are really dangerous, because there is nothing to balance the connection between the minds, no push to counter the pull, if you know what I mean. Which is why, long before I met Sankaran, I had decided never to fall in love.

I met him in America. Janani encouraged me to go there after she heard from a fellow sensitive that Rahul Moghe had been seen in Chandigarh, only a few hours' drive from Delhi. I felt the old, nameless fear again. I had not thought about Rahul Moghe in years. At that time my company was exporting a team of software people to the United States. Urged by a fury of letters from Janani, I joined the exodus to the land of milk and honey.

In America's small towns, with their abnormally clean streets so strangely empty of people and animals, in the surreal, neon-bright canyons of vast sky-scrapered cities, I found that I could further explore my ability to make meta-minds. Despite the much-touted individualism of Americans, I often encountered large groups of people with similar belief systems and mental processes. In the beginning it was vastly entertaining; I walked down Wall Street, peered in at the Stock Exchange. All those people, thinking themselves competitors and rivals, muttering into cell phones and shouting like deranged children—what a seamless, stable meta-mind they made! Then there was suburban America, yuppie-ville, with the over-large houses and multiple cars and boats, where it was just too easy. Teenagers expressing their individuality in their name-brand clothing and angst-ridden looks were easy, too, but there was a dark undercurrent in that meta-mind that disturbed me, hinting of dams upstream about to burst. I amused myself making meta-minds out of warring groups of political opponents and fundamentalist religious types with opposing loyalties. My own community of Indians, with few exceptions, lived in a time warp, adopting conventions and practices that no longer existed in India. Their constant obsession with their status as high-earning professionals was boring. Far more interesting were splinter groups living on the edge of mainstream culture; I made friends with Wiccans, Mexican immigrants, and an Ethiopian gay couple that ran a restaurant in San Francisco. I lived in California at first, working as little as I could get by with, indulging my special ability to the hilt. Despite all this I felt a deep and increasing loneliness at the back of my mind, a longing not just for my old haunts in India, for old friends and people I had known, but for something beyond that. Already I was making a shape, a place, for Sankaran inside me.

Then something happened that drove me from California. One bright Saturday morning I was swimming about in the shallows near a beach when I felt an undertow. I began to struggle against it; then I realized that it was in my mind. A powerful tug, reeling me in as though I were an exhausted fish. I recognized the summons that would not be denied. Rahul Moghe had found me at last.

I emerged from the water and found myself compelled to walk between sunbathers and colorful beach umbrellas toward a car parked on the road above the beach. I tried to stop, or to ask for help, but I was as helpless as a mannequin. As I came near the road one part of my mind noted that the car was a white sedan with tinted windows. A man in sunglasses sat in the driver's seat. He leaned forward to open the passenger side door. I remember that a gold ring flashed on his hand.

There was a sudden squeal of brakes, a shuddering crash. A bus, pulling into its stop just behind the car, hadn't slowed down enough. It rear-ended the parked car, buckling the back and making it rock forward. The pull of Rahul Moghe's mind ceased abruptly.

I took the chance; I ran to where my beach bag lay, picked it up, crossed the road out of sight of the accident, and sprinted furiously through the parking lot on the other side of the road. My bare feet burned on the concrete, but in a minute or two I was in my car, driving off to safety. A police car came in from the other direction, siren wailing.

About twenty minutes later I felt Rahul Moghe's mind reach for me again, but his touch was faint, searching, tentative; a few minutes later I couldn't feel him at all.

Through sheer luck I had gotten away again.

I changed jobs, fled the West Coast, and kept to old, sprawling eastern metropolises like New York and Boston. Nearly a year passed. There was no sign of Rahul Moghe. Janani's letters also did not mention him except to warn me to be vigilant. She hoped I had seen the last of him.

I knew, however, that he would be back, that he would find me. I sensed this in a way that I did not understand. I would dream of him sometimes, of the long arms of his mind reaching for me, drawing me to him, to the abyss of his soul. He terrified me. But there was a part of me that wanted to know him, perhaps the only other person with my ability.

Then one afternoon, in a café in Boston, where I was attempting to drink what Americans fondly believe to be *chai*, I met Sankaran.

I was amusing myself constructing a meta-beast from the very uppity literary crowd in one corner and a dysfunctional family of four at the next table when someone coasted through the whole mess of mental cobwebbing like it wasn't there. Instinctively I looked toward him. He was unmistakably Indian, delicately built, with a thatch of unkempt black hair and an apologetic and neglected mustache. His hands were slender and brown. He sat down with a book and a coffee cup and was soon lost in whatever he was reading.

I went across to him, trying to control my excitement. His being Indian provided an easy excuse to introduce myself.

He was a post-doctoral researcher at one of the universities scattered about this great city. He lived in a hole in Cambridge. While traveling on a bus he had gotten so engrossed in a collection of conference reports that he had gotten off at the wrong stop. Finding himself near a café, he had dropped in for a coffee and a good, long read.

"You mean you don't know where you are?"

He turned his brown eyes to me and smiled. For a moment he really seemed to be there in the café. "Does any body?" he said, separating the "body" from the "any" with the precision of a surgeon. I thought this a deeply philosophical statement until he explained that he meant that since the Earth and the solar system and the entire galaxy were constantly changing their places in space, one had to be very specific about reference frames. I was utterly charmed.

After I helped Sankaran find his way home, we became friends. He never sought me out, but I began to haunt a coffee shop in Cambridge where he turned up nearly every evening like a homing pigeon, armed with books and papers. When aware of the mundane world, he treated it with a bemused, indiscriminate kindness—being the kind of person who, upon bumping into people, doors, or potted plants, apologizes to them with equal courtesy. Much of the time I watched him over my coffee cup, filled with silent wonder. I could explore his mind, embrace it with my own, but I could not draw it to me, play with it, or manipulate it. He was untouched by my mental explorations. He had no need of me; he posed no threat. He filled the emptiness that had been growing in me.

I discovered in Sankaran some of the things that had drawn me to Dulari—but without the pain. His mind had the delicacy of petals about to unfurl and the innocence and wonder of a child beholding a rainbow for the first time. Instead of the white noise of contradictory emotions, the cacophony of thwarted desire and loneliness that makes up a typical human mind, his mind possessed the deep peacefulness found in high places, in the thin air of Himalayan country above the snow line. He did not torture himself with questions about his purpose in life or what other people thought about him—indeed, the obsession with self was quite absent in him. He was beautiful, a being absorbed at play in a universe far vaster than ordinary humans could imagine.

Looking at him, at his thin, mahogany brown body draped without grace on the sofa while his mind saw wonders I could only guess at, I was filled with the sweetness of desire. I wanted to touch his body as well as his mind. I wanted his touch, even if it were only as brief and innocent as a hand on my arm. In India, where platonic friends of the same sex often hold hands or fling arms around each other in public without censure or misunderstanding, it would have been easy. But social mores were different here, and—more to the point—he remained unaware of my need of him.

I spent as much time as I could with Sankaran. Sometimes I would meet him in the physics department and amuse myself looking at star charts on the computer as he finished a colloquium or worked out his equations. He would join me at the computer when he was done and fill me with astronomical lore as we roamed the galaxy. Here was a red giant, there a supernova, a binary star system, a neutron star, a black hole, an extra-solar planet fifteen times the mass of Jupiter. I learned the lexicon of astronomy as a lover learns the body of his love.

Gradually I got to know a little about Sankaran's background. He was from a learned Tamilian family. He was very fond of his mother and his elder brother, who remained in the ancestral home in Chennai after his father's death. I had a mental picture of the faded whitewash on the walls, the banana trees in the courtyard at the back. When he talked about his family, he seemed suddenly to come to earth.

"My mother's cooking, nothing like it." Or, "Unna taught me calculus in eighth class."

"They want for me to get married," he told me once, shyly. He shook his head. "I do not have time for a wife. But it is also tradition to continue your line. Life is not simple." He sighed. But for an accident of gender and the cruelty of convention, I would have married him in a minute.

He was also a devotee of Lord Shiva. He kept a small stone Shiva lingam in his room, a shrine in a bookshelf surrounded by books and papers on astrophysics. There was only one picture on the wall—a photograph of the beautiful and graceful Tamilian actress Shobhana. Sankaran confessed shyly to me that he was a fan.

I feigned an interest in cooking so I could spend more time with him in the privacy of his room. As I stirred eggplant curry on the stove, I would look at him as he lay on the bed, flipping through the latest *Astrophysical Journal*, his eyes dreamy. He would mutter phrases that were meaningless to me, things like "virial theorem" or "off-main-sequence star." Sometimes I would ask him to explain, and I would perch on the bed next to him, feeling the heat of his body, the passion of his intellect. I would glance up at the stone phallus of Shiva and remember how it felt to pretend to be a woman for my old lover, Manek. In the little studio apartment the air would fill with the smell of roasting spices, cumin and coriander, and the sharp, enticing aroma of ginger. I would lean close to Sankaran, looking with him at incomprehensible pages of equations and star charts, conscious only of his nearness, the soft black hairs on his arms stirring in unison with the rhythm of his breath. I would stretch my mind toward his, enclosing him, burying myself between the flanks of his beautiful, oblivious mind. Sleepy with desire, I would remember that one of the manifestations of Shiva is Ardhanarish-waram: half man, half woman. Shiva is the one who dances the world into being and out of it. One day I said:

"Tell me something, Sankaran. If you could ask the Lord Shiva three questions, what would they be?"

He was silent for a while. Then he said, "I would ask if the dark matter problem is truly a question of missing mass. Then I would ask about the

Higgs boson and the accelerating expansion rate. Which may be related to the very failure of the standard model I mentioned at the seminar. You have to consider . . ."

I would distract him gently back to my question. Each time I asked him the question, he would answer as though he had never been asked this before. One day, after he had read a letter from his mother, he sighed.

"I would like to ask Lord Shiva if there is some way I can avoid getting married without hurting my family."

And once:

"I would ask Lord Shiva if there is life on the extra-solar planets we have found. If there is life on other worlds at all."

I found myself falling into Sankaran's gravitational well as inevitably as a star being swallowed by a black hole.

Janani cautioned me not to focus on Sankaran to the exclusion of other things. "Explore your ability," she wrote. "Travel a bit. See the world, Arun. Immerse yourself in it. We think all we have are our paltry possessions and the special people in our lives. But the world is greater than that. . . ."

Her advice came too late. I remember wondering about the tone of Janani's letter—she was not one to wax philosophical as a rule. It occurred to me that she never wrote about her life in Rishikesh, or the woman she worked with—I had never thought to ask about these things. But then I had a new distraction. Sankaran got a phone call from his elder brother in India. The family had found him a bride. He was to go home in a week to tie the knot.

He told me the news with a resigned air. Clearly he saw marriage as a duty to endure with good grace. We sat in silence for a while, my own mind reeling with dismay and resentment. Then Sankaran turned back to his notes and scribbled away at his equations, quite happily lost in his universe of stellar wonders, and I was relieved. The wife would be a nuisance, and I would have to find a way to spend time with Sankaran without her interfering, but she could never truly touch him, never own him. How could one woman compete with a trillion burning suns?

I saw him off at the airport. As I felt the quiet comfort of his mind recede, I staggered out into the warm light of a spring day, a man adrift in a sea of blathering minds, without an island in sight.

The days of his absence are still clear to me: the heat of my apartment, the monotony of the days at work, the stupefying predictability of the minds around me that produced an answering dullness in my own soul.

Then came a letter from Janani that worried and mystified me.

"I am going on a journey to Thailand," she wrote. "I, who have never been out of India! I am very excited to be traveling on a plane and seeing the world, just as you have done. At my age, too! Still, it is not a pleasure trip. I am on an adventure, Arun, the culmination of a life's work. I don't know if I will emerge from it unscathed. Meanwhile I have just sent you a parcel containing the last of your things. When you understand who you are, Arun, I hope you will forgive me. . . ."

There was no way to contact Janani for details. The little shop where she lived and worked as a seamstress did not have a phone. I debated going to India to see her. The thought was tempting. I had not been home in three years. Perhaps later I could go down to Chennai and see Sankaran. I began making inquiries at a travel agent's.

But Providence had other plans.

A few days before I was to pay for my ticket, I woke up in the throes of a nightmare. I sat up in bed in the half-light of dawn, looking around at the familiar chaos of my room, wiping my sweaty hands on the bedclothes. The monster that had been there in my dream was still present, however. I sensed it—a meta-mind of great power. It seemed to be some distance away, a fact that puzzled me. Even the self-generated meta-mind I had encountered at the rally in Delhi had had a fairly short range. I remembered how it had buzzed and hummed in my ears, driving me close to madness. This was something like that, but quieter. It was engaged in some kind of play, like a child absorbed in a toy. Only this play felt dangerous.

I could have walked away from it, but I felt a deep curiosity mingled with fear. Where was this meta-mind? What was taking up its attention so completely? How had such a powerful thing come into being?

I dressed hurriedly, flung myself into the car, and began to drive toward it.

When I was halfway to Boston (having driven about ten miles) I realized it was much farther than I had thought. What could make its presence felt from so far away?

My apprehension mounted the closer I got to it. As I drove between the tall buildings of the city, with the sunlight flashing on tiers of windowpanes, reflecting in my eyes, I realized that the meta-mind was different from any I had encountered. The one at the Red Fort had been a hasty and temporary thing, powerful only because it was made up of seventeen thousand minds. This thing had fewer components and was more focused, like a laser beam.

I came to a stop before an old brick office building. Sirens wailed; as I leaped out of my car, police vehicles and ambulances drove up, disgorging men in uniform. A crowd had collected in front of the building, looking skyward with a mixture of apprehension and ghoulish anticipation. I squinted against the glare of the sun and saw a man standing on a window ledge some seven stories above the street. He teetered, looked behind him, and jumped.

He seemed to fall in slow motion, his arms flung up as though in surrender. About halfway down, his mind, which had been locked in a trancelike state, woke up to screaming terror. Too quickly, a red flower blossomed on the sidewalk, and a splinter of bone buried itself in a watching woman's arm. People screamed, moving back, stumbling over each other. Blood spattered their clothes. TV cameras zoomed in as policemen began to shout orders.

Then the next one fell. A woman, her skirts billowing up. She broke like a cracked egg on the sidewalk.

In the screaming and confusion I darted into an entrance I'd noticed further along the sidewalk.

I took an elevator to the seventh floor. The meta-mind was still quivering with satisfaction. It was composed of not more than twenty minds, twisted and knotted together, not randomly but with the intricacy, order, and beauty of an integrated circuit or a Persian carpet. It was beautiful and deadly, and I sensed its hunger as it felt around for its next victim.

I entered a corridor with plush blue carpeting and chrome and glass décor. The place was cold and smelled of fear. People stood silently in little knots, with wide, frightened eyes. A troop of policemen were trying to force open one of the double doors in the hallway. A large woman in a red business suit was flailing her arms and crying hysterically, "Another one! There must be another one!"

I stood very still, concentrating, stilling my own fears. My mind felt like it was being run over by a convoy of trucks. I thought of Sankaran, took a deep breath, and concentrated on undoing the meta-mind. I slipped into the meta-mind the way a snake enters a marsh, without a ripple, and started to unravel it, thread by thread, mind by mind. The exquisite patterns and symmetries were the work of a master. As I took it apart I regretted having to destroy something so beautifully constructed.

It came loose as though it had been turned off with a switch. I took a breath of relief, and found that my knees were shaking. I trembled all over, and little rivers of sweat dribbled down my face. Untangling it had taken more out of me than I had realized.

I leaned against the wall for support, fighting panic. Meanwhile the hysterical woman had stopped shouting and was looking around her in bewilderment. Tears started running down her face. The double doors that the police had been trying to force opened suddenly, and a man looked out. He seemed dazed. The policemen pushed him aside and ran into the room. Inside, people were getting up from a table, passing hands over their eyes, shaking their heads, as though they were coming out of a trance. Sunlight streamed through an open window; the glass lay smashed on the floor, like diamonds. One of the men at the table looked at the window, the policemen. "What happened?" he asked.

I walked with difficulty to the elevator; every few steps I had to stop to lean against the wall. People around me were shouting, crying, and rushing about, and nobody took any notice of me. As I stumbled into the elevator I realized that only one person could have constructed a meta-mind so powerful.

Now I recognized the familiar swift current of his mind drawing me toward him. I staggered out of the lobby and round the corner of the building to a blue station wagon. I saw the tinted windows, the flash of the gold ring as the door opened. I got into the passenger seat almost thankfully, collapsing in a heap.

Rahul Moghe took off his sunglasses, looked at me, and smiled. I had an impression of largeness, although physically he was not more than average in height and build. Seeing him in his entirety, body and mind, was like looking at a vast ship with the prow head-on. His eyes burned like forest fires in his dark face—his arms reached toward me, pulling me into the seat. I heard the click of the seat belt.

Much later, when I came to, the first thing I saw was his face, leaning over me. We were in a dingy hotel room. I remember the hardness of the bed on which I lay, the sunlight making a pool of brightness on the green carpet. I closed my eyes, but he was still there in my mind.

The feelers of his mind held me close, with an intimacy that terrified me. He spoke.

"You are a coward, Arun. You run from the only person who is like you. Why?"

The fingers of his mind opened every door, every barrier in my mind. He entered my memories, my secret places, the unknown depths of my consciousness. He gathered me to him, and hot pincers of pain gripped my head.

"What you saw just now is only the beginning of what we can do together. You don't know who you are, or how long I have needed you. Together we will build meta-minds that will make this last one look like a child. Come, I will train you, tell you how to use your power. But first let me tell you who you are. At last . . ."

His mind relaxed its hold on mine as he began to caress me. I was so tired; I had struggled for so long. Now I could rest. I had never known what it was like to reach across the void between one person and another and find a hand held out to grasp your own. . . .

I hit him with all the strength I had. I got him squarely on his throat; he rolled off the bed and fell gasping and gurgling to the ground. My mind pushed his away as I leaped off the bed. He lay on the ground, clutching his throat, rolling from side to side.

As my hands fumbled with the doorknob, a searing pain tore through my head. He was sitting on the floor, rubbing his neck, concentrating. Against my will, I turned around and walked back to him and sat helplessly on the bed. The pain receded. He sat beside me, his arms pushing me down until his face was leaning over mine.

"You don't know who you are, Arun. That bitch Janani took your memories away from you. Did you know that? She took away what you were. If I could resurrect you, I would. But all I can do now is share with you . . ."

My vision blanked. I dropped into darkness, into a silence in which my own screams kept echoing. Terrifying images came crowding out of the dark—demonlike visages and shapes that kept morphing from one monstrosity to another. I fell with them toward a pale circle of light that opened up below me like the mouth of a well. Then I lost consciousness.

When I came to, Rahul Moghe was holding me up against his shoulder, trying to spoon something into my mouth. I gagged as chicken soup went down my throat, then licked my cracked lips and tried to struggle out of his grasp. The room spun.

"Take it easy," he said. A dim lamp lit the room; I saw that night had already fallen. I felt weak and spent.

"It was too much for you, too fast," he told me, spooning more soup into my mouth. "I see that I have to work against a great deal of conditioning. So much damage has been done. . . ."

He let me sleep after that, but throughout my incarceration I never truly regained consciousness. I experienced brief periods of wakeful clarity, but for the most part I was in a confused, dreamlike state during which I could not distinguish between reality and the nightmares that plagued me. Held in Rahul Moghe's fierce grip, his face against mine, I thought I heard voices of people I had known. Once it seemed a woman lay by me, painfully thin; she nestled sensuously against my shoulder and spoke in Dulari's voice. Another time I felt Sankaran prop me up to a sitting position. I thought I was being rescued at last, but he was holding a star chart in his hands, pointing at it, saying something insistently. Old friends—the boys I had played with in my teenage years, Manek—walked through my consciousness like ghosts. Always Rahul Moghe was there in my mind, muttering in my ear in Hindi, English, and languages I could not understand. "You belong to me," he would say. "You and I are one of a kind . . . both alien, both lost, both pretending to belong. . . ." And again: "Alone, our powers are nothing. Together we can do things. . . ." Sometimes his words would echo in my head like muffled drumbeats: "power to change . . . to change . . . to change . . ." or "she burned you . . . burned you . . ." He would alternately entreat and reprimand me. "You think you belong, Arun," I remember him muttering against my ear. "But you live in a dangerous place outside the boundaries humans create around themselves. Man-woman. Mind-body . . . If your so-called friends could see you as you are, they would hate and revile you. I am the only friend you have, my love. We owe our allegiance to a different star. . . ."

I saw myself falling again toward a pale sun, surrounded by demonlike wraiths that stretched long fingers toward me. "This is who you are," Rahul Moghe whispered. His hands raked my bare chest. As I bit back a cry of pain, I perceived it—his mind, opening before me like sunrise on a new world. I saw the power, the beauty, the ruthlessness of him—the mountain ranges, the sheer cliffs, vast Escher-like vistas. He was letting me into his soul.

And I turned to him, reaching out exploring arms toward this stupendous geography. As we lay entwined, he changed beside me—his skin paled, then darkened; his hair changed colors like a kaleidoscope. Arms and breasts and thighs moved against my skin—I had a glimpse of a great, hungry creature, all orifices and phalluses—and as I joined with him, I could no longer tell body from mind. Then, just as our bizarre mating reached its climax, he tore into me, tasting and feeding, ripping and slicing.

When eons later I opened my eyes, I was weak but able to think. Rahul Moghe lay beside me, asleep, one arm flung over my chest. Afternoon light filtered through the green plastic curtains. My mind felt as though it had been shredded and trampled on. To my horror I saw that the covers over my chest were stained with blood. Warily I groped about in my mind for him, but he was gone. Slowly and carefully I put myself back together, like an injured animal licking its wounds.

Just then I saw the door open halfway. An olive-skinned woman stood there, holding a pile of clean sheets, her mouth open. She backed out and shut the door behind her. Had I dreamed her? And if not, why had I not felt her mind? Why had Rahul Moghe not stirred, not known she was there? It came to me that she was a blank, one of those whose minds were inaccessible to me. And to him, also, I realized.

I must have fallen into exhausted slumber, because when I woke again the room was dark and the phone was ringing. Moghe stirred beside me, cursed, and turned on the lamp. He grabbed the phone and spoke into it for a few minutes in Hindi. His mind was quivering with excitement.

"Another of our kind has been found," he told me. "You are too weak to travel with me. I must leave you for a few days. Do not think of betraying me. A man in the hotel who is my servant will look after you."

When I found my voice it was barely a whisper.

"Where . . . ?"

"Bangkok," he said.

I fell asleep again and woke some time later to find a strange dark-haired older man in the room, dressed in the hotel livery of white and green. His mind was like a cowering animal. "This is Odylio," Moghe said. "He will feed you and check on you. Perhaps without me you will recover faster." He leaned toward me, and for a moment I saw the mouths of the demons that plagued my sleep. "Wait for me, Arun," he whispered, and then he was gone.

That night Odylio fed me soup. He did not try to talk to me. I was too weak to play any tricks with his mind; besides which, I suspected that whatever Rahul Moghe had done to this man could not be reversed by my poor skill. In Moghe's absence my mind slowly cleared; I began to think of escape, although it seemed impossible. Perhaps the soup had some drug in it—I was still unnaturally weak. I lay helpless, sensing the minds of people passing by outside the door, but I could not even cry out.

Then, next morning after breakfast, the olive-skinned cleaning woman opened the door. She was holding a pile of towels. She gave me a nervous look and began to back out. I raised my hand weakly from the bed. "Help me!" I croaked.

She came slowly into the room, her eyes wide. She looked at me and said something I could not understand. She set the towels down, picked up the phone, and began speaking breathlessly in what I realized must be Portuguese.

I had avoided and feared blanks all my life; the irony of being rescued by one was not lost on me. I was taken to hospital by the police; lying there with the IV in my arm, I closed my eyes to stop the tears of relief and gratitude and to remember the face of my deliverer.

The police did not believe my story. Although I did not think there was much point in telling them the truth—mere forces of law and order could hardly contain a person such as Rahul Moghe—I was too weak to invent something more plausible. The hotel receptionist had said very clearly that the person who had checked in and taken the key of Room 323 was a young white woman called Marie Grenier from Baton Rouge, Louisiana. Nobody knew anything about an Indian man.

I never found out what, if anything, the Brazilian maid told the police, or whether they had believed her.

That night, I sat up in my hospital bed and detached the IV from my arm. I found my clothes folded neatly at the foot of the bed, and changed into them with some difficulty. There were bandages on my chest that hurt every time I moved. I dragged myself from corridor to corridor under garish fluorescent lights, choking on the antiseptic smell, until I came upon a side exit.

The cool night air revived my senses. With the last of my strength I found the nearest subway station, took a train journey that I can no longer remember, and went home to my apartment. I didn't have any of my things with me—I had to find the manager, who was not amused at being woken at four in the morning. I fell onto my bed and slept until noon.

When I woke, my mind was mercifully my own. I was bruised and injured physically and mentally from my ordeal—I thought longingly of Sankaran's healing presence—but at the same time I dared to hope that I would recover.

I resigned from my job, telling my colleagues I had found work in Florida. I withdrew my savings from my bank and rented a room in a ramshackle apartment complex in Cambridge. I requested an unlisted phone number, obtained a post office box under a different name, and immediately wrote Janani to let her know how to reach me.

If it had not been for Sankaran, I would have fled to the ends of the earth. I don't think Moghe understood that. I believe that my subterfuge paid off because he expected me to leave Boston, to run before him as I had done before. I would no longer run.

Within a few weeks, I found a job working with a medical company as a lowly computer technician. It paid enough to keep me alive, and to maintain my car. Now assured of a livelihood and a roof over my head, I could no longer avoid thinking about my ordeal with Rahul Moghe and what it implied about my past. Janani's last parcel, which came a few days after my new job started, confirmed that I had not dreamed up the events in that hotel room.

The parcel contained the usual junk that Janani had sent me over the years, bits of broken metal and shards of ceramic, some with drawings and etchings on them. There was also a letter.

I read it. I looked at the contents of the parcel that I had piled on the bed. I read the letter again. I remembered Rahul Moghe whispering impossible things into my ear.

"Alien, alien, alien," he had said. "You and I owe our allegiance to a different star."

I looked at the strange objects on the bed. Whether I wanted them to or not, they began to make sense. The ceramic pieces, burnt black on one side, red on the other. The strange etchings, the pointillist ones in particular, one of them showing me a pattern I had seen before, not only on Sankaran's computer but also in my fevered dreams: the constellation Sapt-Rishi as seen from Earth. Then the pictures Janani had taken, of the boys so like me—they were all me, I realized, at various stages of formation.

I could no longer avoid the truth of my origin. I sat on my bed, watching night fall, shadows moving out from the corners of the room to fill it with darkness. Headlight beams swept across the curtained window, and through the thin walls I could hear my neighbors having an argument about laundry.

I laughed hysterically. After a while I started to cough, so I got up, turned on the light, and got a drink of water. Looking out of the grimy window at the busy street in front of my apartment complex, I had an impulse to cry.

Instead I went to the local pub and drank myself stupid. I told the bartender I was an alien. He gave me a sad look from beneath long, dark eyelashes and went on polishing glasses. "You won't believe how many people tell me that," he said. This set me off laughing again, until I was weeping large tears onto the bar. I don't remember how I got home. I slept like a dead person until late the next afternoon.

When I woke I had a headache the size of Antarctica; I staggered into the shower with my clothes on. Under the cold water some of my reason returned. I stripped, looking down at my all-too-human body. I thought about the notion that Janani was as much my murderer as my progenitor. She had burned me, Moghe had said. I understood now that I was stuck with this body, this gender, because of that. Unlike him, I could no longer change form; nor could I tell friend from foe. "Damn them all, Moghe and Janani and all," I told myself.

I spent two days in this insane state, staring at the things on my bed, re-reading Janani's letter. Rahul Moghe appeared in my dreams, and sometimes I would wake terrified, feeling as though I was still his prisoner, that my escape had only been a trick of the mind. Then, slowly, sanity would return.

On the third day, a colleague, Rick, called from work to ask why I had not come in. I stammered something about being sick. Rick commiserated and asked when I could come in. They were having a problem with the computer system.

So the world pulled me back. I spent the next few days working out and fixing the glitch. Having to focus helped me a great deal. When two other technicians took me out for pizza after it was all done, I saw myself in the mirrors that ran along two walls of the restaurant. There I was, a skinny Indian guy with stubble on my chin and pizza sauce at the corners of my mouth, grinning and guzzling like everyone else. Rick's people had immigrated here three generations ago from Holland. Aichiro was a second-generation Japanese immigrant. So what if I'd come from a farther shore than anyone else? This was Boston, one of the great melting pots of the world, where nearly everyone was a stranger. My two colleagues were both married, and I, too, had someone I loved, someone to wait for. The revelation about my true identity seemed, all of a sudden, irrelevant.

As soon as I could take leave from my job, I booked a flight to India. It was too late to attend Sankaran's wedding. Much as I wanted to see him, I felt this wasn't the right time. As for Janani, I had no idea what I would say to her, but she owed me some answers. I also had to admit to a growing worry about her silence. Why had she not written to me? What had happened to her in Thailand? Surely it could not be a coincidence that she and Moghe had been headed to the same place?

I did not know how much I had missed being in India until I was in Delhi, taking in great lungfuls of warm air that smelled of car exhaust, roasting corncobs, and 11 million people. From the Inter State Bus Terminus I took a night bus to Rishikesh, traveling with a group of elderly pilgrims who took pity on me and shared their dinner of *parathas* and pickled mangoes. As dawn came I woke from uneasy slumber to find myself breathing in the scent of the Himalayas.

It took the auto-rickshaw man only about ten minutes to locate the address I gave him. He piloted his little vehicle through narrow, twisting streets, past amiable gatherings of cows, goats, and people to a small row of shops. Their shutters were still down, and the shopkeepers were bustling about in front of their shops, putting up the cots they had slept in. At last I came to the place Janani had lived in for the past ten years.

I searched for her with my mind, but she was not there. A handsome, middle-aged woman in a blue cotton sari was raising the shutters. She was chewing on a neem twig. Every few seconds she would rub her teeth with the twig and spit in a corner in front of the shop. (I remembered, with a pang, Janani teaching me how to brush my teeth in just this manner.) Behind the woman I could see two large, old-fashioned sewing machines and a number of finished clothes on racks. An array of grimy bottles stood on a shelf—Janani's herbal concoctions. I smelled the familiar aroma of *tulsi*. *Heeng*. Dried *amla*.

I put my palms together. "Namaste," I said. "My name is Arun. I am looking for Janani-behn. Are you Rinu Devi?"

Her eyes widened; the neem twig fell from her mouth. Her mind was quivering, tense. I found her reaction puzzling.

"Janani is not here," she said with outward composure. "She has moved to foreign lands."

"I know she went to Thailand," I said, coming into the shop. I was aware of a curious urchin or two hanging about, listening. The woman's mind was bristling with fear and dislike.

"I am just a friend," Rinu Devi said, sounding placating. She gave me a wary look. "Janani's helped me run my shop these past few years. Then recently she met someone and got married and went to Thailand."

She was lying. I looked outside. It was still early, and only a slow car or sleepy bullock cart went by. The urchins had gone back to their business for the moment.

"Look, Rinu-ji," I said. "I could be nice and spend the next two days trying to persuade you to tell me the truth. Or I could mess with your mind. Janani must have told you what kind of monster I am."

She gave me a look of loathing.

"If you must know, Janani went to a place near Bangkok, I don't remember the name, because she heard that one of your kind had landed there. Someone new. She went to organize a burning. It's been nearly a month and she has not been back. How can I say what happened to her?"

"Did she leave any message, any note?"

"No. She wasn't one to confide in me about these things. She told me just this: that she might not return. She expected danger." Rinu Devi's mind was calmer now. She was feeling more confident. Yet under the façade I sensed strong emotion.

"That's all she told you? Why didn't she confide in you?"

"She knew I don't like her involvement in the network. I've never understood why she wouldn't just want to kill the aliens instead of . . . of changing them. We . . . we had disagreements."

I took a deep breath.

"What network?"

She raised her eyebrows in mock astonishment.

"Oh, she didn't tell you? There are other people like her who can sense the aliens. Whenever they hear of an unusual event—like reports of strange lights in the sky—they go to that place. If they find one of your kind, they burn them to take away their power. What's left is like an empty gourd."

"Where is this network? Where are the other people like me?"

She curled her lip. Her mind trembled with spite.

"Mostly in mental hospitals," she said. "Or wandering the streets, begging, I don't know. Janani didn't go far enough with you—she said you called out to her, as your old self died. She pulled you out of the fire too early."

I sensed it then: my ghost self. It stood at the edge of my consciousness, a limb raised, as though to beckon. But I am dead, I thought. I am dead.

Into the silence between us came the sounds of shutters being opened, a cot being dragged across the ground. Mingled with the smell of Janani's herbs was the pungent scent of pine. Away and below us the great Ganga rushed frothing toward the plains.

When I spoke, my voice was barely a whisper.

"But why . . . why do they do this to us?"

I already knew the answer. In her last letter Janani had said that they had to burn me to save me, to make me human. Rahul Moghe had escaped this ordeal by fire, she wrote, and look how dangerous he was. But apart from him, she had said nothing about others like me or about a network. Perhaps my species was indeed hostile to humankind. And yet . . . what if that was not the case with every individual? What if some of us were different? What right did Janani and her network have to deny us the chance to be who we were?

"You really don't know much, do you?" said Rinu. Her tone had lost some of its bite. "You are alien—enemy. You want to subdue us, enslave us!"

"But—," I began.

She waved an impatient hand. "I can't answer your questions. I don't know who these network people are. I just wanted her to leave the whole thing, to have a life with me. . . ."

Her eyes filled with tears. I sensed her mind turning over, like a cat turns on its back, exposing the belly. Here she was, vulnerable, all pretense lost. Her hatred of me was not gone but contained, as water is by a dam.

"Did you love her?" I asked.

She wiped her eyes with the free end of her sari.

"How could I not? We were friends as girls." She hesitated, looked at me with defiance, chewing the end of her neem twig with strong white teeth. "We began like sisters, but then we fell in love. She left me to work for the network. When she came back here after years, I thought . . . I thought . . ."

"You thought she had come back to you, but she was still working for the network."

She nodded. Eyes that had once been beautiful peered out from a nest of premature wrinkles. Lines of discontent surrounded the well-shaped lips. Her hair was tied in a bun, the free end of the sari draped over her head. Her sari was blue, not white, but I knew I was looking into the face of a mourner.

"So she said nothing about this network," I said at last. "You didn't see her meet anyone. . . ."

"I don't know anything about those people," she said. "Janani knew I would be upset if she talked about them. Always, letters came for her, and phone calls at the booth in the next lane. I don't know anything."

She made space for me on a mat on the floor. Through the one shutter she had opened, pale light came in. She went to the front and yelled to a boy to bring tea.

The tea came in chipped glasses, milky and strong with the scent of cardamom. I sipped and listened to Rinu talk about her life with Janani. She kept rubbing tears away from the corners of her eyes.

"Why are you so certain she is dead?" I asked her. Without a word she got up, went behind a curtain at the back of the shop, and returned with an envelope that she handed to me. When I opened it I found a piece of newsprint torn from an English-language daily based out of Bangkok. With it was a note in a crude hand that said simply: "Sorry. She was one of our best." It was signed "A.R."

"The man at the tea shop read it to me," she said, pointing to the newspaper fragment. "I don't read English—not enough."

The news brief said only that there had been an explosion in an abandoned warehouse in a locality on the outskirts of Bangkok. Three people had been killed, two of them women. One of them was believed to have been a tourist from India, one Janani Devi. The heat from the explosion had been so great that nothing recognizable had been left of the bodies. Witnesses had seen the three people entering the warehouse just before the explosion.

I stared at the dirty little piece of paper, numb with grief and anger. This only confirmed what I had feared all along—that Janani was dead. I would never be able to confront her now, never have answers to my questions. Never receive letters from her, full of scolding and advice . . .

Rinu leaned forward, patted me on the shoulder. She wiped her face with the end of her sari. I thought of Rahul Moghe in the hotel room, the phone call, and his face filled with hunger and anticipation as he said, "Bangkok."

Who had called him? Who had told him about the next landing? Had he known Janani would be there?

For that matter, how had he known—twice—where to find me?

"You betrayed her, didn't you?" My words came out brokenly.

Her shapely lower lip trembled. Perhaps she thought I could read her mind. But the pieces were slowly coming together.

"You were the one who told Rahul Moghe I had gone to America. Someone must have been telling him. How else would he find me in San Francisco and Boston? You couldn't read the English return addresses on my letters to Janani, but perhaps you could read enough to make out the city I was in. Tell me, did you phone him from somewhere, or did you write?"

She flinched, then gathered herself together and stood up. I stood up also, trembling with rage. She spat at my feet.

"Yes, yes, I betrayed her. I told Rahul Moghe that she was going to Bangkok, that they had found one of his kind. I knew he would find her and confront her, perhaps kill her. So what! She betrayed our love a hundred times. I always came second for her. Even to you—you!"

Tears slid down her face, and a wave of jealous hatred rose in her mind.

"You! A thing, a creature from another world—she loved you better than me! Serve her right! But I never knew what it would be like without her. I thought I could just go back to the time ten years ago before she returned. I had become free of wanting her, you see. . . ."

My mind lashed out at hers like the talons of a predatory bird. I had never been able to do this before. Suddenly, I knew I could hurt her. I drew back. I looked at her, now sobbing at my feet. A face peered around the shutters.

"Anything wrong, Rinu-behn?"

It was the barber's wife from next door; she glared suspiciously at me.

"It's all right," I said. "It's just some bad news I brought. Death in the family. Look after her—I must be on my way."

I left that miserable creature sobbing in the arms of her neighbor and went away, feeling a hundred curious eyes on me.

In my little hotel room I lay on my bed and stared at the ceiling for what seemed like days. The sun rose and set in the two small windows that faced each other, and each time dark fell I saw the stars of Sapt-Rishi burning in a velvet sky.

Sapt-Rishi . . . Sankaran showing me star charts on his computer.

I roused myself, made a phone call to Sankaran's home in Chennai. It would be good to see him, I thought. But he wasn't there. I talked to his mother, who spoke with enthusiasm about the wedding. She told me that Sankaran and his bride had gone to Ootacamund for their honeymoon.

I thought of Sankaran in the blue Nilgiri hills, the stars spreading in the sky above him like a great, sequined quilt. Would he lecture his wife on celestial objects? Would she listen to him as I had? A great wave of envy and loneliness swept over me.

I spent the remaining week of my leave wandering around the hill towns near Rishikesh. I bathed in the holy waters of the Ganga with the other pilgrims. I went to a lonely shrine of Lord Shiva's, high in the mountains. Moved by a strange impulse, I set before the stone lingam a small offering of marigolds. In the little hill towns I walked the crowded streets restlessly, enjoying, despite my grief and loneliness, the anonymity that I had nowhere else in the world.

When I returned to Boston, I was in the lowest of spirits. I had lost everything, including my illusions about myself. Sankaran was my last resort. I needed the healing touch of his mind, the restful pleasure of his company. Meanwhile I wondered uneasily about Rahul Moghe. He seemed to have vanished from my life, but I could never rid myself entirely of his presence. It was as though he had left a splinter lodged in me, a ghost of a voice that called to me with a longing that could not be denied, an endless summons of desire that reminded me of the bull I had seen once on a street in New Delhi.

Sankaran's itinerary was posted on my fridge. As the day of his return approached, I became more and more nervous. What if his wife was a tyrant? What if she restricted his movements so that we could no longer meet? How could I make a claim on him that would be at least equal to that of his wife?

How does a man who is not a man or a woman, not a human or an alien—how does such a being confess his love to another man?

Then it came to me: I would tell him my story.

Not all at once, but with hints and intimations at first.

I shook all over at the thought. With Janani gone, there was nobody in the world excepting Rinu and the network who knew what I was. What better evidence of love and trust could I give Sankaran?

On an impulse I went to the local bookstore and bought the most lavish card I could find. In it I wrote:

> Dear Sankaran,
> Lord Shiva has given me an answer to one of the questions you asked him. There is life on other worlds. Let's talk about this.
> > Your Friend,
> > Arun.

I put the card in an envelope and pushed it under the door of his apartment. Breathlessly I waited for his return, for the time when I could once more sink my mind into the cool streambed of his being. On the day that he was to arrive I decided to surprise him by meeting him and his wife at the airport.

Because there was a traffic pileup on the highway, I was late getting to the airport. When I rushed into the baggage claim area, most of the passengers from his flight had left. I looked around for him for a while. Finally I realized that he must have already gone home.

I drove like a madman to his apartment. When I arrived, I found Sankaran and his wife relaxing over coffee. Sankaran welcomed me and introduced me to his wife.

She was all aglitter in a blue silk sari and gold jewelry. Her eyes were like black beetles. She smiled coldly and disapprovingly at me. With a shock I realized that I could not sense her mind at all. She was a blank.

As for Sankaran, I sensed that the clarity and beauty of his mind was already being undermined by the confusion and contradictions that characterize the ordinary person. There were only hints of damage now, but the clean, clear transparency of his soul that had sustained me was breaking up into bubbles, little patches of opacity. He was dissipating before my eyes.

What had she done to him?

She was holding the card I had put under the door. She wrinkled her nose as though she had picked it up out of the trash and handed it to him.

"What's this?"

He glanced at it without (apparently) noting my untidy scrawl. He shrugged his shoulders, put the card on the desk, and smiled fondly at his wife, following her movements with his eyes as she poured me a cup of coffee. He was already only peripherally aware of me.

My heart clenched in my chest. I drank my coffee in a few gulps, burning my tongue, made my excuses as quickly as I could, and left them to their domestic bliss.

The next time I saw Sankaran, I didn't see him. I was in the café, and he walked in with his wife, and I didn't even feel the quiet, clean wave of his mind wash over and refresh my soul.

I remembered then what physicists say about solitons—eventually they all dissipate.

It is hard for me to recall with composure the days after these events. I lived in a surreal, depressive daze in which night and day blurred into one another. My mind dwelled constantly on death and loss.

When my company folded and I lost my job, I left Boston and began to travel. My depression gave way to the restlessness that had always been a part of me. I moved from port to port, taking up jobs in short spells, staying only as long as the wanderlust let me. I felt as though I was being shadowed—whether it was by my ghost self or Rahul Moghe I could not tell. A footfall on a quiet street in the outskirts of Atlanta. My hotel door in Milan creaking open, then shut, while I lay half-asleep on the bed. A whisper in a darkened street in Ankara, saying my name. Through this troubled time I continued to experiment with mind-weaving, but without the enthusiasm of my earlier days. I was only too aware that whatever pleasure it gave me was temporary—and that it underlined the fact that I was not human.

Eventually I washed up on Indian shores. It was a relief to be back; I took comfort in the small but immutable fact that I looked like everybody else. I knew the sense of belonging was illusory, but it eased my mind a little.

I took up a job as a lecturer at a college in South Delhi. Something about the slow circumlocutions of the ceiling fans, the languor of heat-stupefied students, the cool rush of air-conditioned air in the computer rooms, took me back to my own days as a young student, when I had not a care in the world and Janani was still part of my life. I used my skills with mind-weaving, crude as they were, to settle disputes, to help students understand each other. This should have given me some satisfaction, but at the end of the day when I went up to my two-room flat only the familiar despair awaited me. At times I wanted to end my life, but the same inertia that kept me from living also kept me from dying by my own hand.

Then I met Binodini.

Her mind was muscular, strong, beautiful. Its fluxes and transformations were smooth, controlled, like a dancer executing a familiar turn. Although she could not sense my mind exploring hers, I had difficulty manipulating its topography to make a meta-mind with another. There was a discipline about her that, while quite different from the high-Himalayan feel of a soliton's mind, had a similar, if muted, effect on me—a subtle quieting, a calming. In appearance she was a middle-aged woman with graying hair that she did up carelessly in a bun; her face was calm, her large, sympathetic eyes observant.

She taught sociology. I had seen her at faculty meetings and liked the shape of her mind; one day, when I was nursing a cup of tea alone at a stained wooden table in the café, she asked if she could join me. It turned out she was a divorced single woman without children. She did research on groups that believed in supernatural phenomena including UFO sightings.

"Do you believe in aliens?" I asked her, hoping I sounded jocular.

She smiled. "There are things I've come across in my research that I can't explain. So I keep an open mind." She looked at me over her cup of *chai*. "Something tells me that your question wasn't a casual one. Is there an experience you've had that you can't explain either?"

I wasn't ready to tell her, but it occurred to me with an immense sense of relief that perhaps I had found a confidante.

Life wasn't easy for her. She was not interested in a relationship and had to keep fending off men who couldn't understand that. There was a controlled fierceness about her, a courage and curiosity that kept her going. She kept a little vegetable garden behind her apartment, where she grew red radishes and *brinjal,* and *simla mirch.* I still recall the color and roundness of freshly uprooted radishes in the blue ceramic bowl on her kitchen table, the crunch of her strong white teeth as she bit into one. She did an hour of yoga every morning.

"I'd be dead without yoga," she told me. "Disciplines the mind."

She gave me a shrewd look.

"It's also good if you're in mourning."

It was then that I told her. That morning—classes had been canceled due to some unrest in the city—we'd walked off campus together, and she had invited me into her home.

She listened well. I don't think she necessarily believed me the first time, but she didn't disbelieve me either. To my own ears my story sounded ludicrous, but her sympathy was real, without condescension.

Later I showed her my things, the broken ceramic bits that were presumably the remains of my ship; the photos; Janani's letters. She looked at everything with a scholar's interested gaze, mingled with childlike wonder. When she looked at me her eyes were bright; she hugged me.

"Take me to your leader," I said, to stop my own tears. And we laughed helplessly.

After that we spent a lot of time together. We went to movie theaters and watched bad science fiction films. We sat in the café and talked. I sensed that she was holding off on becoming intimate with me, which at first upset me. But I knew that although our friendship had brought a lightness into my heart, the despair was still there. I was still haunted by what had happened to me, and she knew it.

"You know you have to find him, don't you?" she told me after we emerged from a showing of *Antariksh ki Yatra*.

The crowd was spilling out of the exit doors; my feet crunched on popcorn. A teenager was shouting into her cell phone; somewhere I smelled henna. A man looked at me from the doorway and smiled, apparently mistaking me for someone else. His face changed when I stared at him.

Outside under the neem trees it was dark, quiet. The earth smelled damp from yesterday's rain. Tonight the stars were partly obscured by city haze and light pollution. As was my habit, I looked for the star that was my native sun, but the constellation Sapt-Rishi was lost in the haze.

"Whom do I have to find?" I said, although I knew whom she meant.

"Rahul Moghe."

His name, unspoken for so long, sent an electric shock through me. My ghost self arose in my mind as though it had been waiting for those very syllables. I felt a great wave of fear and longing.

Over the next few days Binodini argued with me, and ultimately I gave in. She was simply repeating to me what my own mind had been trying to tell me: that if I were to have any peace in this life I would have to confront Rahul Moghe, to find the answers to the questions that had plagued me half my life. And then I would have to make a decision.

"All right," I said at last. From pursued I would become the pursuer. But how would I find him?

"You'll find him," Binodini said confidently.

One day I confessed to her my greatest fear. What if I joined forces with Rahul Moghe and turned against humanity as he had done? "He would kill you without a thought," I told her. "Do you want me to become like that?"

"Listen, Arun, whatever decision you make, you will still be you. Alien or human — those are just words, labels. You are what you are."

So I went looking. Because I didn't know where to find Rahul Moghe, I followed the trails of disasters, riots, unexplained violent events. But all these turned out to be the work of human beings alone. Wherever he was, Rahul Moghe was not trying to attract my attention.

One evening I was in a train returning from one of these trips. The Shatabdi Express was tearing through the night across the Gangetic plain. I was in a second-class, air-conditioned compartment; my fellow travelers were asleep, but I was wide awake, leaning against the window, watching my reflection in the glass. The impenetrable night outside made the compartment seem like a cocoon, a world unto itself. Yet as the train swayed and sang in rhythm, it seemed to be singing his name.

Rahul Moghe, wherever you are, let me find you, I said in my mind, with all the fervor of my despair.

I didn't know I had also spoken aloud. The man in front of me, huddled in a blanket, stirred; black eyes snapped open. His mind woke suddenly, but he closed his eyes and feigned sleep. There was a suitcase under his bunk, embossed in gold letters: Amit Rajagopal.

It wasn't him. I would have known Rahul Moghe anywhere from his mind's signature. This man's mind seemed vaguely familiar, but perhaps it was just that he reminded me of someone at the college. I didn't pay much attention to him because something in my own mind woke up when I made my plea.

How can I describe it?

It's like falling asleep with the radio on very low. The sound does not disturb your sleep or your dreams, except perhaps to give them a certain haunted quality, but when you wake up it is there. So I heard his voice in my mind as it woke, calling to me very faintly across a vast distance.

"I'm coming!" I said, and in that moment there was no fear in my heart.

He would not wait but would meet me halfway. I don't know what means he employed to travel from wherever he was, but early that morning I stepped off the train at a tiny station where this train normally did not stop. He must have arranged it by tinkering with the engine driver's mind. The thought made me shudder. I knew this was the place.

The brick station platform was edged with lush bougainvillea bushes with red flowers. Apart from the blanket-wrapped people asleep on the platform in the early morning stillness and a small band of crows raiding the garbage, there was nobody. In the field by the station, men, young and old, squatted at their ablutions, their water pots agleam in the early sun. They watched the train go by and did their business without embarrassment. I walked through the nearly empty station house, where I smelled tea brewing. Lata Mangeshkar was singing a *bhajan* on the radio. I came out into the narrow lanes of a small town.

He was in a ramshackle hotel room not far from the station. Our minds met as I climbed the stairs. I didn't have to knock; he opened the door and let me in. He was in the same form as when I'd seen him last: a wiry Indian man who seemed larger than he was. The room was dingy, with a dressing table and a tarnished mirror in an ornate brass frame. A single, sagging bed was covered with a blue, patterned sheet, and *paan* stains showed through the whitewashed walls. A calendar with a buxom movie star hung on the wall by the window. I could see the street below, already crowded with bicycles, and a few cars lurching behind them, honking. The air was full of the sounds of bicycle bells.

Rahul Moghe did not touch me but bade me sit on the only chair in the room.

How can I describe that meeting? Here was the being I had feared and loathed for so many years of my life, who had killed innocent people, had done to death the one human being who had loved me and cared for me: Janani. And yet . . . he was my own kind. Between our minds there were no barriers. With him I could begin to learn the lexicon of my lost language.

I touched his mind tentatively; I could have lost myself exploring its dizzying contours. But when the whole mass shifted and loomed over me like a great blue whale turning, I withdrew in panic.

"I forgot," he said, and his voice startled me in the room. "Last time. You weren't used to how we communicate. I should have given you more time."

The questions and challenges I had for him dried on my tongue. It took me some time to speak. All the while his eyes looked hungrily at me. Leopard's eyes, burning in that gold-brown face.

"I want to know . . . I need to know more about what I . . . what we are," I said. "Why we are here. Why you've done what you've done."

"Let me touch you," he said. "Not mind-to-mind, if that frightens you still, but I can't explain things very well by speech alone. I must have contact."

I put my hand on his arm. He shivered, and it seemed to me that his arm would change, that he would change form any moment, but he didn't.

"You don't know how long I searched for you," he said. "I went all over the world. . . . Then it came to me that I would have to wait for you to come home to me. All these years I have been waiting."

I don't know what I had expected of this meeting, but the almost anti-climactic quietness of it was something I had not anticipated.

"Let me tell you about our people," he said. "According to the lore, when our species was still young, yet old enough to go out among the stars, we colonized several worlds, this one among them. Then our own world fell into an age of darkness and ignorance. Instead of letting each other meld and fuse and thereby achieve greater harmony, we put up barriers. We fought. We lost ourselves and our history. You must understand that a species such as ours does not record data on stone—we have no need of it. When we die, we simply rejoin the formless substrate that holds all our memories. New ones are born from that substrate with bits and pieces of the old knowledge. When we meld with another, we recover it for all of ourselves.

"When I was young we had recovered some fragments, enough to know how to build ships again to navigate the seas of the sky. But there had been no contact between us and the colonized worlds for eons. Our history would not be complete until the colonizers came home and mingled with us. So some of us set out. I landed on this planet and began my search for our kind."

I could feel his mind straining to speak its own language, to tell me mind-to-mind what those first years had been like. The escape from the first burning. The destruction of the spaceship. The endless wanderings from continent to continent to find the colonizers. And then, a stupendous discovery.

"The first wave of colonizers had taken over the native species as we have done on our own and other worlds," he said. "It is a form of perspective-borrowing, where you get to see from the point of view of the animal what the universe looks like to it. But the colonizers had gone a step further. They had, in fact, joined with the mind-shapes of the natives—turned native, in a manner of speaking, so that they no longer remembered who they were.

"Have you ever wondered why you found it so easy to get into the minds of the animals here? The humans, more than any other species? It is because at some level the colonizers still remember their old language. Why do you think the average human is such a messy mix of contradictory emotions? Why do you think they feel alienated, not only from each other but from their own selves?"

He fell silent.

"But why do you destroy the humans, then," I asked, "if part of them is like us?"

The mountain ranges of his mind quivered, loomed large over me.

"Why? Why? You can ask that?"

He clutched my hand and pulled me to the bed. His hand burned as though with fever. He put his face close to mine. His eyes were empty sockets in which danced a universe of stars.

After a while he could speak again.

"When I made my discovery I realized I had to free our people, the first colonizers, from their bondage to this species. I could not go home; my spaceship had been destroyed. If another of our kind came to this planet we could return on their ship, or we could put our minds together and send forth a beacon into space, a message calling for help.

"But that woman—that viper—destroyed the few who came. So I realized that there was another way.

"If I could do the right kind of mind-weave between human minds, I could project a message into space, a weak one, but enough that it could be picked up. But for that I need your help. I have not succeeded because I need another to hold the structure. It will be the largest structure ever built, at least a hundred thousand human minds. . . ."

It was like making waves on a string, I realized. You need a person at each end.

"I think," he resumed, "that this great melding of minds will free the original colonizers from their current state. They will realize who they really are. They will leave with us when the ship comes. Even if they cannot take corporeal form, we can find some way to take them with us. To go home . . ."

His mindscape convulsed when he said the word "home." All these decades he had experienced the utter loneliness of the foreigner whose language nobody knows.

"I haven't melded with a mind for years," he said. "They left enough of you that I could at least get a taste of what it used to be like. You know, among our species, when we mate, nothing is hidden. We know each other as truly as it is possible to know another being. And then, when we have tired of the world and need rest, we sink into formlessness, to rise again as another consciousness.

"How inadequate this language is! Come, now, let me show you in the way that you will truly understand. I cannot tell you what it is like . . . to actually be there."

We leaned toward each other. I could not help it. I suppose I had made the decision already that I would remain with him, two of a kind, marooned on this world. Perhaps I had hopes of ultimately being able to stop him from wreaking havoc on humankind. I don't know. All I wanted at that moment was to know again what it meant to meet mind-to-mind with my own species.

How can I explain that need? I was trapped in this male, human, unchanging body; only with my mind meeting his could I have the freedom to transcend these boundaries. To taste all the thirty-four states and more, to soar above the barriers that humans make between each other, and between humankind and all else. To know another being in a way that surpasses ordinary intimacy. My human fears dissipated; my ghost self appeared in my mind, beckoning.

Our attention was on each other, so it startled us both when there was a thunderous knocking at the door and shouting outside. We had already drawn together; the top of his pale yellow shirt was unbuttoned and I could smell, incongruously, cologne on his skin. In that moment as we sprang apart, I saw what hung from his neck on a black thread.

It was a human finger. It looked fresh; somehow the nail gleamed pinkly, which seemed unnatural, because it must have hung on his neck these many years, a trophy. It had once graced Janani's hand. I was sure of that.

"Fire!" shouted the man at the door. He left us and ran to the next door, shouting. Downstairs we could hear more yells, confusion. I smelled smoke.

Rahul Moghe stared fiercely at me.

"Have you led those vipers to me? Is this a betrayal, after all?"

"No!" I said. "Let's get out quickly. I don't know, it may just be an ordinary fire."

But even as I said it I knew that it wasn't so. I had been followed. That man on the train . . . his initials, A.R. Like the signature on the note that Rinu had showed me, those years ago in the Himalayas.

They must have been keeping track of me for a long time.

The lower part of the building was in flames. Men were leading cattle out from one of the rooms, which had apparently been used as a barn. Bits of straw floated in the smoke. A crowd of passersby had already collected; some were hauling buckets of water.

Rahul Moghe and I pushed through the crowds. The streets were full of people, bicycles, cattle, and noise. Like him, I wanted to find a quiet place where we could be together. The knowledge of what the string around his neck held throbbed in my consciousness.

We found an empty field behind a house that was being constructed. At this time house and field were both deserted. Great piles of red brick lay in rectangular stacks around us. There was some kind of storage shed in the field, with a massive padlock on its wooden door. We stopped in front of it and looked at each other. His mind quivered with hunger. I nodded.

He put his finger into the padlock keyhole, thinning it into the right shape, and the lock clicked open. We went into the darkness of the hut, which was lit only by a narrow slit of a window. Inside were dusty bags of cement. I sensed a rat mind as the creature slithered away between the bags.

What I had seen, what I hadn't told him, was that a man had slipped behind us as we left the crowds outside the hotel. One man, maybe two. The interesting thing was that they were both blanks. I could not sense their minds, nor could Rahul Moghe.

That finger. That is what stopped me from warning him.

I thought to myself: I will pull him out of the fire before they completely destroy his mind. He will be like me, then, a creature with whom I can meld my own mind, but who will no longer be able to destroy humankind. After all, this world isn't so bad; I don't even remember the other one. We'll be marooned together. . . .

He must have sensed some change in my mindscape; I think it was only his need of me that stopped him from probing too deeply. Perhaps he thought only that I was afraid.

"I will be careful with you," he told me, as he reached toward me. I felt myself go under as the great waves of his loneliness and longing washed over me. Then there I was, sailing with him as though on the waves of a vast sea. He was beginning to change shape, very slowly out of consideration for me.

I opened my mouth to speak, to warn him after all, maybe, but he closed it with his own. Limbs emerged from his trunk, embracing my own body, fitting against me like no human ever could, making allowance for the rigidity of my form. How trapped I felt then, in my human, unchangeable body!

Outside, there was a muffled explosion; I saw that the thatched roof over our heads was on fire. The walls of the hut were mud and straw. People—the

A.R. frowned. "Janani has been dead for years," he said. "That fellow—Rahul Moghe—killed her. I thought you knew."

"But," I began, then gave up.

Someone said "Hush; be still." The man was a doctor; he was leaning over me, applying some kind of ointment. Soothing my burns.

"You suffered smoke inhalation and some pretty bad burns," he said. "But you'll be all right. We dare not take you to a hospital lest questions be asked."

I turned my head, not without pain, to indicate Rahul Moghe. Seeing his face was a shock all over again. I could have been looking into a mirror.

"What about him?"

"He's going to be fine," the doctor said. "He's harmless now."

He was harmless all right. That great mindscape was gone, and in its place . . . a shadow. Nothing left but a ghost. After all this, I had not saved him; I had not pulled him out in time.

He stirred, opened his eyes. They were as vacant as an idiot child's. A thin line of drool trickled down from one corner of his lips.

"Rahul?" I said, and began to weep.

Later they told me that there must always be a human holding the alien in their grasp when the fire is lit, so that the alien would take up the form of that person. In my own burning the person had been a young friend of Janani's, part of the network. He had later been killed by Rahul Moghe.

"How did you know where I was?" I asked my captors. I think it was the second day of my recovery. I lay on a bed, my body covered with bandages. Rahul Moghe drooped in a chair in a corner, looking at nothing.

"We've been . . . keeping track of you," said the man called A.R.

A terrible thought occurred to me.

"Not Binodini?"

"Not Binodini," he said, but I could not tell whether he was, with gentle mockery, simply repeating my words, or whether he meant that she had nothing to do with this. Was it a coincidence that she had been the one to persuade me to look for Rahul Moghe? She had connections to groups that kept track of UFO sightings. If she was part of the network, she would know that the only way they would find him would be through me.

I don't know that I'll ever know.

Rahul Moghe is at a special home for the retarded. I go to see him nearly every month. When he sees me, something like recognition comes into his eyes. Sometimes he laughs; sometimes he sets up a terrible keening, like a child in pain. He can speak a few words of Hindi, use the bathroom, brush his teeth, but he cannot read. He likes it when I tell him stories, though. I tell him about other worlds and their wonders, and sometimes it almost seems to me that he is remembering.

I still don't know if Janani is alive. A.R. swore to me that she died at Rahul Moghe's hands all those years ago, but my memory of her face in the fire, her hands with that missing finger, is so vivid that I have trouble believing she is gone. She may think it best to stay out of my life, knowing what she's done, what I've been through. If we meet someday I have no idea what I'll say to her.

I've often thought about what Rahul Moghe told me that fateful morning in the hotel room: that people of our own kind came to live in and become part of human minds. I've read about that curious organelle, the mitochondrion that inhabits cells. It was once an independent entity, a kind of bacterium, but at some point in human evolutionary history it ceased to become an invader and instead became an essential part of something larger. If you could offer a mitochondrion its freedom, would it take it?

Now when I explore the mindscape of a human, I wonder which part is my species and which was originally human. I wonder if the ancestral memories of my species are buried somewhere in the minds of humans. Perhaps they can access these memories only in their wildest dreams. After all, in dreams you can change form; you can walk among otherworldly wonders. The other thing that occurs to me is that while humans (unlike other animals) cannot normally communicate mind-to-mind, that ability might still be latent. So, for instance, some people can tell that they are being watched, or that there is someone besides them in an apparently empty room. Perhaps these are vestigial remains of the original ability to sense and meld with other minds.

After I recovered physically, I went back to my college in Delhi, although my heart wasn't in it. I needed to earn a living so that I could make sure Rahul Moghe was well taken care of. As for Binodini, I have not yet asked her if she betrayed me. I can sense the contours of her mind, but I cannot tell whether she would lie to me or not—her mind is disciplined enough that she might successfully conceal an untruth. Besides, if I don't ask her, I can still persuade myself, sometimes, that she is innocent.

When I returned she immediately understood that I had been through an ordeal; my still-healing body was proof enough. But she knew also that my mind and heart were broken, and she did not press me with questions. I told her only that I had met Rahul Moghe and that he was no longer a danger to humanity. Perhaps she supposed that I had made my choice and that it had been a difficult one. Perhaps she guessed that the possibility of her betrayal might always stand between us. But we no longer met as often as we used to.

I saw my old friend Sankaran again, some time after my return. He came to Delhi University to deliver a lecture. He was now a well-known cosmologist at an institute in Chennai, but he recognized me at once and greeted me affectionately. His wife seemed a lot more relaxed; she chatted pleasantly with me and introduced their seven-year-old daughter, a shy child with a mind as clear and still as lake water with the most interesting undercurrents. All three of them seemed happy, and despite the pain old memories brought me, I was happy for them.

He was no longer a soliton, of course. But that old curiosity, that childlike openness to the marvels of the universe, remained, as did his complete lack of pretension. He still apologized to potted plants when he bumped into them. My eyes filled with tears when I saw this; I blinked them rapidly away and laughed with him.

Perhaps the shadow of my old love was still there. We parted with promises of keeping in touch.

One evening Binodini came to my little flat. I was just seeing off some students I had been tutoring; they gave me good-natured "aha" glances when she came up the stairs. She had been worrying about my depression, she said. There was a movie in the local theater, a particularly silly science fiction movie we had not yet seen, and would I go with her to see it? I did not want to go, but I let myself be persuaded. In the hot and stuffy theater I sat stiffly in my seat as the drama revealed itself; it was all about aliens on Earth trying to pretend to be human and failing hilariously. Another time it would have sent me into hysterical fits of laughter, but this time I simply felt the sadness come upon me like a wave. Binodini seemed to sense that the movie was not the right one; she pressed my hand as if in apology, and when I stood up to go out, bumping against people's knees and apologizing, she followed.

It was a clear night. The neighborhood next to the theater was suffering a power failure, common in the summer months, so the stars stood out more brightly than they normally did. I looked up at the speck that was my native sun, unfathomably far away.

Binodini took my hand.

I thought of human beings, how they could be, simultaneously, friend and betrayer. Murderer, mother, lover. I, too, had loved and betrayed my own kind.

"You're not alone," Binodini said. "At least, not any more than anyone else."

In that place where we paused, the neon lights of the theater and the sounds of traffic and people were both muted. Under the neem trees the night was thick, so that the candles in the windows of the darkened houses appeared like flickering stars. I could, with a little imagination, see us as adrift in the ocean of space. Home was just a short flight away.

As we gazed up, a meteor seared a path through the black velvet sky and disappeared. A meteor, or a ship.

"Wish a wish, Arun!" Binodini said. Her voice was full of tears.

Her hand was warm in mine. She disengaged it gently, and we walked home together through the star-filled night.

steve fever

GREG EGAN

Here's another highly inventive story by Greg Egan, whose "Glory" appears elsewhere in this anthology. Here he shows us that in the uneasy future that awaits us it'll be possible to catch a lot more than a *cold*. . . .

1

A few weeks after his fourteenth birthday, with the soybean harvest fast approaching, Lincoln began having vivid dreams of leaving the farm and heading for the city. Night after night, he pictured himself gathering supplies, trudging down to the highway, and hitching his way to Atlanta.

There were problems with the way things got done in the dream, though, and each night in his sleep he struggled to resolve them. The larder would be locked, of course, so he dreamed up a side-plot about collecting a stash of suitable tools for breaking in. There were sensors all along the farm's perimeter, so he dreamed about different ways of avoiding or disabling them.

Even when he had a scenario that seemed to make sense, daylight revealed further flaws. The grille that blocked the covered part of the irrigation ditch that ran beneath the fence was too strong to be snipped away with bolt cutters, and the welding torch had a biometric lock.

When the harvest began, Lincoln contrived to get a large stone caught in the combine, and then volunteered to repair the damage. With his father looking on, he did a meticulous job, and when he received the expected praise he replied with what he hoped was a dignified mixture of pride and bemusement, "I'm not a kid anymore. I can handle the torch."

"Yeah." His father seemed embarrassed for a moment; then he squatted down, put the torch into supervisor mode, and added Lincoln's touch to the authorized list.

Lincoln waited for a moonless night. The dream kept repeating itself, thrashing impatiently against his skull, desperate to be made real.

When the night arrived and he left his room, barefoot in the darkness, he felt as if he was finally enacting some long-rehearsed performance: less a play than an elaborate dance that had seeped into every muscle in his body. First he carried his boots to the back door and left them by the step. Then he took his backpack to the larder, the borrowed tools in different pockets so they wouldn't clank against each other. The larder door's hinges were attached on the inside, but he'd marked their positions with penknife scratches in the varnish that he'd practiced finding by touch. His mother had secured the food store years before, after a midnight raid by Lincoln and his younger brother, Sam, but it was still just a larder, not a jewel safe, and the awl bit through the wood easily enough, finally exposing the tip of one of the screws that held the hinges in place. The pliers he tried first couldn't grip the screw tightly enough to get it turning, but Lincoln had dreamed of an alternative. With the awl, he cleared away a little more wood; then he jammed a small hexagonal nut onto the screw's thread and used a T-handled socket wrench to turn them together. The screw couldn't move far, but this was enough to loosen it. He removed the nut and used the pliers; then with a few firm taps from a hammer, delivered via the socket wrench, the screw broke free of the wood.

He repeated the procedure five more times, freeing the hinges completely; then he strained against the door, keeping a firm grip on the handle, until the tongue of the lock slipped from its groove.

The larder was pitch-black, but he didn't risk using his flashlight; he found what he wanted by memory and touch, filling the backpack with enough provisions for a week. *After that?* He'd never wondered, in the dream. Maybe he'd find new friends in Atlanta who'd help him. The idea struck a chord, as if it was a truth he was remembering, not a hopeful speculation.

The toolshed was locked securely, but Lincoln was still skinny enough to crawl through the hole in the back wall, hidden by junk for so long that it had fallen off the end of his father's repair list. This time he risked the flashlight and walked straight to the welding torch, rather than groping his way across the darkness. He maneuvered it through the hole, and didn't bother rearranging the rotting timbers that had concealed the entrance. There was no point covering his tracks. He would be missed within minutes of his parents' rising, no matter what, so the important thing now was speed.

He put on his boots and headed for the irrigation ditch. Their German shepherd, Melville, trotted up and started licking Lincoln's hand. Lincoln stopped and petted him for a few seconds, then firmly ordered him back toward the house. The dog made a soft wistful sound but complied.

Twenty meters from the perimeter fence, Lincoln climbed into the ditch. The enclosed section was still a few meters away, but he crouched down immediately, practicing the necessary constrained gait, and shielding himself from the sensors' gaze. He clutched the torch under one arm, careful to keep it dry. The chill of the water didn't much bother him; his boots grew heavy, but he didn't know what the ditch concealed, and he'd rather have waterlogged boots than a rusty scrap of metal slicing his foot.

He entered the enclosed concrete cylinder; then a few steps brought him to the metal grille. He switched on the torch and oriented himself by the light of its control panel. When he put on the goggles he was blind, but then he squeezed the trigger of the torch and the arc lit up the tunnel around him.

Each bar took just seconds to cut, but there were a lot of them. In the confined space the heat was oppressive; his T-shirt was soon soaked with sweat. Still, he had fresh clothes in his pack, and he could wash in the ditch once he was through. If he was still not respectable enough to get a ride, he'd walk to Atlanta.

"Young man, get out of there immediately."

Lincoln shut off the arc. The voice, and those words, could only belong to his grandmother. For a few pounding heartbeats, he wondered if he'd imagined it, but then in the same unmistakable tone, ratcheted up a notch, she added, "Don't play games with me; I don't have the patience for it."

Lincoln slumped in the darkness, disbelieving. He'd dreamed his way through every detail, past every obstacle. How could she appear out of nowhere and ruin everything?

There wasn't room to turn around, so he crawled backward to the mouth of the tunnel. His grandmother was standing on the bank of the ditch.

"What exactly do you think you're doing?" she demanded.

He said, "I need to get to Atlanta."

"Atlanta? All by yourself, in the middle of the night? What happened? You got a craving for some special kind of food we're not providing here?"

Lincoln scowled at her sarcasm but knew better than to answer back. "I've been dreaming about it," he said, as if that explained everything. "Night after night. Working out the best way to do it."

His grandmother said nothing for a while, and when Lincoln realized that he'd shocked her into silence he felt a pang of fear himself.

She said, "You have no earthly reason to run away. Is someone beating you? Is someone treating you badly?"

"No, ma'am."

"So *why exactly is it* that you need to go?"

Lincoln felt his face grow hot with shame. How could he have missed it? How could he have fooled himself into believing that the obsession was his own? But even as he berated himself for his stupidity, his longing for the journey remained.

"You've got the fever, haven't you? You know where those kind of dreams come from: nanospam throwing a party in your brain. Ten billion idiot robots playing a game called Steve at Home."

She reached down and helped him out of the ditch. The thought crossed Lincoln's mind that he could probably overpower her, but then he recoiled from the idea in disgust. He sat down on the grass and put his head in his hands.

"Are you going to lock me up?" he asked.

"Nobody's turning anybody into a prisoner. Let's go talk to your parents. They're going to be thrilled."

The four of them sat in the kitchen. Lincoln kept quiet and let the others argue, too ashamed to offer any opinions of his own. How could he have let himself sleepwalk like that? Plotting and scheming for weeks, growing ever prouder of his own ingenuity, but doing it all at the bidding of the world's stupidest, most despised dead man.

He still yearned to go to Atlanta. He itched to bolt from the room, scale the fence, and jog all the way to the highway. He could see the whole sequence in his mind's eye; he was already thinking through the flaws in the plan and hunting for ways to correct them.

He banged his head against the table. "Make it stop! Get them out of me!"

His mother put an arm around his shoulders. "You know we can't wave a magic wand and get rid of them. You've got the latest counterware. All we can do is send a sample to be analyzed, do our bit to speed the process along."

The cure could be months away, or years. Lincoln moaned pitifully. "Then lock me up! Put me in the basement!"

His father wiped a glistening streak of sweat from his forehead. "That's not going to happen. If I have to be beside you everywhere you go, we're still going to treat you like a human being." His voice was strained, caught somewhere between fear and defiance.

Silence descended. Lincoln closed his eyes. Then his grandmother spoke.

"Maybe the best way to deal with this is to let him scratch his damned itch."

"What?" His father was incredulous.

"He wants to go to Atlanta. I can go with him."

"*The Stevelets* want him in Atlanta," his father replied.

"They're not going to harm him; they just want to borrow him. And like it or not, they've already done that. Maybe the quickest way to get them to move on is to satisfy them."

Lincoln's father said, "You know they can't be satisfied."

"Not completely. But every path they take has its dead end, and the sooner they find this one, the sooner they'll stop bothering him."

His mother said, "If we keep him here, that's a dead end for them, too. If they want him in Atlanta, and he's not in Atlanta—"

"They won't give up that easily," his grandmother replied. "If we're not going to lock him up and throw away the key, they're not going to take a few setbacks and delays as some kind of proof that Atlanta's beyond all hope."

Silence again. Lincoln opened his eyes. His father addressed Lincoln's grandmother. "Are you sure you're not infected yourself?"

She rolled her eyes. "Don't go all *Body Snatchers* on me, Carl. I know the two of you can't leave the farm right now. So if you want to let him go, I'll look after him." She shrugged and turned her head away imperiously. "I've said my piece. Now it's your decision."

2

Lincoln drove the truck as far as the highway, then reluctantly let his grandmother take the wheel. He loved the old machine, which still had the engine his grandfather had installed, years before Lincoln was born, to run on their home-pressed soybean oil.

"I plan to take the most direct route," his grandmother announced. "Through Macon. Assuming your friends have no objection."

Lincoln squirmed. "Don't call them that!"

"I'm sorry." She glanced at him sideways. "But I still need to know."

Reluctantly, Lincoln forced himself to picture the drive ahead, and he felt a surge of *rightness* endorsing the plan. "No problem with that," he muttered. He was under no illusion that he could prevent the Stevelets from influencing his thoughts, but deliberately consulting them, as if there were a third person sitting in the cabin between them, made him feel much worse.

He turned to look out the window, at the abandoned fields and silos passing by. He had been down this stretch of highway a hundred times, but each piece of blackened machinery now carried a disturbing new poignancy. The Crash had come thirty years ago, but it still wasn't truly over. The Stevelets aspired to do no harm—and supposedly they got better at that year by year—but they were still far too stupid and stubborn to be relied upon to get anything right. They had just robbed his parents of two skilled pairs of hands in the middle of the harvest; how could they imagine that that was harmless? Millions of people around the world had died in the Crash, and that couldn't all be blamed on panic and self-inflicted casualties. The government had been crazy, bombing half the farms in the southeast; everyone agreed now that it had only made things worse. But many other deaths could not have been avoided, except by the actions of the Stevelets themselves.

You couldn't reason with them, though. You couldn't shame them, or punish them. You just had to hope they got better at noticing when they were screwing things up, while they forged ahead with their impossible task.

"See that old factory?" Lincoln's grandmother gestured at a burned-out metal frame drooping over slabs of cracked concrete, standing in a field of weeds. "There was a conclave there, almost twenty years ago."

Lincoln had been past the spot many times, and no one had ever mentioned this before. "What happened? What did they try?"

"I heard it was meant to be a time machine. Some crackpot had put his plans on the Net, and the Stevelets decided they had to check it out. About a hundred people were working there, and thousands of animals."

Lincoln shivered. "How long were they at it?"

"Three years." She added quickly, "But they've learned to rotate the workers now. It's rare for them to hang on to any individual for more than a month or two."

A month or two. A part of Lincoln recoiled, but another part thought: that wouldn't be so bad. A break from the farm, doing something different. Meeting new people, learning new skills, working with animals.

Rats, most likely.

Steve Hasluck had been part of a team of scientists developing a new kind of medical nanomachine, refining the tiny surgical instruments so they could make decisions of their own, on the spot. Steve's team had developed an efficient way of sharing computing power across a whole swarm, allowing them to run large, complex programs known as "expert systems" that codified decades of biological and clinical knowledge into pragmatic lists of rules. The nanomachines didn't really "know" anything, but they could churn through a very long list of "if A and B, there's an eighty percent chance of C" at blistering speed, and a good list gave them a good chance of cutting a lot of diseases off short.

Then Steve found out that he had cancer, and that his particular kind wasn't on anyone's list of rules.

He took a batch of the nanomachines and injected them into a room full of caged rats, along with samples of his tumor. The nanomachines could swarm all over the tumor cells, monitoring their actions constantly. The polymer radio antennas they built beneath the rats' skin let them share their observations and hunches from host to host, like their own high-speed wireless Internet, as well as reporting their findings back to Steve himself. With that much information being gathered, how hard could it be to understand the problem, and fix it? But Steve and his colleagues couldn't make sense of the data. Steve got sicker, and all the gigabytes pouring out of the rats remained as useless as ever.

Steve tried putting new software into the swarms. If nobody knew how to cure his disease, why not let the swarms work it out? He gave them access to vast clinical databases, and told them to extract their own rules. When the cure still failed to appear, he bolted on more software, including expert systems seeded with basic knowledge of chemistry and physics. From this starting point, the swarms worked out things about cell membranes and protein folding that no one had ever realized before, but none of it helped Steve.

Steve decided that the swarms still had too narrow a view. He gave them a general-purpose knowledge acquisition engine and let them drink at will from the entire Web. To guide their browsing and their self-refinement, he gave them two clear goals. The first was to do no harm to their hosts. The second was to find a way to save his life and, failing that, to bring him back from the dead.

That last rider might not have been entirely crazy, because Steve had arranged to have his body preserved in liquid nitrogen. If that had happened, maybe the Stevelets would have spent the next thirty years ferrying memories out of his frozen brain. Unfortunately, Steve's car hit a tree at high speed just outside of Austin, Texas, and his brain ended up as flambé.

This made the news, and the Stevelets were watching. Between their lessons from the Web and whatever instincts their creator had given them, they figured out that they were now likely to be incinerated themselves. That wouldn't have mattered to them, if not for the fact that they'd decided that the game wasn't over. There'd been nothing about resurrecting charred flesh in the online medical journals, but the Web embraced a wider range of opinions. The swarms had read the sites of various groups who were convinced that self-modifying software could find ways to make itself smarter, and then smarter again, until nothing was beyond its reach. Resurrecting the dead was right there on every bullet-pointed menu of miracles.

The Stevelets knew that they couldn't achieve anything as a plume of smoke wafting out of a rat crematorium, so the first thing they engineered was a breakout. From the cages, from the building, from the city. The original nanomachines couldn't replicate themselves, and could be destroyed in an instant by a simple chemical trigger, but somewhere in the sewers or the fields or the silos they had inspected and dissected each other to the point where they were able to reproduce. They took the opportunity to alter some old traits: the new generation of Stevelets lacked the suicide switch, and resisted external meddling with their software.

They might have vanished into the woods to build scarecrow Steves out of sticks and leaves, but their software roots gave their task rigor, of a kind.

From the Net they had taken ten thousand crazy ideas about the world, and though they lacked the sense to see that they were crazy, they couldn't simply take anything on faith either. They had to test these claims, one by one, as they groped their way toward Stevescence. And while the Web had suggested that with their power to self-modify they could achieve anything, they found that in reality there were countless crucial tasks which remained beyond their abilities. Even with the aid of dextrous mutant rats, Steveware Version 2 was never going to reengineer the fabric of space-time, or resurrect Steve in a virtual world.

Within months of their escape, it must have become clear to them that some hurdles could only be jumped with human assistance, because that was when they started borrowing people. Doing them no physical harm, but infesting them with the kinds of ideas and compulsions that turned them into willing recruits.

The panic, the bombings, the Crash, had followed. Lincoln hadn't witnessed the worst of it. He hadn't seen conclaves of harmless sleepwalkers burned to death by mobs, or fields of grain napalmed by the government, lest they feed and shelter nests of rats.

Over the decades, the war had become more subtle. Counterware could keep the Stevelets at bay, for a while. The experts kept trying to subvert the Steveware, spreading modified Stevelets packed with propositions that aimed to cripple the swarms' ability to function, or, more ambitiously, make them believe that their job was done. In response, the Steveware had developed verification and encryption schemes that made it ever harder to corrupt or mislead. Some people still advocated cloning Steve from surviving pathology samples, but most experts doubted that the Steveware would be satisfied with that, or taken in by any misinformation that made the clone look like something more.

The Stevelets aspired to the impossible, and would accept no substitutes, while humanity longed to be left unmolested, to get on with more useful tasks. Lincoln had known no other world, but until now he'd viewed the struggle from the sidelines, save shooting the odd rat and queueing up for his counterware shots.

So what was his role now? Traitor? Double agent? Prisoner of war? People talked about sleepwalkers and zombies, but in truth there was still no right word for what he had become.

3

Late in the afternoon, as they approached Atlanta, Lincoln felt his sense of the city's geography warping, the significance of familiar landmarks shifting. *New information coming through.* He ran one hand over each of his forearms, where he'd heard the antennas often grew, but the polymer was probably too soft to feel beneath the skin. His parents could have wrapped his body in foil to mess with reception, and put him in a tent full of bottled air to keep out any of the slower, chemical signals that the Stevelets also used, but none of that would have rid him of the basic urge.

As they passed the airport, then the tangle of overpasses where the highway from Macon merged with the one from Alabama, Lincoln couldn't stop thinking about the baseball stadium up ahead. Had the Stevelets commandeered the home of the Braves? That would have made the news, surely, and ramped the war up a notch or two.

"Next exit," he said. He gave directions that were half his own, half flowing from an eerie dream logic, until they turned a corner and the place where he knew he had to be came into view. It wasn't the stadium itself; that had merely been the closest landmark in his head, a beacon the Stevelets had used to help guide him. "They booked a whole motel!" his grandmother exclaimed.

"Bought," Lincoln guessed, judging from the amount of visible construction work. The Steveware controlled vast financial assets, some flat-out stolen from sleepwalkers, but much of it honestly acquired by trading the products of the rat factories: everything from high-grade pharmaceuticals to immaculately faked designer shoes.

The original parking lot was full, but there were signs showing the way to an overflow area near what had once been the pool. As they headed for Reception, Lincoln's thoughts drifted weirdly to the time they'd come to Atlanta for one of Sam's spelling competitions.

There were three uniformed government Stevologists in the lobby, seated at a small table with some equipment. Lincoln went to the reception desk first, where a smiling young woman handed him two room keys before he'd had a chance to say a word. "Enjoy the conclave," she said. He didn't know if she was a zombie like him, or a former motel employee who'd been kept on, but she didn't need to ask him anything.

The government people took longer to deal with. His grandmother sighed as they worked their way through a questionnaire; then a woman called Dana took Lincoln's blood. "They usually try to hide," Dana said, "but sometimes your counterware can bring us useful fragments, even when it can't stop the infection."

As they ate their evening meal in the motel dining room, Lincoln tried meeting the eyes of the people around him. Some looked away nervously; others offered him encouraging smiles. He didn't feel as if he was being inducted into a cult, and that was not just from the lack of pamphlets or speeches. He hadn't been brainwashed into worshiping Steve; his opinion of the dead man was entirely unchanged. Like the desire to reach Atlanta in the first place, his task here would be far more focused and specific. To the

Steveware he was a kind of machine, a machine it could instruct and tinker with the way Lincoln could control and customize his phone, but the Steveware no more expected him to share its final goal than he expected his own machines to enjoy his music, or respect his friends.

Lincoln knew that he dreamed that night, but when he woke he had trouble remembering the dream. He knocked on his grandmother's door; she'd been up for hours. "I can't sleep in this place," she complained. "It's quieter than the farm."

She was right, Lincoln realized. They were close to the highway, but traffic noise, music, sirens, all the usual city sounds, barely reached them.

They went down to breakfast. When they'd eaten, Lincoln was at a loss to know what to do. He went to the reception desk; the same woman was there.

He didn't need to speak. She said, "They're not quite ready for you, sir. Feel free to watch TV, take a walk, use the gym. You'll know when you're needed."

He turned to his grandmother. "Let's take a walk."

They left the motel and walked around the stadium, then headed east away from the highway, ending up in a leafy park a few blocks away. All the people around them were doing ordinary things: pushing their kids on swings, playing with their dogs. Lincoln's grandmother said, "If you want to change your mind, we can always go home."

As if his mind were his own to change. Still, at this moment the compulsion that had brought him here seemed to have waned. He didn't know if the Steveware had taken its eyes off him, or whether it was deliberately offering him a choice, a chance to back out.

He said, "I'll stay." He dreaded the idea of hitting the road only to find himself summoned back. Part of him was curious, too. He wanted to be brave enough to step inside the jaws of this whale, on the promise that he would be disgorged in the end.

They returned to the motel, ate lunch, watched TV, ate dinner. Lincoln checked his phone; his friends had been calling, wondering why he hadn't been in touch. He hadn't told anyone where he'd gone. He'd left it to his parents to explain everything to Sam.

He dreamed again, and woke clutching at fragments. Good times, an edge of danger, wide blue skies, the company of friends. It seemed more like a dream he could have had on his own than anything that might have come from the Steveware cramming his mind with equations so he could help test another crackpot idea that the swarms had collected thirty years ago by Googling the physics of immortality.

Three more days passed, just as aimlessly. Lincoln began to wonder if he'd failed some test, or if there'd been a miscalculation leading to a glut of zombies.

Early in the morning of their fifth day in Atlanta, as Lincoln splashed water on his face in the bathroom, he felt the change. Shards of his recurrent dream glistened potently in the back of his mind, while a set of directions through the motel complex gelled in the foreground. He was being summoned. It was all he could do to bang on his grandmother's door and shout out a garbled explanation, before he set off down the corridor.

She caught up with him. "Are you sleepwalking? Lincoln?"

"I'm still here, but they're taking me soon."

She looked frightened. He grasped her hand and squeezed it. "Don't worry," he said. He'd always imagined that when the time came he'd be the one who was afraid, drawing his courage from her.

He turned a corner and saw the corridor leading into a large space that might once have been a room for conferences or weddings. Half a dozen people were standing around; Lincoln could tell that the three teenagers were fellow zombies, while the adults were just there to look out for them. The room had no furniture but contained an odd collection of items, including four ladders and four bicycles. There was cladding on the walls, *soundproofing*, as if the whole building weren't quiet enough already.

Out of the corner of his eye, Lincoln saw a dark mass of quivering fur: a swarm of rats, huddled against the wall. For a moment his skin crawled, but then a heady sense of exhilaration swept his revulsion away. His own body held only the tiniest fragment of the Steveware; at last he could confront the thing itself.

He turned toward the rats and spread his arms. "You called, and I came running. So what is it you want?" Disquietingly, memories of the Pied Piper story drifted into his head. Irresistible music lured the rats away. Then it lured away the children.

The rats gave him no answer, but the room vanished.

4

Ty hit a patch of dust on the edge of the road, and it rose up around him. He whooped with joy and pedaled twice as hard, streaking ahead to leave his friends immersed in the cloud.

Errol caught up with him and reached across to punch him on the arm, as if he'd raised the dust on purpose. It was a light blow, not enough to be worth retribution; Ty just grinned at him.

It was a school day, but they'd all snuck off together before lessons began. They couldn't do anything in town, there were too many people who'd know them, but then Dan had suggested heading for the water tower. His father had some spray paint in the shed. They'd climb the tower and tag it.

There was a barbed-wire fence around the base of the tower, but Dan had already been out here on the weekend and started a tunnel, which didn't take them long to complete. When they were through, Ty looked up and felt his head swimming. Carlos said, "We should have brought a rope."

"We'll be OK."

Chris said, "I'll go first."

"Why?" Dan demanded.

Chris took his fancy new phone from his pocket and waved it at them. "Best camera angle. I don't want to be looking up your ass."

Carlos said, "Just promise you won't put it on the Web. If my parents see this, I'm screwed."

Chris laughed. "Mine, too. I'm not that stupid."

"Yeah, well, you won't be on camera if you're holding the thing."

Chris started up the ladder; then Dan went next, with one paint can in the back pocket of his jeans. Ty followed, then Errol and Carlos.

The air had been still down on the ground, but as they went higher a breeze came out of nowhere, cooling the sweat on Ty's back. The ladder started shuddering; he could see where it was bolted securely to the concrete of the tower, but in between it could still flex alarmingly. He'd treat it like a fairground ride, he decided: a little scary, but probably safe.

When Chris reached the top, Dan let go of the ladder with one hand, took the paint can, and reached out sideways into the expanse of white concrete. He quickly shaped a blue background, a distorted diamond, then called down to Errol, who was carrying the red.

When Ty had passed the can up he looked away, out across the expanse of brown dust. He could see the town in the distance. He glanced up and saw Chris leaning forward, gripping the ladder with one hand behind his back while he aimed the phone down at them.

Ty shouted up at him, "Hey, Scorsese! Make me famous!"

Dan spent five minutes adding finicky details in silver. Ty didn't mind; it was good just being here. He didn't need to mark the tower himself; whenever he saw Dan's tag he'd remember this feeling.

They clambered down, then sat at the base of the tower and passed the phone around, checking out Chris's movie.

5

Lincoln had three rest days before he was called again, this time for four days in succession. He fought hard to remember all the scenes he was sleepwalking through, but even with his grandmother adding her accounts of the "playacting" she'd witnessed, he found it hard to hold on to the details.

Sometimes he hung out with the other actors, shooting pool in the motel's games room, but there seemed to be an unspoken taboo against discussing their roles. Lincoln doubted that the Steveware would punish them even if they managed to overcome the restraint, but it was clear that it didn't want them to piece too much together. It had even gone to the trouble of changing Steve's name—as Lincoln and the other actors heard it, though presumably not Steve himself—as if the anger they felt toward the man in their ordinary lives might have penetrated into their roles. Lincoln couldn't even remember his own mother's face when he was Ty; the farm, the Crash, the whole history of the last thirty years was gone from his thoughts entirely.

In any case, he had no wish to spoil the charade. Whatever the Steveware thought it was doing, Lincoln hoped it would believe it was working perfectly, all the way from Steve's small-town childhood to whatever age it needed to reach before it could write this creation into flesh and blood, congratulate itself on a job well done, and then finally, mercifully, dissolve into rat piss and let the world move on.

A fortnight after they'd arrived, without warning, Lincoln was no longer needed. He knew it when he woke, and after breakfast the woman at Reception asked him, politely, to pack his bags and hand back the keys. Lincoln didn't understand, but maybe Ty's family had moved out of Steve's hometown and the friends hadn't stayed in touch. Lincoln had played his part; now he was free.

When they returned to the lobby with their suitcases, Dana spotted them, and asked Lincoln if he was willing to be debriefed. He turned to his grandmother. "Are you worried about the traffic?" He'd already phoned his father and told him they'd be back by dinnertime.

She said, "You should do this. I'll wait in the truck."

They sat at a table in the lobby. Dana asked his permission to record his words, and he told her everything he could remember.

When Lincoln had finished, he said, "You're the Stevologist. You think they'll get there in the end?"

Dana gestured at her phone to stop recording. "One estimate," she said, "is that the Stevelets now comprise a hundred thousand times the computational resources of all the brains of all the human beings who've ever lived."

Lincoln laughed. "And they still need stage props and extras, to do a little VR?"

"They've studied the anatomy of ten million human brains, but I think they know that they still don't fully understand consciousness. They bring in real people for the bit parts, so they can concentrate on the star. If you gave them a particular human brain, I'm sure they could faithfully copy it into software, but anything more complicated starts to get murky. How do they know their Steve is conscious, when they're not conscious themselves? He never gave them a reverse Turing test, a checklist they could apply. All they have is the judgment of people like you."

Lincoln felt a surge of hope. "He seemed real enough to me." His memories were blurred—and he wasn't even absolutely certain which of Ty's four friends was Steve—but none of them had struck him as less than human.

Dana said, "They have his genome. They have movies; they have blogs; they have e-mails: Steve's, and a lot of people who knew him. They have a thousand fragments of his life. Like the borders of a giant jigsaw puzzle."

"So that's good, right? A lot of data is good?"

Dana hesitated. "The scenes you described have been played out thousands of times before. They're trying to tweak their Steve to write the right e-mails, pull the right faces for the camera—by himself, without following a script like the extras. A lot of data sets the bar very high."

As Lincoln walked out to the parking lot, he thought about the laughing, carefree boy he'd called Chris. Living for a few days, writing an e-mail—then memory-wiped, re-set, started again. Climbing a water tower, making a movie of his friends, but later turning the camera on himself, saying one wrong word—and wiped again.

A thousand times. A million times. The Steveware was infinitely patient, and infinitely stupid. Each time it failed it would change the actors, shuffle a few variables, then run the experiment over again. The possibilities were endless, but it would keep on trying until the sun burned out.

Lincoln was tired. He climbed into the truck beside his grandmother, and they headed for home.

Hellfire at Twilight

KAGE BAKER

One of the most prolific new writers to appear in the late '90s, Kage Baker made her first sale in 1997, to *Asimov's Science Fiction*, and has since become one of that magazine's most frequent and popular contributors with her sly and compelling stories of the adventures and misadventures of the time-traveling agents of the Company; of late, she's started two other linked sequences of stories there as well, one of them set in as lush and eccentric a High Fantasy milieu as any we've ever seen. Her stories have also appeared in *Realms of Fantasy, Sci Fiction,* and *Amazing* and elsewhere. Her first Company novel, *In the Garden of Iden,* was also published in 1997 and immediately became one of the most acclaimed and widely reviewed first novels of the year. More Company novels quickly followed, including *Sky Coyote, Mendoza in Hollywood, The Graveyard Game, The Life of the World to Come,* and *The Machine's Child,* as well as a chapbook novella, *The Empress of Mars,* and her first fantasy novel, *The Anvil of the World.* Her many stories have been collected in *Black Projects, White Knights; Mother Aegypt and Other Stories; The Children of the Company;* and *Dark Mondays.* Her most recent books include a new novel, *The Sons of Heaven.* Coming up is another new novel, *Or Else My Lady Keeps the Key.* In addition to writing, Baker has been an artist, actor, and director at the Living History Center and has taught Elizabethan English as a second language. She lives in Pismo Beach, California.

Here, in company with a time-traveling immortal, she helps us gain entrance to a famous and very exclusive club, one that's very hard to get into—and even harder to get *out* of.

On a certain autumn day in the year 1774, a certain peddler walked the streets of a certain residential district in London.

His pack was full, because he wasn't really making much of an effort to sell any of his wares. His garments were shabby, and rather large for him, but clean, and cut with a style making it not outside the powers of imagination that he might in fact be a dashing hero of some kind. One temporarily down on his luck, perhaps. Conceivably the object of romantic affection.

He whistled as he trudged along; doffed his hat and made a leg when the coaches of the great rumbled by, spattering him with mud. When occasionally hailed by customers, he stopped and rifled through his pack with alacrity, producing sealing wax, bobbins of thread, blotting paper, cheap stockings, penny candles, tinderboxes, soap, pins, and buttons. His prices were reasonable, his manner deferential without being fawning, but he was nonetheless unable to make very many sales.

Indeed, so little notice was taken of him that he might as well have been invisible when he slipped down an alley and came out into one of the back lanes that ran behind the houses. This suited his purposes, however.

He proceeded along the backs of sheds and garden fences with an ease born of familiarity, and went straight to a certain stretch of brick wall. He balanced briefly on tiptoe to peer over, then knocked at the gate in a certain pattern, *rap-a-rap rap*.

The gate was opened by a maid, with such abruptness it was pretty evident she'd been lurking there, waiting for his knock.

"You ain't half behind your time," she said.

"I was assailed by profitable custom," he replied, sweeping off his hat and bowing. "Good morning, my dear! What have you for me today?"

"Gooseberry," she said. "Only it's gone cold, you know."

"I shan't mind that one whit," the peddler replied, swinging his pack round. "And I have brought you something particularly nice in return."

The maid looked at his pack with eager eyes. "Ooooh! You never found one!"

"Wait and see," said the peddler, with a roguish wink. He reached into the very bottom of his pack and brought out an object wrapped in brown paper. Presenting it to the maid with a flourish, he watched as she unwrapped it.

"You *never*!" she cried. She whipped a glass lens out of her apron pocket and held the object up, examining it closely.

"Masanao of Kyoto, that is," she announced. "Here's the cartouche. Boxwood. *Very* nice. Some sort of funny little dog, is it?"

"It's a fox, I believe," said the peddler.

"So it is. Well! What a stroke of luck." The maid tucked both lens and netsuke into her apron pocket. "You might go by Limehouse on your rounds, you know; they do say there's all sorts of curious things to be had there."

"What a good idea," said the peddler. He hefted his pack again and looked at her expectantly.

"Oh! Your pie, to be sure. La! I was that excited, I did forget." The maid ran indoors, and returned a moment later with a small pie wrapped in a napkin. "Extra well lined, just as you asked."

"Not a word to your good master about this, however," said the peddler, laying his finger beside his nose. "Eh, my dear?"

"Right you are," said the maid, repeating the gesture with a knowing wink. "He don't miss all that old parchment, busy as he is, and now there's ever so much more room in that spare cupboard."

The peddler took his leave and walked on. Finding a shady spot with a view of the Thames, he sat down and ever-so-carefully lifted the pie out of its parchment shell, though he was obliged to peel the last sheet free, it having been well gummed with gooseberry leakage. He spread the sheets out across his lap, studying them thoughtfully as he bit into the pie. They were closely written in much-blotted ink, ancient jottings in a quick hand.

"'*Whatte to fleshe out thys foolyshe farye play? Too insubstancyal. Noble courte of Oberon nott unlike Theseus his courte. The contrast invydious. Yet too much wit in that lyne and the M of Revylls lyketh it not. Lovers not sufficienclye pleasing of themseylves. Thinke. Thinke, Will. Thinke,*'" he read aloud, through a full mouth.

"'*How yf a rustick brought in? None can fynde fawlt there by Jesu. Saye a weaver, bellowes-mender or some suche in the woodes by chance. Excellent good meate for Kempe. JESU how yf a companye of rusticks??? As who should bee apying we players? Memo, speake wyth Burbage on thys . . .*'"

At that moment he blinked, frowned, and shook his head. Red letters were dancing in front of his eyes: TOXIC RESPONSE ALERT.

"I *beg* your pardon?" he murmured aloud. Vaguely he waved a hand through the air in front of his face, as though swatting away flies, while he ran a self-diagnostic. The red letters were not shooed away, yet neither did his organic body appear to be having any adverse reactions to anything he was tasting, touching, or breathing.

But the red letters did fade slightly after a moment. He shrugged, had another mouthful of pie, and kept reading.

"'*Cost of properteyes: not so muche an it might be, were we to use agayne the dresses fro thatt Merlyne playe—*'"

TOXIC RESPONSE ALERT, cried the letters again, flashing bright. The peddler scowled in real annoyance, and ran another self-diagnostic. He received back the same result as before. He looked closely at the pie in his hand. It appeared wholesome, with gooseberry filling oozing out between buttery crusts, and he was rather hungry.

With a sigh, he wrapped it in a pocket handkerchief and set it aside. Carefully he packed the Shakespeare notes in a flat folder and slid it into his pack, took up the pie again, and walked away quickly in the direction of St. Paul's.

There was a stately commercial edifice of brick built on a slope, presenting its respectable upper stories level with the busy street above. The side facing downhill to the river, however, looked out on one of the grubbier waste grounds in London, thickly grown with weeds. Little winding dog paths crossed the area, and the peddler followed one to an unobtrusive-looking door set in the cellar wall of the aforementioned edifice. He did not knock but stood patiently, waiting as various unseen devices scanned him. Then the door swung inward and he stepped inside.

He walked down an aisle between rows of desks, at which sat assorted gentlemen or ladies working away at curious blue-glowing devices. One or two people nodded to him as he passed, or waved a languid pen. He smiled pleasantly but proceeded past them to a low flight of stairs and climbed to a half landing, which opened out on private offices. One door bore a sign in gold lettering that read *REPAIRS*.

The peddler opened the door, looked in and called hesitantly:

"Yoo-hoo, Cullender, are you receiving?"

"What the hell is it *now*?" said someone from behind a painted screen. A face rose above the screen, glaring through what appeared to be a pair of exceedingly thick spectacles. "Oh, it's you, Lewis. Sorry, been trying to catch the last episode of *Les Vampires,* and there's an Anthropologist over in Cheapside who keeps transmitting on my channel, all in a panic because he thinks—well, never mind. What can I do for you?"

Lewis set the half-eaten pie down on Cullender's desk blotter. "Would you mind very much scanning this for toxins?"

Cullender blinked in surprise at it. He switched off the ring holo, removed it, and came around the screen to unwrap the handkerchief.

"Gooseberry," he observed. "Looks all right to me."

"Well, but when I take a bite of it, I get this Red Alert telling me it's toxic," said Lewis, holding his fingers up at eye level and making jerky little stabs at the air to signify flashing lights. Cullender frowned, perplexed. He took off his wig, draped it over a corner of the screen, and scratched his scalp.

"You ran a self-diagnostic, I suppose?"

"I certainly did. I appear to be fit as a fiddle."

"Where'd you get it?"

"From the cook of a certain collector of rare documents," said Lewis, lowering his voice.

"Oh! Oh! The, er, Shakespeare correspondence?" Cullender looked at the pie with new respect. He turned it over carefully, as though expecting to find the front page of *Loves Labours Wonne* stuck there.

"I've already peeled the parchment off," said Lewis. "But I did wonder, you know, whether some sort of chemical interaction with old parchment, or the ink perhaps . . . ?"

"To be sure." Cullender took hold of the pie with both hands and held it up. He stared at it intently. His eyes seemed to go out of focus, and in a flat voice he began rattling off a chemical analysis of ingredients.

"No; nothing unusual," he said in a perfectly normal voice, when he had done. He took a bite of the pie and chewed thoughtfully. "Delicious."

"Any flashing red letters?"

"Nary a one. Half a minute—I've thought of something." Cullender went to a shelf and took down what appeared to be a small Majolica ware saucer. He held it out to Lewis. "Spit, there's a good fellow."

"I beg your pardon?"

"Just hoick up a good one. Don't be shy. It's the latest thing in noninvasive personnel chemistry diagnostics."

"But I've already run a diagnostic," said Lewis in tones of mild exasperation, and spat anyway.

"Well, but, you see, this gives us a different profile," said Cullender, studying the saucer as he swirled its contents to and fro. "Yes . . . yes, I thought as much. Ah ha! Perfectly clear now."

"Would you care to enlighten me?"

"It's nothing over which you need be concerned. Merely a cryptoallergy," said Cullender, as he stepped into a back cubicle and rinsed off the dish.

"I'm sorry?"

"Had you lived your life as a mortal man, you'd have been allergic to gooseberries," said Cullender, returning to his desk. "*But* when we underwent the process that made us cyborgs, our organic systems were given the ability to neutralize allergens. Nonetheless, sometimes a little glitch in the software reads the allergen as an active toxin—sends you a warning, when in fact you have nothing to fear from the allergen at all, a mere false alarm. Don't let it trouble you, my friend!"

"But I've eaten gooseberries plenty of times," said Lewis.

"You may have become sensitized," said Cullender. "Had a mortal acquaintance once became allergic to asparagus at the age of forty. One day he's happily wolfing it down with mayonnaise—next day he's covered in hives the size of half crowns at the mere smell of the stuff."

"Yes, but I'm a cyborg," said Lewis, with a certain amount of irritation.

"Well—a minor error in programming, perhaps," said Cullender. "Who knows why these things happen, eh? Could be sunspots."

"There haven't been any," said Lewis.

"Ah. True. Well, been in for an upgrade recently?"

"No."

"Perhaps you ought, then," said Cullender. "And in the meanwhile, just avoid gooseberries! You'll be fine."

"Very well," said Lewis stiffly, tucking his handkerchief back in his pocket. "Good day."

He turned and left the REPAIRS office. Behind him, Cullender surreptitiously picked up the rest of the pie and crammed it into his mouth.

Lewis proceeded down the hall to the cloakroom, where he claimed a change of clothes, and continued to the showers. He bathed, attired himself in a natty ensemble and neat powdered wig that made him indistinguishable from any respectable young clerk in the better offices in London, and went back to the cloakroom to turn in his peddler's outfit. The pack went with it, save for the folder containing the Shakespeare notes.

"Literature Preservation Specialist Grade Three Lewis," said the cloak warden meditatively. "Your case officer's expecting you, you know. Upstairs."

"Ah! I could just do with a cup of coffee," said Lewis. He tucked the folder under his arm, set his tricorn on his head at a rakish angle, and went off down the hall to climb another flight of stairs.

Having reached the top, and having passed through no fewer than three hidden panels, he stepped out into the Thames Street coffee room that sat above the London HQ of Dr. Zeus Incorporated.

The coffee room, in its décor, reflected the Enlightenment: rather than being dark paneled, low beamed, and full of jostling sheep farmers clutching leathern jacks of ale, it was high ceilinged and spacious, with wainscoting painted white, great windows admitting the (admittedly somewhat compromised) light and air of a London afternoon, and full of clerks, politicians, and poets chatting over coffee served in porcelain cups imported from China.

Lewis threaded his way between the tables, smiling and nodding. He heard chatter of Gainsborough's latest painting, and the disquiet in the American colonies. Three periwigged gentlemen in tailored silk of pastel Easter egg colors discussed Goethe's latest. Two red-faced, jolly-looking elders pondered the fall of the Jesuits. A tableful of grim men in snuff-colored

broadcloth debated the fortunes of the British East India Company. Someone else, in a bottle green waistcoat, was declaring that Mesmer was a fraud.
And, over in a secluded nook, a gentleman of saturnine countenance was
watching the room, his features set in an expression compounded of equal
parts disdain and boredom.

Ave, Nennius! Lewis transmitted. The gentlemen turned his head, spotted Lewis, and stifled a yawn.

Ave, Lewis. He took out his watch and looked at it in a rather pointed
fashion, as Lewis came to his table and removed his hat.

"Your servant, sir!" said Lewis, aloud. "Dr. Nennys? I believe I had the
pleasure of your acquaintance at Mr. Dispater's party, some weeks ago."

"I believe you are correct, sir," said Nennius. "Pray have a seat, won't
you? The boy's just bringing a fresh pot."

"Too kind of you," said Lewis, as he settled into a chair. He held up the
folder containing the parchments, waggled his eyebrows in a triumphant
manner, and set it down at Nennius's elbow. "I believe you collect antiquities, sir, do you not? If you will do me the kindness of examining these
papers, I believe you will find much to engage your interest!"

Don't lay it on with a trowel, for gods' sake, transmitted Nennius, but
aloud said merely, "Indeed? Let us see."

He opened the folder and studied its contents, while a waiter brought
another pot of coffee and a fresh cup and saucer for Lewis.

"Would you be dining, sir? Cake or something?"

Lewis felt the pangs of appetite. "Have you any apple pie?"

"Yes, sir," said the waiter, "bring you a nice one," and withdrew.

"We-ell," said Nennius, "very interesting . . . some prime examples here.
Private correspondence, notes, what appears to be a script page or two . . ."
He lifted out one parchment, and pursed his lips in annoyance as it brought
two other pages with it, glued together by fruit filling. "Rather a lot of work
for the conservators, however."

Lewis spread out his hands in a gesture of apology. "At least we have
them. Before I made the contact, she was using them to light the boiler. Poor
old fellow! I expect he'll have apoplexy when he finds out. Still, 'History—'"

"'Cannot Be Changed,'" said Nennius, finishing the statement for him.
"So somebody ought to profit from it. Eh? Not a bad job overall, Lewis." He
closed the folder and studied his nails as the waiter brought a sturdy-looking little apple tart and set it before Lewis. The waiter left, and, as Lewis was happily
breaking into the crust with a fork, Nennius said, "Still, they're pulling you out.
Sending you down to the Chilterns."

"Mm! Lovely country thereabouts," said Lewis, noting in satisfaction
that no red letters flashed in his field of vision. He had another mouthful of
pie. "What's the quarry, pray?"

"*If* it really exists, it's a Greek scroll or codex that would be anywhere from three thousand to seventeen hundred years old," said Nennius. "On the other hand, it may be a fraud. The sort of thing that would be cobbled together and sold to an impressionable young Briton on a grand tour. Your job's to find it—which may in itself be a bit tricky—and obtain it for the Company, which may be more difficult still."

"And determine whether it's authentic or otherwise, I assume," said Lewis.

"Of course, of course." Nennius took out a calfskin folder nearly identical to the one Lewis had given him and deftly switched them. "Your directions and letter of introduction are in there. Scholar wanting employment, highly recommended, encyclopedic knowledge of all things Greek and Latin, expert curator of papyrus, parchment, and et cetera. The gentleman in question has an extensive library." Nennius smiled as he said the last word.

"Sounds easy!" said Lewis, not looking up from his pie. "Hours of browsing through a splendid classical library? Now, that's my idea of a posting!"

"How nice that you bring your customary enthusiasm to the job," Nennius drawled. "Though we don't believe your specific quarry will be in the library, in fact. More likely hidden in a box of some kind, somewhere in one of the tunnels. Perhaps in an altar."

"Tunnels?" Lewis knitted his brows in perplexity. "Wherever am I being sent?"

"West Wycombe," said Nennius, with just a trace of malicious amusement. "To the estate of Baron leDespencer."

"Ah," said Lewis politely, lifting another forkful of flaky pastry crust.

"That would be Baron leDespencer, Sir Francis Dashwood," said Nennius. The bit of pie fell off Lewis's fork.

"I *beg* your pardon?" he stammered. Looking around hastily, he leaned forward and lowered his voice. "Surely you don't mean that fellow with the, the, er—"

"Notorious hellfire club? I'm afraid I do, yes," said Nennius in a leisurely fashion, taking a sip of his coffee.

"But I'm a *Literature Preservation Specialist*," said Lewis.

"So I understand. And Dashwood has one of the most extensive libraries of pornography, both ancient and modern, in the world. I know of some operatives who'd positively leap at the chance to have a peek at it," said Nennius. "You ought to have ample time, whilst you're searching for the scroll. Which is something entirely different, by the way. It may, or may not, contain an account of the rituals performed during the Eleusinian Mysteries."

"But *we* know all about the Eleusinian Mysteries!" said Lewis. "I attended them myself! And managed to record them, I might add."

"Yes, but your old holiday holoshots aren't the sort of thing the Company can sell to wealthy collectors," Nennius pointed out. "He's expecting you on the fifteenth. You'll do famously, I'm quite sure. Good day, sir. You'll excuse me, I trust; I have an engagement at the Cocoa Tree."

He rose, took up a silver-headed walking stick, and strolled out, leaving Lewis with the check.

In the dim gray hours of the fifteenth of the month, Lewis stepped down from the coach, caught his valise as the coachman threw it down to him, and looked blearily around at High Wycombe.

Its appearance lived up to its reputation as the capital of the British chair manufacturing industry.

There was a tavern that looked as though its interior was dark paneled, low beamed, and full of jostling upholsterers clutching leathern jacks of ale. It did not look as though it might be open and serving breakfast, however. Lewis sighed, and started the trudge to West Wycombe.

In spite of his worries, his spirits rose as he went along. The road was good, free of mud holes, the country rolling and wooded, beautiful in the brightening air. The dawn chorus of birds began. When the sun rose at last, it struck an answering gleam from a curious feature high on a hill: what appeared to be the steeple of a church, surmounted not with a cross but with a golden ball, like an echo of the sun itself.

How charmingly neoclassical, Lewis thought to himself, and was surprised, on accessing his database of local information, to discover that it was in fact St. Lawrence's church, and had been "restored and improved" by Sir Francis Dashwood himself.

The birds sang on. The autumn meadows were full of gamboling hares, and fleecy sheep, and the occasional prosperous and happy-looking shepherd. Rose brambles were bright with scarlet fruit. When the great house came into view at last, that too was all sunlight and peace: a great Palladian mansion of golden stone, trimmed with white.

Lewis scanned the countryside for suspicious-looking altars, standing stones, or at least a wicker man or two. There weren't any. No black hounds watched him from behind trees, either. Only, as he entered the park and started down the wide, pleasant drive, an elderly pug limping along on its solitary business stopped to regard him. It coughed at him in a querulous sort of way, and then lost interest in him and wandered on through drifts of fallen leaves.

At the end of the drive Lewis came to the tremendous entrance portico, Greek Revival looking strangely comfortable in its setting. Within, like an immense lawn jockey, a statue of Bacchus towered beside the door. Bacchus too looked comfortable. Lewis smiled nervously up at him as he knocked.

He gazed about as he waited for someone to open the door; there were panels painted with representations of scenes from classical literature, including one of Bacchus crowning Ariadne. Lewis was studying it with his head craned back, mouth agape, when the door was abruptly opened. He looked down and found himself being regarded by an elderly gentleman, far too well dressed to be a butler.

"You're not the postman," he said.

"No, sir. Your servant, sir!" Lewis removed his hat and bowed. "Lewis Owens. Is Lord leDespencer within?"

"He is," said the gentleman. "Owens? You'd be the librarian?"

"I hope to be, sir," said Lewis, drawing forth and offering his letter of introduction. The gentleman took it and waved him within in an absent-minded way, as he broke the seal and perused the letter's contents. Lewis slid past him and set down his valise in the Great Hall.

He scanned but was unable to pick up any currents of mortal agitation, only a droning like a well-run beehive, and fragments of mortal thought: . . . *Just get them geraniums potted . . . it doesn't hurt quite so much now; I shall be better presently . . . he asked for jugged hare special, and here you've gone and used up all the . . . damn, however shall I get that grease spot out? . . . I could quite fancy a cup of chocolate just now . . . see, he put all his money in barley futures, but . . .*

Lewis tended to become enthralled by mortal dramas, however ordinary, so he was startled from his reverie when the gentleman said, without warning:

"'*Vilia miretur vulgus; mihi flavus Apollo—*'"

"'*Pocula Castalia plena ministret aqua,*'" responded Lewis automatically.

The old gentleman smiled at him. "I see your patron is not mistaken in you. My apologies, young man; the last candidate Sir Francis considered for the post was something of an impostor. Paul Whitehead, sir, at your service."

"Whitehead, the author of *Manners* and other celebrated satires!" Lewis cried, bowing low. "Oh, sir, what an honor—"

They were interrupted at this moment by the butler hurrying in, hastily rearranging his cravat.

"I beg your pardon, Mr. Whitehead—so sorry—is the gentleman a friend?"

"I think it likely," said Mr. Whitehead, looking dazed. "You have, in fact, *read* something of mine? Good God, sir! And here I thought myself quite forgotten."

He drew breath to laugh and coughed instead, a hard, racking cough. John hurried forward to take his arm, but he held up his hand.

"I'm quite all right. Never mind, John. Come along, Mr. Owens; Sir Francis will be delighted to see you."

He led Lewis through splendid rooms, all done in a rather old-fashioned Italian Renaissance style and perhaps with too many statues to be in the best of taste.

"My understanding was that the library was in some disarray," said Lewis delicately.

"Well, it ought to be properly catalogued," said Mr. Whitehead. "We never got around to it; and now that so many of the books from Medmenham have been conveyed over here—why, it is in a sad condition."

Lewis cleared his throat. "That would be the, er, famous abbey?"

"Of the monks of St. Francis of Wycombe." The old man rolled his eyes. "*Famous*, is it? I daresay. For a secret society, we had an extraordinary number of tattlers. Not that any of them are up to much lechery nowadays. But there it is: 'In the days of me youth I could bill like a dove . . . tra la la la.'"

They emerged from the house into wide garden acreage, in which the neoclassical theme continued: temples, arches, and yet more statues, crowded around a lake. In the near foreground, however, a small and somewhat wobbly-looking pavilion of pink silk had been pitched on the lawn.

As they approached it, Lewis heard a man's voice saying, "I shouldn't do it, Francis. You will almost certainly have your left hand cut off by the Grand Turk."

"Bad Francis," said a child's voice.

"I believe you've found your librarian, Francis," said Mr. Whitehouse, leading Lewis around to the front of the pavilion. Inside, seated on a Turkish carpet, were two tiny children, a dish of quartered oranges and sweetmeats, and a man in late middle age. He wore a dressing gown and a turban.

"What?" he said. "Oh. Pray excuse me; we're being Arabs."

"Quite all right," said Lewis.

"May I present Mr. Lewis Owens, Sir Francis?" said Mr. Whitehead, not without a certain irony. "Mr. Owens—Lord leDespencer, Sir Francis Dashwood."

Further introduction was delayed at this point, because the little boy lunged for the sweetmeats and crammed a fistful of them in his mouth quick as lightning, occasioning the little girl to scream shrilly, "Papa, he went and done it after all!"

"And may I present my children? Francis and Frances Dashwood." Sir Francis clapped twice, and a nurse came from the portico. "I name them all after me; so like the Roman custom, don't you think? Take them back to the harem, Mrs. Willis. Fanny, remember your manners. What must we do when we meet infidel gentlemen?"

The little girl drew a curtain over her head, then rose to her feet and made an unsteady curtsey. The nurse scooped up the baby, levered the goo ball of sweets out of his mouth with a practiced hand, and bore him away despite his screams of rage. The little girl followed her, tripping only once on the trailing curtain.

"Won't you sit down, Mr. Owens?" said Sir Francis, indicating the carpet beside him. Mr. Whitehead had already gone to the portico and fetched himself a garden chair.

"With gratitude, sir," said Lewis, crawling awkwardly into the tent. Sir Francis offered him the dish, and he helped himself to an orange quarter. Seen close to, Sir Francis looked nothing like a notorious rake and blasphemer; he had a good-natured face, with shrewd eyes and none of the bloated fogginess of the habitual drinker.

"Here's his letter," said Mr. Whitehead, handing it to Sir Francis, who held it out at arm's length and peered at it.

"Why, sir, you come to us highly recommended," he said after a moment. "It would appear you are quite the scholar."

"Dr. Franklin is too kind," said Lewis, doing his best to look abashed.

"And you've some experience restoring old papers! That's an excellent thing, for, you know, some of my library is exceeding rare and, like mortal flesh, prone to crumble with age." Sir Francis tucked the letter into his pocket and gave Lewis a sidelong look. "I suppose you were, er, advised as to its nature?"

"Oh." Lewis blushed. "Yes. Yes, my lord, I was."

"I don't imagine you're a prudish young fellow; Franklin would scarce have sent you if you were inclined that way. Mr. Williams was a sad disappointment, yes indeed; let us hope his successor fares better." Sir Francis took up a piece of orange and bit into it.

"I expect you have heard stories, of course," he added.

"Er—yes," said Lewis.

Sir Francis chortled. "Most of them are wildest exaggeration. Yet we had some rare times in our day, Paul, had we not? Good food, good drink, good company. Taste the sweets of life, my boy, whilst you're able, for all too soon we fade like summer flowers."

"Too soon indeed," said Mr. Whitehead with a sigh. "Albeit a firm belief in eternal life in the hereafter is a great comfort."

"Quite so," Sir Francis agreed, looking solemn. "Still, we're not entirely withered yet, hey? I was thinking only the other evening, we really ought to have another 'Chapter Meeting' with some of our brother monks." He winked broadly at Lewis. "Quite a bit of fun, and really nothing of which to be ashamed. Paul knows of a respectable house with the most agreeable, good-natured girls—charmers all, discreet, free of the pox, but with a certain amount of *intellectual* furniture, you know."

"Ah! Like the hetaerae of Ancient Greece?" Lewis inquired.

"Exactly!" said Sir Francis, and seized his hand and shook it enthusiastically. "Just so. And, after all, in men of our years, good conversation hath its virtue, too. Not that I expect a young man to believe me."

He popped a sweetmeat in his mouth and crawled out of the tent on hands and knees. "Come along," he said briskly. "We'll show you the library."

Lewis found himself employed. It couldn't have been easier; he had a pleasant room, was free to keep his own hours, and had a place at Sir Francis's table. On his second evening in residence he had a difficult encounter with a dish of syllabub that proved to contain gooseberries, but managed to ignore the flashing lights and keep smiling at his host's witticisms.

And the library was a treasure trove.

It was true that a great deal of it consisted of erotica, inclining to the eclectic rather than the perverse. Lewis found a splendid copy of the earliest translation into English of the *Kama Sutra*. And the library certainly needed putting into order: *Gulliver's Travels* jostled for shelf space with books on the Kabbalah, or on architecture, or *Foxe's Book of Martyrs*, or Ovid's *Amores*. There were indeed a couple of fairly ancient scrolls and codices: a second-century copy of Euripides' *The Bacchae*, and a copy of Aristophanes' *The Frogs* that was nearly as old.

There were a few fakes, too, most notably a work on alchemy purporting to have been written by Aristotle; these were well done, clearly by a someone who had had access to a cache of very old papyrus and knew a few tricks for compounding period-formula inks. Lewis recognized the hand of a certain forger active in the last century, who had worked from the Eugenikos manuscripts. This unknown Russian was quite a celebrity in the faked document trade; Lewis, noting that Sir Francis had traveled to Russia in his youth, suspected that he may have been sold a number of phonies from the same artist.

At the end of a week, he sat down at his artfully concealed field credenza and sent the message:

> DASHWOOD MISSION SUCCESS SO FAR. HAVE GAINED ACCESS TO LIBRARY. MUCH TO INTEREST COMPANY INVESTORS! WILL REQUIRE TWO DRUMS PAPYRO-FIX AND ONE OF PARCH-FIX. KINDLY SHIP BY EARLIEST POST.
>
> HOWEVER, NO SIGN OF QUOTE ELEUSINIAN MYSTERY SCROLL UNQUOTE. NO SIGN OF PAGAN ORGIES YET. NO ORGIES OF ANY KIND, IN FACT. SUGGEST INFORMANT MISTAKEN?

After an hour the reply came back, in glaring yellow letters:

PAPYRO-FIX AND PARCH-FIX HAVE SHIPPED.
LOOK HARDER, LEWIS.

"This is excellent bacon, my lord," said Lewis, at the breakfast table.

"Eh?" Sir Francis looked up from watching the nurse attempting to feed his offspring porridge. "Ah. Good pigs hereabouts."

Lewis wondered how to gracefully transition from pigs to the subject at hand, and couldn't think of a way.

"I wondered, my lord, whether, since it is the Sabbath, I might not have the day to walk in the gardens," he said.

"What? Oh, by all means!" said Sir Francis. "Yes, you'll enjoy that. A man of classical education will find much to engage his attention," he added, winking so broadly that his little daughter was fascinated, and sat there at the table practicing outrageous winks, until her nurse quelled her with a deadly look.

Lewis slipped forth after breakfast and had hoped to spend a profitable day spying out likely places where a scroll might be hidden, but he had got no farther than the Temple of Venus when Sir Francis popped out of a folly.

"There you are! It occurred to me that you'd benefit from a guide; there's rather a lot to see," he cried heartily.

"You're too kind, my lord," said Lewis, concealing his irritation.

"Oh, not at all." Sir Francis cleared his throat a little self-consciously and went on: "Well! The Temple of Venus. Note, sir, the statue."

"Which one?" Lewis inquired politely, for there were before him nearly thirty figures decorating the slope up to the temple, among the bright fallen leaves: boys bearing shields, various smaller figures of fauns, nymphs, cherubs, and what looked suspiciously like a contingent of garden gnomes.

"Venus herself," said Sir Francis, leading the way up the hill. "The one actually in the temple, you see? Regard the rather better execution than in all the little figures; I got those at a bargain price, though, by God. Someone's plaster yard in Genoa had gone bankrupt and was closing out its stock. This, sir, is a copy of the Venus de Medici; rather fine, don't you think?"

"Profoundly so," said Lewis, wondering whether Sir Francis was guiding him away from something.

Sir Francis stepped back and swung his hand up to point at the dome of the temple. "And, see there? Look closely. It's a little hard to make out, at this angle, but that's Leda and Jove in the guise of a swan."

Lewis stepped back and looked. "Oh," he said. "Oh! Well. She, er, certainly looks happy."

"I think the sculptor caught perfectly the combination of ecstatic convulsion and divine-regarding reverie," said Sir Francis. "Pity we can't have it down here where it might be better viewed, but . . . well, perhaps better not. Awkward to explain to the children."

"I expect it would be, yes."

"And down *here* we put Venus's Parlor," Sir Francis went on. "That one represents Mercury, you see? Rather an ironic reminder to incautious youth. Observe the many elegant references to sweet Venus's portal of bliss, or, as some have called it, the Gate of Life itself, whence we all are come."

"How evocative, my lord," said Lewis, stammering rather.

"And that yonder is a temple to the nymph Daphne," said Sir Francis, pointing. "Must have the laurels trimmed back somewhat, so as to disclose it with more art. I put that in during my druidical days."

"I beg your pardon?"

"Was going to worship trees, once," said Sir Francis. "Applied to Stukeley—the Head Druid, you know—for initiation and all that. Got a charter to start up a grove, as it happened; but they grew vexed with me and withdrew it. No sense of humor, those fellows."

"Not the eighteenth-century ones, at any rate," Lewis murmured.

"And I don't know that I see much to worship in mere *trees*, in any case," said Sir Francis. "They're not good company, eh?" He nudged Lewis. "Same thing with the Freemasons; I always did my best to behave with them, but 'pon my soul I couldn't keep a straight face. Though I trust I give no offense, sir?"

"Oh, none, I assure you."

"I suppose I ought to have inquired whether you were a Christian," said Sir Francis.

"I frankly own myself a pagan," confided Lewis. "Though I have Christian friends."

"Oh, I too! I'd never mock Christ himself, you know; it's the institution I can't abide. Loathsome, cruel, sanctimonious greedy hypocrites! But regard my little church up there, on the hill; what d'you think of that, sir, hey?"

"I did wonder what the golden ball was for," said Lewis.

"It represents the Sun," said Sir Francis. "To my mind, much the more appropriate symbol for the Light of the World, wouldn't you say? But certain folk took umbrage, of course. Though I expect I only made things worse by having drinking parties up there, for I had it built hollow, you know, with seats inside. Then I slipped and nearly broke my neck climbing down out of it . . . dear, dear." He began to snicker shamefacedly. "Still, you ought to have seen the vicar's expression!"

They walked on a little, and Sir Francis pointed out the lake, with its swans and authentic fleet of small ships, useful for mock sea battles at parties ("though last time a fire broke out—burning wadding flew everywhere—so we haven't fired the cannons in years"). On an island in the center of the lake was another folly, with yet more statues.

"Looks rather like the Temple of Vesta in Rome," Lewis observed. Hastily he added, "At least, as it might have looked before it became a ruin."

"Ah! You saw that, did you?" said Sir Francis. "Very good! That was my intent, you know. You *are* a scholar, sir. I sketched the ruins myself, once. Dearly loved classical Rome when I was a young man. Still think its religion was quite the most sensible men have ever made for themselves."

"You know, I've thought that, too," said Lewis.

"Have you?" Sir Francis turned to him, positively beaming. "Their gods are so like *us*, you know: ordinary people, with faults and family quarrels. Some of them quite dreadful, but others rather endearing. Much more likely to have made this dirty, silly world than some remote Perfection in th' ether. Or wouldn't you say?"

"It has always seemed that way to me," said Lewis, thinking wistfully of his human ancestry. He considered Sir Francis, and decided to cast out a hook. "Of course, there wasn't much prospect of an afterlife for mere mortals in antiquity."

"Not so!" said Sir Francis. "Or what would you make of the Eleusinian Mysteries, then?"

Lewis drew a deep breath and thanked Mercury, god of schemers.

"Well, what can one make, my lord? The Eleusinian rites are unknown, because their initiates were sworn to secrecy," he said.

"Ha! I can tell you how much an oath of secrecy's worth," said Sir Francis, shaking his head. "Depend upon it, my young friend, people blabbed. Life everlasting was offered to mortals long before St. Paul and his cronies claimed the idea."

True enough, thought Lewis, reflecting on the Company's immortality process. "So it's rumored, my lord; but, alas, we've not a shred of proof for that, have we?"

"That's as may be," said Sir Francis blandly. "If I were to tell you that there are certain sacred groves in Italy where satyrs yet dance, you'd think me mad; yet I have seen something pretty near to them. Ay, and nymphs, too!"

Lewis did his best to look like a man of the world. "Well, I could name you a nymph or two here in England, if it comes to that," he said, attempting a nudge and wink.

Sir Francis clapped him on the back. "I dare say you could! Yes, we really must have another Chapter Meeting. I'll sponsor you, if you like."

"Oh, sir, what kindness!"

"Not at all," said Sir Francis, looking immensely pleased. "We've needed some young blood in our ranks. I'll send to Twickenham for Whitehead; he'll arrange it."

Lewis looked at the box of fragments and shook his head sadly. The pornographic papyrus was in shocking condition, nearly as bad as some of the Dead Sea Scrolls would be, though this damage seemed due to recent abuse of some kind. Worse still, some of the little bits were gummed together with something, and it wasn't gooseberry jam. Lewis had begun to have a queasy notion as to the circumstances of his immediate predecessor's departure.

"Well, let's see if we can't put things to rights," he muttered to himself, and set out the larger pieces. Three nymphs, five satyrs, and . . . possibly a horse? And a flute player? And a lot of bunches of grapes. Three sets of unattached, er, bits. Part of a . . . duck?

Frowning, the tip of his tongue between his teeth in intense concentration, Lewis sorted through all the fragments of wildly posturing limbs. With a cyborg's speed in analysis, he began to assemble the bits of the puzzle.

"There . . . and *he* goes there and *she* goes there and . . . no, that doesn't look anatomically possible, does it? Ah. But if this leg goes up *this* way . . . no, that's an elbow . . . oh, it's a *centaur*! Well, that makes much more sense. Silly me."

The door to the library opened, admitting a draft and Sir Francis. Lewis spread out his hands to prevent the reassembled orgy scene from sailing across the tabletop.

"There you are, Owens," Sir Francis said. He sounded a trifle hesitant. Lewis looked up at him sharply, but he did not meet Lewis's gaze; instead he kept his eyes on the papyrus as he approached.

"Well! H'em. What a splendid job you're doing! Deplorable state that one was in; should have had this seen to ages ago, I suppose. But, then, I've been busy these last years bringing myrtles to Venus myself, rather than reading about other people doing it. Eh?"

"Very wise, my lord."

He pulled out a chair and sat at the table, looking on in silence a moment as Lewis went back to fitting fragments together.

"I remember acquiring that one as though it were yesterday," Sir Francis said. "I was seeing Naxos. My guide was a shrewd man; you could trust him to find you absolutely anything. Girls fair or dark, plump or slender, whatever your mood; and the very best houses for drinking, you know, whether you wanted wine or stronger spirits. If you wanted to see temples, he could find those, too; and I had but to mention that I was interested in antiquities, and, by God, sir, he showed me . . ."

"A certain shop?" said Lewis, carefully applying Papyro-Fix from a plain jar, with a tiny brush. He fitted two fragments together. They reunited so perfectly it would have been impossible to say where they had been sundered. "A dark little place down a winding street?"

"Look at that! I declare, sir, you are a very physician of books! . . . But no, it wasn't such a shop. I've seen those places; they're all too eager to snare a young fool on his first Grand Tour, and sell him Homer's very lyre and Caesar's own laurels to boot. All impostures, you may be certain. No . . . this was another sort of place entirely."

Lewis was silent, waiting for him to continue. He looked up and saw Sir Francis gazing out the window, where the autumn forest showed now black branches through the drifting red and gold.

"The man led me up a mountainside," said Sir Francis. "A mountain of golden stone, only thinly greened over with little gnarled holm oaks, and with some sort of herb that gave off an aromatic perfume in the sunlight. And what sunlight! White as diamond, clear and hot. The sunlight of the very morning of the world. Transparent air, and the dome of blue overhead so deep a man could drown in it.

"Well, the path was less than a goat path, and we climbed for the best part of an hour, through thorns half the time, and how I cursed the fellow! He kept pointing out a little white house, far up the mountainside, lonely and abandoned looking. But I followed him, very surly indeed as you may imagine by the time we'd gained the house at last.

"Up there it was a little better; there was a great old fig tree that cast pleasant shade. I threw myself down in the coolness and panted, as an eagle sailed past—at eye level, sir—and the sea so far below was nothing but a blue mist, with little atomies of ships plying to and fro.

"I could hear murmuring coming from the house, but no other noises at all, not so much as the cry of a bird, and the drone of the insects had ceased. It was all very like a dream, you know; and it became more so when I got to my feet and went inside.

"There in the cool and the dark, a row of antique faces regarded me. They were only the heads of statues that had been ranged along a shelf, but upon my life I took them for persons at first, perhaps interrupted in conversation.

"My guide introduced the old man and his daughter. He'd been a scholar, evidently—dug amongst the ruins and through forgotten places to amass his collection—penniless now, and selling off the better pieces when he could find buyers. She was a beauty. Very Greek, gray eyed and proud. Brought me a cup of cold water with all the grace of Hebe.

"Well, we commenced to do business. I'd a well-lined purse—stupid thing to carry in such country, of course, but some god or other protects

KAGE BAKER | 477

young idiots from harm. He sold me the scrolls at once. His daughter brought out a few painted urns, very fine some of them, and I bought one or two. I had my man ask if there were any more. They talked that over between them, the father and his girl, and at last she signed for us to follow her.

"We went out through the back of the house. There was a spring, trickling from the rock, and a sort of pergola joining the back of the house to a grotto there. It was all deep in vine shade, with the little green grapes hanging down. Blessedly refreshing. That Achaean charmer led me back into the shadows, and I was upon point of seeing whether I might coax a kiss from her when—there—on my life and honor, sir, I tell you I looked on the face of God."

"What did you see?" said Lewis, enthralled.

"I think it must have been a little temple, once," said Sir Francis. "It certainly felt sacred to me. There were figures carved at the back of the grotto, into the living rock: Bacchus with all his train of satyrs and nymphs, coming to the rescue of Ariadne. Primitive, but I tell you, sir, the artist *could do faces*. The revelers were so jolly, you wanted to laugh with them—and, oh, the young Divinity, immortal and human all at once, smiling so kindly on that poor girl, seduced and deserted on her island! Holding out his hand to save her, and, in his compassion, granting her the golden crown of eternal life.

"It was a revelation, sir. That's what a god ought to be, I said to myself: wild joy in flesh and blood! And, being flesh and blood, generous enough to preserve we wretched mortals from death's affliction.

"I was desperate to buy the panel, but it wasn't to be had; no indeed. The girl had brought me in there simply to show some few small bronzes, stacked on the floor for want of room in the cottage. I sought by gestures to convey I wished to break the figures free of the wall; she understood well enough, and favored me with a look that nearly froze my blood. You'll think me a booby, sir, but I wept.

"I never close my eyes at night but I see that grotto still. I have had the god's likeness made many times, by some tolerably good painters, and bought me several images of him, yet none can compare with his countenance as I saw it on that bright morning in my youth.

"And I cannot but believe that, for a brief moment on that morning, I escaped this world's confines and walked in the realm of the ineffable."

"An enchanting story, my lord," said Lewis. He looked down at the bits of paper before him, fragments of some long-dead mortal's imagination.

How different their perception is, from ours. How I wish . . .

"Not the story I came in here to tell, alas," said Sir Francis, looking sheepish. "The past rules the present when you reach my age; you'll understand in your time, my boy. I, er, haven't quite been able to arrange the party. Not the initiation party into the Order, in any case. Paul's been ill, and our friend

Dr. Franklin sends his regrets, but he's otherwise engaged—still trying to salvage something from this calamity with the Americans, I've no doubt."

"I quite understand," said Lewis.

"And Bute's quite taken up with his gardening now. . . . Montagu sent word he'd certainly come, but for the entertainment he owes his guest—you've heard of Omai, the wild South Seas fellow? Captain Cook brought him back for show, and he's been feted in all the best homes. I said, 'Bring him with you; we'll initiate a noble savage!' But it seems his time's all bespoke with garden parties . . . well. You see how it is."

"Quite," said Lewis. "Perhaps another time, then."

"Oh, indeed! In point of fact, sir . . ." Sir Francis turned his head to peer at the doorway, then turned back and spoke with lowered voice. "I had contemplated something else, a rather more exclusive affair entirely. We haven't had one in a while; but now and again the need presents itself, and you being such an agreeable pagan, I thought . . ."

Lewis, scarcely believing his luck, put down the brush and leaned forward.

"This wouldn't have anything to do with a certain mystery we spoke of in the garden, would it?"

"Yes! Yes! You understand?" Sir Francis looked desperately hopeful.

"I believe I do, my lord. Trust me, you may count on my discretion," said Lewis, setting a finger beside his nose.

"Oh, good. Although, you know . . ." Sir Francis leaned in and spoke so low that if he hadn't been a cyborg, Lewis couldn't have made out what he was saying. "It won't be quite as, er, jolly as the services at the abbey. Perhaps we'll have a little dinner party first, just to warm us up, but then things will be rather solemn. I hope you won't be disappointed."

"I'm sure I shan't be," said Lewis.

When Sir Francis had left, after several winks, nudges, and hoarse declarations of the need for *utter secrecy*, Lewis jumped up and did a buck-and-wing down the length of the library.

There were certain comings and goings over the next week, nothing to indicate anything out of the ordinary to the unsuspecting observer, but significant. Sir Francis packed his present mistress, the children, and their nurses off to Bath, with a great many sloppy kisses and endearments. Guests arrived at odd hours: Sir Francis's half brother John, and another elderly gentleman who turned out to be a Regius Professor of Civil Law.

Lewis, placidly piecing together ancient carnal acrobatics, scanned the household as he worked and picked up more snippets of information. He learned that the seamstress had been given a great deal of last-minute work to do, because someone's costume hadn't been tried on in three years and didn't fit anymore. A young pig was driven over from an outlying farm and made a nasty mess in the kitchen garden, about which the cook complained; then Sir Francis himself went down and slaughtered it, somewhat inexpertly, judging from the noise and the complaints of the laundress who had to get the blood out of his garments.

The gardener was sent off with a shovel and wheelbarrow, and was gone all day, and grumbled when he returned; the footman and butler loaded a table and several chairs into a wagon, and drove them away somewhere.

Lewis was applying Parch-Fix to a codex purporting to tell the secrets of the Vestal Virgins when he heard the trumpets announcing a coach's arrival. He scanned; yes, a coach was coming up the drive, containing five . . . no, six mortals.

He set the brush down and closed his eyes, the better to focus.

Jingling ring of metal-shod wheels on gravel, with dreadful tooth-grinding clarity. The hollow thunder of the horses' hooves slowing to distinct *clop-clop-clop*, like the final drops in a rain shower, counterpointed by slippered feet crossing the marble floor of the entry hall in the house below.

Boom! Sir Francis seemed incapable of using a door without flinging it wide.

"*Ladies! Ladies, my charmers, my beauties, welcome, welcome one and all! Dear Mrs. Digby, it has been an age! How d'ye do? By Venus and her son, my dear, you're looking well!*"

"*La, bless you, my lord, and ain't you the 'oney-tongued flatterer!*"

"*Never in the world, sweetheart. Sukey! Pretty Bess! My arm, ladies, pray step down, mind your gown there—welcome once again—ah, Joan, you did come after all! We'd have missed you sorely. A kiss for thee, my love—and who's this? A new rose in the bouquet?*"

"*That's our young miss. Ain't been with us long. We reckoned she'd do for—*" And here the voice dropped to a whisper, but Lewis made it out: "*For our you-know-who.*"

"*Ah!*" Sir Francis likewise resorted to an undertone. "*Then a chaste kiss for you, fair child. Welcome! Where's Mr. Whitehead?*"

"*I'm just getting my hat—*"

"*A word in your ear, my lord—'e ain't well. 'ad a fainting fit and frighted us something awful. Sukey brought 'im round with a little gin, but 'e's that pale—*"

"*I know, I know, my dear, but—ah, here you are, Paul! What a rascal you are, swiving yourself into collapse with a carriageful of beauties! Eh? I declare, you're like a spawning salmon. Couldn't wait until tonight, could you?*"

"'Ere then, dearie, you just take my arm—"

"What nonsense. I'm perfectly well—"

"Bess, you take 'is other arm—come now, lovey, we'll just go inside for a bit of a lie-down afore dinner, won't we?"

"Perhaps that would be best—"

"Yes, let's give this rampant stallion a rest before the next jump. John! Have Mrs. Fitton send up a restorative."

"At once, my lord."

The voices louder now, because everyone had come indoors, but more muffled and indistinct. Lewis pushed back from the table and tilted his head this way and that, until he could pick up sounds clearly once more. There was Sir Francis, whispering again:

"—looks dreadful, poor creature. We ought to have done this sooner."

"'E looked well enough this fortnight past, when 'e was down to London. My sister's 'usband, 'e done just the same—sound as a bell at Christmas, and we buried 'im at Twelfth Night. Well, we must just 'ope for the best; that's what my mother used to say, my lord. What think you of the girl?"

"A little obscured by the veil, but she seems a pretty creature. She's observed all the . . . er . . . ?"

"Yes, my lord, you may be sure of that. And you 'ave a boy?"

"A capital boy! You shall meet him presently."

"Oh, good, 'cos I didn't care for t' other young gentleman at all. . . ."

Lewis sneezed, breaking his focus and sending a bit of Vestal Virgin flying. "Drat," he muttered. He got down on hands and knees to retrieve her from under the table and wondered once again, as he did so, just what exactly had happened to his predecessor.

Any unease he might have felt, however, was being rapidly overpowered by a certain sense of hopeful anticipation. A dinner party composed almost entirely of old men and nubile and willing ladies! Was it possible his perpetual bad luck was about to change, if only for an evening's bliss?

He had repaired the Vestal Virgins and was busily pasting the spine back on a copy of A New Description of Merryland when Sir Francis's butler entered the library, bearing a cloak draped over his arm.

"I beg your pardon, sir, but my lord requests your presence in the garden. You are to wear this." He held up the cloak, which had a capacious hood.

"Ah! A fancy-dress party, is it?" Lewis took the cloak and slung it around his shoulders. The hood fell forward, blinding him.

John, unsmiling, adjusted it. "If you say so, sir. You want to go out by the east door."

"Right-ho! I'm on my way," said Lewis, and trooped off with an eager heart.

In the garden he encountered a huddle of other cloaked figures, and was greeted by the foremost of them, who in speaking revealed himself as Sir Francis:

"That you, young Owens? We're just waiting for the ladies, bless 'em. Ah, they approach!"

Indeed, a procession was winding its way around the side of the house. Lewis saw five cloaked figures, and the foremost carried a torch held high. The gentlemen bowed deeply. Lewis followed suit.

"Goddess," said Sir Francis, "we mortals greet you with reverence and longing. Pray grant us your favor!"

"My favor thou shalt 'ave, mortal," said she of the blazing torch. "Come with me to yon 'allowed shrine, and I shall teach thee my 'oly mystery."

"Huzzay!" said the old Regius Professor, under his breath. He gave Lewis a gleeful dig in the ribs. His elbow was rather sharp and Lewis found it quite painful. All discomfort fled, however, when a little cloaked figure came and took his hand.

They paired up, a lady to each gentleman. Sir Francis took the arm of the torchbearer, and led them away through the night in solemn procession, like a troupe of elderly Guy Fawkes pranksters. The line broke only once, when one of the gentlemen stumbled and began to cough; they stopped and waited until he recovered himself, and then moved on.

Lewis, checking briefly by infrared, saw that the procession was moving in the general direction of the high hill crowned by the Church of the Golden Ball. Most of his attention was turned on the girl who walked beside him. Her hand was warm; she was young, and shapely, and walked with a light step. He wondered what she looked like.

The procession did not climb the hill but wound around its base. Presently Lewis was able to drag his attention away from the girl long enough to observe another church that lay straight ahead of them, seemingly dug into the hill. As they drew closer, he saw that it was only a façade of flint, built to conceal the entrance to a tunnel.

The famous Hellfire Caves! thought Lewis, and his heartbeat quickened.

They entered through gates, to a long tunnel cut through chalk, and here they must go single file. To his amazement, Lewis felt his racing heart speed into a full-blown panic attack; it was all he could do not to break from the line and run. He scanned the strata above his head: wet chalk, fractured and unstable. Plenty of rational reasons to fear this place; no need to summon demons from the unconscious . . .

The little girl reached forward and gave his hand a squeeze. It made him feel better.

They followed the tunnel gradually downhill, past niches opening off to the left, and then around in a loop that seemed to have taken them in a complete circle. It was black as pitch but for the torch flaring ahead of them, and silent, and damp, and cold as the grave. Another long straight descent; then a tight maze of turns and multiple openings where anyone but a cyborg might have had difficulty keeping a sense of direction. But now light showed ahead, down a straight passage, and Lewis picked up the scent of food.

They emerged into a great open chamber, well lit by flaring torches. Four figures stood perfectly motionless against the far wall. Each was draped in a black veil that dropped from the crown of the head nearly to the floor, in long straight lines. Each wore a mask. Two were black and featureless; two were painted in black and gold, resembling insect faces.

In the center of the room, looking incongruous, was a dining table set for ten.

Sir Francis's voice boomed into the silence, shattering the tension with echoes:

"And now, a pause in our solemnities! Supper in Hell, my friends! Though I promise you, you shall not be long *tantalized*. Tantalus, hey? In Hades? D'y'get the joke?"

"What a witty fellow you are, my lord, to be sure," said the lady with the torch dryly. She threw back her hood to reveal a svelte woman in early middle age. Her hair was a flaming and unnatural red. Painted, plastered, and upholstered as she was, she had nonetheless maintained a certain charm.

All the party now threw off their cloaks, and Lewis blinked in surprise. The gentlemen, himself excepted, wore white jackets and pantaloons, as well as extraordinary floppy blue and red hats embroidered on the front with the words *Love and Friendship*. The ladies wore white robes, cut in what must have been intended as a Greek fashion; all save the youngest, who, like Lewis, wore ordinary street dress. Her features remained hidden by her veil, however.

"It's cold in here," complained a buxom wench somewhat past her prime. "Why couldn't we done this at the abbey? It's ever so nice there. Remember the times we used to have?"

"I know, my dear, a thousand apologies—," said Sir Francis. "But the abbey's not so convenient as it was, I fear—"

"And we ain't a-doing of our sacred rites in no profane place, Sukey Foster, so just you shut your cake 'ole," reproved her mistress. She cast a somewhat anxious eye upon Sir Francis. "All the same, dearie, I 'ope I'll get a cushion to put under my bum this time? That altar ain't 'arf cold and 'ard."

"Everything has been seen to, dear Demeter," Sir Francis assured her.

"Very kind of you, I'm sure, Lord 'Ermes," she replied. Gazing around at the assembled party, she spotted Lewis. "'Ere now! Is 'e the . . . ?"

"Yes," Sir Frances replied.

"Well, ain't you the pretty fellow!" Demeter pinched Lewis's cheek.

"Might we perhaps sit?" said the old professor. "My leg is positively throbbing, after that march."

"Yes, please," said Whitehead faintly. He looked sweating and sick, a ghastly contrast with his clownish attire. Lewis scanned him, and winced; the mortal was terminally ill.

They shuffled to their places. To his disappointment, Lewis found himself seated far down the table from the little girl in the veil. The masked figures, who had been still as statues until now, came to life and served in eerie silence. A whole roast pig was brought from a side passage, as well as a dish of fruit sauce, loaves of barley bread, and oysters. Chocolate was poured from silver urns. ("No wine?" said the professor in disappointment. Sir Francis and Madam Demeter gave him identical looks of disapproval, and he blushed and muttered, "Oh! So sorry—forgot.")

Lewis, cold, hungry, and depressed, took a reckless gulp of chocolate and at once felt the rush of Theobromine elevating his spirits.

They feasted. Perhaps to make up for the lack of alcoholic cheer, the mortal party became terrifically loud, in riotous laughter and bawdy witticisms that made Lewis blush for the veiled girl. She sat in silence at her end of the table, except for once when she began to lift her veil and:

"'Ere! Just you keep your face covered, girl!" said Madam Demeter.

"'Ow the bloody 'ell am I supposed to eat anything?" the girl demanded.

"You pushes the cloth forward, and slips little bites under, like you was a proper lady," explained Sukey. "That's how I done it, when it was me."

The girl said nothing more but folded her arms in a monumental sulk. Lewis, well into his second cup of chocolate and with his cyborg nervous system now definitely under the influence of Theobromine, regarded her wistfully. He thought she looked enchanting. He wondered if he could rescue her from her degrading life.

How to do it? . . . Not enough money in the departmental budget. They'd all laugh at me anyway. But what if I went to one of the gambling houses? I could count cards. Prohibited, of course, but the Facilitator class operatives do it all the time, for extra pocket money. Nennius himself, in fact. Win enough to set her up with, with a shop or something. Poor child . . .

"Have another slice of this excellent pork, my boy!" roared Sir Frances, reaching across to slap meat on his plate. "And you haven't tried the fruit sauce! It's sublime!"

"Thanks," Lewis shouted back, leaning out of the way as a servant buried the pork in dollops of fruit compote. He leaned back in, took up a spoon, and began shoveling compote into his mouth, aware he needed to take in solid food.

No sooner had he set the spoon down, however, than the red letters began to flash before his eyes with all the vividness of migraine distortion: TOXIC RESPONSE ALERT!

"God Apollo," he groaned. Peering down at his plate, he made out one or two gooseberry seeds in the syrupy mess, when the flashing letters allowed him to see anything. "What have I done to myself?"

He sat very still and waited for the flashing to stop, but it didn't seem to; too late, he wondered if the Theobromine might have combined badly with whatever it was in the gooseberries to which his organic body objected.

Judge, then, with what sense of dread he heard the *ping-ping-ping* of spoon against water glass, and the creaking chair as Sir Francis rose to his feet to say:

"Now, my dears! Now, my esteemed brothers in revelry! Let us put aside our jollity! Our sacred business begins!"

"Huzzay!" shrieked the old professor.

"A little more decorum, sir, if you please," said Madam Demeter. "This is a solemn h'occasion, ain't it?"

"I'm sorry, my dear; it's my sense of enthusiasm—"

"Quite understandable, sir," said Sir Francis. "But we ought to remember that we have a new celebrant amongst us, who, though but a youth, has shown a true spirit of—er—Mr. Owens, are you quite all right?"

Lewis opened his eyes to behold a revolving wheel of faces staring at him, peeping in and out between the flashing red letters.

"Quite," he said, and gave what he hoped was a confident smile. The smile went on longer than he had intended it to; he had the distinct impression it was turning into a leer and dripping down one side of his face.

"Ah; very well then; I think we'll commence. Brothers and sisters! Let us drink together from the cup that will bind us in immortality," said Sir Francis, and Lewis was aware that a servant was stepping up behind him and leaning down to offer something. Blinking at it, he beheld a figured wine krater, a modern copy, showing Bacchus rescuing Ariadne. He took it and drank.

Water, barley, pennyroyal . . . a memory buried for fifteen hundred years floated up into his consciousness. Lewis tasted it again.

"The *kykeon*!" he exclaimed, rather more loudly than he had meant to. "And you've even got the formula right! Well done!"

In the absolute silence that followed, he became aware that everyone was staring at him. *You idiot, Lewis!* he thought, and meekly passed the krater to Sir Francis. All the others at table drank without speaking. When the empty krater had been placed in the center of the table at last, Sir Francis cleared his throat.

"The time has come. Behold my caduceus."

This provoked a shrill giggle from the professor, quickly shushed by the ladies on either side of him.

"If you ain't going to take this seriously, you didn't ought to be here," said Bess severely.

Lewis peered and made out that Sir Francis had produced a staff from somewhere and was holding it up. It was in fact a caduceus, very nicely carved, and the twining serpents' scales had been gilded, and their eyes set with faceted stones that glittered in the torchlight.

"I speak now as Hermes, servant of Jove," said Sir Francis. "I but do his immortal will."

"And I am Demeter, goddess of all that grows," intoned the lady, with a theatrical flourish. "'Ow weary I am, after the bountiful 'arvest! I will sleep. I trust in Jove, no 'arm shall come to my dear daughter Persephone, 'oo wanders on Nysa's flowery plain."

Sir Francis indicated to Lewis that he ought to rise. Lewis got up so hastily his chair fell backward with a crash, and he was only prevented from going with it by the masked servant, who steadied him. The veiled girl rose, too, and dragged from beside her chair a basket.

"I am Persephone, goddess of the spring," she announced. "Blimey, what a lovely great flower do I see! I shall pick it straightaway!"

Sir Francis took Lewis by the arm and led him to the dark mouth of another tunnel, opposite from the one by which they had entered. Persephone followed on tiptoe, grabbing a torch from one of the wall sockets as she came. They went down the tunnel a few yards, and stopped. Persephone drew a deep breath and screamed at the top of her lungs:

"Owwwwww! What dark god is this 'oo ravishes me away from the light of the world? Ow, 'elp, 'elp, will nobody 'ear my distress? Father Jove, where art thou?"

"Quickly now," Sir Francis whispered, and they hurried on through the darkness, around a corner, around another and another, deeper into the labyrinth, and Lewis heard water rushing somewhere ahead. They passed through another, smaller chamber, where there was a low stone altar; Lewis nearly fell over it, but Sir Francis caught him again and the girl took his other arm. Somehow they made it into the next passage and shortly came out into another chamber.

"The River Styx," announced Sir Francis, with a wave of his caduceus. "Here Hermes of the winged heels can conduct no farther. Away! He flits! He flies, back to lofty Olympus!" Throwing out his arms and springing into air with quite a remarkable balletic grace for a man his age, even crossing his ankles before he came down, and landing so lightly that his wig scarcely moved on his head, he turned and ran back up the passageway.

Lewis stood staring after him. The girl tugged on his sleeve.

"We're supposed to get in the boat," she said.

Lewis turned around to look. They stood on the edge of a dark stream that rushed through the cavern. On the farther shore was the entrance to yet another black passage. Before them was moored a quaint little boat, beautifully if morbidly carved with skulls and crossed bones, painted in black and gold.

"Oh," said Lewis. "Yes, of course! But where's Charon?"

"'Oo?" said Persephone.

"The ferryman," said Lewis, making punting motions.

"Oh. Nobody told me nothing about no ferrymen; I reckon you're supposed to get us across," said the girl.

"Right! Yes! In we go, then," said Lewis, who was finding the red flashes subsiding somewhat, but in their place was an increasing urge to giggle. "My hand, madam! Yo-heave-ho and hoist the anchor!"

"'Ere, are you all right?" The girl squinted at him through her veil.

"Never better, fair Persephone!" Lewis cast off and seized up the pole. He propelled them across with such a mighty surge that—

"Bleeding Jesus, mister, look out! You'll—"

The boat ran aground and Lewis toppled backward, falling with a tremendous splash into the dark water. He came up laughing hysterically as he dog-paddled toward the boat, with his wig bobbing eerily in his wake.

"Oh, God Apollo, I've drowned in the River Styx. Well, this *is* a first for me, but I wouldn't be *mister*, you know; the technical term is *mystes*—"

Persephone stuck her torch in a rock crevice, grabbed his collar, and hauled him ashore. "You been drinking, ain't you?" she said in exasperation.

"No, actually—it's the drinking chocolate; it has an odd effect on our nervous systems, we cyb-, I mean, we . . . Owenses," said Lewis through chattering teeth, for the water had been like ice.

"Ow, your shoes'll be ruined and—give me the bleeding pole; we got to fish your wig out. Damn it, I ain't wearing this veil another minute," said Persephone, and tore it off.

Lewis caught his breath.

She was a very young girl, pale by torchlight, but with roses in her cheeks. Her hair was red. Her eyes, rather than the blue or green one might expect, were black as the stream from which she'd pulled him. His heart— not the cyborg mechanism that pumped his blood—contracted painfully.

"*Mendoza?*" he whispered.

"'Oo's that? 'Ere, what's wrong?" she demanded. "You ain't going be sick, are you? You look like you seen a ghost."

"I—you—you look like someone I knew," said Lewis. "I must apologize—"

A throaty scream came echoing down the passage from the banqueting chamber.

"*My child!*" cried Madam Demeter, in tones she had clearly picked up from watching Mr. Garrick at Drury Lane. "*Ooooh, my chiiiiild! She is quite rrrravished away! Ow, somebody 'elp me quick! Wherever could she be?*"

"Bugger," said Persephone. "We got to go on. Come on, get up! You need a 'and?"

"Please—" Lewis let her haul him to his feet. He stood swaying, wondering if she was a hallucination, as she stuck the torch in his nerveless hand, retrieved his sopping wig, and grabbed up the basket. She did not wait but started ahead of him through the dark doorway. Coming to himself, he ran squelching after her.

Only a few yards on they emerged into the last chamber; there was no way to exit but back the way they had come. It was a small room, very cold and damp indeed, and empty but for a squarish stone object in the middle of the floor. There were some carvings on the side; Lewis recognized it for a Roman sarcophagus. Persephone sat down on it and began to rummage through the basket.

"You want to get out of them wet clothes," she advised. She held up one end of a length of white cloth. "This ain't much, but at least it's dry."

He stared at it in incomprehension, trying to clear his wits. She sighed, set the basket down, and began to unbutton his waistcoat.

"Don't tell *me* you ain't drunk. Come on, old dear, we ain't got all night," she said. "'Ark at 'em going on!"

"*I am Hecate, her what rules the night! I know where your daughter got to, Mistress Demeter!*"

"*Pray, speak thou!*"

"*Well, I hears this scream, see? And I says to all-seeing Helios, lord of the Sun, I says, 'Whatever was that noise? Sounded like a virgin pure being carried off!' And Helios says, he says, 'Oh, that was fairest Persephone being ravished. It was that Lord Hades done it!'*"

"*'E never!*"

"*S'welp me God! She's gone to the Otherworld to be Queen of the Dead!*"

"*My CHIIIIILD! Almighty Jove, is there no rrrrremedy!*"

Lewis stood nervelessly, letting the little girl peel off his soaked garments, until she unfastened his trousers.

"I—perhaps I'd better do that," he said, clutching at himself and backing away.

"Please yourself," she said, and matter-of-factly began to strip down.

"*Madam, be content!*" a male voice came echoing down the passageway. "*It is the will of All-Seeing Jove!*"

"*Whaaaaaat? What perfidy is this? It shall not be!*"

"'Ow they do go on," said Persephone. Lewis, hopping on one foot as he tried to get his breeches off, turned to answer her and nearly fell over, for she had skinned out of her garments with the speed of frequent practice and stood unconcernedly brushing out her hair. He stared. She didn't seem to notice.

"*. . . why then, sir, 'Eaven shall learn a goddess may be wrathful, too! I shall with'old my gracious bounty from the woooorld! See if I don't! The green corn shall wither in the field, and mortal men shall staaaarve!*"

"They're getting louder!" said Lewis. "Oh, dear, they're not coming in here, are they?"

"Naow, just as far as the room with the h'altar," said Persephone. "This is the sacred grotto. Nothing in 'ere but the sacred scroll."

Lewis managed to get his breeches off. Clutching them to his lap, he shuffled crabwise to the basket, rummaging for something with which to clothe himself. He pulled out a voluminous length of gauze embroidered with flowers.

"That's mine, ducky," said Persephone, sliding past him to take it. Her bare breast grazed his arm. He started so violently he dropped the sodden bundle he'd been holding. Persephone looked down. Her eyes widened.

"*. . . wander through the barren world, mourning the 'ole time for my dearest daughter! Oooooh, the perfidy of Jove!*"

"I'm sorry," said Persephone. "This ain't 'arf awkward. Look, if we was anyplace else, I'd do you proper, a nice-looking boy like you; only I can't 'ere, on account of it'd be sacrilege."

"It would?" said Lewis piteously.

"*'Ere will I rest awhile amid this sheltering grove, and in the shape of somebody's old wet nurse I will appear. But, soft! 'Oo approaches wretched Demeter? I perceive they are the daughters of some king or other.*"

"*Why, who is this poor old thing as sits beside our washing well? Cheer up, good lady. You shall come home with us and nurse our young brother.*"

"Didn't 'is Lordship h'explain?" Persephone rolled her eyes. "I thought you'd done this afore." She pulled the embroidered shift over her head, and yanked it down smartly to cover herself.

"Well, yes, but—it was a long time ago, and . . ." His distress seemed to aggravate the TOXIC RESPONSE ALERT. He squeezed his eyes tight shut, and made an effort to sober up.

"*Nooooow I am alone with the mortal babe, I will reward the kindness done to me! So! So! 'Ey presto! Another pass through the flaaaaames, and he shall become immortal—*"

"Ow my gawd, lady, you'll burn up my baby!"

"Now look what you went and done, foolish mortal! The spell's broke—"

"I can't do you because I'm being the Queen of h'Avernus," Persephone explained. "Which it would be h'adultery, see, on account of me being married to the Lord of the Dead and all. Do your breechclout up like a nice bloke, won't you? I know it don't seem fair, what with 'is Lordship and that lot getting to fornicate like mad. But it's in aid of Mr. Whitehead, you know."

"Oh," said Lewis, blinking back tears as she fastened his loincloth in place for him and then draped a white scarf over her hair.

"Poor old thing's dying," said Persephone. "Ever such a nice gentleman, 'e is. I wonder why the nice ones always dies on you? But this way 'e won't be scared, see—"

"—build a temple to meee, and so my divine wrath shall be appeeeeeeased! Nay, more! I shall grant eternal life to 'im as performs my sacred rites!"

"We thank thee, merciful goddess!" Now it became an exchange between the woman's voice and the chorus of male voices:

"What 'ave you done?"

"We have feasted; we drank the kykeon!"

"Fasted," Lewis corrected absently.

"What'll you do next?"

"We're taking something out!"

"What'll you do with it?"

"We're going to put it in something else!"

"Then come forward, mortals, and be'old the Sacred Flame! Die in the fire of my h'embrace, to live eternally!"

"Whu-huh-HEY!"

"I'm just as glad I ain't got to watch this part," remarked Persephone, settling down on the tomb lid. "Between you and me, Mrs. Digby ain't so young as she was, and the thought of 'er on that h'altar with 'er knees up—it's enough to curl your 'air, ain't it?"

"I suppose so," said Lewis, sitting down beside her.

Sounds of violent carnal merriment echoed down the passageway. Persephone twiddled her thumbs.

"So, er, 'ow'd you learn about the old gods and all that?" she asked.

Lewis stared into the darkness, through a hazy roil of red letters and memories.

"I was a foundling baby, left in a blanket by a statue of Apollo," he said. "In Aquae Sulis."

"Where's that?"

"I mean, Bath. It's in Bath. I was raised by a . . ." Lewis pondered how to explain a twenty-fourth-century corporation with the ability to time-travel and collect abandoned human children for the purpose of processing them into cyborg operatives. "By a wealthy scholar with no particular religious views. But I always rather liked the idea of the gods of Old Rome."

"Fancy that," said Persephone. "Mrs. Digby, she learned it off His Lordship. Ever such a comfort, for poor working girls, she says."

"You shouldn't be doing this," said Lewis, taking her hand in his. "You should have a better life. If I helped you—if I set you up in business, or something—"

"That's the liquor talking, dearie," said Persephone, not unkindly. "Lord love us, you ain't nothing but a clerk; you ain't got any money. And it ain't such a bad life; things is 'igh-class at Mrs. Digby's, you know. *Much* rather do that than be somebody's scullery maid."

"I'm so sorry," Lewis whispered.

"It's all right; it's what we're born to, ain't it?" she said. She inclined her head to listen to the tumult coming from the altar chamber. "I reckon it's time for the seed, then."

From her basket she produced a pomegranate, and, digging into the rind with her thumbs, prized it open. She picked out a seed and crunched it.

Lewis watched her hopelessly. She offered him the fruit.

"'Ave some?"

"Yes," said Lewis. "Yes, for you. I will." He took a handful of ruby seeds and ate, and the bittersweet juice ran down his chin. She reached up a corner of her veil and wiped it clean. They huddled together for warmth, there on the lid of the tomb.

"Go to it, Paul!"

"Bravo, Whitehead! That's the spirit!"

"Huzzay!"

"That's it, lovey; that's the way, ooh! Lord, plenty of life in this one yet! That's it. You just rest in my arms, my dear. There ain't nothing to be afraid of. Think about them Elysium Fields . . . that's my darling, that's my sweet gentleman. . . ."

"Hup! Ho! Ha! Whitehead's soul is to Heaven fled!"

"I 'ope they don't take all night," said Persephone, a little crossly. "Blimey, I'm cold." She rummaged in her basket again and pulled out a flask. Unstoppering it, she had a gulp of its contents and sighed, wiping her mouth with the back of her hand.

"Nothing like a bit of this to take the chill off," she said, and passed the flask to Lewis. He drank without thinking, and handed it back.

"Oh," he said. "That was gin, wasn't it?"

Chants of rejoicing echoed down the tunnel.

"Eh? Course it was. I think our cue's coming up now—"

"I'm afraid gin combines rather badly with Theobromine," said Lewis unsteadily.

"With what?" Persephone turned her face to him. He watched in fascination as she became an equation of light and shadow, and then an image of stained glass shining with light. She was telling him something; she was rising and taking his hand, leaving trails of colored light where she moved—

He felt a gentle impact at the back of his head and a tremendous happiness. He was flying down the tunnel, bearing her along with him—the sundering water, rippling with subtle colors, was easily bounded across. He roared the ancient hymn as he came, and heard the eternal masses echoing it back from Paradise.

"*Evohe! Evohe! Iacchus! Evohe!*" He was in the cave with the altar, but it was full of light; it was glowing like summer, and no longer cold but warm.

"*I have taken in the seed, and see what I bring into the light!*" Persephone declared. The mortals knelt around him, crowding close, weeping and laughing and catching at his hands.

"*Blessed Iacchus, give us hope!*"
"*Iacchus! The boy Iacchus is come!*"
"*Iacchus, take away our fear!*"
"*Make us immortal, Iacchus!*"

Demeter and Persephone were greeting each other, with elaborate palms-out rapture, and Persephone was saying, "*Behold my son, which is Life come out of Death!*"

"*Please, Iacchus!*" He looked down into old Whitehead's pleading face, sweating and exhausted. "*Let me not be lost in the dark!*"

He wept for the mortal man; he touched his face and promised him the moon; he promised them all the moon; he babbled any comforting nonsense he could think of. He tried to stretch out his hand to Persephone, but she had receded somehow, on the golden sea of faces. Everything was golden. Everything was melting into golden music.

Lewis opened his eyes. He looked up; he looked down; he looked from side to side. Doing anything more ambitious than this seemed a bad idea.

He was in bed in the room allotted to him by Sir Francis. Someone had laid him out as carefully as a carving of a saint on a tomb, with the counterpane drawn up to his chest. They had put one of his nightshirts on him, too. It seemed to be morning.

He closed his eyes again and ran a self-diagnostic. His body told him, quite pointedly, that he'd been extremely stupid. It implied that if he ever subjected it to that kind of abuse again, he was going to find himself in a regeneration tank for at least six months. It stated further that it required complex carbohydrates *right now,* as well as at least two liters of fluid containing high concentrations of calcium, magnesium, and potassium. He opened his eyes again and looked around to see if anything answering that description was within reach.

No; the nearest fluid of any kind was water on a table beside his bed, in a crystal vase containing a few sprays of late hedge roses. It looked exquisitely wet. He wondered whether he could get the roses out and drink from the vase without making too much of a mess. His body told him it didn't care whether he made a mess. Groaning, he prepared to sit up.

At that moment he heard the approach of footsteps, two pair. They were accompanied by a slight rattle of china.

The door opened and Sir Francis stuck his head into the room. Seeing Lewis awake, his face brightened extraordinarily.

"Mr. Owens! Thank all the gods you're with us again at last! You . . . er, that is . . . that *is* you, Mr. Owens?"

"I think so," said Lewis. Little lightning flashes of headache assailed him.

Sir Francis bustled into the room, waving the butler in after him. Lewis found his gaze riveted on the covered tray the butler carried. Sir Francis sat down on the edge of the bed, staring at Lewis no less fixedly.

"D'you recall much, eh?"

"Not a great deal, my lord," said Lewis. "That wouldn't happen to be breakfast, would it?"

The butler lifted the napkin to disclose a pitcher, a small pot of honey, and a dish of little cakes.

Sir Francis twisted his fingers together self-consciously. "That's, er, milk and honey and, ah, the closest my cook could approximate to ambrosia. The honey comes from Delos," he said, with a peculiar tone of entreaty in his voice.

Lewis dragged himself into a sitting position, though his brain quailed against the red-hot lining of his skull. The butler set the tray on his lap; he grabbed up the pitcher, ignoring the crystal tumbler provided with it, and drank two quarts of milk straight down without pausing to breathe. Sir Francis watched with round eyes as he gulped the ambrosia cakes one after another, and, seizing up a spoon, started on the honey.

"Wonderful stuff," said Lewis, remembering his manners. "Might I have a little more?"

"Anything you like," said Sir Francis, beckoning distractedly at John.

Lewis held the pitcher up. "Another round of this, please, and three or four loaves of bread?"

"With jam, sir?"

"No! No jam. Thank you."

John took the pitcher and hurried out of the room.

"I don't wonder you've an appetite," said Sir Francis. "That was an astonishing evening, my boy. We're all greatly indebted to you. Never saw anything quite like that in my life."

"But . . . I received the impression you'd—er, enacted certain rites before," said Lewis, scraping the bottom of the honey jar with the spoon.

"Why, so we had. But never with such remarkable results!" said Sir Francis. "What an improvement on your predecessor. *He* was no fit vessel for Divinity at all! Treated the ladies most disrespectfully. I sent him packing; then we discovered he'd helped himself to the spoons. Apprehended him in the very act of boarding the coach with my best silver coffee urn in his trunk, too, would you credit it?

"Not at all like you. Such Olympian presence! Such efficacy! White-head looked positively well. 'How d'ye feel now, Paul?' I said, and bless me if he didn't reply, 'Why, sir, I declare I could pile Mount Pelion upon Mount Ossa, and straightwise mount to Heaven!'"

"I'm gratified, my lord," said Lewis cautiously. "Though I confess the evening is somewhat indistinct in my memory."

"I expect it would be, sir. I suspect *you* were scarcely there at all! Eh?" Sir Francis winked at him. "But I'll leave you in peace; John will lay out your clothes. All fresh-laundered, though the wig's at the barber's for a fresh setting and powdering. It was in a sad state, I fear. And I've taken the liberty of having a new pair of shoes made; one of yours seems to have gone missing in the Styx. You'll find them in the bottom of your wardrobe."

"New shoes?" Lewis said. "Made overnight?"

"Overnight? Bless you, no! You've slept for three days! A very Endymion," Sir Francis told him. He lingered shyly by the door a moment, his eyes downcast. "You have rendered me a greater service than I can ever repay. Your servant, sir."

Lewis enjoyed an unaccustomed luxury of idleness over the next few days; the servants tiptoed in his presence, looked on him with awe, and leaped to bring him anything he requested. He used the time to access and review his memory, and found, to put it mildly, some difference between what his conscious mind had perceived and what his augmented perception had recorded.

He was chagrined by this, but his embarrassment was ameliorated somewhat by the relaxation of pressure as regarded his mission for the Company.

DASHWOOD OBJECTIVE OBTAINED, he transmitted on his credenza, long past midnight when he was unlikely to be disturbed by a servant. ATTENDED "ELEUSINIAN RITE" AND CAN REPORT THAT IT IS

*NOT, REPEAT, NOT AUTHENTIC. DETAILS WELL-KNOWN IN
ANTIQUITY WORKED INTO A PLAUSIBLE FAKE. SOURCE SCROLL
NOT LOCATED BUT SUSPECT THE EUGENIKOS FORGER. AWAIT-
ING FURTHER ORDERS.*

He sent the message and relaxed, but almost at once a reply shot out of
the ether:

OBTAIN SOURCE SCROLL. CLIENT MADE SUBSTANTIAL
OFFER.

Lewis gnawed his lower lip. He sent:

BUT IT'S A FAKE.

IRRELEVANT.

*BUT IT WOULDN'T FOOL ANYONE WHO'D ATTENDED
THE MYSTERIES.*

CLIENT IS MORTAL. WON'T KNOW DIFFERENCE.

With a certain sense of moral outrage, Lewis transmitted:

ACKNOWLEDGED. UNDER PROTEST. VALE.

He knew well enough, now, where the object of his quest was.

With a heavy heart, in the small hours following an evening during
which Sir Francis had been particularly pleasant company, Lewis packed his
valise. He drew on his cloak and slipped down through the dark house, and
out a side door into the garden. He switched to night vision; the surrounding
countryside leaped into focus, lurid green, unearthly. Pausing only to hide
his bag in a clump of rhododendron, he set out.

He went quickly, though it was a long cold walk just the same. Once, a
bat shrieked overhead; he looked up in time to see its smear of red light vanishing into the trees. Once a fox crossed his path, and stopped to regard him
with eyes like fire. He missed the little girl walking at his side, and wondered
whether he'd be too great a fool if he sought her out once he returned to London. He wondered whether he could bear watching her grow old and die.

This question so preoccupied him that he almost failed to notice that he
was being followed. After a while, however, the laboring mortal heartbeat and
steam-bellows breath distracted him, and he looked back. There, a great way

off, a scarlet blur made its way along the track. Its dark lantern pulsed with heat. A poacher? Lewis shrugged and picked up his pace, until he reached the entrance to the Hellfire Caves.

The gates had been locked; a moment's work with his cloak pin and Lewis had them open. Fighting panic once more, he hurried into true Stygian blackness, rendered more ghostly by his vision. Emerging from the maze into the banqueting chamber, he nearly shouted at what he took at first to be a lurking figure; but it was only a pair of serving tables stacked up on end, draped with oilcloth.

Muttering to himself, Lewis went on. In the chamber with its altar, he was almost surprised to see no spot of residual heat glowing still from Mrs. Digby's bum. At the River Styx he proceeded soberly, poling himself across in the little boat with all the dignity of Charon, and stepped out dry-shod on the other shore. There, trampled and forgotten in the chalk, Lewis spotted Persephone's veil.

He bent and picked it up. He regarded it a long moment before folding it carefully and tucking it away inside his shirt, next to his heart.

In the Inner Temple, he lifted the lid from the sarcophagus. Within was a box of alabaster, something Egyptian from the look of it. He lifted the lid on that and found a box of cypress wood, a modern piece painted with figures of maenads dancing. Within, he found the scroll.

Lewis unrolled it, examined it briefly, and sighed. Yes: the work of the clever Russian. *Let him not speak, he who has witnessed the rites sacred to holy Demeter and her slender-ankled daughter! But bear witness, oh furies, that this scribe breaks no oath in relating the true nature of what he has seen with his silent pen . . .* He returned the scroll to its box, tucked it under his arm, and walked back toward the starlight.

He was on his way to the maze when he heard the crunch of footsteps coming. In a panic, he turned back and dodged into one of the alcoves opening off the banqueting chamber. There he stood, absolutely still as the mortal shuffled into the chamber.

It was Sir Francis, peering about by the single ray of light his lamp gave forth.

Lewis held his breath. *Do not see me, mortal man . . . you will not see me, mortal . . .*

A bat swooped through. Sir Francis gasped and dropped his lantern, which unfortunately did not go out; rather, its shutter was knocked open by the impact. The chamber was flooded with light.

Oh, crumbs.

Sir Francis bent to pick up the lantern, straightened with it, and looked full into Lewis's face. His gaze fell to the box under Lewis's arm.

"Oh, dear," he said. "I was afraid of something like this."

Lewis, ready to babble out an apology, was quite unprepared for what happened next. Scuffing sharp-edged gravel out of the way, Sir Francis knelt down laboriously.

"Please," he said. "Which one are you? Apollo? Hermes? I was sure I recognized you, t'other night. Forgive my old eyes, I pray; I might have seen you more clearly, once."

"I am only a messenger," said Lewis, praying to both gods for help.

"Just as you wish, my lord," said Sir Francis, and he nearly winked. He regarded the scroll box sadly. "Must you take it away? We were idle merry boys once, and we did blaspheme, but only as boys do. I had rather hoped you had come to dwell among us at last. We need you, we poor mortals."

"But you no longer need this." Lewis held up the scroll box, wondering if he could wink out without dropping it.

"I suppose not," said Sir Francis, slumping. He clasped his hands. "Please, tell me, Bright One—will my friend die?"

"You know he must," said Lewis, as gently as he could.

"Oh, Paul," said Sir Francis. He said nothing more for a moment, as a tear rolled down his cheek. He looked up at Lewis hopefully. "But if *you* are here—why then, it's a sign! The gods are not unkind. They must care for us. It's all true, isn't it? We *will* go to Paradise, and revel in the Elysian Fields, just as She promised us."

"Believe, it, mortal man," said Lewis. *For all I know, it may be true.*

He reached down his hand as though in blessing, setting it on Sir Francis's head. Concentrating, he generated a pulse designed to have an effect on the temporal lobe of the mortal brain.

Sir Francis gasped in pleasure. He heard celestial choirs, had visions of glory, and *knew* a sublime truth impossible to put into words. The ecstasy was enough to send him into a dead faint.

Lewis picked him up and staggered out with him, far away through the night fields to the great house, where he laid Sir Francis down before the statue of Bacchus. He paused only a moment, leaning forward with his hand on the wall, gasping for breath; then he knocked, loud enough to rouse the servants.

Long before the fearful mortals had come to the door, he had retrieved his valise from the shrubbery and fled in the direction of London.

No more than a month later, a certain peddler wandered the streets of a certain district of London. The streets were crowded and filthy, even in this somewhat better-class part of the district. The mad king squatted on his throne, the American crisis was going from bad to worse, nay, the whole globe was reeling in chaos that would soon spit forth another age, and the first snow of winter had begun to drift out of a sullen and steely sky.

The peddler's garments were shabby, not really adequate for the weather, and yet he carried himself with a style making it not outside the powers of imagination that he might in fact be a dashing hero of some kind. One temporarily down on his luck, perhaps. Conceivably the object of romantic affection.

He doffed his hat to all he met and, when meeting any who looked as though he or she might know, discreetly inquired whether they knew the way to Mrs. Digby's establishment.

Hoping, even as foolish mortals do, for some sign of a compassionate universe.

The Immortals of Atlantis

BRIAN STABLEFORD

Critically acclaimed British "hard-science" writer Brian Stableford is the author of more than seventy-five books, at least fifty of them novels, including *Cradle of the Sun*, *The Blind Worm*, *The Days of Glory*, *In the Kingdom of the Beasts*, *Day of Wrath*, *The Halcyon Drift*, *The Paradox of the Sets*, *The Realms of Tartarus*, *The Empire of Fear*, *The Angel of Pain*, *The Carnival of Destruction*, *Serpent's Blood*, *Inherit the Earth*, *The Omega Expedition*, *Dark Ararat*, *The Cassandra Complex*, *The Fountains of Youth*, *Architects of Emortality*, *The Gateway of Eternity*, *Streaking*, *Curse of the Coral Bride*, and *Kiss the Goat*, among many others. His many short stories have been collected in *Sexual Chemistry: Sardonic Tales of the Genetic Revolution*, *Salome and Other Decadent Fantasies*, *Fables and Fantasies*, *Complications and Other Science Fiction Stories*, *The Wayward Muse*, and *Designer Genes and Other Stories: Tales of the Biotech Revolution*. His non-fiction books include *The Sociology of Science Fiction* and, with David Langford, *The Third Millennium: A History of the World A.D. 2000–3000*. Stableford's novella *Les Fleurs du Mal* was a finalist for the Hugo Award in 1994. His most recent books are the novels *The Stones of Camelot* and *The New Faust at the Tragicomique* and several new collections, including *The Tree of Life*, *The Haunted Bookshop and Other Apparitions*, and *The Cure for Love and Other Tales of the Biotech Revolution*. A biologist and sociologist by training, Stableford lives in Reading, England.

Stableford may have written more about how the ongoing revolutions in biological and genetic science will change the very nature of humanity itself than any other writer of the last decade, covering the development of posthumanity in story after story, including such stories as "Out of Touch," "The Magic Bullet," "Age of Innocence," "The Tree of Life," "The Pipes of Pan," "Hidden Agendas," and "The Color of Envy," the aforementioned *Les Fleurs du Mal*, and many others. Here he shows us that in the future, refugees may find some very unusual places to hide, including in your own blood.

*S*heila never answered the door when the bell rang because there was never anyone there that she wanted to see and often someone there that she was desperate to avoid. The latter category ranged from debt collectors and the police to Darren's friends, who were all apprentice drug dealers, and Tracy's friends, who were mostly veteran statutory rapists. Not everyone took no for an answer, of course; the fact that debt collectors and policemen weren't really entitled to kick the door in didn't seem to be much of a disincentive. It was, however, very unusual for anyone to use subtler means of entry, so Sheila was really quite surprised when the white-haired man appeared in her sitting room without being preceded by the slightest sound of splintering wood.

"I did ring," he said, labouring the obvious, "but you didn't answer."

"Perhaps," she said, not getting up from her armchair or reaching for the remote, "that was because I didn't want to let you in."

In spite of the fact that she hadn't even reached for the remote, the TV switched itself off. It wasn't a matter of spontaneously flipping into standby mode, as it sometimes did, but of switching itself off. It was eleven o'clock in the morning, so she hadn't so much been watching it as using it to keep her company in the absence of anything better, but the interruption seemed a trifle rude all the same.

"Did you do that?" she asked.

"Yes," he said. "We need to talk."

The phrasing made her wonder if he might be one of her ex-boyfriends, most of whom she could hardly remember because their acquaintance had been so brief, but he certainly didn't look like one. He was wearing a suit and tie. The suit was sufficiently old-fashioned and worn to have come from the bargain end of an Oxfam rail, but it was still a suit. He was also way too old—sixty if he was a day—and way too thin, with hardly an ounce of spare flesh on him. The fact that he was so tall made him look almost skeletal. Sheila would have found it easier to believe in him if he'd been wearing a hooded cloak and carrying a scythe. In fact, he was carrying a huge briefcase—so huge that it was a miracle he'd been able to cross the estate without being mugged.

"What do you want?" Sheila asked, bluntly.

"You aren't who you think you are, Sheila," was his reply to that—which immediately made her think "religious nut." The Mormons and Jehovah's Witnesses had stopped coming to the estate years ago, because there were far easier places in the world to do missionary work—Somalia, for instance, or Iraq—but it wasn't inconceivable that there were people in the world who could still believe that God's protection even extended to places like this.

"Everybody around here is who they think they are," she told him. "Nobody has any illusions about being anybody. This is the end of the world, and I'm not talking Rapture."

"I knew this wasn't going to be easy," the tall man said. "There's no point wasting time. I'm truly sorry to have to do this, but it really is for the best." He put his suitcase down, pounced on her, dragged her to her feet, and bound her hands behind her back with a piece of slender but incredibly strong cord.

She screamed as loudly as she could, but she knew that no one was going to take any notice. He must have known that too, because he didn't try to stop her immediately. He selected the sturdiest of her three dining chairs, set it in the middle of the room and started tying her ankles to the legs of the chair.

"My boyfriend will be home any minute," Sheila said. "He's a bouncer. He'll break you into little pieces."

"You don't have a boyfriend, Shelia," the white-haired man informed her. "You've never had a relationship that lasted longer than a fortnight. You've always claimed that it's because all men are bastards, but you've always suspected that it might be you—and you're right. You really do put them off and drive them away, no matter how hard you try not to."

Sheila was trussed up tightly by now, with more cord passed around her body, holding her tight to the back of the chair. The way she was positioned made it extremely unlikely that he intended to rape her, but that wasn't at all reassuring. Rape she understood; rape she could cope with, and survive.

"I do have a son," she told him. "He may not be as big as you, but he's in a gang, and he's vicious. He carries a knife. He might even have graduated to a gun by now—and if he hasn't, some of his mates certainly have."

"All true," the white-haired man conceded, readily enough, "but it leaves out of account the fact that Darren hardly ever comes home anymore, because he finds you as uncomfortable to be with as all the other men who've briefly passed through your wretched life. To put it brutally, you disgust him."

"Tracy loves me," Sheila retorted, feeling far greater pressure to make that point than to ask the man with the briefcase how he knew Darren's name.

The briefcase was open now, and the tall man was pulling things out at a rate of knots: weird things, like the apparatus of a chemistry set. There were bottles and jars, flasks and tripods, even a mortar and pestle. There was also something that looked like a glorified butane cigarette lighter, whose flame ignited at a touch, and became more intense in response to another.

"That's true too," her remorseless tormentor went on. "There's a lot of love in Tracy, just as there was always a lot of love in you, always yearning for more and better outlets. She can't hang on to relationships either, can she? She hasn't given up hope yet, though. Darren wouldn't be any use, because the mitochondrial supplement atrophies in males long before they reach puberty, but I could have gone to Tracy instead of you, and would probably have found her more cooperative. It wouldn't have been sporting, though. She's still a child, and you're entitled to your chance. It wouldn't be fair simply to pass you over. Her life will change irrevocably, too, once you're fully awake. So will Darren's, although he probably won't be quite as grateful."

That was too much. "What the fuck are you talking about, you stupid fuck?" Sheila demanded, although she knew that he would see that she was cracking up, that he had succeeded in freaking her out with his psychopathic performance.

"My name—my true name, not the one on my driving licence—is Sarmerodach," the tall man said. "This body used to belong to an oceanographer named Arthur Bayliss, Ph.D., but I was able to rescue him from an unbelievably dull life wallowing in clathrate-laden ooze. The predatory DNA that crystallized in my viral avatar dispossessed his native DNA, little by little, in every single cell in his body, and then set about resculpting the neuronal connections in his brain. The headaches were terrible. I wish I could say that you won't have to suffer anything similar, but you will—not for nearly as long, but even more intensely. I wish it were as simple as feeding you a dose of virus-impregnated ooze, but it isn't. Your predatory DNA is already latent in your cells, secreted in mitochondrial supplements, awaiting activation. The activation process is complex, but not very difficult if you have the right raw materials. I have—although it wasn't easy to locate them all. It will take an hour to trigger the process, and six months thereafter to complete the transition."

Sheila had hardly understood a word of the details, but she thought she had got the gist of the plan. "Transition to what?" she asked, thinking of the Incredible Hulk and Mr. Hyde.

"Oh, don't worry," he said. "You'll still look human. Your hair will turn white overnight, but you'll be able to watch the flab and the cellulite melt away. You won't look like a supermodel, but you will live for thousands of years. In a sense, given that the real you is locked away in your mitochondrial supplements, you already have. Your other self is one of the Immortals of Atlantis."

Sheila had always felt that she was fully capable of dealing with psychopaths—she knew so many—but she knew from bitter experience that negotiating with delusional schizophrenics was a different kettle of fish. She started screaming again, just as loudly and even more desperately than before.

In all probability, she thought, there would be at least a dozen people in the neighbouring flats who could hear her. The chances of one of them responding, in any way whatsoever, were pretty remote—screaming passed for normal behaviour in these parts—but it might be her last hope.

Arthur Bayliss, Ph.D., alias Sarmerodach, obviously thought so, too, because he crammed a handkerchief into her open mouth and then used more of his ubiquitous cord to make a gag holding it in place.

Then he got busy with his chemistry set.

Sheila had no idea what the ingredients were that her captor was mixing up in his flasks, but she wouldn't have been at all surprised if she'd been told that they included virgin's blood, adder's venom, and the hallucinogenic slime that American cane toads were rumoured to secrete. There were certainly toadstool caps, aromatic roots, and perfumed flowers among the things he was grinding up in the mortar, and Sheila was prepared to assume that every one of them was as poisonous as deadly nightshade and as dangerous to mental health as the most magical magic mushrooms in the world.

The tall man talked while he worked. "I'd far rather observe the principle of informed consent," he said, "even though I'm not really a Ph.D. anymore, let alone a physician, but it's not really practical in the circumstances. Your false self would be bound to refuse to realise your true self, no matter how worthless a person you presently are or how wretched a life you presently lead, because selves are, by definition, selfish."

He paused to deploy a spatula, measuring out a dose of red powder. He tipped it into the flask whose contents were presently seething away over the burner. He didn't use scales, but the measurement was obviously delicate.

"If caterpillars had the choice," he continued, "they'd never consent to turn into butterflies. Some kinds of larvae don't have to, you know—it's called paedogenesis. Instead of pupating and re-emerging as adults, they can grow sex organs and breed as juveniles, sometimes for several generations. They still transmit the genes their descendants will eventually need to effect metamorphosis, though, in response to the appropriate environmental trigger, so that those descendants, however remote, can eventually recover their true nature, their true glory and their true destiny."

He paused again, this time to dribble a few drops of liquid out of the mortar, where he'd crushed a mixture of plant tissues, into a second flask that had not yet been heated at all.

"That's what the Immortals of Atlantis did," he went on, "when they realised that they were about to lose all their cultural wealth once their homeland disappeared beneath the sea. They knew that the next generation, and many generations thereafter, would have to revert to the cultural level of Stone Age barbarians and take thousands of years to achieve a tolerable level of civilisation, but they wanted to give them the chance to become something better, when circumstances became ripe again. So the Immortals hid themselves away, the best way they could. The Atlantean elite were great biotechnologists, you see; they considered our kind of heavy-metal technology to be inexpressibly vulgar, fit only for the toilsome use of slaves."

This time he stopped to make a careful inspection of some kind of paste he'd been blending, lifting a spoonful to within a couple of inches of his pale grey eyes. He didn't have a microscope either.

"What would our elite do, do you think," he resumed, "if the Antarctic ice melted and the sea swamped their cities, and the methane gushing out of the suboceanic clathrates mopped up all the oxygen and rendered the air unbreathable? I think they'd retreat underground, burrowing deep down and going into cultural hibernation for a thousand or a hundred thousand years, until the ever-loyal plants had restored the breathability of the atmosphere again. But that's not going to happen, because you and I—and the other Immortals, when we've located and restored a sufficient number—are going to see that it doesn't. We'll have the knowledge, once you're fully awake, and we'll have the authority. The only way the world can be saved is for everyone to work together and do what's necessary, and that isn't going to happen unless someone takes control and reinstitutes a sensible system of slavery. The Immortals will be able to do that, once we've resurrected enough of them. This is just the beginning."

He took one flask off the burner and replaced it with another; the pause in his monologue was hardly perceptible.

"As you might be able to see," he said, gesturing expansively to take in all the different compounds he was making up, "the process of revitalisation has five stages—that's five different drugs, all of them freshly prepared to very specific recipes, administered in swift sequence. Don't worry—it doesn't involve any injections, or even swallowing anything with a nasty taste. All you have to do is breathe them in. It's even simpler than smoking crack. I know it looks complicated, and it could all go wrong if I made the slightest mistake in the preparation or administration, but you have to trust me. Dr. Bayliss has never done anything like this before, but Sarmerodach has. He hasn't lost the knack, even though he's spent the last few thousand years lying dormant in the suboceanic ooze encoded as a crystalline supervirus. Everything's just about ready. You mustn't be afraid, Sheila; you really—"

He stopped abruptly as the doorbell rang. For a second or two he seemed seriously disconcerted—but then he relaxed again. He knew her children's names, and more about her than anyone had any right to know. He knew that she never answered the doorbell.

For the first time in her life, Shelia yearned to hear the sound of someone kicking the door in, splintering the wood around the lock and the bolts.

Instead, she heard several sets of shuffling footsteps moving away from the flat. If she'd screamed then it might just have made a difference, but she couldn't.

"Good," said the man with the Ph.D. "We can get on with the job in peace."

The first drug, which the tall man administered simply by holding a loaded spoon beneath her nostrils, made Sheila feel nauseous. It wasn't that it stank—its odour was delicately sweet, like the scent of sugared porridge heating up in the microwave—but that it disturbed her internal equilibrium in a fashion she'd never experienced before.

The second, which he administered by pouring warm liquid onto cotton wool and holding it in the same position, disturbed her even more profoundly. At first, it just tickled—except that she'd never been tickled inside before, in her lungs and liver and intestines instead of on her skin. Then the tickling turned into prickling, and it felt as if a thorn bush were growing inside her, jabbing its spines into every last corner of her soft red flesh. She hadn't known that it was possible to endure such agony without being rendered unconscious by shock and terror.

"Just be patient," he said, infuriatingly. "It will pass. Your cells are coming back to life, Sheila. They've been half-dead for so long—much longer than your own meagre lifetime. A metazoan body is just a single cell's way of making more single cells, you see; sex and death are just means of shuffling the genetic deck, so that cells are capable of evolution. All metazoan cells are partly shut down—they have to be, to specialise them for specific physiological functions—but they can all be reawakened, wholly or partially, by the right stimulus."

The pain abated, but not because her captor's voice had soothed it away. It abated because the second drug had now completed its work, having been scrupulously ferried to every hinterland of her being by her dutiful bloodstream. It had taken time, but that phase was finished.

Sheila felt better, and not just in the way she usually felt better after feeling ill or depressed, which was only a kind of dull relief, comparable to that obtainable by such proverbial means as ceasing to bang one's head against a brick wall. She actually felt better, in a positive sense. It was a very strange sensation, by virtue of its unfamiliarity—but there were still three drugs to go.

The ex-Ph.D. had been measuring her condition with his uncannily skilful eyes. He had to get the timing right, but he was as adept at that as he had been at the mixing and the cooking. He had the third compound ready, and he lifted the whole flask up and swirled its contents around to make the vapour rise up from its neck.

This time, the effect was narcotic, or at least anaesthetic. Sheila felt that she was falling asleep, but she didn't lose consciousness, and she didn't begin to dream. It was a little like getting high, albeit more in the crystal meth vein than a heroin kick, but it was quite distinct. For one thing, it didn't seem that she was only feeling it in her head, or in her nerves. It seemed that she was feeling it in every organic fibre of her being, and then some. It made her feel much bigger than she was, and much more powerful—but not, alas, powerful enough to break the bonds that held her tight to the chair. The anaesthetic effect wasn't dulling, or straightforwardly euphoric, but something that promised to take her far beyond the reach of pain.

It was, alas, flattering only to deceive. It hadn't taken her beyond the reach of pain at all, but merely to some existential plane where pain came in different, previously unknown forms. The fourth drug—the first one whose vapour was hot enough to scald the mucous membranes of her nasal passages and bronchi—was a real bastard. It gave her the migraine to end all migraines, visual distortions and all; it plunged a million daggers into her flesh; it sent waves of agony rippling through her like sound waves, as if she were imprisoned in a gigantic church bell smashed by a sequence of steel hammers—but the vibrations were silent, even though she hadn't gone deaf.

She could still hear Sarmerodach rambling on, and make out every word in spite of her excruciation.

"You'll begin to feel more yourself soon," he said. "You'll begin to feel Sheila slipping away, like the husk of a redundant cocoon. You'll be able to sense your true being and personality—not well enough for a while to put a name to yourself, but well enough to know that you exist. You'll be able to catch glimpses of the possibilities inherent within you—not just the power but the aesthetic sensibility, the awareness of the physiological transactions of hormones and enzymes, the ecstasy of the mitochondria and the triumph of the phagocytes. The agony is just a kind of birth trauma, a necessary shock. As it fades, you'll begin to sense what you truly are, and what you might eventually. . . ."

The last word of the sentence died on his thin lips as the doorbell sounded again. This time, the repeated ring was swiftly followed by the sound of fists pounding on the door. No one shouted, "Police!" though— what they shouted instead was: "Darren! We know you're in there!"

The boys at the door didn't have Sarmerodach's uncanny powers of intuition. What they thought they "knew" was utterly false. Wherever Darren was hiding, it wasn't at home.

As the white-haired man reached for his spoon again, with a hand that had begun, ever so slightly, to tremble, the sound of thumping fists was replaced by the sound of thudding boots. The door had far too little strength left in it to resist for long. It splintered, and crashed against the hallway wall.

Sarmerodach was already holding the spoon up to Sheila's nose. Wisps of vapour were already curling up into her nostrils. She could already sense its exotic odour—which she normally wouldn't have liked at all, but which somehow seemed, at this particular moment, to be the most wonderful scent she'd ever encountered.

Time seemed to slow down. The sitting-room door burst open in slow motion, and the boys stumbled through the doorway in a bizarrely balletic fashion, floating with impossible grace as they got in one another's way. Only one of them had a gun, but the other three had knives, and all four were ready for action.

There was something irredeemably comical about the way they stopped short as they caught sight of the scene unfolding before their eyes. Their jaws dropped; their eyes seemed actually to bulge.

Under normal circumstances, of course, they'd have threatened Sheila with their weapons. They'd have threatened to hit her, and then they would probably have slashed her face, not because she was being uncooperative in refusing to tell them where Darren was, but simply because they were pumped up and incapable of containing their violence. They might even have raped her, and told themselves afterwards that they were "teaching Darren a lesson"—but when they saw her tied up and helpless, apparently being threatened by a man in a suit, if only with a spoon, a different set of reflexes kicked in. Suddenly, Sheila was one of their own at the mercy of a feral bureaucrat.

Somehow, the tall man had crossed the estate with his briefcase without attracting sufficient attention to be mugged, but he wasn't inconspicuous anymore.

The members of the pack hurled themselves upon the outsider. At first, they probably only intended to kick the shit out of him—but three of them were wielding knives. The one with the gun never fired it; he, at least, still had a vestige of self-restraint. The others were not so intimidated by the talismanic power of their own armaments.

The killing would probably have qualified as manslaughter rather than murder, even if it hadn't seemed to its perpetrators to be a clear case of justifiable homicide; not one of the boys was capable of formulating an intention to kill within the very limited time at their disposal. Even so, the tall man was doomed within a matter of seconds—down and out in ten, at the most, and well on his way to extinction after forty, by which time his heart had presumably stopped and his brain was no longer getting sufficient oxygen to function.

The spoon flew from his hand and disappeared from view, taking its cargo of aromatic pulp with it.

Sheila had been saved, in the proverbial nick of time. If the spoon had been held in place for ten seconds more . . .

Sheila really had been saved, and she knew it. If she had breathed in the pre-scribed dose of the fifth perfume, she would have ceased to be herself and would have begun an inexorable process of becoming someone else.

She never believed, even momentarily, that she would actually have become one of the Immortals of Atlantis, ready to take command of her faithful slaves and restore her sisters to life, in order that they could take over the world and save humankind from self-destruction by means of benevolent dictatorship. She wasn't that mad . . . but she knew that, however crazy or deluded Sarmerodach had been, he had been dead right about one thing. She wasn't really the person she thought she was, and never had been. There really was a flab-free, cellulite-free, thinking individual lurking somewhere inside her, in the secret potentialities of her cellular makeup—a person who might have been able to get out, if only four pathetic rivals of Darren's equally pathetic gang hadn't decided that it was his turn to be taken out in their lame and stupid drug war.

Sheila had no idea who that latent person might have been. She cer-tainly couldn't put a name to her. One thing she did know, though, without a shadow of lingering doubt, was that all that hideous pain would somehow have been worthwhile, if only she'd been able to complete the ritual.

It was a ritual, she decided, even though it really was some kind of occult science, and not mere magic at all. It was an initiation ceremony: a symbolic process of existential transition, like marriage or graduation, but a million times better and more accurate.

Whether she had turned out to be one of the Immortals of Atlantis or not, Sheila knew that she would have become somebody. She would have become a butterfly-person instead or a caterpillar-person—or maybe, even better, a dragonfly-person or someone equipped with a deadly sting. She had not seen anything distinctly when she had sucked those first few wisps of vapour number five avidly into her aching lungs, but she had felt such a yearn-ing for sight as she had never conceived before, or ever thought conceivable—and still did.

But she had lost the opportunity, probably forever.

When the police eventually turned up, in the wake of the ambulance she summoned to dispose of the body, she told them what had happened. She didn't identify the boys, of course, but it didn't take long for the police to figure out who had done what to whom, and why. When all the statements had been collected, all the stories matched—which made the police furious, because they really wanted to put the boys away for something meatier than possession of illegal weapons, and Sheila, too, for perverting the course of justice, if nothing else, but they knew that they wouldn't be able to make anything heavy stick, even though the victim had once been a respectable oceanographer before he had flipped his lid and gone round the bend.

In the end, the body was taken away. Sheila was kicked out of the flat, because it was a crime scene, and because the bloodstains and all the "miscellaneous potentially toxic contaminants" would need the careful attention of a specialist cleaning squad before the council could "deem it fit for rehabilitation." Darren couldn't be found, but Social Services managed to locate Tracy so that she could be "temporarily rehoused," along with her mother, in a single room in a run-down B and B.

In the twenty minutes or so before Tracy skipped out again to find somewhere less suitable to sleep, Sheila gave her a big hug.

"There's no need to worry about me, love," she said, unnecessarily. "I'm okay; really I am. But I want you to know, before you go, that I love you very much."

There was, of course, much more that she might have said. She might have said that she also wanted her daughter to know that she was the flesh of her flesh, and that it was very special flesh, and that if ever a mysterious man came into her life who'd been messing about with ooze dragged up from the remote ocean bed, and had picked up some sort of infection from it that had driven him completely round the twist, then maybe she should show a little patience, because it would probably be Sarmerodach, reincarnate again and trying heroically to fulfill his age-long mission, just like the freak in bandages from *The Mummy*, but in a smoother sort of way. She didn't, of course. That would have been ridiculous, and Tracy wouldn't have taken a blind bit of notice.

Once Tracy had gone, though, and Sheila was alone in her filthy and claustrophobic room, with the TV on for company but not really watching it, she couldn't help wondering whether there might be a glimmer of hope, not just for her and Tracy, or Darren, but for the whole ecocatastrophe-threatened world.

She decided, eventually, that she might as well believe that there was.

Nothing personal

PAT CADIGAN

Pat Cadigan was born in Schenectady, New York, and now lives in London with her family. She made her first professional sale in 1980 and has subsequently come to be regarded as one of the best new writers of her generation. Her story "Pretty Boy Crossover" has appeared on several critics' lists as among the best science-fiction stories of the 1980s, and her story "Angel" was a finalist for the Hugo Award, the Nebula Award, *and* the World Fantasy Award (one of the few stories ever to earn that rather unusual distinction). Her short fiction—which has appeared in most of the major markets, including *Omni*, *Asimov's Science Fiction*, and *The Magazine of Fantasy & Science Fiction*—has been gathered in the collections *Patterns* and *Dirty Work: Stories*. Her first novel, *Mindplayers*, was released in 1987 to excellent critical response, and her second novel, *Synners*, released in 1991, won the Arthur C. Clarke Award as the year's best science-fiction novel, as did her third novel, *Fools*, making her one of only two writers (the other is China Mieville) to win the Clarke Award twice. Cadigan's other books include the novels *Tea from an Empty Cup* and *Dervish Is Digital* and, as editor, the anthology *The Ultimate Cyberpunk*. Her most recent book is a new novel, *Reality Used to Be a Friend of Mine*. Her stories have appeared in our First through Sixth and Ninth through Thirteenth Annual Collections.

In the suspenseful story that follows, she takes us on a tour of cyberspace, which turns out to be every bit as dangerous a place as the real world, if not more so.

Detective Ruby Tsung could not say when the Dread had first come over her. It had been a gradual development, taking place over a period of weeks, possibly months, with all the subtlety of any of the more mundane life processes—weight gain, graying hair, aging itself. Time marched on and one day you woke up to find you were a somewhat dumpy, graying, middle-aged homicide detective with twenty-five years on the job and a hefty lump of bad feeling in the pit of your stomach: the Dread.

It was a familiar enough feeling, the Dread. Ruby had known it well in the past. Waiting for the verdict in an officer-involved shooting; looking up from her backlog of paperwork to find a stone-faced IAD officer standing over her; the doctor clearing his throat and telling her to sit down before giving her the results of the mammogram; answering an unknown trouble call and discovering it was a cop's address. Then there were the ever-popular rumors, rumors, rumors: of budget cuts, of forced retirement for everyone with more than fifteen years in, of mandatory transfers, demotions, promotions, stings, grand jury subpoenas, not to mention famine, war, pestilence, disease, and death—business as usual.

After a while she had become inured to a lot of it. You had to or you'd make yourself sick, give yourself an ulcer, or go crazy. As she had grown more experienced, she had learned what to worry about and what she could consign to denial even just temporarily. Otherwise, she would have spent all day with the Dread eating away at her insides and all night with it sitting on her chest crushing the breath out of her.

The last ten years of her twenty-five had been in Homicide, and in that time she had had little reason to feel Dread. There was no point. This was Homicide—something bad *was* going to happen, so there was no reason to dread it. Someone was going to turn up dead today, tomorrow it would be someone else, the next day still someone else, and so forth. Nothing personal, just Homicide.

Nothing personal. She had been coping with the job on this basis for a long time now and it worked just fine. Whatever each murder might have been about, she could be absolutely certain that it wasn't about her. Whatever had gone so seriously wrong as to result in loss of life, it was not meant to serve as an omen, a warning, or any other kind of signifier in her life. Just the facts, ma'am or sir. Then punch out and go home.

Nothing personal. She was perfectly clear on that. It didn't help. She still felt as if she had swallowed something roughly the size and density of a hockey puck.

There was no specific reason that she could think of. She wasn't under investigation—not as far as she knew, anyway, and she made a point of not dreading what she didn't know. She hadn't done anything (lately) that would have called for any serious disciplinary action; there were no questionable medical tests to worry about, no threats of any kind. Her son, Jake, and his wife, Lita, were nested comfortably in the suburbs outside Boston, making an indecent amount of money in computer software and raising her grand-kids in a big old Victorian house that looked like something out of a story-book. The kids e-mailed her regularly, mostly jokes and scans of their crayon drawings. Whether they were all really as happy as they appeared to be was another matter, but she was fairly certain they weren't suffering. But even if she had been inclined to worry unduly about them, it wouldn't have felt like the Dread.

Almost as puzzling to her as when the Dread had first taken up residence was how she had managed not to notice it coming on. Eventually she under-stood that she hadn't—she had simply pushed it to the back of her mind and then, being continuously busy, had kept on pushing it all the way into the *Worry About Later* file, where it had finally grown too intense to ignore.

Which brought her back to the initial question: when the hell had it started? Had it been there when her partner Rita Castillo had retired? She didn't remember feeling anything as unpleasant as the Dread when Rita had made the announcement or later on, at her leaving party. Held in a cop bar, the festivities had gone on till two in the morning, and the only unusual thing about it for Ruby had been that she had gone home relatively sober. Not by design and not for any specific reason. Not even on purpose—she had had a couple of drinks that had given her a nice mellow buzz, after which she had switched to diet cola. Some kind of new stuff—someone had given her a taste and she'd liked it. Who? Right, Tommy DiCenzo; Tommy had fifteen years of sobriety, which was some kind of precinct record.

But the Dread hadn't started that night; it had already been with her then. Not the current full-blown knot of Dread, but in retrospect, she knew that she had felt something and simply refused to think about the bit of dis-quiet that had sunk its barbed hook into a soft place.

But she hadn't been so much in denial that she had gotten drunk. You left yourself open to all sorts of unpleasantness when you tied one on at a cop's retirement party: bad thoughts, bad memories, bad dreams, and real bad mornings after. Of course, knowing that hadn't always stopped her in the past. It was too easy to let yourself be caught up in the moment, in all the moments, and suddenly you were completely shitfaced and wondering how that could have happened. Whereas she couldn't remember the last time she'd heard of anyone staying sober by accident.

Could have been the nine-year-old that had brought the Dread on. That had been pretty bad even for an old hand like herself. Rita had been on vaca-tion and she had been working alone when the boy's body had turned up in the Dumpster on the south side—or south town, which was what everyone seemed to be calling it now. The sudden name change baffled her; she had joked to Louie Levant at the desk across from hers about not getting the memo on renaming the 'hoods. Louie had looked back at her with a mixture of mild surprise and amusement on his pale features. "South town was what we always called it when I was growing up there," he informed her, a bit loftily. "Guess the rest of you finally caught on." Louie was about twenty years younger than she was, Ruby reminded herself, which meant that she had two decades more history to forget; she let the matter drop.

Either way, south side or south town, the area wasn't a crime hotspot. It wasn't as upscale as the parklike west side or as stolidly middle/working class as the northland grid, but it wasn't east midtown, either. Murder in south town was news; the fact that it was a nine-year-old boy was worse news, and worst of all, it had been a sex crime.

Somehow she had known that it would be a sex crime even before she had seen the body, lying small, naked, and broken amid the trash in the bottom of the Dumpster. Just what she hadn't wanted to catch—kiddie sex murder. Kiddie sex murder had something for everyone: nightmares for parents, hysterical ammunition for religious fanatics, and lurid headlines for all. And a very special kind of hell for the family of the victim, who would be forever overshadowed by the circumstances of his death.

During his short life, the boy had been an average student with a talent for things mechanical—he had liked to build engines for model trains and cars. He had told his parents he thought he'd like to be a pilot when he grew up. Had he died in some kind of accident, a car wreck, a fall, or something equally unremarkable, he would have been remembered as the little boy who never got a chance to fly—tragic, what a shame, light a candle. Instead, he would now and forever be defined by the sensational nature of his death. The public memory would link him not with little-kid stuff like model trains and cars but with the pervert who had killed him.

She hadn't known anything about him, none of those specific details about models and flying, when she had first stood gazing down at him; at that point, she hadn't even known his name. But she had known the rest of it as she had climbed into the Dumpster, trying not to gag from the stench of garbage and worse and hoping that the plastic overalls and booties she had on didn't tear.

That had been a bad day. Bad enough that it could have been the day the Dread had taken up residence in her gut.

Except it wasn't.

Thinking about it, remembering the sight, the smell, the awful way it felt when she had accidentally stepped on the dead boy's ankle, she knew the Dread had already been with her. Not so cumbersome at the time, still small enough to snub in favor of more immediate problems, but definitely there.

Had it been Ricky Carstairs, then? About a month before the nine-year-old, she had been on her way out of the precinct house when she had passed two uniformed officers bringing him in and recognized him immediately. She had no idea how she had managed that mental feat—he had been skinny, dirty, and obviously strung out, and she hadn't seen him since he and Jake had been in the seventh grade together, but she had known him at once and it hadn't been a good moment.

"It's just plain wrong," she had said when Rita asked her why she looked as if she had just found half a worm in the middle of an apple. "Your kid's old school friends are supposed go away and live lives with no distinguishing characteristics. Become office workers in someplace like Columbus or Chicago or Duluth."

"And that's just plain *weird*," Rita replied, her plump face wearing a slightly alarmed expression. "Or maybe not weird enough—I don't know. You been watching a lot of TV lately? Like the Hallmark Channel or something?"

"Never mind," she said, making a short dismissive wave with one hand. "It made more sense *before* I said it out loud."

Rita had burst into hearty laughter and that had been that; they'd gone with the rest of the day, whatever that had involved. Probably a dead body.

The dismaying sight of one of Jake's old school friends sweating in hand-cuffs had lodged in her mind more as a curiosity than anything else. Uncomfortable but hardly critical—not the fabled moment of clarity, not a short sharp shock or a reality check or a wake-up call from Planet Earth. Just a moment when she hoped that poor old Ricky hadn't recognized her, too.

So had the Dread already been lodged in her gut then?

She tried, but she honestly couldn't remember one way or the other— the incident was just that too far in the past and it had lasted only a minute, if that—but she thought it was very possible that it had.

It was unlikely, she realized, that she would ever pinpoint the exact moment when something had shifted or slipped or cracked—gone faulty, anyway— and let a sense of something wrong get in and take root. And for all she knew, it might not even matter. Not if she were in the first stage of one of those on-the-job crack-ups that a lot of cops fell victim to. Just what she needed—a slow-motion train wreck. Christ, what the hell was the point of having a breakdown in slow motion unless you could actually do something about it, actually prevent it from happening? Too bad it didn't work that way—every cop she knew who had come out the other side of a crash described it as unstoppable. If it had to happen, why couldn't it be fast? Crack up quick and have an equally rapid recovery, get it over with. She pictured herself going to the department shrink for help: *Overclock me, Doc—I got cases to solve and they're gaining on me.*

Ha-ha, good one; the shrink might even get a chuckle out of it. Unless she had to explain what overclocking was. Would a shrink know enough about computers to get it? Hell, she wouldn't have known herself if she hadn't picked things up from Jake, who had blossomed into a tech head practically in his playpen.

Her mind snagged on the idea of talking to the shrink and wouldn't let go. Why not? She had done it before. Granted, it had been mandatory, then—all cops involved in a shooting had to see the shrink—but she'd had no problem with that. And what the hell, it had done her more good than she'd expected it to. She had known at the time that she'd needed help and if she was honest with herself, she had to admit that she needed help now. Going around with the lead weight of the Dread dragging on her wasn't even on the extreme ass end of acceptably screwed up that was in the range of normal for a homicide detective.

The more she thought about it, the more imperative it seemed that she talk to the department shrink, because she sure hadn't talked to anyone else about it. Not her lieutenant, not Tommy DiCenzo, not even Rita.

Well, she wouldn't have talked to Lieutenant Ostertag—that was a no-brainer. Throughout her career, she had always had the good sense never to believe any my-door-is-always-open bullshit from a superior officer. Ostertag hadn't even bothered with the pretense.

Tommy DiCenzo, on the other hand, she could have talked to and counted on his complete confidence. They'd gone through the academy together and she'd listened to plenty from him, both before and after he'd dried out. Tommy might even have understood enough to tell her whether she was about to derail big-time or just experiencing another side effect of being middle-aged, overworked, and underpaid. But every time she thought about giving him a call or asking him to go for coffee, something stopped her.

Maddeningly, she couldn't think of a single good reason why. Hell, she couldn't even think of a crappy reason. There was no reason. She simply could not bring herself to talk to him about the Dread and that was all there was to it.

And Rita—well, there had been plenty of reasons not to talk to her. They were busy, far too busy to devote any time to anything that didn't have a direct bearing on the cases piling up on their respective desks. Not that Rita wouldn't have listened. But whenever she considered bringing it up, saying, *You know, Rita, lately I've had the damnedest feeling, a sense of being in the middle of something real bad that's about to get a whole lot worse*, the image of the nine-year-old boy in the Dumpster would bloom in her brain and she would clench her teeth together.

Of course, she could go to Rita now. She could trot on over to her neat little fourth floor condo, sit out on the balcony with her amid the jungle of plants with a few beers, and tell her all about it. Only she knew what Rita would probably say, because Rita had already said it. That had been the night before she had put in her retirement papers; she had taken Ruby out to dinner and broken the news to her privately.

"I always planned to put in my twenty and get out while I was still young enough to enjoy it," she said, cheerfully sawing away at a slab of bloody steak. "You could have done that five years ago. Do it now and you'll be in good shape all the way around. Maybe you want to get in thirty, but is putting in another five years really worth it?"

"Five years—" Ruby had shrugged. "What's five years? Blink of an eye, practically."

"All the more reason to get out," Rita had insisted. "Before it's too late to get a life."

Bristling inwardly, Ruby had looked down at her own steak. Why she had ordered that much food was beyond her. The Dread didn't leave anywhere nearly enough room for it. "I have a life."

"The job is *not* a life," Rita said, chewing vigourously and then dragging her napkin across her lips. "The job is the job. What do you do when you're not on the job?"

"Talk to the grandkids on e-mail. Shop. Rent DVDs—"

"You ever go *out* to a movie? Or out to dinner—with anyone *other* than me?" Rita added quickly before she could answer. "Hell, girlfriend, when was the last time you got laid?"

Ruby blinked at her, startled, unsure whether it was by the question itself or by the fact that she didn't know the answer.

"I don't know if you've heard—" Rita leaned over the table and lowered her voice confidentially. "But there are more alternatives for people our age than the cone or the rabbit."

"Yeah, but my idea of sex doesn't involve *typing*." Ruby looked at her sidelong.

"Keeps the fingers nimble." Rita laughed. "No, I wasn't referring to chat room sex. I'm talking about going out and meeting people."

"Dating sites?" Ruby made a pained face.

"*Please.*" Rita mirrored her expression. "Social groups. Meet-ups for people with similar interests. Hobbies, film festivals, shit like that. You know I've got a boyfriend?" Pause. "*And* a girlfriend."

"Sounds exciting," Ruby told her. "But I don't know if that's really for me."

"I didn't know, either," Rita said. "I sure didn't go looking for it. It just happened. That's how it is when you have a life—things happen. You ought to try it."

"Yeah? Well, what I really want to know is how come I haven't gotten to meet these people you've been seeing." Ruby folded her arms and pretended to be stern.

"Well, for one thing—and I've got to be perfectly honest here—" Rita put down her knife and fork. "I wasn't sure how you'd react."

Ruby's eyebrows went up. "What? All this time we've worked together and you don't know I'm not a homophobe?"

"I was referring to the guy," Rita said, deadpan.

"Damn. And I thought I hid it so well," said Ruby, equally deadpan.

Rita gave a laugh and picked up her knife and fork again. "So pull the pin with me. You won't have to hide anything you don't want to."

"I'll give it some thought," Ruby lied.

"I'm asking you again—what're you waiting for?" Rita paused, regarding her expectantly. When she didn't answer, she went on: "They're not gonna promote you, you know. You *do* know that, don't you?"

Ruby dipped her head noncommittally.

"I sure knew they weren't gonna promote *me*. I knew that for a goddam *fact*." Rita took a healthy swig of wine and dragged her napkin across her mouth again.

"So is that why you decided to retire?"

Rita wagged her head emphatically. "I told you, it was my plan all along—get in my twenty and get the hell out. They'd have had to come up with a pretty hefty promotion to make me want to stay."

"Yeah? Like what—chief? Commissioner?"

"Supreme dictator for life. And I'm not so sure I would have said yes." Rita sighed. "What are you holding out for—lieutenant?"

"I passed the exam."

"So did I. So did umpty-hundred other cops ahead of us both and they ain't moving up, either." Rita's expression abruptly turned sad. "I never figured you for a lifer."

"Or maybe you hoped I wasn't?" Ruby said. "Personally, I never thought about it. I just get up and go to work every day."

"Think about it now," Rita said urgently. "Think about it like you've never thought about anything else. Get serious—you're topped out. Whatever you're waiting for, it isn't coming. All you can do is mark time."

"I work on solving murders and putting away the guilty parties," Ruby said, an edge creeping into her voice. "I wouldn't call that marking time."

"For you personally, it is," Rita insisted, unapologetic. "And in case you forgot, you count for something."

"I'm a good cop. That counts for a lot."

"That's not all you are, though. Do you even know that anymore?"

Ruby shifted in her seat, more than a little irritated. "Retiring young isn't for everybody, even if you think it is. When all you have is a hammer, everything looks like a nail."

"Oh, for chrissakes, already—" Rita blew out a short breath. "That's what *I've* been trying to tell *you*."

They sat looking at each other for some unmeasured time and Ruby realized that her soon-to-be-ex-partner was just as irritated with her, possibly more. She tried to come up with something to say to defuse the situation before a serious quarrel developed, but the Dread sitting large and uncomfortable in the middle of her body was eating her brain. The Dread was actually all she ever thought about now, like a pain that never went away, she realized, and there was barely room for anything else anymore.

Then Rita had sat back in her chair, dismay in her plump, round face. "Shit, what the hell am I doing? I'm sorry, Rube."

Ruby stared at her, baffled.

"I'm telling you you don't have a life and I'm browbeating you like I'm trying to get a confession." She shook her head as if trying to clear it. "I think I'm getting out just in time."

"Well, I *was* gonna lawyer up," Ruby said, laughing a little. "Forget it. It's a touchy thing when a partner leaves; we both know that. Things can get a little weird, blown out of proportion."

They had finished their dinner—or rather, Rita had finished hers while Ruby got a doggy bag—and called it a night early, smiles all round, although the smiles were slightly sad.

That was how things still stood between them: smoothed over but not actually resolved. If she went to Rita now and told her about the Dread, growing a little bit bulkier, a little heavier, and a little more uncomfortable every day with no end in sight, Rita would only take that as further proof that she was right about retirement.

And she really did not want to have that conversation with Rita, because she had no intention of retiring. Because she knew, deep in her core and in her bones, that even if she did take Rita's advice to pack it all in, even if she took it a step further, sold everything she owned and went off to a luxury beach condo in the Caribbean to laze around in the sun all day, indulge in fancy food and drink, and get thoroughly, perfectly laid every night by a series of gorgeous men and women, separately and together—despite all of that and a billion dollars besides, she knew with no uncertainty at all that she would still wake up every morning with the Dread that much larger and heavier and unrelenting than it had been the day before.

If she went to Rita, she would have to tell her that, and she didn't want to because she really didn't think Rita would understand. And if she didn't tell her, then Rita would only start harping again on the question of what she was waiting for. Probably accuse her of waiting for the Dread to go away.

Then she would have to confess: *No. I'm waiting to find out. I'm waiting for whatever it is I've been Dreading to show up.* Which was something she hadn't quite admitted to herself yet.

"Coffee?"

The voice cut through the combination of Ruby's usual morning haze and the constant overriding pressure of the Dread, startling her and making her jump a little. She looked up from the open folder she had been staring at unseeingly to find a young guy standing next to her desk, holding out a large cup that definitely had not come from any of the precinct machines.

"I didn't know you guys delivered," she said, smiling as she took the cup from him.

"Don't let it get around," the guy said, "or I'll have to do it for everybody." He was about thirty, just a little too dark to be called olive skinned, with a sprinkling of freckles across the bridge of his nose and a head full of honey-colored dreadlocks that had the potential to become unruly. He was only a couple of inches taller than Ruby herself—five-eight, five-nine at the most—and slightly husky.

"It'll be our secret," she assured him, taking the lid off the cup. A dark roast aroma wafted up with the steam; not her favorite, but she wasn't inclined to find fault. "Am I supposed to know you?"

"When the lieutenant comes in, he'll introduce me as your new partner."

"I see." Ruby studied him. "Transfer from Vice?"

He shook his head.

"Narcotics?"

"Ah." He smiled with half his mouth. "Must be the dreads."

Ruby barely managed not to flinch at the word; it took a quarter of a second before she realized what he was referring to. "Well, it was some kind of undercover work, though. Right?"

"Fraud and cybercrime. Rafe Pasco." He held out his hand and Ruby took it. It was strong and square but as smooth and soft as a woman's.

"Portuguese?" she guessed.

"Filipino, actually. On my father's side." He grinned and half sat on the edge of her desk. "Though as you can see, that's only part of the story. Even on my father's side." His grin widened a bit. "Like you, maybe."

Ruby shrugged. "Everybody had a story in my family and none of them could ever keep them straight. My father claimed they almost named me Kim Toy O'Toole. And I didn't even have freckles."

"Then you grew up deprived." He tilted his head to look at the file on her desk. "What are you working on?"

She had to glance down to remind herself. "Ah. Suspicious drowning.

Wife reported her husband missing; three days later he turns up on the rocks under the Soldiers Road bridge. Coroner says he's pretty sure the guy didn't just happen to wash up there, that someone must have pulled him out and then just left him."

"Anonymous call tipping you off where to find him?"

Ruby shook her head. "Couple of kids found him and told their parents. Can't figure why someone would pull a corpse out of the river and then just leave him."

"The killer?"

"Then why pull him out at all?"

"Well, the wife couldn't collect on any insurance without a body. For instance."

"Could be." Ruby made a face. "But I don't think she killed him. I think he's a suicide and she's trying to make it seem like a murder so she doesn't lose the insurance. The payout isn't much—$25,000. Not enough to inspire murder but not a sum you'd want to have to give up, either."

Pasco nodded, looking thoughtful. "Is she a hardship case?"

"Why?" Ruby asked, frowning.

"Maybe she really needs it."

She gave a short laugh. "Hey, man, who *doesn't* need $25,000? Especially if it's on the verge of dropping right into your lap."

"Yeah, but if she's got kids or she's gonna get evicted or something, it'd be too bad to take it away from her."

Ruby leaned back in her chair and gave him a searching look. "Are you kidding?"

"I'm just saying."

"That's a whole lot of *just saying* about a case I only just now told you about. You always get so deeply invested on such short notice?"

He looked slightly embarrassed. "I'm not invested. This is just something we do in Fraud—think about all the angles. Try to get into the mind-set of the people we're investigating, try to figure out where they're coming from—are they desperate or do they feel entitled for some reason. Stuff like that."

Ruby had to bite her tongue to keep from making an acid remark concerning the mass media image of criminal profiling and other extraordinary popular delusions and the madness of crowds. It wouldn't do any good. Pasco would only get defensive and then expend a lot of effort trying to prove she was wrong instead of just working the cases. In the end, he'd flounder, trying to adapt the job to his methods rather than the other way around.

Abruptly she realized that she had been staring at him in silence for more than just a moment or two. Before she could think of some neutral comment, Lieutenant Ostertag came in and waved them into his office.

"I know, I know—he's a geek," Ostertag said to Ruby after he had waved Pasco out of his office again. "He's got, I dunno, two, three degrees, maybe four. He's been in Fraud and Cybercrime since he joined the department about five years ago."

Ruby nodded. "And somebody thinks he'd make a good homicide detective."

"Apparently he already is. In the course of his last two cases he cleared up two murders, one of which nobody even knew about at the time."

"Good for him," said Ruby. "Has anyone told him that he left all the criminal masterminds back in Cybercrime?"

"He's working another case right now. I'll let him tell you about it." He got up and opened the door for her by way of declaring the meeting over, then caught her arm before she could leave. "You OK?"

Ruby drew back slightly, giving him a surprised look. "Sure I'm OK. Why wouldn't I be?"

Ostertag's mouth twitched. "You OK with getting this guy as a partner so soon after Rita leaving?"

She laughed a little. "Rita retired; she didn't die. I'm not in mourning."

The lieutenant nodded a bit impatiently. "This guy's pretty different than what you're used to."

Ruby tilted her head and frowned. "Are you asking me if I'd rather work with someone else?"

Ostertag's face turned expressionless. "No."

"What I thought," Ruby said good-naturedly, and went back to her desk.

She decided to give Pasco a little while to organize his desk, maybe meet a few of the other detectives, and then go over to ask him about his case. Instead of taking over Rita's old spot, he had opted for the vacant desk by the blocky pillar that served as an unofficial bulletin board for less-than-official notices and items, usually cartoons (which were usually obscene). It was a strange choice; Ruby had never seen anyone actually opt for that particular desk if there was anything else available, and there were two others empty at the moment. It was badly positioned—you had to sit either facing the pillar or with your back to it. Turn the desk sideways and it would obstruct the aisle. The previous lieutenant had tried switching the desk with a set of filing cabinets, but that had been no solution at all and they'd switched things back before the day was up. Moving the desk out altogether would have made more sense, but there were no city employees anywhere who would have been so foolish as to voluntarily give up anything. Someone at City

Hall could get the wrong idea, start thinking that if there was no room for a desk in your area, there were probably other things you could do without as well.

Rafe Pasco obviously had no idea he had picked the lousiest spot in the room, Ruby thought. Maybe he'd had a similar spot in Cybercrime, wherever that was headquartered. Spending all his time on a computer, he might not have noticed or cared where he sat.

"So you get the new guy." Tommy DiCenzo sat down in the chair beside her desk, a bottle of Coke Zero in one big paw. He tilted it toward her, offering her a sip.

She waved it away. "Rafe Pasco. From Cybercrime."

"I heard." Tommy glanced over his shoulder. "What'd you do, tell him to keep his distance?"

"Didn't get a chance to," she said. "He picked it out himself." From where she was sitting, she could actually see him quite well. She watched as he took a shiny black laptop out of a bag and set it on the desk. "I see he brought his own hardware. Maybe he figures he'll have more privacy over there. No one'll be able to see when he's playing solitaire."

Tommy followed her gaze. "Guy's a geek. No offense," he added quickly. "How is Jake, anyway?"

Ruby laughed. "Fine. And he'd take offense if you *didn't* call him a geek. As would he, I imagine." She jerked her chin in Pasco's general direction.

"It's a different world," Tommy said, affecting a heavy sigh. Then his face grew suddenly serious. "You OK?"

"Damn." Ruby gave a short laugh. "You know you're the second person to ask me that today?"

Tommy's steely-gray eyebrows arched. "Oh? Must be something going around." He gazed at her thoughtfully. "So, *are* you OK? Anything bothering you?"

The Dread seemed to reawaken then; it shifted inside of her by way of reasserting itself, reminding her that it was there and it was in charge. "Like what?" she said, hoping the casually offhand tone in her voice didn't sound as forced as it felt.

"Well, like Rita pulling the pin."

She let out a long breath. "It'll take some getting used to. I keep looking around for her. Which is only normal, I guess."

"You weren't prepared for her leaving, were you." It wasn't really a question.

"No," she admitted. "But I'm OK with it."

"I'm sure you are." Tommy's smile was knowing. "But it still took you by surprise. You never thought about her retiring."

"I was busy," she said, and then winced inwardly. Had she ever said anything lamer? "But you know, things, uh, change." Now she had.

"They do that." Tommy pushed himself to his feet. "It's not a steady-state universe."

"No, I guess not." Ruby stared after him as he ambled over to introduce himself to Rafe Pasco, wondering why his words seemed to hang in the air and echo in her brain. Maybe it was just having him and Ostertag ask her if she were OK within a few minutes of each other had put a whole new level of odd over the day.

The call came in about twenty minutes before Ruby had tentatively planned to go to lunch. Which figured, she thought as she and Pasco drove to the east midtown address; it had been a quiet morning. Any time you had a quiet morning, you could just about count on having to skip lunch. Of course, since the Dread had moved in on her, it hadn't left much room in her stomach. Not a whole lot of room in her mind, either—she missed the turn onto the right street and, thanks to the alternating one-ways, had to drive around in a three-block circle. If Pasco noticed, he didn't say anything. Maybe she would let him drive back to the station.

She was a bit surprised to see that patrol cars had almost half the street blocked off, even though there were very few curious onlookers and not much in the way of traffic. The address in question was a six-story tenement that Ruby had visited with Rita a few times in the past.

"Is this an actual residence or a squat?" Pasco asked her as they went up the chipped concrete steps to the front door.

"Both," Ruby told him. She wasn't actually sure anymore herself.

The uniform standing at the entrance was a young guy named Fraley; Ruby thought he looked about twelve years old, despite the thick moustache he was sporting. He opened the door for them as if that were really what he did for a living.

The smell of urine in the vestibule was practically a physical blow; she heard a sharp intake of breath from Pasco behind her.

"Straight from the perfume counter in hell," she said wryly. "Ever wonder why it's always the front of the building, why they don't take a few extra seconds to run to the back?"

"Marking their territory?" Pasco suggested.

"Good answer." Ruby glanced over her shoulder at him, impressed.

There was another uniformed officer in the hallway by the stairs, a tall black woman named Desjean whom Ruby recognized as a friend of Rita's. "Sorry to tell you this," she told them, "but your crime scene's on the roof and there's no elevator."

Ruby nodded, resigned. "Do we know who it is?"

Desjean's dark features turned sad. "Girl about twelve or thirteen. No I.D."

Ruby winced, feeling acid bubbling up in her chest. "Great. Sex crime."

"Don't know yet," the uniform replied. "But, well, up on the roof?"

"Local kid?" Ruby asked.

Desjean shook her head. "Definitely not."

Ruby looked at the stairs and then at Pasco. "You can go first if you think you might go faster."

Pasco blew out a short breath. "I'm a geek, not a track star." He frowned. "Ostertag did tell you that, didn't he?"

"Uh, yeah," Ruby said, unsure as to whether he was kidding around or not. "Before we go up, one thing."

"Don't talk to you on the way?" He nodded. "The feeling's mutual."

She felt a brief moment of warmth toward him. Then the Dread overwhelmed it, crushing it out of existence, and she started up the stairs.

A uniformed sergeant named Papoojian met them just outside the door on the roof. "Kid with a telescope spotted the body and called it in," she told them as they stood catching their breath. "I sent a couple of officers over to get a preliminary statement from him and his very freaked-out parents."

"Kid with a telescope." Ruby sighed. "I don't know if that's an argument for closed-circuit TV surveillance or against it."

The sergeant looked up at the sky worriedly. "I wish the lab guys would hurry up and get here with a tent or we're gonna have regular TV surveillance to deal with. I'm surprised the news helicopters aren't buzzing us already."

As if on cue, there was the faint sound of a chopper in the distance. Immediately, one of the other three uniformed cops on the roof produced a blanket and threw it over the body, then turned to look a question at Papoojian. Papoojian nodded an OK at him and turned back to Ruby. "If the lab has a problem with that, tell them to get in *my* face about it."

Ruby waved a hand. "You got nothing to worry about. No I.D. on the body?"

The sergeant shook her curly head. "Except for a charm on her bracelet with the name *Betty* engraved on it." She spelled it for them.

"There's a name you don't hear much these days." Ruby looked over at the blanket-covered form. She was no longer panting from the long climb, but for some reason she couldn't make herself walk the twenty feet over to where the body lay on the dusty gravel.

"Hey, you caught that other case with the kid," Papoojian said suddenly. "The Dumpster boy."

Ruby winced inwardly at the term. "Yeah."

"They dumping all the murdered kid cases on you now?"

She shrugged, taking an uncomfortable breath against the Dread, which now seemed to be all but vibrating in her midsection.

Was this what she had been dreading? she wondered suddenly. Murdered children?

It almost felt as if she were tearing each foot loose from slow-hardening cement as she urged herself to go over and look at the victim, Pasco at her elbow with an attitude that seemed oddly dutiful.

"Ever see a dead kid?" she asked him in a low voice.

"Not like this," Pasco replied, his tone neutral.

"Well, it's gruesome even when it's not gruesome," she said. "So brace yourself." She crouched down next to the body and lifted the blanket.

The girl was lying faceup, her eyes half-closed and her lips slightly parted, giving her a sort of preoccupied expression. She might have been in the middle of a daydream, except for the pallor.

"Well, I see why Desjean was so sure the girl wasn't local," Ruby said.

"Because she's Japanese?" he guessed.

"Well, there are a few Japanese in east midtown, not many, but I was referring to her clothes." Ruby shifted position, trying to relieve the pressure from the way the Dread was pushing on her diaphragm. It crossed her mind briefly that perhaps what she thought of as the Dread might actually be a physical problem. "That's quality stuff she's got on. Not designer but definitely boutique. You get it in the more upscale suburban malls. I have grandchildren," she added in response to Pasco's mildly curious expression.

She let the blanket drop and pushed herself upright, her knees cracking and popping in protest. Pasco gazed down at the covered body, his smooth, deep gold face troubled.

"You OK?" Ruby asked him.

He took a deep breath and let it out.

"Like I said, kids are gruesome even when they're not—"

"I think this is related to this case I've been working on."

"Really." She hid her surprise. "We'll have to compare notes, then. Soon."

He didn't answer right away, looking from the blanket to her with a strange expression she wasn't sure how to read. There was something defensive about it, with more than a little suspicion as well. "Sure," he said finally, with all the enthusiasm of someone agreeing to a root canal.

Ruby felt a mix of irritation and curiosity, which was quickly overridden by the Dread. She couldn't decide whether to say something reassuring or simply assert her authority and reassure him later, after she knew she had his cooperation.

Then the crime lab arrived, saving her from having to think about anything from the immediate situation. And the Dread.

At the end of the day, Pasco managed to get away without talking about his case. It was possible of course that he had not been purposely trying to elude her. After spending most of the day talking to, or trying to talk to, the people in the building, checking on the results of the door-to-door in the neighborhood, looking over the coroner's shoulder, and through it all pushing the Dread ahead of her like a giant boulder uphill, she was too tired to care.

She made a note about Pasco in her memo book and then dragged herself home to her apartment, where she glanced at an unopened can of vegetable soup before stripping off and falling into bed, leaving her clothes in a heap on the floor.

3:11.

The numbers, glowing danger red, swam out of the darkness and into focus. It was a moment or two before she realized that she was staring at the clock radio on the nightstand.

Odd. She never woke in the middle of the night; even with the Dread pressing relentlessly harder on her every day, she slept too heavily to wake easily or quickly. Therefore, something must have happened, something big or close, or both. She held very still, not even breathing, listening for the sound of an intruder in the apartment, in the bedroom.

A minute passed, then another; nothing. Maybe something had happened in the apartment next door or upstairs, she thought, still listening, barely breathing.

Nothing. Nothing and more nothing. And perhaps that was all it was, a whole lot of nothing. It could have been a car alarm out on the street, an ambulance passing close with its siren on, or someone's bassed-out thump-mobile with the volume set on stun. Just because she didn't usually wake up didn't mean that she couldn't. She took a long deep breath and let it out, rolling onto her back.

There was something strange about the feel of the mattress under her and she realized that she wasn't alone in the bed.

Automatically she rolled onto her right side. Rafe Pasco's head was resting on the other pillow. He was gazing at her with an expression of deep regret.

Shock hit her like an electric jolt. She jumped back, started to scream.

In the next moment she was staring at the empty place next to her in the bed, her own strangled cry dying in her ears as daylight streamed in through the window.

She jumped again and scrambled out of bed, looking around. There was no one in the room except her, no sign that anyone else had been lying in bed with her. She looked at the clock. 7:59.

Still feeling shaky, she knelt on the bed and reached over to touch the pillow Pasco's head had been resting on. She could still see him vividly in her mind's eye, that regretful expression. Or maybe "apologetic" was more like it. Sorry that he had showed up in her bed uninvited? *Hope you'll forgive the intrusion — it was too late to call and there wasn't time to get a warrant.*

The pillow was cool to her touch. Of course. Because she had been dreaming.

She sat down on the edge of the bed, one hand unconsciously pressed to her chest. That had been some crazy dream; her heart was only now starting to slow down from double time.

She stole a glance over her shoulder at the other side of the bed. Nope, still nobody there, not nobody, not nohow, and most especially not Rafe Pasco. What the hell had that been all about, anyway, seeing her new partner in bed with her? Why him, of all the goddam people? Just because he was new? Not to mention young and good-looking. She hadn't thought she'd been attracted to him, but apparently there was a dirty old woman in her subconscious who begged to differ.

Which, now that she thought about it, was kind of pathetic.

"God or whoever, please, save me from that," Ruby muttered, and stood up to stretch. Immediately, a fresh wave of the Dread washed over her, almost knocking her off balance. She clenched her teeth, afraid for a moment that she was going to throw up. Then she steadied herself and stumped off to the bathroom to stand under the shower.

Pasco was already at his desk when Ruby dragged herself in. She found it hard to look at him and she was glad to see that he was apparently too wrapped up in something on his notebook to pay attention to anything else. Probably the mysterious case he was working on and didn't seem to want to tell her about. *Shouldn't have slipped and told me you thought it might be related to the one we caught yesterday,* she admonished him silently, still not looking at him. *Now I'll have to pry it out of you.*

Later. She busied herself with phone calls, setting up some witness interviews, putting in a call to the medical examiner about getting a preliminary report on the Japanese girl, and requesting information from Missing Persons on anyone fitting the girl's description. It wasn't until nearly noon that it occurred to her that he was working just as hard to avoid catching her eye as vice versa.

She drew in an uneasy breath and the Dread seemed to breathe with her. *Maybe he had the same dream you did*, suggested a tiny voice in her mind.

As if he had sensed something, he looked up from his notebook at her. She gave him a nod, intending to turn away and find something else that had to be done before she could talk to him. Instead, she surprised herself by grabbing her memo book and walking over to his desk.

"So tell me about this case of yours," she said, pulling over an empty chair and plumping down in it. "And why you think it might have something to do with the dead girl from yesterday."

"Do we know who she is yet?" he asked.

Ruby shook her head. "I'm still waiting to hear from Missing Persons. I've also put a call into the company that makes the charm bracelet, to find out who sells it in this area."

Pasco frowned. "She could have bought it on the Internet."

"Thanks for that," she said sourly. "You can start with the auction sites if I come up empty."

He nodded a bit absently and then turned his notebook around to show her the screen. The dead girl smiled out from what seemed to be a formal school photo; her eyes twinkled in the bright studio lights and her lips were parted just enough to show the thin gold line of a retainer wire around her front teeth.

"Where'd you get that?" Ruby demanded, incredulous.

"It's not the same girl," he told her.

"Then who is it—her twin?"

"Can't say at this point." He smiled a little. "This girl is Alice Nakamura. I was investigating a case of identity theft involving her parents."

"Perps or victims?"

"To be honest, I'm still not clear on that. They could be either, or even both."

Ruby shook her head slightly. "I don't get it."

"Identity theft is a complex thing and it's getting more complex all the time."

"If that's supposed to be an explanation, it sucks."

Pasco dipped his head slightly in acknowledgment. "That's putting it mildly. The Nakamuras first showed up entering the country from the Cayman Islands. Actually, you might say that's where they popped into existence, as I couldn't find any record of them prior to that."

"Maybe they came from Japan via the Caymans?" Ruby suggested.

"The parents have—had—U.S. passports."

Ruby gave a short laugh. "If they've got passports, then they've got Social Security cards and birth certificates."

"And we looked those up—"

" 'We?' "

"This task force I was on," he said, a bit sheepishly. "It was a state-level operation with a federal gateway."

Here comes the jargon, Ruby thought, willing her eyes not to film over.

"Anyway, we looked up the numbers. They were issued in New York, as were their birth certificates. There was no activity of any kind on the numbers—no salary, no withholding, no income, no benefits. According to the records, these people have never worked and never paid taxes."

"Call the IRS; tell them you've got a lead on some people who've never paid taxes. That'll take care of it."

"Tried that," Pasco said, his half smile faint. "The IRS records show that everything is in order for the Nakamuras. Unfortunately, they can't seem to find any copies of their tax returns."

"That doesn't sound like the IRS *I* know," Ruby said skeptically.

Pasco shrugged. "They're looking. At least, that's what they tell me whenever I call. I have a feeling that it's not a priority for them."

"But what about the rest of it? The birth certificates? You said they were issued in New York?"

"They're not actually the original birth certificates," Pasco said. "They're notarized copies, replacing documents which have been lost. Some of the information is missing—like where exactly each of them was born, the hospital, the attending physician, and, except for Alice, the parents' names."

Ruby glanced heavenward for a moment. "What are they, in witness protection?"

"I'll let you know if I ever get a straight answer one way or another on that one," Pasco said, chuckling a little, "but I'd bet money that they aren't."

"Yeah, me, too." Ruby sat for a few moments, trying to get her mind around everything he had told her. None of it sounded right. Incomplete birth certificates? Even if she bought the stuff about the IRS, she found that completely implausible. "But I still don't understand. Everything's computerized these days, which means everything's recorded. Nobody just *pops* into existence, let alone a whole family."

"It's not against the law to live off the grid," Pasco said. "Some people do. You'd be surprised at how many."

"What—you mean living off the land, generating your own electricity, shit like that?" Ruby gave a short, harsh laugh. "Look at that photo. That's not a picture of a girl whose family has been living off the grid. She's got an orthodontist, for chrissakes."

"I'm not so sure," Pasco said. "We had the Nakamuras on our radar, so to speak, when they entered the state. However they had been covering themselves before they left the Caymans, whatever they'd been doing to stay invisible, they weren't doing it anymore. They left an easy trail to follow. I found them in a northland hotel near the airport. They were there for a week. At the same time, the task force was investigating some fraudulent activity elsewhere in the same area. It seemed that the Nakamura case was going to converge with it."

"What was it, this other activity?" Ruby asked.

Pasco made a face. "More identity theft. I can run you through the long version later if you want, but the short version is, be careful what you do with your utility bills after you pay them, and if you insist on paying them over the phone, don't use a cordless phone or a mobile." He paused; when she nodded, he went on. "Anyway, we had enough evidence for a warrant. But when the police got there, the house was abandoned. The only thing they found was the body of Alice Nakamura in one of the bedrooms. Her birth certificate, school photo, library card, and passport were lying next to her on the floor."

"How did she die?"

"Natural causes. Heart failure. I forget what the conditon's called, but the coroner said that a lot of kids on the transplant lists have it. Alice Nakamura wasn't on any of those. There are no medical records for her anywhere, in fact. And it turned out that her passport was a forgery."

Ruby blinked. "So much for homeland security."

"It was an excellent forgery, but a forgery nonetheless, as there was no record of her ever applying for a passport, let alone receiving one. Unlike her parents."

"If this is some kind of conspiracy, it's the most random and disorganized one I've ever heard of," Ruby said, frowning. "Not to mention that it doesn't make any sense. Unless you've actually been speaking a language that only sounds like English, but all the words mean something entirely different, and I haven't really understood a single thing you've said."

Her words hung in the air between them for a long moment. Pasco's face was deeply thoughtful (not deeply regretful; she stamped down on the memory again), practically contemplative, as if she had set out a significant issue that had to be addressed with care. Inside her, the Dread pushed sharply into the area just under her breastbone.

"I'm sure that's how everything probably looks when you see it from the outside," he said finally. "If you don't know a system, if you don't understand how things work or what the rules are, it won't make any sense. The way a foreign language will sound like gibberish."

Ruby grimaced at him. "But nothing's that strange. If you listen to a foreign language for even just a minute, you start picking up some sense of the patterns in it. You recognize it's a system even if it's one you're not familiar with—"

"Oh?" Pasco's half smile was back. "Ever listened to Hungarian?"

She waved a hand at him. "No, but I've listened to Cantonese and

Mandarin, simultaneously at full volume when my grandparents argued. You know what I mean. For a system, or anything, to be completely incomprehensible, it would have to be something totally—" She floundered, groping for a word. "It would have to be something totally alien. Outside human experience altogether."

Her words replayed themselves in her mind. "Christ," she said, massaging her forehead. "What the hell are we talking about and why?"

Pasco pressed his lips together briefly. "You were saying that there are a lot of things about my case that don't make any sense."

"You got *that* right, my man," she said feelingly, and then let out a long sigh. "I suppose that's the human element at work."

"Pardon?" Now he looked bewildered.

"People are infinitely screwy," she said. "Human beings can make a mess out of chaos."

He surprised her by bursting into loud, hearty laughter. She twisted around in her seat to see that the whole room was staring at them curiously. "Thanks, I'll be here all week," she said a bit self-consciously, and turned back to Pasco, trying to will him to wind down fast. Her gaze fell on the notebook screen again.

"Hey, what about her retainer?" she asked, talking over his guffaws.

"Her what?" Pasco said, slightly breathless and still chuckling a little.

"On her teeth." Ruby tapped the screen with her little finger. It felt spongy. "Were you able to trace it to a particular orthodontist?"

"She wasn't wearing a retainer and they didn't find one in the house," Pasco said, sobering.

"And what about her parents?"

"The Nakamuras have dropped out of sight again."

"*Popped out* of existence?"

"I thought so at first," he said, either oblivious to or ignoring her tone of voice. "But then that girl turned up on the roof yesterday, which leads me to believe they were still around. Up to that point, anyway. They might be gone by now, though."

"Why? You think they had something to do with the girl's death?"

"Not intentionally."

Ruby shook her head. "Intentionally, unintentionally—either way, why? Who is she to them—the long-lost twin of the girl who died of heart failure?" Abruptly the Dread gave her stomach a half twist; she swallowed hard and kept talking. "How long ago was that anyway, when you found Alice Nakamura?"

Pasco hesitated, his face suddenly very serious. "*I* didn't find her. I mean, I only pinpointed the address. I wasn't there when the police entered the house. The geek squad never goes along on things like that. I think the other cops are afraid of geeks with guns."

"But you're cops, too."

"Exactly. Anyway—" He swiveled the notebook around and tapped the keyboard a few times. "That was about five and a half weeks ago, almost six." He looked up again. "Does that suggest anything special to you?"

Ruby shook her head. "You?"

"Just that the Nakamuras have managed to lay pretty low for quite a while. I wonder how. And where."

Ruby wanted to ask him something about that but couldn't quite figure out how to word the question. "And you're absolutely sure that girl—Alice Nakamura, I mean—died of natural causes?"

"None whatsoever. Also, she wasn't abused or neglected in any way before she died, either. She was well taken care of. She just happened to be very sick."

"Uh-huh." Ruby nodded absently. "Then why would they just go off and leave her?"

"If they didn't want to be found—and judging from their behavior, they didn't—then they couldn't carry her dead body along with them."

"All right, *that* makes sense," Ruby said. "But it still leaves the question of why they don't want to be found. Because they're in on this identity theft thing, conspiracy, whatever it is?"

"Or because they're victims of identity theft who have had to steal a new identity themselves."

Ruby closed her eyes briefly. "OK, now we're back to not making sense again."

"No, it's been known to happen," Pasco insisted. "For some people, when their identity gets stolen, the thief does so much damage that they find it's virtually impossible to clear their name. They have to start over."

"But why steal someone else's identity to do that?" Ruby asked. "Why not just create an entirely new identity?"

"Because the created identity would eventually trace back to the old one. Better to get one with completely different connections."

Ruby shook her head obstinately. "You could still do that with a brand-new identity."

Pasco was shaking his own head just as obstinately. "The idea isn't just to steal someone's identity—it's to steal their past, too. If I create a new identity, I really do have to start over in every way. That's pretty hard. It's easier if I can, say, build on your already-excellent credit rating."

"Obviously you've never tried to steal my identity," Ruby said with a short, humorless laugh. "Or you'd know better than to say something like that."

"I was just giving an example."

Ruby let out a long breath. "I think I'll pay the coroner a visit, see if there's anything he can tell me about how Alice Nakamura's twin died. Maybe it'll tell us something about—oh, I don't know, *anything*. In a way that will make sense." She stood up to go back to her desk.

"Hey—" Pasco caught her wrist; the contact startled her and he let go immediately. "What if she died of natural causes?"

"Jesus, you really can dream things up, can't you." Ruby planted her fists on her hips and gave him a hard look. "That would be entirely too much of a coincidence."

"Natural causes," said the coroner's assistant, reading from a clipboard. Her I.D. gave her name as Sheila St. Pierre; there was a tiny Hello Kitty sticker under the "St." She was a plump woman in her midtwenties with short, spiky blond hair and bright red cat's-eye glasses, and while she wasn't chewing gum, Ruby kept expecting to hear it pop every time she opened her mouth. "Aneurysm. Tragic in one so young, you know?"

"You're sure you have the right chart?" Ruby asked tensely.

"Unidentified Oriental adolescent female, brought in yesterday from a rooftop in east midtown, right?" Sheila St. Pierre offered Ruby the clipboard. "See for yourself."

Ruby scanned the form quickly several times before she was able to force herself to slow down and check each detail. "How can a thirteen-year-old girl have a fucking *aneurysm*?" she said finally, handing the clipboard back to the other woman. "The coroner must have screwed up. Where is he? I want to make him do it again."

"There's no do-overs in postmortems," Sheila St. Pierre said, making a face. "What do you think we're working with here, Legos?" She shifted her weight to her right side and folded her arms, hugging the clipboard to her front. "How about a second opinion?"

"Great," Ruby said. "Where can I get one?"

"Right here. I assisted Dr. Levitt on this one and I saw it myself firsthand. It was an aneurysm. Case closed. You know, an aneurysm is one of those things anybody can have without even knowing it. You could have one, or I could. We just go along living our lives day in, day out, everything's swell, and suddenly—boom. Your head blows up and you're history. Or I am. Or we both are. Most people have no idea how thin that membrane between life and death can be. But then, isn't it really better that way? Better living though denial. Who'd want to go around in a constant state of dread?"

Ruby glared at her, but she was turning away to put the clipboard down on a metal table nearby. "At least it isn't all bad news," she said, holding up a small plastic bag between two fingers. There was a retainer in it. "We did manage to identify the girl from her dental records."

"I didn't see that on that report!" Ruby snapped. "Why wasn't it on there? Who is she? When were you going to fucking tell me?"

Sheila St. Pierre tossed the bag with the retainer in it back on the table. "Which question would like me to fucking answer first?"

Ruby hesitated and then looked at the retainer. "Where did that come from, anyway? I didn't see one at the scene."

"Well, it was there. Nobody looked close enough till we got her on the table. Her name is Betty Mura—"

"What's her address?" Ruby demanded. "And why didn't you call me?"

"I did call you," Sheila St. Pierre said with exaggerated patience. "You weren't at your desk, so I left a message."

Ruby had to force herself not to lunge forward and shake the woman. "When was that?"

"As near as I can tell, it was while you were on your way over here."

"Give me that information *now!*" Ruby ordered her, but she was already picking up the clipboard. She slid a piece of paper out from under the form on top and handed it over.

"Thank you," she prompted politely as Ruby snatched it from her.

"You're welcome," Ruby growled over her shoulder, already out of the room.

There was a ticket on her windshield, another skirmish in the struggle to keep the area in front of the municipal complex a strict no-parking zone, this means you, no exceptions, especially cops. Ruby crumpled it up and tossed it in the backseat as she slid behind the wheel. She clipped Betty Mura's home address to her visor. A West Side address, no surprise there considering the girl's clothes. But what had she been doing on a roof in east midtown? What had she been doing *anywhere* in east midtown, and how had she gotten there? She might have died of natural causes, but there had definitely been something unusual going on in the last hours of her life.

She went to start the car and then paused. First she should call Rafe Pasco, tell him she had the girl's name and address and she would pick him up.

The image of his head resting on the pillow beside her flashed in her mind; irritation surged and was immediately overwhelmed by the Dread in a renewed assault. She had a sudden strong urge to close her eyes and let her head fall forward on the steering wheel and stay that way until the next Ice Age or the heat death of the universe, whichever came second.

She took a steadying breath, popped her cell phone into the cradle on the dashboard, put it on speaker, and dialed the squad room. Tommy DiCenzo answered; she asked him to put her through to Pasco.

"Can't, Ruby. He's not here; he left."

"Where'd he go?" she asked, but as soon as the words were out of her mouth, she knew the answer.

"Coroner's office called—they identified your rooftop girl from her dental records. He took the name and address and left."

"Did he say anything about coming to get me first?" Knowing that he hadn't.

Tommy hesitated. "Not to me. But I got the impression he thought you already knew, since you were on your way over to the coroner's anyway."

"*Shit*," she muttered, and started the car. "Hey, you wouldn't happen to know Pasco's cell phone number, would you? I don't have it with me."

"Hang on—"

"Tommy—" But he had already put the phone down. She could hear the tanky background noise of the squad room: footsteps, a phone ringing, and Tommy's voice, distant and indistinct, asking a question. A few seconds later he picked up the phone again.

"OK, ready?"

"Wait—" She found a pen, looked around hurriedly, and then held the point over the back of her other hand. "Go."

He dictated the number to her carefully, saying it twice.

"Thanks, Tommy," she said, disconnecting before he could say anything else. She dialed the number he'd given her, then pulled away from the curb as it began to ring.

To her immense frustration, it kept on ringing for what seemed like a hundred times before she finally heard the click of someone picking up.

"Rafe Pasco speaking—"

"Goddammit, Rafe, why didn't you call me before—"

"I'm in the Bahamas for two weeks," his voice went on cheerfully, cutting into her tirade, "and as you can see, I didn't pack my cell phone. Sorry about that. But you can phone my house sitter and talk to her if you want. It's *your call*." There was another click followed by a mechanical female voice inviting her to leave a message after the beep.

Ruby stabbed the disconnect button and redialed. The same thing happened and she disconnected again, furious. Was Pasco playing some kind of mind game or had he really just forgotten to change his voice-mail message after his last vacation? Either way, she was going to have a hard time not punching him. Weaving in and out of the traffic, she headed for the freeway.

She was merging into traffic from the entrance ramp when all at once she found herself wondering what she was so frantic about. Pasco had been inconsiderate, even rude, but he must have figured she'd get the same information from the coroner. Possibly he had assumed she would head over to the

Mura house directly from the coroner. He was her partner, after all—why should she be concerned about him going to the girl's house without her?

The Dread clutched her stomach like a fist and she swerved halfway into the breakdown lane. Behind her, a horn blared long and hard. She slowed down, pulling all the way into the breakdown lane to let it pass; it whizzed by a fraction of a second later. The Dread maintained its grip on her, flooding her system and leaving no room for even a flash of fear at her close call. She slowed down intending to stop, but the Dread wouldn't let her step on the brake.

"What the *fuck*," she whispered as the car rumbled along. The Dread seemed to have come to life in her with an intensity beyond anything she had felt in the past. The maddening, horrible thing about it, however, was that it had not tipped over into terror or panic, which she realized finally was what she had been waiting for it to do. She had been expecting that as a logical progression—apprehension turned to dread; dread became fear. But it hadn't. She had never suspected it was possible to feel so much dread—Dread—without end. It shouldn't have been. Because it wasn't a steady-state universe.

So what kind of universe was it, then?

This was it, she thought suddenly; this was the crack-up and it was happening in fast motion just like she had wanted. The thing to do now was stop the car, call Tommy DiCenzo, and tell him she needed help.

Then she pressed the accelerator, put on her turn signal, and checked the rearview mirror as she moved back into the travel lane.

The well-groomed west side houses slid through the frame of the car windows as Ruby navigated the wide, clean streets. She didn't know the West Side quite as well as the rest of the city and the layout was looser than the strict, organized northland grid or the logical progressions of midtown and the south side. Developers and contractors had staked out patches of the former meadowlands and put up subdivisions with names like Saddle Hills and Wildflower Dale and filled them with split-level ranches for the young middle class and cookie-cutter mansions for the newly affluent. Ruby had taken small notice of any of it during the years Jake had been growing up. There was no appeal to the idea of moving to the West Side from downtown—it would have meant two hours of sheer commuting every day, time she preferred to spend with her son. The downtown school district had not been cutting-edge, but it hadn't been anywhere near disastrous, either—

She gave her head a quick shake to clear it. *Get a grip,* she ordered herself, and tightened her hands on the steering wheel as if that would help. She checked the address clipped to her visor again, then paused at the end of the street, craning her neck to read the road sign. It would solve a lot of problems, she thought, if the cheap-ass city would just put GPS navigation in all the goddam cars. She turned right onto the cross street and then wondered if she had made a mistake. Had she already driven along this street? The houses looked familiar.

Well, of course they looked familiar, she realized, irritated—they were all alike. She kept going, watching the street signs carefully. Christ, it wasn't only the houses themselves that were all like—it was also the cars in the driveways, the front lawns, even the toys scattered on the grass. The same but not the same. Like Alice Nakamura and Betty Mura.

She came to another intersection and paused again, almost driving on before she realized that the street on her left was the one she wanted. The Dread renewed its intensity as she made the turn, barely noticing the woman pushing a double stroller with two toddlers in it. Both the woman and her children watched her pass with alert curiosity on their unremarkable faces. They were the only people Ruby had seen out walking, but the Dread left no room for her to register as much.

The Mura house was not a cookie-cutter mansion—more like a cookie-cutter update of the kind of big old Victorian Jake and Lita lived in with the kids. Ruby pulled up at the curb instead of parking in the driveway where a shiny black SUV was blocked in by a not-so-shiny car that she knew had to belong to Rafe Pasco.

Ruby sat, staring at the front of the house. It felt as if the Dread were writhing inside her now. The last thing she wanted to do was go inside. Or rather, it should have been the last thing she wanted to do. The Dread, alive everywhere in her all the way to her fingertips, to the soles of her feet, threatened to become even worse if she didn't.

Moving slowly and carefully, she got out of the car and walked up the driveway, pausing at Pasco's car to look in the open driver's side window. The interior was impossibly clean for a cop or a geek—no papers, no old sandwich wrappers or empty drink cups. Hell, even the floor mats were clean, as if they had just been vacuumed. Nothing in the backseat, either, except more clean.

She glanced over at the glove box; then her gaze fell on the trunk release. If she popped it, what would she find in there, she wondered—a portable car-cleaning kit with a hand vac? A carton of secret geek files? Or just more clean nothing?

There would be nothing in the trunk. All the secret geek files would be on Pasco's notebook, and he probably had that with him. She considered popping the trunk anyway and then moved away from the car, stopping again to look inside the SUV. The windows were open and the doors were unlocked—apparently the Muras trusted their neighbors and the people who came to visit them. Even the alarm was off.

There was a hard-shell CD case sitting on the passenger seat and a thin crescent of disk protruding from the slot of the player in the dash. A small string of tiny pink and yellow beads dangled from the rearview mirror along with a miniature pair of fuzzy, hot pink dice. Ruby wondered if Betty Mura had put them there.

She turned toward the front door and then thought better of it. Instead, she made her way around the side of the garage and into the unfenced backyard.

Again she stopped. The yard was empty except for a swing set and a brightly painted jungle gym. Behind the swings was a cement patio with a couple of loungers; under one of them was an empty plastic glass lying on its side, forgotten and probably considered lost.

The sliding glass patio doors were open, Ruby realized suddenly, although the screen door was closed and the curtains were drawn. She edged her way along the rear of the garage and sidled up next to the open door.

". . . less pleading your case with me," she heard Pasco saying. "Both girls are dead. It ends here."

"But the other girls—," a man started.

"There are *no* other girls," Pasco told him firmly. "Not for you. They aren't your daughters."

Ruby frowned. Daughters? So the girls really had been twins?

"But they *are*—," protested a woman.

"You can't think that way," Pasco said. "Once there's been a divergence, those lives—your own, your children's, everyone's—are lost to you. To act as if it were otherwise is the same as if you went next door to your neighbors' house and took over everything they owned. Including their children."

"I told you, we didn't come here to kidnap Betty," the man said patiently. "I saw her records—the man showed me. He told us about her aneurysm. He said it was almost a sure thing that it would kill her before Alice's heart gave out. Then we could get her heart for transplant knowing that it would be a perfect match for Alice—"

"You heartless bastard," said a second male voice identical to the one that had been speaking. How many people were in that room, Ruby wondered.

"She was going to die anyway," said the first man. "There was nothing anyone could do about it—"

"The hell there wasn't. If we had known, we could have taken her to a hospital for emergency surgery," a woman said angrily. "They can fix those things now, you know. Or aren't they as advanced where you come from?"

"It doesn't matter anymore," Pasco said, raising his voice to talk over them. "Because Alice died first after all."

"Yes," said the woman bitterly, speaking through tears. It sounded like the same woman who had been talking so angrily a few moments before, but Ruby had a feeling it wasn't.

"And do you know why that is?" Pasco asked in a stern, almost paternal tone of voice.

"The man was wrong," said the tearful woman.

"Or he lied," said the angry one.

"No, it was because you came here and you brought Alice with you," Pasco said. "Once you did that, all bets, as they say here, were off. The moment you came in, it threw everything out of kilter because you don't belong here. You're extra—surplus. One too many times three. It interrupted the normal flow of progress; things scattered with such force that there were even natural-law anomalies. This morning, a very interesting woman said to me, 'Human beings can make a mess out of chaos.' I couldn't tell her how extraordinarily right she was, of course, so I couldn't stop laughing. She must have thought I was crazy."

Ruby pressed her lips together, thinking that he couldn't be any crazier than she was herself right now; it was just that she was a lot more confused.

Abruptly, she heard the sound of the front door opening, followed by new voices as a few more people entered the house. This was turning into quite a party; too bad Pasco had left her off the guest list.

"Finally," she heard him saying. "I was about to call you again, find out what happened to you."

"These West Side streets are confusing," a woman answered. This was a completely new voice, but Ruby found it strangely familiar. "It's not a nice, neat grid like northland, you know."

"Complain all you want later," Pasco said. "I want to wrap this up as soon as possible."

"I don't know about that," said another man. "Have you looked out front?"

Pasco groaned. "What now?"

"There's a car parked at the curb, right in front of the house," the man said. "I don't think that's a coincidence."

"Oh, hell," Pasco said. She heard his footsteps thumping hurriedly away from the patio door—probably going to look out the window at the car—and then coming back again. She straightened her shoulders and, refusing to give herself time to think about it, she yanked open the screen door and stepped into the house, flinging aside the curtain.

"I'm right h—" Her voice died in her throat and she could only stand, frozen in place, one hand still clutching the edge of the curtain while she stared at Rafe Pasco. And a man who seemed to be his older, much taller brother. And two identical Japanese couples sitting side by side on a long sofa with their hands cuffed in front of them.

And, standing behind the couch, her newly retired ex-partner, Rita Castillo.

"Now, don't panic," Pasco said after might have been ten minutes or ten months.

"I'm not panicking," Ruby managed in a hoarse voice. She drew a long, shaky breath. Inside her, the Dread was no longer vibrating or writing or swelling; it had finally reached full power. This was what she had been Dreading all this time, day after day. Except now that she was finally face-to-face with it, she had no idea what it actually was.

"I can assure you that you're not in any danger," Pasco added.

"I know," she said faintly.

"No, you don't."

"OK," Ruby said. Obviously he was in charge, so she would defer willingly, without protest.

"The sensation you're feeling right now has nothing to do with your actual safety," Pasco went on, speaking carefully and distinctly, as if he were trying to talk her down from a high ledge. Or maybe a bad acid trip was more like it, she thought, glancing at the Japanese couples. The Muras and the Nakamuras, apparently. She wondered which was which. "What it actually is, is a kind of allergic reaction."

"Oh?" She looked around the room. Everyone else seemed to understand what he was talking about, including the Japanese couples. "What am I allergic to?"

"It's something in the nature of a disturbance."

Oh, God, no, she thought, *now he's going to say something about "the force." I'll find out they're all actually a lunatic cult and Pasco's the leader. And I'm trapped in a house with them.* Her gaze drifted over to Rita. No, Rita would never have let herself get sucked into anything like that. Would she?

Rita shifted, becoming slightly uncomfortable under Ruby's gaze. "Do I know you?" she asked finally.

Ruby's jaw dropped. She felt as if Rita had slapped her.

"No, you don't," Pasco said over his shoulder. "She knows someone like you. Where you come from, the two of you never met. Here, you were partners."

"Wow," Rita said, shaking her head. "It never ceases to amaze me, all that what-might-have-been stuff." She smiled at Ruby, giving an apologetic shrug.

"And where does she come from?" Ruby wanted to know. Her voice was a little stronger now.

"That doesn't matter," Pasco told her. "Besides, the less you know, the better you'll feel."

"Really?" She made a skeptical face.

"No," he said, resigned. "Actually, you'll feel not quite so bad. Not quite so much Dread. It may not be much, but any relief is welcome. Isn't it?" He took a small step toward her. "And you've been feeling very bad for a while now, haven't you? Though it wasn't quite so awful in the beginning."

Ruby didn't say anything.

"Only you're not sure exactly when it started," Pasco continued, moving a little closer. Ruby wondered why he was being so cautious with her. Was he afraid of what she might do? "I can tell you. It started when the Nakamuras arrived here. Ostensibly from the Cayman Islands. When they stepped out of their own world and into this one. Into yours."

Ruby took a deep breath and let it out, willing herself to be less tense. She looked around, spotted an easy chair opposite the couch, and leaned on the back of it. "All right," she said to Pasco, "who are you and what the hell are you talking about?"

Pasco hesitated. "I'm a cop."

"No," Ruby said with exaggerated patience, "*I'm* a cop. Try again."

"It's the truth," Pasco insisted. "I really am a cop. Of sorts."

"What sort?" Ruby asked. "Geek squad? Not Homicide."

He hesitated again. "Crimes Against Persons and Property. This includes identity theft, which is not a geek squad job in my line of law enforcement."

Ruby wanted to sit down more than anything in the world now, but she forced herself to stay on her feet. To make Pasco look at her on the same level, as an equal. "Go on."

"It's my job to make sure that people who regret what might've been don't get so carried away that they try to do something unlawful to try to rectify it. Even if that means preventing a young girl from getting the heart transplant that will save her life."

Ruby looked over at the people sitting handcuffed on the sofa. They all looked miserable and angry.

"An unscrupulous provider of illegal goods and services convinced a couple of vulnerable parents that they could save their daughter's life if they went to a place where two other parents very similar to themselves were living a life in which things had gone a bit differently. Where their daughter, who was named Betty instead of Alice, had an undetected aneurysm instead of a heart condition."

Light began to dawn for Ruby. Her mind returned to the idea of being trapped in a house with a bunch of lunatic cultists. Then she looked at Rita. *Where you come from, the two of you never met.*

"Many of my cases are much simpler," Pasco went on. "People who want to win instead of lose—a hand of cards, a race, the lottery. Who think they'd have been better off if they'd turned left instead of right, said yes instead of no." He spread his hands. "But we can't let them do that, of course. We can't let them take something from its rightful owner."

"And by 'we' you mean . . . ?" Ruby waited; he didn't answer. "All right, then let's try this: you can't possibly be the same kind of cop I am. I'm local, equally subject to the laws that I enforce. But you're not. Are you."

"I wouldn't say that, exactly," Pasco replied. "I have to obey those laws, but in order to enforce them, I have to live outside the system they apply to."

She looked at Rita again. Or rather, the woman she had thought was Rita. "And what's your story? He said you're from a place where we never met. Does your being here with him mean you don't live there anymore?"

Not-Rita nodded. "Someone stole my identity and I couldn't get it back. Things didn't end well."

"And all you could do was become a sort of a cop?" Ruby asked.

"We have to go," said Pasco's taller brother before the woman could answer. He could have been an alternative version of Pasco, Ruby thought, from a place where she hadn't met him, either. Would that be the same place that Not-Rita came from? She decided she didn't want to know and hoped none of them would feel compelled to tell her.

"We've still got time," Pasco said, looking at his watch, which seemed to be a very complicated device. "But there's no good in pushing things right down to the wire. Take them out through the garage and put them in the SUV—"

"Where are you taking them?" Ruby asked as taller Pasco and not-Rita got the Japanese couples on their feet.

Pasco looked surprised by the question; it was a moment or two before he could answer. "To court. A kind of court."

"Ah," Ruby said. "Would that be for an arraignment? A sort of arraignment?"

He nodded and Ruby knew he was lying. She had no idea how she knew, but she did, just as she knew it was the first time he had ever lied to her. She let it go, watching as the other two herded the Japanese couples toward the kitchen.

"Wait," she said suddenly. Everyone stopped, turning to look at her. "Which ones are the Nakamuras?"

Judging from the group reaction, she had definitely asked the wrong question. Even the couples looked dismayed, as if she had threatened them in some fashion.

"Does it matter?" Pasco said after a long moment.

"No, I guess not."

And it didn't, not to her or anyone else, she realized, not now, not ever again. When you got caught in this kind of identity theft, you probably had to give identity up completely. Exactly what that meant she had no idea, but she knew it couldn't have been very pleasant.

Pasco nodded and the other two escorted the couples out of the room. A few moments later, Ruby heard the kitchen door leading to the garage open and close.

"How did you know the Nakamuras would come here?" Ruby asked Pasco.

"I didn't. Just dumb luck—they were here when I arrived, so I took them all into custody."

"And they didn't resist or try to get away?"

"There's nowhere for them to go. The Nakamuras can't survive indefinitely here unless they could somehow replace the Muras."

"Then why did you arrest the Muras?"

"They were going to let the Nakamuras supplant them while they moved on to a place where their daughter hadn't died."

The permutations began to pile up in Ruby's brain; she squeezed her eyes shut for a moment, cutting off the train of thought before it made her dizzy.

"All right," she said. "But what about this master criminal who convinced the Nakamuras to do all this in the first place? How could he, she— whatever—know about Betty Mura's aneurysm?"

Pasco's face became thoughtful again and she could practically see his mind working at choosing the right words. "Outside the system, there is access to certain kinds of information about the elements within it. Features are visible outside that can't be discerned inside.

"Unfortunately, making that information available inside never goes well. It's like poison. Things begin to malfunction."

"Is that really why Alice Nakamura died before the other girl?" Ruby asked.

"It was an extra contributing factor, but it also had to do with the Nakamuras being in a world where they didn't belong. As I said." Pasco crossed the room to close the patio door and lock it. "What I was referring to were certain anomalies of time and space."

Ruby shook her head, not understanding.

"It's how Betty Mura ended up on a rooftop in midtown," he clarified. "She just *went* there, from wherever she had been at the time. Undoubtedly the shock blew out the weakness in her brain and killed her."

"Jesus," Ruby muttered under her breath. "Don't think I'll be including that in my report—" Abruptly, the memory of Rafe Pasco lying in bed with her, his head resting on the pillow and looking at her with profound regret, lit up in her mind. *So sorry to have dropped in from nowhere without calling first.* Not a dream? He might tell her if she asked him, but she wasn't sure that was an answer she really wanted.

"That's all right," Pasco said. "I will. Slightly different case, of course, and the report will go elsewhere."

"Of course." Ruby's knees were aching. She finally gave up and sat down on the edge of the chair. "Should I assume that all the information you showed me about the Nakamuras—passports, the IRS, all that—was fabricated?"

"I adapted it from their existing records. Alice's passport worried me, though. It's not exactly a forgery—they brought it with them and I have no idea why they left it or any other identifying materials behind."

"You don't have kids, do you," Ruby said, amused in spite of everything.

"No, I don't," he said, mildly surprised.

"If you did, you'd know why they couldn't just leave her to go nameless into an unmarked grave."

Pasco nodded. "The human factor." Outside, a horn honked. "It's time to go. Or do *you* want to stay here?"

Ruby stood up, looking around. "What's going to happen to this place? And all the other things in the Muras' lives?"

"We have ways of papering over the cracks and stains, so to speak," he told her. "Their daughter was just found dead. If they don't come back here for a while and then decide not to come back at all, I don't think anyone will find that terribly strange."

"But their families—"

"There's a lot to take care of," Pasco said, talking over her. "Even if I had the time to cover every detail for you, I would not. It comes dangerously close to providing information that doesn't belong here. I could harm the system. I'm sure I've told you too much as it is."

"What are you going to do?" she asked. "Take me to 'court,' too?"

"Only if you do something you shouldn't." He ushered her through the house to the front door.

"OK, but just tell me this, then." She put her hand on the doorknob before he could. "What are you going to do when the *real* Rafe Pasco comes back from the Bahamas?"

He stared at her in utter bewilderment. "What?"

"That is what you did, isn't it? Waited for him to go on vacation and then borrowed his identity so you could work on this case?" When he still looked blank, she told him about listening to the message on his cell phone.

"Ah, that," he said, laughing a little. "No, I *am* the real Rafe Pasco. I forgot to change my voice-mail message after I came back from vacation. Then I decided to leave it that way. Just as a joke. It confuses the nuisance callers."

It figured, Ruby thought. She opened the door and stepped outside, Pasco following. Behind his car was a small white van; the print on the side claimed that it belonged to Five-Star Electrical Services, Re-Wiring Specialists, which Ruby thought also figured. Not-Rita was sitting in the driver's seat, drumming her fingers on the steering wheel. The tall guy was sitting in the SUV.

"So that's it?" Ruby said, watching Pasco lock the front door. "You close down your case and I just go home now, knowing everything that I know, and that's all right with you?"

"Shouldn't I trust you?" he asked her.

"Should I trust you?" she countered. "How do I know I'm not going to get a service call from an electrician and end up with all new wiring, too?"

"I told you," he said patiently, "only if you use any of what you know to engage in something illegal. And you won't."

"What makes you so goddam sure about that?" she demanded.

Forehead creasing with concern, Pasco looked into her face. She was about to say something else when something happened.

All at once, her mind opened up and she found that she was looking at an enormous panorama—all the lost possibilities, the missed opportunities, the bad calls, a lifetime of uncorrected mistakes, missteps, and fumbles. All those things were a single big picture—perhaps the proverbial big picture, the proverbial forest you sometimes couldn't see for the proverbial trees. But she was seeing it now and seeing it all at once.

It was too much. She would never be able to recall it as an image, to look at it again in the future. Concentrating, she struggled to focus on portions of it instead:

Jake's father, going back to his wife, unaware that she was pregnant—she had always been sure that had been no mistake, but now she knew there was a world where he had known and stayed with her, and one where he had known and left anyway—

Jake, growing up interested in music, not computers; getting mixed up with drugs with Ricky Carstairs; helping Ricky Carstairs straighten out; coming out to her at sixteen and introducing his boyfriend; marrying his college sweetheart instead of Lita; adopting children with his husband, Dennis; getting the Rhodes Scholarship instead of someone else; moving to California instead of Boston—

The mammogram and the biopsy results; the tests left too late—

Wounding the suspect in the Martinez case instead of killing him; missing her shot and taking a bullet instead while someone else killed him; having the decision by the shooting board go against her; retiring after twenty years instead of staying on; getting fed up and quitting after ten; going to night school to finish her degree—

Jury verdicts, convictions instead of acquittals and vice versa; catching Darren Hightower after the first victim instead of after the seventh—

Or going into a different line of work altogether—

Or finding out about all of this before now, long before now when she was still young and full of energy, looking for an edge and glad to find it. Convincing herself that she was using it not for her own personal gain but as a force for good. Something that would save lives, literally and figuratively, expose the corrupt, and reward the good and the worthy. One person *could* make a difference—wasn't that what everyone always said? The possibilities could stretch so far beyond herself:

Government with a conscience instead of agendas; schools and hospitals instead of wars; no riots, no assassinations, no terror, no Lee Harvey Oswald, no James Earl Ray, no Sirhan Sirhan, no 9/11—

And maybe even no nine-year-old boy found naked and dead in a Dumpster—

Abruptly she found herself leaning heavily against the side of the Mura house, straining to keep from falling down while the Dread tried to turn her inside out.

Rafe Pasco cleared his throat. "How do you feel?"

She looked at him, miserable.

"That's what makes me so certain," he went on. "Your, uh, allergic reaction. If there's any sort of disruption here, no matter how large or small, you'll feel it. And it won't feel good. And if you tried to do something yourself—" He made a small gesture at her. "Well, you see what happened when you only thought about it."

"Great," she said shakily. "What do I do now, spend the rest of my life trying not to think impure thoughts?"

Pasco's expression turned sheepish. "That's not what I meant. You feel this way because of the current circumstances. Once the alien elements have been removed from your world"—he glanced at the SUV—"you'll start to feel better. The bad feeling will fade away."

"And how long is that going to take?" she asked him.

"You'll be all right."

"That's no answer."

"I think I've given you enough answers already." He started for his car and she caught his arm.

"Just one more thing," she said. "Really. Just one."

Pasco looked as if he was deciding whether to shake her off or not. "What?" he said finally.

"This so-called allergic reaction of mine. Is there any reason for it or is it just one of those things? Like hay fever or some kind of weakness."

"Some kind of weakness." Pasco chuckled without humor. "Sometimes when there's been a divergence in one's own line, there's a certain . . . sensitivity."

Ruby nodded with resignation. "Is that another way of saying that you've given me enough answers already?"

Pasco hesitated. "All those could-have-beens, those might-have-dones and if-I-knew-thens you were thinking."

The words were out of her mouth before she even knew what she was going to say. "They all happened."

"I know you won't do anything," he said, lowering his voice and leaning toward her slightly, "because you have. And the conscience that bothers you still bothers you, even at long distance. Even in the hypothetical."

Ruby made a face. "My guilty conscience? Is that really what it is?"

"I don't know how else to put it."

"Well." She took a breath, feeling a little bit steadier. "I guess that'll teach me to screw around with the way things should be."

Pasco frowned impatiently. "It's not should or shouldn't. It's just what *is*."

"With no second chances."

"With second chances, third chances, hundredth chances, millionth chances," Pasco corrected her. "All the chances you want. But not a second chance to have a first chance."

Ruby didn't say anything.

"This is what poisons the system and makes everything go wrong. You live within the system, within the mechanism. It's not meant to be used or manipulated by an individual. To be taken personally. It's a system, a process. It's nothing personal."

"Hey, I thought it was time to go," the man in the SUV called impatiently.

Pasco waved at him and then turned to Ruby again. "I'll see you tomorrow."

"You will?" she said, surprised. But he was already getting into his car and she had no idea whether he had heard her or not. And he had given her enough answers already anyway, she thought, watching all three vehicles drive away. He had given her enough answers already and he would see her tomorrow.

And how would that go, she wondered, now that she knew what she knew? How would it be working with him? Would the Dread really fade away if she saw him every day, knowing and remembering?

Would she be living the rest of her life or was she just stuck with it?

Pasco had given her enough answers already and there was no one else to ask.

Ruby walked across the Muras' front lawn to her car, thinking that it felt as if the Dread had already begun to lift a little. That was something, at least. Her guilty conscience; she gave a small, humorless laugh. Now that was something she had never suspected would creep up on her. Time marched on and one day you woke up to find you were a somewhat dumpy, graying, middle-aged homicide detective with twenty-five years on the job and a hefty lump of guilty conscience and regret. And if you wanted to know why, to understand, well, that was just too bad because you had already been given too many answers already. Nothing personal.

She started the car and drove away from the empty house, through the meandering streets, and did no better finding her way out of the west side than she had finding her way in.

tideline

ELIZABETH BEAR

Here's the poignant story of a battered and limping robot warrior who must struggle to perform one last task for her fallen human comrades. . . .

New writer Elizabeth Bear was born in Hartford, Connecticut, and now lives in the Mohave Desert near Las Vegas. She won the John W. Campbell Award for Best New Writer in 2005. Her short work has appeared in *SCI FICTION*, *Interzone*, *The 3rd Alternative*, *On Spec*, and elsewhere, and she is the author of three highly acclaimed SF novels, *Hammered*, *Scardown*, and *Worldwired*. Her other books include a novel, *Carnival*, and a collection of her short works, *The Chains That You Refuse*. Her most recent books include the novels *Dust*, *Undertow*, *Whiskey & Water*, and, with Sarah Monette, *A Companion to Wolves*, as well as a new collection, *New Amsterdam*. Coming up are more new novels, including *Ink & Steel* and *Hell & Earth*.

Chalcedony wasn't built for crying. She didn't have it in her, not unless her tears were cold tapered glass droplets annealed by the inferno heat that had crippled her.

Such tears as that might slide down her skin over melted sensors to plink unfeeling on the sand. And if they had, she would have scooped them up, with all the other battered pretties, and added them to the wealth of trash jewels that swung from the nets reinforcing her battered carapace.

They would have called her salvage, if there were anyone left to salvage her. But she was the last of the war machines, a three-legged oblate teardrop as big as a main battle tank, two big grabs and one fine manipulator folded like a spider's palps beneath the turreted head that finished her pointed end, her polyceramic armor spiderwebbed like shatterproof glass. Unhelmed by her remote masters, she limped along the beach, dragging one fused limb. She was nearly derelict.

The beach was where she met Belvedere.

Butterfly coquinas unearthed by retreating breakers squirmed into wet grit under Chalcedony's trailing limb. One of the rear pair, it was less of a nuisance on packed sand. It worked all right as a pivot, and as long as she stayed off rocks, there were no obstacles to drag it over.

As she struggled along the tideline, she became aware of someone watching. She didn't raise her head. Her chassis was equipped with targeting sensors which locked automatically on the ragged figure crouched by a weathered rock. Her optical input was needed to scan the tangle of seaweed and driftwood, Styrofoam and sea glass that marked high tide.

He watched her all down the beach, but he was unarmed, and her algorithms didn't deem him a threat.

Just as well. She liked the weird flat-topped sandstone boulder he crouched beside.

The next day, he watched again. It was a good day; she found a moonstone, some rock crystal, a bit of red-orange pottery, and some sea glass worn opalescent by the tide.

"Whatcha picken up?"

"Shipwreck beads," Chalcedony answered. For days, he'd been creeping closer, until he'd begun following behind her like the seagulls, scrabbling the coquinas harrowed up by her dragging foot into a patched mesh bag. Sustenance, she guessed, and indeed he pulled one of the tiny mollusks from the bag and produced a broken-bladed folding knife from somewhere to prize it open with. Her sensors painted the knife pale colors. A weapon, but not a threat to her.

Deft enough—he flicked, sucked, and tossed the shell away in under three seconds—but that couldn't be much more than a morsel of meat. A lot of work for very small return.

He was bony as well as ragged, and small for a human. Perhaps young.

She thought he'd ask *what shipwreck*, and she would gesture vaguely over the bay, where the city had been, and say *there were many*. But he surprised her.

"Whatcha gonna do with them?" He wiped his mouth on a sandy paw, the broken knife projecting carelessly from the bottom of his fist.

"When I get enough, I'm going to make necklaces." She spotted something under a tangle of the algae called dead man's fingers, a glint of light, and began the laborious process of lowering herself to reach it, compensating by math for her malfunctioning gyroscopes.

The presumed-child watched avidly. "Nuh uh," he said. "You can't make a necklace outta that."

"Why not?" She levered herself another decimeter down, balancing against the weight of her fused limb. She did not care to fall.

"I seed what you pick up. They's all different."

"So?" she asked, and managed another few centimeters. Her hydraulics whined. Someday, those hydraulics or her fuel cells would fail and she'd be stuck this way, a statue corroded by salt air and the sea, and the tide would roll in and roll over her. Her carapace was cracked, no longer watertight.

"They's not all beads."

Her manipulator brushed aside the dead man's fingers. She uncovered the treasure, a bit of blue-gray stone carved in the shape of a fat, merry man. It had no holes. Chalcedony balanced herself back upright and turned the figurine in the light. The stone was structurally sound.

She extruded a hair-fine diamond-tipped drill from the opposite manipulator and drilled a hole through the figurine, top to bottom. Then she threaded him on a twist of wire, looped the ends, work-hardened the loops, and added him to the garland of beads swinging against her disfigured chassis.

"So?"

The presumed-child brushed the little Buddha with his fingertip, setting it swinging against shattered ceramic plate. She levered herself up again, out of his reach. "I's Belvedere," he said.

"Hello," Chalcedony said. "I'm Chalcedony."

By sunset, when the tide was lowest, he scampered chattering in her wake, darting between flocking gulls to scoop up coquinas by the fistful, which he rinsed in the surf before devouring raw. Chalcedony more or less ignored him as she activated her floods, concentrating their radiance along the tideline.

A few dragging steps later, another treasure caught her eye. It was a twist of chain with a few bright beads caught on it—glass, with scraps of gold and silver foil imbedded in their twists. Chalcedony initiated the laborious process of retrieval—

Only to halt as Belvedere jumped in front of her, grabbed the chain in a grubby broken-nailed hand, and snatched it up. Chalcedony locked in position, nearly overbalancing. She was about to reach out to snatch the treasure away from the child and knock him into the sea when he rose up on tiptoe and held it out to her, straining over his head. The floodlights cast his shadow black on the sand, illumined each thread of his hair and eyebrows in stark relief.

"It's easier if I get that for you," he said, as her fine manipulator closed tenderly on the tip of the chain.

She lifted the treasure to examine it in the floods. A good long segment, seven centimeters, four jewel-toned shiny beads. Her head creaked when she raised it, corrosion showering from the joints.

She hooked the chain onto the netting wrapped around her carapace. "Give me your bag," she said.

Belvedere's hand went to the soggy net full of raw bivalves dripping down his naked leg. "My bag?"

"Give it to me." Chalcedony drew herself up, akilter because of the ruined limb but still two and a half meters taller than the child. She extended a manipulator, and from some disused file dredged up a protocol for dealing with civilian humans. "Please."

He fumbled at the knot with rubbery fingers, tugged it loose from his rope belt, and held it out to her. She snagged it on a manipulator and brought it up. A sample revealed that the weave was cotton rather than nylon, so she folded it in her two larger manipulators and gave the contents a low-wattage microwave pulse.

She shouldn't. It was a drain on her power cells, which she had no means to recharge, and she had a task to complete.

She shouldn't—but she did.

Steam rose from her claws and the coquinas popped open, roasting in their own juices and the moisture of the seaweed with which he'd lined the net. Carefully, she swung the bag back to him, trying to preserve the fluids.

"Caution," she urged. "It's hot."

He took the bag gingerly and flopped down to sit crosslegged at her feet. When he tugged back the seaweed, the coquinas lay like tiny jewels—pale orange, rose, yellow, green, and blue—in their nest of glass-green *Ulva*, sea lettuce. He tasted one cautiously, and then began to slurp with great abandon, discarding shells in every direction.

"Eat the algae, too," Chalcedony told him. "It is rich in important nutrients."

When the tide came in, Chalcedony retreated up the beach like a great hunched crab with five legs amputated. She was beetle-backed under the moonlight, her treasures swinging and rustling on her netting, clicking one another like stones shivered in a palm.

The child followed.

"You should sleep," Chalcedony said, as Belvedere settled beside her on the high, dry crescent of beach under towering mud cliffs, where the waves wouldn't lap.

He didn't answer, and her voice fuzzed and furred before clearing when she spoke again. "You should climb up off the beach. The cliffs are unstable. It is not safe beneath them."

Belvedere hunkered closer, lower lip protruding. "You stay down here."

"I have armor. And I cannot climb." She thumped her fused leg on the sand, rocking her body forward and back on the two good legs to manage it.

"But your armor's broke."

"That doesn't matter. You must climb." She picked Belvedere up with both grabs and raised him over her head. He shrieked; at first she feared she'd damaged him, but the cries resolved into laughter before she set him down on a slanted ledge that would bring him to the top of the cliff.

She lit it with her floods. "Climb," she said, and he climbed.

And returned in the morning.

Belvedere stayed ragged, but with Chalcedony's help he waxed plumper. She snared and roasted seabirds for him, taught him how to construct and maintain fires, and ransacked her extensive databases for hints on how to keep him healthy as he grew—sometimes almost visibly, fractions of a millimeter a day. She researched and analyzed sea vegetables and hectored him into eating them, and he helped her reclaim treasures her manipulators could not otherwise grasp. Some shipwreck beads were hot, and made Chalcedony's radiation detectors tick over. They were no threat to her, but for the first time she discarded them. She had a human ally; her program demanded she sustain him in health.

She told him stories. Her library was vast—and full of war stories and stories about sailing ships and starships, which he liked best for some inexplicable reason. Catharsis, she thought, and told him again of Roland, and King Arthur, and Honor Harrington, and Napoleon Bonaparte, and Horatio Hornblower, and Captain Jack Aubrey. She projected the words on a monitor as she recited them, and—faster than she would have imagined—he began to mouth them along with her.

So the summer ended.

By the equinox, she had collected enough memorabilia. Shipwreck jewels still washed up and Belvedere still brought her the best of them, but Chalcedony settled beside that twisted flat-topped sandstone rock and arranged her treasures atop it. She spun salvaged brass through a die to make wire, threaded beads on it, and forged links which she strung into garland.

It was a learning experience. Her aesthetic sense was at first undeveloped, requiring her to make and unmake many dozens of bead combinations to find a pleasing one. Not only must form and color be balanced, but there were structural difficulties. First the weights were unequal, so the chains hung crooked. Then links kinked and snagged and had to be redone.

She worked for weeks. Memorials had been important to the human allies, though she had never understood the logic of it. She could not build a tomb for her colleagues, but the same archives that gave her the stories Belvedere lapped up as a cat laps milk gave her the concept of mourning jewelry. She had no physical remains of her allies, no scraps of hair or cloth, but surely the shipwreck jewels would suffice for a treasure?

The only quandary was who would wear the jewelry. It should go to an heir, someone who held fond memories of the deceased. And Chalcedony had records of the next of kin, of course. But she had no way to know if any survived, and if they did no way to reach them.

At first, Belvedere stayed close, trying to tempt her into excursions and explorations. Chalcedony remained resolute, however. Not only were her power cells dangerously low, but with the coming of winter her ability to utilize solar power would be even more limited. And with winter the storms would come, and she would no longer be able to evade the ocean.

She was determined to complete this last task before she failed.

Belvedere began to range without her, to snare his own birds and bring them back to the driftwood fire for roasting. This was positive; he needed to be able to maintain himself. At night, however, he returned to sit beside her, to clamber onto the flat-topped rock to sort beads and hear her stories.

The same thread she worked over and over with her grabs and fine manipulators—the duty of the living to remember the fallen with honor—was played out in the war stories she still told him, though now she'd finished with fiction and history and related him her own experiences. She told him about Emma Percy rescuing that kid up near Savannah, and how Private Michaels was shot drawing fire for Sergeant Kay Patterson when the battle robots were decoyed out of position in a skirmish near Seattle.

Belvedere listened, and surprised her by proving he could repeat the gist, if not the exact words. His memory was good, if not as good as a machine's.

One day when he had gone far out of sight down the beach, Chalcedony heard Belvedere screaming.

She had not moved in days. She hunkered on the sand at an awkward angle, her frozen limb angled down the beach, her necklaces in progress on the rock that served as her impromptu workbench.

Bits of stone and glass and wire scattered from the rock top as she heaved herself onto her unfused limbs. She thrashed upright on her first attempt, surprising herself, and tottered for a moment unsteadily, lacking the stabilization of long-failed gyroscopes.

When Belvedere shouted again, she almost overset.

Climbing was out of the question, but Chalcedony could still run. Her fused limb plowed a furrow in the sand behind her and the tide was coming in, forcing her to splash through corroding seawater.

She barreled around the rocky prominence that Belvedere had disappeared behind in time to see him knocked to the ground by two larger humans, one of whom had a club raised over its head and the other of which was holding Belvedere's shabby net bag. Belvedere yelped as the club connected with his thigh.

Chalcedony did not dare use her microwave projectors.

But she had other weapons, including a pinpoint laser and a chemical-propellant firearm suitable for sniping operations. Enemy humans were soft targets. These did not even have body armor.

She buried the bodies on the beach, for it was her program to treat enemy dead with respect, following the protocols of war. Belvedere was in no immediate danger of death once she had splinted his leg and treated his bruises, but she judged him too badly injured to help. The sand was soft and amenable to scooping, anyway, though there was no way to keep the bodies above water. It was the best she could manage.

After she had finished, she transported Belvedere back to their rock and began collecting her scattered treasures.

The leg was sprained and bruised, not broken, and some perversity connected to the injury made him even more restlessly inclined to push his boundaries once he partially recovered. He was on his feet within a week, leaning on crutches and dragging a leg as stiff as Chalcedony's. As soon as the splint came off, he started ranging even further afield. His new limp barely slowed him, and he stayed out nights. He was still growing, shooting up, almost as tall as a Marine now, and ever more capable of taking care of himself. The incident with the raiders had taught him caution.

Meanwhile, Chalcedony elaborated her funeral necklaces. She must make each one worthy of a fallen comrade, and she was slowed now by her inability to work through the nights. Rescuing Belvedere had cost her more carefully hoarded energy, and she could not power her floods if she meant to finish before her cells ran dry. She could *see* by moonlight, with deadly clarity, but her low-light and thermal eyes were of no use when it came to balancing color against color.

There would be forty-one necklaces, one for each member of her platoon-that-was, and she would not excuse shoddy craftsmanship.

No matter how fast she worked, it was a race against sun and tide.

The fortieth necklace was finished in October while the days grew short. She began the forty-first—the one for her chief operator Platoon Sergeant Patterson, the one with the gray-blue Buddha at the bottom—before sunset. She had not seen Belvedere in several days, but that was acceptable. She would not finish the necklace tonight.

His voice woke her from the quiescence in which she waited the sun. "Chalcedony?"

Something cried as she came awake. *Infant*, she identified, but the warm shape in his arms was not an infant. It was a dog, a young dog, a German shepherd like the ones teamed with the handlers that had sometimes worked with Company L. The dogs had never minded her, but some of the handlers had been frightened, though they would not admit it. Sergeant Patterson had said to one of them, *Oh, Chase is just pretty much a big attack dog herself*, and had made a big show of rubbing Chalcedony behind her telescopic sights, to the sound of much laughter.

The young dog was wounded. Its injuries bled warmth across its hind leg.

"Hello, Belvedere," Chalcedony said.

"Found a puppy." He kicked his ragged blanket flat so he could lay the dog down.

"Are you going to eat it?"

"Chalcedony!" he snapped, and covered the animal protectively with his arms. "S'hurt."

She contemplated. "You wish me to tend to it?"

He nodded, and she considered. She would need her lights, energy, irreplaceable stores. Antibiotics and coagulants and surgical supplies, and the animal might die anyway. But dogs were valuable; she knew the handlers held them in great esteem, even greater than Sergeant Patterson's esteem for Chalcedony. And in her library, she had files on veterinary medicine.

She flipped on her floods and accessed the files.

She finished before morning, and before her cells ran dry. Just barely.

When the sun was up and young dog was breathing comfortably, the gash along its haunch sewn closed and its bloodstream saturated with antibiotics, she turned back to the last necklace. She would have to work quickly, and

Sergeant Patterson's necklace contained the most fragile and beautiful beads, the ones Chalcedony had been most concerned with breaking and so had saved for last, when she would be most experienced.

Her motions grew slower as the day wore on, more laborious. The sun could not feed her enough to replace the expenditures of the night before. But bead linked into bead, and the necklace grew—bits of pewter, of pottery, of glass and mother of pearl. And the chalcedony Buddha, because Sergeant Patterson had been Chalcedony's operator.

When the sun approached its zenith, Chalcedony worked faster, benefiting from a burst of energy. The young dog slept on in her shade, having wolfed the scraps of bird Belvedere gave it, but Belvedere climbed the rock and crouched beside her pile of finished necklaces.

"Who's this for?" he asked, touching the slack length draped across her manipulator.

"Kay Patterson," Chalcedony answered, adding a greenish brown pottery bead mottled like a combat uniform.

"Sir Kay," Belvedere said. His voice was changing, and sometimes it abandoned him completely in the middle of words, but he got that phrase out entire. "She was King Arthur's horse-master, and his adopted brother, and she kept his combat robots in the stable," he said, proud of his recall.

"They were different Kays," she reminded. "You will have to leave soon." She looped another bead onto the chain, closed the link, and work-hardened the metal with her fine manipulator.

"You can't leave the beach. You can't climb."

Idly, he picked up a necklace, Rodale's, and stretched it between his hands so the beads caught the light. The links clinked softly.

Belvedere sat with her as the sun descended and her motions slowed. She worked almost entirely on solar power now. With night, she would become quiescent again. When the storms came, the waves would roll over her, and then even the sun would not awaken her again. "You must go," she said, as her grabs stilled on the almost-finished chain. And then she lied and said, "I do not want you here."

"Who's this'n for?" he asked. Down on the beach, the young dog lifted its head and whined. "Garner," she answered, and then she told him about Garner, and Antony, and Javez, and Rodriguez, and Patterson, and White, and Woszczyna, until it was dark enough that her voice and her vision failed.

In the morning, he put Patterson's completed chain into Chalcedony's grabs. He must have worked on it by firelight through the darkness. "Couldn't harden the links," he said, as he smoothed them over her claws.

Silently, she did that, one by one. The young dog was on its feet, limping, nosing around the base of the rock and barking at the waves, the birds, a scuttling crab. When Chalcedony had finished, she reached out and draped the necklace around Belvedere's shoulders while he held very still. Soft fur downed his cheeks. The male Marines had always scraped theirs smooth, and the women didn't grow facial hair.

"You said that was for Sir Kay." He lifted the chain in his hands and studied the way the glass and stones caught the light.

"It's for somebody to remember her," Chalcedony said. She didn't correct him this time. She picked up the other forty necklaces. They were heavy, all together. She wondered if Belvedere could carry them all. "So remember her. Can you remember which one is whose?"

One at a time, he named them, and one at a time she handed them to him. Rogers, and Rodale, and van Metier, and Percy. He spread a second blanket out—and where had he gotten a second blanket? Maybe the same place he'd gotten the dog—and laid them side by side on the navy blue wool.

They sparkled.

"Tell me the story about Rodale," she said, brushing her grab across the necklace. He did, sort of, with half of Roland-and-Oliver mixed in. It was a pretty good story anyway, the way he told it. Inasmuch as she was a fit judge.

"Take the necklaces," she said. "Take them. They're mourning jewelry. Give them to people and tell them the stories. They should go to people who will remember and honor the dead."

"Where'd I find alla these people?" he asked, sullenly, crossing his arms. "Ain't on the beach."

"No," she said, "they are not. You'll have to go look for them."

But he wouldn't leave her. He and the dog ranged up and down the beach as the weather chilled. Her sleeps grew longer, deeper, the low angle of the sun not enough to awaken her except at noon. The storms came, and because the table rock broke the spray, the salt water stiffened her joints but did not— yet—corrode her processor. She no longer moved and rarely spoke, even in daylight, and Belvedere and the young dog used her carapace and the rock for shelter, the smoke of his fires blackening her belly.

She was hoarding energy.

By mid-November, she had enough, and she waited and spoke to Belvedere when he returned with the young dog from his rambling. "You must go," she said, and when he opened his mouth to protest, she added, "It is time you went on errantry."

His hand went to Patterson's necklace, which he wore looped twice around his neck, under his ragged coat. He had given her back the others, but that one she had made a gift of. "Errantry?"

Creaking, powdered corrosion grating from her joints, she lifted the necklaces off her head. "You must find the people to whom these belong."

He deflected her words with a jerk of his hand. "They's all dead."

"The warriors are dead," she said. "But the stories aren't. Why did you save the young dog?"

He licked his lips, and touched Patterson's necklace again. "'Cause you saved me. And you told me the stories. About good fighters and bad fighters. And so, see, Percy woulda saved the dog, right? And so would Hazel-rah."

Emma Percy, Chalcedony was reasonably sure, would have saved the dog if she could have. And Kevin Michaels would have saved the kid. She held the remaining necklaces out. "Who's going to protect the other children?"

He stared, hands twisting before him. "You can't climb."

"I can't. You must do this for me. Find people to remember the stories. Find people to tell about my platoon. I won't survive the winter." Inspiration struck. "So I give you this quest, Sir Belvedere."

The chains hung flashing in the wintry light, the sea combed gray and tired behind them. "What kinda people?"

"People who would help a child," she said. "Or a wounded dog. People like a platoon should be."

He paused. He reached out, stroked the chains, let the beads rattle. He crooked both hands, and slid them into the necklaces up to the elbows, taking up her burden.

the accord

KEITH BROOKE

British writer and editor Keith Brooke is the founder and longtime editor of acclaimed Internet Web site Infinity Plus (he recently stepped down from this position to concentrate on his fiction-writing career). His novels include *Keepers of the Peace*, *Expatria*, *Expatria Incorporated*, *Lord of Stone*, and, most recently, *Genetopia*. He also writes as "Nick Gifford," under which name he's published *Piggies*, *Flesh & Blood*, *Incubus*, and *Erased*. As editor, he has produced the anthologies *Infinity Plus One* and *Infinity Plus Two*, edited with Nick Gevers; his most recent book is the anthology *Infinity Plus*, also edited with Nick Gevers. He's had two chapbooks published, *Head Shots*, and, with Eric Brown, *Parallax View*.

Here he takes us to an intricate far-future world, where races and peoples live in uneasy equilibrium, for a tale of love, obsession, and intrigue that just might throw everything out of whack.

1. TISH GOLDENHAWK

Tish Goldenhawk watched the gaudy Daguerran vessel slide into the harbour. If she had known then what she was soon to learn, she might even have settled for her humdrum existence, and even now she and Milton would be living a quiet life, seeing out their days before finally joining the Accord.

But no, unblessed with foresight, Tish stood atop the silver cliffs of

Penhellion and watched—no, *marvelled*—as the *Lady Cecilia* approached the crooked arm of the dock.

The ship was unlike any she had seen. Far taller than it was long, it rose out of the mirrored waters like some kind of improbable island. Its flanks were made of polished wood and massed ranks of high arched windows, these revealing bodies within, faces pressed against glass as the grand touristas took in yet more of the sights of the worlds.

He might have been among them. Another face staring out, its perfect features only distinguished by a crooked incisor. But no, he wouldn't have been part of that gawping crowd. She would have known that if she had been blessed with foresight, if she had somehow known that there was a "he" of whom she could speculate just so at this moment.

The ship, the *Lady Cecilia* . . . It towered unfeasibly. Only vastly advanced engineering could keep it from toppling this way or that. The thing defied gravity by its very existence. It sailed, a perfect vertical, its array of silken sails bulging picturesquely, its crew scrambling over the rigging like squirrels.

At a distant screech, Tish tipped her head back and stared until she had picked out the tiny scimitar shapes of gliding pterosaurs. It was a clear day, and the world's rings slashed a ribbon across the southern sky. Why did beauty make her sad?

Tish breathed deep, and she knew she should be back at the Falling Droplet helping Milton and their fifteen-year-old son Druce behind the bar.

And then she looked again at the golden, jewelled, bannered sailing ship now secured in the harbour and she felt an almighty welling of despair that this should be her lot in a world of such beauty and wonder.

She walked back along a road cut into the face of the cliff. She was lucky. She lived in a beautiful place. She had a good husband, a fine son. She could want for nothing. Nobody starved or suffered in the worlds of the Diaspora, unless it was their choice to do so. People were born to different lots and hers was a good one.

She was lucky, she told herself again. Blessed by the Accord.

The Falling Droplet was set into the silver cliffs of Penhellion, its floor-to-ceiling windows giving breathtaking views out across the bay to where the coast hooked back on itself and the Grand Falls plunged more than a thousand metres into the sea.

Rainbows played and flickered across the bay, an ever-changing colour masque put on by the interplay of the Falls and the sun. Pterosaurs and gulls and flying fish cut and swooped through the spray, while dolphins and merfolk arced and flipped in the waves.

Tish was staring at the view, again, when the stranger approached the bar. "I . . . Erm . . ." He placed coins on the age-polished flutewood surface.

Tish dragged her gaze away from the windows. She smiled at him, another anonymous grand tourista with perfect features, flawless skin, silky hair, a man who might as easily have been twenty as a century or more.

He smiled back.

The crooked tooth was a clever touch. A single tooth at the front, just a little angled so that there was a gap at the top, a slight overlap at the bottom. An imperfection in the perfect, a mote in the diamond.

In that instant Tish Goldenhawk was transfixed, just as she had been by the sight of the *Lady Cecilia* earlier.

She knew who he was, or rather, *what* he was, this stranger, this not quite perfect visitor. A made man should always have a flaw, if he were not to look, immediately, like a made man.

"I . . . Erm . . ." she said, inadvertently repeating his own words from a moment before. "What'll it be?"

"I . . ." He gestured at one of the pumps.

"Roly's Scrumpy?" she said, reaching for a long glass. "You'd better be watching your head in the morning, if you're not used to it. That stuff's an ass: drink it full in the face and you're fine, but as soon as you turn your back it'll kick you."

She put the drink before him and helped herself to some of the coins he had spread out.

"Been on Laverne for long?" she said, knowing the answer he would give. He had just landed, along with all these other touristas. Struggling with the dialect and the coins. These poor over-rich sods must be constantly disoriented, she realised, as they took their grand tours of the known. The poor lambs.

He shook his head, smiled again. A day ago—even a few hours ago—he had probably been in a jungle, or in a seething metropolis, or deep in an undersea resort, ten, a hundred, a thousand light years away, along with others on the grand tour.

Or that, at least, was probably what she was supposed to think. But Tish stuck with her hunch instead. She often constructed stories about the people she served in the Falling Droplet. The spies, the adulterers, the scag addicts, and the gender-confused. Sometimes she even turned out to be right, but usually she never confirmed her hunches one way or the other. This man was no grand tourista, although he might indeed be a new arrival.

"You on the *Lady Cecilia*?" she asked him, hoping he would give himself away but knowing he wouldn't.

"I am," he said, and then dipped his head to take a long draw of the cider. He glanced around. "Or at least," he added, "I *was* . . ."

"Tish?"

Milton. He gestured. They had customers lined up at the bar. The Droplet had grown crowded and Tish had barely noticed. She moved away from the stranger, and served old Ruth with her usual Brewer's Gold and nuts.

Later, she noticed the three men as they came in from the darkening evening. They were strangers, too, as were many of this evening's clientele, but they didn't look like they were on any kind of grand tour. Their eyes scanned the crowd, and as one of the men fixed on her for the briefest of instants she felt skewered, scanned by some kind of machine.

But no, these three were men, if clearly enhanced. They wore identical dark grey outfits, and now she saw what appeared to be weapons at their belts.

Tish had never seen a weapon before, unless you counted harpoons and ginny traps and the like. She had never seen men who looked like machines, although up in Daguerre she had seen machines like men and women.

One of the men pointed, and the other two swivelled their heads in unison until all three looked in the same direction, motionless like a sandfisher poised to drop. The pointing man opened his hand and a beam of light shone from it across the crowded bar.

Tish turned and saw a single man picked out by the beam, a long glass poised partway to his mouth, a mouth which revealed one imperfection in its otherwise flawless ranks of teeth.

The stranger dropped his glass, ducked down, darted into the pack of bodies near to the bar.

The three . . . they were no longer there by the door, they were across the room, standing where the stranger had been, motionless again, robot eyes surveying the crowd.

Tish revised her earlier assessment. These men could not be mere humans—enhanced or not—and move as they did. They must be more than that. Other than that.

The stranger . . . a tussle by the far door, and there he was, reaching for the handle.

But the handle vanished, the door blurred, its boundaries softening, merging . . . and it was wall, not door. There was no exit there. There never had been.

The stranger's hand slid across a smooth surface, and he staggered. Why was he scratching at the wall like that?

The three stood, watching, eyes locked on the stranger . . .

. . . on nothing.

The stranger had ducked into the crowd again.

Tish leaned against the bar, her heart pounding, her mind swirling, her brain playing catch-up with the succession of images crammed into the merest of seconds that had passed since the door had opened and the three more-than-men had appeared.

Another disturbance.

The stranger.

He had a wooden chair raised above his head.

Beyond him, the sun was setting, heavy and swollen over the rainbowed water. The sky was cast in bands of the deepest of crimsons, a staggering gold, shading up to a high, dreamy purple. Laverne's rings slashed darkly across this vivid sunset.

The sky shattered. Crazed lines divided it up into an enormous, jagged jigsaw.

Someone screamed, someone else shouted, someone else . . .

Tish could no longer see the three men, and she could no longer see the stranger. She could see the chair embedded in one of the big windows, though, the glass crazed but still holding in its frame.

Then she saw him, a silhouette against the fiery sky, diving.

He hit the glass and for an instant it held and she thought he would end up embedded like the chair. And then the moment had passed and the glass shifted, bulged, and it, the chair, and the man tumbled out into the air.

Someone screamed again, and the shouting continued, as the crowd shuffled back from the abyss.

Tish looked away. They were half a kilometre up here, nothing but an awful lot of air between them and the rocks and waves below. No one could survive such a fall.

She looked up again. The three were standing by the opening, peering out into the gloom. They were not talking, but she could tell from the poise of their bodies that they were somehow communicating. Was this a satisfactory outcome for them, or was it not?

And then she thought, why would they do such a thing? What was it that had brought them here, on this evening, to do this?

Why would they come here, to her normally peaceful cliff-hanging bar, and pursue this stranger in so startling and violent a manner?

Why would anyone want to chase God, or even a very small fragment of God?

Tish dropped in an air-shaft to Fandango Way, Penhellion's main thoroughfare. The Way was cut into the base of the cliff, and ran from the docks to where it wound its way up the cliff face three kilometres east.

She stepped out among the stalls of itinerant traders. She nodded and smiled and exchanged words here and there. She was not here to buy, and most of the traders knew that anyway: these same traders delivered supplies direct to the Falling Droplet. Tish had little need of market shopping.

She carried a basket, though, and in the basket, beneath a checkered cloth, there was a crust of bread and a fistful of feathers from a quetzal.

She crossed the road, dodging rickshaws and scooters. Lifting her feet daintily over the low wall, she stepped out onto the rocks.

Down by the water's edge, first of all she looked at the gentle chop of the waves, and then she craned her neck to peer upward, but she could not pick out the Falling Droplet's frontage from all the others. So many dwellings and other establishments set into the cliff here. It was a very desirable place to live. She was lucky.

She knelt on a big rounded boulder and wondered why she should be so sad also. She knew this feeling from the months after Druce was born. Back then she had been offered medication but had refused. Such feelings were part of the full spectrum of being and she had felt it her duty to endure them, so that one day she could carry them into the Accord: her contribution, a droplet of despair in the ocean of human experience.

But this . . . this weight. She could not remember when it had started, and she suspected that there could be no such neat line: in some ways it had started in the mixing of genetic material used at her conception, while in others it might be quite recent.

This melancholy was different than the postnatal darkness. Not so deep, yet somehow more pervasive. A flatness that smothered everything, a tinge of desperation in her thoughts, a clutching at the straws of strangers' imagined lives.

She told herself to stop being so maudlin.

She pulled the cover from her basket and took out the crust of bread. She broke it into three pieces and hurled each as far as she could manage out onto the waves. Then she took the quetzal feathers and cast them into the breeze, watching them as they fluttered, some onto the water and some onto the rocks.

Food for the journey and feathers for the passage. An old family tradition, perhaps even one that came from Earth.

Softly, she wished the stranger a peaceful transition into the Accord.

Milton had square shoulders and a square face. Most often, if you caught him unawares, you would see him smiling, because that was the way his features settled themselves.

He was a good man.

Tish came into the bar of the Falling Droplet just as Hilary and Dongsheng were leaving, having replaced the picture window through which the stranger and one of their bar chairs had plummeted the night before.

Milton was looking out through the new glass, relaxed, smiling gently.

Tish came up behind him, put her hands on his shoulders and turned him, kissed him, first close-mouthed and then, briefly, allowing her tongue to press between his lips.

He stepped back, smiling more broadly now—a sure sign that he was unsettled by her ways. "Steady, steady!" he said. "What's got into you, then, eh? Won that grand tour ticket or something?"

"No," she said. "Not that." She took hold of a handful of his shirt and smiled. "No," she went on, "I just want to fuck you, Milton."

He looked scared, like a small animal. Once, she had found that endearing.

"But . . . ," he said. "What if someone comes in?"

"We're closed." She toyed with the handful of shirt she still had, knowing she was pulling at the hairs on his chest, knowing how that turned him on.

"But Druce—"

"Isn't here," she said.

"But he might—"

"So you'd better be quick."

But the moment was going, had gone. Had maybe never really been there at all.

She released his shirt, moved away.

"You're a good man, Milton," she said, looking out over the bay.

When she glanced back over her shoulder, Milton was smiling, because that's how his features tended to settle themselves.

It would have ended there, if she had not gone up top to the Shelf: the window repaired, the stranger and his three pursuers gone, the spark just beginning to return to Tish Goldenhawk's life—and to Milton's, whether he wanted it or not.

But no, four days after paying tribute to the stranger's passing over into the Accord, Tish took a shaft up to the top of the cliffs again, to the Shelf, and there she saw what her first response told her must be a ghost.

Here, a row of homes and bars and shops lined the cliff top, so that one had to enter a building in order to enjoy the view over the bay to the Grand Falls.

Tish had been in a bar called the Vanguard, sharing gossip with Billi Narwhal, a multicentenarian who was currently wearing his hair white on the principle that it advertised his many years of experience to any of the youngsters wanting lessons in love. The Vanguard was busy, with another two cruise ships in harbour having replaced the *Lady Cecilia*, now two days south.

A little tipsy from Billi's ruby port, Tish left the bar. A little way ahead of her was a man and there was something about the way he held himself, something about the slight taste of cinnamon on her lips—on the air, a scent.

He turned. The stranger. Undamaged, unblemished by his fall.

Tish clutched at the door frame and blamed the ruby port, both for her unsteadiness and for the apparition.

The stranger was no longer there. For a few seconds Tish was able to convince herself that he never had been.

She gathered herself and tried to remember what she had come up to the Shelf to do. She hadn't just come up here to gossip with Billi Narwhal and flatter herself with his attention.

She pushed through the crowd. She was following him. Following so quickly that it was more pursuit than passive following.

She paused, thinking of the three men in the Falling Droplet. Had it been like this for them? Were they mere innocents suddenly overcome with the urge to pursue? She knew such things were possible: the Accord could reach out to any individual and guide their actions.

But why? Why pursue this man? She was convinced now that he was a part of the Accord, a fragment of God made flesh. What, then, were the men pursuing him? Or rather, what was it that was guiding them?

She sensed no dark presence lurking in her mind, no external force appropriating her body, her senses.

She started to walk again, eyes scanning the faces.

She found him at a cafe, sipping jasmine tea while a newscast spoke to him from the middle of the table. She sat across from him. "May I?" she asked.

He smiled, and blanked the 'cast with a pass of his hand. He looked quizzical.

"The Falling Droplet," she explained. "You . . . left rather abruptly."

Understanding crossed his face. "I'm sorry," he said. "I did not anticipate that. I should have known."

She smiled. He should.

"There are expenses?"

"Oh no," she said. "Well, yes, actually, but they're covered by the city." Acts of God.

They sat quietly for a while, and Tish started to think he might prefer to be left alone. "How did you survive?" she blurted out, eventually.

"There are ways," he said. "It's not important."

She smiled. So far he had said nothing to deny her belief about his true nature, her fantasy.

"How do you find all this?" she asked him now, making conversation, prolonging their exchange. "The world of Laverne?"

"It's a mystery to me. The place, the people. You. It's beautiful. You're beautiful. Being chased by men who wish me harm—it's all beautiful."

That last bit rather detracted from what he was saying, Tish felt. Here, sitting at a table with a strange and handsome man, telling her she was beautiful . . . yet, he was like a child, eyes newly opened to the world.

"Shall we walk?" he asked.

They walked. Out past the last of the cliff-top dwellings, to where the road became a track, became an ill-defined path.

They walked: Tish Goldenhawk, hand in hand with God.

"Why did you come after me if there is no debt?" the man asked, after a time.

"I've never met anyone like you before," Tish told him. Then, brave, she added, "Anyone of your kind."

He was shaking his head, smiling as if at the wonder of the world, of this simple exchange. "You people," he said. "Always drawn to me. . . ."

She knew what he meant. Their touch—her small hand in his larger, smoother, stronger hand—was like a wick in an oil lamp, energy flowing through it, always from her to him. It made her buzz, made her feel alive.

Later, stopping on a promontory, breathing salt, cinnamon, grass, with butterflies flitting about the flowers in the turf and gulls raucously occupying the cliff below, they stopped. Picking up the thread of their conversation as if there had been no gap, he said, "My kind. What did you mean by that?"

Suddenly shy, Tish looked away, then lowered herself to the springy grass, spreading her skirts out across her legs, smoothing the fabric down.

"You," she said, wondering how to shape her words, "you're no grand tourista. Even without the goons chasing you through my bar it was obvious that you're different."

He nodded, smiled, waited for her to continue. A bee hummed nearby.

"You're of the Accord, aren't you?"

That single question embodied so much more. The Accord—the Diaspora-spanning networked supermind where we all go when our time in the real world is up, the amalgam of all past human experience, a super-city of the mind, of minds, of souls, even. The Accord.

"I don't understand."

"Your body," she said, "grown somewhere, budded off a clone of a clone, just waiting for an emissary of the Accord to occupy it. Don't worry: we all know it happens—the Accord reaching out to the real world." All that stored experience and individuality was nothing without a connection to real life.

Not nothing, but something other—the Accord sent out men and women like this stranger all the time. The process kept it human.

"If the Accord is our God, then you are a part of God," she told him. As he kneeled before her, she added, "You are God, too—God in . . . in a man's body."

And she hoped desperately that he would not correct her, not now. She reached for him and in her mind she pleaded that he should let her believe, for now, at least.

Afterwards, she lay back, enjoying the play of the cliff-top breeze on her body.

She had never done this before. Never taken one of her fantasies and played it out. Never betrayed poor, dull Milton, whom she had once, long ago, loved and now merely liked.

She turned onto her side as this man—this God—rose to a squatting position.

"Let me show you something," he said.

She laughed. "I'm not sure I'm quite ready yet," she joked.

He stood, wearing only a creamy cotton smock top that buttoned to halfway down. He reached down, arms crossing, took its hem and pulled the top over his head, discarding it so that now he stood over her, fully naked.

She looked at him, enjoying what she saw, his nakedness somehow adding to the frisson of sheer *badness* that touched every aspect of this engagement.

He turned, and she saw a strange lump between his shoulder blades. She was sure that had not been there moments before, when she had held him. As she watched, it bulged, grew, bifurcated.

As she watched, feathered wings sprouted from his back.

With a shake, he settled his flight feathers and held his wings out stiffly behind him. He turned and stepped off the cliff and, moments later, was soaring, swooping, cutting back heavenward in an updraft like a giant gull, like an angel.

Her angel.

Tish returned to the Falling Droplet late, unwashed.

Milton smiled at her, because that was how he was, and she wondered if he could tell, if she was that changed by what had happened.

She certainly felt different. She felt like something had been added, something taken away. She was not the woman she had been this morning.

She kissed Milton, willing him to taste the salt on her lips, to smell the cinnamon scent on her hair, her clothes.

She had arranged to meet her angel again the following day, and she knew she would keep the appointment.

"Customers," murmured her husband, drifting away.

She turned, looked out across the bay to where birds and pterosaurs flew, wondering if he might be out there too.

It couldn't last, of course. It could never last.

Ever more brazen, Tish had brought her lover to the Vanguard to eat the renowned dipped crabs. They had met in the street, like passing friends, with a smile and a few words, with not a single touch exchanged. Even now, sitting across a table from each other, their hands did not touch, their feet did not brush against each other. Only their eyes met, filled with promise, anticipation.

Billi came across before their food had come out, unable to resist finding out more. Tish was tempting fate, and she knew it. If Billi put two and two together, word would be all over Penhellion before nightfall.

"Going to introduce me to your friend?"

Tish looked up, and casually stroked a hand across her lover's wrist, their touch like electricity. "Hello, Billi," she said. "This is—" barely a pause "—Angelo. Angelo, meet Billi."

She saw Billi's eyes narrow, a slight nod. "You like my bar, Angelo, eh?" he said. "What're you eating? Crab's good. Crab's always good here. Don't touch the lobster, though. Trust me on that."

"Crab," said Angelo—the name fitted, the name stuck. "I took Tish Goldenhawk's advice."

Billi's eyes narrowed again, and Tish wondered what connection he was making now. Then his eyes widened, turned more fully on Angelo.

She had seen that look before, that mechanical movement.

Billi raised a hand, held it palm-out toward Angelo with the fingers stiffly pointing.

His palm glowed.

Angelo ducked, dived forward, knocking the table aside, hard against Tish's knee so that she screamed, then gasped as his weight struck her, sending her back off her chair.

She looked up from the floor, as voices rose around them.

The chair where Angelo had been seated was a blackened lump, smoking furiously.

Billi was turning slowly from the burnt chair to where Angelo and Tish lay on the floor. He had a puzzled expression on his face, a smooth, mechanical glide to his movements.

He was not Billi. Not for now, at least. Billi had been pushed aside and someone—the Accord, presumably—had taken over.

Why try to kill one of your own angels?

Billi raised a hand and Angelo stood, hauling Tish to her feet, kicking a chair and table back at the old man to stop him pursuing.

They were standing by one of the Vanguard's big picture windows.

Tish looked out, suddenly dizzy at the height.

Angelo took a chair and raised it.

"You're making a habit of this," she said, as he swung it down against the window, crazing the glass.

This time, he gave the chair a twist, and the glass gave way.

Salty air leapt in through the opening.

Angelo opened his arms and wrapped them around Tish as she stepped into his embrace, and then he jumped clear, taking her with him.

They fell, air rushing, whistling in Tish's ears.

They were going to die on the rocks this time, she felt sure. This was a lovers' end, and they would move on into the Accord for eternity.

Fabric ripped, wings broke free, and their fall became a graceful swoop taking them out across the water, towards the place where the rainbows filled the air and the gulls and the pterosaurs flew.

"You need to escape," she told him. "You need to get away from here. Why ever did you stay here in the first place after they found you?"

He shrugged. "I don't think they expected me to still be here," he explained.

They were on an island, one of the many islands where the Grand River became the Grand Falls and tumbled over the cliffs to the sea far below.

"If you want to get away why can't you just . . . I don't know . . . snap your fingers? If you're of the Accord then you should be able to just slip away and reappear somewhere else."

"Like a god?" he laughed. He raised a hand and snapped his fingers. Nothing happened.

Tish stood and looked down at the seated Angelo. Time to confront things.

"If you're no god, then who are you? What are you? Who are these people chasing after you? If they're agents of the Accord, then why is this happening? What have you done?"

He let her finish. He smiled. He shrugged. "I don't know," he told her. "I don't know who or what I am. I don't know why these people are chasing me or who they are. I don't know what I have done, if I've done anything at all. I don't remember much before a few tens of days ago. I don't understand at all, but I can tell you one thing."

He waited. She asked: "What's that?"

"I love every moment of this existence. Every last detail. I'm soaking it up. I'm a sponge. I want more. I want ever and ever more."

Tish heard the buzz of a motor—a flyer, perhaps. "You have to get away from here," she said. "They'll destroy you."

"Will you come with me? Will you share it with me?"

She nodded. She remembered that moment, walking back into the Falling Droplet and realising that she was irrevocably changed. She felt that again, only more so. She hoped it would carry on happening, because she wasn't finished yet.

2. ER-JIAN-DIE

I have no past. I have no future. Only now.

I have many pasts and many futures, but as me, as *this*, there is only now. I am a composite. I have been cast for this occasion, for this task.

I am of the Accord.

I am assembled from the many, from the multitude. I will go back to the multitude.

I am of the Accord.

I am male, in this body. My skin is dark, my hair short, straight. I am slim and strong and fast, of course. Why would I be anything else?

I am enhanced. In many ways.

I am not alone. I will not be alone when I step out of this cabin. There are two others. Two like me: Ee and Sen. We are a team.

I step out through the cabin door, having opened it first. My others are here already. Their heads turn, we nod simultaneously. I join them at the rail.

We are high up, on the deck of a faux sailing ship that is really powered by twinned gravity-wave microgenerators below decks. Above us, sails bulge in a manner designed to appeal to the grand touristas.

We are only a few hours from port. I know this for a fact, like I know much for a fact.

I close my eyes. We close our eyes. Together.

Data flashes.

We open our eyes.

He is here, on the *Lady Cecilia*. The anomaly.

In a realm where everything is known to the Accord—where everything, by its nature, *must* be known to the Accord—he is different. He is unknown. He, by his very nature, does not conform with the rules that govern our existence, your existence, everyone's existence.

He must be found.

He must be stopped.

He must be reabsorbed before he becomes self-propagating.

I turn. We turn. Together.

We smell him.

He has been here, on this deck, recently. He must be nearby.

We will seek him out, find him, reabsorb him, before the *Lady Cecilia* docks. We know this for a fact.

The *Lady Cecilia* docks at Penhellion, sliding smoothly into her space in the harbour.

We have not found him, the anomaly.

We have found places where he has been, places where he has spent long hours alone, no doubt doing battle with his perverse nature. They do that. They don't understand, but they try. They are you and me, us; it is their nature.

It is their nature to hide, and to run. This one has been here, in this world called Laverne, for longer than initial data indicated. Re-run analyses give him perhaps twenty more days' existence in which to accumulate knowledge, experience, before he was first detected.

His development is not linear. Those twenty days are days in which every aspect of his self has become exponentially more complex and data-rich.

This one is no babe in arms, then. He is a whirlwind, a destroyer of worlds.

He does not know it, of course.

Our task is to stop him from finding out.

Penhellion is a city built into a cliff. They could have built it on top of the cliff. They could have built it a few kilometres along the coast where the cliffs are not anything up to 1,200 metres high. Human nature is not such, and they built it in the cliff. We built it in the cliff. We are of the Accord.

Data flashes.

There are agents in this city. Many agents. They will look out for him and their reports will be relayed to us whenever they hold anything of relevance.

They do not know they are agents. They do not know they have been selected. Sanji Roseway does not know that she is watching, as she happily stocks her fabric stall on Fandango Way. Neither do the street musician, Mo

Yous, or the bar owner, Milton Goldenhawk, or the dreamcaster, Serendip Jones. They will not know when they are reporting, or when they have reported. That is not their place.

We did not see him leaving the *Lady Cecilia*, but he has done so. Those extra days, that logarithmic escalation of his survival instinct and wiles, have made a difference.

We must not underrate him.

But first, we must find him.

He has been quiet, which has not helped us in our task. He should be like a whirlpool, drawing in the human debris of this society, feeding on it. Such activity sends out signals, leaves traces, a pebble dropped in our collective pool.

But with experience comes guile and with guile, restraint. Perhaps he has stabilised. That would be unusual, but not a first.

We remain in Penhellion, studying and using our agents to study. He will break cover. He will reveal himself by his actions. They always do.

We proxy into a bar—a bar through the eyes of another.

There has been a ripple—only the slightest of ripples, but detectable nonetheless. He has emerged.

We look across the bar. We are behind the bar, its surface finely polished flutewood. The barroom is crowded, which is good. Picture windows show sunlight splitting into separate colours through water droplets. I like rainbows. I am not an artist, but once I think a part of me was a part of an artist. Alizarin crimson. Venetian red. Monastral blue. Yellow ochre. I could paint that view a million times and in every instance it would be different.

My team, my others, are also proxying this bartender, and our gaze is drawn away from the picture windows, and we look along the bar.

Another bartender is serving, or rather, not serving, but leaning on the flutewood bar top, chatting. She is of indeterminate age, as are most adult humans. She has long auburn hair with natural wave, wide eyes with burnt umber irises.

She is talking to him. The anomaly. He has the shape of a man, but we find it hard to focus our eyes—this proxy's eyes—on that shape and determine any detail. He swirls and flows. He is drawing her in.

"Tish?" we say, addressing the bartender. She looks, we nod toward the crowded room. This proxy is not communicative, but his meaning gets across even so.

Tish moves off to serve other customers.

We withdraw, as data flashes.

The Falling Droplet. We are several levels away, in this cliff-face city. We open a channel through the consensus, arriving in seconds.

We enter the bar. It looks different from this perspective, from the crowd rather than from behind the bar. I took around, orientating myself. We each look around. We scan faces, locating Milton the bartender and then Tish the other bartender.

I see him. I point.

He is intense. I feel dizzy, sick, as if I am being sucked in even though I know that cannot be so, due to the heavy levels of security built into my being.

I am aware of the others, Ee-jian-die and Sen-jian-die, turning to look. I sense their turmoil.

I open my hand and spotlight him. That should stun him, lock him into a pool of slowed time so that he will be swimming through perceptual treacle.

He is unaffected.

He drops a glass, ducks, moves, is gone.

We channel, and are standing where he was.

We know of the other exit. We look, and he is there, reaching for the door.

We close our eyes, lock minds, shift consensus. There is no door there. There never has been a door there.

He ducks, vanishes again. He is channeling, too, although he does not know it. Short, desperate hops. He reappears by the windows, snatching a chair.

He does not understand what is happening. He is resorting to violence, the chair his only weapon against us.

I smile. He is making it easy.

He swings the chair—but not at us, at the window. It shatters, he turns, he throws himself after the chair.

We look out of the smashed window at the sea and rocks below.

He is not dead.

He cannot be dead.

He can only be reabsorbed.

We remain in Penhellion, even though our anomaly has probably moved on now. He would be foolish to remain, after our first contact. We do not think he is a fool.

He is still here. Or rather, he has not gone far: only as far as the cliff-top community.

We tackle him immediately contact is made, through our proxy Billi Narwhal.

He pulls the same trick and evades us.

He is fast, but he appears to be a creature of habit.

He has another weakness, too: the woman, Tish Goldenhawk. She is with him. She appears to have retained her integrity, too, which is a bonus.

He is an anomaly. He can be detected by his disruption patterns, but equally, he can lie low. That is the nature of an anomaly. Or *one* of its natures.

But Tish Goldenhawk . . . If we find her, there is a high probability that we find him.

3. TISH GOLDENHAWK

"Who are you? *What* are you?"

Tish Goldenhawk has travelled the length of Laverne's main continent with the man she calls Angelo, and finally she realises that her invented name for him, "Angelo," is a more appropriate label than "man."

She has travelled the length of the continent with him, but today is the first time she has seen him kill, although she suspects it is not the first time he has killed. She has dispensed bread and feathers for his victim before confronting Angelo.

She has travelled the length of the continent with him and she is ill, drained both physically and mentally, like a scag addict.

He smiles. He shrugs. He says, "I don't know. I did not know the first time you asked me and I have not yet made that discovery. You are beautiful. Death is beautiful. I soak up beauty. That is as close as I have come to defining myself: I am a receptacle."

Death. Tish had never witnessed violent death until today. She hoped young Ferdinand would find peace in his absorption into the Accord.

They were walking, Tish and Angelo at the front, and his ragged band of followers, now numbering some twenty-four, doing as their role demanded: following.

Angelo accumulated followers. It was his nature. People he encountered, people with a sharp enough sense of perception, of distinction, were always able to detect his special nature, his divinity, the fact that he had been touched by the Accord.

They wanted to be with him.

They wanted to share with him.

They wanted to give to him.

And he, like a child with toys made of flesh and not even the slightest sense of responsibility, took.

The first time Tish had found him with another, she had ranted and raved, and he had smiled and looked puzzled, and she had seen that he had no concept of what she was feeling, and anyway, she could never be the first to cast stones in matters of infidelity.

Blind to herself, Tish had first seen the weakness in others. In Maggie and Li, who had joined the group late but had given so wholeheartedly, she had first seen the addict look in the eye, the transformation of devotion into something physical, something living. They each of them carried a cancer, and that cancer was Angelo.

Ferdinand had been one of the first to join. Tish and Angelo and three or four others had stayed the night in a grand ranch house somewhere a few days to the northwest of Daguerre. The welcome was warm—as welcomes for Angelo tended to be—and the seventeen-year-old son of the owner had been cute and, instantly, devoted.

Ferdinand had come with them. Told his parents he was guiding them to the river crossing and just carried on with them, and then they'd had to speed up a bit, hitching a ride on a goods wagon, because their welcome at that ranch would never be as warm again.

Ferdinand supplanted Tish as Angelo's favourite, if he could be said to have such a thing. To be honest, she was not too put out by this development: already she was starting to feel that psychic leaching that would only get worse.

Ferdinand went from fresh-faced disciple to hollowed devotee to shuffling, skeletal wreck in only twenty or so days.

It happened among them—it was happening to all of them, only at a slower rate—and yet it had taken far too long for Tish to notice. In the worlds of the Diaspora suffering had long since been banished. It was not even something readily recognised, like a language newly encountered. There was a whole new syntax of suffering for them to learn.

"What am I? I don't know. But I can tell you that it is like flying: I wish to fly and I fly, but once I am up there it is only the air and a few feathers that prevent me from plummeting. So tenuous the thread of existence!

"You are strong, Tish. So much stronger than the others. You hold me together. You are my air, my feathers. Without you . . . well, I don't know what would *be* without you to support me, to contain me."

She was growing weak. Had been growing weak.

But not as rapidly as Ferdinand.

She came up on them early that morning, when the sun was still heavy over the mountains, painting them gold and pink.

Angelo was holding him, his arms easily enfolding the wasted frame.

Tish almost turned away. She had seen this kind of encounter often enough by now. She closed her eyes and thought back to those few precious nights when it had just been the two of them, sleeping rough, both enfolded by his wings.

She had been strong then.

She opened her eyes just as Ferdinand started to vanish.

She watched. She could see through him. See the stones, the thorn bush, the tussock grass, the inside of Angelo's embracing left arm, previously obscured by Ferdinand's bony torso.

Things blurred. Things dissolved, melted, slipped away from this existence.

He was gone.

Angelo turned to her, his expression startled, as if he did not know what had happened, had not expected it to happen; but beneath the surprise there was satisfaction, a thrill of pleasure, of strength, and the first hint of that crooked-toothed smile.

4. ER-JIAN-DIE

"Your air, your feathers . . . so poetic. If you weren't such an innocent I'd say you had the crassest line in smooth-talk, but you don't have a clue, do you?"

We have her. We have him. I see him through the eyes of Tish Golden-hawk and it is as if a distorting lens has been removed. He is male, of indeterminate age, of mid-brown skin tone and dark hair. He is beautiful and engaging.

He draws you in.

Even at this remove—proxied and many hundred kilometres distant—he draws you in.

We debate, as he moves out of view. Act now, via proxy, or attend in body, allowing a short interval in which he might detect our approach and take evasive action? We do not know how much his powers have grown.

Data flashes.

Ee-jian-die takes the proxy, turns her head so that he is back in our field of view. Sen-jian-die and I withdraw, lock, open a channel through the consensus, step through.

There is momentary disorientation and then we are standing on a plain, surrounded by cacti and thorn bushes and oddly balanced round boulders.

The two of them are there, locked in conflict. A short distance away there is an encampment of bubble tents and track trikes. The people there look on, too damaged to stir.

She has him in the beam. She stands, knees slightly bent, body tipped forward, one arm stretched out, palm first, fingers straight, and a beam of white light lances from her hand to him, the anomaly.

He stands there smiling.

He looks at us, as we materialise, although he should not be able to turn his head at all.

He raises a hand so that he mirrors Tish Goldenhawk's stance and his palm cuts out the beam, reflects it.

It shines on her face and she crumples, sobbing, more damaged than she had been before.

Ee-jian-die appears at my side, his proxying of Tish abandoned.

He looks ashen, damaged by the encounter, even at a proxy.

I allow myself to be identified as leader, even though we three are equal, we three are far greater than we three alone. "Your time is up," I tell the anomaly. "Let these people go. Come back with us. Allow yourself to be reabsorbed."

He smiles in a way that indicates he is both amused and puzzled. "Reabsorbed?" he said. "*Re?*"

I nod. "You are a glitch," I tell him. "A chaotic anomaly. The Accord contains all the individuals who have lived and then died since its inception. You are a bug in that process, a self-resonant fluctuation in the billions upon billions of human elements within the Accord. A remix error. You're a strange attractor and you need to be smoothed over. Come with us: you will not be lost, you will simply be reabsorbed."

"But how? . . . How can I be reabsorbed if I am not yet dead?"

He doesn't know. He has grown, but he does not know.

"This *is* the Accord," I tell him. "We are living the afterlife. The afterlives."

"What happens if I say 'no'?"

"We will force you."

"And if you fail?"

"You will carry on growing. Like a leak in a pool, you will continue to drag in those about you, soaking them up until they are husks. They are drawn to you. *We* are drawn to you. You are like a black hole in human form. You will suck us all in and the Accord will fail to be. It will crash on a galaxy-wide scale."

He—this thing, this entity, this *it*—is smiling. "So, if I believe you, then

I—" he thumped his chest in apelike display "—am an alternative to the Accord? An alternative reality?"

It laughs. "I like this," it says. "It is all so beautiful. So, so beautiful."

We strike, synchronised.

Ee locks him in the immobilising beam, far more powerful than we have used so far. I lock him in a second, our combined beams more than doubling their intensity in combination. Sen moves in to interface, a physical connection with the Accord.

The anomaly is still smiling.

It turns and lashes out a beam of light and Sen flies through the air in several pieces.

It turns again, and lashes at Ee, and I sense our hold—if ever we had had a hold—weakening.

And then . . . light, dark, an absence that is where the pain would have been if my body had not immediately shut down those pathways. A lot of absence.

Mental silence. Ee-jian-die and Sen-jian-die have been returned to the Accord. They will reappear, but not here, not now.

I am still here, though. I have not been returned.

I open the eye that I am able to control.

I see sky, a thorn bush.

I see her. Tish Goldenhawk. Looking down at me.

"What can I do?" she says.

"Nothing," I tell her. The body that carries me is too fundamentally damaged. It could be repaired, of course, but what is the point? My task is over, I have failed. I will be reabsorbed. Someone else will be sent, and they will try again. The anomaly will have grown, but it will be fought, only not by me next time, or at least, not by the combination of traits that is this me.

"What happens to us when he has sucked us dry?"

She is strong, this one.

"If this is the Accord, then where does the data go when he has absorbed it? You said he's some kind of black hole—what's inside him?"

"Who knows?" I say. "The physically dead enter the Accord and we live on, again and again, for eternity. But attractant anomalies like this remove us from the afterlife. It's like asking where the dead went before there was an Accord. They died. They stopped being. They ended. If he takes us from the Accord, we end."

"What can I do?" she repeats, and I realise that she does not mean to ask what she can do to help my mortally damaged body, but rather what can she do to stop the anomaly, the attractor, her lover.

"He said I was his air, his feathers, that I held him together," she said. "I want that to stop."

In that instant I want to paint her. Like the rainbows, I could paint her a million times and each would be different, but always her strength, her purity, would come through.

"You have to get close to him," I tell her.

5. TISH GOLDENHAWK

"You have to get close to him," this wreck of a human construct tells her. "Hold him."

Tish Goldenhawk nods. In her mind she can see Angelo holding Ferdinand, absorbing him. She knows exactly what this agent of the Accord means. "What then?"

"That's all," he tells her. "I will do the rest."

Angelo waits for her in the encampment, smiling. She should have known he would not go on without her.

"I'm sorry," he says. His words have no meaning. They are just vibrations in the air. "They tried to kill me."

She nods. "They're dead now," she says, wondering then at the lie— whether she has made a fatal mistake already.

He shakes his head. "One lives," he says, "but only tenuously. He does not have long, I think."

He turns. "We must move on," he says. "There will be more of them. Another day and we will reach a city, I think. A city would be good."

She looks at him, tries to see him as she had once seen him, a charming, exciting escape. That had only ever been one of her fantasies. She tries to see him as her lover, but cannot. Tries to see him even as human, but no.

"I can't," she says in a quiet voice.

He turns, raises an eyebrow.

"I can't go on." Getting stronger. "I'm leaving. Going home. You don't need me anymore."

"But . . ."

"No buts," she says. "I can't do this. I'm exhausted. Drained. I'm leaving."

He is not human, but there is so much in him that *is*.

"You can't," he says. "I . . . You're my support. My feathers, the air that holds me up. The air that I breathe!"

"I'm tired," she says. "You can't lean on me anymore. I'm none of those things. . . . I'm not strong enough. Can't you see? It's *me* who needs supporting!"

"I will always support you," he says.

He opens his arms, just as he had for Ferdinand, who had been too weak to continue.

He steps forward.

She waits for him to come to her, to hold her.

Scent of cinnamon, of dry, dusty feathers. She holds him.

She senses the flow, the seething mass of energies. They came from . . . beyond.

He gasps, straightens.

She holds on.

He is looking down at her. He knows. He dips his head and kisses her on the brow.

She holds nothing, holds air, hugs herself. She drops to her knees.

There are feathers, nothing else. She gathers some. She will cast them for him, with bread, when she gets back to Penhellion.

She does not doubt that she will go there, go home.

Poor Milton. Poor Druce. She has changed. She does not know what can be salvaged, but she will go home now and she will see.

She stands.

Even if nothing can be repaired, she has no regrets. She would do it all again.

She is of the Accord.

They all are of the Accord.

Laws of Survival

NANCY KRESS

Nancy Kress began selling her elegant and incisive stories in the mid-seventies, and has since become a frequent contributor to *Asimov's Science Fiction*, *The Magazine of Fantasy & Science Fiction*, *Omni*, *SCI FICTION*, and elsewhere. Her books include the novel version of her Hugo and Nebula-winning story, *Beggars in Spain*, and a sequel, *Beggars and Choosers*, as well as *The Prince of Morning Bells*, *The Golden Grove*, *The White Pipes*, *An Alien Light*, *Brain Rose*, *Oaths and Miracles*, *Stinger*, *Maximum Light*, *Crossfire*, *Nothing Human*, and the Space Opera trilogy *Probability Moon*, *Probability Sun*, and *Probability Space*. Her short work has been collected in *Trinity and Other Stories*, *The Aliens of Earth*, and *Beaker's Dozen*. Her most recent book is the novel *Crucible*. Coming up is a new novel, *Dogs*, and a new collection, *Nano Comes to Clifford Falls and Other Stories*. In addition to the awards for "Beggars in Spain," she has also won Nebula Awards for her stories "Out of All Them Bright Stars" and "The Flowers of Aulit Prison."

Here she tells us the story of someone who quite literally has gone to the dogs—and must somehow learn to live with them if she wants to survive.

M y name is Jill. I am somewhere you can't imagine, going somewhere even more unimaginable. If you think I like what I did to get here, you're crazy. Actually, I'm the one who's crazy. You—any "you"—will never read this. But I have paper now, and a sort of pencil, and time. Lots and lots of time. So I will write what happened, all of it, as carefully as I can.

After all—why the hell not?

I went out very early one morning to look for food. Before dawn was safest for a woman alone. The boy-gangs had gone to bed, tired of attacking each other. The trucks from the city hadn't arrived yet. That meant the garbage was pretty picked over, but it also meant most of the refugee camp wasn't out scavenging. Most days I could find enough: a carrot stolen from somebody's garden patch, my arm bloody from reaching through the barbed wire. Over-looked potato peelings under a pile of rags and glass. A can of stew thrown away by one of the soldiers on the base, but still half full. Soldiers on duty by the Dome were often careless. They got bored, with nothing to do.

That morning was cool but fair, with a pearly haze that the sun would burn off later. I wore all my clothing, for warmth, and my boots. Yesterday's garbage load, I'd heard somebody say, was huge, so I had hopes. I hiked to my favorite spot, where garbage spills almost to the Dome wall. Maybe I'd find bread, or even fruit that wasn't too rotten.

Instead I found the puppy.

Its eyes weren't open yet and it squirmed along the bare ground, a scrawny brown-and-white mass with a tiny fluffy tail. Nearby was a fluid-soaked towel. Some sentimental fool had left the puppy there, hoping . . . what? It didn't matter. Scrawny or not, there was some meat on the thing. I scooped it up.

The sun pushed above the horizon, flooding the haze with golden light.

I hate it when grief seizes me. I hate it and it's dangerous, a violation of one of Jill's Laws of Survival. I can go for weeks, months without thinking of my life before the War. Without remembering or feeling. Then something will strike me—a flower growing in the dump, a burst of birdsong, the stars on a clear night—and grief will hit me like the maglevs that no longer exist, a grief all the sharper because it contains the memory of joy. I can't afford joy, which always comes with an astronomical price tag. I can't even afford the grief that comes from the memory of living things, which is why it is only the flower, the birdsong, the morning sunlight that starts it. My grief was not for that puppy. I still intended to eat it.

But I heard a noise behind me and turned. The Dome wall was opening.

Who knew why the aliens put their Domes by garbage dumps, by waste pits, by radioactive cities? Who knew why aliens did anything?

There was a widespread belief in the camp that the aliens started the War. I'm old enough to know better. That was us, just like the global warming and the bio-crobes were us. The aliens didn't even show up until the War was over and Raleigh was the northernmost city left on the East Coast and refugees poured south like mudslides. Including me. That's when the ships landed and then turned into the huge gray Domes like upended bowls. I heard there were many Domes, some in other countries. The Army, what was left of it, threw tanks and bombs at ours. When they gave up, the refugees threw bullets and Molotov cocktails and prayers and graffiti and candlelight vigils and rain dances. Everything slid off and the Domes just sat there. And sat. And sat. Three years later, they were still sitting, silent and closed, although of course there were rumors to the contrary. There are always rumors. Personally, I'd never gotten over a slight disbelief that the Dome was there at all. Who would want to visit us?

The opening was small, no larger than a porthole, and about six feet above the ground. All I could see inside was a fog the same color as the Dome. Something came out, gliding quickly toward me. It took me a moment to realize it was a robot, a blue metal sphere above a hanging basket. It stopped a foot from my face and said, "This food for this dog."

I could have run, or screamed, or at the least—the very least—looked around for a witness. I didn't. The basket held a pile of fresh produce, green lettuce and deep purple eggplant and apples so shiny red they looked lacquered. And *peaches* . . . My mouth filled with sweet water. I couldn't move.

The puppy whimpered.

My mother used to make fresh peach pie.

I scooped the food into my scavenger bag, laid the puppy in the basket, and backed away. The robot floated back into the Dome, which closed immediately. I sped back to my corrugated-tin and windowless hut and ate until I couldn't hold any more. I slept, woke, and ate the rest, crouching in the dark so nobody else would see. All that fruit and vegetables gave me the runs, but it was worth it.

Peaches.

Two weeks later, I brought another puppy to the Dome, the only survivor of a litter deep in the dump. I never knew what happened to the mother. I had to wait a long time outside the Dome before the blue sphere took the puppy in exchange for produce. Apparently the Dome would only open when there was no one else around to see. What were they afraid of? It's not like PETA was going to show up.

The next day I traded three of the peaches to an old man in exchange for a small, mangy poodle. We didn't look each other in the eye, but I nonetheless knew that his held tears. He limped hurriedly away. I kept the dog, which clearly wanted nothing to do with me, in my shack until very early morning and then took it to the Dome. It tried to escape but I'd tied a bit of rope onto its frayed collar. We sat outside the Dome in mutual dislike, waiting, as the sky paled slightly in the east. Gunshots sounded in the distance.

I have never owned a dog.

When the Dome finally opened, I gripped the dog's rope and spoke to the robot. "Not fruit. Not vegetables. I want eggs and bread."

The robot floated back inside.

Instantly I cursed myself. Eggs? Bread? I was crazy not to take what I could get. That was Law of Survival #1. Now there would be nothing. Eggs, bread . . . *crazy*. I glared at the dog and kicked it. It yelped, looked indignant, and tried to bite my boot.

The Dome opened again and the robot glided toward me. In the gloom I couldn't see what was in the basket. In fact, I couldn't see the basket. It wasn't there. Mechanical tentacles shot out from the sphere and seized both me and the poodle. I cried out and the tentacles squeezed harder. Then I was flying through the air, the stupid dog suddenly howling beneath me, and we were carried through the Dome wall and inside.

Then nothing.

A nightmare room made of nightmare sound: barking, yelping, whimpering, snapping. I jerked awake, sat up, and discovered myself on a floating platform above a mass of dogs. Big dogs, small dogs, old dogs, puppies, sick dogs, dogs that looked all too healthy, flashing their forty-two teeth at me—why did I remember that number? From where? The largest and strongest dogs couldn't quite reach me with their snaps, but they were trying.

"You are operative," the blue metal sphere said, floating beside me. "Now we must begin. Here."

Its basket held eggs and bread.

"Get them away!"

Obediently it floated off.

"Not the food! The dogs!"

"What to do with these dogs?"

"Put them in cages!" A large black animal—German shepherd or boxer or something—had nearly closed its jaws on my ankle. The next bite might do it.

"Cages," the metal sphere said in its uninflected mechanical voice. "Yes."

"Son of a bitch!" The shepherd, leaping high, had grazed my thigh; its spittle slimed my pants. "Raise the goddamn platform!"

"Yes."

The platform floated so high, so that I had to duck my head to avoid hitting the ceiling. I peered over the edge and . . . no, that wasn't possible. But it was happening. The floor was growing upright sticks, and the sticks were growing crossbars, and the crossbars were extending themselves into mesh tops. . . . Within minutes, each dog was encased in a cage just large enough to hold its protesting body.

"What to do now?" the metal sphere asked.

I stared at it. I was, as far as I knew, the first human being to ever enter an alien Dome, I was trapped in a small room with feral caged dogs and a robot . . . *what to do now?*

"Why . . . why am I here?" I hated myself for the brief stammer and vowed it would not happen again. Law of Survival #2: Show no fear.

Would a metal sphere even recognize fear?

It said, "These dogs do not behave correctly."

"Not behave correctly?"

"No."

I looked down again at the slavering and snarling mass of dogs; how strong was that mesh on the cage tops? "What do you want them to do?"

"You want to see the presentation?"

"Not yet." Law #3: Never volunteer for anything.

"What to do now?"

How the hell should I know? But the smell of the bread reached me and my stomach flopped. "Now to eat," I said. "Give me the things in your basket."

It did, and I tore into the bread like a wolf into deer. The real wolves below me increased their howling. When I'd eaten an entire loaf, I looked back at the metal sphere. "Have those dogs eaten?"

"Yes."

"What did you give them?"

"Garbage."

"*Garbage?* Why?"

"In hell they eat garbage."

So even the robot thought this was Hell. Panic surged through me; I pushed it back. Surviving this would depend on staying steady. "Show me what you fed the dogs."

"Yes." A section of wall melted and garbage cascaded into the room, flowing greasily between the cages. I recognized it: It was exactly like the garbage I picked through every day, trucked out from a city I could no longer imagine and from the Army base I could not approach without being shot. Bloody rags, tin cans from before the War, shit, plastic bags, dead flowers, dead animals, dead electronics, cardboard, eggshells, paper, hair, bone, scraps of decaying food, glass shards, potato peelings, foam rubber, roaches, sneakers with holes, sagging furniture, corn cobs. The smell hit my stomach, newly distended with bread.

"You fed the dogs *that?*"

"Yes. They eat it in hell."

Outside. Hell was outside, and of course that's what the feral dogs ate, that's all there was. But the metal sphere had produced fruit and lettuce and bread for me.

"You must give them better food. They eat that in . . . in hell because they can't get anything else."

"What to do now?"

It finally dawned on me—slow, I was too slow for this, only the quick survive—that the metal sphere had limited initiative along with its limited vocabulary. But it had made cages, made bread, made fruit—hadn't it? Or was this stuff grown in some imaginable secret garden inside the Dome? "You must give the dogs meat."

"Flesh?"

"Yes."

"No."

No change in that mechanical voice, but the "no" was definite and quick. Law of Survival #4: Notice everything. So—no flesh-eating allowed here. Also no time to ask why not; I had to keep issuing orders so that the robot didn't start issuing them. "Give them bread mixed with . . . with soy protein."

"Yes."

"And take away the garbage."

"Yes."

The garbage began to dissolve. I saw nothing poured on it, nothing rise from the floor. But all that stinking mass fell into powder and vanished. Nothing replaced it.

I said, "Are you getting bread mixed with soy powder?" *Getting* seemed the safest verb I could think of.

"Yes."

The stuff came then, tumbling through the same melted hole in the wall, loaves of bread with, presumably, soy powder in them. The dogs, barking insanely, reached paws and snouts and tongues through the bars of their cages. They couldn't get at the food.

"Metal sphere—do you have a name?"

No answer.

"Okay. Blue, how strong are those cages? Can the dogs break them? Any of the dogs?"

"No."

"Lower the platform to the floor."

My safe perch floated down. The aisles between the cages were irregu-lar, some wide and some so narrow the dogs could reach through to touch each other, since each cage had "grown" wherever the dog was at the time. Gingerly I picked my way to a clearing and sat down. Tearing a loaf of bread into chunks, I pushed the pieces through the bars of the least dangerous—looking dogs, which made the bruisers howl even more. For them, I put chunks at a distance they could just reach with a paw through the front bars of their prisons.

The puppy I had first brought to the Dome lay in a tiny cage. Dead.

The second one was alive but just barely.

The old man's mangy poodle looked more mangy than ever, but otherwise alert. It tried to bite me when I fed it.

"What to do now?"

"They need water."

"Yes."

Water flowed through the wall. When it had reached an inch or so, it stopped. The dogs lapped whatever came into their cages. I stood with wet feet—a hole in my boot after all, I hadn't known—and a stomach roiling from the stench of the dogs, which only worsened as they got wet. The dead puppy smelled especially horrible. I climbed back onto my platform.

"What to do now?"

"You tell me," I said.

"These dogs do not behave correctly."

"Not behave correctly?"

"No."

"What do you want them to do?"

"Do you want to see the presentation?"

We had been here before. On second thought, a "presentation" sounded more like acquiring information ("Notice everything") than like undertaking action ("Never volunteer"). So I sat cross-legged on the platform, which was easier on my uncushioned bones, breathed through my mouth instead of my nose, and said, "Why the hell not?"

Blue repeated, "Do you want to see the presentation?"

"Yes." A one-syllable answer.

I didn't know what to expect. Aliens, spaceships, war, strange places barely comprehensible to humans. What I got was scenes from the dump.

A beam of light shot out from Blue and resolved into a three-dimensional holo, not too different from one I'd seen in a science museum on a school field trip once (*no, push memory away*), only this was far sharper and detailed. A ragged and unsmiling toddler, one of thousands, staggered toward a cesspool. A big dog with a patchy coat dashed up, seized the kid's dress, and pulled her back just before she fell into the waste.

A medium-sized brown dog in a guide-dog harness led around someone tapping a white-headed cane.

An Army dog, this one sleek and well-fed, sniffed at a pile of garbage, found something, pointed stiffly at attention.

A group of teenagers tortured a puppy. It writhed in pain, but in a long lingering close-up, tried to lick the torturer's hand.

A thin, small dog dodged rocks, dashed inside a corrugated tin hut, and laid a piece of carrion beside an old lady lying on the ground.

The holo went on and on like that, but the strange thing was that the people were barely seen. The toddler's bare and filthy feet and chubby knees, the old lady's withered cheek, a flash of a camouflage uniform above a brown boot, the hands of the torturers. Never a whole person, never a focus on people. Just on the dogs.

The "presentation" ended.

"These dogs do not behave correctly," Blue said.

"These dogs? In the presentation?"

"These dogs here do not behave correctly."

"These dogs *here*." I pointed to the wet, stinking dogs in their cages. Some, fed now, had quieted. Others still snarled and barked, trying their hellish best to get out and kill me.

"These dogs here. Yes. What to do now?"

"You want these dogs to behave like the dogs in the presentation."

"These dogs here must behave correctly. Yes."

"You want them to . . . do what? Rescue people? Sniff out ammunition dumps? Guide the blind and feed the hungry and love their torturers?"

Blue said nothing. Again I had the impression I had exceeded its thought processes, or its vocabulary, or its something. A strange feeling gathered in my gut.

"Blue, you yourself didn't build this Dome, or the starship that it was before, did you? You're just a . . . a computer."

Nothing.

"Blue, who tells you what to do?"

"What to do now? These dogs do not behave correctly."

"Who wants these dogs to behave correctly?" I said, and found I was holding my breath.

"The masters."

The masters. I knew all about them. Masters were the people who started wars, ran the corporations that ruined the Earth, manufactured the bioweapons that killed billions, and now holed up in the cities to send their garbage out to us in the refugee camps. Masters were something else I didn't think about, but not because grief would take me. Rage would.

Law of Survival #5: Feel nothing that doesn't aid survival.

"Are the masters here? In this . . . inside here?"

"No."

"Who is here inside?"

"These dogs here are inside."

Clearly. "The masters want these dogs here to behave like the dogs in the presentation."

"Yes."

"The masters want these dogs here to provide them with loyalty and protection and service."

No response.

"The masters aren't interested in human beings, are they? That's why they haven't communicated at all with any government."

Nothing. But I didn't need a response; the masters' thinking was already clear to me. Humans were unimportant—maybe because we had, after all, destroyed each other and our own world. We weren't worth contact. But dogs: companion animals capable of selfless service and great unconditional love, even in the face of abuse. For all I knew, dogs were unique in the universe. For all I know.

Blue said, "What to do now?"

I stared at the mangy, reeking, howling mass of animals. Some feral, some tamed once, some sick, at least one dead. I chose my words to be as simple as possible, relying on phrases Blue knew. "The masters want these dogs here to behave correctly."

"Yes."

"The masters want *me* to make these dogs behave correctly."

"Yes."

"The masters will make me food, and keep me inside, for to make these dogs behave correctly."

Long pause; my sentence had a lot of grammatical elements. But finally Blue said, "Yes."

"If these dogs do not behave correctly, the masters—what to do then?"

Another long pause. "Find another human."

"And *this* human here?"

"Kill it."

I gripped the edges of my floating platform hard. My hands still trembled. "Put me outside now."

"No."

"I must stay inside."

"These dogs do not behave correctly."

"I must make these dogs behave correctly."

"Yes."

"And the masters want these dogs to display . . ." I had stopped talking to Blue. I was talking to myself, to steady myself, but even that I couldn't manage. The words caromed around in my mind—loyalty, service, protection—but none came out of my mouth. I couldn't do this. I was going to die. The aliens had come from God-knew-where to treat the dying Earth like a giant pet store, intrigued only by a canine domestication that had happened ten thousand years ago and by nothing else on the planet, nothing else humanity had or might accomplish. Only dogs. *The masters want these dogs to display—*

Blue surprised me with a new word. "Love," it said.

Law #4: Notice everything. I needed to learn all I could, starting with Blue. He'd made garbage appear, and food and water and cages. What else could he do?

"Blue, make the water go away." And it did, just sank into the floor, which dried instantly. I was fucking Moses, commanding the Red Sea. I climbed off the platform, inched among the dog cages, and studied them individually.

"You called the refugee camp and the dump 'hell.' Where did you get that word?"

Nothing.

"Who said 'hell'?"

"Humans."

Blue had cameras outside the Dome. Of course he did; he'd seen me find that first puppy in the garbage. Maybe Blue had been waiting for someone like me, alone and nonthreatening, to come close with a dog. But it had watched before that, and it had learned the word "hell," and maybe it had recorded the incidents in the "presentation." I filed this information for future use.

"This dog is dead." The first puppy, decaying into stinking pulp. "It is killed. Non-operative."

"What to do now?"

"Make the dead dog go away."

A long pause: thinking it over? Accessing data banks? Communicating with aliens? And what kind of moron couldn't figure out by itself that a dead dog was never going to behave correctly? So much for artificial intelligence.

"Yes," Blue finally said, and the little corpse dissolved as if it had never been.

I found one more dead dog and one close to death. Blue disappeared the first, said no to the second. Apparently we had to just let it suffer until it died. I wondered how much the idea of "death" even meant to a robot. There were twenty-three live dogs, of which I had delivered only three to the Dome.

"Blue—did another human, before you brought me here, try to train the dogs?"

"These dogs do not behave correctly."

"Yes. But did a human *not me* be inside? To make these dogs behave correctly?"

"Yes."

"What happened to him or her?"

No response.

"What to do now with the other human?"

"Kill it."

I put a hand against the wall and leaned on it. The wall felt smooth and slick, with a faint and unpleasant tingle. I removed my hand.

All computers could count. "How many humans did you kill?"

"Two."

Three's the charm. But there were no charms. No spells, no magic wards, no cavalry coming over the hill to ride to the rescue; I'd known that ever since the War. There was just survival. And, now, dogs.

I chose the mangy little poodle. It hadn't bit me when the old man had surrendered it, or when I'd kept it overnight. That was at least a start. "Blue, make this dog's cage go away. But *only* this one cage!"

The cage dissolved. The poodle stared at me distrustfully. Was I supposed to stare back, or would that get us into some kind of canine pissing contest? The thing was small but it had teeth.

I had a sudden idea. "Blue, show me how this dog does not behave correctly." If I could see what it wasn't doing, that would at least be a start.

Blue floated to within a foot of the dog's face. The dog growled and backed away. Blue floated away and the dog quieted but it still stood in what would be a menacing stance if it weighed more than nine or ten pounds: ears raised, legs braced, neck hair bristling. Blue said, "Come." The dog did nothing. Blue repeated the entire sequence and so did Mangy.

I said, "You want the dog to follow you. Like the dogs in the presentation."

"Yes."

"You want the dog to come when you say 'Come.'"

"Love," Blue said.

"What is 'love,' Blue?"

No response.

The robot didn't know. Its masters must have had some concept of "love," but fuck-all knew what it was. And I wasn't sure I knew anymore, either. That left Mangy, who would never "love" Blue or follow him or lick his hand because dogs operated on smell—even I knew that about them—and Blue, a machine, didn't smell like either a person or another dog. Couldn't the aliens who sent him here figure that out? Were they watching this whole farce, or had they just dropped a half-sentient computer under an upturned bowl on Earth and told it, "Bring us some loving dogs"? Who knew how aliens thought?

I didn't even know how dogs thought. There were much better people for this job—professional trainers, or that guy on TV who made tigers jump through burning hoops. But they weren't here, and I was. I squatted on my haunches a respectful distance from Mangy and said, "Come."

It growled at me.

"Blue, raise the platform this high." I held my hand at shoulder height. The platform rose.

"Now make some cookies on the platform."

Nothing.

"Make some . . . cheese on the platform."

Nothing. You don't see much cheese in a dump.

"Make some bread on the platform."

Nothing. Maybe the platform wasn't user-friendly.

"Make some bread."

After a moment, loaves tumbled out of the wall. "Enough! Stop!"

Mangy had rushed over to the bread, tearing at it, and the other dogs were going wild. I picked up one loaf, put it on the platform, and said, "Make the rest of the bread go away."

It all dissolved. No wonder the dogs were wary; I felt a little dizzy myself. A sentence from a so-long-ago child's book rose in my mind: *Things come and go so quickly here!*

I had no idea how much Blue could, or would, do on my orders. "Blue, make another room for me and this one dog. Away from the other dogs."

"No."

"Make this room bigger."

The room expanded evenly on all sides. "Stop." It did. "Make only this end of the room bigger."

Nothing.

"Okay, make the whole room bigger."

When the room stopped expanding, I had a space about forty feet square, with the dog cages huddled in the middle. After half an hour of experimenting, I got the platform moved to one corner, not far enough to escape the dog stench but better than nothing. (Law #1: Take what you can get.) I got a depression in the floor filled with warm water. I got food, drinking water, soap, and some clean cloth, and a lot of rope. By distracting Mangy with bits of bread, I got rope onto her frayed collar. After I got into the warm water and scrubbed myself, I pulled the poodle in. She bit me. But somehow I got her washed, too. Afterwards she shook herself, glared at me, and went to sleep on the hard floor. I asked Blue for a soft rug.

He said, "The other humans did this."

And Blue killed them anyway.

"Shut up," I said.

The big windowless room had no day, no night, no sanity. I slept and ate when I needed to, and otherwise I worked. Blue never left. He was an over-sized, all-seeing eye in the corner. Big Brother, or God.

Within a few weeks—maybe—I had Mangy trained to come when called, to sit, and to follow me on command. I did this by dispensing bits of bread and other goodies. Mangy got fatter. I didn't care if she ended up the Fat Fiona of dogs. Her mange didn't improve, since I couldn't get Blue to wrap his digital mind around the concept of medicines, and even if he had I wouldn't have known what to ask for. The sick puppy died in its cage.

I kept the others fed and watered and flooded the shit out of their cages every day, but that was all. Mangy took all my time. She still regarded me warily, never curled up next to me, and occasionally growled. Love was not happening here.

Nonetheless, Blue left his corner and spoke for the first time in a week, scaring the hell out of me. "This dog behaves correctly."

"Well, thanks. I tried to . . . no, Blue . . ."

Blue floated to within a foot of Mangy's face, said, "Follow," and floated away. Mangy sat down and began to lick one paw. Blue rose and floated toward me.

"This dog does not behave correctly."

I was going to die.

"No, listen to me—listen! The dog can't smell you! It behaves for humans because of humans' smell! Do you understand?"

"No. This dog does not behave correctly."

"Listen! How the hell can you learn anything if you don't listen? You have to have a smell! Then the dog will follow you!"

Blue stopped. We stood frozen, a bizarre tableau, while the robot consid-ered. Even Mangy stopped licking her paw and watched, still. They say dogs can smell fear.

Finally Blue said, "What is smell?"

It isn't possible to explain smell. Can't be done. Instead I pulled down my pants, tore the cloth I was using as underwear from between my legs, and rubbed it all over Blue, who did not react. I hoped he wasn't made of the same stuff as the Dome, which even spray paint had just slid off of. But, of course, he was. So I tied the strip of cloth around him with a piece of rope, my fingers trembling. "Now try the dog, Blue."

"Follow," Blue said, and floated away from Mangy.

She looked at him, then at me, then back at the floating metal sphere. I held my breath from some insane idea that I would thereby diminish my own smell. Mangy didn't move.

"This dog does not be—"

"She will if I'm gone!" I said desperately. "She smells me *and* you . . .

and we smell the same so it's confusing her! But she'll follow you fine if I'm gone, do you understand?"

"No."

"Blue . . . I'm going to get on the platform. See, I'm doing it. Raise the platform *very high*, Blue. Very high."

A moment later my head and ass both pushed against the ceiling, squishing me. I couldn't see what was happening below. I heard Blue say, "Follow," and I squeezed my eyes shut, waiting. My life depended on a scrofulous poodle with a gloomy disposition.

Blue said, "This dog behaves correctly."

He lowered my platform to a few yards above the floor, and I swear that—eyeless as he is and with part of his sphere obscured by my underwear—he looked right at me.

"This dog does behave correctly. This dog is ready."

"Ready? For . . . for what?"

Blue didn't answer. The next minute the floor opened and Mangy, yelping, tumbled into it. The floor closed. At the same time, one of the cages across the room dissolved and a German shepherd hurtled toward me. I shrieked and yelled, "Raise the platform!" It rose just before the monster grabbed me.

Blue said, "What to do now? This dog does not behave correctly."

"For God's sakes, Blue—"

"This dog must love."

The shepherd leapt and snarled, teeth bared.

I couldn't talk Blue out of the shepherd, which was as feral and vicious and unrelenting as anything in a horror movie. Or as Blue himself, in his own mechanical way. So I followed the First Law: Take what you can get.

"Blue, make garbage again. A lot of garbage, right here." I pointed to the wall beside my platform.

"No."

Garbage, like everything else, apparently was made—or released, or whatever—from the opposite wall. I resigned myself to this. "Make a lot of garbage, Blue."

Mountains of stinking debris cascaded from the wall, spilling over until it reached the dog cages.

"Now stop. Move my platform above the garbage."

The platform moved. The caged dogs howled. Uncaged, the shepherd poked eagerly in the refuse, too distracted to pay much attention to me. I had Blue lower the platform and I poked among it, too, keeping one eye on Vicious. If Blue was creating the garbage and not just trucking it in, he was doing a damn fine job of duplication. Xerox should have made such good copies.

I got smeared with shit and rot, but I found what I was looking for. The box was nearly a quarter full. I stuffed bread into it, coated the bread thoroughly, and discarded the box back onto the pile.

"Blue, make the garbage go away."

It did. Vicious glared at me and snarled. "Nice doggie," I said, "have some bread." I threw pieces and Vicious gobbled them.

Listening to the results was terrible. Not, however, as terrible as having Vicious tear me apart or Blue vaporize me. The rat poison took all "night" to kill the dog, which thrashed and howled. Throughout, Blue stayed silent. He had picked up some words from me, but he apparently didn't have enough brain power to connect what I'd done with Vicious's death. Or maybe he just didn't have enough experience with humans. What does a machine know about survival?

"This dog is dead," Blue said in the "morning."

"Yes. Make it go away." And then, before Blue could get there first, I jumped off my platform and pointed to a cage. "This dog will behave correctly next."

"No."

"Why not this dog?"

"Not big."

"Big. You want big." Frantically I scanned the cages, before Blue could choose another one like Vicious. "This one, then."

"Why the hell not?" Blue said.

It was young. Not a puppy but still frisky, a mongrel of some sort with short hair of dirty white speckled with dirty brown. The dog looked liked something I could handle: big but not too big, not too aggressive, not too old, not too male. "Hey, Not-Too," I said, without enthusiasm, as Blue dissolved her cage. The mutt dashed over to me and tried to lick my boot.

A natural-born slave.

I had found a piece of rotten, moldy cheese in the garbage, so Blue could now make cheese, which Not-Too went crazy for. Not-Too and I stuck with the same routine I used with Mangy, and it worked pretty well. Or the cheese did. Within a few "days" the dog could sit, stay, and follow on command.

Then Blue threw me a curve. "What to do now? The presentation."

"We had the presentation," I said. "I don't need to see it again."

"What to do now? The presentation."

"Fine," I said, because it was clear I had no choice. "Let's have the presentation. Roll 'em."

I was sitting on my elevated platform, combing my hair. A lot of it had fallen out during the malnourished years in the camp, but now it was growing again. Not-Too had given up trying to jump up there with me and gone to sleep on her pillow below. Blue shot the beam out of his sphere and the holo played in front of me.

Only not the whole thing. This time he played only the brief scene where the big, patchy dog pulled the toddler back from falling into the cesspool. Blue played it once, twice, three times. Cold slid along my spine.

"You want Not-Too . . . you want this dog here to be trained to save children."

"This dog here does not behave correctly."

"Blue . . . How can I train a dog to save a child?"

"This dog here does not behave correctly."

"Maybe you haven't noticed, but we haven't got any fucking children for the dog to practice on!"

Long pause. "Do you want a child?"

"No!" Christ, he would kidnap one or buy one from the camp and I would be responsible for a kid along with nineteen semi-feral dogs. No.

"This dog here does not behave correctly. What to do now? The presentation."

"No, not the presentation. I saw it, *I saw it*. Blue . . . the other two humans who did not make the dogs behave correctly . . ."

"Killed."

"Yes. So you said. But they did get one dog to behave correctly, didn't they? Or maybe more than one. And then you just kept raising the bar higher. Water rescues, guiding the blind, finding lost people. Higher and higher."

But to all this, of course, Blue made no answer.

I wracked my brains to remember what I had ever heard, read, or seen about dog training. Not much. However, there's a problem with opening the door to memory: you can't control what strolls through. For the first time in years, my sleep was shattered by dreams.

I walked through a tiny garden, picking zinnias. From an open window came music, full and strong, an orchestra on CD. A cat paced beside me, purring. And there was someone else in the window, someone who called my name and I turned and—

I screamed. Clawed my way upright. The dogs started barking and howling. Blue floated from his corner, saying something. And Not-Too made a mighty leap, landed on my platform, and began licking my face.

"Stop it! Don't do that! I won't remember!" I shoved her so hard she fell off the platform onto the floor and began yelping. I put my head in my hands.

Blue said, "Are you not operative?"

"Leave me the fuck alone!"

Not-Too still yelped, shrill cries of pain. When I stopped shaking, I crawled off the platform and picked her up. Nothing seemed to be broken—although how would I know? Gradually she quieted. I gave her some cheese and put her back on her pillow. She wanted to stay with me but I wouldn't let her.

I would not remember. *I would not.* Law #5: Feel nothing.

We made a cesspool, or at least a pool. Blue depressed part of the floor to a depth of three feet and filled it with water. Not-Too considered this a swimming pool and loved to be in it, which was not what Blue wanted ("This water does not behave correctly"). I tried having the robot dump various substances into it until I found one that she disliked and I could tolerate: light-grade motor oil. A few small cans of oil like those in the dump created a polluted pool, not unlike Charleston Harbor. After every practice session I needed a bath.

But not Not-Too, because she wouldn't go into the "cesspool." I curled myself as small as possible, crouched at the side of the pool, and thrashed. After a few days, the dog would pull me back by my shirt. I moved into the pool. As long as she could reach me without getting any liquid on her, Not-Too happily played that game. As soon as I moved far enough out that I might actually need saving, she sat on her skinny haunches and looked away.

"This dog does not behave correctly."

I increased the cheese. I withheld the cheese. I pleaded and ordered and shunned and petted and yelled. Nothing worked. Meanwhile, the dream continued. The same dream, each time not greater in length but increasing in intensity. *I walked through a tiny garden, picking zinnias. From an open window came music, full and strong, an orchestra on CD. A cat paced beside me, purring. And there was someone else in the window, someone who called my name and I turned and—*

And woke screaming.

A cat. I had had a cat, before the War. Before everything. I had always had cats, my whole life. Independent cats, aloof and self-sufficient, admirably disdainful. Cats—

The dog below me whimpered, trying to get onto my platform to offer comfort I did not want.

I would not remember.

"This dog does not behave correctly," day after day.

I had Blue remove the oil from the pool. But by now Not-Too had been conditioned. She wouldn't go into even the clear water that she'd reveled in before.

"This dog does not behave correctly."

Then one day Blue stopped his annoying mantra, which scared me even more. Would I have any warning that I'd failed, or would I just die?

The only thing I could think of was to kill Blue first.

Blue was a computer. You disabled computers by turning them off, or cutting the power supply, or melting them in a fire, or dumping acid on them, or crushing them. But a careful search of the whole room revealed no switches or wires or anything that looked like a wireless control. A fire in this closed room, assuming I could start one, would kill me, too. Every kind of liquid or solid slid off Blue. And what would I crush him with, if that was even possible? A piece of cheese?

Blue was also—sort of—an intelligence. You could kill those by trapping them somewhere. My prison-or-sanctuary (depending on my mood) had no real "somewheres." And Blue would just dissolve any structure he found himself in.

What to do now?

I lay awake, thinking, all night, which at least kept me from dreaming. I came up with two ideas, both bad. Plan A depended on discussion, never Blue's strong suit.

"Blue, this dog does not behave correctly."

"No."

"This dog is not operative. I must make another dog behave correctly. Not this dog."

Blue floated close to Not-Too. She tried to bat at him. He circled her slowly, then returned to his position three feet above the ground. "This dog is operative."

"No. This dog *looks* operative. But this dog is not operative inside its head. I cannot make this dog behave correctly. I need a different dog."

A very long pause. "This dog is not operative inside its head."

"Yes."

"You can make another dog behave correctly. Like the presentation."

"Yes." It would at least buy me time. Blue must have seen "not operative" dogs and humans in the dump; God knows there were enough of them out there. Madmen, rabid animals, druggies raving just before they died or were shot. And next time I would add something besides oil to the pool; there must be something that Blue would consider noxious enough to simulate a cesspool but that a dog would enter. If I had to, I'd use my own shit.

"This dog is not operative inside its head," Blue repeated, getting used to the idea. "You will make a different dog behave correctly."

"Yes!"

"Why the hell not?" And then, "I kill this dog."

"No!" The word was torn from me before I knew I was going to say anything. My hand, of its own volition, clutched at Not-Too. She jumped but didn't bite. Instead, maybe sensing my fear, she cowered behind me, and I started to yell.

"You can't just kill everything that doesn't behave like you want! People, dogs . . . you can't just kill everything! You can't just . . . I had a cat . . . I never wanted a dog, but this dog . . . she's behaving correctly for her! For a fucking traumatized dog and you can't just—I had a dog I mean a cat I had . . . I had . . ."

—from an open window came music, full and strong, an orchestra on CD. A cat paced beside me, purring. And there was someone else in the window, someone who called my name and I turned and—

"I had a child!"

Oh, God no no no . . . It all came out then, the memories and the grief and the pain I had pushed away for three solid years in order to survive . . . *Feel nothing* . . . Zack Zack *Zack* shot down by soldiers like a dog *Look, Mommy, here I am Mommy look* . . .

I curled in a ball on the floor and screamed and wanted to die. Grief had been postponed so long that it was a tsunami. I sobbed and screamed; I don't know for how long. I think I wasn't quite sane. No human should ever have to experience that much pain. But of course they do.

However, it can't last too long, that height of pain, and when the flood passed and my head was bruised from banging it on the hard floor, I was still alive, still inside the Dome, still surrounded by barking dogs. Zack was still dead. Blue floated nearby, unchanged, a casually murderous robot who would not supply flesh to dogs as food but who would kill anything he was programmed to destroy. And he had no reason not to murder me.

Not-Too sat on her haunches, regarding me from sad brown eyes, and I did the one thing I told myself I never would do again. I reached for her warmth. I put my arms around her and hung on. She let me.

Maybe that was the decision point. I don't know.

When I could manage it, I staggered to my feet. Taking hold of the rope that was Not-Too's leash, I wrapped it firmly around my hand. "Blue," I said, forcing the words past the grief clogging my throat, "make garbage."

He did. That was the basis of Plan B; that Blue made most things I asked of him. Not release, or mercy, but at least rooms and platforms and pools and garbage. I walked toward the garbage spilling from the usual place in the wall.

"More garbage! Bigger garbage! I need garbage to make this dog behave correctly!"

The reeking flow increased. Tires, appliances, diapers, rags, cans, furniture. The dogs' howling rose to an insane, deafening pitch. Not-Too pressed close to me.

"Bigger garbage!"

The chassis of a motorcycle, twisted beyond repair in some unimaginable accident, crashed into the room. The place on the wall from which the garbage spewed was misty gray, the same fog that the Dome had become when I had been taken inside it. Half a sofa clattered through. I grabbed Not-Too, dodged behind the sofa, and hurled both of us through the onrushing garbage and into the wall.

A broken keyboard struck me in the head, and the gray went black.

Chill. Cold with a spot of heat, which turned out to be Not-Too lying on top of me. I pushed her off and tried to sit up. Pain lanced through my head and when I put a hand to my forehead, it came away covered with blood. The same blood streamed into my eyes, making it hard to see. I wiped the blood away with the front of my shirt, pressed my hand hard on my forehead, and looked around.

Not that there was much to see. The dog and I sat at the end of what appeared to be a corridor. Above me loomed a large machine of some type with a chute pointed at the now-solid wall. The machine was silent. Not-Too quivered and pressed her furry side into mine, but she, too, stayed silent. I couldn't hear the nineteen dogs on the other side of the wall, couldn't see Blue, couldn't smell anything except Not-Too, who had made a small yellow puddle on the floor.

There was no room to stand upright under the machine, so I moved away from it. Strips ripped from the bottom of my shirt made a bandage that at least kept blood out of my eyes. Slowly Not-Too and I walked along the corridor.

No doors. No openings or alcoves or machinery. Nothing until we reached the end, which was the same uniform material as everything else. Gray, glossy, hard. Dead. Blue did not appear. Nothing appeared, or disappeared, or lived. We walked back and studied the overhead bulk of the machine. It had no dials or keys or features of any kind.

I sat on the floor, largely because I couldn't think what else to do, and Not-Too climbed into my lap. She was too big for this and I pushed her away. She pressed against me, trembling.

"Hey," I said, but not to her. Zack in the window *Look, Mommy, here I am Mommy look. . . .* But if I started down that mental road, I would be lost. Anger was better than memory. Anything was better than memory. "Hey!" I screamed. "Hey, you bastard Blue, what to do now? What to do now, you Dome shits, whoever you are?"

Nothing except, very faint, an echo of my own useless words.

I lurched to my feet, reaching for the anger, cloaking myself in it. Not-Too sprang to her feet and backed away from me.

"What to do now? What bloody fucking hell to do *now?*"

Still nothing, but Not-Too started back down the empty corridor. I was glad to transfer my anger to something visible, real, living. "There's nothing there, Not-Too. *Nothing*, you stupid dog!"

She stopped halfway down the corridor and began to scratch at the wall.

I stumbled along behind her, one hand clamped to my head. What the hell was she doing? This piece of wall was identical to every other piece of wall. Kneeling slowly—it hurt my head to move fast—I studied Not-Too. Her scratching increased in frenzy and her nose twitched, as if she smelled something. The wall, of course, didn't respond; nothing in this place responded to anything. Except—

Blue had learned words from me, had followed my commands. Or had he just transferred my command to the Dome's unimaginable machinery, instructing it to do anything I said that fell within permissible limits? Feeling like an idiot, I said to the wall, "Make garbage." Maybe if it complied and the garbage contained food . . .

The wall made no garbage. Instead it dissolved into the familiar gray fog, and Not-Too immediately jumped through, barking frantically.

Every time I had gone through a Dome wall, my situation had gotten worse. But what other choices were there? Wait for Blue to find and kill me, starve to death, curl up and die in the heart of a mechanical alien mini-world I didn't understand. Not-Too's barking increased in pitch and volume. She was terrified or excited or thrilled. . . . How would I know? I pushed through the gray fog.

Another gray metal room, smaller than Blue had made my prison but with the same kind of cages against the far wall. Not-Too saw me and raced from the cages to me. Blue floated toward me. . . . No, not Blue. This metal sphere was dull green, the color of shady moss. It said, "No human comes into this area."

"Guess again," I said and grabbed the trailing end of Not-Too's rope. She'd jumped up on me once and then had turned to dash back to the cages.

"No human comes into this area," Green repeated. I waited to see what the robot would do about it. Nothing.

Not-Too tugged on her rope, yowling. From across the room came answering barks, weirdly off. Too uneven in pitch, with a strange undertone. Blood, having saturated my makeshift bandage, once again streamed into my eyes. I swiped at it with one hand, turned to keep my gaze on Green, and let Not-Too pull me across the floor. Only when she stopped did I turn to look at the mesh-topped cages. Vertigo swooped over me.

Mangy was the source of the weird barks, a Mangy altered not beyond recognition but certainly beyond anything I could have imagined. Her mange was gone, along with all her fur. The skin beneath was now gray, the same gunmetal gray as everything else in the Dome. Her ears, the floppy poodle ears, were so long they trailed on the floor of her cage, and so was her tail. Holding on to the tail was a gray grub.

Not a grub. Not anything Earthly. Smooth and pulpy, it was about the size of a human head and vaguely oval. I saw no openings on the thing but Mangy's elongated tail disappeared into the doughy mass, and so there must have been at least one orifice. As Mangy jumped at the bars, trying to get at Not-Too, the grub was whipped back and forth across the cage floor. It left a slimy trail. The dog seemed oblivious.

"This dog is ready," Blue had said.

Behind me Green said, "No human comes into this area."

"Up yours."

"The human does not behave correctly."

That got my attention. I whirled around to face Green, expecting to be vaporized like the dead puppy, the dead Vicious. I thought I was already dead—and then I welcomed the thought. *Look, Mommy, here I am Mommy look.* . . . The laws of survival that had protected me for so long couldn't protect me against memory, not anymore. I was ready to die.

Instead, Mangy's cage dissolved, she bounded out, and she launched herself at me.

Poodles are not natural killers, and this one was small. However, Mangy was doing her level best to destroy me. Her teeth closed on my arm. I screamed and shook her off, but the next moment she was biting my leg above my boot, darting hysterically toward and away from me, biting my legs at each lunge. The grub, or whatever it was, lashed around at the end of her new tail. As I flailed at the dog with both hands, my bandage fell off. Fresh blood from my head wound blinded me. I stumbled and fell and she was at my face.

Then she was pulled off, yelping and snapping and howling.

Not-Too had Mangy in her jaws. Twice as big as the poodle, she shook Mangy violently and then dropped her. Mangy whimpered and rolled over on her belly. Not-Too sprinted over to me and stood in front of me, skinny legs braced and scrawny hackles raised, growling protectively.

Dazed, I got to my feet. Blood, mine and the dogs', slimed everything. The floor wasn't trying to reabsorb it. Mangy, who'd never really liked me, stayed down with her belly exposed in submission, but she didn't seem to be badly hurt. The grub still latched onto the end of her tail like a gray tumor. After a moment she rolled onto her feet and began to nuzzle the grub, one baleful eye on Not-Too: *Don't you come near this thing!* Not-Too stayed in position, guarding me.

Green said—and I swear its mechanical voice held satisfaction, no one will ever be able to tell me any different—"These dogs behave correctly."

The other cages held grubs, one per cage. I reached through the front bars and gingerly touched one. Moist, firm, repulsive. It didn't respond to my touch, but Green did. He was beside me in a flash. "No!"

"Sorry." His tone was dog-disciplining. "Are these the masters?"

No answer.

"What to do now? One dog for one . . ." I waved at the cages.

"Yes. When these dogs are ready."

This dog is ready, Blue had said of Mangy just before she was tumbled into the floor. Ready to be a pet, a guardian, a companion, a service animal to alien . . . what? The most logical answer was "children." Lassie, Rin Tin Tin, Benji, Little Guy. A boy and his dog. The aliens found humans dangerous or repulsive or uncaring or whatever, but dogs . . . You could count on dogs for your kids. Almost, and for the first time, I could see the point of the Domes.

"Are the big masters here? The adults?"

No answer.

"The masters are not here," I said. "They just set up the Domes as . . . as nurseries-slash-obedience schools." And to that statement I didn't even expect an answer. If the adults had been present, surely one or more would have come running when an alien blew into its nursery wing via a garbage delivery. There would have been alarms or something. Instead there was only Blue and Green and whatever 'bots inhabited whatever place held the operating room. Mangy's skin and ears and tail had been altered to fit the needs of these grubs. And maybe her voice box, too, since her barks now had that weird undertone, like the scrape of metal across rock. Somewhere there was an OR.

I didn't want to be in that somewhere.

Green seemed to have no orders to kill me, which made sense because he wasn't programmed to have me here. I wasn't on his radar, which raised other problems.

"Green, make bread."

Nothing.

"Make water."

Nothing.

But two indentations in a corner of the floor, close to a section of wall, held water and dog-food pellets. I tasted both, to the interest of Not-Too and the growling of Mangy. Not too bad. I scooped all the rest of the dog food out of the trough. As soon as the last piece was out, the wall filled it up again. If I died, it wasn't going to be of starvation.

A few minutes ago, I had wanted to die. *Zack* . . .

No. Push the memory away. Life was shit, but I didn't want death, either. The realization was visceral, gripping my stomach as if that organ had been laid in a vise, or . . . There is no way to describe it. The feeling just was, its own justification. I wanted to live.

Not-Too lay a short distance away, watching me. Mangy was back in her cage with the grub on her tail. I sat up and looked around. "Green, this dog is not ready."

"No. What to do now?"

Well, that answered one question. Green was programmed to deal with dogs, and you didn't ask dogs "what to do now." So Green must be in some sort of communication with Blue, but the communication didn't seem to include orders about me. For a star-faring advanced race, the aliens certainly weren't very good at LANs. Or maybe they just didn't care—how would I know how an alien thinks?

I said, "I make this dog behave correctly." The all-purpose answer.

"Yes."

Did Green know details—that Not-Too refused to pull me from oily pools and thus was an obedience-school failure? It didn't seem like it. I could pretend to train Not-Too—I could actually train her, only not for water rescue—and stay here, away from the killer Blue, until . . . until what? As a survival plan, this one was shit. Still, it followed Laws #1 and #3: Take what you can get and never volunteer. And I couldn't think of anything else.

"Not-Too," I said wearily, still shaky from my crying jag, "sit."

"Days" went by, then weeks. Not-Too learned to beg, roll over, bring me a piece of dog food, retrieve my thrown boot, lie down, and balance a pellet of dog food on her nose. I had no idea if any of these activities would be useful to an alien, but as long as Not-Too and I were "working," Green left us alone. No threats, no presentations, no objections. We were behaving correctly. I still hadn't thought of any additional plan. At night I dreamed of Zack and woke in tears, but not with the raging insanity of my first day of memory. Maybe you can only go through that once.

Mangy's grub continued to grow, still fastened onto her tail. The other grubs looked exactly the same as before. Mangy growled if I came too close to her, so I didn't. Her grub seemed to be drying out as it got bigger. Mangy licked it and slept curled around it and generally acted like some mythical dragon guarding a treasure box. Had the aliens bonded those two with some kind of pheromones I couldn't detect? I had no way of knowing.

Mangy and her grub emerged from their cage only to eat, drink, or shit, which she did in a far corner. Not-Too and I used the same corner, and all of our shit and piss dissolved odorlessly into the floor. Eat your heart out, Thomas Crapper.

As days turned into weeks, flesh returned to my bones. Not-Too also lost her starved look. I talked to her more and more, her watchful silence preferable to Green's silence or, worse, his inane and limited repertoires of answers. *"Green, I had a child named Zack. He was shot in the war. He was five." "This dog is not ready."*

Well, none of us ever are.

Not-Too started to sleep curled against my left side. This was a problem because I thrashed in my sleep, which woke her, so she growled, which woke me. Both of us became sleep-deprived and irritable. In the camp, I had slept twelve hours a day. Not much else to do, and sleep both conserved energy and kept me out of sight. But the camp was becoming distant in my mind. Zack was shatteringly vivid, with my life before the war, and the Dome was vivid, with Mangy and Not-Too and a bunch of alien grubs. Everything in between was fading.

Then one "day"—after how much time? I had no idea—Green said, "This dog is ready."

My heart stopped. Green was going to take Not-Too to the hidden OR, was going to—"No!"

Green ignored me. But he also ignored Not-Too. The robot floated over to Mangy's cage and dissolved it. I stood and craned my neck for a better look.

The grub was hatching.

Its "skin" had become very dry, a papery gray shell. Now it cracked along the top, parallel to Mangy's tail. She turned and regarded it quizzically, this thing wriggling at the end of her very long tail, but didn't attack or even growl. Those must have been some pheromones.

Was I really going to be the first and only human to see a Dome alien?

I was not. The papery covering cracked more and dropped free of the dog's tail. The thing inside wiggled forward, crawling out like a snake shedding its skin. It wasn't a grub but it clearly wasn't a sentient being, either. A larva? I'm no zoologist. This creature was as gray as everything else in the Dome but it had legs, six, and heads, two. At least, they might have been heads. Both had various indentations. One "head" crept forward, opened an orifice, and fastened itself back onto Mangy's tail. She continued to gaze at it. Beside me, Not-Too growled.

I whirled to grab frantically for her rope. Not-Too had no alterations to make her accept this . . . thing as anything other than a small animal to attack. If she did—

I turned just in time to see the floor open and swallow Not-Too. Green said again, "This dog is ready," and the floor closed.

"No! Bring her back!" I tried to pound on Green with my fists. He bobbed in the air under my blows. "Bring her back! Don't hurt her! Don't . . ." do what?

Don't turn her into a nursemaid for a grub, oblivious to me.

Green moved off. I followed, yelling and pounding. Neither one, of course, did the slightest good. Finally I got it together enough to say, "When will Not-Too come back?"

"This human does not behave correctly."

I looked despairingly at Mangy. She lay curled on her side, like a mother dog nursing puppies. The larva wasn't nursing, however. A shallow trough had appeared in the floor and filled with some viscous glop, which the larva was scarfing up with its other head. It looked repulsive.

Law #4: Notice everything.

"Green . . . okay. Just . . . okay. When will Not-Too come back here?"

No answer; what does time mean to a machine?

"Does the other dog return here?"

"Yes."

"Does the other dog get a . . ." A what? I pointed at Mangy's larva.

No response. I would have to wait.

But not, apparently, alone. Across the room another dog tumbled, snarling, from the same section of wall I had once come through. I recognized it as one of the nineteen left in the other room, a big black beast with powerful-looking jaws. It righted itself and charged at me. There was no platform, no place to hide.

"No! Green, no, it will hurt me! This dog does not behave—"

Green didn't seem to do anything. But even as the black dog leapt toward me, it faltered in mid-air. The next moment, it lay dead on the floor.

The moment after that, the body disappeared, vaporized.

My legs collapsed under me. That was what would happen to me if I failed in my training task, was what had presumably happened to the previous two human failures. And yet it wasn't fear that made me sit so abruptly on the gray floor. It was relief, and a weird kind of gratitude. Green had protected me, which was more than Blue had ever done. Maybe Green was brighter, or I had proved my worth more, or in this room as opposed to the other room, all dog-training equipment was protected. I was dog-training equipment. It was stupid to feel grateful.

I felt grateful.

Green said, "This dog does not—"

"I know, *I know.* Listen, Green, what to do now? Bring another dog here?"

"Yes."

"*I* choose the dog. I am the . . . the dog leader. Some dogs behave correctly, some dogs do not behave correctly. I choose. Me."

I held my breath. Green considered, or conferred with Blue, or consulted its alien and inadequate programming. Who the hell knows? The robot had been created by a race that preferred Earth dogs to whatever species usually nurtured their young, if any did. Maybe Mangy and Not-Too would replace parental care on the home planet, thus introducing the idea of babysitters. All I wanted was to not be eaten by some canine nanny-trainee.

"Yes," Green said finally, and I let out my breath.

A few minutes later, eighteen dog cages tumbled through the wall like so much garbage, the dogs within bouncing off their bars and mesh tops, furious and noisy. Mangy jumped, curled more protectively around her oblivious larva, and added her weird, rock-scraping bark to the din. A cage grew up around her. When the cages had stopped bouncing, I walked among them like some kind of tattered lord, choosing.

"This dog, Green." It wasn't the smallest dog but it had stopped barking the soonest. I hoped that meant it wasn't a grudge holder. When I put one hand into its cage, it didn't bite me, also a good sign. The dog was phenomenally ugly, the jowls on its face drooping from small, rheumy eyes into a sort of folded ruff around its short neck. Its body seemed to be all front, with stunted and short back legs. When it stood, I saw it was male.

"This dog? What to do now?"

"Send all the other dogs back."

The cages sank into the floor. I walked over to the feeding trough, scooped up handfuls of dog food, and put the pellets into my only pocket that didn't have holes. "Make all the rest of the dog food go away."

It vaporized.

"Make this dog's cage go away."

I braced myself as the cage dissolved. The dog stood uncertainly on the floor, gazing toward Mangy, who snarled at him. I said, as commandingly as possible, "Ruff!"

He looked at me.

"Ruff, come."

To my surprise, he did. Someone had trained this animal before. I gave him a pellet of dog food.

Green said, "This dog behaves correctly."

"Well, I'm really good," I told him, stupidly, while my chest tightened as I thought of Not-Too. The aliens, or their machines, did understand about anesthetic, didn't they? They wouldn't let her suffer too much? I would never know.

But now I *did* know something momentous. I had choices. I had chosen which room to train dogs in. I had chosen which dog to train. I had some control.

"Sit," I said to Ruff, who didn't, and I set to work.

Not-Too was returned to me three or four "days" later. She was gray and hairless, with an altered bark. A grub hung onto her elongated tail, undoubtedly the same one that had vanished from its cage while I was asleep. But unlike Mangy, who'd never liked either of us, Not-Too was ecstatic to see me. She wouldn't stay in her grub-cage against the wall but insisted on sleeping curled up next to me, grub and all. Green permitted this. I had become the alpha dog.

Not-Too liked Ruff, too. I caught him mounting her, her very long tail conveniently keeping her grub out of the way. Did Green understand the significance of this behavior? No way to tell.

We settled into a routine of training, sleeping, playing, eating. Ruff turned out to be sweet and playful but not very intelligent, and training took a long time. Mangy's grub grew very slowly, considering the large amount of glop it consumed. I grew, too; the waistband of my ragged pants got too tight and I discarded them, settling for a loin cloth, shirt, and my decaying boots. I talked to the dogs, who were much better conversationalists than Green since two of them at least pricked up their ears, made noises back at me, and wriggled joyfully at attention. Green would have been a dud at a cocktail party.

I don't know how long this all went on. Time began to lose meaning. I still dreamed of Zack and still woke in tears, but the dreams grew gentler and farther apart. When I cried, Not-Too crawled onto my lap, dragging her grub, and licked my chin. Her brown eyes shared my sorrow. I wondered how I had ever preferred the disdain of cats.

Not-Too got pregnant. I could feel the puppies growing inside her distended belly.

"Puppies will be easy to make behave correctly," I told Green, who said nothing. Probably he didn't understand. Some people need concrete visuals in order to learn.

Eventually, it seemed to me that Ruff was almost ready for his own grub. I mulled over how to mention this to Green but before I did, everything came to an end.

Clang! Clang! Clang!

I jerked awake and bolted upright. The alarm—a very human-sounding alarm—sounded all around me. Dogs barked and howled. Then I realized that it was a human alarm, coming from the Army camp outside the Dome, on the opposite side to the garbage dump. I could *see* the camp—in outline and faintly, as if through heavy gray fog. The Dome was dissolving.

"Green—what—no!"

Above me, transforming the whole top half of what had been the Dome, was the bottom of a solid saucer. Mangy, in her cage, floated upwards and disappeared into a gap in the saucer's underside. The other grub cages had already disappeared. I glimpsed a flash of metallic color through the gap: Blue. Green was halfway to the opening, drifting lazily upward. Beside me, both Not-Too and Ruff began to rise.

"No! No!"

I hung onto Not-Too, who howled and barked. But then my body froze. I couldn't move anything. My hands opened and Not-Too rose, yowling piteously.

"No! No!" And then, before I knew I was going to say it, "Take me, too!"

Green paused in mid-air. I began babbling.

"Take me! Take me! I can make the dogs behave correctly—I can—you need me! Why are you going? Take me!"

"Take this human?"

Not Green but Blue, emerging from the gap. Around me the Dome walls thinned more. Soldiers rushed toward us. Guns fired.

"Yes! What to do? Take this human! The dogs want this human!"

Time stood still. Not-Too howled and tried to reach me. Maybe that's what did it. I rose into the air just as Blue said, "Why the hell not?"

Inside—inside *what*?—I was too stunned to do more than grab Not-Too, hang on, and gasp. The gap closed. The saucer rose.

After a few minutes, I sat up and looked around. Gray room, filled with dogs in their cages, with grubs in theirs, with noise and confusion and the two robots. The sensation of motion ceased. I gasped, "Where . . . where are we going?"

Blue answered. "Home."

"Why?"

"The humans do not behave correctly." And then, "What to do now?"

We were leaving Earth in a flying saucer, and it was asking *me?*

Over time—I have no idea how much time—I actually got some answers from Blue. The humans "not behaving correctly" had apparently succeeding in breaching one of the Domes somewhere. They must have used a nuclear bomb, but that I couldn't verify. Grubs and dogs had both died, and so the aliens had packed up and left Earth. Without, as far as I could tell, retaliating. Maybe.

If I had stayed, I told myself, the soldiers would have shot me. Or I would have returned to life in the camp, where I would have died of dysentery or violence or cholera or starvation. Or I would have been locked away by whatever government still existed in the cities, a freak who had lived with aliens none of my story believed. I barely believed it myself.

I *am* a freak who lives with aliens. Furthermore, I live knowing that at any moment Blue or Green or their "masters" might decide to vaporize me. But that's really not much different from the uncertainty of life in the camp, and here I actually have some status. Blue produces whatever I ask for, once I get him to understand what that is. I have new clothes, good food, a bed, paper, a sort of pencil.

And I have the dogs. Mangy still doesn't like me. Her larva hasn't as yet done whatever it will do next. Not-Too's grub grows slowly, and now Ruff has one, too. Their three puppies are adorable and very trainable. I'm not so sure about the other seventeen dogs, some of whom look wilder than ever after their long confinement in small cages. Aliens are not, by definition, humane.

I don't know what it will take to survive when, and if, we reach "home" and I meet the alien adults. All I can do is rely on Jill's Five Laws of Survival:

#1: Take what you can get.
#2: Show no fear.
#3: Never volunteer.
#4: Notice everything.

But the Fifth Law has changed. As I lie beside Not-Too and Ruff, their sweet warmth and doggie-odor, I know that my first formulation was wrong. "Feel nothing"—that can take you some ways toward survival, but not very far. Not really.

Law #5: Take the risk. Love something.

The dogs whuff contentedly and we speed toward the stars.

the mists of time

TOM PURDOM

Tom Purdom made his first sale in 1957, to *Fantastic Universe*, and has subsequently sold to *Analog, The Magazine of Fantasy & Science Fiction, Star*, and most of the major magazines and anthologies. In recent years, he's become a frequent contributor to *Asimov's Science Fiction*. He is the author of one of the most unfairly forgotten SF novels of the '60s, the powerful and still-timely *Reduction in Arms*, about the difficulties of disarmament in the face of the mad proliferation of nuclear weapons, as well as such novels as *I Want the Stars, The Tree Lord of Imeten, Five Against Arlane*, and *The Barons of Behavior*. Purdom lives in Philadelphia, where he reviews classical music concerts for a local newspaper, and is at work on several new novels.

Here he takes us adventuring on the high seas in the dangerous sail-and-broadside days when the British Navy was slugging it out with slave traders, and tells a compelling and morally complex story that demonstrates that—like the present—the past is a more diverse and complicated place than we like to think of it having been, and that few people have just one motive for doing anything.

The cry from the lookout perked up every officer, rating, and common seaman on deck. The two-masted brig they were intercepting was being followed by sharks—a sure sign it was a slaver. Slave ships fouled the ocean with a trail of bodies as they worked their way across the Atlantic.

John Harrington was standing in front of the rear deckhouse when the midshipman's yell floated down from the mast. His three officers were loitering around him with their eyes fixed on the sails three miles off their port bow—a mass of wind-filled cloth that had aroused, once again, the hope that their weeks of tedious, eventless cruising were coming to an end.

The ship rolling under their own feet, HMS *Sparrow*, was a sixty-foot schooner—one of the smallest warships carried on the rolls of Her Majesty's navy. There was no raised quarterdeck her commander could pace in majestic isolation. The officers merely stood in front of the deckhouse and looked down a deck crowded with two boats, spare spars, and the sweating bodies of crewmen who were constantly working the big triangular sails into new positions in response to the shipmaster's efforts to draw the last increment of movement from the insipid push of the African coastal breezes. A single six-pound gun, mounted on a turntable, dominated the bow.

Sub-lieutenant Bonfors opened his telescope and pointed it at the other ship. He was a broad, well-padded young man, and he beamed at the image in his lenses with the smile of a gourmand who was contemplating a particularly interesting table.

"*Niggers*, gentlemen. She's low in the water, too. I believe a good packer can squeeze five hundred prime niggers into a hull that long—twenty-five hundred good English pounds if they're all still breathing and pulsing."

It was the paradox of time travel. You were there and you weren't there, the laws of physics prohibited it and it was the laws of physics that got you there. You were the cat that was neither dead nor alive, the photon that could be in two places at once, the wave function that hadn't collapsed. You slipped through a world in which you could see but not be seen, exist and not exist. Sometimes there was a flickering moment when you really were there—a moment, oddly enough, when they could see you and you couldn't see them. It was the paradox of time travel—a paradox built upon the contradictions and inconsistencies that lie at the heart of the sloppy, fundamentally unsolvable mystery human beings call the physical universe.

For Emory FitzGordon the paradox meant that he was crammed into an invisible, transparent space/time bubble, strapped into a two-chair rig shoulder to shoulder with a bony, hyperactive young woman, thirty feet above the tepid water twenty miles off the coast of Africa, six years after the young Princess Victoria had become Queen of England, Wales, Scotland, Ireland, and all the heathen lands Her government ruled beyond the seas. The hyperactive young woman, in addition, was an up-and-coming video auteur who possessed all the personality quirks traditionally associated with the arts.

"Four minute check completed," the hal running the bubble said. "Conditions on all four coordinates register satisfactory and stable. You have full clearance for two hours, provisional clearance for five hours."

Giva Lombardo's hands had already started bustling across the screen-bank attached to her chair. The cameras attached to the rig had started recording as soon as the bubble had completed the space/time relocation.

Giva was obviously rearranging the angles and magnifications chosen by the hal's programming.

"It didn't take them long to start talking about that twenty-five hundred pounds, did it?" Giva murmured.

John Harrington glanced at the other two officers. A hint of mischief flickered across his face. He tried to maintain a captainly gravity when he was on deck but he was, after all, only twenty-three.

"So how does that break down, Mr. Bonfors?"

"For the slaves alone," the stout sub-lieutenant said, "*conservatively*, it's two hundred and sixty pounds for you, eighty-nine for your hardworking first lieutenant, seventy-two for our two esteemed colleagues here, sixteen for the young gentleman in the lookout, and two and a half pounds for every hand in the crew. The value of the ship itself might increase every share by another fifth, depending on the judgement of our lords at the Admiralty."

The sailing master, Mr. Whitjoy, rolled his eyes at the sky. The gunnery officer, Sub-lieutenant Terry, shook his head.

"I see there's one branch of mathematics you seem to have thoroughly mastered, Mr. Bonfors," Terry said.

"I may not have your knowledge of the calculus and other arcane matters, Mr. Terry," Bonfors said, "but I know that the quantity of roast beef and claret a man can consume is directly related to the mass of his purse."

Harrington raised his head. His eyes ranged over the rigging as if he were inspecting every knot. It would take them two hours—perhaps two and a half—to close with the slave ship. *Sparrow* was small and lightly armed but he could at least be thankful she was faster than her opposition. Most of the ships the Admiralty assigned to the West African antislavery squadron were two-masted brigs that wallowed through the water like sick whales.

How would they behave when the shooting started? Should he be glad they were still bantering? This would be the first time any of them had actually faced an armed enemy. Mr. Whitjoy was a forty-year-old veteran of the struggle against the Corsican tyrant but his seagoing service had been limited to blockade duty in the last three years of the Napoleonic wars. For the rest of them—including their captain and all the hands—"active service" had been a placid round of uneventful cruises punctuated by interludes in the seamier quarters of foreign ports.

"We'll keep flying the Portuguese flag until we come into range," Harrington said. "We still have a bit of ship handling ahead of us. We may sail a touch faster than an overloaded slaver but let's not forget they have four guns on each side. Let's make sure we're positioned straight across their bow when we bring them to, Mr. Whitjoy."

Giva had leaped on the prize money issue during their first planning session. She hadn't known the British sailors received special financial bonuses when she had applied for the job. She had circled around the topic, once she became aware of it, as if she had been tethered to it with a leash.

The scholar assigned to oversee the project, Dr. Peter LeGrundy, was a specialist in the cultural and social history of the Victorian British Empire. Peter claimed he normally avoided the details of Victorian military history—a subject his colleagues associated with excessive popular appeal—but in this case he had obviously had to master the relevant complexities. The ships assigned to the West African antislavery patrol had received five pounds for every slave they liberated, as a substitute for the prize money they would have received if they had been fighting in a conventional nation-state war. Prize money had been a traditional wartime incentive. The wages the Crown paid its seaborne warriors had not, after all, been princely. The arbitrary five pound figure had actually been a rather modest compensation, in Peter's opinion, compared to the sums the *Sparrow*'s crew would have received in wartime, from a cargo the government could actually sell.

Peter had explained all that to Giva—several times. And received the same reaction each time.

"There were five hundred captives on that ship," Giva said. "Twenty-five hundred pounds would be what—two or three million today? Audiences aren't totally stupid, Peter. I think most of them will manage to see that the great antislavery crusade could be a very profitable little business."

John Harrington had been reading about the Napoleonic Wars ever since his youngest uncle had given him a biography of Lord Nelson for his ninth birthday. None of the books he had read had captured the stately tempo of naval warfare. He knew the British had spent three hours advancing toward the Franco-Spanish fleet at Trafalgar but most authors covered that phase of the battle in a handful of paragraphs and hurried straight to the thunder that followed. Lieutenant Bonfors and Lieutenant Terry both made two trips to their quarters while *Sparrow* plodded across the gentle African waves toward their quarry. They were probably visiting their chamber pots, Harrington presumed. Mr. Whitjoy, on the other hand, directed the handling of the ship with his usual stolid competence. Harrington thought he caught Whitjoy praying at one point, but the master could have been frowning at a patch of deck that needed a touch of the hollystone.

Harrington had stifled his own urge to visit the chamber pot. He had caught two of the hands smiling the second time Bonfors had trudged off the deck.

It had been Midshipman Montgomery who had spotted the sharks. The other midshipman, Davey Clarke, had replaced Montgomery in the lookout. Montgomery could have gone below but he was circling the deck instead. He stopped at the gun every few minutes and gave it a thorough inspection. Montgomery would be assisting Mr. Terry when the time came to open fire.

Giva had started defending her artistic integrity at the very beginning of her pre-hiring interview. "I get the final edit," Giva had advised the oversight committee. "I won't work under any other conditions. If it's got my name on it, it represents my take on the subject."

Giva had been in Moscow, working on a historical drama. Emory had been staring at seven head-and-shoulder images on his living room imaging stage and Giva had been the only participant in the montage who had chosen a setting that accented her status. All the other participants had selected neutral backdrops. Giva had arranged herself so the committee could see, just beyond her shoulder, two actors who were dressed in flat, twenty-first-century brain-link hats.

"There's one thing I absolutely have to say, Mr. FitzGordon," Giva said. "I appreciate your generosity. I will try to repay you by turning out the best possible product I can. But please don't think you can expect to have any influence on the way I do it. I'm not interested in creating public relations fog jobs for wealthy families."

Emory had listened to Giva's tirade with the thin, polite smile a tolerant parent might bestow on a child. "I wouldn't expect you to produce a fog job," Emory responded. "I believe the facts in this case will speak for themselves. I can't deny that I specified this particular incident when I offered the agency this grant partly because my ancestor was involved in it. I wouldn't have known the Royal Navy had engaged in an antislavery campaign if it hadn't been part of our family chronicles. But I also feel this episode is a typical example of the courage and devotion of a group of men who deserve to be remembered and honored. The crews of the West African antislavery patrol saved a hundred thousand human beings from slavery. They deserve a memorial that has been created by an honest, first-class artist."

The committee had already let Emory know Giva Lombardo was the candidate they wanted to hire. Giva had friends in the Agency for Chronautical Studies, it seemed.

She also had ability and the kind of name recognition that would attract an audience. Emory had been impressed with both the docs that had catapulted Giva out of the would-be class. The first doc had been a one-hour essay on women who bought sexually enhancing personality modifications. The second had been a rhapsodic portrait of a cruise on a fully automated sailing ship; the cruise doc was essentially an advertisement funded by the cruise company but it had aroused the enthusiasm of the superaesthete audience.

Emory's family had been dealing with artists for a hundred and fifty years. His great-grandfather's encounter with the architect who designed his primary residence was a standard item in popular accounts of the history of architecture. It had become a family legend encrusted with advice and observations. *All interactions between artists and the rich hinge on one basic fact*, Emory's great-grandfather had said. *You need the creatives. The creatives need your money.*

Harrington placed his hands behind his back. The approach was coming to an end. Mr. Whitjoy had placed *Sparrow* on a course that would cross the slaver's bow in just four or five minutes.

He took a deep breath and forced the tension out of his neck muscles. He was the captain of a ship of war. He must offer his crew a voice that sounded confident and unperturbed.

"Let's show them our true colors, Mr. Whitjoy. You may advise them of our request as soon as we start to raise our ensign, Mr. Terry."

Lieutenant Bonfors led the boarding party. The slaver hove to in response to Lieutenant Terry's shot across its bow and Lieutenant Bonfors settled his bulk in the stern of a longboat and assumed a rigid, upright dignity that reminded Emory of the recordings of his great-grandfather he had viewed when he had been a child. Harrison FitzGordon had been an ideal role model, in the opinion of Emory's father. He was courteous to everyone he encountered, according to the family catechism, but he never forgot his position in society. He always behaved like someone who assumed the people around him would treat him with deference—just as Lieutenant Bonfors obviously took it for granted that others would row and he would be rowed.

Bonfors maintained the same air of haughty indifference when he hauled himself aboard the slaver and ran his eyes down its guns. Two or three crewmen were lounging near the rear of each gun. Most of them had flintlock pistols stuck in their belts.

A tall man in a loose blue coat hurried across the deck. He held out his hand and Bonfors put his own hands behind his back.

"I am Sub-lieutenant Barry Richard Bonfors of Her Majesty's Ship *Sparrow*. I am here to inspect your ship and your papers in accordance with the treaties currently in effect between my government and the government of the nation whose flag is flying from your masthead."

"I am William Zachary," the officer in the blue coat said, "and I am the commander of this ship. If you will do me the honor of stepping into my cabin, I will be happy to present you with our papers."

"I would prefer to start with an inspection of your hold."

"I'm afraid that won't be possible, Sub-lieutenant. I assure you our papers will give you all the information you need."

"The treaties in effect between our countries require the inspection of your entire ship, sir. I would be neglecting my duties if I failed to visit your hold."

Captain Zachary gestured at the guns. "I have two twelve-pound guns and two eighteen pounders on each side of my ship, Sub-lieutenant. You have, as far as I can tell, one six pounder. I have almost fifty hands. What do you have? Twenty-five? And some of them boys? I'm certain a visit to my cabin and an inspection of my papers will provide you with a satisfactory report to your superiors. As you will see from our papers, our hold is stuffed with jute and bananas."

Zachary was speaking with an accent that sounded, to Emory's ear, a lot like some of the varieties of English emitted by the crew on the *Sparrow*. Giva's microphone arrangement had picked up some of the cries coming from the slaver's crew as Bonfors had made his progress across the waters and Emory had heard several examples of the best-known English nouns and verbs. The ship was flying a Brazilian flag, Emory assumed, because it offered the crew legal advantages they would have missed if they had sailed under their true colors. British citizens who engaged in the slave trade could be hanged as pirates.

The legal complexities of the antislavery crusade had been one of the subjects that had amused Emory when he had been a boy. The officers of the West African Squadron had operated under legal restrictions that were so complicated the Admiralty had issued them an instruction manual they could carry in their uniforms. The Royal Navy could stop the ships of some nations and not others and it could do some things on one country's ships and other things on others.

Emory had been five when he had first heard about John Harrington's exploits off the African coast. Normally the FitzGordon adults just mentioned it now and then. You were reminded you had an ancestor who had liberated slaves when your elders felt you were spending too much time thinking about some of the other things your ancestors had done, such as their contributions to the coal mining and timber cutting industries. In Emory's case, it had become a schoolboy enthusiasm. He had scoured the data banks for information on Lieutenant John Harrington and the great fifty-year struggle in which Harrington had participated. Almost no one outside of his family had heard about the Royal Navy's antislavery campaign, but the historians who had studied it had all concluded it was one of the great epics of the sea. Young officers in small ships had fought the slavers for over half a century. They had engaged in hotly contested ship-to-ship actions. They had ventured up the rivers that communicated with the interior and attacked fortified slaveholding pens. Thousands of British seamen had died from the diseases that infested the African coast. The African slave markets north of the equator had been shut down. One hundred thousand men, women, and children had been rescued from the horrors of the slave ships.

The campaign had been promoted by a British politician, Lord Palmerston, who had tried to negotiate a general international treaty outlawing the slave trade. Palmerston had failed to achieve his goal and British diplomats had been forced to negotiate special agreements country by country. The officers on the spot were supposed to keep all the agreements straight and remember they could be fined, or sued, if they looked in the wrong cupboard or detained the wrong ship.

In this case, the situation was relatively straightforward. The ship was flying the flag of Brazil and the *Sparrow* therefore had the right to examine its papers and search its hull. If the searchers found any evidence the ship was engaging in the slave trade—such as the presence of several hundred chained Africans—the *Sparrow* could seize the slaver and bring the ship, its crew, and all its contents before the courts the navy had established in Freetown, Sierra Leone.

"Look at that," Emory said. "Look at the way he's handling himself."

Bonfors had turned his back on Captain Zachary. He was walking toward the ladder on the side of the ship with the same unhurried serenity he had exhibited when he came aboard.

Did Bonfors's back itch? Was he counting the number of steps that stretched between his present position and the minimal safety he would enjoy when he reached the boat? For Emory it was a thrilling moment—a display of the values and attitudes that had shaped his own conduct since he had been a child. Most of the officers on the *Sparrow* shared a common heritage. Their family lines had been molded, generation after generation, by the demands of the position they occupied in their society.

"You are now provisionally cleared for six hours total," the hal said. "All coordinates register satisfactory and stable."

The slaver was turning. Harrington noted the hands in the rigging making minor adjustments to the sails and realized the slaver's bow was shifting to the right—so it could bring its four starboard guns to bear on *Sparrow*.

Mr. Whitjoy had seen the movement, too. His voice was already bellowing orders. He had been told to hold *Sparrow* lined up across the slaver's bows. He didn't need further instructions.

Conflicting courses churned across Harrington's brain. Bonfors had reboarded his boat and he was still crossing the gap between the ships. The slave ship couldn't hit the boat with the side guns but it had a small chaser on the bow—a four pounder that could shatter the boat with a single lucky shot. The wind favored the slaver, too. The two ships had hove to with the wind behind the slaver, hitting its sails at a twenty degree angle. . . .

He hurried down the narrow deck toward the bow. Terry and Montgomery both looked at him expectantly. The swivel gun was loaded with chain shot. The slow match smoldered in a bucket.

"Let's give our good friend Mr. Bonfors time to get aboard," Harrington said.

"Aren't you afraid they'll fire on the boat with their chaser?" Montgomery said. "Sir."

Terry started to say something and Harrington stopped him with his hand. Montgomery should have kept his thoughts to himself but this wasn't the time to rebuke him.

"It's obvious Mr. Bonfors didn't finish the inspection," Harrington said. "But we won't be certain they refused to let him go below until he makes his report. We don't want to give the lawyers any unnecessary grounds for complaint."

He glanced around the men standing near the gun. "Besides, everybody says these slavers tend to be poor shots. They're businessmen. They go to sea to make money."

He paused for what he hoped would be an effect. "We go to sea to make *war*."

Montgomery straightened. Harrington thought he saw a light flash in the eyes of one of the seamen in the gun crew. He turned away from the gun and made his way toward the stern with his hands behind his back, in exactly the same pose his second commanding officer, Captain Ferris, would have assumed. A good commander had to be an actor. Good actors never ruined an exit line with too much talk.

Emory had started campaigning for Giva's removal a week after he had audited the first planning meeting. Giva had nagged at the prize money issue for a tiresome fifteen minutes at the end of the fourth meeting and Emory had maintained his link to Peter LeGrundy after she had exited. Giva had still been in Russia at that state of their association. Emory was staying at his New York residence, where he was sampling the opening premieres of the entertainment season. Peter had based himself in London so he could take a firsthand look at the Royal Navy archives.

"Are you really sure we can't do anything about her supporters in the chronautical bureaucracy?" Emory said. "It seems to me there should be some *small* possibility we can overcome their personal predilections and convince them she has a bias that is obviously incompatible with scholarship. A ten-minute conversation with her would probably be sufficient."

"She's peppery, Emory. She feels she has to assert herself. She's young and she's an artist."

"And what's she going to be like when she's actually recording? We'll only have one opportunity, Peter—the only opportunity anybody will ever have. Whatever she records, that's it."

Under the rules laid down by the chrono bureaucrats, the *Sparrow*'s encounter with the slaver was surrounded by a restricted zone that encompassed hundreds of square miles of ocean and twenty hours of time. No one knew what would happen if a bubble entered a space/time volume occupied by another bubble—and the bureaucrats had decided they would avoid the smallest risk they would ever find out. The academics and fund-raisers who had written the preamble to the agency's charter had decreed that its chrononauts would "dispel the mists of time with disciplined on-site observations," and the careerists and political appointees who ran the agency had decreed each site would receive only one dispelling. Once their bubble left the restricted zone, no one else would ever return to it.

"She's what they want," Peter said. "I've counted the votes. There's only one way you can get her out of that bubble—withdraw your grant and cancel the project."

"And let the media have a fiesta reporting on the rich idler who tried to bribe a committee of dedicated scholars."

Peter was being cautious, in Emory's opinion. He could have changed the committee's mind if he had made a determined effort. Giva had flaunted her biases as if she thought they were a fashion statement. But Peter also knew he would make some permanent enemies among the losing minority if he pressed his case.

Peter was a freelance scholar who lived from grant to grant. He had never managed to land a permanent academic position. He was balancing two forces that could have a potent impact on his future: a rich individual who could be a fertile source of grants and a committee composed of scholars who could help him capture a permanent job.

Emory could, of course, offer Peter some inducements that might overcome his respect for Giva's supporters. But that was a course that had its own risks. You never knew when an academic might decide his scholarly integrity had to be asserted. In the end, Emory had adopted a more straightforward approach and applied for a seat in the bubble under the agency's Chrono Tourist program. The extra passenger would cost the agency nothing and the fee would increase his grant by thirty percent. Giva would still control the cameras on the bubble but he could make his own amateurish record with his personal recording implant. He would have evidence he could use to support any claim that she had distorted the truth.

Harrington could have leaned over the side of the ship and called for a report while Bonfors was still en route but he was certain Captain Ferris would never have done that. Neither would Nelson. Instead, he stood by the deck-house and remained at his post while Bonfors climbed over the side, saluted the stern, and marched across the deck.

"He threatened me," Bonfors said. "He pointed at his guns and told me I could learn all I needed to know from his account books."

"He refused to let you visit the hold?"

"He told me I could learn all I needed from his books. He told me he had eight guns and fifty hands and we only had one gun and twenty-five."

Harrington frowned. Would a court interpret that as a threat? Could a lawyer claim Bonfors had deliberately misinterpreted the slave captain's words?

"It was a clear refusal," Bonfors said. "He gave me no indication he was going to let me inspect the hold."

Harrington turned toward the gun. He sucked in a good lungful and enjoyed a small pulse of satisfaction when he heard his voice ring down the ship.

"You may fire at your discretion, Mr. Terry."

Montgomery broke into a smile. Terry said something to his crew and the lead gunner drew the slow match from its bucket.

Terry folded his arms over his chest and judged the rise and fall of the two ships. Chain shot consisted of two balls connected by a length of chain. It could spin through the enemy rigging and wreak havoc on any rope or wood that intersected its trajectory.

Terry moved his arm. The lead gunner laid the end of the match across the touchhole.

It was the first time in his life Harrington had stood on a ship that was firing on other human beings. It was the moment he had been preparing for since he had been a twelve-year-old novice at the Naval School at Portsmouth, but the crash of the gun still caught him by surprise.

Montgomery was standing on tiptoe staring at the other ship. Terry was already snapping out orders. The sponger was pulling his tool out of its water bucket. Drill and training were doing their job. On the entire ship, there might have been six men who could feel the full weight of the moment, undistracted by the demands of their posts—and one of them was that supreme idler, the commanding officer.

The slaver's foremast quivered. A rip spread across a topsail. Bonfors pulled his telescope out of his coat and ran it across the slaver's upper rigging.

"I can see two lines dangling from the foretopsail," Bonfors said.

Harrington was playing his own telescope across the slaver's deck. Four men had gathered around the bowchaser. The two ships were positioned so its ball would hit the *Sparrow* toward the rear midships—a little forward of the exact spot where he was standing.

He had assumed they should start by destroying the slaver's sails. Then, when there was no danger their quarry could slip away, they could pick it off at their leisure, from positions that kept them safe from its broadsides. Should he change that plan merely because he was staring at the muzzle of the enemy gun? Wouldn't it make more sense to fire at the gun? Even though it was a small, hard-to-hit target?

It was a tempting thought. The slavers might even strike their colors if the shot missed the stern gun and broke a few bodies as it hurtled down the deck.

It was a thought generated by fear.

"Well started, Mr. Terry. Continue as you are."

The slaver's gun flashed. There was a short pause—just time enough to feel himself stiffen—and then, almost simultaneously, his brain picked up the crash of the gun and the thud of the ball striking the side of *Sparrow*'s hull.

The ball had hit the ship about where he had guessed it would. If it had been aimed a few degrees higher, it would have crossed the deck three steps to his right.

The *Sparrow*'s gun fired its second shot moments after the slaver's ball hit the hull. The sponger shoved his tool down the gun barrel, the crew fell into their drill, and the *Sparrow* hurled a third ball across the gap while the slaver's crew was still loading their second shot.

"The slaver's got a crew working on the rear boat," Giva said.

Emory had been watching the two gun crews and looking for signs they were actually creating some damage. The third shot from the *Sparrow*'s gun had drawn an excited, arms-raised leap from the midshipman posted with the gun crew. The upper third of the slaver's forward mast had bounced away from the lower section, and sagged against the rigging.

Harrington's report to the Admiralty said the slaver had brought out a boat and used it to pull the ship around to bring its broadside into play. Harrington hadn't said when they had lowered the boat. Emory had assumed they had done it after the battle had raged for a while.

"It looks like they're going to lower it on the other side of their ship," Emory said. "Is that going to cause any problems?"

"The rotation program can correct for most of the deficiencies. We can always have a talking head explain some of the tactics—some professor who's goofy about old weapons. We could even have you do it, Emory. You probably know more about the antislavery patrol than Peter and all the rest of the committee combined. That could be a real tingler—the hero's descendant talking about the ancestor he hero-worshiped as a boy. After he had actually seen him in action."

Harrington was making another calculation. The slaver's boat was pulling the slaver's bow into the wind. There was no way Mr. Whitjoy could stay with the bow as it turned and avoid a broadside. Should he pull out of range, circle around, and place *Sparrow* across the enemy's stern? Or should he hold his current position, take the broadside, and inflict more damage on their sails?

The blow to the slaver's mast had weakened its sailing capabilities but it wasn't decisive. He wanted them dead in the water—totally at his mercy.

The slaver's bow gun was already pointing away from *Sparrow*. There would be a period—who knew how long?—when *Sparrow* could fire on the slaver and the slaver couldn't fire back.

"Hold position, Mr. Whitjoy. Keep up the good work, Mr. Terry."

Harrington was holding his pocket watch in his hand. The swivel gun roared again and he noted that Terry's crew was firing a shot every minute and twenty seconds.

He put his hands behind his back and watched the enemy ship creep around. It was all a matter of luck. The balls from the slaver's broadside would fly high or low—or pass over the deck at the height of a young commander's belly. They would intersect the place where you were standing or pass a few feet to your right or left. The odds were on your side.

And there was nothing you could do about it.

Bonfors glanced back. He saw what Harrington was doing and resumed his telescopic observations of the enemy ship.

Terry's crew fired three more times while the slaver made its turn. The second shot cut the broken topmast free from its support lines and sent it sliding through the rigging to the deck. The third shot slammed into the main mast with an impact that would have made every captive in the hold howl with joy if they could have seen the result—and understood what it meant. The top of the mast lurched to the right. The whole structure, complete with spars and furled sails, toppled toward the deck and sprawled over the slaver's side.

Harrington felt himself yield to an uncontrollable rush of emotion. *"Take her about, Mr. Whitjoy! Take us out of range."*

Whitjoy barked orders. Hands raced to their stations. The big triangular main sail swung across *Sparrow*'s deck. The hand at the wheel adjusted the angle of the rudder and Harrington's ship began to turn away from the wind.

Some of the crew on the other ship had left their guns and rushed to the fallen sail. With luck, one or two of their compatriots would be lying under the wreckage.

If there was one virtue the Navy taught you, it was patience. You stood your watches, no matter how you felt. You endured storms that went on and on, for days at a time, without any sign they were coming to an end. You waited out calms. And now you locked yourself in your post and watched the elephantine motions of the ships, as *Sparrow* turned away from the wind, and the muzzles of the enemy guns slowly came to bear on the deck you were standing on. . . .

The flash of the first gun caught him by surprise. He would have waited at least another minute before he fired if he had been commanding the other ship. A huge noise whined past Sparrow's stern. The second gun lit up a few seconds later, and he realized they were firing one gun at a time.

This time the invisible Thing passed over his head, about fifty feet up. Mr. Terry fired the swivel gun and he heard Montgomery's treble shout a word of encouragement at the ball.

The slaver hurled its third shot. A tremendous bang shook the entire length of *Sparrow*'s hull. He looked up and down the deck, trying to find some sign of damage, and saw Montgomery covering his face with both hands.

A gunner grabbed Montgomery's shoulders. Terry stepped in front of the boy and seized his wrists. The rest of the gun crew gathered around.

"Mr. Bonfors—please see what the trouble is. See if you can get the gun back in action."

Bonfors shot him one of the most hostile looks he had ever received from another human being. It only lasted a moment but Harrington knew exactly what his second in command was thinking. The captain had seen an unpleasant duty and passed it to the appropriate subordinate. They both knew it was the right thing to do—the only thing a captain *could* do—but that didn't alter the basic fact that the coldhearted brute had calmly handed you a job that both of you would have given almost anything to avoid.

A crewman was standing by the railing near the bow. He pointed at the railing and Harrington understood what had happened. The big bang had been a glancing blow from a cannonball. Wooden splinters had flown off the rail at the speed of musket balls. One of the splinters had apparently hit Montgomery in the face.

"It looks like we now know who Montgomery is," Emory said.

Giva was looking at a rerun on her display. "I got it all. The camera had him centered the whole time. I lost him when they all crowded around him. But I got the moment he was hit."

Lieutenant Bonfors had reached the gun and started easing the crew away from Montgomery with a mixture of jovial comments and firm pushes. "Let's keep our minds on our work, gentlemen. Take Mr. Montgomery to the captain's cabin, Hawksbill. I believe we've got time for one more shot before we pull away from our opponent, Mr. Terry."

Their planning sessions had contained one moment of pure harmony. They had all agreed Giva would have two cameras continuously tracking both midshipmen. They knew one of the boys was going to be hit but they didn't know which one. They knew the boy was referred to as Mr. Montgomery in Harrington's report but they didn't know what he looked like or when it would happen. They only knew *Mr. Montgomery and Mr. Clarke acquitted themselves with courage and competence. I regret to report that Mr. Montgomery has lost the sight of his left eye. He is bearing his misfortune with commendable cheerfulness.*

Sparrow put a solid half mile between its stern and the slaver before it turned into a long, slow curve that ended with it bearing down on the slaver's stern. The men in the slaver's boat tried to turn with it, but Mister Whitjoy outmaneuvered them. The duel between sail power and oar power came to an abrupt end as soon as *Sparrow* drew within firing range. Harrington ordered Terry to fire on the boat, the second shot raised a fountain of water near the boat's bow, and every slaver in the boat crew lunged at the ladder that hung from the side of their ship.

Bonfors chuckled as he watched them scramble onto the deck. "They don't seem to have much tolerance for being shot at, do they?"

Harrington was eyeing the relative positions of the two ships. In another five minutes *Sparrow* would be lying directly behind the slaver's stern, poised to hurl ball after ball down the entire length of the other ship.

"You may fire at the deck as you see fit, Mr. Terry. We'll give them three rounds. And pause to see if they strike."

"They're opening the hatch," Emory said.

Captain Zachary and four of his men were crouching around the hatch in the center of the slave ship. They had drawn their pistols and they were all holding themselves close to the deck, in anticipation of the metal horror that could fly across their ship at any moment.

The four crewmen dropped through the hatch. Captain Zachary slithered backward and crouched on one knee, with his pistol clutched in both hands.

Harrington threw out his arm as soon as he saw the first black figures stumble into the sunlight. "Hold your fire, Mr. Terry."

The slavers had arranged themselves so he could enjoy an unobstructed view of the slaves. The Africans were linked together with chains but the captain and his crew were still training guns on them. Two of the slaves slumped to the deck as they came out of the hold. Their companions picked them up and dragged them away from the hatch.

"I'd say a third of them appear to be women," Bonfors said.

Harrington raised his telescope and verified Bonfors's estimate. One of the women was holding a child.

He lowered his telescope and pushed it closed. "Organize a boarding party, Mr. Bonfors. I will lead it. You will take command of the ship."

"My God," Emory said. "He didn't waste a second."

They had known what Harrington was going to do. It was in his report. But nothing in the written record had prepared Emory for the speed of his decision.

I ascertained that we could no longer punish their crew with our gun, Harrington had written, *and I therefore determined to take their ship by assault, with one of our boats. The presence of the unfortunate innocents meant that our adversaries could repair their masts before our very eyes and perhaps slip away in the night. There was, in addition, the danger they would adopt the infamous course others have taken in such a situation and avoid prosecution by consigning their cargo to the sea.*

Terry volunteered at once. Davey Clarke wanted to go, but Harrington decreed they couldn't risk another midshipman.

"We'd have a fine time keeping the ship afloat with both of our young gentlemen laid up, Davey."

The hands obviously needed encouragement. Four men stepped forward. The expressions on the rest of them convinced Harrington he had to give Bonfors some support.

"A double share for every man who volunteers," Harrington called out. "Taken from the captain's portion."

A ball from the slaver's stern gun ploughed into the water forty feet from *Sparrow*'s port side. Bonfors's arm shot toward the splash while it was still hanging over the waves. "It's the easiest money you'll ever earn, lads. You've seen how these fellows shoot."

In the end, fifteen men shuffled up to the line. That would leave ten on the *Sparrow*—enough to get the ship back to port if worse came to worst.

Giva smiled. "He just doubled their profit, didn't he? He didn't mention that in his report."

Harrington placed himself in the front of the boat. Terry sat in the back, where the ranking officer would normally sit.

Their positions wouldn't matter that much during the approach. The slavers would be firing down from the deck. They would all be equally exposed. When they initiated the assault, however, he had to be in front. The whole enterprise might fail if he went down—but it was certain to fail if the men felt their captain was huddling in the rear. The assault had been his idea, after all.

They had boarded the boat on *Sparrow*'s starboard side, with *Sparrow*'s hull between them and the enemy guns. For the first few seconds after Terry gave the order, they traveled along the hull. Then they cleared the bow.

And there it was. There was nothing between him and the stern gun of the enemy ship but a hundred yards of sunlight and water.

Terry was supposed to steer them toward the rear of the slaver's starboard side. They had agreed he would aim them at a point that would accomplish two objectives. He would keep the boat outside the angle the slaver's broadside could cover and he would minimize the time they would spend inside the stern gun's field of fire. Terry was the best man to hold the tiller. No one on *Sparrow* had a better understanding of the strengths and limitations of nautical artillery.

They had overcome their boat's initial resistance as they had slid down *Sparrow*'s hull. Terry called out his first firm "*Stroke!*" and the bow shot toward its destination. Terry gave the rowers two cycles of *stroke* and *lift* at a moderate pace. Then he upped the pace and kept increasing it with every cycle.

Every push of the oars carried them out of the danger presented by the stern gun. But it also carried them toward the armed men who were crowding around the rail.

Harrington's hands tightened on the weapons he was holding—a pistol in his right hand, a cutlass in his left. He was keeping his fingers on the butt of the pistol, well away from the trigger and the possibility he would fire the gun by accident and leave himself one bullet short and looking like a fool. Two more pistols were tucked into his belt, right and left. The men behind him were all equipped with two pistols, two loaded muskets wrapped in oil-cloth, and a cutlass laid across their feet.

The stern gun flashed. The impulse to squeeze himself into a package the size of his hat seemed irresistible but he focused his eyes on the side of the slaver and discovered he could hold himself fixed in place until he heard the bang of the gun reaching him from a distance that seemed as remote as the moons of Jupiter.

"*Stroke* . . . lift . . . *stroke* . . . lift."

Was there anything more beautiful than the crash of a gun that had just fired in your direction? The noise had made its way across the water and you were still alive. You could be certain four pounds of iron had sailed harmlessly past you, instead of slamming into your bones or knocking holes in your boat and mutilating your shipmates.

"That should be the last we'll hear from that thing," a voice muttered behind him.

"I should hope so," a brasher voice said. "Unless these niggerwhippers have picked up some pointers from Mr. Terry in the last half hour."

The second voice belonged to a hand named Bobby Dawkins—a veteran in his fourth decade who was noted for his monkeyish agility and the stream of good-natured comments he bestowed on everything that happened around him. Dawkins had been the first man to volunteer after Harrington had augmented the cash reward.

Armed men were lining up along the rail of the slave ship. More men were falling in behind them.

Emory ran his eyes down the rail picking out faces that looked particularly vicious or threatening. He had begun his recording as a weapon in his contest with Giva but he was beginning to think along other lines. He wanted a personal record of this—the kind of record a tourist would make. It wouldn't be as sharp as Giva's work but it would be *his*—a personal view of his ancestor's courage.

The slavers started firing their muskets when the boat was still fifty yards from its destination. Harrington had been hoping they would waste a few of their shots but he still felt himself flinch when he saw the first flash. Everybody else in the boat had something to do. The hands had to row. Terry had to steer. He had to sit here and be a target.

He knew he should give his men a few words of encouragement but he couldn't think of a single phrase. His mind had become a blank sheet. Was he afraid? Was this what people meant when they said someone was *paralyzed*?

The slavers shoved two African women up to the rail. The men in the center of the firing line stepped aside and more slaves took their place.

"The swine," Dawkins said. "Bloody. Cowardly. *Bastards*."

Black faces stared at the oncoming boat. Harrington peered at their stupefied expressions and realized they didn't have the slightest idea they were being used as shields. They had been pushed in chains along trails that might be hundreds of miles long. They had been packed into a hold as if they were kegs of rum. They were surrounded by men who didn't speak their language. By now they must be living in a fog.

"*Make sure you aim before you shoot. Make these animals feel every ball you fire.*"

He was bellowing with rage. He would have stood up in the boat if he hadn't been restrained by years of training. He knew he was giving his men a stupid order. He knew there was no way they could shoot with that kind of accuracy. It didn't matter. The slavers had provoked emotions that were as uncontrollable as a hurricane.

More slaves were shoved to the railing. Muskets banged. Slavers were actually resting their guns on the shoulders of the slaves they were using for cover.

"We're inside their guns," Terry yelled. "I'll take us forward."

Harrington pointed at a spot just aft of the forward gun. "Take us there. Between one and two. First party—stow your oars. Shoulder your muskets. Wait for my order."

They had worked this out before they had boarded the boat. Half the men would guide the boat during the final approach. The other half would pick up their muskets and prepare to fight.

Giva had stopped making comments. Her face had acquired the taut, focused lines of a musician or athlete who was working at the limits of her capacity. She was scanning the drama taking place outside the bubble while she simultaneously tracked the images on six screens and adjusted angles and subjects with quick, decisive motions of her hands.

Emory had noted the change in her attitude and turned his attention to his own record. What difference did it make how she felt? The people who saw the finished product would see brave men hurling themselves into danger. Would anybody really care why they did it?

Musket balls cracked in the air around the boat. Metal hammered on the hull. Four members of the slaver crew were running toward the spot where

Harrington planned to board. The rest of them were staying near the middle and firing over their human shields.

"Hold her against the side," Harrington yelled. "Throw up the grappling hooks."

The four hands who had been given the job threw their grappling hooks at the rail. The man beside Harrington tugged at the rope, to make sure it was firm, and Harrington fired his first pistol at the ship and handed the gun to one of the rowers. He grabbed the rope and walked himself up the side of the hull, past the gun that jutted out of the port on his left. His cutlass dangled from a loop around his wrist.

He knew he would be most vulnerable when he went over the rail. His hands would be occupied. He would be exposed to gunfire and hand-to-hand attacks. He seized the rail with both hands as soon as he came in reach and pulled himself over before he could hesitate.

Four men were crouching on the roof of the rear deckhouse. A gun flamed. Harrington jerked his left pistol out of his belt and fired back. He charged at the deckhouse with his cutlass raised.

The slavers fired their guns and scampered off the deckhouse. Harrington turned toward the bow, toward the men who were using the slaves as shields. His boarding party was crowding over the rails. He had half a dozen men scattered beside him. Most of them were firing their muskets at the slavers and their flesh and blood bulwarks.

"Use your cutlasses! Make these bastards bleed!"

He ran across the deck with his cutlass held high. He could hear himself screaming like a wild man. He had tried to think about the best way to attack while they had been crossing the water. Now he had stopped thinking. They couldn't stand on the deck and let the animals shoot at them.

The Africans' eyes widened. They twisted away from the lunatics rushing toward them and started pushing against the bodies behind them. The slavers had overlooked an important fact—they were hiding behind a wall that was composed of conscious, intelligent creatures.

The African directly in front of Harrington was a woman. She couldn't turn her back on him because of her chains but she had managed to make a half turn. The man looming behind her was so tall she didn't reach his shoulder. The man was pointing a pistol at Harrington and the woman was clawing at his face with one hand.

The pistol sounded like a cannon when it fired. Harrington covered the deck in front of him in two huge leaps—the longest leaps he had ever taken—and brought his cutlass down on the slaver with both hands.

Steel sliced through cloth and bit into the slaver's collarbone. The man's mouth gaped open. He fell back and Harrington shouldered the female slave aside and hoisted his legs over the chain dangling between her and the captive on her right.

Emory was clamping his jaw on the kind of bellow overwrought fans emitted at sports events. Giva had shifted the bubble to a location twenty-five meters from the side of the slave ship. He could see and hear every detail of Harrington's headlong rush.

Half a dozen men had joined Harrington's assault. More had fallen in behind as they had come over the side. Most of the men in the first rank were running at a crouch, about a step behind their captain. One sailor was holding his hand in front of his face, as if he thought he could stop a bullet with his palm. Emory had been watching combat scenes ever since he was a boy but no actor had ever captured the look on these men's faces—the intense, white-faced concentration of men who knew they were facing real bullets.

A slaver backed away from the pummeling fists of a tall, ribby slave and fired at the oncoming sailors. For a moment Emory thought the shot had gone wild. Then he glanced toward the rear of the assault. A sailor who had just pulled himself over the side was sagging against the rail.

Giva had expanded her display to eight monitors. Her hands were flying across her screens as if she were conducting the action taking place on the ship.

The slavers in front of Harrington were all falling back. Most of them seemed to be climbing the rigging or ducking behind boats and deck gear. On his right, his men had stopped their rush and started working their muskets with a ragged, hasty imitation of the procedure he had drilled into them when he had decided it would be a useful skill if they ever actually boarded a ship. They would never load and fire like three-shots-to-the-minute redcoats but they were doing well enough for a combat against a gang who normally fought unarmed primitives.

The slaver captain—Captain Zachary?—was standing on the front deckhouse, just behind the rail. He stared at Harrington across the heads of the slavers who were scattered between them and Harrington realized he was pulling a rod out of the pistol he was holding in his left hand.

It was one of those moments when everything around you seems to stand still. Harrington's cutlass dropped out of his hand. He reached for the pistol stuck in his belt. He pulled it out and cocked it—methodically, with no haste—with the heel of his left hand.

On the deckhouse, Zachary had poured a dab of powder into the firing pan without taking his eyes off Harrington. He cocked the gun with his thumb and clutched it in a solid two-handed grip as he raised it to the firing position.

"Look at that!" Emory said. "Are you getting that, Giva? They're facing each other like a pair of duelists."

If this had been a movie, Emory realized, the director would have captured the confrontation between Harrington and Zachary from at least three angles—one long shot to establish that they were facing each other, plus a close-up for each combatant. How did you work it when you were shooting the real thing and you couldn't reenact it several times with the camera placed in different positions? He turned his head and peered at Giva's screens.

Giva's hands were hopping across her screens. She had centered the gunfight in a wide-view, high angle shot in the second screen in her top row.

Zachary's hands flew apart. The tiny figure on Giva's screen sagged. The life-size figure standing on the real ship clutched at his stomach with both palms.

The captain of the slaver received a mortal bullet wound during the fray, Harrington had written. *His removal from the mêlée soon took the fight out of our adversaries.* There had been no mention that Harrington himself had fired the decisive shot.

"Is that all you got?" Emory said. "That one long shot?"

He had searched her screens twice, looking for a closeup of the duel. Half of Giva's screens seemed to be focused on the slaves.

Giva jabbed at her number three screen. Emory glanced at the scene on the ship and saw the African woman Harrington had shoved aside stiffening as if she were having a fit. The image on the screen zoomed to a close-up and the camera glimpsed a single glassy eye before the woman's head slumped forward.

Giva pulled the camera back and framed the body sprawling on the deck. The woman's only garment had been a piece of blue cloth she had wrapped around her breasts and hips. The big wound just above her left breast was clearly visible.

"You got him, sir! Right in the bastard's stomach!"

Bobby Dawkins was moving into a position on Harrington's right. He had a raised cutlass in his right hand and he was waving a pistol with his left.

More men took their places beside Dawkins. Nobody was actually stepping *between* Harrington and the enemy but they were all making some effort to indicate they were willing to advance with their captain.

Harrington's hands had automatically stuffed the empty pistol into his belt. He dropped into an awkward crouch and picked up his cutlass. Most of the slavers in front of him were looking back at the deckhouse.

"You just lost the most dramatic event of the whole assault—something we'd never have guessed from the printed record."

"I can zoom in on the scene when I'm editing," Giva muttered. "I'm a pro, Emory. Let me work."

"So why do you need the close-up you just got? Why do you have so many cameras focused on the slaves? Couldn't you edit that later, too?"

Four hands were standing beside Harrington. Three more hands were standing a pair of steps behind them. Three of them had muskets pressed into their shoulders. The other four were cursing and grunting as they worked their way through various sections of the reloading drill.

"*Hold your fire!*" Harrington snapped. "Train your piece on a target but hold your fire."

He heard the jumpy excitement in his voice and knew it would never do. Use the voice you use when the wind is whipping across the deck, he told himself. Pretend you're thundering at the mast and Davey Clarke has the lookout.

His right arm was raising his sword above his head. "Your captain has fallen! *Yield. Lay down your arms*. Lay down your arms or I'll order my men to keep firing."

"Is that your idea of *scholarship*, Giva—another weepy epic about suffering victims?"

John Harrington knew he would be talking about this moment for the rest of his life. He knew he had managed to sound like a captain was supposed to sound—like a man who had absolute control of the situation and assumed everyone who heard him would obey his orders. Now he had to see if they really would submit. He had to stand here, fully exposed to a stray shot, and give them time to respond.

Captain Zachary was slumping against the railing of the deckhouse with his hands clutching his stomach. The two slavers who were standing directly in front of him had turned toward Harrington when they had heard his roar. Their eyes settled on the muskets leveled at their chests.

Zachary raised his head. He muttered something Harrington couldn't understand. One of the slavers immediately dropped to one knee. He placed his pistol on the deck.

"The captain says to surrender," the sailor yelled. "He says get it over with."

Harrington lowered his sword. He pushed himself across the deck—it was one of the hardest things he had ever done—and picked up the musket.

"You have my sincerest thanks, Captain Zachary. You have saved us all much discomfort."

"This is *my* project, Emory. I was given complete control of the cameras and the final product. Do you have any idea what you and the whole chrono bureaucracy would look like if I handed in my resignation because you tried to bully me while I was doing my job?"

"I'm not trying to bully you. You're the one with the power in this situation. No one has to draw me a power flowchart. I've got my own record of the dueling incident. Anybody who looks at my recording—or yours for that matter—can see you've ignored a dramatic, critical event and focused on a peripheral incident."

"Don't you think those *niggers* deserve a little attention, too? Do you think they're having a fun time caught between two groups of money-hungry berserkers?"

Dawkins was picking up the slavers' weapons as they collected near the starboard rail. Five other hands were aiming their muskets over the slavers' heads. Harrington had positioned the musket men six paces from their potential targets—close enough they couldn't miss, far enough none of their prisoners could convince themselves they could engage in a rush before the muskets could fire.

The regulations said the slavers had to be transported to *Sparrow*. The prize crew he assigned to the slaver would have enough trouble looking after the Africans. How many prisoners could he put in each boatload as they made the transfer, given the number of men he could spare for guard duty? He could put the prisoners in irons, of course. But that might be too provocative. They had been operating in a milieu in which chains were associated with slavery and racial inferiority.

He turned to Terry, who had taken up a position behind the musket men. "Keep an eye on things, Mr. Terry. I think it's time I ventured into the hold."

The world around the space/time bubble turned black—the deepest blackness Emory had ever experienced. They had known it could happen at any time—they had even been exposed to simulations during their pre-location training—but the reality still made him freeze. There was nothing outside the bubble. *Nothing.*

The world snapped back. A male slave near the front of the ship was staring their way with his mouth gaping. He gestured with a frantic right hand and the elderly man beside him squinted in their direction.

Harrington had known the hold would stink. Every officer who had ever served in the West African squadron agreed on that. He had picked up the stench when the boat had approached the ship's side but he had been too preoccupied to react to it. Now his stomach turned as soon as he settled his feet on the ladder.

In theory, the slavers were supposed to wash their cargo down to fight disease and keep it alive until they could take their profit. In practice, nothing could eliminate the stink of hundreds of bodies pressed into their storage shelves like bales of cotton.

The noise was just as bad as the odor. Every captive in the hold seemed to be jabbering and screaming. The slaves in a cargo could come from every section of the continent. They were brought to the coast from the places where they had been captured—or bought from some native chief who had taken them prisoner during a tribal war—and assembled in big compounds before they were sold to the European slave traders. It would be a miracle if fifty of them spoke the same language.

He paused at the bottom of the ladder and stared at the patch of blue sky over the hatch. He was the commander of a British warship. Certain things were required.

He unhooked the lamp that hung beside the ladder and peered into the din. White eyes stared at him out of the darkness. A glance at the captives he saw told him Captain Zachary had adapted one of the standard plans. Each slave had been placed with his back between the legs of the slave behind him.

He had been listening to descriptions of slave holds since he had been a midshipman. He had assumed he had been prepared. The slaves had been arranged on three shelves, just as he had expected. They would spend most of the voyage staring at a ceiling a few inches above their faces. The passage that ran down the center of the hold was only a little wider than his shoulders.

"We have encountered a space/time instability," the hal said. "I must remind you an abort is strongly recommended."

"We have to stay," Emory said. "We haven't captured the liberation of the slaves. There's no finale."

The mission rules were clear. Two flickers and the hal would automatically abort. One, and they could stay if they thought it was worth the risk.

No one knew if those rules were necessary. The bureaucrats had established them and their electronic representative would enforce them. Time travel was a paradox and an impossibility. Intelligent people approached it with all the caution they would confer on a bomb with an unknown detonating mechanism.

Giva kept her eyes focused on her screens. If she voted with him, they would stay. If they split their vote, the hal would implement the "strong recommendation" it had received from its masters.

The slave who had pointed at them seemed to have been the only person who had seen the instability. There was no indication anyone else had noticed the apparition that had flickered beside the hull.

"I think we should stay," Giva said. "For now."

"The decision will be mandatorily reconsidered once every half hour. A termination may be initiated at any time."

Harrington made himself walk the entire length of the passage. He absorbed the odor. He let the clamor bang on his skull. He peered into the shelves on both sides every third step. He couldn't make his men come down here if he wasn't willing to do it himself.

On the deck, he had yielded to a flicker of sympathy for Zachary. Stomach wounds could inflict a painful slow death on their victims. Now he hoped Zachary took a whole month to die. And stayed fully conscious up to the last moment.

He marched back to the ladder with his eyes fixed straight ahead. He had lost his temper in the boat when he had seen Zachary's cutthroats using their captives as human shields. It had been an understandable lapse but it couldn't happen twice in the same day. His ship and his crew depended on his judgment.

Terry glanced at him when he assumed his place on the deck. Most of the slaver's crew had joined the cluster of prisoners. Some of them even looked moderately cheerful. They all knew the court at Freetown would set them free within a month at the most. An occasional incarceration was one of the inconveniences of their trade.

"There should be at least four hundred," Harrington said. "Two thousand pounds minimum. And the value of the ship."

Emory made a mental calculation as he watched the first boatload of prisoners crawl toward the *Sparrow*. At the rate the boat was moving, given the time it had taken to load it, they were going to sit here for at least two more hours.

Giva was devoting half her screens to the crew and half to the Africans but he knew he would look like a fool if he objected. The crew were stolidly holding their guns on their prisoners. The Africans were talking among themselves. The two Africans who were chained on either side of the fallen woman had dropped to their knees beside her.

The moment when the slaves would be brought into the sunlight was the moment Emory considered the emotional climax of the whole episode. He had been so enthusiastic when he described it during their planning sessions that Peter LeGrundy had told him he sounded like he had already seen it.

I ordered the liberated captives brought to the deck as circumstances allowed, Harrington had written. *They did not fully comprehend their change in status, and I could not explain it. Our small craft does not contain a translator among its complement. But the sight of so many souls rescued from such a terrible destiny stimulated the deepest feelings of satisfaction in every heart capable of such sentiments.*

"You think we could press this lad, Captain? We could use some of that muscle."

Harrington turned his head. He had decided he should let the men standing guard take a few minutes rest, one at a time. Dawkins had wandered over the deck to the Africans and stopped in front of a particularly muscular specimen.

"I wouldn't get too close if I were you," Harrington said. "We still haven't given him any reason to think we're his friends."

Dawkins raised his hands in mock fright. He scurried back two steps and Harrington let himself yield to a smile.

"We'd get a sight more than five pounds for you if we took you to Brazil," Dawkins said to the African. "A nigger like you would fetch three hundred clean if he scowled at white people like that for the rest of his black life."

Giva was smiling again. She hadn't said anything about the way the British sailors used the word *nigger* but Emory was certain she was noting every use she recorded. Emory had first encountered the word when he had started collecting memoirs and letters penned by men who had served in the anti-slavery patrol. He had assumed it was simply a derivative of the River Niger or a corruption of the French for black. He had been very surprised when

Peter LeGrundy had told him it was a pejorative that had once been associated with a deep contempt for dark-skinned humans. Peter had claimed the British tended to think up insulting terms for every kind of foreigner they met, including Europeans.

"Frenchmen were called frogs," Peter had said. "Apparently because there was some belief they were especially fond of eating frogs. People from Asian countries were called wogs—an ironic acronym for Worthy Oriental Gentlemen."

Harrington watched the next to last boatload pull away from the slaver. The mob of prisoners had been reduced to a group of seven. Three of the prisoners were crouching beside their captain and offering him sips of water and occasional words of encouragement.

"Mr. Terry—will you please take a party below and bring about fifty of the unfortunates on deck? Concentrate on women and children. We don't have the strength to handle too many restless young bucks."

"Your ancestor doesn't seem to have much confidence in his ability to handle the animals," Giva said. "What do they call the African women? Does?"

"If you will do a little research before you edit your creation," Emory said, "I believe you'll discover *British* young men were called young bucks, too. It was just a term for young men with young attitudes. They would have called *you* a restless young buck if you'd been born male, Giva."

Harrington hadn't tried black women yet. His sexual experience had been limited to encounters with the kind of females who lifted their skirts for sailors in the Italian and South American ports he had visited on his first cruises. Bonfors claimed black women were more ardent than white women but Bonfors liked to talk. It had been Harrington's experience that most of his shipmates believed *all* foreign women were more ardent than their English counterparts.

Some of the women Terry's men were ushering on deck looked like they were younger than his sisters. Several were carrying infants. Most of them were wearing loose bits of cloth that exposed their legs and arms and other areas civilized women usually covered.

Harrington had read William Pitt's great speech on the abolition of the slave trade when he had been a boy, and he had read it again when his uncle had advised him the Admiralty had agreed to give him this command. There had been a time, Pitt had argued, when the inhabitants of ancient Britain had been just as savage and uncivilized as the inhabitants of modern Africa, "a time when even human sacrifices were offered on this island."

In those days, Pitt had suggested, some Roman senator could have pointed to *British barbarians* and predicted "*There* is a people that will never rise to civilization—there is a people destined never to be free—a people without the understanding necessary for the attainment of useful arts, depressed by the hand of nature below the level of the human species, and created to form a supply of slaves for the rest of the world."

The women in front of him might be barbarians. But they had, as Pitt had said, the potential to rise to the same levels the inhabitants of Britain had achieved. They had the right to live in freedom, so they might have the same opportunity to develop.

A woman sprawled on the deck as she emerged from the hatch. Two of the hands were pulling the captives through the opening. Two were probably pushing them from below.

One of the sailors on the deck bent over the fallen woman. His hand closed over her left breast.

"Now there's a proper young thing," the sailor said.

The sailor who was working with him broke out in a smile. "I can't say I'd have any objection to spending a few days on *this* prize crew."

The officer who was supposed to be supervising the operation—the gunnery officer, Mr. Terry—was standing just a step away. John Harrington had been watching the slaves stumble into the sunlight but now he turned toward the bow and eyed the seven prisoners lounging in front of the forward deckhouse.

The next African out of the hatch was a scrawny boy who looked like he might be somewhere around seven or eight, in Emory's unpracticed judgment. The woman who followed him—his mother?—received a long stroke on the side of her hip as she balanced herself against the roll of the ship.

"The African males don't seem to be the only restless young bucks," Giva said. "These boys have been locked up in that little ship for several weeks now, as I remember it."

"It has been one half hour since your last mandatory stay/go decision," the hal said. "Do you wish to stay or go, Mr. FitzGordon?"

"Stay."

"Do you wish to stay or go, Ms. Lombardo?"

"Stay, of course. We're getting some interesting insights into the attractions of African cruises."

Harrington ran his eyes over the rigging of the slaver. He should pick the most morally fastidious hands for the prize crew. But who could that be? Could any of them resist the opportunity after all these months at sea?

He could proclaim strict rules, of course. And order Terry to enforce them. But did he really want to subject his crew to the lash and the chain merely because they had succumbed to the most natural of urges? They were good men. They had just faced bullets and cannonballs to save five hundred human souls from the worst evil the modern world inflicted on its inhabitants.

And what if some of the women were willing? What if some of them offered themselves for money?

He could tell Terry to keep carnal activity to a minimum. But wouldn't that be the same as giving him permission to let the men indulge? He was the captain. Anything he said would have implications.

"Mr. Terry. Will you come over here, please?"

Harrington was murmuring but the microphones could still pick up the conversation.

"I'm placing you in command of the prize, Mr. Terry. I am entrusting its cargo to your good sense and decency."

"I understand," Terry said.

"These people may be savages but they are still our responsibility."

Emory nodded. Harrington was staring at the two men working the hatch as he talked. The frown on his face underlined every word he was uttering.

"That should take care of that matter," Emory said.

Giva turned away from her screens. "You really think that little speech will have an effect, Emory?"

"Is there any reason to think it won't? He won't be riding with the prize crew. But that lieutenant knows what he's supposed to do."

"It was a standard piece of bureaucratic vagueness! It was exactly the kind of thing slot-fillers always say when they want to put a fence around their precious little careers."

"It was just as precise as it needed to be, Giva. Harrington and his officers all come from the same background. That lieutenant knows exactly what he's supposed to do. He doesn't need a lot of detail."

"When was the last time you held a job? I've been dealing with *managers* all my life. They always say things like that. The only thing you know when they're done is that you're going to be the one who gets butchered if anything goes wrong."

Harrington stood by the railing as the last group of prisoners took their places in the boat. A babble of conversation rang over the deck. The African captives they had brought out of the hold had mingled with the captives who had been used as shields and they were all chattering away like guests at a lawn party.

It was an exhilarating sight. He had never felt so completely satisfied with the world. Five hours ago the people standing on the deck had been crowded into the hell belowdecks, with their future lives reduced to weeks of torment in the hold, followed by years of brutal servitude when they finally made land. Now they merely had to endure a three- or four-day voyage to the British colony in Freetown. Half of them would probably become farmers in the land around Freetown. Some would join British regiments. Many would go to the West Indies as laborers—but they would be indentured laborers, not slaves, free to take up their own lives when they had worked off their passage. A few would even acquire an education in the schools the missionaries had established in Freetown and begin their own personal rise toward civilization.

He had raised the flag above the slaver with his own hands. Several of the Africans had pointed at it and launched into excited comments when it was only a third of the way up the mast. He could still see some of them pointing and obviously explaining its significance to the newcomers. Some of them had even pointed at *him*. Most liberated slaves came from the interior. The captives who came from the coast would know about the antislavery patrol. They would understand the significance of the flag and the blue coat.

"We're all loaded and ready, sir."

Harrington turned away from the deck. The last prisoner had settled into his seat in the boat.

He nodded at Terry and Terry nodded back. The hands had managed to slip in a few more pawings under the guise of being helpful, but Terry seemed to have the overall situation under control.

"She's your ship, Mr. Terry. I'll send you the final word on your prize crew as soon as I've conferred with Mr. Bonfors."

"It looks to me like it's about time we hopped for home," Giva said.

"Now? He's only brought one load of slaves on deck."

"You don't really think he's going to decorate the deck with more Africans, do you? Look at my screens. I'm getting two usable images of your ancestor returning to his ship. It's a high feel closure. All we need is a sunset."

"There's five hundred people in that hold. Don't you think he's going to give the rest of them a chance to breathe?"

"He exaggerated his report. Use your head, Emory. Would you go through all the hassle involved in controlling five hundred confused people when you knew they were only four or five days away from Freetown?"

"You are deliberately avoiding the most important scene in the entire drama. We'll never know what happened next if we go now."

"You're clinging to a fantasy. We're done. It's time to go. Hal—I request relocation to home base."

"I have a request for relocation to home base. Please confirm."

"I do not confirm. I insist that we—"

"Request confirmed, Hal. Request confirmed."

Time stopped. The universe blinked. A technology founded on the best contemporary scientific theories did something the best contemporary scientific theories said it couldn't do.

The rig dropped onto the padded stage in Transit Room One. The bubble had disappeared. Faces were peering at them through the windows that surrounded the room.

Gina jabbed her finger at the time strip mounted on the wall. They had been gone seven minutes and thirty-eight seconds local time.

"We were pushing it," Gina said. "We were pushing it more than either of us realized."

The average elapsed local time was three minutes—a fact they had both committed to memory the moment they had heard it during their first orientation lecture. The bump when they hit the stage had seemed harder than the bumps they had experienced during training, too. The engineers always set the return coordinates for a position two meters above the stage—a precaution that placed the surface of the stage just outside the margin of error and assured the passengers they wouldn't relocate *below* it. They had come home extra late and extra high. Gina would have some objective support for her decision to return.

The narrow armored hatch under the time strip swung open. An engineer hopped through it with a medic right behind her.

"Is everything all right?"

"I can't feel anything malfunctioning," Giva said. "We had a flicker about two hours before we told Hal to shoot us home."

Emory ripped off his seat belt. He jumped to his feet and the medic immediately dropped into his soothe-the-patient mode. "You really should sit down, Mr. FitzGordon. You shouldn't stand up until we've checked you out."

The soft, controlled tones only added more points to the spurs driving Emory's rage. Giva was sprawling in her chair, legs stretched in front of her, obviously doing her best to create the picture of the relaxed daredevil who had courageously held off until the last minute. And now the medic was treating him like he was some kind of disoriented patient. . . .

He swung toward the medic and the man froze when he saw the hostility on Emory's face. He was a solid, broad-shouldered type with a face that probably looked pleasant and experienced when he was helping chrononauts disembark. Now he slipped into a stance that looked like a slightly disguised on-guard.

"You're back, Mr. FitzGordon. Everything's okay. We'll have you checked out and ready for debriefing before you know it."

Peter LeGrundy crouched through the hatch. He flashed his standard-issue smile at the two figures on the rig and Emory realized he had to get himself under control.

"So how did it go?" Peter said. "Did you have a nice trip?"

Emory forced his muscles to relax. He lowered his head and settled into the chair as if he was recovering from a momentary lapse—the kind of thing any normal human could feel when he had just violated the laws of physics and traveled through three centuries of time. He gave the medic a quick thumbs-up and the medic nodded.

He had his own record of the event. He had Giva's comments. Above all, he had Peter LeGrundy. And Peter LeGrundy's ambitions. He could cover every grant Peter could need for the rest of Peter's scholarly career if he had to. The battle wasn't over. Not yet.

You need the creatives. The creatives need your money.

I ordered the liberated captives brought to the deck as circumstances allowed. They did not fully comprehend their change in status, and I could not explain it. Our small craft does not contain a translator among its complement. But the sight of so many souls rescued from such a terrible destiny stimulated the deepest feelings of satisfaction in every heart capable of such sentiments.

Two well-placed candles illuminated the paper on John Harrington's writing desk without casting distracting shadows. The creak of *Sparrow's* structure created a background that offered him a steady flow of information about the state of his command.

He lowered his pen. He had been struggling with his report for almost two hours. The emotions he had ignored during the battle had flooded over him as soon as he had closed the door of his cabin. The pistol that had roared in his face had exploded half a dozen times.

He shook his head and forced out a sentence advising the Admiralty he had placed Mr. Terry in command of the prize. He had already commended Terry's gunnery and his role in the assault. He had given Bonfors due mention. Dawkins and several other hands had been noted by name. The dead and the wounded had been properly honored.

It had been a small battle by the standards of the war against Napoleon. A skirmish really. Against an inept adversary. But the bullets had been real.

Men had died. *He* could have died. He had boarded an enemy ship under fire. He had led a headlong assault at an enemy line. He had exchanged shots with the captain of the enemy.

The emotions he was feeling now would fade. One hard, unshakeable truth would remain. He had faced enemy fire and done his duty.

He had met the test. He had become the kind of man he had read about when he was a boy.

craters

KRISTINE KATHRYN RUSCH

Kristine Kathryn Rusch started out the decade of the '90s as one of the fastest-rising and most prolific young authors on the scene, took a few years out in mid-decade for a very successful turn as editor of *The Magazine of Fantasy & Science Fiction*, and, since stepping down from that position, has returned to her old standards of production here in the 21st century, publishing a slew of novels in four genres, writing fantasy, mystery, and romance novels under various pseudonyms, as well as science fiction. She has published more than twenty novels under her own name, including *The White Mists of Power, The Disappeared, Extremes*, and *Fantasy Life*, the four-volume *Fey* series, the *Black Throne* series, *Alien Influences*, and several *Star Wars, Star Trek*, and other media tie-in books, both solo and written with husband Dean Wesley Smith and with others. Her most recent books (as Rusch, anyway) are the SF novels of the popular "Retrieval Artist" series, which include *The Disappeared, Extreme, Consequences, Buried Deep, Paloma, Recovery Man*, and a collection of "Retrieval Artist" stories, *The Retrieval Artist and Other Stories*. Her copious short fiction has been collected in *Stained Black: Horror Stories, Stories for an Enchanted Afternoon, Little Miracles and Other Tales of Murder*, and *Millennium Babies*. In 1999, she won Readers Award polls from the readerships of both *Asimov's Science Fiction* and *Ellery Queen's Mystery Magazine*, an unprecedented double honor! As an editor, she was honored with the Hugo Award for her work on *The Magazine of Fantasy & Science Fiction*, and shared the World Fantasy Award with Dean Wesley Smith for her work as editor of the original hardcover anthology version of *Pulphouse*. As a writer, she has won the Herodotus Award for Best Historical Mystery (for *A Dangerous Road*, written as Kris Nelscott) and the Romantic Times Reviewer's Choice Award (for *Utterly Charming*, written as Kristine Grayson); as Kristine Kathryn Rusch, she has won the John W. Campbell Award, been a finalist for the Arthur C. Clarke Award, and took home a Hugo Award in

2000 for her story "Millennium Babies," making her one of the few people in genre history to win Hugos for both editing *and* writing.

Let's hope that the harrowing future that she portrays here *doesn't* come to pass—although looking around the modern world, I get the uneasy feeling that it just might.

W hat they don't tell you when you sign up is that the work takes a certain amount of trust. The driver, head covered by a half-assed turban, smiles a little too much, and when he yes-ma'ams you and no ma'ams you, you can be lulled into thinking he actually works for you.

Then he opens the side door of his rusted jeep and nods at the dirt-covered seat. You don't even hesitate as you slide in, backpack filled with water bottles and purifying pills, vitamins and six days' dry rations.

You sit in that jeep, and you're grateful, because you never allow yourself to think that he could be one of them, taking you to some roadside bunker, getting paid an advance cut of the ransom they anticipate. Or worse, getting paid to leave you there so that they can all take turns until you're bleeding and catatonic and don't care when they put the fifty-year-old pistol to your head.

You can't think about the risks, not as you're getting in that jeep, or letting some so-called civilian lead you down sunlit streets that have seen war for centuries almost nonstop.

You trust, because if you don't you can't do your job.

You trust, and hope you get away from this place before your luck runs out.

I still have luck. I know it because today we pull into the camp. This camp's just like all the others I've seen in my twenty-year career. The ass-end of nowhere, damn near unbearable heat. Barbed wire, older than God, fences in everything, and at the front, soldiers with some kind of high-tech rifle, some sort of programmable thing I don't understand.

My driver pulls into a long line of oil-burning cars, their engines only partly modified to hydrogen. The air stinks of gasoline, a smell I associate with my childhood, not with now.

We sit in the heat. Sweat pours down my face. I nurse the bottle of water I brought from the Green Zone—a misnomer we've applied to the American base in every "war" since Iraq. The Green Zone doesn't have a lick of green in it. It just has buildings that are theoretically protected from bombs and suicide attacks.

Finally, we pull up to the checkpoint. I clutch my bag against my lap, even though the canvas is heavy and hot.

My driver knows the soldiers. "Reporter lady," he tells them in English. The English is for my benefit, to prove once again that he is my friend. I haven't let him know that I know parts (the dirty parts mostly) of two dozen languages. "Very famous. She blog, she do vid, you see her on CNN, no?"

The soldiers lean in. They have young faces covered in sand and mud and three-day-old beards. The same faces I've been seeing for years—skin an indeterminate color, thanks to the sun and the dirt, eyes black or brown or covered with shades, expressions flat—the youth visible only in the body shape, the lack of wrinkles and sun-lines, the leftover curiosity undimmed by too much death over too much time.

I lean forward so they can see my face. They don't recognize me. CNN pays me, just like *The New York Times News Service*, just like the Voice of the European Union. But none of them broadcast or replicate my image.

The woman everyone thinks of as me is a hired face, whose features get digitized over mine before anything goes out public. Too many murdered journalists. Too many famous targets.

The military brass, they know to scan my wrist, send the code into the Reporter Registry, and get the retinal download that they can double-check against my eye. But foot soldiers, here on crap duty, they don't know for nothing.

So they eyeball me, expecting a pretty face—all the studio hires are skinny and gorgeous—and instead, getting my shoe-leather skin, my dishwater blond going on steel gray hair, and my seen-too-much eyes. They take in the sweat and the khakis and the pinkie jacks that look like plastic fingernails.

I wait.

They don't even confer. The guy in charge waves the jeep forward, figuring, I guess, that I clean up startlingly well. Before I can say anything, the jeep roars through the barbed wire into a wide flat street filled with people.

Most cultures call them refugees, but I think of them as the dregs— unwanted and unlucky, thrown from country to country, or locked away in undesirable land, waiting for a bit of charity, a change of political fortune, waiting for an understanding that will never, ever come.

The smell hits you first: raw sewage combined with vomit and dysentery. Then the bugs, bugs like you've never seen, moving in swarms, sensing fresh meat.

After your first time with those swarms, you slather illegal bug spray on your arms, not caring that developed countries banned DDT as a poison/nerve toxin long ago. Anything to keep those creatures off you, anything to keep yourself alive.

You get out of your jeep, and immediately, the children who aren't dying surround you. They don't want sweets—what a quaint old idea that is—they want to know what kind of tech you have, what's buried in your skin, what you carry under your eyes, what you record from that hollow under your chin. You give them short answers, wrong answers, answers you'll regret in the quiet of your hotel room days later, after you know you've made it out to report once more. You remember them, wonder how they'll do, hope that they won't become the ones you see farther into the camp, sprawled outside thin government-issue tents, those bug swarms covering their faces, their stomachs distended, their limbs pieces of scrap so thin that they don't even look like useful sticks.

Then you set the memories—the knowledge—aside. You're good at setting things aside. That's a skill you acquire in this job, if you didn't already have it when you came in. The I'll-think-about-it-later skill, a promise to the self that is never fulfilled.

Because if you do think about it later, you get overwhelmed. You figure out pretty damn quickly that if you do think about all the things you've seen—all the broken bodies, all the dying children—you'll break, and if you break you won't be able to work, and if you can't work, you can no longer be.

After a while, work is all that's left to you. Between the misplaced trust and the sights no human should have to bear, you stand, reporting, because you believe someone will care, someone stronger will Do Something.

Even though, deep down, you know, there is no one stronger, and nothing ever gets done.

5:15 UPLOAD: **SUICIDE SQUADRON PART I**
BY MARTHA TRUMANTE

General Amanda Pedersen tells the story as if it happened two days ago instead of twenty years ago. She's sitting in one of the many cafeterias in the Louvre, this one just beneath the glass pyramid where the tourists enter. She's an American soldier on leave, spending a week with her student boyfriend at the Sorbonne. He has classes. She's seeing the sights.

She's just resting her feet, propping them up—American-style— on the plastic chair across from her. From her vantage, she can't see the first round of security in the pyramid itself, but she can see the second set of metal detectors, the ones installed after the simultaneous attacks of '19 that leveled half the Prado in Madrid and the Tate in London.

She likes watching security systems—that's what got her to enlist in the first place, guaranteeing a sense of security in an insecure world—and she likes watching people go through them.

The little boy and his mother are alone on the escalator coming down. They reach the security desk, the woman opening her palm to reveal the number embedded under the skin, her son—maybe four, maybe five—bouncing with excitement beside her.

A guard approaches him, says something, and the boy extends his arms—European, clearly, used to high levels of security. The guard runs his wand up the boy's legs, over his crotch, in front of his chest—

And the world collapses.

That's how she describes it. The world collapses. The air smells of blood and smoke and falling plaster. Her skin is covered in dust and goo and she has to pull some kind of stone off her legs. Miraculously, they're not broken, but as the day progresses, part of her wishes they were, so she wouldn't be carrying dead through the ruins of the Roman area, up the back stairs, and into the thin Paris sunlight.

She can't go to the rebuilt pyramid, even now, nor to the Tuileries Garden, or even look at the Seine without thinking of that little boy, the smile on his face as he bounces, anticipating a day in the museum, a day with his mother, a day without cares, like five-year-olds are supposed to have.

Were supposed to have.

Before everything changed.

The driver has left me. He will be back in two days, he says, waiting for me near the checkpoint, but I do not believe him. My trust only goes so far, and I will not pay him in advance for the privilege of ferrying me out of this place. So he will forget, or die, or think I have forgotten, or died, whatever eases his conscience if a shred of his conscience still remains.

I walk deep into the camp, my pack slung over my shoulder. My easy walk, my relatively clean clothing, and my pack mark me as a newcomer, as someone who doesn't belong.

The heat is oppressive. There's no place out of the sun except the tents the Red Cross and its relative out here, the Red Crescent, have put up. People sit outside those tents, some clutching babies, other supervising children who dig in the dirt.

Rivulets of mud run across the path. Judging by the flies and the smell, the mud isn't made by water. It's overflowing sewage, or maybe it's urine from the lack of a good latrine system, or maybe it's blood.

There's a lot of blood here.

I do no filming, record no images. The Western world has seen these places before, countless times. When I was a child, late-night television had infomercials featuring cheerful men who walked through such places with a single well-dressed child, selling some religious charity that purported to help people.

Charities don't help people here. They merely stem the tide, stop the preventable deaths, keep the worst diseases at bay. But they don't find real homes for these people, don't do job training, don't offer language lessons, and more importantly, don't settle the political crises or the wars that cause the problems in the first place.

The aid worker has a harder job than I do, because the aid worker—the real aid worker—goes from country to country from camp to camp from crisis to crisis, knowing that for each life saved a thousand more will be lost.

I prefer my work, focused as it can be.

I have been on this assignment for six months now. Writing side pieces. Blogging about the bigger events. Uploading pieces that give no hint of my actual purpose.

My editors fear it will make me a target.

I know that I already am.

Whoever called these places camps had a gift for euphemism. These are villages, small towns with a complete and evolved social system.

You learn that early, in your first camp, when you ask the wrong person the wrong question. Yes, violence is common here—it's common in any human enclave—but it is also a means of crowd control.

Usually you have nothing to do with the extended social system. Usually you speak to the camp leaders—not the official leaders, assigned by the occupying power (whoever that may be), but the de facto leaders, the ones who ask for extra water, who discipline the teenagers who steal hydrogen from truck tanks, who kill the occasional criminal (as an example, always as an example).

You speak to these leaders, and then you leave, returning to the dumpy hotel in the dumpy (and often bombed-out) city, and lie on the shallow mattress behind the thin wooden door, and thank whatever god you know that you have a job, that your employer pays the maximum amount to ensure your safety, that you are not the people you visited that afternoon.

But sometimes, you must venture deep into the enclave, negotiate the social strata without any kind of assistance. You guess which tents are the tents of the privileged (the ones up front, nearest the food?), which tents are the tents of the hopelessly impoverished (in the middle, where the mud runs deep and the smells overwhelm?), and which tents belong to the outcasts, the ones no one speaks to, the ones that make you unclean when you speak to them.

Never assume they're the tents farthest away from the entrance. Never assume they're the ones nearest the collapsing latrines.

Never assume.

Watch, instead. Watch to see which areas the adults avoid, which parts the parents grab their children away from in complete and utter panic.

Watch.

It is the only way you'll survive.

The people I have come to see live in a row near the back of the medical tent. The medical tent has open sides to welcome easy cases, and a smaller, air-conditioned tent farther inside the main one for difficult cases. There is no marking on the main tent—no garish red cross or scythe-like red crescent. No initials for Doctors Without Borders, no flag from some sympathetic and neutral country.

Just a medical tent, which leads me to believe this camp is so unimportant that only representatives from the various charitable organizations come here. Only a few people even know how bad things are here, are willing to see what I can see.

Even though I will not report it.

I'm here for this group within the camp, an enclave within the enclave. I must visit them and leave. I have, maybe, eight hours here—seven hours of talk, and one hour to get away.

I'm aware that when I'm through, I may not be able to find a ride close to the camp. I must trust again or I must walk.

Neither is a good option.

The tents in this enclave are surprisingly clean. I suspect these people take what they need and no one argues with them. No children lay outside the flaps covered in bugs. No children have distended stomachs or too-thin limbs.

But the parents have that hollow-eyed look. The one that comes when the illusions are gone, the one that comes to people who have decided their god has either asked too much of them or has abandoned them.

I stand outside the tent, my questions suddenly gone. I haven't felt real fear for twenty years. It takes a moment to recognize it.

Once I go inside one of these tents, I cannot go back. My interest—my story—gets revealed.

Once revealed, I am through here. I cannot stay in this camp, in this country, in this region. I might even have to go stateside—some place I haven't been in years—and even then I might not be safe.

When I came here, I was hoping to speak a truth.

Now I'm not even sure I can.

6:15 UPLOAD: **SUICIDE SQUADRON PART 2**
BY MARTHA TRUMANTE

Two other devastating explosions occurred in Paris that day: 150 people died as the elevator going up the Eiffel Tower exploded; and another 20 died when a bomb went off in one of the spires near the top of Notre Dame Cathedral.

France went into an unofficial panic. The country had just updated all its security systems in all public buildings. The systems, required by the European Union, were state-of-the-art. No explosives could get into any building undetected—or so the creators of the various systems claimed.

Armand de Monteverde had supervised the tests. He is a systems analyst and security expert with fifteen years experience in the most volatile areas—Iraq, Russia, and Saudi Arabia. The United States hired him to establish security at its borders with Mexico and Canada, as well as oversee security at the various harbors along the East, West, and Gulf Coasts.

He consulted with the French, went in as a spoiler—someone who tried to break the system—and declared the new process temporarily flawless.

"Why temporarily?" some British tabloid reporter asked him.

"Because," Monteverde said, "systems can always be beat."

But not usually so quickly, and not without detection. What bothered Monteverde as he pored over the data from all three Paris explosions was that he couldn't find, even then, the holes in the system.

He couldn't find who had brought the explosives in, how they'd been set off, or even what type they were.

No one else had those answers either, and they should have.

Until the Paris bombings, explosives left traces—some kind of fingerprints or signature. Until the Paris bombings, explosives were easy to understand.

I slip into the third tent to my left. It's cool inside, not just from the lack of sun, but also because some tiny computerized system runs air-conditioning out of mesh covering the canvas. It's a rich person's tent, installed at great expense.

The tent has furniture, which surprises me. Chairs, blanket-covered beds, two small tables for meals. A woman, sitting cross-legged on a rug near the back, wears western clothing—a thin black blouse and black pants—her black hair cut in a stylish wedge. An eleven-year-old boy, clearly her son, sits beside her. He glances at me, his eyes dark and empty, then goes back to staring straight ahead.

I know he has no internal downloads. The camp doesn't allow any kind of net coverage, even if he has the personal chips. There's some kind of blocking technology that surrounds everything, including the medical tent. International agreements allow medical facilities to have net links at all times, but these camps often exist outside an established international perimeter. Even though it straddles the borders of three separate countries, it is in none or all of them, depending on which international law the people in charge of the camp are trying to avoid.

I introduce myself. The woman gives me the look of disbelief that the soldiers should have given me. I slide her my plastic i.d., since we have no systems to log on to here.

She stares at it, then turns it over, sees the hologram of the woman who plays me on the vids, and sighs.

"They warned me," she says, and I do not ask who they are. They are the people who arranged our meeting, the ones who use dozens of intermediaries, and who probably, even now, believe they are using me for some nefarious purpose. "They warned me you would not be what I expect."

A shiver runs through me. Even though I am impersonated on purpose so that the "bad guys," as our president calls them, do not know who I am, someone out there does. Maybe many someones. Maybe many someones connected to the "bad guys."

We go through preliminaries, she and I. I sit across from her, slightly out of range of her child's empty eyes. She offers tea, which I take but do not intend to drink. The cup is small and dainty, trimmed with gold. She has not yet had to trade it for a meal.

Then she slides a chip to me. I press it. A smiling man wearing a western business suit, his head uncovered, his hair as stylishly cut as the woman's, grins at me. He holds the hand of a young girl, maybe five, who is the image of her mother. The girl laughs, one of those floaty childish laughs that some people never outgrow. The sound fills the tent, and the boy, sitting across from me, flinches.

"That's her?" I ask.

"Them," she says. "He died too."

I made it a point to know the case. There are so many cases that sometimes the details are irrelevant to all except the people involved. He had just parked his car outside a café in Cairo. He had told his wife he was taking his daughter to a special class—and indeed, an English-language class for the children of businessmen who had dealings with the West, was meeting just a block away.

He opened his door and the car exploded, killing him, his daughter, and three people on the sidewalk. If they had made it to class as was the plan, over fifty children would have died.

"She's so beautiful," I say. Hard to believe, even now, that a child like that can carry a bomb inside her. Hard to believe she exists only to kill others, at a specified place, at her own designated time.

I have promised myself I will not ask the standard question—*how can you do this? How can you do this to your own child?*

Instead, I say, "Did you know?"

"None of us knew." Her gaze meets mine. It is fierce, defiant. She has answered this question a hundred times, and her answer has never varied. Like so many survivors, she cannot believe her husband doomed his own child.

But I have promised myself I will get the real story, the story no one else has told. I want to know what it's like to be part of a society where children are tools, not people to be loved. I want to know how these people believe so much in a cause—any cause—that it is worth not only their own lives, but their child's as well.

So I must take her initial answers at face value. Perhaps I will challenge them later, but for now, I will see where they lead.

"If neither you nor your husband knew," I say.

"My son didn't know either." Just as fierce. Maybe fiercer. She puts her hand on her son's head. He closes his eyes, but doesn't acknowledge her in any other way.

"If none of you knew," I say, trying hard not to let my disbelief into my voice, "then how did this happen?"

"Like it always does," she snaps. "They put the chips in at the hospital. On the day she was born."

The job is strange. It cannot be work because you cannot leave at the end of the day. It becomes part of you and you become part of it. That's why you and your colleagues label it a calling, put it on par with other religions, other callings that deal with ethics.

You sit across from murderers and ask, what made you decide to kill? as if that's a valid question. You sit across from mass murderers and ask, what is it about your political philosophy that makes your methods so attractive to others? as if you care about the answer.

You think: we need to know, as if knowing's enough to make the problem go away. As if you did the right thing when you were granted the only meeting ever with some charismatic leader—this generation's Vlad the Impaler or Hitler or Osama bin Laden—and interviewed him as if he were a reasonable person. As if you did the right thing when you failed to grab a guard's old-fashioned pistol, and blow the charismatic leader away.

Later you discuss ethics as if they are an important concept.

You say: your job prevents you from judging other people.

You say: other reporters could not get interviews if we take such lethal sides.

You do not say: I lacked the courage to die for my beliefs.

And that is the bottom line. Behind the talk of ethics and jobs and callings lies a simple truth.

You can look. You can see.

But you cannot feel.

If you feel, you will see that your calling is simply a job, a dirty and often disgusting one at that, and you realize there were times when you should have acted. When you could have saved one life or a dozen or maybe even a hundred, but you chose not to.

You chose not to—you say—for the greater good.

7:15 UPLOAD: SUICIDE SQUADRON PART 3
BY MARTHA TRUMANTE

Investigations always seem to hinge on luck. The Paris investigations are no different.

Three months into sorting the Louvre wreckage, the authorities find a chip, its information largely undamaged. Curiously, its technology was five years old, a detail that stumped the investigators more than anything else.

But not General Pedersen.

"I was watching the news that day," she says. "I don't know why. It's not something I normally do. I usually scan the relevant feeds. But that day, I was watching, and it hit me. I had seen the bomb come into the museum. I'd seen him laugh and rock back and forth and smile in anticipation. I'd thought he was looking forward to his day when really, he was looking forward to his death."

At first, other security experts would not listen to Pedersen. In a world where suicide bombers had become commonplace—when child suicide bombers packed with explosives were part of the norm—no one could believe that a child could have had a chip implanted years before with enough high density explosives to destroy an entire building.

People could not plan ahead that far, the common wisdom went. People could not be that cruel.

But they were. That was the new truth—or maybe it was an old truth.

They were.

She shows me the documents the hospital had her sign. She shows me the diagrams, the little marking some doctor made on a chart of a newborn baby, showing where the chips would be—"chips that will enable her to live in the modern world," the doctors told her.

She shows me computer downloads, bank accounts her husband set up in her daughter's name, the college enrollment forms—required for a wealthy child of age four to get into some of Cairo's best private schools—the plans she and her husband had for her daughter's future, her son's future, *their* future.

The authorities, she tells me, believe her husband created all these accounts and family documents to protect her, to prove that she and her son had nothing to do with the family's patriotic explosion.

Only he is not political, she tells me. He never was, and no one believes her.

They believe her enough to send her here instead of kill her as so many other families have been killed in the past. They don't even try or imprison her. They just disown her, her and her son, make them people without a country, refugees in a world filled with refugees.

She can afford this tent on this sandy piece of land. She pays for the space closest to the medical tent. She hoped that someone would befriend her, that the medical personnel—the aid workers—would help her and her unjustly accused son.

Instead, they shun her like everyone else does. They shun her for failing to protect her daughter. They shun her for failing to participate in her husband's crime. They shun her for being naïve, for forcing the so-called patriots to ignore her husband and daughter's martyrdom, for failing to die with her family.

They shun her because they cannot understand her.

Or because they do not want to.

8:15 UPLOAD: SUICIDE SQUADRON PART 4
BY MARTHA TRUMANTE

Experts spend their entire career studying this new bombing phenomenon. Some experts who specialized in suicide bombing have moved to this new area of research.

One, Miguel Franq, wanted to know how three families decided to murder their five-year-olds in well-known Paris landmarks on the same day. Initially, he believed he would find a link that would lead him to a terror cell.

When he did not find the link, he worked with some of the scientists to see if the bomb-chips were set to activate on a certain day, then detonate when they were hit with X-rays, laser beams, or sonar equipment—all three being the main items used in security scans.

The intact chip revealed nothing like that. Only a detonator that was set to go off on a particular time on a particular day.

After much research, many hours of survivor interviews, and that inevitable lucky break, Franq found the link. Someone had given the families free tickets to each site. That all three children did not end up at the same tourist attraction is another matter of luck, although what kind of luck no one can say.

Would it have been better to lose more of the Louvre? Or the Eiffel Tower? Or Notre Dame?

Would it have been better to lose one monument instead of damage three? Would more lives have been saved? Lost? Would more people have noticed? Or would less?

I speak to all the parents in this part of the enclave. All of them survivors—some male, some female—of a once-intact family. All of them claiming to be non-political, claiming they did not know—nor did their spouse—that their child was programmed to die.

I ask for proof. They give me similar documents. They give me bank accounts. But, tellingly—at least to me—the names of the hospitals vary, the names of the doctors vary.

"It is the nursing staff," one man says to me.

"It is an out-patient procedure," says another woman.

"Anyone could do it," says a second man. "Even you."

The rules of journalism have tightened in the past forty years. The scandals of fifty years ago, the tales of made-up sources, or badly researched material or political bias—true or not—nearly destroyed the profession.

When you were hired, you were reminded of those past scandals, told that any story with less than three *verifiable* sources (sources that have proof of their claims, sources that can be reinterviewed by the fact checker—no listening to vids, which can be manipulated, no scanning of notes), any story with less than three will not be run. Any such stories appearing in blogs or personal writings will be considered the same as a published or viewed newspiece.

Hire an editor for your own work, you're told. You will be watched.

We're all watched.

So you become an observer and a detective, a recorder of your facts and a disbeliever in someone else's. You need to verify and if you cannot, you risk losing your job.

You risk damaging the profession.

You risk losing your calling—because you might believe.

Finally, they take me to the person I had hoped to see. They take me into the medical tent to see a six-year-old girl.

She has her own air-conditioned section. It has a hospital bed, a holo-vid player (nothing new; only old downloads), several comfortable chairs, and a table covered with playing cards. Someone is teaching her poker, the international game.

An aid worker accompanies me. He whispers, "No one outside the family visits her. We're not supposed to say she's here."

Until now, she has existed primarily as a rumor.

You know, right, of the little girl? The one who lived?

Permanently blind, she is . . .

They pay her millions of Euros just to remain quiet . . .

She lives in a palace in Switzerland . . .

. . . in Baghdad . . .

. . . in Singapore . . .

She lives in a corner of a medical tent in a refugee camp. Her face is crisscrossed with scars and the shiny tissue of a dozen different plastic surgeries. She has only one arm. You don't realize until you come close that half her torso is a kind of clear plastic, one designed for the medical interns to monitor the fake parts inside her, the miracles that keep her alive.

As I say hello, her eyes move toward me. She can see, then. She says hello in return, her accent upper-class British with a touch of India in it. She looks wary.

I don't blame her.

No parent watches over her. Her mother committed suicide—the real kind, the kind that's personal, and lonely, and takes no one else with it— when she heard the news. The blast killed her father.

She was an only child.

I sit next to her, on her right side so that I don't have to see that clear torso, the workings of her rebuilt interior, that missing—and soon-to-be-replaced—arm.

She is being rebuilt as if she were a machine. Someone is paying for this, real money that keeps this medical tent, and hence the people in the camp, alive.

Someone who, no matter how hard I investigate, manages to remain anonymous.

"Do you know who I am?" I ask.

"Reporter lady," she says, just like my driver, which makes me nervous. I will not stay here two days. I will leave tonight, maybe even on foot. There are too many connections, too many people who know what I'm doing. Not enough ways to make me safe.

"That's right," I say. "Reporter lady. Can I talk to you about your accident?"

She makes a face, but half of her skin does not move. "Not an accident," she says. "I sploded."

The words, said so flatly, as if it is a fact of life. And, if I think about it, it is. A fact of her life.

A fact of all the lives I've touched here today. Every single one of them knew someone who became a bomb.

"Do you know why you exploded?" I ask.

She nods, runs her remaining hand over her stomach. "Someone put something in me."

So flat. Like a child discussing rape.

"Did your daddy know about this?" I ask. Her father took her to an open-air market that day almost one year ago.

She shakes her head. Those bright, inquisitive eyes have moved away from me. Despite the flat tone, she hates talking about this. Or maybe hates talking about her father, the man who decided she was going to be a weapon.

"What did he say when he took you to the market?" I ask.

"Mommy wasn't feeling so good," she says. "We had to get her some medicine and a flower."

"Nothing else?" I ask.

She shrugs.

"Nothing about going to a better place?" I don't know what euphemism to use. I don't know enough about her or her past, being unable to research much of it. I don't know if she was raised Christian or Muslim or Jewish, since that open-air market catered to all three. I don't even know what nationality she is, something these camps like to keep as quiet as they can.

"No," she says.

"He didn't hug you extra hard? Tell you he loved you? Act strange in any way?"

"No," she says.

"Did your mom?"

"No!"

"Did they ever tell you that you were special?" I ask.

She looks at me again. A frown creases her brow, creating a line between the scars. "Yes."

My heart starts to pound. "What did they say?"

She shrugs.

"It's all right to tell me," I say.

She bites her lower lip. This is a question she clearly hasn't been asked much. "Special," she says, "because I'm the only one."

"The only one what?" I ask.

"The only one they ever wanted." Her voice shakes. "Everyone else, they have two, three, four."

I blink for a moment, trying to find the context.

She sees my confusion. Color runs up her cheeks, and I wonder if I've made her angry.

That fear returns—that odd sensation. Afraid twice in one day, after years without it. Afraid, of a damaged six-year-old girl.

"My daddy said I was so perfect, they only wanted me. Only me." Her voice rises, and she squeezes something in her hand.

The aid worker appears at the door. He looks sadly at me. I stand. My time is up.

As I walk out, he says, "She was an only child, in a culture that frowns on it. Her parents were trying to make her feel good about that."

"Is that what you think?" I ask.

"You're not the first she's told that to," he says. "Investigators, officials, everyone tries to find the two, three, and four others. You people never seem to remember that she's a lonely little girl, in a lot of pain, who can't understand why everyone thinks she's evil."

I look over my shoulder at her. Her lower lip trembles, but her eyes are dry.

I want to go back, ask her different questions, but the aid worker doesn't let me.

I am done here. I had hoped I would find my proof. Instead, I found a child whose parents told her she was special—because she was an only child? Or because they had planted a time-release bomb-chip in her?

Or both?

9:15 UPLOAD: **SUICIDE SQUADRON PART 5**
BY MARTHA TRUMANTE

The Paris bombings were the first and last time more than one child detonated in the same city on the same day. Ever since, these explosions have occurred at all times of the day, at hundreds of locations across the globe, at thousands of targets—some large, like the Eiffel Tower, and some small, like a deceptively normal home in a tiny suburban neighborhood.

The small bombings lend credence to the rumors that have plagued this weapon from the beginning: that these children and their parents are innocent victims of fanatics who have wormed their way into the medical establishment, that the true bombers aren't suicidal at all. Instead they are nurses, doctors, interns, who piggyback the detonator chip onto a relatively normal chipping procedure—giving a child an identity chip, for example, or the standard parental notification chip that must now be inserted into every newborn—a procedure that's a law in more than 120 countries.

Hospitals insist that medical personnel are screened. Each chip brought into the building is scanned for foreign technology. Each chip has its own identification number so that it can be traced to its source.

None of the chips found at the thousands of bomb sites since the Paris bombings have had hospital identification. Yet the rumors persist.

Perhaps it is wishful thinking on the part of all involved. How much easier it is to blame a nameless, faceless person hidden in the impersonal medical system than a parent who knowingly pays someone to place a bomb inside a child—a bomb that will not go off in days or even weeks, but years later, after that parent spends time feeding, clothing, and raising that child.

Bonding with that child.

Treating her as if she's normal.

Treating her as if she's loved.

One of the soldiers gives you a ride back to the Green Zone. You lean your head against the back of his modern, hydrogen-powered, air-conditioned behemoth—too big to even call a truck—and close your eyes.

The little girl has shaken you. Some stories do that—some interviews do that—and the key is to hold onto your professionalism, to remember what you can prove.

But in that space between wakefulness and sleep, you find yourself thinking that you live your life in three distinct ways: You have your everyday experiences, which are so different from most people's. How many people travel from war zone to war zone, from danger spot to danger spot, running toward the crisis instead of away from it? Such behavior is now second nature to you. You think of it only at odd moments, like this one, when you should be asleep.

You also live through your articles, your "live" reports, your blogs. People who see/read/hear those things believe they know the real you. They believe they have walked with you into the valley of the shadow of death, and they believe that they, like you, have survived some kind of evil.

Really, however, you live inside your head, in the things you're afraid to write down, afraid to record, afraid to even feel. You lied when you implied that fear hasn't been in your life in decades. Fear is in your every movement. But you speak truth when you say you haven't *felt* fear.

You haven't felt anything in a long, long time.

That's the most important thing they fail to tell you when you sign up for this job. Not that it could kill you or that you might even want it to kill you.

But that you can look at a little girl who has lost everything—her health, her family, her belief that someone once loved her—and you think she does not measure up to the rumor. She isn't the story that will save you, the news that will make you even more famous than you already are.

She doesn't even merit a mention in your long piece on suicide squads because she doesn't change anything. She is, to you, another body—another item—another fact in a lifetime of useless facts.

She is not a child, any more than you are a woman.

She is a weapon, and you are a reporter.

And that's all you'll ever be.

The Prophet of Flores

Ted Kosmatka

New writer Ted Kosmatka has been a zookeeper, a chem tech, and a steelworker, and is now a self-described "lab rat" who gets to play with electron microscopes all day. He made his first sale, to *Asimov's*, in 2005, and has since made several subsequent sales there, as well as to *Ideomancer*, *City Slab*, and *Kindred Voices*.

Here he takes us sideways in time to a world where a certain pesky Theory was "disproved" early on, even though facts in support of it stubbornly continue to appear . . . facts that can be extremely dangerous to mention.

> If this is the best of all possible worlds, what are the others like?
>
> — *Voltaire*

When Paul was a boy, he played God in the attic above his parents' garage. That's what his father called it, playing God, the day he found out. That's what he called it the day he smashed it all down.

Paul built the cages out of discarded two-by-fours he'd found behind the garage and quarter-inch mesh he bought from the local hardware store. While his father was away speaking at a scientific conference on divine cladistics, Paul began constructing his laboratory from plans he'd drawn during the last day of school.

Because he wasn't old enough to use his father's power tools, he had to use a hand saw to cut the wood for the cages. He used his mother's sturdy black scissors to snip the wire mesh. He borrowed hinges from old cabinet doors, and he borrowed nails from the rusty coffee can that hung over his father's unused workbench.

One evening his mother heard the hammering and came out to the garage. "What are you doing up there?" she asked, speaking in careful English, peering up at the rectangle of light that spilled down from the attic.

Paul stuck his head through the opening, all spiky black hair and sawdust. "I'm just playing around with some tools," he said. Which was, in some sense, the truth. Because he couldn't lie to his mother. Not directly.

"Which tools?"

"Just a hammer and some nails."

She stared up at him, her delicate face a broken Chinese doll—pieces of porcelain re-glued subtly out of alignment. "Be careful," she said, and he understood she was talking both about the tools, and about his father.

"I will."

The days turned into weeks as Paul worked on the cages. Because the materials were big, he built the cages big—less cutting that way. In reality, the cages were enormous, overengineered structures, ridiculously outsized for the animals they'd be holding. They weren't mouse cages so much as mouse cities—huge tabletop-sized enclosures that could have housed German Shepherds. He spent most of his paper route money on the project, buying odds and ends that he needed: sheets of plexi, plastic water bottles, and small dowels of wood he used for door latches. While the other children in the neighborhood played basketball or wittedandu, Paul worked.

He bought exercise wheels and built walkways; he hung loops of yarn the mice could climb to various platforms. The mice themselves he bought from a pet store near his paper route. Most were white feeder mice used for snakes, but a couple were of the more colorful, fancy variety. And there were even a few English mice—sleek, long-bodied show mice with big tulip ears and glossy coats. He wanted a diverse population, so he was careful to buy different kinds.

While he worked on their permanent homes, he kept the mice in little aquariums stacked on a table in the middle of the room. On the day he finished the last of the big cages, he released the mice into their new habitats one by one—the first explorers on a new continent. To mark the occasion, he brought his friend John Long over, whose eyes grew wide when he saw what Paul had made.

"You built all this?" John asked.

"Yeah."

"It must have taken you a long time."

"Months."

"My parents don't let me have pets."

"Neither do mine," Paul answered. "But anyway, these aren't pets."

"Then what are they?"

"An experiment."

"What kind of experiment?"

"I haven't figured that out yet."

Mr. Finley stood at the projector, marking a red ellipse on the clear plastic sheet. Projected on the wall, it looked like a crooked half-smile between the X and Y axis.

"This represents the number of daughter atoms. And *this* . . ." He drew the mirror image of the first ellipse. "This is the number of parent atoms." He placed the marker on the projector and considered the rows of students. "Can anyone tell me what the point of intersection represents?"

Darren Michaels in the front row raised his hand. "It's the element's half-life."

"Exactly. Johnson, in what year was radiometric dating invented?"

"1906."

"By whom?"

"Rutherford."

"What method did he use?"

"Uranium lead—"

"No. Wallace, can you tell us?"

"He measured helium as an intermediate decay product of uranium."

"Good, so then who used the uranium-lead method?"

"That was Boltwood, in 1907."

"And how were these initial results viewed?"

"With skepticism."

"By whom?"

"By the evolutionists."

"Good." Mr. Finley turned to Paul. "Carlson, can you tell us what year Darwin wrote *On the Origin of Species*?"

"1867," Paul said.

"Yes, and in what year did Darwin's theory finally lose the confidence of the larger scientific community?"

"That was 1932." Anticipating his next question, Paul continued. "When Kohlhorster invented potassium-argon dating. The new dating method proved the earth wasn't as old as the evolutionists thought."

"And in what year was the theory of evolution finally debunked completely?"

"1954, when Willard F. Libby invented carbon-14 dating at the University of Chicago. He won the Nobel prize in 1960 when he used carbon dating to prove, once and for all, that the Earth was 5,800 years old."

Paul wore a white lab coat when he entered the attic. It was one of his father's old coats, so he had to cut the sleeves to fit his arms. Paul's father was a doctor, the Ph.D. kind. He was blond and big and successful. He'd met Paul's mother after grad school while consulting for a Chinese research firm. They had worked on the same projects for a while, but there was never any doubt that Paul's father was the bright light of the family. The genius, the famous man. He was also crazy.

Paul's father liked breaking things. He broke telephones, and he broke walls, and he broke tables. He broke promises not to hit again. One time, he broke bones, and the police were called by the ER physicians who did not believe the story about Paul's mother falling down the stairs. They did not believe the weeping woman of porcelain who swore her husband had not touched her.

Paul's father was a force of nature, a cataclysm as unpredictable as a comet strike or a volcanic eruption. The attic was a good place to hide, and Paul threw himself into his hobby.

Paul studied his mice as though they were Goodall's chimps. He documented their social interactions in a green spiral notebook. He found that, within the large habitats, they formed packs like wolves, with a dominant male and a dominant female—a structured social hierarchy involving mating privileges, territory, and almost-ritualized displays of submission by males of lower rank. The dominant male bred most of the females, and mice, Paul learned, could kill each other.

Nature abhors a vacuum, and the mouse populations expanded to fill the new worlds he'd created for them. The babies were born pink and blind, but as their fur came in, Paul began documenting colors in his notebook. There were fawns, blacks, and grays. Occasional agoutis. There were Irish spotted, and banded, and broken marked. In later generations, colors appeared that he hadn't purchased, and he knew enough about genetics to realize these were recessive genes cropping up.

Paul was fascinated by the concept of genes, the stable elements through which God provided for the transfer of heritable characteristics from one generation to the next. In school they called it divine transmission.

Paul did research and found that the pigmentation loci of mice were well-mapped and well-understood. He categorized his population by phenotype and found one mouse, a pale, dark-eyed cream that must have been a triple recessive: bb, dd, ee. But it wasn't enough to just have them, to observe them, to run the Punnett squares. He wanted to do real science. And because real scientists used microscopes and electronic scales, Paul asked for these things for Christmas.

Mice, he quickly discovered, did not readily yield themselves to microscopy. They tended to climb down from the stand. The electronic scale, however, proved useful. He weighed every mouse and kept meticulous records. He considered developing his own inbred strain—a line with some combination of distinctive characteristics, but he wasn't sure what characteristics to look for.

He was going over his notebook when he saw it. January-17. Not a date, but a mouse—the seventeenth mouse born in January. He went to the cage and opened the door. A flash of sandy fur, and he snatched it up by its tail— a brindle specimen with large ears. There was nothing really special about the mouse. It was made different from the other mice only by the mark in his notebook. Paul looked at the mark, looked at the number he'd written there. Of the more than ninety mice in his notebook, January-17 was, by two full grams, the largest mouse he'd ever weighed.

In school they taught him that through science you could decipher the truest meaning of God's words. God wrote the language of life in four letters—A, T, C, and G. That's not why Paul did it though, to get closer to God. He did it for the simplest reason, because he was curious.

It was early spring before his father asked him what he spent his time doing in the attic.

"Just messing around."

They were in his father's car on the way home from piano lessons. "Your mother said you built something up there."

Paul fought back a surge of panic. "I built a fort a while ago."

"You're almost twelve now. Aren't you getting a little old for forts?'

"Yeah, I guess I am."

"I don't want you spending all your time up there."

"All right."

"I don't want your grades slipping."

Paul, who hadn't gotten a B in two years, said, "All right."

They rode the rest of the way in silence, and Paul explored the walls of his newly shaped reality. Because he knew foreshocks when he felt them.

He watched his father's hands on the steering wheel. Though large for his age, like his father, Paul's features still favored his Asian mother, and he sometimes wondered if that was part of it, this thing between his father and him, this gulf he could not cross. Would his father have treated a freckled, blond son any differently? No, he decided. His father would have been the same. The same force of nature; the same cataclysm. He couldn't help being what he was.

Paul watched his father's hand on the steering wheel, and years later, when he thought of his father, even after everything that happened, that's how he thought of him. That moment frozen. Driving in the car, big hands on the steering wheel, a quiet moment of foreboding that wasn't false, but was merely what it was, the best it would ever be between them.

"What have you done?" There was wonder in John's voice. Paul had snuck him up to the attic, and now Paul held Bertha up by her tail for John to see. She was a beautiful golden brindle, long whiskers twitching.

"She's the most recent generation, an F4."

"What does that mean?"

Paul smiled. "She's kin to herself."

"That's a big mouse."

"The biggest yet. Fifty-nine grams, weighed at a hundred days old. The average weight is around forty."

Paul put the mouse on John's hand.

"What have you been feeding her?" John asked.

"Same as the other mice. Look at this." Paul showed him the charts he'd graphed, like Mr. Finley, a gentle upward ellipse between the X and Y axis — the slow upward climb in body weight from one generation to the next.

"One of my F2s tipped the scales at forty-five grams, so I bred him to the biggest females, and they made more than fifty babies. I weighed them all at a hundred days and picked the biggest four. I bred them and did the same thing the next generation, choosing the heaviest hundred-day weights. I got the same bell-curve distribution — only the bell was shifted slightly to the right. Bertha was the biggest of them all."

John looked at Paul in horror. "That works?"

"Of course it works. It's the same thing people have been doing with domestic livestock for the last five thousand years."

"But this didn't take you thousands of years."

"No. Uh, it kind of surprised me it worked so well. This isn't even subtle. I mean, look at her, and she's only an F4. Imagine what an F10 might look like."

"That sounds like evolutionism."

"Don't be silly. It's just directional selection. With a diverse enough population, it's amazing what a little push can do. I mean, when you think about it, I hacked off the bottom ninety-five percent of the bell curve for five generations in a row. Of course the mice got bigger. I probably could have gone the other way if I wanted, made them smaller. There's one thing that surprised me though, something I only noticed recently."

"What?"

"When I started, at least half of the mice were albino. Now it's down to about one in ten."

"Okay."

"I never consciously decided to select against that."

"So?"

"So, when I did culls . . . when I decided which ones to breed, some-times the weights were about the same, and I'd just pick. I think I just hap-pened to pick one kind more than the other."

"So what's your point?"

"So what if it happens that way in nature?"

"What do you mean?"

"It's like the dinosaurs. Or woolly mammoths, or cavemen. They were here once; we know that because we find their bones. But now they're gone. God made all life about six thousand years ago, right?"

"Yeah."

"But some of it isn't here anymore. Some died out along the way."

It happened on a weekend. Bertha was pregnant, obscenely, monstrously. Paul had isolated her in one of the aquariums, an island unto herself, sitting on a table in the middle of the room. A little tissue box sat in the corner of her small glass cage, and Bertha had shredded bits of paper into a comfort-able nest in which to give birth to the next generation of goliath mice.

Paul heard his father's car pull into the garage. He was home early. Paul considered turning off the attic lights but knew it would only draw his father's suspicion. Instead he waited, hoping. The garage was strangely quiet—only the ticking of the car's engine. Paul's stomach dropped when he heard the creak of his father's weight on the ladder.

There was a moment of panic then—a single hunted moment when Paul's eyes darted for a place to hide the cages. It was ridiculous; there was no place to go.

"What's that smell?" his father asked as his head cleared the attic floor. He stopped and looked around. "Oh."

And that was all he said at first. That was all he said as he climbed the rest of the way. He stood there like a giant, taking it in. The single bare bulb draped his eyes in shadow. "What's this?" he said finally. His dead voice turned Paul's stomach to ice.

"What's this?" Louder now, and something changed in his shadow eyes. Paul's father stomped toward him, above him.

"What's this?" The words more shriek than question now, spit flying from his mouth.

"I, I thought—"

A big hand shot out and slammed into Paul's chest, balling his T-shirt into a fist, yanking him off his feet.

"What the fuck is this? Didn't I tell you no pets?" The bright light of the family, the famous man.

"They're not pets, they're—"

"God, it fucking stinks up here. You brought these things into the house? You brought this *vermin* into the house? Into my house!"

The arm flexed, sending Paul backward into the cages, toppling one of the tables—wood and mesh crashing to the floor, the squeak of mice and twisted hinges, months and months and months of work.

His father saw Bertha's aquarium and grabbed it. He lifted it high over his head—and there was a moment when Paul imagined he could almost see it, almost see Bertha inside, and the babies inside her, countless generations that would never be born. Then his father's arms came down like a force of nature, like a cataclysm. Paul closed his eyes against exploding glass, and all he could think was, *this is how it happens. This is exactly how it happens.*

Paul Carlson left for Stanford at seventeen. Two years later, his father was dead.

At Stanford he double-majored in genetics and anthropology, taking eighteen credit hours a semester. He studied transcripts of the Dead Sea Scrolls and the Apocryphal verses; he took courses in Comparative Interpretation and Biblical Philosophy. He studied fruit flies and amphioxus and, while still an undergraduate, won a prestigious summer internship working under renowned geneticist Michael Poore.

Paul sat in classrooms while men in dark suits spun theories about Kibra and T-variants; about microcephalin-1 and haplogroup D. He learned researchers had identified structures within a family of proteins called AAA+ that were shown to initiate DNA replication, and he learned these genetic structures were conserved across all forms of life, from men to archaebacteria—the very calling card of the great designer.

Paul also studied the banned texts. He studied balancing equilibriums and Hardy-Weinburg; but alone at night, walking the dark halls of his own head, it was the trade-offs that fascinated him most. Paul was a young man who understood trade-offs.

He learned of the recently discovered Alzheimer's gene, APOE4—a gene common throughout much of the world; and he learned theories about how deleterious genes grew to such high frequencies. Paul learned that although APOE4 caused Alzheimer's, it also protected against the devastating cognitive consequences of early childhood malnutrition. The gene that destroys the mind at seventy, saves it at seven months. He learned that people with sickle cell trait are resistant to malaria; and heterozygotes for cystic fibrosis are less susceptible to cholera; and people with type A blood survived the plague at higher frequencies than other blood types, altering forever, in a single generation, the frequency of blood types in Europe. A process, some said, now being slow-motion mimicked by the gene CKR5 and HIV.

In his anthropology courses, Paul learned that all humans alive today could trace their ancestry back to Africa, to a time almost six thousand years ago when the whole of human diversity existed within a single small population. And there had been at least two dispersions out of Africa, his professors said, if not more—a genetic bottleneck in support of the Deluvian Flood Theory. But each culture had its own beliefs. Muslims called it Allah. Jews, Yahweh. The science journals were careful not to call it God anymore; but they spoke of an intelligent designer—an architect, lowercase a. Though in his heart of hearts, Paul figured it all amounted to the same thing.

Paul learned they'd scanned the brains of nuns, looking for the God spot, and couldn't find it. He learned about evolutionism. Although long debunked by legitimate science, adherents of evolutionism still existed—their beliefs enjoying near immortality among the fallow fields of pseudo-science, cohabitating the fringe with older belief systems like astrology, phrenology, and acupuncture. Modern evolutionists believed the various dating systems were all incorrect; and they offered an assortment of unscientific explanations for how the isotope tests could all be wrong. In hushed tones, some even spoke of data tampering and conspiracies.

The evolutionists ignored the accepted interpretation of the geological record. They ignored the miracle of the placenta and the irreducible complexity of the eye.

During his junior and senior years, Paul studied archaeology. He studied the ancient remains of Homo erectus, and Homo neanderthalensis. He studied the un-Men; he studied afarensis, and Australopithecus, and Pan.

In the world of archeology, the line between Man and un-Man could be fuzzy—but it was never unimportant. To some scientists, Homo erectus was a race of Man long dead, a withered branch on the tree of humanity. To those more conservative, he wasn't Man at all; he was other, a hiccup of the creator, an independent creation made from the same toolbox. But that was an extreme viewpoint. Mainstream science, of course, accepted the use of stone tools as the litmus test. Men made stone tools. Soulless beasts didn't. Of course there were still arguments, even in the mainstream. The fossil KNM ER 1470, found in Kenya, appeared so perfectly balanced between Man and un-Man that a new category had to be invented: near-Man. The arguments could get quite heated, with both sides claiming anthropometric statistics to prove their case.

Like a benevolent teacher swooping in to stop a playground fight, the science of genetics arrived on the scene. Occupying the exact point of intersection between Paul's two passions in life—genetics and anthropology—the field of paleometagenomics was born.

Paul received a bachelor's degree in May and started a graduate program in September. Two years and an advanced degree later, he moved to the East Coast to work for Westin Genomics, one of the foremost genetics research labs in the world.

Three weeks after that, he was in the field in Tanzania, learning the proprietary techniques of extracting DNA from bones 5,800 years old. Bones from the very dawn of the world.

Two men stepped into the bright room.

"So this is where the actual testing is done?" It was a stranger's voice, the accent urban Australian.

Paul lifted his eyes from the microscope and saw his supervisor accompanied by an older man in a gray suit.

"Yes," Mr. Lyons said.

The stranger shifted weight to his teak cane. His hair was short and gray, parted neatly on the side.

"It never ceases to amaze," the stranger said, glancing around. "How alike laboratories are across the world. Cultures who cannot agree on anything agree on this: how to design a centrifuge, where to put the test tube rack, what color to paint the walls—white, always. The bench tops, black."

Mr. Lyons nodded. Mr. Lyons was a man who wore his authority like a uniform two sizes too large; it required constant adjustment to look presentable.

Paul stood, pulled off his latex gloves.

"Gavin McMaster," the stranger said, sticking out a hand. "Pleased to make your acquaintance, Mr. Carlson."

They shook.

"Paul. You can call me Paul."

"I apologize for interrupting your work," Gavin said.

"It's time I took a break anyway."

"I'll leave you two to your discussion," Mr. Lyons said and excused himself.

"Please," Paul said, gesturing to a nearby worktable. "Take a seat."

Gavin sank onto the stool and set his briefcase on the table. "I promise I won't take much of your time," he said. "But I did need to talk to you. We've been leaving messages for the last few days and—"

"Oh." Paul's face changed. "You're from—"

"Yes."

"This is highly unusual for you to contact me here."

"I can assure you these are very unusual circumstances."

"Still, I'm not sure I like being solicited for one job while working at another."

"I can see there's been a misunderstanding."

"How's that?"

"You called it a job. Consider it a consulting offer."

"Mr. McMaster, I'm very busy with my current work. I'm in the middle of several projects, and to be honest, I'm surprised Westin let you through the door."

"Westin is already onboard. I took the liberty of speaking to the management before contacting you today."

"How did you . . ." Paul looked at him, and Gavin raised an eyebrow. With corporations, any question of "how" was usually rhetorical. The answer was always the same. And it always involved dollar signs.

"Of course, we'll match that bonus to you, mate." McMaster slid a check across the counter. Paul barely glanced at it.

"As I said, I'm in the middle of several projects now. One of the other samplers here would probably be interested."

McMaster smiled. "Normally I'd assume that was a negotiating tactic. But that's not the case here, is it?"

"No."

"I was like you once. Hell, maybe I still am."

"Then you understand." Paul stood.

"I understand you better than you think. It makes it easier, sometimes, when you come from money. Sometimes I think that only people who come from it realize how worthless it really is."

"That hasn't been my experience. If you'll excuse me." Politeness like a wall, a thing he'd learned from his mother.

"Please," Gavin said. "Before you leave, I have something for you." He opened the snaps on his briefcase and pulled out a stack of glossy 8 × 10 photographs.

For a moment Paul just stood there. Then he took the photos from Gavin's extended hand. Paul looked at the pictures. Paul looked at them for a long time.

Gavin said, "These fossils were found last year on the island of Flores, in Indonesia."

"Flores," Paul whispered, still studying the photos. "I heard they found strange bones there. I didn't know anybody had published."

"That's because we haven't. Not yet, anyway."

"These dimensions can't be right. A six-inch ulna."

"They're right."

Paul looked at him. "Why me?" And just like that, the wall was gone. What lived behind it had hunger in its belly.

"Why not?"

It was Paul's turn to raise an eyebrow.

"Because you're good," Gavin said.

"So are others."

"Because you're young and don't have a reputation to risk."

"Or one to stand on."

Gavin sighed. "Because I don't know if archaeology was ever meant to be as important as it has become. Will that do for an answer? We live in a world where zealots become scientists. Tell me, boy, are you a zealot?"

"No."

"That's why. Or close enough."

> There were a finite number of unique creations at the beginning of the world—a finite number of species which has, since that time, decreased dramatically through extinction. Speciation is a special event outside the realm of natural processes, a phenomena relegated to the moment of creation, and to the mysteries of Allah.
>
> —Expert witness, heresy trials,
> Ankara, Turkey

The flight to Bali was seventeen hours, and another two to Flores by chartered plane—then four hours by Jeep over the steep mountains and into the heart of the jungle. To Paul, it might have been another world. Rain fell, stopped, then fell again, turning the road into a thing which had to be reasoned with.

"Is it always like this?" Paul asked.

"No," Gavin said. "In the rainy season, the roads are much worse."

Flores, isle of flowers. From the air it had looked like a long ribbon of jungle thrust from blue water, part of a rosary of islands between Australia and Java. The Wallace Line—a line more real than any on a map—lay kilometers to the west, toward Asia and the empire of placental mammals. A stranger emperor ruled here.

Paul was exhausted by the time they pulled into Ruteng. He rubbed his eyes. Children ran alongside the Jeep, their faces some combination of Malay and Papuan—brown skin, strong white teeth like a dentist's dream. The hill town crouched one foot in the jungle, one on the mountain. A valley flung itself from the edge of the settlement, a drop of kilometers.

The men checked into their hotel. Paul's room was basic, but clean, and Paul slept like the dead. The next morning he woke, showered, and shaved. Gavin met him in the lobby.

"It's a bit rustic, I apologize," Gavin said.

"No, it's fine," Paul said. "There was a bed and a shower. That's all I needed."

"We use Ruteng as a kind of base camp for the dig. Our future accommodations won't be quite so luxurious."

Back at the Jeep, Paul checked his gear. It wasn't until he climbed into the passenger seat that he noticed the gun, its black leather holster duct-taped to the driver's door. It hadn't been there the day before.

Gavin caught him staring. "These are crazy times we live in, mate. This is a place history has forgotten till now. Recent events have made it remember."

"Which recent events are those?"

"Religious events to some folks' view. Political to others." Gavin waved his hand. "More than just scientific egos are at stake with this find."

They drove north, descending into the valley and sloughing off the last pretense of civilization. "You're afraid somebody will kidnap the bones?" Paul asked.

"Yeah, that's one of the things I'm afraid of."

"One?"

"It's easy to pretend that it's just theories we're playing with—ideas dreamed up in some ivory tower between warring factions of scientists. Like it's all some intellectual exercise." Gavin looked at him, his dark eyes grave. "But then you see the actual bones; you feel their weight in your hands, and sometimes theories die between your fingers."

The track down to the valley floor was all broken zigzags and occasional, rounding turns. For long stretches, overhanging branches made a tunnel of the roadway—the jungle a damp cloth slapping at the windshield. But here and there that damp cloth was yanked aside, and out over the edge of the drop you could see a valley like Hollywood would love, an archetype to represent all valleys, jungle floor visible through jungle haze. In those stretches of muddy road, a sharp left pull on the steering wheel would have gotten them there quicker, deader.

"Liange Bua," Gavin called their destination. "The Cold Cave." And Gavin explained that was how they thought it happened—the scenario. This steamy jungle all around, so two or three of them went inside to get cool, to sleep. Or maybe it was raining, and they went in the cave to get dry—only the rain didn't stop, and the river flooded, as it sometimes still did, and they were trapped inside the cave by the rising waters, their drowned bodies buried in mud and sediment.

The men rode in silence for a while before Gavin said it, a third option Paul felt coming. "Or they were eaten there."

"Eaten by what?"

"*Homo homini lupus est*," Gavin said. "Man is wolf to man."

They crossed a swollen river, water rising to the bottom of the doors. For a moment Paul felt the current grab the Jeep, pull, and it was a close thing, Gavin cursing and white-knuckled on the wheel, trying to keep them to the shallows. When they were past it he said, "You've got to keep it to the north; if you slide a few feet off straight, the whole bugger'll go tumbling downriver."

Paul didn't ask him how he knew.

Beyond the river was the camp. Researchers in wide-brimmed hats or bandannas. Young and old. Two or three shirtless. A dark-haired woman in a white shirt sat on a log outside her tent. The one feature unifying them all, good boots.

Every head followed the Jeep, and when the jeep pulled to a stop, a small crowd gathered to help unpack. Gavin introduced him around. Eight researchers, plus two laborers still in the cave. Australian mostly. Indonesian. One American.

"Herpetology, mate," one of them said when he shook Paul's hand. Small, stocky, red-bearded; he couldn't have been more than twenty-two. Paul forgot his name the moment he heard it, but the introduction, "Herpetology mate," stuck with him. "That's my specialty," the small man continued. "I got mixed up in this because of professor McMaster here. University of New England, Australia." His smile was two feet wide under a sharp nose that pointed at his own chin. Paul liked him instantly.

When they'd finished unpacking the Jeep, Gavin turned to Paul. "Now I think it's time we made the most important introductions," he said.

It was a short walk to the cave. Jag-toothed limestone jutted from the jungle, an overhang of vine, and beneath that, a dark mouth. The stone was the brown-white of old ivory. Cool air enveloped him, and entering Liange Bua was a distinct process of stepping down. Once inside, it took Paul's eyes a moment to adjust. The chamber was thirty meters wide, open to the jungle in a wide crescent — mud floor, low-domed ceiling. There was not much to see at first. In the far corner, two sticks angled from the mud, and when he looked closer, Paul saw the hole.

"Is that it?"

"That's it."

Paul took off his backpack and stripped the white paper suit out of its plastic wrapper. "Who else has touched it?"

"Talford, Margaret, me."

"I'll need blood samples from everybody for comparison assays."

"DNA contamination?"

"Yeah."

"We stopped the dig when we realized the significance."

"Still. I'll need blood samples from anybody who has dug here, anybody who came anywhere near the bones. I'll take the samples myself tomorrow."

"I understand. Is there anything else you need?"

"Solitude." Paul smiled. "I don't want anybody in the cave for this part."

Gavin nodded and left. Paul broke out his tarps and hooks. It was best if the sampler was the person who dug the fossils out of the ground—or better yet, if the DNA samples were taken when the bones were still *in* the ground. Less contamination that way. And there was always contamination. No matter what precautions were taken, no matter how many tarps, or how few people worked at the site, there was still always contamination.

Paul slid down into the hole, flashlight strapped to his forehead, white paper suit slick on the moist earth. From his perspective, he couldn't tell what the bones were—only that they were bones, half buried in earth. From his perspective, that's all that mattered. The material was soft, unfossilized; he'd have to be careful.

It took nearly seven hours. He snapped two dozen photographs, careful to keep track of which samples came from which specimens. Whoever these things were, they were small. He sealed the DNA samples into small, sterile lozenges for transport.

It was night when he climbed from under the tarp.

Outside the cave, Gavin was the first to find him in the firelight. "Are you finished?"

"For tonight. I have six different samples from at least two different individuals. Shouldn't take more than a few more days."

McMaster handed him a bottle of whiskey.

"Isn't it a little early to celebrate?"

"Celebrate? You've been working in a grave all night. In America, don't they drink after funerals?"

That night over the campfire, Paul listened to the jungle sounds and to the voices of scientists, feeling history congeal around him.

"Suppose it isn't," Jack was saying. Jack was thin and American and very drunk. "Suppose it isn't in the same lineage with us, then what would that mean?"

The red-bearded herpetologist groaned. His name was James. "Not more of that doctrine of descent bullshit," he said.

"Then what is it?" someone added.

They passed the drink around, eyes occasionally drifting to Paul like he was a priest come to grant absolution—his sample kit just an artifact of his priestcraft. Paul swigged the bottle when it came his way. They'd finished off the whiskey long ago; this was some local brew brought by laborers, distilled from rice. Paul swallowed fire.

Yellow-haired man saying, "It's the truth," but Paul had missed part of the conversation, and for the first time he realized how drunk they all were; and James laughed at something, and the woman with the white shirt turned and said, "Some people have nicknamed it the 'hobbit.'"

"What?"

"Flores Man—the hobbit. Little people three feet tall."

"Tolkien would be proud," a voice contributed.

"A mandible, a fairly complete cranium, parts of a right leg and left inominate."

"But what is it?"

"Hey, are you staying on?"

The question was out there for two beasts before Paul realized it was aimed at him. The woman's eyes were brown and searching across the fire. "Yeah," he said. "A few more days."

Then the voice again, "But what is it?"

Paul took another swallow—trying to cool the voice of panic in his head.

Paul learned about her during the next couple of days, the girl with the white shirt. Her name was Margaret. She was twenty-eight. Australian. Some fraction aborigine on her mother's side, but you could only see it for sure in her mouth. The rest of her could have been Dutch, English, whatever. But that full mouth: teeth like Ruteng children, teeth like dentists might dream. She tied her brown hair back from her face, so it didn't hang in her eyes while she worked in the hole. This was her sixth dig, she told him. "This is the one." She sat on the stool while Paul took her blood, a delicate index finger extended, red pearl rising to spill her secrets. "Most archaeologists go a whole lifetime without a big find," she said. "Maybe you get one. Probably none. But this is the one I get to be a part of."

"What about the Leakeys?" Paul asked, dabbing her finger with cotton.

"Bah." She waved at him in mock disgust. "They get extra. Bloody Kennedys of Archaeology."

Despite himself, Paul laughed.

> This brings us to the so-called doctrine of common descent, whereby each species is seen as a unique and individual creation. Therefore all men, living and dead, are descended from a common one-time creational event. To be outside of this lineage, no matter how similar in appearance, is to be other than Man.
>
> —Journal of Heredity

That evening, Paul helped Gavin pack the Jeep for a trek back up to Ruteng. "I'm driving our laborers back to town," Gavin told him. "They work one week on, one off. You want me to take your samples with me?"

Paul shook his head. "Can't. There are stringent protocols for chain of possession."

"Where are they now?"

Paul patted the cargo pocket of his pant leg.

"So when you get those samples back, what happens next?"

"I'll hand them over to an evaluation team."

"You don't test them yourself?"

"I'll assist, but there are strict rules. I test animal DNA all the time, and the equipment is all the same. But genus *Homo* requires a license and oversight."

"All right, mate, then I'll be back tomorrow evening to pick you up." Gavin went to the Jeep and handed Paul the sat phone. "In case anything happens while I'm gone."

"Do you think something will?"

"No," Gavin said. Then, "I don't know."

Paul fingered the sat phone, a dark block of plastic the size of a shoe. "What are you worried about?"

"To be honest, bringing you here has brought attention we didn't want yet. I received a troubling call today. So far, we've shuffled under the radar, but now . . . now we've flown in an outside tech, and people want to know why."

"What people?"

"Official people. Indonesia is suddenly very interested."

"Are you worried they'll shut down the dig?"

Gavin smiled. "Have you studied theology?"

"Why?"

"I've long been fascinated by the figure of Abraham. Are you familiar with Abraham?"

"Of course," Paul said, unsure where this was going.

"From this one sheepherder stems the entire natural history of monotheism. He's at the very foundation of all three Abrahamic faiths—Judaism, Christianity, and Islam. When Jews, Christians, and Muslims get on their knees for their One True God, it is to Abraham's God they pray." Gavin closed his eyes. "And still there is such fighting over steeples."

"What does this have to do with the dig?"

"The word 'prophet' comes from the Greek, *prophetes*. In Hebrew, the word is *nabi*. I think Abraham Heschel said it best when he wrote 'the prophet is the man who feels fiercely.' What do you think, Paul? Do you think prophets feel fiercely?"

"Why are you asking me this?"

"Oh, never mind." Gavin smiled again and shook his head. "It's just the rambling of an old man."

"You never answered if you thought they'd shut down the dig."

"We come onto their land, their territory; we come into this place and we find bones that contradict their beliefs; what do you think might happen? Anything."

"Contradict their beliefs?" Paul said. "What do you believe about these bones? You've never said."

"I don't know. They could be pathological."

"That's what they said about the first Neanderthal bones. Except they kept finding them."

"It could be microcephaly."

"What kind of microcephaly makes you three feet tall?"

"The odd skull shape and small body size could be unrelated. Pygmies aren't unknown to theses islands."

"There are no pygmies this small."

"But perhaps the two things together . . . perhaps the bones are a microcephalic representation of . . ." His voice trailed off. Gavin sighed. He looked suddenly defeated.

"That's not what you believe, is it?" Paul said.

"These are the smallest bones discovered that look anything like us. Could they just be pathological humans? I don't know. Maybe. Pathology could happen anywhere, so you can't rule it out when you've only got a few specimens to work with. But what my mind keeps coming back to is that these bones weren't found just anywhere."

"What do you mean?"

"These bones weren't found in Africa or Asia. These tiny bones were found on a tiny island. Near the bones of dwarf elephants. And that's a coincidence? They hunted dwarf elephants, for God's sake."

"So if not pathological, what do you believe they were? You still haven't said."

"That's the powerful thing about genetics, my friend. One does not have to believe. One can know. And that's precisely what is so dangerous."

"Strange things happen on islands." Margaret's white shirt was gone. She sat slick-armed in overalls. Skin like a fine coat of gloss. The firelight beat the night back, lighting candles in their eyes. It was nearly midnight, and the researchers sat in a circle, listening to the crackle of the fire. Listening to the jungle.

"Like the Galápagos," she said. "The finches."

"Oh come on," James said. "The skulls we found are small, with brains the size of chimps. Island dwarfing of genus Homo; is that what you're proposing? Some sort of local adaptation over the last five thousand years?"

"It's the best we have."

"Those bones are too different. They're not of our line."

"But they're younger than the other archaics. It's not like erectus, some branch cut down at the dawn of time. These things survived here for a long time. The bones aren't even fossilized."

"It doesn't matter, they're still not us. Either they share common descent from Man, or they were a separate creation at the beginning. There is no in-between. And they're only a meter tall don't forget."

"That's just an estimate."

"A good estimate."

"Achondroplasia—"

"Those skulls are as achondroplastic as I am. I'd say the sloped frontal bone is *anti*-achondroplastic."

"Some kind of growth hormone deficiency would—"

"No," Paul said, speaking for the first time. Every face turned toward him.

"No, what?"

"Pygmies have normal growth hormone levels," Paul said. "Every population studied—the negritos, the Andaman, the Congolese. All normal."

The faces stared. "It's the circulating domain of their receptors that are different," Paul continued. "Pygmies are pygmies because of their GH receptors, not the growth hormone itself. If you inject a pygmy child with growth hormone, you still get a pygmy."

"Well still," Margaret said. "I don't see how that impacts whether these bones share common descent or not."

James turned to the circle of faces. "So are they on our line? Are they us, or other?"

"Other."

"Other."

"Other."

Softly, the girl whispered in disbelief, "But they had stone tools."

The faces turned to Paul, but he only watched the fire and said nothing.

The next morning started with a downpour. The dig team huddled in tents, or under the tarped lean-to near the fire pit. Only James braved the rain, stomping off into the jungle. He was back in an hour, smiling ear to ear.

"Well, will you look at that," James said, holding something out for Paul to see.

"What is it?"

"Partially eaten monitor. A species only found here."

Paul saw now that it was a taloned foot that James held. "That's a big lizard."

"Oh, no. This was just a juvenile. Mother nature is odd this side of the Wallace Line. Not only are most of the species on this side not found anywhere else. A lot of them aren't even vaguely related to anything else. It's like God started from scratch to fill all the niches."

"How'd you get interested in herpetology?" Paul asked.

"By His creations shall ye know God."

"McMaster mentioned a dwarf elephant."

"Yeah, stegadon. They're extinct now though."

"What killed them off?"

"Same thing that killed off a lot of the ancient fauna on the island. Classic catastrophism, a volcanic eruption. We found the ash layer just above the youngest bones."

Once, lying in bed with a woman, Paul had watched the moon through the window. The woman traced his scars with her finger.

"Your father was brutal."

"No," Paul had said. "He was broken, that's all."

"There's a difference?"

"Yeah."

"What?"

"He was always sorry afterward."

"That mattered?"

"Every single time."

> A: Incidences of local adaptation have occurred, sure. Populations adapt to changing conditions all the time.
>
> Q: Through what process?
>
> A: Differential reproductive success. Given genetic variability, it almost has to happen. It's just math and genes. Fifty-eight hundred years is a long time.
>
> Q: Can you give an example?
>
> A: Most dogs would fall into this category, having been bred by man to suit his needs. While physically different from each other, when you study their genes, they're all one species—though admittedly divided into several distinct clades.
>
> Q: So you're saying God created the original dog, but Man bred the different varieties?
>
> A: You called it God, not me. And for the record, honey, God created the gray wolf. Man created dogs.
>
> —excerpted from the trial of geneticist Michael Poore.

It came the next morning in the guise of police action. It came in shiny new Daihatsus with roll bars and off-road tires. It came with guns. Mostly, it came with guns.

Paul heard them before he saw them, men shouting in a language he could not understand. He was with James at the cave's entrance. When Paul saw the first assault rifle, he sprinted for the tents. He slid the DNA lozenges into a pouch in his belt and punched numbers on the sat phone. Gavin picked up on the second ring. "The police are here," Paul said.

"Good Lord, I just spoke to officials today," Gavin said. There was shouting outside the tents—angry shouts. "They assured me nothing like this would happen."

"They lied."

Behind him, James said, "This is bad. This is very bad."

"Where are you?" Paul asked.

"I'm still in Ruteng," Gavin said.

"Then this will be over by the time you can get here."

"Paul, it's not safe for you th—"

Paul hung up. *Tell me something I don't know.*

He took his knife from his sample kit and slit the back of the tent open. He slid through, James following close behind. Paul saw Margaret standing uncertain at the edge of the jungle. Their eyes met and Paul motioned toward the Jeeps; on the count of three, they all ran for it.

They climbed in and shut the doors. The soldiers—for that's what Paul knew they were now—the soldiers didn't notice them until Paul started the engine. Malay faces swung around, mouths open in shouts of outrage.

"You'll probably want your seat belts on for this," Paul said. Then he gunned it, spitting dirt.

"Don't shoot," James whispered in the backseat, eyes closed in prayer.

"What?" Paul said.

"If they shoot, they're not police."

A round smashed through the rear window and blew out a chunk of the front windshield, spidering the safety glass.

"Shit!" Margaret screamed.

A quick glance in the rearview, and Paul saw soldiers climbing into one of the Daihatsus. Paul yanked the wheel right.

"Not that way!" Margaret shouted. Paul ignored her and floored the accelerator.

Jungle whipped past, close enough to touch. Ruts threatened to buck them from the cratered roadway. The Daihatsu whipped into view behind them. Shots rang out, a sound like Chinese firecrackers, the ding of metal. They rounded the bend, and the river came into view—big and dumb as the sky. Paul gunned the engine.

"We're not going to make it across!" James shouted.

"We only need to get halfway."

Another shot slammed into the back of the Jeep.

They hit the river like a slow-speed crash, water roaring up and over the broken windshield—the smell of muck suddenly overpowering.

Paul stomped his foot to the floor.

The Jeep chugged, drifted, caught gravel. They got about halfway across before Paul yanked the steering wheel to the left. The world came unstuck and started to shift. The right front fender came up, rocking with the current. The engine died. They were floating.

Paul looked back. The pursuing vehicle skidded to a halt at the shoreline, and men jumped out. The Jeep heaved, one wheel pivoting around a submerged rock.

"Can you swim?" Paul asked.

"Now you ask us?"

"I'd unbuckle if I were you."

The Jeep hit another rock, metal grinding on stone, then sky traded places with water, and everything went dark.

They dragged themselves out of the water several miles downriver, where a bridge crossed the water. They followed the dirt road to a place called Rea. From there they took a bus. Margaret had money.

They didn't speak about it until they arrived at Bajawa.

"Do you think they're okay?" Margaret asked.

"I think it wouldn't serve their purpose to hurt the dig team. They only wanted the bones."

"They shot at us."

"Because they assumed we had something they wanted. They were shooting at the tires."

"No," she said. "They weren't."

Three rented nights in the hotel room, and James couldn't leave—that hair like a great big handle anybody could pick up and carry, anybody with eyes and a voice. Some of the locals hadn't seen red hair in their lives, and James's description was prepackaged for easy transport. Paul, however, blended—just another vaguely Asian set of cheekbones in the crowd, even if he was a half a foot taller than the locals.

That night, staring at the ceiling from one of the double beds, James said, "If those bones aren't us . . . then I wonder what they were like."

"They had fire and stone tools," Paul said. "They were probably a lot like us."

"We act like we're the chosen ones, you know? But what if it wasn't like that?"

"Don't think about it," Margaret said.

"What if God had all these different varieties . . . all these different walks, these different options at the beginning, and we're just the ones who killed the others off?"

"Shut up," she said.

"What if there wasn't just one Adam, but a hundred Adams?"

"Shut the fuck up, James."

There was a long quiet, the sound of the street filtering through the thin walls. "Paul," James said. "If you get your samples back to your lab, you'll be able to tell, won't you?"

Paul was silent. He thought of the evaluation team and wondered.

"The winners write the history books," James said. "Maybe the winners write the bibles, too. I wonder what religion died with them."

The next day, Paul left to buy food. When he returned Margaret was gone.

"Where is she?"

"She left to find a phone. She said she'd be right back."

"Why didn't you stop her?"

"I couldn't."

Day turned into evening. By darkness, they both knew she wasn't coming back.

"How are we going to get home?" James asked.

"I don't know."

"And your samples. Even if we got to an airport, they'd never let you get on the plane with them. You'll be searched. They'll find them."

"We'll find a way once things have settled down."

"Things are never going to settle down."

"They will."

"No, you still don't get it. When your entire culture is predicated on an idea, you can't afford to be proven wrong."

Out of deep sleep, Paul heard it. Something.

He'd known this was coming, though he hadn't been aware that he'd known, until that moment. The creak of wood, the gentle breeze of an open door. Shock and awe would have been better—an inrush of soldiers, an arrest of some kind, expulsion, deportation, the legal system. A silent man in the dark meant many things. None of them good. The word assassin rose up in his mind.

Paul breathed. There was a cold in him—a part of him that was dead, a part of him that could never be afraid. A part of him his father had put there. Paul's eyes searched the shadows and found it, the place where shadow moved, a breeze that eased across the room. If there was only one of them, then there was a chance.

Paul thought of making a run for it, sprinting for the door, leaving the samples and this place behind; but James, still sleeping, stopped him. He made up his mind.

Paul exploded from the bed, flinging the blanket ahead of him, wrapping that part of the darkness; and a shape moved, darkness like a puma's spots, black on black—there even though you can't see it. And Paul knew he'd surprised him, that darkness, and he knew, instantly, that it wouldn't be enough. A blow rocked Paul off his feet, forward momentum carrying him into the wall. The mirror shattered, glass crashing to the floor.

"What the fuck?" James hit the light, and suddenly the world snapped into existence, a flashbulb stillness—and the assassin was Indonesian, preternatural silence coming off him like a heat shimmer. He carried endings with him, nothingness in a long blade. The insult of it hit home. The shocking fucking insult, standing there, knees bent, bright blade in one hand—blood on reflective steel. That's when Paul felt the pain. It was only then he realized he'd already been opened.

And the Indonesian moved fast. He moved so fast. He moved faster than Paul's eyes could follow, covering distance like thought, across the room to James, who had time only to flinch before the knife parted him. Such a professional, and James's eyes went wide in surprise. Paul moved using the only things he had, size, strength, momentum. He hit the assassin like a linebacker, sweeping him into his arms, crushing him against the wall. Paul felt something snap, a twig, a branch, something in the Indonesian's chest—and they rolled apart, the assassin doing something with his hands; the rasp of blade on bone, a new blackness, and Paul flinched from the blow, feeling the steel leave his eye socket.

There was no anger. It was the strangest thing. To be in a fight for his life and not be angry. The assassin came at him again, and it was only Paul's size that saved him. He grabbed the arm and twisted, bringing the fight to the floor. A pushing down of his will into three square inches of the Indonesian's throat—a caving-in like a crumpling aluminum can, but Paul still held on, still pushed until the lights went out of those black eyes.

"I'm sorry," he said. "I'm sorry."

Paul rolled off him and collapsed to the floor. He crawled over to James. It wasn't a pool of blood. It was a swamp, the mattress soggy with it. James lay on the bed, still conscious.

"Don't bleed on me, man," James said. "No telling what you Americans might carry. Don't want to have to explain it to my girlfriend."

Paul smiled at the dying man, crying and bleeding on him, wiping the blood from his beard with a pillowcase. He held James's hand until he stopped breathing.

Paul's eye opened to white. He blinked. A man in a suit sat in the chair next to the hospital bed. A man in a police uniform stood near the door. "Where am I?" Paul asked. He didn't recognize his own voice. It was an older man. Who'd eaten glass.

"Maumere," the suited man said. He was white, mid-thirties, lawyer written all over him.

"How long?"

"A day."

Paul touched the bandage over his face. "Is my eye . . ."

"I'm sorry."

Paul took the news with a nod. "How did I get here?"

"They found you naked in the street. Two dead men in your room."

"So what happens now?"

"Well, that depends on you." The man in the suit smiled. "I'm here at the behest of certain parties interested in bringing this to a quiet close."

"Quiet?"

"Yes."

"Where is Margaret? Mr. McMaster?"

"They were put on flights back to Australia this morning."

"I don't believe you."

"Whether you believe or not is of no consequence to me. I'm just answering your questions."

"What about the bones?"

"Confiscated for safekeeping, of course. The Indonesians have closed down the dig. It is their cave, after all."

"What about my DNA samples in the hotel room, the lozenges?"

"They've been confiscated and destroyed."

Paul sat quietly.

"How did you end up in the street?" the suit asked.

"I walked."

"How did you end up naked?"

"I figured it was the only way they'd let me live. The only way to prove I didn't have the samples. I was bleeding out. I knew they'd still be coming."

"You are a smart man, Mr. Carlson. So you figured you'd let them have the samples?"

"Yeah," Paul said.

The suited man stood and left the room.

"Mostly," Paul said.

On the way to the airport, Paul told the driver to pull over. He paid the fare and climbed out. He took a bus to Bengali, and from there took a cab to Rea.

He climbed on a bus in Rea, and as it bore down the road, Paul yelled, "Stop!"

The driver hit the breaks. "I'm sorry," Paul said. "I've forgotten something." He climbed off the bus and walked back to town. No car followed.

Once in town, down one of the small side streets, he found it, the flower pot with the odd pink plant. He scooped dirt out of the base.

The old woman shouted something at him. He held out money. "For the plant," he said. "I'm a flower lover." She might not have understood English, but she understood money.

He walked with the plant under his arm. James had been right about some things. Wrong about others. Not a hundred Adams, no. Just two. All of Australoid creation like some parallel world. *And you shall know God by His creations.* But why would God create two Adams? That's what Paul had wondered. The answer was that He wouldn't.

Two Adams. Two gods. One on each side of the Wallace Line.

Paul imagined it began as a competition. A line drawn in the sand, to see whose creations would dominate.

Paul understood the burden Abraham carried, to witness the birth of a religion.

As Paul walked through the streets he dug his fingers through the dirt. His fingers touched it, and he pulled the lozenge free. The lozenge no evaluation team would ever lay eyes on. He would make sure of that.

He passed a woman in a doorway, an old woman with a beautiful, full mouth. He thought of the bones in the cave, and of the strange people who had once crouched on this island.

He handed her the flower. "For you," he said.

He hailed a cab and climbed inside. "Take me to the airport."

As the old cab bounced along the dusty roads, Paul took off his eye patch. He saw the cabby glance into his rearview and then look away, repulsed.

"They lied, you see," Paul told the cabbie. "About the irreducible complexity of the eye. Oh, there are ways."

The cabbie turned his radio up, keeping his face forward. Paul grimaced as he unpacked his eye, pulling white gauze out in long strips—pain exploding in his skull.

"A prophet is one who feels fiercely," he said, then slid the lozenge into his empty eye socket.

stray

BENJAMIN ROSENBAUM
DAVID ACKERT

New writer Benjamin Rosenbaum has made sales to *The Magazine of Fantasy & Science Fiction*, *Asimov's Science Fiction*, *Argosy*, *The Infinite Matrix*, *Strange Horizons*, *Harper's*, *McSweeney's*, *Lady Churchill's Rosebud Wristlet*, and elsewhere. He has been a party clown, a day care worker on a kibbutz in the Galilee, a student in Italy, a stay-at-home dad, and a programmer for Silicon Valley start-ups, the U.S. government, online fantasy games, and the Swiss banks of Zurich. His story "Embracing-the-New" was on last year's Nebula Ballot. Recently returned from a long stay in Switzerland, he now lives with his family in Falls Church, Virginia. Coming up is his first collection, *The Ant King and Other Stories*. He has a Web site at: www.benjaminrosenbaum.com.

New writer David Ackert is an actor whose credits include television shows such as *CSI: Miami* and *JAG*, as well as the films *Suckers* and *Cool Crime*, and a short film entitled *Blue Plate* that he also produced. He is currently producing and appearing in a documentary entitled *Voices of Uganda*.

Here they join forces to demonstrate that sometimes the hardest thing about having power is *not* using it. . . .

She'd found him by the side of the road: Ivan, who had been prince of the immortals, lying in the long grass. Ivan, against whose knees weeping kings had laid their cheeks; who had collected popes, khans, prophets, martyrs, minstrels, whores, revolutionaries, poets, anarchists, and industrial magnates; who could send armies into the sea with a movement of his hand.

She'd stopped her Model T where he lay by the side of the road. He was shell-shocked, marooned at the end of one kind of life, an empty carapace, soul-dry. There were a million drifters and Okies and ruined men cluttering the gutters of Franklin Delano Roosevelt's America, and Muriel had taken him for a white man at first. Colored doctor's daughter stopping for what looked like a white hobo; the wild danger of that. On that improbable fulcrum, his life had turned.

He'd told her what he was. She was a mortal; of course she was afraid. But she'd listened, and at the end of that long, mad tale, she'd gotten up from her cedar kitchen table, cleared the teacups, washed them in the sink, and dried her hands.

"I believe you," she'd said, and some strange sweet leviathan had moved through the dark water within him. He'd studied the grain of the polished cedar wood, not meeting her eyes. She was like a glass he was afraid of dropping. But even without looking, every creak of the floorboards, every clink of the dishes told him: stay.

The wedding had been a long Sunday in June. The church was bright, with thick white paint over the boards. It seated forty, squeezed together on pine benches—two rows of out-of-town relatives and Muriel's father's old patients had to stand in the back. There was potato salad and coleslaw and grits and greens on the benches outside. The rich smell of the barbecue, the smoke from the grill. Mosquitoes dancing in the afternoon light.

Muriel smiling and crying and laughing. With Muriel set into the center of his world like a jewel, Ivan was home; when she touched his hand, his enemies became God's wounded children, his centuries of pain and crime a fireside tale to wonder at. In her embrace, Ivan's bitter knowledge was refuted. He was a fool in a garden.

Without her, the world was a desert of evil beings.

And he was full of fear—full of fear, that she would go.

Aunt Gertrude was saying, "No no no, the Monroes, from the *other* side of the family, you know—I think they out in Kansas. Very respectable. Well, let me tell you *this*, child—I knew that man was perfect for Muriel *before* she told me he was family. The moment I laid eyes . . ."

The women fluttered about Ivan and fussed at him. The men tried out their jokes and stories on him. He nodded and laughed, and watched what their bodies told each other. Yes, he was an out-of-towner, strange, his past unknown; drifter, some said, the kind you want to keep on moving past your town. But that kind settled down sometimes—now look how hard he worked at the mill, when there was work. And she was so happy, look how happy she was. And you know that's what Muriel needed to be satisfied: someone with an air of strangeness, like this green-eyed ageless second cousin who had probably been in the Great War.

And he hadn't pulled any of his puppeteer's strings. Not one. All on their own, they had chosen him.

Except Li'l Wallace.

Li'l Wallace was polite. He complimented Muriel's dress and he told the men the one about the sailor and the Dutchman. But to Ivan, the man's thoughts were as loud as a siren: How had this stranger, this high yellow "second cousin" with city manners and slippery ways, won Muriel? Li'l Wallace was strong and good-looking and a steady day-shift man at the mill, and he was from around here. Sure, he was dark, but he couldn't believe all Muriel wanted was a light-skinned man! After ten years of patient and chivalrous wooing, he had a right to the heart of the doctor's daughter. He couldn't fathom how the stranger had gotten by him.

All through the reception, Li'l Wallace's eyes tracked across Ivan's face, hands, clothes, looking for a weakness. Ivan squirmed. It would be so easy: to shift the cadence of his voice to match Li'l Wallace's; to hold his shoulders in a certain way that would remind Li'l Wallace of his dead brother; to be silent at the right moment, then say the words Li'l Wallace was thinking; so that Li'l Wallace would feel suddenly an unreasonable rush of affection for him, would grin, shake his head ruefully, give up his desire for Muriel and love Ivan.

Ivan felt like a cripple. Like a man trying to feed himself with a fork held in his toes. And he was afraid. Eventually, Li'l Wallace would find something out of place. What if he found out enough to hate and fear Ivan? To turn these people against him? Part of Ivan seethed with rage that any human would look at him with those suspicious eyes. How good it would feel to turn that resentment and suspicion, in an instant, to adoration.

But if Ivan was going to be human, to be here, he would have to leave the puppeteer's strings alone.

Ivan had been sitting on a picnic bench in the churchyard, smearing his last piece of cornbread into the cooling dabs of gravy, when Li'l Wallace approached.

"You smoke?"

Ivan blinked up at him. What was this? "I have," he said. He watched the resentment and mistrust brewing in the mortal, calculating its trajectory, aching to banish it.

"Good," Li'l Wallace said, and pressed something small, square, and cold into Ivan's hand. Then nodded, and walked away.

Ivan looked at the lighter. And up at Li'l Wallace's retreating back, and in it, the decision, simple and sweet: that Muriel deserved to be happy.

A shiver raced through Ivan's body. He thought: this human has surprised me. This human has surprised me! Ivan's heart beat large within him and he looked up at Muriel in her white dress, swinging a niece in slow circles in the air. How can this be?

And then Ivan answered himself: because in ten thousand years, this is what you have never seen: what happens, what they choose, if only you leave them alone.

There were moments when he suddenly felt lost in this new life. Sitting by the pond with Li'l Wallace, a checkerboard between them, throwing bread to the ducks, his heart would abruptly begin to race and he would think, what am I doing here? I am wasting time, there is something terribly important I must do, and first of all I must take this human—make sure he is mine, under my control, safe. He'd squeeze his eyes shut and wait for the feeling to pass.

Or he'd be in a church pew singing David's psalms and be overcome with a memory: walking through a walled city to the court of a hill-country half-nomad potentate, asses braying in the evening, a crowd of slaves falling onto their bellies before him. Scowling at the princes and lords in disgust—this one too passive, this one low and mean, this one dissolute, none of them souls he'd want pressed close to him. And then turning to see the hard eyes and wild grin of the minstrel boy sitting in the corner with a harp in his goatherd's hands. Thinking: ah, yes. You. On you I will build an empire, and a path to God. Whatever you were before, now you are mine; now you are the arrow that pierces Heaven. And seeing the yearning begin in the boy's eyes, the yearning that would never end, that only Ivan could fulfill.

And in the middle of the mill floor, a fifty-pound sack of flour on one shoulder, Ivan would stop, remembering the shadow the roach cast. After he'd feasted on a hundred centuries of human devotion and need, when he was full of power and empty of fear, he'd forced his way past the Last Door of Dream. And beyond the door, where he'd expected answers and angels—in that terrible light, he'd seen a roach skittering across a wall. And he'd known that that automaton, that empty dead machine creeping on and on and on over the bodies of the dead—that insect was Ivan.

He'd burned his castle. Burned his library of relics—the jade knife that killed this one, the lock of that one's hair. Abandoned his living prizes to madness. He'd vanished into a Europe descending into hell: walked through fields of corpses amidst the whistling of shells, on dusty roads by the tinkling and bleating of starving goats. Stared at the blue walls of the sanitorium, seeing the eyes of all those he'd taken. A wall of eyes in darkness. Years that were all one long moment of terror and rage and shame, before he'd crossed the Atlantic.

Now, when it came upon him, he shouldered the bag and moved his feet. One, then the other. Watched the men at their work of stacking, looked at each one, whispering their names. That's Henry. That's Roy. That's Li'l Wallace.

Thought of Muriel waiting at home. Of ham and collard greens. Coffee. Checkers. Lucky Strikes.

The eyes still watched him, from their wall.

Ivan loved positioning the checkers, sacrificing one to save another, cornering, crowning, collecting. He loved pretending to make a stupid mistake, giving his last piece to Li'l Wallace with a show of effort and disappointment. And if Ivan kept his eyes carefully on the ducks in the pond and hummed a song from the radio silently to himself, sometimes he could distract himself enough that Li'l Wallace's moves would actually surprise him.

The sun was touching the horizon now. Li'l Wallace finished his smoke and handed the lighter back to Ivan. "How's married life?"

"Can't complain," Ivan said, and looked over at Li'l Wallace. The question was guileless, friendly. But Ivan felt uneasy.

"I guess y'all gon' be working on children now," Li'l Wallace said with an easy smile, his eyes on the lake.

Blood rushed to Ivan's face and he turned away. He closed his eyes and remembered Muriel crying in the kitchen. "Shush," she'd said, pushing him away, "shush, Ivan, yes, I *knew*, I know what life I chose, now you just let me be, you let me be." Her cheeks glistening, the bedroom door slamming. (And he could make her laugh again, make her happy again, instantly, so easily! He'd closed his eyes, knowing where that road led: a madman in an empty palace, a lock of hair in a ribbon, burning.)

Ivan heard Li'l Wallace shift in his chair.

So there you are, you bastard, Ivan thought. You were right all along. You are the right one for Muriel. You could have given her a real life, a real family. I can only give her a parody.

He opened his eyes and saw, in Li'l Wallace's, only compassion.

And that was too much for Ivan to bear. He pushed himself out of his chair and headed for the woods. Li'l Wallace said something; Ivan kept walking. He didn't speak, he didn't gesture. He didn't trust what he might do to Li'l Wallace if he did.

Ivan pissed against a tree, buttoned up, and walked deeper into the woods, toward the abandoned graveyard at its heart. He slowed his heartbeat and watched the shadows among the leaves. Then, at the graveyard's edge, he saw the girl.

She had dirty blond hair and wore a dress stitched from old calico rags. She was about eleven years old. She knelt in the dirt, her eyes closed, framed in the sun's last light filtering green through the trees. She was praying. Her lips moved, clumsy, honest. There were tears on her cheeks.

Ivan felt her prayer, like a beam piercing through the veil. That veil that had been like a wall of stone for him, that door he had opened at such cost, was like a cobweb to her. She was whispering in God's ear.

Ivan shifted his posture to become a white man, made himself calm, comforting. He knelt by her and put his hand on her shoulder. She opened her eyes but she was not startled. She smiled at him.

"I'm Ivan. What's your name?"

"Sarah," said the girl.

She bit her lip. The question she was expecting was, what are you doing out in these woods alone? Instead he asked: "What are you praying for?"

Sarah drew in a deep and shuddering breath, but she didn't cry. "I live with my sick grandma. When she dies, I'll be alone. Ain't nobody else to take me in. But I'm not afraid. I'm not afraid. God's gonna send someone."

Ivan stroked his hand across her hair. This girl's eyes were a speckled blue. And yet their shape was so familiar. Where had he seen them before? He wondered if a little manipulation in a good cause might be permitted him. Surely he could arrange for a family of whites to take her in. Maybe he would ask Muriel to bend their rules. Maybe—

There was a crunch of boots on leaves in the forest behind him. "Ivan?" Li'l Wallace said.

Ivan jumped up. Damn, damn, he'd been lost in the little girl's eyes. Sarah looked wildly around. Li'l Wallace stared at them and frowned. They were both looking at him, and there was no time.

Maybe he could have crafted a way to look that would have set them both at ease. In the old days, when he was powerful. But he was so tired now, and he couldn't risk losing his new home. So he looked as Li'l Wallace expected him to—Negro.

The girl screamed.

"Oh my God!" she shouted. She stumbled back against a gravestone and grabbed at her hair where Ivan had touched it. "You're a *nigger!* Oh my God, no, you're gonna—"

Li'l Wallace hissed in breath, and in it Ivan heard their future. The girl running, crying, found on the road, her imagination feverish. Torches. Guns. Dogs. Crosses of fire. Li'l Wallace's feet kicking in the air, kicking, finding no purchase, nowhere to stand.

Sarah drew another breath to scream and—

Ivan took her.

She ran to him and collapsed into his arms, buried her face against his stomach, sobbing. Ivan lifted her up gently, nestled her face against his neck.

For Li'l Wallace's benefit, he said, "Shush now, little miss, you know no one gonna hurt you here, we're decent folk here, no one gonna treat you with any disrespect, come now, Ivan's gonna take you back to your home."

And when he looked up into Li'l Wallace's eyes, suspicion and fear were fading. Li'l Wallace blinked and smiled uneasily and let a breath out. His eyes said: you handled that well. I hope.

Ivan nodded and walked back toward the pond. Li'l Wallace stood behind him, uncertain whether to follow, and Ivan said, "I'll see you tomorrow, brother."

The brown duck quacked at him by the side of the pond. Wanting bread. But he had no bread left. Sarah's little body was warm and light against his. He leaned his head back a little to look in her eyes. She would follow him anywhere. She didn't care if he was white or black. He was her sent angel.

Ivan felt the sting of tears.

Could it be different, this time? What if there was no shaping, no manipulation, no harvesting; what if he gardened her soul, not for himself, but for her? She was his now: very well, he would be hers. His heart was racing; he felt her total attention, the silence in her mind, the way the collected clear themselves away to make room for the master's will, and it sickened him. He could cherish her, like a daughter. Would it bring her back to herself? He'd freed prizes before, abandoned them to collapse into madness. Not this time. Too late to turn back. He steeled himself: this time there would be only love, a father's love!

He put Sarah on her feet as they approached the porch steps. She leaned in toward him, inhaled the scent of him as it breezed off his shirt, his jacket, his skin. He looked down at her, scratching his jaw, and opened the door.

"Muriel?" he called in, escorting the girl inside. He sat Sarah down at the kitchen table and scooped generous curls of ice cream into a bowl. He heard Muriel coming down the stairs as he handed Sarah a spoon.

Muriel stopped when she saw the girl. She had not expected a third person in the house. The two of them locked eyes.

"This here is our new friend, Sarah," Ivan said.

"Hello, Sarah." Muriel nodded, a nod of extreme politeness, a nod in which no one could find any insolence at all. Her spine was knotted tense. She looked around the room at the chairs, wondering if she should sit down. Smiled broadly. Tried not to wonder where this girl's people were, if they were looking for her, what they would do if they found her here. Trying to trust Ivan. Just a little girl eating ice cream, Ivan saw Muriel tell herself, trying not to think of torches and dogs.

Sarah shrank back a little. She glanced at Ivan, looking for some cue or instruction. She found it in his expression and put down the spoon.

"I don't mean to be any bother, ma'am. Your husband was kind enough to help me after I took a fall on the road. He kept saying nice things about you and so we thought I might like to meet you is all." Sarah sparkled at her hostess. Her smile was warm and innocent, smudged with vanilla.

"Oh," Muriel said, relaxing a little. "Of course." She stepped forward and opened the napkin drawer. "Well, you're certainly welcome here."

Sarah flicked a look back to Ivan. He smiled to reassure her. Well done, little one. We will convince my Muriel. She needs a little time for these fears of hers, fears from the world beyond this house. They don't belong in this house anymore; they don't matter now.

Sarah stroked her chin, mock serious.

"Now if I had to guess, I'd say you made this delicious ice cream yourself, am I right, ma'am?"

Muriel laughed and turned back to the girl. "Oh yes, and it's kind of you to . . ." She stopped and looked at Ivan. He realized he was stroking his chin in exactly the same way, and jerked his hand from his face. Muriel handed the girl a checkered napkin. "Sarah, would you excuse us for a minute?"

Sarah did not move. Not until Ivan dismissed her. Then she collected her bowl, flashed a jealous glance in Muriel's direction, and went out to the porch.

Muriel waited until she heard the screen door swing shut. "Ivan, what in Heaven's name is going on here?"

"I'm sorry, Muriel," he said.

Maybe Muriel hadn't believed Ivan's stories until now, not all the way. She'd listened attentively to all he told her about what he was, what he had been, while she fell in love with him. But for her it was just a bad old life he'd led, as if she'd married a man who had fought his way up from being a back-alley drunk. She hadn't thought too much about the people he'd left behind. "You're *sorry?*"

"I just wanted to talk to her, Muriel—I was curious, and then—she was in a bad way, and I thought we could help her—" He gritted his teeth with the effort of leaving alone the tension knotting the muscles of Muriel's neck, the panic in her eyes. A mortal man would soothe her, wouldn't he? Li'l Wallace would soothe her. But where was the line? Did he err, in keeping his face flat, his movements drained of their power to unravel her fear? She turned her face away. "Li'l Wallace came up and I had to be Negro again. The child panicked, so I . . . I had to . . ."

"How could you?" Muriel whispered.

"Muriel, it ain't like that. I don't want a prize or a tool. It's—it was just— the girl's about to be orphaned. We could . . . she needs us."

"You promised me, Ivan," Muriel whispered. It burned like a bullet through Ivan's heart.

"Muriel, I know it was wrong. But it's done. We can do this with love, Muriel, as a family—"

She whipped around to face him. "Ivan, how can you be what you are and be such a fool? Look in that little white girl's eyes, look at how she looks at me. That's not a daughter, Ivan. That's a slave. Is that what you think I want?"

It would be so easy, so easy. "Oh Ivan," she would say. "You're right, I'm just shocked is all—but that poor little girl—bring her back in. Let's make this work."

And then he'd have lost her. He'd have two slaves.

"This is what I am, Muriel," he hissed. "Should I just abandon her? I'm responsible for her—"

Muriel walked to the sink and held onto it, seeking purchase. "You're responsible to me, too, Ivan. You chose me, too. You said 'I do.'" She wiped at the corner of her eye a few times as if something were stuck there. "So what, then? Are we going to run away from my home and family? Set up a new life for you and your white daughter, with me as the maid?" She leaned forward at him, her face flushed dark as wine, her voice shaking. "Or are you just gonna *change* everybody so they don't mind any that she's white? Or so they don't know no more? Are you going to just work some of your tricks on Aunt Gertrude and Li'l Wallace and the preacher and the police? Are we all gonna end up as your trained puppies?"

He stood up from his chair, his hands at his sides. He put his ice cream spoon down on the table. If the others of his kind had been there, they would have heard volumes in the clatter of that spoon. Muriel just looked at him. So he said, "I can never give you what you want."

Muriel burst out crying.

That surprised him, and for a moment he felt a little surge of terror from an ancient part of him. What was he losing, that mortals started surprising him? He hadn't been paying attention. It had been easy to see them clearly, in the old days, like dangling string above a kitten, knowing how the kitten would jump. Now he'd fallen into a mysterious country.

He put his arms around her, and she bowed her head to push her forehead into his shoulder.

"You fool, you fool," she sobbed, "I don't need no baby, I just want you."

Like a fist, some kind of joy or sadness forced its way from Ivan's chest up through his throat and out through his face. Its passage was sudden and unexpected, and Ivan sighed. He did not know who he was anymore.

They held each other. Her tears cooled his shoulder, and he could feel the tremors dancing through her. And then he tasted his own tears, unbidden, cool on his cheeks.

"Ivan," Muriel said in a throaty whisper, "you tell me straight now. I don't want your good intentions, I want the truth. Is there any hope for that little girl? Can you undo what you did?"

It was safe here, in Muriel's arms. In this safe place, he thought about the plan he'd made on the walk back home, and he could smell its stink of pride—the pride of princes. Muriel felt it in the silence, and she stiffened.

"You mortals," he said, the words muddy in his throat, "you walk around with this huge—emptiness in you, like wanting back into the womb. You think we'll fill it. Once you get that hunger . . . you don't let go. You'll die for us, but you won't leave us. Maybe I can make her forget, but the hunger stays."

"And if you keep her here? Or we go off with her?" She shook her head. "Or you go off with her alone? Is she going to get better?"

"I don't know."

Muriel pulled away. "Good Lord, Ivan! Guess!"

He looked at his hands. "I think she'll be something like a child, and something like a prize, and maybe that'll twist her up." He could feel his cheeks get hot. "No. She won't get better. And I'll have to be . . . what I was."

Muriel shook, her eyes closed. She put her hands over her face. "Oh Jesus, oh Jesus," she said.

Ivan said nothing.

She wiped her tears on her apron. "I can't give you up willingly," she said. "God forgive me. I can't make you stay. And I can't follow you into that."

"I know," he said. He thought of Aunt Gertrude, of Li'l Wallace, of Henry, of the preacher, of Bob Pratchett the white foreman at the mill. How long before he damned them all? He was a fool.

She saw it in his face. "Ivan. Listen to me. You got to leave folks alone." She reached a hand out to touch his cheek. "And you can, I know you can. You ain't no demon, Ivan. You're just a sinner like everybody else."

He kissed her and took her close. He squeezed his eyes shut and smelled the salt of her tears, mixed in with dish soap and sweat and vanilla and the spice of cedar wood.

Then he blew his nose into the paper napkin and wiped the sweat from his brow. She looked away from him, down at the table, as he got up and left the kitchen.

Sarah was sitting dutifully in the twilight, looking out onto the dark oval of water and the first eager stars that blinked above it. She heard the screen door swing open and turned, bright with anticipation.

"It's time to go home," Ivan said.

She shook her head, unsure if she had heard him correctly. He offered his hand and she took it. Her fingers were cold from the outside air and the ice cream inside her. They walked through the ragged grass over the hill.

In her face was a wolfish joy—she was soaking him in with her eyes. Somewhere behind that need was that lonely little girl, brave enough to pray in a lonely cemetery. His chest throbbed with pain.

Her lips shivered and her teeth clicked together. He wanted to give her his jacket, but how could she forget him then?

They reached the road. He let go her hand.

He stepped back from her and slouched, scratching his head. He spoke in a new tone that was neither paternal nor comforting, but like that green-eyed nigger who lived in the house by the pond.

"Well, I hope you enjoyed your dessert. Now run along afore anyone sees you hangin' round here."

He saw the arrow of panic as it stabbed through her. Where was her Ivan? Where was her angel sent? Who was this man? "No, no," she said, looking around her. Her head was foggy. She wiped at her eyes. She looked at him: some harmless nigger standing with her under the cold night sky. She stepped away. "What—"

Ivan forced himself to turn and wave respectfully, to walk away.

When he glanced back, Sarah was hugging herself. Her thoughts burned the air. A moment ago she had been saved, she had had a father and a home. Had she been with Jesus? No, she'd eaten with some niggers—shame leapt burning to her cheeks.

She pushed past a fence post and began to run. God had seen her, seen her naked soul, seen everything there was of her to love, and abandoned her. He did not love her at all.

The lost soul fell into the night.

Coldness made a fist in Ivan's belly as he crossed over the hill to his house.

He pulled his jacket around him and stared ahead. Muriel had turned the porch light on so that he would not stumble.

ROXIE

ROBERT REED

Robert Reed sold his first story in 1986 and quickly established himself as a frequent contributor to *The Magazine of Fantasy & Science Fiction* and *Asimov's Science Fiction*, as well as selling many stories to *Science Fiction Age, Universe, New Destinies, Tomorrow, Synergy, Starlight*, and elsewhere. Reed may be one of the most prolific of today's young writers, particularly at short fiction lengths, seriously rivaled for that position only by authors such as Stephen Baxter and Brian Stableford. And—also like Baxter and Stableford—he manages to keep up a very high standard of quality *while* being prolific, something that is not at all easy to do. Reed stories such as "Sister Alice," "Brother Perfect," "Decency," "Savior," "The Remoras," "Chrysalis," "Whiptail," "The Utility Man," "Marrow," "Birth Day," "Blind," "The Toad of Heaven," "Stride," "The Shape of Everything," "Guest of Honor," "Waging Good," and "Killing the Morrow," among at least a half-dozen others equally as strong, count as among some of the best short work produced by anyone in the '80s and '90s; many of his best stories were assembled in his first collection, *The Dragons of Springplace*. Nor is he nonprolific as a novelist, having turned out ten novels since the end of the '80s, including *The Lee Shore, The Hormone Jungle, Black Milk, The Remarkables, Down the Bright Way, Beyond the Veil of Stars, An Exaltation of Larks, Beneath the Gated Sky, Marrow*, and *Sister Alice*. His most recent books include two chapbook novellas, *Mere* and *Flavors of My Genius*; a collection, *The Cuckoo's Boys*; and a novel, *The Well of Stars*. Reed lives with his family in Lincoln, Nebraska.

As the wistful, gentle, regretful story that follows explains, a man's best friend should be with him until the end—whether it's his own, or the end of all things.

She wakes me at five minutes before five in the morning, coming into the darkened bedroom with tags clinking and claws skating across the old oak floor, and then she uses a soft whine that nobody else will hear.

I sit up and pull myself to the end of the bed, dressing in long pants and new walking shoes—the old shoes weren't helping my balky arch and Achilles—and then I stop at the bathroom before pulling a warm jacket from the front closet. My dog keeps close track of my progress. In her step and the big eyes is enthusiasm and single-minded focus. At the side door, I tell her to sit and hold still please, and in the dark, I fasten the steel pinch collar and six-foot leash around a neck that has grown alarmingly thin.

Anymore our walks are pleasant, even peaceful events—no more hard tugging or challenging other dogs. A little after five in the morning, early in March, the world is black and quiet beneath a cold, clear sky. Venus is brilliant, the moon cut thin. Crossing the empty four-lane road to the park, we move south past the soccer field and then west, and then south again on a narrow asphalt sidewalk. A hundred dogs pass this ground daily. The city has leash laws, and I have always obeyed them. But the clean-up laws are new, and only a fraction of the dog-walkers carry plastic sacks and flashlights. Where my dog has pooped for thirteen years, she poops now, and I kneel to stare at what she has done, convincing myself that the stool is reasonably firm, if exceptionally fragrant.

A good beginning to our day.

We continue south to a set of white wooden stairs. She doesn't like stairs anymore, but she climbs them easily enough. Then we come back again on the wide bike path—a favorite stretch of hers. In the spring, rabbits will nest in the mowed grass, and every year she will find one or several little holes stuffed with tiny, half-formed bunnies.

On this particular morning, nothing is caught and killed.

An older man and his German shepherd pass us on the sidewalk below. Tony is a deep-voiced gentleman who usually waves from a distance and chats when we're close. He loves to see Roxie bounce about, and she very much likes him. But in the darkness he doesn't notice us, and I'm not in the mood to shout. He moves ahead and crosses the four-lane road, and when we reach that place, Roxie pauses, smelling where her friend has just been and leaking a sorry little whine.

Home again, I pill my dog. She takes Proin to control bedwetting, plus half a metronidazole to fight diarrhea. She used to take a full metro, but there was an endless night a few weeks ago when she couldn't rest, not indoors or out. She barked at nothing, which is very strange for her. Maybe a high-pitched sound was driving her mad. But our vet warned that she could have a tendency toward seizures, and the metro can increases their likelihood and severity. Which is why I pulled her back to just half a pill in the morning.

I pack the medicine into a handful of canned dog food, stinky and prepared with the senior canine in mind. She waits eagerly and gobbles up the treat in a bite, happily licking the linoleum where I dropped it, relishing that final taste.

Before six in the morning, I pour orange juice and go down to my basement office. My PC boots up without incident. I discover a fair amount of e-mail, none of it important. Then I start jumping between sites that offer a good look at science and world events. *Sky & Telescope* has a tiny article about an asteroid of uncertain size and imprecise orbit. But after a couple nights of observation, early estimates describe an object that might be a kilometer in diameter, and in another two years, it seems that this intruder will pass close to the Earth, bringing with it a one-in-six-thousand chance of an impact.

"But that figure won't stand up," promises one astronomer. "This happens all the time. Once we get more data, this danger is sure to evaporate to nothing."

My future wife was a reporter for the Omaha newspaper. I knew her because in those days, a lot of my friends were reporters. On a sultry summer evening, she and I went to the same Fourth of July party; and over the smell of gunpowder, Leslie mentioned that she'd recently bought a husky puppy.

Grinning, I admitted that I'd always been intrigued by sled dogs.

"You should come meet Roxie sometime," she said.

"Why Roxie?" I asked.

"Foxie Roxie," she explained. "She's a red husky. To me, she sort of looks like an enormous fox."

Her dog was brownish red and white, with a dark red mask across her narrow face, accenting her soulful blue eyes. Leslie wasn't home when I first visited, but her dog was in the backyard, absolutely thrilled to meet me. (Huskies are the worst guard dogs in the world.) Roxie was four or five months old, with a short coat and a big, long-legged frame. Sitting behind the chain-link gate, she licked the salt off my offered fingers. And then she hunkered down low, feigning submission. But her human was elsewhere, and I didn't want the responsibility of opening gates and possibly letting this wolfish puppy escape. So I walked away, triggering a string of plaintive wails that caused people for a mile in every direction to ask, "Now who's torturing that poor, miserable creature?"

Leslie and I started dating in late October. But the courtship always had a competitive triangular feel about it.

My new girlfriend worked long hours and drove a two-hour commute to and from Omaha. She didn't have enough time for a hyperactive puppy. Feeling sorry for both of them, I would drop by to tease her dog with brief affections. Or if I stayed the night, I'd get up at some brutally early hour—before seven o'clock, some mornings—and dripping with fatigue, I'd join the two of them on a jaunt through the neighborhood and park and back again.

In those days, Roxie lived outside as much as she lived in. But the backyard gate proved inadequate; using her nose, she would easily flip the latch up and out of the way. Tying the latch only bought a few more days of security. Leaping was easy work, and a four-foot chain-link fence was no barrier at all. A series of ropes and lightweight chains were used and discarded. Finally Leslie went to a farm supply store and bought a steel chain strong enough to yank cars out of ditches. Years later, a friend from Alaska visited, and I asked sheepishly if our chain was overkill. No, it was pretty standard for sled dogs, she conceded. Then she told me what I already knew: "These animals love to run."

One morning, somebody's dog was barking, and Leslie asked me to make sure it wasn't hers. Peering out the dining room window, I found a beautiful red-and-white husky dancing on the patio, happy as can be.

"It's not your dog," I told my girlfriend.

Even burdened with the heavy chain, Roxie had killed a squirrel, and now she was happily flinging the corpse into the air and catching it again. The game was delicious fun until the limp squirrel fell out of reach, and then the wailing began. I got dressed and found a shovel in the garage, and when I picked up her prize by its tail, the dog leaped happily. Oh, I was saving her day! But with the first spade of earth, she saw my betrayal for what it was, and the wailing grew exponentially.

Two nights later, Leslie called for help. Again, her dog had killed an animal. She didn't know what kind; despite being a farmer's kid, Leslie has an exceptionally weak stomach, and she didn't want to look too closely. But if I could drop over and take care of the situation . . .

It was late, and I was very tired. But I stopped by that next afternoon, when no humans were home. A half-grown opossum was baking in the sun. Using my growing puddle of wisdom, I gave my girlfriend's dog a quick walk and put her inside before burying the bloated body. Then I let Roxie back out on her chain, and she hurried to the spot where the opossum had been, sniffing and digging, and then flinging herself down on her back to roll on the ripe, wondrous ground.

After a year of dating, I moved in with both of them, and that next spring, Leslie and I dug a pond below the patio. That's where we found the opossum's grave. Rot and time had eaten the flesh from the skull, and I put the prize in a little jar that I set on a shelf in the spare bedroom that had become my office.

After several days, the new asteroid surfaces again on the Web, this time wearing an official designation. The bolide is found to be exceptionally dark, lending evidence that this could be a short-term comet with most of its volatiles bled away. A tiny albedo means it must be larger than it appears in the images. Two black kilometers across, and maybe more. As promised, the one-in-six-thousand chance of an impact has been discarded. Extra data allow astronomers to plot a lovely elliptical orbit that reaches out past Saturn and then dives inside the Earth's orbit. Calculations are still in flux, I read online. If the object starts to act like a comet, watery fountains and gaseous vents will slow it down or speed it up, depending on chaotic factors. These are complications that will mean much, or nothing. But for the moment, the odds of an impact with the Earth have shifted by a factor of twenty.

"One-in-three-hundred," I read at the ScienceDaily site.

In other words, it is easier to fill an inside straight in poker. And if the object's trajectory makes any substantial change, the chance of an impact will probably—probably—drop to one-in-infinity.

I grew up with black Labradors in the house. They were docile animals, a little foolish but always good-hearted, and each one began his day by asking, "How can I make my owner proud of me?"

No husky thinks in those subservient, dim-witted terms.

Leslie grew up on a farm full of dogs and cats, but those pets lived outdoors. Because of that and because she wasn't home during the day, she'd had limited success housebreaking Roxie. Of course I like to tell myself that once I had moved in, the chaos turned to discipline. But the truth is a more complex, less edifying business: To make certain our dog was drained in the morning, I walked her. Since I worked at home, taking Roxie outside for the midday pee was easily done. And when my girlfriend was tired in the evening, I would throw a thirty-foot lead on the beast and take her up to the park and back again.

But "Who trained who?" is a valid question.

The evening walk came after the human dinner. When I put down the fork, the dog would begin to whine and leap, sometimes poking me in the gut with her paw. Disciplining her was endless work, and often futile. She was too quick to grab, too graceful to corral. One night, watching some favorite TV show, I got a little too clever and lured her upstairs. Then after a few words about what a spoiled bitch she was, I shut the door between us, and after a few seconds of loud thumping, the house went quiet. At the first commercial break, I peeked through the door to find my dog sitting in the kitchen, waiting patiently. "Good girl," I said, and as a reward, I let her come downstairs. She sat at my feet, as patient as I had ever seen her act, sometimes glancing my way with an expression full of meanings that I couldn't quite read.

When I went upstairs again, I discovered what she had done. In my office, on the throw rug, she had emptied her bladder. Here was a message, and the lesson was learned; and after that, our walks were a priority, and I tried to avoid treating her like inconvenient luggage.

The dead comet surfaces in newspaper articles and on television. Its soulless official designation has been replaced by "Shelby," which happens to be the off-the-cuff name given to it by its discoverers. The odds of an impact are fluctuating between one in three hundred and one in one thousand, depending on the expert being quoted. But even the most alarming voice sounds calm, particularly when he or she repeats the undeniable truth: The bolide is a long ways out and still traveling toward the sun. Any day now, Shelby will start to vent, and its orbit will shift some significant distance.

Meanwhile, what has been an unnaturally mild winter ends with a single heavy snow. Fifteen wet inches fall in less than a day. Cars wear white pillars. The warm earth melts the first several inches, but what remains is impressive. With my four-year-old daughter's help, I build a snowman in the front yard— my first snowman in forty years. And Roxie appreciates the snow, though she can't leap into those places that aren't plowed or shoveled. For several days, our walks are limited to the plowed streets, and it takes persistence and some coaxing before she finds a place worthy of her poop.

I still run with her on the cool days. For several years, we haven't gone farther than a mile. There is one course she accepts without complaint, knowing the turnaround point to the inch. One blustery afternoon, when the last snow has melted, I take her into a stand of old pines growing beside the park's nine-hole golf course, and then I lure her past that point, tricking her into running a course that is slightly longer than normal.

Together, we maintain a comfortable nine-minute gait. And at the one-mile mark, almost exactly, she begins to limp. She looks pained and pitiful, right up to the moment when we start to walk home, and then her limp vanishes as quickly as it appeared.

A few days later, she wakes me at four-thirty in the morning. Our walk is uneventful, but I can't relax when I come home. Online, I jump to the *New Scientist* site, reading that somebody has uncovered photographic plates taken several decades ago. These old images show Shelby moping along near its perigee—a forgotten speck moving just outside Venus's orbit. Astronomers now have fresh data to plug into their equations, refining their predictions. And more important, they don't see any evidence of a coma or tail. During its last fiery summer, this old comet didn't spill any significant volatiles.

Worse still, between then and now our bolide has been moving along an exceptionally predictable line.

Overnight, the odds of an impact with the Earth have shifted, jumping from a comforting one in three hundred, at their very worst, to a one-miserable-chance-in-thirteen.

I used to be a semi-fast runner, and except in summer, Roxie was good for a six- or eight-mile adventure. And in late fall and winter, when temperatures dipped to a bearable chill, we would run twelve miles at a shot, or farther. She adored the snow. I think she knew every course by heart, even when drifts obscured the trails. We ran with human friends, and she always worked harder around new people, trying to impress them. But the real fun was to get out and smell the smells, and she relished her chances to pee against fresh trees and important fences.

Roxie often lifted one hind leg like a boy dog would; but better than that, she occasionally did the canine equivalent of a handstand, throwing her piss high to fool strange dogs into thinking, "What a big bad bitch was here!"

And she was exceptionally competitive. When we saw another dog up ahead, or human runners, or even a slow cyclist, it was critically important to put on a sprint and pass your opponent. And not only pass them, but look back at them too, laughing happily, flashing the canine equivalent of a "Beat your ass" grin.

People who know me—family and friends, and even passing acquaintances—start to ask, "What do you think the real odds are?"

Of an impact, they mean.

Sad to say, being a science-fiction writer doesn't give a person special knowledge. It should, but it doesn't. All I can offer is the standard figure. One-in-thirteen. The most likely scenario is that Shelby will cross the Earth's orbit at a distance far closer to us than we are to the moon. If there is a collision, it will happen in a little less than two years: on March 11, at approximately 3:45 AM local time. And because of the orbital dynamics, if the object does strikes, it will plunge down somewhere in the Northern Hemisphere.

But like the talking heads on television, I remind my audience that these numbers are certain to change.

In mid-April, I am a guest at a little SF convention held at one of our state colleges. Going in, I imagine an event where people talk openly about murderous asteroids and comets. But I keep forgetting that most fans today read nothing but fantasy and media tie-in books. They don't want to invest much breath in what is a very depressing subject. And the rest of us— including me, I discover—have convinced ourselves that in the end, nothing will come of this.

I enjoy the convention. Best of all, I relish the change in routine: I don't have a dog to listen for in the wee hours. I can sleep all the way to a lazy seven-thirty, if I want. Though I can't manage that trick, since my body isn't geared for so much leisure.

On Monday morning, I retrieve my dog from the kennel. As always, Roxie gives me a quick hello before heading for the car. Her poop has been fine, I learn, and she's eaten every pill and every bite of food that I brought for her.

The week turns summery warm. On Thursday morning, at one o'clock, I jump awake when Roxie begins to lick herself. She isn't licking her privates, but instead she is obsessively wetting down her paws and legs, working hard until she has to stop to pant. Then she climbs to her feet and gets a drink from the toilet, then returns to the bedroom to lick her legs some more.

I could push her into the hall and shut the door, but that would only make her whine. So I lie awake for two or three hours, thinking about work. I play with unfinished stories. I dance with a novel that still hasn't sold. And when I don't have anything else to consider, I think about Shelby. If this is the murderer of human civilization, doesn't the bastard deserve a better name?

By four in the morning, I am exhausted and anxious.

Shutting the windows, I turn on the air conditioning. The cool air doesn't seem to help my dog, but at least the noise covers up the sounds of licking. And by four-thirty, I manage to drift into sleep, fifteen minutes of dreamy slumber enjoyed before Roxie comes to the foot of the bed and starts to whine.

One winter, my dog took an extraordinary interest in one portion of a local bike path. The path dove under a bridge. That bridge had three tunnels: The pedestrian tunnel was narrow and dark. Beside it was a wider tunnel where a peaceful stream flowed through. And on the far side was a second, equally wide tunnel meant for the overflow during high water. I usually gave Roxie a chance to drink, but suddenly she got it into her head that we needed to investigate the far tunnel. She would stand in the freezing creek, looking back at me with a questioning insistence. This was important; this mattered. We really need to cross over here, she was telling me. But there was no way to convince me to wade through shin-deep water, only to reach an empty tunnel floored with packed clay and trash.

More than most humans, my dog is woven into her world. Drop a cardboard box anywhere near the bike path, and she will leap and woof until she is convinced that the new object isn't dangerous. The same can be true for a kid's bike left in a front yard, or a snowman that wasn't there yesterday.

One evening, years ago, Leslie and I were walking the dog together. One of our neighbors had been enjoying too much partying that night, and his wife had refused to let him inside. So he lay down on the front walk and fell asleep. At a glance, Roxie knew this was unusual. Somebody needed to be alerted. She began to bark and whine, and then dance, very much troubled by the fact we were dragging her away from what was clearly somebody in distress.

She often notices details that the observant writer beside her has completely missed.

One calm, cool afternoon, Roxie and I were running on a bike path when she suddenly, inexplicably went mad, running circles around me while staring up at the sky, her blue eyes huge and terrified.

I looked up, and ugly me, I laughed.

Floating directly above our heads was an enormous white spiral. It looked ominous, yes. To Roxie, this apparition must have been ready to drop on us, which was why we broke into a hard sprint. Off in the distance, a little biplane was spitting out random letters; a skywriter was practicing his trade. I was breathless and laughing, my strides pulled long by the panicked tugs. But the wind happened to be out of the north, and since we were racing south, the spiral hovered above us for another half mile before the trail mercifully bent westward, allowing us to escape. (Though I noticed that she never stopped watching the busy plane, having wisely decided that it must be to blame for this travesty of Nature.)

Roxie often knew what I didn't know. But when she tried to coax me into the mysterious tunnel, I ignored her. "You're not the only stubborn creature in the family," I warned. Then the weather grew warm, and a couple local kids went exploring. In the tunnel was the body of a teenager, a young man who had been buried in a shallow grave. Police were summoned, and for a week the underpass was cordoned off. Piles of excavated earth were left in the streambed, and when we could run through again, Roxie would stop and shamelessly sniff at the dirt, burying her nose in the ripest parts, every breath telling her stories about what was still, judging by her interest, vividly real.

As it happened, the dead boy had vanished months ago from a group home for troubled youth. His two best friends in the world were arrested. It came out that there had been a fight over cigarettes. One boy confessed to being present at the murder, but he swore the other fellow had bashed in their buddy's skull. With no other witnesses and only sketchy forensics, the state had to give a free pass in exchange for a testimony. But then at trial, the boy recanted his story. In the end, a brutal crime was committed and nobody went to prison. And I occasionally have to ask myself, "What would have happened if I'd listened to my dog? If we'd crossed that stream, and if I let her unearth the grave, would the police, given a fresher trail, have been able to make their case?"

By week's end, one spent comet has pushed everything else out of the news. Most of a dozen runners gather at the YMCA early Saturday morning, and Shelby is our first topic. I explain what I know about its delicate motion through the sky. I report that the venerable Hubble has spotted what looks like a tiny eruption of gas—probably carbon monoxide—from its equator. Will this make any difference? Maybe, I admit, and maybe not for the best. On the Torino scale, our enemy presently wears an ominous 7. 10 means doom, and the group wrings some comfort in the gulf between 7 and 10. But the Torino scale is misleading. Only rocks and tiny asteroids can earn 8s or 9s. And the fatal 10 won't kick in until a massive object—Shelby, for instance—has a 99 percent chance of impacting on the Earth's face.

For the last few days, the published odds of the horrific are hovering around one in eleven.

"We're going to have to blow it up," one runner announces. "Stuff a thousand nukes on a missile, and hit the bastard hard."

"But that's not going to help," I mention.

"Why not?"

I don't respond.

But the other runners are listening, and our lone female—a little ex-gymnast—comes up beside me, asking, "Why won't bombs work?"

Small bolides aren't brittle rocks ready to shatter to dust under a single hammer blow; they are usually soft, stubborn rubble piles filled with considerable empty space. "It'll be like kicking a snowdrift," I mention. Besides, we don't have a fleet of rockets strong enough to fling hydrogen bombs across the solar system. Even with a crash program, no workable bomb could be launched for months. And without years of lead time, we won't be able to carefully map Shelby's surface before putting down at the best possible location. What we'll have to do is attack it straight on, one or several tiny bullets battering one gigantic cannonball. Sure, the rubble pile might break into pieces. But that might turn a near-collision into a shotgun blast, hill-sized chunks raining down on everybody. And even if we are very lucky—if Shelby holds together and we trigger the perfect outgassing—that won't happen until late next year. "Which won't leave us any time, if we make a mistake then," I remind them.

My lecture finished, I discover that I'm out of breath, my stomach aching and throat parched.

For a long moment, the others say nothing. Then the CPA in our group points out, "Ten times out of eleven, Shelby misses us."

That is a fair point.

"And the odds can get better," says an optimistic voice. My voice, as it happens. I don't want everyone left as miserable as I feel, which is why I promise, "One-in-eleven isn't the final word."

My dog isn't comfortable. That afternoon, I'm sitting at my computer and reading about orbital dynamics, and Roxie lies nearby, licking at her paws and feet. I can't stand the sound of it, and when she finally quits, I breathe easier. But she only quits because she is exhausted, and after half an hour nap, she wakes and begins the process over again.

My vet's office is closed until Monday. I call the emergency clinic, and the assistant says that it sounds like allergies, which isn't too unexpected with the warm spring weather. She suggests Benadryl, though I don't have any in the house. Or, if I want, I could bring my dog over for an examination.

I lead Roxie outside and open the back of my CRV, and she leaps in, but with nothing to spare. It's a five-minute drive to the clinic. I'm the only customer. The veterinarian is a heavy middle-aged fellow with big hands and a matching voice. He asks if my dog has arthritis. "No," I say, and immediately I'm remembering every slow trip up the stairs. Yet she managed to jump into my car, which is impressive for a thirteen-year-old lady. He tells me that her heart is strong. It shows that she gets plenty of exercise. Then he points out the redness in her eyes—a telltale sign of allergies. He recommends a cortisone shot and pills. The hypodermic needle is only a little smaller than a pool cue, and he injects a bucket of oily goo into her back and both hind legs, leaving her whining, trembling from the stress.

Returning to the waiting room, we find a patient in genuine trouble—a little mutt who got into a one-sided fight with a pit bull. Seeing that dog's misery, I feel better. Roxie suddenly looks to be in pretty good shape. The prescription is for twenty tabs of prednisone, and the total bill is nearly one hundred and fifty dollars. But the licking stops immediately, and she sleeps hard until nearly seven that next morning, waking refreshed and ready to walk.

Her pee comes in rivers, but I was warned about that side effect.

The watery diarrhea that arrives later is a big surprise. By Monday morning, I call my own vet to ask questions and complain. The pred dosage is quite high, I learn. But I have to wean Roxie off the medication slowly or risk the catastrophic failure of her adrenal gland.

For the rest of the week, my sleep is broken, full of dreams and abrupt moments of wakefulness. Someone in the house groans, and I find myself alert and exhausted. And if I can't hear my dog, I start to wonder if she has died. It astonishes me how I seem to want that to happen. In the middle of the night, when she whines and demands to go outside, I feel trapped. Nobody else is going to take care of this dog. Leslie claims that Roxie is just getting old, slowing down but generally happy, and I worry about her too much. But at three in the morning, shaking with fatigue, it isn't worry that I'm feeling. I am angry. I feel trapped. With nothing else to do, I can't help but imagine the days to come when I won't have to get up at all hours, when I won't have to tend to this animal; and it scares me when I realize just how much I am looking forward to this one inevitable end.

When Leslie became pregnant, certain people in both of our families worried. We were sharing the house with a wolfish dog, and did we appreciate the risks? That summer, we went out of town on short notice and couldn't get Roxie into her usual kennel. But my mother-in-law offered to take her, promising us that our sled dog would live in air conditioning, safe from the July heat.

When we returned to the farm, we discovered Roxie in the yard, chained to a tree and looking miserable. My father-in-law had us sit down in the kitchen, and with urgency, he asked if we knew that our dog was vicious. It seemed that everything had been fine until this morning, and then for no reason, Roxie attacked one of his dogs and killed a cat.

This was ominous news, yes.

We asked questions, both of us trying to put these incidents into context. What I kept thinking was that Roxie had decided we weren't coming home, and she was trying to establish dominance. Leslie asked if the other dog was hurt.

"Not too bad," my father-in-law conceded. "She's a little stiff, is all."

"Which cat?" I wanted to know.

He described this sweet little calico that I'd noticed before.

"Where's the body?"

"Oh, she ran off to die," he reported. Then in the next breath, he added, "I don't care about the cats. That's not the point. But they're little animals, and your baby is going to be a little animal too. Who knows what that dog might do?"

Leslie and I were shaken. But when I went outside to rescue the forlorn, thoroughly pissed-off dog, I saw a familiar calico walking beside our car. Going back inside, I pointed out the window and asked, "Is that the dead cat?"

"Huh," he responded. "I guess she didn't die."

And at that point my best defense was to say, "If my dog wanted that cat dead, believe me, she would have killed it."

Roxie goes off the pred early, and for the next couple days, she seems fine. She seems perfect. But then the licking resumes. I give her Benadryl, and not just a little taste. Six tablets go inside her—three times the usual dosage—but she continues moving from place to place, licking at her miserable legs. Late on Sunday night, I call the emergency clinic, explaining symptoms and mentioning that I still have half of the original prescription. Ten tabs. Their advice is to feed her one pred to help her through the night. But the effects aren't immediate. I can't sleep with Roxie in this mood, which is why I take refuge in the basement. If she follows me, I decide, at least the white noise of the aquariums will help mask any chaos.

But thank goodness, my dog leaves me alone. This little vacation lasts until six—an exceptionally late hour—and then she pees rivers while we slowly, contentedly make our usual one-mile walk.

When Jessie was a newborn, we would set her on the floor, on her back, and Roxie would come close to investigate, never quite allowing the tiny hands to grab hold of her. Sometimes she brought our daughter gifts—tennis balls or one of the plastic snowmen with its head chewed off—and she would put the toys at Jessie's feet, waiting for the kick that would start their little game.

The violence came later. Teeth and nails inflicted pain, and there were some hard body blows delivered in weak moments. But as I explained to others, I couldn't euthanize the guilty party. She was my daughter, after all, and not even two years old.

When we return from day care, Roxie always makes a point of greeting Jessie. I rarely get such treatment, which is another way huskies aren't anything like Labradors. She is smart enough and secure enough to take me for granted. And if my dog decides to come when I call her—a huge crapshoot as it is—she usually stops short, forcing me take the final few steps.

"You're describing a cat," one lady exclaimed upon hearing our stories.

A fifty-pound cat, yes. With blue eyes and a curled tail, a graying coat, and a predator's fierce instincts.

My haphazard research into huskies gave me one explanation into their nature: Come summer, the Siberian humans would let their dogs run free. With no work for the animals to do, they could feed themselves on the three-month bounty. Then with the first snows, the happy survivors would return to camp, ready to pull sleds in exchange for easy food.

I can't count all of the rabbits Roxie has killed. She has also butchered mice and at least one nest of shrews, and there have been a few birds snapped out of the air. But rabbits are prizes above all others. When she was young, she nabbed a half-grown bunny and happily brought it home. But I refused to let her prize come indoors, and after giving me a long baleful stare, she ate it whole. And for the rest of the day, there was an extra bounce to her always-bouncy step.

Over the years, Roxie developed a taste for breadsticks and pizza. Sloppy people and my nephews often found their hands suddenly empty. But when Jessie was in the house, I tried to put an end to everybody's misbehavior. One night, Roxie snatched the bread from my wife's grip, missing her fingers by nothing. My response was abrupt and passionate. I asserted my dominance, and my dog responded by baring her teeth, telling me quite clearly to back off. But I tried to grab her collar anyway, wanting to drag her outside, and when she snapped, a long sharp canine punctured the meat between my thumb and index finger.

After that, both of us were exceptionally careful with one another.

More than once, tension would erupt and I would see my dog willfully holding back. I would do the same, or at least I tried to. One morning when Roxie picked up a road-killed squirrel—a putrid, half-grown marvel—she looked at me with a wishful expression. I didn't reach for her mouth, but with a calm voice, I warned her that as soon as we were home, I was going to stick a hose in her mouth and flush that ugliness out of there.

Maybe she understood. More likely, she remembered when I had done that trick with another edible treasure. Either way, she stopped in front of our driveway and crunched on the carcass, and then she gave me a long smile, letting me smell the rancid wonders riding on her breath.

A week later, she was living at the vet's.

When I finally retrieved her, I found her lying on her side inside a wire cage, looking depressed and painfully skinny. But when the cage door opened, she sprang out, evading every reaching hand and trying to leap up on a table where a squawking parrot sat inside its cage.

That illness was followed by several months of acting happy and comfortable. Roxie would follow me around the house until I settled, and then she would sleep nearby. She ate well, and she pooped quite a lot, and there were a few bouts of diarrhea, but things always resolved themselves within a day or two.

Roxie often slept in the exact place where she had bitten me. And sometimes when she dreamed, her legs would run fast, little woofs leaking out as she chased the most delicious prey.

Then one day, it occurred to me that I hadn't seen her running in her sleep in some time.

My dog sleeps almost constantly now, but with very few dreams.

While for me, sleep comes in brief snatches that are filled with the most lucid and awful nightmares.

In less than two years, Shelby will reach the Earth. The most likely scenario has the black body dipping below the geosynchronous satellites and then plunging even closer. The space station is in a relatively high orbit, and if it happens to be in the proper position, its crew will be able to watch an irregularly shaped body streaking between them and their home world. From a distance, Shelby won't look particularly large or ominous. But the sun will light it up its black crust, even when North America still lies in darkness. And then after kissing the atmosphere's upper reaches, it will head back out into space, its orbit nudged slightly by our gravity's sturdy tug.

Just as I once predicted, the odds of the worst are continuing to evolve.

One-in-eleven has become a rather worse one-in-nine. But unless there is a major outgassing event, these numbers won't move much further, at least for the next year or so. Shelby exists in a strange territory where it is mostly harmless. More often than not, astronomers will decide in the final weeks that it won't hit, and everybody will get up in the wee hours and step outside to watch a dull little star passing overhead. The asteroid will miss us by miles and miles before continuing on its mindless way, following a new orbit that is our big old world's little gift to it.

My wife and I discuss what to do if the odds worsen. My mother lives in Yuma during the winter. We could pay a visit then, bringing her granddaughter as well as a few tons of canned goods as gifts.

Our four-year-old hears us talking and sees pictures on the news, and she repeats little fragments of what she hears, in a mangled form. Yet she is an unapologetic optimist, assuring me, "It will be pretty, this meteor thing. We'll go out and watch it. You and me. And Roxie too."

"What about Mommy?" I ask.

"She'll be sleeping," Jessie confides, obviously having given this issue some thought. "She has go to work tomorrow, Daddy. Remember?"

One day, coming home from day care, NPR is giving details about a Mars probe that's being quickly reconfigured. With less than perfect equipment, it is going to be launched early and sent on a near-collision course with Shelby, skimming low over its surface while snapping a few thousand pictures that will help us aim a nuke mission that may or may not launch in August. Or September. We need milk tonight, and pulling up in front of the local grocery store, I turn off the car and listen to the rest of the story before getting out and unbuckling my daughter.

A man is walking past, his German shepherd striding beside him.

I don't often see Tony during the day, and rarely up close. Watching Jessie more than him, I say, "We don't cross paths much anymore."

The man holds his dog leash with both hands. I sense his eyes even as I hold my daughter's hand. This isn't easy, but I thought I should tell him my news. A few years ago, when Tony's original German shepherd was failing, he would share updates while working through the usual emotions.

I explain, "Roxie's walking earlier and earlier. And she's starting to lose strength, I'm afraid." That's when I look up, staring directly at the man's face, and I honestly don't recognize him.

The man says, "That's too bad," with a voice that I don't know. Tony's voice is thick and hearty—an FM radio voice—while this man has a faint, almost girlish tenor. He is also quite skinny and overly dressed for what isn't a terribly cool afternoon.

"Are you Tony?" I have to ask.

He smiles and nods, saying, "Yes."

He says, "It's the chemo. It does this to me."

I feel silly and lost, and I am quite sad.

"But I'm still vertical," he adds with a ramshackled pride.

I wish him all the luck in the world, and then I take my daughter into the store for milk and a little tube of M&M's.

A few mornings later, well before five, Roxie stops a few feet short of our usual turnaround point. She gives me one of her meaningful stares, and when she has my undivided attention, she glances at the big white stairs. She isn't tired, at least no more tired than usual. But she tells me that she isn't in the mood to climb those stairs, which is why we turn and start back home again.

It is a starry chill morning, with Venus and the remnants of the moon.

I don't know why I'm crying while I walk. But I am, blubbering myself sick, hoping to hell no other dog walkers come by and see me this way.

My hope was to someday invite Roxie to a road race. A small town five-miler seemed like the perfect candidate—held in February and named, appropriately, the Animal Run. But one year proved too warm, while the next winter left me in the mood to run a serious, undistracted race. But eventually a timely Arctic front arrived, ending any thought of racing, and before bed, I told my dog to sleep hard because we had a very busy morning coming.

But the cold was even worse than predicted. Digging out from under my blankets, I discovered it was ten below, with a brutal wind sure to cut through any exposed flesh. Being rather fond of my nose, I didn't want to lose it for fifteenth place in some little survival run. That's why I stayed home, telling myself and my dog that maybe next year would be our year.

Except soon after that, Roxie quit running long miles.

She told me her wishes by various means: She wouldn't come when I called. She would feign sleep or a limp. Or, if another runner visited the house, she would greet him joyfully and then make a show of diving into the window well, hunkering down in the delicious shade.

My wife says it's crazy how much I talk to my dog.

Leslie hears my end of the conversation, and with a palpable tension, she'll ask, "How do you know that's what she wants?"

"The eyes. The body. Everything about this dog is talking. Can't you see?"

Not at all, no.

For more than a year, Roxie would run nothing but little, lazy-day runs. Then on an autumn afternoon, while I was dressing in the basement, she suddenly came to the side door and gave me a long look. When I returned the stare, she glanced up at the leashes hanging from the hook on the wall.

"No, hun," I said. "I'm going long today."

She knows the difference between "long" and "little."

Yet those blue eyes danced, and again she stared up at the salt-crusted six-foot running leash.

I told her the course I wanted to run.

She knows our routes by name.

"You're sure?" I asked.

She stepped back into the kitchen and stretched, front paws out ahead while the body extended, teasing out the kinks.

"Okay then. Let's go."

Until the following spring, she ran twenty miles every week. And then the weather got warm, and she quit again. For good.

But in that final youth, one run stands out: A different Arctic front was pushing through. We began by heading toward the southeast, letting the bitter wind push us along. But then we had no choice but to turn and head for home. For some reason, I was using her twenty-foot leash—probably to let her cavort in the snowdrifts. Roxie was as far ahead as possible, nose to the wind and her leash pulled taut. We eventually reached that place where the path split two ways. To the left was home and warmth, while straight on meant adding miles in a numbing cold. When Roxie reached the intersection, she looked back at me, making a request with her eyes. I said, "No, girl." I told her it was time to finish. But she trotted ahead anyway, stopping only when I stopped. And then she turned and stared stubbornly back at me, making absolutely certain that I understood what she wanted.

"I'm cold," I confessed. "This isn't fun anymore."

"Are you sure?" she asked by lifting her paws and putting them down again.

"No, girl. We're heading in."

And this is why that one run is my favorite: Just then, Roxie gave me a look. A disappointed, disgruntled glare. Those pale blue eyes spoke volumes.

Behind them lived a vivid soul, passionate and secure. And to my dog, in ways that still make me bleed, I was such a fucking, miserable disappointment.

I really don't know what to do about Shelby.

For now, we do nothing. When our daughter is elsewhere, my wife and I will have to talk about the possibilities. The practicalities. And the kinds of choices we must work to avoid. The latest guesses claim that if the asteroid strikes, the hammer blow comes either to the western Atlantic or the East Coast. The president promises that the government will do everything possible to help its citizens—a truthful statement, if ever there was, and full of ominous warnings. We probably won't run far from home, I'm thinking. Two years from now, California and New Zealand will be jammed with refugees. But most people would never think of coming to Nebraska. If it's a wet March, with ample snow cover and rain, the firestorm won't reach us. At least that's what these very preliminary computer models are saying. There won't be any crops that year, what with the sun choked out by airborne dust and acids, but by then we'll have collected tons of canned goods and bottled water. Leslie's family farm seems like a suitable refuge, although I can't take comfort imagining myself as only a son-in-law, surrounded by strong-willed souls who feud in the best of times.

Chances are, Shelby misses us.

Vegas odds say that nothing changes on this little world.

Not for now, at least.

It is a warm perfect evening in early May, and my dog needs her post-dinner walk. A baby gate blocks the basement door; if Roxie wanders downstairs, she won't have the strength to climb back up by herself. She waits patiently for me to move the gate and clip her six-foot leash to her purple collar with the tags. The metal pinch-collar sits on a hook, unnecessary now. The prednisone makes her hungry and patient, sweet and sleepy. I had a rather tearful discussion with the vet about dosages and the prognosis. For today, she gets half a pill in the morning, then half a pill at night. But if she acts uncomfortable, I'll bump it up. Whatever is needed, and don't worry about any long-term health effects.

She has become an absolutely wonderful dog. Her mind remains sharp and clear. One morning, she acts a little confused about where we are going, but that's the lone exception to an exceptionally lucid life. When I give commands, she obeys. But there is very little need to tell her what to do. Every walk has something worth smelling. The weather has been perfect, and neither of us is in a hurry anymore. Halfway to the park, we come upon an elderly couple climbing out of an enormous sedan. They're in their eighties, maybe their nineties, and the frail little woman says to my dog, "You are so beautiful, honey."

I thank her for both of us and go on.

The park lies to our right, beginning with a triangle of public ground where people bring their dogs throughout the day. Roxie does her business in one of the traditional places. I congratulate her on a fine-looking poop. Then we continue walking, heading due north, and at some point it occurs to me that it would be fun to change things up. We could walk down into the pine trees standing beside the golf course. But since I'm not sure that she's strong enough, I say nothing. Not a hint about what I want to do. Yet when we reach our usual turnaround point, Roxie keeps on walking, not looking back at me as we pass the old maintenance building and start down a brief steep slope.

Coincidence, or did she read my mind?

Whatever the reason, we move slowly into the pines, down where the long shadows make the grass cool and inviting, and I am crying again, thinking what a blessing this is, being conjured out of nothingness, and even when that nothingness reclaims us, there remains that unvanquished honor of having once, in some great way or another, having been alive. . . .

Dark Heaven

GREGORY BENFORD

Gregory Benford is one of the modern giants of the field. His 1980 novel *Timescape* won the Nebula Award, the John W. Campbell Memorial Award, the British Science Fiction Association Award, and the Australian Ditmar Award, and is widely considered to be one of the classic novels of the last two decades. His other novels include *Jupiter Project*, *The Stars in Shroud*, *In the Ocean of Night*, *Against Infinity*, *Artifact*, and *Across the Sea of Suns*, *Great Sky River*, *Tides of Light*, *Furious Gulf*, *Sailing Bright Eternity*, *Cosm*, *Foundation's Fear*, *The Martian Race*, *Beyond Infinity*, and *The Sunborn*. His short work has been collected in *Matter's End*, *Worlds Vast and Various*, and *Immersion and Other Short Novels*; his essays have been assembled in a nonfiction collection, *Deep Time*. His most recent book is another nonfiction study of future possibilities, *Beyond Human: The New World of Cyborgs and Androids*, cowritten with Elizabeth Malartre. Benford is a professor of physics at the University of California, Irvine.

In the white-knuckle thriller that's up next, he follows a hard-nosed cop investigating a murder down some mean streets in the humid subtropical night of the American Gulf Coast, a night that turns out to be alive with creatures a lot more dangerous than rattlesnakes and alligators.

The body was bloated and puckered. The man looked to be in his thirties maybe, but with the bulging face and goggle eyes it was hard to tell. His pants and shirt were gone so he was down to his skivvies. They were grimy on the mud beach.

That wasn't unusual at all. Often the Gulf currents pulled the clothes off. Inquisitive fish or sharks came to visit, and indeed there was a chunk out of the left calf and thigh. Someone had come for a snack. Along the chest and belly were long raised red marks, and that was odd. McKenna hadn't seen anything like that before.

McKenna looked around but the muddy beach and stands of reeds held nothing of interest. As the first homicide detective there it was his case, and they were spread so thin he got no backup beyond a few uniforms. Those were mostly just standing around. The photo/video guy was just finishing with his systematic sweep of the area.

The body didn't smell. It had been in the salt water at least a day, the medical examiner had said, judging from the swelling. McKenna listened to the drone of the ME's summary as he circled around the body, his boots scrunching on the beach.

Outside Mobile and the coastal towns, most bodies get found by a game warden or fisherman or by somebody on a beach party who wanders off into the cattails. This one was apparently a wash-up, left by the tide for a cast fisherman to find. A kid had called it in. There was no sign of a boating accident and no record of men missing off a fishing boat; McKenna had checked before leaving his office.

The sallow-faced ME pointed up to a pine limb. "Buzzards get the news first." There were three up there in the cypress.

"What are those long scars?" McKenna asked, ignoring the buzzards.

"Not a propeller, not knife wounds. Looks swole up." A shrug. "I dunno for now."

"Once you get him on the table, let me know."

The ME was sliding the corpse's hands into a metal box with a battery pack on the end. He punched in a command and a flash of light lit the hand for an instant.

"What's that?" McKenna pointed.

The ME grinned up at him as he fitted the left hand in, dropping the right. "I thought the perfessor was up on all the new tech."

McKenna grimaced. Back at the beginning of his career he had been the first in the department to use the Internet very much, when he had just been promoted into the ranks that could wear a suit to work. He read books too, so for years everybody called him the "perfessor." He never corrected their pronunciation and they never stopped calling him that. So for going on plenty years now he was the "perfessor" because he liked to read and listen to music in the evenings rather than hang out in bars or go fishing. Not that he didn't like fishing. It gave a body time to think.

The ME took his silence as a mild rebuke and said finally, as the light flashed again, "New gadget, reads fingerprints. Back in the car I connect it and it goes wireless to the FBI database, finds out who this guy is. Maybe."

McKenna was impressed but decided to stay silent. It was better to be known as a guy who didn't talk much. It increased the odds that when you did say something, people listened. He turned and asked a uniform, "Who called it in?"

It turned out to be one of the three kids standing by a prowl car. The kid had used a cell phone, of course, and knew nothing more. He and his buddies were just out here looking, he said. For what, he didn't say.

The ME said, "I'd say we wait for the autopsy before we do more." He finished up. Homicide got called in on accidental deaths, suicides, even deaths by natural causes, if there was any doubt. "How come you got no partner?" the ME asked.

"He's on vacation. We're shorthanded."

McKenna turned back to the beach for a last look. So the case was a man in his thirties, brown hair cropped close, a moustache, no scars. A tattoo of a dragon adorned the left shoulder. Except for the raised red stripes wrapped around the barrel chest, nothing unusual that McKenna could spot. But those red ridges made it a possible homicide, so here he was.

Anything more? The camera guy took some more shots and some uniforms were searching up and down the muddy beach but they weren't turning up anything. McKenna started to walk away along the long curve of the narrow beach and then turned back. The ME was already supervising two attendants, the three of them hauling the body onto a carry tarp toward the morgue ambulance. "Was it a floater?" McKenna called.

The ME turned and shouted back, "Not in long enough, I'd say."

So maybe in the Gulf for a day, tops, McKenna figured as his boots squished through the mud back to his car. Without air in the lungs, bodies sank unless a nylon jacket or shirt held a bubble and kept them on the surface. More often a body went straight down to the sand and mud until bacteria in the gut did its work and the gas gave lift, bringing the dead soul back into sunshine and more decay. But that took days here so this one was fresh. He didn't have to wait on the ME to tell him that, and except for fingerprints and the teeth that was probably all the physical evidence they would ever get from the poor bastard back there.

The ME caught up to him and said, "He's real stiff, too, so I'd say he struggled in the water a while."

McKenna nodded. A drowning guy burns up his stored sugar and the muscles go rigid quickly.

Two uniforms were leaning against his car, picking their teeth, and he answered their nods but said nothing. This far from Mobile McKenna was technically working beyond his legal limits, but nobody stood on procedure this far into the woods. Not on the coast. The body might be from Mississippi or even Louisiana or Florida, given the Gulf currents, so jurisdiction was uncertain, and might never be decided. A body was a body was a body, as an old New Orleans cop had told him once. Gone to rest. It belongs to no one anymore.

People started out in life looking different. But they ended up a lot alike. Except this one had some interesting ridges.

McKenna recalled being called out for bodies that turned out to be parts of long-drowned deer, the hair gone missing from decay. People sometimes mistook big dogs and even cows for people. But he had never seen any body with those long ridges of reddened, puckering flesh on anything. At least those made this case interesting.

He paused in the morning mist that gathered up from the bayou nearby and watched the impromptu funeral cortège escort the body away, prowl cars going first, crunching along the narrow oyster shell road. The kids were staring at the body, the uniforms, eyeing every move.

Routine, really, probably leading to nothing at all. But something about this bothered him and he could not say what.

He drove back toward Mobile with the window open to the pine-scented spring breezes. To get back from Bayou La Batre, you turn north toward U.S. 90. But he kept going east on two-lane blacktop. At a Citgo station a huge plastic chicken reared up from the bed of a rusted-out El Camino, pointing to a Sit 'n Rest Restaurant that featured shrimp and oysters and fresh catch, the proceeds of the Gulf that had long defined Bayou La Batre.

The book that turned into the movie *Forrest Gump* was set partly around there and the whole place looked it. But Katrina and the hurricanes that came after, pounding the coast like an angry Climate God, had changed the terms of discussion. As if the aliens hadn't, too.

He watched people walking into the Sit 'n Rest and wondered if he should stop and eat. The sunset brimmed the empty sky with rosy fingers, but he didn't feel like eating yet. There was a bottle of Pinot Grigio waiting at home and he somehow didn't want to see people tonight. But he did want to swing by the Centauri Center. The ones around here regarded everybody else as "farmers," as locals along the coast refer to anyone who lives inland. Tough and hard-working people, really, and he respected them. They could handle shrimp, hurricanes, civil rights, Federal drug agents, so why should aliens from another star be any more trouble? At least the aliens didn't want to raise taxes.

And he had taken this case off the board right away, back in Mobile, because it gave him a chance to go by the Centauri Center. He kept going across the long flat land toward the bay, looking for the high building he had read about but never seen. The Feds kept people away from here, but he was on official business.

There were boats in the trees. Two shrimpers, eighty feet long at least, lying tilted on their hulls in scrub oak and pine, at least half a mile from their bayou. Bows shoved into the green, their white masts and rigging rose like bleached treetops. Still not pulled out, nine months since the last hurricane had howled through here. The Feds had other things to do, like hosting amphibians from another star.

That, and discounting insurance for new construction along the Gulf Coast. Never mind that the glossy apartments and condos were in harm's way just by being there.

Just barely off-road, a trawler had its bow planting a hard kiss on a pine. He drove through a swarm of yellow flies, rolling up the windows though he liked the aroma of the marsh grass.

He had heard the usual story, a Federal acronym agency turned into a swear word. A county health officer had the boats declared a public hazard, so the Coast Guard removed the fuel and batteries, which prompted FEMA to say it no longer had reason to spend public money on retrieving private property, and it followed as the night the day that the state and the city submitted applications to "rescue" the boats. Sometime real soon now.

Wind dimpled the bays beside the causeway leading to Mobile Bay. Willow flats and drowned cypress up the far inlets gave way to cattails, which blunted the marching whitetops of the bay's hard chop. They were like endless regiments that had defeated oil platforms and shipping fleets but broke and churned against the final fortress of the land.

He drove toward Mobile Bay and soon he could see what was left of the beachfront.

The sun sparkled on the bay and heat waves rose from the beaches so the new houses there seemed to flap in the air like flags of gaudy paper.

They were pricey, with slanted roofs and big screened porches, rafts supported meters above the sand on tall stilts. They reminded him of ladies with their skirts hoisted to step over something disagreeable.

He smiled at the thought and then felt a jolt as he saw for the first time the alien bunker near the bay. It loomed over the center of Dauphin Island, where Fed money had put it up with round-the-clock labor, to Centauri specs. The big dun-colored stucco frame sloped down toward the south. Ramps led onto the sand where waves broke a few meters away. Amphibian access, he guessed. It had just been finished, though the papers said the Centauri delegation to this part of the Gulf Coast had been living in parts of it for over a year.

He slowed as the highway curved past and nosed into a roadblock. A woman Fed officer in all black fatigues came over to the window. McKenna handed out his ID and the narrow-faced woman asked, "You have business here?"

"Just following a lead on a case."

"Going to need more than that to let you get closer."

"I know." She kept her stiff face and he said, "Y'know, these wrinkles I got at least show that I smiled once upon a time."

Still the flat look. He backed away and turned along a curve taking him inland. He was a bit irked with himself, blundering in like that, led only by curiosity, when his cell phone chimed with the opening bars of "Johnny B. Goode." He wondered why he'd said that to her, and recalled an article he had read this week. Was he a dopamine-rich nervous system pining for its serotonin heartthrob? Could be, but what use was knowing that?

He thumbed the phone on and the ME's voice said, "You might like to look at this."

"Or maybe not. Seen plenty."

"Got him on the table, IDed and everything. But there's something else."

The white tile running up to the ceiling reminded him that this place got hosed down every day. You did that in damp climates because little life forms you could barely see came through even the best air conditioning and did awful things to dead matter. Otherwise it was like all other autopsy rooms. Two stainless steel tables, overhead spray hoses on auto, counters of gleaming stainless, cabinets and gear on three walls. The air conditioning hummed hard but the body smell layered the room in a damp musk. The ME was working and barely glanced up. The county couldn't afford many specialists so the ME did several jobs.

Under the relentless ceramic lights the body seemed younger. Naked, tanned legs and arms and face, the odd raised welts. The ME was at home with bodies, touching and probing and squeezing. Gloved fingers combing the fine brown hair. Fingers in the mouth and throat, doubtless after probing the other five openings with finer tools. The ME used a magnifying glass to look carefully at the throat, shook his head as if at another idea gone sour, then picked up a camera.

He studied the extremities, feet and hands and genitalia. The magnifier swept over the palms and fingers and he took pictures, the flash startling McKenna, adding a sudden whiteness to the ceramic room.

The ME looked up as if noticing McKenna for the first time. "Wanna help?"

They turned the body after McKenna pulled on rubber gloves. A head-to-foot search, careful attention to the tracery of raised yellow-white marks that now had deep purple edges. The bruises lay under the skin and were spreading like oozing ink. The ME took notes and samples and then stepped back and sighed.

"Gotta say I just dunno. He has two clear signatures. Drowning in the lungs, but his heart stopped before that."

"From what?"

"Electrocution. And there's these—" He showed five small puncture wounds on both arms. Puckered and red. "Funny, not like other bites I've seen. So I got to do the whole menu, then."

The county had been going easy on full autopsies. They cost and budgets were tight. "At least you have his name."

"Ethan Anselmo. No priors, FBI says. Married, got the address."

"Wounds?"

"The big welts, I dunno. Never seen such. I'll send samples to the lab. Those punctures on the hands, like he was warding something off. That sure didn't work."

"Torture?"

"Not any kind I know."

"Anybody phone the widow?"

He looked up from his notes, blinking back sweat though the air conditioning was running full blast. "Thought that was your job."

It was. McKenna knocked on the door of the low-rent apartment and it swung open to reveal a woman in her thirties with worried eyes. He took a deep breath and went into the ritual. Soon enough he saw again the thousand-yard stare of the new widow. It came over her after he got only a few sentences into his description. Ordinary people do not expect death's messenger to be on the other side of the knock. Marcie Anselmo got a look at the abyss and would never be the same.

McKenna never wanted to be the intruder into others' pain. He didn't like asking the shell-shocked widow details about their life, his job, where he'd been lately. All she knew was he hadn't come home last night. He did some night jobs but he had never stayed out all night like this before.

He spent a long hour with her. She said he sometimes hung out at The Right Spot. McKenna nodded, recognizing the name. Then they talked some more and he let the tensions rise and fall in her, concluding that maybe it was time to call their relatives. Start the process. Claim the body, the rest. Someone would be calling with details.

He left his card. This part went with the job. It was the price you paid to get to do what came next. Figure out. Find out.

Ethan Anselmo had worked as a pickup deck man on shrimpers out of Bayou La Batre. She hadn't asked which one he went out on lately. They came and went, after all.

McKenna knew The Right Spot, an ancient bar that had once sported decent food and that knew him, too. He forgot about the Pinot Grigio chilling at home and drove through the soft night air over to the long line of run-down docks and sheds that had avoided the worst of the last hurricane. The Right Spot had seen better days but then so had he.

He changed in the darkness to his down-home outfit. Dirty jeans, blue work shirt with snaps instead of buttons, baseball cap with salt stains. Last time he had been here he had sported a moustache, so maybe clean-shaven he would look different. Older, too, by half of a pretty tough year. *Showtime* . . .

Insects shrilled in the high grass of the wiped-out lot next door and frogs brayed from the swampy pond beyond. There was even a sort-of front yard to it, since it had once been a big rambling house, now canted to the left by decay. Night creeper and cat's claw smothered the flowerbeds and flavored the thick air.

There was a separate bar to the side of the restaurant and he hesitated. The juke joint music was pump and wail and crash, sonic oblivion for a few hours. Food first, he decided. Mercifully, there were two rooms and he got away from the noise into the restaurant, a room bleached out by the flat ceramic light. A sharp smell of disinfectant hiding behind the fried food aroma. New South, all right. A sign on the wall in crude type said FRIENDS DON'T LET FRIENDS EAT FOREIGN SHRIMP.

The joint had changed. He sat at a table and ordered jambalaya. When it came, too fast, he knew what to expect before the first mouthful.

It was a far, forlorn cry from the semi-Cajun coast food he knew as a boy, spicy if you wanted and not just to cover the taste of the ingredients. The shrimp and okra and oysters were fresh then, caught or picked that day. That was a richer time, when people ate at home and grew or caught much of what they ate. Paradise, and as usual, nobody had much noticed it at the time.

He looked around and caught the old flavor. Despite his disguise, he saw that some people notice you're a cop. After a few minutes their eyes slide away and they go back to living their lives whether he was watching them or not. Their talk followed the meandering logic of real talk or the even more wayward path of stoned talk. Half-lowered eyelids, gossip, beer smells mingling with fried fish and nose-crinkling popcorn shrimp. Life.

He finished eating, letting the place get used to him. Nobody paid him much attention. The Right Spot was now an odd combination, a restaurant in steep decline with a sleazy bar one thin wall away. Maybe people only ate after they'd guzzled enough that the taste didn't matter anyway.

When he cut through the side door two Cajun women at the end of the bar gave him one glance that instantly said *cop* at the same time his eyes registered *hookers*. But they weren't full-on pros. They looked like locals in fluffy blouses and skinny pants who made a little extra on the side and told themselves they were trying out the talent for the bigger game, a sort of modern style of courtship, free of hypocrisy. Just over the line. He had seen plenty of them when he worked vice. It was important to know the difference, the passing tide of women versus the real hard core who made up the true business. These were just true locals. Fair enough.

The woman bartender leaned over to give him a look at the small but nicely shaped breasts down the top of her gold lame vest. She had a rose tattoo on one.

"Whiskey rocks, right?" She gave him a thin smile.

"Red wine." She had made him as a cop, too. Maybe he had even ordered whiskey last time he was here.

"You been gone a while."

Best to take the polite, formal mode, southern Cary Grant. "I'm sure you haven't lacked for attention." Now that he thought about it, he had gotten some good information here about six months back, and she had pointed out the source.

"I could sure use some." A smile and a slow wink.

"Not from me. Too old. I can remember when the air was clean and sex was dirty."

She laughed, showing a lot of bright teeth, even though it was an old line, maybe as ancient as the era it referred to. But this wasn't what he was here for, no. He took the wine, paid and turned casually to case the room.

Most of the trade here was beer. Big TVs showed talking heads with thick necks against a backdrop of a football field. Guys in jeans and work shirts watched, rapt eyes above the bottles pressed to their mouths. He headed for the back with the glass of indifferent wine, where an old juke strummed with Springsteen singing "There's a darkness on the edge of town."

The fishermen sat along the back. He could tell by the work boots, worn hands, and salt-rimmed cuffs of their jeans and by something more, a squinty look from working in the sea glare. He walked over and sat down at the only open table, at the edge of maybe a dozen of the men sipping on beers.

It took a quarter of an hour before he could get into their conversation. It helped that he had spent years working on his family's boat. He knew the rhythms and lingo, the subtle lurch of consonants and soft vowels that told them he was from around here. He bought the next table over a round of Jax beers and that did it. Only gradually did it dawn on him that they already knew about Ethan Anselmo's death. The kids on the beach had spread the story, naturally.

But most of them here probably didn't know he was a cop, not yet. He sidled along and sat in a squeaky oak chair. Several of the guys were tired and loaded up with beer, stalling before going home to the missus. Others were brighter and on a guess he asked one, "Goin' out tonight?"

"Yeah, night dredgin'. All I can get lately."

The man looked like he had, in his time, quite probably eaten dinner in lot of poolrooms, or out of vending machines, and washed off using a garden hose. Working a dredger at night was mean work. Also, the easiest way to avoid the rules about damaging the sea bottom. Getting caught at that was risky and most men wouldn't take it.

McKenna leaned back and said in slow syllables, "This guy Ethan, the dead guy, know him?"

A nod, eyes crinkling with memory. "He worked the good boat. That one the Centauris hired, double money."

"I hadn't heard they hired anybody other than on Dauphin Island."

"This was some special work. Not dredgin'. Hell, he'd be here right now gettin' ready if he hadn't fell off that boat."

"He fell?" McKenna leaned forward a little and then remembered to look casual.

"They say."

"Who says?" Try not to seem too urgent.

A slow blink, sideways glance, a decision made. "Merv Pitscomb, runs the *Busted Flush*. Now and then they went out together on night charter."

"Really? Damn." He let it ride a little, then asked, "They go out last night?"

"I dunno."

"What they usually go for? Night fishin'?"

Raised eyebrows, shrug. "No bidness of mine."

"Pitscomb works for the Centauris?"

"Not d'rectly. They got a foreman kinda, big guy named Durrer. He books work for the Centauris when they need it."

"Regular work?"

A long tug at his beer. "Comes an' goes. Top dollar, I hear."

McKenna had to go slow here. The man's face was closing in, suspicion written in the tight mouth. McKenna always had a problem pressing people for information, and that got around, but apparently not to The Right Spot just yet. One suspect had once named him, Man Who Ax Questions More'n He Should. True, but the suspect got ten to twenty upstate just the same.

McKenna backed off and talked football until the guy told him his name, Fred Godwin. Just then, by pure luck that at first didn't look like it, a woman named Irene came over to tell them both that she'd all heard about the body and all, and to impart her own philosophy on the matter.

The trouble with teasing information out of people was you get interrupted. It felt like losing a fish from a line, knowing it would never fall for the hook again. Irene went on about how it was a tragedy of course and she knew it weighed upon everybody. That went without saying, only she said it. She looked to be about forty going on fifty pretty hard, and unsteady on her shimmering gold high heels.

"Look at it this way," she said profoundly, eyes crinkling up above her soulful down-turned lips, "Ethan was young, so that as he was taken up on an angel's wing to the Alabaster City, he will be still brimming with what he could be. See? Set down at the Lord's Table, he will have no true regret. There will be no time for that. Another life will beckon to him while he is still full of energy, without memories of old age. No fussing with medicine and fear and failed organs, none. No such stations of duress on the way to Glory."

He could hear the capitals. Godwin looked like he was waiting for the right moment to escape. Which meant it was the right moment to buy him a beer, which McKenna did. To keep control of the conversation, maybe hinting at an invitation to sit with them, Irene volunteered that she'd heard Ethan had been working on the *Busted Flush* the night before his body washed up. *Bingo*.

McKenna bought Godwin the beer anyway.

Up toward the high end districts of Mobile the liquor stores stocked decades-old single malt Scotch and groceries had goat yoghurt and five kinds of oregano and coffee from nations you never heard of since high school. You could sip it while you listened to Haydn in their coffee shops and maybe scan the latest *New Yorker* for an indie film review.

But down by the coast the stores had Jim Beam if you asked right and the only seasoning on their shelves was salt and pepper, usually lots of pepper for Cajun tastes, and coffee came in cans. There was no music at all where he shopped and he was grateful. Considering what it might have been.

He got a bottle of a good California red to wash away the taste of the stuff he'd had earlier and made his way to the dock near the *Busted Flush* mooring. From his trunk he got out his rod and tackle and bait and soon enough was flipping his lure toward the lily pads in the nearby bayou. He pulled it lazily back, letting the dark water savor it. In a fit of professional rigor he had left the good California red in the car.

The clapboard shack beside the mooring was gray, the nail holes trailing rust and the front porch sagging despite the cinder blocks loyally holding it up from the damp sand. There was a big aluminum boathouse just beyond but no lights were on. He guessed it was too austere and indeed the only murmur of talk came from the shack. A burst of cackling laughter from the fishing crew leaked out of the walls.

He sat in the shadows. An old Dr Pepper sign was almost gone but you could still see the holes from buckshot. Teenagers love targets.

It made no real good sense to fish at night but the moon was coming up like a cat's yellow smile over the shimmering gulf and some thought that drew the fish out. Like a false dawn, an old fisherman had said to him long ago, and maybe it was true. All he needed was the excuse anyway so he sat and waited. He always kept worms in a moist loam pail in the car trunk and maybe they would work tonight even if this stakeout didn't.

The *Busted Flush* crew was hauling out the supplies for a night run. There was always something to do on a boat, as McKenna knew from working them as a teenager, but these guys were taking longer than it should.

He had learned long ago the virtues of waiting. At his distance of about a hundred meters simple binoculars told him all he needed, and they had an IR filter to bring out the detail if he needed it. The amber moonlight glanced off the tin-roofed shotgun shacks down along the curve of the bay. Night-blooming flowers perfumed the night air and bamboo rattled in the distance like a whisper in his ear.

Then a big van rumbled up. Two guys got out, then a woman. They wore black and moved with crisp efficiency, getting gear out of the back. This didn't fit.

The team went to the dock and Merv Pitscomb ambled along to greet them. McKenna recognized him as skipper of the *Busted Flush* from a car fax he had gotten from the Mobile Main library, after leaving the restaurant. His car was more his office now than the desk he manned; electronics had changed everything.

The team and Pitscomb went together back to the van, talking. Pitscomb slid open the side door and everyone stepped back. A dark shape came out—large, moving slowly and in a silence from the Feds that was like reverence.

McKenna froze. He knew immediately it was a Centauri. Its arms swung slowly, as if heavily muscled. The oddly jointed elbow swung freely like a pendulum, going backward. In water that would be useful, McKenna imagined. The arm tapered down to a flat four-fingered hand that he knew could be shaped to work like the blade of an oar.

The amphibians were slow and heavy, built for a life spent moving from water to land. It walked solidly behind the two guys in black, who were forming a screen of what had to be Federal officers. No talk. Centauris' palate could not manage the shaped human sounds, so all communication was written.

It shuffled toward *Busted Flush* on thick legs that had large, circular feet. With help at the elbows from the Feds it mounted the gangplank. This was the first he had seen for real, not on TV, and it struck him that it waddled more than walked. It was slow here, in a slightly stronger gravity. Centauris had evolved from a being that moved on sand, seldom saw rock, and felt more at home in the warm waters of a world that was mostly sea.

He realized as it reached the boat that he had been holding his breath. It was *strange* in a way he could not define. The breeze blew his way. He sniffed and wondered if that rank flavoring was the alien.

It went aboard, the Federal officers' eyes swiveling in all directions. McKenna was under a cypress and hard to spot and their eyes slid right over him. He wondered why they didn't use infrared goggles.

Busted Flush started up with a hammering turbo engine. It turned away from the dock and headed straight out into the gulf. McKenna watched it go but he could not see the alien. The shrimp nets hung swaying on their high rocker arms and *Busted Flush* looked like any other dredge shrimper going out for the night. That was the point, McKenna guessed.

When he finally got home down the oyster-shell road and parked under the low pines, he walked out onto his dock to look at the stars above the gulf. It always helped. He did not want to go right away into the house where he and his lost wife had lived. He had not moved away, because he loved this place, and though she was not here at least the memories were.

He let the calm come over him and then lugged his briefcase up onto the porch and was slipping a key into the lock when he heard a scraping. He turned toward the glider where he had swung so many happy times and someone was getting up from it. A spike of alarm shot through him, the one you always have once you work the hard criminals, and then he saw it was a woman in a pale yellow dress. Yellow hair, too, blond with a ribbon in it. Last time it had been red.

"John! Now, you did promise you'd call."

At first he could not tell who she was, but he reached inside the door and flipped on the porch light and her face leaped out of the darkness. "Ah, uh, Denise?"

"Why yes, did you forget me already?" Humorous reproach, coquettish and a little strained.

She swayed toward him, her hair bouncing as if just washed. Which it probably was. He felt his spirits sinking. If the average woman would rather have beauty than brains, it's because the average man can see better than he can think. Denise believed that and so was even more dolled up than on their first date. Also, last date.

"I figured out where you lived, so stopped by." Her broad smile was wise and enticing. "You didn't call, you know."

The vowels rolled off her tongue like sugar and he remembered why he had found her so intriguing.

"I've been awful busy."

"So've I, but you cain't just let life go by, y'know."

What to say to that? She was here for a clear purpose, her large red handbag on a shoulder strap and probably packed with cosmetics and a change of underwear. Yet he had no easy counter to it.

"Denise, I'm . . . seeing someone else." Easy, reasoned.

Her expression shifted subtly, the smile still in place but now glassy. "I . . . I didn't know that."

"It didn't make the papers."

No, that was wrong, humor wouldn't work here. He decided on the physical instead and held out a hand, edge on, thumb straight up, for a shake. A long moment passed while her eyelashes batted beneath the yellow porch light and he could hear frogs croaking in the night marsh.

She looked at his hand and blinked and the smile collapsed. "I . . . I thought . . ."

It was his duty to make this as easy as possible so he took her half-offered hand and put an arm around her shoulders. He turned her delicately, murmuring something that made sense at the time but that he could not remember ten seconds later. With a sweeping arm he ushered her down the wooden stairs, across the sandy lawn in the moist sea air. Without more than soft words they both got to the car he had not even seen parked far back under the big oak tree aside the house. He said nothing that meant anything and she did the same and they got through the moment with something resembling their dignity.

He helped her into her car and turned back toward his house. A year ago, in a momentary fit, one member of the sorority of such ladies of a certain age had tried to run him down. This time, though, her Chevy started right off, growling like a late model, and turned toward the oyster driveway that shimmered in the silvery moon glow. He walked away from it, the noise pushing him.

The lie about seeing someone settled in him. His social graces were rusty. He mounted the steps as her headlights swept across the porch, spotlighting him momentarily, like an angry glare. To jerk open the front door and finally get inside felt like a forgiveness.

McKenna got into work early. It had bothered him to usher Denise off like that and he had stayed up too late thinking about it. Also, there was that good California red. Not that he had failed to enjoy Denise and the others in their mutual nonjudgmental rejection of middle class values. Not at all.

But that style wasn't working for him anymore. He had set out vaguely searching for someone who could bring that light back into his life, the oblivious glow he had basked in for decades of a happy marriage. He had thought that if it happened once it could happen again. But since Linda's death nothing had that magic to it. Not dating—a term he hated, preferring "courtship"—and most of the time not even sex, his old standby.

So Denise's sad approach, the stuff of every teenage boy's dream, had been too little, too late.

He was still musing about this when he got to his desk. Homicide was a big squad room in worn green industrial carpet. The work pods had five desks each and he walked past these because he at last had gained a sheltered cubicle. The sergeant's desk was nearby his lieutenant's cubicle and framing the whole array was a rank of file cabinets. No paperless office here, no. Maybe never. At least there was no smoking anymore, but the carpet remembered those days. Especially after a rain, which meant usually.

The morning squad room buzzed with movement, talk, caffeine energy. Homicide detectives always run because it's a timed event. You close in on the perp inside two weeks or it's over.

And here was the ME folder on Ethan Anselmo. Once you've studied a few hundred autopsy reports you know you can skip the endless pages of organs, glands, general chemistry, and just go to the conclusions. Forensic analysis had a subreport labeled GSR, which meant gunshot residue, that was blank.

The ME was confused. Heart stopped, lungs full, much like a drowning victim who had fought the ocean to his last. But the strange ridges on his skin looked like nerve damage, seared as if in an electrocution. The punctures McKenna had seen just obscured the case further.

McKenna hated muddy cases. Now he had to assign cause, focusing the ME report and the background he had gotten last night. He didn't hesitate. *Probable homicide*, he wrote.

The usual notices had gone through, assigning case and ME numbers, letting the Squad and Precinct Captains know, asking if there seemed any link to other cases—all routine. Section Command and District Office heard, all by standard e-mail heads-up forms, as did Photo and Latent and Lab.

He took out a brown loose-leaf binder and made up a murder book. First came the Homicide Occurrence Report with Mobile Main as the address in the right upper corner. Then the basics. A door that opened wide with no sure destination beyond.

McKenna sat back and let his mind rove. Nothing. Sometimes an idea lurked there after he had reviewed the case; not now.

He knew he had to finish up a report on a domestic slaying from two days back, so he set to it. Most murders were by guys driven crazy by screeching kids and long-term debt and bipolar wives. Alcohol helped. They had figured out their method about ten seconds before doing it and had no alibi, no plausible response to physical evidence, and no story that didn't come apart under a two-minute grilling. When you took them out to the car in cuffs the neighbors just nodded at each other and said they'd always figured on this, hadn't they said so?

This was a no-brainer case. He finished the paperwork, longing for that paperless office, and dispatched it to the prosecutor's office. They would cut the deal and McKenna would never hear of it again. Unless the perp showed up in fifteen years on his front porch, demanding vengeance. That had happened, too. Now McKenna went armed, even on Sundays to church.

Then he sat and figured.

The ME thought the odd marks on Ethan Anselmo might be electrocution. Torture? Yet the guy was no lowlife. He had no history of drug-running using shrimp boats, the default easy way for a fisherman to bring in extra income all along the Gulf. For a moment McKenna idly wondered when the War on Drugs would end, as so many failed American adventures had, with admission that the war was clearly lost. It would certainly be easier to legalize, tax, and control most drugs than it was to chase after them. He had at first figured Anselmo for a drug gang killing. There were plenty of them along the Gulf shore. But now that felt wrong.

His desktop computer told him that the Anselmo case was now online in the can't-crack site Mobile used to coordinate police work now. There were some additions from the autopsy and a background report on Anselmo, but nothing that led anywhere.

He sighed. Time to do some shoe-leather work.

The *Busted Flush* was back at its dock. McKenna had changed into a beat-up work shirt and oil-stained jeans. Sporting a baseball cap, he found the crew hosing off a net rig inside the big aluminum boathouse nearby. "Pitscomb around?" he asked them, rounding the vowels to fit the local accent.

A thirty-something man walked over to McKenna. One cheek had a long, ugly scar now gone to dirty pink. His hair was blond and ratty, straight and cut mercifully short. But the body was taut and muscular and ready; the scrollwork tattoos of jailhouse vintage showed he had needed for much of his life. He wore a snap-button blue work shirt with a stuck-on nameplate that said Buddy Johnson. Completing the outfit was a hand-tooled belt with carry hooks hanging and half-topped boots that needed a polish pretty bad.

"Who wants to know?"

The stern, gravel voice closed a switch in McKenna's head. He had seen this guy a decade before when he helped make an arrest. Two men tried to pull the front off a cash machine by running a chain from the machine to the bumper of their pickup truck. Instead of pulling the front panel off the machine, though, they yanked the bumper off the truck. They panicked and fled, leaving the chain still attached to the machine, their bumper still attached to the chain, and their license plate still attached to the bumper.

"Lookin' for work," McKenna said. This guy couldn't be heading up the operation, so he needed to go higher.

"We got none." The eyes crinkled as if Buddy was trying to dredge up a memory.

McKenna shifted his own tone from soft to medium. "I need to see your boss."

Still puzzling over the memory, Johnson waved toward the boathouse. McKenna walked away, feeling Johnson's eyes on his back.

Pitscomb was at the back of the building, eating hog cracklings from a greasy bag, brushing the crumbs into the lagoon. Carrion birds eyed him as they drifted by on the soft slurring wind, keeping just above the gnarled tops of the dead cypress, just in case they saw some business below that needed doing.

Pitscomb was another matter. Lean, angular, intelligent blue eyes. McKenna judged that he might as well come clean. He showed his badge and said with a drawl, "Need to talk about Ethan Anselmo."

Pitscomb said, "Already heard. He didn't come to work that night."

"Your crew, they'll verify that?"

He grinned. "They'd better."

"Why you have an ex-con working your boat?"

"I don't judge people, I just hire 'em. Buddy's worked out fine."

"What do you do for the Centauris?"

"That's a Federal matter, I was told to say."

McKenna leaned against a pier stay. "Why do they use you, then? Why not take the Centuri out on their own boat?"

Pitscomb brushed his hands together, sending the last of the cracklings into the water. "You'd have to ask them. Way I see it, the Feds want to give the Centauris a feel for our culture. And spread the money around good an' local, too."

"What's the Centauri do out there?"

"Just looks, swims. A kind of night off, I guess."

"They live right next to the water."

"Swimming out so far must be a lot of work, even for an amphibian." By now Pitscomb had dropped the slow-South accent and was eyeing McKenna.

"How far out?"

"A few hours."

"Just to swim?"

"The Feds don't want me to spread gossip."

"This is a murder investigation."

"Just gossip, far as I'm concerned."

"I can take this to the Feds."

Again the sunny smile, as sincere as a postage stamp. "You do that. They're not backwoods coon-asses, those guys."

Meaning, pretty clearly, that McKenna was. He turned and walked out through the machine oil smells of the boathouse. Buddy Johnson was waiting in the moist heat. He glowered but didn't say anything.

As he walked past McKenna said, using hard vowels, "Don't worry, now. I haven't chewed off anybody's arm in nearly a week."

Buddy still didn't say anything, just smiled slyly. When McKenna got to his car he saw the reason.

A tire was flat, seeming to ooze into the blacktop. McKenna glanced back at Buddy, who waved and went back inside. McKenna thought about following him but it was getting warm and he was sticking to his shirt. Buddy would wait until he knew more, he figured.

He got his gloves from the trunk, then lifted out the jack, lug wrench, and spare. He squatted down and started spinning the nuts off, clattering them into the hubcap. By the time he fitted the spare on the axle and tightened the wheel nuts with the jack, then lowered it, he had worked up a sweat and smelled himself sour and fragrant.

The work had let him put his mind on cruise and as he drove away he felt some connections link up.

The Pizottis. One of them was a real professor, the kind he needed. Was that family fish fry tonight? He could just about make it.

Since Linda died he had seen little of the Pizotti family. Their shared grief seemed to drive them apart. The Pizottis always kept somewhat distant anyway, an old country instinct.

He drove over the causeway to the eastern shore of the bay and then down through Fairhope to the long reaches south of the Grand Hotel. He had grown up not far away, spending summers on the Fish River at Grammaw McKenzie's farm. To even reach the fish fry, on an isolated beach, he decided to take a skiff out across Weeks Bay.

The Pizottis had invited him weeks ago, going through the motions of pretending he was family. They weren't the reason, of course. He let himself forget about all that as he poled along amid the odors of reeds and sour mud, standing in the skiff. In among the cattails lurked alligators, one with three babies a foot and a half long. They scattered away from the skiff, nosing into the muddy fragrant water, the mother snuffing as she sank behind the young ones. He knew the big legendary seventeen-footers always lay back in the reeds, biding their time. As he coasted forward on a few oar strokes, he saw plenty of lesser lengths lounging in the late sun like metallic sculptures. A big one ignored the red-tailed hawk on a log nearby, knowing it was too slow to ever snare the bird. By a cypress tree, deep in a thick tangle of matted saw grass, a gray possum was picking at something and sniffing like it couldn't decide whether to dine or not. The phosphorus-loving cattails had moved in further up the bay, stealing away the skiff's glide so he came to a stop. He didn't like the cattails and felt insulted by their presence. Cattails robbed sunlight from the paddies and fish below, making life harder for the water-feeding birds.

He cut toward Mobile Bay where the fish fry should be and looked in among the reeds. There were lounging gators like logs sleeping in the sun. One rolled over in the luxury of the warm mud and gave off a moaning grunt, an *umph-umph-umph* with mouth closed. Then it opened in a yawn and achieved a throaty, bellowing roar. He had seen alligators like that before in Weeks Bay where the Fish River eased in, just below the old arched bridge. Gators seemed to like bridges. They would lie in the moist heat and sleep, the top predators here, unafraid. He admired their easy assurance that nothing could touch them, their unthinking arrogance.

Until people came along, only a few centuries before, with their rifles. He suddenly wondered if the Centauris were like this at all. They were amphibians, not reptiles. What would they make of gators?

A gator turned and looked up at him for a long moment. It held the gaze, as if figuring him out. It snuffed and waddled a little in the mud to get more comfortable and closed its big eyes. McKenna felt an odd chill. He paddled faster.

The other wing of the Pizotti family was on the long sand bar at the end of Weeks Bay, holding forth in full cry. He came ashore, dragged the skiff up to ground it, and tried to mix. The Pizottis' perfunctory greetings faded and they got back to their social games.

He had loved Linda dearly but these were not truly his kind of people. She had been serene, savoring life while she had it. The rest of the Pizottis were on the move. Nowadays the Gulf's Golden Coast abounded with Masters of the Universe. They sported excellently cut hair and kept themselves slim, casually elegant, and carefully muscled. Don't want to look like a *laborer*, after all, never mind what their grandfathers did for a living. The women ran from platinum blond through strawberry, quite up to the minute. Their plastic surgery was tasteful: eye-smoothings and maybe a discreet wattle tuck. They carried themselves with that look not so much of energetic youth but rather of expert maintenance, like a Rolls with the oil religiously changed every 1500 miles. Walking in their wake made most working stiffs feel just a touch shabby.

One of them eyed him and professed fascination with a real detective. He countered with enthusiasm for the fried flounder and perch a cousin had brought. Food was a good dodge, though these were fried in too much oil. He held out for a polite ten minutes and then went to get one of the crab just coming off the grill. And there, waiting for the next crab to come sizzling off, was Herb. Just in time. McKenna could have kissed him.

It didn't take too long to work around to the point of coming here. Herb was an older second cousin of Linda, and had always seemed to McKenna like the only other Pizotti who didn't fit in with the rest. He had become an automatic friend as soon as McKenna started courting her.

"It's a water world," Herb said, taking the bit immediately. He had been a general science teacher at Faulkner State in Fairhope, handling the chemistry and biology courses. "You're dead on, I've been reading all I could get about them."

"So they don't have much land?" McKenna waved to the woman who loved detectives and shrugged comically to be diplomatic. He got Herb and himself a glass of red, a Chianti.

"I figure that's why they're amphibians. Best to use what there's plenty of. Their planet's a moon, right?—orbiting around a gas giant like Jupiter. It gets sunlight from both Centauri stars, plus infrared from the gas giant. So it's always warm and they don't seem to have plate tectonics, so their world is real, real different."

McKenna knew enough from questioning witnesses to nod and look interested. Herb was already going beyond what he'd gotten from TV and newspapers and *Scientific American*. McKenna tried to keep up. As near as he could tell, plate tectonics was something like the grand unified theory of geology. Everything from the deep plains of the ocean to Mount Everest came from the waltz of continents, butting together and churning down into the deep mantle. Their dance rewrote climates and geographies, opening up new possibilities for life and at times closing down old ones. But that was here, on Earth.

The other small planets of our solar system didn't work that way. Mars had been rigid for billions of years. Venus upchucked its mantle and buried its crust often enough to leave it barren.

So planets didn't have to work like Earth, and the Centauri water world was another example. It rotated slowly, taking eight days to get around its giant neighbor. It had no continents, only strings of islands. And it was *old*— more than a billion years older than Earth. Life arose there from nothing more than chemicals meeting in a warm sea while sunlight boomed through a blanket of gas.

"So they got no idea about continents?" McKenna put in.

Herb said. He sure seemed to miss lecturing, ever since he retired, and it made him a dinner companion not exactly sought after here among the Pizottis. McKenna had never thought he could be useful, like now. "They took one up in an airplane, with window blinds all closed, headphones on its ears. Turns out it liked Bach! Great, huh?"

McKenna nodded, kept quiet. None of the other Pizottis was paying any attention to Herb. They seemed to be moving away, even.

"The blindfold was so it wouldn't get scared, I guess. They took off the blindfold and showed it mountains, river valleys, all that. Centauris got no real continents, just strings of islands. It could hardly believe its clamshell eyes."

"But they must've seen those from space, coming in. Continents and all."

"Not the same, close up."

"So maybe they're thinking to move inland, explore?"

"I doubt it. They got to stick close to warm, salty water."

McKenna wondered if they had any global warming there and then said, "They got no oil, I guess. No place for all those ferns to grow, so long ago."

Herb blinked. "Hadn't figured that. S'pose so. But they say they got hurricanes alla time, just the way we do now."

McKenna poked a finger up and got them another glass of the Chianti. Herb needed fueling.

"It's cloudy alla time there, the astro boys say. They can never see through the clouds. Imagine, not knowing for thousands of years that there are stars."

McKenna imagined never having a sunny day. "So how'd they ever get a space program going?"

"Slow and steady. Their civilization is way old, y'know, millions of years. They say their spaceships are electric, somehow."

McKenna couldn't imagine electric rockets. "And they've got our kind of DNA."

Herb brightened. "Yeah, what a surprise. Spores brought it here, *Scientific American* figures."

"Amazing. What sort of biology do amphibians have?"

Herb shrugged and pushed a hush puppy into his mouth, then chewed thoughtfully. The fish fry was a babble all around them and McKenna had to concentrate. "Dunno. There's nothing in the science press about that. Y'know, Centauris are mighty private about that stuff."

"They give away plenty of technology, the financial pages say."

"You bet, whole new products. Funny electrical gadgets, easy to market."

"So why are they here? Not to give us gifts." Might as well come out and say it.

"Just like Carl Sagan said, right? Exchange cultures and all. A great adventure, and we get it without spending for starships or anything."

"So they're tourists? Who pay with gadgets?"

Herb knocked back the rest of his Chianti. "Way I see it, they're lonely. They heard our radio a century back and started working on a ship to get here."

"Just like us, you think about it. Why else do we make up ghosts and angels and the like? Somebody to talk to."

"Only they can't talk."

"At least they write."

"Translation's hard, though. The Feds are releasing a little of it, but there'll be more later. You see those Centauri poems?"

He vaguely recalled some on the front page of the paper. "I couldn't make sense of it."

Herb grinned brightly. "Me either, but it's fascinating. All about the twin suns. Imagine!"

When he got home he showered, letting the steam envelop him and ease away the day. His mind had too much in it, tired from the day. Thinking about sleep, when he often got his best ideas, he toweled off.

The shock came when he wiped the steam from the mirror and saw a smeary old man, blotchy skin, gray hair pasted to the skull, ashen whiskers sprouting from deep pores. He had apparently gone a decade or two without paying attention to mirrors.

Fair enough, if they insult you this deeply. He slapped some cream on the wrinkles hemming in his eyes, dressed, sucked in his belly, and refused to check himself out in the mirror again. Insults enough, for one day. Growing older he couldn't do much about, but Buddy Johnson was another matter.

At dawn he quite deliberately went fishing. He needed to think.

He sat on his own wharf and sipped orange juice. He had to wash off the reels with the hose from the freshwater tank as waves came rolling in and burst in sprays against the creaking pilings. He smelled the salty tang of bait fish in his bucket and, as if to tantalize him, a speckled fish broke from a curling wave, plunging headfirst into the foam. He had never seen a fish do that and it proved yet again that the world was big and strange and always changing. Other worlds, too.

He sat at his desk and shuffled paper for the first hour of the morning shift. He knew he didn't have long before the Ethan Anselmo case hit a dead end. Usually a homicide not wrapped up in two weeks had a less-than-even chance of ever getting solved at all. After two weeks the case became an unclaimed corpse in the files, sitting there in the dark chill of neglect.

Beyond the autopsy you go to the evidence analysis reports. Computer printouts, since most detectives still worked with paper. Tech addenda and photos. All this under a time and cost constraint, the clock and budget always ticking along. "Investigative prioritizing," the memos called it. Don't do anything expensive without your supe's nod.

So he went to see his supe, a black guy two months in from Vice, still learning the ropes. And got nothing back.

"The Feds, you let them know about the Centauri connection, right?" the supe asked.

"Sure. There's a funnel to them through the Mobile FBI office."

Raised eyebrows. "And?"

"Nothing so far."

"Then we wait. They want to investigate, they will."

"Not like they don't know the Centauris are going out on civilian boats." McKenna was fishing to see if his supe knew anything more but the man's eyes betrayed nothing.

The supe said, "Maybe the Centauris want it this way. But why?"

"Could be they want to see how ordinary people work the sea?"

"We gotta remember they're aliens. Can't think of them as like people."

McKenna couldn't think of how that idea could help so he sat and waited. When the supe said nothing more, McKenna put in, "I'm gonna get a call from the Anselmo widow."

"Just tell her we're working on it. When's your partner get back?"

"Next week. But I don't want a stand-in."

A shrug. "Okay, fine. Just don't wait for the Feds to tell you anything. They're just like the damn FBI over there."

McKenna was in a meeting about new arrest procedures when the watch officer came into the room and looked at him significantly.

The guy droning on in front was a city government lawyer and most of his audience was nodding off. It was midafternoon and the coffee had long run out but not the lawyer.

McKenna ducked outside and the watch officer said, "You got another, looks like. Down in autopsy."

It had washed up on Orange Beach near the Florida line, so Baldwin County Homicide had done the honors. Nobody knew who it was and the fingerprints went nowhere. It had on jeans and no underwear, McKenna read in the Baldwin County report.

When the Baldwin County sheriff saw on the Internet cross-correlation index that it was similar to McKenna's case they sent it over for the Mobile ME. That had taken a day, so the corpse was a bit more rotted. It was already gutted and probed, and the ME had been expecting him.

"Same as your guy," the ME said. "More of those raised marks, all over the body."

Suited up and wearing masks, they went over the swollen carcass. The rot and swarming stink caught in McKenna's throat but he forced down the impulse to vomit. He had never been good at this clinical stuff. He made himself focus on what the ME was pointing out, oblivious to McKenna's rigidity.

Long ridges of reddened, puckering flesh laced around the trunk and down the right leg. A foot was missing. The leg was drained white, and the ME said it looked like a shark bite. Something had nibbled at the genitals. "Most likely a turtle," the ME said. "They go for the delicacies."

McKenna let this remark pass by and studied the face. Black eyes, broad nose, weathered brown skin. "Any punctures?"

"Five, on top of the ridges. Not made by teeth or anything I know."

"Any dental ID?"

"Not yet."

"I need pictures," McKenna said. "Cases like this cool off fast."

"Use my digital, I'll e-mail them to you. He looks like a Latino," the ME said. "Maybe that's why no known fingerprints or dental. Illegal."

Ever since the first big hurricanes, Katrina and Rita, swarms of Mexicans had poured in to do the grunt work. Most stayed, irritating the working class who then competed for the construction and restaurant and fishing jobs. The ME prepared his instruments for further opening the swollen body and McKenna knew he could not take that. "Where . . . where's the clothes?"

The ME looked carefully at McKenna's eyes. "Over there. Say, maybe you should sit down."

"I'm okay." It came out as a croak. McKenna went over to the evidence bag and pulled out the jeans. Nothing in the pockets. He was stuffing them back in when he felt something solid in the fabric. There was a little inner pocket at the back, sewed in by hand. He fished out a key ring with a crab-shaped ornament and one key on it.

"They log this in?" He went through the paperwork lying on the steel table. The ME was cutting but came over. Nothing in the log.

"Just a cheap plastic thingy," the ME said, holding it up to the light. "Door key, maybe. Not a car."

"Guy with one key on his ring. Maybe worked boats, like Anselmo."

"That's the first guy, the one who had those same kinda marks?"

McKenna nodded. "Any idea what they are?"

The ME studied the crab ornament. "Not really. Both bodies had pretty rough hands, too. Manual labor."

"Workin' stiffs. You figure he drowned?"

"Prob'ly. Got all the usual signs. Stick around, I'll know soon."

McKenna very carefully did not look back at the body. The smell was getting to him even over the air conditioning sucking air out of the room with a loud hum. "I'll pick up the report later." He left right away.

His supe sipped coffee, considered the sound-absorbing ceiling, and said, "You might see if VICAP got anything like this."

The Violent Criminal Apprehension Program computer would cross-filter the wounds and tell him if anything like that turned up in other floaters. "Okay. Thought I'd try to track that crab thing on the key chain."

The supe leaned back and crossed his arms, showing scars on both like scratches on ebony. "Kinda unlikely."

"I want to see if anybody recognizes it. Otherwise this guy's a John Doe."

"It's a big gulf. The ME think it could've floated from Mexico?"

"No. Local, from the wear and tear."

"Still a lot of coastline."

McKenna nodded. The body had washed up about forty miles to the east of Bayou La Batre, but the currents could have brought it from anywhere. "I got to follow my hunches on this."

The supe studied McKenna's face like it was a map. He studied the ceiling again and sighed. "Don't burn a lot of time, okay?"

There were assorted types working in homicide but he broke them into two different sorts.

Most saw the work as a craft, a skill they learned. He counted himself in those, though wondered lately if he was sliding into the second group: those who thought it was a mission in life, the only thing worth doing. Speakers for the dead, he called them.

At the crime scene a bond formed, a promise from the decaying corpse to the homicide detective: that this would be avenged. It went with the job.

The job was all about death, of course. He had shot only two perps in his career. Killed one in a messy attempt at an arrest, back when he was just getting started. A second when a smart guy whose strategy had gone way wrong decided he could still shoot his way out of his confusion. All he had done was put a hole through McKenna's car.

But nowadays he felt more like an avenging angel than he had when young. Closer to the edge. Teetering above the abyss.

Maybe it had something to do with his own wife's death, wasting away, but he didn't go there anymore. Maybe it was just about death itself, the eternal human problem without solution. If you can't solve it you might as well work at it anyway.

Murderers were driven, sometimes just for a crazed moment that shaped all the rest of their lives. McKenna was a cool professional, calm and sure—or so he told himself.

But something about the Anselmo body—drowned and electrocuted both—got to him. And now the anonymous illegal, apparently known to nobody, silent in his doom.

Yet he, the seasoned professional, saw no place to go next. No leads. This was the worse part of any case, where most of them went cold and stayed that way. Another murder file, buried just like the bodies.

McKenna started in the west, at the Mississippi state line. The Gulf towns were much worse off after getting slammed with Katrina and Rita and the one nobody could pronounce right several years after. The towns never got off the ropes. The Gulf kept punching them hard, maybe fed by global warming and maybe just out of some kind of natural rage. Mother Earth Kicks Ass, part umpty-million.

He had the tech guy Photoshop the photos of the Latino's face, taking away the swelling and water bleaching. With eyes open he looked alive. Then he started showing it around.

He talked to them all—landlords and labor in-between men, Mexicans who worked the fields, labor center types. Nothing. So he went to the small-time boosters, hookers, creeps in alleys, button men, strong-arm types slow and low of word, addicts galore, those who thrived on the dark suffering around them—the underlife of the decaying coast. He saw plenty of thick-bodied, smoldering anger that would be bad news someday for someone, of vascular crew-cut slick boys, stained jeans, arms ridged with muscle that needed to be working. Some had done time in the bucket and would again.

Still, nothing. The Latino face rang no bells.

He was coming out of a gardening shop that used a lot of Latinos when the two suits walked up. One wore a Marine-style bare-skull haircut and the other had on dark glasses and both those told him *Federal*.

"You're local law?" the Marine type said.

Without a word McKenna showed them his badge. Dark Glasses and Marine both showed theirs, FBI, and Dark Glasses said, "Aren't you a long way beyond Mobile city lines?"

"We're allowed to follow cases out into the county," McKenna said levelly.

"May we see the fellow you're looking for?" Mr. Marine asked, voice just as flat.

McKenna showed the photo. "What did he do?" Mr. Marine asked.

"Died. I'm Homicide."

"We had a report you were looking in this community for someone who worked boats," Dark Glasses said casually.

"Why would that interest the FBI?"

"We're looking for a similar man," Mr. Marine said. "On a Federal issue."

"So this is the clue that I should let you know if I see him? Got a picture?"

Dark Glasses started a smile and thought better of it. "Since there's no overlap, I think not."

"But you have enough sources around here that as soon as I show up, you get word." McKenna said it flatly and let it lie there in the sun.

"We have our ways," Dark Glasses said. "How'd this guy die?"

"Drowned."

"Why think it's homicide?" Mr. Marine came in.

"Just a hunch."

"Something tells me you have more than that," Mr. Marine shot back.

"You show me yours, I'll show you mine."

They looked at each other and McKenna wondered if they got the joke. They turned and walked away without a word.

His bravado with them made him feel good but it didn't advance his case. His mind spun with speculations about the FBI and then he put them away. The perpetual rivalry between local and federal always simmered, since the Feds could step in and capture a case when they thought they could profit from it. Or solve it better. Sometimes they were even right.

He prowled the Latino quarters. Hurricane damage was still common all along the Gulf Coast, years after the unpronounceable hurricane that had made Katrina and Rita look like mere overtures. He worked his way east and saw his fill of wrecked piers, abandoned houses blown out when the windows gave in, groves of pines snapped off halfway up, roofs ripped away, homes turned to flooded swamps. Weathered signs on damaged walls brought back to mind the aftermath: LOOTERS SHOT; on a roof: HELP; a plaintive WE'RE HERE; an amusing FOR SALE: SOME WATER DAMAGE on a condo completely gutted. Historical documents, now.

Hurricanes had hammered the coast so hard that in the aftermath businesses got pillaged by perfectly respectable people trying to hang on, and most of those stores were still closed. Trucks filled with scrap rumbled along the pitted roads. Red-shirted crews wheelbarrowed dark debris out of good brick homes. Blue tarp-covered breached roofs, a promise that eventually they would get fixed. Near the beaches, waterline marks of scummy yellow remained, head high.

Arrival of aliens from another star had seemed less important to the coast people. Even though the Centauris had chosen the similar shores in Thailand, Africa, and India to inhabit, the Gulf was their focus, nearest an advanced nation. McKenna wondered what they thought of all the wreckage.

The surge of illegal Mexicans into the Gulf Coast brought a migration of some tough gangs from California. They used the illegal worker infrastructure as shelter, and occupied the drug business niches. Killings along the Mobile coast dropped from an average of three or four a day before to nearly zero, then rose in the next two years. Those were mostly turf wars between the druggies and immigrant heist artists of the type who prey on small stores.

So he moved among them in jeans, dog-eared hat, and an old shirt, listening. Maybe the Centauris were making people think about the stars and all, but he worked among a galaxy of losers: beat-up faces, hangdog scowls, low-hanging pants, and scuffed brown shoes. They would tell you a tearful life story in return for just looking at them. Every calamity that might befall a man had landed on them: turncoat friends, deadbeat buddies, barren poverty, cold fathers, huge bad luck, random inexplicable diseases, prison, car crashes, and of course the eternal forlorn song: treacherous women. It was a seminar in the great themes of Johnny Cash.

Then a droopy-eyed guy at a taco stand said he had seen the man in the picture over in a trailer park. McKenna approached it warily. If he got figured for a cop the lead would go dead.

Nearby were Spanish-language graffiti splashed on the minimart walls, and he passed Hispanic mothers and toddlers crowding into the county's health clinic. But the shabby mobile homes were not a wholly Hispanic enclave. There was a lot of genteel poverty making do here. Pensioners ate in decrepit diners that gave seniors a free glass of anonymous domestic wine with the special. Workers packed into nearby damaged walk-ups with no air conditioning. On the corners clumps of men lounged, rough-handed types who never answered questions, maybe because they knew no English.

McKenna worked his way down the rows of shabby trailers. Welfare mothers blinked at him and he reassured them he was not from the county office. It was hard to read whether anybody was lying because they seemed dazed by the afternoon heat. Partway through the trailer park a narrow-chested guy in greasy shorts came up and demanded, "Why you bothering my tenants?"

"Just looking for a friend."

"What for?"

"I owe him money."

A sarcastic leer snaked across the narrow face. "Yeah, right."

"Okay, I got a job for him." McKenna showed the photo.

A flicker in the man's eyes came and went. "Huh."

"Know him?"

"Don't think so."

"You don't lie worth a damn."

The mouth tightened. "You ax me an I tole you."

McKenna sighed and showed the badge. After a big storm a lot of fake badges sprouted on the chests of guys on the make, so this guy's caution was warranted. County sheriffs and state police tried to enforce the law and in byways like this they gave up. Time would sort it out, they figured. Some of the fakes became hated, then dead.

To his surprise, the man just stiffened and jutted his chin out. "Got nothin' to say."

McKenna leaned closer and said very fast, "You up to code here? Anybody in this trailer park got an outstanding warrant? How 'bout illegals? Safety code violations? I saw that extension cord three units back, running out of a door and into a side shed. You charge extra for the illegals under that tent with power but no toilet? Bet you do. Or do you just let it happen on the side and pick up some extra for being blind?"

The man didn't even blink.

McKenna was enjoying this. "So suppose we deport some of these illiterates, say. Maybe call in some others here, who violated their parole, uh? So real quick your receivables drop, right? Maybe a lot. Child support could come in here, too, right? One phone call would do it. There's usually a few in a trailer park who don't want to split their check with the bitch that keeps hounding them with lawyers, right? So with them gone, you got open units, buddy. Which means no income, so you're lookin' worse to the absentee landlord who cuts your check, you get me?"

McKenna could hear the gears grind and the eyes got worried. "Okay, look, he left a week back."

"Where to?"

"You know that bayou east about two miles, just before Angel Point? He went to an island just off there, some kind of boat work."

Floating lilies with lotus flowers dotted the willow swamp. Tupelo gums hung over the brown water as he passed, flavoring the twilight. The rented skiff sent its bow wash lapping at half-sunken logs with hides like dead manatees.

His neck felt sunburned from the sour day and his throat was raspy-dry. He cut the purring outboard and did some oar work for the last half mile. The skiff drifted silently up to the stilt house. It leaned a little on slender pilings, beneath a vast canopy of live oaks that seemed centuries old. The bow thumped at the tiny gray-wood dock, wood piling brushing past as he stepped softly off, lashing the stay rope with his left hand while he pulled his 9mm out and forward. No point in being careless.

Dusk settled in. A purple storm hung on the southern horizon and sheet lighting worked yellow magic at its edges. A string of lights hung along the wharf, glowing dimly in the murk, and insects batted at them. Two low pirogues drifted on the tide and clanked rusty chains.

The lock was antique and took him ten seconds.

The room smelled of damp dogs. He searched it systematically but there was nothing personal beyond worn clothes and some letters in Spanish. The postmarks were blurred by the moisture that never left the old wooden drawers. But in another drawer one came through sharp, three weeks old from Veracruz. That was a port town down the long curve of the eastern Mexican coast. From his knowledge of the Civil War era, which was virtually a requirement of a Southern man when he grew up, Veracruz was where Grant and Lee nearly got killed. Together they went out in a small boat to survey the shore in the Mexican war and artillery fire splashed within ten yards of them.

Lots of fishing in Veracruz. A guy from there would know how to work nets.

He kept the letters and looked in the more crafty places. No plastic bag in the commode water closet. Nothing under the filthy pine floor. No hollow legs on the flimsy wooden chairs. In his experience, basically no perp hid anything in smart-ass places or even planned their murders. No months of pondering, of painstaking detail work, alibi prep, escape route, weapon disposal. Brilliant murders were the stuff of television, where the cop played dumb and tripped up the canny murderer, ha ha.

The storm came in off the Gulf and rattled the shack's tin roof. In the musty two-roomer he thought as mist curled up from great steaming sheets of rain. Drops tapped on leaves outside the window and the air mixed with sharp, moist smells of bird droppings. He stood in the scrappy kitchen and wondered if this was a phony lead. The Spanish letters probably wouldn't help but they were consistent at least with the Latino body. Still, he was getting nowhere.

His intuition was fuzzy with associations, a fog that would not condense. The battering shower made him think of the oceans rising and warming from the greenhouse gases and how the world might come to be more like the Centauris' moon, more tropical sea and the land hammered with storms. Out the streaked front window he wondered if aliens swam among the quilted waves, living part of their lives among the schools of fishes.

This thinking went nowhere and his ankle had acquired red dots of flea bites. He looked out the back window. The rain tapered off and he saw now the gray of a FEMA trailer back in the woods. A breeze came from it. Frying peppers and onions flavored the air with pungent promise.

He knocked on the front door and a scrawny white man wearing jeans and nothing else answered. "Hello, sir," plus the badge got him inside.

In a FEMA trailer even words take up room. You have to stand at a conversational distance in light-metal boxes that even a tropical storm could flip like playing cards. His initial urge was to hunch, then to make a joke about it. Mr. Fredson, a gangly six foot two, stretched out his arms to show how he could at the same time touch the ceiling with one hand and the floor with the other. Hangers in the small closet were tilted sideways to fit and beside them stood a short bronze-skinned woman who was trying not to look at him.

"I was wondering if you knew who lived up front there."

"He been gone more'n a week."

"Did he look like this?" McKenna showed the picture.

"Yeah, that's Jorge."

"Jorge what?"

"Castan," the woman said in a small, thin voice. Her hands twisted at the pale pink fabric of the shift she wore. "You *la migra?*"

"No ma'm. Afraid I got some bad news about Jorge though."

"He dead?" Mr. Fredson said, eyes downcast.

"'Fraid so. He washed up on a beach east of here."

"He worked boats," Fredson said, shaking his head. "Lot of night work, fillin' in.

"Mexican, right? Wife in Veracruz?"

"Yeah, he said. Sent money home. Had two other guys livin' up there for a while, nice fellas, all worked the boats. They gone now."

McKenna looked around, thinking. The Latino woman went stiffly into the kitchen and rearranged paper plates and plastic cups from Wal-Mart, cleaned a Reed & Barton silver coffeepot. Fredson sighed and sat on a small, hard couch. The woman didn't look like a good candidate to translate the Veracruz letter, judging from her rigid back. To unlock her he had to ask the right question

"Jorge seem okay? Anything bother him?"

Fredson thought, shrugged. "I'd look in over there sometimes when he was out on the Gulf for a few days. He axed me to. Lately his baidclose all tangled up come mornin'."

"Maybe afraid of *la migra?*" McKenna glanced at the woman. She had stopped pretending to polish the coffeepot and was staring at them.

"Lotsa people are." Fredson jutted his chin out. "They come for the work, we make out they be criminals."

"We do have a justice system." McKenna didn't know how to work this so he stalled.

"Jorge, he get no justice in the nex' world either." Fredson looked defiantly at him. "I'm not religious, like some."

"I'm not sayin' Jorge was doin' anything dishonest." McKenna was dropping into the coast accent, an old strategy to elicit trust. "Just want to see if he died accidentally of drowning."

Fredson said flatly, knotting his hands, "Dishonest ain't same as dishonorable."

He was getting nowhere here. "I'll need to report his death to his wife. Do you have any papers on him, so I can send them?"

The woman said abruptly, "*Documento.*"

Fredson stared at her and nodded slowly. "Guess we ought to."

He got up and reached back into the packed closet. How they had gotten a FEMA trailer would be an interesting story, but McKenna knew not to press his luck. Fredson withdrew a soiled manila envelope and handed it to McKenna. "I kept this for him. He weren't too sure about those other two guys he was renting floor space to, I guess."

McKenna opened it and saw inside a jumble of odd-sized papers. "I sure thank you. I'll see this gets to her."

"How you know where she is?" Fredson asked.

"Got the address."

"Searched his place, did ya?"

"Of course. I'll be leaving—"

"Have a warrant?"

McKenna smiled slowly. "Have a law degree, do you?" His eyes slid toward the woman and he winked. Fredson's mouth stiffened and McKenna left without another word.

He crunched down his oyster-shell road in the dark. Coming around the bend he barely saw against the yard light two people sitting in the glider swing on his porch. He swung his car off into the trees. He wanted to get inside and study the papers he had from Fredson, but he had learned caution and so put his hand on his 9mm as he walked toward them. The gulf salt tang hung under the mimosa tree. A breeze stirred the smell of salt and fish and things dead, others spawning. Sugarcane near the house rattled in the breeze as he worked around to the back.

He let himself silently into his back door. When he snapped on the porch light the two figures jumped. It was Denise and his distant relative, Herb. Unlikely they knew each other.

McKenna opened the front door and let them in, a bit embarrassed at his creeping around. Denise made great fun of it and Herb's confused scowl said he had been rather puzzled by why this woman was here. McKenna wondered, too. He thought he had been pretty clear last time Denise showed up. He didn't like pushy women, many with one eye on his badge and the other on his pension. Even coming to his front door, like they were selling something. Well, maybe they were. He grew up when women didn't ask for dates. Whatever happened to courtship?

Not that he was all that great with women. In his twenties he had been turned down more times than an old blanket. He got them drinks and let the question of why Denise was here lie.

They traded pleasantries and McKenna saw maybe a way to work this. Herb said he'd been in the neighborhood and just stopped by to say hello. Fine. He asked Herb if he knew anything new about the Centauris, since the Pizotti fish fry, and that was enough. Herb shifted into lecture mode and McKenna sat back and watched Denise's reaction.

"There's all kinda talk on the Internet 'bout this," Herb said with relish. "Seems the Centauris deliberately suppressed their radio stations, once they picked up Marconi's broadcasts. They'd already spotted Earth as a biological planet centuries ago, see?—from studying the atmosphere. They'd already spent more centuries building those electric starships."

"My, my," Denise said softly.

Herb beamed at her, liking the audience. "Some think they're the origin of UFOs!"

Denise blinked, mouth making a surprised O. "The UFOs are theirs?"

"The UFOs we see, they're not solid, see? The Centauris sent them as a kind of signaling device. Pumped some kind of energy beams into our atmosphere, see, made these UFO images. Radar could pick them up 'cause they ionized the gas. That's why we never found anything solid."

McKenna was enjoying this. "Beams?"

Herb nodded, eyes dancing. "They excited some sorta atmospheric resonance effects. They projected the beams from our own asteroid belt."

Denise frowned. "But they got here only a few years back."

"They sent robot probes that got here in the 1940s. They'd already planned to send a one here and land to take samples. So they used the beams somehow to, I dunno, maybe let us know somethin' was up."

"Seems odd," Denise said. "And what about all those people the UFOs kidnapped? They did all kinds of experiments on 'em!"

Herb's mouth turned down scornfully. "That's just *National Enquirer* stuff, Denise."

McKenna smiled so he could control the laugh bubbling up in his throat. "Learn any biology?"

Herb said, "We've got plenty land-dwelling reptiles, plenty fish. Not many species use both land and sea."

Herb took a breath to launch into a lecture and Denise put in, "How about gators?"

Herb blinked, gave a quick polite smile and said, "The bio guys figure the Centauris had some reptile predators on the islands, gave what they call selection pressure. Centauris developed intelligence to beat them down when they came ashore, could be. Maybe like frogs, start out as larvae in the water."

Denise said wonderingly, eyeing Herb, "So they're like tadpoles at first?"

"Could be, could be." Herb liked feedback and McKenna guessed he didn't get a lot from women. Maybe they were too polite to interrupt. "They grow and develop lungs, legs, those funny hand-like fins, big opposable thumbs. Then big brains to deal with the reptiles when they go ashore."

McKenna asked, "So they're going to hate our gators."

"S'pose so," Herb allowed. "They sure seem hostile to 'em around Dauphin Island. Could be they're like frogs, put out lots of offspring. Most tadpoles don't survive, y'know, even after they get ashore."

Denise said brightly, "But once one does crawl ashore, the adults would have to help it out a lot. Defend it against reptiles. Teach it how to make tools, maybe. Cooperation, but social competition, too."

Both men looked at her and she read their meaning. "I majored in sociology, minor in biology."

Herb nodded respectfully, looking at her with fresh eyes. "Hard to think that something like frogs maybe could bring down big reptiles, eh?"

Denise tittered at the very thought, eyes glistening eagerly, and McKenna got up to get them more drinks. By the time he came back out, though, they were getting up. Herb said he had to get home and they discovered that they didn't live all that far from each other, what a surprise then to meet out here at this distance, and barely noticed McKenna's good-byes.

He watched them stand beside Denise's car and exchange phone numbers. Now if only he could be as good a matchmaker for himself. But something in him wasn't ready for that yet.

And what else have you got in your life? the unwelcome thought came.

Work. *Oh yes, the Jorge papers from the FEMA people.*

Jorge had stuffed all sorts of things into the envelope. Receipts, check stubs, unreadables, some telephone numbers, a Mexican passport with a picture that looked a lot like the corpse.

He was stacking these when a thin slip fell out. A note written on a rubber-stamped sheet from Bayside Boats.

It wasn't that far to Bayside Boats. He went there at dawn and watched a shrimp boat come in. When he showed every man in the place Jorge's photo, nobody recognized it. But the manager and owner, a grizzled type named Rundorf, hesitated just a heartbeat before answering. Then shook his head.

Driving away, he passed by the *Busted Flush* mooring. It was just coming in from a run and Merv Pitscomb stood at the prow.

His supervisor said, "You get anything from SIU on these cases?"

"Nope." The Special Investigations Unit was notoriously jammed up and in love with the FBI.

"Any statewide CAPs?"

CAPs, Crimes Against Persons, was the latest correct acronym that shielded the mind from the bloody reality, kept you from thinking about the abyss. "Nope."

"So you got two drowned guys who worked boats out of the same town. Seems like a stretch."

McKenna tried to look judicious. "I want a warrant to look at their pay records. Nail when these two worked, and work from there."

The supervisor shook his head. "Seems pretty thin."

"I doubt I'll get much more."

"You've been workin' this one pretty hard. Your partner LeBouc, he's due back tomorrow."

"So?"

A level gaze. "Maybe you should work it with him. This FBI angle, these guys coming up to you like that. Maybe this really should be their game."

"They're playing close to their vest. No help there for sure. And waiting for LeBouc won't help, not without more substance."

"Ummm." The supervisor disliked the FBI, of course, but he didn't want to step on their toes. "Lessee. This would have to go through Judge Preston. He's been pretty easy on us lately, must be gettin' laid again. . . ."

"Let me put it in the batch going up to him later this morning."

"Okay, but then you got to get onto some more cases. They're piling up."

He had boilerplate for the warrant application. He called it up and pasted in *I respectfully request that the Court issue a Warrant and Order of Seizure in the form annexed, authorizing a search of premises at . . . And such as is found shall be brought before the Court, together with such other and further relief that the Court may deem proper.* The lawyers loved such stuff.

Merv Pitscomb's face knotted with red rage. The slow-witted Buddy Johnson, ex-con and tire deflator, stood beside Pitscomb and wore a smirk. Neither liked the warrant and they liked it still less when he took their pay company records.

Ethan Anselmo was there, of course, and had gone out on the *Busted Flush*, a night job two days before the body washed up. No entry for Jorge Castan. But some initials from the bookkeeper a week before the last Anselmo entry, and two days after it, had a total, $178. One initial was GB and the other JC.

Bookkeepers have to write things down, even if they're supposed to keep quiet. Illegals were off the books, of course, usually with no Social Security numbers. But you had to balance your books, didn't you? McKenna loved bookkeepers.

"Okay," his supervisor said, "we got reasonable grounds to bring in this Pitscomb and the other one —"

"Rundorf."

"—to bring them in and work them a little. Maybe they're not wits, maybe these are just accidents the skippers don't want to own up to. But we got probable cause here. Bring them in tomorrow morning. It's near end of our shift."

There was always some paperwork confusion at quitting time. McKenna made up the necessaries and was getting some other, minor cases straightened out, thinking of heading home.

Then he had an idea.

He had learned a good trick a decade back, from a sergeant who had busted a lot of lowlife cases open.

If you had two different suspects for a murder, book them both. Hold them overnight. Let the system work on them.

In TV lawyer shows the law was a smart, orderly machine that eventually—usually about an hour—punished the guilty.

But the system was not about that at all. The minute you stepped into its grinder you lost control of your life and became a unit. You sat in holding cells thinking your own fevered thoughts. Nobody knew you. You stared at the drain hole in the gray concrete floor where recent stains got through even the bleaching disinfectant sprayed over them. On the walls you saw poorly scrawled drawings of organs and acts starkly illuminated by the actinic, buzzing lights that never went out. You heard echoing yells and cops rapping their batons on the bars to get some peace. Which never came. So you sat some more with your own fevered thoughts.

You had to ask permission to go to the toilet rather than piss down that hole. There was the phone call you could make and a lawyer you chose out of the phone book, and the fuzzed voice said he'd be down tomorrow. Maybe he would come and maybe not. It was not like you had a whole lot of money.

The cops referred to you by your last name and moved you like walking furniture to your larger stinking cell with more guys in it. None of them looked at you except the ones you didn't like the look of at all. Then it was night and the lights dimmed, but not much.

That was where the difference between the two suspects came in. One would sleep, the other wouldn't.

Anybody who kills someone doesn't walk away clean. Those movies and TV lawyer shows made out that murderers were smart, twisted people. Maybe twisted was right but not smart, and for sure they were not beasts. Some even dressed better than anyone he had ever seen.

But like it or not, they were people. Murderers saw all the same movies as ordinary folk, and a lot more TV. They sat around daytime making drug deals or waiting for nighttime to do second-story jobs. Plenty of time to think about their business. Most of them could quote from *The Godfather*. The movie, of course. None of them read novels or anything else. They were emotion machines running all the time and after a job they blew their energy right away. Drank, went out cruising for pussy, shot up.

Then, if you timed it right, they got arrested.

So then the pressure came off. The hard weight of tension, the slow-building stress fidgeting at the back of the mind—all that came home to roost. They flopped down on the thin pad of their bunk and pulled the rough wool blanket over their faces and fell like the coming of heaven into a deep sleep. Many of them barely made it to the bunk before the energy bled out of them.

But now think about the guy who didn't do it. He *knows* he didn't do it even if the goddamn world doesn't. He is scared, sure, because he is far enough into the downstreet culture to know that justice is a whore and lawyers run the whorehouse. And so he is in real danger here. But he also for sure knows that he has to fight hard now, think, pay attention. And he is mad too because *he didn't do it* and shouldn't that matter?

So he frets and sits and doesn't sleep. He is ragged-eyed and slurring his words when he tries to tell the other guys in the cell—who have rolled over and gone to sleep—that he didn't do it. It would be smart to be some kind of Zen samurai and sleep on this, he knows that, but he can't. Because *he didn't do it*.

On a cell surveillance camera you can see the difference immediately. Get the cell assignments and go to the room where a bored overweight uniform watched too many screens. Check out the numbers on the screens, find the cells, watch the enhanced-light picture. The sleepers faced away from the lights, coiled up in their blankets. The ones who wouldn't or couldn't— it didn't matter much which—ignored the lights and you could see their eyes clicking around as they thought all this through.

Next morning, he leaned on the sleeper and released the guy who had stayed up all night. Sometimes the innocent ones could barely walk. But at least they were out in the sun.

The sleepers sometimes took days to break. Some of them had the smarts or the clout lawyers, to lawyer up. But he had them and that was the point.

He had learned all this, more years back than he wanted to think about, and it would still be true when he was long gone from this Earth.

He brought in Pitscomb and Rundorf at sunset. Got them booked, photoed, fingerprinted. They gave him plenty of mouth and he just stayed silent, doing his job.

Into the overnight holding cell they went.

He had a bottle of Zinfandel and slept well that night.

Back in at sunup, Pitscomb and Rundorf were red-eyed and irritated.

His supervisor was irritated, too. "I didn't tell you to bring them in late."

"You didn't? I must have misheard." McKenna kept his face absolutely still while he said it. He had practiced that in the mirror when he first made detective and it was a valuable skill.

He made the best of interrogating Pitscomb and Rundorf but the simple fact that they had stayed awake most of the night took McKenna's confidence away. The two gave up nothing. He booked them out and had some uniforms drive them home.

His partner came in that afternoon. LeBouc was a burly man who liked detail, so McKenna handed off some stickup shootings to him. They had been waiting for attention and McKenna knew they would get no leads. The perps were the same black gang that had hit the minimarkets for years and they knew their stuff. The videotapes showed only rangy guys in animal masks. LeBouc didn't seem to mind. McKenna filled him in on the drowned cases but he couldn't make an argument for where to go next. The cases were cooling off by the minute now, headed for the storage file.

McKenna had never been as systematic as LeBouc, who was orderly even when he was fishing. So when LeBouc said, "How'd those phone numbers from the illegal turn out?" McKenna felt even worse. He had noticed them in the stack of paper at Castan's shack, just before he found the Bayside

Boats notepaper. Like a hound dog, he chased that lead down and forgot the telephone numbers.

He got right on them. One was the Mexican consulate in New Orleans, probably for use if Jorge got picked up.

One number answered in a stony voice saying only, "Punch in your code." The rest answered in Spanish and he got nowhere with them. He thought of getting a Spanish speaker but they were in high demand and he would have to wait for days. Nobody in Homicide knew more than restaurant Spanish. He went back to the stony voice, a Mobile number.

Usually, to break a number you use a reverse directory of published numbers. McKenna found nothing there. There were lesser-known electronic directories of unpublished numbers that link phone numbers to people and addresses. He found those in the Mobile Police database. They were built up nationally, working from anyone who used the number to place a phone order. So he considered pretexting. To pretext, you call the phone company repair department, saying there's a problem on the line and getting them to divulge the address associated with the account. But you needed a warrant to do that and his credit had run out with Judge Preston.

If he couldn't pretend to be someone else, maybe he could pretend that his phone was someone else's. That would be caller-ID spoofing—making it seem as if a phone call is coming from another phone, rather than his Homicide number. That made it more likely that the target person would answer the call, even if they had the new software that back-tracked the caller in less than a second. McKenna's office number was not in the phone book but for sure it was in any sophisticated database software. And the stony voice sounded professional, smart.

Spoofing used to require special equipment, but now with Internet phone calling and other Web services it was relatively easy to do. So easy, in fact, that just about anyone can do it. But McKenna hadn't. It took an hour of asking guys and gals in the office to get it straight. Everybody had a fine time making fun of "the Perfesser" coming to them for help, of course. He developed a fixed grin.

Once you burned an hour to know how, it took less than a minute.

The site even had a code breakdown for the number, too. When stony voice answered, McKenna typed in the last four digits of the number again and in a few more seconds he got a ring. "Hello?"

McKenna said nothing. "Hello?" the voice of Dark Glasses said.

It took a while for his supervisor to go through channels and pin a name on Dark Glasses. The next morning Dark Glasses was in Federal court, the FBI office said. So McKenna found him, waiting to testify.

"May I have a word in the hallway?" McKenna sat down in the chair at the back of the court. Somebody was droning on in front and the judge looked asleep.

"Who are you?" Dark Glasses said, nose up in the air. He wasn't wearing the glasses now and it was no improvement.

McKenna showed the badge. "Remember me? You were with Mr. Marine."

"Who?"

"You didn't say you were a lawyer, too."

"Who told you that?"

"Your office. The FBI, remember?"

The lawyer inched away but kept his chin out, first line of defense. "I'm waiting to testify on a Federal case."

"Murder crosses boundaries."

The bailiff was looking at them. He jerked a thumb toward the doors. In the hallway Dark Glasses had revived his lawyerly presence. "Make it quick."

"This is about one of your cases, Jorge Castan."

"I don't discuss my cases."

He moved to go past and McKenna casually put a hand on his chest.

"You have no right to touch me. Move away."

McKenna just shook his head. "You know what's up. Your case got himself murdered, looks like. The second one like that in a week. And the Bar Association Web site says that before you got hired into the FBI you were an immigration lawyer. And you must know that your case was an illegal or else you're dumber than you look."

"I do not take a liking to insult. You touch me—"

"You're in serious trouble if you know what's really up. See, murder is a local crime unless you can show it has a proper Federal issue that trumps local. Do you?"

"I do not have to—"

"Yes you do."

"There is not one scintilla of evidence—"

"Save it for the judge. Wrong attitude, counselor."

"I don't know what—"

"What I'm talking about, yeah. I hear it all the time. You guys must all watch the same movies."

"I am an attorney." He drew himself up.

"Yeah, and I know the number of the Bar Association. Being FBI won't protect you."

"I demand to know—"

Dark Glasses went on but little by little McKenna had been backing him up against the marble walls until the man's shoulder blades felt it. Then his expression changed. McKenna could see in the lawyer's face the schoolboy threatened by bullies. So he had gone into the law, which meant good ol' safe words and paper, to escape the real world where the old primate signals held sway. Dark Glasses held his briefcase in front of his body in defense, but the shield wasn't thick enough to stop McKenna from poking a finger into the surprisingly soft Dark Glasses bicep. "You're up at bat now, lawyer."

"As an attorney—"

"You're assumed to be a liar. For hire. Almost rhymes, don't it?"

"I do not respond to insults." He was repeating his material and he tilted his chin up again. McKenna felt his right hand come halfway up, balling into a fist, wanting so much to hit this clown hard on the point of that chin.

"You knew to go looking for Jorge in jig time. Or maybe for the people who knew him. Why's that?"

"I—I'm going to walk away now."

"Not if you're smart. One of those who knew him is an illegal, too. Maybe you wanted to use that to shut her up?"

"That's speculative—"

"Not really, considering your expression. No, you're working for somebody else. Somebody who has influence."

"My clients and cases are Bureau—"

"Confidential, I know."

"I have every assurance that my actions will prove victorious in this matter."

McKenna grinned and slapped an open palm against the briefcase, a hard smack. The lawyer jumped, eyebrows shooting up, back on the playground during recess. "I—I have an attorney-client relationship that by the constitution—"

"How 'bout the Bible?"

"—demands that you respect his . . . protection."

"The next one who dies is on you, counselor."

In a shaky voice the lawyer pulled his briefcase even closer and nodded, looking at the floor as if he had never seen it before. A small sigh came from him, filled with gray despair.

It was a method McKenna had worked out years ago, once he understood that lawyers were all talk and no muscle. Good cop/bad cop is a cliché, only the lawyer keeps looking for the good cop to show up and the good cop doesn't. Bluff is always skin deep.

The lawyer backed away once McKenna let him. "You better think about who you choose to represent. And who might that be, really?"

"My client is—"

"No, I mean who, really? Whose interest?"

"I . . . I don't know what you mean. I—"

"You know more than you've said. I expect that. But you still have to think about what you do." A rogue smile. "We all do."

"Look, we can handle this issue in a nice way—"

"I'll try being nicer if you'll try being smarter."

McKenna slid a business card into the suit handkerchief pocket of Dark Glasses Lawyer. "Call me. I find out the same stuff before you do, and that you knew it—well, I'll be without mercy, Counselor. No quarter."

McKenna stepped aside and let the lawyer flee from the playground. Dark Glasses didn't look back.

McKenna's supervisor leaned back and scowled. "And you did this because? . . ."

"Because two drowned men with strange scars don't draw FBI without a reason, for starters."

"Not much to go on."

"The ME says he can't identify the small puncture marks. Or what made those funny welts."

His supervisor made a sour grin. "You know how much physical evidence is worth. It has to fit a filled-in story."

"And I don't have enough story."

He spread his hands, the cuff sliding up to expose part of his arm tattoo, rosy barbed wire.

McKenna had read somewhere that an expert is one who has made all the possible mistakes in a narrow field. A wise man is one who has made them widely. It was supposed to be funny but it was too true for that.

So he followed his good ole friend Buddy Johnson home from work that evening. Buddy liked his pleasures and spent the first hour of his night in a bar. Then he went out back to smoke a joint. It was dark and Buddy jumped a foot when McKenna shined the flashlight straight into his eyes.

"Gee, that cigarette sure smells funny."

"What? Who you?"

"The glare must be too much for you. Can't you recognize my voice?"

"What the— Look, I—"

McKenna slipped behind him, dropping the flashlight to distract him, and got the cuffs on. "We're gonna take a little ride."

McKenna took him in cuffs down a scruffy side alley and got him into Buddy's own convertible. Puffing, feeling great, he strapped Buddy in with the seat belt, passenger side. Then McKenna drove two quick miles and turned into a car wash. The staff was out front finishing up and when they came out McKenna showed them the badge and they turned white. All ille-gals, of course, no English. But they knew the badge. They vanished like the dew after the dawn.

Game time, down south.

Even with cuffs behind his back, Buddy kept trying to say something.

"Remember letting the air out of my tires?" McKenna hit him hard in the nose, popped some blood loose and Buddy shut up. McKenna drove the convertible onto the ratchet conveyor and went back to the control panel. It was in English and the buttons were well-thumbed, some of the words gone in the worn plastic. McKenna ran up a SUPER CLEAN and HOT WAX and LIGHT BUFF. Then he gave a little laugh and sent Buddy on his way.

Hissing pressure hoses came alive. Big black brushes lowered into the open seats and whirred up to speed. They ripped Buddy full on. He started yelling and the slapping black plastic sheets slammed into him hard and he stopped screaming. McKenna hit the override and the brushes lifted away. Silence, only the dripping water on the convertible's leather seats.

McKenna shouted a question and waited. No answer. He could see the head lolling back and wondered if the man was conscious.

McKenna thought about the two drowned men and hit the buttons again.

The brushes hardly got started before a shrill cry came echoing back. McKenna stopped the machine. The brushes rose. He walked forward into the puddles, splashing and taking his time.

"You're nearly clean for the first time in your life, Buddy. Now I'm gonna give you a chance to come full clean with me."

"I . . . They ain't gonna like . . ." His mouth opened expectantly, rimmed with drool. The eyes flickered, much too white.

"Just tell me."

"They really ain't gonna like—"

McKenna turned and started back toward the control board. The thin, plaintive sobbing told him to turn around again. You could always tell when a man was broke clean through.

"Where'd they go?"

"Nearly to Chandeleur."

"The islands?"

"Yeah . . . long way out . . . takes near all night. Oil rigs . . . the wrecked ones."

"What'd you take out?"

"Centauris. Usually one, sometimes two."

"The same one?"

"Who can tell? They all look alike to me. Pitscomb, he bowed and scraped to the Centauri and the Feds with him, but he don't know them apart either."

"Pitscomb have anything to do with Ethan's death?"

"Man, I weren't workin' that night."

"Damn. What'd the rest of the crew say about it?"

"Nothin'. All I know is that Ethan was on the boat one night and he didn't come back to work next day."

"Who else was with the Centauri?"

"Just Feds."

"What was the point of going out?"

"I dunno. We carried stuff in big plastic bags. Crew went inside for 'bout an hour while we circled round the messed-up oil rigs. FBI and Centauri were out there. Dunno what they did. Then we come back."

McKenna took the cuffs off Buddy and helped him out of the car. To his surprise, Buddy could walk just fine. "You know Jorge?"

"Huh? Yeah, that wetback?"

"Yeah. You're a wetback too now."

"Huh? Oh." Buddy got the joke and to his credit, grinned. "Look, you don't nail me on the dope, it's even, okay?"

"You're a gentleman and a scholar, Buddy."

"Huh?"

"It's fine. Keep your nose clean from here on out or I'll bring you back here to clean it myself."

He hung his head. "Y'know, you're right. I got to straighten up."

"You're straight with me right now."

They even shook hands.

A take-charge raccoon was working the trash when he hauled in on the oyster shell road. He shooed it away and then tossed it a watermelon that had gone old anyway.

Then he sat on the porch and sipped a Cabernet and worked himself over about the car wash stunt. His wife had once told him, after he had worked up through being a uniform, then Vice and then bunko and finally Homicide, that the process had condensed him into a hard man. He had never said to her that maybe it was her long illness that had made him quiet around the house, wary and suspicious . . . but in the end maybe it was both. He had never been interested in small talk but had picked up the skill for getting witnesses to open up.

Now he felt very little after working Buddy over. He had done it with a vague intuition that the kid needed a wake-up call, sure, but mostly because he was blocked in this case. And he couldn't let it go. Maybe it helped fill the emptiness in him, one he felt without shame or loss, as not a lack but as a blank space—an openness that made him hear the wind sigh and waves slosh not as mere background but as life passing while most people ignored it, talked over it, trying to pin life down with their words. He listened at nightfall, sitting out here on the warped planking of his wharf, to the planet breathing in its sleep. A world never fully revealed, a planet with strangeness at its core.

The next day he and LeBouc worked some ordinary gang-related cases. And planned. LeBouc was a fisherman and would go out for just about any reason. Not a hard sell. And neither of them could think of anything else to do. The FBI had called up their supervisor and bad-mouthed McKenna, of course. But they wouldn't reveal anything more and tried to pry loose what McKenna knew. The supe stonewalled. A Mexican standoff.

Just before twilight McKenna sprayed on exercise shorts plus shirt. This was a semi-new techie product, snug and light, and he wanted to try them. The shorts were black, the cheapest spray-on, with spaced breather holes to respire sweat through. His belly was a bit thick and his calves stringy, but nobody was going to see him anyway if he could help it. The smart fibers itched as they linked up to form the hems, contouring to his body, the warmth from their combining getting him in the mood. He drove to the boat ramp just west of Bayou La Batre, huffing the salty sunset breeze into his lungs with a liberating zest.

LeBouc was there with an aluminum boat and electric motor and extra batteries, rented from a Mobile fishing company. Great for quiet night work, spotlights and radiophone, the works. LeBouc was pumped, grinning and stowing gear.

"Thought I'd do some line trawling on the way," he said, bringing on a big pole and a tackle box. He carried a whole kit of cleaning knives and an ice chest. "Never know when you might bag a big one."

McKenna's shoes grated on the concrete boat ramp as the water lapped against the pilings. The boat rose on the slow, lumbering tide. A dead nutria floated by, glassy-eyed and with a blue crab gouging at it. Business as usual at the Darwin Café.

They used a gas outboard to reach the estimated rendezvous point, to save on the batteries. McKenna had planted a directional beeper on the *Busted Flush* in late afternoon, using a black guy he hired in Bayou La Batre to pretend to be looking for work. Right away they picked up the microwave beeper, using their tracking gear. With GPS geared into the tracker they could hang back a mile away and follow them easily. LeBouc was a total non-tech type and had never once called McKenna "the Perfesser."

LeBouc flipped on the Raytheon acoustic radar and saw the sandy bottom sliding away into deeper vaults of mud. Velvet air slid by. The night swallowed them.

It was exciting at first, but as they plowed through the slapping swells the rhythm got to McKenna. He hadn't been sleeping all that well lately, so LeBouc took the first watch, checking his trailing line eagerly. LeBouc had spent his vacation deep-sea fishing off Fort Lauderdale and was happy to be back on the water again.

LeBouc shook McKenna awake three hours later. "Thought you were gonna wake me for a watch," McKenna mumbled.

"Nemmine, I was watchin' my line. Almost got one too."

"What's up?"

"They hove to, looks like from the tracker."

They quietly approached the *Busted Flush* using the electric motor. The tracker picked up a fixed warning beacon. "Maybe an oil platform," McKenna said. LeBouc diverted slightly toward it.

Out of the murk rose a twisted skeleton. Above the waterline the main platform canted at an angle on its four pylons. A smashed carcass of a drilling housing lay scattered across its steel plates. Three forlorn rotating beacons winked into the seethe of the sea.

LeBouc asked, "How far's the shrimper?"

McKenna studied the tracker screen, checked the scale. "About three hundred yards. Not moving."

LeBouc said, "Let's tuck in under that platform. Make us hard to see."

"Don't know if I can see much in IR at this range."

"Try now."

The IR goggles LeBouc had wangled out of Special Operations Stores fit on McKenna's head like a fat parasite. In them he could see small dots moving, the infrared signature blobs of people on the shrimper deck. "Barely," McKenna said.

"Lemme try it."

They carefully slid in under the steel twenty feet above. LeBouc secured them with two lines to the pylon cleats and the boat did not rock with the swell so much. McKenna could make out the *Busted Flush* better here in the deeper dark. He studied it and said, "They're moving this way. Slow, though."

"Good we're under here. Wonder why they chose a platform area."

Many of the steel bones had wrenched away down on the shoreward side of the platform and now hung down beneath the waves. The enviros made the best of it, calling these wrecks fish breeders, and maybe they were.

"Fish like it here, maybe."

"Too far offshore to fish reg'lar."

McKenna looked up at the ripped and rusted steel plates above, underpinned by skewed girders. His father had died on one of these twelve years back, in the first onslaught of a hurricane. When oil derricks got raked in a big storm and started to get worked, you hooked your belt to a Geronimo wire and bailed out from the top—straight into the dark sea, sliding into hope and kersplash. He had tried to envision it, to see what his father had confronted.

When you hit the deck of the relief hauler it was awash. Your steel-toed boots hammered down while you pitched forward, face down, with your hard hat to save the day, or at least some memories. But his father's relief hauler had caught a big one broadside and the composite line had snapped and his father went into the chop. They tried to get to him but somehow he didn't have his life jacket on and they lost him.

With his inheritance from his father McKenna bought their house on the water. He recalled how it felt getting the news, the strange sensation that he had dropped away into an abyss. How his father had always hated life jackets and didn't wear them to do serious work.

McKenna realized abruptly that he didn't have his own life jacket on. Maybe it was genetic. He found some in the rear locker and pulled one on, tossing another to LeBouc, who was fooling with his tackle and rod.

LeBouc said, "You watch, I'll try a bait line."

McKenna opened his mouth and heard a faint rumble in the distance. The boat shuttled back and forth on its cleat lines. Waves smacked against steel and shed a faint luminous glow. He could see nothing in the distance though and sat to pull down the IR goggles. A hazy shimmer image. The *Busted Flush* was coming closer, on a course that angled to the left. "They're moving."

There was a lot of splashing nearby as currents stirred among the pylons. The three figures on the deck of the shrimper were easier to see now.

The IR blobs were right at the edge of definition. Then one of them turned into the illumination cone of a pale running light, making a jabbing gesture to another blob. He couldn't quite resolve the face, but McKenna recognized the man instantly.

Dark Glasses stood out like a clown at a funeral.

The man next to him must be Pitscomb, McKenna figured. The third form was fainter and taller and with a jolt McKenna knew it was a Centauri. It moved more gracefully at sea than on land as it walked along the railing. Its sliding gait rocked with the ship, better than the men. It held a big dark lump and seemed to be throwing something from the lump over the side.

McKenna focused to make sense of the image. The Centauri had a bag, yes—

A grunt from nearby told him LeBouc was casting and an odd splash came and then thumping. The boat shifted and jerked as he tried to focus on the IR images and another big splash came.

He jerked off the goggles. His eyes took a few seconds to adjust. There was fitful radiance from the surf. LeBouc was not in the boat.

A leg jerked up in the water, arms flailed in a white churn. Long swift things like ropes whipped around the leg. McKenna reached for the oars secured along the boatline. A sudden pain lurched up in his right calf and he looked down. A furred cord was swiftly wrapping itself up his leg, over his knee, starting on his calf. Needles of pain shot into his leg. The sting of it ran up his spine and provoked a shudder through his torso. His leg twitched, out of his control.

The wrapping rope stopped at his thigh and yanked. He fell over and his knee slammed hard on the bottom of the boat. Another cord came over and hit his shoulder. It clung tight and snarled around him. The shoulder muscles thrashed wildly as the thing bit through his plastic all-weather jacket and his shirt. Pain jabbed into his chest.

Other wriggling strands came snaking across the bowed deck. He wrenched around and hit his head on LeBouc's tackle box. He thought one of the things had grabbed his ear but it was the latch on the box, caught in his hair. A hollering came and he realized it was his own ragged voice.

His hands beat at the cord but prickly spines jutting out of it stung him. That jolted him badly and he tried to pull himself up to get a tool. The tackle box. He grabbed a gutting knife. With both hands he forced it under the edge of the cord across his chest. The ropy thing was strong and fought against the blade. He got some leverage and pulled up and the blade bit. The pink cord suddenly gave way. It flailed around and the main body lashed back at him. He caught it on the point of the knife and drove it into the side of the boat. That gave him a cutting surface and he worked the knife down the length of the thing. He sawed with all his strength. It split into two splices that went still. Stroking along it he sliced it in two, clear up to the housing at the stern.

The shooting pain in his calf he had made himself ignore and now he turned to it. The cord had sunk into his jeans. He pried it up as before and turned the blade. This one popped open and drooled milky fluid. He hacked away at it, free of the lancing pain. It took a moment to cut away chunks. They writhed on the boat bottom. With stinging hands he reached into the tackle box and found the workman's gloves. That made it easier to pick up and toss the long strands into the sea. They struggled weakly.

Numbness crept up his leg and across his chest. He felt elated and sleepy and wanted to rest. His eyes flickered and he realized that his face was numb too. Everything was moving too fast. He needed a rest. Then he could think about this. Figure it out.

Then another pink rope came sliding over the gunnel. It felt around and snaked toward him as if it could sense his heat or smell. He felt the tip of it touch his deck shoe. Sharp fear cleared his mind.

The knife came down on it and he pounded the point along its length. Without cutting it into pieces he lurched toward the gunwale. With a swipe the tie line popped away from its cleat. He leaped over a section of pink rope and cut the second line. He could barely see. With hands he felt along the stern and found the starter button and helm. The outboard caught right away. With a strum the engines turned over and he slid the throttles forward to rev the engines into a quick-start warmup.

He veered among the pylons. With a click the flashlight glare made the scene jump out at him. There were pink strands in the water.

No sign at all of LeBouc.

He hit the throttle and shot out into open water and reached for the radiophone.

The worst of it was the wait.

He stung in running sheets of fire all over the right leg and chest. The thing had wrapped around his calf like a bracelet. He wondered why the ME never said anything about the corpses being pumped full of venom and only then realized that he had felt electrical shocks, not stings. His leg and arm had been jerking on their own. He fingered the trembling muscles, remembering through a fog.

He got away from there into the darkness, not caring any more about the *Busted Flush*. Eventually he thought that they might be following the sound of the outboard. He shut it off and drifted. Then he called the shore and said he was headed in on the electric. By then he was flopping on the deck as debilitating cramps swept through him. Breath came hard and he passed out several times.

Then a chopper came out of the murk. It hovered over him like an angel with spotlights and an unfurling ladder. Men in wet suits dropped onto the deck. They harnessed him up and he spun away into the black sky. On the hard floor of the chopper a woman stood over him with a big needle of epinephrine, her face lined with concern. He could not get his thick tongue to tell her that this case was something else. She shot him full of it and his heart pounded. That did clear his sluggish mind but it did not stop the shooting jolts that would come up suddenly in his leg and chest and in other places he had no memory of the pink rope being at all.

She gave him other injections though and those made the whole clattering chopper back away. It was like a scene on late night television, mildly interesting and a plot you could vaguely remember seeing somewhere. She barked into her helmet mike and asked him questions but it was all theory now, not really his concern.

The next few hours went by like a movie you can't recall the next day. A cascading warm shower lined in gray hospital tile, McKenna lying on the tiles. A doctor in white explaining how they had to denature something, going on and on, just about as interesting as high school chemistry. They said they needed his consent for some procedure and he was happy to give it so long as they agreed to leave him alone.

He slowly realized the ER whitecoats were not giving him painkillers because of the War on Drugs and its procedural requirements. A distant part of him considered how it would be for a lawman to die of an excess of law. Doctors X and then Y and finally Z had to sign off. Time equaled pain and dragged on tick by tick.

Then there was Demerol, which settled the arguments nicely.

The next day he found a striping of tiny holes along his leg. More across his chest. He guessed the corpses had sealed up most of these when they swelled, so they showed only a few tiny holes.

The ME came by and talked to McKenna as though he were an unusually fascinating museum exhibit. At least he brought some cortisone cream to see if it would help and it did. He recalled distantly that the ME was actually a doctor of some sort. Somehow he had always thought of the ME as a cop.

Two days later a team of Fed guys led him out of the hospital and into a big black van. They had preempted local law, of course, so McKenna barely got to see his supervisor or the Mobile Chief of Police, who was there mostly for a photo op anyway.

In the van a figure in front turned and gave him a smile without an ounce of friendliness in it. Mr. Marine.

"Where's Dark Glasses?" McKenna asked but Mr. Marine looked puzzled and then turned away and watched the road. Nobody said anything until they got to Dauphin Island.

They took him up a ramp and down a corridor and then through some sloping walkways and odd globular rooms and finally to a little cell with pale glow coming from the walls. It smelled dank and salty and they left him there.

A door he hadn't known was there slid open in the far wall. A man all in white stepped in carrying a big, awkward laptop and behind him shuffled a Centauri.

McKenna didn't know how he knew it, but this was the same Centauri he had seen getting onto the *Busted Flush*. It looked at him with the famous slitted eyes and he caught a strange scent that wrinkled his nose.

The man in white sat down in one of two folding chairs he had brought and gestured for McKenna to sit in the other. The Centauri did not sit. It carefully put a small device on the floor, a bulb and nozzle. Then it stood beside the man and put its flipper-hands on the large keyboard of the laptop.

McKenna had heard about these devices shaped to the Centauri movements.

"It will reply to questions," the man in white said. "Then it types a reply. This computer will translate on-screen."

"It can't pronounce our words, right?" McKenna had read that.

"It has audio pickups that transduce our speech into its own sounds. But it can't speak our words, no. This is the best we've been able to get so far." The man seemed nervous.

The Centauri held up one flipper-hand and with the device sprayed itself, carefully covering its entire skin. Or at least it seemed more like skin now, and not the reptile armor McKenna had first thought it might be.

"It's getting itself wetted down," the man said. "This is a dry room, easier for us to take."

"The wet rooms have—"

"Ceiling sprays, yeah. They gotta stay moist 'cause they're amphibians. That's why they didn't like California. It's too dry, even at the beach."

The Centauri was finished with its spraying. McKenna thought furiously and began. "So, uh, why were you going out on the shrimp boat?"
Its jointed flippers were covered in a mesh hide. They moved in circular passes over pads on the keyboard. The man had to lift the awkward computer a bit to the alien, who was shorter than an average man. On the screen appeared:

<<Feed our young.>>

"Is that what attacked me?"

<<Yes. Friend died.>>

"Your young are feeding?"

<<Must. Soon come to land.>>

"Why don't we know of this?"

<<Reproducing private for you also.>>

He could not look away from those eyes. The scaly skin covered its entire head. The crusty deep green did not stop at the big spherical eyes, but enclosed nearly all of it, leaving only the pupil open in a clamshell slit. He gazed into the unreadable glittering black depths of it. The eyes swiveled to follow him as he fidgeted. McKenna couldn't think of anything to say.

"I, I can't read your expression. Like *Star Trek* and that stuff, we expect aliens to be like humans, really."

The alien wrote:

>> <<I know of your vision programs. The Trek drama we studied.
To discern how you would think of us.>>

"You don't have our facial expressions."

<<We have our own.>>

"Of course. So I can't tell if you care whether your young killed two men on fishing boats."

<<They were close to water. Young. Hungry. Your kind stay away is best.>>

"We don't know! Our government has not told us. Why?"

The man holding the computer opened his mouth to say something and thought better of it. The alien wrote:

<<Change is hard for both our kinds. Ideas should come slowly
to be understood.>>

"People are okay with your visit. They might not like your seeding our oceans and moving in. Plus killing us."

This time it took a while to answer:

<<Those you call dead live on now in the dark heaven.>>

McKenna blinked. "Is that a religious idea?"

<<No. It arises from our skystorians.>>

"Uh, sky? . . . "

The computer guy said, "Mistranslation. I saw that one with the astro guys last week. The software combines two concepts, see. Sky—means astronomy, 'cause their world is always cloudy, so the night sky is above that—and history. Closest word is cosmology, astronomy of the past."

McKenna looked at the alien's flat, unreadable gaze. "So it's . . . science."

<<Your term for this bedrock of the universe is the dark energy. I modify these words to show the nature of your dark energy. It forces open the universe.>>

McKenna could not see where this was going. He had read some pop science about something called dark energy, sure. It supposedly was making the whole universe expand faster and faster. "So what's it . . . this dark heaven . . . do?"

<<It is the . . . substrate. Entangled information propagates as waves in it. Organized minds of high level emit probability waves in packets of great complexity. These persist long after the original emitter is dead.>>

McKenna blinked. "You mean we . . . our minds . . . send out their . . ."

<<Their presence, that is a better term. Minds emit presence. This persists as waves in the dark heaven that is everywhere in the universe. All minds join it.>>

"This sounds like religion."

<<Your distinction between fears for your fate and the larger category of science is not one we share. This required long study by us to understand since you are a far younger life-form. You have not yet had the time and experience to study the universe for long.>>

McKenna was getting in over his head. He felt light-headed, taking shallow breaths, clenching his hands. "You don't regret that those men died?"

<<Our emotions do not fit in your categories, either. We sorrow, yes. While also knowing that the loss is only a transition, as when our young come to shore. One gives up one form for another. Beyond the dark heaven perhaps there is something more but we do not know. Probably that is a question beyond our categories. We have limits just as do you, though not so great. You are young. There is time.>>

"Around here murder is a crime."

<<We are not from here.>>

"Look, even if spirits or whatever go someplace else, that doesn't excuse murder."

<<Our young do not murder. They hunt and eat and grow. Again, a category difference between our kinds.>>

"Being dead matters to us."

<<Our young that you attacked. By your own terms you murdered them.>>

The Centauri blinked slowly at McKenna with its clamshell opening in the leathery, round eyes. Then it stooped to get its sprayer. From its wheezing spout moisture swirled around all of them.

The giddy swirl of this was getting to him. "I, I don't know where to go with this. Your young have committed a crime."

<<The coming together between stars of intelligence has a cost.
We all pay it.>>

McKenna stood up. The damp scent of the alien swarmed around him. "Some more than others."

He barely made it to LeBouc's funeral. It was a real one, with a burial plot. At the church he murmured soft words to the widow, who clung to him, sobbing. He knew that she would later ask how her husband had died. It was in her pleading eyes. He would not know what to say. Or what he would be allowed to say. So he sat in the back of the whitewashed Baptist church and tried to pay attention to the service. As LeBouc's partner he had to say something in the eulogies. A moment after he sat down again he had no idea what he had said. People looked oddly at him. In the graveyard, as protocol demanded he stood beside the phalanx of uniforms, who fired a popping salute.

At least LeBouc got buried. He had washed up on a beach while McKenna was in the hospital. McKenna had never liked the other ways, especially after his wife went away into cremation. One dealt with death, he felt, by dealing with the dead. Now bodies did not go into the earth but rather the air through cremation or then the ashes into the sea. People were less grounded, more scattered. With the body seldom present, the wheel working the churn between the living and dead could not truly spin.

God had gone out of it, too. LeBouc's fishing friends got up and talked about that. For years McKenna had noticed how his friends in their last profile became not dead Muslims or Methodists but dead bikers, golfers, surfers. That said, a minister inserted talk about the afterlife at the grave site and then the party, a respectable several hundred, went to the reception. There the tone shifted pretty abruptly. McKenna heard some guy in a seersucker suit declare "closure" just before the Chardonnay ran out.

On his sunset drive back down by the Bay he rolled down the windows to catch the sea breeze tang. He tried to think about the alien.

It had said they wanted privacy in their reproductive cycle. But was that it? Privacy was a human concept. The Centauris knew that because they had been translating human radio and TV dramas for a century. Privacy might not be a Centauri category at all, though. Maybe they were using humans' own preconceptions to get some maneuvering room?

He needed to rest and think. There would for sure come a ton of questions about what happened out there in the dark Gulf. He did not know what he would or could say to LeBouc's widow. Or what negotiations would come between Mobile PD and the Feds. Nothing was simple, except maybe his slow-witted self.

What he needed was some Zinfandel and an hour on his wharf.

A black Ford sedan was parked on the highway a hundred yards from his driveway. It looked somehow official, deliberately anonymous. Nobody around here drove such a dull car, one without blemish or rust. Such details probably meant nothing, but he had learned what one of the desk sergeants called "street sense" and he never ignored it.

He swung onto the oyster drive, headed toward home, and then braked. He cut his lights and engine, shifting into neutral, and eased the car down the sloping driveway, gliding along behind a grove of pines.

In the damp night air rushing by he heard the crunching of the tires and wondered if anybody up ahead heard them too. Around the bend before the house he stopped and let the motor tick, cooling, while he just listened. Breeze whispered through the pines and he was upwind from the house. He eased open the car door and pulled his 9mm. from the glove compartment, not closing it, letting the silence settle.

No bird calls, none of the rustle and scurry of early night.

He slid out of the car, keeping low under the window of the door. No moon yet. Clouds scudded off the Gulf, masking the stars.

He circled around behind the house. On the Gulf side a man stood in shadows just around the corner from the porch. He wore jeans and a dark shirt and cradled a rifle. McKenna eased up on him, trying to ID the profile from the dim porch light. At the edge of the pines he surveyed the rest of his yard and saw no one.

Nobody carries a rifle to make an arrest. The smart way to kill an approaching target was to bracket him, so if there was a second guy he would be on the other side of the house, under the oak tree.

McKenna faded back into the pines and circled left to see the other side of his house. He was halfway around when he saw the head of another man stick around the corner. There was something odd about the head as it turned to survey the backyard but in the dim light he could not make it out.

McKenna decided to walk out to the road and call for backup. He stepped away. This caught the man's attention and brought up another rifle and aimed straight at him. McKenna brought his pistol up.

The recoil rocked his hand back and high as the 9mm snapped away, two shots. Brass casings curled back past his vision, time in slow-mo. The man went down and McKenna saw he was wearing IR goggles.

McKenna turned to his right in time to see the other man moving. McKenna threw himself to the side and down and a loud report barked from the darkness. McKenna rolled into a low bush and lay there looking out through the pines. The man was gone. McKenna used both hands to steady his pistol, elbows on the sandy ground, knowing that with a rifle the other man had the advantage at this distance, maybe twenty yards.

He caught a flicker of movement at his right. The second man was well away from the wall now, range maybe thirty yards, bracing his rifle against the old cypress trunk. McKenna fired fast, knowing the first shot was off but following it with four more. He could tell he was close but the hammering rounds threw off his judgment. He stopped, the breech locking open on the last one. He popped the clip and slid in another, a stinging smell in his widened nostrils.

The flashes had made him night blind. He lay still, listening, but his ears hummed from the shooting. This was the hardest moment, when he did not know what had happened. Carefully he rolled to his left and behind a thick pine tree. No sounds, as near as he could tell.

He wondered if the neighbors had heard this, called some uniforms.

He should do the same, he realized. Quietly he moved further left.

The clouds had cleared and he could see better. He looked toward the second guy's area and saw a shape lying to the left of the tree. Now he could make out both the guys, down.

He called the area dispatcher on his cell phone, whispering.

Gingerly he worked around to the bodies. One was Dark Glasses, the other Mr. Marine. They were long gone.

They both carried M-1A rifles, the semiauto version for civilians of the old M-14. Silenced and scoped, fast and sure, the twenty-round magazines were packed firm with snub-nosed .308s. A perfectly deniable, non-Federal weapon.

So the Feds wanted knowledge of the aliens tightly contained. And Dark Glasses had a grudge, no doubt. The man had been a stack of anxieties walking around in a suit.

He walked out onto the wharf, nerves jumping in the salty air, and looked up at the glimmering stars. So beautiful.

Did some dark heaven lurk out there? As nearly as he could tell, the alien meant that it filled the universe. If it carried some strange wave packets that minds emitted, did that matter?

That Centauri had seemed to say that murder didn't matter so much because it was just a transition, not an ending.

So was his long-lost wife still in this universe, somehow? Were all the minds that had ever lived?

Minds that had lived beneath distant suns? Mingled somehow with Dark Glasses and Mr. Marine?

This might be the greatest of all possible revelations. A final confirmation of the essence of religion, of the deepest human hopes.

Or it might be just an alien theology, expressed in an alien way.

A heron flapped overhead and the night air sang with the chirps and scurries of the woods. Nature was getting back to business, after all the noise and death.

Business as usual.

But he knew that this night sky would never look the same again.

Daniel Abraham, "The Cambist and Lord Iron: A Fairy Tale of Economics," *Logorrhea*.

Brian W. Aldiss, "Life, Learning, Leipzig and a Librarian," *Postscripts 12*.

Erik Amundssen, "Bufo Rex," *Weird Tales*, December.

Kim Antieau, "The Señorita and the Cactus Thorn," *Coyote Road*.

Lou Antonelli, "Avatar," *Darker Matter*, April.

Madeline Ashby, "In Which Joe and Laurie Save Rock and Roll," *Tesseracts Eleven*.

Neal Asher, "Bioship," *The Solaris Book of New SF*.

A.A. Attanasio, "Telefunken Remix," *Fantasy & Science Fiction*, May.

Kate Bachus, "Ferryman's Reprieve," *Strange Horizons*, 28 April.

Paolo Bacigalupi, "Small Offerings," *Fast Forward 1*.

_____, "Softer," *Logorrhea*.

Kage Baker, "Maelstrom," *The New Space Opera*.

_____, "Plotters and Shooters," *Fast Forward 1*.

_____, "The Ruby Incomparable," *Wizards*.

_____, "Rude Mechanicals," *Rude Mechanicals*.

_____, "To the Land Beyond the Sunset," *Gods and Pawns*.

Tony Ballantyne, "Aristotle OS," *Fast Forward 1*.

_____, "Third Person," *The Solaris Book of New Science Fiction*.

John Barnes, "Ron Rapid and His Electric Chair," *Helix 3*.

Jamie Barras, "Pale Saints and Dark Madonnas," *Black Static*.

_____, "Winter," *Interzone*, April.

Neal Barrett, Jr., "Eating Crow," *Subterranean Online*, Spring.

_____, "Getting Dark," *Subterranean 5*.

Laird Barron, "The Forest," *Inferno*.

William Barton, "The Rocket into Planetary Space," *Asimov's*, April–May.

Christopher Barzak, "Realer Than You," *Coyote Road*.

Stephen Baxter, "No More Stories," *Fast Forward 1*.

_____, "Remembrance," *The New Space Opera*.

Peter S. Beagle, "Barrens Dance," *Wizards*.

_____, "The Last and Only, or, Mr. Moscowitz Becomes French," *Eclipse*.

_____, "We Never Talk About My Brother," *OSC's InterGalactic Medicine Show*, July.

Elizabeth Bear, "Black Is the Color," *Subterranean Online*, Summer.

_____, "Cryptic Coloration," *JBU*. June.

_____, "The Ladies," *Coyote Wild*, December.

_____, "Limerent," *Subterranean* 6.

_____, "Lucifugous," *Subterranean* 5.

_____, "Orm the Beautiful," *Clarkesworld*, January.

_____, "The Rest of Your Life in a Day," *JBU*, October.

_____, "The Something-Dreaming Game," *Fast Forward 1*.

_____, "War Stories," *Jim Baen Universe*, February.

Gregory Benford, "Reasons Not to Publish," *Nature Physics*, November.

_____, "The Worm Turns," *The New Space Opera*.

Judith Berman, "Awakenings," *Black Gate*, Spring.

Beth Bernobich, "A Handful of Pearls," *Interzone*, October.

_____, "Marsdog," *Coyote Wild*, December.

Terry Bisson, "Billy and the Wizard," *Wizards*.

Holly Black, "Paper Cuts Scissors," *Realms of Fantasy*, October.

Jenny Blackford, "Python," *Ruins Terra*.

Sue Blalock, "Charybdis," *Ruins Extraterrestrial*.

Jayme Lynn Blaschke, "The Final Voyage of *La Riaza*," *Interzone*, June.

Leah Bobet, "The Sorceress's Assistant," *On Spec*, Fall.

Keith Brooke & Eric Brown, "In Transit," *The Parallax View*.

Eric Brown, "The Farewell Party," *The Solaris Book of New Science Fiction*.

_____, "Starship Summer," *PS Publishing*.

_____, "Three's a Crowd," *Thrilling Wonder Stories*, Summer.

Leslie Brown, "Wake-Up Call," *Strange Horizons*, 30 July.

Simon Brown, "Reiteration," *Man Vs Machine*.

Tobias S. Buckell, "Io, Robot," *Visual Journeys*.

Stephanie Burgis, "It's All About the Shoes," *Flytrap 8*.

Stephen L. Burns, "The Face of Hate," *Analog*, January–February.

Pat Cadigan, "Among Strangers," *disLOCATIONS*.

_____, "Stilled Life," *Inferno*.

Orson Scott Card, "A Young Man with Prospects," OSC's *InterGalactic Medicine Show*, February.

_____, "The Gold Bug," OSC's *InterGalactic Medicine Show*, July.

_____, "Stonefather," *Wizards*.

Lisa Carreiro, "The Azure Sky," *Tesseracts Eleven*.

James L. Cambias, "The Barbary Shore," *Shimmer, The Pirate Issue*.

Bruce Carlson, "Dogs of War," *Cosmos*, June–July.

_____, "The Frozen Sky," *Writers of the Future, XXIII*.

Tim Casson, "Lady of the Crows," *Black Static*.

Michael Cassutt, "Skull Valley," *Asimov's*, October–November.

Jay Caselberg, "The Garden of Earthly Delights," *Electric Velocipede 12*.

Sarah K. Castle, "Kukulkan," *Analog*, December.

_____, "The Mechanical Mechanic, His Apprentice, and the Judge," *Helix 6*.

Fred Chappell, "Dance of Shadows," *Fantasy & Science Fiction*, March.

——, "The Diamond Shadow," *Fantasy & Science Fiction*, October–November.

Robert R. Chase, "'Domo Arigato,' Says Mr. Roboto," *Analog*, December.

Richard Chwedyk, "Where We Go," *Visual Journeys*.

Brenda Clough, "A Mighty Fortress," *Helix*, Summer.

James H. Cobb, "The First Cup of Coffee War," *Future Weapons of War*.

Eoin Colfer, "A Fowl Tale," *Wizards*.

Albert E. Cowdrey, "Envoy Extraordinary," *Fantasy & Science Fiction*, September.

——, "Murder in the Flying Vatican," *Fantasy & Science Fiction*, August.

——, "The Recreation Room," *Fantasy & Science Fiction*, October–November.

Ian Creasey, "Strawberry Thief," *Weird Tales*, June–July.

——, "Memories of the Knacker's Yard," *Apex 10*.

Tony Daniel, "The Valley of the Gardens," *The New Space Opera*.

Jack Dann, "Café Culture," *Asimov's*, January.

Aliette de Bodard, "The Lost Xuyan Bride," *Interzone*, October–November.

——, "Obsidian Shards," *Writers of the Future, XXIII*.

Stephen Dedman, "Centenary," *Cosmos*, April–May.

A.M. Dellamonica, "Time of the Snake," *Fast Forward 1*.

Paul Di Filippo, "The End of the Great Continuity," *Postscripts 13*.

——, "Personal Jesus," *The Solaris Book of New Science Fiction*.

——, "Wikiworld," *Fast Forward 1*.

Jetse de Vries, "Qubit Conflicts," *Clarkesworld*, May.

Cory Doctorow, "After the Siege," *The Infinite Matrix*, 1/8.

Candas Jane Dorsey, "Seven in a Boat, No Dog," *Tesseracts Eleven*.

Terry Dowling, "The Magikkers," *Wizards*.

——, "The Suits at Auderlene," *Inferno*.

Noreen Doyle, "The Rope," *Realms of Fantasy*, April.

Brendan DuBois, "The Unplug War," *Man Vs Machine*.

Grace Dugan, "Somewhere in Central Queensland," *Strange Horizons*, 22 January.

Andy Duncan, "A Diorama of the Infernal Regions, or The Devil's Ninth Question," *Wizards*.

——, "Unique Chicken Goes in Reverse," *Eclipse*.

Hal Duncan, "The Drifter's Tale," *disLOCATIONS*.

——, "The Island of the Pirate Gods," *Postscripts 13*.

Frederic S. Durbin, "The Bone Man," *Fantasy & Science Fiction*, December.

Greg Egan, "Dark Integers," *Asimov's*, October–November.

——, "Induction," *Foundation 100*.

M.P. Ericson, "Lost Soul," *Clarkesworld*, September.

Melanie Fazi, "In the Shape of a Dragon," *Black Static 2*.

Sheila Finch, "First Was the Word," *Fantasy & Science Fiction*, June.

Charles Coleman Finlay, "An Eye For An Eye," *Fantasy & Science Fiction*, June.

Eliot Fintushel, "How the Little Rabbi Grew," *Strange Horizons*, 17 September.

Michael F. Flynn, "Quaestiones Super Caelo et Mundo," *Analog*, July–August.

Jeffrey Ford, "The Bedroom Light," *Inferno*.

_____, "The Dreaming Wind," *Coyote Road*.

_____, "The Manticore Spell," *Wizards*.

Eugie Foster, "The Center of the Universe," *Helix*, Summer.

Karen Joy Fowler, "Always," *Asimov's*, April/May.

_____, "The Last Worders," *Lady Churchill's Rosebud Wristlet*, June.

Carl Frederick, "Double Helix, Downward Gyre," *Analog*, January/February.

Dave Freer, "Thin Ice," *JBU*, June.

Peter Friend, "Miniature," *OSC's InterGalactic Medicine Show*, February.

Esther M. Friesner, "At These Prices," *Fantasy & Science Fiction*, August.

Neil Gaiman, "The Witch's Headstone," *Wizards*.

Stephen Gallagher, "The Blackwood Oak," *Subterranean Online*, Fall.

R. Garcia y Robertson, "The Good Ship Lollypop," *Asimov's*, September.

Sara Genge, "Family Values," *Cosmos 16*.

Lisa Goldstein, "Dark Rooms," *Asimov's*, October–November.

_____, "Lilyanna," *Asimov's*, April–May.

Kathleen Ann Goonan, "The Bridge," *Asimov's*, August.

_____, "Electric Rains," *Eclipse*.

_____, "What Science Fiction Is All About, or, The Dancing Chairs," *Flurb*, Fall–Winter.

B. Gordon, "The King of Elfland's Stepdaughter," *Coyote Wild*, Spring.

Theodora Goss, "Catherine and the Satyr," *Strange Horizons*, 1 October.

_____, "Princess Lucinda and the Hound of the Moon," *Realms of Fantasy*, June.

_____, "Singing of Mount Abora," *Logorrhea*.

Gavin J. Grant, "'Janet, Meet Bob,'" *Lone Star Stories*, February.

John Grant, "Lives," *Inferno*.

Andrew Gray, "Tofino," *Tesseracts Eleven*.

Daryl Gregory, "Dead Horse Point," *Asimov's*, August.

_____, "Unpossible," *Fantasy & Science Fiction*, October–November.

Jim Grimsley, "The Sanguine," *Asimov's*, March.

_____, "Wendy," *Subterranean 5*.

Jon Courtenay Grimwood, "Angel of the Waters," *Foundation 100*.

Eileen Gunn, "Michael Swanwick and Samuel R. Delany at the Joyce Kilmer Service Area, March 2005," *Foundation 101*.

_____, "Up the Fire Road," *Eclipse*.

Joseph Paul Haines, "The Man Behind the Curtain," *Abyss & Apex*, First Quarter.

Peter F. Hamilton, "Blessed By An Angel," *The New Space Opera*.

_____, "If at First . . . ," *The Solaris Book of New Science Fiction*.

Elizabeth Hand, "Illyria," *PS Publishing*.

_____, "Winter's Wife," *Wizards*.

M. John Harrison, "The Good Detective," *Interzone*, April.

John G. Hemry, "These Are the Times," *Analog*, November.
Samantha Henderson, "Starry Night," *Helix 3*.
Howard V. Hendrix, "Palimpset," *Analog*, September.
Glen Hirshberg, "The Janus Tree," *Inferno*.
M.K. Hobson, "The Hotel Astarte," *Realms of Fantasy*, June.
Nina Kiriki Hoffman, "A Soul Cake," *Lone Star Stories*, 1 December.
_____, "The Listeners," *Coyote Road*.
Andrew Hook, "The Glass Football," *disLOCATIONS*.
Dave Hoing, "Servant of the Stone," *Postscripts 11*.
Nalo Hopkinson, "Soul Case," *Foundation 100*.
Paul Hosek, "Made," *On Spec*, Spring.
Gorg Huff & Paula Goodlett, "From the Badlands," *Jim Baen Universe*, October.
Matthew Hughes, "The Helper and His Hero," *Fantasy & Science Fiction*, February–March.
_____, "Sweet Trap," *Fantasy & Science Fiction*, June.
Alex Irvine, "Semaphore," *Logorrhea*.
_____, "Wizard's Six," *Fantasy & Science Fiction*, June.
Alexander Jablokov, "Brain Raid," *Fantasy & Science Fiction*, February.
_____, "Wrong Number," *Fantasy & Science Fiction*, September.
Michael J. Jasper, "A Miracle in Shreveport," *Electric Velocipede 12*.
C.W. Johnson, "Icarus Beach," *Analog*, December.
Kij Johnson, "The Evolution of Trickster Stories Among the Dogs of North Park After the Change," *Coyote Road*.
Gwyneth Jones, "Big Cat," *Interzone*, April.
_____, "In the Forest of the Queen," *Eclipse*.
_____, "The Tomb Wife," *Fantasy & Science Fiction*, August.
Andrea Kail, "Soft, Like a Rabbit," *Fantasy Magazine Online*, 28 October.
_____, "The Sun God at Dawn, Rising from a Lotus Blossom," *Writers of the Future*, XXIII.
William H. Keith, "The Weapon," *Future Weapons of War*.
James Patrick Kelly, "Dividing the Sustain," *The New Space Opera*.
_____, "Don't Stop," *Asimov's*, May.
Lucy Kemnitzer, "The Boulder," *Fantasy Magazine*, 6.
_____, "John Brown's Body," *Glorifying Terrorism*.
John Kessel, "Downtown," *Flurb*, Fall–Winter.
_____, "The Last American," *Foundation 100*.
Caitlín R. Kiernan, "A Season of Broken Dolls," *Subterranean Online*, Spring.
_____, "In the Dreamtime of Lady Resurrection," *Subterranean Online*, Fall.
_____, "The Ape's Wife," *Clarkesworld 12*.
_____, "Zero Summer," *Subterranean 6*.
James Killus, "Vamp in the Middle," *Helix*, Spring.
Stephen King, "Graduation Day," *Postscripts 10*.

Ellen Klages, "Mrs. Zeno's Paradox," *Eclipse*.

Ted Kosmatka, "Deadnauts," *Ideomancer*, August.

Mary Robinette Kowal, "For Solo Cello, p. 12," *Cosmos*, February–March.

Nancy Kress, "Art of War," *The New Space Opera*.

____, "By Fools Like Me," *Asimov's*, September.

____, "End Game," *Asimov's*, April–May.

____, "Fountain of Age," *Asimov's*, July.

____, "The Rules," *Asimov's*, December.

____, "Safeguard," *Asimov's*, January.

____, "Stone Man," *Wizards*.

Ellen Kushner, "Honored Guest," *Coyote Road*.

Marc Laidlaw, "The Vicar of R'lyeh," *Flurb*, Fall–Winter.

Jay Lake, "A Very Old Man with No Wings At All," *Aeon Eleven*.

____, "After Bonestell," *Visual Journeys*.

____, "Eating Their Sins and Ours," *Lone Star Stories*, 1 June.

____, "Chewing Up the Innocent," *Clarkesworld*, February.

____, "Crossing the Seven," *Logorrhea*.

____, "The Fly and Die Ticket," *Subterranean Online*, Fall.

____, "The Golden Whip," *Helix 6*.

____, "The Leopard's Paw," *Subterranean*, Spring.

____, "Tom Edison and His Telegraphic Harpoon," *Weird Tales*, June.

____, "Where the Water Meets the Sky," *Interzone*, February.

____ and Greg van Eekhout, "C-Rock City," *Solaris Book of New Science Fiction*.

Claude Lalumière, "Hochelaga and Sons," *Electric Velocipede 13*.

____, "The Object of Worship," *Tesseracts Eleven*.

Margo Lanagan, "Reflecting Glory," *Foundation 100*.

____, "She Creatures," *Eclipse*.

Geoffrey A. Landis, "David in the Lion's Den," *Future Weapons of War*.

____, "Vectoring," *Analog*, June.

Joe R. Lansdale, "Deadman's Road," *Subterranean*, Spring.

Chris Lawson, "Screening Test," *Agog! Ripping Reads*.

Tanith Lee, "Cold Fire," *Asimov's*, February.

____, "Zinder," *Wizards*.

Yoon Ha Lee, "Screamers," *Ideomancer*, Vol. 6, Issue 2.

____, "The Shadow Postulates," *Helix*, Summer.

G.D., Leeming, "Empty Clouds," *Interzone*, February.

Tim Lees, "Preachers," *Interzone*, June.

Edward M. Lerner, "A Stranger in Paradise," *Jim Baen Universe*, February.

David D. Levine, "Babel Probe," *Darker Matter*, March.

____, "Moonlight on the Carpet," *Aeon Twelve*.

____, "Titanium Mike Saves the Day," *Fantasy & Science Fiction*, April.

Marissa Lingen, "Pirates by Adeline Thromb Age 8," *Shimmer, The Pirate Issue*.

Kelly Link, "The Constable of Abal," *Coyote Road*.

Richard A. Lovett, "The Last of the Weathermen," *Analog*, July–August.

____, "The Sands of Titan," *Analog*, June.

____, "The Unrung Bells of the *Marie Celeste*," *Analog*, January–February.

Ian R. MacLeod, "The Master Miller's Tale," *Fantasy & Science Fiction*, May.

Ken MacLeod, "Jesus Christ, Reanimator," *Fast Forward 1*.

____, "Who's Afraid of Wolf 359?," *The New Space Opera*.

Bruce McAllister, "His Wife," *Fantasy Magazine*, 6.

____, "The Lion," *Asimov's*, March.

____, "Poison," *Asimov's*, January.

Paul McAuley, "Rocket Boy," *Future Weapons of War*.

____, "Winning Peace," *The New Space Opera*.

Wil McCarthy, "The Necromancer in Love," *Jim Baen Universe*, October.

Una McCormack, "Torch Song," *Glorifying Terrorism*.

Tim McDaniel, "The Lonesome Planet Travelers' Advisory," *Asimov's*, December.

____, "Teacher's Lounge," *Asimov's*, August.

Jack McDevitt, "Fifth Day," *Asimov's*, April/May.

____, "Tweak," *Jim Baen Universe*, October.

Maureen McHugh, "The Lost Boy: A Reporter at Large," *Eclipse*.

Will McIntosh, "Perfect Violet," *On Spec*, Summer.

Christopher McKitterick, "The Empty Utopia," *Ruins Extraterrestrial*.

____, "Jupiter Whispers," *Visual Journeys*.

Elizabeth Malartre, "Darwin's Suitcase," *Jim Baen Universe*, December.

Darja Malcolm-Clarke, "The Beacon," *Clarkesworld*, August.

Geoffrey Maloney, "Blonde on Blonde: An American Fable," *Albedo 33*.

____, "When the World Was Flat," *Agog! Ripping Reads*.

Barry N. Malzberg & Jack Dann, "The Art of Memory," *Jim Baen Universe*, December.

Lisa Mantchev, "A Dance Across Embers," *Clarkesworld*, October.

Louise Marley, "p dolce," *Fast Forward 1*.

____, "The Spiral Road," *Jim Baen Universe*, February.

David Marusek, "HealthGuard," *Foundation 100*.

____, "Osama Phone Home," *MIT Technology Review*, March–April.

Donald Mead, "A Thing Forbidden," *Fantasy & Science Fiction*, April.

John Meaney, "Sideways From Now," *Fast Forward 1*.

Charles Midwinter, "A Portrait of the Artist," *Asimov's*, February.

Jeremy Minton, "The Darkness Between," *Fantasy & Science Fiction*, January.

Manek Mistry, "Stories of the Alien Invasion," *Abyss & Apex*, First Quarter.

Judith Moffett, "The Bird Shaman's Girl," *Fantasy & Science Fiction*, October–November.

Sarah Monette, "Under the Beansidhe's Pillow," *Lone Star Stories 22*.

John Morressy, "Fool," *Fantasy & Science Fiction*, February.

January Mortimer, "Brighton Bay," *Aeon Eleven*.

Richard Mueller, "I Read the News Today, Oh Boy," *Paradox*, Autumn.

Pat Murphy, "One Odd Shoe," *Coyote Road*.

Steven Francis Murphy, "Tearing Down Tuesday," *Interzone*, June.

Pati Nagle, "Draw," *Asimov's*, September.

Ruth Nestvold, "Far Side of the Moon," *Ideomancer*, Vol. 6, Issue 2.

_____, "The Leaving Sweater," *Strange Horizons*, 25 June.

_____ & Jay Lake, "Roger Lambelin," *Realms of Fantasy*, October.

R. Neube, "Battlefield Games," *Asimov's*, January.

_____, "Studies in the Field," *Asimov's*, May.

Garth Nix, "Bad Luck, Trouble, Death, and Vampire Sex," *Eclipse*.

_____, "Holly and Iron," *Wizards*.

_____, "Sir Hereward and Master Fitz Go to War Again," *Jim Baen Universe*, April.

Larry Niven & Brenda Cooper, "The Terror Bard," *Fast Forward 1*.

G. David Nordley, "Hell Orbit," *Visual Journeys*.

Patrick O'Leary, "The Cane," *Postscripts 12*.

John Philip Olson, "The Men in the Attic," *Interzone*, October–November.

Jerry Oltion, "Salvation," *Analog*, December.

Rebecca Ore, "Acid and Stoned Reindeer," *Clarkesworld*, November.

Paul Park, "Fragrant Goddess," *Fantasy & Science Fiction*, October–November.

Richard Parks, "A Garden in Hell," *Fantasy Magazine*, 5.

_____, "Directional Drift," *Postscripts 13*.

_____, "Hot Water," *Realms of Fantasy*, December.

_____, "The Man Who Carved Skulls," *Weird Tales*, April–May.

Michael Payne, "They Call Me Mr. Goddamn Happy," *Helix 3*.

Jennifer Pelland, "The Last Stand of the Elephant Man," *Helix 6*.

_____, "Mercytanks," *Helix 4*.

Holly Phillips, "The Oracle Spoke," *Clarkesworld*, June.

_____, "Three Days of Rain," *Asimov's*, May.

Tony Pi, "Metamorphoses in Amber," *Abyss & Apex*, Fourth Quarter.

Cherie Priest, "Finding Piper," *Subterranean 6*.

Brian Plante, "The Astronaut," *Analog*, May.

Tim Pratt, "Artifice and Intelligence," *Strange Horizons*, 6 August.

_____, "From Around Here," *Logorrhea*.

_____, "Restless in My Hand," *Realms of Fantasy*, August.

Cat Rambo, "Foam on the Water," *Strange Horizons*, 19 February.

_____, "I'll Gnaw Your Bones, the Manticore Said," *Clarkesworld*, July.

Marta Randall, "The Dark Boy," *Fantasy & Science Fiction*, January.

_____, "Lázaro y Antonio," *Fantasy & Science Fiction*, June.

Kit Reed, "What Wolves Know," *Asimov's*, September.

Marguerite Reed, "Angels of a Desert Heaven," *Lone Star Stories*, December 1.

Robert Reed, "The Caldera of Good Fortune," *Asimov's*, September.

____, "Hatch," *The New Space Opera*.

____, "The Hoplite," *Helix 4*.

____, "If We Can Save Just One Child . . . ," *Fantasy & Science Fiction*, September.

____, "Magic with Thirteen-Year-Old Boys," *Fantasy & Science Fiction*, March.

____, "Night Calls," *Asimov's*, October–November.

____, "X-Country," *Fantasy & Science Fiction*, January.

Mike Resnick, "A Locked-Planet Mystery," *Alien Crimes*.

____, "The Big Guy," *Jim Baen Universe*, June.

____, "Distant Replay," *Asimov's*, April–May.

____& Nancy Kress, "Solomon's Choice," *Fast Forward 1*.

Alastair Reynolds, "Minla's Flowers," *The New Space Opera*.

M. Rickert, "Don't Ask," *Fantasy & Science Fiction*, December.

____, "Holiday," *Subterranean 7*.

____, "Memoir of a Deer Woman," *Fantasy & Science Fiction*, March.

Uncle River, "Ginger Ear and Elephant Hair," *Analog*, September.

Chris Roberson, "Fire in the Lake," *Subterranean Online*, Fall.

____, "Metal Dragon Year," *Interzone*, October–November.

Adam Roberts, "A Distillation of Grace," *Solaris Book of New SF*.

____, "Here Comes the Flood," *Glorifying Terrorism*.

____, "Remorse," *disLOCATIONS*.

Margaret Ronald, "Goat Eschatologies," *Strange Horizons*, 19 November.

Benjamin Rosenbaum, "Molly and the Red Hat," *Interzone*, October–November.

Mary Rosenblum, "Breeze from the Stars," *Asimov's*, March.

____, "Color Vision," *Wizards*.

____, "Splinters of Glass," *The New Space Opera*.

Rudy Rucker & Bruce Sterling, "Hormiga Canyon," *Asimov's*, August.

Kristine Kathryn Rusch, "Dark Corners," *Jim Baen Universe*, August.

____, "The End of the World," *Alien Crimes*.

____, "Recovering Apollo 8," *Asimov's*, February.

____, "The Taste of Miracles," *Analog*, January–February.

Richard Paul Russo, "The King's Physician," *Postscripts 11*.

William Sanders, "The Contractors," *Helix 3*.

Jason Sanford, "Rumspringa," *OSC's InterGalactic Medicine Show*, July.

Pamela Sargent, "A Smaller Government," *Fast Forward 1*.

Erica L. Satifka, "Automatic," *Clarkesworld*, January.

John Scalzi, "How I Proposed to My Wife: An Alien Sex Story," *Subterranean Publishing*.

____, "The Sagan Diary," *Subterranean Online*, Fall.

Ken Scholes, "Summer in Paris, Light from the Sky," *Clarkesworld*, November.

Ekaterina Sedia, "Virus Changes Skin," *Analog*, October.

Lori Selke, "Dead. Nude. Girls.," *Strange Horizons*, February 12.

Michael Shara & Jack McDevitt, "Cool Neighbor," *Analog*, March.

Delia Sherman, "The Fiddler of Bayou Teche," *Coyote Road*.

Lucius Shepard, "Dagger Key," *Dagger Key*.

_____, "Dead Money," *Asimov's*, April–May.

_____, "The Ease With Which We Freed the Beast," *Inferno*.

_____, "Larissa Miusov," *Eclipse*.

_____, "Stars Seen through Stone," *Fantasy & Science Fiction*, July.

_____, "Vacancy," *Subterranean 7*.

Marc Shultz, "Practicing My Sad Face," *Strange Horizons*, 27 August.

William Shunn, "Not of This Fold," *An Alternate History of the 21st Century*.

_____, "Objective Impermeability in a Closed System," *An Alternate History of the 21st Century*.

Robert Silverberg, "The Eater of Dreams," *Asimov's*, April–May.

_____, "The Emperor and the Maula," *The New Space Opera*.

Dan Simmons, "Muse of Fire," *The New Space Opera*.

Vandana Singh, "Life-Pod," *Foundation 100*.

Jack Skillingstead, "The Chimera Transit," *Asimov's*, February.

_____, "Scrawl Daddy," *Asimov's*, May.

_____, "Strangers on a Bus," *Asimov's*, December.

_____, "Two," *Talebones*, Summer.

_____, "Thank You, Mr. Whiskers," *Asimov's*, August.

Alan Smale, "A Trade in Serpents," *Realms of Fantasy*, August.

Cat Sparks, "Hollywood Roadkill," *On Spec*, Summer.

Katharine Sparrow, "Welcome to Oceanopia!," *Aeon Twelve*.

Hugh A.D. Spencer, "(Coping With) Norm Deviation," *Tesseracts Eleven*.

William Browning Spencer, "Stone and the Librarian," *Fantasy & Science Fiction*, February.

_____, "The Tenth Muse," *Subterranean 6*.

Brian Stableford, "Casualty," *Future Weapons of War*.

_____, "Doctor Muffet's Island," *Asimov's*, March.

_____, "The Trial," *Asimov's*, July.

Justin Stanchfield, "Exile's Child," *Visual Journeys*.

_____, "Prodigal," *Asimov's*, August.

Allen M. Steele, "The River Horses," *Asimov's*, April–May.

Bruce Sterling, "A Plain Tale from Our Hills," Subterranean, Spring.

_____, "The Interoperation," *MIT Technology Review* November–December.

_____, "The Lustration," *Eclipse*.

Jason Stoddard, "The Best of Your Life," *Interzone*, October–November.

_____, "Fermi Packet," *Talebones*, Winter.

_____, "Softly Shining in the Forbidden Dark," *Interzone*, February.

_____, "True History," *Darker Matter*, August.

Charles Stross, "Minutes of the Labour Party Conference, 2016," *Glorifying Terrorism*.

_____, "Trunk and Disorderly," *Asimov's*, January.

Beverly Suarez-Beard, "A Thing Brilliant and Fine," *Cricket*, June–July.

Tricia Sullivan, "The Spirit of Radio," *Foundation 100*.

Michael Swanwick, "A Small Room in Koboldtown," *Asimov's*, April–May.

____, "Congratulations from the Future!," *Asimov's*, July.

____, "Urdumheim," *Fantasy & Science Fiction*, October–November.

Rachel Swirsky, "Dispersed by the Sun, Melting in the Wind," *Subterranean Online*, Summer.

Anna Tambour, "The Jeweller of Second-Hand Roe," *Subterranean 7*.

Jeffrey Thomas, "In His Sights," *Solaris Book of New SF*.

Lavie Tidhar, "Bophuthatswana," *Glorifying Terrorism*.

____, "Elsbeth Rose," *Fantasy Magazine Online*, 28 October.

____, "The Fateful Voyage of the Madame Liberté," *Ruins Extraterrestrial*.

____, "The Master," *Strange Horizons*, 8 October.

____, "The Prisoner in the Forest," *Electric Velocipede 12*.

____, "What the Thunder Said," *Strange Horizons*, 2 April.

Jeremiah Tolbert, "Captain Blood's Booty," *Shimmer, The Pirate Issue*.

Harry Turtledove, "Hoxbomb," *Alien Crimes*.

Mary A. Turzillo, "Pride," *Fast Forward 1*.

____, "Zora and the Land Ethic Nomads," *The Solaris Book of New SF*.

Lisa Tuttle, "Closet Dreams," *Postscripts 10*.

____, "Old Mr. Boudreaux," *Subterranean 7*.

____ & Steven Utley, "In the Hole," *Black Static 2*.

Melissa Tyler, "The Sky Spider," *Aeon Eleven*.

Rajnar Vajra, "Emerald River, Pearl Sky," *Analog*, January–February.

Jeff VanderMeer, "The Third Bear," *Clarkesworld*, April.

____ & Cat Rambo, "The Surgeon's Tale," *Subterranean Online*, Winter.

Greg Van Eekhout, "Hermod's Ride," *Flytrap 8*.

Mark L. Van Name, "Broken Bits," *Future Weapons of War*.

James Van Pelt, "How Music Begins," *Asimov's*, September.

Carrie Vaughn, "Marrying In," *Asimov's*, May.

____, "Swing Time," *Jim Baen Universe*, June.

Edd Vick, "Rebel the First," *Jim Baen Universe*, February.

Elisabeth Vonarburg, "Language of the Night," *Tesseracts Eleven*.

Jo Walton, "Tradition," *Lone Star Stories*, June 1.

William John Watkins, "The Polka Man," *OSC's InterGalactic Medicine Show*, July.

Ian Watson, "Cages," *Solaris Book of New Science Fiction*.

K.D. Wentworth, "Kaleidoscope," *Fantasy & Science Fiction*, May.

Leslie What, "Tsuris," *Logorrhea*.

Ysabeau S. Wilce, "Quartermaster Returns," *Eclipse*.

Jan Wildt, "The After-Life," *Flytrap 6*.

Donna Glee Williams, "Limits," *Strange Horizons*, 23 July.

Liz Williams, "Debatable Lands," *Asimov's*, October–November.

_____, "The Hide," *Strange Horizons*, 7 May.

_____, "Lyceum," *Logorrhea*.

_____, "Wolves of the Spirit," *Asimov's*, April–May.

Sean Williams, "Cenotaxis," *MonkeyBrain Books*.

Tad Williams, "The Stranger's Hands," *Wizards*.

Walter Jon Williams, "Send Them Flowers," *The New Space Opera*.

_____, "Womb of Every World," *Alien Crimes*.

Michael Z. Williamson, "Humans Call It Duty," *Future Weapons of War*.

Connie Willis, "All Seated on the Ground," *Asimov's*, December.

Chris Willrich, "A Wizard of the Old School," *Fantasy & Science Fiction*, August.

Robert Charles Wilson, "YFL-500," *Fast Forward 1*.

Eric Witchey, "Running Water for L.A.," *Jim Baen Universe*, June.

Gene Wolfe, "Green Glass," *Asimov's*, April–May.

_____, "The Hour of the Sheep," *Fast Forward 1*.

_____, "The Magic Animal," *Wizards*.

_____, "Memorare," *Fantasy & Science Fiction*, April.

_____, "Unrequited Love," *Foundation 100*.

John C. Wright, "Silence of the Night," *Night Lands*, 21 May.

Jane Yolen, "Slipping Sideways through Eternity," *Wizards*.

Marly Youmans, "The Comb," *Fantasy Magazine Online*, 24 December.

_____, "Drunk Bay," *Postscripts 13*.

_____, "Prologomenon to the Adventures of Childe Phoenix," *Lady Churchill's Rose-bud Wristlet*, June.

George Zebrowski, "Settlements," *Fast Forward 1*.

Kim Zimring, "My Heart as Dry as Dust," *Asimov's*, September.